Classic Short Stories

CLASSIC
SHORT
STORIES

Selection by
ROSEMARY GRAY

Wordsworth Editions

For my husband
ANTHONY JOHN RANSON
with love from your wife, the publisher.
Eternally grateful for your unconditional love.

Readers who are interested in other titles from
Wordsworth Editions are invited to visit our website at
www.wordsworth-editions.com

For our latest list and a full mail-order service, contact
Bibliophile Books, 5 Datapoint, South Crescent, London E16 4TL
TEL: +44 (0)20 7474 2474 FAX: +44 (0)20 7474 8589
ORDERS: orders@bibliophilebooks.com
WEBSITE: www.bibliophilebooks.com

This edition published in 2007
by Wordsworth Editions Limited
8B East Street, Ware, Hertfordshire SG12 9HJ

ISBN 978 1 84022 270 8

Text © Wordsworth Editions Limited 2007

Wordsworth Editions
is the company founded in 1987 by
MICHAEL TRAYLER

Typeset in Great Britain by Antony Gray
Printed and bound by Clays Ltd, St Ives plc

Contents

ARNOLD BENNETT

Arnold Bennett was born on 27 May 1867. He grew up in the
environs of Hanley, Staffordshire, one of the Midlands pottery
towns that later served as a backdrop for his celebrated *Five
Towns* novels. The son of a solicitor, Bennett received a secondary
education but was forced to leave school at the age of sixteen to
be a clerk in his father's firm. Having twice failed his legal
examinations, Bennett escaped to London in 1889 to work in
law offices. Gradually drawn into literary and artistic circles, he
abandoned the law in 1894 and embarked on a writing career,
securing an editorial position with the weekly magazine *Woman*.
The following year his story 'A Letter Home' appeared in the
fashionable *Yellow Book*, and he soon brought out an autobiographical first novel, *A Man from the North* (1898). In 1902
Bennett completed two highly popular works: *The Grand Babylon
Hotel* and *Anna of the Five Towns*. In 1903 Bennett settled in Paris,
where he lived for much of the next decade. He scored a
triumphant success in 1908 with the publication of *The Old
Wives' Tale*, a masterful portrayal of English provincial life that
rivals the novels of Flaubert and other French realists. Bennett
enhanced his renown with the *Clayhanger* trilogy (1910–16) and
enjoyed theatrical success in London with the plays *Milestones*
(1912) and *The Great Adventure* (1913). Bennett's prominence
declined temporarily following World War 1 but experienced a
resurgence of popularity with *Riceyman Steps* (1923) and *Lord
Raingo* (1926). In 1926 he began contributing a weekly book
review to the London *Evening Standard*. His final novel, *Imperial
Palace*, came out in 1930. Arnold Bennett died in London of
typhoid fever on 27 March 1931.

In a New Bottle

Commercial travellers are rather like bees; they take the seed of a good story from one district and deposit it in another.

Thus several localities, imperfectly righteous, have within recent years appropriated this story to their own annals. I once met an old herbalist from Wigan – Wigan of all places in beautiful England! – who positively asserted that the episode occurred just outside the London and North-Western main line station at Wigan.

This old herbalist was no judge of the value of evidence. An undertaker from Hull told me flatly, little knowing who I was and where I came from, that he was the undertaker concerned in the episode. This undertaker was a liar. I use this term because there is no other word in the language which accurately expresses my meaning. Of persons who have taken the trouble to come over from the United States in order to inform me that the affair happened at Harper's Ferry, Poughkeepsie, Syracuse, Allegheny, Indianapolis, Columbus, Charlotte, Tabernacle, Alliance, Wheeling, Lynchburg, and Chicago it would be unbecoming to speak – they are best left to silence themselves by mutual recrimination. The fact is that the authentic scene of the affair was a third-class railway carriage belonging to the North Staffordshire Railway Company and rolling on that company's loop-line between Longshaw and Hanbridge. The undertaker is now dead – it is a disturbing truth that even undertakers die sometimes – and since his widow has given me permission to mention his name, I shall mention his name. It was Edward Till. Of course everybody in the Five Towns knows who the undertaker was, and if anybody in the Five Towns should ever chance to come across this book, I offer him my excuses for having brought coals to Newcastle.

Mr Till used to be a fairly well-known figure in Hanbridge, which is the centre of undertaking, as it is of everything else, in the Five Towns. He was in a small but a successful way of business, had one leg a trifle shorter than the other (which slightly deteriorated the majesty of his demeanour on solemn occasions), played the fiddle, kept rabbits, and was of a forgetful disposition. It was possibly this forgetful disposition which had prevented him from rising into a large way of business. All admired his personal character and tempered geniality; but there are some things that will not bear forgetting. However, the story touches but lightly that side of his individuality.

One morning Mr Till had to go to Longshaw to fetch a baby's coffin which had been ordered under the mistaken impression that a certain baby was dead. This baby, I may mention, was the hero of the celebrated scare of Longshaw about the danger of being buried alive. The little thing had apparently passed away; and, what is more, an inquest had been held on it and its parents had been censured by the jury for criminal carelessness in overlaying it; and it was within five minutes of being nailed up, when it opened its eyes! You may imagine the enormous sensation that there was in the Five Towns. One doctor lost his reputation, naturally. He emigrated to the Continent, and now, practising at Lucerne in the summer and Mentone in the winter, charges fifteen shillings a visit (instead of three and six at Longshaw) for informing people who have nothing the matter with them that they must take care of themselves. The parents of the astonished baby moved the heaven and earth of the Five Towns to force the coroner to withdraw the stigma of the jury's censure; but they did not succeed, not even with the impassioned aid of two London halfpenny dailies.

To resume, Mr Till had to go to Longshaw. Now, unless you possess a most minute knowledge of your native country, you are probably not aware that in Aynsley Street, Longshaw, there is a provision dealer whose reputation for cheeses would be national and supreme if the whole of England thought as the Five Towns think.

'Teddy,' Mrs Till said, as Mr Till was starting, 'you might as well bring back with you a pound of Gorgonzola.' (Be it noted that I had the details of the conversation from the lady herself.)

'Yes,' said he enthusiastically, 'I will.'

'Don't go and forget it,' she enjoined him.

'No,' he said. 'I'll tie a knot in my handkerchief.'

'A lot of good that'll do!' she observed. 'You'd tied a knot in your handkerchief when you forgot that Councillor Barker's wife's funeral was altered from Tuesday to Monday.'

'Ah!' he replied. 'But now I've got a bad cold.'

'So you have!' she agreed, reassured.

He tied the knot in his handkerchief and went.

Thanks to his cold he did not pass the cheesemonger's without entering.

He adored Gorgonzola, and he reckoned that he knew a bit of good Gorgonzola when he met with it. Moreover, he and the cheesemonger were old friends, he having buried three of the cheesemonger's children. He emerged from the cheesemonger's with a pound of the perfectest Gorgonzola that ever greeted the senses.

The abode of the censured parents was close by, and also close to the station. He obtained the coffin without parley, and told the mother, who showed him the remarkable child with pride, that under the circumstances he should make no charge at all. It was a ridiculously small coffin. He was quite accustomed to coffins.

Hence he did the natural thing. He tucked the little coffin under one arm, and, dangling the cheese (neat in brown paper and string) from the other hand, he hastened to the station. With his unmatched legs he must have made a somewhat noticeable figure.

A loop-line train was waiting, and he got into it, put the cheese on the rack in a corner, and the coffin next to it, assured himself that he had not mislaid his return ticket, and sat down under his baggage. It was the slackest time of day, and, as the train started at Longshaw, there were very few passengers. He had the compartment to himself.

He was just giving way to one of those moods of vague and pleasant meditation which are perhaps the chief joy of such a temperament, when he suddenly sprang up as if in fear. And fear had in fact seized him. Suppose he forgot those belongings on the rack? Suppose, sublimely careless, he descended from the train and left them there? What a calamity! And similar misadventures had happened to him before. It was the cheese that disquieted him. No one would be sufficiently unprincipled to steal the coffin, and he would ultimately recover it at the lost luggage office, babies' coffins not abounding on the North Staffordshire Railway. But the cheese! He would never see the cheese again! No integrity would be able to withstand the blandishments of that cheese. Moreover, his wife would be saddened. And for her he had a sincere and profound affection.

His act of precaution was to lift the coffin down from the rack, and place it on the seat beside him, and then to put the parcel of cheese on the coffin. He surveyed the cheese on the coffin; he surveyed it with the critical and experienced eye of an undertaker, and he decided that, if anyone else got into the carriage, it would not look quite decent, quite becoming – in a word, quite nice. A coffin is a coffin, and people's feelings have to be considered.

So he whipped off the lid of the coffin, stuck the cheese inside, and popped the lid on again. And he kept his hand on the coffin that he might not forget it. When the train halted at Knype, Mr Till was glad that he had put the cheese inside, for another passenger got into the compartment. And it was a clergyman. He recognised the clergyman, though the clergyman did not recognise him. It was the Reverend Claud ffolliott, famous throughout the Five Towns as the man who begins his name with a small letter, doesn't smoke, of course doesn't drink, but goes to football matches, has an average of eighteen at cricket, and makes a very pretty show with the gloves, in spite of his thirty-eight years; celibate, very High, very natty and learned about vestments, terrific at sick couches and funerals. Mr Till inwardly trembled to think what the Reverend Claud ffolliott might have said had he seen the cheese reposing in the coffin, though the coffin was empty.

The parson, whose mind was apparently occupied, dropped into the nearest corner, which chanced to be the corner farthest away from Mr Till. He then instantly opened a copy of the *Church Times* and began to read it, and the train went forward. The parson sniffed, absently, as if he had been dozing and a fly had tickled his nose. Shortly afterwards he sniffed again, but without looking up from his perusals. He sniffed a third time, and glanced over the top edge of the *Church Times* at Mr Till. Calmed by the innocuous aspect of Mr Till, he bent once more to the paper. But after an interval he was sniffing furiously. He glanced at the window; it was open. Finally he lowered the *Church Times*, as who should say: 'I am a long-suffering man, but really this phenomenon which assaults my nostrils must be seriously enquired into.'

Then it was that he caught sight of the coffin, with Mr Till's hand caressing it, and Mr Till all in black and carrying a funereal expression. He straightened himself, pulled himself together on account of his cloth, and said to Mr Till in his most majestic and sympathetic graveside voice, 'Ah! my dear friend, I see that you have suffered a sad, sad bereavement.'

That rich, resonant voice was positively thrilling when it addressed hopeless grief. Mr Till did not know what to say, nor where to look.

'You have, however, one thing to be thankful for, very thankful for,' said the parson after a pause, 'you may be sure the poor thing is not in a trance.'

During Dinner

The lounge, a large apartment of irregular shape, full of cosy corners and grouped easy-chairs inviting to intimacies, and lit by rose-shaded lamps embedded in the carved ceiling, and screened from the outer world by thick, rosy curtains, was perfectly empty. Warm and well-cushioned and softly carpeted, it waited in silence with its discreetly voluptuous engravings and statuettes, its silver trophies of sport and its gigantic ferns and palms, for the end of dinner, when it would be comfortably filled by ladies and gentlemen who, until they went up in the lift to bed, had nothing to do except digest and play cards.

The dining-room was separated from the lounge by a glass wall, through which the diners, aided by their high-priests, priests and acolytes, could be seen dining with dignity and ceremony. Not a sound came from the dining-room through the glass wall; its inhabitants might have been an optical illusion.

On the other side of the lounge was a much smaller apartment, called by the hotel proprietor the sun-room, and by certain facetious guests the grill-room. Its semi-circular front-wall was wholly window, and if there was any sunshine this room caught it and imprisoned it and presented it to the persons who cared to occupy the row of easy-chairs ranged in front of the vast expanse of glass. The sun-room was cold at night. On this night its curtains had not been drawn, nor its lamps lit. Through the window the nocturnal pleasure-town offered itself with its piers and its promenade all festooned and jewelled in electricity, and its motors gliding to and fro, and a little ragged boy crying evening papers in the east wind just under the window.

The sun-room was not quite dark, partly because of the radiance from the streets and partly because of the radiance from the glowing lounge. Within it, gazing forth at the magic spectacle of the town, could be seen a young man in a dinner-jacket. He was tall, with a small head; he had race and distinction; he had evidently done all that was proper to his station and age, from fighting in the trenches to joining the right clubs. And although he held himself carelessly and was ever so little negligent of his attire (but not of his glossy hair) he had the authentic *chic* which the most meticulous and earnest dandies in Paris try in vain to match. He gazed at the town for quite a long time and then turned and gazed into the brightness of the lounge. He was waiting. The lounge was waiting.

Then a fat middle-aged woman, with dirty dress and dirty apron, sidled apologetically into the lounge, carrying a dirty tool-box. Her tools consisted chiefly of various brushes and rags. She knelt down before the great patent stove that burnt coal economically and yet brightly near the middle of the lounge, and burnished and tidied and rubbed the stove and swept its hearth, and sidled apologetically out again. She knew she was an eyesore in the rich room and ought to be ashamed of herself for being visible in paradise.

And once more the lounge and the young man waited. Then a bell rang and the lift went up. The lift-shaft, surrounded by the staircase, ended in the lounge itself, so that the traffic and burdens of the lift might provide interest for the loungers in the lounge. The lift descended, bearing a young woman. It was a pity that the lounge happened to be empty of sightseers, for the young woman was worth witnessing. A blonde, rather plump, and not very tall, she had a face lovely in form and tints, glinting, light brown eyes and hair, a large richly promising mouth, and a smile that was habitual. The arched curve of her eyebrows added to her agreeable and eager expression a note of constant slightly thrilled surprise. Having a perfect complexion and lips, she had of course plentifully employed rouge and powder. Having the most adorable fingernails she had of course most elaborately painted them. It would not have been decent for her to show herself as nature had so exquisitely made her. She was magnificently dressed; her jewels, though few, might have been pawned for at least a thousand pounds.

She emerged from the lift well aware of her costly perfection but not a bit conceited about it. She glanced questioningly round the empty lounge with a look half-innocent and half-initiated, half-jaunty and half-bashful. The truth was that she had been married nearly three weeks, and this was not the first hotel of her honeymoon; therefore she considered herself an old hand, learned in the world's ways, omniscient on the subject of love and husbands, and not on any account to be mistaken for part of a honeymoon couple. But also she had doubts concerning her competence as a woman of experience, and her great knowledge sometimes frightened her. Nevertheless she knew that she was utterly delicious and all-powerful, and that the whole earth ought to be grateful to her for residing on it.

Satisfied that there really was nobody in the lounge, she tripped up to the glass partition and spied cautiously upon the dining-room. Then, puzzled, she crossed the lounge again and peered into the twilight of the sun-room.

'Ah! There you are! I was wondering where you'd got to.'

She spoke so vivaciously and charmingly and lovingly that you would have thought that, the place being quite deserted, the young husband would have sprung at the young wife, whom less than a month ago he had snatched away in all her virginal innocence from her weeping parents, and kissed her on the spot.

But no! The young husband did not move. He did not even look at the young wife. He glared aside – at nothing. His mouth worked. He bit his lip. His hands dug themselves into the very deeps of his pockets. He was in a state of considerable emotional disturbance. Whereas the young wife, whose intimate acquaintance with the male sex was limited to a week or two, and who surely ought to have been seriously agitated – the wife maintained a beautiful calm.

'Aren't you coming in to dinner?' she asked sweetly and simply.

'No!' grunted the husband, and then after a little pause added: 'I'm not.'

'But what's the matter?' she demanded in gentle, complete amazement. 'Phil, what *is* the matter?'

In that moment Philip, as hundreds of millions of young men and old men before him, stood absolutely astounded at woman's power of duplicity. Here was a young woman whom he had really believed to be quite different in her nature from all other women whatsoever, an honest, sincere, genuine, straight young woman, a pal as well as a wife; and now every tone of her voice and every word she said and every movement of her hands lied to him – lied foolishly without the least hope of deceiving him! She asked what was the matter, but she knew what was the matter, exactly and entirely what was the matter. She knew that he was profoundly hurt and anxious. Her odious tranquillity proved that she was insensible to his suffering.

'I am not going in to dinner until that fellow at the next table has come out,' Philip announced with finality. And then the little pause, and then the clinching phrase: 'And so now you know!'

She gave a low, light laugh.

'Oh! It's *that*? You're still worrying about *that*?' she said, just as though ten minutes earlier they had not had quite a scene in the bedroom about the fellow who sat by himself at the next table. Her method of conducting an argument was exasperating to the last degree.

'I told you I shouldn't,' said Philip, with restrained savageness. He was in such spiritual pain that her extraordinary physical attractiveness became loathsome to him. His evident extreme distress alarmed her somewhat, and she thought she would do well to repeat what she had said upstairs and what she had sworn never to repeat: 'But don't I tell you I've never even spoken to him? I don't know his name even.'

'The man's a cad. That's certain.'

'I don't see that he's a cad.'

'No. Women often like cads. But he's a cad all the same. He makes eyes at you all the time, at every meal. And upon my soul you smile at him. Do you think I'm blind?'

'I think you're very silly,' she replied, this time with conviction. 'I can't understand you at all. I never heard of such a thing! I suppose you think I ought to feel flattered by your jealousy –'

'Jealousy!' he sneered.

'But I'm not.' She still spoke evenly and kindly, somewhat like a mother to a child, though she was by six years his junior.

She imagined that her equanimity was very clever. But it maddened Philip. He began to lose control of himself, and found a terrible satisfaction in doing so. The dreadful thoughts – suspicions, accusations, criticisms, condemnations – about our best friends which lie hidden at the bottom of the hearts of all of us, and upon the concealment of which depends the safety and decency of human relations, rose up unchecked to the surface and escaped in speech. He called his wife a flirt; he referred to her ruthless hunger for pleasure and luxury, to her egotism, to her vanity, to her faulty upbringing, to the absurdities of her parents and other relatives, and to his own confiding, trustful, foolish nature, which his wicked wife had known how to deceive.

'I'm afraid I've married a jealous monster,' said she in reply sadly, and then with an assumption of courage: 'Still, there it is, and I expect I must make the best of it. Anyhow, if you aren't going in to dinner, I am. You'd better take a stroll. The exercise will calm you and pull you together . . . '

'Smiled at the man!' How grotesque! She had never smiled at the man. She had smiled at the room, smiled generally – nothing more. The man was absolutely nothing to her. Must she scowl, to please Phil? He had gone clean off his head? She had always suspected that he was inclined to be a bit jealous; but this scene was indeed too much. It was incredible, tragic, catastrophic. It was the ruin of all her chances of happiness. She thought of the wedding – only the other day – and of his tenderness and his passion . . . She turned away with a fixed, expressionless smile, towards the dining-room. She would see the thing through. She would eat and drink, though she choked for it. She did not guess that if she had burst into tears and fled upstairs he would have followed her, furious at first – and then contrite.

Philip watched her depart. His hand behind him touched a blind-cord. He pulled at it, and it broke, and a large blind rattled down with a noise astonishingly like thunder. A stout cord, a cord nearly a quarter of an inch in diameter, and he had (he thought) scarcely touched it; and yet it had broken between his fingers as a bit of cotton might have broken! The noise and confusion of the blind seemed to him somehow to symbolise what had happened to his marriage. He suddenly felt exhausted and also frightened, and he dropped into a chair as after a long, harrowing night he had ducked back into some sort of semi-safety in the Ypres salient. He was quite alone. Ethel had disappeared into the distant dining-room. The whole brooding expanse of the deserted lounge lay between him and humanity. He ought, according to his own code, to have sworn and raged manfully. But there was no occasion to keep up appearances, and he moaned to himself weakly, despairingly: 'Oh, dear! Oh, dear! Oh, dear!'

That was all.

Then he was aware in the gloom of a face peering at him round the flap of a huge easy-chair that was slightly turned from the direction of the window.

He was not alone! He had not been alone! The episode from beginning to end had had an unseen, unguessed spectator. Philip, discountenanced and wondering how he ought to behave in the very startling circumstances, did not move.

'I know exactly how you feel,' said the spectator in a quiet, worn voice, and so naturally, so simply and amicably, that Philip could not take offence at the unheard-of familiarity.

The man rose from his chair and slowly approached Philip and stood close to him. A little grey-haired man, apparently about sixty. Philip had seen him once or twice in the hotel; he always came very late into the dining-room for meals, eating by himself. He was well dressed and of good deportment, and yet there was something queer, disconcerting, about him – about his demeanour, his accent, and about the very quality of his voice; he was both apologetic and haughty, both hard and sensitive, both common and distinguished; as for his accent, Phil could not put a name to it; further, when he spoke his lips scarcely moved.

'There's nobody can understand you better than I can,' the man continued. 'And there's nobody got a better right than me to warn you that if you can't control that insane jealousy of yours you have a fair chance of a tragedy in your life. Look at you! Look at your face! You're all shaking. You aren't a man. You're what remains of a man after a devil has had possession of him and devastated him.'

'See here – ' Philip began in sharp but feeble protest; he was somehow over-awed, as much by the man's choice of words as by his extraordinary self-assurance.

'You won't mind me talking to you like this,' the man stopped him, almost grandly, 'when I tell you that I'm Crary.'

He spoke as though he were announcing a fact of terrific, dazzling, unique interest.

'Crary?' Philip repeated the name murmuringly, as he might have repeated 'Smith' or 'Jones'.

'*The* Crary.'

'I'm afraid – '

'Do you mean to say you've never heard of the Crary Case, the Crary-Hamwich Case?'

Mr Crary still spoke quietly, but in his tone there was utter amazement, and some resentment. His sensitive pride had been wounded by Philip's ignorance. He was really hurt. Plainly he felt that he had a grievance.

'I'm afraid I haven't.'

'Oh, well!' Mr Crary gloomily accepted the situation. 'I suppose you're too young to remember even the greatest public events of the nineties. But believe me that for weeks, once, I was the most celebrated man in this country . . . And now you don't even . . . Such is fame! Such is fame! Good

God, sir! I'm in the "Famous Trials" series. And even today I stand alone. Nobody else has been through what I've been through. Nobody!'

'Oh! What was it?'

'Well, I can't tell it you all. Take too long. So you've never heard of the murder of Mr Hamwich! . . . I murdered him. From jealousy. That's why I thought I must speak to you. Will you listen? Nobody'll come into the lounge for twenty minutes yet.' He glanced round.

'Yes,' answered Philip, still shakily. He did not want to listen, but he was intimidated by the singular mien of the little man, and by the conjunction of the words 'jealousy' and 'murder', and by the horror of his own frightful feelings only a few minutes earlier . . . A murderer in front of him! Why had the murderer not been hung? How came he to be at large, a guest in high-class hotels?

The little man proceeded.

'I was in love with Mrs Hamwich as much as you are with that young lady who's just gone. I assume she's your wife.'

'She is.'

'Mrs Hamwich was young.' Mr Crary's voice trembled. 'And I was a bit younger. Mr Hamwich was forty-five. I say I was in love with Mrs Hamwich desperately. And Mrs Hamwich was in love with me. We couldn't help it. We didn't know what to do. She wouldn't do anything wrong. She wouldn't leave her husband. A Jewess, I ought to explain. They're like that, Jewesses are. I had to give her up. That was in the afternoon in a tea-shop. Mr and Mrs Hamwich lived at Canonbury, you know – North London. I don't know why I went up to Canonbury that night, and into their street. I saw them walking home together. He held her arm. He was owning her. A very correct gentle-man, in business. I'd nothing against him except that he was her husband and owning her. I couldn't stand the way he owned her. It drove me mad. I was so moved that I could not bear my emotion. It was unbearable. I *had* to ease it, and there was only one way. The devil rushed me across the road, and I stabbed Mr Hamwich in the back – twenty-two times, they said afterwards. With a pair of scissors that Delphine – that was Mrs Hamwich – had given me for a keepsake. Oh, I knew what I was doing! Only it wasn't me, it was somebody else in me. I enjoyed doing it. Yes, I enjoyed it. I'd never been so happy in my life. It was awful – my happiness was. Awful! Awful! Afterwards I was very ill. Of course they arrested me. But they arrested Mrs Hamwich as well. They made out that she had planned the murder with me – urged me to do it. They brought evidence for that. Scissors and so on. Letters. But it was an absolute lie. An absolute lie. I was staggered. Neither she nor I had had the slightest idea that I was going to kill him. *You* don't think *you're* ever going to kill anybody, do you? No more did I, till the moment came. They tried us together. I had money, lots, and I spent a lot of it on the trial. Not for myself. No hope for me. But for her. We were both convicted and sentenced to death.

I thought the jury was insane. I fainted in the dock. She didn't faint. I never saw her again. There was no appeal in those days. There was only the Home Secretary to go to. The newspapers were full of us for a fortnight. Tremendous petitions for reprieve. Then at last I heard that the Home Secretary had refused to interfere in my case. That was the day before the day. They wouldn't tell me anything about Delphine. Prison rules. Not a word could I get. And I was allowed no visits. I was sure she was reprieved. They'd put me in another cell. Nobody said anything, but I knew it was the condemned cell. I was never left alone. Two special warders all the time. Very friendly fellows. That is, they got friendly after a day or two. But they wouldn't talk about her – not a word. Had orders, I suppose. Only I didn't want to talk about anything else.

'It wasn't being hanged that troubled me so much. No, it was remorse. You don't know what remorse is. You can't. It's the most dreadful thing can happen to a man. Remorse for killing Mr Hamwich, of course. But far more, far more, *far* more, for having got Delphine into this ghastly ruin. This ghastly ruin, I say. I raged about that. I couldn't believe the stupidity of the jury, or the unscrupulousness of the Crown Counsel. I couldn't believe it was all true. I had one thought in my head all day, and nearly all night. Injustice! Monstrous injustice to her! And I'd done it. I'd brought it about! In two minutes – a minute! And what had made me do it I didn't know. Sometimes I couldn't credit that I *had* done it. It was rather as if it was something I had read about in a paper.

'Well, it was the governor himself came to tell me my petition for a reprieve was refused. I asked him about the petition for Mrs Hamwich. He got stiff and awkward at once. He said: "I know nothing about Mrs Hamwich. She is not in my charge, and I've no responsibility for her." I said: "But she's *bound* to be reprieved!" He said: "Yes."

'Well then I was sure that she *was* reprieved. They couldn't hang her, couldn't! A woman, and innocent! I went easier in my mind. I wondered how I could ever have doubted that she'd get off in the end.'

Mr Crary ceased and turned from Philip, seated in front of him, and looked out of the half of the window not covered by the fallen blind. Not a sound from the empty, illuminated lounge. It seemed as if the lounge was waiting for Mr Crary to be executed.

'But what next?' Philip demanded, now impatient, excited, feverish.

'I'm not telling this well,' said Mr Crary. 'I've never told it before to a soul, and I'm forgetting things. I'm mixing things up. I'd forgotten about chapel on Execution Sunday – that's the last Sunday before the execution. I was taken into chapel by myself then, after the others, and I sat in the red pew at the back, pew with red curtains across it. The condemned pew. Nobody could see I was there. But all the other prisoners knew I was there, and they knew I knew. And once when I met a convict in a corridor – how he turned his head away! I asked my warders why he did that. They both blushed. One of them told me afterwards the reason. It isn't etiquette in a prison for convicts to look at a condemned man. Not nice. They think he won't like it, you see.'

Another pause. Mr Crary had not faced Philip again. He was talking quietly, but with slight emphases now and then, to the street, to the glittering piers and the promenade and the motors gliding to and fro in the pleasure town. Philip sat up in his easy-chair and leaned forward and glared intently at Mr Crary's back.

'Well, all that's nothing after all. After he'd been to see me in my cell, the governor sent for me to his office. At night. So I was taken to his office. My warders stayed outside. The governor said to me: "Crary," he said, "sit down and have a cigar." So I did. I was as calm as calm. Then he said: "Crary, I'm not a religious man. I don't know anything about heaven, and I don't know anything about hell. That's the chaplain's business, not mine, and I dare say this last few days you've had to listen to all you wanted in that line," he said. "But," he said, "you're going to die tomorrow morning. Before you die," he said, "I *should* like to know you're sorry for having killed that man." "Sir," I said, "I'm damned sorry." And so I was. So I am.

'When I got back to my cell they lighted the lamp outside that shines through the little window into the cell. No other light. I might have written things on the slate that they give you. But I didn't. Didn't want to do anything. One of my warders asked me to play draughts, and I did, just to please him. Then I lay down on the bed without taking off my clothes. The other warder came back. He said: "Aren't you going to undress, Crary?" "No," I said. "I'm not." They didn't say anything to that. I slept all night Next morning when I woke up I said: "What time is it?" They said: "You've got two hours yet. Try to sleep a bit more." But I didn't try. One of the warders went out and came back in a minute or two with a bundle. It was my clothes, my dark-grey suit. I was to be hung in my own clothes. I liked that. But they wouldn't let me put on my collar and necktie. You see.

' "How do you feel?" they asked me. "All right?" "Yes," I said, "all right." Then they brought me my breakfast, which I'd asked for, two poached eggs, and the tea in a can, and the mug. I ate it all. And a cigarette. "Is it raining?" I said. "No," they said, "but it has been." I didn't feel as if anything was real. I felt as if it was a tale – fairy-tale, yes, fairy-tale. Then the prison clock struck. I had another hour yet. Then it was the chaplain in his surplice came in. The warders went out. Don't I remember the keys rattling! When the chaplain had finished the governor came in, and the chief warder and the assistant-executioner and the doctor. Cell was full of people. They gave me some brandy. They were all very nice, and I told 'em so. I didn't ask about Delphine or anything. Then the assistant-executioner fastened my arms. I began to feel queer. But that was nothing to when the chaplain started to say the burial service at me as if I was dead.

'Another thing I forgot to tell you. There were two doors to my cell. One of them had never been opened. It was opened now. We went out in a procession and the chaplain went on with the burial service, and there was the execution shed or whatever they call it, just outside! And the under-sheriff and one or two others were waiting there, and the executioner was waiting for me on the scaffold – he had a red moustache, and I thought he looked terribly ill and queer. So I went up on the scaffold – I tell you I couldn't believe it was true – and the executioner put a bag over my head and I couldn't see, of course. And then there was a thud and I couldn't make out what had happened. I heard the governor's voice, very excited and nervous. He said: "Never mind *him*, never mind *him*! *You* must do it; *you* must do it." And the assistant-executioner said, "No, sir. Not after that I won't do it. Not if it was fifteen hundred pounds instead of fifteen. Not after *that*."

'I only found out afterwards what it was *had* happened. The executioner had had a fit. They took the bag off my head again, and I went back to the cell. And they were all as white as a sheet, every one of them. My sentence was commuted to penal servitude for life. I needn't tell you there's no such thing really as a life-sentence. After about a quarter of a century you're let out. A quarter of a century! *You*, sir, must have been aged about three when my executioner had a fit. All the time you were growing up, governess, school, college, I suppose, fighting, I suppose, falling in love, I suppose, I was in prison, thinking about what mad jealousy leads to. And I'm still thinking about it, and after what I've seen and heard of you tonight I'm thinking about it now more than I have for years. I'm not fifty – '

'Not fifty!' exclaimed Philip in amazement.

'Not fifty. But I've lived through whole centuries. And I haven't told you all yet. I haven't told you the worst part. At the very moment when my executioner had his fit, my innocent Delphine was executed in another prison-yard in London. She hadn't been reprieved. They'd allowed me to deceive myself, for fear I might go mad. Someone actually proposed that the other executioner who had dealt with Delphine should come along the next morning and deal with me. The scheme "fell through" as they say. For one thing the fellow refused. Executioners are very superstitious.

'I've had all that to think over for a quarter of a century. Of course I don't feel it so much now – not nearly so much. I'm numbed. You do get numbed. I go about the world numbed. Nobody knows me. Naturally I don't call myself Crary.' He turned at last sharply to face Philip and said with a sort of explosion: 'If I wasn't numbed I should have smashed this plate-glass window with my fists long before I'd finished telling you my story.'

At this point there was a thud just outside the sun-room, in the lounge. Philip gave an involuntary cry. For an instant he thought it was the executioner in a fit – astounding delusion on his part!

The thud was the noise of the fall of Philip's young wife. Girlishly repenting her resolution to dine alone and leave Philip to recover unaided from his madness, Ethel had quitted the dining-room, crossed silently the silent lounge, and, intimidated and enthralled by the discourse of Mr Crary to the window, had hidden herself behind the wall which separated the sun-room from the easternmost part of the lounge. She had withstood the terror of the recital as long as she could, and then, just after the climax, had faltered and dropped in the arched opening between the rooms. She lay there in an ineffective posture, rather bunched up, with her lovely raiment and jewels all disordered, and her face as dead-white as the faces of the officials at the execution where the criminal was not executed. Mr Crary saw her first and pointed to her. Philip turned in obedience to Mr Crary's searing finger. He sprang from his chair to the archway and knelt beside her, not in the least knowing what to do.

'Let her lie. She'll come round in a minute,' said Mr Crary proudly, with his unmoving lips.

Philip was himself ready to faint under the fearful shocks of Mr Crary's tale with its tremendous moral for the jealous. Mr Crary had put Philip in terror of the possibilities of his own instincts. The husband felt as though he had just escaped a catastrophe for which none but himself could have been blamed, and as though the catastrophe avoided might recur soon or late in the future if he did not watch over himself night and day. He was nearly stunned by the revelation of himself to himself.

And also he was exquisitely and profoundly touched by the yielding compunction of his wife, who, after leaving him to his folly, had out of sheer loving good-nature come back to wheedle and cajole him out of his folly. His passion for his wife flamed up burning white in those moments; it was as overpowering as the passion of Mr Crary for Delphine.

He stroked her cold cheek, marvelling at the fineness of it and at the complex and delicate perfection of the organism which was she. His sensations had the surpassing inexpressible intensity of which people, it is said, sometimes die.

And the empty lounge brooded with its rosy lamps and its flickering fire, indifferent and yet warmly indulgent, upon the group. And outside the gleaming motor-cars glided in curves against the glittering electric back-ground of the promenade and the piers. And through the glass wall of the dining-room waiters, attentive and deferential, could be seen passing to and fro. And there was not a sound.

And Mr Crary contemplated with pride what he had done, the stupendous impression he had made, the mighty lesson he had taught. After a quarter of a century of martyrised subjection Mr Crary had risen suddenly to majesty, to domination, to sovereignty. He had imprinted himself upon his fellow-creatures. He was saved from futility. The sublime horror of his tragedy clothed him. He lived again.

Returning life-blood tinged the young girl's cheeks. Philip kissed them with abandoned and tender violence. His passion was to shield and cherish her, to surround her with protective affection, to exist uniquely in and for her. His passion was by extraordinary deeds of devotion to earn her forgiveness.

'I'm all right,' she murmured feebly.

He picked her up in his arms. Light! Light as down! She had no weight in his arms. He carried her off swiftly towards the lift, the pale wisp of the train of her dress dragging along the carpet. The auburn girl and the yellow girl in their tight-fitting black, caged in the reception office before vast books of account, these saw the pair first and caught their breath. Then the hall-porter, meditating between notices of theatres, trains and charabancs, saw them, and started officiously. He was too late. They were in the lift. The gate banged. The lift shot up, showing through its bars a glimpse of a white skirt against a black coat. It was gone aloft . . .

The doors of the dining-room opened.

'You can say what you like,' the voice of a young woman emerging was heard, breaking the enchantment of the lounge, 'I prefer *crème de menthe* to green chartreuse.'

The Box-Office Girl

I

The Rotunda Royal, as everyone who knows the world knows, lifts its immense mass of yellow masonry (not really masonry but iron thinly faced with stone) right in the middle of London. It is the largest music-hall in London, and the most successful music-hall in London, and it burns more electricity than any other place of amusement in London. Its upper parts are glitteringly outlined in green and yellow electricity; its high tower can be glimpsed from all manner of streets, and the rich glow of the whole affair illuminates a cloudy sky for the whole of central London to see. Though entirely respectable, it has an altar of its own in the hearts of the young and the old bloods of provincial cities who come to town strictly on business. It is the Mecca of suburban inhabitants with a dull afternoon in front of them and ten shillings in their pockets to squander. To have his, or her, name printed in fire on the façade of the Rotunda is the ambition of every music-hall artist in the world, and of many another artist besides. In brief, the Rotunda is a very important, grandiose and impressive organism, an organism which emphatically 'functions'. And it is a household world. Even judges of the High Court have heard of the Rotunda. No daily paper in London ever appears without some mention of it somewhere.

Now daily and nightly behind a counter on your left as you enter by the main entrance into the grand foyer stood, until lately, a girl named Elaine Edar. She was a blonde, with bright hair, an attractive, pretty and benevolent face, and a good figure – because these attributes were essential to her position. Her simple, smart dress was of black, but it had touches of fantasy and of colour – because Mr Walter King (managing director – risen from call-boy, as he openly stated about ten times every day) had said that he did not care for his girls to look like hotel-clerks. Elaine's face and hair were known to tens of thousands of people. Often in the street such people would start at the sight of her and murmur something to a companion, and Elaine knew that they were saying: 'That's the box-office girl at the Rotunda.'

So she had a certain importance on earth, and assuredly at the Rotunda. For she gathered in money, and to Mr Walter King ('Old Wal' behind his back, to his employees, and 'Wally', without concealment, to those proud persons who had the great privilege of his intimacy) – to Mr Walter King the Rotunda was in the end nothing but a machine for gathering in more money than it paid out. Not that Elaine was the sole instrument for gathering in

26

money. Far from it! Above her counter were displayed the words: 'Box-office for this performance only. Boxes. Royal Fauteuils. Royal Stalls. Stalls. Grand Balcony'. All advance booking was done in a special office up the street, and each of the unreserved parts of the house had its own entrance, with turnstile and money-taker. Still, Elaine took a goodish bit of money twice a day, and she was easily the most prominent of all the human machines that received silver coins and notes in exchange for bits of coloured paper or base-metal discs.

Twelve performances a week – and Elaine had to be on duty ten minutes before the doors opened and to remain on duty until one hour before the end of each performance. Then she had to check her money and prove to the cashier's department that the total was correct. An anxious job, especially during the 'rush' quarter of an hour, when she had to read with the glance of an eagle the numbers on the 'sheet' of the performance, treat every patron as a benefactor, return good for evil, give change like a flash of lightning, detect spurious coins in the tenth of a second, and render sweet smiles to louts, curmudgeons and cats! Happily she was by nature profoundly and universally benevolent – and in this respect indeed a wonder to her assistant, who did the telephoning and lent a general hand. It was her benevolent air that had recommended her to Mr Walter King, who had sacked her predecessor for being hoity-toity to patrons whenever business was abnormally good. She was devoted to the theatre. Nobody thought of her apart from the theatre, and in fact she had little private life. Mr Walter King was himself passionately devoted to the theatre, and he expected all the staff to be passionately devoted to the theatre; but whereas his own devotion brought in a large share of the profits, Elaine's devotion brought in only a small fixed salary, which Mr King did not dream of passionately increasing when business grew fabulous. Elaine saw nothing odd in this arrangement.

It was a quarter to ten. The day's work was nearly over. Elaine's assistant had gone. The entrance-hall and foyer blazed, deserted, with their super-lavish electricity. When an idle programme-girl swung open a door at the end of a vast corridor and peeped forth, Elaine could faintly catch the sound of clapping. She rarely got more of a performance than these brief distant rumours of applause. For her the Rotunda was not an auditorium but a foyer with box-office; and the artists were mere names on bills. She estimated the quality of the applause and glanced at the clock and the timetable to know who was being applauded, for she had to be in a position to inform patrons what artist was 'on' at any given moment. Then she proceeded with the secret counting of notes on a shelf beneath the counter. In view of the absence of a grille to protect the counter and of the prevalence of gangs of robbers in London, her situation with all that money for Mr Walter King might seem perilous. But it was not so in reality. Elaine and her treasure were well guarded by formidable giants and astute dwarfs in the shape of gorgeous doormen and pages. Though he disapproved of grilles, Mr Walter King took no chances with the night's receipts. Elaine was as safe as a priestess in a temple, dedicated, imprisoned, inviolate.

Then a dark and elegant young man in full evening panoply appeared from the street. The guardians saluted him. He saluted Elaine. This unidentified and mysterious gentleman came nearly every night towards ten o'clock. Elaine guessed that he came to witness the performance of the Russian dancer, the incomparably illustrious Feodora.

'Did you keep the *fauteuil* for me, Miss Edar?' (He had picked up her name from somewhere, it seemed.)

She nodded, kindly smiling. She liked the regular visitant, not in the least because he was regular, but because he was dark, elegant, slim, and had a sad, wistful smile. Yes, she had kept the stall for him, despite the fact that if he had not come to claim it she would have had to pay for it out of her own pocket. He usually telephoned just before the rush, and Elaine had accepted the risk of his not coming quite a dozen times. Occasionally, as tonight, he would try to get a box, and if successful would pay for both the box and the stall. And he would show amazing indecision. Tonight she had no box to sell; the sole empty seat in the house was the one she had retained for him; and yet in his rich, low voice he would keep talking about a box, and also she had to repeat to him several times precisely where the stall was in regard to the stage.

At length he paid, raised his hat again, and went off towards the auditorium, followed by her benedictory, sympathetic smile. The head-doorman, his pocket gaping for the harvest of sixpences which he would shortly garner for putting patrons into cars and taxis, winked at her rather broadly, as if to indicate that the dark gentleman was queer in the head. But Elaine gently deprecated the wink, seeing in the dark gentleman a victim of hopeless love for a Russian dancer. Silence fell upon the foyer, whose ceiling was upheld by the immobile figures of pink, nude girls.

Elaine had taken out the self-locking steel cash-drawer from its niche, detached and hidden the telephone, and was about to disappear through the little door behind the counter, when Rachel Gordon hurried up rather breathless from somewhere. 'I'm the publicity lady,' Rachel would introduce herself to the new artists in the wings and in dressing-rooms when she wanted material for piquant press-paragraphs. She did all the day-to-day publicity work for the Rotunda. A pretty Jewess, with full lips and eyes, waved hair, striking clothes, carefully tended complexion, and a general air of knowing all that was worth knowing; not quite young, but far from old! She spent every evening in the theatre, and little in it escaped her attention.

'Feo asked me to give you this note,' said she. 'I'm so glad I've caught you before you'd gone.'

She handed the note, with a characteristic, sparkling glance that was full of chicane and the spirit of plotting. 'Feo!' Thus she familiarly referred to the great, the unique Feodora! But then she managed to be very friendly with all, and she could be highly useful even to the greatest.

As Elaine read the note she showed extreme astonishment. It ran: 'My dear Miss Edar, I give a party tomorrow night at the Fantasy Club; some friends, dancing, fun. Will you come? I do hope. Your obliged Feo.' Indeed the thing was enough to astonish a box-office girl. 'Your obliged.' Elaine knew what that referred to. A fortnight earlier, when a not uncommon state of war existed between Feodora and Mr Walter King, Feodora had been unable to get two free seats for friends. She had most particularly wanted those seats, even if it should be necessary to pay for them. But she was too haughty to tell Mr King that she would pay for them, and so she had herself run round (furs and pearls and all – as described by Rachel for the press) to implore Elaine to allot seats to her even though all seats were sold. And Elaine, by methods known to box-office keepers only, had bestowed upon her the two desired seats – and Mr Walter King not a penny the wiser! Feodora, in the generosity of her impulsive, poetic heart, had not forgotten.

'Shall you come?' asked Rachel, who evidently knew what was in the scrawled note.

'I – I haven't a rag to wear,' answered Elaine, much flustered.

'Oh, stuff!' observed Rachel simply. 'You're always awfully well turned out. Everybody knows that.'

'But evening wear –' protested Elaine, despite a secret mistrust of Rachel.

'Oh, stuff!' Rachel repeated.

Elaine could scarcely sleep that night. It was an incredible happening. She rose early to look through her wardrobe.

2

The Fantasy Club, scene of Feodora's party, was in Goodge Street, off Tottenham Court Road. Elaine had never heard of it, and indeed had some difficulty in finding it, since its portal was hidden at the end of a long covered passage and showed no signs of festivity. No wonder the conductor of the motor-bus by which she travelled could give her no information about it! In the lobby she saw a printed notice: 'Breakfasts served from 4 a.m.' This frightened her, but she was re-assured by the sight of Rachel Gordon in the cloakroom.

Rachel gave the names of sundry high-brow novelists and painters and musicians who regularly frequented the club, and she said that in the art of turning night into day they were the greatest experts in London. Rachel laughed at the nocturnal pretensions of the more famous dancing-clubs – she scorned them as 'bourgeois'. Anyone could join them, but according to Rachel not anyone could join the Fantasy. You had to be someone or the approved friend of someone to be admitted to the Fantasy.

The dancing-room was large, low and very bare – compared to the ornate interiors of the Rotunda. It had no decorations except electric lights in Chinese lanterns, and the costumes of the ladies. These decorations, however, were extremely effective. The room was full; it was also noisy and torrid. Revellers were eating, drinking, dancing, chattering, laughing and giggling, with much gusto.

'There's Feo's table,' said Rachel, pointing to the biggest and busiest table in the place, and led Elaine towards it. Elaine was nervous.

'How sweet of you!' the slim and gorgeous Feo greeted her. 'How sweet you look! No! It is more than sweet. I understand now when Carly does say how you are *exotique*. It is so. Yes. Sit down. Have drink? Have chicken? Or soup? Yes. Soup first. Rachel, occupy yourself with Miss Edar.' Feodora turned to two young men, who kissed her hand.

Elaine listened eagerly to the confused talk at the table, but, though all laughed or giggled, she heard nothing that struck her as amusing. No doubt the humour was being accomplished in French or Russian, of which languages Elaine had no knowledge. However, all the ladies looked either lovely or strange. She was still very shy, but she was mysteriously happy too – somehow uplifted.

'Who is Carly?' she murmured to Rachel, and Rachel by a discreet turn of the head indicated a young man who stood behind Feodora against the wall. Elaine started and flushed. It was the nightly visitant for whom she reserved stalls. The word 'exotic' in the tiny mouth of Feodora had already exercised Elaine, who could not comprehend how anybody could regard her as deserving of such an adjective. That the nightly visitant should deem her exotic, and should have said so to a high goddess like Feodora, almost disturbed her – while enchanting her! Rachel beckoned to the nightly visitant, who approached.

'Mr Lyeskov,' said Rachel. 'Miss Edar. I think you have met.'

She laughed. Mr Lyeskov blushed.

The next moment Elaine became aware that her hand had been kissed. A unique experience. Hand-kissing was of course 'foreign' and somewhat foolish, but it was surprisingly delicious, even flattering. So this was the young man who, while paying for stalls from which to worship Feodora, had found time to examine herself and to decide that she was exotic. Yes, disturbing! Disturbing!

He now asked her to dance. Could she refuse? How ridiculous! Unfortunately in the dance she could not think of a single thing to say to him. He was a fine dancer, but scarcely cleverer as a talker than Elaine. They just danced, yielded themselves to the music and the movement. It was exquisite.

'You are a natural dancer. You have the gift,' he remarked.

She smiled. She knew that she was a natural dancer. She had no more learnt to dance than she had learnt to breathe; she rarely danced – and only in suburban resorts with one or two dull acquaintances; yet she knew all the steps and never erred, never hesitated. They danced two consecutive dances. As he restored her to the table he asked if he might dance again with her very soon. Feodora called to him.

'How did you get on?' Rachel demanded of Elaine, with a peculiar glance.

'Oh, splendid! He's asked me for another dance.'

'And did you refuse?'

'Ought I?'

'Don't be silly. Can't you see he's mad about you? Why do you suppose he comes to get tickets off you every night? Why do you suppose he got Feo to ask you here tonight? And let me tell you – he may be a French-Russian, but he's very serious and very rich. *He* didn't lose anything in the Revolution, he didn't! Pity he's so shy, isn't it?'

Elaine's face burned again. The fact is, she was overwhelmed, absolutely overwhelmed, as she realised bit by bit that 'Carly' came nightly to the Rotunda not to worship Feodora but to worship her! It was staggering! She was glad when a male performer in Feodora's troupe invited her on to the floor. She did not care for his face nor for his coarse manners, nor yet for his dancing – how different from Carly's! – but he enabled her to escape from Rachel Gordon's enigmatic scrutiny. As she went round the room with the professional dancer something happened to her and she half stumbled and turned wholly pale. It was a night of sensations, blushes and pallors, such a night as she had never before known. The dancer looked at his faltering partner enquiringly, but said no word, and Elaine recovered herself. No one knew, no one could guess, what had happened to her. And after all it was naught. She had only caught sight of Ned seated at a table with another man, and he had seemed to be somewhat unprosperous and defiant, in his shabby evening-dress. And he looked older, thinner, worn.

Ned was the one man who had entered into that private life of hers, the existence of which none of the patrons of the Rotunda could visualise. It was six years ago, when she was twenty-one, and before her connection with the life of music-halls. Ned was an advertising-agent and lots of things beside – he had had a hand in promoting one or two of the earlier dance clubs. He was up one month and down the next. He had defects, but he had made love to her, proposed to her, been accepted. She gave him all her heart; she learnt rapturously to love love. The world became magical. The date of the wedding was fixed. Then Ned came one day and said that candour was best, and that the sole manly course was to confess to her. What? What? That he had mistaken his feelings. That he had found that he did not care for her 'in that way'. Whereas he did care for Alice 'in that way' and Alice cared for him 'in that way'. That of course he was hers to command, but would it not be better for her sake and for the sake of them all, if she . . . ? He was extremely sorry. He did not and could not defend himself . . . Alice was a friend of hers, had but a few months before been congratulating her on her betrothal to nice Ned. Ned married Alice. And so that was that. Elaine's tragic grief softened gradually into vague regret, and vague regret changed into a vague feeling that perhaps she had done well to lose Ned. Such stories lie buried in the memory of numberless girls who go through life apparently as though butter had never melted in their mouths. And you dig up the stories with difficulty, with amazement . . .

Well, she had caught sight of Ned Haltright.

The next minute his table was empty. She hoped he had not seen her, and could not help thinking that he had. Undoubtedly she had had a shock. But when, after powdering herself anew and drinking some champagne, she put her hand once again in the hand of Carly Lyeskov, and felt his right hand lightly on her back, and resumed the dance with him, the effects of the shock soon disappeared. She glimpsed herself in a mirror and was satisfied with the vision. Idle to deny that she was pretty, had a good figure, or that her frock was not smart! She was as presentable as most, and more so than a lot of them, though her only trinket was a necklace of Chinese-dyed mother-of-pearl. Carly's worship of her blossomed like a flower. It was heavenly to be worshipped, to be able to confer a favour by merely consenting to exist. She had a sense of dominion which intoxicated. And then there was the band, the colours, the movement, the feeling of being surrounded by illustrious and witty artists – she wondered who was who! And Carly was so distinguished. His very shirt-front was a miracle. And he was so deferential.

'May I ask where you live?'

She told him Fulham.

'I suppose you would not let me drive you home in my car?'

Yes, she would – he was really too kind! Romance ! Romance! Soon she was thinking that Carly was unique in the whole world – so sympathetic he was! And he worshipped her. He had gone off his head about her. Triumph! Power! Dizziness! It was silently established between them that they would dance every dance together. And they did. The Fantasy faded to a dim background for their emotions. And Elaine looked with pity at her past life, at the horrid grind and daily work, at her loneliness – because behind her counter she was nearly as lonely as a bus-driver, and at home in her rooms she was terribly lonely. How had she supported it? Could she possibly continue to support it?

At three o'clock, when the gaiety was at its apogee she said she thought she must go home. Not that she wanted to go home or had any reason for going home. She wanted simply to command him and to prove to the entire Fantasy Club that he was hers to command. She took leave of Feodora, who poured over her a delicious cascade of protests. And Carly did drive her to Fulham – Parson's Green it was. No little 'liberties' in the large, smooth-gliding car, such as are expected and condoned by the primmest maidens after such ecstasies, in such circumstances, at such an hour! Nothing but the deepest respect! Yes, he was 'serious . . .' She leaned forward suddenly and tapped on the window. The car stopped. Mr Lyeskov sprang to the pavement, handed her out, removed his hat, kissed her hand, and was richly rewarded by her smile under the lamp-post. He waited until she had found her latchkey and opened her door. Of course It was a poor little suburban house. But she knew that that didn't matter. It was where she lived. Her presence in it transformed it for him. Another smile from her; another bow from him. She shut the door. The car drove off.

3

Elaine went to bed in a state of ecstatic, blissful excitement. No sooner had she laid herself down than she heard the prolonged trill of the front-door bell in the back-room. She occupied the two rooms which constituted the third or top-floor of the old house. (In earlier days she had had only one room, but destiny had been fairly kind to her.) The front-room was a sort of bed-sitting-room; the back was a kitchen-scullery-dining-room. The floor was her home and held all that she possessed. Compared to many young and ageing women in her situation of life she was affluent and of luxurious habit. Now there were four bells on the front-door, each labelled. Sometimes, and especially at night, visitors got confused and rang the wrong bell. Elaine thought that on this occasion the wrong bell had been rung.

'They'll have to keep on ringing,' she said. After all, the bell did not make a great deal of noise. The bell continued to ring.

'Nobody can possibly be wanting me at this time of night,' she said.

Nevertheless she put on her dressing-gown and opened the window and looked forth and down. But she could not see who was ringing because of the wide, leaded eave of the old-fashioned porch. She shut the window and shut out the invading chill of the dark night. At length the persistent bell began to exasperate her fatigued nerves, and with an annoyed, apprehensive shrug, she crept step by creaking step all the way downstairs and softly undid the front-door.

Ned Haltrlght was standing in the porch. She gave a start, and instinctively drew the thin peignoir more tightly round her shoulders. As she did so, she stiffened, looking at him. She was affronted, angered, by this inexcusable visitation. Nothing but sheer good-nature prevented her from shutting the door in Ned's face.

'I saw you at the club – ' he commenced.

'Not so loud, *please!*' She stopped him in a sharp whisper, thinking of her immaculate reputation in the crowded house that so often buzzed with gossip. To have come home at God knows what hour in a car was bad enough, but to receive male callers still later . . . !

'I want to see you. I must talk to you,' Ned whispered plaintively.

'Not now,' she whispered.

'Yes, now.'

She shook her head firmly.

'Fancy coming here now!' she whispered, in still colder reproof. 'And how on earth did you get here, at this time?'

'Walked,' he whispered.

'Walked?' she whispered.

'Yes.'

He must certainly have walked over six miles. The whispering seemed to render them intimate in spite of her aggrieved attitude towards him. It struck her as strange and affecting that she had once been his affianced sweetheart, that they used to kiss each other with long kisses, and that now they were nothing to each other . . . She made a sign for him to enter. She very gently and cautiously closed the door.

'I'm on the top-floor now,' she murmured, scarcely audible.

He nodded. The fanlight over the door let through the ray of the street-lamp, so that the first flight of stairs was fairly plain. The higher flights were dark. But Ned knew the staircase. Ned followed her on tiptoe, and every now and then a stair creaked with a thunderous sound that no prudence of tread could avoid. Elaine had the horrid illusion that behind every door as they passed it women with slanderous tongues were greedily listening.

At the summit of the perilous climb she led him into the kitchen-scullery-dining-room, and found the matches, lit the gas, lit the gas-stove. She put her fingers to her lips. They must still exist and communicate without sound. No sound-proof floors in that house! She motioned him to the wicker easy-chair. He sank into it. She looked at him and looked round the room. Happily it was very tidy and cosy. He was pale, pathetic, with his pointed, exhausted, weak-charactered features. He wore a blue Burberry, strapped close at the waist and bulging out above and below over his evening clothes. In his hand he held an ordinary bowler hat. No style! What a contrast with Mr Lyeskov! He had the air of defeat, even of being a prisoner-of-war. And he had walked more than six miles in his madness. Without a word she turned away, lit the gas-ring, and began to make some tea. She had to do it from simple humanity. And there she was with him, sharing surreptitiously the room with him, in nightdress, peignoir and slippers. And their tender intimacy emerged towards them out of the past, indestructible. Somehow, what had been still was. How could she treat him as a stranger? She could not. Moreover, she felt far superior to him in moral force; she felt, despite her resentment, almost protective in a casual condescending way. She had the adoration of Carly Lyeskov at her back.

'Well?' she whispered.

Ned gazed at the rug under his feet. Silence. Hiss of the gas-stove; hiss of the gas-ring; fizzing of the blue-yellow gas-jet within its mantle.

'Well, how's Alice?' she whisperingly questioned, in a rather indifferent, half-quizzing tone, as if saying: 'Well, you got your Alice. How does it work now you've had her six years?'

He whispered solemnly: 'Poor Alice died two years ago, and the baby's two years old. Hadn't you heard?'

She shook her head. She could not speak; her throat was suddenly constricted; tears glittered in her eyes. At length: 'I'm sorry to hear it.' How poor the words! Then after a pause, while Ned stared at the inside of his hat: 'Is it a girl or a boy?'

'A girl.'

'What have you called her?'

'Alice.'

'And how do you manage about the poor little thing?'

'Ah! That's the trouble. How *do* I manage?' He looked up suddenly, and he was crying.

'Ellie' – nobody else had ever called her 'Ellie' – 'Ellie, I made a frightful mistake when I broke it off with you, and I've known it for years. And then when I saw you tonight . . . It was too much for me. Yes. I had to talk to you.' His whispered utterance was so obscure and feeble that she had to guess what he said; but she guessed right. The water boiled. She turned from him again to fill the teapot.

How weak he was! So impulsive! But so enterprising, too! Full of initiative as usual! He had had the wild idea of coming to her and he had come. He had arrived. He had wanted to talk to her, and he was talking to her.

'And how's business?' she asked, extinguishing the gas-ring. She was bound to say something – and something ordinary, banal, off the point.

'Oh, pretty fair,' he whispered. 'Not bad. Changeable, of course. But you rub along, you know.'

She was confirmed in her notion that he was out of luck. He drank the hot tea, which seemed to revive him – he was a man easy to revive and easy to deject. She took some tea herself. As an afterthought she cut some bread-and-butter; she gave him a slice with her hand, as there was no plate save the wooden bread-platter. He ate it savagely, and several more slices. The scene was domestic. The night, the enforced whispering, his trouble, her peignoir, the informality of the little meal, made it domestic. She stood near the fire in order to keep warm in her thin raiment.

'Ellie,' he said, rising vivaciously to put his cup and saucer on the table, and standing near to her, 'I've always been in love with you. I know there's no excuse for me. I didn't treat you right. But there it is. And when I saw you tonight – ' He had raised his voice.

'Hsh!' she warned him.

She spoke gently, keeping resentment out of her voice, partly because she was flattered by the realisation of her power over him (and she had the same power over Carly Lyeskov), and partly because he was so wistful and she pitied him in his unhappiness. Nevertheless in her heart she was indignant. And she thought of her independence, of the stability of her position as a self-maintained woman beholden to none. She did not see Elaine Edar abandoning her independent situation for the status of the wife of a Ned Haltright, asking a Ned Haltright for money when she needed it, considering his wishes in regard to her own conduct, sacrificing herself to the baby of the girl who had supplanted her, sharing the material vicissitudes which must inevitably result from his character. He might love her, admire her, but that could not compensate. Moreover the whole idea was absurd, monstrous. His suggestion amounted to effrontery. And Carly Lyeskov existed and worshipped. However, she offered no reasoned reply. Her daily traffic with all sorts of human beings had taught her when to argue and when not to argue.

'Please don't say any more,' she murmured firmly. 'You can't burst out like this.'

'But I've had it on my mind for years, I tell you.'

'Please don't say any more.'

He seemed to wither.

'I'll go. Better go. Sorry I spoke.'

The wicker easy-chair, empty, complained with creakings of the burden which it had had to bear. The dawn began delicately to announce itself in silver-grey gleams through the interstice between the curtains of the window.

'You mustn't go yet,' Elaine whispered.

'Why not?'

'Because it's getting light, and the people on the first floor will be about, and I can't have a man, especially in evening-dress, leaving my rooms at this time. Besides, there's no buses or trams yet. You must wait till everyone's up and people have begun to go up and downstairs, and you must cover up your shirt-front properly. Then you can slip out.' She whispered soberly, with the sagacity of a young woman who has learnt her world. She added: 'I shall lie down. I'm frightfully tired, and you must be too. Try to sleep in the chair.' She left him for the front-room, and locked the door, and dropped on to her bed. She was indeed exhausted, but she could not sleep. Her eyes burned. She reflected that dancers were still dancing at the Fantasy. Then she slept.

4

When she woke the alarm-clock (which never alarmed) showed the hour of ten. The memory of the night gradually re-established itself in her mind. How fortunate that her charwoman came only at eleven-thirty! She thought gladly: 'Yesterday it was the day after tomorrow that I was to see Carly. Now it is tomorrow. Tea at the Regent Palace at five.' It was she who had chosen the Regent Palace. She arose, washed, dressed deliberately, gave particular attention to the toilette of her face. Cautiously she unlocked her door and cautiously went into the back-room. Ned was fast asleep, in a twisted, uncomfortable posture in the wicker-chair. His pallid face had the pathos of a corpse. He appeared tragically defenceless, so much so that she could have cried at the sight of him and at the thought of his weaknesses, his perils, his incompetency to deal with the responsibilities attached to little Alice the baby. Much gas had been burned, but she did not care. She drew the curtains back and the entire room became pathetic – the tea-cups, the teapot, crumbs on the floor. The image of Carly Lyeskov was obscured in her soul. She turned off the gas-jet. Ned awoke with a jump.

'You're all dressed. Shall I go now?'

'Where's little Alice?'

'She's with some people in Canonbury.'

'Who are they? Relations?'

'No. Not relations. I'm not strong in relations. *You* know that. I think they're very decent people. She seems to be pretty well looked after.'

'Oh, Ned! You must give me the address. I'll go and see her tomorrow morning. I'll have a look at things a bit.'

The images of Carly Lyeskov, automobiles, luxury, distinction, worship, adoration, passion, eternal romance, began to slip away from her. She clutched at them, drew them back, held them fast, hugged them, but the next moment they were wriggling away again like eels.

'Oh, Ellie! There's nobody like you, and there never was. You're an angel and nothing else.'

She wept. She let the tears fall – drop, drop; they slipped down her cheeks and fell into space. Perhaps she was sorry as much for herself as for little Alice and little Alice's father. She saw vistas of effort, struggle, reverses, obstinate recommencings, narrownesses, dependence, despairs, fluttering hopes, quarrels, reconciliations, disillusions and illusions. People would cease to stare at her in the streets of the West End because she would never be in the West End. She would be withdrawn from the vast world of pleasure and excitement and electricity, where tinted statues of nymphs supported heavily carved ceilings on their frail shoulders. Yet an immense peace took possession of her disturbed soul and stilled it.

'This is my fate,' she thought. 'I was born for it. I wasn't really born for the other thing.'

The immense peace in her was warmed and lighted with tenderness, and by the memory of far-off kisses. It was a strange sort of happiness, austere, purposeful, braced; but she was happy. She smiled kindly. Ned advanced towards her. She lifted her chin and stopped him. Did he suppose that things were as simple as all that, that the virgin fortress would yield like that at the first summons of the trumpet? Her smile changed to a look of self-possession and extreme gravity.

'Meet me this afternoon for tea at the Regent Palace, will you?' she said. 'After the matinée. Then you can tell me just how matters stand.'

And Carly Lyeskov went back to his Paris.

The Umbrella

I

Although the village of Slipcup was larger and more opulent and more beautiful than he had gathered from his sister's rare letters, although it had a quite imposing bank and a cinema (open one night a week – *this* night), although its railway station was a junction, with three platforms and four tracks, Mr Arthur Malpatent felt as he passed up the steep main road as if he was passing out of the world, his world, into something unknown, strange, queerly romantic.

He was a man of fifty or so, grey, thin, lively, with a mobile and highly expressive face, elastic lips, vague eyes. He talked confidentially to himself and smiled to himself, now and then flourishing his umbrella. Anybody with any knowledge of the physiognomy of professions would have seen at once that he was an actor – who dreamed when he was not acting. He was neatly dressed in a lounge suit to match his ample hair, and wore buttoned boots, a grey wideawake hat, and a club necktie carelessly knotted.

It was a beautiful warm evening, and at half-past nine night had not yet fallen. Mr Malpatent had enquired the way to 'The Weald', his sister's house. He had to continue up the main road and then take the second on the left. He did so. If the main road was steep, the by-road was steeper, with a bad surface for frail buttoned boots. He saw two low bungalows (semi-detached) and then he saw a house, and an inscription on its open garden-gate named it The Weald. It was the last house, the highest house, and it stood in its own garden on the moor. (The moor, however, was pleasingly covered with shrubs and small trees.) Mr Malpatent mounted the steep slope of the small front-garden and rang his sister's bell. He then turned round to view the scene from the doorstep, and saw a marvellous panorama of the distant estuary.

'Charming! Charming!' he ejaculated. 'But in winter it must be deuced bleak up here.'

So this was the abode, and this the situation, which Muriel had chosen for herself! Here she lived with one servant. Her letters had announced that her neighbours were without exception very odd people, but Mr Malpatent thought that few of them could be odder than his queer, beloved Muriel. The door did not open. No sound within the house. Mr Malpatent rang again. He rang thrice. Still no answer.

'Yes,' he reflected, impartially. 'It might have been better to warn her.

Still, what does it matter, after all? Man's life's a vapour. One is here today and gone tomorrow.'

An immense, semi-clouded moon was approaching him over the summit of the hill. Indeed, all was romantic. Accidentally he pressed with his back against the door and it opened.

'Tut-tut!'

He saw the dim hall of Muriel's house.

'Anybody about?' he cried. No response. 'Have I the right to enter my sister's house merely because it is my sister's?' he asked, and answered the question by entering, and clinched it by shutting the door. 'Why not?' said he. 'We have always been on the very best of terms. But how astonishingly careless timid women are!' He cried once more, 'Anybody about?' His voice resounded in a sinister manner. No response. 'Well!' he said, and walked first into the drawing-room on the left, and second into the dining-room on the right.

Nice rooms; full – too full – of old furniture, engravings, knick-knacks; some of which he recognised with a gentle thrill. Yes, Muriel evidently knew how to make herself comfortable. He came back into the hall. The stairs invited him.

'Well!' And he went up the stairs, into the even more unknown. 'Perhaps the poor dear is in bed and asleep,' he said.

Four doors on the landing at the top of the stairs, all shut, all as it were hiding secrets! He knocked at one of the doors and opened it and peeped in. A bedroom, empty. This happened twice. The two rooms were swathed in dust-sheets.

'She can put me up handsomely,' said Mr Malpatent.

The third door was locked. Mr Malpatent's skin crept.

The fourth door proved to be the door of the largest and richest bedroom – crammed with a miscellany of furniture. Empty, but the state of the dressing-table indicated use!

'I am alone in this house,' said Mr Malpatent, impressed, and he invaded the room boldly.

From one of the windows he could see the large back-garden. It was much better tended than the small front-garden, whose drive, indeed, showed a deplorable array of weeds. But the back-garden was as deserted as the front-garden and as the house. Turning again into the room, he noticed, to his astonishment, a telephone by the bedside.

'Telephones out on the moor!' he murmured. 'The world does revolve after all. But what does Muriel want with a telephone?'

Of course, he did not know that his sister had inherited the instrument from a previous tenant, and that she had kept it on account of its con-venience for giving orders to the chief village tradesmen.

'Well,' said he, brightly, to the room. 'If my darling sister thinks I'm going to wait here all night for her the chit is mistaken.'

He had not yet been in the house for more than a quarter of an hour; but he was an impatient man, if genial and kindly. He dropped his umbrella on the floor by the bed and picked up the telephone-receiver.

'Please give me the station,' he said, sitting carelessly on the bed.

The exchange asked him whether he wanted the police station or the railway station.

'The railway station.'

'What railway station?' the exchange demanded.

'Slipcup, naturally.'

It did not occur to him that the exchange was situated in a big seaside town five miles off and had at least a dozen railway stations on its list of subscribers.

When he got Slipcup Junction he blandly enquired: 'Have you any trains tonight?'

'Where for, sir?'

'Oh, anywhere. Doesn't matter.'

He was like that. He learnt that in twenty-five minutes there was a train whose chief destination was Bristol.

'Oh, Bristol!' said he. 'Very well, then. I'll go to Bristol. I've never been there, but I think Bristol will do quite nicely, thank you. I left my luggage with the head-porter in the porters' room.' (Slipcup, though a junction, was rural and informal and had no left-luggage office.) 'Will you please ask him to get it out on to the platform ready for me?'

'What name, sir?'

'Malpatent. Professor Malpatent. It's all labelled.'

The student of the physiognomy of professions would have been wrong in putting him down as an actor. He merely resembled an actor. He was a professor of mathematics in the University of Leeds. There is, however, a marked similarity between the appearance of actors and the appearance of professors who have abandoned themselves utterly and passionately to mathematics.

In five minutes he had departed from his sister's house. He might have encountered Muriel in the road, in which case he would have returned with her, and probably sent down to the station for his luggage. But as he did not happen to meet her, he allowed her to fade out of his mind. He was extremely casual. Finding himself on the coast not many miles from Slipcup, he had had, suddenly and unexpectedly, the idea of paying a visit to his sister. A charming and brotherly idea! She was not at home. He dropped the idea, forgot it completely; and it was as though it had never been! He was like that.

Not till well on the way to Bristol did he observe that he had left his umbrella behind at The Weald. Regrettable, perhaps; but what did it matter? He could do without an umbrella. He had the temperament which makes for happiness.

The next morning, which was a marvellously beautiful morning, a slim and somewhat elegant lady, dressed entirely in white and dangling a pair of white gloves, might have been seen issuing from the front-door of The Weald. This was Miss Malpatent. Even in Bond Street, or on a Sunday forenoon in Hyde Park, she would have passed as being quite presentable. As a fact, she made a point of being presentable – even to powder and rouge (though these aids rather clouded her reputation in Slipcup). But she did so in order to disprove the detestable masculine theory that women only dress 'for' men.

A quarter of a century earlier Miss Malpatent had been jilted by a rake with whom she had most foolishly permitted herself to fall passionately in love. From that moment all men, except possibly her brother – whom she rarely saw – were alike to Miss Malpatent. At first she hated them; then she loftily pitied them; but she never distinguished between them. She was delighted when a strange man glanced at her with admiration. All admiration is good, and doubtless Miss Malpatent liked to be admired, but what she liked far more was the opportunity to return the admiring glance with a glance of cold contempt.

She was fifty, and despite grey hair did not nearly look it, because she had retained her figure, and because the charm of her pretty face depended not on complexion but on the excellent shape of its bones and the sparkling beauty of the eyes. She had a secret dread – common to all slim women – the dread of getting too thin; and she was always trying to achieve plumpness and never succeeding. She envied her servant Annie, who was a big, bouncing wench of forty or so. Annie looked older than her mistress, but she possessed what was for Miss Malpatent the incomparable charm of magnitude. There is a moral lesson to be drawn here.

Annie was cleaning the drawing-room window as Miss Malpatent issued forth on to the weed-encumbered gravel.

'I shan't be long, Annie,' said Miss Malpatent, with the sweetest, most sisterly smile, as of a pearl of mistresses to a pearl of servants. 'I'm only going down to see about the weedkiller.'

Annie nodded. An ideal relationship, you would have said, between those two women who lived their solitary lives in appreciative amity together at The Weald.

Miss Malpatent stopped outside the first of the two semi-detached bungalows. A Mrs Pastow lived in the first one and a Mr Pastow lived in the second one. They were man and wife, and they were friends, yet they lived in separate houses! Slipcup, however, as Miss Malpatent always maintained, was inhabited by odd people. Mrs Pastow, gloved and aproned, was polishing the brass of the front-door. She was a downright lady, who had no shame. Her husband kept a servant, but she didn't – and didn't want one – and her bungalow was assuredly the cleaner and neater of the twain.

'Can I come in?' asked Miss Malpatent, deliciously, if abruptly.

Now Mrs Pastow in her downright way objected to morning callers. She held that friendship and nearness and the general simplicity of village life could in no wise justify informality of intercourse, and especially the informality of morning calls – save for very pressing reasons. She knew that Miss Malpatent shared this view with her. Hence she divined at once that Miss Malpatent had something urgent on her mind.

'Come right in, Muriel,' said she, heartily, and removed her thick gloves.

Her robust common sense, her time, and her knowledge of human nature were always at the disposal of her friends when her friends needed them, though she was apt to be curt with those who made merely frivolous demands on her sound qualities and her leisure.

'Here, sit here,' she said, picking up a book that lay on an easy-chair. 'I'm halfway through the second volume of *Orley Farm*. I couldn't help reading a bit this morning in the middle of my work. I shall beat you if you don't buck up.'

Both of them were fervent admirers and students of Anthony Trollope. Indeed, they read little else, and were rather scornful of the Brontë and Jane Austen sects in the district.

'Now I can see you're a bit upset.'

Thus did Mrs Pastow enjoin Muriel Malpatent to begin the recital of her woe. Twelve years younger than the spinster, she nevertheless treated her as a niece. Both women sat.

'Am I upset?' Muriel's tone was a little weak, uncertain. She knew that it was useless to try any pretences with Mrs Pastow. 'Well, it's about Annie.'

'O–oh! The model maid! She's not taken to drink, has she? I always said she would, remember. Here! I shall take my apron off too.' Mrs Pastow took her apron off and put it under her chair.

'Oh, no! It's worse than that.'

'Worse than drink? No, it isn't. Because there's nothing worse, my dear.'

Muriel Malpatent shook her head and smiled sadly. 'That girl,' said she, 'was determined to get me out of the house last night. It was cinema night, you know. She went last week and saw something called *Daughters of the Storm*, and liked it. And it was such a success last week they brought it again yesterday, and the girl would have me go to it. Never was anything so beautiful, and so on and so on! She knows quite well I don't care for films. However, she was so insistent that I said I'd go. I didn't want to hurt her feelings. Anyhow, she got me out of the house. But I didn't go to the film after all. It was such a lovely evening I walked over the hill instead, right down into Mersington. When I came home her ladyship was in bed – at least, she was in her room and no light burning. But do you know what I found in *my* bedroom?'

'No. What?'

'I found a man's umbrella! Yes, my dear! A man's umbrella in my bed-room!' Miss Malpatent's voice shook as she announced the outrage. 'And what's more, it was lying by the side of my bed. She must have had a man in the house. Of course, I saw at once then why she'd been so anxious to get me out of the house. She'd arranged a rendezvous.'

'But are you sure?'

'Well, the umbrella couldn't have walked upstairs by itself, could it?'

'But why in your bedroom?'

'My *dear*! The telephone, of course. He'd wanted to use the telephone. I do wish I'd had that telephone moved long ago, as I said I would. It's frightfully inconvenient. And I'll tell you something else. The umbrella is a very good umbrella. Which seems to me to prove either that Annie's carrying on with some rake above her own class, or, if he's of her own class, he's a thief and stole the umbrella . . . Well, what do you make of it?'

'I don't know what to make of it. Have you tackled her about it?'

'Indeed I haven't tackled her about it! It was for her to speak. I simply put the umbrella on a chair and left it there. I needn't tell you I had very little sleep. A man being in my bedroom and using my telephone and probably sitting on my bed! When she came in with the tea this morning, naturally she saw the umbrella. You should have seen the start she gave – though she tried to cover it as well as she could. She blushed. And I felt so queer and nervous I'm afraid I blushed too. Still, I said nothing. I was most sweet to her, as I always am. I gave her every chance to make some explanation. But did she? Not a word! She knows she's in a hole and there's no escape – all through her gentleman forgetting his umbrella – and yet she doesn't say anything! Talk about an ostrich. She didn't even ask me how I liked the film. Yesterday afternoon she was all film, film. This morning not a syllable about the film! Can you conceive it, my dear? That woman has always pretended she's got no use for men – silly thing that she is! One would have thought she had a positive sex-complex against men! And I believe she had, too! But not now! Now she's carrying on. I've treated her more like a friend than a servant – '

'That's always a mistake.'

'I know! I know!' cried Miss Malpatent, admitting guilt. 'But I have. And this is how she rewards me! But I've noticed several little things lately. In her work. Forgetful. A bit capricious. Careless. I understand now! Instead of getting on with her work she was thinking about the owner of the umbrella. Of course, she'll have to go. I couldn't possibly keep her. She was *perfect*, that woman was! So devoted, so thoughtful. *And* punctual.'

'There's no such thing as a perfect servant, and I've always said so,' put in Mrs Pastow. 'Where's the umbrella now?'

'It's where I put it – on the chair. But she's done the room. Oh, yes, if you please, she's done the room and left the umbrella where it was. Can you imagine it? The brazenness! I don't know what to do, I really don't.'

'I know what I should do,' said Mrs Pastow, with characteristic robust decisiveness.

'What?'

'I should tackle her about it. I should have it out with her, and at once.'

'Never!' Miss Malpatent protested. 'It's her place to speak. She knows all about the umbrella and she owes me an explanation.'

'Well, she does. I admit that. But supposing she doesn't give you the explanation? Supposing she lets it drag on? You know what servants are.'

'I was wondering whether – '

'What?'

'Whether Amelia mightn't know something.'

The ancient Amelia was Mr Pastow's servant, in the adjoining bungalow.

'Oh, I never talk to Amelia more than's necessary,' said Mrs Pastow, curtly.

'But she talks to Mr Pastow, doesn't she? I know he's often made me laugh repeating the things she says to him.'

'Well, Charlie's coming in for lunch today. When he gets so sick of Amelia's cooking he can't stand it any longer, then he asks me to ask him to lunch. I'll see whether he's heard anything, if you like. Not that I'd trust anything Amelia says!'

'No, of course not.'

'It's very trying for you, my dear,' said Mrs Pastow, kindly, as Miss Malpatent rose to leave. 'But I'm sure I'm right. You ought to tackle her straight.'

Miss Malpatent sadly shook her head. You would have thought that she was broken by misfortune. Nevertheless, she held herself proudly enough as she passed down the road towards the village. And when she returned to The Weald her charming manner to Annie was absolutely faultless – so faultless that umbrellas might never have been invented. But Annie, for her part, was startlingly and disconcertingly glum – to the point of rudeness. It was a hard world for mistresses.

3

Mr Pastow came to his wife's lunch in a particularly jolly mood. He was a stoutish man of forty-two, with a reddish, rural face; brown beard and moustache; fairly robust voice; country clothes. He was not always jolly; on the contrary, like many fat men, he was addicted to moods of grave depression, when his conscience or something of the sort got hold of him and worried him. It was in such moods that his wife preferred him; when he was jolly she was apt to be a bit sardonic, and he never knew why; she never told him, being well aware that it advantages a woman to practise mystery with a man. There were only two things in him to which she objected; his beard and his irresponsibility. As to his beard, he clung to it because it saved the terrible daily task of shaving. He had held the chair of psychology in University College; but when he inherited some solid money he gave up the chair, saying that he could conceive no reason why he should work when he need not. He still published pamphlets and small books on his own subject; his wife smiled indulgently at them and asserted that the worst novel of Anthony Trollope's was a better textbook of psychology than any that any lecturer on psychology ever issued.

The twin-bungalow arrangement was one of the fruits of his irresponsibility. Looking for houses, they had seen the twin bungalows.

'Let's each have our own home,' he had suggested humorously.

His wife had laughed disdainfully.

'But why not?' he had demanded, defending the sudden, capricious, unconsidered notion.

Whereupon his wife quickly agreed, just to try him. He was entirely ready to enter on the wild experiment. She wondered how far he would let it continue. He had now been letting it continue for four years. To her surprise it suited her at least as well as it suited him. It seemed to combine most of the blessing of marriage with very few of the drawbacks.

They lunched in the kitchen, for reasons of cookery, Mrs Pastow being cook as well as wife on these occasions.

'You'll never believe it, Sally,' he began, as he put the first mouthful of Welsh rabbit into his eager mouth, 'but Muriel's losing her sex-complex.'

'What on earth do you mean, boy?'

'She's getting herself tangled up with some man.'

Mrs Pastow did not believe it, but she was startled and, as always when startled, she grew cautious.

'Oh!' said she, dryly.

'Yes,' said he. 'I've had such a morning as I think I've never had. Muriel's Annie was down confabulating with old Amelia at eight o'clock or soon after, and, of course, I had it all – no, not all, but a lot of it – with my bacon at nine. I should say this must have been the greatest morning, the most dramatic, in the whole history of Slipcup.'

'Oh!'

'Yes. It seems that our dear Miss Malpatent pretended to go to the cinema last night; only she didn't go. We know she didn't go – when I say "we" I mean, as usual, Annie and Amelia – we know she didn't go because the girl that takes the money is a friend of ours, and she swore last night that Miss Malpatent had not been in. Now, the question is: Where was Muriel last evening? Well, we can answer the question. Annie was out; it wasn't her night out, but she went out, as there was nothing to do at home – she went down to the village; that was how she learnt from the cinema girl that Miss Malpatent hadn't been where she set out for. When she came home – it was rather late – she saw Miss Malpatent coming down the hill, from the moor. "Oh!" says Annie to herself, "this is rather odd." And she hid in the hedge until Miss Malpatent had got into the house, because she wasn't sure if Miss Malpatent would quite care for her taking a night off without leave. Then she crept in afterwards – quietly. But Miss Malpatent must have known she'd been out all the evening, and counted on it, because this morning, when Annie took up the tea, she found absolutely convincing, undeniable evidence that there'd been a person of the male sex in Miss Malpatent's bedroom last night. When she saw the evidence she didn't say a word, and Miss Malpatent didn't say a word, but Miss Malpatent blushed, I can tell you, blushed like anything. The theory is that Miss Malpatent, guessing that Annie *would* go out, surreptitiously introduced a man into the house and then got him away and accompanied him over the moor – probably to Mersington.'

'Oh!'

'Yes.'

'And what was the absolutely convincing, undeniable evidence?'

'The fellow forgot his umbrella – left it in the bedroom! The pair had no doubt been up there to use the telephone. Hence I say that Miss Malpatent is losing her sex-complex. I say further that she is somewhat ashamed of losing it. Otherwise, why should she make a secret of her man, why should she pretend to go to the cinema and not go? Why should she blush when Annie catches sight of the male umbrella?'

Silence fell between husband and wife. Mrs Pastow snatched, rather than removed, the empty plates from the table, and threw, rather than placed, the clean plates on the table for the ham and salad.

'My dear,' said Mr Pastow, 'you are strangely moved.'

Mrs Pastow burst out laughing.

'My poor boy,' said she, 'I wonder how you can interest yourself in such ridiculous tittle-tattle. That's all.' And she laughed again.

'It's nothing to laugh at, believe me!' the husband reproved her. 'From all I can gather the excellent Annie regards herself as positively insulted and outraged by what has occurred. After all, she and Muriel have been most beautifully at one in their attitude towards the sex which – which is not theirs. And now the male umbrella! Personally I am delighted at the news. It would be idyllic to see Muriel philandering – perhaps marrying. I should attend her wedding with the utmost satisfaction. I should esteem Muriel's marriage as the greatest lark that ever was or could be.' He smiled thought-fully. 'Ah!' he said, reflectively. 'For fun, for real fun, give me village life every time. For pure diversion, no town is in it with a village.'

'If you want fruit,' said Mrs Pastow, 'it's there on the dresser.'

'Are you leaving me, my dear?'

'I am. I'm going out – now, this instant.'

'But you haven't eaten your delicious ham and salad.'

'No, and I shan't; at any rate, not at *this* meal.'

4

'My dear!' exclaimed Mrs Pastow, when she reached The Weald and found Miss Malpatent walking to and fro somewhat agitatedly in the front-garden. Tears, she noticed, stood in Miss Malpatent's eyes. She had hurried up the hill in order to tell Miss Malpatent without the loss of one moment that some mistake, some misunderstanding, some misapprehension, had occurred on somebody's part, and that assuredly Annie was not guilty of the umbrella. If this mistress and this servant both lacked the ordinary sense to talk plainly to one another, and so clear up a silly and dangerous situation, then Mrs Pastow was determined to talk plainly to each of them for their joint good and their earthly salvation.

'What is it now?' Miss Malpatent demanded curtly, almost rudely, in a broken voice, stifling a hysterical sob.

'I've found out one thing,' answered Mrs Pastow, in a tone intended to tranquillise the disturbed. 'Annie knows no more of the umbrella than you do yourself. She was just as astonished as you were to see it in your bedroom.'

Whereupon Miss Malpatent's glance blazed down destructively upon the robust Mrs Pastow.

'My good woman,' said she, with extraordinary bitterness and resentment and rudeness. 'My good woman, I've no doubt you mean well, but please don't annoy me any more than you can help by such a silly tale. *Of course* Annie knows more about the umbrella than I do. I asked you before and I ask you again: Could the umbrella have walked upstairs – or couldn't it? You don't accuse me of putting it where I found it, I hope?'

'No. Certainly not.'

'Well, then?'

Mrs Pastow was wise enough to know when she was beaten, and so she strategically withdrew with the minimum of loss. She perceived that reason had vacated the throne of Muriel's intelligence. And, therefore, she decided on the spot that she would, and indeed must, postpone any further remarks until reason had returned to its seat. She laughed sadly at human nature as she went back to the bungalow, and the first thing she did on arriving was to snub Mr Pastow.

Later in the afternoon Miss Malpatent, having eaten nothing at lunch, and having recovered some of her self-control, rang for tea, which was brought into the drawing-room by stout Annie in a defiant style.

'Wait one moment, Annie.' Miss Malpatent stopped her at the door as she was going out. 'This milk has turned.' Miss Malpatent's voice was a sugary masterpiece of dissimulation.

'And what if it is turned?' Annie retorted. 'Can I help the weather? There's no pleasing you, miss, and that's all there is to it. Look at the lunch I cooked for you, and you snorting at every dish. I've got my feelings same as other people. And now it's the milk, *if* you please.'

Inflammable matter had at last caught fire and exploded. It was bound to happen.

'I will not permit you or anybody to talk to me in that way,' said Miss Malpatent.

'You mean you'd like me to leave?'

'You must do as you choose, Annie.' Pathetic attempt of Miss Malpatent to be indifferent!

'So I will leave!' said Annie, with excessive heat. 'So I will leave! This is no house for me nowadays, this house isn't. I'll leave now, and you can keep my wages in loo of notice.'

She slammed the door and went upstairs. A moment later Miss Malpatent also went upstairs and came down again bearing the umbrella. In twenty minutes Annie, in all her best clothes, hot, flustered and very warlike, came down in turn. The drawing-room door was open.

'I'm off, miss,' she nearly shouted from the hall. 'I'll send up a man with a barrow for my box.'

'Annie,' said Miss Malpatent, approaching her, 'you'll take away this umbrella,' and she held forth the umbrella.

Both women gazed in horror at the incriminating object, origin of an immense disaster.

'I'll take no umbrella, let alone that one.'

'*You will take away this umbrella,*' Miss Malpatent repeated, with icy and devastating authority.

It was a duel. By sheer force of will Miss Malpatent won. Annie took away the umbrella.

Alone in the house the victor tragically wept.

Now, as she was descending the hill into Slipcup Annie met a gentleman ascending. He had grey hair and was harmoniously clad in grey. His manner of walking was flamboyant. And he was singing to himself. He looked at Annie and then at the umbrella, and then he stopped, and under some strange influence Annie also stopped.

'What are you doing with that umbrella, madam?' the gentleman enquired, looking Annie straight in the face and frightening her.

'Nothing, sir,' she faltered.

'I say, what are you doing with that umbrella?'

'Miss Malpatent told me to take it away, sir.'

'Well, you'll just take it back, then! Quick! March! That umbrella's mine.

I left it behind last night, by inadvertence. I am Professor Malpatent. Are you the perfect "Annie" that I've heard about from my sister?'

Annie was somehow glad of the excuse to return to The Weald. But she let the professor precede her.

5

'I do think, Arthur, you might have left a note to say you'd called,' said Miss Malpatent to her brother.

The reconciliation between the mistress and the servant was one of those intimate and elemental affairs in which the barriers of class break down utterly.

'We mistrusted one another,' murmured Miss Malpatent to Annie. 'Never let us do it again. It's too serious.'

'Yes, miss.'

Mrs Pastow benevolently smiled. The village laughed. Mr Pastow roared.

Nine o'Clock Tomorrow

James Devra descended from his car at the entrance to the club. The same adjective applied to himself as to the car – he was perfectly appointed. A dark and handsome Jew, with riches increasing every month, he had the face of a kind, capable, clear-thinking, orderly, masterful and successful man. In the Jewish community he was much respected for strict orthodoxy, broad generosity and artistic taste. His pride of race was intense. Charitable in estimating mankind, he excepted only one type of individual from his benevolence; he had nothing but scorn – a scorn fierce, cold and taciturn – for the renegade Jew.

'Nine forty-five,' he said to the chauffeur. He said it with a friendly, reliant smile, as one human being to another. But in the firm features and gaze there was somehow the warning implication that he did not mean nine forty-six.

He crossed the pavement of Pall Mall, walked up the noble and massive steps of the club, glanced at the encaged hall-porter, who by a sign indicated that there were no letters for him, hung his hat in the cloakroom on peg no. 58 (mnemonics: five eights are forty, his age), passed into the lavatory to wash, and then through the great dim tessellated and pillared hall to the coffee-room – as the restaurant of the club was still called. The long apartment, severe, beautiful, magnificent, disfigured only by bad portraits of statesmen, had just been lighted for the evening. It had tables for a hundred and fifty, and at lunch nearly every chair was occupied; but now there were fewer diners than stewards, cashiers, waiters, waitresses and page-girls. Devra with an enquiring eye sought among the infrequent guests for an acquaintance whose company might attract him, found none, sat down solitary at a table for four, and ordered some food and half a bottle of champagne from an old congenial steward, who devolved part of the command to a pale and high-heeled waitress.

'Rather dark here, Corser. I shan't be able to see my plate for my shadow,' said Devra cheerfully.

'Yes, sir,' the old steward replied, and his manner showed that he had the deep sentiment of Pall Mall in his bones. 'They have talked of putting in extra chandeliers, but it seems it wouldn't suit the architecture.'

'We must resign ourselves, I suppose. You might bring me the *Westminster Gazette*, will you?'

'Certainly, sir.'

Corser went off to get the wine and the paper.

51

When the waitress arrived with the soup, Devra slily examined the face, which he could not recall. It was a sad, pretty face, blonde and brainless, with a foolish little mouth.

He thought: 'Why is she here, with her high heels? No tips, Nothing. She ought to be in the front row of a theatre chorus.'

For a moment he imaginatively conceived her as a living creature with desires and sorrows. The whole room was as melancholy as the girl's face. What a contrast with the same room in the lunch-hour, when friends and acquaintances and enemies sat close together in amiable and playful conversations, teasing one another, firing off scandal, innuendos, indictments, satire, sarcasm – all in utmost good humour. You could say anything then, simply anything, provided you used the right club-tone. The lunch-hour was the apogee of the club's day. To lunch at the club was the proper thing, far better and more amusing than to lunch anywhere else. But the diners, chiefly old, dull and preoccupied, had the air of dining at the club because they could dine nowhere else, an air neglected, desolate and gloomy. They did not in fact dine; they solemnly nourished themselves. And the attendants, prisoners of the club, seemed to partake of the desolation of the diners, as was indeed correct behaviour on their part, for it was their business to reflect the club's mood as it changed from morn to eve.

Devra lodged the *Westminster Gazette* in front of the cruet, but to read it was too much trouble. He preferred to savour the vast despondency of the room. Not that he shared it. No! His own cheerfulness quite uninfected, he merely commiserated the diners and with benign urbanity disdained them. Nor did he object to dining alone. Being a man of very varied interests, sentimental and otherwise, he was accustomed to evenings over-full, and occasional solitude made a piquant change for him.

Raphael Field, RA, came vaguely in: a tall, stout, stooping, slouching old man with white hair and a boyish look on his rather rugged, red, carelessly shaven face, and pale hands whose joints were much enlarged. He wore shabby but well-cut tweeds, clumsy black boots, a low collar, and a little black tie of the last insignificance. Raphael Field's career had been a series of triumphs, not the least of which was the triumph over his fond father, an excessively bad mid-Victorian painter, who had baptised his offspring with that absurd Christian name and insisted that he must and would be a great artist. That anyone so handicapped should – especially after having commenced as an author – become the most distinguished and successful painter of his epoch, redeeming his Christian name from its absurdity and reluctantly joining the Academy late in life in order to oblige the Academy and to give lustre to that poor old body – this was miraculously against all the chances and an astounding demonstration of the man's native force. Raphael Field would have been a first-rate lion at any West End party, and the chief lion at most. But in the club, which was a club of celebrities, rich men, high officials, expensive professionals, prominent statesmen, he was just an individual like the rest of the members. Indeed he had a naïve, semi-apologetic demeanour, as though acknowledging that the renown of a painter, however wealthy and successful, could not truly be as authentic and imposing as that of a millionaire, a specialist doctor, a gladiator of the bar, or a transient cabinet minister. He was wandering at large, rather like an ox on a high road, past Devra's table when Devra stopped him.

'Good-evening, Mr Field,' said Devra, with his well-known bright smile, and the respect due to genius and to a man not far off thirty years older than himself.

The sound of his name seemed to recall Raphael Field from another world. He marshalled his strayed faculties, in the manner of the old, and stooped hugely over Devra and the table.

'Ah! Mr Devra!' His faint answering smile showed the ruined, irregular teeth.

'Have you forgiven me for outbidding you for that Queen Anne table at Christie's?'

Raphael Field suddenly beamed. 'Ah!' he said in his rich, deep voice, the voice of a strong, vital energy that was not yet quite spent. 'Ah! You city men always get what you want. We others are content with your leavings.'

'Now, now, Mr Field,' Devra protested flatteringly, 'that's irony. It's common knowledge you've got one of the finest collections in London. And, d'you know, I've been ashamed of myself ever since last Thursday. I'll be delighted to send you round that table at the price of your last bid. I was carried away – with your experience as a collector you must know the feeling – and I forgot myself. Otherwise I shouldn't have dreamed of bidding against you. Let me send you the table. I should feel privileged.'

'But this is exceedingly generous of you,' said Field simply and sincerely. 'I don't know that I shouldn't take you at your word – I'm an awful brigand – only that yesterday I happened to pick up an even more interesting table than the one you carried off under my guns – popguns, shall we say?'

'I'm so glad.' Devra put genuine relief into his tone. 'You've lifted a weight off my conscience . . . I expect you're dining with someone or I'd ask you to sit here.'

'May I?' murmured the eternal boy.

Devra quickly cast the *Westminster Gazette* on to the floor.

'I shall be honoured,' he said earnestly.

And he meant it. Genuises are rare. He had only a slight acquaintance with Raphael Field and was eager enough to strengthen it. After all, his own title to distinction was slender. True, he had a house in Cavendish Square, and there were ten gardeners on his place in Oxfordshire; and he enjoyed great consideration in the City and in restaurants and in auction-rooms ; and he knew a thing or two about all the arts, which is more than could be said of most artists! But Field was the unique Raphael Field. Field would receive an obituary notice of at least two columns in *The Times* – yea, and in the New York and Chicago papers also – and his biography, when it came to be written, would run to a couple of volumes and perhaps eight hundred pages.

They talked about the menu. Field examined the card as though it were a cuneiform inscription – and yet he seemed to know all about it. Devra soon saw, however, that the old gentleman was incapable of composing a meal artistically. And he thought how strange and pitiful it was that a man should know brilliant triumph and go down to the grave without having acquired the skill to compose a meal artistically. Devra had the respect of all the chief head-waiters in London. He was gathering courage to say, 'May I suggest?' when the competent and soothing Corser came to Field's assistance. Evidently Corser knew Field's weaknesses.

After a colloquy with Corser, Field blew out breath.

'That's done,' he said, eased.

And then he said: 'This room's very dull and dark at night, don't you think?'

'I agree,' Devra responded with a grimmish smile. 'I usually lunch here. It's quite different then. I'm surprised to find it is so empty. It's nearly as empty as the library. By the way, Mr Field, what are your views about the suggestion for turning the library into the smoking-room and vice versa ? The present smoking-room's uncomfortably small. The library's twice as big, and is only used as a dormitory.'

'I did hear something about the suggestion,' Field replied with slow negligence. 'But I don't know that I care for all these changes. I remember this club for thirty years. I remember it when you could get a meal and a tankard of ale for a shilling – or was it one and twopence. I don't find many changes for the better.'

'I dare say you're right,' Devra concurred deferentially. 'We mustn't forget the claims of tradition in a place like this.' But he was thinking sadly: 'Here is one of that tribe of obstinate old mummies who keep all good clubs a quarter of a century behind the times.'

'Do you dine here often?' he asked in a diplomatic tone that dismissed the delicate subject.

'Every night – nearly,' said Field.

'Really! I'm never here at night, myself. Mr Field, if it won't bore you, I wish you'd tell me something about picture prices. I'm very ignorant. I've often wanted to pick your brains, but I never hoped to get the chance.'

And he skilfully led the old man into the enchanting domain of prices, especially the history of the prices of Field's own early pictures. And he made Field feel glorious, and, so doing, realised with elation that he was once more casting the spell of his personal charm over a fellow-creature. Nevertheless, while he listened interested and talked interestingly he was saying in his heart: 'If I hadn't asked the old fellow to sit here he'd have been dining by himself. And he dines here every night – generally by himself, I bet. What a life! What's the use of being a genius and successful and famous if you're driven to eat in this catacomb every night? Why doesn't he accept invitations? Must have lots. Simply doesn't want to, I suppose.'

He grew very sad in secret. The evening despondency of the big room had at last infected him. He was filled with painful compassion for the distinguished celebrity, Raphael Field. More, he was filled with compassion for the whole human race, of which so few members had any sound comprehension of the great art of life as he understood it.

Just then he detected the waitress delivering a comic naughty grimace to the impassible Corser. This shocking and delightful phenomenon modified his mood of pity for all mankind. He hated waste.

At the end of the dinner Raphael sighed and announced that he was going home.

'I'm going too,' said Devra on a sudden impulse.

'Which way do you go ?'

'Cavendish Square.'

'I'm on your route then.'

'If I might walk with you,' Devra suggested respectfully.

'I walk so damned slowly.'

'I'm not a runner myself.'

Field's eye gleamed. The friendship was growing.

Field said deliberately: 'Would you care to look in at my place? I'd show you some bits of Queen Anne.'

'Mr Field, you're too kind. It's an unexpected pleasure, and I jump at it,' said Devra with eagerness.

A renewed realisation of the fact that he possessed a most singular power of captivating people began to mingle with an exciting sense of anticipation. He had an earnest desire to probe more deeply into Field's existence, and he was about to gratify it. Perhaps it was a morbid desire, but there it was – and he was an amateur of human nature! As they left the club he murmured discreetly to the hall porter: 'When my car comes just tell the chauffeur I shan't want him any more tonight, will you? Thanks.'

2

Raphael Field wore a curious short cape, thrown lightly on his shoulders in the cool summer evening. This cape, flowing out under his rather long dishevelled white hair, added to the pathos of his appearance as he anxiously undertook the feat of threading himself between the taxi-cabs in the dark dusk of Pall Mall. Devra thought with pain: 'And if I were not with him the old gentleman would be crossing Pall Mall alone.' When they reached

Orange Square, the whole of which had been built at the end of the seventeenth century, Field drew out a bunch of keys and turned into a side-street. Although his address was Orange Square, his front-door was in the side-street. He spent half a minute in selecting his latchkey and another half minute in getting the door open. Then he stumbled up two steps and, groaning slightly, switched on the electric light in the staircase, and Devra had a glimpse of pictures rising in slopes above him. They were obviously fine pictures, but the stair-carpet lacked distinction.

'We'll take the lift,' said Raphael Field, banging the front-door. 'It's my exclusive property, but I never use it at night for fear it should jam halfway and I shouldn't be able to make my people hear. However, as you're with me . . . It never does jam, you know, but it might.' He laughed uneasily.

They took the lift, which Field manipulated. It barely held the two of them. When they emerged from it in safety, Field seemed surprised and Devra had a feeling of relief.

'Shall we go into the studio?'

But when Field pulled the switch down no light resulted in the studio.

'That fuse must have gone again,' said he. 'Let's try the drawing-room.'

In the drawing-room he rang the bell. Devra heard the sound of it in the distance above.

No answer.

'Hm!' grunted Field, and rang again.

No answer.

'Hm!' grunted Field, and went out to the corridor and called: 'Higginbotham.'

No answer.

He returned to the drawing-room.

'In bed and asleep, I suppose,' he said. 'I keep a man and his wife here. But I suppose one can't expect servants to work more than fourteen hours a day seven days a week.' He laughed uneasily once more. 'Oh! Here *are* the drinks! He's put them in the other corner tonight.'

'You've lived here for about forty years, haven't you, Mr Field?' said Devra. 'At least, so it's generally understood. How central you are!' he added falteringly. 'Equidistant from Regent Street, Bond Street, Piccadilly and Oxford Street. It puts Cavendish Square quite in the suburbs.'

'Oh, no, no!' answered Field. 'Funny how that story got about of me living here for forty years! It's true I first had the place forty years ago, but I gave it up after seven or eight years. I had the whole house then. There were no business houses in Orange Square then. Now nearly every house is wholly or partly let for business purposes. The two floors under us are occupied by a very fashionable dressmaker. She is a limited company, and she has the main entrance and the main staircase. I use now what used to be the servants' entrance and staircase in my time. Yes, I gave up the place.

Couldn't stand it somehow. When I came back to England after living in Paris about ten years ago, I heard that the upper floors were to let, and so I took them. Thought I might as well. As you say, it's very central. What'll you have?'

'A little soda-water, if I may . . . Can't keep my eyes off your pictures. Mr Field. You'll excuse me if I look round.'

'Do, my dear fellow. Do! Most of 'em were given to me by the painters. I've got some furniture here, as you see; but very little. The fact is, most of my furniture's stored in Paris. I couldn't be bothered to bring it over.'

They examined a magnificent picture by Cezanne together.

'It's one of the three or four very finest I've seen,' said Devra earnestly.

Instead of replying Raphael Field opened a little drawer, and pulled out a duster, and delicately dusted the frame.

'I keep my own private duster in every room,' said he, with his uneasy laugh.

They passed from room to empty room, all the walls lined with pictures. Field in a rather childish way returned to the studio door and tried the ineffectual switch again; and Devra vaguely made out a large, bare interior, with the statue of a woman that in the gloom resembled a living woman so startlingly as to cause his flesh to creep for an instant. 'Do you paint every day?'

'Most days. Some days I can't be bothered, and I just sit about or go to the National Gallery.'

Field displayed the whole floor, even to the bathroom.

'Fairly spacious, considering its situation, isn't it?'

'It is indeed.'

'Hm!'

Devra had offered appropriate remarks in front of the principal pictures. But in fact he was not thinking about the pictures at all. The existence of Raphael Field preoccupied him and desolated him. He saw the old man in his queer cape walking home solitary every night from his solitary dinner, and fumbling with his bunch of keys and fumbling at the keyhole, and puffing up the stairs (the servants' stairs) on his antique legs because he was afraid of the lift, and ringing vainly for servants, and sitting silent and lonely now in this room, now in that, and probably fumbling with the old-fashioned geyser in the bathroom with the linoleum floor; and finally undressing alone and getting into bed and lying awake alone.

But the most heart-rending thing of all was the private duster kept in every room to remedy the negligence of servants. Devra was waited on hand and foot by servants in Cavendish Square. If Devra came home at 3 a.m. and rang a bell that was unanswered he would have thought the Day of Judgement was at hand. As for switches that wouldn't work, as for geysers, as for linoleum in a bathroom, as for private dusters hidden in drawers – his imagination simply refused to conceive the phenomena in connection with his own existence. Of course the pictures were superb, far finer than Devra's. The sale of them would be a notable event after Field's death. But they were chiefly gifts. Field had not bought them, and Devra somehow could not attach a genuine value to that which had not cost money. The furniture was first-rate – there were several museum-pieces – but the quantity of it was disappointing. What in the name of common sense and efficiency was the point of keeping beautiful furniture stored away in Paris? The flat was large, but it was only large for a flat. Devra's house in Cavendish Square would hold three of it; his place in Oxfordshire would hold six of it. And the flat was not clean. The one indisputable quality it possessed was an impeccable tidiness.

Here was Raphael Field, world-renowned, his name familiar and sacred to the lips of every connoisseur throughout Christendom! What had he got out of life? The pathos of him was tragic, shattering.

They wandered back through the emptiness of the flat, with the mystery of the servants' rooms above them, and the mystery of the dressmaker's atelier below them, to the drawing-room.

'Oh! Here's that Queen Anne table I was telling you of,' said the old man. 'Pretty good, isn't it?'

'Very interesting! Very interesting!' said Devra responsively, after he had inspected the piece with polite thoroughness. But he did not really think that it was very interesting. It was indeed indisputably second-rate, and he wondered that the old man should have been deceived by it. Still, he went on praising it quite convincingly, for he could never resist the temptation to be agreeable.

'Curious thing,' said Field. 'Very curious thing! I picked that up in Mortimer Street on Monday for less than I gave for it in the eighteen eighties!'

'Then it belonged to you before?' Devra's tone was positively eager.

'It did. And there's a very curious incident connected with it.'

'May I hear it? . . . Or is it a secret?'

'It would bore you.'

'Mr Field! Mr *Field*!' Devra's dark eyes glinted a discreet flattery.

'It used to be a secret. But the thing happened so long ago it needn't be a secret any more. I wrote it all down at the time. Did you know I once had literary ambitions?'

' "Ambitions", Mr Field. "Did I know?" I have all your three books in my library.'

The old man flushed with satisfaction, and his face was more boyish, more naïve, than ever.

'Like me to read it to you?'

'I shall insist, Mr Field.'

Slowly and clumsily the old man produced his keys, unlocked a bookcase, adjusted his eyeglasses anew, and chose a calf-bound book from the shelves.

'The first volume of a journal that I used to keep – for practice,' said he, and sat down under a light, and turned pages backwards and forwards, breathing rather heavily.

'Here it is. I was looking at it on Monday night. It's very jejune, I'm afraid. Perhaps I ought to explain . . . No! Let's let it explain itself. I'll only say that at the time I wrote it I had almost given up my literary ambitions.'

This is what he read in his rich, deep voice.

3

'Friday morning I was in my beautiful new old house all by myself, just finishing my packing ready to go away for the weekend to Harry's. There was a terrible state of dirt and mess, because the workmen weren't finally leaving until next day. The front-door bell rang. At first I thought I'd let it ring; but it rang several times. The ringing of the bell made the house seem very large and empty and me very lonely in it. My charwoman had gone. I wouldn't let her stay in the house after me. At last I went downstairs. The front-door was locked and the key was gone. The workmen had taken it away, by arrangement. I was supposed to be using the servants' entrance. So I had to go out into the street by the side-door and round the corner to the front-door. A girl was standing in the portico. She was dressed in black. I had made a movement as if to raise my hat, before I remembered that I wasn't wearing a hat. I asked her what she wanted, and she said she wanted to see Mr Raphael Field. Then she said, "You're Mr Field, aren't you?" I explained how I was situated and brought her round to the side-entrance, and upstairs to the second-floor, nothing else being even half habitable – no carpets down, naturally.'

('It was to this room I brought her,' Field interjected.)

'There were two kitchen chairs, my easel, dais, and so on, a floor-sweeper, and the Queen Anne table I'd found a fortnight ago; that was all, except some planks and trestles that the workmen hadn't removed. She was extremely nervous, and I was rather nervous too. She said she wanted me to paint her portrait, at once – she was leaving England the next day. Just a sketch-portrait. She had come to me because I had painted a portrait of a friend of hers, and she wanted the portrait of herself to give to the mother of that friend. What friend? She preferred not to say, and hoped I would excuse her.

'I told her that I was just going out of London – should be gone in half an hour – had a train to catch. But some other day I'd be delighted. She didn't speak, and I perceived she couldn't speak. The tears were falling from her eyes. I was considerably upset. In fact I had the most extraordinary sensations. There I was alone in the big house with her! I felt very sad and depressed. I'm a successful man, but I wondered whether I should continue to be successful, and whether I could afford the big house and the servants I'd engaged, and pay the rent and everything. I felt very solitary in the world. It was very curious how I felt. All at once, and without quite intending to do so, I told her I'd go out and send a telegram to say that I couldn't leave London until tomorrow, and I'd do her a sketch-portrait immediately. She didn't protest. No! She just looked at me, quietly crying. It was a rather wild thing for me to do, and I shouldn't have done it, only she was a most beautiful young girl, with very fair hair, and dressed in half-mourning: which suited her. I knew nothing whatever about her except that she was a most beautiful young girl with fair hair. I had very little desire to know anything else about her. I ran off. I was kept a long time at the Regent Street Post Office telegraphing to Harry.

'When I returned she was sweeping the floor. Indeed, she'd practically swept it. Her bonnet was hung on the back of a chair. I was thrilled; couldn't utter a word. I had a prickly feeling all over my skin. She smiled. I told her I'd paint her in her bonnet, and I put a chair on the dais and asked her to take a pose.

'While I was fixing the easel and arranging my palette, she looked silently out of the window. Suddenly she said: "How much will the portrait be?" I said that didn't matter, and we'd talk about that afterwards. The things one does usually say. But she insisted that the price must be fixed before I began. So I told her to fix it. She said she could pay fifty pounds. I agreed. If she'd said five I should have agreed. She took the money in notes out of her purse. She said: "You don't know anything about me, and I prefer to pay in advance." I objected. The argument ended by her leaving the dais and placing the notes on the mantelpiece.

'After I'd been painting about three-quarters of an hour I decided that the portrait should be more than a sketch and that I should paint all day. But between twelve and one I began to feel terribly hungry. I never felt so hungry before. I suggested to her that we should go out and have lunch at Verrey's. She told me to go, but she declined to go herself. She said she wasn't hungry and couldn't eat. Then I said that I wasn't hungry and that I wouldn't go either. I said I'd see whether there were any leavings in the kitchen. I went upstairs to the kitchen. The fire in the range wasn't quite out. The charwoman's apron hung on the knob of a cupboard door. I searched about and discovered three eggs and then half a loaf. I was startled by a noise behind me. It was she. She said: "If there's anything, let me cook it for you!" I pointed to what I'd found. She put on the charwoman's apron, made up the fire, looked into all the cupboards, found some tea, washed a saucepan. Her movements were simply exquisite. I think that these were the most marvellous moments I had ever lived. She was young and extremely beautiful, with fair hair. She was an absolute mystery. I thought what a fool I should have been if I hadn't sent the telegram to Harry. It made me almost sick to think what I should have missed if I hadn't stayed.

'When the meal was ready, she put everything on a tray, and I carried the tray downstairs, and we had lunch opposite each other at the Queen Anne table.'

('This table,' Field interjected, pointing.)

'A kind of intimacy developed. But we only talked about painting. She evidently knew something about painting. She didn't really know, but she had that charming superficial knowledge that women acquire of things. She must have had acquaintances among painters. I had been working about an hour after lunch when the light failed very quickly. It was impossible to continue. We heard thunder. Then came a proper heavy thunderstorm. The darkness was such that we could plainly see the lightning. She turned pale. The regular traffic of the square ceased. Only occasionally a horse trotted by. We looked out of the window. The rain rebounded from the pavements, which were deserted. A few people were sheltering in porticoes. Charles James Fox in his tight coat of granite glittered with wet. And the beautiful mysterious young girl with fair hair and I were safely under cover in the big empty unfurnished house.

'We thought the rain would cease, but it didn't. It settled into an obstinate downpour. There was no hope of continuing the portrait. The church clock boomed. I moved the easel to the window so that we could examine it. She was enraptured with it. I also was satisfied. But it was far from finished. She said: "I can come again tomorrow." I reminded her that she was leaving England tomorrow. She said: "Yes, but only in the afternoon. Supposing I came very early." Thus we arranged for a final sitting. Then the rain ceased. Dusk, however, had now begun to fall. When we looked back from the window into the room, shadows were gathering in the corners.

'She put on her mantle and her gloves and picked up her reticule. She would go. She would not let me find a four-wheeler for her. She said she must take an omnibus. I followed her down the stairs. On the first-floor landing she stopped and I stopped. She said: "Mr Field, you've been very, very good to me and I've not thanked you at all. You haven't even asked anything about me. It's only right that you should know my name." She opened her reticule. And then she melted into tears. She was so extremely beautiful, and so benign, and so movingly sad, and so seductive, and so enigmatic, and I was so close to her that I kissed her. She did not resent the kiss, but she gave a little sob. Her mouth was wet and cool. My feelings could not possibly be described. A piece of paper was pushed into my hand. She murmured: "Nine o'clock tomorrow." She ran down the remaining stairs. The door banged.'

4

The old man's rich voice ceased; he shut the book, and turned to replace it in the bookcase. With his back to Devra he said, in a self-conscious, excusing tone: 'I was under thirty then.'

'And what happened next?' Devra cautiously asked.

'Nothing.'

'Nothing?'

'Nothing. She never came. The first hours of the following day were the most joyously exciting I ever spent. But she never came. The last hours of the day were the most terrible I ever spent.' Raphael Field gave one of his short nervous laughs.

'But you had her address.'

'I couldn't find the paper. Neither that night nor the next day. Looked everywhere. Thought I'd stuffed it into my pocket. Cut open the lining of my jacket. Couldn't find it. Only a very small paper. Never did find it.'

'But hadn't you even looked at the paper?'

'No. You see, at first I just sat down and – er – thought about her. I didn't worry about her name at first.'

'And you never had the least idea who she was?'

Field hesitated before replying.

'You remember the Ollinson case?'

'No.'

'You wouldn't. Before your time. Ollinson was a painter. Pretty good in his day. I painted his portrait. He killed himself in his studio in Chelsea. That would be in the autumn of 1879 about. He was always queer. And usually mixed up with women. There was a rumour that he was violently in love – he was violent in everything, but this was said to be more violent than usual, and the girl wouldn't look at him. Well, it occurred to me that the girl who came to me that night might be the girl who wouldn't look at Ollinson.'

'I see,' Devra said. 'She said you'd painted a portrait of a friend of hers and she wanted her own portrait for his mother. Perhaps the mother had a sort of morbid interest in the girl that her son had killed himself for – '

'Just so. The mother and she might even have been friendly. Sorrow drawing 'em together and so on. Because naturally Ollinson's suicide must have upset the young woman tremendously. Perhaps it was on account of the suicide that she was leaving England. Who knows? All mere supposition, of course. I tried to get hold of Ollinson's mother. She'd died. I tried everything. I got on the traces of about nineteen girls that Ollinson was supposed to have been interested in. But mine didn't happen to be among them. And I can tell you that none of the others was the least bit like her, either.'

A silence.

'*Why* didn't she come back the next day?' Devra said, half to himself.

'God knows. Perhaps afraid. Perhaps she had a sense of duty elsewhere . . . She may have been run over. People are run over every day . . . If she's alive now she's over sixty – she's just a ruin of the girl I knew. She may be a grandmother. It's forty years ago. A long time.'

Another silence.

'I think you've never married, Mr Field?' said Devra, lapsing slightly from good taste. Devra had his moments of crudity.

'No.'

'It's so long ago I suppose it seems to you now as if it had happened to somebody else and not to you.'

'Nothing of the kind,' Field answered with strange curtness. 'It happened to *me*.'

Soon afterwards Devra rose to depart.

'We may as well walk down,' said Field, as he switched on the staircase lights.

Devra followed slowly, glancing at the pictures on the staircase walls, which Field had not as yet shown to him.

'This is it,' said Field, halting on the first-floor landing.

There hung the unfinished portrait. Devra examined it intently. A work youthful but masterly . . . Yes, a lovely creature in the demoded frock and funny bonnet – tantalising, mysterious, virginal, voluptuous, acquiescent . . . The wet mouth! . . . Worth no doubt a couple of thousand pounds at Christie's.

'I hung it there,' said Field, 'because it was just there – it was just there – she stopped and – told me I'd been very good to her. There was no carpet on the stairs.'

Outside Devra stood and looked at the beautiful silhouetted Corinthian façade of the famous church rising from the silence of the square hugely against a soft sky. And he heard Raphael Field shooting the bolts within. Tomorrow night the decrepit old fellow with his dignified smile, half-boyish and half-senile, would no doubt be dining forlornly alone once more at the club. What a life! What a career! What a memory! The decrepit old fellow had created masterpieces; and he had lived. Devra, walking thoughtfully in the direction of his immense and perfectly appointed home, reflected that though he, Devra, had got much in this world he had not got quite every-thing. He was a little disturbed in his complacency to find himself envying Raphael Field.

Last Love

'Don't you hate ugly undies, Miss Osyth?' Minnie demanded vehemently, and without any warning.

The piano-lesson was finished. Teacher and pupil sat at the window of Miss Osyth's small parlour, which looked out over Mozewater, where the bright sea was creeping furtively in the dusk across the salt-marshes.

'I don't like anything that's ugly,' said Miss Osyth cautiously in her soft, weak voice, and gave a characteristic little cough. She felt a responsibility towards Minnie's somewhat indifferent parents because Minnie adored her more than them. 'You're not getting that edge straight,' she added.

Their heads approached one another above the fine needlework. Though Minnie showed much natural facility upon the piano, more indeed than her teacher had ever had, Miss Osyth did not enjoy the piano-lessons, for the reason that the pupil seemed to be incapable of musical emotion. This was strange, seeing that she was an emotional young girl. In the matter of needlework, for example, Minnie could be rapturous. At times she was quite obviously thrilled by the beauty of Miss Osyth's achievements in crocheting and drawn-thread work. Needlework united them far more effectively than music; and Miss Osyth, who had a passion for needlework, was thereby made glad and proud and enthusiastic. Nevertheless Minnie's emphatic tendency to lavish ornamental stitchery upon flimsy garments invisible to the world disturbed Miss Osyth. She glanced anxiously at the head of bobbed brown hair and at the down-turned pretty face, and at the slim, soft, flexible, apparently undeveloped body. A boyish body. A boyish quality in the face and in the free gestures! The girl was twenty and looked seventeen. The girl's attitude towards the world was one of frank, fresh, possibly rash investigation. Nothing perverse or secretive or morbid in her! She was innocence itself. And yet this utterly unboyish preoccupation with unseen attire, which she never attempted to explain or justify! Miss Osyth was alarmed, and at the same time curiously conscious of an agreeable excitement.

Minnie dropped the work and leaned upon a third chair that was in the bay of the window. She was always adopting the strangest sprawling positions, and could seldom sit on one chair if there was a chance of sitting on two simultaneously; her body seemed to be more than she could manage, to be somehow superfluous and cumbersome, despite its frequent startling grace.

'Miss Osyth.'

'Yes, darling?'

'Do you mind if I ask you a question?' Minnie intoned these words. When she was not quite at ease she would intone, chant, or even sing instead of speaking.

'Well?'

'I've been dying to ask you heaps and heaps of times.'

Minnie lived in a violent and extravagant universe of her own. In this universe time existed in aeons or it did not exist at all. The same with every other commodity. There were heaps, tons, stacks; or there was not a single scrap. In this universe Minnie died continually, from the mere acuteness of her sensations. She did not like or dislike. She hated; she loved and adored; no intermediate degrees of feeling! In fact a superlative universe, and dangerous to inhabit!

'Well?' repeated Miss Osyth.

'Have you ever been in love?'

A short silence.

'No,' answered Miss Osyth truthfully, in a smothered voice, realising first how the girl was mysteriously growing up and then the shock of the question to her own mind.

To hide her constraint she looked steadily out of the window.

In a creek about fifty yards in front of the cottage were three yachts; the two smaller ones were already afloat on the rising tide; the third and largest, dismantled, was still aground. Miss Osyth saw those yachts float and take the mud every day and often twice in a day. At any hour she could tell without looking whether any or all of them were afloat or aground. She lived day and night with the ceaseless tides. This evening, as she replied to Minnie, the largest yacht with its green sagging chain and weed-clad undersides suddenly appeared to her forlorn and pathetic.

She knew that Minnie, misjudging her tone, thought that she was annoyed. She was not annoyed, but she could not say so because to say so would prolong the topic, which she wished to close at once. It was a disconcerting topic. She could not conceive herself discussing love with the blossoming girl. Instinct warned her against such a perilous course.

'I must rush home,' said Minnie, after a moment.

'I'll go with you part of the way,' said Miss Osyth.

'You *are* an angel!' (Minnie's universe was peopled with angels and fiends.)

They set out, shutting but not locking the door of the solitary cottage. Two hundred yards over hummocks of grass, and they reached the hamlet of Flittering – a row of white cottages, an inn, a larger private house, and on the rough cobbled quay two antique buildings in the nature of warehouses which were in process of demolition. From Flittering, as from all the coast villages and towns of that East Anglian peninsula, there was only one road inland, and the road from tiny Flittering was no more than a broadish track, nearly impassable by footfarers for days together in winter, but now dry and dusty.

Minnie nervously skipped and ran, playing round the sedate Miss Osyth as a porpoise round a ship. When they had passed the disused little eighteenth-century lighthouse and come to the corner where the track mounted towards the village of Hoe (Flittering's metropolis) and the highroad to the vast Babylon with a music-hall and three cinemas called Colchester, Miss Osyth stopped. Lilly's farm, the home of Minnie, began at the corner. Minnie leaped passionately at Miss Osyth and gave her an intense kiss.

'I do like you!' Minnie exclaimed, thus, and without another word, begging forgiveness for the indiscreet inquiry into her angel's past. Miss Osyth fondly returned the kiss . . . The child receded, a glimmer of white in the dusk.

Miss Osyth faced eastwards again. She passed through white Flittering, calling out good-night to the landlord of the inn as she went. She passed the beautiful antique warehouses, whose slow demolition, always painful to her, now struck her as unbearably tragic. A Thames barge, with all its sails lowered or brailed except the topsail, which hung like a ghost in the sombre sky, was very slowly moving up the channel on the night-tide. And in this approach of a phantom to the quay soon to be deserted for ever there was also a quality unbearably tragic.

She climbed over the hummocks of grass. The immense inlet, which at low tide was a waste of land with little lakes, had been transformed into a sea with little islands. The sea gleamed in a strange light. She entered her small garden, and looked at the roosting fowls. She opened the door and went into the five-roomed cottage, which was the end of the inhabited world, and according to her custom she glanced into each room. Then, in the parlour, she lit a candle and drew the blind.

Her mother had bought the cottage after her father's death, more than twenty years earlier. Mrs Drine was a stern old lady, who would sit in the garden in black gloves. She talked very, very quietly, and had always expected and received absolute obedience and entire devotion from Osyth. They had kept a servant, who was the only human being with any power over Mrs Drine. They had also a dog. Mrs Drine died. Osyth was free, and had not the force to use her freedom. The servant ruled. The dog died. The servant died. Osyth then became the slave of the cottage, which she could not sell without loss, and would not leave. She was afraid of servants, would not engage another one, and did everything for herself. She had a very small income and slightly increased it by giving piano-lessons – she had 'learnt' at Colchester – and by the sale at low prices of her lovely needlework. An appreciable part of the income was spent in small surgical operations on her nose and throat. She was frequently indisposed, and often her face gave signs of the dyspepsia and neuralgia which everlastingly tortured her. The east wind which blew for two months each spring over the saltings was her enemy. She was thirty-nine. At Minnie's age she had been called pretty; and she was still slim, without being desiccated; only she was round-shouldered. Having good judgement and an unusually sound and detached sense of proportion, she knew the cause of her failure in life. She had never been able to assert herself, never had the strength to assert herself.

She would not have called her existence an unhappy one. But now Minnie's crude question seemed to have precipitated all the unperceived misery which her life had as it were held in solution. She was shocked by the swift vision of all that she had missed. Self-pity agonised her. She slipped on to the hard sofa, and cried in the loneliness as softly as she talked and as her mother had talked. She did not sob. The tears flowed quietly. She had the illusion of hearing Minnie's fresh boyish voice: 'Have you ever been in love?' No! She had never been in love. Rarely had she had the chance to be in love; and never the courage to take advantage of the rare chance.

2

In the middle of the night Miss Osyth was awakened by the noise of a quarrel in front of her cottage. She had, strangely enough for a woman of her timid temperament, not the slightest fear of solitude, but now the sound of men's angry tones frightened her; for never once in twenty years' residence at the cottage had she heard any human voices in the night on the marshes. The cottage was indeed the end of the world. Nobody could safely wander at dark on the marshes intersected by innumerable creeks. The night sounds round about Miss Osyth's cottage were the uncanny calls of birds, the wind over the rushes and in the chimneys, and during the great Christmas gales the fringes of the sea in the larger creeks. However, though she was alarmed, Miss Osyth did not bury her head. She arose and lit the candle for companionship. She dared not draw the blind aside and look out of the window. In one of the voices she recognised the gruff fierce accents of the landlord of the Flittering inn.

'And I tell *you* you've no business in that yacht,' shouted the landlord. 'I've had my eye on you for three hours past.'

'Oh! Have you?'

'Yes, I have. That yacht belongs to Mr Beaumont, and he don't want no dirty tramps in her.'

'And supposing *my* name's Beaumont?'

It seemed to be a young voice.

Miss Osyth heard no more. She listened for a long time to the hammering of her own heart, and at last blew out the candle and went to sleep again, thinking of the history of the Beaumonts. She was roused once more by a new and fainter noise which at first she thought was her heart, but which ultimately explained itself as an intermittent knocking on the front-door.

She now pulled the bedclothes over her head. The sound would not be silenced; it was like a conscience penetrating the defences of a shameful sloth. She sprang up nervously, re-lit the candle, put on a wrap, and looked out between the muslin curtains of the window. The night, which had been clear, was very dark indeed. Miss Osyth shook with apprehensions. But in a moment, as she listened, she seemed to say to herself: 'I'm in a dreadful predicament. I may as well *be* in it.' And she yielded, acquiescent and relieved, to the situation. There were steps on the gravel.

'Ah!' called a calm voice, of one who had probably noticed at last the candlelight above him and the shadow of a head on the muslin curtains. 'Please come down, you up there! I'm all bleeding!' It was the voice of the inn-landlord's late antagonist.

3

'I think I'd better light the big lamp, and I think I'd better warm some water before I begin on *that*,' said Miss Osyth faintly and timidly, and yet somehow sturdily too, facing the visitor whom she had let into her parlour, where only a candle was burning.

If not precisely ashamed of her little parlour, she was concerned about his probable contempt for it, with its queer bits of Victorian furniture – hand-painted tables, comic chairs, frayed glaring carpet, her mother's crewel work and watercolours, and incredible photographs and engravings. She knew well enough that the room was enough to make a modern cat laugh. She knew that it was a pathetic exile in the implacable welter of the twentieth century. But she would not, could not, have had it altered. She would forlornly stand by it.

Also she was concerned about her own attire, which was very summary and incomplete: whereas the young man was fully and elegantly dressed, though a little ruffled. The young man had a waistline which was created by the lowest button of his jacket and which became him admirably. Miss Osyth suddenly felt more virginal than she had ever felt. She was flushed and thrilling with virginity. She was eager and defensive. She seemed to dare and to run away, to invite and to repulse, to care and not to care. Extremely unused to men, chance had thrown her close against a man, and in the most singular circumstances. However, as she had encouraged herself before, she was in a predicament, and there she was! And the roughly bandaged hand was enough in itself to reassure the sensitive primness of her virginity. The bandage had noticeably reddened. She wanted to look at the man's face, but looked at the bandage instead. All she knew about the face was that it was fair and impossibly handsome; it was as unique as the face of the Angel Gabriel. In addition to feeling virginal, she felt extraordinarily and absurdly young.

'Do sit down! Do sit down!' she urged nervously, and in her nervousness bungled the lighting of the lamp, which first smelt because the wick was too low and then smoked because the wick was too high. 'Dear! Dear! . . . And I must warm some water.'

Even alone in the kitchen igniting the spirit-lamp with which she always made her morning tea, she was flurried.

'What a ridiculous idiot I am!' she thought. The young man followed her into the kitchen. 'I don't want to make a mess in your sitting-room,' he said. He took off the bandage himself and held his hand under the tap at the sink. He didn't know it, but he was being frightfully extravagant with her precious rainwater from the tank beneath the eave. The wound was on the back of the hand. A fairly bad wound, an inch and a half in length! The cold water soon stopped the bleeding. She was too diffident to enquire as to the origin of the wound, but she connected it with the inn-landlord. Then she had to hold his wrist, and bathe the wound in warm water coloured pink with Condy fluid. How unfortunate that she kept her cast-off linen and oddments in a drawer of the kitchen dresser, and so was forced to cut and tear the new bandage in his presence! Still, she was getting hardened now.

'I suppose you're Alexis Beaumont?' she ventured, after he had thanked her for the dressing, which indeed she had accomplished very well. She was quite sure of his identity.

He nodded, with a mysterious smile. The Beaumonts had bought a house and grounds near Hoe some fifteen years earlier. They had invaded Hoe from London, which is equal to nowhere. They were rich, and they were determined, in their ignorance of the fundamentals of English country life, to wake up Hoe. Everybody above a certain station called on them, and they called on everybody. They organised flower-shows and tennis-tournaments, and they gave dances and established a club for the civilisation of labourers. Hoe accepted all. They were marvellous in the war and after the war. Then events compelled them to leave. They imagined that the great departure would stir Hoe to its foundations. They imagined that the painted notice at the august front entrance-gates: '*This property to be sold*', would cause Hoe to shed poignant tears. Not a bit! They left amid perfect calm. Their seven bright busy years of occupation had made no more impression upon Hoe than the passage of a strange motor-car down the village high street. In the life of the indifferent and insensitive populace, whose roots were buried centuries deep in the social history of the district, the sojourn of the Beaumonts had about the same importance as the picking up of half a crown in the gutter. It was better than a bat in the eye with a burnt stick, and that was all. The yacht alone remained to testify that the Beaumonts really had existed. An agent from Colchester occasionally let it for duck-shooting on Mozewater, but he had never succeeded in selling it. Miss Osyth had caught sight of Alexis once or twice as a boy when he was home from school for the holidays. He then had the reputation of being a spoilt boy who created strife between his parents.

'I'll go back to the yacht now. You've been most awfully kind, and skilful.' He said it neatly, in distinguished tones. He had a rather dazzling style with him.

'But are you going to try to sleep on the yacht?'

'Where else? There's a bed. Two beds, in fact. It's rather cosy.' He smiled easily.

'But the beds must be dreadfully damp!'

'Oh, no!'

'But they must be!' Miss Osyth pitied the simplicity of the man, of all men, in practical details of daily existence.

'It's of no consequence,' he said casually, and added: *'But if you'd like to spoil me'* – he uttered this phrase with a disturbing, irresistible confidence, ever so softly and gently – 'I'll tell you what you might do. You might give me a bucket of water – there's soap and towels on board – and a candle.'

'Yes,' said she.

When the preparations were done Miss Osyth lit her outdoor lantern and they issued forth into the warm night. A loose punt was the means of transport to the yacht. One push and they were alongside. They both moved quietly, as though afraid of being overheard. To Miss Osyth's surprise the cabin of the yacht actually did have an air of cosiness; when illuminated by the lantern and a candle it revealed all sorts of handy contraptions and some food, and it was roomier than she would have thought possible. She made up the bed; she poured the water into the brass-bound barrel, which had a brass tap.

'Now have you got everything you want?'

'No, but I shall have. I shall run over to Colchester tomorrow and get a toothbrush, and a razor, and some blacking, and a boot-brush and a clothes-brush and a shirt or two. I shall take the motor-bus.'

Miss Osyth laughed, enigmatically excited by this glimpse into a man's private life.

'I can let you have everything for your boots,' she said.

He shook his head in refusal. They extricated themselves one after the other from the close confinement of the cabin, Miss Osyth going first with the lantern. She got into the punt and in a moment was on the bank of the creek.

'I say,' cried Alexis, low, 'I must tell you you're a splendid girl. You positively are!' Enthusiasm was in his fresh, strong voice.

'Girl!' She blushed peacefully in the immense, faintly rustling darkness of the reedy marshes. She thrilled peacefully. Well, she felt like a girl. She did not feel like thirty-nine, and could scarcely believe that she was thirty-nine. She said nothing in answer. In the parlour she regarded herself in the glass, moving the lantern up and down. Of course the inadequacy of her attire was terrible, but it did not seem to matter. And honestly she was convinced that she did not look nearly her age. She *was* a girl. She had all the sensations of a girl. How old was Alexis? She made a calculation and decided that he was twenty-five. In her bedroom she sat by the window and gazed at the candlelight steadily shining through the cabin porthole of the yacht. Mysterious! Fascinating! . . . He had given no explanation at all of his visit to the yacht.

'Oh, dear! Oh, dear!' she reflected. 'What a good thing this kind of thing doesn't happen every day! It's most upsetting, and I don't know where I am. And I don't know *what* people would say!' She smiled very happily, expectantly, shakily. She cried.

4

'Oh, Miss Osyth!' cried Minnie the next day. 'You look simply frightfully young today! I can't think how you do it. *I* feel a hundred.'

Miss Osyth blushed slightly. Whereon Minnie added: 'And you look so charming, too. But then of course you always do look charming . . . Well, it beats me, that's what it does. It beats me.'

Miss Osyth blushed a little more. She felt inexplicably happy, but constrained too; she didn't know what to say. The sincerity and enthusiasm of the young girl's praise gave her a confidence in herself which she had never had before. Obviously Minnie would not burst out at first sight of her into these impassioned praises without some very striking cause. And Minnie's observations were richly corroborated by Miss Osyth's own feelings. She indeed did feel young; and though she was tired and ought therefore according to custom to have been suffering from neuralgia, she had a strange new physical condition of good health. Had a miracle happened to Miss Osyth? Miss Osyth, being usually a person of strong common sense, had no belief in miracles. What she at the moment believed was that she had got into the habit of regarding herself as old when she was not old. Thirty-nine! Thirty-nine was nothing. The phrase: 'You're a splendid girl,' glowed in her memory and heart, glowed steadily, beautifully, inspiringly; it was the magic phrase of rejuvenation.

Always, in her hidden happiness, Miss Osyth was disquieted by the visit of Minnie. This was not Minnie's day, and though Minnie did sometimes appear unexpectedly, why should she appear on just this day? Minnie had something on her mind, and she had to get it off; she had come with the sole intention of getting it off.

'Oh, Miss Osyth,' she exclaimed, gazing through the window, 'of course you've heard all about Alexis Beaumont? I see he doesn't seem to be on the yacht now. In fact, I know he isn't, because I saw him go past the farm this morning. He took the motor-bus to Colchester in Hoe High Street. *I* think he's *too* handsome. I'd never seen him before, at least since he was a mere school-kid. But isn't it funny, him living in the yacht like that? I can't make it out. No one can. They say he's quarrelled with his father about something, and he's waiting here till Mrs Beaumont brings his father round. But how does he *manage*? I wonder if it's true that he had a fight with Mr Cossange? I suppose he did, but I'm told they've made it up, and he's going to have his meals at the Maid's Head. Of course Cossange hasn't been in the district long enough to know who he was.'

Minnie had without an effort collected all the rumours connected with Alexis. She was clearly obsessed by him.

'I can tell you this,' said Miss Osyth, in response to Minnie's persistency. 'He came here last night and asked me to let him have some fresh water.'

'And did you?'

'Naturally.'

'And don't *you* think he's too good looking for words!'

'It was nearly dark.' Such extreme and calculated duplicity was very unlike Miss Osyth. It ought to have disturbed her conscience, but it did not. She was delighted when Minnie reluctantly left. She desired above everything to think her thoughts in solitude – to think the same thoughts over and over again. She had her wish. No one called at the cottage, not even a tradesman; and she did not go into Flittering. She scarcely even went into her garden – lest, if he came by, Alexis might suspect that she had been lying in wait, for he could not reach the yacht without being seen from the garden. A queer, a touching modesty on her part! But perhaps also it was pride. She did no needlework. She sat. She moved, restless and purposeless, from room to room. She sat. She talked to the cat, and to the fowls, not about herself but about themselves. Like most solitaries she had the habit of talking aloud to herself; but today she said not a word aloud to herself. If she had talked to herself she would have heard things that would have made her uncomfortable, that would have abashed her. And she was supersensitive; the virgin instinctive and watchful in her heart was ready at any moment to leap up like a young and uncontrollably impulsive savage and do strange deeds.

The day was glorious, perfect, endless. The memories of the sun would not leave the evening sky until at last they were annihilated by the enormous moon rising out of the sea. It would be high tide, and a very high tide, just before midnight.

Miss Osyth sat late in her bedroom. But she did not undress. She had dressed with care in the afternoon – not in her best clothes. Oh, no! That would have been absurd. Quietly. But more carefully than usual. And a lovely collarette of her own creation!

'I must go to bed. I cannot go to bed. I must go to bed,' her thoughts circled round and round . . . She looked cautiously between the drawn blind and the side of the window, not for the first time, and started. The light was burning in the yacht's cabin. Unimaginable! Unimaginable that the vibrations of light from one little candle should transpierce the glass of the porthole and the glass of her window, transpierce her head, energise her brain and cause her brain to energise the physical mechanism of her heart till it thumped, thumped, thumped against her tight-fitting blue frock! Frightening! . . .

He had mysteriously returned. How? When? She knew not. But he was there, alone, solitary as herself, within fifty yards of her, enfolded in the tremendous night of the marshes.

She sank to her knees at the window, would not move. She would wait till the light went out. She was now very sad and resentful against herself. She was utterly exhausted too; she was old . . . She heard sounds on the gravel. She heard an ominous, delicious, soft, authoritative knocking at the door below . . . He had come. It was impossible that he should come; but he had come. Young again, strong, eager, and fresh as though she had just risen from a long night's rest, she pushed up the window.

'I suppose you don't happen to have any aspirin?' said the calm, firm voice of Alexis. 'I know it's rotten of me to trouble you; but this hand of mine's throbbing like the deuce.'

5

'No,' Miss Osyth said, holding the wounded hand in her two hands, and examining it by the light of the candle in the cabin, 'it's going on perfectly all right. Of course it's still a bit inflamed, but that's because you've been doing too much today – carrying parcels and things, I expect, and walking a lot.' She spoke reassuringly, with knowledge, and as if there could not possibly be any appeal from her verdict.

'Oh, well, that's fine,' he murmured, admitting her authority by his relieved tone.

She was proud. She at once took charge of the cabin. This interior was about seven feet long by six feet broad. In certain places, under the open flaps of the skylight, Miss Osyth could stand up straight in it, but Alexis could not. A narrow table occupied the centre, and two couches, or beds, flanked the table. It was small, but it was habitable; and the diminutive cosiness of it ravished Miss Osyth. While she dressed the hand with a new bandage which she had brought from the cottage, she kept exclaiming upon the cabin's quality of cosiness. And it was picturesque too: the sides and the top were a dead white, touched here and there with gilt; the table was of teak, which set off the white; the crumpled blankets were highly coloured; and the floor was covered with linoleum in a pattern to imitate large black and white tiles.

'It's a regular little home,' said Miss Osyth. 'It's delicious.' Her voice was ecstatic.

The place was warm, in spite of the open skylight; but she loved the warmth of it. She enquired almost menacingly about his meals, and he replied that he was eating at the inn.

'Yes,' she said. 'I heard you'd made it up with the landlord.'

She laughed. He laughed.

'Things do get about quick, don't they?' he said

'Oh! They do.'

The two exchanged a glance.

'You'd better take the aspirin in hot water.'

'But I haven't got any hot water.'

'But I've brought my thermos,' she said, superiorly. She had laid it in a corner of the empty couch. It was wrapped in white linen.

'What's that?' he said, as she undid the wrapping.

'A clean pillowslip. I don't mind you sleeping in blankets but you oughtn't to have a bare pillow. Tick is horrid against the cheek.'

'You're a wonderful girl,' he observed simply.

'But that's not all,' she said, and crept out of the cabin to the steep stairs leading to the deck. She groped with her hand on the surface of the deck, and brought down a small bunch of flowers which she had left there on entering.

All these little matters she had prepared in advance in the hope of a summons from him. The entry of the garden flowers had quite a sensationally dramatic effect.

'They'll have to have hot water, like you,' she said.

'I've got plenty of cold water now,' said Alexis. 'The landlord was very decent. After all, I couldn't blame him for making a fuss at the start, could I? How should *he* know who I was?'

Miss Osyth said nothing. She was busy with the pillowslip, and the blankets, and turning over the mattress, and the tin mug for the flowers and the smaller tin mug with the hot water for Alexis to drink from. She moved to and fro like a real girl, with the flexibility of a girl and perhaps also the grace. She was acutely aware of her body and rather proud of its shapeliness beneath the thin, nice frock and stockings, and of her fair complexion and soft hair. She bent over the bunk with a wilful sinuosity of movement.

'There ! Now the aspirin at last.'

The pillowslip, immaculate as Miss Osyth herself, gleamed smoothly with a heavenly invitation. The coloured blankets were straightened out, and one corner of the upper one turned back with geometrical precision. The flowers bloomed on the dark table. The small tin mug steamed. Miss Osyth had the tablet of aspirin in her hand. Alexis suddenly and startlingly opened his mouth, advancing the tongue, just like a clever, spoilt child. Miss Osyth trembled at the irresistible gesture, hesitated an instant, and then shakily placed the tablet on the tongue and offered the mug. Alexis blinked. Her excitement was extreme, unique to her, and she was exquisitely troubled. Alexis's gesture was the most marvellous and disturbing phenomenon in her experience. Her finger remembered the thrilling moisture of his tongue.

'I'll go now,' she said, with forced but apparently successful quietude, after he had drunk the water.

'Oh! But you haven't seen my purchases at Colchester. You must tell me what you think of them. Won't take a minute.'

She would have refused to stay one second longer, but could not. She had no will-power. All fortitude had been drawn out of her by felicity. He was so fair and handsome and frank; his movements and voice were so distinguished; and he had been so obedient to her. And they were alone, and necessarily so close together in the warm bright cosiness of the cabin. And the cabin was hidden in the night of the salt-marshes. They were safe. None knew, nor could know, of this intimacy. The sanctions of society stopped short at the tiny paradise of the cabin.

And Miss Osyth handled his small purchases and savoured the masculinity of them. The safety razor, for instance. What a strange and dangerous contrivance! She tried it on the down of her delicate cheek. She took it to pieces, oh, so fearfully. She put it together again.

'No, no!' she cried, as she rose swiftly and unexpectedly to depart. 'Don't move. I can get ashore by myself.' She was gone.

Four nights later – to Miss Osyth the intervening period seemed more like a month than four days, a month in which her nights had become days and her days nights, and her whole existence turned rapturously upside down – Alexis without warning began in the secrecy of the yacht's cabin to tell his companion about the cause of his estrangement from the home in Dorset. He had resolved to join some youthful friends in an expedition, for commercial purposes, to an uninhabited island some hundreds of miles off the west coast of South America. Five hundred pounds was to be his contribution to the general funds of the enterprise, and his rich father had absolutely refused to provide the sum. But he was sure from experience that his mother would wheedle his father into a surrender. To Miss Osyth, Alexis painted his own martyrdom in affecting colours. Tears came into her eyes as she sat by his side on the couch. He was moved by her quick generous sympathy and never guessed that she wept at the prospect of his departure to the other end of the world. He turned his face to hers, and, looking into her wet eyes, gently kissed her unresisting lips. The kiss was a sacrament for her. She bowed her head and held it bowed. He was spellbound by her fair and pure charm. Had she bowed her head in shame, or in acquiescence, or in both? He was intimidated by her innocence. She had no age then; she was neither old nor young, neither mature nor unripe. She was simply that which had been immaculate. Alexis averted his gaze. Before he could decide what he should do next she had risen with a hysterical, instinctive swiftness and vanished. How beautiful and exciting, he thought, was the whirl of her white skirt as she flew up the steep stairs into the dark world of the salt-marshes!

6

The next morning – but it was the same morning – after receiving from the postman a letter which agitated her from the moment she saw the Brussels postmark on the envelope, Miss Osyth went forth towards the yacht with a pencilled note in her hand. She hurried and yet was undecided. No sign of life on the yacht. Alexis must be in the deep sleep of youth. She dared not call, and moreover she was too modest to wake him. The tide was low. Taking off her shoes and stockings she padded through the sticky mud to the yacht's side. She listened and heard faintly the regular breathing of the unseen sleeper, to her a sacred and a beautiful sound. Life had never seemed to her more romantic or more terrible. She was mysteriously afraid of her excessively strange situation, and the immense hitherto unsuspected power of her instincts. The porthole of the little cabin was open. She ledged the note on the lower rim of the porthole and put a stone on it to keep it in place. She knew well enough, with her capacity for detachment, that Alexis must sooner or later involve her in some kind of tragedy. Nevertheless her ecstasy had not abated; it had increased; and it had only been exasperated by the letter from Brussels. Her unsigned note to Alexis ran thus: 'One of my uncles is very ill in Brussels. I have to go. Shall be back as soon as possible. Please do take care of yourself.'

Then began the awful fever of the expedition of a woman who had never travelled. She had to go all the way to London to obtain a passport, and then return all the way to Harwich (whose highest chimney rose on the other side of Mozewater in sight of her cottage) to catch the evening boat for Antwerp . . .

The uncle died. She was hustled in a tram in Brussels and all her money stolen. With the amazing audacity of the timid she made a scene about this, though she could not speak a word of French, at the police station in Brussels. The staff there showed keen curiosity as to herself, and would do nothing until she had revealed, among other things, the maiden name of her mother. And they did nothing afterwards either. They caused her to understand that there were half a dozen pocket robberies a day in the trams of Brussels.

Miss Osyth reached Harwich one morning in black, poorer, but with the prospect of an inheritance. She drove by the curling road round the edge of Mozewater back to her cottage, which smelt fusty and was, to her eyes, intolerably dirty. Some letters awaited, but nothing from Alexis. She was in an agony. She could not conceivably ask for news of him. The yacht, with an air enigmatic and secretive, lay as usual in the hollow of the creek. The weather was still magnificent. In the afternoon she went out for a walk in her salt-marshes; they were hers because she knew them better than any other living person. The tide was at lowest ebb. On the caked margin of the creek she saw an envelope all brown and green. It was unopened and contained her note to Alexis. No doubt in closing the porthole he had without noticing it pushed it into the water. It looked inexpressibly forlorn.

Clutching it in her hand, she moved onwards into the lonely maze of the marshes. She crossed little bridges of an incredible frailness, climbed and descended slopes, jumped the dry beds of rivulets, skirted the marvellous bright greens of treacherous moss, strode through high, sturdy rushes, dusted her shoes in clumps of bracken, startled fowl and ground-game, yielded herself to the vast powers of breeze and sunlight. The landscape was as primeval as the sun and the wind. Scarcely any foot but hers ever ventured into that tremendous waste, which indeed was dangerous enough for the unwary and ignorant. On those walks she always ultimately made for the same objective, a bowl of grass-green land protected equally from the wind and from the water.

In the hollow she saw Alexis and Minnie sitting side by side, and their lips were joined in a long kiss. They were so young, so graceful, so natural, so ingenuous, so innocent in loving gesture, so fitted to the wild and lovely landscape, that Miss Osyth stood entranced, as much by admiration as by a shocked astonishment. They were pure creatures of the golden age which never was and never will be, but which flickers now and then for a moment into a half-existence and vanishes. They had probably been there all day, and nothing but dusk would arouse them to the reality of time. They were sure of their solitude. And it was Miss Osyth herself who had taught Minnie the intricate geography of the marshes.

Miss Osyth turned and ran. She ran, lest she should be seen. She ran because she was ashamed before these two of her age and her disillusion. The memory of the exquisite movements of Minnie's lithe body shamed her . . . These two were bound to meet, and, once met, neither could resist the other.

'But do your father and mother know?' Miss Osyth asked when Minnie feverishly gave her the news.

'Well, it only happened yesterday. Alexis is going to see them today. They'll be all right.'

'And his people?'

'Well, they've *got* to be all right,' said Minnie confidently.

'But isn't there a quarrel?'

'It'll be fixed up. He isn't going on that Pacific island business.'

'Oh! He's given it up?'

'You don't suppose I'd agree to such madness, do you? Oh, Miss Osyth! I love you more than ever because he says you were so frightfully kind to him.' She clung round Miss Osyth's neck. 'I'm so happy I might die of it any minute. I might, really. You can't imagine how happy I am!'

'Oh, yes, I can!' said Miss Osyth firmly.

Minnie, wondering, surveyed her.

'Can you?'

When the beautiful girl had gone, Miss Osyth sat down to the piano and played all alone in the cottage a little prelude of Bach's. And as she played she resolved passionately to be the tireless guardian angel of the two youths. She forgot herself. She was poignantly happy, with a vicarious happiness.

AMBROSE BIERCE

Born in 1842, Ambrose Bierce was the author of supernatural stories that have secured his place in both the weird tradition and in the wider world of American letters. He is also noted for his tales of the Civil War, which drew on his own experience as a Union cartographer and officer. His first job in journalism was as editor for the *San Francisco News-Letter* and *California Advertiser* (1868–72). In time, Bierce established himself a kind of literary dictator of the West Coast and was so respected and feared as a critic that his judgement could 'make or break' an aspiring author's reputation. Well known by his mere initials, A. G. B., he was called by his enemies and detractors 'Almighty God Bierce'. He was also nicknamed 'Bitter Bierce' and his nihilistic motto was, 'Nothing matters.' Bierce is best remembered for his cynical but humorous *Devil's Dictionary*. In 1913, at the age of seventy-one, Bierce disappeared into revolution-torn Mexico to fight alongside the bandit Pancho Villa. Although a popular theory is that Bierce argued with Villa over military strategy and was subsequently shot, he probably perished in the battle of Ojinaga on 11 January 1914.

The Man and the Snake

It is of veritabyll report, and attested of so many that there be nowe of wyse and learned none to gaynsaye it, that ye serpente hys eye hath a magnetick propertie that whosoe falleth into its vasion is drawn forwards in despyte of his wille, and perisheth miserabyll by ye creature hys byte.

Stretched at ease upon a sofa, in gown and slippers, Harker Brayton smiled as he read the foregoing sentence in old Morryster's *Marvells of Science*. 'The only marvel in the matter,' he said to himself, 'is that the wise and learned in Morryster's day should have believed such nonsense as is rejected by most of even the ignorant in ours.'

A train of reflections followed – for Brayton was a man of thought – and he unconsciously lowered his book without altering the direction of his eyes. As soon as the volume had gone below the line of sight, something in an obscure corner of the room recalled his attention to his surroundings. What he saw, in the shadow under his bed, were two small points of light, apparently about an inch apart. They might have been reflections of the gas jet above him in metal nail heads; he gave them but little thought and resumed his reading. A moment later something – some impulse which it did not occur to him to analyse – impelled him to lower the book again and seek for what he saw before. The points of light were still there. They seemed to have become brighter than before, shining with a greenish luster which he had not at first observed. He thought, too, that they might have moved a trifle – were somewhat nearer. They were still too much in the shadow, however, to reveal their nature and origin to an indolent attention, and he resumed his reading. Suddenly something in the text suggested a thought which made him start and drop the book for the third time to the side of the sofa, whence, escaping from his hand, it fell sprawling to the floor, back upward. Brayton, half-risen, was staring intently into the obscurity beneath the bed, where the points of light shone with, it seemed to him, an added fire. His attention was now fully aroused, his gaze eager and imperative. It disclosed, almost directly beneath the foot rail of the bed, the coils of a large serpent – the points of light were its eyes! Its horrible head, thrust flatly forth from the innermost coil and resting upon the outermost, was directed straight toward him, the definition of the wide, brutal jaw and the idiot-like forehead serving to show the direction of its malevolent gaze. The eyes were no longer merely luminous points; they looked into his own with a meaning, a malign significance.

2

A snake in a bedroom of a modern city dwelling of the better sort is, happily, not so common a phenomenon as to make explanation altogether needless. Harker Brayton, a bachelor of thirty-five, a scholar, idler, and something of an athlete, rich, popular and of sound health, had returned to San Francisco from all manner of remote and unfamiliar countries. His tastes, always a trifle luxurious, had taken on an added exuberance from long privation; and the resources of even the Castle Hotel being inadequate for their perfect gratification, he had gladly accepted the hospitality of his friend, Dr Druring, the distinguished scientist. Dr Druring's house, a large, old-fashioned one in what was now an obscure quarter of the city, had an outer and visible aspect of reserve. It plainly would not associate with the contiguous elements of its altered environment, and appeared to have developed some of the eccent-ricities which come of isolation. One of these was a 'wing', conspicuously irrelevant in point of architecture, and no less rebellious in the matter of purpose; for it was a combination of laboratory, menagerie and museum. It was here that the doctor indulged the scientific side of his nature in the study of such forms of animal life as engaged his interest and comforted his taste – which, it must be confessed, ran rather to the lower forms. For one of the higher types nimbly and sweetly to recommend itself unto his gentle senses, it had at least to retain certain rudimentary characteristics allying it to such 'dragons of the prime' as toads and snakes. His scientific sympathies were distinctly reptilian; he loved nature's vulgarians and described himself as the Zola of zoology. His wife and daughters, not having the advantage to share his enlightened curiosity regarding the works and ways of our ill-starred fellow-creatures, were, with needless austerity, excluded from what he called the Snakery, and doomed to companionship with their own kind; though, to soften the rigours of their lot, he had permitted them, out of his great wealth, to outdo the reptiles in the gorgeousness of their surroundings and to shine with a superior splendour.

Architecturally, and in point of 'furnishing', the Snakery had a severe simplicity befitting the humble circumstances of its occupants, many of whom, indeed, could not safely have been entrusted with the liberty which is necessary to the full enjoyment of luxury, for they had the troublesome peculiarity of being alive. In their own apartments, however, they were under as little personal restraint as was compatible with their protection from the baneful habit of swallowing one another; and, as Brayton had thoughtfully been apprised, it was more than a tradition that some of them had at divers times been found in parts of the premises where it would have embarrassed them to explain their presence. Despite the Snakery and its uncanny associations – to which, indeed, he gave little attention – Brayton found life at the Druring mansion very much to his mind.

3

Beyond a smart shock of surprise and a shudder of mere loathing, Mr Brayton was not greatly affected. His first thought was to ring the call-bell and bring a servant; but, although the bell-cord dangled within easy reach, he made no movement toward it; it had occurred to his mind that the act might subject him to the suspicion of fear, which he certainly did not feel. He was more keenly conscious of the incongruous nature of the situation than affected by its perils; it was revolting, but absurd.

The reptile was of a species with which Brayton was unfamiliar. Its length he could only conjecture; the body at the largest visible part seemed about as thick as his forearm. In what way was it dangerous, if in any way? Was it venomous? Was it a constrictor? His knowledge of nature's danger signals did not enable him to say; he had never deciphered the code.

If not dangerous, the creature was at least offensive. It was *de trop* – 'matter out of place' – an impertinence. The gem was unworthy of the setting. Even the barbarous taste of our time and country, which had loaded the walls of the room with pictures, the floor with furniture, and the furniture with bric-a-brac, had not quite fitted the place for this bit of the savage life of the jungle. Besides – insupportable thought! – the exhalations of its breath mingled with the atmosphere which he himself was breathing!

These thoughts shaped themselves with greater or less definition in Brayton's mind, and begot action. The process is what we call consideration and decision. It is thus that we are wise and unwise. It is thus that the withered leaf in an autumn breeze shows greater or less intelligence than its fellows, falling upon the land or upon the lake. The secret of human action is an open one – something contracts our muscles. Does it matter if we give to the preparatory molecular changes the name of will?

Brayton rose to his feet and prepared to back softly away from the snake, without disturbing it, if possible, and through the door. People retire so from the presence of the great, for greatness is power, and power is a menace. He knew that he could walk backward without obstruction, and find the door without error. Should the monster follow, the taste which had plastered the walls with paintings had consistently supplied a rack of murderous Oriental weapons from which he could snatch one to suit the occasion. In the meantime the snake's eyes burned with a more pitiless malevolence than ever.

Brayton lifted his right foot free of the floor to step backward. That moment he felt a strong aversion to doing so.

'I am accounted brave,' he murmured; 'is bravery, then, no more than pride? Because there are none to witness the shame shall I retreat?'

He was steadying himself with his right hand upon the back of a chair, his foot suspended.

'Nonsense!' he said aloud; 'I am not so great a coward as to fear to seem to myself afraid.'

He lifted the foot a little higher by slightly bending the knee, and thrust it sharply to the floor – an inch in front of the other! He could not think how that occurred. A trial with the left foot had the same result; it was again in advance of the right. The hand upon the chair back was grasping it; the arm was straight, reaching somewhat backward. One might have seen that he was reluctant to lose his hold. The snake's malignant head was still thrust forth from the inner coil as before, the neck level. It had not moved, but its eyes were now electric sparks, radiating an infinity of luminous needles.

The man had an ashy pallor. Again he took a step forward, and another, partly dragging the chair, which, when finally released, fell upon the floor with a crash. The man groaned; the snake made neither sound nor motion, but its eyes were two dazzling suns. The reptile itself was wholly concealed by them. They gave off enlarging rings of rich and vivid colours, which at their greatest expansion successively vanished like soap bubbles; they seemed to approach his very face, and anon were an immeasurable distance away. He heard, somewhere, the continual throbbing of a great drum, with desultory bursts of far music, inconceivably sweet, like the tones of an Aeolian harp. He knew it for the sunrise melody of Memnon's statue, and thought he stood in the Nileside reeds, hearing, with exalted sense, that immortal anthem through the silence of the centuries.

The music ceased; rather, it became by insensible degrees the distant roll of a retreating thunderstorm. A landscape, glittering with sun and rain, stretched before him, arched with a vivid rainbow, framing in its giant curve a hundred visible cities. In the middle distance a vast serpent, wearing a crown, reared its head out of its voluminous convolutions and looked at him with his dead mother's eyes. Suddenly this enchanting landscape seemed to rise swiftly upward, like the drop scene at a theatre, and vanished in a blank. Something struck him a hard blow upon the face and breast. He had fallen to the floor; the blood ran from his broken nose and his bruised lips. For a moment he was dazed and stunned, and lay with closed eyes, his face against the door. In a few moments he had recovered, and then realised that his fall, by withdrawing his eyes, had broken the spell which held him. He felt that now, by keeping his gaze averted, he would be able to retreat. But the thought of the serpent within a few feet of his head, yet unseen – perhaps in the very act of springing upon him and throwing its coils about his throat – was too horrible. He lifted his head, stared again into those baleful eyes, and was again in bondage.

The snake had not moved, and appeared somewhat to have lost its power upon the imagination; the gorgeous illusions of a few moments before were not repeated. Beneath that flat and brainless brow its black, beady eyes simply glittered, as at first, with an expression unspeakably malignant. It was as if the creature, knowing its triumph assured, had determined to practice no more alluring wiles.

Now ensued a fearful scene. The man, prone upon the floor, within a yard of his enemy, raised the upper part of his body upon his elbows, his head thrown back, his legs extended to their full length. His face was white between its gouts of blood; his eyes were strained open to their uttermost expansion. There was froth upon his lips; it dropped off in flakes. Strong convulsions ran through his body, making almost serpentine undulations. He bent himself at the waist, shifting his legs from side to side. And every movement left him a little nearer to the snake. He thrust his hands forward to brace himself back, yet constantly advanced upon his elbows.

4

Dr Druring and his wife sat in the library. The scientist was in rare good humour.

'I have just obtained, by exchange with another collector,' he said, 'a splendid specimen of the *Ophiophagus*.'

'And what may that be?' the lady enquired with a somewhat languid interest.

'Why, bless my soul, what profound ignorance! My dear, a man who ascertains after marriage that his wife does not know Greek, is entitled to a divorce. The *Ophiophagus* is a snake which eats other snakes.'

'I hope it will eat all yours,' she said, absently shifting the lamp. 'But how does it get the other snakes? By charming them, I suppose.'

'That is just like you, dear,' said the doctor, with an affectation of petulance. 'You know how irritating to me is any allusion to that vulgar superstition about the snake's power of fascination.'

The conversation was interrupted by a mighty cry which rang through the silent house like the voice of a demon shouting in a tomb. Again and yet again it sounded, with terrible distinctness. They sprang to their feet, the man confused, the lady pale and speechless with fright. Almost before the echoes of the last cry had died away the doctor was out of the room, springing up the staircase two steps at a time. In the corridor, in front of Brayton's chamber, he met some servants who had come from the upper floor. Together they rushed at the door without knocking. It was unfastened, and gave way. Brayton lay upon his stomach on the floor, dead. His head and arms were partly concealed under the foot rail of the bed. They pulled the body away, turning it upon the back. The face was daubed with blood and froth, the eyes were wide open, staring – a dreadful sight!

'Died in a fit,' said the scientist, bending his knee and placing his hand upon the heart. While in that position he happened to glance under the bed. 'Good God!' he added; 'how did this thing get in here?'

He reached under the bed, pulled out the snake, and flung it, still coiled, to the centre of the room, whence, with a harsh, shuffling sound, it slid across the polished floor till stopped by the wall, where it lay without motion. It was a stuffed snake; its eyes were two shoe buttons.

The Suitable Surroundings

The Night

One midsummer night a farmer's boy living about ten miles from the city of Cincinnati was following a bridle path through a dense and dark forest. He had lost himself while searching for some missing cows, and near midnight was a long way from home, in a part of the country with which he was unfamiliar. But he was a stout-hearted lad, and knowing his general direction from his home, he plunged into the forest without hesitation, guided by the stars. Coming into the bridle path, and observing that it ran in the right direction, he followed it.

The night was clear, but in the woods it was exceedingly dark. It was more by the sense of touch than by that of sight that the lad kept the path. He could not, indeed, very easily go astray; the undergrowth on both sides was so thick as to be almost impenetrable. He had gone into the forest a mile or more when he was surprised to see a feeble gleam of light shining through the foliage skirting the path on his left. The sight of it startled him and set his heart beating audibly.

'The old Breede house is somewhere about here,' he said to himself. 'This must be the other end of the path which we reach it by from our side. Ugh! what should a light be doing there?'

Nevertheless, he pushed on. A moment later he had emerged from the forest into a small, open space, mostly upgrown to brambles. There were remnants of a rotting fence. A few yards from the trail, in the middle of the 'clearing', was the house from which the light came, through an unglazed window. The window had once contained glass, but that and its supporting frame had long ago yielded to missiles flung by hands of venturesome boys to attest alike their courage and their hostility to the supernatural; for the Breede house bore the evil reputation of being haunted. Possibly it was not, but even the hardiest sceptic could not deny that it was deserted – which in rural regions is much the same thing.

Looking at the mysterious dim light shining from the ruined window the boy remembered with apprehension that his own hand had assisted at the destruction. His penitence was of course poignant in proportion to its tardiness and inefficacy. He half expected to be set upon by all the unworldly and bodiless malevolences whom he had outraged by assisting to break alike their windows and their peace. Yet this stubborn lad, shaking in every limb, would not retreat. The blood in his veins was strong and rich with the iron of the frontiersman. He was but two removes from the generation that had

87

subdued the Indian. He started to pass the house.

As he was going by he looked in at the blank window space and saw a strange and terrifying sight – the figure of a man seated in the centre of the room, at a table upon which lay some loose sheets of paper. The elbows rested on the table, the hands supporting the head, which was uncovered. On each side the fingers were pushed into the hair. The face showed dead-yellow in the light of a single candle a little to one side. The flame illuminated that side of the face, the other was in deep shadow. The man's eyes were fixed upon the blank window space with a stare in which an older and cooler observer might have discerned something of apprehension, but which seemed to the lad altogether soulless. He believed the man to be dead.

The situation was horrible, but not without its fascination. The boy stopped to note it all. He was weak, faint and trembling; he could feel the blood forsaking his face. Nevertheless, he set his teeth and resolutely advanced to the house. He had no conscious intention – it was the mere courage of terror. He thrust his white face forward into the illuminated opening. At that instant a strange harsh cry, a shriek, broke upon the silence of the night – the note of a screech-owl. The man sprang to his feet, overturning the table and extinguishing the candle. The boy took to his heels.

The Day Before

'Good-morning, Colston. I am in luck, it seems. You have often said that my commendation of your literary work was mere civility, and here you find me absorbed – actually merged – in your latest story in the *Messenger*. Nothing less shocking than your touch upon my shoulder would have roused me to consciousness.'

'The proof is stronger than you seem to know,' replied the man addressed: 'so keen is your eagerness to read my story that you are willing to renounce selfish considerations and forgo all the pleasure that you could get from it.'

'I don't understand you,' said the other, folding the newspaper that he held and putting it into his pocket. 'You writers are a queer lot, anyhow. Come, tell me what I have done or omitted in this matter. In what way does the pleasure that I get, or might get, from your work depend on me?'

'In many ways. Let me ask you how you would enjoy your breakfast if you took it in this street car. Suppose the phonograph so perfected as to be able to give you an entire opera – singing, orchestration, and all; do you think you would get much pleasure out of it if you turned it on at your office during business hours? Do you really care for a serenade by Schubert when you hear it fiddled by an untimely Italian on a morning ferryboat? Are you always cocked and primed for enjoyment? Do you keep every mood on tap, ready to any demand? Let me remind you, sir, that the story which you have done me the honour to begin as a means of becoming oblivious to the discomfort of this car is a ghost story!'

'Well?'

'Well! Has the reader no duties corresponding to his privileges? You have paid five cents for that newspaper. It is yours. You have the right to read it when and where you will. Much of what is in it is neither helped nor harmed by time and place and mood; some of it actually requires to be read at once – while it is fizzing. But my story is not of that character. It is not "the very latest advices" from Ghostland. You are not expected to keep yourself *au courant* with what is going on in the realm of spooks. The stuff will keep until you have leisure to put yourself into the frame of mind appropriate to the sentiment of the piece – which I respectfully submit that you cannot do in a street car, even if you are the only passenger. The solitude is not of the right sort. An author has rights which the reader is bound to respect.'

'For specific example?'

'The right to the reader's undivided attention. To deny him this is immoral. To make him share your attention with the rattle of a street car, the moving panorama of the crowds on the sidewalks, and the buildings beyond – with any of the thousands of distractions which make our customary environment – is to treat him with gross injustice. By God, it is infamous!'

The speaker had risen to his feet and was steadying himself by one of the straps hanging from the roof of the car. The other man looked up at him in sudden astonishment, wondering how so trivial a grievance could seem to justify so strong language. He saw that his friend's face was uncommonly pale and that his eyes glowed like living coals.

'You know what I mean,' continued the writer, impetuously crowding his words – 'you know what I mean, Marsh. My stuff in this morning's *Messenger* is plainly sub-headed "A Ghost Story". That is ample notice to all. Every honorable reader will understand it as prescribing by implication the conditions under which the work is to be read.'

The man addressed as Marsh winced a trifle, then asked with a smile: 'What conditions? You know that I am only a plain businessman who cannot be supposed to understand such things. How, when, where should I read your ghost story?'

'In solitude – at night – by the light of a candle. There are certain emotions which a writer can easily enough excite – such as compassion or merriment. I can move you to tears or laughter under almost any circumstances. But for my ghost story to be effective you must be made to feel fear – at least a strong sense of the supernatural--and that is a difficult matter. I have a right to expect that if you read me at all you will give me a chance; that you will make yourself accessible to the emotion that I try to inspire.'

The car had now arrived at its terminus and stopped. The trip just completed was its first for the day and the conversation of the two early passengers had not been interrupted. The streets were yet silent and desolate; the house tops were just touched by the rising sun. As they stepped from the car and walked away together Marsh narrowly eyed his companion, who was reported, like most men of uncommon literary ability, to be addicted to various destructive vices. That is the revenge which dull minds take upon bright ones in resentment of their superiority. Mr Colston was known as a man of genius. There are honest souls who believe that genius is a mode of excess. It was known that Colston did not drink liquor, but many said that he ate opium. Something in his appearance that morning – a certain wildness of the eyes, an unusual pallor, a thickness and rapidity of speech – were taken by Mr Marsh to confirm the report. Nevertheless, he had not the self-denial to abandon a subject which he found interesting, however it might excite his friend.

'Do you mean to say,' he began, 'that if I take the trouble to observe your directions – place myself in the conditions that you demand: solitude, night and a tallow candle – you can with your ghostly work give me an uncomfortable sense of the supernatural, as you call it? Can you accelerate my pulse, make me start at sudden noises, send a nervous chill along my spine and cause my hair to rise?'

Colston turned suddenly and looked him squarely in the eyes as they walked. 'You would not dare – you have not the courage,' he said. He emphasised the words with a contemptuous gesture. 'You are brave enough to read me in a street car, but – in a deserted house – alone – in the forest – at night! Bah! I have a manuscript in my pocket that would kill you.'

Marsh was angry. He knew himself courageous, and the words stung him. 'If you know such a place,' he said, 'take me there tonight and leave me your story and a candle. Call for me when I've had time enough to read it and I'll tell you the entire plot and – kick you out of the place.'

That is how it occurred that the farmer's boy, looking in at an unglazed window of the Breede house, saw a man sitting in the light of a candle.

The Day After

Late in the afternoon of the next day three men and a boy approached the Breede house from that point of the compass toward which the boy had fled the preceding night. The men were in high spirits; they talked very loudly and laughed. They made facetious and good-humored ironical remarks to the boy about his adventure, which evidently they did not believe in. The boy accepted their raillery with seriousness, making no reply. He had a sense of the fitness of things and knew that one who professes to have seen a dead man rise from his seat and blow out a candle is not a credible witness.

Arriving at the house and finding the door unlocked, the party of investigators entered without ceremony. Leading out of the passage into which this door opened was another on the right and one on the left. They entered the room on the left – the one which had the blank front window. Here was the dead body of a man.

It lay partly on one side, with the forearm beneath it, the cheek on the floor. The eyes were wide open; the stare was not an agreeable thing to encounter. The lower jaw had fallen; a little pool of saliva had collected beneath the mouth. An overthrown table, a partly burned candle, a chair and some paper with writing on it were all else that the room contained. The men looked at the body, touching the face in turn. The boy gravely stood at the head, assuming a look of ownership. It was the proudest moment of his life. One of the men said to him, 'You're a good 'un' – a remark which was received by the two others with nods of acquiescence. It was Scepticism apologising to Truth. Then one of the men took from the floor the sheet of manuscript and stepped to the window, for already the evening shadows were glooming the forest. The song of the whippoorwill was heard in the distance and a monstrous beetle sped by the window on roaring wings and thundered away out of hearing. The man read:

> Before committing the act which, rightly or wrongly, I have resolved on and appearing before my Maker for judgement, I, James R. Colston, deem it my duty as a journalist to make a statement to the public. My name is, I believe, tolerably well known to the people as a writer of tragic tales, but the somberest imagination never conceived anything so tragic as my own life and history. Not in incident: my life has been destitute of adventure and action. But my mental career has been lurid with experiences such as kill and damn. I shall not recount them here – some of them are written and ready for publication elsewhere. The object of these lines is to explain to whomsoever may be interested that my death is voluntary – my own act. I shall die at twelve o'clock on the night of the 15th of July – a significant anniversary to me, for it was on that day, and at that hour, that my friend in time and eternity, Charles Breede, performed his vow to me by the same act which his fidelity to our pledge now entails upon me. He took his life in his little house in the Copeton woods. There was the customary verdict of 'temporary insanity'. Had I testified at that inquest – had I told all I knew, they would have called *me* mad!

Here followed an evidently long passage which the man reading read to himself only. The rest he read aloud.

> I have still a week of life in which to arrange my worldly affairs and prepare for the great change. It is enough, for I have but few affairs and it is now four years since death became an imperative obligation.
>
> I shall bear this writing on my body; the finder will please hand it to the coroner.
>
> James R. Colston
>
> PS Willard Marsh, on this the fatal fifteenth day of July I hand you this manuscript, to be opened and read under the conditions agreed upon, and

at the place which I designated. I forgo my intention to keep it on my body to explain the manner of my death, which is not important. It will serve to explain the manner of yours. I am to call for you during the night to receive assurance that you have read the manuscript. You know me well enough to expect me. But, my friend, it *will be after twelve o'clock*. May God have mercy on our souls!

J. R. C.

Before the man who was reading this manuscript had finished, the candle had been picked up and lighted. When the reader had done, he quietly thrust the paper against the flame and despite the protestations of the others held it until it was burnt to ashes. The man who did this, and who afterward placidly endured a severe reprimand from the coroner, was a son-in-law of the late Charles Breede. At the inquest nothing could elicit an intelligent account of what the paper had contained.

[From *The Times*] Yesterday the Commissioners of Lunacy committed to the asylum Mr James R. Colston, a writer of some local reputation, connected with the *Messenger*. It will be remembered that on the evening of the 15th inst. Mr Colston was given into custody by one of his fellow-lodgers in the Baine House, who had observed him acting very suspiciously, baring his throat and whetting a razor – occasionally trying its edge by actually cutting through the skin of his arm, etc. On being handed over to the police, the unfortunate man made a desperate resistance, and has ever since been so violent that it has been necessary to keep him in a strait-jacket.

A Resumed Identity

I

One summer night a man stood on a low hill overlooking a wide expanse of forest and field. By the full moon hanging low in the west he knew what he might not have known otherwise: that it was near the hour of dawn. A light mist lay along the earth, partly veiling the lower features of the landscape, but above it the taller trees showed in well-defined masses against a clear sky. Two or three farmhouses were visible through the haze, but in none of them, naturally, was a light. Nowhere, indeed, was any sign or suggestion of life except the barking of a distant dog, which, repeated with mechanical iteration, served rather to accentuate than dispel the loneliness of the scene.

The man looked curiously about him on all sides, as one who among familiar surroundings is unable to determine his exact place and part in the scheme of things. It is so, perhaps, that we shall act when, risen from the dead, we await the call to judgment.

A hundred yards away was a straight road, showing white in the moonlight. Endeavouring to orient himself, as a surveyor or navigator might say, the man moved his eyes slowly along its visible length and at a distance of a quarter-mile to the south of his station saw, dim and grey in the haze, a group of horsemen riding to the north. Behind them were men afoot, marching in column, with dimly gleaming rifles aslant above their shoulders. They moved slowly and in silence. Another group of horsemen, another regiment of infantry, another and another – all in unceasing motion toward the man's point of view, past it, and beyond. A battery of artillery followed, the cannoneers riding with folded arms on limber and caisson. And still the interminable procession came out of the obscurity to south and passed into the obscurity to north, with never a sound of voice, nor hoof, nor wheel.

The man could not rightly understand: he thought himself deaf; said so, and heard his own voice, although it had an unfamiliar quality that almost alarmed him; it disappointed his ears' expectancy in the matter of timbre and resonance. But he was not deaf, and that for the moment sufficed.

Then he remembered that there are natural phenomena to which someone has given the name 'acoustic shadows'. If you stand in an acoustic shadow there is one direction from which you will hear nothing. At the battle of Gaines's Mill, one of the fiercest conflicts of the Civil War, with a hundred guns in play, spectators a mile and a half away on the opposite side of the Chickahominy valley heard nothing of what they clearly saw. The bombardment of Port Royal, heard and felt at St Augustine, a hundred and fifty miles to the south, was inaudible two miles to the north in a still atmosphere. A few days before the surrender at Appomattox a thunderous engagement between the commands of Sheridan and Pickett was unknown to the latter commander, a mile in the rear of his own line.

These instances were not known to the man of whom we write, but less striking ones of the same character had not escaped his observation. He was profoundly disquieted, but for another reason than the uncanny silence of that moonlight march.

'Good Lord!' he said to himself – and again it was as if another had spoken his thought – 'if those people are what I take them to be we have lost the battle and they are moving on Nashville!'

Then came a thought of self – an apprehension – a strong sense of personal peril, such as in another we call fear. He stepped quickly into the shadow of a tree. And still the silent battalions moved slowly forward in the haze.

The chill of a sudden breeze upon the back of his neck drew his attention to the quarter whence it came, and turning to the east he saw a faint grey light along the horizon – the first sign of returning day. This increased his apprehension.

'I must get away from here,' he thought, 'or I shall be discovered and taken.'

He moved out of the shadow, walking rapidly toward the greying east. From the safer seclusion of a clump of cedars he looked back. The entire column had passed out of sight: the straight white road lay bare and desolate in the moonlight!

Puzzled before, he was now inexpressibly astonished. So swift a passing of so slow an army! – he could not comprehend it. Minute after minute passed unnoted; he had lost his sense of time. He sought with a terrible earnestness a solution of the mystery, but sought in vain. When at last he roused himself from his abstraction the sun's rim was visible above the hills, but in the new conditions he found no other light than that of day; his understanding was involved as darkly in doubt as before.

On every side lay cultivated fields showing no sign of war and war's ravages. From the chimneys of the farmhouses thin ascensions of blue smoke signalled preparations for a day's peaceful toil. Having stilled its immemorial allocution to the moon, the watchdog was assisting a negro who, prefixing a team of mules to the plough, was flatting and sharping contentedly at his task. The hero of this tale stared stupidly at the pastoral picture as if he had never seen such a thing in all his life; then he put his hand to his head, passed it through his hair and, withdrawing it, attentively considered the palm – a singular thing to do. Apparently reassured by the act, he walked confidently toward the road.

Dr Stilling Malson, of Murfreesboro, having visited a patient six or seven miles away, on the Nashville road, had remained with him all night. At daybreak he set out for home on horseback, as was the custom of doctors of the time and region. He had passed into the neighbourhood of Stone's River battlefield when a man approached him from the roadside and saluted in the military fashion, with a movement of the right hand to the hat-brim. But the hat was not a military hat, the man was not in uniform and had not a martial bearing. The doctor nodded civilly, half thinking that the stranger's uncommon greeting was perhaps in deference to the historic surroundings. As the stranger evidently desired speech with him he courteously reined in his horse and waited.

'Sir,' said the stranger, 'although a civilian, you are perhaps an enemy.'

'I am a physician,' was the noncommittal reply.

'Thank you,' said the other. 'I am a lieutenant, of the staff of General Hazen . . .' he paused a moment and looked sharply at the person whom he was addressing, then added, 'of the Federal army.'

The physician merely nodded.

'Kindly tell me,' continued the other, 'what has happened here. Where are the armies? Which has won the battle?'

The physician regarded his questioner curiously with half-shut eyes. After a professional scrutiny, prolonged to the limit of politeness, 'Pardon me,' he said; 'one asking information should be willing to impart it. Are you wounded?' he added, smiling.

'Not seriously – it seems.'

The man removed the unmilitary hat, put his hand to his head, passed it through his hair and, withdrawing it, attentively considered the palm.

'I was struck by a bullet and have been unconscious. It must have been a light, glancing blow: I find no blood and feel no pain. I will not trouble you for treatment, but will you kindly direct me to my command – to any part of the Federal army – if you know?'

Again the doctor did not immediately reply: he was recalling much that is recorded in the books of his profession – something about lost identity and the effect of familiar scenes in restoring it. At length he looked the man in the face, smiled and said: 'Lieutenant, you are not wearing the uniform of your rank and service.'

At this the man glanced down at his civilian attire, lifted his eyes, and said with hesitation: 'That is true. I – I don't quite understand.'

Still regarding him sharply but not unsympathetically the man of science bluntly enquired: 'How old are you?'

'Twenty-three – if that has anything to do with it.'

'You don't look it; I should hardly have guessed you to be just that.'

The man was growing impatient. 'We need not discuss that,' he said; 'I want to know about the army. Not two hours ago I saw a column of troops moving northward on this road. You must have met them. Be good enough to tell me the colour of their clothing, which I was unable to make out, and I'll trouble you no more.'

'You are quite sure that you saw them?'

'Sure? My God, sir, I could have counted them!'

'Why, really,' said the physician, with an amusing consciousness of his own resemblance to the loquacious barber of *The Arabian Nights*, 'this is very interesting. I met no troops.'

The man looked at him coldly, as if he had himself observed the likeness to the barber. 'It is plain,' he said, 'that you do not care to assist me. Sir, you may go to the devil!'

He turned and strode away, very much at random, across the dewy fields, his half-penitent tormentor quietly watching him from his point of vantage in the saddle till he disappeared beyond an array of trees.

3

After leaving the road the man slackened his pace, and now went forward, rather deviously, with a distinct feeling of fatigue. He could not account for this, though truly the interminable loquacity of that country doctor offered itself in explanation. Seating himself upon a rock, he laid one hand upon his knee, back upward, and casually looked at it. It was lean and withered. He lifted both hands to his face. It was seamed and furrowed; he could trace the lines with the tips of his fingers. How strange! – a mere bullet-stroke and a brief unconsciousness should not make one a physical wreck.

'I must have been a long time in hospital,' he said aloud. 'Why what a fool I am! The battle was in December, and it is now summer!' He laughed. 'No wonder that fellow thought me an escaped lunatic. He was wrong: I am only an escaped patient.'

At a little distance a small plot of ground enclosed by a stone wall caught his attention. With no very definite intent he rose and went to it. In the centre was a square, solid monument of hewn stone. It was brown with age, weather-worn at the angles, spotted with moss and lichen. Between the massive blocks were strips of grass the leverage of whose roots had pushed them apart. In answer to the challenge of this ambitious structure Time had laid his destroying hand upon it, and it would soon be 'one with Nineveh and Tyre'. In an inscription on one side his eye caught a familiar name. Shaking with excitement, he craned his body across the wall and read:

HAZEN'S BRIGADE

*to the memory of its
soldiers who fell at*

Stone River, December 31, 1862

The man fell back from the wall, faint and sick. Almost within an arm's length was a little depression in the earth; it had been filled by a recent rain – a pool of clear water. He crept to it to revive himself, lifted the upper part of his body on his trembling arms, thrust forward his head and saw the reflection of his face, as in a mirror. He uttered a terrible cry. His arms gave way; he fell, face downward, into the pool and yielded up the life that had spanned another life.

My Favourite Murder

Having murdered my mother under circumstances of singular atrocity, I was arrested and put upon trial, which lasted seven years. In summing up, the judge of the Court of Acquittal remarked that it was one of the most ghastly crimes that he had ever been called upon to explain away.

At this my counsel rose and said:

'May it please your honour, crimes are ghastly or agreeable only by comparison. If you were familiar with the details of my client's previous murder of his uncle, you would discern in his later offence something in the nature of tender forbearance and filial consideration for the feelings of the victim. The appalling ferocity of the former assassination was indeed inconsistent with any hypothesis but that of guilt; and had it not been for the fact that the honourable judge before whom he was tried was the president of a life insurance company which took risks on hanging, and in which my client held a policy, it is impossible to see how he could have been decently acquitted. If your honour would like to hear about it for the instruction and guidance of your honour's mind, this unfortunate man, my client, will consent to give himself the pain of relating it under oath.'

The district attorney said: 'Your honour, I object. Such a statement would be in the nature of evidence, and the testimony in this case is closed. The prisoner's statement should have been introduced three years ago, in the spring of 1881.'

'In a statutory sense,' said the judge, 'you are right, and in the Court of Objections and Technicalities you would get a ruling in your favour. But not in a Court of Acquittal. The objection is overruled.'

'I except,' said the district attorney.

'You cannot do that,' the judge said. 'I must remind you that in order to take an exception you must first get this case transferred for a time to the Court of Exceptions upon a formal motion duly supported by affidavits. A motion to that effect by your predecessor in office was denied by me during the first year of this trial.

'Mr. Clerk, swear the prisoner.'

The customary oath having been administered, I made the following statement, which impressed the judge with so strong a sense of the comparative triviality of the offence for which I was on trial that he made no further search for mitigating circumstances, but simply instructed the jury to acquit, and I left the court without a stain upon my reputation.

'I was born in 1856 in Kalamakee, Michigan, of honest and reputable parents, one of whom heaven has mercifully spared to comfort me in my later years. In 1867 the family came to California and settled near Nigger Head, where my father opened a road agency and prospered beyond the dreams of avarice. He was a silent, saturnine man then, though his increasing years have now somewhat relaxed the austerity of his disposition, and I believe that nothing but his memory of the sad event for which I am now on trial prevents him from manifesting a genuine hilarity.

'Four years after we had set up the road agency an itinerant preacher came along, and having no other way to pay for the night's lodging which we gave him, favoured us with an exhortation of such power that, praise God, we were all converted to religion. My father at once sent for his brother, the Honourable William Ridley of Stockton, and on his arrival turned over the agency to him, charging him nothing for the franchise or plant – the latter consisting of a Winchester rifle, a sawn-off shot gun and an assortment of masks made out of flour sacks. The family then moved to Ghost Rock and opened a dance house. It was called The Saints' Rest Hurdy-Gurdy, and the proceedings each night began with a prayer. It was there that my now sainted mother, by her grace in the dance, acquired the sobriquet of The Bucking Walrus.

'In the fall of '75 I had occasion to visit Coyote, on the road to Mahala, and took the stage at Ghost Rock. There were four other passengers. About three miles beyond Nigger Head, persons whom I identified as my Uncle William and his two sons held up the stage. Finding nothing in the express box, they went through the passengers. I acted a most honourable part in the affair, placing myself in line with the others, holding up my hands and permitting myself to be deprived of forty dollars and a gold watch. From my behaviour no one could have suspected that I knew the gentlemen who gave the entertainment. A few days later, when I went to Nigger Head and asked for the return of my money and watch, my uncle and cousins swore they knew nothing of the matter, and they affected a belief that my father and I had done the job ourselves in dishonest violation of commercial good faith. Uncle William even threatened to retaliate by starting an opposition dance house at Ghost Rock. As The Saints' Rest had become rather unpopular, I saw that this would assuredly ruin it and prove a paying enterprise, so I told my uncle that I was willing to overlook the past if he would take me into the scheme and keep the partnership a secret from my father. This fair offer he rejected, and I then perceived that it would be better and more satisfactory if he were dead.

'My plans to that end were soon perfected, and communicating them to my dear parents, I had the gratification of receiving their approval. My father said he was proud of me, and my mother promised that, although her religion forbade her to assist in taking human life, I should have the advantage of her prayers for my success. As a preliminary measure, looking to my security in case of detection, I made an application for membership in that powerful order the Knights of Murder, and in due course was received as a member of the Ghost Rock Commandery. On the day that my probation ended I was for the first time permitted to inspect the records of the order and learn who belonged to it – all the rites of initiation having been conducted in masks. Fancy my delight, when, in looking over the roll of membership, I found the third name to be that of my uncle, who indeed was junior vice-chancellor of the order! Here was an opportunity exceeding my wildest dreams – to murder I could add insubordination and treachery. It was what my good mother would have called "a special Providence".

'At about this time something occurred which caused my cup of joy, already full, to overflow on all sides, a circular cataract of bliss. Three men, strangers in that locality, were arrested for the stage robbery in which I had lost my money and watch. They were brought to trial and, despite my efforts to clear them and fasten the guilt upon three of the most respectable and worthy citizens of Ghost Rock, convicted on the clearest proof. The murder would now be as wanton and reasonless as I could wish.

'One morning I shouldered my Winchester rifle and, going over to my uncle's house, near Nigger Head, asked my Aunt Mary, his wife, if he were at home, adding that I had come to kill him. My aunt replied with a peculiar smile that so many gentlemen called on the same errand and were afterward carried away without having performed it that I must excuse her for doubting my good faith in the matter. She said it did not look as if I would kill anybody, so, as a guarantee of good faith, I levelled my rifle and wounded a Chinaman who happened to be passing the house. She said she knew whole families who could do a thing of that kind, but Bill Ridley was a horse of another colour. She said, however, that I would find him over on the other side of the creek in the sheep lot; and she added that she hoped the best man would win.

'My Aunt Mary was one of the most fair-minded women whom I have ever met.

'I found my uncle down on his knees engaged in skinning a sheep. Seeing that he had neither gun nor pistol handy, I had not the heart to shoot him, so I approached him, greeted him pleasantly, and struck him a powerful blow on the head with the butt of my rifle. I have a very good delivery, and Uncle William lay down on his side, then rolled over on his back, spread out his fingers, and shivered. Before he could recover the use of his limbs I seized the knife that he had been using and cut his ham strings. You know, doubtless, that when you sever the *tendo Achillis* the patient has no further use of his leg; it is just the same as if he had no leg. Well, I parted them both, and when he revived he was at my service. As soon as he comprehended the situation, he said: "Samuel, you have got the drop on me, and can afford to be liberal. I have only one thing to ask of you, and that is that you carry me to the house and finish me in the bosom of my family."

'I told him I thought that a pretty reasonable request, and I would do so if he would let me put him in a wheat sack; he would be easier to carry that way, and if we were seen by the neighbours *en route* it would cause less remark. He agreed to that, and, going to the barn, I got a sack. This, however, did not fit him; it was too short and much wider than he was; so I bent his legs, forced his knees up against his breast, and got him into it that way, tying the sack above his head. He was a heavy man, and I had all I could do to get him on my back, but I staggered along for some distance until I came to a swing which some of the children had suspended to the branch of an oak. Here I had laid him down and sat upon him to rest, and the sight of the rope gave me a happy inspiration. In twenty minutes my uncle, still in the sack, swung free to the sport of the wind. I had taken down the rope, tied one end tightly about the mouth of the bag, thrown the other across the limb, and hauled him up about five feet from the ground. Fastening the other end of the rope also to the mouth of the sack, I had the satisfaction to see my uncle converted into a huge pendulum. I must add that he was not himself entirely aware of the nature of the change which he had undergone in his relation to the exterior world, though in justice to a brave man's memory I ought to say that I do not think he would in any case have wasted much of my time in vain remonstrance.

'Uncle William had a ram which was famous in all that region as a fighter. It was in a state of chronic constitutional indignation. Some deep disappointment in early life had soured its disposition, and it had declared war upon the whole world. To say that it would butt anything accessible is but faintly to express the nature and scope of its military activity; the universe was its antagonist; its method was that of a projectile. It fought, like the angels and devils, in mid-air, cleaving the atmosphere like a bird, describing a parabolic curve and descending upon its victim at just the exact angle of incidence to make the most of its velocity and weight. Its momentum, calculated in foot-tons, was something incredible. It had been seen to destroy a four-year-old bull by a single impact upon that animal's gnarly forehead. No stone wall had ever been known to resist its downward swoop; there were no trees tough enough to stay it; it would splinter them into matchwood and defile their leafy honours in the dust. This irrascible and implacable brute – this incarnate thunderbolt – this monster of the upper deep, I had seen reposing in the shade of an adjacent tree, dreaming dreams of conquest and glory. It was with a view of summoning it forth to the field of honour that I suspended its master in the manner described.

'Having completed my preparations, I imparted to the avuncular pendulum a gentle oscillation, and retiring to cover behind a contiguous rock, lifted up my voice in a long, rasping cry, whose diminishing final note was drowned in a noise like that of a swearing cat, which emanated from the sack. Instantly that formidable sheep was upon its feet and had taken in the military situation at a glance. In a few moments it had approached, stamping, to within fifty yards of the swinging foeman who, now retreating and anon advancing, seemed to invite the fray. Suddenly I saw the beast's head drop earthward as if depressed by the weight of its enormous horns; then a dim, white, wavy streak of sheep prolonged itself from that spot in a generally horizontal direction to within about four yards of a point immediately beneath the enemy. There it struck sharply upward, and before it had faded from my gaze at the place whence it had set out I heard a horrible thump and a piercing scream, and my poor uncle shot forward with a slack rope, higher than the limb to which he was attached. Here the rope tautened with a jerk, arresting his flight, and back he swung in a breathless curve to the other end of his arc. The ram had fallen, a heap of indistinguishable legs, wool, and horns, but, pulling itself together and dodging as its antagonist swept downward, it retired at random, alternately shaking its head and stamping its fore-feet. When it had backed about the same distance as that from which it had delivered the assault, it paused again, bowed its head as if in prayer for victory, and again shot forward, dimly visible as before – a prolonging white streak with monstrous undulations, ending with a sharp ascension. Its course this time was at a right angle to its former one, and its impatience so great that it struck the enemy before he had nearly reached the lowest point of his arc. In consequence he went flying around and around in a horizontal circle, whose radius was about equal to half the length of the rope, which I forgot to say was nearly twenty feet long. His shrieks, crescendo in approach and diminuendo in recession, made the rapidity of his revolution more obvious to the ear than to the eye. He had evidently not yet been struck in a vital spot. His posture in the sack and the distance from the ground at which he hung compelled the ram to operate upon his lower extremities and the end of his back. Like a plant that has struck its root into some poisonous mineral, my poor uncle was dying slowly upward.

'After delivering its second blow the ram had not again retired. The fever of battle burned hot in its heart; its brain was intoxicated with the wine of strife. Like a pugilist who in his rage forgets his skill and fights ineffectively at half-arm's length, the angry beast endeavoured to reach its fleeting foe by awkward vertical leaps as he passed overhead, sometimes, indeed, succeeding in striking him feebly, but more frequently overthrown by its own misguided eagerness. But as the impetus was exhausted and the man's circles narrowed in scope and diminished in speed, bringing him nearer to the ground, these tactics produced better results and elicited a superior quality of screams, which I greatly enjoyed.

'Suddenly, as if the bugles had sung truce, the ram suspended hostilities and walked away, thoughtfully wrinkling and smoothing its great aquiline nose, and occasionally cropping a bunch of grass and slowly munching it. It seemed to have tired of war's alarms and resolved to beat the sword into a ploughshare and cultivate the arts of peace. Steadily it held its course away from the field of fame until it had gained a distance of nearly a quarter of a mile. There it stopped and stood with its rear to the foe, chewing its cud and apparently half asleep. I observed, however, an occasional slight turn of its head, as if its apathy were more affected than real.

'Meanwhile, Uncle William's shrieks had abated with his emotion, and nothing was heard from him but long, low moans, and at long intervals my name, uttered in pleading tones exceedingly gratifying to my ear. Evidently the man had not the faintest notion of what was being done to him, and was inexpressibly terrified. When Death comes cloaked in mystery he is terrible indeed. Little by little my uncle's oscillations diminished, and finally he hung motionless. I went to him and was about to give him the *coup de grâce*, when I heard and felt a succession of smart shocks which shook the ground like a series of light earthquakes, and turning in the direction of the ram, saw a cloud of dust approaching me with inconceivable rapidity and alarming effect. At a distance of some thirty yards away it stopped short, and from the near end of it rose into the air what I at first thought a great white bird. Its ascent was so smooth and easy and regular that I could not realise its extraordinary celerity, and was lost in admiration of its grace. To this day the impression remains that it was a slow, deliberate movement, the ram – for it was that animal – being upborne by some power other than its own impetus, and supported through the successive stages of its flight with infinite tenderness and care. My eyes followed its progress through the air with unspeakable pleasure, all the greater by contrast with my former terror of its approach by land. Onward and upward the noble animal sailed, its head bent down almost between its knees, its fore-feet thrown back, its hinder legs trailing to rear like the legs of a soaring heron. At a height of forty or fifty feet, as near as I could judge, it attained its zenith and appeared to remain an instant stationary; then, tilting suddenly forward without altering the relative position of its parts, it shot downward on a steeper and steeper course with augmenting velocity, passed immediately above me with a noise like the rush of a cannon shot, and struck my poor uncle almost squarely on top of the head! So frightful was the impact that not only the neck was broken, but the rope, too; and the body of the deceased, forced against the earth, was crushed to pulp beneath the awful front of that meteoric sheep. The concussion stopped all the clocks between Lone Hand and Dutch Dan's, and Professor Davidson, who happened to be in the vicinity, promptly explained that the vibrations were from the north to south.

'Altogether, I cannot help thinking that in point of atrocity my murder of Uncle William has seldom been excelled.'

WILKIE COLLINS

The eldest son of the landscape painter William Collins, Wilkie Collins was born in London in 1824. Educated for a few years at private schools in London, he moved with his family to Italy when he was thirteen and it was there that he gained his real education. Rebelling against his father's strict religious code and conservative values, Wilkie Collins refused to settle into life in either the tea business or as a barrister and remained adamant that he wanted to write. He went on to become one of the most popular novelists of his day. His reputation now rests on his novels *The Woman in White* and *The Moonstone*. Because in his work he explored the realms of mystery, suspense and crime, he is often regarded as the inventor of the detective story. Collins never married and his private life remains a mixture of the romantic and the raffish. Living with his mother until he was thirty-two, Collins then left to set up home with a young woman, Caroline Graves, and her daughter by another man. Remaining with Caroline on and off for the rest of his life, he also fathered three illegitimate children by Martha Rudd. This scandalous arrangement led to Collins being ostracised by smart Victorian society. Plagued by gout from his thirties, Collins was often in great pain, which he attempted to dull with increasing amounts of opium. He died in 1889.

The Black Cottage

To begin at the beginning, I must take you back to the time after my mother's death, when my only brother had gone to sea, when my sister was out at service, and when I lived alone with my father, in the midst of a moor in the West of England.

The moor was covered with great limestone rocks, and intersected here and there by streamlets. The nearest habitation to ours was situated about a mile and a half off, where a strip of the fertile land stretched out into the waste, like a tongue. Here the outbuildings of the great Moor Farm, then in the possession of my husband's father, began. The farm lands stretched down gently into a beautiful rich valley, lying nicely sheltered by the high platform of the moor. When the ground began to rise again, miles and miles away, it led up to a country house, called Holme Manor, belonging to a gentleman named Knifton. Mr Knifton had lately married a young lady whom my mother had nursed, and whose kindness and friendship for me, her foster-sister, I shall remember gratefully to the last day of my life. These, and other slight particulars, it is necessary to my story that I should tell you; and it is also necessary that you should be especially careful to bear them well in mind.

My father was by trade a stonemason. His cottage stood a mile and a half from the nearest habitation. In all other directions we were four or five times that distance from neighbours. Being very poor people, this lonely situation had one great attraction for us – we lived rent free on it. In addition to that advantage, the stones, by shaping which my father gained his livelihood, lay all about him at his very door; so that he thought his position, solitary as it was, quite an enviable one. I can hardly say that I agreed with him, though I never complained. I was very fond of my father, and managed to make the best of my loneliness with the thought of being useful to him. Mrs Knifton wished to take me into her service when she married, but I declined – unwillingly enough – for my father's sake. If I had gone away, he would have had nobody to live with him; and my mother made me promise on her deathbed, that he should never be left to pine away alone in the midst of the bleak moor. Our cottage, small as it was, was stoutly and snugly built, with stone from the moor, as a matter of course. The walls were lined inside and fenced outside with wood, the gift of Mr Knifton's father to my father. This double covering of cracks and crevices, which would have been superfluous in a sheltered position, was absolutely necessary in our exposed situation to keep out the cold winds which, excepting just the summer months, swept over us continually, all the year round. The outside boards covering our roughly-built stone walls my father protected against the wet with pitch and tar. This gave to our little abode a curiously dark, dingy look, especially when it was seen from a distance, and so it had come to be called in the neighbourhood, even before I was born, the Black Cottage.

I have now related the preliminary particulars which it is desirable that you should know, and may proceed at once to the pleasanter task of telling you my story.

One cloudy autumn day, when I was rather more than eighteen years old, a herdsman walked over from Moor Farm with a letter which had been left there for my father. It came from a builder, living at our county town, half a day's journey off, and it invited my father to come to him and give his judgement about an estimate for some stonework on a very large scale. My father's expenses for loss of time were to be paid, and he was to have his share of employment afterwards in preparing the stone. He was only too glad, therefore, to obey the directions which the letter contained, and to prepare at once for his long walk to the county town.

Considering the time at which he received the letter, and the necessity of resting before he attempted to return, it was impossible for him to avoid being away from home for one night at least. He proposed to me, in case I disliked being left alone in the Black Cottage, to lock the door, and to take me to Moor Farm to sleep with any of the milkmaids who would give me a share of her bed. I by no means liked the notion of sleeping with a girl whom I did not know, and I saw no reason to feel afraid of being left alone for only one night: so I declined. No thieves had ever come near us; our poverty was sufficient protection against them: and of other dangers there were none that even the most timid person could apprehend. Accordingly, I got my father's dinner, laughing at the notion of my taking refuge under the protection of a milkmaid at Moor Farm. He started for his walk as soon as he had done, saying he should try and be back by dinner-time the next day, and leaving me and my cat Polly to take care of the house.

I had cleared the table and brightened up the fire, and had sat down to my work, with the cat dozing at my feet, when I heard the trampling of horses and, running to the door, saw Mr and Mrs Knifton, with their groom behind them, riding up to the Black Cottage. It was part of the young lady's kindness never to neglect an opportunity of coming to pay me a friendly visit; and her husband was generally willing to accompany her for his wife's sake. I made my best curtsey, therefore, with a great deal of pleasure, but with no particular surprise at seeing them. They dismounted and entered the cottage, laughing and talking in great spirits. I soon heard that they were riding to the same county town for which my father was bound and that they intended to stay with some friends there for a few days, and to return home on horseback, as they went out.

I heard this, and I also discovered that they had been having an argument, in jest, about money matters, as they rode along to our cottage. Mrs Knifton had accused her husband of inveterate extravagance, and of never being able to go out with money in his pocket without spending it all, if he possibly could, before he got home again. Mr Knifton had laughingly defended himself by declaring that all his pocket-money went in presents for his wife, and that, if he spent it lavishly, it was under her sole influence and superintendence.

'We are going to Cliverton now,' he said to Mrs Knifton, naming the county town, and warming himself at our poor fire just as pleasantly as if he had been standing on his own grand hearth. 'You will stop to admire every pretty thing in every one of the Cliverton shop-windows; I shall hand you the purse, and you will go in and buy. When we have reached home again, and you have had time to get tired of your purchases, you will clasp your hands in amazement, and declare that you are quite shocked at my habits of extravagance. I am only the banker who keeps the money – you, my love, are the spendthrift who throws it all away!'

'Am I, sir?' said Mrs Knifton, with a look of mock indignation. 'We will see if I am to be misrepresented in this way with impunity. Bessie, my dear' (turning to me), 'you shall judge how far I deserve the character which my husband has just given to me. *I* am the spendthrift, am I? And you are only the banker? Very well. Banker, give me my money at once, if you please!'

Mr Knifton laughed, and took some gold and silver from his waistcoat pocket.

'No, no,' said Mrs Knifton. 'You may want what you have got there for necessary expenses. Is that all the money you have about you? What do I feel here?' and she tapped her husband on the chest, just over the breast-pocket of his coat.

Mr Knifton laughed again, and produced his pocket-book. His wife snatched it out of his hand, opened it, drew out some banknotes, put them back again immediately, and closing the pocket-book, stepped across the room to my poor mother's little walnut-wood bookcase – the only bit of valuable furniture we had in the house.

'What are you going to do there?' asked Mr Knifton, following his wife.

Mrs Knifton opened the glass door of the bookcase, put the pocket-book in a vacant place on one of the lower shelves, closed and locked the door again, and gave me the key.

'You called me a spendthrift just now,' she said. 'There is my answer. Not one farthing of that money shall you spend at Cliverton on *me*. Keep the key in your pocket, Bessie, and, whatever Mr Knifton may say, on no account let him have it until we call again on our way back. No, sir, I won't trust you with that money in your pocket in the town of Cliverton. I will make sure of your taking it all home again by leaving it here in more trustworthy hands than yours until we ride back. Bessie, my dear, what do you say to that, as a lesson in economy inflicted on a prudent husband by a spendthrift wife?'

She took Mr Knifton's arm while she spoke, and drew him away to the door. He protested, and made some resistance, but she easily carried her point, for he was far too fond of her to have a will of his own in any trifling matter between them. Whatever the men might say, Mr Knifton was a model husband in the estimation of all the women who knew him.

'You will see us as we come back, Bessie. Till then, you are our banker, and the pocket-book is yours,' cried Mrs Knifton gaily, at the door. Her husband lifted her into the saddle, mounted himself, and away they both galloped over the moor, as wild and happy as a couple of children.

Although my being trusted with money by Mrs Knifton was no novelty (in her maiden days she always employed me to pay her dressmaker's bills), I did not feel quite easy at having a pocket-book full of banknotes left by her in my charge. I had no positive apprehension about the safety of the deposit placed in my hands, but it was one of the odd points in my character then (and I think it is still) to feel an unreasonably strong objection to charging myself with money responsibilities of any kind, even to suit the convenience of my dearest friends. As soon as I was left alone, the very sight of the pocket-book behind the glass door of the bookcase began to worry me; and, instead of returning to my work, I puzzled my brains about finding a place to lock it up in, where it would not be exposed to the view of any chance passer-by who might stray into the Black Cottage.

This was not an easy matter to compass in a poor house like ours, where we had nothing valuable to put under lock and key. After running over various hiding-places in my mind, I thought of my tea-caddy, a present of Mrs Knifton's, which I always kept out of harm's way in my own bedroom. Most unluckily – as it afterwards turned out – instead of taking the pocket-book to the tea-caddy, I went into my room first, to take the tea-caddy to the pocket-book. I only acted in this roundabout way from sheer thought-essness, and severely enough I was punished for it, as you will acknowledge yourself when you have read a page or two more of my story.

I was just getting the unlucky tea-caddy out of my cupboard, when I heard footsteps in the passage, and running out immediately, saw two men walk into the kitchen – the room in which I had received Mr and Mrs Knifton. I enquired what they wanted, sharply enough, and one of them answered immediately that they wanted my father. He turned towards me, of course, as he spoke, and I recognised him as a stonemason, going among his comrades by the name of Shifty Dick. He bore a very bad character for everything but wrestling – a sport for which the working men of our parts were famous all through the county. Shifty Dick was champion, and he had got his name from some tricks in wrestling, for which he was celebrated. He was a tall, heavy man, with a lowering, scarred face, and huge hairy hands –

the last visitor in the whole world that I should have been glad to see under any circumstances. His companion was a stranger, whom he addressed by the name of Jerry – a quick, dapper, wicked-looking man, who took off his cap to me with mock politeness, and shewed, in so doing, a very bald head, with some very ugly-looking knobs on it. I distrusted him worse than I did Shifty Dick, and managed to get between his leering eyes and the bookcase, as I told the two that my father was gone out, and that I did not expect him back till the next day.

The words were hardly out of my mouth before I repented of having spoken them. My anxiety to get rid of my unwelcome visitors had made me incautious enough to acknowledge that my father would be away from home for the whole night.

Shifty Dick and his companion looked at each other when I unwisely let out the truth, but made no remark, except to ask me if I would give them a drop of cider. I answered, sharply, that I had no cider in the house – having no fear of the consequences of refusing them drink, because I knew that plenty of men were at work within hail, in a neighbouring quarry. The two looked at each other again, when I denied having any cider to give them; and Jerry (as I am obliged to call him, knowing no other name by which to distinguish the fellow) took off his cap to me once more, and, with a kind of blackguard gentility upon him, said they would have the pleasure of calling the next day, when my father was at home. I said good afternoon as ungraciously as possible: and, to my great relief, they both left the cottage immediately afterwards.

As soon as they were well away, I watched them from the door. They trudged off in the direction of Moor Farm; and as it was beginning to get dusk, I soon lost sight of them.

Half an hour afterwards I looked out again.

The wind had lulled with the sunset, but the mist was rising and a heavy rain was beginning to fall. Never did the lonely prospect of the moor look so dreary as it looked to my eyes that evening. Never did I regret any slight thing more sincerely than I then regretted the leaving of Mr Knifton's pocketbook in my charge. I cannot say that I suffered under any actual alarm, for I felt next to certain that neither Shifty Dick nor Jerry had got a chance of setting eyes on so small a thing as the pocket book, while they were in the kitchen: but there was a kind of vague distrust troubling me – a suspicion of the night – a dislike at being left by myself, which I never remember having experienced before. This feeling so increased, after I had closed the door and gone back to the kitchen, that, when I heard the voices of the quarrymen, as they passed our cottage on their way home to the village in the valley below Moor Farm, I stepped out into the passage with a momentary notion of telling them how I was situated, and asking them for advice and protection.

I had hardly formed this idea, however, before I dismissed it. None of the quarrymen were intimate friends of mine. I had a nodding acquaintance with them, and believed them to be honest men, as times went. But my own common sense told me that what little knowledge of their characters I had was by no means sufficient to warrant me in admitting them into my confidence in the matter of the pocket-book. I had seen enough of poverty and poor men to know what a terrible temptation a large sum of money is to those whose whole lives are passed in scraping up sixpences by weary hard work. It is one thing to write fine sentiments in books about incorruptible honesty, and another thing to put those sentiments in practice, when one day's work is all that a man has to set up in the way of an obstacle between starvation and his own fireside.

The only resource that remained was to carry the pocket-book with me to Moor Farm, and ask permission to pass the night there. But I could not persuade myself that there was any real necessity for taking such a course as this; and, if the truth must be told, my pride revolted at the idea of presenting myself in the character of a coward before the people at the farm. Timidity is thought rather a graceful attraction among ladies, but among poor women it is something to be laughed at. A woman with less spirit of her own than I had, and always shall have, would have considered twice in my situation before she made up her mind to encounter the jokes of ploughmen and the jeers of milkmaids. As for me, I had hardly considered about going to the farm before I despised myself for entertaining any such notion. 'No, no,' I thought, 'I am not the woman to walk a mile and a half through rain, and mist, and darkness, to tell a whole kitchenful of people that I am afraid. Come what may, here I stop till father gets back.'

Having arrived at that valiant resolution, the first thing I did was to lock and bolt the back and front doors, and see to the security of every shutter in the house.

That duty performed, I made a blazing fire, lighted my candle, and sat down to tea, as snug and comfortable as possible. I could hardly believe now, with the light in the room, and the sense of security inspired by the closed doors and shutters, that I had ever felt even the slightest apprehension earlier in the day. I sang as I washed up the tea-things: and even the cat seemed to catch the infection of my good spirits. I never knew the pretty creature more playful than she was that evening.

The tea-things put by, I took up my knitting and worked away at it so long that I began at last to get drowsy. The fire was so bright and comforting that I could not muster resolution enough to leave it and go to bed. I sat staring lazily into the blaze, with my knitting on my lap – sat till the splashing of the rain outside, and the fitful, sullen sobbing of the wind, grew fainter and fainter on my ear. The last sounds I heard before I fairly dozed off to sleep were the cheerful crackling of the fire and the steady purring of the cat, as she basked luxuriously in the warm light on the hearth. Those were the last sounds before I fell asleep.

The sound that woke me was a loud bang at the front door.

I started up, with my heart (as the saying is) in my mouth, with a frightful momentary shuddering at the roots of my hair – I started up, breathless and cold; waiting in the silence, I hardly knew for what; doubtful, at first, whether I had dreamed about the bang at the door, or whether the blow had really been struck on it.

In a minute, or less, there came a second bang, louder than the first. I ran into the passage.

'Who's there?'

'Let us in,' answered a voice, which I recognised immediately as the voice of Shifty Dick.

'Wait a bit, my dear, and let me explain,' said a second voice, in the low, oily, jeering tones of Dick's companion – the wickedly clever little man whom he called Jerry. 'You are alone in the house, my pretty little dear. You may crack your sweet voice with screeching, but there's nobody near to hear you. Listen to reason, my love, and let us in. We don't want cider this time – we only want a very neat-looking pocket-book which you happen to have, and your late excellent mother's four silver teaspoons, which you keep so nice and clean on the chimney-piece. If you let us in, we won't hurt a hair of your head, my cherub, and we promise to go away the moment we have got what we want, unless you particularly wish us to stop to tea. If you keep us out, we shall be obliged to break into the house, and then – '

'And then,' burst in Shifty Dick, 'we'll *mash* you!'

'Yes,' said Jerry, 'we'll mash you, my beauty. But you won't drive us to doing that, will you? You will let us in?'

This long parley gave me time to recover from the effect which the first bang at the door had produced on my nerves. The threats of the two villains would have terrified some women out of their senses; but the only result produced on *me* was violent indignation. I had, thank God, a strong spirit of my own: and the cool, contemptuous insolence of the man Jerry effectually roused it.

'You cowardly villains!' I screamed at them through the door. 'You think you can frighten me because I am only a poor girl left alone in the house. You ragamuffin thieves, I defy you both! Our bolts are strong, our shutters are thick. I am here to keep my father's house safe, and keep it I will against an army of you!'

You may imagine what a passion I was in when I vapoured and blustered in that way. I heard Jerry laugh, and Shifty Dick swear a whole mouthful of oaths. Then there was a dead silence for a minute or two; and then the two ruffians attacked the door.

I rushed into the kitchen and seized the poker, and then heaped wood on the fire, and lighted all the candles I could find: for I felt as though I could keep up my courage better if I had plenty of light. Strange and improbable as it may appear, the next thing that attracted my attention was my poor pussy, crouched up, panic-stricken, in a corner. I was so fond of the little creature that I took her up in my arms and carried her into my bedroom, and put her inside my bed. A comical thing to do in a situation of deadly peril, was it not? But it seemed quite natural and proper at the time.

All this while the blows were falling faster and faster on the door. They were dealt, as I conjectured, with heavy stones picked up from the ground outside. Jerry sang at his wicked work, and Shifty Dick swore. As I left the bedroom, after putting the cat under cover, I heard the lower panel of the door begin to crack.

I ran into the kitchen and huddled our four silver spoons into my pocket; then took the unlucky book with the bank-notes and put it into the bosom of my dress. I was determined to defend the property confided to my care with my life. Just as I had secured the pocket-book I heard the door splintering, and rushed into the passage again with my heavy kitchen poker lifted in both hands.

I was in time to see the bald head of Jerry, with the ugly-looking knobs on it, pushed into the passage through a great rent in one of the lower panels of the door.

'Get out, you villain, or I'll brain you on the spot!' I screeched, threatening him with the poker.

Mr Jerry took his head out again much faster than he put it in.

The next thing that came through the rent was a long pitchfork, which they darted at me from the outside, to move me from the door. I struck at it with all my might, and the blow must have jarred the hand of Shifty Dick up to his very shoulder, for I heard him give a roar of rage and pain. Before he could catch at the fork with his other hand, I had drawn it inside. By this time, even Jerry lost his temper, and swore more awfully than Dick himself.

Then there came another minute of respite. I suspected they had gone to get bigger stones, and I dreaded the giving way of the whole door.

Running into the bedroom as this fear beset me, I laid hold of my chest of drawers, dragged it into the passage, and threw it down against the door. On the top of that I heaped my father's big tool chest, three chairs, and a scuttle-full of coals – and last, I dragged out the kitchen table and rammed it as hard as I could against the whole barricade. They heard me as they were coming up to the door with fresh stones. Jerry said, 'Stop a bit,' and then the two consulted together in whispers. I listened eagerly, and just caught these words: 'Let's try it the other way.'

Nothing more was said, but I heard their footsteps retreating from the door.

Were they going to besiege the back-door now?

I had hardly asked myself that question when I heard their voices at the other side of the house. The back-door was smaller than the front; but it had this advantage in the way of strength – it was made of two solid oak boards, joined longwise, and strengthened inside by heavy cross pieces. It had no bolts like the front door, but was fastened by a bar of iron, running across it in a slanting direction, and fitting at either end into the wall.

'They must have the whole cottage down before they can break in at that door,' I thought to myself. And they soon found out as much for themselves. After five minutes of banging at the back door, they gave up any further attack in that direction, and cast their heavy stones down with curses of fury awful to hear.

I went into the kitchen and dropped on the window-seat to rest for a moment. Suspense and excitement together were beginning to tell upon me. The perspiration broke out thick on my forehead, and I began to feel the bruises I had inflicted on my hands in making the barricade against the front door. I had not lost a particle of my resolution, but I was beginning to lose strength. There was a bottle of rum in the cupboard, which my brother the sailor had left with us the last time he was ashore. I drank a drop of it. Never before or since have I put anything down my throat that did me half so much good as that precious mouthful of rum.

I was still sitting in the window-seat drying my face, when I suddenly heard their voices close behind me.

They were feeling the outside of the window against which I was sitting. It was protected, like all the other windows in the cottage, by iron bars. I listened in dreadful suspense for the sound of filing, but nothing of the sort was audible. They had evidently reckoned on frightening me easily into letting them in, and had come unprovided with housebreaking tools of any kind. A fresh burst of oaths informed me that they had recognised the obstacle of the iron bars. I listened breathlessly for some warning of what they were going to do next, but their voices seemed to die away in the distance. They were retreating from the window. Were they also retreating from the house altogether? Had they given up the idea of effecting an entrance in despair?

A long silence followed – a silence which tried my courage even more severely than the tumult of their first attack on the cottage.

Dreadful suspicions now beset me of their being able to accomplish by treachery what they had failed to effect by force. Well as I knew the cottage, I began to doubt whether there might not be ways of cunningly and silently entering it against which I was not provided. The ticking of the clock annoyed me; the crackling of the fire startled me. I looked out twenty times in a minute into the dark corners of the passage, straining my eyes, holding my breath, anticipating the most unlikely events, the most impossible dangers. Had they really gone? or were they still prowling about the house? Oh, what a sum of money I would have given only to have known what they were about in that interval of silence!

I was startled at last out of my suspense in the most awful manner.

A shout from one of them reached my ears on a sudden down the kitchen chimney. It was so unexpected and so horrible in the stillness, that I screamed for the first time since the attack on the house. My worst forebodings had never suggested to me that the two villains might mount upon the roof.

'Let us in, you she-devil!' roared a voice down the chimney.

There was another pause. The smoke from the wood fire, thin and light as it was in the red state of the embers at that moment, had evidently obliged the man to take his face from the mouth of the chimney. I counted the seconds while he was, as I conjectured, getting his breath again. In less than half a minute there came another shout: 'Let us in, or we'll burn the place down over your head.'

Burn it? Burn what? There was nothing easily combustible but the thatch on the roof; and that had been well soaked by the heavy rain which had now fallen incessantly for more than six hours. Burn the place over my head? How?

While I was still casting about wildly in my mind to discover what possible danger there could be of fire, one of the heavy stones placed on the thatch to keep it from being torn up by high winds, came thundering down the chimney. It scattered the live embers on the hearth all over the room. A richly furnished place, with knickknacks and fine muslin about it, would have been set on fire immediately. Even our bare floor and rough furniture gave out a smell of burning at the first shower of embers which the first stone scattered.

For an instant I stood quite horror-struck before this new proof of the devilish ingenuity of the villains outside. But the dreadful danger I was now in recalled me to my senses immediately. There was a large canful of water in my bedroom, and I ran in at once to fetch it. Before I could get back to the kitchen, a second stone had been thrown down the chimney, and the floor was smouldering in several places.

I had wit enough to let the smouldering go on for a moment or two more, and to pour the whole of my canful of water over the fire before the third stone came down the chimney. The live embers on the floor I easily disposed of after that. The man on the roof must have heard the hissing of the fire as I put it out and have felt the change produced in the air at the mouth of the chimney; for after the third stone had descended, no more followed it. As for either of the ruffians themselves dropping down by the same road along which the stones had come, that was not to be dreaded. The chimney, as I well knew by our experience in cleaning it, was too narrow to give passage to anyone above the size of a small boy.

I looked upwards as that comforting reflection crossed my mind – I looked up, and saw, as plainly as I see the paper I am now writing on, the point of a knife coming through the inside of the roof, just over my head. Our cottage had no upper story, and our rooms had no ceilings. Slowly and wickedly the knife wriggled its way through the dry inside thatch between the rafters. It stopped for a while, and there came a sound of tearing. That, in its turn, stopped too; there was a great fall of dry thatch on the floor; and I saw the heavy, hairy hand of Shifty Dick, armed with the knife, come through after the fallen fragments. He tapped at the rafters with the back of the knife, as if to test their strength. Thank God, they were substantial and close together! Nothing lighter than a hatchet would have sufficed to remove any part of them.

The murderous hand was still tapping with the knife, when I heard a shout from the man Jerry, coming from the neighbourhood of my father's stone-shed in the back-yard. The hand and knife disappeared instantly. I went to the back-door, and put my ear to it and listened.

Both men were now in the shed. I made the most desperate efforts to call to mind what tools and other things were left in it, which might be used against me. But my agitation confused me. I could remember nothing except my father's big stone saw, which was far too heavy and unwieldy to be used on the roof of the cottage. I was still puzzling my brains and making my head swim to no purpose, when I heard the men dragging something out of the shed. At the same instant when the noise caught my ear, the remembrance flashed across me like lightning of some beams of wood which had lain in the shed for years past. I had hardly time to feel certain that they were removing one of these beams, before I heard Shifty Dick say to Jerry: 'Which door?'

'The front,' was the answer. 'We've cracked it already; we'll have it down now in no time.'

Senses less sharpened by danger than mine would have understood but too easily, from these words, that they were about to use the beam as a battering-ram against the door. When that conviction overcame me, I lost courage at last. I felt that the door must come down. No such barricade as I had constructed could support it for more than a few minutes against such shocks as it was now to receive.

'I can do no more to keep the house against them,' I said to myself, with my knees knocking together, and the tears at last beginning to wet my cheeks. 'I must trust to the night and the thick darkness, and save my life by running for it, while there is yet time.'

I huddled on my cloak and hood, and had my hand on the bar of the back-door, when a piteous mew from the bedroom reminded me of the existence of poor pussy. I ran in, and huddled the creature up in my apron. Before I was out in the passage again, the first shock from the beam fell on the door.

The upper hinge gave way. The chairs and the coal-skuttle forming the top of my barricade were hurled, rattling, on to the floor; but the lower hinge of the door, and the chest of drawers and tool-chest, still kept their places.

'One more,' I heard the villains cry – 'one more run with the beam, and down it comes!'

Just as they must have been starting for that 'one more run', I opened the back door and fled out into the night, with the banknotes in my bosom, the silver spoons in my pocket, and the cat in my arms. I threaded my way easily enough through the familiar obstacles in the back-yard, and was out in the pitch darkness of the moor before I heard the second shock, and the crash which told me that the whole door had given way.

In a few minutes they must have discovered the fact of my flight with the pocket-book, for I heard shouts in the distance as if they were running out to pursue me. I kept on at the top of my speed, and the noise soon died away. It was so dark, that twenty thieves, instead of two, would have found it useless to follow me.

How long it was before I reached the farmhouse – the nearest place to which I could fly for refuge – I cannot tell you. I remember that I had just sense enough to keep the wind at my back (having observed in the beginning of the evening that it blew towards Moor Farm), and to go on resolutely through the darkness. In all other respects, I was by this time half crazed by what I had gone through. If it had so happened that the wind had changed after I had observed its direction early in the evening, I should have gone astray, and have probably perished of fatigue and exposure on the moor. Providentially, it still blew steadily, as it had blown for hours past, and I reached the farmhouse with my clothes wet through, and my brain in a high fever. When I made my alarm at the door, they had all gone to bed but the farmer's eldest son, who was sitting up late over his pipe and newspaper. I just mustered strength enough to gasp out a few words, telling him what was the matter, and then fell down at his feet, for the first time in my life in a dead swoon.

That swoon was followed by a severe illness. When I got strong enough to look about me again, I found myself in one of the farmhouse beds – my father, Mrs Knifton and the doctor were all in the room – my cat was asleep at my feet, and the pocket-book that I had saved lay on the table by my side.

There was plenty of news for me to hear, as soon as I was fit to listen to it. Shifty Dick and the other rascal had been caught, and were in prison, waiting their trial at the next assizes. Mr and Mrs Knifton had been so shocked at the danger I had run – for which they blamed their own want of thoughtfulness in leaving the pocket-book in my care – that they had insisted on my father's removing from our lonely home to a cottage on their land, which we were to inhabit rent free. The banknotes that I had saved were given to me to buy furniture with, in place of the things that the thieves had broken. These pleasant tidings assisted so greatly in promoting my recovery that I was soon able to relate to my friends at the farmhouse the particulars that I have written here. They were all surprised and interested; but no one, as I thought, listened to me with such breathless attention as the farmer's eldest son. Mrs Knifton noticed this, too, and began to make jokes about it, in her lighthearted way, as soon as we were alone. I thought little of her jesting at the time; but when I got well, and we went to live at our new home, 'the young farmer', as he was called in our parts, constantly came to see us, and constantly managed to meet me out of doors. I had my share of vanity, like other young women, and I began to think of Mrs Knifton's jokes with some attention. To be brief, the young farmer managed one Sunday – I never could tell how – to lose his way with me in returning from church, and before we found out the right road home again, he had asked me to be his wife.

His relations did all they could to keep us asunder, and break off the match, thinking a poor stonemason's daughter no fit wife for a prosperous yeoman. But the farmer was too obstinate for them. He had one form of answer to all their objections. 'A man, if he is worth the name, marries according to his own notions, and to please himself,' he used to say. 'My notion is that when I take a wife I am placing my character and my happiness – the most precious things I have to trust – in one woman's care. The woman I mean to marry had a small charge confided to her care, and showed herself worthy of it at the risk of her life. That is proof enough for me that she is worthy of the greatest charge I can put into her hands. Rank and riches are fine things, but the certainty of getting a good wife is something better still. I'm of age, I know my own mind, and I mean to marry the stonemason's daughter.'

And he did marry me. Whether I proved myself worthy or not of his good opinion is a question which I must leave you to ask my husband. All that I had to relate about myself and my doings is now told. Whatever interest my perilous adventure may excite, ends, I am well aware, with my escape to the farmhouse. I have only ventured on writing these few additional sentences, because my marriage is the moral of my story. It has brought me the choicest blessings of happiness and prosperity; and I owe them all to my night-adventure in the Black Cottage.

The Family Secret

I

Was it an Englishman or a Frenchman who first remarked that every family had a skeleton in its cupboard? I am not learned enough to know; but I reverence the observation, whoever made it. It speaks a startling truth through an appropriately grim metaphor – a truth which I have discovered by practical experience. Our family had a skeleton in the cupboard, and its name was Uncle George.

I arrived at the knowledge that this skeleton existed, and I traced it to the particular cupboard in which it was hidden, by slow degrees. I was a child when I first began to suspect that there was such a thing, and a grown man when I at last discovered that my suspicions were true.

My father was a doctor, having an excellent practice in a large country town. I have heard that he married against the wishes of his family. They could not object to my mother on the score of birth, breeding, or character – they only disliked her heartily. My grandfather, grandmother, uncles and aunts, all declared that she was a heartless, deceitful woman; all disliked her manners, her opinions, and even the expression of her face – all, with the one exception of my father's youngest brother George.

George was the unlucky member of our family. The rest were all clever; he was slow in capacity. The rest were all remarkably handsome; he was the sort of man that no woman ever looks at twice. The rest succeeded in life; he failed. His profession was the same as my father's; but he never got on when he started in practice for himself.

The sick poor, who could not choose, employed him, and liked him. The sick rich, who could – especially the ladies – declined to call him in when they could get anybody else. In experience he gained greatly by his profession; in money and reputation he gained nothing.

There are very few of us, however dull and unattractive we may be to outward appearance, who have not some strong passion, some germ of what is called romance, hidden more or less deeply in our natures. All the passion and romance in the nature of my Uncle George lay in his love and admiration for my father.

He sincerely worshipped his eldest brother, as one of the noblest of human beings. When my father was engaged to be married, and when the rest of the family, as I have already mentioned, did not hesitate to express their unfavourable opinion of the disposition of his chosen wife, Uncle

George, who had never ventured on differing with anyone before, to the amazement of everybody undertook the defence of his future sister-in-law in the most vehement and positive manner.

In his estimation, his brother's choice was something sacred and indisputable. The lady might, and did, treat him with unconcealed contempt, laugh at his awkwardness, grow impatient at his stammering – it made no difference to Uncle George. It was enough for him that she was to be his brother's wife.

When my father had been married a little while, he took his youngest brother to live with him as his assistant. If Uncle George had been made president of the College of Surgeons, he could not have been prouder and happier than he was in his new position.

I am afraid my father never understood the depth of his brother's affection for him. All the hard work fell to George's share: the long journeys at night, the physicking of wearisome poor people, the drunken cases, the revolting cases – all the drudging, dirty business of surgery, in short, was turned over to him; and day after day, month after month, he struggled through it without a murmur.

When his brother and sister-in-law went out to dine with the country gentry, it never entered his head to feel disappointed at being left unnoticed at home. When the return dinners were given, and he was asked to come in at tea-time and left to sit unregarded in a corner, it never occurred to him to imagine that he was treated with any want of consideration or respect. He was part of the furniture of the house, and it was the business, as well as the pleasure of his life, to turn himself to any use to which his brother might please to put him.

So much for what I have heard from others on the subject of my Uncle George. My own personal experience of him is limited to what I remember as a mere child. Let me say something however, first, about my parents, my sister, and myself. My sister was the eldest born, and the best loved. I did not come into the world till four years after her birth; and no other child followed me.

Caroline, from her earliest days, was the perfection of beauty and health. I was small, weakly, and if the truth must be told, almost as plain-featured as Uncle George himself. It would be ungracious and undutiful in me to presume to decide whether there was any foundation or not for the dislike that my father's family always felt for my mother. All I can venture to say is that her children never had any cause to complain of her.

Her passionate affection for my sister, her pride in the child's beauty, I remember well; as also her uniform kindness and indulgence towards me. My personal defects must have been a sore trial to her in secret, but neither she nor my father ever showed me that they perceived any difference between Caroline and myself. When presents were made to my sister, presents were made to me. When my father and mother caught my sister up in their arms and kissed her, they scrupulously gave me my turn afterwards.

My childish instinct told me that there was a difference in their smiles when they looked at me and looked at her; that the kisses given to Caroline were warmer than the kisses given to me; that the hands which dried her tears in our childish griefs, touched her more gently than the hands which dried mine.

But these, and other small signs of preference like them, were such as no parents could be expected to control. I noticed them at the time rather with wonder than with repining. I recall them now, without a harsh thought, either towards my father or my mother. Both loved me, and both did their duty by me. If I seem to speak constrainedly about them here, it is not on my own account. I can honestly say that, with all my heart and soul.

Even Uncle George, fond as he was of me, was fonder of my beautiful child-sister. When I used mischievously to pull at his lank, scanty hair, he would gently and laughingly take it out of my hands; but he would let Caroline tug at it till his dim, wandering grey eyes winked and watered again with pain. He used to plunge perilously about the garden, in awkward imitation of the cantering of a horse, while I sat on his shoulders; but he would never proceed at any pace beyond a slow and safe walk when Caroline had a ride in her turn.

When he took us out walking, Caroline was always on the side next the wall. When we interrupted him over his dirty work in the surgery, he used to tell me to go and play until he was ready for me; but he would put down his bottles, and clean his clumsy fingers on his coarse apron, and lead Caroline out again, as if she had been the greatest lady in the land. Ah, how he loved her! – and, let me be honest and grateful, and add, how he loved me too!

When I was eight years old, and Caroline was twelve, I was separated from home for some time. I had been ailing for many months previously, had got benefit from being taken to the seaside, and had shown symptoms of relapsing on being brought home again to the midland county in which we resided. After much consultation it was at last resolved that I should be sent to live, until my constitution got stronger, with a maiden-sister of my mother's, who had a house at a watering-place on the south coast.

I left home, I remember, loaded with presents, rejoicing over the prospect of looking at the sea again, as careless of the future and as happy in the present as any boy could be. Uncle George petitioned for a holiday to take me to the seaside, but he could not be spared from the surgery. He consoled himself and me by promising to make me a magnificent model of a ship.

I have that model before my eyes now, while I write. It is dusty with age; the paint on it is cracked, the ropes are tangled, the sails are moth-eaten and yellow. The hull is all out of proportion, and the rig has been smiled at by every nautical friend of mine who has ever looked at it. Yet, worn out and inferior to every vessel nowadays in any toyshop window – I hardly know a possession of mine in this world that I would not sooner part with than Uncle George's ship.

My life at the seaside was a very happy one. I remained with my aunt more than a year. My mother often came to see how I was going on; and, at first, always brought my sister with her. But, during the last eight months of my stay, Caroline never once appeared. I noticed also at the same period a change in my mother's manner. She looked paler and more anxious at each succeeding visit, and always had long conferences in private with my aunt. At last she ceased to come and see us altogether, and only wrote to know how my health was getting on.

My father, too, who had at the earlier periods of my absence from home travelled to the seaside to watch the progress of my recovery, as often as his professional engagements would permit, now kept away like my mother. Even Uncle George, who had never been allowed a holiday to come and see me, but who had hitherto often written, and begged me to write to him, broke off our correspondence.

I was naturally perplexed and amazed by these changes, and persecuted my aunt to tell me the reason of them. At first she tried to put me off with excuses; then she admitted that there was trouble in our house; and finally she confessed that the trouble was caused by the illness of my sister. When I enquired what that illness was, my aunt said it was useless to attempt to explain it to me.

I next applied to the servants. One of them was less cautious than my aunt, and answered my question, but in terms that I could not comprehend. After much explanation, I was made to understand that 'something was growing on my sister's neck which would spoil her beauty for ever, and perhaps kill her, if it could not be got rid of'.

How well I remember the shudder of horror that ran through me at the vague idea of this deadly 'something!' An awestruck curiosity to see what Caroline's illness was with my own eyes troubled my inmost heart; and I begged to be allowed to go home and help to nurse her. The request was, it is almost needless to say, refused. Weeks passed away, and still I heard nothing, except that my sister continued to be ill.

One day I privately wrote a letter to Uncle George, asking him, in my childish way, to come and tell me about Caroline's illness. I knew where the post-office was, and slipped out in the morning unobserved, and dropped my letter into the box. I stole home again by the garden, and climbed in at the window of a back parlour on the ground floor. The room above was my aunt's bedchamber, and the moment I was inside the house I heard moans and loud convulsive sobs proceeding from it. My aunt was a singularly quiet, composed woman. I could not imagine that the loud sobbing and moaning came from her; and I ran down terrified into the kitchen to ask the servants who was crying so violently in my aunt's room.

I found the housemaid and the cook talking together in whispers, with serious faces. They started when they saw me, as if I had been a grown-up master who had caught them neglecting their work.

'He is too young to feel it much,' I heard one say to the other. 'So far as he is concerned, it seems like a mercy that it happened no later.'

In a few minutes they had told me the worst. It was my aunt who had been crying in the bedroom. Caroline was dead.

I felt the blow more severely than the servants or anyone else about me supposed. Still, I was a child in years, and I had the blessed elasticity of a child's nature. If I had been older, I might have been too much absorbed in grief to observe my aunt so closely as I did, when she was composed enough to see me, later in the day.

I was not surprised by the swollen state of her eyes, the paleness of her cheeks, or the fresh burst of tears that came from her when she took me in her arms at meeting. But I was both amazed and perplexed by the look of terror that I detected in her face. It was natural enough that she should grieve and weep over my sister's death; but why should she have that frightened look, as if some other catastrophe had happened?

I asked if there was any more dreadful news from home besides the news of Caroline's death? My aunt said, 'No,' in a strange stifled voice, and suddenly turned her face from me. Was my father dead? No. My mother? No. Uncle George? My aunt trembled all over as she said No to that also, and bade me cease asking any more questions. She was not fit to bear them yet, she said; and signed to the servant to lead me out of the room.

The next day I was told that I was to go home after the funeral, and was taken out towards evening by the housemaid, partly for a walk, partly to be measured for my mourning clothes. After we had left the tailor's, I persuaded the girl to extend our walk for some distance along the seabeach, telling her, as we went, every little anecdote connected with my lost sister that came tenderly back to my memory in those first days of sorrow. She was so interested in hearing, and I in speaking, that we let the sun go down before we thought of turning back.

The evening was cloudy, and it got on from dusk to dark by the time we approached the town again. The housemaid was rather nervous at finding herself alone with me on the beach, and once or twice looked behind her distrustfully as we went on. Suddenly she squeezed my hand hard, and said – 'Let's get up on the cliff as fast as we can.'

The words were hardly out of her mouth before I heard footsteps behind me – a man came round quickly to my side, snatched me away from the girl, and catching me up in his arms, without a word, covered my face with kisses. I knew he was crying, because my cheeks were instantly wet with his tears;

but it was too dark for me to see who it was, or even how he was dressed. He did not, I should think, hold me half a minute in his arms. The housemaid screamed for help, I was put down gently on the sand, and the strange man instantly disappeared in the darkness.

When this extraordinary adventure was related to my aunt, she seemed at first merely bewildered at hearing of it; but in a moment more there came a change over her face, as if she had suddenly recollected or thought of something. She turned deadly pale, and said in a hurried way, very unusual with her, 'Never mind; don't talk about it any more. It was only a mischievous trick to frighten you, I dare say. Forget all about it, my dear; forget all about it.'

It was easier to give this advice than to make me follow it. For many nights after, I thought of nothing but the strange man who had kissed me and cried over me. Who could he be? Somebody who loved me very much, and who was very sorry. My childish logic carried me to that length. But when I tried to think over all the grown-up gentlemen who loved me very much, I could never get on, to my own satisfaction, beyond my father and my Uncle George.

2

I was taken home on the appointed day to suffer the trial – a hard one, even at my tender years – of witnessing my mother's passionate grief, and my father's mute despair. I remember that the scene of our first meeting after Caroline's death was wisely and considerately shortened by my aunt, who took me out of the room. She seemed to have a confused desire to keep me from leaving her after the door had closed behind us, but I broke away and ran downstairs to the surgery, to go and cry for my lost playmate with the sharer of all our games, Uncle George.

I opened the surgery door, and could see nobody. I dried my tears, and looked all round the room: it was empty. I ran upstairs again to Uncle George's garret-bedroom – he was not there; his cheap hairbrush and old cast-off razor-case, that had belonged to my grandfather, were not on the dressing-table. Had he got some other bedroom? I went out on the landing, and called softly, with an unaccountable terror and sinking at my heart, 'Uncle George!'

Nobody answered; but my aunt came hastily up the garret-stairs.

'Hush!' she said. 'You must never mention that name here again.'

She stopped suddenly, and looked as if her own words had frightened her.

'Is Uncle George dead?' I asked.

My aunt turned red and pale, and stammered.

I did not wait to hear what she said – I brushed past her, down the stairs – my heart was bursting – my flesh felt cold. I ran breathlessly and recklessly into the room where my father and mother had received me. They were both sitting there still. I ran up to them, wringing my hands, and crying out in a passion of tears –

'Is Uncle George dead?'

My mother gave a scream that terrified me into instant silence and stillness. My father looked at her for a moment, rang the bell that summoned the maid, then seized me roughly by the arm, and dragged me out of the room.

He took me down into the study, seated himself in his accustomed chair, and got me before him between his knees. His lips were awfully white, and I felt his two hands, as they grasped my shoulders, shaking violently.

'You are never to mention the name of Uncle George again,' he said in a quick, angry, trembling whisper. 'Never to me, never to your mother, never to your aunt, never to anybody in this world! Never, never, never!'

The repetition of the word terrified me even more than the suppressed vehemence with which he spoke. He saw that I was frightened, and softened his manner a little before he went on.

'You will never see Uncle George again,' he said. 'Your mother and I love you dearly; but if you forget what I have told you, you will be sent away from home. Never speak that name again – mind, never! Now kiss me, and go away.'

How his lips trembled – and, oh, how cold they felt on mine!

I shrank out of the room the moment he had kissed me, and went and hid myself in the garden.

'Uncle George is gone; I am never to see him any more, I am never to speak of him again.' Those were the words I repeated to myself, with indescribable terror and confusion, the moment I was alone. There was something unspeakably horrible to my young mind in this mystery which I was commanded always to respect, and which, so far as I then knew, I could never hope to see revealed. My father, my mother, my aunt all appeared to be separated from me now by some impassable barrier. Home seemed home no longer, with Caroline dead, Uncle George gone, and a forbidden subject of talk perpetually and mysteriously interposing between my parents and me.

Though I never infringed the command my father had given me in his study (his words and looks, and that dreadful scream of my mother's, which seemed to be still ringing in my ears, were more than enough to ensure my obedience), I also never lost the secret desire to penetrate the darkness which clouded over the fate of Uncle George.

For two years I remained at home, and discovered nothing. If I asked the servants about my uncle, they could only tell me that one morning he disappeared from the house. Of the members of my father's family, I could make no enquiries. They lived far away, and never came to see us – and the idea of writing to them, at my age and in my position was out of the question.

My aunt was as unapproachably silent as my father and mother; but I never forgot how her face had altered, when she reflected for a moment, after hearing of my extraordinary adventure while going home with the servant over the sands at night. The more I thought of that change of countenance, in connection with what had occurred on my return to my father's house, the more certain I felt that the stranger who had kissed me and wept over me must have been no other than Uncle George.

At the end of my two years at home, I was sent to sea in the merchant navy by my own earnest desire. I had always determined to be a sailor from the time when I first went to stay with my aunt at the seaside – and I persisted long enough in my resolution to make my parents recognise the necessity of acceding to my wishes.

My new life delighted me: and I remained away on foreign stations more than four years. When I at length returned home, it was to find a new affliction darkening our fireside. My father had died on the very day when I sailed for my return voyage to England.

Absence and change of scene had in no respect weakened my desire to penetrate the mystery of Uncle George's disappearance. My mother's health was so delicate that I hesitated for some time to approach the forbidden subject in her presence. When I at last ventured to refer to it, suggesting to her that any prudent reserve, which might have been necessary while I was a child, need no longer be persisted in, now that I was growing to be a young man, she fell into a violent fit of trembling, and commanded me to say no more. It had been my father's will, she said, that the reserve to which I referred should be always adopted towards me; he had not authorised her, before he died, to speak more openly; and, now that he was gone, she would not so much as think of acting on her own unaided judgement.

My aunt said the same thing in effect when I appealed to her. Determined not to be discouraged even yet, I undertook a journey, ostensibly to pay my respects to my father's family, but with the secret intention of trying what I could learn in that quarter on the subject of Uncle George.

My investigations led to some results, though they were by no means satisfactory. George had always been looked upon with something like contempt by his handsome sisters and his prosperous brothers; and he had not improved his position in the family by his warm advocacy of his brother's cause at the time of my father's marriage.

I found that my uncle's surviving relatives now spoke of him slightingly and carelessly. They assured me that they had never heard from him, and that they knew nothing about him, except that he had gone away to settle, as they supposed, in some foreign place, after having behaved very basely and badly to my father. He had been traced to London, where he had sold out of the funds the small share of money which he had inherited after his father's death, and he had been seen on the deck of a packet bound for France later on the same day. Beyond this, nothing was known about him.

In what the alleged baseness of his behaviour consisted, none of his brothers and sisters could tell me. My father had refused to pain them by going into particulars, not only at the time of his brother's disappearance, but afterwards, whenever the subject was mentioned. George had always been the black sheep of the flock, and he must have been conscious of his own baseness, or he would certainly have written to explain and to justify himself.

Such were the particulars which I gleaned during my visit to my father's family. To my mind they tended rather to deepen than to reveal the mystery. That such a gentle, docile, affectionate creature as Uncle George should have injured the brother he loved, by word or deed, at any period of their intercourse, seemed incredible; but that he should have been guilty of an act of baseness at the very time when my sister was dying was simply and plainly impossible.

And yet there was the incomprehensible fact staring me in the face that the death of Caroline and the disappearance of Uncle George had taken place in the same week! Never did I feel more daunted and bewildered by the family secret than after I had heard all the particulars in connection with it that my father's relatives had to tell me.

I may pass over the events of the next few years of my life briefly enough.

My nautical pursuits filled up all my time, and took me far away from my country and my friends. But, whatever I did, and wherever I went, the memory of Uncle George, and the desire to penetrate the mystery of his disappearance, haunted me like familiar spirits. Often, in the lonely watches of the night at sea, did I recall the dark evening on the beach, the strange man's hurried embrace, the startling sensation of feeling his tears on my cheeks, the disappearance of him before I had breath or self-possession enough to say a word.

Often did I think over the inexplicable events that followed, when I had returned, after my sister's funeral, to my father's house; and oftener still did I puzzle my brains vainly, in the attempt to form some plan for inducing my mother or my aunt to disclose the secret which they had hitherto kept from me so perseveringly. My only chance of knowing what had really happened to Uncle George, my only hope of seeing him again, rested with those two near and dear relatives. I despaired of ever getting my mother to speak on the forbidden subject after what had passed between us; but I felt more sanguine about my prospects of ultimately inducing my aunt to relax in her discretion.

My anticipations, however, in this direction were not destined to be fulfilled. On my next visit to England I found my aunt prostrated by a paralytic attack, which deprived her of the power of speech. She died soon afterwards in my arms, leaving me her sole heir. I searched anxiously among her papers for some reference to the family mystery, but found no clue to guide me. All my mother's letters to her sister at the time of Caroline's illness and death had been destroyed.

3

More years passed; my mother followed my aunt to the grave; and still I was as far as ever from making any discoveries in relation to Uncle George. Shortly after the period of this last affliction, my health gave way, and I departed, by my doctor's advice, to try some baths in the South of France. I travelled slowly to my destination, turning aside from the direct road, and stopping wherever I pleased. One evening, when I was not more than two or three days' journey from the baths to which I was bound, I was struck by the picturesque situation of a little town placed on the brow of a hill at some distance from the main road and resolved to have a nearer look at the place, with a view of stopping there for the night, if it pleased me.

I found the principal inn clean and quiet; ordered my bed there, and after dinner strolled out to look at the church. No thought of Uncle George was in my mind when I entered the building; and yet, at the very moment, chance was leading me to the discovery which, for so many years past, I had vainly endeavoured to make – the discovery which I had given up as hopeless since the day of my mother's death.

I found nothing worth notice in the church, and was about to leave it again, when I caught a glimpse of a pretty view through a side door, and stopped to admire it.

The churchyard formed the foreground, and below it the hillside sloped away gently into the plain, over which the sun was setting in full glory. The curé of the church was reading his breviary, walking up and down a gravel path that parted the rows of graves. In the course of my wanderings I had learnt to speak French as fluently as most Englishmen; and when the priest came near me I said a few words in praise of the view, and complimented him on the neatness and prettiness of the churchyard. He answered with great politeness, and we got into conversation together immediately.

As we strolled along the gravel-walk, my attention was attracted by one of the graves standing apart from the rest. The cross at the head of it differed remarkably, in some points of appearance, from the crosses on the other graves. While all the rest had garlands hung on them, this one cross was quite bare; and, more extraordinary still, no name was inscribed on it.

The priest, observing that I stopped to look at the grave, shook his head and sighed.

'A countryman of yours is buried there,' he said, 'I was present at his death. He had borne the burden of a great sorrow among us, in this town, for many weary years, and his conduct had taught us to respect and pity him with all our hearts.'

'How is it that his name is not inscribed over his grave?' I enquired.

'It was suppressed by his own desire,' answered the priest, with some little hesitation. 'He acknowledged to me in his last moments that he had lived here under an assumed name. I asked his real name, and he told it to me, with the particulars of his sad story. He had reason for desiring to be forgotten after his death. Almost the last words he spoke were. "Let my name die with me!" Almost the last request he made was, that I would keep that name a secret from all the world, excepting only one person.'

'Some relative, I suppose?' said I.

'Yes – a nephew,' said the priest.

The moment the last word was out of his mouth, my heart gave a strange answering bound. I suppose I must have changed colour also, for the curé looked at me with sudden attention and interest.

'A nephew,' the priest went on, 'whom he had loved like his own child. He told me that if this nephew ever traced him to his burial-place, and asked about him, I was free in that case to disclose all I knew. "I should like my little Charley to know the truth," he said. "In spite of the difference in our ages, Charley and I were playmates years ago." '

My heart beat faster and I felt a choking sensation at the throat the moment I heard the priest unconsciously mention my Christian name in reporting the dying man's last words.

As soon as I could steady my voice, and feel certain of my self-possession, I communicated my family name to the curé, and asked him if that was not part of the secret that he had been requested to preserve?

He started back several steps, and clasped his hands amazedly.

'Can it be?' he said in low tones, gazing at me earnestly, with something like dread in his face.

I gave him my passport, and looked away towards the grave. The tears came into my eyes as the recollections of past days crowded back on me. Hardly knowing what I did, I knelt down by the grave, and smoothed the grass over it with my hand. Oh, Uncle George, why not have told your secret to your old playmate? Why leave him to find you here?

The priest raised me gently, and begged me to go with him into his own house. On our way there, I mentioned persons and places that I thought my uncle might have spoken of, in order to satisfy my companion that I was really the person I represented myself to be. By the time we had entered his little parlour, and had sat down alone in it, we were almost like old friends together.

I thought it best that I should begin by telling all that I have related here on the subject of Uncle George, and his disappearance from home. My host listened with a very sad face, and said, when I had done: 'I can understand your anxiety to know what I am authorised to tell you, but pardon me if I say first that there are circumstances in your uncle's story which it may pain you to hear – ' he stopped suddenly.

'Which it may pain me to hear, as a nephew?' I asked.

'No,' said the priest, looking away from me, ' – as a son.'

I gratefully expressed my sense of the delicacy and kindness which had prompted my companion's warning, but I begged him at the same time to keep me no longer in suspense, and to tell me the stern truth, no matter how painfully it might affect me as a listener.

'In telling me all you know about what you term the Family Secret,' said the priest, 'you have mentioned as a strange coincidence that your sister's death and your uncle's disappearance took place at the same time. Did you ever suspect what cause it was that occasioned your sister's death?'

'I only knew what my father told me, and what all our friends believed – that she died of a tumour in the neck; or, as I sometimes heard it stated, from the effect on her constitution of a tumour in the neck.'

'She died under an operation for the removal of that tumour,' said the priest, in low tones. 'And the operator was your Uncle George.'

In those few words all the truth burst upon me.

'Console yourself with the thought that the long martyrdom of his life is over,' the priest went on.

'He rests: he is at peace. He and his little darling understand each other, and are happy now. That thought supported him to the last, on his death-bed. He always spoke of your sister as his "little darling". He firmly believed that she was waiting to forgive and console him in the other world – and who shall say he was deceived in that belief?'

Not I! Not anyone who has ever loved and suffered, surely!

'It was out of the depth of his self-sacrificing love for the child that he drew the fatal courage to undertake the operation,' continued the priest. 'Your father naturally shrank from attempting it. His medical brethren, whom he consulted, all doubted the propriety of taking any measures for the removal of the tumour, in the particular condition and situation of it when they were called in. Your uncle alone differed with them. He was too modest a man to say so, but your mother found it out. The deformity of her beautiful child horrified her; she was desperate enough to catch at the faintest hope of remedying it that anyone might hold out to her; and she persuaded your uncle to put his opinion to the proof. Her horror at the deformity of the child, and her despair at the prospect of its lasting for life, seem to have utterly blinded her to all natural sense of the danger of the operation.

It is hard to know how to say it to you, her son, but it must be told, nevertheless, that one day, when your father was out, she untruly informed your uncle that his brother had consented to the performance of the operation, and that he had gone purposely out of the house because he had not nerve enough to stay and witness it. After that, your uncle no longer hesitated. He had no fear of results, provided he could be certain of his own courage. All he dreaded was the effect on him of his love for the child, when he first found himself face to face with the dreadful necessity of touching her skin with the knife.

I tried hard to control myself; but I could not repress a shudder at those words.

'It is useless to shock you by going into particulars,' said the priest, considerately. 'Let it be enough if I say that your uncle's fortitude failed to support him when he wanted it most. His love for the child shook the firm hand which had never trembled before. In a word, the operation failed. Your father returned, and found his child dying. The frenzy of his despair, when the truth was told him, carried him to excesses which it shocks me to mention – excesses which began in his degrading his brother by a blow, which ended in his binding himself by an oath to make that brother suffer public punishment for his fatal rashness, in a court of law.

Your uncle was too heartbroken by what had happened to feel those outrages as some men might have felt them. He looked for one moment at his sister-in-law (I do not like to say your mother, considering what I have now to tell you), to see if she would acknowledge that she had encouraged him to attempt the operation, and that she had deceived him in saying that he had his brother's permission to try it. She was silent, and when she spoke, it was to join her husband in denouncing him as the murderer of their child. Whether fear of your father's anger or revengeful indignation against your uncle most actuated her, I cannot presume to enquire in your presence. I can only state facts.'

The priest paused, and looked at me anxiously. I could not speak to him at that moment – I could only encourage him to proceed by pressing his hand.

He resumed in these terms: 'Meanwhile, your uncle turned to your father, and spoke the last words he was ever to address to his eldest brother in this world. He said, "I have deserved the worst your anger can inflict on me, but I will spare you the scandal of bringing me to justice in open court. The law, if it found me guilty, could at the worst but banish me from my country and my friends. I will go of my own accord. God is my witness that I honestly believed I could save the child from deformity and suffering. I have risked all and lost all. My heart and spirit are broken. I am fit for nothing but to go and hide myself and my misery from all eyes that have ever looked on me. I shall never come back, never expect your pity or forgiveness. If you think less harshly of me when I am gone, keep secret what has happened; let no other lips say of me what yours and your wife's have said. I shall think that forbearance atonement enough, atonement greater than I have deserved. Forget me in this world. May we meet in another, where the secrets of all hearts are opened, and where the child who is gone before may make peace between us!" He said those words and went out. Your father never saw him or heard from him again.'

I knew the reason now why my father had never confided the truth to anyone, his own family included. My mother had evidently confessed all to her sister, under the seal of secrecy. And there the dreadful disclosure had been arrested.

'Your uncle told me,' the priest continued, 'that before he left England, he took leave of you by stealth, in a place you were staying at by the seaside. He had not the heart to quit his country and his friends for ever, without kissing you for the last time. He followed you in the dark, and caught you up in his arms, and left you again before you had a chance of discovering him. The next day he quitted England.'

'For this place?' I asked.

'Yes: he had spent a week here once with a student friend, at the time when he was a pupil in the Hôtel Dieu. And to this place he returned to hide, to suffer, and to die. We all saw that he was a man crushed and broken by some great sorrow, and we respected him and his affliction. He lived alone, and only came out of doors towards evening, when he used to sit on the brow of the hill yonder, with his head on his hand, looking towards England. That place seemed a favourite with him, and he is buried close by it. He revealed the story of his past life to no living soul here but me; and to me he only spoke when his last hour was approaching. What he had suffered during his long exile, no man can presume to say. I, who saw more of him than anyone, never heard a word of complaint fall from his lips. He had the courage of the martyrs while he lived, and the resignation of the saints when he died. Just at the last his mind wandered. He said he saw his little darling waiting by the bedside to lead him away; and he died with a smile on his face – the first I had ever seen there.'

The priest ceased, and we went out together in the mournful twilight, and stood for a little while on the brow of the hill where Uncle George used to sit, with his face turned towards England. How my heart ached for him, as I thought of what he must have suffered in the silence and solitude of his long exile! Was it well for me that I had discovered the Family Secret at last? I have sometimes thought not. I have sometimes wished that the darkness had never been cleared away which once hid from me the fate of Uncle George.

Mr Lismore and the Widow

Late in the autumn, not many years since, a public meeting was held at the Mansion House, London, under the direction of the Lord Mayor.

The list of gentlemen invited to address the audience had been chosen with two objects in view. Speakers of celebrity, who would rouse public enthusiasm, were supported by speakers connected with commerce, who would be practically useful in explaining the purpose for which the meeting was convened. Money wisely spent in advertising had produced the customary result: every seat was occupied before the proceedings began.

Among the late arrivals, who had no choice but to stand or to leave the hall, were two ladies. One of them at once decided on leaving the hall.

'I shall go back to the carriage,' she said, 'and wait for you at the door.'

Her friend answered, 'I shan't keep you long. He is advertised to support the second resolution; I want to see him, and that is all.'

An elderly gentleman, seated at the end of a bench, rose and offered his place to the lady who remained. She hesitated to take advantage of his kindness, until he reminded her that he had heard what she said to her friend. Before the third resolution was proposed his seat would be at his own disposal again. She thanked him, and without further ceremony took his place. He was provided with an opera-glass, which he more than once offered to her when famous orators appeared on the platform. She made no use of it until a speaker, known in the City as a ship-owner, stepped forward to support the second resolution.

His name (announced in the advertisements) was Ernest Lismore.

The moment he rose the lady asked for the opera-glass. She kept it to her eyes for such a length of time, and with such evident interest in Mr Lismore, that the curiosity of her neighbours was aroused. Had he anything to say in which a lady (evidently a stranger to him) was personally interested? There was nothing in the address that he delivered which appealed to the enthusiasm of women. He was undoubtedly a handsome man, whose appearance proclaimed him to be in the prime of life, midway, perhaps, between thirty and forty years of age. But why a lady should persist in keeping an opera-glass fixed on him all through his speech was a question which found the general ingenuity at a loss for a reply.

Having returned the glass with an apology, the lady ventured on putting a question next. 'Did it strike you, sir, that Mr Lismore seemed to be out of spirits?' she asked.

'I can't say it did, ma'am.'

'Perhaps you noticed that he left the platform the moment he had done?'

This betrayal of interest in the speaker did not escape the notice of a lady seated on the bench in front. Before the old gentleman could answer she volunteered an explanation.

'I am afraid Mr Lismore is troubled by anxieties connected with his business,' she said. 'My husband heard it reported in the City yesterday that he was seriously embarrassed by the failure – '

A loud burst of applause made the end of the sentence inaudible. A famous member of Parliament had risen to propose the third resolution. The polite old man took his seat, and the lady left the hall to join her friend.

'Well, Mrs Callender, has Mr Lismore disappointed you?'

'Far from it! But I have heard a report about him which has alarmed me: he is said to be seriously troubled about money matters. How can I find out his address in the City?'

'We can stop at the first stationer's shop we pass, and ask to look at the directory. Are you going to pay Mr Lismore a visit?'

'I am going to think about it.'

The next day a clerk entered Mr Lismore's private room at the office, and presented a visiting-card. Mrs Callender had reflected, and had arrived at a decision. Underneath her name she had written these explanatory words: 'An important business.'

'Does she look as if she wanted money?' Mr Lismore enquired.

'Oh dear, no! She comes in her carriage.'

'Is she young or old?'

'Old, sir.'

To Mr Lismore, conscious of the disastrous influence occasionally exercised over busy men by youth and beauty, this was a recommendation in itself. He said, 'Show her in.'

Observing the lady as she approached him with the momentary curiosity of a stranger, he noticed that she still preserved the remains of beauty. She had also escaped the misfortune, common to persons at her time of life, of becoming too fat. Even to a man's eye, her dressmaker appeared to have made the most of that favourable circumstance. Her figure had its defects concealed, and its remaining merits set off to advantage. At the same time she evidently held herself above the common deceptions by which some women seek to conceal their age. She wore her own grey hair, and her complexion bore the test of daylight. On entering the room, she made her apologies with some embarrassment. Being the embarrassment of a stranger (and not of a youthful stranger) it failed to impress Mr Lismore favourably.

'I am afraid I have chosen an inconvenient time for my visit,' she began.

'I am at your service,' he answered, a little stiffly, 'especially if you will be so kind as to mention your business with me in few words.'

She was a woman of some spirit, and that reply roused her.

'I will mention it in one word,' she said, smartly. 'My business is – gratitude.'

He was completely at a loss to understand what she meant, and he said so plainly. Instead of explaining herself she put a question.

'Do you remember the night of the 11th of March, between five and six years since?'

He considered for a moment.

'No,' he said, 'I don't remember it. Excuse me, Mrs Callender, I have affairs of my own to attend to which cause me some anxiety – '

'Let me assist your memory, Mr Lismore, and I will leave you to your affairs. On the date that I have referred to you were on your way to the railway station at Bexmore, to catch the night express from the north to London.'

As a hint that his time was valuable the ship-owner had hitherto remained standing. He now took his customary seat, and began to listen with some interest. Mrs Callender had produced her effect on him already.

'It was absolutely necessary,' she proceeded, 'that you should be on board your ship in the London docks at nine o'clock the next morning. If you had lost the express the vessel would have sailed without you.'

The expression of his face began to change to surprise.

'Who told you that?' he asked.

'You shall hear directly. On your way into the town your carriage was stopped by an obstruction on the highroad. The people of Bexmore were looking at a house on fire.'

He started to his feet.

'Good heavens! are you the lady?'

She held up her hand in satirical protest.

'Gently, sir! You suspected me just now of wasting your valuable time. Don't rashly conclude that I am the lady until you find that I am acquainted with the circumstances.'

'Is there no excuse for my failing to recognise you?' Mr Lismore asked. 'We were on the dark side of the burning house; you were fainting, and I – '

'And you,' she interposed, 'after saving me at the risk of your own life, turned a deaf ear to my poor husband's entreaties when he asked you to wait till I had recovered my senses.'

'Your poor husband? Surely, Mrs Callender, he received no serious injury from the fire?'

'The firemen rescued him under circumstances of peril,' she answered, 'and at his great age he sank under the shock. I have lost the kindest and best of men. Do you remember how you parted from him – burned and bruised in saving me? He liked to talk of it in his last illness. "At least,' he said to you, "tell me the name of the man who preserved my wife from a dreadful death." You threw your card to him out of the carriage window, and away you went at a gallop to catch your train. In all the years that have passed I have kept that card, and have vainly enquired for my brave sea-captain. Yesterday I saw your name on the list of speakers at the Mansion House. Need I say that I attended the meeting? Need I tell you now why I come here and interrupt you in business hours?'

She held out her hand. Mr Lismore took it in silence, and pressed it warmly.

'You have not done with me yet,' she resumed, with a smile. 'Do you remember what I said of my errand when I first came in?'

'You said it was an errand of gratitude.'

'Something more than the gratitude which only says "thank you",' she added. 'Before I explain myself, however, I want to know what you have been doing, and how it was that my enquiries failed to trace you after that terrible night.' The appearance of depression which Mrs Callender had noticed at the public meeting showed itself again in Mr Lismore's face. He sighed as he answered her.

'My story has one merit,' he said: 'it is soon told. I cannot wonder that you failed to discover me. In the first place, I was not captain of my ship at that time; I was only mate. In the second place, I inherited some money, and ceased to lead a sailor's life, in less than a year from the night of the fire. You will now understand what obstacles were in the way of your tracing me. With my little capital I started successfully in business as a ship-owner. At the time I naturally congratulated myself on my own good fortune. We little know, Mrs Callender, what the future has in store for us.'

He stopped. His handsome features hardened, as if he were suffering (and concealing) pain. Before it was possible to speak to him there was a knock at the door. Another visitor without an appointment had called; the clerk appeared again with a card and a message.

'The gentleman begs you will see him, sir. He has something to tell you which is too important to be delayed.'

Hearing the message, Mrs Callender rose immediately.

'It is enough for today that we understand each other,' she said. 'Have you any engagement tomorrow after the hours of business?'

'None.'

She pointed to her card on the writing-table. 'Will you come to me tomorrow evening at that address? I am like the gentleman who has just called: I too have my reason for wishing to see you.'

He gladly accepted the invitation. Mrs Callender stopped him as he opened the door for her.

'Shall I offend you,' she said, 'if I ask a strange question before I go? I have a better motive, mind, than mere curiosity. Are you married?'

'No.'

'Forgive me again,' she resumed. 'At my age you cannot possibly mis-understand me; and yet – '

She hesitated. Mr Lismore tried to give her confidence. 'Pray don't stand on ceremony, Mrs Callender. Nothing that *you* can ask me need be prefaced by an apology.'

Thus encouraged, she ventured to proceed. 'You may be engaged to be married?' she suggested. 'Or you may be in love?'

He found it impossible to conceal his surprise, but he answered without hesitation.

'There is no such bright prospect in *my* life,' he said. 'I am not even in love.'

She left him with a little sigh. It sounded like a sigh of relief.

Ernest Lismore was thoroughly puzzled. What could be the old lady's object in ascertaining that he was still free from a matrimonial engagement? If the idea had occurred to him in time he might have alluded to her domestic life, and might have asked if she had children. With a little tact he might have discovered more than this. She had described her feeling toward him as passing the ordinary limits of gratitude, and she was evidently rich enough to be above the imputation of a mercenary motive. Did she propose to brighten those dreary prospects to which he had alluded in speaking of his own life? When he presented himself at her house the next evening would she introduce him to a charming daughter?

He smiled as the idea occurred to him. 'An appropriate time to be thinking of my chances of marriage!' he said to himself. 'In another month I may be a ruined man.'

The gentleman who had so urgently requested an interview was a devoted friend who had obtained a means of helping Ernest at a serious crisis in his affairs.

It had been truly reported that he was in a position of pecuniary embarrassment, owing to the failure of a mercantile house with which he had been intimately connected. Whispers affecting his own solvency had followed on the bankruptcy of the firm. He had already endeavoured to obtain advances of money on the usual conditions, and had been met by excuses for delay. His friend had now arrived with a letter of introduction to a capitalist, well known in commercial circles for his daring speculations and for his great wealth.

Looking at the letter, Ernest observed that the envelope was sealed. In spite of that ominous innovation on established usage in cases of personal introduction, he presented the letter. On this occasion he was not put off with excuses. The capitalist flatly declined to discount Mr Lismore's bills unless they were backed by responsible names.

Ernest made a last effort.

He applied for help to two mercantile men whom he had assisted in *their* difficulties, and whose names would have satisfied the money-lender. They were most sincerely sorry, but they too refused.

The one security that he could offer was open, it must be owned, to serious objections on the score of risk. He wanted an advance of twenty thousand pounds, secured on a homeward-bound ship and cargo. But the vessel was not insured, and at that stormy season she was already more than a month overdue. Could grateful colleagues be blamed if they forgot their obligations when they were asked to offer pecuniary help to a merchant in this situation? Ernest returned to his office without money and without credit.

A man threatened by ruin is in no state of mind to keep an engagement at a lady's tea-table. Ernest sent a letter of apology to Mrs Callender, alleging extreme pressure of business as the excuse for breaking his engagement.

'Am I to wait for an answer, sir?' the messenger asked.

'No; you are merely to leave the letter.'

In an hour's time, to Ernest's astonishment, the messenger returned with a reply.

'The lady was just going out, sir, when I rang at the door,' he explained, 'and she took the letter from me herself. She didn't appear to know your handwriting, and she asked me who I came from. When I mentioned your name I was ordered to wait.'

Ernest opened the letter.

DEAR MR LISMORE – One of us must speak out, and your letter of apology forces me to be that one. If you are really so proud and so distrustful as you seem to be, I shall offend you; if not, I shall prove myself to be your friend.

Your excuse is 'pressure of business'; the truth (as I have good reason to believe) is 'want of money'. I heard a stranger at that public meeting say that you were seriously embarrassed by some failure in the City.

Let me tell you what my own pecuniary position is in two words: I am the childless widow of a rich man – '

Ernest paused. His anticipated discovery of Mrs Callender's 'charming daughter' was in his mind for the moment. 'That little romance must return to the world of dreams,' he thought, and went on with the letter.

After what I owe to you, I don't regard it as repaying an obligation; I consider myself as merely performing a duty when I offer to assist you by a loan of money.

Wait a little before you throw my letter into the waste-paper basket.

Circumstances (which it is impossible for me to mention before we meet) put it out of my power to help you – unless I attach to my most sincere offer of service a very unusual and very embarrassing condition. If you are on the brink of ruin that misfortune will plead my excuse – and your excuse too, if you accept the loan on my terms. In any case, I rely on the sympathy and forbearance of the man to whom I owe my life.

After what I have now written, there is only one thing to add: I beg to decline accepting your excuses, and I shall expect to see you tomorrow evening, as we arranged. I am an obstinate old woman, but I am also your faithful friend and servant,

MARY CALLENDER

Ernest looked up from the letter. 'What can this possibly mean?' he wondered.

But he was too sensible a man to be content with wondering; he decided on keeping his engagement.

What Dr Johnson called 'the insolence of wealth' appears far more frequently in the houses of the rich than in the manners of the rich. The reason is plain enough. Personal ostentation is, in the very nature of it, ridiculous; but the ostentation which exhibits magnificent pictures, priceless china, and splendid furniture, can purchase good taste to guide it, and can assert itself without affording the smallest opening for a word of depreciation or a look of contempt. If I am worth a million of money, and if I am dying to show it, I don't ask you to look at me, I ask you to look at my house.

Keeping his engagement with Mrs Callender, Ernest discovered that riches might be lavishly and yet modestly used.

In crossing the hall and ascending the stairs, look where he might, his notice was insensibly won by proofs of the taste which is not to be purchased, and the wealth which uses, but never exhibits, its purse. Conducted by a manservant to the landing on the first floor, he found a maid at the door of the boudoir waiting to announce him. Mrs Callender advanced to welcome her guest, in a simple evening dress, perfectly suited to her age. All that had looked worn and faded in her fine face by daylight was now softly obscured by shaded lamps. Objects of beauty surrounded her, which glowed with subdued radiance from their background of sober colour. The influence of appearances is the strongest of all outward influences, while it lasts. For the moment the scene produced its impression on Ernest, in spite of the terrible anxieties which consumed him. Mrs Callender in his office was a woman who had stepped out of her appropriate sphere. Mrs Callender in her own house was a woman who had risen to a new place in his estimation.

'I am afraid you don't thank me for forcing you to keep your engagement,' she said, with her friendly tones and her pleasant smile.

'Indeed I do thank you,' he replied. 'Your beautiful house and your gracious welcome have persuaded me into forgetting my troubles – for a while.'

The smile passed away from her face. 'Then it is true,' she said, gravely.

'Only too true.'

She led him to a seat beside her, and waited to speak again until her maid had brought in the tea.

'Have you read my letter in the same friendly spirit in which I wrote it?' she asked, when they were alone again.

'I have read your letter gratefully, but – '

'But you don't know yet what I have to say. Let us understand each other before we make any objections on either side. Will you tell me what your present position is – at its worst? I can, and will, speak plainly when my turn comes, if you will honour me with your confidence. Not if it distresses you,' she added, observing him attentively. He was ashamed of his hesitation, and he made amends for it.

'Do you thoroughly understand me?' he asked, when the whole truth had been laid before her without reserve.

She summed up the result in her own words: 'If your overdue ship returns safely within a month from this time, you can borrow the money you want without difficulty. If the ship is lost, you have no alternative, when the end of the month comes, but to accept a loan from me or to suspend payment. Is that the hard truth?'

'It is.'

'And the sum you require is – twenty thousand pounds?'

'Yes.'

'I have twenty times as much money as that, Mr Lismore, at my sole disposal – on one condition.'

'The condition alluded to in your letter?'

'Yes.'

'Does the fulfilment of the condition depend in some way on any decision of mine?'

'It depends entirely on you.'

That answer closed his lips.

With a composed manner and a steady hand, she poured herself out a cup of tea. 'I conceal it from you,' she said, 'but I want confidence. Here' (she pointed to the cup) 'is the friend of women, rich or poor, when they are in trouble. What I have now to say obliges me to speak in praise of myself. I don't like it; let me get it over as soon as I can. My husband was very fond of me; he had the most absolute confidence in my discretion, and in my sense of duty to him and to myself. His last words before he died were words that thanked me for making the happiness of his life. As soon as I had in some degree recovered after the affliction that had fallen on me, his lawyer and executor produced a copy of his will, and said there were two clauses in it which my husband had expressed a wish that I should read. It is needless to say that I obeyed.'

She still controlled her agitation – but she was now unable to conceal it. Ernest made an attempt to spare her.

'Am I concerned in this?' he asked.

'Yes. Before I tell you why, I want to know what you would do – in a certain case which I am unwilling even to suppose. I have heard of men, unable to pay the demands made on them, who began business again, and succeeded, and in course of time paid their creditors.'

'And you want to know if there is any likelihood of my following their example?' he said. 'Have you also heard of men who have made that second effort – who have failed again – and who have doubled the debts they owed to their brethren in business who trusted them? I knew one of those men myself. He committed suicide.'

She laid her hand for a moment on his.

'I understand you,' she said. 'If ruin comes – '

'If ruin comes,' he interposed, 'a man without money and without credit can make but one last atonement. Don't speak of it now.'

She looked at him with horror.

'I didn't mean that!' she said.

'Shall we go back to what you read in the will?' he suggested.

'Yes – if you will give me a minute to compose myself.'

In less than the minute she had asked for, Mrs Callender was calm enough to go on.

'I now possess what is called a life-interest in my husband's fortune,' she said. 'The money is to be divided, at my death, among charitable institutions; excepting a certain event – '

'Which is provided for in the will?' Ernest added, helping her to go on.

'Yes. I am to be absolute mistress of the whole of the four hundred thousand pounds – ' her voice dropped, and her eyes looked away from him as she spoke the next words – 'on this one condition, that I marry again.'

He looked at her in amazement.

'Surely I have mistaken you,' he said. 'You mean on this one condition, that you do *not* marry again?'

'No, Mr Lismore; I mean exactly what I have said. You now know that the recovery of your credit and your peace of mind rests entirely with yourself.'

After a moment of reflection he took her hand and raised it respectfully to his lips. 'You are a noble woman!' he said.

She made no reply. With drooping head and downcast eyes she waited for his decision. He accepted his responsibility.

'I must not, and dare not, think of the hardship of my own position,' he said; 'I owe it to you to speak without reference to the future that may be in store for me. No man can be worthy of the sacrifice which your generous forgetfulness of yourself is willing to make. I respect you; I admire you; I thank you with my whole heart. Leave me to my fate, Mrs Callender – and let me go.'

He rose. She stopped him by a gesture.

'A young woman,' she answered, 'would shrink from saying – what I, as an old woman, mean to say now. I refuse to leave you to your fate. I ask you to prove that you respect me, admire me, and thank me with your whole heart. Take one day to think – and let me hear the result. You promise me this?'

He promised. 'Now go,' she said.

Next morning Ernest received a letter from Mrs Callender. She wrote to him as follows:

There are some considerations which I ought to have mentioned yesterday evening, before you left my house.

I ought to have reminded you – if you consent to reconsider your decision – that the circumstances do not require you to pledge yourself to me absolutely.

At my age, I can with perfect propriety assure you that I regard our marriage simply and solely as a formality which we must fulfill, if I am to carry out my intention of standing between you and ruin.

Therefore – if the missing ship appears in time, the only reason for the marriage is at an end. We shall be as good friends as ever; without the encumbrance of a formal tie to bind us.

In the other event, I should ask you to submit to certain restrictions, which, remembering my position, you will understand and excuse.

'We are to live together, it is unnecessary to say, as mother and son. The marriage ceremony is to be strictly private, and you are so to arrange our affairs that, immediately afterward, we leave England for any foreign place which you prefer. Some of my friends, and (perhaps) some of your friends, will certainly misinterpret our motives, if we stay in our own country, in a manner which would be unendurable to a woman like me.

As to our future lives, I have the most perfect confidence in you, and I should leave you in the same position of independence which you occupy now. When you wish for my company you will always be welcome. At other times you are your own master. I live on my side of the house, and you live on yours; and I am to be allowed my hours of solitude every day in the pursuit of musical occupations, which have been happily associated with all my past life, and which I trust confidently to your indulgence.

A last word, to remind you of what you may be too kind to think of yourself.

At my age, you cannot, in the course of nature, be troubled by the society of a grateful old woman for many years. You are young enough to look forward to another marriage, which shall be something more than a mere form. Even if you meet with the happy woman in my lifetime, honestly tell me of it, and I promise to tell her that she has only to wait.

In the meantime, don't think, because I write composedly, that I write heartlessly. You pleased and interested me when I first saw you at the public meeting. I don't think I could have proposed what you call this sacrifice of myself to a man who had personally repelled me, though I had felt my debt of gratitude as sincerely as ever. Whether your ship is safe or whether your ship is lost, old Mary Callender likes you, and owns it without false shame.

Let me have your answer this evening, either personally or by letter, whichever you like best.

Mrs Callender received a written answer long before the evening. It said much in few words:

A man impenetrable to kindness might be able to resist your letter. I am not that man. Your great heart has conquered me.

The few formalities which precede marriage by special licence were observed by Ernest. While the destiny of their future lives was still in suspense, an unacknowledged feeling of embarrassment on either side kept Ernest and Mrs Callender apart. Every day brought the lady her report of the state of affairs in the City, written always in the same words: 'No news of the ship.'

On the day before the ship-owner's liabilities became due the terms of the report from the City remained unchanged, and the special licence was put to its contemplated use. Mrs Callender's lawyer and Mrs Callender's maid were the only persons trusted with the secret. Leaving the chief clerk in charge of the business, with every pecuniary demand on his employer satisfied in full, the strangely married pair quitted England.

They arranged to wait for a few days in Paris, to receive any letters of importance which might have been addressed to Ernest in the interval. On the evening of their arrival a telegram from London was waiting at their hotel. It announced that the missing ship had passed up channel – undiscovered in a fog until she reached the Downs – on the day before Ernest's liabilities fell due.

'Do you regret it?' Mrs Lismore said to her husband.

'Not for a moment!' he answered.

They decided on pursuing their journey as far as Munich.

Mrs Lismore's taste for music was matched by Ernest's taste for painting. In his leisure hours he cultivated the art, and delighted in it. The picture-galleries of Munich were almost the only galleries in Europe which he had not seen. True to the engagements to which she had pledged herself, his wife was willing to go wherever it might please him to take her. The one suggestion she made was that they should hire furnished apartments. If they lived at a hotel friends of the husband or the wife (visitors like themselves to the famous city) might see their names in the book or might meet them at the door.

They were soon established in a house large enough to provide them with every accommodation which they required. Ernest's days were passed in the galleries, Mrs Lismore remaining at home, devoted to her music, until it was time to go out with her husband for a drive. Living together in perfect amity and concord, they were nevertheless not living happily. Without any visible reason for the change, Mrs Lismore's spirits were depressed. On the one occasion when Ernest noticed it she made an effort to be cheerful, which it distressed him to see. He allowed her to think that she had relieved him of any further anxiety. Whatever doubts he might feel were doubts delicately concealed from that time forth.

But when two people are living together in a state of artificial tranquillity, it seems to be a law of nature that the element of disturbance gathers unseen, and that the outburst comes inevitably with the lapse of time.

In ten days from the date of their arrival at Munich the crisis came. Ernest returned later than usual from the picture-gallery, and, for the first time in his wife's experience, shut himself up in his own room.

He appeared at the dinner hour with a futile excuse. Mrs Lismore waited until the servant had withdrawn.

'Now, Ernest,' she said, 'it's time to tell me the truth.'

Her manner, when she said those few words, took him by surprise. She was unquestionably confused, and, instead of looking at him, she trifled with the fruit on her plate. Embarrassed on his side, he could only answer: 'I have nothing to tell.'

'Were there many visitors at the gallery?' she asked.

'About the same as usual.'

'Any that you particularly noticed?' she went on. 'I mean among the ladies.'

He laughed uneasily.

'You forget how interested I am in the pictures,' he said.

There was a pause. She looked up at him, and suddenly looked away again; but – he saw it plainly – there were tears in her eyes.

'Do you mind turning down the gas?' she said. 'My eyes have been weak all day.'

He complied with her request the more readily, having his own reasons for being glad to escape the glaring scrutiny of the light.

'I think I will rest a little on the sofa,' she resumed. In the position which he occupied his back would have been now turned on her. She stopped him when he tried to move his chair. 'I would rather not look at you, Ernest,' she said, 'when you have lost confidence in me.'

Not the words, but the tone, touched all that was generous and noble in his nature. He left his place and knelt beside her, and opened to her his whole heart.

'Am I not unworthy of you?' he asked, when it was over.

She pressed his hand in silence.

'I should be the most ungrateful wretch living,' he said, 'if I did not think of you, and you only, now that my confession is made. We will leave Munich tomorrow, and, if resolution can help me, I will only remember the sweetest woman my eyes ever looked on as the creature of a dream.'

She hid her face on his breast, and reminded him of that letter of her writing which had decided the course of their lives.

'When I thought you might meet the happy woman in my lifetime I said to you, "Tell me of it, and I promise to tell her that she has only to wait." Time must pass, Ernest, before it can be needful to perform my promise, but you might let me see her. If you find her in the gallery tomorrow you might bring her here.'

Mrs Lismore's request met with no refusal. Ernest was only at a loss to know how to grant it.

'You tell me she is a copyist of pictures,' his wife reminded him. 'She will be interested in hearing of the portfolio of drawings by the great French artists which I bought for you in Paris. Ask her to come and see them, and to tell you if she can make some copies; and say, if you like, that I shall be glad to become acquainted with her.'

He felt her breath beating fast on his bosom. In the fear that she might lose all control over herself, he tried to relieve her by speaking lightly.

'What an invention yours is!' he said. 'If my wife ever tries to deceive me, I shall be a mere child in her hands.'

She rose abruptly from the sofa, kissed him on the forehead, and said wildly, 'I shall be better in bed!' Before he could move or speak she had left him.

The next morning he knocked at the door of his wife's room, and asked how she had passed the night.

'I have slept badly,' she answered, 'and I must beg you to excuse my absence at breakfast-time.' She called him back as he was about to withdraw. 'Remember,' she said, 'when you return from the gallery today I expect that you will not return alone.'

Three hours later he was at home again. The young lady's services as a copyist were at his disposal; she had returned with him to look at the drawings.

The sitting-room was empty when they entered it. He rang for his wife's maid, and was informed that Mrs Lismore had gone out. Refusing to believe the woman, he went to his wife's apartments. She was not to be found.

When he returned to the sitting-room the young lady was not unnaturally offended. He could make allowances for her being a little out of temper at the slight that had been put on her; but he was inexpressibly disconcerted by the manner – almost the coarse manner – in which she expressed herself.

'I have been talking to your wife's maid while you have been away,' she said. 'I find you have married an old lady for her money. She is jealous of me, of course?'

'Let me beg you to alter your opinion,' he answered. 'You are wronging my wife; she is incapable of any such feeling as you attribute to her.'

The young lady laughed. 'At any rate, you are a good husband,' she said, satirically. 'Suppose you own the truth: wouldn't you like her better if she was young and pretty like me?'

He was not merely surprised, he was disgusted. Her beauty had so completely fascinated him when he first saw her that the idea of associating any want of refinement and good breeding with such a charming creature never entered his mind. The disenchantment to him was already so complete that he was even disagreeably affected by the tone of her voice; it was almost as repellent to him as this exhibition of unrestrained bad temper which she seemed perfectly careless to conceal.

'I confess you surprise me,' he said, coldly.

The reply produced no effect on her. On the contrary, she became more insolent than ever.

'I have a fertile fancy,' she went on, 'and your absurd way of taking a joke only encourages me! Suppose you could transform this sour old wife of yours, who has insulted me, into the sweetest young creature that ever lived by only holding up your finger, wouldn't you do it?'

This passed the limits of his endurance. 'I have no wish,' he said, 'to forget the consideration which is due to a woman. You leave me but one alternative.' He rose to go out of the room.

She ran to the door as he spoke, and placed herself in the way of his going out.

He signed to her to let him pass.

She suddenly threw her arms round his neck, kissed him passionately, and whispered, with her lips at his ear, 'Oh Ernest, forgive me! Could I have asked you to marry me for my money if I had not taken refuge in a disguise?'

When he had sufficiently recovered to think he put her back from him. 'Is there an end of the deception now?' he asked, sternly. 'Am I to trust you in your new character?'

'You are not to be harder on me than I deserve,' she answered, gently. 'Did you ever hear of an actress named Miss Max?'

He began to understand her. 'Forgive me if I spoke harshly,' he said. 'You have put me to a severe trial.'

She burst into tears. 'Love,' she murmured, 'is my only excuse.'

From that moment she had won her pardon. He took her hand and made her sit by him.

'Yes,' he said, 'I have heard of Miss Max, and of her wonderful powers of personation; and I have always regretted not having seen her while she was on the stage.'

'Did you hear anything more of her, Ernest?'

'Yes; I heard that she was a pattern of modesty and good conduct, and that she gave up her profession at the height of her success to marry an old man.'

'Will you come with me to my room?' she asked. 'I have something there which I wish to show you.'

It was the copy of her husband's will.

'Read the lines, Ernest, which begin at the top of the page. Let my dead husband speak for me.'

The lines ran thus:

My motive in marrying Miss Max must be stated in this place, in justice to her, and, I will venture to add, in justice to myself. I felt the sincerest sympathy for her position. She was without father, mother, or friends, one of the poor forsaken children whom the mercy of the foundling hospital provides with a home. Her afterlife on the stage was the life of a virtuous woman, persecuted by profligates, insulted by some of the baser creatures associated with her, to whom she was an object of envy. I offered her a home and the protection of a father, on the only terms which the world would recognise as worthy of us. My experience of her since our marriage has been the experience of unvarying goodness, sweetness, and sound sense. She has behaved so nobly in a trying position that I wish her (even in this life) to have her reward. I entreat her to make a second choice in marriage, which shall not be a mere form. I firmly believe that she will choose well and wisely, that she will make the happiness of a man who is worthy of her, and that, as wife and mother, she will set an example of inestimable value in the social sphere that she occupies. In proof of the heartfelt sincerity with which I pay my tribute to her virtues, I add to this, my will, the clause that follows.

With the clause that followed Ernest was already acquainted.

'Will you now believe that I never loved till I saw your face for the first time?' said his wife. 'I had no experience to place me on my guard against the fascination – the madness, some people might call it – which possesses a woman when all her heart is given to a man. Don't despise me, my dear! Remember that I had to save you from disgrace and ruin. Besides, my old stage remembrances tempted me. I had acted in a play in which the heroine did – what I have done. It didn't end with me as it did with her in the story. *She* was represented as rejoicing in the success of her disguise. I have known some miserable hours of doubt and shame since our marriage. When I went to meet you in my own person at the picture-gallery, oh, what relief, what joy I felt when I saw how you admired me! It was not because I could no longer carry on the disguise; I was able to get hours of rest from the effort, not only at night, but in the daytime, when I was shut up in my retirement in the music-room, and when my maid kept watch against discovery. No, my love! I hurried on the disclosure because I could no longer endure the hateful triumph of my own deception. Ah, look at that witness against me! I can't bear even to see it.'

She abruptly left him. The drawer that she had opened to take out the copy of the will also contained the false grey hair which she had discarded. It had only that moment attracted her notice. She snatched it up and turned to the fireplace.

Ernest took it from her before she could destroy it. 'Give it to me,' he said.

'Why?'

He drew her gently to his bosom, and answered, 'I must not forget my old wife.'

The Dead Hand

When this present nineteenth century was younger by a good many years than it is now, a certain friend of mine, named Arthur Holliday, happened to arrive in the town of Doncaster exactly in the middle of the race-week, or, in other words, in the middle of the month of September.

He was one of those reckless, rattle-pated, open-hearted, and open-mouthed young gentlemen who possess the gift of familiarity in its highest perfection, and who scramble carelessly along the journey of life, making friends, as the phrase is, wherever they go. His father was a rich manu-facturer, and had bought landed property enough in one of the midland counties to make all the born squires in his neighbourhood thoroughly envious of him. Arthur was his only son, possessor in prospect of the great estate and the great business after his father's death; well supplied with money, and not too rigidly looked after, during his father's lifetime. Report, or scandal, whichever you please, said that the old gentleman had been rather wild in his youthful days, and that, unlike most parents, he was not disposed to be violently indignant when he found that his son took after him. This may be true or not. I myself only knew the elder Mr Holliday when he was getting on in years, and then he was as quiet and as respectable a gentleman as ever I met with.

Well, one September, as I told you, young Arthur comes to Doncaster, having suddenly decided, in his hare-brained way, that he would go to the races. He did not reach the town till towards the close of evening, and he went at once to see about his dinner and bed at the principal hotel. Dinner they were ready enough to give him; but as for a bed, they laughed when he mentioned it. In the race-week at Doncaster, it is no uncommon thing for visitors who have not bespoken apartments to pass the night in their carriages at the inn doors. As for the lower sort of strangers, I myself have often seen them, at that full time, sleeping out on the doorsteps for want of a covered place to creep under. Rich as he was, Arthur's chance of getting a night's lodging (seeing that he had not written beforehand to secure one) was more than doubtful. He tried the second hotel, and the third hotel, and two of the inferior inns after that; and was met everywhere with the same form of answer. No accommodation for the night of any sort was left. All the bright golden sovereigns in his pocket would not buy him a bed at Doncaster in the race-week.

To a young fellow of Arthur's temperament, the novelty of being turned away into the street like a penniless vagabond, at every house where he asked for a lodging, presented itself in the light of a new and highly amusing piece of experience. He went on with his carpet-bag in his hand, applying for a bed at every place of entertainment for travellers that he could find in Doncaster, until he wandered into the outskirts of the town.

By this time the last glimmer of twilight had faded out, the moon was rising dimly in a mist, the wind was getting cold, the clouds were gathering heavily, and there was every prospect that it was soon going to rain.

The look of the night had rather a lowering effect on young Holliday's good spirits. He began to contemplate the houseless situation in which he was placed from the serious rather than the humorous point of view; and he looked about him for another public-house to enquire at with something very like downright anxiety in his mind on the subject of a lodging for the night.

The suburban part of the town towards which he had now strayed was hardly lighted at all, and he could see nothing of the houses as he passed them, except that they got progressively smaller and dirtier the farther he went. Down the winding road before him shone the dull gleam of an oil lamp, the one faint lonely light that struggled ineffectually with the foggy darkness all round him. He resolved to go on as far as this lamp; and then, if it showed him nothing in the shape of an inn, to return to the central part of the town, and to try if he could not at least secure a chair to sit down on, through the night, at one of the principal hotels.

As he got near the lamp, he heard voices; and, walking close under it, found that it lighted the entrance to a narrow court, on the wall of which was painted a long hand in faded flesh colour, pointing, with a lean forefinger, to this inscription: 'The Two Robins'.

Arthur turned into the court without hesitation, to see what the Two Robins could do for him. Four or five men were standing together round the door of the house, which was at the bottom of the court, facing the entrance from the street. The men were all listening to one other man, better dressed than the rest, who was telling his audience something, in a low voice, in which they were apparently very much interested.

On entering the passage, Arthur was passed by a stranger with a knapsack in his hand, who was evidently leaving the house.

'No,' said the traveller with the knapsack, turning round and addressing himself cheerfully to a fat, sly-looking, bald-headed man, with a dirty white apron on, who had followed him down the passage. 'No, Mr Landlord, I am not easily scared by trifles; but I don't mind confessing that I can't quite stand *that*.'

It occurred to young Holliday, the moment he heard these words, that the stranger had been asked an exorbitant price for a bed at the Two Robins; and that he was unable, or unwilling to pay it. The moment his back was turned, Arthur, comfortably conscious of his own well-filled pockets, addressed himself in a great hurry, for fear any other benighted traveller should slip in and forestall him, to the sly-looking landlord with the dirty apron and the bald head.

'If you have got a bed to let,' he said, 'and if that gentleman who has just gone out won't pay your price for it, I will.'

The sly landlord looked hard at Arthur.

'Will you, sir?' he asked, in a meditative, doubtful way.

'Name your price,' said young Holliday, thinking that the landlord's hesitation sprang from some boorish distrust of him. 'Name your price, and I'll give you the money at once, if you like.'

'Are you game for five shillings?' enquired the landlord, rubbing his stubbly double chin, and looking up thoughtfully at the ceiling above him.

Arthur nearly laughed in the man's face; but thinking it prudent to control himself, offered the five shillings as seriously as he could. The sly landlord held out his hand, then suddenly drew it back again.

'You're acting all fair and above-board by me,' he said; 'and, before I take your money, I'll do the same by you. Look here, this is how it stands. You can have a bed all to yourself for five shillings; but you can't have more than a half share of the room it stands in. Do you see what I mean, young gentleman?'

'Of course I do,' returned Arthur, a little irritably. 'You mean that it is a double-bedded room, and that one of the beds is occupied?'

The landlord nodded his head, and rubbed his double chin harder than even. Arthur hesitated, and mechanically moved back a step or two towards the door. The idea of sleeping in the same room with a total stranger did not present an attractive prospect to him. He felt more than half inclined to drop his five shillings into his pocket, and to go out into the street once more.

'Is it yes, or no?' asked the landlord. 'Settle it as quick as you can, because there's lots of people wanting a bed at Doncaster, tonight, besides you.'

Arthur looked towards the court, and heard the rain falling heavily in the street outside. He thought he would ask a question or two before he rashly decided on leaving the shelter of the Two Robins.

'What sort of man is it who has got the other bed?' he enquired. 'Is he a gentleman? I mean is he a quiet, well-behaved person?'

'The quietest man I ever came across,' said the landlord, rubbing his fat hands stealthily one over the other. 'As sober as a judge, and as regular as clockwork in his habits. It hasn't struck nine, not ten minutes ago, and he's in his bed already. I don't know whether that comes up to your notion of a quiet man – it goes a long way ahead of mine, I can tell you.'

'Is he asleep, do you think?' asked Arthur.

'I know he's asleep,' returned the landlord. 'And what's more, he's gone off so fast, that I'll warrant you don't wake him. This way, sir,' said the landlord, speaking over young Holliday's shoulder, as if he was addressing some new guest who was approaching the house.

'Here you are,' said Arthur, determined to be beforehand with the stranger, whoever he might be. 'I'll take the bed.' And he handed the five shillings to the landlord, who nodded, dropped the money carelessly into his waistcoat-pocket, and lighted a candle.

'Come up and see the room,' said the host of the Two Robins, leading the way to the staircase quite briskly, considering how fat he was.

They mounted to the second floor of the house. The landlord half opened a door, fronting the landing, then stopped, and turned round to Arthur.

'It's a fair bargain, mind, on my side as well as on yours,' he said. 'You give me five shillings; I will give you in return a clean, comfortable bed; and I warrant, beforehand, that you won't be interfered with, or annoyed in any way, by the man who sleeps in the same room with you.' Saying those words, he looked hard, for a moment, in young Holliday's face, and then led the way into the room.

It was larger and cleaner than Arthur expected it would be. The two beds stood parallel with each other – a space of about six feet intervening between them. They were both of the same medium size, and both had the same plain white curtains, made to draw, if necessary, all round them.

The occupied bed was the bed nearest the window. The curtains were all drawn round it, except the half curtain at the bottom, on the side of the bed farthest from the window. Arthur saw the feet of the sleeping man raising the scanty clothes into a sharp little eminence, as if he were lying flat on his back. He took the candle, and advanced softly to draw the curtain – stopped halfway, and listened for a moment – then turned to the landlord.

'He is a very quiet sleeper,' said Arthur.

'Yes,' said the landlord, 'very quiet.'

Young Holliday advanced with the candle, arid looked in at the man cautiously.

'How pale he is,' said Arthur.

'Yes,' returned the landlord, 'pale enough, isn't he?'

Arthur looked closer at the man. The bedclothes were drawn up to his chin, and they lay perfectly still over the region of his chest. Surprised and vaguely startled, as he noticed this, Arthur stooped down closer over the stranger; looked at his ashy, parted lips; listened breathlessly for an instant; looked again at the still face, and the motionless lips and chest; and turned round suddenly on the landlord, with his own cheeks as pale, for the moment, as the hollow cheeks of the man on the bed.

'Come here,' he whispered, under his breath. 'Come here, for God's sake! The man's not asleep – he is dead.'

'You have found that out sooner than I thought you would,' said the landlord composedly. 'Yes, he's dead, sure enough. He died at five o'clock today.'

'How did he die? Who is he?' asked Arthur, staggered for the moment by the audacious coolness of the answer.

'As to who he is,' rejoined the landlord, 'I know no more about him than you do. There are his books and letters and things, all sealed up in that brown-paper parcel, for the coroner's inquest to open tomorrow or next day. He's been here a week, paying his way fairly enough, and stopping indoors, for the most part, as if he was ailing. My girl brought up his tea at five today, and as he was pouring of it out, he fell down in a faint, or a fit, or a compound of both, for anything I know. We couldn't bring him to – and I said he was dead. And the doctor couldn't bring him to – and the doctor said he was dead. And there he is. And the coroner's inquest's coming as soon as it can. And that's as much as I know about it.'

Arthur held the candle close to the man's lips. The flame still burnt straight up, as steadily as ever. There was a moment of silence; and the rain pattered drearily through it against the panes of the window.

'If you haven't got nothing more to say to me,' continued the landlord, 'I suppose I may go. You don't expect your five shillings back, do you? There's the bed I promised you, clean and comfortable. There's the man I warranted not to disturb you, quiet in this world for ever. If you're frightened to stop alone with him, that's not my lookout. I've kept my part of the bargain, and I mean to keep the money. I'm not Yorkshire myself, young gentleman; but I've lived long enough in these parts to have my wits sharpened; and I shouldn't wonder if you found out the way to brighten up yours, next time you come among us.'

With those words, the landlord turned towards the door, and laughed to himself softly, in high satisfaction at his own sharpness.

Startled and shocked as he was, Arthur had by this time sufficiently recovered himself to feel indignant at the trick that had been played on him, and at the insolent manner in which the landlord exulted in it.

'Don't laugh, till you are quite sure you have got the laugh against me,' he said sharply. 'You shan't have the five shillings for nothing, my man. I'll keep the bed.'

'Will you?' said the landlord. 'Then I wish you a good night's rest.'

With that brief farewell, he went out, and shut the door after him.

A good night's rest The words had hardly been spoken, the door had hardly been closed, before Arthur half repented the hasty words that had just escaped him. Though not naturally over-sensitive, and not wanting in courage of the moral as well as the physical sort, the presence of the dead man had an instantaneously chilling effect on his mind when he found himself alone in the room – alone, and bound by his own rash words to stay there till the next morning. An older man would have thought nothing of those words, and would have acted without reference to them, as his calmer sense suggested. But Arthur was too young to treat the ridicule, even of his inferiors, with contempt – too young not to fear the momentary humiliation of falsifying his own foolish boast more than he feared the trial of watching out the long night in the same chamber with the dead.

'It is but a few hours,' he thought to himself, 'and I can get away the first thing in the morning.'

He was looking towards the occupied bed as that idea passed through his mind, and the sharp angular eminence made in the clothes by the dead man's upturned feet again caught his eye. He advanced and drew the curtains, purposely abstaining, as he did so, from looking at the face of the corpse, lest he might unnerve himself at the outset by fastening some ghastly impression of it on his mind. He drew the curtain very gently, and sighed involuntarily as he closed it.

'Poor fellow!' he said, almost as sadly as if he had known the man. 'Ah, poor fellow!'

He went next to the window. The night was black and he could see nothing from it. The rain still pattered heavily against the glass. He inferred, from hearing it, that the window was at the back of the house; remembering that the front was sheltered from the weather by the court and the buildings over it.

While he was still standing at the window – for even the dreary rain was a relief, because of the sound it made; a relief, also, because it moved, and had some faint suggestion, in consequence, of life and companionship in it – while he was standing at the window, and looking vacantly into the black darkness outside, he heard a distant church-clock strike ten. Only ten! How was he to pass the time till the house was astir the next morning?

Under any other circumstances, he would have gone down to the public-house parlour, would have called for his grog, and would have laughed and talked with the company assembled as familiarly as if he had known them all his life. But the very thought of whiling away the time in this manner was now distasteful to him. The new situation in which he was placed seemed to have altered him to himself already. Thus far, his life had been the common, trifling, prosaic surface-life of a prosperous young man, with no troubles to conquer, and no trials to face. He had lost no relation whom he loved, no friend whom he treasured. Till this night, what share he had of the immortal inheritance that is divided amongst us all, had lain dormant with him. Till this night, Death and he had not once met, even in thought.

He took a few turns up and down the room – then stopped. The noise made by his boots on the poorly carpeted floor jarred on his ear. He hesitated a little, and ended by taking the boots off, and walking backwards and forwards noiselessly.

All desire to sleep or to rest had left him. The bare thought of lying down on the unoccupied bed instantly drew the picture on his mind of a dreadful mimicry of the position of the dead man. Who was he? What was the story of his past life? Poor he must have been or he would not have stopped at such a place as the Two Robins Inn – and weakened, probably, by long illness, or he could hardly have died in the manner which the landlord had described. Poor, ill, lonely – dead in a strange place; dead, with nobody but a stranger to pity him. A sad story: truly, on the mere face of it, a very sad story.

While these thoughts were passing through his mind, he had stopped insensibly at the window, close to which stood the foot of the bed with the closed curtains. At first he looked at it absently; then he became conscious that his eyes were fixed on it; and then, a perverse desire took possession of him to do the very thing which he had resolved not to do, up to this time – to look at the dead man.

He stretched out his hand towards the curtains; but checked himself in the very act of undrawing them, turned his back sharply on the bed, and walked towards the chimney-piece, to see what things were placed on it, and to try if he could keep the dead man out of his mind that way.

There was a pewter inkstand on the chimney-piece, with some mildewed remains of ink in the bottle. There were two coarse china ornaments of the commonest kind; and there was a square of embossed card, dirty and fly-blown, with a collection of wretched riddles printed on it, in all sorts of zigzag directions, and in variously coloured inks. He took the card and went away to read it at the table on which the candle was placed; sitting down, with his back resolutely turned to the curtained bed.

He read the first riddle, the second, the third, all in one corner of the card – then turned it round impatiently to look at another. Before he could begin reading the riddles printed here, the sound of the church clock stopped him.

Eleven.

He had got through an hour of the time, in the room with the dead man.

Once more he looked at the card. It was not easy to make out the letters printed on it in consequence of the dimness of the light which the landlord had left him – a common tallow candle, furnished with a pair of heavy old-fashioned steel snuffers. Up to this time, his mind had been too much occupied to think of the light. He had left the wick of the candle unsnuffed, till it had risen higher than the flame, and had burnt into an odd penthouse shape at the top, from which morsels of the charred cotton fell off, from time to time, in little flakes. He took up the snuffers now, and trimmed the wick. The light brightened directly, and the room became less dismal.

Again he turned to the riddles; reading them doggedly and resolutely, now in one corner of the card, now in another. All his efforts, however, could not fix his attention on them. He pursued his occupation mechanically, deriving no sort of impression from what he was reading. It was as if a shadow from the curtained bed had got between his mind and the gaily printed letters – a shadow that nothing could dispel. At last, he gave up the struggle, threw the card from him impatiently, and took to walking softly up and down the room again.

The dead man, the dead man, the *hidden* dead man on the bed!

There was the one persistent idea still haunting him. Hidden! Was it only the body being there – or was it the body being there, *concealed*, that was preying on his mind? He stopped at the window, with that doubt in him; once more listening to the pattering rain, once more looking out into the black darkness.

Still the dead man!

The darkness forced his mind back upon itself, and set his memory at work, reviving, with a painfully vivid distinctness, the momentary impression it had received from his first sight of the corpse. Before long, the face seemed to be hovering out in the middle of the rain and darkness, confronting him through the window – with the paleness whiter – with the dreadful dull line of light between the imperfectly closed eyelids broader than he had seen it – with the parted lips slowly dropping farther and farther away from each other – with the features growing larger and moving closer, till they seemed to fill the window, and silence the rain, and shut out the night.

The sound of a voice shouting below stairs woke him suddenly from the dream of his own distempered fancy. He recognised it as the voice of the landlord.

'Shut up at twelve, Ben,' he heard it say. 'I'm off to bed.'

He wiped away the damp that had gathered on his forehead, reasoned with himself for a little while, and resolved to shake his mind free of the ghastly counterfeit which still clung to it by forcing himself to confront, if it was only for a moment, the solemn reality. Without allowing himself an instant to hesitate, he parted the curtains at the foot of the bed, and looked through.

There was the sad, peaceful, white face, with the awful mystery of stillness on it, laid back upon the pillow. No stir, no change there! He only looked at it for a moment before he closed the curtains again; but that moment steadied him, calmed him, restored him – mind and body – to himself.

He returned to his old occupation of walking up and down the room; persevering in it, this time, till the clock struck again.

Twelve.

As the sound of the clock bell died away, it was succeeded by the confused noise, downstairs, of the drinkers in the tap-room leaving the house. The next sound, after an interval of silence, was caused by the barring of the door, and the closing of the shutters at the back of the inn. Then the silence followed again, and was disturbed no more.

He was alone now – absolutely, hopelessly alone with the dead man, till the next morning.

The wick of the candle wanted trimming again. He took up the snuffers –

but paused suddenly on the very point of using them, and looked attentively at the candle – then back, over his shoulder, at the curtained bed – then again at the candle. It had been lighted, for the first time, to show him the way upstairs, and three parts of it, at least, were already consumed. In another hour it would be burnt out. In another hour – unless he called at once to the man who had shut up the inn, for a fresh candle – he would be left in the dark.

Strongly as his mind had been affected since he had entered the room, his unreasonable dread of encountering ridicule, and of exposing his courage to suspicion, had not altogether lost its influence over him yet.

He lingered irresolutely by the table, waiting till he could prevail on himself to open the door and call from the landing to the man who had shut up the inn. In his present hesitating frame of mind, it was a kind of relief to gain a few moments only by engaging in the trifling occupation of snuffing the candle. His hand trembled a little, and the snuffers were heavy and awkward to use. When he closed them on the wick, he closed them a hair's breadth too low. In an instant the candle was out, and the room was plunged in pitch darkness.

The one impression which the absence of light immediately produced on his mind, was distrust of the curtained bed – distrust which shaped itself into no distinct idea, but which was powerful enough, in its very vagueness, to bind him down to his chair, to make his heart beat fast, and to set him listening intently. No sound stirred in the room but the familiar sound of the rain against the window, louder and sharper now than he had heard it yet.

Still the vague distrust, the inexpressible dread, possessed him, and kept him in his chair. He had put his carpet-bag on the table when he first entered the room; and he now took the key from his pocket, reached out his hand softly, opened the bag, and groped in it for his travelling writing-case, in which he knew there was a small store of matches. When he had got one of the matches, he waited before he struck it on the coarse wooden table, and listened intently again, without knowing why. Still there was no sound in the room but the steady, ceaseless, rattling sound of the rain.

He lighted the candle again, without another moment of delay; and, on the instant of its burning up, the first object in the room that his eyes sought for was the curtained bed.

Just before the light had been put out, he had looked in that direction, and had seen no change, no disarrangement of any sort, in the folds of the closely drawn curtains.

When he looked at the bed now, he saw, hanging over the side of it – a long white hand.

It lay perfectly motionless, midway on the side of the bed, where the curtain at the head and the curtain at the foot met. Nothing more was visible. The clinging curtains hid everything but the long white hand.

He stood looking at it, unable to stir, unable to call out; feeling nothing, knowing nothing; every faculty he possessed gathered up and lost in the one seeing faculty. How long that first panic held him, he never could tell afterwards. It might have been only for a moment; it might have been for many minutes together. How he got to the bed – whether he ran to it headlong, or whether he approached it slowly – how he wrought himself up to unclose the curtains and look in, he never has remembered, and never will remember, to his dying day. It is enough that he did go to the bed, and that he did look inside the curtains.

The man had moved. One of his arms was outside the clothes; his face was turned a little on the pillow; his eyelids were wide open. Changed as to position, and as to one of the features, the face was otherwise fearfully and wonderfully unaltered. The dead paleness and the dead quiet were on it still.

One glance showed Arthur this – one glance before he flew breathlessly to the door, and alarmed the house.

The man whom the landlord called 'Ben' was the first to appear on the stairs. In three words, Arthur told him what had happened, and sent him for the nearest doctor.

I, who tell you this story, was then staying with a medical friend of mine, in practice at Doncaster, taking care of his patients for him during his absence in London; and I, for the time being, was the nearest doctor. They had sent for me from the inn when the stranger was taken ill in the afternoon; but I was not at home, and medical assistance was sought for elsewhere. When the man from the Two Robins rang the night-bell, I was just thinking of going to bed. Naturally enough, I did not believe a word of his story about 'a dead man who had come to life again'. However, I put on my hat, armed myself with one or two bottles of restorative medicine, and ran to the inn, expecting to find nothing more remarkable, when I got there, than a patient in a fit.

My surprise at finding that the man had spoken the literal truth was almost, if not quite, equalled by my astonishment at finding myself face to face with Arthur Holliday as soon as I entered the bedroom. It was no time then for giving or seeking explanations. We just shook hands amazedly; and then I ordered everybody but Arthur out of the room, and hurried to the man on the bed.

The kitchen fire had not been long out. There was plenty of hot water in the boiler, and plenty of flannel to be had. With these, with my medicines, and with such help as Arthur could render under my direction, I dragged the man, literally, out of the jaws of death. In less than an hour from the time when I had been called in, he was alive and talking, in the bed on which he had been laid out to wait for the coroner's inquest.

You will naturally ask me what had been the matter with him; and I might treat you, in reply, to a long theory, plentifully sprinkled with what the children call hard words. I prefer telling you that, in this case, cause and effect could not be satisfactorily joined together by any theory whatever.

There are mysteries in life, and in the conditions of it, which human science has not fathomed yet; and I candidly confess to you that, in bringing that man back to existence, I was, morally speaking, groping haphazard in the dark. I know (from the testimony of the doctor who attended him in the afternoon) that the vital machinery, so far as its action is appreciable by our senses, had, in this case, unquestionably stopped; and I am equally certain (seeing that I recovered him) that the vital principle was not extinct. When I add that he had suffered from a long and complicated illness, and that his whole nervous system was utterly deranged, I have told you all I really know of the physical condition of my dead-alive patient at the Two Robins Inn.

When he 'came to', as the phrase goes, he was a startling object to look at, with his colourless face, his sunken cheeks, his wild black eyes, and his long black hair. The first question he asked me about himself, when he could speak, made me suspect that I had been called in to a man in my own profession. I mentioned to him my surmise, and he told me that I was right.

He said he had come last from Paris, where he had been attached to a hospital. That he had lately returned to England, on his way to Edinburgh to continue his studies; that he had been taken ill on the journey; and that he had stopped to rest and recover himself at Doncaster. He did not add a word about his name, or who he was, and of course I did not question him on the subject. All I enquired, when he ceased speaking, was what branch of the profession he intended to follow.

'Any branch,' he said, bitterly, 'which will put bread into the mouth of a poor man.'

At this, Arthur, who had been hitherto watching him in silent curiosity, burst out impetuously in his usual good-humoured way: 'My dear fellow!' (everybody was 'my dear fellow' with Arthur) 'now you have come to life again, don't begin by being downhearted about your prospects. I'll answer for it, I can help you to some capital thing in the medical line – or, if I can't, I know my father can.'

The medical student looked at him steadily.

'Thank you,' he said coldly; then added, 'May I ask who your father is?'

'He's well enough known all about this part of the country,' replied Arthur. 'He is a great manufacturer, and his name is Holliday.'

My hand was on the man's wrist during this brief conversation. The instant the name of Holliday was pronounced, I felt the pulse under my fingers flutter, stop, go on suddenly with a bound, and beat afterwards for a minute or two at the fever rate.

'How did you come here?' asked the stranger – quickly, excitably, passionately almost.

Arthur related briefly what had happened from the time of his first taking the bed at the inn.

'I am indebted to Mr Holliday's son, then, for the help that has saved my life,' said the medical student, speaking to himself, with a singular sarcasm in his voice. 'Come here!'

He held out, as he spoke, his long, white, bony right hand.

'With all my heart,' said Arthur, taking his hand cordially. 'I may confess it now,' he continued, laughing; 'upon my honour you almost frightened me out of my wits.'

The stranger did not seem to listen. His wild black eyes were fixed with a look of eager interest on Arthur's face, and his long bony fingers kept tight hold of Arthur's hand. Young Holliday, on his side, returned the gaze, amazed and puzzled by the medical student's odd language and manners. The two faces were close together; I looked at them; and, to my amazement, I was suddenly impressed by the sense of a likeness between them – not in features or complexion, but solely in expression. It must have been a strong likeness, or I should certainly not have found it out, for I am naturally slow at detecting resemblances between faces.

'You have saved my life,' said the strange man, still looking hard in Arthur's face, still holding tightly by his hand. 'If you had been my own brother, you could not have done more for me than that.'

He laid a singularly strong emphasis on those three words, 'my own brother', and a change passed over his face as he pronounced them – a change that no language of mine is competent to describe.

'I hope I have not done being of service to you yet,' said Arthur. 'I'll speak to my father as soon as I get home.'

'You seem to be fond and proud of your father,' said the medical student. 'I suppose, in return, he is fond and proud of you?'

'Of course he is,' answered Arthur, laughing. 'Is there anything wonderful in that? Isn't *your* father fond –'

The stranger suddenly dropped young Holliday's hand, and turned his face away.

'I beg your pardon,' said Arthur. 'I hope I have not unintentionally pained you. I hope you have not lost your father?'

'I can't well lose what I have never had,' retorted the medical student, with a harsh mocking laugh.

'What you have never had!'

The strange man suddenly caught Arthur's hand again, suddenly looked once more hard in his face.

'Yes,' he said, with a repetition of the bitter laugh. 'You have brought a poor devil back into the world, who has no business there. Do I astonish you? Well! I have a fancy of my own for telling you what men in my situation generally keep a secret. I have no name and no father. The merciful law of Society tells me I am Nobody's son! Ask your father if he will be my father too, and help me on in life with the family name.'

Arthur looked at me more puzzled than ever.

I signed to him to say nothing, and then laid my fingers again on the man's wrist. No! In spite of the extraordinary speech that he had just made, he was not, as I had been disposed to suspect, beginning to get light-headed. His pulse, by this time, had fallen back to a quiet, slow beat, and his skin was moist and cool. Not a symptom of fever or agitation about him.

Finding that neither of us answered him, he turned to me, and began talking of the extraordinary nature of his case, and asking my advice about the future course of medical treatment to which he ought to subject himself. I said the matter required careful thinking over, and suggested that I should send him a prescription a little later. He told me to write it at once, as he would, most likely, be leaving Doncaster in the morning before I was up. It was quite useless to represent to him the folly and danger of such a proceeding as this. He heard me politely and patiently, but held to his resolution, without offering any reasons or explanations, and repeated to me, that if I wished to give him a chance of seeing my prescription, I must write it at once.

Hearing this, Arthur volunteered the loan of a travelling writing-case, which, he said, he had with him; and, bringing it to the bed, shook the note-paper out of the pocket of the case forthwith in his usual careless way. With the paper, there fell out, on the counterpane of the bed, a small packet of sticking-plaster and a little watercolour drawing of a landscape.

The medical student took up the drawing and looked at it. His eye fell on some initials, neatly written in cipher, in one corner. He started, and trembled; his pale face grew whiter than ever; his wild black eyes turned on Arthur, and looked through and through him.

'A pretty drawing,' he said, in a remarkably quiet tone of voice.

'Ah! and done by such a pretty girl,' said Arthur. 'Oh, such a pretty girl! I wish it was not a landscape – I wish it was a portrait of her!'

'You admire her very much?'

Arthur, half in jest, half in earnest, kissed his hand for answer.

'Love at first sight,' said young Holliday, putting the drawing away again. 'But the course of it doesn't run smooth. It's the old story. She's monopolised, as usual. Trammelled by a rash engagement to some poor man who is never likely to get money enough to marry her. It was lucky I heard of it in time, or I should certainly have risked a declaration when she gave me that drawing. Here, doctor. Here is pen, ink and paper, all ready for you.'

'When she gave you that drawing! Gave it. Gave it.'

He repeated the words slowly to himself, and suddenly closed his eyes. A momentary distortion passed across his face, and I saw one of his hands clutch up the bedclothes and squeeze them hard. I thought he was going to be ill again, and begged that there might be no more talking. He opened his eyes when I spoke, fixed them once more, searchingly, on Arthur, and said, slowly and distinctly: 'You like her, and she likes you. The poor man may die out of your way. Who can tell that she may not give you herself as well as her drawing, after all?'

Before young Holliday could answer, he turned to me, and said in a whisper, 'Now for the prescription.' From that time, though he spoke to Arthur again, he never looked at him more.

When I had written the prescription, he examined it, approved of it, and then astonished us both by abruptly wishing us good-night. I offered to sit up with him, and he shook his head. Arthur offered to sit up with him, and he said, shortly, with his face turned away, 'No.' I insisted on having somebody left to watch him. He gave way when he found I was determined, and said he would accept the services of the waiter at the Inn.

'Thank you both,' he said, as we rose to go. 'I have one last favour to ask – not of you, doctor, for I leave you to exercise your professional discretion – but of Mr Holliday.' His eyes, while he spoke, still rested steadily on me, and never once turned towards Arthur. 'I beg that Mr Holliday will not mention to anyone – least of all to his father – the events that have occurred, and the words that have passed, in this room. I entreat him to bury me in his memory, as, but for him, I might have been buried in my grave. I cannot give my reasons for making this strange request. I can only implore him to grant it.'

His voice faltered for the first time, and he hid his face on the pillow. Arthur, completely bewildered, gave the required pledge. I took young Holliday away with me, immediately afterwards, to the house of my friend; determining to go back to the inn, and to see the medical student again before he left in the morning.

I returned to the inn at eight o'clock, purposely abstaining from waking Arthur, who was sleeping off the past night's excitement on one of my friend's sofas. A suspicion had occurred to me, as soon as I was alone in my bedroom, which made me resolve that Holliday and the stranger whose life he had saved should not meet again, if I could prevent it.

I have already alluded to certain reports, or scandals, which I knew of, relating to the early life of Arthur's father. While I was thinking, in my bed, of what had passed at the inn – of the change in the student's pulse when he heard the name of Holliday; of the resemblance of expression that I had discovered between his face and Arthur's; of the emphasis he had laid on those three words, 'my own brother'; and of his incomprehensible acknowledgment of his own illegitimacy – while I was thinking of these things, the reports I have mentioned suddenly flew into my mind, and linked themselves fast to the chain of my previous reflections. Something within me whispered, 'It is best that those two young men should not meet again.' I felt it before I slept; I felt it when I woke; and I went, as I told you, alone to the inn the next morning.

I had missed my only opportunity of seeing my nameless patient again. He had been gone nearly an hour when I enquired for him.

I have now told you everything that I know for certain, in relation to the man whom I brought back to life in the double-bedded room of the inn at Doncaster. What I have next to add is matter for inference and surmise, and is not, strictly speaking, matter of fact.

I have to tell you, first, that the medical student turned out to be strangely and unaccountably right in assuming it as more than probable that Arthur Holliday would marry the young lady who had given him the watercolour drawing of the landscape. That marriage took place a little more than a year after the events occurred which I have just been relating.

The young couple came to live in the neighbourhood in which I was then established in practice. I was present at the wedding, and was rather surprised to find that Arthur was singularly reserved with me, both before and after his marriage, on the subject of the young lady's prior engagement. He only referred to it once, when we were alone, merely telling me, on that occasion, that his wife had done all that honour and duty required of her in the matter, and that the engagement had been broken off with the full approval of her parents. I never heard more from him than this. For three years he and his wife lived together happily. At the expiration of that time, the symptoms of a serious illness first declared themselves in Mrs Arthur Holliday. It turned out to be a long, lingering, hopeless malady. I attended her throughout. We had been great friends when she was well, and we became more attached to each other than ever when she was ill. I had many long and interesting conversations with her in the intervals when she suffered least. The result of one of those conversations I may briefly relate, leaving you to draw any inferences from it that you please.

The interview to which I refer, occurred shortly before her death.

I called one evening, as usual, and found her alone, with a look in her eyes which told me she had been crying. She only informed me, at first, that she had been depressed in spirits; but, by little and little, she became more communicative and confessed to me that she had been looking over some old letters, which had been addressed to her, before she had seen Arthur, by a man to whom she had been engaged to be married. I asked her how the engagement came to be broken off. She replied that it had not been broken off, but that it had died out in a very mysterious manner. The person to whom she was engaged – her first love, she called him – was poor, and there was no immediate prospect of their being married. He followed my profession, and went abroad to study. They had corresponded regularly, until the time when, as she believed, he had returned to England. From that period she heard no more of him. He was of a fretful, sensitive temperament; and she feared that she might have inadvertently done or said something to offend him. However that might be, he had never written to her again; and, after waiting a year, she had married Arthur. I asked when the first estrangement had begun, and found that the time at which she ceased to hear anything of her first lover, exactly corresponded with the time at which I had been called in to my mysterious patient at the Two Robins Inn.

A fortnight after that conversation, she died. In the course of time Arthur married again. Of late years, he has lived principally in London, and I have seen little or nothing of him.

I have some years to pass over before I can approach to anything like a conclusion of this fragmentary narrative. And even when that later period is reached, the little that I have to say will not occupy your attention for more than a few minutes.

One rainy autumn evening, while I was still practising as a country doctor, I was sitting alone, thinking over a case then under my charge which sorely perplexed me, when I heard a low knock at the door of my room.

'Come in,' I cried, looking up curiously to see who wanted me.

After a momentary delay, the lock moved, and a long, white, bony hand stole round the door as it opened, gently pushing it over a fold in the carpet which hindered it from working freely on the hinges. The hand was followed by a man whose face instantly struck me with a very strange sensation. There was something familiar to me in the look of him, and yet it was also something that suggested the idea of change.

He quietly introduced himself as 'Mr Lorn', presented to me some excellent professional recommendations, and proposed to fill the place, then vacant, of my assistant. While he was speaking, I noticed it as singular that we did not appear to be meeting each other like strangers; and that, while I was certainly startled at seeing him, he did not appear to be at all startled at seeing me.

It was on the tip of my tongue to say that I thought I had met with him before. But there was something in his face, and something in my recollections – I can hardly say what – which unaccountably restrained me from speaking, and which, as unaccountably, attracted me to him at once, and made me feel ready and glad to accept his proposal.

He took my assistant's place on that very day. We got on together as if we had been old friends from the first; but, throughout the whole time of his residence in my house, he never volunteered any confidences on the subject of his past life; and I never approached the forbidden topic except by hints, which he resolutely refused to understand.

I had long had a notion that my patient at the inn might have been a natural son of the elder Mr Holliday's, and that he might also have been the man who was engaged to Arthur's first wife. And now, another idea occurred to me, that Mr Lorn was the only person in existence who could, if he chose, enlighten me on both those doubtful points. But he never did choose – and I was never enlightened. He remained with me till I removed to London to try my fortune there, as a physician, for the second time; and then he went his way, and I went mine, and we have never seen one another since.

I can add no more. I may have been right in my suspicion, or I may have been wrong. All I know is that, in those days of my country practice, when I came home late, and found my assistant asleep, and woke him, he used to look, in coming to, wonderfully like the stranger at Doncaster, as he raised himself in the bed on that memorable night.

The Fatal Cradle

There has never yet been discovered a man with a grievance who objected to mention it. I am no exception to this general human rule. I have got a grievance, and I don't object to mention it. Compose your spirits to hear a pathetic story, and kindly picture me in your own mind as a baby five minutes old.

Do I understand you to say that I am too big and too heavy to be pictured in anybody's mind as a baby? Perhaps I may be – but don't mention my weight again, if you please. My weight has been the grand misfortune of my life. It spoiled all my prospects (as you will presently hear) before I was two days old.

My story begins thirty-one years ago, at eleven o'clock in the forenoon, and starts with the great mistake of my first appearance in this world, at sea, on board the merchant ship *Adventure* – Captain Gillop, five hundred tons burden, coppered, and carrying an experienced surgeon.

In presenting myself to you (which I am now about to do) at that eventful period of my life when I was from five to ten minutes old, and in withdrawing myself again from your notice (so as not to trouble you with more than a short story) before the time when I cut my first tooth, I need not hesitate to admit that I speak on hearsay knowledge only. It is knowledge, however, that may be relied on, for all that. My information comes from Captain Gillop, commander of the *Adventure* (who sent it to me in the form of a letter); from Mr Jolly, experienced surgeon of the *Adventure* (who wrote it for me – most unfeelingly, as I think – in the shape of a humorous narrative); and from Mrs Drabble, stewardess of the *Adventure* (who told it me by word of mouth). Those three persons were, in various degrees, spectators – I may say astonished spectators – of the events which I have now to relate.

The *Adventure*, at the time I speak of, was bound out from London to Australia. I suppose you know without my telling you that thirty years ago was long before the time of the gold-finding and the famous clipper ships. Building in the new colony and sheep-farming far up inland were the two main employments of those days, and the passengers on board our vessel were consequently builders or sheep-farmers, almost to a man.

A ship of five hundred tons, well loaded with cargo, doesn't offer first-rate accommodation to a large number of passengers. Not that the gentlefolk in the cabin had any great reason to complain. There the passage-money, which was a good round sum, kept them what you call select. One or two berths in this part of the ship were even empty and going a-begging, in consequence of there being only four cabin passengers. These are their names and descriptions: Mr Sims, a middle-aged man, going out on a building speculation; Mr Purling, a weakly young gentleman, sent on a long sea-voyage, for the benefit of his health; and Mr and Mrs Smallchild, a young married couple, with a little independence, which Mr Smallchild proposed to make a large one by sheep-farming.

This latter gentleman was reported to the captain as being very good company when on shore. But the sea altered him to a certain extent. When Mr Smallchild was not sick, he was eating and drinking; and when he was not eating and drinking, he was fast asleep. He was perfectly patient and good-humoured, and wonderfully nimble at running into his cabin when the qualms took him on a sudden; but, as for his being good company, nobody heard him say ten words together all through the voyage. And no wonder. A man can't talk in the qualms; a man can't talk while he is eating and drinking; and a man can't talk when he is asleep. And that was Mr Smallchild's life. As for Mrs Smallchild, she kept her cabin from first to last. But you will hear more of her presently.

These four cabin passengers, as I have already remarked, were well enough off for their accommodation. But the miserable people in the steerage – a poor place at the best of times on board the *Adventure* – were all huddled together, men and women and children, higgledy-piggledy, like sheep in a pen, except that they hadn't got the same quantity of fine fresh air to blow over them. They were artisans and farm-labourers, who couldn't make it out in the Old Country. I have no information either of their exact numbers or of their names. It doesn't matter; there was only one family among them which need be mentioned particularly – namely, the family of the Heavysides. To wit, Simon Heavysides, intelligent and well-educated, a carpenter by trade; Susan Heavysides, his wife; and seven little Heavysides, their unfortunate offspring. My father and mother and brothers and sisters, did I understand you to say? Don't be in a hurry! I recommend you to wait a little before you make quite sure of that circumstance.

Though I myself had not, perhaps, strictly speaking, come on board when the vessel left London, my ill luck, as I firmly believe, had shipped in the *Adventure* to wait for me – and decided the nature of the voyage accordingly.

Never was such a miserable time known. Stormy weather came down on us from all points of the compass, with intervals of light, baffling winds or dead calms. By the time the *Adventure* had been three months out, Captain Gillop's naturally sweet temper began to get soured. I leave you to say whether it was likely to be much improved by a piece of news which reached him from the region of the cabin on the morning of the ninety-first day. It had fallen to a dead calm again and the ship was rolling about helpless, with her head all round the compass, when Mr Jolly (from whose facetious narrative I repeat all conversations exactly as they passed) came on deck to the captain, and addressed him in these words:

'I have got some news that will rather surprise you,' said Mr Jolly, smiling and rubbing his hands. (Although the experienced surgeon has not shown much sympathy for my troubles, I won't deny that his disposition was as good as his name. To this day no amount of bad weather or hard work can upset Mr Jolly's temper.)

'If it's news of a fair wind coming,' grumbled the captain, 'that would surprise me on board this ship, I can promise you!'

'It's not exactly a wind coming,' said Mr Jolly. 'It's another cabin passenger.'

The captain looked round at the empty sea, with the land thousands of miles away, and with not a ship in sight – turned sharply on the experienced surgeon – eyed him hard – changed colour suddenly – and asked what he meant.

'I mean there's a fifth cabin passenger coming on board,' persisted Mr Jolly, grinning from ear to ear – 'introduced by Mrs Smallchild – likely to join us, I should say, towards evening – size, nothing to speak of – sex, not known at present – manners and customs, probably squally.'

'Do you really mean it?' asked the captain, backing away, and turning paler and paler.

'Yes, I do,' answered Mr Jolly, nodding hard at him.

'Then I'll tell you what,' cried Captain Gillop, suddenly flying into a violent passion, 'I won't have it! the infernal weather has worried me out of my life and soul already – and I won't have it! Put it off, Jolly – tell her there isn't room enough for that sort of thing on board my vessel. What does she mean by taking us all in in this way? Shameful! Shameful!'

'No! no!' remonstrated Mr Jolly. 'Don't look at it in that light. It's her first child, poor thing. How should *she* know? Give her a little more experience, and I dare say – '

'Where's her husband?' broke in the captain, with a threatening look. 'I'll speak my mind to her husband, at any rate.'

Mr Jolly consulted his watch before he answered.

'Half-past eleven,' he said. 'Let me consider a little. It's Mr Smallchild's regular time just now for squaring accounts with the sea. He'll have done in a quarter of an hour. In five minutes more he'll be fast asleep. At one o'clock he'll eat a hearty lunch, and go to sleep again. At half-past two he'll square accounts as before – and so on till night. You'll make nothing out of Mr Smallchild, captain. Extraordinary man – wastes tissue, and repairs it again perpetually, in the most astonishing manner. If we are another month at sea, I believe we shall bring him into port totally comatose. – Halloo! What do *you* want?'

The steward's mate had approached the quarter-deck while the doctor was speaking. Was it a curious coincidence? This man also was grinning from ear to ear, exactly like Mr Jolly.

'You're wanted in the steerage, sir,' said the steward's mate to the doctor. 'A woman taken bad, name of Heavysides.'

'Nonsense!' cried Mr Jolly 'Ha, ha, ha! You don't mean – eh?'

'That's it, sir, sure enough,' said the steward's mate, in the most positive manner.

Captain Gillop looked all around him in silent desperation; lost his sea-legs for the first time these twenty years; staggered back till he was brought up all standing by the side of his own vessel; dashed his fist on the bulwark, and found language to express himself in, at the same moment.

'This ship is bewitched,' said the captain, wildly. 'Stop!' he called out, recovering himself a little as the doctor bustled away to the steerage. 'Stop! If it's true, Jolly, send her husband here aft to me. Damme, I'll have it out with one of the husbands!' said the captain, shaking his fist viciously at the empty air.

Ten minutes passed; and then there came staggering toward the captain, tottering this way and that with the rolling of the becalmed vessel, a long, lean, melancholy, light-haired man, with a Roman nose, a watery blue eye, and a complexion profusely spotted with large brown freckles. This was Simon Heavysides, the intelligent carpenter, with the wife and the family of seven small children on board.

'Oh! you're the man, are you?' said the captain.

The ship lurched heavily; and Simon Heavysides staggered away with a run to the opposite side of the deck, as if he preferred going straight overboard into the sea to answering the captain's question.

'You're the man – are you?' repeated the captain, following him, seizing him by the collar, and pinning him up fiercely against the bulwark. 'It's your wife – is it? You infernal rascal! what do you mean by turning my ship into a lying-in hospital? You have committed an act of mutiny; or, if it isn't mutiny, it's next door to it. I've put a man in irons for less! I've more than half a mind to put *you* in irons! Hold up, you slippery lubber! What do you mean by bringing passengers I don't bargain for on board my vessel? What have you got to say for yourself, before I clap the irons on you?'

'Nothing, sir,' answered Simon Heavysides, accepting the captain's strong language without a word of protest. 'As for the punishment you mentioned just now, sir,' continued Simon, 'I wish to say – having seven children more than I know how to provide for, and an eighth coming to make things worse – I respectfully wish to say, sir, that my mind is in irons already; and I don't know as it will make much difference if you put my body in irons along with it.'

The captain mechanically let go of the carpenter's collar; the mild despair of the man melted him in spite of himself.

'Why did you come to sea? Why didn't you wait ashore till it was all over?' asked the captain, as sternly as he could.

'It's no use waiting, sir,' remarked Simon. 'In our line of life, as soon as it's over it begins again. There's no end to it that I can see,' said the miserable carpenter, after a moment's meek consideration – 'except the grave.'

'Who's talking about the grave?' cried Mr Jolly, coming up at that moment. 'It's births we've got to do with on board this vessel – not burials. Captain Gillop, this woman, Mrs Heavysides, can't be left in your crowded steerage in her present condition. She must be moved off into one of the empty berths – and the sooner the better, I can tell you!'

The captain began to look savage again. A steerage passenger in one of his 'state-rooms' was a nautical anomaly subversive of all discipline. He eyed the carpenter once more, as if he was mentally measuring him for a set of irons.

'I'm very sorry, sir,' Simon remarked, politely – 'very sorry that any inadvertence of mine or Mrs Heavysides – '

'Take your long carcass and your long tongue forward!' thundered the captain. 'When talking will mend matters, I'll send for you again. Give your own orders, Jolly,' he went on, resignedly, as Simon staggered off. 'Turn the ship into a nursery as soon as you like!'

Five minutes later – so expeditious was Mr Jolly – Mrs Heavysides appeared horizontally on deck, shrouded in blankets and supported by three men. When this interesting procession passed the captain, he shrank aside from it with as vivid an appearance of horror as if a wild bull was being carried by him instead of a British matron.

The sleeping-berths below opened on either side out of the main cabin. On the left-hand side (looking towards the ship's bowsprit) was Mrs Small-child. On the right-hand side, opposite to her, the doctor established Mrs Heavysides. A partition of canvas was next run up, entirely across the main cabin. The smaller of the two temporary rooms thus made lay nearest the stairs leading on deck, and was left free to the public. The larger was kept sacred to the doctor and his mysteries. When an old clothes-basket, emptied, cleaned, and comfortably lined with blankets (to serve for a makeshift cradle), had been in due course of time carried into the inner cabin, and had been placed midway between the two sleeping-berths, so as to be easily producible when wanted, the outward and visible preparations of Mr Jolly were complete; the male passengers had all taken refuge on deck; and the doctor and the stewardess were left in undisturbed possession of the lower regions.

While it was still early in the afternoon the weather changed for the better. For once in a way, the wind came from a fair quarter, and the *Adventure* bowled along pleasantly before it, almost on an even keel. Captain Gillop mixed with the little group of male passengers on the quarter-deck, restored to his sweetest temper; and set them his customary example, after dinner, of smoking a cigar.

'If this fine weather lasts, gentlemen,' he said, 'we shall make out very well with our meals up here, and we shall have our two small extra cabin passengers christened on dry land in a week's time, if their mothers approve of it. How do you feel in your mind, sir, about your good lady?'

Mr Smallchild (to whom the enquiry was addressed) had his points of external personal resemblance to Simon Heavysides. He was neither so tall nor so lean, certainly – but he, too, had a Roman nose, and light hair, and watery blue eyes. With careful reference to his peculiar habits at sea, he had been placed conveniently close to the bulwark, and had been raised on a heap of old sails and cushions, so that he could easily get his head over the ship's side when occasion required. The food and drink which assisted in 'restoring his tissue', when he was not asleep and not 'squaring accounts with the sea', lay close to his hand. It was then a little after three o'clock, and the snore with which Mr Smallchild answered the captain's enquiry showed that he had got round again, with the regularity of clockwork, to the period of the day when he recruited himself with sleep.

'What an insensible blockhead that man is!' said Mr Sims, the middle-aged passenger, looking across the deck contemptuously at Mr Smallchild.

'If the sea had the same effect on you that it has on him,' retorted the invalid passenger, Mr Purling, 'you would be just as insensible yourself.'

Mr Purling (who was a man of sentiment) disagreed with Mr Sims (who was a man of business) on every conceivable subject, all through the voyage. Before, however, they could continue the dispute about Mr Smallchild, the doctor surprised them by appearing from the cabin.

'Any news from below, Jolly?' asked the captain, anxiously.

'None whatever,' answered the doctor. 'I've come to idle the afternoon away up here, along with the rest of you.'

As events turned out, Mr Jolly idled away an hour and a half exactly. At the end of that time Mrs Drabble, the stewardess, appeared with a face of mystery, and whispered, nervously, to the doctor,

'Please to step below directly, sir.'

'Which of them is it?' asked Mr Jolly.

'*Both* of them,' answered Mrs Drabble, emphatically.

The doctor looked grave; the stewardess looked frightened. The two immediately disappeared together.

'I suppose, gentlemen,' said Captain Gillop, addressing Mr Purling, Mr Sims, and the first mate, who had just joined the party – 'I suppose it's only fit and proper, in the turn things have taken, to shake up Mr Smallchild? And I don't doubt but what we ought to have the other husband handy, as a sort of polite attention under the circumstances. Pass the word forward there, for Simon Heavysides. Mr Smallchild, sir! rouse up! Here's your good lady – Hang me, gentlemen, if I know exactly how to put it to him.'

'Yes. Thank you,' said Mr Smallchild, opening his eyes drowsily. 'Biscuit and cold bacon, as usual – when I'm ready. I'm not ready yet. Thank you. Good-afternoon.' Mr Smallchild closed his eyes again, and became, in the doctor's phrase, 'totally comatose'.

Before Captain Gillop could hit on any new plan for rousing this imperturbable passenger, Simon Heavysides once more approached the quarter-deck.

'I spoke a little sharp to you, just now, my man,' said the captain, 'being worried in my mind by what's going on on board this vessel. But I'll make it up to you, never fear. Here's your wife in what they call an interesting situation. It's only right you should be within easy hail of her. I look upon you, Heavysides, as a steerage passenger in difficulties; and I freely give you leave to stop here along with us till it's all over.'

'You are very good, sir,' said Simon, 'and I am indeed thankful to you and to these gentlemen. But please to remember, I have seven children already in the steerage – and there's nobody left to mind 'em but me. My wife has got over it uncommonly well, sir, on seven previous occasions – and I don't doubt but what she'll conduct herself in a similar manner on the eighth. It will be a satisfaction to her mind, Captain Gillop and gentlemen, if she knows I'm out of the way, and minding the children. For which reason, I respectfully take my leave.' With those words Simon made his bow, and returned to his family.

'Well, gentlemen, these two husbands take it easy enough, at any rate!' said the captain. 'One of them is used to it, to be sure; and the other is –'

Here a banging of cabin doors below, and a hurrying of footsteps, startled the speaker and his audience into momentary silence and attention.

'Ease her with the helm, Williamson!' said Captain Gillop, addressing the man who was steering the vessel. 'In my opinion, gentlemen, the less the ship pitches the better, in the turn things are taking now.'

The afternoon wore on into evening, and evening into night.

Mr Smallchild performed the daily ceremonies of his nautical existence as punctually as usual. He was aroused to a sense of Mrs Smallchild's situation when he took his biscuit and bacon; lost the sense again when the time came round for 'squaring his accounts'; recovered it in the interval which ensued before he went to sleep; lost it again, as a matter of course, when his eyes closed once more – and so on through the evening and early night. Simon Heavysides received messages occasionally (through the captain's care), telling him to keep his mind easy; returned messages mentioning that his mind was easy, and that the children were pretty quiet, but never approached the deck in his own person. Mr Jolly now and then showed himself, said, 'All right – no news,' took a little light refreshment, and disappeared again as cheerful as ever. The fair breeze still held; the captain's temper remained unruffled; the man at the helm eased the vessel, from time to time, with the most anxious consideration. Ten o'clock came; the moon rose and shone superbly; the nightly grog made its appearance on the quarter-deck; the captain gave the passengers the benefit of his company; and still nothing happened. Twenty minutes more of suspense slowly succeeded each other – and then, at last, Mr Jolly was seen suddenly to ascend the cabin stairs.

To the amazement of the little group on the quarter-deck, the doctor held Mrs Drabble, the stewardess, fast by the arm, and, without taking the slightest notice of the captain or the passengers, placed her on the nearest seat he could find. As he did this his face became visible in the moonlight and displayed to the startled spectators an expression of blank consternation.

'Compose yourself, Mrs Drabble,' said the doctor, in tones of unmistakable alarm. 'Keep quiet, and let the air blow over you. Collect yourself, ma'am – for heaven's sake, collect yourself!'

Mrs Drabble made no answer. She beat her hands vacantly on her knees, and stared straight before her, like a woman panic-stricken.

'What's wrong?' asked the captain, setting down his glass of grog in dismay. 'Anything amiss with those two unfortunate women?'

'Nothing,' said the doctor. 'Both doing admirably well.'

'Anything queer with their babies?' continued the captain. 'Are there more than you bargained for, Jolly? Twins, for instance?'

'No! no!' replied Mr Jolly, impatiently. 'A baby apiece – both boys – both in first-rate condition. Judge for yourselves,' added the doctor, as the two new cabin passengers tried their lungs below for the first time, and found that they answered their purpose in the most satisfactory manner.

'What the devil's amiss, then, with you and Mrs Drabble?' persisted the captain, beginning to lose his temper again.

'Mrs Drabble and I are two innocent people, and we have got into the most dreadful scrape that ever you heard of!' was Mr Jolly's startling answer.

The captain, followed by Mr Purling and Mr Sims, approached the doctor with looks of horror. Even the man at the wheel stretched himself over it as far as he could to hear what was coming next. The only uninterested person present was Mr Smallchild. His time had come round for going to sleep again, and he was snoring peacefully, with his biscuit and bacon close beside him.

'Let's hear the worst of it at once, Jolly,' said the captain, a little impatiently.

The doctor paid no heed to his request. His whole attention was absorbed by Mrs Drabble. 'Are you better now, ma'am?' he asked, anxiously.

'No better in my mind,' answered Mrs Drabble, beginning to beat her knees again. 'Worse, if anything.'

'Listen to me,' said Mr Jolly, coaxingly. 'I'll put the whole case over again to you, in a few plain questions. You'll find it all come back to your memory, if you only follow me attentively, and if you take time to think and collect yourself before you attempt to answer.'

Mrs Drabble bowed her head in speechless submission – and listened. Everybody else on the quarter-deck listened, except the impenetrable Mr Smallchild.

'Now, ma'am!' said the doctor. 'Our troubles began in Mrs Heavysides's cabin, which is situated on the starboard side of the ship?'

'They did, sir,' replied Mrs Drabble.

'Good! We went backwards and forwards, an infinite number of times, between Mrs Heavysides (starboard) and Mrs Smallchild (larboard) – but we found that Mrs Heavysides, having got the start, kept it – and when I called out, "Mrs Drabble! here's a chopping boy for you; come and take him!" – I called out starboard, didn't I?'

'Starboard, sir – I'll take my oath of it,' said Mrs Drabble.

'Good again! "Here's a chopping boy," I said. "Take him, ma'am, and make him comfortable in the cradle." And you took him, and made him comfortable in the cradle, accordingly? Now where was the cradle?'

'In the main cabin, sir,' replied Mrs Drabble.

'Just so! In the main cabin, because we hadn't got room for it in either of the sleeping cabins. You put the starboard baby (otherwise Heavysides) in the clothes-basket cradle in the main cabin. Good once more. How was the cradle placed?'

'Crosswise to the ship, sir,' said Mrs Drabble.

'Crosswise to the ship? That is to say, with one side longwise towards the stern of the vessel, and one side longwise towards the bows. Bear that in mind – and now follow me a little further. No! no! don't say you can't, and your head's in a whirl. My next question will steady it. Carry your mind on half an hour, Mrs Drabble. At the end of half an hour you heard my voice again; and my voice called out, "Mrs Drabble! here's another chopping boy for you; come and take him!" – and you came and took him larboard, didn't you?'

'Larboard, sir, I don't deny it,' answered Mrs Drabble.

'Better and better! "Here is another chopping boy," I said. "Take him, ma'am, and make him comfortable in the cradle, along with number one." And you took the larboard baby (otherwise Smallchild), and made him comfortable in the cradle along with the starboard baby (otherwise Heavysides), accordingly! Now what happened after that?'

'Don't ask me, sir!' exclaimed Mrs Drabble, losing her self-control, and wringing her hands desperately.

'Steady, ma'am! I'll put it to you as plain as print. Steady! and listen to me. Just as you had made the larboard baby comfortable I had occasion to send you into the starboard (or Heavysides) cabin to fetch something which I wanted in the larboard (or Smallchild) cabin; I kept you there a little while along with me; I left you and went into the Heavysides cabin, and called to you to bring me something I wanted out of the Smallchild cabin, but before you got halfway across the main cabin I said, "No; stop where you are, and

I'll come to you;" immediately after which Mrs Smallchild alarmed you, and you came across to me of your own accord; and thereupon I stopped you in the main cabin, and said, "Mrs Drabble, your mind's getting confused; sit down and collect your scattered intellects;" and you sat down and tried to collect them – '

('And couldn't, sir,' interposed Mrs Drabble, parenthetically. 'Oh, my head! my head!')

– "And tried to collect your scattered intellects, and couldn't?' continued the doctor. 'And the consequence was, when I came out from the Smallchild cabin to see how you were getting on, I found you with the clothes-basket cradle hoisted up on the cabin table, staring down at the babies inside, with your mouth dropped open, and both your hands twisted in your hair? And when I said, "Anything wrong with either of those two fine boys, Mrs Drabble?" you caught me by the coat collar, and whispered in my right ear these words, "Lord save us and help us, Mr Jolly, I've confused the two babies in my mind, and I don't know which is which!" '

'And I don't know now!' cried Mrs Drabble, hysterically. 'Oh, my head! my head! I don't know now!'

'Captain Gillop and gentlemen,' said Mr Jolly, wheeling round and addressing his audience with the composure of sheer despair, 'that is the Scrape – and, if you ever heard of a worse one, I'll trouble you to compose this miserable woman by mentioning it immediately.'

Captain Gillop looked at Mr Purling and Mr Sims. Mr Purling and Mr Sims looked at Captain Gillop. They were all three thunderstruck – and no wonder.

'Can't *you* throw any light on it, Jolly?' enquired the captain, who was the first to recover himself.

'If you knew what I have had to do below you wouldn't ask me such a question as that,' replied the doctor. 'Remember that I have had the lives of two women and two children to answer for – remember that I have been cramped up in two small sleeping-cabins, with hardly room to turn round in, and just light enough from two miserable little lamps to see my hand before me; remember the professional difficulties of the situation, the ship rolling about under me all the while, and the stewardess to compose into the bargain; bear all that in mind, will you, and then tell me how much spare time I had on my hands for comparing two boys together inch by inch – two boys born at night, within half an hour of each other, on board a ship at sea. Ha, ha! I only wonder the mothers and the boys and the doctor are all five of them alive to tell the story!'

'No marks on one or other of them that happened to catch your eye?' asked Mr Sims.

'They must have been strongish marks to catch my eye in the light I had to work by, and in the professional difficulties I had to grapple with,' said the doctor. 'I saw they were both straight, well-formed children – and that's all I saw.'

'Are their infant features sufficiently developed to indicate a family likeness?' enquired Mr Purling. 'Should you say they took after their fathers or their mothers?'

'Both of them have light eyes, and light hair – such as it is,' replied Mr Jolly, doggedly. 'Judge for yourself.'

'Mr Smallchild has light eyes and light hair,' remarked Mr Sims.

'And Simon Heavysides has light eyes and light hair,' rejoined Mr Purling.

'I should recommend waking Mr Smallchild, and sending for Heavysides, and letting the two fathers toss up for it,' suggested Mr Sims.

'The parental feeling is not to be trifled with in that heartless manner,' retorted Mr Purling. 'I should recommend trying the Voice of Nature.'

'What may that be, sir?' enquired Captain Gillop, with great curiosity.

'The maternal instinct,' replied Mr Purling. 'The mother's intuitive knowledge of her own child.'

'Ay, ay!' said the captain. 'Well thought of. What do you say, Jolly, to the Voice of Nature?'

The doctor held up his hand impatiently. He was engaged in resuming the effort to rouse Mrs Drabble's memory by a system of amateur cross-examination, with the unsatisfactory result of confusing her more helplessly than ever.

Could she put the cradle back, in her own mind, into its original position? No. Could she remember whether she laid the starboard baby (otherwise Heavysides) on the side of the cradle nearest the stern of the ship, or nearest the bows? No. Could she remember any better about the larboard baby (otherwise Smallchild)? No. Why did she move the cradle on to the cabin table, and so bewilder herself additionally, when she was puzzled already? Because it came over her, on a sudden, that she had forgotten, in the dreadful confusion of the time, which was which; and of course she wanted to look closer at them, and see; and she couldn't see; and to her dying day she should never forgive herself; and let them throw her overboard, for a miserable wretch, if they liked – and so on, till the persevering doctor was wearied out at last, and gave up Mrs Drabble, and gave up, with her, the whole case.

'I see nothing for it but the Voice of Nature,' said the captain, holding fast to Mr Purling's idea. 'Try it, Jolly – you can but try it.'

'Something must be done,' said the doctor. 'I can't leave the women alone any longer, and the moment I get below they will both ask for their babies. Wait here till you're fit to be seen, Mrs Drabble, and then follow me. Voice of Nature!' added Mr Jolly, contemptuously, as he descended the cabin stairs. 'Oh yes, I'll try it – much good the Voice of Nature will do us, gentlemen. You shall judge for yourselves.'

Favoured by the night, Mr Jolly cunningly turned down the dim lamps in the sleeping-cabins to a mere glimmer, on the pretext that the light was bad for his patients' eyes. He then took up the first of the two unlucky babies that came to hand, marked the clothes in which it was wrapped with a blot of ink, and carried it in to Mrs Smallchild, choosing her cabin merely because he happened to be nearest to it. The second baby (distinguished by having no mark) was taken by Mrs Drabble to Mrs Heavysides. For a certain time the two mothers and the two babies were left together. They were then separated again by medical order; and were afterwards reunited, with the difference that the marked baby went on this occasion to Mrs Heavysides, and the unmarked baby to Mrs Smallchild – the result, in the obscurity of the sleeping-cabins, proving to be that one baby did just as well as the other, and that the Voice of Nature was (as Mr Jolly had predicted) totally incompetent to settle the existing difficulty.

'While night serves us, Captain Gillop, we shall do very well,' said the doctor, after he had duly reported the failure of Mr Purling's suggested experiment. 'But when morning comes, and daylight shows the difference between the children, we must be prepared with a course of some kind. If the two mothers below get the slightest suspicion of the case as it stands, the nervous shock of the discovery may do dreadful mischief. They must be kept deceived, in the interests of their own health. We must choose a baby for each of them when tomorrow comes, and then hold to the choice, till the mothers are well and up again. The question is, who's to take the responsibility? I don't usually stick at trifles – but I candidly admit that I'm afraid of it.'

'I decline meddling in the matter, on the ground that I am a perfect stranger,' said Mr Sims.

'And I object to interfere, from precisely similar motives,' added Mr Purling, agreeing for the first time with a proposition that emanated from his natural enemy all through the voyage.

'Wait a minute, gentlemen,' said Captain Gillop. 'I've got this difficult matter, as I think, in its right bearings. We must make a clean breast of it to the husbands, and let *them* take the responsibility.'

'I believe they won't accept it,' observed Mr Sims.

'And I believe they will,' asserted Mr Purling, relapsing into his old habits.

'If they won't,' said the captain, firmly, 'I'm master on board this ship – and, as sure as my name is Thomas Gillop, I'll take the responsibility!'

This courageous declaration settled all difficulties for the time being and a council was held to decide on future proceedings. It was resolved to remain passive until the next morning, on the last faint chance that a few hours' sleep might compose Mrs Drabble's bewildered memory. The babies were to be moved into the main cabin before the daylight grew bright – or, in other words, before Mrs Smallchild or Mrs Heavysides could identify the infant who had passed the night with her. The doctor and the captain were to be assisted by Mr Purling, Mr Sims, and the first mate, in the capacity of witnesses; and the assembly so constituted was to meet, in consideration of the emergency of the case, at six o'clock in the morning, punctually. At six o'clock, accordingly, with the weather fine, and the wind still fair, the proceedings began. For the last time Mr Jolly cross-examined Mrs Drabble, assisted by the captain, and supervised by the witnesses. Nothing whatever was elicited from the unfortunate stewardess. The doctor pronounced her confusion to be chronic, and the captain and the witnesses unanimously agreed with him.

The next experiment tried was the revelation of the true state of the case to the husbands.

Mr Smallchild happened, on this occasion, to be 'squaring his accounts' for the morning; and the first articulate words which escaped him in reply to the disclosure were, 'Deviled biscuit and anchovy paste.' Further perseverance merely elicited an impatient request that they would 'pitch him overboard at once, and the two babies along with him'. Serious remonstrance was tried next, with no better effect. 'Settle it how you like,' said Mr Smallchild, faintly. 'Do you leave it to me, sir, as commander of this vessel?' asked Captain Gillop. (No answer.) 'Nod your head, sir, if you can't speak.' Mr Smallchild nodded his head roundwise on his pillow – and fell asleep. 'Does that count for leave to me to act?' asked Captain Gillop of the witnesses. And the witnesses answered, decidedly, 'Yes.'

The ceremony was then repeated with Simon Heavysides, who responded, as became so intelligent a man, with a proposal of his own for solving the difficulty.

'Captain Gillop and gentlemen,' said the carpenter, with fluent and melancholy politeness, 'I should wish to consider Mr Smallchild before myself in this matter. I am quite willing to part with my baby (whichever he is); and I respectfully propose that Mr Smallchild should take *both* the children, and so make quite sure that he has really got possession of his own son.'

The only immediate objection to this ingenious proposition was started by the doctor, who sarcastically enquired of Simon, 'what he thought Mrs Heavysides would say to it?' The carpenter confessed that this consideration had escaped him, and that Mrs Heavysides was only too likely to be an irremovable obstacle in the way of the proposed arrangement. The witnesses all thought so too; and Heavysides and his idea were dismissed together after Simon had first gratefully expressed his entire readiness to leave it all to the captain.

'Very well, gentlemen,' said Captain Gillop. 'As commander on board, I reckon next after the husbands in the matter of responsibility. I have considered this difficulty in all its bearings, and I'm prepared to deal with it. The

Voice of Nature (which you proposed, Mr Purling) has been found to fail. The tossing up for it (which you proposed, Mr Sims) doesn't square altogether with my notions of what's right in a very serious business. No, sir! I've got my own plan; and I'm now about to try it. Follow me below, gentlemen, to the steward's pantry.'

The witnesses looked round on one another in the profoundest astonishment – and followed.

'Pickerel,' said the captain, addressing the steward, 'bring out the scales.'

The scales were of the ordinary kitchen sort, with a tin tray on one side to hold the commodity to be weighed, and a stout iron slab on the other to support the weights. Pickerel placed these scales upon a neat little pantry table, fitted on the ball-and-socket principle, so as to save the breaking of crockery by swinging with the motion of the ship.

'Put a clean duster in the tray,' said the captain. 'Doctor,' he continued, when this had been done, 'shut the doors of the sleeping-berths (for fear of the women hearing anything), and oblige me by bringing those two babies in here.'

'Oh, sir!' exclaimed Mrs Drabble, who had been peeping guiltily into the pantry – 'oh, don't hurt the little dears! If anybody suffers, let it be me!'

'Hold your tongue, if you please, ma'am,' said the captain. 'And keep the secret of these proceedings, if you wish to keep your place. If the ladies ask for their children, say they will have them in ten minutes' time.'

The doctor came in, and set down the clothes-basket cradle on the pantry floor. Captain Gillop immediately put on his spectacles, and closely examined the two unconscious innocents who lay beneath him.

'Six of one and half a dozen of the other,' said the captain. 'I don't see any difference between them. Wait a bit, though! Yes, I do. One's a bald baby. Very good. We'll begin with that one. Doctor, strip the bald baby, and put him in the scales.'

The bald baby protested – in his own language – but in vain. In two minutes he was flat on his back in the tin tray, with the clean duster under him to take the chill off.

'Weigh him accurately, Pickerel,' continued the captain. 'Weigh him, if necessary, to an eighth of an ounce. Gentlemen! watch this proceeding closely; it's a very important one.'

While the steward was weighing and the witnesses were watching, Captain Gillop asked his first mate for the log-book of the ship, and for pen and ink.

'How much, Pickerel?' asked the captain, opening the book.

'Seven pounds one ounce and a quarter,' answered the steward.

'Right, gentlemen?' pursued the captain.

'Quite right,' said the witnesses.

'Bald child – distinguished as Number One – weight, seven pounds one ounce and a quarter (avoirdupois),' repeated the captain, writing down the entry in the log-book. 'Very good. We'll put the bald baby back now, doctor, and try the hairy one next.'

The hairy one protested – also in his own language – and also in vain.

'How much, Pickerel?' asked the captain.

'Six pounds fourteen ounces and three-quarters,' replied the steward.

'Right, gentlemen?' enquired the captain.

'Quite right,' answered the witnesses.

'Hairy child – distinguished as Number Two – weight, six pounds fourteen ounces and three-quarters (avoirdupois),' repeated and wrote the captain. 'Much obliged to you, Jolly – that will do. When you have got the other baby back in the cradle, tell Mrs Drabble neither of them must be taken out of it till further orders; and then be so good as to join me and these gentlemen on deck. If anything of a discussion rises up among us, we won't run the risk of being heard in the sleeping-berths.' With these words Captain Gillop led the way on deck, and the first mate followed with the log-book and the pen and ink.

'Now, gentlemen,' began the captain, when the doctor had joined the assembly, 'my first mate will open these proceedings by reading from the log a statement which I have written myself, respecting this business, from beginning to end. If you find it all equally correct with the statement of what the two children weigh, I'll trouble you to sign it, in your quality of witnesses, on the spot.'

The first mate read the narrative, and the witnesses signed it, as perfectly correct. Captain Gillop then cleared his throat, and addressed his expectant audience in these words: 'You'll all agree with me, gentlemen, that justice is justice, and that like must to like. Here's my ship of five hundred tons, fitted with her spars accordingly. Say she's a schooner of a hundred and fifty tons, the veriest landsman among you, in that case, wouldn't put such masts as these into her. Say, on the other hand, she's an Indiaman of a thousand tons, would our spars (excellent good sticks as they are, gentlemen) be suitable for a vessel of that capacity? Certainly not. A schooner's spars to a schooner, and a ship's spars to a ship, in fit and fair proportion.'

Here the captain paused, to let the opening of his speech sink well into the minds of the audience. The audience encouraged him with the parliamentary cry of, 'Hear! hear!'

The captain went on: 'In the serious difficulty which now besets us, gentlemen, I take my stand on the principle which I have just stated to you. My decision is as follows. Let us give the heaviest of the two babies to the heaviest of the two women; and let the lightest then fall, as a matter of course, to the other. In a week's time, if this weather holds, we shall all (please God) be in port; and if there's a better way out of this mess than *my* way, the parsons and lawyers ashore may find it, and welcome.'

With those words the captain closed his oration; and the assembled council immediately sanctioned the proposal submitted to them with all the unanimity of men who had no idea of their own to set up in opposition.

Mr Jolly was next requested (as the only available authority) to settle the question of weight between Mrs Smallchild and Mrs Heavysides, and decided it, without a moment's hesitation, in favour of the carpenter's wife, on the indisputable ground that she was the tallest and stoutest woman of the two. Thereupon the bald baby, 'distinguished as Number One', was taken into Mrs Heavysides' cabin; and the hairy baby, 'distinguished as Number Two', was accorded to Mrs Smallchild; the Voice of Nature, neither in the one case nor in the other, raising the slightest objection to the captain's principle of distribution. Before seven o'clock Mr Jolly reported that the mothers and sons, larboard and starboard, were as happy and comfortable as any four people on board ship could possibly wish to be; and the captain thereupon dismissed the council with these parting remarks: 'We'll get the studding-sails on the ship now, gentlemen, and make the best of our way to port. Breakfast, Pickerel, in half an hour, and plenty of it! I doubt if that unfortunate Mrs Drabble has heard the last of this business yet. We must all lend a hand, gentlemen, and pull her through if we can. In other respects the job's over, so far as we are concerned; and the parsons and lawyers must settle it ashore.'

The parsons and the lawyers did nothing of the sort, for the plain reason that nothing was to be done. In ten days the ship was in port, and the news was broken to the two mothers. Each one of the two adored her baby, after ten day's experience of it – and each one of the two was in Mrs Drabble's condition of not knowing which was which.

Every test was tried. First, the test by the doctor, who only repeated what he had told the captain. Secondly, the test by personal resemblance; which failed in consequence of the light hair, blue eyes, and Roman noses shared in common by the fathers, and the light hair, blue eyes, and no noses worth mentioning shared in common by the children. Thirdly, the test of Mrs Drabble, which began and ended in fierce talking on one side and floods of tears on the other. Fourthly, the test by legal decision, which broke down through the total absence of any instructions for the law to act on. Fifthly, and lastly, the test by appeal to the husbands, which fell to the ground in consequence of the husbands knowing nothing about the matter in hand. The captain's barbarous test by weight remained the test still – and here am I, a man of the lower order, without a penny to bless myself with, in consequence.

Yes! I was the bald baby of that memorable period. My excess in weight settled my destiny in life. The fathers and mothers on either side kept the babies according to the captain's principle of distribution, in despair of knowing what else to do. Mr Smallchild, who was sharp enough when not seasick, made his fortune. Simon Heavysides persisted in increasing his family, and died in the workhouse.

Judge for yourself (as Mr Jolly might say) how the two boys born at sea fared in afterlife. I, the bald baby, have seen nothing of the hairy baby for years past. He may be short, like Mr Smallchild – but I happen to know that he is wonderfully like Heavysides, deceased, in the face. I may be tall, like the carpenter – but I have the Smallchild eyes, hair, and expression, notwithstanding. Make what you can of that! You will find it comes, in the end, to the same thing. Smallchild, junior, prospers in the world, because he weighed six pounds, fourteen ounces and three-quarters. Heavysides, junior, fails in the world, because he weighed seven pounds one ounce and a quarter. Such is destiny, and such is life. I'll never forgive *my* destiny as long as I live. There is my grievance. I wish you good-morning.

The Fatal Fortune

I

One fine morning more than three months since, you were riding with your brother, Miss Anstell, in Hyde Park. It was a hot day, and you had allowed your horses to fall into a walking pace. As you passed the railing on the right-hand side, near the eastern extremity of the lake in the park, neither you nor your brother noticed a solitary woman loitering on the footpath to look at the riders as they went by.

The solitary woman was my old nurse, Nancy Connell. And these were the words she heard exchanged between you and your brother, as you slowly passed her.

Your brother said, 'Is it true that Mary Brading and her husband have gone to America?'

You laughed, as if the question amused you, and answered, 'Quite true.'

'How long will they be away?' your brother asked next.

'As long as they live,' you answered, with another laugh.

By this time you had passed beyond Nancy Connell's hearing. She owns to having followed your horses a few steps to hear what was said next. She looked particularly at your brother. He took your reply seriously; he seemed to be quite astonished by it.

'Leave England and settle in America!' he exclaimed. 'Why should they do that?'

'Who can tell why?' you answered. 'Mary Brading's husband is mad, and Mary Brading herself is not much better.'

You touched your horse with the whip, and in a moment more you and your brother were out of my old nurse's hearing. She wrote and told me what I here tell you, by a recent mail. I have been thinking of those last words of yours, in my leisure hours, more seriously than you would suppose. The end of it is that I take up my pen, on behalf of my husband and myself, to tell you the story of our marriage, and the reason for our emigration to the United States of America.

It matters little or nothing to him or to me whether our friends in England think us both mad or not. Their opinions, hostile or favourable, are of no sort of importance to us. But you are an exception to the rule. In bygone days at school we were fast and firm friends; and – what weighs with me even more than this – you were heartily loved and admired by my dear mother. She spoke of you tenderly on her deathbed. Events have separated us of late years.

But I cannot forget the old times; and I cannot feel indifferent to your opinion of me and of my husband, though an ocean does separate us, and though we are never likely to look on one another again. It is very foolish of me, I dare say, to take seriously to heart what you said in one of your thoughtless moments. I can only plead in excuse that I have gone through a great deal of suffering, and that I was always (as you may remember) a person of sensitive temperament, easily excited and easily depressed.

Enough of this. Do me the last favour I shall ever ask of you. Read what follows, and judge for yourself whether my husband and I are quite so mad as you were disposed to think us when Nancy Connell heard you talking to your brother in Hyde Park.

2

It is now more than a year since I went to Eastbourne, on the coast of Sussex, with my father and my brother James.

My brother had then, as we hoped, recovered from the effects of a fall in the hunting-field. He complained, however, at times, of pain in his head; and the doctors advised us to try the sea air. We removed to Eastbourne, without a suspicion of the serious nature of the injury that he had received. For a few days all went well. We liked the place; the air agreed with us; and we determined to prolong our residence for some weeks to come.

On our sixth day at the seaside – a memorable day to me, for reasons which you have still to hear – my brother complained again of the old pain in his head. He and I went out together to try what exercise would do towards relieving him. We walked through the town to the fort at one end of it, and then followed a footpath running by the side of the sea, over a dreary waste of shingle, bounded at its inland extremity by the road to Hastings and by the marshy country beyond.

We had left the fort at some little distance behind us. I was walking in front, and James was following me. He was talking as quietly as usual, when he suddenly stopped in the middle of a sentence. I turned round in surprise, and discovered my brother prostrate on the path, in convulsions terrible to see.

It was the first epileptic fit I had ever witnessed. My presence of mind entirely deserted me. I could only wring my hands in horror, and scream for help. No one appeared either from the direction of the fort or of the high road. I was too far off, I suppose, to make myself heard. Looking ahead of me along the path, I discovered, to my infinite relief, the figure of a man running towards me. As he came nearer, I saw that he was unmistakably a gentleman – young, and eager to be of service to me.

'Pray compose yourself,' he said, after a look at my brother. 'It is very dreadful to see, but it is not dangerous. We must wait until the convulsions are over, and then I can help you.'

He seemed to know so much about it that I thought he might be a medical man. I put the question to him plainly.

He coloured, and looked a little confused.

'I am not a doctor,' he said. 'I happen to have seen persons afflicted with epilepsy; and I have heard medical men say that it is useless to interfere until the fit is over. See!' he added. 'Your brother is quieter already. He will soon feel a sense of relief which will more than compensate him for what he has suffered. I will help him to get to the fort, and, once there, we can send for a carriage to take him home.'

In five minutes more we were on our way to the fort; the stranger supporting my brother as attentively and tenderly as if he had been an old friend. When the carriage had been obtained, he insisted on accompanying us to our own door, on the chance that his services might still be of some use. He left us, asking permission to call and enquire after James's health the next day. A more modest, gentle, and unassuming person I never met with. He not only excited my warmest gratitude; he interested me at my first meeting with him.

I lay some stress on the impression which this young man produced on me – why, you will soon find out.

The next day the stranger paid his promised visit of enquiry. His card, which he sent upstairs, informed us that his name was Roland Cameron. My father – who is not easily pleased – took a liking to him at once. His visit was prolonged, at our request. He said just enough about himself to satisfy us that we were receiving a person who was at least of equal rank with ourselves. Born in England, of a Scotch family, he had lost both his parents. Not long since, he had inherited a fortune from one of his uncles. It struck us as a little strange that he spoke of this fortune with a marked change to melancholy in his voice and his manner. The subject was, for some inconceivable reason, evidently distasteful to him. Rich as he was, he acknowledged that he led a simple and solitary life. He had little taste for society, and no sympathies in common with the average young men of his age. But he had his own harmless pleasures and occupations; and past sorrow and suffering had taught him not to expect too much from life. All this was said modestly, with a winning charm of look and voice which indescribably attracted me. His personal appearance aided the favourable impression which his manner and his conversation produced. He was of the middle height, lightly and firmly built; his complexion pale; his hands and feet small, and finely shaped; his brown hair curling naturally; his eyes large and dark, with an occasional indecision in their expression which was far from being an objection to them, to my taste. It seemed to harmonise with an occasional indecision in his talk; proceeding, as I was inclined to think, from some passing confusion in his thoughts which it always cost him a little effort to discipline and overcome. Does it surprise you to find how closely I observed a man who was only a chance acquaintance, at my first interview with him? Or do your suspicions enlighten you, and do you say to yourself, She has fallen in love with Mr Roland Cameron at first sight? I may plead in my own defence that I was not quite romantic enough to go that length. But I own I waited for his next visit with an impatience which was new to me in my experience of my sober self. And, worse still, when the day came, I changed my dress three times before my newly developed vanity was satisfied with the picture which the looking-glass presented to me of myself.

In a fortnight more, my father and my brother began to look on the daily companionship of our new friend as one of the settled institutions of their lives. In a fortnight more, Mr Roland Cameron and I – though we neither of us ventured to acknowledge it – were as devotedly in love with each other as two young people could well be. Ah, what a delightful time it was! and how cruelly soon our happiness came to an end!

During the brief interval which I have just described, I observed certain peculiarities in Roland Cameron's conduct, which perplexed and troubled me when my mind was busy with him in my lonely moments.

For instance, he was subject to the strangest lapses into silence, when he and I were talking together. At these times his eyes assumed a weary, absent look, and his mind seemed to wander away – far from the conversation, and far from me. He was perfectly unaware of his own infirmity; he fell into it unconsciously, and came out of it unconsciously. If I noticed that he had not been attending to me, or if I asked why he had been silent, he was completely at a loss to comprehend what I meant; I puzzled and distressed him. What he was thinking of in these pauses of silence, it was impossible to guess. His face, at other times singularly mobile and expressive, became almost a perfect blank. Had he suffered some terrible shock at some past period of his life and had his mind never quite recovered from it? I longed to ask him the question, and yet I shrank from doing it, I was so sadly afraid of distressing him; or, to put it in plainer words, I was so truly and so tenderly fond of him.

Then, again, though he was ordinarily, I sincerely believe, the most gentle and most lovable of men, there were occasions when he would surprise me by violent outbreaks of temper, excited by the merest trifles. A dog barking suddenly at his heels, or a boy throwing stones in the road, or an importunate shopkeeper trying to make him purchase something that he did not want, would throw him into a frenzy of rage which was, without exaggeration, really frightful to see. He always apologised for these outbreaks, in terms which showed that he was sincerely ashamed of his own violence. But he could never succeed in controlling himself. The lapses into passion, like the lapses into silence, took him into their own possession, and did with him, for the time being, just what they pleased.

One more example of Roland's peculiarities, and I have done. The strangeness of his conduct in this case was noticed by my father and my brother, as well as by me.

When Roland was with us in the evening, whether he came to dinner or to tea, he invariably left us exactly at nine o'clock. Try as we might to persuade him to stay longer, he always politely but positively refused. Even I had no influence over him in this matter. When I pressed him to remain, though it cost him an effort, he still retired exactly as the clock struck nine. He gave no reason for this strange proceeding; he only said that it was a habit of his, and begged us to indulge him in it without asking for an explanation. My father and my brother (being men) succeeded in controlling their curiosity. For my part (being a woman) every day that passed only made me more and more eager to penetrate the mystery. I privately resolved to choose my time, when Roland was in a particularly accessible humour, and then to appeal to him for the explanation which he had hitherto refused – as a special favour to myself.

In two days more I found my opportunity.

Some friends of ours, who had joined us at Eastbourne, proposed a picnic party to the famous neighbouring cliff called Beachey Head. We accepted the invitation. The day was lovely, and the gypsy dinner was, as usual, infinitely preferable (for once in a way) to a formal dinner indoors. Towards evening, our little assembly separated into parties of twos and threes to explore the neighbourhood. Roland and I found ourselves together, as a matter of course. We were happy, and we were alone. Was it the right or the wrong time to ask the fatal question? I am not able to decide; I only know that I asked it.

3

'Mr Cameron,' I said, 'will you make allowances for a weak woman? And will you tell me something that I am dying to know?'

He walked straight into the trap, with that entire absence of ready wit, or small suspicion (I leave you to choose the right phrase), which is so much like men, and so little like women.

'Of course I will,' he answered.

'Then tell me,' I asked, 'why you always insist on leaving us at nine o'clock?'

He started, and looked at me so sadly, so reproachfully, that I would have given everything I possessed to recall the rash words that had just passed my lips.

'If I consent to tell you,' he replied, after a momentary struggle with himself, 'will you let me put a question to you first, and will you promise to answer it?'

I gave him my promise, and waited eagerly for what was coming next.

'Miss Brading,' he said, 'tell me honestly, do you think I am mad?'

It was impossible to laugh at him: he spoke those strange words seriously – sternly, I might almost say.

'No such thought ever entered my head,' I answered.

He looked at me very earnestly.

'You say that on your word of honour?'

'On my word of honour.'

I answered with perfect sincerity, and I evidently satisfied him that I had spoken the truth.

He took my hand, and lifted it gratefully to his lips. 'Thank you,' he said, simply. 'You encourage me to tell you a very sad story.'

'Your own story?' I asked.

'My own story. Let me begin by telling you why I persist in leaving your house always at the same early hour. Whenever I go out, I am bound by a promise to the person with whom I am living at Eastbourne to return at a quarter-past nine o'clock.'

'The person with whom you are living?' I repeated. 'You are living at a boarding-house, are you not?'

'I am living, Miss Brading, under the care of a doctor who keeps an asylum for the insane. He has taken a house for some of his wealthier patients at the seaside; and he allows me liberty in the daytime, on condition that I faithfully perform my promise at night. It is a quarter of an hour's walk from your house to the doctor's, and it is a rule that the patients retire at half-past nine o'clock.'

Here was the mystery which had so sorely perplexed me revealed at last! The disclosure literally struck me speechless. Unconsciously and instinctively I drew back from him a few steps. He fixed his sad eyes on me with a touching look of entreaty.

'Don't shrink away from me,' he said. '*You* don't think I am mad.'

I was too confused and distressed to know what to say, and, at the same time, I was too fond of him not to answer that appeal. I took his hand and pressed it in silence. He turned his head aside for a moment. I thought I saw a tear on his cheek. I felt his hand close tremblingly on mine. He mastered himself with surprising resolution; he spoke with perfect composure when he looked at me again.

'Do you care to know my story,' he asked, 'after what I have just told you?'

'I am eager to hear it,' I answered. 'You don't know how I feel for you. I am too distressed to be able to express myself in words.'

'You are the kindest and dearest of women!' he said, with the utmost fervour, and at the same time with the utmost respect.

We sat down together in a grassy hollow of the cliff, with our faces towards the grand grey sea. The daylight was beginning to fade as I heard the story which made me Roland Cameron's wife.

4

'My mother died when I was an infant in arms,' he began. 'My father, from my earliest to my latest recollections, was always hard towards me. I have been told that I was an odd child, with strange ways of my own. My father detested anything that was strongly marked, anything out of the ordinary way, in the characters and habits of the persons about him. He himself lived (as the phrase is) by line and rule; and he determined to make his son follow his example. I was subjected to severe discipline at school, and I was carefully watched afterwards at college. Looking back on my early life, I can see no traces of happiness, I can find no tokens of sympathy. Sad submission to a hard destiny, weary wayfaring over unfriendly roads – such is the story of my life, from ten years old to twenty.

'I passed one autumn vacation at the Cumberland lakes; and there I met by accident with a young French lady. The result of that meeting decided my whole afterlife.

'She filled the position of nursery governess in the house of a wealthy Englishman. I had frequent opportunities of seeing her. We took an innocent pleasure in each other's society. Her little experience of life was strangely like mine. There was a perfect sympathy of thought and feeling between us. We loved, or thought we loved. I was not twenty-one, and she was not eighteen, when I asked her to be my wife.

'I can understand my folly now, and can laugh at it, or lament over it, as the humour moves me. And yet I can't help pitying myself when I look back at myself at that time – I was so young, so hungry for a little sympathy, so weary of my empty, friendless life. Well! everything is comparative in this world. I was soon to regret, bitterly to regret, that friendless life – wretched as it was.

'The poor girl's employer discovered our attachment, through his wife. He at once communicated with my father.

'My father had but one word to say – he insisted on my going abroad, and leaving it to him to release me from my absurd engagement in my absence. I answered him that I should be of age in a few months, and that I was determined to marry the girl. He gave me three days to reconsider that resolution. I held to my resolution. In a week afterwards I was declared insane by two medical men; and I was placed by my father in a lunatic asylum.

'Was it an act of insanity for the son of a gentleman, with great expectations before him, to propose marriage to a nursery governess? I declare, as heaven is my witness, I know of no other act of mine which could justify my father, and justify the doctors, in placing me under restraint.

'I was three years in that asylum. It was officially reported that the air did not agree with me. I was removed, for two years more, to another asylum in a remote part of England. For the five best years of my life I have been herded with madmen – and my reason has survived it. The impression I produce on you, on your father, on your brother, on all our friends at this picnic, is that I am as reasonable as the rest of my fellow-creatures. Am I rushing to a hasty conclusion when I assert myself to be now, and always to have been, a sane man?

'At the end of my five years of arbitrary imprisonment in a free country, happily for me – I am ashamed to say it, but I must speak the truth – happily for me, my merciless father died. His trustees, to whom I was now consigned, felt some pity for me. They could not take the responsibility of granting me my freedom. But they placed me under the care of a surgeon, who received me into his private residence, and who allowed me free exercise in the open air.

'A year's trial of this new mode of life satisfied the surgeon, and satisfied everyone else who took the smallest interest in me, that I was perfectly fit to enjoy my liberty. I was freed from all restraint, and was permitted to reside with a near relative of mine, in that very Lake country which had been the scene of my fatal meeting with the French girl, six years before.'

5

'I lived happily in the house of my relative, satisfied with the ordinary pursuits of a country gentleman. Time had long since cured me of my boyish infatuation for the nursery governess. I could revisit with perfect composure the paths along which we had walked, the lake on which we had sailed together. Hearing by chance that she was married in her own country, I could wish her all possible happiness, with the sober kindness of a disinterested friend. What a strange thread of irony runs through the texture of the simplest human life! The early love for which I had sacrificed and suffered so much was now revealed to me in its true colours, as a boy's passing fancy – nothing more!

'Three years of peaceful freedom passed; freedom which, on the uncontradicted testimony of respectable witnesses, I never abused. Well, that long and happy interval, like all intervals, came to its end – and then the great misfortune of my life fell upon me. One of my uncles died and left me inheritor of his whole fortune. I alone, to the exclusion of the other heirs, now received, not only the large income derived from the estates, but seventy thousand pounds in ready money as well.

'The vile calumny which had asserted me to be mad was now revived by the wretches who were interested in stepping between me and my inheritance. A year ago, I was sent back to the asylum in which I had been last imprisoned. The pretence for confining me was found in an act of violence (as it was called), which I had committed in a momentary outbreak of anger, and which it was acknowledged had led to no serious results. Having got me into the asylum, the conspirators proceeded to complete their work. A Commission in Lunacy was issued against me. It was held by one commissioner, without a jury, and without the presence of a lawyer to assert my interests. By one man's decision I was declared to be of unsound mind. The custody of my person, as well as the management of my estates, was confided to men chosen from among the conspirators who had declared me to be mad. I am here through the favour of the proprietor of the asylum, who has given me my holiday at the seaside, and who humanely trusts me with my liberty, as you see. At barely thirty years old, I am refused the free use of my money and the free management of my affairs. At barely thirty years old, I am officially declared to be a lunatic for life!'

6

He paused; his head sank on his breast; his story was told.

I have repeated his words as nearly as I can remember them; but I can give no idea of the modest and touching resignation with which he spoke. To say that I pitied him with my whole heart, is to say nothing. I loved him with my whole heart – and I may acknowledge it now!

'Oh, Mr Cameron,' I said, as soon as I could trust myself to speak, 'can nothing be done to help you? Is there no hope?'

'There is always hope,' he answered, without raising his head. 'I have to thank *you*, Miss Brading, for teaching me that.'

'To thank me?' I repeated. 'How have I taught you to hope?'

'You have brightened my dreary life. When I am with you, all my bitter remembrances leave me. I am a happy man again; and a happy man can always hope. I dream now of finding what I have never yet had – a dear and devoted friend, who will rouse the energy that has sunk in me under the martyrdom that I have endured. Why do I submit to the loss of my rights and my liberty, without an effort to recover them? I was alone in the world until I met with you. I had no kind hand to raise me, no kind voice to encourage me. Shall I ever find the hand? Shall I ever hear the voice? When I am with you, the hope that you have taught me answers yes. When I am by myself, the old despair comes back, and says no.'

He lifted his head for the first time. If I had not understood what his words meant, his look would have enlightened me. The tears came into my eyes; my heart heaved and fluttered wildly; my hands mechanically tore up and scattered the grass round me. The silence became unendurable. I spoke, hardly knowing what I was saying; tearing faster and faster at the poor harmless grass, as if my whole business in life was to pull up the greatest quantity in the shortest possible space of time!

'We have only known each other a little while,' I said; 'and a woman is but a weak ally in such a terrible position as yours. But useless as I may be, count on me, now and always, as your friend – '

He moved close to me before I could say more, and took my hand. He murmured in my ear,

'May I count on you one day as the nearest and dearest friend of all? Will you forgive me, Mary, if I own that I love you? You have taught me to love, as you have taught me to hope. It is in your power to lighten my hard lot. *You* can recompense me for all that I have suffered; *you* can rouse me to struggle for my freedom and my rights. Be the good angel of my life! Forgive me, love me, rescue me – be my wife!'

I don't know how it happened. I found myself in his arms – and I answered him in a kiss. Taking all the circumstances into consideration, I dare say I was guilty, in accepting him, of the rashest act that ever a woman committed. Very good. I didn't care then – I don't care now. I was then, and I am now, the happiest woman living.

7

It was necessary that either he or I should tell my father of what had passed between us. On reflection, I thought it best that I should make the disclosure. The day after the picnic, I repeated to my father Roland's melancholy narrative, as a necessary preface to the announcement that I had promised to be Roland's wife.

My father saw the obvious objections to the marriage. He warned me of the imprudence which I had contemplated committing in the strongest terms. Our prospect of happiness, if we married, would depend entirely on our capacity legally to supersede the proceedings of the Lunacy Commission. Success in this arduous undertaking was, to say the least of it, uncertain. The commonest prudence pointed to the propriety of delaying our marriage until the doubtful experiment had been put to the proof.

This reasoning was unanswerable. It was, nevertheless, completely thrown away upon me.

When did a woman in love ever listen to reason? I believe there is no instance of it on record. My father's wise words of caution had no chance against Roland's fervent entreaties. The days of his residence at Eastbourne were drawing to a close. If I let him return to the asylum an unmarried man, months, years perhaps, might pass before our union could take place. Could I expect him, could I expect any man, to endure that cruel separation, that unrelieved suspense? His mind had been sorely tried already; his mind might give way under it. These were the arguments that carried weight with them, in my judgement! I was of age, and free to act as I pleased. You are welcome, if you like, to consider me the most foolish and the most obstinate of women.

In sixteen days from the date of the picnic Roland and I were privately married at Eastbourne.

My father – more grieved than angry, poor man – declined to be present at the ceremony; in justice to himself. My brother gave me away at the altar.

Roland and I spent the afternoon of the wedding-day and the earlier part of the evening together. At nine o'clock he returned to the doctor's house, exactly as usual; having previously explained to me that he was in the power of the Court of Chancery, and that until we succeeded in setting aside the proceedings of the Lunacy Commission there was a serious necessity for keeping the marriage strictly secret. My husband and I kissed, and said goodbye till tomorrow, as the clock struck the hour. I little thought, while I looked after him from the street-door, that months on months were to pass before I saw Roland again.

A hurried note from my husband reached me the next morning. Our marriage had been discovered (we never could tell by whom), and we had been betrayed to the doctor. Roland was then on his way back to the asylum. He had been warned that force would be used if he resisted. Knowing that resistance would be interpreted, in his case, as a new outbreak of madness, he had wisely submitted. 'I have made the sacrifice,' the letter concluded; 'it is now for you to help me. Attack the Commission in Lunacy, and be quick about it!'

We lost no time in preparing for the attack. On the day when I received the news of our misfortune we left Eastbourne for London, and at once took measures to obtain the best legal advice.

My dear father – though I was far from deserving his kindness – entered into the matter heart and soul. In due course of time, we presented a petition to the Lord Chancellor, praying that the decision of the Lunacy Commission might be set aside.

We supported our petition by quoting the evidence of Roland's friends and neighbours, during his three years' residence in the Lake country, as a free man. These worthy people (being summoned before the Lunacy Commission) had one and all agreed that he was, as to their judgement and experience, perfectly quiet, harmless, and sane. Many of them had gone out shooting with him. Others had often accompanied him in sailing excursions on the lake. Do people trust a madman with a gun, and with the management of a boat? As to the 'act of violence', which the heirs at law and the next of kin had made the means of imprisoning Roland in the mad-house, it amounted to this: he had lost his temper, and had knocked a man down who had offended him. Very wrong, no doubt; but if that is a proof of madness, what thousands of lunatics are still at large! Another instance produced to prove his insanity was still more absurd. It was solemnly declared that he put an image of the Virgin Mary in his boat when he went out on his sailing excursions! I have seen the image – it was a very beautiful work of art. Was Roland mad to admire it, and take it with him? His religious convictions leaned toward Catholicism. If he betrayed insanity in adorning his boat with an image of the Virgin Mary, what is the mental condition of most of the ladies in Christendom who wear the cross as an ornament round their necks? We advanced these arguments in our petition, after quoting the evidence of the witnesses. And more than this, we even went the length of admitting, as an act of respect toward the Court, that my poor husband might be eccentric in some of his opinions and habits. But we put it to the authorities, whether better results might not be expected from placing him under the care of a wife who loved him, and whom he loved, than from shutting him up in an asylum, among incurable madmen as his companions for life.

Such was our petition, so far as I am able to describe it.

The decision rested with the Lords Justices. They decided against us.

Turning a deaf ear to our witnesses and our arguments, these merciless lawyers declared that the doctor's individual assertion of my husband's insanity was enough for them. They considered Roland's comfort to be sufficiently provided for in the asylum with an allowance of seven hundred pounds a year – and to the asylum they consigned him for the rest of his days.

So far as I was concerned, the result of this infamous judgement was to deprive me of the position of Roland's wife; no lunatic being capable of contracting marriage by law. So far as my husband was concerned, the result may be best stated in the language of a popular newspaper, which published an article on the case. 'It is possible' (said the article – I wish I could personally thank the man who wrote it!) 'for the Court of Chancery to take a man who has a large fortune, and is in the prime of life, but is a little touched in the head, and make a monk of him, and then report to itself that the comfort and happiness of the lunatic have been effectually provided for at the expenditure of seven hundred pounds a year.'

Roland was determined, however, that they should *not* make a monk of him – and, you may rely upon it, so was I!

But one alternative was left to us. The authority of the Court of Chancery (within its jurisdiction) is the most despotic authority on the face of the earth. Our one hope was in taking to flight. The price of our liberty, as citizens of England, was exile from our native country, and the entire abandonment of Roland's fortune. We accepted those hard conditions. Hospitable America offered us a refuge, beyond the reach of doctors of the insane and Lords Justices. To hospitable America our hearts turned, as to our second country. The serious question was, How were we to get there?

We had attempted to correspond, and had failed. Our letters had been discovered and seized by the proprietor of the asylum. Fortunately we had taken the precaution of writing in a 'cipher' of Roland's invention, which he had taught me before our marriage. Though our letters were illegible, our purpose was suspected, as a matter of course; and a watch was kept on my husband night and day.

Foiled in our first effort at making arrangements secretly for our flight, we continued our correspondence (still in cipher) by means of advertisements in the newspapers. This second attempt was discovered in its turn. Roland was refused permission to subscribe to the newspapers, and was forbidden to enter the reading-room at the asylum. These tyrannical prohibitions came too late. Our plans had already been communicated; we understood each other, and we had now only to bide our time. We had arranged that my brother and a friend of his, on whose discretion we could thoroughly rely, should take it in turns to watch every evening, for a given time, at an appointed meeting-place, three miles distant from the asylum. The spot had been carefully chosen. It was on the bank of a lonely stream, and close to the outskirts of a thick wood. A waterproof knapsack, containing a change of clothes, a false beard and wig, and some biscuits and preserved meat, was hidden in a hollow tree. My brother and his friend always took their fishing-rods with them, and presented themselves as engaged in the innocent occupation of angling to any chance strangers who might pass within sight of them. On one occasion the proprietor of the asylum himself rode by my brother, on the opposite bank of the stream, and asked politely if he had had good sport!

For a fortnight these stanch allies of ours relieved each other regularly on their watch – and no sign of the fugitive appeared. On the fifteenth evening, just as the twilight was changing into night, and just as my brother (whose turn it was) had decided on leaving the place, Roland suddenly joined him on the bank of the stream.

Without wasting a moment in words, the two at once entered the wood, and took the knapsack from its place of shelter in the hollow tree. In ten minutes more my husband was dressed in a suit of workman's clothes, and was further disguised in the wig and beard. The two then set forth down the course of the stream, keeping in the shadow of the wood until the night had fallen and the darkness hid them. The night was cloudy; there was no moon. After walking two miles or a little more, they altered their course, and made for the high road to Manchester, entering on it at a point some thirty miles distant from the city.

On their way from the wood, Roland described the manner in which he had effected his escape.

The story was simple enough. He had assumed to be suffering from nervous illness, and had requested to have his meals in his own room. For the first fortnight, the two men appointed to wait upon him in succession, week by week, were both more than his match in strength. The third man employed, at the beginning of the third week, was physically a less for-midable person than his predecessors. Seeing this, Roland decided, when evening came, on committing another 'act of violence'. In plain words, he sprang upon the keeper waiting on him in his room, and gagged and bound the man.

This done, he laid the unlucky keeper, face to the wall, on his own bed, covered with his own cloak, so that anyone entering the room might suppose he was lying down to rest. He had previously taken the precaution to remove the sheets from the bed, and he had now only to tie them together to escape by the window of his room, situated on the upper floor of the house. The sun was setting, and the inmates of the asylum were then at tea. After narrowly missing discovery by one of the labourers employed in the grounds, he had climbed the garden enclosure, and had dropped on the other side – a free man!

Arrived on the high road to Manchester, my husband and my brother parted.

Roland, who was an excellent walker, set forth on his way to Manchester on foot. He had food in his knapsack, and he proposed to walk some twelve or fifteen miles on the road to the city before he stopped at any town or village to rest. My brother, who was physically unable to accompany him, returned to the place in which I was then residing, to tell me the good news.

By the first train the next morning I travelled to Manchester, and took a lodging in a suburb of the city known to my husband as well as to me. A prim, smoky little square was situated in the immediate neighbourhood; and we had arranged that whichever of us first arrived in Manchester should walk round that square, between twelve and one in the afternoon, and between six and seven in the evening. In the evening I kept my appointment. A dusty, foot-sore man, in shabby clothes, with a hideous beard, and a knapsack on his back, met me at my first walk round. He smiled as I looked at him. Ah! I knew that smile through all disguises. In spite of the Court of Chancery and the Lords Justices, I was in my husband's arms once more.

We lived quietly in our retreat for a month. During that time (as I heard by letters from my brother), nothing that money and cunning could do toward discovering Roland was left untried by the proprietor of the asylum, and by the persons acting with him. But where is the cunning which can trace a man who, escaping at night in disguise, has not trusted himself to a railway or a carriage, and who takes refuge in a great city in which he has no friends? At the end of our month in Manchester we travelled northward, crossed the Channel to Ireland, and passed a pleasant fortnight in Dublin. Leaving this again, we made our way to Cork and Queenstown, and embarked from that latter place (among a crowd of steerage passengers) in a steamship for America.

My story is told. I am writing these lines from a farm in the west of the United States. Our neighbours may be homely enough; but the roughest of them is kinder to us than a doctor of the insane or a Lord Justice. Roland is happy in those agricultural pursuits which have always been favourite pursuits with him; and I am happy with Roland. Our sole resources consist of my humble little fortune, inherited from my dear mother. After deducting our traveling expenses, the sum total amounts to between seven and eight hundred pounds; and this, as we find, is amply sufficient to start us well in the new life that we have chosen. We expect my father and my brother to pay us a visit next summer; and I think it is just possible that they may find our family circle increased by the presence of a new member in long clothes. Are there no compensations here for exile from England and the loss of a fortune? *We* think there are! But then, my dear Miss Anstell, 'Mary Brading's husband is mad, and Mary Brading herself is not much better.'

If you feel inclined to alter this opinion, and if you remember our old days at school as tenderly as I remember them, write and tell me so. Your letter will be forwarded, if you send it to the enclosed address at New York.

In the meantime, the moral of our story seems to be worth serious consideration. A certain Englishman legally inherits a large fortune. At the time of his inheritance, he has been living as a free man for three years – without once abusing his freedom, and with the express sanction of the medical superintendent who has had experience and charge of him. His next of kin and his heirs at law (who are left out of the fortune) look with covetous eyes at the money, and determine to get the management and the ultimate possession of it. Assisted by a doctor, whose honesty and capacity must be taken on trust, these interested persons, in this nineteenth century of progress, can lawfully imprison their relative for life, in a country which calls itself free, and which declares that its justice is equally administered to all alike.

NOTE The reader is informed that this story is founded, in all essential particulars, on a case which actually occurred in England, eight years since.

W. C.

JOSEPH CONRAD

Joseph Conrad was born in the Ukraine to Polish parents in 1857 and orphaned as a child. He longed for a life at sea from an early age and in 1874 began a twenty-year career as a sailor. In 1886 he became a British subject and eight years later devoted himself to being a full-time writer. He married Jessie George – the mother of his two sons – in 1895. Publication of his first novel, *Almayer's Folly*, when he was thirty-eight, marked the beginning of a career as a novelist that was to produce such classics as *Lord Jim* (1900), *Nostromo* (1904) and *Under Western Eyes* (1911). Conrad died in 1924 at a point when his stature as a writer of considerable significance was firmly established.

The Brute

Dodging in from the rainswept street, I exchanged a smile and a glance with Miss Blank in the bar of the Three Crows. This exchange was effected with extreme propriety. It is a shock to think that, if still alive, Miss Blank must be something over sixty now. How time passes!

Noticing my gaze directed enquiringly at the partition of glass and varnished wood, Miss Blank was good enough to say, encouragingly: 'Only Mr Jermyn and Mr Stonor in the parlour with another gentleman I've never seen before.'

I moved towards the parlour door. A voice discoursing on the other side (it was but a matchboard partition) rose so loudly that the concluding words became quite plain in all their atrocity.

'That fellow Wilmot fairly dashed her brains out, and a good job, too!'

This inhuman sentiment, since there was nothing profane or improper in it, failed to do as much as to check the slight yawn Miss Blank was achieving behind her hand. And she remained gazing fixedly at the window-panes, which streamed with rain.

As I opened the parlour door the same voice went on in the same cruel strain: 'I was glad when I heard she got the knock from somebody at last. Sorry enough for poor Wilmot, though. That man and I used to be chums at one time. Of course that was the end of him. A clear case if there ever was one. No way out of it. None at all.'

The voice belonged to the gentleman Miss Blank had never seen before. He straddled his long legs on the hearthrug. Jermyn, leaning forward, held his pocket-handkerchief spread out before the grate. He looked back dismally over his shoulder, and as I slipped behind one of the little wooden tables, I nodded to him. On the other side of the fire, imposingly calm and large, sat Mr Stonor, jammed tight into a capacious Windsor armchair. There was nothing small about him but his short, white side-whiskers. Yards and yards of extra superfine blue cloth (made up into an overcoat) reposed on a chair by his side. And he must just have brought some liner from sea, because another chair was smothered under his black waterproof, ample as a pall, and made of three-fold oiled silk, double-stitched throughout. A man's hand-bag of the usual size looked like a child's toy on the floor near his feet.

I did not nod to him. He was too big to be nodded to in that parlour. He was a senior Trinity pilot and condescended to take his turn in the cutter only during the summer months. He had been many times in charge of royal yachts in and out of Port Victoria. Besides, it's no use nodding to a monument. And he was like one. He didn't speak, he didn't budge. He just sat there, holding his handsome old head up, immovable, and almost bigger than life. It was extremely fine. Mr Stonor's presence reduced poor old Jermyn to a mere shabby wisp of a man, and made the talkative stranger in tweeds on the hearthrug look absurdly boyish. The latter must have been a few years over thirty, and was certainly not the sort of individual that gets abashed at the sound of his own voice, because gathering me in, as it were, by a friendly glance, he kept it going without a check.

'I was glad of it,' he repeated, emphatically. 'You may be surprised at it, but then you haven't gone through the experience I've had of her. I can tell you, it was something to remember. Of course, I got off scot free myself – as you can see. She did her best to break up my pluck for me tho'. She jolly near drove as fine a fellow as ever lived into a madhouse. What do you say to that – eh?'

Not an eyelid twitched in Mr Stonor's enormous face. Monumental! The speaker looked straight into my eyes.

'It used to make me sick to think of her going about the world murdering people.'

Jermyn approached the handkerchief a little nearer to the grate and groaned. It was simply a habit he had. 'I've seen her once,' he declared, with mournful indifference. 'She had a house – '

The stranger in tweeds turned to stare down at him, surprised.

'She had three houses,' he corrected, authoritatively. But Jermyn was not to be contradicted.

'She had a house, I say,' he repeated, with dismal obstinacy. 'A great, big, ugly, white thing. You could see it from miles away – sticking up.'

'So you could,' assented the other readily. 'It was old Colchester's notion, though he was always threatening to give her up. He couldn't stand her racket any more, he declared; it was too much of a good thing for him; he would wash his hands of her, if he never got hold of another – and so on. I dare say he would have chucked her, only – it may surprise you – his missus wouldn't hear of it. Funny, eh? But with women, you never know how they will take a thing, and Mrs Colchester, with her moustaches and big eyebrows, set up for being as strong-minded as they make them. She used to walk about in a brown silk dress, with a great gold cable flopping about her bosom. You should have heard her snapping out: "Rubbish!" or "Stuff and nonsense!" I dare say she knew when she was well off. They had no children, and had never set up a home anywhere. When in England she just made shift to hang out anyhow in some cheap hotel or boarding-house. I dare say she liked to get back to the comforts she was used to. She knew very well she couldn't gain by any change. And, moreover, Colchester, though a first-rate man, was not what you may call in his first youth, and, perhaps, she may have thought that he wouldn't be able to get hold of another (as he used to say) so easily. Anyhow, for one reason or another, it was "Rubbish!" and "Stuff and nonsense!" for the good lady. I overheard once young Mr Apse himself say to her confidentially: "I assure you, Mrs Colchester, I am beginning to feel quite unhappy about the name she's getting for herself." "Oh," says she, with her deep little hoarse laugh, "if one took notice of all the silly talk," and she showed Apse all her ugly false teeth at once. "It would take more than that to make me lose my confidence in her, I assure you," says she.'

At this point, without any change of facial expression, Mr Stonor emitted a short, sardonic laugh. It was very impressive, but I didn't see the fun. I looked from one to another. The stranger on the hearthrug had an ugly smile.

'And Mr Apse shook both Mrs Colchester's hands, he was so pleased to hear a good word said for their favourite. All these Apses, young and old, you know, were perfectly infatuated with that abominable, dangerous – '

'I beg your pardon,' I interrupted, for he seemed to be addressing himself exclusively to me; 'but who on earth are you talking about?'

'I am talking of the *Apse Family*,' he answered, courteously.

I nearly let out a damn at this. But just then the respected Miss Blank put her head in, and said that the cab was at the door, if Mr Stonor wanted to catch the eleven-three up.

At once the senior pilot arose in his mighty bulk and began to struggle into his coat, with awe-inspiring upheavals. The stranger and I hurried impulsively to his assistance, and directly we laid our hands on him he became perfectly quiescent. We had to raise our arms very high, and to make efforts. It was like caparisoning a docile elephant. With a, 'Thanks, gentlemen,' he dived under and squeezed himself through the door in a great hurry.

We smiled at each other in a friendly way.

'I wonder how he manages to hoist himself up a ship's side-ladder,' said the man in tweeds; and poor Jermyn, who was a mere North Sea pilot, without official status or recognition of any sort, pilot only by courtesy, groaned, 'He makes eight hundred a year.'

'Are you a sailor?' I asked the stranger, who had gone back to his position on the rug.

'I used to be till a couple of years ago, when I got married,' answered this communicative individual. 'I even went to sea first in that very ship we were speaking of when you came in.'

'What ship?' I asked, puzzled. 'I never heard you mention a ship.'

'I've just told you her name, my dear sir,' he replied. 'The *Apse Family*. Surely you've heard of the great firm of Apse & Sons, shipowners. They had a pretty big fleet. There was the *Lucy Apse*, and the *Harold Apse*, and *Anne*, *John*, *Malcolm*, *Clara*, *Juliet*, and so on – no end of Apses. Every brother, sister, aunt, cousin, wife – and grandmother, too, for all I know – of the firm had a ship named after them. Good, solid, old-fashioned craft they were, too, built to carry and to last. None of your new-fangled, labour-saving appliances in them, but plenty of men and plenty of good salt beef and hard tack put aboard – and off you go to fight your way out and home again.'

The miserable Jermyn made a sound of approval, which sounded like a groan of pain. Those were the ships for him. He pointed out in doleful tones that you couldn't say to labour-saving appliances: 'Jump lively now, my hearties.' No labour-saving appliance would go aloft on a dirty night with the sands under your lee.

'No,' assented the stranger, with a wink at me. 'The Apses didn't believe in them either, apparently. They treated their people well – as people don't get treated nowadays, and they were awfully proud of their ships. Nothing ever happened to them. This last one, the *Apse Family*, was to be like the others, only she was to be still stronger, still safer, still more roomy and comfortable. I believe they meant her to last for ever. They had her built composite – iron, teak-wood and greenheart, and her scantling was something fabulous. If ever an order was given for a ship in a spirit of pride this one was. Everything of the best. The commodore captain of the employ was to command her, and they planned the accommodation for him like a house on shore under a big, tall poop that went nearly to the mainmast. No wonder Mrs Colchester wouldn't let the old man give her up. Why, it was the best home she ever had in all her married days. She had a nerve, that woman.

'The fuss that was made while that ship was building! Let's have this a little stronger, and that a little heavier; and hadn't that other thing better be changed for something a little thicker. The builders entered into the spirit of the game, and there she was, growing into the clumsiest, heaviest ship of her size right before all their eyes, without anybody becoming aware of it somehow. She was to be 2,000 tons register, or a little over; no less on any account. But see what happens. When they came to measure her she turned out 1,999 tons and a fraction. General consternation! And they say old Mr Apse was so annoyed when they told him that he took to his bed and died. The old gentleman had retired from the firm twenty-five years before, and was ninety-six years old if a day, so his death wasn't, perhaps, so surprising. Still Mr Lucian Apse was convinced that his father would have lived to a hundred. So we may put him at the head of the list. Next comes the poor devil of a shipwright that brute caught and squashed as she went off the ways. They called it the launch of a ship, but I've heard people say that, from the wailing and yelling and scrambling out of the way, it was more like letting a devil loose upon the river. She snapped all her checks like packthread, and went for the tugs in attendance like a fury. Before anybody could see what she was up to she sent one of them to the bottom, and laid up another for three months' repairs. One of her cables parted, and then, suddenly – you couldn't tell why – she let herself be brought up with the other as quiet as a lamb.

'That's how she was. You could never be sure what she would be up to next. There are ships difficult to handle, but generally you can depend on them behaving rationally. With that ship, whatever you did with her you never knew how it would end. She was a wicked beast. Or, perhaps, she was only just insane.'

He uttered this supposition in so earnest a tone that I could not refrain from smiling. He left off biting his lower lip to apostrophise me.

'Eh! Why not? Why couldn't there be something in her build, in her lines corresponding to – What's madness? Only something just a tiny bit wrong in the make of your brain. Why shouldn't there be a mad ship – I mean mad in a shiplike way, so that under no circumstances could you be sure she would do what any other sensible ship would naturally do for you. There are ships that steer wildly, and ships that can't be quite trusted always to stay; others want careful watching when running in a gale; and, again, there may be a ship that will make heavy weather of it in every little blow. But then you expect her to be always so. You take it as part of her character, as a ship, just as you take account of a man's peculiarities of temper when you deal with him. But with her you couldn't. She was unaccountable. If she wasn't mad, then she was the most evil-minded, underhand, savage brute that ever went afloat. I've seen her run in a heavy gale beautifully for two days, and on the third broach to twice in the same afternoon. The first time she flung the helmsman clean over the wheel, but as she didn't quite manage to kill him she had another try about three hours afterwards. She swamped herself fore and aft, burst all the canvas we had set, scared all hands into a panic, and even frightened Mrs Colchester down there in these beautiful stern cabins that she was so proud of. When we mustered the crew there was one man missing. Swept overboard, of course, without being either seen or heard, poor devil! and I only wonder more of us didn't go.

'Always something like that. Always. I heard an old mate tell Captain Colchester once that it had come to this with him, that he was afraid to open his mouth to give any sort of order. She was as much of a terror in harbour as at sea. You could never be certain what would hold her. On the slightest provocation she would start snapping ropes, cables, wire hawsers, like carrots. She was heavy, clumsy, unhandy – but that does not quite explain that power for mischief she had. You know, somehow, when I think of her I can't help remembering what we hear of incurable lunatics breaking loose now and then.'

He looked at me inquisitively. But, of course, I couldn't admit that a ship could be mad.

'In the ports where she was known,' he went on, 'they dreaded the sight of her. She thought nothing of knocking away twenty feet or so of solid stone facing off a quay or wiping off the end of a wooden wharf. She must have lost miles of chain and hundreds of tons of anchors in her time. When she fell aboard some poor unoffending ship it was the very devil of a job to haul her off again. And she never got hurt herself – just a few scratches or so, perhaps. They had wanted to have her strong. And so she was. Strong enough to ram Polar ice with. And as she began so she went on. From the day she was launched she never let a year pass without murdering somebody. I think the owners got very worried about it. But they were a stiff-necked generation all these Apses; they wouldn't admit there could be anything wrong with the *Apse Family*. They wouldn't even change her name. "Stuff and nonsense," as Mrs Colchester used to say. They ought at least to have shut her up for life in some dry dock or other, away up the river, and never let her smell salt water again. I assure you, my dear sir, that she invariably did kill someone every voyage she made. It was perfectly well known. She got a name for it, far and wide.'

I expressed my surprise that a ship with such a deadly reputation could ever get a crew.

'Then, you don't know what sailors are, my dear sir. Let me just show you by an instance. One day in dock at home, while loafing on the forecastle head, I noticed two respectable salts come along, one a middle-aged, competent, steady man, evidently, the other a smart, youngish chap. They read the name on the bows and stopped to look at her. Says the elder man: "*Apse Family*. That's the sanguinary female dog" (I'm putting it in that way) "of a ship, Jack, that kills a man every voyage. I wouldn't sign in her – not for Joe, I wouldn't." And the other says: "If she were mine, I'd have her towed on the mud and set on fire, blame if I wouldn't." Then the first man chimes in: "Much do they care! Men are cheap, God knows." The younger one spat in the water alongside. "They won't have me – not for double wages."

'They hung about for some time and then walked up the dock. Half an hour later I saw them both on our deck looking about for the mate, and apparently very anxious to be taken on. And they were.'

'How do you account for this?' I asked.

'What would you say?' he retorted. 'Recklessness! The vanity of boasting in the evening to all their chums: "We've just shipped in that there *Apse Family*. Blow her. She ain't going to scare us." Sheer sailorlike perversity! A sort of curiosity. Well – a little of all that, no doubt. I put the question to them in the course of the voyage. The answer of the elderly chap was: "A man can die but once." The younger assured me in a mocking tone that he wanted to see "how she would do it this time". But I tell you what, there *was* a sort of fascination about the brute.'

Jermyn, who seemed to have seen every ship in the world, broke in sulkily: 'I saw her once out of this very window towing up the river; a great black ugly thing, going along like a big hearse.'

'Something sinister about her looks, wasn't there?' said the man in tweeds, looking down at old Jermyn with a friendly eye. 'I always had a sort of horror of her. She gave me a beastly shock when I was no more than fourteen, the very first day – nay, hour – I joined her. Father came up to see me off, and was to go down to Gravesend with us. I was his second boy to go to sea. My big brother was already an officer then. We got on board about eleven in the morning, and found the ship ready to drop out of the basin, stern first. She had not moved three times her own length when, at a little pluck the tug gave her to enter the dock gates, she made one of her rampaging starts, and put such a weight on the check rope – a new six-inch hawser – that forward there they had no chance to ease it round in time, and it parted. I saw the broken end fly up high in the air, and the next moment that brute brought her quarter against the pier-head with a jar that staggered everybody about her decks. She didn't hurt herself. Not she! But one of the boys the mate had sent aloft on the mizzen to do something, came down on the poop-deck – thump – right in front of me. He was not much older than myself. We had been grinning at each other only a few minutes before. He must have been handling himself carelessly, not expecting to get such a jerk. I heard his startled cry – Oh! – in a high treble as he felt himself going, and looked up in time to see him go limp all over as he fell. Ough! Poor father was remarkably white about the gills when we shook hands in Gravesend. "Are you all right?" he says, looking hard at me. "Yes, father." "Quite sure?" "Yes, father." "Well, then goodbye, my boy." He told me afterwards that for half a word he would have carried me off home with him there and then. I am the baby of the family – you know,' added the man in tweeds, stroking his moustache with an ingenuous smile.

I acknowledged this interesting communication by a sympathetic murmur. He waved his hand carelessly.

'This might have utterly spoiled a chap's nerve for going aloft, you know – utterly. He fell within two feet of me, cracking his head on a mooring-bitt. Never moved. Stone dead. Nice looking little fellow, he was. I had just been thinking we would be great chums. However, that wasn't yet the worst that brute of a ship could do. I served in her three years of my time, and then I got transferred to the *Lucy Apse*, for a year. The sailmaker we had in the *Apse Family* turned up there, too, and I remember him saying to me one evening, after we had been a week at sea: "Isn't she a meek little ship?" No wonder we thought the *Lucy Apse* a dear, meek, little ship after getting clear of that big, rampaging savage brute. It was like heaven. Her officers seemed to me the restfullest lot of men on earth. To me who had known no ship but the *Apse Family*, the *Lucy* was like a sort of magic craft that did what you wanted her to do of her own accord. One evening we got caught aback pretty sharply from right ahead. In about ten minutes we had her full again, sheets aft, tacks down, decks cleared, and the officer of the watch leaning against the weather-rail peacefully. It seemed simply marvellous to me. The other would have stuck for half an hour in irons, rolling her decks full of water, knocking the men about – spars cracking, braces snapping, yards taking charge, and a confounded scare going on aft because of her beastly rudder, which she had a way of flapping about fit to raise your hair on end. I couldn't get over my wonder for days.

'Well, I finished my last year of apprenticeship in that jolly little ship – she wasn't so little either, but after that other heavy devil she seemed but a plaything to handle. I finished my time and passed; and then just as I was thinking of having three weeks of real good time on shore I got at breakfast a letter asking me the earliest day I could be ready to join the *Apse Family* as third mate. I gave my plate a shove that shot it into the middle of the table; dad looked up over his paper, mother raised her hands in astonishment, and I went out bare-headed into our bit of garden, where I walked round and round for an hour.

'When I came in again mother was out of the dining-room, and dad had shifted berth into his big armchair. The letter was lying on the mantelpiece.

' "It's very creditable to you to get the offer, and very kind of them to make it," he said. "And I see also that Charles has been appointed chief mate of that ship for one voyage."

'There was, overleaf, a P.S. to that effect in Mr Apse's own handwriting, which I had overlooked. Charley was my big brother.

'I don't like very much to have two of my boys together in one ship,' father goes on, in his deliberate, solemn way. "And I may tell you that I would not mind writing Mr Apse a letter to that effect."

'Dear old dad! He was a wonderful father. What would you have done? The mere notion of going back (and as an officer, too), to be worried and bothered, and kept on the jump night and day by that brute, made me feel sick. But she wasn't a ship you could afford to fight shy of. Besides, the most genuine excuse could not be given without mortally offending Apse & Sons. The firm, and I believe the whole family down to the old unmarried aunts in Lancashire, had grown desperately touchy about that accursed ship's character. This was the case for answering "Ready now" from your very deathbed if you wished to die in their good graces. And that's precisely what I did answer – by wire, to have it over and done with at once.

'The prospect of being shipmates with my big brother cheered me up considerably, though it made me a bit anxious, too. Ever since I remember myself as a little chap he had been very good to me, and I looked upon him as the finest fellow in the world. And so he was. No better officer ever walked the deck of a merchant ship. And that's a fact. He was a fine, strong, upstanding, sun-tanned, young fellow, with his brown hair curling a little, and an eye like a hawk. He was just splendid. We hadn't seen each other for many years, and even this time, though he had been in England three weeks already, he hadn't showed up at home yet, but had spent his spare time in Surrey somewhere making up to Maggie Colchester, old Captain Colchester's niece. Her father, a great friend of dad's, was in the sugar-broking business, and Charley made a sort of second home of their house. I wondered what my big brother would think of me. There was a sort of sternness about Charley's face which never left it, not even when he was larking in his rather wild fashion.

'He received me with a great shout of laughter. He seemed to think my joining as an officer the greatest joke in the world. There was a difference of ten years between us, and I suppose he remembered me best in pinafores. I was a kid of four when he first went to sea. It surprised me to find how boisterous he could be.

' "Now we shall see what you are made of," he cried. And he held me off by the shoulders, and punched my ribs, and hustled me into his berth. "Sit down, Ned. I am glad of the chance of having you with me. I'll put the finishing touch to you, my young officer, providing you're worth the trouble. And, first of all, get it well into your head that we are not going to let this brute kill anybody this voyage. We'll stop her racket."

'I perceived he was in dead earnest about it. He talked grimly of the ship, and how we must be careful and never allow this ugly beast to catch us napping with any of her damned tricks.

'He gave me a regular lecture on special seamanship for the use of the *Apse Family*; then changing his tone, he began to talk at large, rattling off the wildest, funniest nonsense, till my sides ached with laughing. I could see very well he was a bit above himself with high spirits. It couldn't be because of my coming. Not to that extent. But, of course, I wouldn't have dreamt of asking what was the matter. I had a proper respect for my big brother, I can tell you. But it was all made plain enough a day or two afterwards, when I heard that Miss Maggie Colchester was coming for the voyage. Uncle was giving her a sea-trip for the benefit of her health.

'I don't know what could have been wrong with her health. She had a beautiful colour, and a deuce of a lot of fair hair. She didn't care a rap for wind, or rain, or spray, or sun, or green seas, or anything. She was a blue-eyed, jolly girl of the very best sort, but the way she cheeked my big brother used to frighten me. I always expected it to end in an awful row. However, nothing decisive happened till after we had been in Sydney for a week. One day, in the men's dinner hour, Charley sticks his head into my cabin. I was stretched out on my back on the settee, smoking in peace.

' "Come ashore with me, Ned," he says, in his curt way.

'I jumped up, of course, and away after him down the gangway and up George Street. He strode along like a giant, and I at his elbow, panting. It was confoundedly hot. "Where on earth are you rushing me to, Charley?" I made bold to ask.

' "Here," he says.

' "Here" was a jeweller's shop. I couldn't imagine what he could want there. It seemed a sort of mad freak. He thrusts under my nose three rings, which looked very tiny on his big, brown palm, growling out – "For Maggie! Which?"

'I got a kind of scare at this. I couldn't make a sound, but I pointed at the one that sparkled white and blue. He put it in his waistcoat pocket, paid for it with a lot of sovereigns, and bolted out. When we got on board I was quite out of breath. "Shake hands, old chap," I gasped out. He gave me a thump on the back. "Give what orders you like to the boatswain when the hands turn-to," says he; "I am off duty this afternoon."

'Then he vanished from the deck for a while, but presently he came out of the cabin with Maggie, and these two went over the gangway publicly, before all hands, going for a walk together on that awful, blazing-hot day, with clouds of dust flying about. They came back after a few hours looking very staid, but didn't seem to have the slightest idea where they had been. Anyway, that's the answer they both made to Mrs Colchester's question at tea-time.

'And didn't she turn on Charley, with her voice like an old night-cabman's! "Rubbish. Don't know where you've been! Stuff and nonsense. You've walked the girl off her legs. Don't do it again."

'It's surprising how meek Charley could be with that old woman. Only on one occasion he whispered to me, "I'm jolly glad she isn't Maggie's aunt, except by marriage. That's no sort of relationship." But I think he let Maggie have too much of her own way. She was hopping all over that ship in her yachting skirt and a red tam o' shanter like a bright bird on a dead black tree. The old salts used to grin to themselves when they saw her coming along, and offered to teach her knots or splices. I believe she liked the men, for Charley's sake, I suppose.

'As you may imagine, the fiendish propensities of that cursed ship were never spoken of on board. Not in the cabin, at any rate. Only once on the homeward passage Charley said, incautiously, something about bringing all her crew home this time. Captain Colchester began to look uncomfortable at once, and that silly, hard-bitten old woman flew out at Charley as though he had said something indecent. I was quite confounded myself; as to Maggie, she sat completely mystified, opening her blue eyes very wide. Of course, before she was a day older she wormed it all out of me. She was a very difficult person to lie to.

' "How awful," she said, quite solemn. "So many poor fellows. I am glad the voyage is nearly over. I won't have a moment's peace about Charley now."

'I assured her Charley was all right. It took more than that ship knew to get over a seaman like Charley. And she agreed with me.

'Next day we got the tug off Dungeness; and when the tow-rope was fast

Charley rubbed his hands and said to me in an undertone: "We've baffled her, Ned."

' "Looks like it," I said, with a grin at him. It was beautiful weather, and the sea as smooth as a millpond. We went up the river without a shadow of trouble except once, when off Hole Haven, the brute took a sudden sheer and nearly had a barge anchored just clear of the fairway. But I was aft, looking after the steering, and she did not catch me napping that time. Charley came up on the poop, looking very concerned. "Close shave," says he.

' "Never mind, Charley," I answered, cheerily. "You've tamed her."

'We were to tow right up to the dock. The river pilot boarded us below Gravesend, and the first words I heard him say were: "You may just as well take your port anchor inboard at once, Mr Mate."

'This had been done when I went forward. I saw Maggie on the forecastle head enjoying the bustle and I begged her to go aft, but she took no notice of me, of course. Then Charley, who was very busy with the head gear, caught sight of her and shouted in his biggest voice: "Get off the forecastle head, Maggie. You're in the way here." For all answer she made a funny face at him, and I saw poor Charley turn away, hiding a smile. She was flushed with the excitement of getting home again, and her blue eyes seemed to snap electric sparks as she looked at the river. A collier brig had gone round just ahead of us, and our tug had to stop her engines in a hurry to avoid running into her.

'In a moment, as is usually the case, all the shipping in the reach seemed to get into a hopeless tangle. A schooner and a ketch got up a small collision all to themselves right in the middle of the river. It was exciting to watch, and, meantime, our tug remained stopped. Any other ship than that brute could have been coaxed to keep straight for a couple of minutes – but not she! Her head fell off at once, and she began to drift down, taking her tug along with her. I noticed a cluster of coasters at anchor within a quarter of a mile of us, and I thought I had better speak to the pilot. "If you let her get amongst that lot," I said, quietly, "she will grind some of them to bits before we get her out again."

' "Don't I know her!" cries he, stamping his foot in a perfect fury. And he outs with his whistle to make that bothered tug get the ship's head up again as quick as possible. He blew like mad, waving his arm to port, and presently we could see that the tug's engines had been set going ahead. Her paddles churned the water, but it was as if she had been trying to tow a rock – she couldn't get an inch out of that ship. Again the pilot blew his whistle, and waved his arm to port. We could see the tug's paddles turning faster and faster away, broad on our bow.

'For a moment tug and ship hung motionless in a crowd of moving shipping, and then the terrific strain that evil, stony-hearted brute would always put on everything tore the towing-chock clean out. The tow-rope surged over, snapping the iron stanchions of the head-rail one after another as if they had been sticks of sealing-wax. It was only then I noticed that in order to have a better view over our heads, Maggie had stepped upon the port anchor as it lay flat on the forecastle deck.

'It had been lowered properly into its hardwood beds, but there had been no time to take a turn with it. Anyway, it was quite secure as it was, for going into dock; but I could see directly that the tow-rope would sweep under the fluke in another second. My heart flew up right into my throat, but not before I had time to yell out: "Jump clear of that anchor!"'

'But I hadn't time to shriek out her name. I don't suppose she heard me at all. The first touch of the hawser against the fluke threw her down; she was up on her feet again quick as lightning, but she was up on the wrong side. I heard a horrid, scraping sound, and then that anchor, tipping over, rose up like something alive; its great, rough iron arm caught Maggie round the waist, seemed to clasp her close with a dreadful hug, and flung itself with her over and down in a terrific clang of iron, followed by heavy ringing blows that shook the ship from stem to stern – because the ring stopper held!'

'How horrible!' I exclaimed.

'I used to dream for years afterwards of anchors catching hold of girls,' said the man in tweeds, a little wildly. He shuddered. 'With a most pitiful howl Charley was over after her almost on the instant. But, Lord! he didn't see as much as a gleam of her red tam o' shanter in the water. Nothing! nothing whatever! In a moment there were half a dozen boats around us, and he got pulled into one. I, with the boatswain and the carpenter, let go the other anchor in a hurry and brought the ship up somehow. The pilot had gone silly. He walked up and down the forecastle head wringing his hands and muttering to himself: "Killing women, now! Killing women, now!" Not another word could you get out of him.

'Dusk fell, then a night black as pitch; and peering upon the river I heard a low, mournful hail, "Ship, ahoy!" Two Gravesend watermen came alongside. They had a lantern in their wherry, and looked up the ship's side, holding on to the ladder without a word. I saw in the patch of light a lot of loose, fair hair down there.'

He shuddered again.

'After the tide turned poor Maggie's body had floated clear of one of them big mooring buoys,' he explained. 'I crept aft, feeling half-dead, and managed to send a rocket up – to let the other searchers know, on the river. And then I slunk away forward like a cur, and spent the night sitting on the heel of the bowsprit so as to be as far as possible out of Charley's way.'

'Poor fellow!' I murmured.

'Yes. Poor fellow,' he repeated, musingly. 'That brute wouldn't let him – not even him – cheat her of her prey. But he made her fast in dock next morning. He did. We hadn't exchanged a word – not a single look for that matter. I didn't want to look at him. When the last rope was fast he put his hands to his head and stood gazing down at his feet as if trying to remember something. The men waited on the main deck for the words that end the voyage. Perhaps that is what he was trying to remember. I spoke for him. "That'll do, men."

'I never saw a crew leave a ship so quietly. They sneaked over the rail one after another, taking care not to bang their sea chests too heavily. They looked our way, but not one had the stomach to come up and offer to shake hands with the mate as is usual.

'I followed him all over the empty ship to and fro, here and there, with no living soul about but the two of us, because the old ship-keeper had locked himself up in the galley – both doors. Suddenly poor Charley mutters, in a crazy voice: "I'm done here," and strides down the gangway with me at his heels, up the dock, out at the gate, on towards Tower Hill. He used to take rooms with a decent old landlady in America Square, to be near his work.

'All at once he stops short, turns round, and comes back straight at me. "Ned," says he, "I am going home." I had the good luck to sight a four-wheeler and got him in just in time. His legs were beginning to give way. In our hall he fell down on a chair, and I'll never forget father's and mother's amazed, perfectly still faces as they stood over him. They couldn't under-stand what had happened to him till I blubbered out, "Maggie got drowned, yesterday, in the river."

'Mother let out a little cry. Father looks from him to me, and from me to him, as if comparing our faces – for, upon my soul, Charley did not resemble himself at all. Nobody moved; and the poor fellow raises his big brown hands slowly to his throat, and with one single tug rips everything open – collar, shirt, waistcoat – a perfect wreck and ruin of a man. Father and I got him upstairs somehow, and mother pretty nearly killed herself nursing him through a brain fever.'

The man in tweeds nodded at me significantly.

'Ah! there was nothing that could be done with that brute. She had a devil in her.'

'Where's your brother?' I asked, expecting to hear he was dead. But he was commanding a smart steamer on the China coast, and never came home now.

Jermyn fetched a heavy sigh, and the handkerchief being now sufficiently dry, put it up tenderly to his red and lamentable nose.

'She was a ravening beast,' the man in tweeds started again. 'Old Col-chester put his foot down and resigned. And would you believe it? Apse & Sons wrote to ask whether he wouldn't reconsider his decision! Anything to save the good name of the *Apse Family*.' Old Colchester went to the office then and said that he would take charge again but only to sail her out into the North Sea and scuttle her there. He was nearly off his chump. He used to be darkish iron-grey, but his hair went snow-white in a fortnight. And Mr Lucian Apse (they had known each other as young men) pretended not to notice it. Eh? Here's infatuation if you like! Here's pride for you!

'They jumped at the first man they could get to take her, for fear of the scandal of the *Apse Family* not being able to find a skipper. He was a festive soul, I believe, but he stuck to her grim and hard. Wilmot was his second mate. A harum-scarum fellow, and pretending to a great scorn for all the girls. The fact is he was really timid. But let only one of them do as much as lift her little finger in encouragement, and there was nothing that could hold the beggar. As apprentice, once, he deserted abroad after a petticoat, and would have gone to the dogs then if his skipper hadn't taken the trouble to find him and lug him by the ears out of some house of perdition or other.

'It was said that one of the firm had been heard once to express a hope that this brute of a ship would get lost soon. I can hardly credit the tale, unless it might have been Mr Alfred Apse, whom the family didn't think much of. They had him in the office, but he was considered a bad egg altogether, always flying off to race meetings and coming home drunk. You would have thought that a ship so full of deadly tricks would run herself ashore someday out of sheer cussedness. But not she! She was going to last for ever. She had a nose to keep off the bottom.'

Jermyn made a grunt of approval.

'A ship after a pilot's own heart, eh?' jeered the man in tweeds. 'Well, Wilmot managed it. He was the man for it, but even he, perhaps, couldn't have done the trick without the green-eyed governess, or nurse, or whatever she was to the children of Mr and Mrs Pamphilius.

'Those people were passengers in her from Port Adelaide to the Cape. Well, the ship went out and anchored outside for the day. The skipper – hospitable soul – had a lot of guests from town to a farewell lunch – as usual with him. It was five in the evening before the last shore-boat left the side, and the weather looked ugly and dark in the gulf. There was no reason for him to get under way. However, as he had told everybody he was going that day, he imagined it was proper to do so anyhow. But as he had no mind after all these festivities to tackle the straits in the dark, with a scant wind, he gave orders to keep the ship under lower topsails and foresail as close as she would lie, dodging along the land till the morning. Then he sought his virtuous couch. The mate was on deck, having his face washed very clean with hard rain squalls. Wilmot relieved him at midnight.

'The *Apse Family* had, as you observed, a house on her poop . . .'

'A big, ugly white thing, sticking up,' Jermyn murmured, sadly, at the fire.

'That's it: a companion for the cabin stairs and a sort of chart-room combined. The rain drove in gusts on the sleepy Wilmot. The ship was then surging slowly to the southward, close hauled, with the coast within three miles or so to windward. There was nothing to look out for in that part of the gulf, and Wilmot went round to dodge the squalls under the lee of that chart-room, whose door on that side was open. The night was black, like a barrel of coal-tar. And then he heard a woman's voice whispering to him.

'That confounded green-eyed girl of the Pamphilius people had put the kids to bed a long time ago, of course, but it seems couldn't get to sleep herself. She heard eight bells struck, and the chief mate come below to turn in. She waited a bit, then got into her dressing-gown and stole across the empty saloon and up the stairs into the chart-room. She sat down on the settee near the open door to cool herself, I dare say.

'I suppose when she whispered to Wilmot it was as if somebody had struck a match in the fellow's brain. I don't know how it was they had got so very thick. I fancy he had met her ashore a few times before. I couldn't make it out, because, when telling the story, Wilmot would break off to swear something awful at every second word. We had met on the quay in Sydney, and he had an apron of sacking up to his chin, a big whip in his hand. A wagon-driver. Glad to do anything not to starve. That's what he had come down to.

'However, there he was, with his head inside the door, on the girl's shoulder as likely as not – officer of the watch! The helmsman, on giving his evidence afterwards, said that he shouted several times that the binnacle lamp had gone out. It didn't matter to him, because his orders were to "sail her close". "I thought it funny," he said, "that the ship should keep on falling off in squalls, but I luffed her up every time as close as I was able. It was so dark I couldn't see my hand before my face, and the rain came in bucketfuls on my head."

'The truth was that at every squall the wind hauled aft a little, till gradually the ship came to be heading straight for the coast, without a single soul in her being aware of it. Wilmot himself confessed that he had not been near the standard compass for an hour. He might well have confessed! The first thing he knew was the man on the lookout shouting blue murder forward there.

'He tore his neck free, he says, and yelled back at him: "What do you say?"

' "I think I hear breakers ahead, sir," howled the man, and came rushing aft with the rest of the watch, in the "awfullest blinding deluge that ever fell from the sky", Wilmot says. For a second or so he was so scared and bewildered that he could not remember on which side of the gulf the ship was. He wasn't a good officer, but he was a seaman all the same. He pulled himself together in a second, and the right orders sprang to his lips without thinking. They were to hard up with the helm and shiver the main and mizzen-topsails.

'It seems that the sails actually fluttered. He couldn't see them, but he heard them rattling and banging above his head. "No use! She was too slow in going off," he went on, his dirty face twitching, and the damn'd carter's whip shaking in his hand. "She seemed to stick fast." And then the flutter of the canvas above his head ceased. At this critical moment the wind hauled aft again with a gust, filling the sails and sending the ship with a great way upon the rocks on her lee bow. She had overreached herself in her last little game. Her time had come – the hour, the man, the black night, the treacherous gust of wind – the right woman to put an end to her. The brute deserved nothing better. Strange are the instruments of providence. There's a sort of poetical justice – '

The man in tweeds looked hard at me.

'The first ledge she went over stripped the false keel off her. Rip! The skipper, rushing out of his berth, found a crazy woman, in a red flannel dressing-gown, flying round and round the cuddy, screeching like a cockatoo.

'The next bump knocked her clean under the cabin table. It also started the stern-post and carried away the rudder, and then that brute ran up a shelving, rocky shore, tearing her bottom out, till she stopped short, and the foremast dropped over the bows like a gangway.'

'Anybody lost?' I asked.

'No one, unless that fellow, Wilmot,' answered the gentleman, unknown to Miss Blank, looking round for his cap. 'And his case was worse than drowning for a man. Everybody got ashore all right. Gale didn't come on till next day, dead from the west, and broke up that brute in a surprisingly short time. It was as though she had been rotten at heart.' . . . He changed his tone, 'Rain left off? I must get my bike and rush home to dinner. I live in Herne Bay – came out for a spin this morning.'

He nodded at me in a friendly way, and went out with a swagger.

'Do you know who he is, Jermyn?' I asked.

The North Sea pilot shook his head, dismally. 'Fancy losing a ship in that silly fashion! Oh, dear! oh dear!' he groaned in lugubrious tones, spreading his damp handkerchief again like a curtain before the glowing grate.

On going out I exchanged a glance and a smile (strictly proper) with the respectable Miss Blank, barmaid of the Three Crows.

The Duel

I

Napoleon I, whose career had the quality of a duel against the whole of Europe, disliked duelling between the officers of his army. The great military emperor was not a swashbuckler, and had little respect for tradition.

Nevertheless, a story of duelling, which became a legend in the army, runs through the epic of imperial wars. To the surprise and admiration of their fellows, two officers, like insane artists trying to gild refined gold or paint the lily, pursued a private contest through the years of universal carnage. They were officers of cavalry, and their connection with the high-spirited but fanciful animal which carries men into battle seems particularly appropriate. It would be difficult to imagine for heroes of this legend two officers of infantry of the line, for example, whose fantasy is tamed by much walking exercise, and whose valour necessarily must be of a more plodding kind. As to gunners or engineers, whose heads are kept cool on a diet of mathematics, it is simply unthinkable.

The names of the two officers were Feraud and D'Hubert, and they were both lieutenants in a regiment of hussars, but not in the same regiment.

Feraud was doing regimental work, but Lieutenant D'Hubert had the good fortune to be attached to the person of the general commanding the division, as *officier d'ordonnance*. It was in Strasbourg, and in this agreeable and important garrison they were enjoying greatly a short interval of peace. They were enjoying it, though both intensely warlike, because it was a sword-sharpening, firelock-cleaning peace, dear to a military heart and undamaging to military prestige, inasmuch that no one believed in its sincerity or duration.

Under those historical circumstances, so favourable to the proper appreciation of military leisure, Lieutenant D'Hubert, one fine afternoon, made his way along a quiet street of a cheerful suburb towards Lieutenant Feraud's quarters, which were in a private house with a garden at the back, belonging to an old maiden lady.

His knock at the door was answered instantly by a young maid in Alsatian costume. Her fresh complexion and her long eyelashes, lowered demurely at the sight of the tall officer, caused Lieutenant D'Hubert, who was accessible to aesthetic impressions, to relax the cold, severe gravity of his face. At the same time he observed that the girl had over her arm a pair of hussar's breeches, blue with a red stripe.

'Lieutenant Feraud in?' he enquired, benevolently.

'Oh, no, sir! He went out at six this morning.'

The pretty maid tried to close the door. Lieutenant D'Hubert, opposing this move with gentle firmness, stepped into the ante-room, jingling his spurs.

'Come, my dear! You don't mean to say he has not been home since six o'clock this morning?'

Saying these words, Lieutenant D'Hubert opened without ceremony the door of a room so comfortably and neatly ordered that only from internal evidence in the shape of boots, uniforms, and military accoutrements did he acquire the conviction that it was Lieutenant Feraud's room. And he saw also that Lieutenant Feraud was not at home. The truthful maid had followed him, and raised her candid eyes to his face.

'H'm!' said Lieutenant D'Hubert, greatly disappointed, for he had already visited all the haunts where a lieutenant of hussars could be found of a fine afternoon. 'So he's out? And do you happen to know, my dear, why he went out at six this morning?'

'No,' she answered, readily. 'He came home late last night, and snored. I heard him when I got up at five. Then he dressed himself in his oldest uniform and went out. Service, I suppose.'

'Service? Not a bit of it!' cried Lieutenant D'Hubert. 'Learn, my angel, that he went out thus early to fight a duel with a civilian.'

She heard this news without a quiver of her dark eyelashes. It was very obvious that the actions of Lieutenant Feraud were generally above criticism. She only looked up for a moment in mute surprise, and Lieutenant D'Hubert concluded from this absence of emotion that she must have seen Lieutenant Feraud since the morning. He looked around the room.

'Come!' he insisted, with confidential familiarity. 'He's perhaps some-where in the house now?'

She shook her head.

'So much the worse for him!' continued Lieutenant D'Hubert, in a tone of anxious conviction. 'But he has been home this morning.'

This time the pretty maid nodded slightly.

'He has!' cried Lieutenant D'Hubert. 'And went out again? What for? Couldn't he keep quietly indoors! What a lunatic! My dear girl – '

Lieutenant D'Hubert's natural kindness of disposition and strong sense of comradeship helped his powers of observation. He changed his tone to a most insinuating softness, and, gazing at the hussar's breeches hanging over the arm of the girl, he appealed to the interest she took in Lieutenant Feraud's comfort and happiness. He was pressing and persuasive. He used his eyes, which were kind and fine, with excellent effect. His anxiety to get hold at once of Lieutenant Feraud, for Lieutenant Feraud's own good, seemed so genuine that at last it overcame the girl's unwillingness to speak.

Unluckily she had not much to tell. Lieutenant Feraud had returned home shortly before ten, had walked straight into his room, and had thrown himself on his bed to resume his slumbers. She had heard him snore rather louder than before far into the afternoon. Then he got up, put on his best uniform, and went out. That was all she knew.

She raised her eyes, and Lieutenant D'Hubert stared into them incredulously.

'It's incredible. Gone parading the town in his best uniform! My dear child, don't you know he ran that civilian through this morning? Clean through, as you spit a hare.'

The pretty maid heard the gruesome intelligence without any signs of distress. But she pressed her lips together thoughtfully.

'He isn't parading the town,' she remarked in a low tone. 'Far from it.'

'The civilian's family is making an awful row,' continued Lieutenant D'Hubert, pursuing his train of thought. 'And the general is very angry. It's one of the best families in the town. Feraud ought to have kept close at least – '

'What will the general do to him?' enquired the girl, anxiously.

'He won't have his head cut off, to be sure,' grumbled Lieutenant D'Hubert. 'His conduct is positively indecent. He's making no end of trouble for himself by this sort of bravado.'

'But he isn't parading the town,' the maid insisted in a shy murmur.

'Why, yes! Now I think of it, I haven't seen him anywhere about. What on earth has he done with himself?'

'He's gone to pay a call,' suggested the maid, after a moment of silence.

Lieutenant D'Hubert started.

'A call! Do you mean a call on a lady? The cheek of the man! And how do you know this, my dear?'

Without concealing her woman's scorn for the denseness of the masculine mind, the pretty maid reminded him that Lieutenant Feraud had arrayed himself in his best uniform before going out. He had also put on his newest dolman, she added, in a tone as if this conversation were getting on her nerves, and turned away brusquely.

Lieutenant D'Hubert, without questioning the accuracy of the deduction, did not see that it advanced him much on his official quest. For his quest after Lieutenant Feraud had an official character. He did not know any of the women this fellow, who had run a man through in the morning, was likely to visit in the afternoon. The two young men knew each other but slightly. He bit his gloved finger in perplexity.

'Call!' he exclaimed. 'Call on the devil!'

The girl, with her back to him, and folding the hussars breeches on a chair, protested with a vexed little laugh: 'Oh, dear, no! On Madame de Lionne.'

Lieutenant D'Hubert whistled softly. Madame de Lionne was the wife of a high official who had a well-known salon and some pretensions to sensibility and elegance. The husband was a civilian, and old; but the society of the salon was young and military. Lieutenant D'Hubert had whistled, not because the idea of pursuing Lieutenant Feraud into that very salon was disagreeable to him, but because, having arrived in Strasbourg only lately, he had not had the time as yet to get an introduction to Madame de Lionne. And what was that swashbuckler Feraud doing there, he wondered. He did not seem the sort of man who –

'Are you certain of what you say?' asked Lieutenant D'Hubert.

The girl was perfectly certain. Without turning round to look at him, she explained that the coachman of their next-door neighbours knew the *maître-d'hôtel* of Madame de Lionne. In this way she had her information. And she was perfectly certain. In giving this assurance she sighed. Lieutenant Feraud called there nearly every afternoon, she added.

'Ah, bah!' exclaimed D'Hubert, ironically. His opinion of Madame de Lionne went down several degrees. Lieutenant Feraud did not seem to him specially worthy of attention on the part of a woman with a reputation for sensibility and elegance. But there was no saying. At bottom they were all alike – very practical rather than idealistic. Lieutenant D'Hubert, however, did not allow his mind to dwell on these considerations.

'By thunder!' he reflected aloud. 'The general goes there sometimes. If he happens to find the fellow making eyes at the lady there will be the devil to pay! Our general is not a very accommodating person, I can tell you.'

'Go quickly, then! Don't stand here now I've told you where he is!' cried the girl, colouring to the eyes.

'Thanks, my dear! I don't know what I would have done without you.'

After manifesting his gratitude in an aggressive way, which at first was repulsed violently, and then submitted to with a sudden and still more repellent indifference, Lieutenant D'Hubert took his departure.

He clanked and jingled along the streets with a martial swagger. To run a comrade to earth in a drawing-room where he was not known did not trouble him in the least. A uniform is a passport. His position as *officier d'ordonnance* of the general added to his assurance. Moreover, now that he knew where to find Lieutenant Feraud, he had no option. It was a service matter.

Madame de Lionne's house had an excellent appearance. A man in livery, opening the door of a large drawing-room with a waxed floor, shouted his name and stood aside to let him pass. It was a reception day. The ladies wore big hats surcharged with a profusion of feathers; their bodies, sheathed in clinging white gowns from the armpits to the tips of the low satin shoes, looked sylph-like and cool in a great display of bare necks and arms. The men who talked with them, on the contrary, were arrayed heavily in multi-coloured garments with collars up to their ears and thick sashes round their waists. Lieutenant D'Hubert made his unabashed way across the room and, bowing low before a sylph-like form reclining on a couch, offered his apologies for this intrusion, which nothing could excuse but the extreme urgency of the service order he had to communicate to his comrade Feraud. He proposed to himself to return presently in a more regular manner and beg forgiveness for interrupting the interesting conversation . . .

A bare arm was extended towards him with gracious nonchalance even before he had finished speaking. He pressed the hand respectfully to his lips, and made the mental remark that it was bony. Madame de Lionne was a blonde, with too fine a skin and a long face.

'*C'est ça!*' she said, with an ethereal smile, disclosing a set of large teeth. 'Come this evening to plead for your forgiveness.'

'I will not fail, madame.'

Meantime, Lieutenant Feraud, splendid in his new dolman and the extremely polished boots of his calling, sat on a chair within a foot of the couch, one hand resting on his thigh, the other twirling his moustache to a point. At a significant glance from D'Hubert he rose without alacrity, and followed him into the recess of a window.

'What is it you want with me?' he asked, with astonishing indifference. Lieutenant D'Hubert could not imagine that in the innocence of his heart and simplicity of his conscience Lieutenant Feraud took a view of his duel in which neither remorse nor yet a rational apprehension of consequences had any place. Though he had no clear recollection how the quarrel had originated (it was begun in an establishment where beer and wine are drunk late at night), he had not the slightest doubt of being himself the outraged party. He had had two experienced friends for his seconds. Everything had been done according to the rules governing that sort of adventures. And a duel is obviously fought for the purpose of someone being at least hurt, if not killed outright. The civilian got hurt. That also was in order. Lieutenant Feraud was perfectly tranquil; but Lieutenant D'Hubert took it for affectation, and spoke with a certain vivacity.

'I am directed by the general to give you the order to go at once to your quarters, and remain there under close arrest.'

It was now the turn of Lieutenant Feraud to be astonished. 'What the devil are you telling me there?' he murmured, faintly, and fell into such profound wonder that he could only follow mechanically the motions of Lieutenant D'Hubert. The two officers, one tall, with an interesting face and a moustache the colour of ripe corn, the other, short and sturdy, with a hooked nose and a thick crop of black curly hair, approached the mistress of the house to take their leave. Madame de Lionne, a woman of eclectic taste, smiled upon these armed young men with impartial sensibility and an equal share of interest. Madame de Lionne took her delight in the infinite variety of the human species. All the other eyes in the drawing-room followed the departing officers; and when they had gone out one or two men, who had already heard of the duel, imparted the information to the sylph-like ladies, who received it with faint shrieks of humane concern.

Meantime, the two hussars walked side by side, Lieutenant Feraud trying to master the hidden reason of things which in this instance eluded the grasp of his intellect, Lieutenant D'Hubert feeling annoyed at the part he had to play, because the general's instructions were that he should see personally that Lieutenant Feraud carried out his orders to the letter, and at once.

'The chief seems to know this animal,' he thought, eyeing his companion, whose round face, round eyes and even the twisted-up jet-black little moustache seemed animated by a mental exasperation against the incomprehensible. And aloud he observed rather reproachfully, 'The general is in a devilish fury with you!'

Lieutenant Feraud stopped short on the edge of the pavement, and cried in accents of unmistakable sincerity, 'What on earth for?' The innocence of the fiery Gascon soul was depicted in the manner in which he seized his head in both hands as if to prevent it bursting with perplexity.

'For the duel,' said Lieutenant D'Hubert, curtly. He was annoyed greatly by this sort of perverse fooling.

'The duel! The . . .'

Lieutenant Feraud passed from one paroxysm of astonishment into another. He dropped his hands and walked on slowly, trying to reconcile this information with the state of his own feelings. It was impossible. He burst out indignantly, 'Was I to let that sauerkraut-eating civilian wipe his boots on the uniform of the 7th Hussars?'

Lieutenant D'Hubert could not remain altogether unmoved by that simple sentiment. This little fellow was a lunatic, he thought to himself, but there was something in what he said.

'Of course, I don't know how far you were justified,' he began, soothingly. 'And the general himself may not be exactly informed. Those people have been deafening him with their lamentations.'

'Ah! the general is not exactly informed,' mumbled Lieutenant Feraud, walking faster and faster as his choler at the injustice of his fate began to rise. 'He is not exactly . . . And he orders me under close arrest, with God knows what afterwards!'

'Don't excite yourself like this,' remonstrated the other. 'Your adversary's people are very influential, you know, and it looks bad enough on the face of it. The general had to take notice of their complaint at once. I don't think he means to be over-severe with you. It's the best thing for you to be kept out of sight for a while.'

'I am very much obliged to the general,' muttered Lieutenant Feraud through his teeth. 'And perhaps you would say I ought to be grateful to you, too, for the trouble you have taken to hunt me up in the drawing-room of a lady who – '

'Frankly,' interrupted Lieutenant D'Hubert, with an innocent laugh, 'I think you ought to be. I had no end of trouble to find out where you were. It wasn't exactly the place for you to disport yourself in under the circumstances. If the general had caught you there making eyes at the goddess of the temple . . . oh, my word! . . . He hates to be bothered with complaints against his officers, you know. And it looked uncommonly like sheer bravado.'

The two officers had arrived now at the street door of Lieutenant Feraud's lodgings. The latter turned towards his companion. 'Lieutenant D'Hubert,' he said, 'I have something to say to you, which can't be said very well in the street. You can't refuse to come up.'

The pretty maid had opened the door. Lieutenant Feraud brushed past her brusquely, and she raised her scared and questioning eyes to Lieutenant D'Hubert, who could do nothing but shrug his shoulders slightly as he followed with marked reluctance.

In his room Lieutenant Feraud unhooked the clasp, flung his new dolman on the bed, and, folding his arms across his chest, turned to the other hussar.

'Do you imagine I am a man to submit tamely to injustice?' he enquired, in a boisterous voice.

'Oh, do be reasonable!' remonstrated Lieutenant D'Hubert.

'I am reasonable! I am perfectly reasonable!' retorted the other with ominous restraint. 'I can't call the general to account for his behaviour, but you are going to answer me for yours.'

'I can't listen to this nonsense,' murmured Lieutenant D'Hubert, making a slightly contemptuous grimace.

'You call this nonsense? It seems to me a perfectly plain statement. Unless you don't understand French.'

'What on earth do you mean?'

'I mean,' screamed suddenly Lieutenant Feraud, 'to cut off your ears to teach you to disturb me with the general's orders when I am talking to a lady!'

A profound silence followed this mad declaration; and through the open window Lieutenant D'Hubert heard the little birds singing sanely in the garden. He said, preserving his calm, 'Why! If you take that tone, of course I shall hold myself at your disposition whenever you are at liberty to attend to this affair; but I don't think you will cut my ears off.'

'I am going to attend to it at once,' declared Lieutenant Feraud, with extreme truculence. 'If you are thinking of displaying your airs and graces tonight in Madame de Lionne's salon you are very much mistaken.'

'Really!' said Lieutenant D'Hubert, who was beginning to feel irritated, 'you are an impracticable sort of fellow. The general's orders to me were to put you under arrest, not to carve you into small pieces. Good-morning!' And turning his back on the little Gascon, who, always sober in his potations, was as though born intoxicated with the sunshine of his vine-ripening country, the northman, who could drink hard on occasion but was born sober under the watery skies of Picardy, made for the door. Hearing, however, the unmistakable sound behind his back of a sword drawn from the scabbard, he had no option but to stop.

'Devil take this mad southerner!' he thought, spinning round and surveying with composure the warlike posture of Lieutenant Feraud, with a bare sword in his hand.

'At once! – at once!' stuttered Feraud, beside himself.

'You had my answer,' said the other, keeping his temper very well.

At first he had been only vexed, and somewhat amused; but now his face got clouded. He was asking himself seriously how he could manage to get away. It was impossible to run from a man with a sword, and as to fighting him, it seemed completely out of the question. He waited awhile, then said exactly what was in his heart.

'Drop this! I won't fight with you. I won't be made ridiculous.'

'Ah, you won't?' hissed the Gascon. 'I suppose you prefer to be made infamous. Do you hear what I say? . . . Infamous! Infamous! Infamous!' he shrieked, rising and falling on his toes and getting very red in the face.

Lieutenant D'Hubert, on the contrary, became very pale at the sound of the unsavoury word for a moment, then flushed pink to the roots of his fair hair. 'But you can't go out to fight; you are under arrest, you lunatic!' he objected, with angry scorn.

'There's the garden: it's big enough to lay out your long carcass in,' spluttered the other with such ardour that somehow the anger of the cooler man subsided.

'This is perfectly absurd,' he said, glad enough to think he had found a way out of it for the moment. 'We shall never get any of our comrades to serve as seconds. It's preposterous.'

'Seconds! Damn the seconds! We don't want any seconds. Don't you worry about any seconds. I shall send word to your friends to come and bury you when I am done. And if you want any witnesses, I'll send word to the old girl to put her head out of a window at the back. Stay! There's the gardener. He'll do. He's as deaf as a post, but he has two eyes in his head. Come along! I will teach you, my staff officer, that the carrying about of a general's orders is not always child's play.'

While thus discoursing he had unbuckled his empty scabbard. He sent it flying under the bed, and, lowering the point of the sword, brushed past the perplexed Lieutenant D'Hubert, exclaiming, 'Follow me!' Directly he had flung open the door a faint shriek was heard and the pretty maid, who had been listening at the keyhole, staggered away, putting the backs of her hands over her eyes. Feraud did not seem to see her, but she ran after him and seized his left arm. He shook her off, and then she rushed towards Lieutenant D'Hubert and clawed at the sleeve of his uniform.

'Wretched man!' she sobbed. 'Is this what you wanted to find him for?'

'Let me go,' entreated Lieutenant D'Hubert, trying to disengage himself gently. 'It's like being in a madhouse,' he protested, with exasperation. 'Do let me go! I won't do him any harm.'

A fiendish laugh from Lieutenant Feraud was his comment on that assurance. 'Come along!' he shouted, with a stamp of his foot.

And Lieutenant D'Hubert did follow. He could do nothing else. Yet in vindication of his sanity it must be recorded that as he passed through the ante-room the notion of opening the street door and bolting out presented itself to this brave youth, only of course to be instantly dismissed, for he felt sure that the other would pursue him without shame or compunction. And the prospect of an officer of hussars being chased along the street by another officer of hussars with a naked sword could not be for a moment entertained. Therefore he followed into the garden. Behind them the girl tottered out, too. With ashy lips and wild, scared eyes, she surrendered herself to a dreadful curiosity. She had also the notion of rushing if need be between Lieutenant Feraud and death.

The deaf gardener, utterly unconscious of approaching footsteps, went on watering his flowers till Lieutenant Feraud thumped him on the back. Beholding suddenly an enraged man flourishing a big sabre, the old chap trembling in all his limbs dropped the watering-pot. At once Lieutenant Feraud kicked it away with great animosity, and, seizing the gardener by the throat, backed him against a tree. He held him there, shouting in his ear, 'Stay here, and look on! You understand? You've got to look on! Don't dare budge from the spot!'

Lieutenant D'Hubert came slowly down the walk, unclasping his dolman with unconcealed disgust. Even then, with his hand already on the hilt of his sword, he hesitated to draw till a roar, *'En garde, fichtre!* What do you think you came here for?' and the rush of his adversary forced him to put himself as quickly as possible in a posture of defence.

The clash of arms filled that prim garden, which hitherto had known no more warlike sound than the click of clipping shears; and presently the upper part of an old lady's body was projected out of a window upstairs. She tossed her arms above her white cap, scolding in a cracked voice. The gardener remained glued to the tree, his toothless mouth open in idiotic astonishment, and a little farther up the path the pretty girl, as if spellbound to a small grass plot, ran a few steps this way and that, wringing her hands and muttering crazily. She did not rush between the combatants: the onslaughts of Lieutenant Feraud were so fierce that her heart failed her. Lieutenant D'Hubert, his faculties concentrated upon defence, needed all the skill and science of the sword to stop the rushes of his adversary. Twice already he had to break ground. It bothered him to feel his foothold made insecure by the round, dry gravel of the path rolling under the hard soles of his boots. This was most unsuitable ground, he thought, keeping a watchful, narrowed gaze, shaded by long eyelashes, upon the fiery stare of his thick-set adversary. This absurd affair would ruin his reputation of a sensible, well-behaved, promising young officer. It would damage, at any rate, his immediate prospects, and lose him the good-will of his general. These worldly preoccupations were no doubt misplaced in view of the solemnity of the moment. A duel, whether regarded as a ceremony in the cult of honour, or even when reduced in its moral essence to a form of manly sport, demands a perfect singleness of intention, a homicidal austerity of mood. On the other hand, this vivid concern for his future had not a bad effect inasmuch as it began to rouse the anger of Lieutenant D'Hubert. Some seventy seconds had elapsed since they had crossed blades, and Lieutenant D'Hubert had to break ground again in order to avoid impaling his reckless adversary like a beetle for a cabinet of specimens. The result was that misapprehending the motive, Lieutenant Feraud with a triumphant sort of snarl pressed his attack.

'This enraged animal will have me against the wall directly,' thought Lieutenant D'Hubert. He imagined himself much closer to the house than he was, and he dared not turn his head; it seemed to him that he was keeping his adversary off with his eyes rather more than with his point. Lieutenant Feraud crouched and bounded with a fierce tigerish agility fit to trouble the stoutest heart. But what was more appalling than the fury of a wild beast, accomplishing in all innocence of heart a natural function, was the fixity of savage purpose man alone is capable of displaying. Lieutenant D'Hubert in the midst of his worldly preoccupations perceived it at last. It was an absurd and damaging affair to be drawn into, but whatever silly intention the fellow had started with, it was clear enough that by this time he meant to kill – nothing less. He meant it with an intensity of will utterly beyond the inferior faculties of a tiger.

As is the case with constitutionally brave men, the full view of the danger interested Lieutenant D'Hubert. And directly he got properly interested, the length of his arm and the coolness of his head told in his favour. It was the turn of Lieutenant Feraud to recoil, with a bloodcurdling grunt of baffled rage. He made a swift feint, and then rushed straight forward.

'Ah! you would, would you?' Lieutenant D'Hubert exclaimed, mentally. The combat had lasted nearly two minutes, time enough for any man to get embittered, apart from the merits of the quarrel. And all at once it was over. Trying to close breast to breast under his adversary's guard Lieutenant Feraud received a slash on his shortened arm. He did not feel it in the least, but it checked his rush, and his feet slipping on the gravel he fell backwards with great violence. The shock jarred his boiling brain into the perfect quietude of insensibility. Simultaneously with his fall the pretty servant-girl shrieked; but the old maiden lady at the window ceased her scolding, and began to cross herself piously.

Beholding his adversary stretched out perfectly still, his face to the sky, Lieutenant D'Hubert thought he had killed him outright. The impression of having slashed hard enough to cut his man clean in two abode with him for a while in an exaggerated memory of the right good-will he had put into the blow. He dropped on his knees hastily by the side of the prostrate body. Discovering that not even the arm was severed, a slight sense of disappointment mingled with the feeling of relief. The fellow deserved the worst. But truly he did not want the death of that sinner. The affair was ugly enough as it stood, and Lieutenant D'Hubert addressed himself at once to the task of stopping the bleeding. In this task it was his fate to be ridiculously impeded by the pretty maid. Rending the air with screams of horror, she attacked him from behind and, twining her fingers in his hair, tugged back at his head. Why she should choose to hinder him at this precise moment he could not in the least understand. He did not try. It was all like a very wicked and harassing dream. Twice to save himself from being pulled over he had to rise and fling her off. He did this stoically, without a word, kneeling down again at once to go on with his work. But the third time, his work being done, he seized her and held her arms pinned to her body. Her cap was half off, her face was red, her eyes blazed with crazy boldness. He looked mildly into them while she called him a wretch, a traitor and a murderer many times in succession. This did not annoy him so much as the conviction that she had managed to scratch his face abundantly. Ridicule would be added to the scandal of the story. He imagined the adorned tale making its way through the garrison of the town, through the whole army on the frontier, with every possible distortion of motive and sentiment and circumstance, spreading a doubt upon the sanity of his conduct and the distinction of his taste even to the very ears of his honourable family. It was all very well for that fellow Feraud, who had no connections, no family to speak of, and no quality but courage, which, anyhow, was a matter of course, and possessed by every single trooper in the whole mass of French cavalry. Still holding down the arms of the girl in a strong grip, Lieutenant D'Hubert glanced over his shoulder. Lieutenant Feraud had opened his eyes. He did not move. Like a man just waking from a deep sleep he stared without any expression at the evening sky.

Lieutenant D'Hubert's urgent shouts to the old gardener produced no effect – not so much as to make him shut his toothless mouth. Then he remembered that the man was stone deaf. All that time the girl struggled, not with maidenly coyness, but like a pretty, dumb fury, kicking his shins now and then. He continued to hold her as if in a vice, his instinct telling him that were he to let her go she would fly at his eyes. But he was greatly humiliated by his position. At last she gave up. She was more exhausted than appeased, he feared. Nevertheless, he attempted to get out of this wicked dream by way of negotiation.

'Listen to me,' he said, as calmly as he could. 'Will you promise to run for a surgeon if I let you go?'

With real affliction he heard her declare that she would do nothing of the kind. On the contrary, her sobbed out intention was to remain in the garden, and fight tooth and nail for the protection of the vanquished man. This was shocking.

'My dear child!' he cried in despair, 'is it possible that you think me capable of murdering a wounded adversary? Is it . . . Be quiet, you little wild cat, you!'

They struggled. A thick, drowsy voice said behind him, 'What are you after with that girl?'

Lieutenant Feraud had raised himself on his good arm. He was looking sleepily at his other arm, at the mess of blood on his uniform, at a small red pool on the ground, at his sabre lying a foot away on the path. Then he laid himself down gently again to think it all out, as far as a thundering headache would permit of mental operations.

Lieutenant D'Hubert released the girl who crouched at once by the side of the other lieutenant. The shades of night were falling on the little trim garden with this touching group, whence proceeded low murmurs of sorrow and compassion, with other feeble sounds of a different character, as if an imperfectly awake invalid were trying to swear. Lieutenant D'Hubert went away.

He passed through the silent house, and congratulated himself upon the dusk concealing his gory hands and scratched face from the passers-by. But this story could by no means be concealed. He dreaded the discredit and ridicule above everything, and was painfully aware of sneaking through the back streets in the manner of a murderer. Presently the sounds of a flute coming out of the open window of a lighted upstairs room in a modest house interrupted his dismal reflections. It was being played with a persevering virtuosity, and through the fioriture of the tune one could hear the regular thumping of the foot beating time on the floor.

Lieutenant D'Hubert shouted a name, which was that of an army surgeon whom he knew fairly well. The sounds of the flute ceased, and the musician appeared at the window, his instrument still in his hand, peering into the street.

'Who calls? You, D'Hubert? What brings you this way?'

He did not like to be disturbed at the hour when he was playing the flute. He was a man whose hair had turned grey already in the thankless task of tying up wounds on battlefields where others reaped advancement and glory.

'I want you to go at once and see Feraud. You know Lieutenant Feraud? He lives down the second street. It's but a step from here.'

'What's the matter with him?'

'Wounded.'

'Are you sure?'

'Sure!' cried D'Hubert. 'I come from there.'

'That's amusing,' said the elderly surgeon. Amusing was his favourite word; but the expression of his face when he pronounced it never corresponded. He was a stolid man. 'Come in,' he added. 'I'll get ready in a moment.'

'Thanks! I will. I want to wash my hands in your room.'

Lieutenant D'Hubert found the surgeon occupied in unscrewing his flute, and packing the pieces methodically in a case. He turned his head. 'Water there – in the corner. Your hands do want washing.'

'I've stopped the bleeding,' said Lieutenant D'Hubert. 'But you had better make haste. It's rather more than ten minutes ago, you know.'

The surgeon did not hurry his movements.

'What's the matter? Dressing came off? That's amusing. I've been at work in the hospital all day but I've been told this morning by somebody that he had come off without a scratch.'

'Not the same duel probably,' growled moodily Lieutenant D'Hubert, wiping his hands on a coarse towel.

'Not the same . . . What? Another. It would take the very devil to make me go out twice in one day.' The surgeon looked narrowly at Lieutenant D'Hubert. 'How did you come by that scratched face? Both sides, too – and symmetrical. It's amusing.'

'Very!' snarled Lieutenant D'Hubert. 'And you will find his slashed arm amusing, too. It will keep both of you amused for quite a long time.'

The doctor was mystified and impressed by the brusque bitterness of Lieutenant D'Hubert's tone. They left the house together, and in the street he was still more mystified by his conduct.

'Aren't you coming with me?' he asked.

'No,' said Lieutenant D'Hubert. 'You can find the house by yourself. The front door will be standing open very likely.'

'All right. Where's his room?'

'Ground floor. But you had better go right through and look in the garden first.'

This astonishing piece of information made the surgeon go off without further parley. Lieutenant D'Hubert regained his quarters nursing a hot and uneasy indignation. He dreaded the chaff of his comrades almost as much as the anger of his superiors. The truth was confoundedly grotesque and embarrassing, even putting aside the irregularity of the combat itself, which made it come abominably near a criminal offence. Like all men without much imagination, a faculty which helps the process of reflective thought, Lieutenant D'Hubert became frightfully harassed by the obvious aspects of his predicament. He was certainly glad that he had not killed Lieutenant Feraud outside all rules, and without the regular witnesses

proper to such a transaction. Uncommonly glad. At the same time he felt as
though he would have liked to wring his neck for him without ceremony.

*   *   *

He was still under the sway of these contradictory sentiments when the
surgeon amateur of the flute came to see him. More than three days had
elapsed. Lieutenant D'Hubert was no longer *officier d'ordonnance* to the
general commanding the division. He had been sent back to his regiment.
And he was resuming his connection with the soldiers' military family by
being shut up in close confinement, not at his own quarters in town, but in a
room in the barracks. Owing to the gravity of the incident, he was forbidden
to see anyone. He did not know what had happened, what was being said, or
what was being thought. The arrival of the surgeon was a most unexpected
thing to the worried captive. The amateur of the flute began by explaining
that he was there only by a special favour of the colonel.

'I represented to him that it would be only fair to let you have some
authentic news of your adversary,' he continued. 'You'll be glad to hear he's
getting better fast.'

Lieutenant D'Hubert's face exhibited no conventional signs of gladness.
He continued to walk the floor of the dusty bare room.

'Take this chair, doctor,' he mumbled.

The doctor sat down.

'This affair is variously appreciated – in town and in the army. In fact, the
diversity of opinions is amusing.'

'Is it!' mumbled Lieutenant D'Hubert, tramping steadily from wall to
wall. But within himself he marvelled that there could be two opinions on
the matter. The surgeon continued.

'Of course, as the real facts are not known – '

'I should have thought,' interrupted D'Hubert, 'that the fellow would
have put you in possession of facts.'

'He said something,' admitted the other, 'the first time I saw him. And, by
the by, I did find him in the garden. The thump on the back of his head had
made him a little incoherent then. Afterwards he was rather reticent than
otherwise.'

'Didn't think he would have the grace to be ashamed!' mumbled
D'Hubert, resuming his pacing while the doctor murmured, 'It's very
amusing. Ashamed! Shame was not exactly his frame of mind. However,
you may look at the matter otherwise.'

'What are you talking about? What matter?' asked D'Hubert, with a
sidelong look at the heavy-faced, grey-haired figure seated on a wooden
chair.

'Whatever it is,' said the surgeon a little impatiently, 'I don't want to
pronounce any opinion on your conduct – '

'By heavens, you had better not!' burst out D'Hubert.

'There! – there! Don't be so quick in flourishing the sword. It doesn't pay in the long run. Understand once for all that I would not carve any of you youngsters except with the tools of my trade. But my advice is good. If you go on like this you will make for yourself an ugly reputation.'

'Go on like what?' demanded Lieutenant D'Hubert, stopping short, quite startled. 'I! – I! – make for myself a reputation . . . What do you imagine?'

'I told you I don't wish to judge of the rights and wrongs of this incident. It's not my business. Nevertheless – '

'What on earth has he been telling you?' interrupted Lieutenant D'Hubert, in a sort of awed scare.

'I told you already, that at first, when I picked him up in the garden, he was incoherent. Afterwards he was naturally reticent. But I gather at least that he could not help himself.'

'He couldn't?' shouted Lieutenant D'Hubert in a great voice. Then, lowering his tone impressively, 'And what about me? Could I help myself?'

The surgeon stood up. His thoughts were running upon the flute, his constant companion with a consoling voice. In the vicinity of field ambulances, after twenty-four hours' hard work, he had been known to trouble with its sweet sounds the horrible stillness of battlefields, given over to silence and the dead. The solacing hour of his daily life was approaching, and in peacetime he held on to the minutes as a miser to his hoard.

'Of course! – of course!' he said, perfunctorily. 'You would think so. It's amusing. However, being perfectly neutral and friendly to you both, I have consented to deliver his message to you. Say that I am humouring an invalid if you like. He wants you to know that this affair is by no means at an end. He intends to send you his seconds directly he has regained his strength – providing, of course, the army is not in the field at that time.'

'He intends, does he? Why, certainly,' spluttered Lieutenant D'Hubert in a passion.

The secret of his exasperation was not apparent to the visitor; but this passion confirmed the surgeon in the belief which was gaining ground outside that some very serious difference had arisen between these two young men, something serious enough to wear an air of mystery, some fact of the utmost gravity. To settle their urgent difference about that fact, those two young men had risked being broken and disgraced at the outset almost of their career. The surgeon feared that the forthcoming inquiry would fail to satisfy the public curiosity. They would not take the public into their confidence as to that something which had passed between them of a nature so outrageous as to make them face a charge of murder – neither more nor less. But what could it be?

The surgeon was not very curious by temperament; but that question haunting his mind caused him twice that evening to hold the instrument off his lips and sit silent for a whole minute – right in the middle of a tune – trying to form a plausible conjecture.

2

He succeeded in this object no better than the rest of the garrison and the whole of society. The two young officers, of no especial consequence till then, became distinguished by the universal curiosity as to the origin of their quarrel. Madame de Lionne's salon was the centre of ingenious surmises; that lady herself was for a time assailed by enquiries as being the last person known to have spoken to these unhappy and reckless young men before they went out together from her house to a savage encounter with swords, at dusk, in a private garden. She protested she had not observed anything unusual in their demeanour. Lieutenant Feraud had been visibly annoyed at being called away. That was natural enough; no man likes to be disturbed in a conversation with a lady famed for her elegance and sensibility. But in truth the subject bored Madame de Lionne, since her personality could by no stretch of reckless gossip be connected with this affair. And it irritated her to hear it advanced that there might have been some woman in the case. This irritation arose, not from her elegance or sensibility, but from a more instinctive side of her nature. It became so great at last that she peremptorily forbade the subject to be mentioned under her roof. Near her couch the prohibition was obeyed, but farther off in the salon the pall of the imposed silence continued to be lifted more or less. A personage with a long, pale face, resembling the countenance of a sheep, opined, shaking his head, that it was a quarrel of long standing envenomed by time. It was objected to him that the men themselves were too young for such a theory. They belonged also to different and distant parts of France. There were other physical impossibilities, too. A sub-commissary of the Intendence, an agreeable and cultivated bachelor in kerseymere breeches, Hessian boots, and a blue coat embroidered with silver lace, who affected to believe in the transmigration of souls, suggested that the two had met perhaps in some previous existence. The feud was in the forgotten past. It might have been something quite inconceivable in the present state of their being; but their souls remembered the animosity, and manifested an instinctive antagonism. He developed this theme jocularly. Yet the affair was so absurd from the worldly, the military, the honourable, or the prudential point of view, that this weird explanation seemed rather more reasonable than any other.

The two officers had confided nothing definite to anyone. Humiliation at having been worsted arms in hand, and an uneasy feeling of having been involved in a scrape by the injustice of fate, kept Lieutenant Feraud savagely dumb. He mistrusted the sympathy of mankind. That would, of course, go to that dandified staff officer. Lying in bed, he raved aloud to the pretty maid who administered to his needs with devotion, and listened to his horrible imprecations with alarm. That Lieutenant D'Hubert should be made to 'pay for it', seemed to her just and natural. Her principal care was that Lieutenant Feraud should not excite himself. He appeared so wholly admirable and fascinating to the humility of her heart that her only concern was to see him get well quickly, even if it were only to resume his visits to Madame de Lionne's salon.

Lieutenant D'Hubert kept silent for the immediate reason that there was no one, except a stupid young soldier servant, to speak to. Further, he was aware that the episode, so grave professionally, had its comic side. When reflecting upon it, he still felt that he would like to wring Lieutenant Feraud's neck for him. But this formula was figurative rather than precise, and expressed more a state of mind than an actual physical impulse. At the same time, there was in that young man a feeling of comradeship and kindness which made him unwilling to make the position of Lieutenant Feraud worse than it was. He did not want to talk at large about this wretched affair. At the inquiry he would have, of course, to speak the truth in self-defence. This prospect vexed him.

But no inquiry took place. The army took the field instead. Lieutenant D'Hubert, liberated without remark, took up his regimental duties; and Lieutenant Feraud, his arm just out of the sling, rode unquestioned with his squadron to complete his convalescence in the smoke of battlefields and the fresh air of night bivouacs. This bracing treatment suited him so well that at the first rumour of an armistice being signed he could turn without mis-givings to the thoughts of his private warfare.

This time it was to be regular warfare. He sent two friends to Lieutenant D'Hubert, whose regiment was stationed only a few miles away. Those friends had asked no questions of their principal. 'I owe him one, that pretty staff officer,' he had said, grimly, and they went away quite contentedly on their mission. Lieutenant D'Hubert had no difficulty in finding two friends equally discreet and devoted to their principal. 'There's a crazy fellow to whom I must give a lesson,' he had declared curtly; and they asked for no better reasons.

On these grounds an encounter with duelling-swords was arranged one early morning in a convenient field. At the third set-to Lieutenant D'Hubert found himself lying on his back on the dewy grass with a hole in his side. A serene sun rising over a landscape of meadows and woods hung on his left. A surgeon – not the flute player, but another – was bending over him, feeling around the wound.

'Narrow squeak. But it will be nothing,' he pronounced.

Lieutenant D'Hubert heard these words with pleasure. One of his seconds, sitting on the wet grass, and sustaining his head on his lap, said, 'The fortune of war, *mon pauvre vieux*. What will you have? You had better make it up like two good fellows. Do!'

'You don't know what you ask,' murmured Lieutenant D'Hubert, in a feeble voice. 'However, if he . . .'

In another part of the meadow the seconds of Lieutenant Feraud were urging him to go over and shake hands with his adversary.

'You have paid him off now – *que diable*. It's the proper thing to do. This D'Hubert is a decent fellow.'

'I know the decency of these generals' pets,' muttered Lieutenant Feraud through his teeth, and the sombre expression of his face discouraged further efforts at reconciliation. The seconds, bowing from a distance, took their men off the field. In the afternoon Lieutenant D'Hubert, very popular as a good comrade uniting great bravery with a frank and equable temper, had many visitors. It was remarked that Lieutenant Feraud did not, as is customary, show himself much abroad to receive the felicitations of his friends. They would not have failed him, because he, too, was liked for the exuberance of his southern nature and the simplicity of his character. In all the places where officers were in the habit of assembling at the end of the day the duel of the morning was talked over from every point of view. Though Lieutenant D'Hubert had got worsted this time, his sword play was commended. No one could deny that it was very close, very scientific. It was even whispered that if he got touched it was because he wished to spare his adversary. But by many the vigour and dash of Lieutenant Feraud's attack were pronounced irresistible.

The merits of the two officers as combatants were frankly discussed; but their attitude to each other after the duel was criticised lightly and with caution. It was irreconcilable, and that was to be regretted. But after all they knew best what the care of their honour dictated. It was not a matter for their comrades to pry into over-much. As to the origin of the quarrel, the general impression was that it dated from the time they were holding garrison in Strasbourg. The musical surgeon shook his head at that. It went much farther back, he thought.

'Why, of course! You must know the whole story,' cried several voices, eager with curiosity. 'What was it?'

He raised his eyes from his glass deliberately. 'Even if I knew ever so well, you can't expect me to tell you, since both the principals choose to say nothing.'

He got up and went out, leaving the sense of mystery behind him. He could not stay any longer, because the witching hour of flute-playing was drawing near.

After he had gone a very young officer observed solemnly, 'Obviously, his lips are sealed!'

Nobody questioned the high correctness of that remark. Somehow it added to the impressiveness of the affair. Several older officers of both regiments, prompted by nothing but sheer kindness and love of harmony, proposed to form a Court of Honour, to which the two young men would leave the task of their reconciliation. Unfortunately they began by approaching Lieutenant Feraud, on the assumption that, having just scored heavily, he would be found placable and disposed to moderation.

The reasoning was sound enough. Nevertheless, the move turned out unfortunate. In that relaxation of moral fibre, which is brought about by the ease of soothed vanity, Lieutenant Feraud had condescended in the secret of his heart to review the case, and even had come to doubt not the justice of his cause, but the absolute sagacity of his conduct. This being so, he was disinclined to talk about it. The suggestion of the regimental wise men put him in a difficult position. He was disgusted at it, and this disgust, by a paradoxical logic, reawakened his animosity against Lieutenant D'Hubert. Was he to be pestered with this fellow for ever – the fellow who had an infernal knack of getting round people somehow? And yet it was difficult to refuse point blank that mediation sanctioned by the code of honour.

He met the difficulty by an attitude of grim reserve. He twisted his moustache and used vague words. His case was perfectly clear. He was not ashamed to state it before a proper Court of Honour, neither was he afraid to defend it on the ground. He did not see any reason to jump at the suggestion before ascertaining how his adversary was likely to take it.

Later in the day, his exasperation growing upon him, he was heard in a public place saying sardonically, 'that it would be the very luckiest thing for Lieutenant D'Hubert, because the next time of meeting he need not hope to get off with the mere trifle of three weeks in bed'.

This boastful phrase might have been prompted by the most profound Machiavellism. Southern natures often hide, under the outward impulsiveness of action and speech, a certain amount of astuteness.

Lieutenant Feraud, mistrusting the justice of men, by no means desired a Court of Honour; and the above words, according so well with his temperament, had also the merit of serving his turn. Whether meant so or not, they found their way in less than four-and-twenty hours into Lieutenant D'Hubert's bedroom. In consequence Lieutenant D'Hubert, sitting propped up with pillows, received the overtures made to him next day by the statement that the affair was of a nature which could not bear discussion.

The pale face of the wounded officer, his weak voice which he had yet to use cautiously, and the courteous dignity of his tone had a great effect on his hearers. Reported outside all this did more for deepening the mystery than the vapourings of Lieutenant Feraud. This last was greatly relieved at the issue. He began to enjoy the state of general wonder, and was pleased to add to it by assuming an attitude of fierce discretion.

The colonel of Lieutenant D'Hubert's regiment was a grey-haired, weather-beaten warrior, who took a simple view of his responsibilities. 'I can't,' he said to himself, 'let the best of my subalterns get damaged like this for nothing. I must get to the bottom of this affair privately. He must speak out if the devil were in it. The colonel should be more than a father to these youngsters.' And indeed he loved all his men with as much affection as a father of a large family can feel for every individual member of it. If human beings by an oversight of providence came into the world as mere civilians, they were born again into a regiment as infants are born into a family, and it was that military birth alone which counted.

At the sight of Lieutenant D'Hubert standing before him very bleached and hollow-eyed the heart of the old warrior felt a pang of genuine compassion. All his affection for the regiment – that body of men which he held in his hand to launch forward and draw back, who ministered to his pride and commanded all his thoughts – seemed centred for a moment on the person of the most promising subaltern. He cleared his throat in a threatening manner, and frowned terribly. 'You must understand,' he began, 'that I don't care a rap for the life of a single man in the regiment. I would send the eight hundred and forty-three of you men and horses galloping into the pit of perdition with no more compunction than I would kill a fly!'

'Yes, colonel. You would be riding at our head,' said Lieutenant D'Hubert with a wan smile.

The colonel, who felt the need of being very diplomatic, fairly roared at this. 'I want you to know, Lieutenant D'Hubert, that I could stand aside and see you all riding to Hades if need be. I am a man to do even that if the good of the service and my duty to my country required it from me. But that's unthinkable, so don't you even hint at such a thing.' He glared awfully, but his tone softened. 'There's some milk yet about that moustache of yours, my boy. You don't know what a man like me is capable of. I would hide behind a haystack if . . . Don't grin at me, sir! How dare you? If this were not a private conversation I would . . . Look here! I am responsible for the proper expenditure of lives under my command for the glory of our country and the honour of the regiment. Do you understand that? Well, then, what the devil do you mean by letting yourself be spitted like this by that fellow of the 7th Hussars? It's simply disgraceful!'

Lieutenant D'Hubert felt vexed beyond measure. His shoulders moved slightly. He made no other answer. He could not ignore his responsibility.

The colonel veiled his glance and lowered his voice still more. 'It's deplorable!' he murmured. And again he changed his tone. 'Come!' he went on, persuasively, but with that note of authority which dwells in the throat of a good leader of men, 'this affair must be settled. I desire to be told plainly what it is all about. I demand, as your best friend, to know.'

The compelling power of authority, the persuasive influence of kindness, affected powerfully a man just risen from a bed of sickness. Lieutenant D'Hubert's hand, which grasped the knob of a stick, trembled slightly. But his northern temperament, sentimental yet cautious and clear-sighted, too, in its idealistic way, checked his impulse to make a clean breast of the whole deadly absurdity. According to the precept of transcendental wisdom, he turned his tongue seven times in his mouth before he spoke. He made then only a speech of thanks.

The colonel listened, interested at first, then looked mystified. At last he frowned. 'You hesitate? – *mille tonnerres*! Haven't I told you that I will condescend to argue with you – as a friend?'

'Yes, colonel!' answered Lieutenant D'Hubert, gently. 'But I am afraid that after you have heard me out as a friend you will take action as my superior officer.'

The attentive colonel snapped his jaws. 'Well, what of that?' he said, frankly. 'Is it so damnably disgraceful?'

'It is not,' negatived Lieutenant D'Hubert, in a faint but firm voice.

'Of course, I shall act for the good of the service. Nothing can prevent me doing that. What do you think I want to be told for?'

'I know it is not from idle curiosity,' protested Lieutenant D'Hubert. 'I know you will act wisely. But what about the good fame of the regiment?'

'It cannot be affected by any youthful folly of a lieutenant,' said the colonel, severely.

'No. It cannot be. But it can be by evil tongues. It will be said that a lieutenant of the 4th Hussars, afraid of meeting his adversary, is hiding behind his colonel. And that would be worse than hiding behind a haystack – for the good of the service. I cannot afford to do that, colonel.'

'Nobody would dare to say anything of the kind,' began the colonel very fiercely, but ended the phrase on an uncertain note. The bravery of Lieutenant D'Hubert was well known. But the colonel was well aware that the duelling courage, the single-combat courage, is rightly or wrongly supposed to be courage of a special sort. And it was eminently necessary that an officer of his regiment should possess every kind of courage – and prove it, too. The colonel stuck out his lower lip, and looked far away with a peculiar glazed stare. This was the expression of his perplexity – an expression practically unknown to his regiment; for perplexity is a sentiment which is incompatible with the rank of colonel of cavalry. The colonel himself was overcome by the unpleasant novelty of the sensation. As he was not accustomed to think except on professional matters connected with the welfare of men and horses, and the proper use thereof on the field of glory, his intellectual efforts degenerated into mere mental repetitions of profane language. '*Mille tonnerres!* . . . *Sacre nom de nom* . . .' he thought.

Lieutenant D'Hubert coughed painfully, and added in a weary voice: 'There will be plenty of evil tongues to say that I've been cowed. And I am sure you will not expect me to pass that over. I may find myself suddenly with a dozen duels on my hands instead of this one affair.'

The direct simplicity of this argument came home to the colonel's understanding. He looked at his subordinate fixedly. 'Sit down, lieutenant!' he said, gruffly. 'This is the very devil of a . . . Sit down!'

'*Mon colonel*,' D'Hubert began again, 'I am not afraid of evil tongues. There's a way of silencing them. But there's my peace of mind, too. I wouldn't be able to shake off the notion that I'd ruined a brother officer. Whatever action you take, it is bound to go further. The inquiry has been dropped – let it rest now. It would have been absolutely fatal to Feraud.'

'Hey! What! Did he behave so badly?'

'Yes. It was pretty bad,' muttered Lieutenant D'Hubert. Being still very weak, he felt a disposition to cry.

As the other man did not belong to his own regiment the colonel had no difficulty in believing this. He began to pace up and down the room. He was a good chief, a man capable of discreet sympathy. But he was human in other ways, too, and this became apparent because he was not capable of artifice.

'The very devil, lieutenant,' he blurted out, in the innocence of his heart, 'is that I have declared my intention to get to the bottom of this affair. And when a colonel says something . . . you see . . .'

Lieutenant D'Hubert broke in earnestly: 'Let me entreat you, colonel, to be satisfied with taking my word of honour that I was put into a damnable position where I had no option; I had no choice whatever, consistent with my dignity as a man and an officer . . . After all, colonel, this fact is the very bottom of this affair. Here you've got it. The rest is mere detail. . . .'

The colonel stopped short. The reputation of Lieutenant D'Hubert for good sense and good temper weighed in the balance. A cool head, a warm heart, open as the day. Always correct in his behaviour. One had to trust him. The colonel repressed manfully an immense curiosity. 'H'm! You affirm that as a man and an officer . . . No option? Eh?'

'As an officer – an officer of the 4th Hussars, too,' insisted Lieutenant D'Hubert, 'I had not. And that is the bottom of the affair, colonel.'

'Yes. But still I don't see why, to one's colonel . . . A colonel is a father – *que diable!*'

Lieutenant D'Hubert ought not to have been allowed out as yet. He was becoming aware of his physical insufficiency with humiliation and despair. But the morbid obstinacy of an invalid possessed him, and at the same time he felt with dismay his eyes filling with water. This trouble seemed too big to handle. A tear fell down the thin, pale cheek of Lieutenant D'Hubert.

The colonel turned his back on him hastily. You could have heard a pin drop. 'This is some silly woman story – is it not?'

Saying these words the chief spun round to seize the truth, which is not a beautiful shape living in a well, but a shy bird best caught by stratagem. This was the last move of the colonel's diplomacy. He saw the truth shining unmistakably in the gesture of Lieutenant D'Hubert raising his weak arms and his eyes to heaven in supreme protest.

'Not a woman affair – eh?' growled the colonel, staring hard. 'I don't ask you who or where. All I want to know is whether there is a woman in it?'

Lieutenant D'Hubert's arms dropped, and his weak voice was pathetically broken.

'Nothing of the kind, *mon colonel.*'

'On your honour?' insisted the old warrior.

'On my honour.'

'Very well,' said the colonel, thoughtfully, and bit his lip. The arguments of Lieutenant D'Hubert, helped by his liking for the man, had convinced him. On the other hand, it was highly improper that his intervention, of which he had made no secret, should produce no visible effect. He kept Lieutenant D'Hubert a few minutes longer, and dismissed him kindly.

'Take a few days more in bed. Lieutenant. What the devil does the surgeon mean by reporting you fit for duty?'

On coming out of the colonel's quarters, Lieutenant D'Hubert said nothing to the friend who was waiting outside to take him home. He said nothing to anybody. Lieutenant D'Hubert made no confidences. But on the evening of that day the colonel, strolling under the elms growing near his quarters, in the company of his second in command, opened his lips.

'I've got to the bottom of this affair,' he remarked. The lieutenant-colonel, a dry, brown chip of a man with short side-whiskers, pricked up his ears at that without letting a sign of curiosity escape him.

'It's no trifle,' added the colonel, oracularly. The other waited for a long while before he murmured:

'Indeed, sir!'

'No trifle,' repeated the colonel, looking straight before him. 'I've, however, forbidden D'Hubert either to send to or receive a challenge from Feraud for the next twelve months.'

He had imagined this prohibition to save the prestige a colonel should have. The result of it was to give an official seal to the mystery surrounding this deadly quarrel. Lieutenant D'Hubert repelled by an impassive silence all attempts to worm the truth out of him. Lieutenant Feraud, secretly uneasy at first, regained his assurance as time went on. He disguised his ignorance of the meaning of the imposed truce by slight sardonic laughs, as though he were amused by what he intended to keep to himself. 'But what will you do?' his chums used to ask him. He contented himself by replying, '*Qui vivra verra,*' with a little truculent air. And everybody admired his discretion.

Before the end of the truce Lieutenant D'Hubert got his troop. The promotion was well earned, but somehow no one seemed to expect the event. When Lieutenant Feraud heard of it at a gathering of officers, he muttered through his teeth, 'Is that so?' At once he unhooked his sabre from a peg near the door, buckled it on carefully, and left the company without another word. He walked home with measured steps, struck a light with his flint and steel, and lit his tallow candle. Then snatching an unlucky glass tumbler off the mantelpiece he dashed it violently on the floor.

Now that D'Hubert was an officer of superior rank there could be no question of a duel. Neither of them could send or receive a challenge without rendering himself amenable to a court-martial. It was not to be thought of. Lieutenant Feraud, who for many days now had experienced no real desire to meet Lieutenant D'Hubert arms in hand, chafed again at the systematic injustice of fate. 'Does he think he will escape me in that way?' he thought, indignantly. He saw in this promotion an intrigue, a conspiracy, a cowardly manoeuvre. That colonel knew what he was doing. He had hastened to recommend his favourite for a step. It was outrageous that a man should be able to avoid the consequences of his acts in such a dark and tortuous manner.

Of a happy-go-lucky disposition, of a temperament more pugnacious than military, Lieutenant Feraud had been content to give and receive blows for sheer love of armed strife, and without much thought of advancement; but now an urgent desire to get on sprang up in his breast. This fighter by vocation resolved in his mind to seize showy occasions and to court the favourable opinion of his chiefs like a mere worldling. He knew he was as brave as anyone, and never doubted his personal charm. Nevertheless, neither the bravery nor the charm seemed to work very swiftly. Lieutenant Feraud's engaging, careless truculence of a *beau sabreur* underwent a change. He began to make bitter allusions to 'clever fellows who stick at nothing to get on'. The army was full of them, he would say; you had only to look round. But all the time he had in view one person only, his adversary, D'Hubert. Once he confided to an appreciative friend: 'You see, I don't know how to fawn on the right sort of people. It isn't in my character.'

He did not get his step till a week after Austerlitz. The Light Cavalry of the Grand Army had its hands very full of interesting work for a little while. Directly the pressure of professional occupation had been eased Captain Feraud took measures to arrange a meeting without loss of time. 'I know my bird,' he observed, grimly. 'If I don't look sharp he will take care to get himself promoted over the heads of a dozen better men than himself. He's got the knack for that sort of thing.'

This duel was fought in Silesia. If not fought to a finish, it was, at any rate, fought to a standstill. The weapon was the cavalry sabre, and the skill, the science, the vigour, and the determination displayed by the adversaries compelled the admiration of the beholders. It became the subject of talk on both shores of the Danube, and as far as the garrisons of Gratz and Laybach. They crossed blades seven times. Both had many cuts which bled profusely. Both refused to have the combat stopped, time after time, with what appeared the most deadly animosity. This appearance was caused on the part of Captain D'Hubert by a rational desire to be done once for all with this worry; on the part of Captain Feraud by a tremendous exaltation of his pugnacious instincts and the incitement of wounded vanity. At last, dishevelled, their shirts in rags, covered with gore and hardly able to stand, they were led away forcibly by their marvelling and horrified seconds. Later on, besieged by comrades avid of details, these gentlemen declared that they could not have allowed that sort of hacking to go on indefinitely. Asked whether the quarrel was settled this time, they gave it out as their conviction that it was a difference which could only be settled by one of the parties remaining lifeless on the ground. The sensation spread from army corps to army corps, and penetrated at last to the smallest detachments of the troops cantoned between the Rhine and the Save. In the cafés in Vienna it was generally estimated, from details to hand, that the adversaries would be able to meet again in three weeks' time on the outside. Something really transcendent in the way of duelling was expected.

These expectations were brought to naught by the necessities of the service which separated the two officers. No official notice had been taken of their quarrel. It was now the property of the army, and not to be meddled with lightly. But the story of the duel, or rather their duelling propensities, must have stood somewhat in the way of their advancement, because they were still captains when they came together again during the war with Prussia. Detached north after Jena, with the army commanded by Marshal Bernadotte, Prince of Ponte Corvo, they entered Lübeck together.

It was only after the occupation of that town that Captain Feraud found leisure to consider his future conduct in view of the fact that Captain D'Hubert had been given the position of third aide-de-camp to the marshal. He considered it a great part of a night, and in the morning summoned two sympathetic friends.

'I've been thinking it over calmly,' he said, gazing at them with blood-shot, tired eyes. 'I see that I must get rid of that intriguing personage. Here he's managed to sneak on to the personal staff of the marshal. It's a direct provocation to me. I can't tolerate a situation in which I am exposed any day to receive an order through him. And God knows what order, too! That sort of thing has happened once before – and that's once too often. He under-stands this perfectly, never fear. I can't tell you any more. Now you know what it is you have to do.'

This encounter took place outside the town of Lübeck, on very open ground, selected with special care in deference to the general sentiment of the cavalry division belonging to the army corps that this time the two officers should meet on horseback. After all, this duel was a cavalry affair, and to persist in fighting on foot would look like a slight on one's own arm of the service. The seconds, startled by the unusual nature of the suggestion, hastened to refer to their principals. Captain Feraud jumped at it with alacrity. For some obscure reason, depending, no doubt, on his psychology, he imagined himself invincible on horseback. All alone within the four walls of his room he rubbed his hands and muttered triumphantly, 'Aha! my pretty staff officer, I've got you now.'

Captain D'Hubert on his side, after staring hard for a considerable time at his friends, shrugged his shoulders slightly. This affair had hopelessly and unreasonably complicated his existence for him. One absurdity more or less in the development did not matter – all absurdity was distasteful to him; but, urbane as ever, he produced a faintly ironical smile, and said in his calm voice, 'It certainly will do away to some extent with the monotony of the thing.'

When left alone, he sat down at a table and took his head into his hands. He had not spared himself of late and the marshal had been working all his aides-de-camp particularly hard. The last three weeks of campaigning in horrible weather had affected his health. When over-tired he suffered from a stitch in his wounded side, and that uncomfortable sensation always depressed him. 'It's that brute's doing, too,' he thought bitterly.

The day before he had received a letter from home, announcing that his only sister was going to be married. He reflected that from the time she was nineteen and he twenty-six, when he went away to garrison life in Strasbourg, he had had but two short glimpses of her. They had been great friends and confidants; and now she was going to be given away to a man whom he did not know – a very worthy fellow no doubt, but not half good enough for her. He would never see his old Léonie again. She had a capable little head, and plenty of tact; she would know how to manage the fellow, to be sure. He was easy in his mind about her happiness but he felt ousted from the first place in her thoughts which had been his ever since the girl could speak. A melancholy regret for the days of his childhood settled upon Captain D'Hubert, third aide-de-camp to the Prince of Ponte Corvo.

He threw aside the letter of congratulation he had begun to write as in duty bound but without enthusiasm. He took a fresh piece of paper, and traced on it the words: 'This is my last will and testament.' Looking at these words he gave himself up to unpleasant reflection; a presentiment that he would never see the scenes of his childhood weighed down the equable spirits of Captain D'Hubert. He jumped up, pushing his chair back, yawned elaborately in sign that he didn't care anything for presentiments, and throwing himself on the bed went to sleep. During the night he shivered from time to time without waking up. In the morning he rode out of town between his two seconds, talking of indifferent things, and looking right and left with apparent detachment into the heavy morning mists shrouding the flat green fields bordered by hedges. He leaped a ditch, and saw the forms of many mounted men moving in the fog. 'We are to fight before a gallery, it seems,' he muttered to himself, bitterly.

His seconds were rather concerned at the state of the atmosphere, but presently a pale, sickly sun struggled out of the low vapours, and Captain D'Hubert made out, in the distance, three horsemen riding a little apart from the others. It was Captain Feraud and his seconds. He drew his sabre, and assured himself that it was properly fastened to his wrist. And now the seconds, who had been standing in close group with the heads of their horses together, separated at an easy canter, leaving a large, clear field between him and his adversary. Captain D'Hubert looked at the pale sun, at the dismal fields, and the imbecility of the impending fight filled him with desolation. From a distant part of the field a stentorian voice shouted commands at proper intervals: *Au pas – Au trot – Charrrgez!* . . . Presentiments of death don't come to a man for nothing he thought at the very moment he put spurs to his horse.

And therefore he was more than surprised when, at the very first set-to, Captain Feraud laid himself open to a cut over the forehead, which, blinding him with blood, ended the combat almost before it had fairly begun. It was impossible to go on. Captain D'Hubert, leaving his enemy swearing horribly and reeling in the saddle between his two appalled friends, leaped the ditch again into the road and trotted home with his two seconds, who seemed rather awestruck at the speedy issue of that encounter. In the evening Captain D'Hubert finished the congratulatory letter on his sister's marriage.

He finished it late. It was a long letter. Captain D'Hubert gave reins to his fancy. He told his sister that he would feel rather lonely after this great change in her life; but then the day would come for him, too, to get married. In fact, he was thinking already of the time when there would be no one left to fight with in Europe and the epoch of wars would be over. 'I expect then,' he wrote, 'to be within measurable distance of a marshal's baton, and you will be an experienced married woman. You shall look out a wife for me. I will be, probably, bald by then, and a little blasé. I shall require a young girl, pretty of course, and with a large fortune, which should help me to close my glorious career in the splendour befitting my exalted rank.' He ended with the information that he had just given a lesson to a worrying, quarrelsome fellow who imagined he had a grievance against him. 'But if you, in the depths of your province,' he continued, 'ever hear it said that your brother is of a quarrelsome disposition, don't you believe it on any account. There is no saying what gossip from the army may reach your innocent ears. Whatever you hear you may rest assured that your ever-loving brother is not a duellist.' Then Captain D'Hubert crumpled up the blank sheet of paper headed with the words 'This is my last will and testament', and threw it in the fire with a great laugh at himself. He didn't care a snap for what that lunatic could do. He had suddenly acquired the conviction that his adversary was utterly powerless to affect his life in any sort of way; except, perhaps, in the way of putting a special excitement into the delightful, gay intervals between the campaigns.

From this on there were, however, to be no peaceful intervals in the career of Captain D'Hubert. He saw the fields of Eylau and Friedland, marched and countermarched in the snow, in the mud, in the dust of Polish plains, picking up distinction and advancement on all the roads of north-eastern Europe. Meantime, Captain Feraud, despatched southwards with his regiment, made unsatisfactory war in Spain. It was only when the preparations for the Russian campaign began that he was ordered north again. He left the country of mantillas and oranges without regret.

The first signs of a not unbecoming baldness added to the lofty aspect of Colonel D'Hubert's forehead. This feature was no longer white and smooth as in the days of his youth; the kindly open glance of his blue eyes had grown a little hard as if from much peering through the smoke of battles. The ebony crop on Colonel Feraud's head, coarse and crinkly like a cap of horsehair, showed many silver threads about the temples. A detestable warfare of ambushes and inglorious surprises had not improved his temper. The beak-like curve of his nose was unpleasantly set off by a deep fold on each side of his mouth. The round orbits of his eyes radiated wrinkles. More than ever he recalled an irritable and staring bird – something like a cross between a parrot and an owl. He was still extremely outspoken in his dislike of 'intriguing fellows'. He seized every opportunity to state that he did not pick up his rank in the ante-rooms of marshals. The unlucky persons, civil or military, who, with an intention of being pleasant, begged Colonel Feraud to tell them how he came by that very apparent scar on the forehead, were astonished to find themselves snubbed in various ways, some of which were simply rude and others mysteriously sardonic. Young officers were warned kindly by their more experienced comrades not to stare openly at the colonel's scar. But indeed an officer need have been very young in his profession not to have heard the legendary tale of that duel originating in a mysterious, unforgivable offence.

3

The retreat from Moscow submerged all private feelings in a sea of disaster and misery. Colonels without regiments, D'Hubert and Feraud carried the musket in the ranks of the so-called sacred battalion – a battalion recruited from officers of all arms who had no longer any troops to lead.

In that battalion promoted colonels did duty as sergeants; the generals captained the companies; a marshal of France, Prince of the Empire, commanded the whole. All had provided themselves with muskets picked up on the road, and with cartridges taken from the dead. In the general destruction of the bonds of discipline and duty holding together the companies, the battalions, the regiments, the brigades and divisions of an armed host, this body of men put its pride in preserving some semblance of order and formation. The only stragglers were those who fell out to give up to the frost their exhausted souls. They plodded on, and their passage did not disturb the mortal silence of the plains, shining with the livid light of snows under a sky the colour of ashes. Whirlwinds ran along the fields, broke against the dark column, enveloped it in a turmoil of flying icicles, and subsided, disclosing it creeping on its tragic way without the swing and rhythm of the military pace. It struggled onwards, the men exchanging neither words nor looks; whole ranks marched touching elbow, day after day, and never raising their eyes from the ground, as if lost in despairing reflections. In the dumb, black forests of pines the cracking of overloaded branches was the only sound they heard. Often from daybreak to dusk no one spoke in the whole column. It was like a macabre march of struggling corpses towards a distant grave. Only an alarm of Cossacks could restore to their eyes a semblance of martial resolution. The battalion faced about and deployed, or formed a square under the endless fluttering of snowflakes. A cloud of horsemen with fur caps on their heads, levelled long lances, and yelled 'Hurrah! Hurrah!' around their menacing immobility whence, with muffled detonations, hundreds of dark red flames darted through the air thick with falling snow. In a very few moments the horsemen would disappear, as if carried off yelling in the gale, and the sacred battalion standing still, alone in the blizzard, heard only the howling of the wind, whose blasts searched their very hearts. Then, with a cry or two of '*Vive l'Empereur!*' it would resume its march, leaving behind a few lifeless bodies lying huddled up, tiny black specks on the white immensity of the snows.

Though often marching in the ranks, or skirmishing in the woods side by side, the two officers ignored each other; this not so much from inimical intention as from a very real indifference. All their store of moral energy was expended in resisting the terrific enmity of nature and the crushing sense of irretrievable disaster. To the last they counted among the most active, the least demoralised of the battalion; their vigorous vitality invested them both with the appearance of an heroic pair in the eyes of their comrades. And they never exchanged more than a casual word or two, except one day, when skirmishing in front of the battalion against a worrying attack of cavalry, they found themselves cut off in the woods by a small party of Cossacks. A score of fur-capped, hairy horsemen rode to and fro, brandishing their lances in ominous silence; but the two officers had no mind to lay down their arms, and Colonel Feraud suddenly spoke up in a hoarse, growling voice, bringing his firelock to the shoulder. 'You take the nearest brute, Colonel D'Hubert; I'll settle the next one. I am a better shot than you are.'

Colonel D'Hubert nodded over his levelled musket. Their shoulders were pressed against the trunk of a large tree; on their front enormous snowdrifts protected them from a direct charge. Two carefully aimed shots rang out in the frosty air, two Cossacks reeled in their saddles. The rest, not thinking the game good enough, closed round their wounded comrades and galloped away out of range. The two officers managed to rejoin their battalion halted for the night. During that afternoon they had leaned upon each other more than once, and towards the end, Colonel D'Hubert, whose long legs gave him an advantage in walking through soft snow, peremptorily took the musket of Colonel Feraud from him and carried it on his shoulder, using his own as a staff.

On the outskirts of a village half-buried in the snow an old wooden barn burned with a clear and an immense flame. The sacred battalion of skeletons, muffled in rags, crowded greedily the windward side, stretching hundreds of numbed, bony hands to the blaze. Nobody had noted their approach. Before entering the circle of light playing on the sunken, glassy-eyed, starved faces, Colonel D'Hubert spoke in his turn: 'Here's your musket, Colonel Feraud. I can walk better than you.'

Colonel Feraud nodded, and pushed on towards the warmth of the fierce flames. Colonel D'Hubert was more deliberate, but not the less bent on getting a place in the front rank. Those they shouldered aside tried to greet with a faint cheer the reappearance of the two indomitable companions in activity and endurance. Those manly qualities had never perhaps received a higher tribute than this feeble acclamation.

This is the faithful record of speeches exchanged during the retreat from Moscow by Colonels Feraud and D'Hubert. Colonel Feraud's taciturnity was the outcome of concentrated rage. Short, hairy, black faced, with layers of grime and the thick sprouting of a wiry beard, a frost-bitten hand wrapped up in filthy rags carried in a sling, he accused fate of unparalleled perfidy towards the sublime Man of Destiny. Colonel D'Hubert, his long moustaches pendent in icicles on each side of his cracked blue lips, his eyelids inflamed with the glare of snows, the principal part of his costume consisting of a sheepskin coat looted with difficulty from the frozen corpse of a camp follower found in an abandoned cart, took a more thoughtful view of events. His regularly handsome features, now reduced to mere bony lines and fleshless hollows, looked out of a woman's black velvet hood, over which was rammed forcibly a cocked hat picked up under the wheels of an empty army *fourgon*, which must have contained at one time some general officer's luggage. The sheepskin coat being short for a man of his inches ended very high up, and the skin of his legs, blue with the cold, showed through the tatters of his nether garments. This under the circumstances provoked neither jeers nor pity. No one cared how the next man felt or looked. Colonel D'Hubert himself, hardened to exposure, suffered mainly in his self-respect from the lamentable indecency of his costume. A thought-less person may think that with a whole host of inanimate bodies bestrewing the path of retreat there could not have been much difficulty in supplying the deficiency. But to loot a pair of breeches from a frozen corpse is not so easy as it may appear to a mere theorist. It requires time and labour. You must remain behind while your companions march on. Colonel D'Hubert had his scruples as to falling out. Once he had stepped aside he could not be sure of ever rejoining his battalion; and the ghastly intimacy of a wrestling match with the frozen dead opposing the unyielding rigidity of iron to your violence was repugnant to the delicacy of his feelings. Luckily, one day, grubbing in a mound of snow between the huts of a village in the hope of finding there a frozen potato or some vegetable garbage he could put between his long and shaky teeth, Colonel D'Hubert uncovered a couple of mats of the sort Russian peasants use to line the sides of their carts with. These, beaten free of frozen snow, bent about his elegant person and fastened solidly round his waist, made a bell-shaped nether garment, a sort of stiff petticoat, which rendered Colonel D'Hubert a perfectly decent, but a much more noticeable figure than before.

Thus accoutred, he continued to retreat, never doubting of his personal escape, but full of other misgivings. The early buoyancy of his belief in the future was destroyed. If the road of glory led through such unforeseen passages, he asked himself – for he was reflective – whether the guide was altogether trustworthy. It was a patriotic sadness, not unmingled with some personal concern, and quite unlike the unreasoning indignation against men and things nursed by Colonel Feraud. Recruiting his strength in a little German town for three weeks, Colonel D'Hubert was surprised to discover within himself a love of repose. His returning vigour was strangely pacific in its aspirations. He meditated silently upon this bizarre change of mood. No doubt many of his brother officers of field rank went through the same moral experience. But these were not the times to talk of it. In one of his letters home Colonel D'Hubert wrote, 'All your plans, my dear Léonie, for marrying me to the charming girl you have discovered in your neighbour-hood, seem farther off than ever. Peace is not yet. Europe wants another lesson. It will be a hard task for us, but it shall be done, because the emperor is invincible.'

Thus wrote Colonel D'Hubert from Pomerania to his married sister Léonie, settled in the south of France. And so far the sentiments expressed would not have been disowned by Colonel Feraud, who wrote no letters to anybody, whose father had been in life an illiterate blacksmith, who had no sister or brother, and whom no one desired ardently to pair off for a life of peace with a charming young girl. But Colonel D'Hubert's letter con-tained also some philosophical generalities upon the uncertainty of all personal hopes, when bound up entirely with the prestigious fortune of one incomparably great it is true, yet still remaining but a man in his greatness. This view would have appeared rank heresy to Colonel Feraud. Some melancholy forebodings of a military kind, expressed cautiously, would have been pronounced as nothing short of high treason by Colonel Feraud. But Léonie, the sister of Colonel D'Hubert, read them with profound satisfaction, and, folding the letter thoughtfully, remarked to herself that 'Armand was likely to prove eventually a sensible fellow'. Since her marriage into a southern family she had become a convinced believer in the return of the legitimate king. Hopeful and anxious she offered prayers night and morning, and burnt candles in churches for the safety and prosperity of her brother.

She had every reason to suppose that her prayers were heard. Colonel D'Hubert passed through Lutzen, Bautzen, and Leipzig losing no limb, and acquiring additional reputation. Adapting his conduct to the needs of that desperate time, he had never voiced his misgivings. He concealed them under a cheerful courtesy of such pleasant character that people were inclined to ask themselves with wonder whether Colonel D'Hubert was aware of any disasters. Not only his manners, but even his glances remained untroubled. The steady amenity of his blue eyes disconcerted all grumblers, and made despair itself pause.

This bearing was remarked favourably by the emperor himself; for Colonel D'Hubert, attached now to the major-general's staff, came on several occasions under the imperial eye. But it exasperated the higher strung nature of Colonel Feraud. Passing through Magdeburg on service, this last allowed himself, while seated gloomily at dinner with the *commandant de place*, to say of his life-long adversary: 'This man does not love the emperor,' and his words were received by the other guests in profound silence. Colonel Feraud, troubled in his conscience at the atrocity of the aspersion, felt the need to back it up by a good argument. 'I ought to know him,' he cried, adding some oaths. 'One studies one's adversary. I have met him on the ground half a dozen times, as all the army knows. What more do you want? If that isn't opportunity enough for any fool to size up his man, may the devil take me if I can tell what is.' And he looked around the table, obstinate and sombre.

Later on in Paris, while extremely busy reorganising his regiment, Colonel Feraud learned that Colonel D'Hubert had been made a general. He glared at his informant incredulously, then folded his arms and turned away muttering, 'Nothing surprises me on the part of that man.'

And aloud he added, speaking over his shoulder, 'You would oblige me greatly by telling General D'Hubert at the first opportunity that his advancement saves him for a time from a pretty hot encounter. I was only waiting for him to turn up here.'

The other officer remonstrated.

'Could you think of it, Colonel Feraud, at this time, when every life should be consecrated to the glory and safety of France?'

But the strain of unhappiness caused by military reverses had spoiled Colonel Feraud's character. Like many other men, he was rendered wicked by misfortune.

'I cannot consider General D'Hubert's existence of any account either for the glory or safety of France,' he snapped viciously. 'You don't pretend, perhaps, to know him better than I do – I who have met him half a dozen times on the ground – do you?'

His interlocutor, a young man, was silenced. Colonel Feraud walked up and down the room.

'This is not the time to mince matters,' he said. 'I can't believe that that man ever loved the emperor. He picked up his general's stars under the boots of Marshal Berthier. Very well. I'll get mine in another fashion, and then we shall settle this business which has been dragging on too long.'

General D'Hubert, informed indirectly of Colonel Feraud's attitude, made a gesture as if to put aside an importunate person. His thoughts were solicited by graver cares. He had had no time to go and see his family. His sister, whose royalist hopes were rising higher every day, though proud of her brother, regretted his recent advancement in a measure, because it put on him a prominent mark of the usurper's favour, which later on could have an adverse influence upon his career. He wrote to her that no one but an inveterate enemy could say he had got his promotion by favour. As to his career, he assured her that he looked no farther forward into the future than the next battlefield.

Beginning the campaign of France in this dogged spirit, General D'Hubert was wounded on the second day of the battle under Laon. While being carried off the field he heard that Colonel Feraud, promoted this moment to general, had been sent to replace him at the head of his brigade. He cursed his luck impulsively, not being able at the first glance to discern all the advantages of a nasty wound. And yet it was by this heroic method that providence was shaping his future. Travelling slowly south to his sister's country home under the care of a trusty old servant, General D'Hubert was spared the humiliating contacts and the perplexities of conduct which assailed the men of the Napoleonic empire at the moment of its downfall. Lying in his bed, with the windows of his room open wide to the sunshine of Provence, he perceived the undisguised aspect of the blessing conveyed by that jagged fragment of a Prussian shell, which, killing his horse and ripping open his thigh, saved him from an active conflict with his conscience. After the last fourteen years spent sword in hand in the saddle, and with the sense of his duty done to the very end, General D'Hubert found resignation an easy virtue. His sister was delighted with his reasonableness. 'I leave myself altogether in your hands, my dear Léonie,' he had said to her.

He was still laid up when, the credit of his brother-in-law's family being exerted on his behalf, he received from the royal government not only the confirmation of his rank, but the assurance of being retained on the active list. To this was added an unlimited convalescent leave. The unfavourable opinion entertained of him in Bonapartist circles, though it rested on nothing more solid than the unsupported pronouncement of General Feraud, was directly responsible for General D'Hubert's retention on the active list. As to General Feraud, his rank was confirmed, too. It was more than he dared to expect; but Marshal Soult, then minister of war to the restored king, was partial to officers who had served in Spain. Only not even the marshal's protection could secure for him active employment. He remained irreconcilable, idle and sinister. He sought in obscure restaurants the company of other half-pay officers who cherished dingy but glorious old tricolour cockades in their breast-pockets, and buttoned with the forbidden eagle buttons their shabby uniforms, declaring themselves too poor to afford the expense of the prescribed change.

The triumphant return from Elba, an historical fact as marvellous and incredible as the exploits of some mythological demi-god, found General D'Hubert still quite unable to sit a horse. Neither could he walk very well. These disabilities, which Madame Léonie accounted most lucky, helped to keep her brother out of all possible mischief. His frame of mind at that time, she noted with dismay, became very far from reasonable. This general officer, still menaced by the loss of a limb, was discovered one night in the stables of the château by a groom, who, seeing a light, raised an alarm of thieves. His crutch was lying half-buried in the straw of the litter, and the general was hopping on one leg in a loose box around a snorting horse he was trying to saddle. Such were the effects of imperial magic upon a calm temperament and a pondered mind. Beset in the light of stable lanterns, by the tears, entreaties, indignation, remonstrances and reproaches of his family, he got out of the difficult situation by fainting away there and then in the arms of his nearest relatives, and was carried off to bed. Before he got out of it again, the second reign of Napoleon, the Hundred Days of feverish agitation and supreme effort, passed away like a terrifying dream. The tragic year 1815, begun in the trouble and unrest of consciences, was ending in vengeful proscriptions.

How General Feraud escaped the clutches of the Special Commission and the last offices of a firing squad he never knew himself. It was partly due to the subordinate position he was assigned during the Hundred Days. The emperor had never given him active command, but had kept him busy at the cavalry depot in Paris, mounting and dispatching hastily drilled troopers into the field. Considering this task as unworthy of his abilities, he had discharged it with no offensively noticeable zeal; but for the greater part he was saved from the excesses of royalist reaction by the interference of General D'Hubert.

This last, still on convalescent leave, but able now to travel, had been dispatched by his sister to Paris to present himself to his legitimate sovereign. As no one in the capital could possibly know anything of the episode in the stable he was received there with distinction. Military to the very bottom of his soul, the prospect of rising in his profession consoled him for finding himself the butt of Bonapartist malevolence, which pursued him with a persistence he could not account for. All the rancour of that embittered and persecuted party pointed to him as the man who had never loved the emperor – a sort of monster essentially worse than a mere betrayer.

General D'Hubert shrugged his shoulders without anger at this ferocious prejudice. Rejected by his old friends, and mistrusting profoundly the advances of royalist society, the young and handsome general (he was barely forty) adopted a manner of cold, punctilious courtesy, which at the merest shadow of an intended slight passed easily into harsh haughtiness. Thus prepared, General D'Hubert went about his affairs in Paris feeling inwardly very happy with the peculiar uplifting happiness of a man very much in love. The charming girl looked out by his sister had come upon the scene, and had conquered him in the thorough manner in which a young girl by merely existing in his sight can make a man of forty her own. They were going to be married as soon as General D'Hubert had obtained his official nomination to a promised command.

One afternoon, sitting on the terrasse of the Café Tortoni, General D'Hubert learned from the conversation of two strangers occupying a table near his own, that General Feraud, included in the batch of superior officers arrested after the second return of the king, was in danger of passing before the Special Commission. Living all his spare moments, as is frequently the case with expectant lovers, a day in advance of reality, and in a state of bestarred hallucination, it required nothing less than the name of his perpetual antagonist pronounced in a loud voice to call the youngest of Napoleon's generals away from the mental contemplation of his betrothed. He looked round. The strangers wore civilian clothes. Lean and weather-beaten, lolling back in their chairs, they scowled at people with moody and defiant abstraction from under their hats pulled low over their eyes. It was not difficult to recognise them for two of the compulsorily retired officers of the Old Guard. As from bravado or carelessness they chose to speak in loud tones, General D'Hubert, who saw no reason why he should change his seat, heard every word. They did not seem to be the personal friends of General Feraud. His name came up amongst others. Hearing it repeated, General D'Hubert's tender anticipations of a domestic future adorned with a woman's grace were traversed by the harsh regret of his warlike past, of that one long, intoxicating clash of arms, unique in the magnitude of its glory and disaster – the marvellous work and the special possession of his own generation. He felt an irrational tenderness towards his old adversary and appreciated emotionally the murderous absurdity their encounter had introduced into his life. It was like an additional pinch of spice in a hot dish. He remembered the flavour with sudden melancholy. He would never taste it again. It was all over. 'I fancy it was being left lying in the garden that had exasperated him so against me from the first,' he thought, indulgently.

The two strangers at the next table had fallen silent after the third mention of General Feraud's name. Presently the elder of the two, speaking again in a bitter tone, affirmed that General Feraud's account was settled. And why? Simply because he was not like some bigwigs who loved only themselves. The royalists knew they could never make anything of him. He loved The Other too well.

The Other was the Man of St Helena. The two officers nodded and touched glasses before they drank to an impossible return. Then the same who had spoken before, remarked with a sardonic laugh, 'His adversary showed more cleverness.'

'What adversary?' asked the younger, as if puzzled.

'Don't you know? They were two hussars. At each promotion they fought a duel. Haven't you heard of the duel going on ever since 1801?'

The other had heard of the duel, of course. Now he understood the allusion. General Baron D'Hubert would be able now to enjoy his fat king's favour in peace.

'Much good may it do him,' mumbled the elder. 'They were both brave men. I never saw this D'Hubert – a sort of intriguing dandy, I am told. But I can well believe what I've heard Feraud say of him – that he never loved the emperor.'

They rose and went away.

General D'Hubert experienced the horror of a somnambulist who wakes up from a complacent dream of activity to find himself walking on a quagmire. A profound disgust of the ground on which he was making his way overcame him. Even the image of the charming girl was swept from his view in the flood of moral distress. Everything he had ever been or hoped to be would taste of bitter ignominy unless he could manage to save General Feraud from the fate which threatened so many braves. Under the impulse of this almost morbid need to attend to the safety of his adversary, General D'Hubert worked so well with hands and feet (as the French saying is) that in less than twenty-four hours he found means of obtaining an extraordinary private audience from the minister of police.

General Baron D'Hubert was shown in suddenly without preliminaries. In the dusk of the minister's cabinet, behind the forms of writing-desk, chairs and tables, between two bunches of wax candles blazing in sconces, he beheld a figure in a gorgeous coat posturing before a tall mirror. The old *conventionnel* Fouché, senator of the empire, traitor to every man, to every principle and motive of human conduct, Duke of Otranto, and the wily artisan of the second restoration, was trying the fit of a court suit in which his young and accomplished fiancée had declared her intention to have his portrait painted on porcelain. It was a caprice, a charming fancy which the first minister of police of the second restoration was anxious to gratify. For that man, often compared in wiliness of conduct to a fox, but whose ethical side could be worthily symbolised by nothing less emphatic than a skunk, was as much possessed by his love as General D'Hubert himself.

Startled to be discovered thus by the blunder of a servant, he met this little vexation with the characteristic impudence which had served his turn so well in the endless intrigues of his self-seeking career. Without altering his attitude a hair's-breadth, one leg in a silk stocking advanced, his head twisted over his left shoulder, he called out calmly, 'This way, general. Pray approach. Well? I am all attention.'

While General D'Hubert, ill at ease as if one of his own little weaknesses had been exposed, presented his request as shortly as possible, the Duke of Otranto went on feeling the fit of his collar, settling the lapels before the glass, and buckling his back in an effort to behold the set of the gold embroidered coat-skirts behind. His still face, his attentive eyes, could not have expressed a more complete interest in those matters if he had been alone.

'Exclude from the operations of the Special Court a certain Feraud, Gabriel Florian, general of brigade of the promotion of 1814?' he repeated, in a slightly wondering tone, and then turned away from the glass. 'Why exclude him precisely?'

'I am surprised that your excellency, so competent in the evaluation of men of his time, should have thought it worth while to have that name put down on the list.'

'A rabid Bonapartist!'

'So is every grenadier and every trooper of the army, as your excellency well knows. And the individuality of General Feraud can have no more weight than that of any casual grenadier. He is a man of no mental grasp, of no capacity whatever. It is inconceivable that he should ever have any influence.'

'He has a well-hung tongue, though,' interjected Fouché.

'Noisy, I admit, but not dangerous.'

'I will not dispute with you. I know next to nothing of him. Hardly his name, in fact.'

'And yet your excellency has the presidency of the commission charged by the king to point out those who are to be tried,' said General D'Hubert, with an emphasis which did not miss the minister's ear.

'Yes, general,' he said, walking away into the dark part of the vast room, and throwing himself into a deep armchair that swallowed him up, all but the soft gleam of gold embroideries and the pallid patch of the face – 'yes, general. Take this chair there.'

General D'Hubert sat down.

'Yes, general,' continued the arch-master in the arts of intrigue and betrayals, whose duplicity, as if at times intolerable to his self-knowledge, found relief in bursts of cynical openness. 'I did hurry on the formation of the proscribing commission, and I took its presidency. And do you know why? Simply from fear that if I did not take it quickly into my hands my own name would head the list of the proscribed. Such are the times in which we live. But I am minister of the king yet, and I ask you plainly why I should take the name of this obscure Feraud off the list? You wonder how his name got there! Is it possible that you should know men so little? My dear general, at the very first sitting of the commission names poured on us like rain off the roof of the Tuileries. Names! We had our choice of thousands. How do you know that the name of this Feraud, whose life or death don't matter to France, does not keep out some other name?'

The voice out of the armchair stopped. Opposite General D'Hubert sat still, shadowy and silent. Only his sabre clinked slightly. The voice in the armchair began again. 'And we must try to satisfy the exigencies of the allied sovereigns, too. The Prince de Talleyrand told me only yesterday that Nesselrode had informed him officially of His Majesty the Emperor Alexander's dissatisfaction at the small number of examples the government of the king intends to make – especially amongst military men. I tell you this confidentially.'

'Upon my word!' broke out General D'Hubert, speaking through his teeth, 'if your excellency deigns to favour me with any more confidential information I don't know what I will do. It's enough to make one break one's sword over one's knee, and fling the pieces. . . .'

'What government do you imagine yourself to be serving?' interrupted the minister, sharply.

After a short pause the crestfallen voice of General D'Hubert answered, 'The Government of France.'

'That's paying your conscience off with mere words, general. The truth is that you are serving a government of returned exiles, of men who have been without country for twenty years. Of men also who have just got over a very bad and humiliating fright . . . Have no illusions on that score.'

The Duke of Otranto ceased. He had relieved himself, and had attained his object of stripping some self-respect off that man who had inconveniently discovered him posturing in a gold-embroidered court costume before a mirror. But they were a hot-headed lot in the army; it occurred to him that it would be inconvenient if a well-disposed general officer, received in audience on the recommendation of one of the princes, were to do something rashly scandalous directly after a private interview with the minister. In a changed tone he put a question to the point: 'Your relation – this Feraud?'

'No. No relation at all.'

'Intimate friend?'

'Intimate . . . yes. There is between us an intimate connection of a nature which makes it a point of honour with me to try . . .'

The minister rang a bell without waiting for the end of the phrase. When the servant had gone out, after bringing in a pair of heavy silver candelabra for the writing-desk, the Duke of Otranto rose, his breast glistening all over with gold in the strong light, and taking a piece of paper out of a drawer, held it in his hand ostentatiously while he said with persuasive gentleness: 'You must not speak of breaking your sword across your knee, general. Perhaps you would never get another. The emperor will not return this time . . . *Diable d'homme*! There was just a moment, here in Paris, soon after Waterloo, when he frightened me. It looked as though he were ready to begin all over again. Luckily one never does begin all over again, really. You must not think of breaking your sword, general.'

General D'Hubert, looking on the ground, moved his hand slightly in a hopeless gesture of renunciation. The minister of police turned his eyes away from him, and scanned deliberately the paper he had been holding up all the time.

'There are only twenty general officers selected to be made an example of. Twenty. A round number. And let's see, Feraud . . . Ah, he's there. Gabriel Florian. *Parfaitement*. That's your man. Well, there will be only nineteen examples made now.'

General D'Hubert stood up feeling as though he had gone through an infectious illness. 'I must beg your excellency to keep my interference a profound secret. I attach the greatest importance to his never learning . . .'

'Who is going to inform him, I should like to know?' said Fouché, raising his eyes curiously to General D'Hubert's tense, set face. 'Take one of these pens, and run it through the name yourself. This is the only list in existence. If you are careful to take up enough ink no one will be able to tell what was the name struck out. But, *par exemple*, I am not responsible for what Clarke will do with him afterwards. If he persists in being rabid he will be ordered by the minister of war to reside in some provincial town under the supervision of the police.'

*   *   *

A few days later General D'Hubert was saying to his sister, after the first greetings had been got over: 'Ah, my dear Léonie! it seemed to me I couldn't get away from Paris quick enough.'

'Effect of love,' she suggested, with a malicious smile.

'And horror,' added General D'Hubert, with profound seriousness. 'I have nearly died there of . . . of nausea.'

His face was contracted with disgust. And as his sister looked at him attentively he continued, 'I have had to see Fouché. I have had an audience. I have been in his cabinet. There remains with one who has had the misfortune to breathe the air of the same room with that man a sense of diminished dignity, an uneasy feeling of being not so clean, after all, as one hoped one was . . . But you can't understand.'

She nodded quickly several times. She understood very well, on the contrary. She knew her brother thoroughly, and liked him as he was. Moreover, the scorn and loathing of mankind were the lot of the Jacobin Fouché, who, exploiting for his own advantage every weakness, every virtue, every generous illusion of mankind, made dupes of his whole generation, and died obscurely as Duke of Otranto.

'My dear Armand,' she said, compassionately, 'what could you want from that man?'

'Nothing less than a life,' answered General D'Hubert. 'And I've got it. It had to be done. But I feel yet as if I could never forgive the necessity to the man I had to save.'

General Feraud, totally unable (as is the case with most of us) to comprehend what was happening to him, received the minister of war's order to proceed at once to a small town of Central France with feelings whose natural expression consisted in a fierce rolling of the eye and savage grinding of the teeth. The passing away of the state of war, the only condition of society he had ever known, the horrible view of a world at peace, frightened him. He went away to his little town firmly convinced that this could not last. There he was informed of his retirement from the army, and that his pension (calculated on the scale of a colonel's rank) was made dependent on the correctness of his conduct, and on the good reports of the police. No longer in the army! He felt suddenly strange to the earth, like a disembodied spirit. It was impossible to exist. But at first he reacted from sheer incredulity. This could not be. He waited for thunder, earthquakes, natural cataclysms; but nothing happened. The leaden weight of an irremediable idleness descended upon General Feraud, who having no resources within himself sank into a state of awe-inspiring hebitude. He haunted the streets of the little town, gazing before him with lacklustre eyes, disregarding the hats raised on his passage; and people, nudging each other as he went by, whispered, 'That's poor General Feraud. His heart is broken. Behold how he loved the emperor.'

The other living wreckage of the Napoleonic tempest clustered round General Feraud with infinite respect. He, himself, imagined his soul to be crushed by grief. He suffered from quickly succeeding impulses to weep, to howl, to bite his fists till blood came, to spend days on his bed with his head thrust under the pillow; but these arose from sheer ennui, from the anguish of an immense, indescribable, inconceivable boredom. His mental inability to grasp the hopeless nature of his case as a whole saved him from suicide. He never even thought of it once. He thought of nothing. But his appetite abandoned him, and the difficulty he experienced to express the over-whelming nature of his feelings (the most furious swearing could do no justice to it) induced gradually a habit of silence – a sort of death to a southern temperament.

Great, therefore, was the sensation amongst the *anciens militaires* frequenting a certain little café full of flies when one stuffy afternoon 'that poor General Feraud' let out suddenly a volley of formidable curses.

He had been sitting quietly in his own privileged corner looking through the Paris gazettes with just as much interest as a condemned man on the eve of execution could be expected to show in the news of the day. 'I'll find out presently that I am alive yet,' he declared, in a dogmatic tone. 'However, this is a private affair. An old affair of honour. Bah! Our honour does not matter. Here we are driven off with a split ear like a lot of cast troop horses – good only for a knacker's yard. But it would be like striking a blow for the emperor . . . Messieurs, I shall require the assistance of two of you.'

Every man moved forward. General Feraud, deeply touched by this demonstration, called with visible emotion upon the one-eyed veteran *cuirassier* and the officer of the Chasseurs à Cheval who had left the tip of his nose in Russia. He excused his choice to the others. 'A cavalry affair this – you know.'

He was answered with a varied chorus of, '*Parfaitement, mon général . . . C'est juste . . . Parbleu, c'est connu . . .*' Everybody was satisfied. The three left the café together, followed by cries of '*Bonne chance.*'

Outside they linked arms, the general in the middle. The three rusty cocked hats worn *en bataille* with a sinister forward slant barred the narrow street nearly right across. The overheated little town of grey stones and red tiles was drowsing away its provincial afternoon under a blue sky. The loud blows of a cooper hooping a cask reverberated regularly between the houses. The general dragged his left foot a little in the shade of the walls.

'That damned winter of 1813 got into my bones for good. Never mind. We must take pistols, that's all. A little lumbago. We must have pistols. He's game for my bag. My eyes are as keen as ever. You should have seen me in Russia picking off the dodging Cossacks with a beastly old infantry musket. I have a natural gift for firearms.'

In this strain General Feraud ran on, holding up his head, with owlish eyes and rapacious beak. A mere fighter all his life, a cavalry man, a *sabreur*, he conceived war with the utmost simplicity, as, in the main, a massed lot of personal contests, a sort of gregarious duelling. And here he had in hand a war of his own. He revived. The shadow of peace passed away from him like the shadow of death. It was the marvellous resurrection of the named Feraud, Gabriel Florian, *engagé volontaire* of 1793, general of 1814, buried without ceremony by means of a service order signed by the war minister of the second restoration.

No man succeeds in everything he undertakes. In that sense we are all failures. The great point is not to fail in ordering and sustaining the effort of our life. In this matter vanity is what leads us astray. It hurries us into situations from which we must come out damaged; whereas pride is our safeguard, by the reserve it imposes on the choice of our endeavour as much as by the virtue of its sustaining power.

General D'Hubert was proud and reserved. He had not been damaged by his casual love affairs, successful or otherwise. In his war-scarred body his heart at forty remained unscratched. Entering with reserve into his sister's matrimonial plans, he had felt himself falling irremediably in love as one falls off a roof. He was too proud to be frightened. Indeed, the sensation was too delightful to be alarming.

The inexperience of a man of forty is a much more serious thing than the inexperience of a youth of twenty, for it is not helped out by the rashness of hot blood. The girl was mysterious, as young girls are by the mere effect of their guarded ingenuity; and to him the mysteriousness of that young girl appeared exceptional and fascinating. But there was nothing mysterious about the arrangements of the match which Madame Léonie had promoted. There was nothing peculiar, either. It was a very appropriate match, commending itself extremely to the young lady's mother (the father was dead) and tolerable to the young lady's uncle – an old *emigré* lately returned from Germany, and pervading, cane in hand, a lean ghost of the *ancien régime*, the garden walks of the young lady's ancestral home.

General D'Hubert was not the man to be satisfied merely with the woman and the fortune – when it came to the point. His pride (and pride aims always at true success) would be satisfied with nothing short of love. But as true pride excludes vanity, he could not imagine any reason why this mysterious creature with deep and brilliant eyes of a violet colour should have any feeling for him warmer than indifference. The young lady (her name was Adèle) baffled every attempt at a clear understanding on that point. It is true that the attempts were clumsy and made timidly, because by then General D'Hubert had become acutely aware of the number of his years, of his wounds, of his many moral imperfections, of his secret unworthiness – and had incidentally learned by experience the meaning of the word funk. As far as he could make out she seemed to imply that, with an unbounded confidence in her mother's affection and sagacity, she felt no unsurmountable dislike for the person of General D'Hubert; and that this was quite sufficient for a well-brought-up young lady to begin married life upon. This view hurt and tormented the pride of General D'Hubert. And yet he asked himself, with a sort of sweet despair, what more could he expect? She had a quiet and luminous forehead. Her violet eyes laughed while the lines of her lips and chin remained composed in admirable gravity. All this was set off by such a glorious mass of fair hair, by a complexion so marvellous, by such a grace of expression, that General D'Hubert really never found the opportunity to examine with sufficient detachment the lofty exigencies of his pride. In fact, he became shy of that line of enquiry since it had led once or twice to a crisis of solitary passion in which it was borne upon him that he loved her enough to kill her rather than lose her. From such passages, not unknown to men of forty, he would come out broken, exhausted, remorseful, a little dismayed. He derived, however, considerable comfort from the quietist practice of sitting now and then half the night by an open window and meditating upon the wonder of her existence, like a believer lost in the mystic contemplation of his faith.

It must not be supposed that all these variations of his inward state were made manifest to the world. General D'Hubert found no difficulty in appearing wreathed in smiles. Because, in fact, he was very happy. He followed the established rules of his condition, sending over flowers (from his sister's garden and hot-houses) early every morning, and a little later following himself to lunch with his intended, her mother, and her *emigré* uncle. The middle of the day was spent in strolling or sitting in the shade. A watchful deference, trembling on the verge of tenderness, was the note of their intercourse on his side – with a playful turn of the phrase concealing the profound trouble of his whole being caused by her inaccessible nearness. Late in the afternoon General D'Hubert walked home between the fields of vines, sometimes intensely miserable, sometimes supremely happy, sometimes pensively sad; but always feeling a special intensity of existence, that elation common to artists, poets and lovers – to men haunted by a great passion, a noble thought or a new vision of plastic beauty.

The outward world at that time did not exist with any special distinctness for General D'Hubert. One evening, however, crossing a ridge from which he could see both houses, General D'Hubert became aware of two figures far down the road. The day had been divine. The festal decoration of the inflamed sky lent a gentle glow to the sober tints of the southern land. The grey rocks, the brown fields, the purple, undulating distances harmonised in luminous accord, exhaled already the scents of the evening. The two figures down the road presented themselves like two rigid and wooden silhouettes all black on the ribbon of white dust. General D'Hubert made out the long, straight, military *capotes* buttoned closely right up to the black stocks, the cocked hats, the lean, carven, brown countenances – old soldiers – *vieilles moustaches*! The taller of the two had a black patch over one eye; the other's hard, dry countenance presented some bizarre, disquieting peculiarity, which on nearer approach proved to be the absence of the tip of the nose. Lifting their hands with one movement to salute the slightly lame civilian walking with a thick stick, they enquired for the house where the General Baron D'Hubert lived, and what was the best way to get speech with him quietly.

'If you think this quiet enough,' said General D'Hubert, looking round at the vine-fields, framed in purple lines, and dominated by the nest of grey and drab walls of a village clustering around the top of a conical hill, so that the blunt church tower seemed but the shape of a crowning rock – 'if you think this spot quiet enough, you can speak to him at once. And I beg you, comrades, to speak openly, with perfect confidence.'

They stepped back at this, and raised again their hands to their hats with marked ceremoniousness. Then the one with the chipped nose, speaking for both, remarked that the matter was confidential enough, and to be arranged discreetly. Their general quarters were established in that village over there, where the infernal clodhoppers – damn their false, royalist hearts! – looked remarkably cross-eyed at three unassuming military men. For the present he should only ask for the names of General D'Hubert's friends.

'What friends?' said the astonished General D'Hubert, completely off the track. 'I am staying with my brother-in-law over there.'

'Well, he will do for one,' said the chipped veteran.

'We're the friends of General Feraud,' interjected the other, who had kept silent till then, only glowering with his one eye at the man who had never loved the emperor. That was something to look at. For even the gold-laced Judases who had sold him to the English, the marshals and princes, had loved him at some time or other. But this man had never loved the emperor. General Feraud had said so distinctly.

General D'Hubert felt an inward blow in his chest. For an infinitesimal fraction of a second it was as if the spinning of the earth had become perceptible with an awful, slight rustle in the eternal stillness of space. But this noise of blood in his ears passed off at once. Involuntarily he murmured, 'Feraud! I had forgotten his existence.'

'He's existing at present, very uncomfortably, it is true, in the infamous inn of that nest of savages up there,' said the one-eyed *cuirassier*, drily. 'We arrived in your parts an hour ago on post horses. He's awaiting our return with impatience. There is hurry, you know. The general has broken the ministerial order to obtain from you the satisfaction he's entitled to by the laws of honour, and naturally he's anxious to have it all over before the gendarmerie gets on his scent.'

The other elucidated the idea a little further. 'Get back on the quiet – you understand? Phitt! No one the wiser. We have broken out, too. Your friend the king would be glad to cut off our scurvy pittances at the first chance. It's a risk. But honour before everything.'

General D'Hubert had recovered his powers of speech. 'So you come here like this along the road to invite me to a throat-cutting match with that – that . . .' A laughing sort of rage took possession of him. 'Ha! ha! ha! ha!'

His fists on his hips, he roared without restraint, while they stood before him lank and straight, as though they had been shot up with a snap through a trap door in the ground. Only four-and-twenty months ago the masters of Europe, they had already the air of antique ghosts; they seemed less substantial in their faded coats than their own narrow shadows falling so black across the white road: the military and grotesque shadows of twenty years of war and conquests. They had an outlandish appearance of two imperturbable bonzes of the religion of the sword. And General D'Hubert, also one of the ex-masters of Europe, laughed at these serious phantoms standing in his way.

Said one, indicating the laughing general with a jerk of the head: 'A merry companion, that.'

'There are some of us that haven't smiled from the day The Other went away,' remarked his comrade.

A violent impulse to set upon and beat those unsubstantial wraiths to the ground frightened General D'Hubert. He ceased laughing suddenly. His desire now was to get rid of them, to get them away from his sight quickly before he lost control of himself. He wondered at the fury he felt rising in his breast. But he had no time to look into that peculiarity just then.

'I understand your wish to be done with me as quickly as possible. Don't let us waste time in empty ceremonies. Do you see that wood there at the foot of that slope? Yes, the wood of pines. Let us meet there tomorrow at sunrise. I will bring with me my sword or my pistols, or both if you like.'

The seconds of General Feraud looked at each other.

'Pistols, general,' said the *cuirassier*.

'So be it. *Au revoir* – tomorrow morning. Till then let me advise you to keep close if you don't want the gendarmerie making enquiries about you before it gets dark. Strangers are rare in this part of the country.'

They saluted in silence. General D'Hubert, turning his back on their retreating forms, stood still in the middle of the road for a long time, biting his lower lip and looking on the ground. Then he began to walk straight before him, thus retracing his steps till he found himself before the park gate of his intended's house. Dusk had fallen. Motionless he stared through the bars at the front of the house, gleaming clear beyond the thickets and trees. Footsteps scrunched on the gravel, and presently a tall stooping shape emerged from the lateral alley following the inner side of the park wall.

Le Chevalier de Valmassigue, uncle of the adorable Adèle, ex-brigadier in the army of the princes, bookbinder in Altona, afterwards shoemaker (with a great reputation for elegance in the fit of ladies' shoes) in another small German town, wore silk stockings on his lean shanks, low shoes with silver buckles, a brocaded waistcoat. A long-skirted coat, *à la française*, covered loosely his thin, bowed back. A small three-cornered hat rested on a lot of powdered hair, tied in a queue.

'Monsieur le Chevalier,' called General D'Hubert, softly.

'What? You here again, *mon ami*? Have you forgotten something?'

'By heavens! that's just it. I have forgotten something. I am come to tell you of it. No – outside. Behind this wall. It's too ghastly a thing to be let in at all where she lives.'

The chevalier came out at once with that benevolent resignation some old people display towards the fugue of youth. Older by a quarter of a century than General D'Hubert, he looked upon him in the secret of his heart as a rather troublesome youngster in love. He had heard his enigmatical words very well, but attached no undue importance to what a mere man of forty so hard hit was likely to do or say. The turn of mind of the generation of Frenchmen grown up during the years of his exile was almost unintelligible to him. Their sentiments appeared to him unduly violent, lacking fineness and measure, their language needlessly exaggerated. He joined calmly the general on the road, and they made a few steps in silence, the general trying to master his agitation, and get proper control of his voice.

'It is perfectly true; I forgot something. I forgot till half an hour ago that I had an urgent affair of honour on my hands. It's incredible, but it is so!'

All was still for a moment. Then in the profound evening silence of the countryside the clear, aged voice of the chevalier was heard trembling slightly: 'Monsieur! That's an indignity.'

It was his first thought. The girl born during his exile, the posthumous daughter of his poor brother murdered by a band of Jacobins, had grown since his return very dear to his old heart, which had been starving on mere memories of affection for so many years. 'It is an inconceivable thing, I say! A man settles such affairs before he thinks of asking for a young girl's hand. Why! If you had forgotten for ten days longer, you would have been married before your memory returned to you. In my time men did not forget such things – nor yet what is due to the feelings of an innocent young woman. If I did not respect them myself, I would qualify your conduct in a way which you would not like.'

General D'Hubert relieved himself frankly by a groan. 'Don't let that consideration prevent you. You run no risk of offending her mortally.'

But the old man paid no attention to this lover's nonsense. It's doubtful whether he even heard. 'What is it?' he asked. 'What's the nature of . . . ?'

'Call it a youthful folly, Monsieur le Chevalier. An inconceivable, incredible result of . . .' He stopped short. 'He will never believe the story,' he thought. 'He will only think I am taking him for a fool, and get offended.' General D'Hubert spoke up again: 'Yes, originating in youthful folly, it has become . . .'

The chevalier interrupted: 'Well, then it must be arranged.'

'Arranged?'

'Yes, no matter at what cost to your *amour propre*. You should have remembered you were engaged. You forgot that, too, I suppose. And then you go and forget your quarrel. It's the most hopeless exhibition of levity I ever heard of.'

'Good heavens, monsieur! You don't imagine I was picking up this quarrel last time I was in Paris, or anything of the sort, do you?'

'Eh! What matters the precise date of your insane conduct,' exclaimed the chevalier, testily. 'The principal thing is to arrange it.'

Noticing General D'Hubert getting restive and trying to place a word, the old *emigré* raised his hand, and added with dignity, 'I've been a soldier, too. I would never dare suggest a doubtful step to the man whose name my niece is to bear. I tell you that *entre galants hommes* an affair can always be arranged.'

'But *saperlotte*, Monsieur le Chevalier, it's fifteen or sixteen years ago. I was a lieutenant of hussars then.'

The old chevalier seemed confounded by the vehemently despairing tone of this information. 'You were a lieutenant of hussars sixteen years ago?' he mumbled in a dazed manner.

'Why, yes! You did not suppose I was made a general in my cradle like a royal prince.'

In the deepening purple twilight of the fields spread with vine leaves, backed by a low band of sombre crimson in the west, the voice of the old ex-officer in the army of the princes sounded collected, punctiliously civil.

'Do I dream? Is this a pleasantry? Or am I to understand that you have been hatching an affair of honour for sixteen years?'

'It has clung to me for that length of time. That is my precise meaning. The quarrel itself is not to be explained easily. We met on the ground several times during that time, of course.'

'What manners! What horrible perversion of manliness! Nothing can account for such inhumanity but the sanguinary madness of the Revolution which has tainted a whole generation,' mused the returned *emigré* in a low tone. 'Who's your adversary?' he asked a little louder.

'My adversary? His name is Feraud.'

Shadowy in his tricorne and old-fashioned clothes, like a bowed, thin ghost of the *ancien régime*, the chevalier voiced a ghostly memory. 'I can remember the feud about little Sophie Derval, between Monsieur de Brissac, captain in the bodyguards, and d'Anjorrant (not the pock-marked one, the other – the Beau d'Anjorrant, as they called him). They met three times in eighteen months in a most gallant manner. It was the fault of that little Sophie, too, who would keep on playing . . .'

'This is nothing of the kind,' interrupted General D'Hubert. He laughed a little sardonically. 'Not at all so simple,' he added. 'Nor yet half so reasonable,' he finished, inaudibly, between his teeth, and ground them with rage.

After this sound nothing troubled the silence for a long time, till the chevalier asked, without animation: 'What is he – this Feraud?'

'Lieutenant of hussars, too – I mean, he's a general. A Gascon. Son of a blacksmith, I believe.'

'There! I thought so. That Bonaparte had a special predilection for the *canaille*. I don't mean this for you, D'Hubert. You are one of us, though you have served this usurper, who . . .'

'Let's leave him out of this,' broke in General D'Hubert.

The chevalier shrugged his peaked shoulders. 'Feraud of sorts. Offspring of a blacksmith and some village troll. See what comes of mixing yourself up with that sort of people.'

'You have made shoes yourself, chevalier.'

'Yes. But I am not the son of a shoemaker. Neither are you, Monsieur D'Hubert. You and I have something that your Bonaparte's princes, dukes, and marshals have not, because there's no power on earth that could give it to them,' retorted the *emigré*, with the rising animation of a man who has got hold of a hopeful argument. 'Those people don't exist – all these Ferauds. Feraud! What is Feraud? A *va-nu-pieds* disguised into a general by a Corsican adventurer masquerading as an emperor. There is no earthly reason for a D'Hubert to *s'encanailler* by a duel with a person of that sort. You can make your excuses to him perfectly well. And if the *manant* takes into his head to decline them, you may simply refuse to meet him.'

'You say I may do that?'

'I do. With the clearest conscience.'

'Monsieur le Chevalier! To what do you think you have returned from your emigration?'

This was said in such a startling tone that the old man raised sharply his bowed head, glimmering silvery white under the points of the little tricorne. For a time he made no sound.

'God knows!' he said at last, pointing with a slow and grave gesture at a tall roadside cross mounted on a block of stone, and stretching its arms of forged iron all black against the darkening red band in the sky – 'God knows! If it were not for this emblem, which I remember seeing on this spot as a child, I would wonder to what we who remained faithful to God and our king have returned. The very voices of the people have changed.'

'Yes, it is a changed France,' said General D'Hubert. He seemed to have regained his calm. His tone was slightly ironic. 'Therefore I cannot take your advice. Besides, how is one to refuse to be bitten by a dog that means to bite? It's impracticable. Take my word for it – Feraud isn't a man to be stayed by apologies or refusals. But there are other ways. I could, for instance, send a messenger with a word to the brigadier of the gendarmerie in Senlac. He and his two friends are liable to arrest on my simple order. It would make some talk in the army, both the organised and the disbanded –

especially the disbanded. All *canaille*! All once upon a time the companions in arms of Armand D'Hubert. But what need a D'Hubert care what people that don't exist may think? Or, better still, I might get my brother-in-law to send for the mayor of the village and give him a hint. No more would be needed to get the three "brigands" set upon with flails and pitchforks and hunted into some nice, deep, wet ditch – and nobody the wiser! It has been done only ten miles from here to three poor devils of the disbanded Red Lancers of the Guard going to their homes. What says your conscience, chevalier? Can a D'Hubert do that thing to three men who do not exist?'

A few stars had come out on the blue obscurity, clear as crystal, of the sky. The dry, thin voice of the chevalier spoke harshly: 'Why are you telling me all this?'

The general seized the withered old hand with a strong grip. 'Because I owe you my fullest confidence. Who could tell Adèle but you? You understand why I dare not trust my brother-in-law nor yet my own sister. Chevalier! I have been so near doing these things that I tremble yet. You don't know how terrible this duel appears to me. And there's no escape from it.'

He murmured after a pause, 'It's a fatality,' dropped the chevalier's passive hand, and said in his ordinary conversational voice, 'I shall have to go without seconds. If it is my lot to remain on the ground, you at least will know all that can be made known of this affair.'

The shadowy ghost of the *ancien régime* seemed to have become more bowed during the conversation. 'How am I to keep an indifferent face this evening before these two women?' he groaned. 'General! I find it very difficult to forgive you.'

General D'Hubert made no answer.

'Is your cause good, at least?'

'I am innocent.'

This time he seized the chevalier's ghostly arm above the elbow, and gave it a mighty squeeze. 'I must kill him!' he hissed, and opening his hand strode away down the road.

The delicate attentions of his adoring sister had secured for the general perfect liberty of movement in the house where he was a guest. He had even his own entrance through a small door in one corner of the orangery. Thus he was not exposed that evening to the necessity of dissembling his agitation before the calm ignorance of the other inmates. He was glad of it. It seemed to him that if he had to open his lips he would break out into horrible and aimless imprecations, start breaking furniture, smashing china and glass. From the moment he opened the private door and while ascending the twenty-eight steps of a winding staircase, giving access to the corridor on which his room opened, he went through a horrible and humiliating scene in which an infuriated madman with bloodshot eyes and a foaming mouth played inconceivable havoc with everything inanimate that may be found in a well-appointed dining-room. When he opened the door of his apartment the fit was over, and his bodily fatigue was so great that he had to catch at the backs of the chairs while crossing the room to reach a low and broad divan on which he let himself fall heavily. His moral prostration was still greater. That brutality of feeling which he had known only when charging the enemy, sabre in hand, amazed this man of forty, who did not recognise in it the instinctive fury of his menaced passion. But in his mental and bodily exhaustion this passion got cleared, distilled, refined into a sentiment of melancholy despair at having, perhaps, to die before he had taught this beautiful girl to love him.

That night, General D'Hubert stretched out on his back with his hands over his eyes, or lying on his breast with his face buried in a cushion, made the full pilgrimage of emotions. Nauseating disgust at the absurdity of the situation, doubt of his own fitness to conduct his existence, and mistrust of his best sentiments (for what the devil did he want to go to Fouché for?) – he knew them all in turn. 'I am an idiot, neither more nor less,' he thought – 'A sensitive idiot. Because I overheard two men talking in a café . . . I am an idiot afraid of lies – whereas in life it is only truth that matters.'

Several times he got up and, walking in his socks in order not to be heard by anybody downstairs, drank all the water he could find in the dark. And he tasted the torments of jealousy, too. She would marry somebody else. His very soul writhed. The tenacity of that Feraud, the awful persistence of that imbecile brute, came to him with the tremendous force of a relentless destiny. General D'Hubert trembled as he put down the empty water ewer. 'He will have me,' he thought. General D'Hubert was tasting every emotion that life has to give. He had in his dry mouth the faint sickly flavour of fear, not the excusable fear before a young girl's candid and amused glance, but the fear of death and the honourable man's fear of cowardice.

But if true courage consists in going out to meet an odious danger from which our body, soul and heart recoil together, General D'Hubert had the opportunity to practise it for the first time in his life. He had charged exultingly at batteries and at infantry squares, and ridden with messages through a hail of bullets without thinking anything about it. His business now was to sneak out unheard, at break of day, to an obscure and revolting death. General D'Hubert never hesitated. He carried two pistols in a leather bag which he slung over his shoulder. Before he had crossed the garden his mouth was dry again. He picked two oranges. It was only after shutting the gate after him that he felt a slight faintness.

He staggered on, disregarding it, and after going a few yards regained the command of his legs. In the colourless and pellucid dawn the wood of pines detached its columns of trunks and its dark green canopy very clearly against the rocks of the grey hillside. He kept his eyes fixed on it steadily, and sucked at an orange as he walked. That temperamental good-humoured coolness in the face of danger which had made him an officer liked by his men and appreciated by his superiors was gradually asserting itself. It was like going into battle. Arriving at the edge of the wood he sat down on a boulder, holding the other orange in his hand, and reproached himself for coming so ridiculously early on the ground. Before very long, however, he heard the swishing of bushes, footsteps on the hard ground, and the sounds of a disjointed, loud conversation. A voice somewhere behind him said boastfully, 'He's game for my bag.'

He thought to himself, 'Here they are. What's this about game? Are they talking of me?' And becoming aware of the other orange in his hand, he thought further, 'These are very good oranges. Léonie's own tree. I may just as well eat this orange now instead of flinging it away.'

Emerging from a wilderness of rocks and bushes, General Feraud and his seconds discovered General D'Hubert engaged in peeling the orange. They stood still, waiting till he looked up. Then the seconds raised their hats, while General Feraud, putting his hands behind his back, walked aside a little way.

'I am compelled to ask one of you, messieurs, to act for me. I have brought no friends. Will you?'

The one-eyed cuirassier said judicially, 'That cannot be refused.'

The other veteran remarked, 'It's awkward all the same.'

'Owing to the state of the people's minds in this part of the country there was no one I could trust safely with the object of your presence here,' explained General D'Hubert, urbanely.

They saluted, looked round, and remarked both together: 'Poor ground.'

'It's unfit.'

'Why bother about ground, measurements, and so on? Let us simplify matters. Load the two pairs of pistols. I will take those of General Feraud, and let him take mine. Or, better still, let us take a mixed pair. One of each pair. Then let us go into the wood and shoot at sight, while you remain outside. We did not come here for ceremonies, but for war – war to the death. Any ground is good enough for that. If I fall, you must leave me where I lie and clear out. It wouldn't be healthy for you to be found hanging about here after that.'

It appeared after a short parley that General Feraud was willing to accept these conditions. While the seconds were loading the pistols, he could be heard whistling, and was seen to rub his hands with perfect contentment. He flung off his coat briskly, and General D'Hubert took off his own and folded it carefully on a stone.

'Suppose you take your principal to the other side of the wood and let him enter exactly in ten minutes from now,' suggested General D'Hubert, calmly, but feeling as if he were giving directions for his own execution. This, however, was his last moment of weakness. 'Wait. Let us compare watches first.'

He pulled out his own. The officer with the chipped nose went over to borrow the watch of General Feraud. They bent their heads over them for a time.

'That's it. At four minutes to six by yours. Seven to by mine.'

It was the *cuirassier* who remained by the side of General D'Hubert, keeping his one eye fixed immovably on the white face of the watch he held in the palm of his hand. He opened his mouth, waiting for the beat of the last second, long before he snapped out the word, '*Avancez.*'

General D'Hubert moved on, passing from the glaring sunshine of the Provençal morning into the cool and aromatic shade of the pines. The ground was clear between the reddish trunks, whose multitude, leaning at slightly different angles, confused his eye at first. It was like going into battle. The commanding quality of confidence in himself woke up in his breast. He was all to his affair. The problem was how to kill the adversary. Nothing short of that would free him from this imbecile nightmare. 'It's no use wounding that brute,' thought General D'Hubert. He was known as a resourceful officer. His comrades years ago used also to call him The Strategist. And it was a fact that he could think in the presence of the enemy. Whereas Feraud had been always a mere fighter – but a dead shot, unluckily.

'I must draw his fire at the greatest possible range,' said General D'Hubert to himself.

At that moment he saw something white moving far off between the trees – the shirt of his adversary. He stepped out at once between the trunks, exposing himself freely; then, quick as lightning, leaped back. It had been a risky move but it succeeded in its object. Almost simultaneously with the pop of a shot a small piece of bark chipped off by the bullet stung his ear painfully.

General Feraud, with one shot expended, was getting cautious. Peeping round the tree, General D'Hubert could not see him at all. This ignorance of the foe's whereabouts carried with it a sense of insecurity. General D'Hubert felt himself abominably exposed on his flank and rear. Again something white fluttered in his sight. Ha! The enemy was still on his front, then. He had feared a turning movement. But apparently General Feraud was not thinking of it. General D'Hubert saw him pass without special haste from one tree to another in the straight line of approach. With great firmness of mind General D'Hubert stayed his hand. Too far yet. He knew he was no marksman. His must be a waiting game – to kill.

Wishing to take advantage of the greater thickness of the trunk, he sank down to the ground. Extended at full length, head on to his enemy, he had his person completely protected. Exposing himself would not do now, because the other was too near by this time. A conviction that Feraud would presently do something rash was like balm to General D'Hubert's soul. But to keep his chin raised off the ground was irksome, and not much use either. He peeped round, exposing a fraction of his head with dread, but really with little risk. His enemy, as a matter of fact, did not expect to see anything of him so far down as that. General D'Hubert caught a fleeting view of General Feraud shifting trees again with deliberate caution. 'He despises my shooting,' he thought, displaying that insight into the mind of his antagonist which is of such great help in winning battles. He was confirmed in his tactics of immobility. 'If I could only watch my rear as well as my front!' he thought anxiously, longing for the impossible.

It required some force of character to lay his pistols down; but, on a sudden impulse, General D'Hubert did this very gently – one on each side of him. In the army he had been looked upon as a bit of a dandy because he used to shave and put on a clean shirt on the days of battle. As a matter of fact, he had always been very careful of his personal appearance. In a man of nearly forty, in love with a young and charming girl, this praiseworthy self-respect may run to such little weaknesses as, for instance, being provided with an elegant little leather folding-case containing a small ivory comb, and fitted with a piece of looking-glass on the outside. General D'Hubert, his hands being free, felt in his breeches' pockets for that implement of innocent vanity excusable in the possessor of long, silky moustaches. He drew it out, and then with the utmost coolness and promptitude turned himself over on his back. In this new attitude, his head a little raised, holding the little looking-glass just clear of his tree, he squinted into it with his left eye, while the right kept a direct watch on the rear of his position. Thus was proved Napoleon's saying, that 'for a French soldier, the word impossible does not exist'. He had the right tree nearly filling the field of his little mirror.

'If he moves from behind it,' he reflected with satisfaction, 'I am bound to see his legs. But in any case he can't come upon me unawares.'

And sure enough he saw the boots of General Feraud flash in and out, eclipsing for an instant everything else reflected in the little mirror. He shifted its position accordingly. But having to form his judgement of the change from that indirect view he did not realise that now his feet and a portion of his legs were in plain sight of General Feraud.

General Feraud had been getting gradually impressed by the amazing cleverness with which his enemy was keeping cover. He had spotted the right tree with bloodthirsty precision. He was absolutely certain of it. And yet he had not been able to glimpse as much as the tip of an ear. As he had been looking for it at the height of about five feet ten inches from the ground it was no great wonder – but it seemed very wonderful to General Feraud.

The first view of these feet and legs determined a rush of blood to his head. He literally staggered behind his tree, and had to steady himself against it with his hand. The other was lying on the ground, then! On the ground! Perfectly still, too! Exposed! What could it mean? . . . The notion that he had knocked over his adversary at the first shot entered then General Feraud's head. Once there it grew with every second of attentive gazing, overshadowing every other supposition – irresistible, triumphant, ferocious.

'What an ass I was to think I could have missed him,' he muttered to himself. 'He was exposed *en plein* – the fool! – for quite a couple of seconds.'

General Feraud gazed at the motionless limbs, the last vestiges of surprise fading before an unbounded admiration of his own deadly skill with the pistol.

'Turned up his toes! By the god of war, that was a shot!' he exulted mentally. 'Got it through the head, no doubt, just where I aimed, staggered behind that tree, rolled over on his back, and died.'

And he stared! He stared, forgetting to move, almost awed, almost sorry. But for nothing in the world would he have had it undone. Such a shot! – such a shot! Rolled over on his back and died!

For it was this helpless position, lying on the back, that shouted its direct evidence at General Feraud! It never occurred to him that it might have been deliberately assumed by a living man. It was inconceivable. It was beyond the range of sane supposition. There was no possibility to guess the reason for it. And it must be said, too, that General D'Hubert's turned-up feet looked thoroughly dead. General Feraud expanded his lungs for a stentorian shout to his seconds, but, from what he felt to be an excessive scrupulousness, refrained for a while.

'I will just go and see first whether he breathes yet,' he mumbled to himself, leaving carelessly the shelter of his tree. This move was immediately perceived by the resourceful General D'Hubert. He concluded it to be another shift, but when he lost the boots out of the field of the mirror he became uneasy. General Feraud had only stepped a little out of the line, but his adversary could not possibly have supposed him walking up with perfect unconcern. General D'Hubert, beginning to wonder what had become of the other, was taken unawares so completely that the first warning of danger consisted in the long, early-morning shadow of his enemy falling aslant on his outstretched legs. He had not even heard a footfall on the soft ground between the trees!

It was too much even for his coolness. He jumped up thoughtlessly, leaving the pistols on the ground. The irresistible instinct of an average man (unless totally paralysed by discomfiture) would have been to stoop for his weapons, exposing himself to the risk of being shot down in that position. Instinct, of course, is irreflective. It is its very definition. But it may be an inquiry worth pursuing whether in reflective mankind the mechanical promptings of instinct are not affected by the customary mode of thought. In his young days, Armand D'Hubert, the reflective, promising officer, had emitted the opinion that in warfare one should 'never cast back on the lines of a mistake'. This idea, defended and developed in many discussions, had settled into one of the stock notions of his brain, had become a part of his mental individuality. Whether it had gone so inconceivably deep as to affect the dictates of his instinct, or simply because, as he himself declared afterwards, he was 'too scared to remember the confounded pistols', the fact is that General D'Hubert never attempted to stoop for them. Instead of going back on his mistake, he seized the rough trunk with both hands, and swung himself behind it with such impetuosity that, going right round in the very flash and report of the pistol-shot, he reappeared on the other side of the tree face to face with General Feraud. This last, completely unstrung by such a show of agility on the part of a dead man, was trembling yet. A very faint mist of smoke hung before his face which had an extraordinary aspect, as if the lower jaw had come unhinged.

'Not missed!' he croaked, hoarsely, from the depths of a dry throat.

This sinister sound loosened the spell that had fallen on General D'Hubert's senses. 'Yes, missed – *à bout portant*,' he heard himself saying, almost before he had recovered the full command of his faculties. The revulsion of feeling was accompanied by a gust of homicidal fury, resuming in its violence the accumulated resentment of a lifetime. For years General D'Hubert had been exasperated and humiliated by an atrocious absurdity imposed upon him by this man's savage caprice. Besides, General D'Hubert had been in this last instance too unwilling to confront death for the reaction of his anguish not to take the shape of a desire to kill. 'And I have my two shots to fire yet,' he added, pitilessly.

General Feraud snapped-to his teeth, and his face assumed an irate, undaunted expression. 'Go on!' he said, grimly.

These would have been his last words if General D'Hubert had been holding the pistols in his hands. But the pistols were lying on the ground at the foot of a pine. General D'Hubert had the second of leisure necessary to remember that he had dreaded death not as a man, but as a lover; not as a danger, but as a rival; not as a foe to life, but as an obstacle to marriage. And behold! there was the rival defeated! – utterly defeated, crushed, done for!

He picked up the weapons mechanically, and, instead of firing them into General Feraud's breast, he gave expression to the thoughts uppermost in his mind, 'You will fight no more duels now.'

His tone of leisurely, ineffable satisfaction was too much for General Feraud's stoicism. 'Don't dawdle, then, damn you for a cold-blooded staff-coxcomb!' he roared out, suddenly, out of an impassive face held erect on a rigidly still body.

General D'Hubert uncocked the pistols carefully. This proceeding was observed with mixed feelings by the other general. 'You missed me twice,' the victor said, coolly, shifting both pistols to one hand; 'the last time within a foot or so. By every rule of single combat your life belongs to me. That does not mean that I want to take it now.'

'I have no use for your forbearance,' muttered General Feraud, gloomily.

'Allow me to point out that this is no concern of mine,' said General D'Hubert, whose every word was dictated by a consummate delicacy of feeling. In anger he could have killed that man, but in cold blood he recoiled from humiliating by a show of generosity this unreasonable being – a fellow-soldier of the Grande Armée, a companion in the wonders and terrors of the great military epic. 'You don't set up the pretension of dictating to me what I am to do with what's my own.'

General Feraud looked startled, and the other continued. 'You've forced me on a point of honour to keep my life at your disposal, as it were, for fifteen years. Very well. Now that the matter is decided to my advantage, I am going to do what I like with your life on the same principle. You shall keep it at my disposal as long as I choose. Neither more nor less. You are on your honour till I say the word.'

'I am! But, *sacré bleu*! This is an absurd position for a general of the empire to be placed in!' cried General Feraud, in accents of profound and dismayed conviction. 'It amounts to sitting all the rest of my life with a loaded pistol in a drawer waiting for your word. It's – it's idiotic; I shall be an object of – of – derision.'

'Absurd? – idiotic? Do you think so?' queried General D'Hubert with sly gravity. 'Perhaps. But I don't see how that can be helped. However, I am not likely to talk at large of this adventure. Nobody need ever know anything about it. Just as no one to this day, I believe, knows the origin of our quarrel . . . Not a word more,' he added, hastily. 'I can't really discuss this question with a man who, as far as I am concerned, does not exist.'

When the two duellists came out into the open, General Feraud walking a little behind, and rather with the air of walking in a trance, the two seconds hurried towards them, each from his station at the edge of the wood. General D'Hubert addressed them, speaking loud and distinctly, 'Messieurs, I make it a point of declaring to you solemnly, in the presence of General Feraud, that our difference is at last settled for good. You may inform all the world of that fact.'

'A reconciliation, after all!' they exclaimed together.

'Reconciliation? Not that exactly. It is something much more binding. Is it not so, general?'

General Feraud only lowered his head in sign of assent. The two veterans looked at each other. Later in the day, when they found themselves alone out of their moody friend's earshot, the *cuirassier* remarked suddenly, 'Generally speaking, I can see with my one eye as far as most people; but this beats me. He won't say anything.'

'In this affair of honour I understand there has been from first to last always something that no one in the army could quite make out,' declared the *chasseur* with the imperfect nose. 'In mystery it began, in mystery it went on, in mystery it is to end, apparently.'

General D'Hubert walked home with long, hasty strides, by no means uplifted by a sense of triumph. He had conquered, yet it did not seem to him that he had gained very much by his conquest. The night before he had grudged the risk of his life which appeared to him magnificent, worthy of preservation as an opportunity to win a girl's love. He had known moments when, by a marvellous illusion, this love seemed to be already his, and his threatened life a still more magnificent opportunity of devotion. Now that his life was safe it had suddenly lost its special magnificence. It had acquired instead a specially alarming aspect as a snare for the exposure of unworthiness. As to the marvellous illusion of conquered love that had visited him for a moment in the agitated watches of the night which might have been his last on earth, he comprehended now its true nature. It had been merely a paroxysm of delirious conceit. Thus to this man, sobered by the victorious issue of a duel, life appeared robbed of its charm, simply because it was no longer menaced.

Approaching the house from the back, through the orchard and the kitchen garden, he could not notice the agitation which reigned in front. He never met a single soul. Only while walking softly along the corridor, he became aware that the house was awake and more noisy than usual. Names of servants were being called out down below in a confused noise of coming and going. With some concern he noticed that the door of his own room stood ajar, though the shutters had not been opened yet. He had hoped that his early excursion would have passed unperceived. He expected to find some servant just gone in; but the sunshine filtering through the usual cracks enabled him to see lying on the low divan something bulky, which had the appearance of two women clasped in each other's arms. Tearful and desolate murmurs issued mysteriously from that appearance. General D'Hubert pulled open the nearest pair of shutters violently. One of the women then jumped up. It was his sister. She stood for a moment with her hair hanging down and her arms raised straight up above her head, and then flung herself with a stifled cry into his arms. He returned her embrace, trying at the same time to disengage himself from it. The other woman had not risen. She seemed, on the contrary, to cling closer to the divan, hiding her face in the cushions. Her hair was also loose; it was admirably fair. General D'Hubert recognised it with staggering emotion. Mademoiselle de Valmassigue! Adèle! In distress!

He became greatly alarmed, and got rid of his sister's hug definitely. Madame Léonie then extended her shapely bare arm out of her peignoir, pointing dramatically at the divan. 'This poor, terrified child has rushed here from home, on foot, two miles – running all the way.'

'What on earth has happened?' asked General D'Hubert in a low, agitated voice.

But Madame Léonie was speaking loudly. 'She rang the great bell at the gate and roused all the household – we were all asleep yet. You may imagine what a terrible shock . . . Adèle, my dear child, sit up.'

General D'Hubert's expression was not that of a man who 'imagines' with facility. He did, however, fish out of the chaos of surmises the notion that his prospective mother-in-law had died suddenly, but only to dismiss it at once. He could not conceive the nature of the event or the catastrophe which would induce Mademoiselle de Valmassigue, living in a house full of servants, to bring the news over the fields herself, two miles, running all the way.

'But why are you in this room?' he whispered, full of awe.

'Of course, I ran up to see, and this child . . . I did not notice it . . . she followed me. It's that absurd chevalier,' went on Madame Léonie, looking towards the divan . . . 'Her hair is all come down. You may imagine she did not stop to call her maid to dress it before she started . . . Adèle, my dear, sit up . . . He blurted it all out to her at half-past five in the morning. She woke up early and opened her shutters to breathe the fresh air, and saw him sitting collapsed on a garden bench at the end of the great alley. At that hour – you may imagine! And the evening before he had declared himself indisposed. She hurried on some clothes and flew down to him. One would be anxious for less. He loves her, but not very intelligently. He had been up all night, fully dressed, the poor old man, perfectly exhausted. He wasn't in a state to invent a plausible story . . . What a confidant you chose there! My husband was furious. He said, "We can't interfere now." So we sat down to wait. It was awful. And this poor child running with her hair loose over here publicly! She has been seen by some people in the fields. She has roused the whole household, too. It's awkward for her. Luckily you are to be married next week . . . Adèle, sit up. He has come home on his own legs . . . We expected to see you coming on a stretcher, perhaps – what do I know? Go and see if the carriage is ready. I must take this child home at once. It isn't proper for her to stay here a minute longer.'

General D'Hubert did not move. It was as though he had heard nothing. Madame Léonie changed her mind. 'I will go and see myself,' she cried. 'I want also my cloak. Adèle – ' she began, but did not add 'sit up'. She went out saying, in a very loud and cheerful tone: 'I leave the door open.'

General D'Hubert made a movement towards the divan, but then Adèle sat up, and that checked him dead. He thought, 'I haven't washed this morning. I must look like an old tramp. There's earth on the back of my coat and pine-needles in my hair.' It occurred to him that the situation required a good deal of circumspection on his part.

'I am greatly concerned, mademoiselle,' he began, vaguely, and abandoned that line. She was sitting up on the divan with her cheeks unusually pink and her hair, brilliantly fair, falling all over her shoulders – which was a very novel sight to the general. He walked away up the room, and looking out of the window for safety said, 'I fear you must think I behaved like a madman,' in accents of sincere despair. Then he spun round, and noticed that she had followed him with her eyes. They were not cast down on meeting his glance. And the expression of her face was novel to him also. It was, one might have said, reversed. Those eyes looked at him with grave thoughtfulness, while the exquisite lines of her mouth seemed to suggest a restrained smile. This change made her transcendental beauty much less mysterious, much more accessible to a man's comprehension. An amazing ease of mind came to the general – and even some ease of manner. He walked down the room with as much pleasurable excitement as he would have found in walking up to a battery vomiting death, fire and smoke; then stood looking down with smiling eyes at the girl whose marriage with him (next week) had been so carefully arranged by the wise, the good, the admirable Léonie.

'Ah! mademoiselle,' he said, in a tone of courtly regret, 'if only I could be certain that you did not come here this morning, two miles, running all the way, merely from affection for your mother!'

He waited for an answer imperturbable but inwardly elated. It came in a demure murmur, eyelashes lowered with fascinating effect. 'You must not be *méchant* as well as mad.'

And then General D'Hubert made an aggressive movement towards the divan which nothing could check. That piece of furniture was not exactly in the line of the open door. But Madame Léonie, coming back wrapped up in a light cloak and carrying a lace shawl on her arm for Adèle to hide her incriminating hair under, had a swift impression of her brother getting up from his knees.

'Come along, my dear child,' she cried from the doorway.

The general, now himself again in the fullest sense, showed the readiness of a resourceful cavalry officer and the peremptoriness of a leader of men. 'You don't expect her to walk to the carriage,' he said, indignantly. 'She isn't fit. I shall carry her downstairs.'

This he did slowly, followed by his awed and respectful sister; but he rushed back like a whirlwind to wash off all the signs of the night of anguish and the morning of war, and to put on the festive garments of a conqueror before hurrying over to the other house. Had it not been for that, General D'Hubert felt capable of mounting a horse and pursuing his late adversary in order simply to embrace him from excess of happiness. 'I owe it all to this stupid brute,' he thought. 'He has made plain in a morning what might have taken me years to find out – for I am a timid fool. No self-confidence whatever. Perfect coward. And the chevalier! Delightful old man!' General D'Hubert longed to embrace him also.

The chevalier was in bed. For several days he was very unwell. The men of the empire and the post-Revolution young ladies were too much for him. He got up the day before the wedding, and, being curious by nature, took his niece aside for a quiet talk. He advised her to find out from her husband the true story of the affair of honour, whose claim, so imperative and so persistent, had led her to within an ace of tragedy. 'It is right that his wife should be told. And next month or so will be your time to learn from him anything you want to know, my dear child.'

Later on, when the married couple came on a visit to the mother of the bride, Madame la Générale D'Hubert communicated to her beloved old uncle the true story she had obtained without any difficulty from her husband.

The chevalier listened with deep attention to the end, took a pinch of snuff, flicked the grains of tobacco from the frilled front of his shirt, and asked, calmly, 'And that's all it was?'

'Yes, uncle,' replied Madame la Générale, opening her pretty eyes very wide. 'Isn't it funny? *C'est insense* – to think what men are capable of!'

'H'm!' commented the old *emigré*. 'It depends what sort of men. That Bonaparte's soldiers were savages. It is *insense*. As a wife, my dear, you must believe implicitly what your husband says.'

But to Léonie's husband the chevalier confided his true opinion. 'If that's the tale the fellow made up for his wife, and during the honeymoon, too, you may depend on it that no one will ever know now the secret of this affair.'

Considerably later still, General D'Hubert judged the time come, and the opportunity propitious to write a letter to General Feraud. This letter began by disclaiming all animosity. 'I've never,' wrote the General Baron D'Hubert, 'wished for your death during all the time of our deplorable quarrel. Allow me,' he continued, 'to give you back in all form your forfeited life. It is proper that we two, who have been partners in so much military glory, should be friendly to each other publicly.'

The same letter contained also an item of domestic information. It was in reference to this last that General Feraud answered from a little village on the banks of the Garonne, in the following words:

If one of your boy's names had been Napoléon – or Joseph – or even Joachim, I could congratulate you on the event with a better heart. As you have thought proper to give him the names of Charles Henri Armand, I am confirmed in my conviction that you never loved the emperor. The thought of that sublime hero chained to a rock in the middle of a savage ocean makes life of so little value that I would receive with positive joy your instructions to blow my brains out. From suicide I consider myself in honour debarred. But I keep a loaded pistol in my drawer.

Madame la Générale D'Hubert lifted up her hands in despair after perusing that answer.

'You see? He won't be reconciled,' said her husband. 'He must never, by any chance, be allowed to guess where the money comes from. It wouldn't do. He couldn't bear it.'

'You are a brave *homme*, Armand,' said Madame la Générale, appreciatively.

'My dear, I had the right to blow his brains out; but as I didn't, we can't let him starve. He has lost his pension and he is utterly incapable of doing anything in the world for himself. We must take care of him, secretly, to the end of his days. Don't I owe him the most ecstatic moment of my life? . . . Ha! ha! ha! Over the fields, two miles, running all the way! I couldn't believe my ears! . . . But for his stupid ferocity, it would have taken me years to find you out. It's extraordinary how in one way or another this man has managed to fasten himself on my deeper feelings.'

The Warrior's Soul

The old officer with long white moustaches gave rein to his indignation.

'Is it possible that you youngsters should have no more sense than that! Some of you had better wipe the milk off your upper lip before you start to pass judgement on the few poor stragglers of a generation which has done and suffered not a little in its time.'

His hearers having expressed much compunction, the ancient warrior became appeased. But he was not silenced.

'I am one of them – one of the stragglers, I mean,' he went on patiently. 'And what did we do? What have we achieved? He – the great Napoleon – started upon us to emulate the Macedonian Alexander, with a ruck of nations at his back. We opposed empty spaces to French impetuosity, then we offered them an interminable battle so that their army went at last to sleep in its positions, lying down on the heaps of its own dead. Then came the wall of fire in Moscow. It toppled down on them.

'Then began the long rout of the Grand Army. I have seen it stream on, like the doomed flight of haggard, spectral sinners across the innermost frozen circle of Dante's Inferno, ever widening before their despairing eyes.

'They who escaped must have had their souls doubly riveted inside their bodies to carry them out of Russia through that frost fit to split rocks. But to say that it was our fault that a single one of them got away is mere ignorance. Why! Our own men suffered nearly to the limit of their strength. Their Russian strength!

'Of course our spirit was not broken; but then our cause was good – it was holy. But that did not temper the wind much to men and horses.

'The flesh is weak. Good or evil purpose, humanity has to pay the price. Why! In that very fight for that little village of which I have been telling you we were fighting for the shelter of those old houses as much as victory. And with the French it was the same.

'It wasn't for the sake of glory, or for the sake of strategy. The French knew that they would have to retreat before morning and we knew perfectly well that they would go. As far as the war was concerned there was nothing to fight about. Yet our infantry and theirs fought like wild cats, or like heroes if you like that better, amongst the houses – hot work enough – while the supports out in the open stood freezing in a tempestuous north wind which drove the snow on earth and the great masses of clouds in the sky at a terrific pace. The very air was inexpressibly sombre by contrast with the white earth. I have never seen God's creation look more sinister than on that day.

'We, the cavalry (we were only a handful), had not much to do except turn our backs to the wind and receive some stray French round shot. This, I may tell you, was the last of the French guns and it was the last time they had their artillery in position. Those guns never went away from there either. We found them abandoned next morning. But that afternoon they were keeping up an infernal fire on our attacking column; the furious wind carried away the smoke and even the noise but we could see the constant flicker of the tongues of fire along the French front. Then a driving flurry of snow would hide everything except the dark red flashes in the white swirl.

'At intervals when the line cleared we could see away across the plain to the right a sombre column moving endlessly; the great rout of the Grand Army creeping on and on all the time while the fight on our left went on with a great din and fury. The cruel whirlwind of snow swept over that scene of death and desolation. And then the wind fell as suddenly as it had arisen in the morning.

'Presently we got orders to charge the retreating column; I don't know why unless they wanted to prevent us from getting frozen in our saddles by giving us something to do. We changed front half right and got into motion at a walk to take that distant dark line in flank. It might have been half-past two in the afternoon.

'You must know that so far in this campaign my regiment had never been on the main line of Napoleon's advance. All these months since the invasion the army we belonged to had been wrestling with Oudinot in the north. We had only come down lately, driving him before us to the Beresina.

'This was the first occasion, then, that I and my comrades had a close view of Napoleon's Grand Army. It was an amazing and terrible sight. I had heard of it from others; I had seen the stragglers from it: small bands of marauders, parties of prisoners in the distance. But this was the very column itself! A crawling, stumbling, starved, half-demented mob. It issued from the forest a mile away and its head was lost in the murk of the fields. We rode into it at a trot, which was the most we could get out of our horses, and we stuck in that human mass as if in a moving bog. There was no resistance. I heard a few shots, half a dozen perhaps. Their very senses seemed frozen within them. I had time for a good look while riding at the head of my squadron. Well, I assure you, there were men walking on the outer edge so lost to everything but their misery that they never turned their heads to look at our charge. Soldiers!

'My horse pushed over one of them with his chest. The poor wretch had a dragoon's blue cloak, all torn and scorched, hanging from his shoulders and he didn't even put his hand out to snatch at my bridle and save himself. He just went down. Our troopers were pointing and slashing; well, and of course at first I myself ... What would you have! An enemy's an enemy. Yet a sort of sickening awe crept into my heart. There was no tumult – only a low deep murmur dwelt over them interspersed with louder cries and groans while that mob kept on pushing and surging past us, sightless and without feeling. A smell of scorched rags and festering wounds hung in the air. My horse staggered in the eddies of swaying men. But it was like cutting down galvanised corpses that didn't care. Invaders! Yes . . . God was already dealing with them.

'I touched my horse with the spurs to get clear. There was a sudden rush and a sort of angry moan when our second squadron got into them on our right. My horse plunged and somebody got hold of my leg. As I had no mind to get pulled out of the saddle I gave a back-handed slash without looking. I heard a cry and my leg was let go suddenly.

'Just then I caught sight of the subaltern of my troop at some little distance from me. His name was Tomassov. That multitude of resurrected bodies with glassy eyes was seething round his horse as if blind, growling crazily. He was sitting erect in his saddle, not looking down at them and sheathing his sword deliberately.

'This Tomassov, well, he had a beard. Of course we all had beards then. Circumstances, lack of leisure, want of razors, too. No, seriously, we were a wild-looking lot in those unforgotten days which so many, so very many of us did not survive. You know our losses were awful, too. Yes, we looked wild. *Des Russes sauvages* – what!

'So he had a beard – this Tomassov I mean; but he did not look *sauvage*. He was the youngest of us all. And that meant real youth. At a distance he passed muster fairly well, what with the grime and the particular stamp of that campaign on our faces. But directly you were near enough to have a good look into his eyes, that was where his lack of age showed, though he was not exactly a boy.

'Those same eyes were blue, something like the blue of autumn skies, dreamy and gay, too – innocent, believing eyes. A topknot of fair hair decorated his brow like a gold diadem in what one would call normal times.

'You may think I am talking of him as if he were the hero of a novel. Why, that's nothing to what the adjutant discovered about him. He discovered that he had a "lover's lips" – whatever that may be. If the adjutant meant a nice mouth, why, it was nice enough, but of course it was intended for a sneer. That adjutant of ours was not a very delicate fellow. "Look at those lover's lips," he would exclaim in a loud tone while Tomassov was talking.

'Tomassov didn't quite like that sort of thing. But to a certain extent he had laid himself open to banter by the lasting character of his impressions which were connected with the passion of love and, perhaps, were not of such a rare kind as he seemed to think them. What made his comrades tolerant of his rhapsodies was the fact that they were connected with France, with Paris!

'You of the present generation, you cannot conceive how much prestige there was then in those names for the whole world. Paris was the centre of wonder for all human beings gifted with imagination. There we were, the majority of us young and well connected, but not long out of our hereditary nests in the provinces; simple servants of God; mere rustics, if I may say so. So we were only too ready to listen to the tales of France from our comrade Tomassov. He had been attached to our mission in Paris the year before the war. High protections very likely – or maybe sheer luck.

'I don't think he could have been a very useful member of the mission because of his youth and complete inexperience. And apparently all his time in Paris was his own. The use he made of it was to fall in love, to remain in that state, to cultivate it, to exist only for it in a manner of speaking.

'Thus it was something more than a mere memory that he had brought with him from France. Memory is a fugitive thing. It can be falsified, it can be effaced, it can be even doubted. Why! I myself come to doubt sometimes that I, too, have been in Paris in my turn. And the long road there with battles for its stages would appear still more incredible if it were not for a certain musket ball which I have been carrying about my person ever since a little cavalry affair which happened in Silesia at the very beginning of the Leipzig campaign.

'Passages of love, however, are more impressive perhaps than passages of danger. You don't go affronting love in troops as it were. They are rarer, more personal and more intimate. And remember that with Tomassov all that was very fresh yet. He had not been home from France three months when the war began.

'His heart, his mind were full of that experience. He was really awed by it, and he was simple enough to let it appear in his speeches. He considered himself a sort of privileged person, not because a woman had looked at him with favour, but simply because, how shall I say it, he had had the wonderful illumination of his worship for her, as if it were heaven itself that had done this for him.

'Oh yes, he was very simple. A nice youngster, yet no fool; and with that, utterly inexperienced, unsuspicious and unthinking. You will find one like that here and there in the provinces. He had some poetry in him too. It could only be natural, something quite his own, not acquired. I suppose Father Adam had some poetry in him of that natural sort. For the rest *un Russe sauvage* as the French sometimes call us, but not of that kind which, they maintain, eats tallow candle for a delicacy. As to the woman, the French woman, well, though I have also been in France with a hundred thousand Russians, I have never seen her. Very likely she was not in Paris then. And in any case hers were not the doors that would fly open before simple fellows of my sort, you understand. Gilded salons were never in my way. I could not tell you how she looked, which is strange considering that I was, if I may say so, Tomassov's special confidant.

'He very soon got shy of talking before the others. I suppose the usual camp-fire comments jarred his fine feelings. But I was left to him and truly I had to submit. You can't very well expect a youngster in Tomassov's state to hold his tongue altogether; and I – I suppose you will hardly believe me – I am by nature a rather silent sort of person.

'Very likely my silence appeared to him sympathetic. All the month of September our regiment, quartered in villages, had come in for an easy time. It was then that I heard most of that – you can't call it a story. The story I have in my mind is not in that. Outpourings, let us call them.

'I would sit quite content to hold my peace, a whole hour perhaps, while Tomassov talked with exaltation. And when he was done I would still hold my peace. And then there would be produced a solemn effect of silence which, I imagine, pleased Tomassov in a way.

'She was of course not a woman in her first youth. A widow, maybe. At any rate I never heard Tomassov mention her husband. She had a salon, something very distinguished; a social centre in which she queened it with great splendour.

'Somehow, I fancy her court was composed mostly of men. But Tomassov, I must say, kept such details out of his discourses wonderfully well. Upon my word I don't know whether her hair was dark or fair, her eyes brown or blue; what was her stature, her features, or her complexion. His love soared above mere physical impressions. He never described her to me in set terms; but he was ready to swear that in her presence everybody's thoughts and feelings were bound to circle round her. She was that sort of woman. Most wonderful conversations on all sorts of subjects went on in her salon: but through them all there flowed unheard like a mysterious strain of music the assertion, the power, the tyranny of sheer beauty. So apparently the woman was beautiful. She detached all these talking people from their life interests, and even from their vanities. She was a secret delight and a secret trouble. All the men when they looked at her fell to brooding as if struck by the thought that their lives had been wasted. She was the very joy and shudder of felicity and she brought only sadness and torment to the hearts of men.

'In short, she must have been an extraordinary woman, or else Tomassov was an extraordinary young fellow to feel in that way and to talk like this about her. I told you the fellow had a lot of poetry in him and observed that all this sounded true enough. It would be just about the sorcery a woman very much out of the common would exercise, you know. Poets do get close to truth somehow – there is no denying that.

'There is no poetry in my composition, I know, but I have my share of common shrewdness, and I have no doubt that the lady was kind to the youngster, once he did find his way inside her salon. His getting in is the real marvel. However, he did get in, the innocent, and he found himself in distinguished company there, amongst men of considerable position. And you know what that means: thick waists, bald heads, teeth that are not – as some satirist puts it. Imagine amongst them a nice boy, fresh and simple, like an apple just off the tree; a modest, good-looking, impressionable, adoring young barbarian. My word! What a change! What a relief for jaded feelings! And with that, having in his nature that dose of poetry which saves even a simpleton from being a fool.

'He became an artlessly, unconditionally devoted slave. He was rewarded by being smiled on and in time admitted to the intimacy of the house. It may be that the unsophisticated young barbarian amused the exquisite lady. Perhaps – since he didn't feed on tallow candles – he satisfied some need of tenderness in the woman. You know, there are many kinds of tenderness highly civilised women are capable of. Women with heads and imagination, I mean, and no temperament to speak of, you understand. But who is going to fathom their needs or their fancies? Most of the time they themselves don't know much about their innermost moods, and blunder out of one into another, sometimes with catastrophic results. And then who is more surprised than they? However, Tomassov's case was in its nature quite idyllic. The fashionable world was amused. His devotion made for him a kind of social success. But he didn't care. There was his one divinity, and there was the shrine where he was permitted to go in and out without regard for official reception hours.

'He took advantage of that privilege freely. Well, he had no official duties, you know. The Military Mission was supposed to be more complimentary than anything else, the head of it being a personal friend of our Emperor Alexander; and he, too, was laying himself out for successes in fashionable life exclusively – as it seemed. As it seemed.

'One afternoon Tomassov called on the mistress of his thoughts earlier than usual. She was not alone. There was a man with her, not one of the thick-waisted, bald-headed personages, but a somebody all the same, a man over thirty, a French officer who to some extent was also a privileged intimate. Tomassov was not jealous of him. Such a sentiment would have appeared presumptuous to the simple fellow.

'On the contrary he admired that officer. You have no idea of the French military men's prestige in those days, even with us Russian soldiers who had managed to face them perhaps better than the rest. Victory had marked them on the forehead – it seemed for ever. They would have been more than human if they had not been conscious of it; but they were good comrades and had a sort of brotherly feeling for all who bore arms, even if it was against them.

'And this was quite a superior example, an officer of the major-general's staff, and a man of the best society besides. He was powerfully built, and thoroughly masculine, though he was as carefully groomed as a woman. He had the courteous self-possession of a man of the world. His forehead, white as alabaster, contrasted impressively with the healthy colour of his face.

'I don't know whether he was jealous of Tomassov, but I suspect that he might have been a little annoyed at him as at a sort of walking absurdity of the sentimental order. But these men of the world are impenetrable, and outwardly he condescended to recognise Tomassov's existence even more distinctly than was strictly necessary. Once or twice he had offered him some useful worldly advice with perfect tact and delicacy. Tomassov was completely conquered by that evidence of kindness under the cold polish of the best society.

'Tomassov, introduced into the *petit salon*, found these two exquisite people sitting on a sofa together and had the feeling of having interrupted some special conversation. They looked at him strangely, he thought; but he was not given to understand that he had intruded. After a time the lady said to the officer – his name was De Castel – "I wish you would take the trouble to ascertain the exact truth as to that rumour."

' "It's much more than a mere rumour," remarked the officer. But he got up submissively and went out. The lady turned to Tomassov and said: "You may stay with me."

'This express command made him supremely happy, though as a matter of fact he had had no idea of going.

'She regarded him with her kindly glances, which made something glow and expand within his chest. It was a delicious feeling, even though it did cut one's breath short now and then. Ecstatically he drank in the sound of her tranquil, seductive talk full of innocent gaiety and of spiritual quietude. His passion appeared to him to flame up and envelop her in blue fiery tongues from head to foot and over her head, while her soul reposed in the centre like a big white rose . . .

'H'm, good this. He told me many other things like that. But this is the one I remember. He himself remembered everything because these were the last memories of that woman. He was seeing her for the last time though he did not know it then.

'M. De Castel returned, breaking into that atmosphere of enchantment Tomassov had been drinking in even to complete unconsciousness of the external world. Tomassov could not help being struck by the distinction of his movements, the ease of his manner, his superiority to all the other men he knew, and he suffered from it. It occurred to him that these two brilliant beings on the sofa were made for each other.

'De Castel sitting down by the side of the lady murmured to her discreetly, "There is not the slightest doubt that it's true," and they both turned their eyes to Tomassov. Roused thoroughly from his enchantment he became self-conscious; a feeling of shyness came over him. He sat smiling faintly at them.

'The lady without taking her eyes off the blushing Tomassov said with a dreamy gravity quite unusual to her: "I should like to know that your generosity can be supreme – without a flaw. Love at its highest should be the origin of every perfection."

'Tomassov opened his eyes wide with admiration at this, as though her lips had been dropping real pearls. The sentiment, however, was not uttered for the primitive Russian youth but for the exquisitely accomplished man of the world, De Castel.

'Tomassov could not see the effect it produced because the French officer lowered his head and sat there contemplating his admirably polished boots. The lady whispered in a sympathetic tone: "You have scruples?"

'De Castel, without looking up, murmured: "It could be turned into a nice point of honour."

'She said vivaciously: "That surely is artificial. I am all for natural feelings. I believe in nothing else. But perhaps your conscience . . . "

'He interrupted her: "Not at all. My conscience is not childish. The fate of those people is of no military importance to us. What can it matter? The fortune of France is invincible."

' "Well then . . . " she uttered, meaningly, and rose from the couch. The French officer stood up, too. Tomassov hastened to follow their example. He was pained by his state of utter mental darkness. While he was raising the lady's white hand to his lips he heard the French officer say with marked emphasis: "If he has the soul of a warrior" (at that time, you know, people really talked in that way), "if he has the soul of a warrior he ought to fall at your feet in gratitude."

'Tomassov felt himself plunged into even denser darkness than before. He followed the French officer out of the room and out of the house; for he had a notion that this was expected of him.

'It was getting dusk, the weather was very bad, and the street was quite deserted. The Frenchman lingered in it strangely. And Tomassov lingered, too, without impatience. He was never in a hurry to get away from the house in which she lived. And besides, something wonderful had happened to him. The hand he had reverently raised by the tips of its fingers had been pressed against his lips. He had received a secret favour! He was almost frightened. The world had reeled – and it had hardly steadied itself yet. De Castel stopped short at the corner of the quiet street.

' "I don't care to be seen too much with you in the lighted thoroughfares, M. Tomassov," he said in a strangely grim tone.

' "Why?" asked the young man, too startled to be offended.

' "From prudence," answered the other curtly. "So we will have to part here; but before we part I'll disclose to you something of which you will see at once the importance."

'This, please note, was an evening in late March of the year 1812. For a long time already there had been talk of a growing coolness between Russia and France. The word war was being whispered in drawing-rooms louder and louder, and at last was heard in official circles. Thereupon the Parisian police discovered that our military envoy had corrupted some clerks at the Ministry of War and had obtained from them some very important confidential documents. The wretched men (there were two of them) had confessed their crime and were to be shot that night. Tomorrow all the town would be talking of the affair. But the worst was that the Emperor Napoleon was furiously angry at the discovery, and had made up his mind to have the Russian envoy arrested.

'Such was De Castel's disclosure; and though he had spoken in low tones, Tomassov was stunned as by a great crash.

' "Arrested," he murmured, desolately.

' "Yes, and kept as a state prisoner – with everybody belonging to him . . . "

'The French officer seized Tomassov's arm above the elbow and pressed it hard.

' "And kept in France," he repeated into Tomassov's very ear, and then letting him go stepped back a space and remained silent.

' "And it's you, you, who are telling me this!" cried Tomassov in an extremity of gratitude that was hardly greater than his admiration for the generosity of his future foe. Could a brother have done for him more! He sought to seize the hand of the French officer, but the latter remained wrapped up closely in his cloak. Possibly in the dark he had not noticed the attempt. He moved back a bit and in his self-possessed voice of a man of the world, as though he were speaking across a card table or something of the sort, he called Tomassov's attention to the fact that if he meant to make use of the warning the moments were precious.

' "Indeed they are," agreed the awed Tomassov. "Goodbye then. I have no word of thanks to equal your generosity; but if ever I have an opportunity, I swear it, you may command my life . . . "

'But the Frenchman retreated, had already vanished in the dark lonely street. Tomassov was alone, and then he did not waste any of the precious minutes of that night.

'See how people's mere gossip and idle talk pass into history. In all the memoirs of the time if you read them you will find it stated that our envoy had a warning from some highly placed woman who was in love with him. Of course it's known that he had successes with women, and in the highest spheres, too, but the truth is that the person who warned him was no other than our simple Tomassov – an altogether different sort of lover from himself.

'This then is the secret of our emperor's representative's escape from arrest. He and all his official household got out of France all right – as history records.

'And amongst that household there was our Tomassov of course. He had, in the words of the French officer, the soul of a warrior. And what more desolate prospect for a man with such a soul than to be imprisoned on the eve of war; to be cut off from his country in danger, from his military family, from his duty, from honour, and – well – from glory, too.

'Tomassov used to shudder at the mere thought of the moral torture he had escaped; and he nursed in his heart a boundless gratitude to the two people who had saved him from that cruel ordeal. They were wonderful! For him love and friendship were but two aspects of exalted perfection. He had found these fine examples of it and he vowed them indeed a sort of cult. It affected his attitude towards Frenchmen in general, great patriot as he was. He was naturally indignant at the invasion of his country, but this indignation had no personal animosity in it. His was fundamentally a fine nature. He grieved at the appalling amount of human suffering he saw around him. Yes, he was full of compassion for all forms of mankind's misery in a manly way.

'Less fine natures than his own did not understand this very well. In the regiment they had nicknamed him the Humane Tomassov.

'He didn't take offence at it. There is nothing incompatible between humanity and a warrior's soul. People without compassion are the civilians, government officials, merchants and suchlike. As to the ferocious talk one hears from a lot of decent people in wartime – well, the tongue is an unruly member at best and when there is some excitement going on there is no curbing its furious activity.

'So I had not been very surprised to see our Tomassov sheathe deliberately his sword right in the middle of that charge, you may say. As we rode away after it he was very silent. He was not a chatterer as a rule, but it was evident that this close view of the Grand Army had affected him deeply, like some sight not of this earth. I had always been a pretty tough individual myself – well, even I . . . and there was that fellow with a lot of poetry in his nature! You may imagine what he made of it to himself. We rode side by side without opening our lips. It was simply beyond words.

'We established our bivouac along the edge of the forest so as to get some shelter for our horses. However, the boisterous north wind had dropped as quickly as it had sprung up, and the great winter stillness lay on the land from the Baltic to the Black Sea. One could almost feel its cold, lifeless immensity reaching up to the stars.

'Our men had lighted several fires for their officers and had cleared the snow around them. We had big logs of wood for seats; it was a very tolerable bivouac upon the whole, even without the exultation of victory. We were to feel that later, but at present we were oppressed by our stern and arduous task.

'There were three of us round my fire. The third one was that adjutant. He was perhaps a well-meaning chap but not so nice as he might have been had he been less rough in manner and less crude in his perceptions. He would reason about people's conduct as though a man were as simple a figure as, say, two sticks laid across each other; whereas a man is much more like the sea whose movements are too complicated to explain, and whose depths may bring up God only knows what at any moment.

'We talked a little about that charge. Not much. That sort of thing does not lend itself to conversation. Tomassov muttered a few words about a mere butchery. I had nothing to say. As I told you I had very soon let my sword hang idle at my wrist. That starving mob had not even *tried* to defend itself. Just a few shots. We had two men wounded. Two! . . . and we had charged the main column of Napoleon's Grand Army.

'Tomassov muttered wearily: "What was the good of it?" I did not wish to argue, so I only just mumbled: "Ah, well!" But the adjutant struck in unpleasantly: "Why, it warmed the men a bit. It has made me warm. That's a good enough reason. But our Tomassov is so humane! And besides he has been in love with a French woman, and thick as thieves with a lot of Frenchmen, so he is sorry for them. Never mind, my boy, we are on the Paris road now and you shall soon see her!' This was one of his usual, as we believed them, foolish speeches. None of us but believed that the getting to Paris would be a matter of years – of years. And lo! less than eighteen months afterwards I was rooked of a lot of money in a gambling hell in the Palais Royal.

'Truth, being often the most senseless thing in the world, is sometimes revealed to fools. I don't think that adjutant of ours believed in his own words. He just wanted to tease Tomassov from habit. Purely from habit. We of course said nothing, and so he took his head in his hands and fell into a doze as he sat on a log in front of the fire.

'Our cavalry was on the extreme right wing of the army, and I must confess that we guarded it very badly. We had lost all sense of insecurity by this time; but still we did keep up a pretence of doing it in a way. Presently a trooper rode up leading a horse and Tomassov mounted stiffly and went off on a round of the outposts. Of the perfectly useless outposts.

'The night was still, except for the crackling of the fires. The raging wind had lifted far above the earth and not the faintest breath of it could be heard. Only the full moon swam out with a rush into the sky and suddenly hung high and motionless overhead. I remember raising my hairy face to it for a moment. Then, I verily believe, I dozed off, too, bent double on my log with my head towards the fierce blaze.

'You know what an impermanent thing such slumber is. One moment you drop into an abyss and the next you are back in the world that you would think too deep for any noise but the trumpet of the Last Judgement. And then off you go again. Your very soul seems to slip down into a bottomless black pit. Then up once more into a startled consciousness. A mere plaything of cruel sleep one is, then. Tormented both ways.

'However, when my orderly appeared before me, repeating: "Won't your honour be pleased to eat? . . . Won't your honour be pleased to eat? . . . " I managed to keep my hold of it – I mean that gaping consciousness. He was offering me a sooty pot containing some grain boiled in water with a pinch of salt. A wooden spoon was stuck in it.

'At that time these were the only rations we were getting regularly. Mere chicken food, confound it! But the Russian soldier is wonderful. Well, my fellow waited till I had feasted and then went away carrying off the empty pot.

'I was no longer sleepy. Indeed, I had become awake with an exaggerated mental consciousness of existence extending beyond my immediate surroundings. Those are but exceptional moments with mankind, I am glad to say. I had the intimate sensation of the earth in all its enormous expanse wrapped in snow, with nothing showing on it but trees with their straight stalk-like trunks and their funeral verdure; and in this aspect of general mourning I seemed to hear the sighs of mankind falling to die in the midst of a nature without life. They were Frenchmen. We didn't hate them; they did not hate us; we had existed far apart – and suddenly they had come rolling in with arms in their hands, without fear of God, carrying with them other nations, and all to perish together in a long, long trail of frozen corpses. I had an actual vision of that trail: a pathetic multitude of small dark mounds stretching away under the moonlight in a clear, still and pitiless atmosphere – a sort of horrible peace.

'But what other peace could there be for them? What else did they deserve? I don't know by what connection of emotions there came into my head the thought that the earth was a pagan planet and not a fit abode for Christian virtues.

'You may be surprised that I should remember all this so well. What is a passing emotion or half-formed thought to last in so many years of a man's changing, inconsequential life? But what has fixed the emotion of that evening in my recollection so that the slightest shadows remain indelible was an event of strange finality, an event not likely to be forgotten in a lifetime – as you shall see.

'I don't suppose I had been entertaining those thoughts more than five minutes when something induced me to look over my shoulder. I can't think it was a noise; the snow deadened all the sounds. Something it must have been, some sort of signal reaching my consciousness. Anyway, I turned my head, and there was the event approaching me, not that I knew it or had the slightest premonition. All I saw in the distance were two figures approaching in the moonlight. One of them was our Tomassov. The dark mass behind him which moved across my sight were the horses which his orderly was leading away. Tomassov was a very familiar appearance, in long boots, a tall figure ending in a pointed hood. But by his side advanced another figure. I mistrusted my eyes at first. It was amazing! It had a shining crested helmet on its head and was muffled up in a white cloak. The cloak was not as white as snow. Nothing in the world is. It was white more like mist, with an aspect that was ghostly and martial to an extraordinary degree. It was as if Tomassov had got hold of the God of War himself. I could see at once that he was leading this resplendent vision by the arm. Then I saw that he was holding it up. While I stared and stared, they crept on – for indeed they were creeping – and at last they crept into the light of our bivouac fire and passed beyond the log I was sitting on. The blaze played on the helmet. It was extremely battered and the frost-bitten face, full of sores, under it was framed in bits of mangy fur. No God of War this, but a French officer. The great white *cuirassier*'s cloak was torn, burnt full of holes. His feet were wrapped up in old sheepskins over remnants of boots. They looked monstrous and he tottered on them, sustained by Tomassov who lowered him most carefully on to the log on which I sat.

'My amazement knew no bounds.

' "You have brought in a prisoner," I said to Tomassov, as if I could not believe my eyes.

'You must understand that unless they surrendered in large bodies we made no prisoners. What would have been the good? Our Cossacks either killed the stragglers or else let them alone, just as it happened. It came really to the same thing in the end.

'Tomassov turned to me with a very troubled look.

' "He sprang up from the ground somewhere as I was leaving the out-post," he said. "I believe he was making for it, for he walked blindly into my horse. He got hold of my leg and of course none of our chaps dared touch him then."

' "He had a narrow escape," I said.

' "He didn't appreciate it," said Tomassov, looking even more troubled than before. "He came along holding to my stirrup leather. That's what made me so late. He told me he was a staff officer; and then talking in a voice such, I suppose, as the damned alone use, a croaking of rage and pain, he said he had a favour to beg of me. A supreme favour. Did I understand him, he asked in a sort of fiendish whisper.

' "Of course I told him that I did. I said: *Oui, je vous comprends.*"

' "Then," said he, "do it. Now! At once – in the pity of your heart."

'Tomassov ceased and stared queerly at me above the head of the prisoner. 'I said, "What did he mean?"

' "That's what I asked him," answered Tomassov in a dazed tone, "and he said that he wanted me to do him the favour to blow his brains out. As a fellow soldier, he said. As a man of feeling – as – as a humane man."

'The prisoner sat between us like an awful gashed mummy as to the face, a martial scarecrow, a grotesque horror of rags and dirt, with awful living eyes, full of vitality, full of unquenchable fire, in a body of horrible affliction, a skeleton at the feast of glory. And suddenly those shining unextinguishable eyes of his became fixed upon Tomassov. He, poor fellow, fascinated, returned the ghastly stare of a suffering soul in that mere husk of a man. The prisoner croaked at him in French.

' "I recognise you, you know. You are her Russian youngster. You were very grateful. I call on you to pay the debt. Pay it, I say, with one liberating shot. You are a man of honour. I have not even a broken sabre. All my being recoils from my own degradation. You know me."

'Tomassov said nothing.

' "Haven't you got the soul of a warrior?" the Frenchman asked in an angry whisper, but with something of a mocking intention in it.

' "I don't know," said poor Tomassov.

'What a look of contempt that scarecrow gave him out of his unquenchable eyes. He seemed to live only by the force of infuriated and impotent despair. Suddenly he gave a gasp and fell forward, writhing in the agony of cramp in all his limbs; a not unusual effect of the heat of a camp-fire. It resembled the application of some horrible torture. But he tried to fight against the pain at first. He only moaned low, while we bent over him so as to prevent him rolling into the fire, and muttered feverishly at intervals: "*Tuez moi, tuez moi . . .* " till, vanquished by the pain, he screamed in agony, time after time, each cry bursting out through his compressed lips.

'The adjutant woke up on the other side of the fire and started swearing awfully at the beastly row that Frenchman was making.

' "What's this? More of your infernal humanity, Tomassov," he yelled at us. "Why don't you have him thrown out of this to the devil on the snow?"

'As we paid no attention to his shouts, he got up, cursing shockingly, and went away to another fire. Presently the French officer became easier. We propped him up against the log and sat silent on each side of him till the bugles started their call at the first break of day. The big flame, kept up all through the night, paled on the livid sheet of snow, while the frozen air all round rang with the brazen notes of cavalry trumpets. The Frenchman's eyes, fixed in a glassy stare, which for a moment made us hope that he had died quietly sitting there between us two, stirred slowly to right and left, looking at each of our faces in turn. Tomassov and I exchanged glances of dismay. Then De Castel's voice, unexpected in its renewed strength and ghastly self-possession, made us shudder inwardly.

' "*Bonjour, messieurs.*"

'His chin dropped on his breast. Tomassov addressed me in Russian.

' "It is he, the man himself . . . " I nodded and Tomassov went on in a tone of anguish: "Yes, he! Brilliant, accomplished, envied by men, loved by that woman – this horror – this miserable thing that cannot die. Look at his eyes. It's terrible."

'I did not look, but I understood what Tomassov meant. We could do nothing for him. This avenging winter of fate held both the fugitives and the pursuers in its iron grip. Compassion was but a vain word before that unrelenting destiny. I tried to say something about a convoy being no doubt collected in the village – but I faltered at the mute glance Tomassov gave me. We knew what those convoys were like: appalling mobs of hopeless wretches driven on by the butts of Cossacks' lances back to the frozen inferno, with their faces set away from their homes.

'Our two squadrons had been formed along the edge of the forest. The minutes of anguish were passing. The Frenchman suddenly struggled to his feet. We helped him almost without knowing what we were doing.

' "Come," he said, in measured tones. "This is the moment." He paused for a long time, then with the same distinctness went on: "On my word of honour, all faith is dead in me."

'His voice lost suddenly its self-possession. After waiting a little while he added in a murmur: "And even my courage . . . Upon my honour."

'Another long pause ensued before, with a great effort, he whispered hoarsely: "Isn't this enough to move a heart of stone? Am I to go on my knees to you?"

'Again a deep silence fell upon the three of us. Then the French officer flung his last word of anger at Tomassov.

' "Milksop!"

'Not a feature of the poor fellow moved. I made up my mind to go and fetch a couple of our troopers to lead that miserable prisoner away to the village. There was nothing else for it. I had not moved six paces towards the group of horses and orderlies in front of our squadron when . . . but you have guessed it. Of course. And I, too, I guessed it, for I give you my word that the report of Tomassov's pistol was the most insignificant thing imaginable. The snow certainly does absorb sound. It was a mere feeble pop. Of the orderlies holding our horses I don't think one turned his head round.

'Yes. Tomassov had done it. Destiny had led that De Castel to the man who could understand him perfectly. But it was poor Tomassov's lot to be the predestined victim. You know what the world's justice and mankind's judgement are like. They fell heavily on him with a sort of inverted hypocrisy. Why! That brute of an adjutant, himself, was the first to set going horrified allusions to the shooting of a prisoner in cold blood! Tomassov was not dismissed from the service of course. But after the siege of Dantzig he asked for permission to resign from the army, and went away to bury himself in the depths of his province, where a vague story of some dark deed clung to him for years.

'Yes. He had done it. And what was it? One warrior's soul paying its debt a hundredfold to another warrior's soul by releasing it from a fate worse than death – the loss of all faith and courage. You may look on it in that way. I don't know. And perhaps poor Tomassov did not know himself. But I was the first to approach that appalling dark group on the snow: the Frenchman extended rigidly on his back, Tomassov kneeling on one knee rather nearer to the feet than to the Frenchman's head. He had taken his cap off and his hair shone like gold in the light drift of flakes that had begun to fall. He was stooping over the dead in a tenderly contemplative attitude. And his young, ingenuous face, with lowered eyelids, expressed no grief, no sternness, no horror – but was set in the repose of a profound, as if endless and endlessly silent, meditation.'

HUBERT CRACKANTHORPE

Hubert Montague Crackanthorpe was born Hubert Montague Cookson on 12 May 1870. He changed his surname in 1888, as did his father, in order to inherit a legacy. In 1893, he married Leila Macdonald, another writer. The couple moved to France, where they shared a literary life. Crackanthorpe was associated with the avant-garde literary magazine known as *The Yellow Book* and some of the pieces Crackanthorpe published in that journal were ultimately collected in his most significant work, *Sentimental Studies and a Set of Village Tales* (1895). The state of his marriage to Leila began to disintegrate after 1895. Leila miscarried in 1896 because of a venereal infection she had contracted from Hubert; after this, she left Hubert who promptly began an affair with a woman named Sissie Welch. After a few months, Hubert managed a reunion with Leila, who was now living in Paris with a lover of her own. Hubert and Leila thus set up house once more with their respective lovers in tow, but the situation did not last long and Leila left Hubert in November 1896. Hubert Crackanthorpe was never seen alive again after his wife left him for the second time. She boarded a boat for London a few weeks later. Hubert's body was found in the Seine on Christmas Eve; it is unknown whether he was a victim of foul play or had committed suicide. In subsequent years the aristocratic Crackanthorpe family were eager that the story did not come to public attention. His literary legacy consists largely of three volumes of short stories published during his lifetime; contemporary opinions of his talent as a writer varied widely, though one of his works appeared with an appreciation by none other than Henry James.

Anthony Garstin's Courtship

I

A stampede of huddled sheep, wildly scampering over the slaty shingle, emerged from the leaden mist that muffled the fell-top, and a shrill shepherd's whistle broke the damp stillness of the air. And presently a man's figure appeared, following the sheep down the hillside. He halted a moment to whistle curtly to his two dogs, who, laying back their ears, chased the sheep at top speed beyond the brow; then, his hands deep in his pockets, he strode vigorously forward. A streak of white smoke from a toiling train was creeping silently across the distance; the great, grey, desolate undulations of treeless country showed no other sign of life.

The sheep hurried in single file along a tiny track worn threadbare amid the brown, lumpy grass; and, as the man came round the mountain's shoulder, a narrow valley opened out beneath him – a scanty patchwork of green fields, and, here and there, a whitewashed farm, flanked by a dark cluster of sheltering trees.

The man walked with a loose, swinging gait. His figure was spare and angular: he wore a battered, black-felt hat and clumsy, iron-bound boots: his clothes were dingy from long exposure to the weather. He had close-set, insignificant eyes, much wrinkled, and stubbly eyebrows streaked with grey. His mouth was close-shaven and drawn by his abstraction into hard and taciturn lines; beneath his chin bristled an unkempt fringe of sandy-coloured hair.

When he reached the foot of the fell, the twilight was already blurring the distance. The sheep scurried, with a noisy rustling, across a flat, swampy stretch, overgrown with rushes, while the dogs headed them towards a gap in a low, ragged wall built of loosely heaped boulders. The man swung the gate to after them, and waited, whistling peremptorily, recalling the dogs. A moment later, the animals reappeared, cringing as they crawled through the bars of the gate. He kicked out at them contemptuously, and mounting a stone stile a few yards farther up the road, dropped into a narrow lane.

Presently, as he passed a row of lighted windows, he heard a voice call to him. He stopped, and perceived a crooked, white-bearded figure, wearing clerical clothes, standing in the garden gateway.

'Good-evening, Anthony. A raw evening this.'

'Ay, Mr Blencarn, it is a bit frittish,' he answered. 'I've jest bin gittin' a few

297

lambs off t'fell. I hope ye're keepin' fairly, an' Miss Rosa too.' He spoke briefly, with a loud, spontaneous cordiality.

'Thank ye, Anthony, thank ye. Rosa's down at the church, playing over the hymns for tomorrow. How's Mrs Garstin?'

'Nicely, thank ye, Mr Blencarn. She's wonderful active, is mother.'

'Well, good-night to ye, Anthony,' said the old man, clicking the gate.

'Good-night, Mr Blencarn,' he called back.

A few minutes later the twinkling lights of the village came in sight, and from within the sombre form of the square-towered church, looming by the roadside, the slow, solemn strains of the organ floated out on the evening air. Anthony lightened his tread: then paused, listening; but, presently, becoming aware that a man stood, listening also, on the bridge some few yards distant, he moved forward again. Slackening his pace, as he approached, he eyed the figure keenly; but the man paid no heed to him, remaining, with his back turned, gazing over the parapet into the dark, gurgling stream.

Anthony trudged along the empty village street, past the gleaming squares of ruddy gold, starting on either side out of the darkness. Now and then he looked furtively backwards. The straight open road lay behind him, glimmering wanly; the organ seemed to have ceased; the figure on the bridge had left the parapet, and appeared to be moving away towards the church. Anthony halted, watching it till it had disappeared into the blackness beneath the churchyard trees. Then, after a moment's hesitation, he left the road, and mounted an upland meadow towards his mother's farm.

It was a bare, oblong house. In front, a whitewashed porch, and a narrow garden-plot, enclosed by a low iron railing, were dimly discernible; behind, the steep fell-side loomed like a monstrous, mysterious curtain hung across the night. He passed round the back into the twilight of a wide yard, cobbled and partially grass-grown, vaguely flanked by the shadowy outlines of long, low farm-buildings. All was wrapped in darkness; somewhere overhead a bat fluttered, darting its puny scream.

Inside, a blazing peat-fire scattered capering shadows across the smooth, stone floor, flickered among the dim rows of hams suspended from the ceiling and on the panelled cupboards of dark, glistening oak. A servant-girl, spreading the cloth for supper, clattered her clogs in and out of the kitchen; old Mrs Garstin was stooping before the hearth, tremulously turning some girdle-cakes that lay roasting in the embers.

At the sound of Anthony's heavy tread in the passage, she rose, glancing sharply at the clock above the chimney-piece. She was a heavy-built woman, upright, stalwart almost, despite her years. Her face was gaunt and sallow; deep wrinkles accentuated the hardness of her features. She wore a black widow's cap above her iron-grey hair, gold-rimmed spectacles, and a soiled, chequered apron.

'Ye're varra late, Tony,' she remarked querulously.

He unloosened his woollen neckerchief, and when he had hung it methodically with his hat behind the door, answered: ' 'Twas terrible thick on t' fell-top, an' them two bitches be that senseless.'

She caught his sleeve, and, through her spectacles, suspiciously scrutinised his face.

'Ye did na meet wi' Rosa Blencarn?'

'Nay, she was in church, hymn-playin', wi' Luke Stock hangin' roond door,' he retorted bitterly, rebuffing her with rough impatience.

She moved away, nodding sententiously to herself. They began supper; neither spoke; Anthony sat slowly stirring his tea, and staring moodily into the flames: the bacon on his plate lay untouched. From time to time his mother, laying down her knife and fork, looked across at him in unconcealed asperity, pursing her wide, ungainly mouth. At last, abruptly setting down her cup, she broke out: 'I wonder ye hav'na mare pride, Tony. For hoo lang are ye goin' t' continue settin' mopin' and broodin' like a seck sheep? Ye'll jest mak yesself ill, an' then I reckon what ye'll prove satisfied. Ay, but I wonder ye hav'na more pride.'

But he made no answer, remaining unmoved, as if he had not heard.

Presently, half to himself, without raising his eyes, he murmured: 'Luke be goin' south, Monday.'

'Well, ye canna tak' oop wi' his leavin's anyways. It hasna coom't that, has it? Ye doan't intend settin' all t' parish a-laughin' at ye a second occasion?'

He flushed dully, and bending over his plate, mechanically began his supper.

'Wa dang it,' he broke out a minute later, 'd'ye think I heed the cacklin' o' fifty parishes? Na, not I,' and, with a short, grim laugh, he brought his fist down heavily on the oak table.

'Ye're daft, Tony,' the old woman blurted.

'Daft or na daft, I tell ye this, mother, that I be forty-six year o' age this back-end, and there be some things I will na listen to. Rosa Blencarn's bonny enough for me.'

'Ay, bonny enough – I've na patience wi' ye. Bonny enough – tricked oot in her furbelows, gallivantin' wi' every royster fra Pe'rith. Bonny enough – that be all ye think on. She's bin a proper parson's niece, the giddy, feckless creature, an she'd mak' ye a proper sort o' wife, Tony Garstin, ye great, fond booby.'

She pushed back her chair, and, hurriedly clattering the crockery, began to clear away the supper.

'T' hoose be mine, t' Lord be praised,' she continued in a loud, hard voice, 'an' as long as he spare me, Tony, I'll na see Rosa Blencarn set foot inside it.'

Anthony scowled, without replying, and drew his chair to the hearth.

His mother bustled about the room behind him. After a while she asked: 'Did ye pen t' lambs in t' back field?'

'Na, they're in Hullam bottom,' he answered curtly.

The door closed behind her, and by and by he could hear her moving overhead. Meditatively blinking, he filled his pipe clumsily, and pulling a crumpled newspaper from his pocket, sat on over the smouldering fire, reading and stolidly puffing.

2

The music rolled through the dark, empty church. The last, leaden flicker of daylight glimmered in through the pointed windows, and beyond the level rows of dusky pews, tenanted only by a litter of prayer-books, two guttering candles revealed the organ pipes, and the young girl's swaying figure.

She played vigorously. Once or twice the tune stumbled, and she recovered it impatiently, bending over the key-board, showily flourishing her wrists as she touched the stops. She was bare-headed (her hat and cloak lay beside her on a stool). She had fair, fluffy hair, cut short behind her neck; large, round eyes, heightened by a fringe of dark lashes; rough, ruddy cheeks, and a rosy, full-lipped, unstable mouth. She was dressed quite simply, in a black, close-fitting bodice, a little frayed at the sleeves. Her hands and neck were coarsely fashioned: her comeliness was brawny, literal, unfinished, as it were.

When at last the ponderous chords of the Amen faded slowly into the twilight, flushed, breathing a little quickly, she paused, listening to the stillness of the church. Presently a small boy emerged from behind the organ.

'Good-evenin', Miss Rosa,' he called, trotting briskly away down the aisle.

'Good-night, Robert,' she answered, absently.

After a while, with an impatient gesture, as if to shake some importunate thought from her mind, she rose abruptly, pinned on her hat, threw her cloak round her shoulders, blew out the candles, and groped her way through the church, towards the half-open door. As she hurried along the narrow pathway that led across the churchyard, of a sudden, a figure started out of the blackness.

'Who's that?' she cried, in a loud, frightened voice.

A man's uneasy laugh answered her.

'It's only me, Rosa. I didna' think t' scare ye. I've bin waitin' for ye, this hoor past.'

She made no reply, but quickened her pace. He strode on beside her.

'I'm off, Monday, ye know,' he continued. And, as she said nothing, 'Will ye na stop jest a minnit? I'd like t' speak a few words wi' ye before I go, an tomorrow I hev t' git over t' Scarsdale betimes,' he persisted.

'I don't want t' speak wi' ye: I don't want ever to see ye agin. I jest hate the sight o' ye.' She spoke with a vehement, concentrated hoarseness.

'Nay, but ye must listen to me. I will na be put off wi' fratchin speeches.' And gripping her arm, he forced her to stop.

'Loose me, ye great beast,' she broke out.

'I'll na hould ye, if ye'll jest stand quiet-like. I meant t' speak fair t' ye, Rosa.'

They stood at a bend in the road, face to face quite close together. Behind his burly form stretched the dimness of a grey, ghostly field.

'What is't ye hev to say to me? Hev done wi' it quick,' she said sullenly.

'It be jest this, Rosa,' he began with dogged gravity. 'I want t' tell ye that ef any trouble comes t'ye after I'm gone – ye know t' what I refer – I want t' tell ye that I'm prepared t' act square by ye. I've written out on an envelope my address in London. Luke Stock, care o' Purcell and Co., Smithfield Market, London.'

'Ye're a bad, sinful man. I jest hate t' sight o' ye. I wish ye were dead.'

'Ay, but I reckon what ye'd ha best thought o' that before. Ye've changed yer whistle considerably since Tuesday. Nay, hould on,' he added, as she struggled to push past him. 'Here's t' envelope.'

She snatched the paper, and tore it passionately, scattering the fragments on to the road. When she had finished, he burst out angrily: 'Ye cussed, unreasonable fool.'

'Let me pass, ef ye've nought mare t'say,' she cried.

'Nay, I'll na part wi' ye this fashion. Ye can speak soft enough when ye choose.' And seizing her shoulders, he forced her backwards against the wall.

'Ye do look fine, an' na mistake, when ye're jest ablaze wi' ragin','he laughed bluntly, lowering his face to hers.

'Loose me, loose me, ye great coward,' she gasped, striving to free her arms.

Holding her fast, he expostulated: 'Coom, Rosa, can we na part friends?'

'Part friends, indeed,' she retorted bitterly. 'Friends wi' the likes o' you. What d'ye tak me for? Let me git home, I tell ye. An' please God I'll never set eyes on ye again. I hate t' sight o' ye.'

'Be off wi' ye, then,' he answered, pushing her roughly back into the road. 'Be off wi' ye, ye silly. Ye canna say I hav na spak fair t' ye, an', by goom, ye'll na see me shally-wallyin' this fashion agin. Be off wi' ye: ye can jest shift for yerself, since ye canna keep a civil tongue in yer head.'

The girl, catching at her breath, stood as if dazed, watching his retreating figure; then starting forward at a run, disappeared up the hill, into the darkness.

3

Old Mr Blencarn concluded his husky sermon. The scanty congregation, who had been sitting, stolidly immobile in their stiff, Sunday clothes, shuffled to their feet, and the pewful of schoolchildren, in clamorous chorus, intoned the final hymn. Anthony stood near the organ, absently contemplating, while the rude melody resounded through the church, Rosa's deft manipulation of the keyboard. The rugged lines of his face were relaxed to a vacant, thoughtful limpness that aged his expression not a little: now and then, as if for reference, he glanced questioningly at the girl's profile.

A few minutes later the service was over, and the congregation sauntered out down the aisle. A gawky group of men remained loitering by the church door: one of them called to Anthony; but, nodding curtly, he passed on, and strode away down the road, across the grey upland meadows, towards home. As soon as he had breasted the hill, however, and was no longer visible from below, he turned abruptly to the left, along a small, swampy hollow, till he had reached the lane that led down from the fell-side.

He clambered over a rugged, moss-grown wall, and stood, gazing expectantly down the dark, disused roadway; then, after a moment's hesitation, perceiving nobody, seated himself beneath the wall, on a projecting slab of stone.

Overhead hung a sombre, drifting sky. A gusty wind rollicked down from the fell – huge masses of chilly grey, stripped of the last night's mist. A few dead leaves fluttered over the stones, and from off the fell-side there floated the plaintive, quavering rumour of many bleating sheep.

Before long, he caught sight of two figures coming towards him, slowly climbing the hill. He sat awaiting their approach, fidgeting with his sandy beard, and abstractedly grinding the ground beneath his heel. At the brow they halted: plunging his hands deep into his pockets, he strolled sheepishly towards them.

'Ah! good day t' ye, Anthony,' called the old man, in a shrill, breathless voice. ' 'Tis a long hill, an' my legs are not what they were. Time was when I'd think nought o' a whole day's tramp on t' fells. Ay, I'm gittin' feeble, Anthony, that's what 'tis. And if Rosa here wasn't the great, strong lass she is, I don't know how her old uncle'd manage;' and he turned to the girl with a proud, tremulous smile.

'Will ye tak my arm a bit, Mr Blencarn? Miss Rosa'll be tired, likely,' Anthony asked.

'Nay, Mr Garstin, but I can manage nicely,' the girl interrupted sharply.

Anthony looked up at her as she spoke. She wore a straw hat, trimmed with crimson velvet, and a black, fur-edged cape, that seemed to set off mightily the fine whiteness of her neck. Her large, dark eyes were fixed upon him. He shifted his feet uneasily, and dropped his glance.

She linked her uncle's arm in hers, and the three moved slowly forward. Old Mr Blencarn walked with difficulty, pausing at intervals for breath. Anthony, his eyes bent on the ground, sauntered beside him, clumsily kicking at the cobbles that lay in his path.

When they reached the vicarage gate, the old man asked him to come inside.

'Not jest now, thank ye, Mr Blencarn. I've that lot o' lambs t' see to before dinner. It's a grand marnin', this,' he added, inconsequently.

'Uncle's bought a nice lot o' Leghorns, Tuesday,' Rosa remarked. Anthony met her gaze; there was a grave, subdued expression on her face this morning, that made her look more of a woman, less of a girl.

'Ay, do ye show him the birds, Rosa. I'd be glad to have his opinion on 'em.'

The old man turned to hobble into the house, and Rosa, as she supported his arm, called back over her shoulder: 'I'll not be a minute, Mr Garstin.'

Anthony strolled round to the yard behind the house, and waited, watching a flock of glossy-white poultry that strutted, perkily pecking, over the grass-grown cobbles.

'Ay, Miss Rosa, they're a bonny lot,' he remarked, as the girl joined him.

'Are they not?' she rejoined, scattering a handful of corn before her.

The birds scuttled across the yard with greedy, outstretched necks. The two stood, side by side, gazing at them.

'What did he give for 'em?' Anthony asked.

'Fifty-five shillings.'

'Ay,' he assented, nodding absently.

'Was Dr Sanderson na seein' o' yer uncle yesterday?' he asked, after a moment.

'He came in t' forenoon. He said he was jest na worse.'

'Ye knaw, Miss Rosa, as I'm still thinkin' on ye,' he began abruptly, without looking up.

'I reckon it ain't much use,' she answered shortly, scattering another handful of corn towards the birds. 'I reckon I'll never marry. I'm jest weary o' bein' courted – '

'I would na weary ye wi' courtin',' he interrupted.

She laughed noisily.

'Ye are a queer customer, an' na mistake.'

'I'm a match for Luke Stock anyway,' he continued fiercely. 'Ye think nought o' taking oop wi' him – about as ranty, wild a young feller as ever stepped.'

The girl reddened, and bit her lip.

'I don't know what you mean, Mr Garstin. It seems to me ye're might hasty in jumpin' t' conclusions.'

'Mabbe I kin see a thing or two,' he retorted doggedly.

'Luke Stock's gone to London, anyway.'

'Ay, an' a powerful good job too, in t' opinion o' some folks.'

'Ye're jest jealous,' she exclaimed, with a forced titter. 'Ye're jest jealous o' Luke Stock.'

'Nay, but ye need na fill yer head wi' that nonsense. I'm too deep set on ye t' feel jealousy,' he answered, gravely.

The smile faded from her face, as she murmured: 'I canna mak ye out, Mr Garstin.'

'Nay, that ye canna. An' I suppose it's natural, considerin' ye're little more than a child, an' I'm a'most old enough to be yer father,' he retorted, with blunt bitterness.

'But ye know yer mother's took that dislike t' me. She'd never abide the sight o' me at Hootsey.'

He remained silent a moment, moodily reflecting. 'She'd jest ha' t' git ower it. I see nought in that objection,' he declared.

'Nay, Mr Garstin, it canna be. Indeed it canna be at all. Ye'd best jest put it right from yer mind, once and for all.'

'I'd jest best put it off my mind, had I? Ye talk like a child!' he burst out scornfully. 'I intend ye t' coom t' love me, an' I will na tak ye till ye do. I'll jest go on waitin' for ye, an', mark my words, my day 'ull coom at last.'

He spoke loudly, in a slow, stubborn voice, and stepped suddenly towards her. With a faint, frightened cry she shrank back into the doorway of the hen-house.

'Ye talk like a prophet. Ye sort o' skeer me.'

He laughed grimly, and paused, reflectively scanning her face. He seemed about to continue in the same strain; but, instead, turned abruptly on his heel, and strode away through the garden gate.

4

For three hundred years there had been a Garstin at Hootsey: generation after generation had tramped the grey stretch of upland, in the springtime scattering their flocks over the fell-sides, and, at the 'back-end', on dark, winter afternoons, driving them home again, down the broad bridle-path that led over the 'raise'. They had been a race of few words, 'keeping themselves to themselves', as the phrase goes; beholden to no man, filled with a dogged, churlish pride – an upright, old-fashioned race, stubborn, long-lived, rude in speech, slow of resolve.

Anthony had never seen his father, who had died one night, upon the fell-top, he and his shepherd, engulfed in the great snowstorm of 1849. Folks had said that he was the only Garstin who had failed to make old man's bones.

After his death, Jake Atkinson, from Ribblehead in Yorkshire, had come to live at Hootsey. Jake was a fine farmer, a canny bargainer, and very handy among the sheep, till he took to drink and roystering every week with the town wenches up at Carlisle. He was a corpulent, deep-voiced, free-handed fellow: when his time came, though he died very hardly, he remained festive and convivial to the last. And for years afterwards, in the valley, his memory lingered: men spoke of him regretfully, recalling his quips, his feats of strength, and his choice breed of Herdwicke rams. But he left behind him a host of debts up at Carlisle, in Penrith, and in almost every market town – debts that he had long ago pretended to have paid with money that belonged to his sister. The widow Garstin sold the twelve Herdwicke rams, and nine acres of land: within six weeks she had cleared off every penny, and for thirteen months, on Sundays, wore her mourning with a mute, forbidding grimness; the bitter thought that, unbeknown to her, Jake had acted dishonestly in money matters, and that he had ended his days in riotous sin, soured her pride, imbued her with a rancorous hostility against all the world. For she was a very proud woman, independent, holding her head high, so folks said, like a Garstin bred and born; and Anthony, although some reckoned him quiet and of little account, came to take after her as he grew into manhood.

She took into her own hands the management of the Hootsey farm, and set the boy to work for her along with the two farm servants. It was twenty-five years now since his Uncle Jake's death: there were grey hairs in his sandy beard; but he still worked for his mother, as he had done when a growing lad.

And now that times were grown to be bad (of late years the price of stock had been steadily falling; and the hay harvests had drifted from bad to worse), the widow Garstin no longer kept any labouring men; but lived, she and her son, year in and year out, in a close parsimonious way.

That had been Anthony Garstin's life – a dull, eventless sort of business, the sluggish incrustation of monotonous years. And until Rosa Blencarn had come to keep house for her uncle, he had never thought twice on a woman's face.

The Garstins had always been good churchgoers, and Anthony, for years, had acted as churchwarden. It was one summer evening, up at the vicarage, whilst he was checking the offertory account, that he first set eyes upon her. She was fresh back from school at Leeds: she was dressed in a white dress: she looked, he thought, like a London lady.

She stood by the window, tall and straight and queenly, dreamily gazing out into the summer twilight, whilst he and her uncle sat over their business. When he rose to go, she glanced at him with quick curiosity; he hurried away, muttering a sheepish good-night.

The next time that he saw her was in church on Sunday. He watched her shyly, with a hesitating, reverential discretion: her beauty seemed to him wonderful, distant, enigmatic. In the afternoon, young Mrs Forsyth, from Longscale, dropped in for a cup of tea with his mother, and the two set off gossiping of Rosa Blencarn, speaking of her freely, in tones of acrimonious contempt. For a long while he sat silent, puffing at his pipe; but at last, when his mother concluded with, 'She looks t' me fair stuck-oop, full o' toonish airs an' graces,' despite himself, he burst out: 'Ye're jest wastin' yer breath wi' that cackle. I reckon Miss Blencarn's o' a different clay to us folks.' Young Mrs Forsyth tittered immoderately, and the next week it was rumoured about the valley that 'Tony Garstin was gone luny over t' parson's niece'.

But of all this he knew nothing – keeping to himself, as was his wont, and being, besides, very busy with the hay harvest – until one day, at dinner-time, Henry Sisson asked if he'd started his courting; Jacob Sowerby cried that Tony'd been too slow in getting to work, for that the girl had been seen spooning in Crosby Shaws with Curbison the auctioneer, and the others (there were half a dozen of them lounging round the hay-waggon) burst into a boisterous guffaw. Anthony flushed dully, looking hesitatingly from the one to the other; then slowly put down his beer-can, and of a sudden, seizing Jacob by the neck, swung him heavily on the grass. He fell against the waggon-wheel, and when he rose the blood was streaming from an ugly cut in his forehead. And henceforward Tony Garstin's courtship was the common jest of all the parish.

As yet, however, he had scarcely spoken to her, though twice he had passed her in the lane that led up to the vicarage. She had given him a frank, friendly smile; but he had not found the resolution to do more than lift his hat. He and Henry Sisson stacked the hay in the yard behind the house; there was no further mention made of Rosa Blencarn; but all day long Anthony, as he knelt thatching the rick, brooded over the strange sweetness of her face, and on the fell-top, while he tramped after the ewes over the dry, crackling heather, and as he jogged along the narrow, rickety road, driving his cartload of lambs into the auction mart.

Thus, as the weeks slipped by, he was content with blunt, wistful ruminations upon her indistinct image. Jacob Sowerby's accusation, and several kindred innuendoes let fall by his mother, left him coolly incredulous; the girl still seemed to him altogether distant; but from the first sight of her face he had evolved a stolid, unfaltering conception of her difference from the ruck of her sex.

But one evening, as he passed the vicarage on his way down from the fells, she called to him, and with a childish, confiding familiarity asked for advice concerning the feeding of the poultry. In his eagerness to answer her as best he could, he forgot his customary embarrassment, and grew, for the moment, almost voluble, and quite at his ease in her presence. Directly her flow of questions ceased, however, the returning perception of her rosy, hesitating smile, and of her large, deep eyes looking straight into his face, perturbed him strangely, and, reddening, he remembered the quarrel in the hay-field and the tale of Crosby Shaws.

After this, the poultry became a link between them – a link which he regarded in all seriousness, blindly unconscious that there was aught else to bring them together, only feeling himself in awe of her, because of her schooling, her townish manners, her ladylike mode of dress. And soon, he came to take a sturdy, secret pride in her friendly familiarity towards him. Several times a week he would meet her in the lane, and they would loiter a moment together; she would admire his dogs, though he assured her earnestly that they were but sorry curs; and once, laughing at his staidness, she nicknamed him 'Mr Churchwarden'.

That the girl was not liked in the valley he suspected, curtly attributing her unpopularity to the women's senseless jealousy. Of gossip concerning her he heard no further hint; but instinctively, and partly from that rugged, natural reserve of his, shrank from mentioning her name, even incidentally, to his mother.

Now, on Sunday evenings, he often strolled up to the vicarage, each time quitting his mother with the same awkward affectation of casualness; and, on his return, becoming vaguely conscious of how she refrained from any comment on his absence, and appeared oddly oblivious of the existence of Parson Blencarn's niece.

She had always been a sour-tongued woman; but, as the days shortened with the approach of the long winter months, she seemed to him to grow more fretful than ever; at times it was almost as if she bore him some smouldering, sullen resentment. He was of stubborn fibre, however, toughened by long habit of a bleak, unruly climate; he revolved the matter in his mind deliberately, and when, at last, after much plodding thought, it dawned upon him that she resented his acquaintance with Rosa Blencarn, he accepted the solution with an unflinching phlegm, and merely shifted his attitude towards the girl, calculating each day the likelihood of his meeting her, and making, in her presence, persistent efforts to break down, once for all, the barrier of his own timidity. He was a man not to be clumsily driven, still less, so he prided himself, a man to be craftily led.

It was close upon Christmastime before the crisis came. His mother was just home from Penrith market. The spring-cart stood in the yard, the old grey horse was steaming heavily in the still, frosty air.

'I reckon ye've come fast. T' ould horse is over hot,' he remarked bluntly, as he went to the animal's head.

She clambered down hastily, and, coming to his side, began breathlessly: 'Ye ought t' hev coom t' market, Tony. There's bin pretty goin's on in Pe'rith today. I was helpin' Anna Forsyth t' choose six yards o' sheetin' in Dockroy, when we sees Rosa Blencarn coom oot o' t' Bell and Bullock in company we' Curbison and young Joe Smethwick. Smethwick was fair reelin' drunk, and Curbison and t' girl were a-houldin' on to him, to keep him fra fallin'; and then, after a bit, he puts his arm round the girl t' stiddy hisself, and that fashion they goes off, right oop t' public street – '

He continued to unload the packages, and to carry them mechanically one by one into the house. Each time, when he reappeared, she was standing by the steaming horse, busy with her tale.

'An' on t' road hame we passed t' three on' em in Curbison's trap, with Smethwick leein' in t' bottom, singin' maudlin' songs. They were passin' Dunscale village, an' t' folks coom runnin' oot o' houses t' see 'em go past – '

He led the cart away towards the stable, leaving her to cry the remainder after him across the yard.

Half an hour later he came in for his dinner. During the meal not a word passed between them, and directly he had finished he strode out of the house. About nine o'clock he returned, lit his pipe, and sat down to smoke it over the kitchen fire.

'Where've ye bin, Tony?' she asked.

'Oop t' vicarage, courtin',' he retorted defiantly, with his pipe in his mouth.

This was ten months ago; ever since he had been doggedly waiting. That evening he had set his mind on the girl, he intended to have her; and while his mother gibed, as she did now upon every opportunity, his patience remained grimly unflagging. She would remind him that the farm belonged to her, that he would have to wait till her death before he could bring the hussy to Hootsey; he would retort that as soon as the girl would have him, he intended taking a smallholding over at Scarsdale. Then she would give way, and for a while piteously upbraid him with her old age, and with the memory of all the years she and he had spent together, and he would comfort her with a display of brusque, evasive remorse.

But, none the less, on the morrow, his thoughts would return to dwell on the haunting vision of the girl's face, while his own rude, credulous chivalry, kindled by the recollection of her beauty, stifled his misgivings concerning her conduct.

Meanwhile she dallied with him, and amused herself with the younger men. Her old uncle fell ill in the spring, and could scarcely leave the house. She declared that she found life in the valley intolerably dull, that she hated the quiet of the place, that she longed for Leeds, and the exciting bustle of the streets; and in the evenings she wrote long letters to the girl-friends she had left behind there, describing with petulant vivacity her tribe of rustic admirers. At the harvest-time she went back on a fortnight's visit to friends; the evening before her departure she promised Anthony to give him her answer on her return. But, instead, she avoided him, pretended to have promised in jest, and took up with Luke Stock, a cattle-dealer from Wigton.

5

It was three weeks since he had fetched his flock down from the fell.

After dinner he and his mother sat together in the parlour: they had done so every Sunday afternoon, year in and year out, as far back as he could remember.

A row of mahogany chairs, with shiny, horse-hair seats, were ranged round the room. A great collection of agricultural prize-tickets were pinned over the wall; and, on a heavy, highly-polished sideboard stood several silver cups. A heap of gilt-edged shavings filled the unused grate; there were gaudily tinted roses along the mantelpiece, and, on a small table by the window, beneath a glass-case, a gilt basket filled with imitation flowers. Every object was disposed with a scrupulous precision; the carpet and the red-patterned cloth on the centre table were much faded. The room was spotlessly clean, and wore, in the chilly winter sunlight, a rigid, comfortless air.

Neither spoke or appeared conscious of the other's presence. Old Mrs Garstin, wrapped in a woollen shawl, sat knitting. Anthony dozed fitfully on a stiff-backed chair.

Of a sudden, in the distance, a bell started tolling. Anthony rubbed his eyes drowsily, and taking from the table his Sunday hat, strolled out across the dusky fields. Presently, reaching a rude wooden seat, built beside the bridle-path, he sat down and relit his pipe. The air was very still; below him a white filmy mist hung across the valley: the fell-sides, vaguely grouped, resembled hulking masses of sombre shadow; and, as he looked back, three squares of glimmering gold revealed the lighted windows of the square-towered church.

He sat smoking; pondering, with placid and reverential contemplation, on the Mighty Maker of the world – a world majestically and inevitably ordered; a world where, he argued, each object – each fissure in the fells, the winding course of each tumbling stream – possesses its mysterious purport, its inevitable signification . . .

At the end of the field two rams were fighting: retreating, then running together, and, leaping from the ground, butting head to head and horn to horn. Anthony watched them absently, pursuing his rude meditations.

. . . And the succession of bad seasons, the slow ruination of the farmers throughout the country, were but punishment meted out for the accumulated wickedness of the world. In the olden time God rained plagues upon the land; nowadays, in His wrath, He spoiled the produce of the earth, which, with His own hands, He had fashioned and bestowed upon men.

He rose and continued his walk along the bridle-path. A multitude of rabbits scuttled up the hill at his approach; and a great cloud of plovers, rising from the rushes, circled overhead, filling the air with a profusion of their querulous cries. All at once he heard a rattling of stones, and perceived a number of small pieces of shingle bounding in front of him down the grassy slope.

A woman's figure was moving among the rocks above him. The next moment, by the trimming of crimson velvet on her hat, he had recognised her. He mounted the slope with springing strides, wondering the while how it was she came to be there, why she was not in church playing the organ at afternoon service.

Before she was aware of his approach, he was beside her.

'I thought ye'd be in church – ' he began.

She started, then, gradually regaining her composure, answered, weakly smiling: 'Mr Jenkinson, the new schoolmaster, wanted to try the organ.'

He came towards her impulsively; she saw the odd flickers in his eyes as she stepped back in dismay.

'Nay, but I will na harm ye,' he said. 'Only I reckon what 'tis a special turn o' providence, meetin' wi' ye oop here. I reckon what ye'll hev t' give me a square answer noo. Ye canna dilly-dally everlastingly.'

He spoke almost brutally; and she stood, white and gasping, staring at him with large, frightened eyes. The sheep-walk was but a tiny threadlike track: the slope of the shingle on either side was very steep: below them lay the valley, distant, lifeless, all blurred by the evening dusk. She looked about her helplessly for a means of escape.

'Miss Rosa,' he continued, in a husky voice, 'can ye na coom t' think on me? Think ye, I've bin waitin' nigh upon two year for ye. I've watched ye tak oop, first wi' this young fellar, and then wi' that, till soomtimes my heart's fit t' burst. Many a day, oop on t' fell-top, t' thought o' ye's nigh driven me daft, and I've left my shepherdin' jest t' set on a cairn in t' mist, picturin' an' broodin' on yer face. Many an evenin' I've started oop t' vicarage, wi' t' resolution t' speak right oot t' ye; but when it coomed t' point, a sort o' timidity seemed t' hould me back, I was that feared t' displease ye. I knaw I'm na scholar, an' mabbe ye think I'm rough-mannered. I knaw I've spoken sharply to ye once or twice lately. But it's jest because I'm that mad wi' love for ye: I jest canna help myself soomtimes – '

He waited, peering into her face. She could see the beads of sweat above his bristling eyebrows; the damp had settled on his sandy beard; his horny fingers were twitching at the buttons of his black Sunday coat.

She struggled to summon a smile; but her underlip quivered, and her large dark eyes filled slowly with tears.

And he went on: 'Ye've coom t' mean jest everything to me. Ef ye will na hev me, I care for nought else. I canna speak t' ye in phrases: I'm jest a plain, unscholarly man: I canna wheedle ye, wi' cunnin' after t' fashion o' toon folks. But I can love ye wi' all my might, an' watch over ye, and work for ye better than any one o' em – '

She was crying to herself, silently, while he spoke. He noticed nothing, however: the twilight hid her face from him.

'There's nought against me,' he persisted. 'I'm as good a man as any one on 'em. Ay, as good a man as any one on 'em,' he repeated defiantly, raising his voice.

'It's impossible, Mr Garstin, it's impossible. Ye've been very kind to me – ' she added, in a choking voice.

'Wa dang it, I didna mean t' mak ye cry, lass,' he exclaimed, with a softening of his tone. 'There's nought for ye t' cry ower.'

She sank on to the stones, passionately sobbing in hysterical and defence-less despair. Anthony stood a moment, gazing at her in clumsy perplexity; then, coming close to her, he put his hand on her shoulder, and said gently: 'Coom, lass, what's trouble? Ye can trust me.'

She shook her head faintly.

'Ay, but ye can though,' he asserted, firmly. 'Come, what is't?'

Heedless of him, she continued to rock herself to and fro, crooning in her distress: 'Oh! I wish I were dead . . . I wish I could die!'

'Wish ye could die?' he repeated. 'Why, whatever can 't be that's troublin' ye like this? There, there, lassie, give ower: it 'ull all coom right, whatever it be – '

'No, no,' she wailed. 'I wish I could die! . . . I wish I could die!'

Lights were twinkling in the village below; and across the valley darkness was draping the hills. The girl lifted her face from her hands, and looked up at him with a scared, bewildered expression.

'I must go home. I must be getting home,' she muttered.

'Nay, but there's sommut mighty amiss wi' ye.'

'No, it's nothing . . . I don't know – I'm not well . . . I mean it's nothing . . . it'll pass over . . . you mustn't think anything of it.'

'Nay, but I canna stand by an see ye in sich trouble.'

'It's nothing, Mr Garstin, indeed it's nothing,' she repeated.

'Ay, but I canna credit that,' he objected stubbornly.

She sent him a shifting, hunted glance. 'Let me get home . . . you must let me get home.' She made a tremulous, pitiful attempt at firmness.

Eyeing her keenly, he barred her path: she flushed scarlet, and looked hastily away across the valley. 'If ye'll tell me yer distress, mabbe I can help ye.'

'No, no, it's nothing . . . it's nothing.'

'If ye'll tell me yer distress, mabbe I can help ye,' he repeated, with a solemn, deliberate sternness.

She shivered, and looked away again, vaguely, across the valley. 'You can do nothing: there's nought to be done,' she murmured drearily.

'There's a man in this business,' he declared.

'Let me go! Let me go!' she pleaded desperately.

'Who is't that's bin puttin' ye into this distress?' His voice sounded loud and harsh.

'No one, no one. I canna tell ye, Mr Garstin . . . It's no one,' she protested weakly.

The white, twisted look on his face frightened her. 'My God!' he burst out, gripping her wrist, 'an' a proper soft fool ye've made o' me. Who is't, I tell ye? Who's t' man?'

'Ye're hurtin' me. Let me go. I canna tell ye.'

'And ye're fond o' him?'

'No, no. He's a wicked, sinful man. I pray God I may never set eyes on him again. I told him so.'

'But ef he's got ye into trouble, he'll hev t' marry ye,' he persisted with a brutal bitterness.

'I will not. I hate him!' she cried fiercely.

'But is he *willin'* t' marry ye?'

'I don't know . . . I don't care . . . he said so before he went away . . . But I'd kill myself sooner than live with him.'

He let her hands fall and stepped back from her. She could only see his figure, like a sombre cloud, standing before her. The whole fell-side seemed still and dark and lonely.

Presently she heard his voice again: 'I reckon what there's one road oot o' yer distress.'

She shook her head drearily. 'There's none. I'm a lost woman.'

'An' ef ye took me instead?' he said eagerly.

'I – I don't understand – '

'Ef ye married me instead of Luke Stock?'

'But that's impossible – the – the – '

'Ay, t' child. I know. But I'll tak t' child as mine.'

She remained silent. After a moment he heard her voice answer in a queer, distant tone: 'You mean that – that ye're ready to marry me, and adopt the child?'

'I do,' he answered doggedly.

'But people – your mother – ?'

'Folks 'ull jest know nought about it. It's none o' their business. T' child 'ull pass as mine. Ye'll accept that?'

'Yes,' she answered, in a low, rapid voice.

'Ye'll consent t' hev me, ef I git ye oot o' yer trouble?'

'Yes,' she repeated, in the same tone.

She heard him draw a long breath.

'I said 't was a turn o' providence, meetin' wi' ye oop here,' he exclaimed, with half-suppressed exultation.

Her teeth began to chatter a little; she felt that he was peering at her, curiously, through the darkness.

'An' noo,' he continued briskly, 'ye'd best be gettin' home. Give me ye're hand, an' I'll stiddy ye ower t' stones.'

He helped her down the bank of shingle, exclaiming: 'By goom, ye're stony cauld.' Once or twice she slipped: he supported her, roughly gripping her knuckles. The stones rolled down the steps, noisily, disappearing into the night.

Presently they struck the turf bridle-path, and, as they descended silently towards the lights of the village, he said gravely: 'I always reckoned what my day 'ud coom.' She made no reply; and he added grimly: 'There'll be terrible work wi' mother over this.'

He accompanied her down the narrow lane that led past her uncle's house. When the lighted windows came in sight he halted.

'Good night, lassie,' he said kindly. 'Do ye give ower distressin' yeself.'

'Good night, Mr Garstin,' she answered, in the same low, rapid voice in which she had given him her answer up on the fell.

'We're man an' wife plighted now, are we not?' he blurted timidly.

She held her face to his, and he kissed her on the cheek, clumsily.

6

The next morning the frost had set in. The sky was still clear and glittering: the whitened fields sparkled in the chilly sunlight: here and there, on high, distant peaks, gleamed dainty caps of snow. All the week Anthony was to be busy at the fell-foot, wall-building against the coming of the winter storms: the work was heavy, for he was single-handed, and the stone had to be fetched from off the fell-side. Two or three times a day he led his rickety, lumbering cart along the lane that passed the vicarage gate, pausing on each journey to glance furtively up at the windows. But he saw no sign of Rosa Blencarn; and, indeed, he felt no longing to see her: he was grimly exultant over the remembrance of his wooing of her, and over the knowledge that she was his. There glowed within him a stolid pride in himself: he thought of the others who had courted her, and the means by which he had won her seemed to him a fine stroke of cleverness.

And so he refrained from any mention of the matter; relishing, as he worked, all alone, the days through, the consciousness of his secret triumph, and anticipating, with inward chucklings, the discomforted cackle of his mother's female friends. He foresaw, without misgiving, her bitter opposition: he felt himself strong; and his heart warmed towards the girl. And when, at intervals, the brusque realisation that, after all, he was to possess her swept over him, he gripped the stones, and swung them almost fiercely into their places.

All around him the white, empty fields seemed slumbering breathlessly. The stillness stiffened the leafless trees. The frosty air flicked his blood: singing vigorously to himself he worked with a stubborn, unflagging resolution, methodically postponing, till the length of the wall should be completed, the announcement of his betrothal.

After his reticent, solitary fashion, he was very happy, reviewing his future prospects with a plain and steady assurance, and, as the weekend approached, coming to ignore the irregularity of the whole business; coming almost to assume, in the exaltation of his pride, that he had won her honestly, and to discard, stolidly, all thought of Luke Stock, of his relations with her and his connection with the coming child that was to pass for his own.

And there were moments too, when, as he sauntered homewards through the dusk at the end of his day's work, his heart grew full to overflowing of a rugged, superstitious gratitude towards God in heaven who had granted his desires.

About three o'clock on the Saturday afternoon he finished the length of wall. He went home, washed, shaved, put on his Sunday coat; and, avoiding the kitchen, where his mother sat knitting by the fireside, strode up to the vicarage.

It was Rosa who opened the door to him. On recognising him she started, and he followed her into the dining-room. He seated himself, and began, brusquely: 'I've coom, Miss Rosa, t' speak t' Mr Blencarn.' Then added, eyeing her closely: 'Ye're lookin' sick, lass.'

Her faint smile accentuated the worn, white look on her face.

'I reckon ye've been frettin' yeself,' he continued gently, 'leein' awake o' nights, hev'n't yee, noo?'

She smiled vaguely.

'Well, but ye see I've coom t' settle t' whole business for ye. Ye thought mabbe that I was na a man o' my word.'

'No, no, not that,' she protested, 'but – but – '

'But what then?'

'Ye must not do it, Mr Garstin . . . I must just bear my own trouble the best I can – ' she broke out.

'D'ye fancy I'm takin' ye oot of charity? Ye little reckon the sort o' stuff my love for ye's made of. Nay, Miss Rosa, but ye canna draw back noo.'

'But ye cannot do it, Mr Garstin. Ye know your mother will na have me at Hootsey . . . I could na live there with your mother . . . I'd sooner bear my trouble alone, as best I can . . . She's that stern is Mrs Garstin. I couldn't look her in the face . . . I can go away somewhere . . . I could keep it all from uncle.'

Her colour came and went; she stood before him, looking away from him, dully, out of the window.

'I intend ye t' coom t' Hootsey. I'm na lad: I reckon I can choose my own wife. Mother'll hev ye at t' farm, right enough: ye need na distress yeself on that point – '

'Nay, Mr Garstin, but indeed she will not, never . . . I know she will not. She always set herself against me, right from the first.'

'Ay, but that was different. T' case is all changed noo,' he objected doggedly.

'She'll support the sight of me all the less,' the girl faltered.

'Mother'll hev ye at Hootsey – receive ye willin' of her own free wish – of her own free wish, d'ye hear? I'll answer for that.'

He struck the table with his fist heavily. His tone of determination awed her: she glanced at him hurriedly, struggling with her irresolution.

'I knaw hoo t' manage mother. An' now,' he concluded, changing his tone, 'is yer uncle about t' place?'

'He's up the paddock, I think,' she answered.

'Well, I'll jest step oop and hev a word wi' him.'

'Ye're . . . ye will na tell him.'

'Tut, tut, na harrowin' tales, ye need na fear, lass. I reckon ef I can tackle mother, I can accommodate myself t' Parson Blencarn.'

He rose, and coming close to her, scanned her face.

'Ye must git t' roses back t' yer cheeks,' he exclaimed, with a short laugh, 'I canna be takin' a ghost t' church.'

She smiled tremulously, and he continued, laying one hand affectionately on her shoulder:

'Nay, but I was but jestin'. Roses or na roses, ye'll be t' bonniest bride in all Coomberland. I'll meet ye in Hullam Lane, after church time, tomorrow,' he added, moving towards the door.

After he had gone, she hurried to the back-door furtively. His retreating figure was already mounting the grey upland field. Presently, beyond him, she perceived her uncle, emerging through the paddock gate. She ran across the poultry yard, and mounting a tub, stood watching the two figures as they moved towards one another along the brow, Anthony vigorously trudging, with his hands thrust deep in his pockets; her uncle, his wideawake tilted over his nose, hobbling, and leaning stiffly on his pair of sticks. They met; she saw Anthony take her uncle's arm and the two, turning together, strolled away towards the fell.

She went back into the house. Anthony's dog came towards her, slinking along the passage. She caught the animal's head in her hands, and bent over it caressingly, in an impulsive outburst of almost hysterical affection.

7

The two men returned towards the vicarage. At the paddock gate they halted, and the old man concluded: 'I could not have wished a better man for her, Anthony. Mabbe the Lord'll not be minded to spare me much longer. After I'm gone Rosa'll hev all I possess. She was my poor brother Isaac's only child. After her mother was taken, he, poor fellow, went altogether to the bad, and until she came here she mostly lived among strangers. It's been a wretched sort of childhood for her – a wretched sort of childhood. Ye'll take care of her, Anthony, will ye not? . . . Nay, but I could not hev wished for a better man for her, and there's my hand on 't.'

'Thank ee, Mr Blencarn, thank ee,' Anthony answered huskily, gripping the old man's hand.

And he started off down the lane homewards.

His heart was full of a strange, rugged exaltation. He felt with a swelling pride that God had entrusted to him this great charge – to tend her; to make up to her, tenfold, for all that loving care, which, in her childhood, she had never known. And together with a stubborn confidence in himself, there welled up within him a great pity for her – a tender pity, that, chastening with his passion, made her seem to him, as he brooded over that lonely childhood of hers, the more distinctly beautiful, the more profoundly precious. He pictured to himself, tremulously, almost incredulously, their married life – in the winter, his return home at nightfall to find her awaiting him with a glad, trustful smile; their evenings, passed together, sitting in silent happiness over the smouldering logs; or, in summertime, the midday rest in the hayfields when, wearing perhaps a large-brimmed hat fastened with a red ribbon beneath her chin, he would catch sight of her, carrying his dinner, coming across the upland.

She had not been brought up to be a farmer's wife: she was but a child still, as the old parson had said. She should not have to work as other men's wives worked: she should dress like a lady, and on Sundays, in church, wear fine bonnets, and remain, as she had always been, the belle of all the parish.

And, meanwhile, he would farm as he had never farmed before, watching his opportunities, driving cunning bargains, spending nothing on himself, hoarding every penny that she might have what she wanted . . . And, as he strode through the village, he seemed to foresee a general brightening of prospects, a sobering of the fever of speculation in sheep, a cessation of the insensate glutting, year after year, of the great winter marts throughout the north, a slackening of the foreign competition followed by a steady revival of the price of fatted stocks – a period of prosperity in store for the farmer at last . . . And the future years appeared to open out before him, spread like a distant, glittering plain, across which, he and she, hand in hand, were called to travel together . . .

And then, suddenly, as his iron-bound boots clattered over the cobbled yard, he remembered, with brutal determination, his mother, and the stormy struggle that awaited him.

He waited till supper was over, till his mother had moved from the table to her place by the chimney corner. For several minutes he remained, debating with himself the best method of breaking the news to her. Of a sudden he glanced up at her: her knitting had slipped on to her lap; she was sitting, bunched of a heap in her chair, nodding with sleep. By the flickering light of the wood fire, she looked worn and broken; he felt a twinge of clumsy compunction. And then he remembered the piteous, hunted look in the girl's eyes, and the old man's words when they had parted at the paddock gate, and he blurted out: 'I doot but what I'll hev t' marry Rosa Blencarn after all.'

She started, and blinking her eyes, said: 'I was jest takin' a wink o' sleep. What was 't ye were saying, Tony?'

He hesitated a moment, puckering his forehead into coarse rugged lines, and fidgeting noisily with his tea-cup. Presently he repeated: 'I doot but what I'll hev t' marry Rosa Blencarn after all.'

She rose stiffly, and stepping down from the hearth, came towards him. 'Mabbe I did na hear ye aright, Tony.' She spoke hurriedly, and though she was quite close to him, steadying herself with one hand clutching the back of his chair, her voice sounded weak, distant almost. 'Look oop at me. Look oop into my face,' she commanded fiercely.

He obeyed sullenly.

'Noo oot wi 't. What's yer meanin', Tony?'

'I mean what I say,' he retorted doggedly, averting his gaze.

'What d'ye mean by sayin' that ye've *got* t' marry her?'

'I tell yer I mean what I say,' he repeated dully.

'Ye mean ye've bin an' put t' girl in trouble?'

He said nothing; but sat staring stupidly at the floor.

'Look oop at me, and answer,' she commanded, gripping his shoulder and shaking him.

He raised his face slowly, and met her glance. 'Ay, that's aboot it,' he answered.

'This'll na be truth. It'll be jest a piece o' wanton trickery!' she cried.

'Nay, but 'tis t' truth,' he answered deliberately.

'Ye will na swear t' it?' she persisted.

'I see na necessity for swearin'.'

'Then ye canna swear t' it,' she burst out triumphantly.

He paused an instant; then said quietly: 'Ay, but I'll swear t' it easy enough. Fetch t' Book.'

She lifted the heavy, tattered Bible from the chimney-piece, and placed it before him on the table. He laid his lumpish fist on it.

'Say,' she continued with a tense tremulousness, 'say, I swear t' ye, mother, that 't is t' truth, t' whole truth, and noat but t' truth, s'help me God.'

'I swear t' ye, mother, 't is t' truth, t' whole truth, and nothin' but t' truth, s'help me God,' he repeated after her.

'Kiss t' Book,' she ordered.

He lifted the Bible to his lips. As he replaced it on the table, he burst out into a short laugh: 'Be ye satisfied noo?'

She went back to the chimney corner without a word. The logs on the hearth hissed and crackled. Outside, amid the blackness the wind was rising, hooting through the firs and past the windows.

After a long while he roused himself, and drawing his pipe from his pocket almost steadily, proceeded leisurely to pare in the palm of his hand a lump of black tobacco.

'We'll be asked in church Sunday,' he remarked bluntly.

She made no answer.

He looked across at her.

Her mouth was drawn tight at the corners; her face wore a queer, rigid aspect. She looked, he thought, like a figure of stone.

'Ye're not feeling poorly, are ye, mother?' he asked.

She shook her head grimly; then, hobbling out into the room, began to speak in a shrill, tuneless voice.

'Ye talked at one time o' takin' a farm over Scarsdale way. But ye'd best stop here. I'll no hinder ye. Ye can have t' large bedroom in t' front, and I'll move ower to what used to be my brother Jake's room. Ye knaw I've never had no opinion of t' girl, but I'll do what's right by her, ef I break my sperrit in t' doin' on't. I'll mak' t' girl welcome here: I'll stand by her proper-like: mebbe I'll finish by findin' soom good in her. But from this day forward, Tony, ye're na son o' mine. Ye've dishonoured yeself: ye've laid a trap for me – ay, laid a trap, that's t' word. Ye've brought shame and bitterness on yer ould mother in her ould age. Ye've made me despise t' varra sect o' ye. Ye can stop on here, but ye shall niver touch a penny of my money; every shillin' of 't shall go t' yer child, or to your child's children. Ay,' she went on, raising her voice, 'ay, ye've got yer way at last, and mebbe ye reckon ye've chosen a mighty smart way. But time 'ull coom when ye'll regret this day, when ye eat oot yer repentance in doost an' ashes. Ay, Lord 'ull punish ye, Tony, chastise ye properly. Ye'll learn that marriage begun in sin can end in nought but sin. Ay,' she concluded, as she reached the door, raising her skinny hand prophetically, 'ay, after I'm deed and gone, ye mind ye o' t' words o' t' apostle – "For them that hev sinned without t' law, shall also perish without t' law." '

And she slammed the door behind her.

STEPHEN CRANE

Stephen Crane was born in Newark, New Jersey, in 1871, the youngest son of a Methodist minister. After failing to settle at university, Crane moved to New York where he worked as a journalist and wrote his first novel *Maggie: A Girl of the Streets* in 1893. His second novel, *The Red Badge of Courage*, was far more successful, critically and commercially, and after its publication in 1895 he travelled as a newspaper correspondent to Mexico, to Cuba and to Greece. In 1897 he settled in England, where he met Joseph Conrad and Henry James. He died in Germany in 1900, aged twenty-eight.

The Little Regiment

I

The fog made the clothes of the men of the column in the roadway seem of a luminous quality. It imparted to the heavy infantry overcoats a new colour, a kind of blue which was so pale that a regiment might have been merely a long, low shadow in the mist. However, a muttering, one part grumble, three parts joke, hovered in the air above the thick ranks, and blended in an undertoned roar, which was the voice of the column.

The town on the southern shore of the little river loomed spectrally, a faint etching upon the grey cloud-masses which were shifting with oily languor. A long row of guns upon the northern bank had been pitiless in their hatred, but a little battered belfry could be dimly seen still pointing with invincible resolution toward the heavens.

The enclouded air vibrated with noises made by hidden colossal things. The infantry tramplings, the heavy rumbling of the artillery, made the earth speak of gigantic preparation. Guns on distant heights thundered from time to time with sudden, nervous roar, as if unable to endure in silence a knowledge of hostile troops massing, other guns going to position. These sounds, near and remote, defined an immense battleground, described the tremendous width of the stage of the prospective drama. The voices of the guns, slightly casual, unexcited in their challenges and warnings, could not destroy the unutterable eloquence of the word in the air, a meaning of impending struggle which made the breath halt at the lips.

The column in the roadway was ankle-deep in mud. The men swore piously at the rain which drizzled upon them, compelling them to stand always very erect in fear of the drops that would sweep in under their coat-collars. The fog was as cold as wet cloths. The men stuffed their hands deep in their pockets, and huddled their muskets in their arms. The machinery of orders had rooted these soldiers deeply into the mud, precisely as almighty nature roots mullein stalks.

They listened and speculated when a tumult of fighting came from the dim town across the river. When the noise lulled for a time they resumed their descriptions of the mud and graphically exaggerated the number of hours they had been kept waiting. The general commanding their division rode along the ranks, and they cheered admiringly, affectionately, crying out to him gleeful prophecies of the coming battle. Each man scanned him with a peculiarly keen personal interest, and afterward spoke of him with unquestioning devotion and confidence, narrating anecdotes which were mainly untrue.

When the jokers lifted the shrill voices which invariably belonged to them, flinging witticisms at their comrades, a loud laugh would sweep from rank to rank, and soldiers who had not heard would lean forward and demand repetition. When were borne past them some wounded men with grey and blood-smeared faces, and eyes that rolled in that helpless beseeching for assistance from the sky which comes with supreme pain, the soldiers in the mud watched intently, and from time to time asked of the bearers an account of the affair. Frequently they bragged of their corps, their division, their brigade, their regiment. Anon they referred to the mud and the cold drizzle. Upon this threshold of a wild scene of death they, in short, defied the proportion of events with that splendour of heedlessness which belongs only to veterans.

'Like a lot of wooden soldiers,' swore Billie Dempster, moving his feet in the thick mass, and casting a vindictive glance indefinitely: 'standing in the mud for a hundred years.'

'Oh, shut up!' murmured his brother Dan. The manner of his words implied that this fraternal voice near him was an indescribable bore.

'Why should I shut up?' demanded Billie.

'Because you're a fool,' cried Dan, taking no time to debate it; 'the biggest fool in the regiment.'

There was but one man between them, and he was habituated. These insults from brother to brother had swept across his chest, flown past his face, many times during two long campaigns. Upon this occasion he simply grinned first at one, then at the other.

The way of these brothers was not an unknown topic in regimental gossip. They had enlisted simultaneously, with each sneering loudly at the other for doing it. They left their little town, and went forward with the flag, exchanging protestations of undying suspicion. In the camp life they so openly despised each other that, when entertaining quarrels were lacking, their companions often contrived situations calculated to bring forth display of this fraternal dislike.

Both were large-limbed, strong young men, and often fought with friends in camp unless one was near to interfere with the other. This latter happened rather frequently, because Dan, preposterously willing for any manner of combat, had a very great horror of seeing Billie in a fight; and Billie, almost odiously ready himself, simply refused to see Dan stripped to his shirt and with his fists aloft. This sat queerly upon them, and made them the objects of plots.

When Dan jumped through a ring of eager soldiers and dragged forth his raving brother by the arm, a thing often predicted would almost come to pass. When Billie performed the same office for Dan, the prediction would again miss fulfilment by an inch. But indeed they never fought together, although they were perpetually upon the verge.

They expressed longing for such conflict. As a matter of truth, they had at one time made full arrangement for it, but even with the encouragement and interest of half of the regiment they somehow failed to achieve collision.

If Dan became a victim of police duty, no jeering was so destructive to the feelings as Billie's comment. If Billie got a call to appear at the headquarters, none would so genially prophesy his complete undoing as Dan. Small misfortunes to one were, in truth, invariably greeted with hilarity by the other, who seemed to see in them great re-enforcement of his opinion.

As soldiers, they expressed each for each a scorn intense and blasting. After a certain battle, Billie was promoted to corporal. When Dan was told of it, he seemed smitten dumb with astonishment and patriotic indignation. He stared in silence, while the dark blood rushed to Billie's forehead, and he shifted his weight from foot to foot. Dan at last found his tongue, and said: 'Well, I'm durned!' If he had heard that an army mule had been appointed to the post of corps commander, his tone could not have had more derision in it. Afterward, he adopted a fervid insubordination, an almost religious reluctance to obey the new corporal's orders, which came near to developing the desired strife.

It is here finally to be recorded also that Dan, most ferociously profane in speech, very rarely swore in the presence of his brother; and that Billie, whose oaths came from his lips with the grace of falling pebbles, was seldom known to express himself in this manner when near his brother Dan.

At last the afternoon contained a suggestion of evening. Metallic cries rang suddenly from end to end of the column. They inspired at once a quick, businesslike adjustment. The long thing stirred in the mud. The men had hushed, and were looking across the river. A moment later the shadowy mass of pale blue figures was moving steadily toward the stream. There could be heard from the town a clash of swift fighting and cheering. The noise of the shooting coming through the heavy air had its sharpness taken from it, and sounded in thuds.

There was a halt upon the bank above the pontoons. When the column went winding down the incline, and streamed out upon the bridge, the fog had faded to a great degree, and in the clearer dusk the guns on a distant ridge were enabled to perceive the crossing. The long whirling out-cries of the shells came into the air above the men. An occasional solid shot struck the surface of the river and dashed into view a sudden vertical jet. The distance was subtly illuminated by the lightning from the deep-booming guns. One by one the batteries on the northern shore aroused, the innumerable guns bellowing in angry oration at the distant ridge. The rolling thunder crashed and reverberated as a wild surf sounds on a still night, and to this music the column marched across the pontoons.

The waters of the grim river curled away in a smile from the ends of the great boats, and slid swiftly beneath the planking. The dark, riddled walls of the town upreared before the troops, and from a region hidden by these hammered and tumbled houses came incessantly the yells and firings of a prolonged and close skirmish.

When Dan had called his brother a fool, his voice had been so decisive, so brightly assured, that many men had laughed, considering it to be great humour under the circumstances. The incident happened to rankle deep in Billie. It was not any strange thing that his brother had called him a fool. In fact, he often called him a fool with exactly the same amount of cheerful and prompt conviction, and before large audiences, too. Billie wondered in his own mind why he took such profound offence in this case; but, at any rate, as he slid down the bank and on to the bridge with his regiment, he was searching his knowledge for something that would pierce Dan's blithesome spirit. But he could contrive nothing at this time, and his impotency made the glance which he was once able to give his brother still more malignant.

The guns far and near were roaring a fearful and grand introduction for this column which was marching upon the stage of death. Billie felt it, but only in a numb way. His heart was cased in that curious dissonant metal which covers a man's emotions at such times. The terrible voices from the hills told him that in this wide conflict his life was an insignificant fact, and that his death would be an insignificant fact. They portended the whirlwind to which he would be as necessary as a butterfly's waved wing. The solemnity, the sadness of it came near enough to make him wonder why he was neither solemn nor sad. When his mind vaguely adjusted events according to their importance to him, it appeared that the uppermost thing was the fact that upon the eve of battle, and before many comrades, his brother had called him a fool.

Dan was in a particularly happy mood. 'Hurray! Look at 'em shoot,' he said, when the long witches' croon of the shells came into the air. It enraged Billie when he felt the little thorn in him, and saw at the same time that his brother had completely forgotten it.

The column went from the bridge into more mud. At this southern end there was a chaos of hoarse directions and commands. Darkness was coming upon the earth, and regiments were being hurried up the slippery bank. As Billie floundered in the black mud, amid the swearing, sliding crowd, he suddenly resolved that, in the absence of other means of hurting Dan, he would avoid looking at him, refrain from speaking to him, pay absolutely no heed to his existence; and this done skilfully would, he imagined, soon reduce his brother to a poignant sensitiveness.

At the top of the bank the column again halted and rearranged itself, as a man after a climb rearranges his clothing. Presently the great steel-backed brigade, an infinitely graceful thing in the rhythm and ease of its veteran movement, swung up a little narrow, slanting street.

Evening had come so swiftly that the fighting on the remote borders of the town was indicated by thin flashes of flame. Some building was on fire, and its reflection upon the clouds was an oval of delicate pink.

2

All demeanour of rural serenity had been wrenched violently from the little town by the guns and by the waves of men which had surged through it. The hand of war laid upon this village had in an instant changed it to a thing of remnants. It resembled the place of a monstrous shaking of the earth itself. The windows, now mere unsightly holes, made the tumbled and blackened dwellings seem skeletons. Doors lay splintered to fragments. Chimneys had flung their bricks everywhere. The artillery fire had not neglected the rows of gentle shade-trees which had lined the streets. Branches and heavy trunks cluttered the mud in driftwood tangles, while a few shattered forms had contrived to remain dejectedly, mournfully upright. They expressed an innocence, a helplessness, which perforce created a pity for their happening into this cauldron of battle. Furthermore, there was underfoot a vast collection of odd things reminiscent of the charge, the fight, the retreat. There were boxes and barrels filled with earth, behind which riflemen had lain snugly, and in these little trenches were the dead in blue with the dead in grey, the poses eloquent of the struggles for possession of the town, until the history of the whole conflict was written plainly in the streets.

And yet the spirit of this little city, its quaint individuality, poised in the air above the ruins, defying the guns, the sweeping volleys; holding in contempt those avaricious blazes which had attacked many dwellings. The hard earthen sidewalks proclaimed the games that had been played there during long lazy days, in the careful shadows of the trees. 'General Merchandise', in faint letters upon a long board, had to be read with a slanted glance, for the sign dangled by one end; but the porch of the old store was a palpable legend of wide-hatted men, smoking.

This subtle essence, this soul of the life that had been, brushed like invisible wings the thoughts of the men in the swift columns that came up from the river.

In the darkness a loud and endless humming arose from the great blue crowds bivouacked in the streets. From time to time a sharp spatter of firing from far picket lines entered this bass chorus. The smell from the smouldering ruins floated on the cold night breeze.

Dan, seated ruefully upon the doorstep of a shot-pierced house, was proclaiming the campaign badly managed. Orders had been issued forbidding campfires.

Suddenly he ceased his oration, and scanning the group of his comrades, said: 'Where's Billie? Do you know?'

'Gone on picket.'

'Get out! Has he?' said Dan. 'No business to go on picket. Why don't some of them other corporals take their turn?'

A bearded private was smoking his pipe of confiscated tobacco, seated comfortably upon a horsehair trunk which he had dragged from the house. He observed: 'Was his turn.'

'No such thing,' cried Dan. He and the man on the horsehair trunk held discussion in which Dan stoutly maintained that if his brother had been sent on picket it was an injustice. He ceased his argument when another soldier, upon whose arms could faintly be seen the two stripes of a corporal, entered the circle. 'Humph,' said Dan, 'where you been?'

The corporal made no answer. Presently Dan said: 'Billie, where you been?'

His brother did not seem to hear these enquiries. He glanced at the house which towered above them, and remarked casually to the man on the horsehair trunk: 'Funny, ain't it? After the pelting this town got, you'd think there wouldn't be one brick left on another.'

'Oh,' said Dan, glowering at his brother's back. 'Getting mighty smart, ain't you?'

The absence of campfires allowed the evening to make apparent its quality of faint silver light in which the blue clothes of the throng became black, and the faces became white expanses, void of expression. There was considerable excitement a short distance from the group around the door-step. A soldier had chanced upon a hoop-skirt, and arrayed in it he was performing a dance amid the applause of his companions. Billie and a greater part of the men immediately poured over there to witness the exhibition.

'What's the matter with Billie?' demanded Dan of the man upon the horsehair trunk.

'How do I know?' rejoined the other in mild resentment. He arose and walked away. When he returned he said briefly, in a weather-wise tone, that it would rain during the night.

Dan took a seat upon one end of the horsehair trunk. He was facing the crowd around the dancer, which in its hilarity swung this way and that way. At times he imagined that he could recognise his brother's face.

He and the man on the other end of the trunk thoughtfully talked of the army's position. To their minds, infantry and artillery were in a most precarious jumble in the streets of the town; but they did not grow nervous over it, for they were used to having the army appear in a precarious jumble to their minds. They had learned to accept such puzzling situations as a consequence of their position in the ranks, and were now usually in possession of a simple but perfectly immovable faith that somebody understood the jumble. Even if they had been convinced that the army was a headless monster, they would merely have nodded with the veteran's singular cynicism. It was none of their business as soldiers. Their duty was to grab sleep and food when occasion permitted, and cheerfully fight wherever their feet were planted until more orders came. This was a task sufficiently absorbing.

They spoke of other corps, and this talk being confidential, their voices dropped to tones of awe. 'The Ninth' – 'The First' – 'The Fifth' – 'The Sixth' – 'The Third' – the simple numerals rang with eloquence, each having a meaning which was to float through many years as no intangible arithmetical mist, but as pregnant with individuality as the names of cities.

Of their own corps they spoke with a deep veneration, an idolatry, a supreme confidence which apparently would not blanch to see it match against everything.

It was as if their respect for other corps was due partly to a wonder that organisations not blessed with their own famous numeral could take such an interest in war. They could prove that their division was the best in the corps, and that their brigade was the best in the division. And their regiment – it was plain that no fortune of life was equal to the chance which caused a man to be born, so to speak, into this command, the keystone of the defending arch.

At times Dan covered with insults the character of a vague, unnamed general to whose petulance and busy-body spirit he ascribed the order which made hot coffee impossible.

Dan said that victory was certain in the coming battle. The other man seemed rather dubious. He remarked upon the fortified line of hills, which had impressed him even from the other side of the river. 'Shucks,' said Dan. 'Why, we – ' He pictured a splendid overflowing of these hills by the sea of men in blue. During the period of this conversation Dan's glance searched the merry throng about the dancer. Above the babble of voices in the street a fairway thunder could sometimes be heard – evidently from the very edge of the horizon – the boom-boom of restless guns.

3

Ultimately the night deepened to the tone of black velvet. The outlines of the fireless camp were like the faint drawings upon ancient tapestry. The glint of a rifle, the shine of a button, might have been of threads of silver and gold sewn upon the fabric of the night. There was little presented to the vision, but to a sense more subtle there was discernible in the atmosphere something like a pulse; a mystic beating which would have told a stranger of the presence of a giant thing – the slumbering mass of regiments and batteries.

With fires forbidden, the floor of a dry old kitchen was thought to be a good exchange for the cold earth of December, even if a shell had exploded in it, and knocked it so out of shape that when a man lay curled in his blanket his last waking thought was likely to be of the wall that bellied out above him, as if strongly anxious to topple upon the score of soldiers.

Billie looked at the bricks ever about to descend in a shower upon his face, listened to the industrious pickets plying their rifles on the border of the town, imagined some measure of the din of the coming battle, thought of Dan and Dan's chagrin, and rolling over in his blanket went to sleep with satisfaction.

At an unknown hour he was aroused by the creaking of boards. Lifting himself upon his elbow, he saw a sergeant prowling among the sleeping forms. The sergeant carried a candle in an old brass candlestick. He would have resembled some old farmer on an unusual midnight tour if it were not for the significance of his gleaming buttons and striped sleeves.

Billie blinked stupidly at the light until his mind returned from the journeys of slumber. The sergeant stooped among the unconscious soldiers, holding the candle close, and peering into each face.

'Hello, Haines,' said Billie. 'Relief?'

'Hello, Billie,' said the sergeant. 'Special duty.'

'Dan got to go?'

'Jameson, Hunter, McCormack, D. Dempster. Yes. Where is he?'

'Over there by the winder,' said Billie, gesturing. 'What is it for, Haines?'

'You don't think I know, do you?' demanded the sergeant. He began to pipe sharply but cheerily at men upon the floor. 'Come, Mac, get up here. Here's a special for you. Wake up, Jameson. Come along, Dannie, me boy.'

Each man at once took this call to duty as a personal affront. They pulled themselves out of their blankets, rubbed their eyes, and swore at whoever was responsible. 'Them's orders,' cried the sergeant. 'Come! Get out of here.' An undetailed head with dishevelled hair thrust out from a blanket, and a sleepy voice said: 'Shut up, Haines, and go home.'

When the detail clanked out of the kitchen, all but one of the remaining men seemed to be again asleep. Billie, leaning on his elbow, was gazing into darkness. When the footsteps died to silence, he curled himself into his blanket.

At the first cool lavender lights of daybreak he aroused again, and scanned his recumbent companions. Seeing a wakeful one he asked: 'Is Dan back yet?'

The man said: 'Hain't seen 'im.'

Billie put both hands behind his head, and scowled into the air. 'Can't see the use of these cussed details in the night-time,' he muttered in his most unreasonable tones. 'Darn nuisances. Why can't they – ' He grumbled at length and graphically.

When Dan entered with the squad, however, Billie was convincingly asleep.

The regiment trotted in double time along the street, and the colonel seemed to quarrel over the right of way with many artillery officers. Batteries were waiting in the mud, and the men of them, exasperated by the bustle of this ambitious infantry, shook their fists from saddle and caisson, exchanging all manner of taunts and jests. The slanted guns continued to look reflectively at the ground.

On the outskirts of the crumbled town a fringe of blue figures were firing into the fog. The regiment swung out into skirmish lines, and the fringe of blue figures departed, turning their backs and going joyfully around the flank.

The bullets began a low moan off toward a ridge which loomed faintly in the heavy mist. When the swift crescendo had reached its climax, the missiles zipped just overhead, as if piercing an invisible curtain. A battery on the hill was crashing with such tumult that it was as if the guns had quarrelled and had fallen pell-mell and snarling upon each other. The shells howled on their journey toward the town. From short-range distance there came a spatter of musketry, sweeping along an invisible line, and making faint sheets of orange light.

Some in the new skirmish lines were beginning to fire at various shadows discerned in the vapour, forms of men suddenly revealed by some humour of the laggard masses of clouds. The crackle of musketry began to dominate the purring of the hostile bullets. Dan, in the front rank, held his rifle poised, and looked into the fog keenly, coldly, with the air of a sportsman. His nerves were so steady that it was as if they had been drawn from his body, leaving him merely a muscular machine; but his numb heart was somehow beating to the pealing march of the fight.

The waving skirmish line went backward and forward, ran this way and that way. Men got lost in the fog, and men were found again. Once they got too close to the formidable ridge, and the thing burst out as if repulsing a general attack. Once another blue regiment was apprehended on the very edge of firing into them. Once a friendly battery began an elaborate and scientific process of extermination. Always as busy as brokers, the men slid here and there over the plain, fighting their foes, escaping from their friends, leaving a history of many movements in the wet yellow turf, cursing the atmosphere, blazing away every time they could identify the enemy.

In one mystic changing of the fog, as if the fingers of spirits were drawing aside these draperies, a small group of the grey skirmishers, silent, statuesque, were suddenly disclosed to Dan and those about him. So vivid and near were they that there was something uncanny in the revelation.

There might have been a second of mutual staring. Then each rifle in each group was at the shoulder. As Dan's glance flashed along the barrel of his weapon, the figure of a man suddenly loomed as if the musket had been a telescope. The short black beard, the slouch hat, the pose of the man as he sighted to shoot, made a quick picture in Dan's mind. The same moment, it would seem, he pulled his own trigger, and the man, smitten, lurched forward, while his exploding rifle made a slanting crimson streak in the air, and the slouch hat fell before the body. The billows of the fog, governed by singular impulses, rolled between.

'You got that feller sure enough,' said a comrade to Dan. Dan looked at him absent-mindedly.

5

When the next morning calmly displayed another fog, the men of the regiment exchanged eloquent comments; but they did not abuse it at length, because the streets of the town now contained enough galloping aides to make three troops of cavalry, and they knew that they had come to the verge of the great fight.

Dan conversed with the man who had once possessed a horsehair trunk; but they did not mention the line of hills which had furnished them in more careless moments with an agreeable topic. They avoided it now as condemned men do the subject of death, and yet the thought of it stayed in their eyes as they looked at each other and talked gravely of other things.

The expectant regiment heaved a long sigh of relief when the sharp call: 'Fall in,' repeated indefinitely, arose in the streets. It was inevitable that a bloody battle was to be fought, and they wanted to get it off their minds. They were, however, doomed again to spend a long period planted firmly in the mud. They craned their necks, and wondered where some of the other regiments were going.

At last the mists rolled carelessly away. Nature made at this time all provisions to enable foes to see each other, and immediately the roar of guns resounded from every hill. The endless cracking of the skirmishers swelled to rolling crashes of musketry. Shells screamed with panther-like noises at the houses. Dan looked at the man of the horsehair trunk, and the man said: 'Well, here she comes!'

The tenor voices of younger officers and the deep and hoarse voices of the older ones rang in the streets. These cries pricked like spurs. The masses of men vibrated from the suddenness with which they were plunged into the situation of troops about to fight. That the orders were long-expected did not concern the emotion.

Simultaneous movement was imparted to all these thick bodies of men and horses that lay in the town. Regiment after regiment swung rapidly into the streets that faced the sinister ridge.

This exodus was theatrical. The little sober-hued village had been like the cloak which disguises the king of drama. It was now put aside, and an army, splendid thing of steel and blue, stood forth in the sunlight.

Even the soldiers in the heavy columns drew deep breaths at the sight, more majestic than they had dreamed. The heights of the enemy's position were crowded with men who resembled people come to witness some mighty pageant. But as the column moved steadily to their positions, the guns, matter-of-fact warriors, doubled their number, and shells burst with red thrilling tumult on the crowded plain. One came into the ranks of the regiment, and after the smoke and the wrath of it had faded, leaving motionless figures, everyone stormed according to the limits of his vocabulary, for veterans detest being killed when they are not busy.

The regiment sometimes looked sideways at its brigade companions composed of men who had never been in battle; but no frozen blood could withstand the heat of the splendour of this army before the eyes on the plain, these lines so long that the flanks were little streaks, this mass of men of one intention. The recruits carried themselves heedlessly. At the rear was an idle battery, and three artillerymen in a foolish row on a caisson nudged each other and grinned at the recruits. 'You'll catch it pretty soon,' they called out. They were impersonally gleeful, as if they themselves were not also likely to catch it pretty soon. But with this picture of an army in their hearts, the new men perhaps felt the devotion which the drops may feel for the wave; they were of its power and glory; they smiled jauntily at the foolish row of gunners, and told them to go to blazes.

The column trotted across some little bridges, and spread quickly into lines of battle. Before them was a bit of plain, and back of the plain was the ridge. There was no time left for considerations. The men were staring at the plain, mightily wondering how it would feel to be out there, when a brigade in advance yelled and charged. The hill was all grey smoke and fire-points.

That fierce elation in the terrors of war, catching a man's heart and making it burn with such ardour that he becomes capable of dying, flashed in the faces of the men like coloured lights, and made them resemble leashed animals, eager, ferocious, daunted by nothing. The line was really in its first leap before the wild, hoarse crying of the orders.

The greed for close quarters, which is the emotion of a bayonet charge, came then into the minds of the men and developed until it was a madness. The field, with its faded grass of a Southern winter, seemed to this fury miles in width.

High, slow-moving masses of smoke, with an odour of burning cotton, engulfed the line until the men might have been swimmers. Before them the ridge, the shore of this grey sea, was outlined, crossed, and recrossed by sheets of flame. The howl of the battle arose to the noise of innumerable wind demons.

The line, galloping, scrambling, plunging like a herd of wounded horses, went over a field that was sown with corpses, the records of other charges.

Directly in front of the black-faced, whooping Dan, carousing in this onward sweep like a new kind of fiend, a wounded man appeared, raising his shattered body, and staring at this rush of men down upon him. It seemed to occur to him that he was to be trampled; he made a desperate, piteous effort to escape; then finally huddled in a waiting heap. Dan and the soldier near him widened the interval between them without looking down, without appearing to heed the wounded man. This little clump of blue seemed to reel past them as boulders reel past a train.

Bursting through a smoke-wave, the scampering, unformed bunches came upon the wreck of the brigade that had preceded them, a floundering mass stopped afar from the hill by the swirling volleys.

It was as if a necromancer had suddenly shown them a picture of the fate which awaited them; but the line with muscular spasm hurled itself over this wreckage and onward, until men were stumbling amid the relics of other assaults, the point where the fire from the ridge consumed.

The men, panting, perspiring, with crazed faces, tried to push against it; but it was as if they had come to a wall. The wave halted, shuddered in an agony from the quick struggle of its two desires, then toppled, and broke into a fragmentary thing which has no name.

Veterans could now at last be distinguished from recruits. The new regiments were instantly gone, lost, scattered, as if they never had been. But the sweeping failure of the charge, the battle, could not make the veterans forget their business. With a last throe, the band of maniacs drew itself up and blazed a volley at the hill, insignificant to those iron entrenchments, but nevertheless expressing that singular final despair which enables men coolly to defy the walls of a city of death.

After this episode the men renamed their command. They called it the Little Regiment.

6

'I seen Dan shoot a feller yesterday. Yes, sir. I'm sure it was him that done it. And maybe he thinks about that feller now, and wonders if he tumbled down just about the same way. Them things come up in a man's mind.'

Bivouac fires upon the sidewalks, in the streets, in the yards, threw high their wavering reflections, which examined, like slim, red fingers, the dingy, scarred walls and the piles of tumbled brick. The droning of voices again arose from great blue crowds.

The odour of frying bacon, the fragrance from countless little coffee-pails floated among the ruins. The rifles, stacked in the shadows, emitted flashes of steely light. Wherever a flag lay horizontally from one stack to another was the bed of an eagle which had led men into the mystic smoke.

The men about a particular fire were engaged in holding in check their jovial spirits. They moved whispering around the blaze, although they looked at it with a certain fine contentment, like labourers after a day's hard work.

There was one who sat apart. They did not address him save in tones suddenly changed. They did not regard him directly, but always in little sidelong glances.

At last a soldier from a distant fire came into this circle of light. He studied for a time the man who sat apart. Then he hesitatingly stepped closer, and said: 'Got any news, Dan?'

'No,' said Dan.

The newcomer shifted his feet. He looked at the fire, at the sky, at the other men, at Dan. His face expressed a curious despair; his tongue was plainly in rebellion. Finally, however, he contrived to say: 'Well, there's some chance yet, Dan. Lots of the wounded are still lying out there, you know. There's some chance yet.'

'Yes,' said Dan.

The soldier shifted his feet again, and looked miserably into the air. After another struggle he said: 'Well, there's some chance yet, Dan.' He moved hastily away.

One of the men of the squad, perhaps encouraged by this example, now approached the still figure. 'No news yet, hey?' he said, after coughing behind his hand.

'No,' said Dan.

'Well,' said the man, 'I've been thinking of how he was fretting about you the night you went on special duty. You recollect? Well, sir, I was surprised. He couldn't say enough about it. I swan, I don't believe he slep' a wink after you left, but just lay awake cussing special duty and worrying. I was surprised. But there he lay cussing. He – '

Dan made a curious sound, as if a stone had wedged in his throat. He said: 'Shut up, will you?'

Afterward the men would not allow this moody contemplation of the fire to be interrupted.

'Oh, let him alone, can't you?'

'Come away from there, Casey!'

'Say, can't you leave him be?'

They moved with reverence about the immovable figure, with its countenance of mask-like invulnerability.

After the red round eye of the sun had stared long at the little plain and its burden, darkness, a sable mercy, came heavily upon it, and the wan hands of the dead were no longer seen in strange frozen gestures.

The heights in front of the plain shone with tiny campfires, and from the town in the rear, small shimmerings ascended from the blazes of the bivouac. The plain was a black expanse upon which, from time to time, dots of light, lanterns, floated slowly here and there. These fields were long steeped in grim mystery.

Suddenly, upon one dark spot, there was a resurrection. A strange thing had been groaning there, prostrate. Then it suddenly dragged itself to a sitting posture, and became a man.

The man stared stupidly for a moment at the lights on the hill, then turned and contemplated the faint colouring over the town. For some moments he remained thus, staring with dull eyes, his face unemotional, wooden.

Finally he looked around him at the corpses dimly to be seen. No change flashed into his face upon viewing these men. They seemed to suggest merely that his information concerning himself was not too complete. He ran his fingers over his arms and chest, bearing always the air of an idiot upon a bench at an almshouse door.

Finding no wound in his arms nor in his chest, he raised his hand to his head, and the fingers came away with some dark liquid upon them. Holding these fingers close to his eyes, he scanned them in the same stupid fashion, while his body gently swayed.

The soldier rolled his eyes again toward the town. When he arose, his clothing peeled from the frozen ground like wet paper. Hearing the sound of it, he seemed to see reason for deliberation. He paused and looked at the ground, then at his trousers, then at the ground.

Finally he went slowly off toward the faint reflection, holding his hands palm outward before him, and walking in the manner of a blind man.

8

The immovable Dan again sat unaddressed in the midst of comrades, who did not joke aloud. The dampness of the usual morning fog seemed to make the little campfires furious.

Suddenly a cry arose in the streets, a shout of amazement and delight. The men making breakfast at the fire looked up quickly. They broke forth in clamorous exclamation: 'Well! Of all things! Dan! Dan! Look who's coming! Oh, Dan!'

Dan the silent raised his eyes and saw a man, with a bandage of the size of a helmet about his head, receiving a furious demonstration from the company. He was shaking hands, and explaining, and haranguing to a high degree.

Dan started. His face of bronze flushed to his temples. He seemed about to leap from the ground, but then suddenly he sank back, and resumed his impassive gazing.

The men were in a flurry. They looked from one to the other. 'Dan! Look! See who's coming!' some cried again. 'Dan! Look!'

He scowled at last, and moved his shoulders sullenly. 'Well, don't I know it?'

But they could not be convinced that his eyes were in service. 'Dan, why can't you look! See who's coming!'

He made a gesture then of irritation and rage. 'Curse it! Don't I know it?'

The man with a bandage of the size of a helmet moved forward, always shaking hands and explaining. At times his glance wandered to Dan, who saw with his eyes riveted.

After a series of shiftings, it occurred naturally that the man with the bandage was very near to the man who saw the flames. He paused, and there was a little silence. Finally he said: 'Hello, Dan.'

'Hello, Billie.'

An Experiment in Misery

It was late at night, and a fine rain was swirling softly down, causing the pavements to glisten with hue of steel and blue and yellow in the rays of the innumerable lights. A youth was trudging slowly, without enthusiasm, with his hands buried deep in his trousers pockets, toward the downtown places where beds can be hired for coppers. He was clothed in an aged and tattered suit, and his derby was a marvel of dust-covered crown and torn rim. He was going forth to eat as the wanderer may eat, and sleep as the homeless sleep. By the time he had reached City Hall Park he was so completely plastered with yells of 'bum' and 'hobo', and with various unholy epithets that small boys had applied to him at intervals, that he was in a state of the most profound dejection. The sifting rain saturated the old velvet collar of his overcoat, and as the wet cloth pressed against his neck, he felt that there no longer could be pleasure in life. He looked about him searching for an outcast of highest degree that they two might share miseries, but the lights threw a quivering glare over rows and circles of deserted benches that glistened damply, showing patches of wet sod behind them. It seemed that their usual freights had fled on this night to better things. There were only squads of well-dressed Brooklyn people who swarmed toward the bridge.

The young man loitered about for a time and then went shuffling off down Park Row. In the sudden descent in style of the dress of the crowd he felt relief, as if he were at last in his own country. He began to see tatters that matched his tatters. In Chatham Square there were aimless men strewn in front of saloons and lodging-houses, standing sadly, patiently, reminding one vaguely of the attitudes of chickens in a storm. He aligned himself with these men, and turned slowly to occupy himself with the flowing life of the great street.

Through the mists of the cold and storming night, the cable cars went in silent procession, great affairs shining with red and brass, moving with formidable power, calm and irresistible, dangerful and gloomy, breaking silence only by the loud fierce cry of the gong. Two rivers of people swarmed along the sidewalks, spattered with black mud which made each shoe leave a scar-like impression. Overhead, elevated trains with a shrill grinding of the wheels stopped at the station, which upon its leg-like pillars seemed to resemble some monstrous kind of crab squatting over the street. The quick fat puffings of the engines could be heard. Down an alley there were sombre curtains of purple and black, on which street lamps dully glittered like embroidered flowers.

A saloon stood with a voracious air on a corner. A sign leaning against the front of the doorpost announced 'Free hot soup tonight!' The swing doors, snapping to and fro like ravenous lips, made gratified smacks as the saloon gorged itself with plump men, eating with astounding and endless appetite, smiling in some indescribable manner as the men came from all directions like sacrifices to a heathenish superstition.

Caught by the delectable sign, the young man allowed himself to be swallowed. A bartender placed a schooner of dark and portentous beer on the bar. Its monumental form upreared until the froth atop was above the crown of the young man's brown derby.

'Soup over there, gents,' said the bartender affably. A little yellow man in rags and the youth grasped their schooners and went with speed toward a lunch-counter, where a man with oily but imposing whiskers ladled genially from a kettle until he had furnished his two mendicants with a soup that was steaming hot, and in which there were little floating suggestions of chicken. The young man, sipping his broth, felt the cordiality expressed by the warmth of the mixture, and he beamed at the man with oily but imposing whiskers, who was presiding like a priest behind an altar. 'Have some more, gents?' he enquired of the two sorry figures before him. The little yellow man accepted with a swift gesture, but the youth shook his head and went out, following a man whose wondrous seediness promised that he would have a knowledge of cheap lodging-houses.

On the sidewalk he accosted the seedy man. 'Say, do you know a cheap place to sleep?'

The other hesitated for a time, gazing sideways. Finally he nodded in the direction of the street. 'I sleep up there,' he said, 'when I've got the price.'

'How much?'

'Ten cents.'

The young man shook his head dolefully. 'That's too rich for me.'

At that moment there approached the two a reeling man in strange garments. His head was a fuddle of bushy hair and whiskers, from which his eyes peered with a guilty slant. In a close scrutiny it was possible to distinguish the cruel lines of a mouth which looked as if its lips had just closed with satisfaction over some tender and piteous morsel. He appeared like an assassin steeped in crimes performed awkwardly.

But at this time his voice was tuned to the coaxing key of an affectionate puppy. He looked at the men with wheedling eyes, and began to sing a little melody for charity. 'Say, gents, can't yeh give a poor feller a couple of cents t' git a bed? I got five, an' I gits anudder two I gits me a bed. Now, on th' square, gents, can't yeh jest gimme two cents t' git a bed? Now, yeh know how a respecterble gentlem'n feels when he's down on his luck, an' I – '

The seedy man, staring with imperturbable countenance at a train which clattered overhead, interrupted in an expressionless voice: 'Ah, go t' hell!'

But the youth spoke to the prayerful assassin in tones of astonishment and enquiry. 'Say, you must be crazy! Why don't yeh strike somebody that looks as if they had money?'

The assassin, tottering about on his uncertain legs, and at intervals brushing imaginary obstacles from before his nose, entered into a long explanation of the psychology of the situation. It was so profound that it was unintelligible.

When he had exhausted the subject, the young man said to him: 'Let's see th' five cents.'

The assassin wore an expression of drunken woe at this sentence, filled with suspicion of him. With a deeply pained air he began to fumble in his clothing, his red hands trembling. Presently he announced in a voice of bitter grief, as if he had been betrayed: 'There's on'y four.'

'Four,' said the young man thoughtfully. 'Well, looka here, I'm a stranger here, an' if ye'll steer me to your cheap joint I'll find the other three.'

The assassin's countenance became instantly radiant with joy. His whiskers quivered with the wealth of his alleged emotions. He seized the young man's hand in a transport of delight and friendliness.

'B' Gawd,' he cried, 'if ye'll do that, b' Gawd, I'd say yeh was a damned good fellow, I would, an' I'd remember yeh all m' life, I would, b' Gawd, an' if I ever got a chance I'd return the compliment,' he spoke with drunken dignity: 'b' Gawd, I'd treat yeh white, I would, an' I'd allus remember yeh.'

The young man drew back, looking at the assassin coldly. 'Oh, that's all right,' he said. 'You show me th' joint – that's all you've got t' do.'

The assassin, gesticulating gratitude, led the young man along a dark street. Finally he stopped before a little dusty door. He raised his hand impressively. 'Look-a here,' he said, and there was a thrill of deep and ancient wisdom upon his face, 'I've brought yeh here, an' that's my part, ain't it? If th' place don't suit yeh, yeh needn't git mad at me, need yeh? There won't be no bad feelin', will there?'

'No,' said the young man.

The assassin waved his arm tragically, and led the march up the steep stairway. On the way the young man furnished the assassin with three pennies. At the top a man with benevolent spectacles looked at them through a hole in a board. He collected their money, wrote some names on a register, and speedily was leading the two men along a gloom-shrouded corridor.

Shortly after the beginning of this journey the young man felt his liver turn white, for from the dark and secret places of the building there suddenly came to his nostrils strange and unspeakable odours that assailed him like malignant diseases with wings. They seemed to be from human bodies closely packed in dens; the exhalations from a hundred pairs of reeking lips; the fumes from a thousand bygone debauches; the expression of a thousand present miseries.

A man, naked save for a little snuff-coloured undershirt, was parading sleepily along the corridor. He rubbed his eyes and, giving vent to a prodigious yawn, demanded to be told the time.

'Half-past one.'

The man yawned again. He opened a door, and for a moment his form was outlined against a black, opaque interior. To this door came the three men, and as it was again opened the unholy odours rushed out like fiends, so that the young man was obliged to struggle as against an overpowering wind.

It was some time before the youth's eyes were good in the intense gloom within, but the man with benevolent spectacles led him skilfully, pausing but a moment to deposit the limp assassin upon a cot. He took the youth to a cot that lay tranquilly by the window, and showing him a tall locker for clothes that stood near the head with the ominous air of a tombstone, left him.

The youth sat on his cot and peered about him. There was a gas-jet in a distant part of the room, that burned a small flickering orange-hued flame. It caused vast masses of tumbled shadows in all parts of the place, save where, immediately about it, there was a little grey haze. As the young man's eyes became used to the darkness, he could see upon the cots that thickly littered the floor the forms of men sprawled out, lying in deathlike silence, or heaving and snoring with tremendous effort, like stabbed fish.

The youth locked his derby and his shoes in the mummy-case near him, and then lay down with an old and familiar coat around his shoulders. A blanket he handled gingerly, drawing it over part of the coat. The cot was covered with leather, and as cold as melting snow. The youth was obliged to shiver for some time on this affair, which was like a slab. Presently, however, the chill gave him peace, and during this period of leisure from it he turned his head to stare at his friend the assassin, whom he could dimly discern where he lay sprawled on a cot in the abandon of a man filled with drink. He was snoring with incredible vigour. His wet hair and beard dimly glistened, and his inflamed nose shone with subdued lustre like a red light in a fog.

Within reach of the youth's hand was one who lay with yellow breast and shoulders bare to the cold draughts. One arm hung over the side of the cot, and the fingers lay full length upon the wet cement floor of the room. Beneath the inky brows could be seen the eyes of the man, exposed by the partly opened lids. To the youth it seemed that he and this corpse-like being were exchanging a prolonged stare, and that the other threatened with his eyes. He drew back, watching his neighbour from the shadows of his blanket-edge. The man did not move once through the night, but lay in this stillness as of death like a body stretched out expectant of the surgeon's knife.

And all through the room could be seen the tawny hues of naked flesh, limbs thrust into the darkness, projecting beyond the cots; upreared knees, arms hanging long and thin over the cot-edges. For the most part they were statuesque, carven, dead. With the curious lockers standing all about like tombstones, there was a strange effect of a graveyard where bodies were merely flung.

Yet occasionally could be seen limbs wildly tossing in fantastic nightmare gestures, accompanied by guttural cries, grunts, oaths. And there was one fellow off in a gloomy corner, who in his dreams was oppressed by some frightful calamity, for of a sudden he began to utter long wails that went almost like yells from a hound, echoing wailfully and weird through this chill place of tombstones where men lay like the dead.

The sound, in its high piercing beginnings that dwindled to final melancholy moans, expressed a red and grim tragedy of the unfathomable possibilities of the man's dreams. But to the youth these were not merely the shrieks of a vision-pierced man: they were an utterance of the meaning of the room and its occupants. It was to him the protest of the wretch who feels the touch of the imperturbable granite wheels, and who then cries with an impersonal eloquence, with a strength not from him, giving voice to the wail of a whole section, a class, a people. This, weaving into the young man's brain, and mingling with his views of the vast and sombre shadows that, like mighty black fingers, curled around the naked bodies, made the young man so that he did not sleep, but lay carving the biographies for these men from his meagre experience. At times the fellow in the corner howled in a writhing agony of his imaginations.

Finally a long lance-point of grey light shot through the dusty panes of the window. Without, the young man could see roofs drearily white in the dawning. The point of light yellowed and grew brighter, until the golden rays of the morning sun came in bravely and strong. They touched with radiant colour the form of a small fat man who snored in stuttering fashion. His round and shiny bald head glowed suddenly with the valour of a decoration. He sat up, blinked at the sun, swore fretfully, and pulled his blanket over the ornamental splendours of his head.

The youth contentedly watched this rout of the shadows before the bright spears of the sun, and presently he slumbered. When he awoke he heard the voice of the assassin raised in valiant curses. Putting up his head, he perceived his comrade seated on the side of the cot engaged in scratching his neck with long fingernails that rasped like files.

'Hully Jee, dis is a new breed. They've got can-openers on their feet,' he continued in a violent tirade.

The young man hastily unlocked his closet and took out his shoes and hat. As he sat on the side of the cot lacing his shoes, he glanced about and saw that daylight had made the room comparatively commonplace and uninteresting. The men, whose faces seemed stolid, serene, or absent, were engaged in dressing, while a great crackle of bantering conversation arose.

A few were parading in unconcerned nakedness. Here and there were men of brawn, whose skins shone clear and ruddy. They took splendid poses, standing massively like chiefs. When they had dressed in their ungainly garments there was an extraordinary change. They then showed bumps and deficiencies of all kinds.

There were others who exhibited many deformities. Shoulders were slanting, humped, pulled this way and pulled that way. And notable among these latter men was the little fat man who had refused to allow his head to be glorified. His pudgy form, builded like a pear, bustled to and fro, while he swore in fishwife fashion. It appeared that some article of his apparel had vanished.

The young man attired himself speedily, and went to his friend the assassin. At first the latter looked dazed at the sight of the youth. This face seemed to be appealing to him through the cloud-wastes of his memory. He scratched his neck and reflected. At last he grinned, a broad smile gradually spreading until his countenance was a round illumination. 'Hello, Willie,' he cried cheerily.

'Hello,' said the young man 'Are yeh ready t' fly?'

'Sure.' The assassin tied his shoe carefully with some twine and came ambling.

When he reached the street the young man experienced no sudden relief from unholy atmospheres. He had forgotten all about them, and had been breathing naturally, and with no sensation of discomfort or distress.

He was thinking of these things as he walked along the street, when he was suddenly startled by feeling the assassin's hand, trembling with excitement, clutching his arm, and when the assassin spoke, his voice went into quavers from a supreme agitation.

'I'll be hully, bloomin' blowed if there wasn't a feller with a nightshirt on up there in that joint.'

The youth was bewildered for a moment, but presently he turned to smile indulgently at the assassin's humour. 'Oh, you're a damned liar,' he merely said.

Whereupon the assassin began to gesture extravagantly and take oath by strange gods. He frantically placed himself at the mercy of remarkable fates if his tale were not true. 'Yes, he did! I cross m' heart thousan' times!' he protested, and at the moment his eyes were large with amazement, his mouth wrinkled in unnatural glee. 'Yessir! A nightshirt! A hully white nightshirt!'

'You lie!'

'No, sir! I hope ter die b'fore I kin git anudder ball if there wasn't a jay wid a hully, bloomin' white nightshirt!"

His face was filled with the infinite wonder of it. 'A hully white night-shirt,' he continually repeated.

The young man saw the dark entrance to a basement restaurant. There was a sign which read 'No mystery about our hash !' and there were other age-stained and world-battered legends which told him that the place was within his means. He stopped before it and spoke to the assassin: 'I guess I'll git somethin' t' eat.'

At this the assassin, for some reason, appeared to be quite embarrassed. He gazed at the seductive front of the eating place for a moment. Then he started slowly up the street. 'Well, goodbye, Willie,' he said bravely.

For an instant the youth studied the departing figure. Then he called out, 'Hol' on a minnet.' As they came together he spoke in a certain fierce way, as if he feared that the other would think him to be charitable. 'Look-a here, if yeh wan ta git some breakfas' I'll lend yeh three cents t' do it with. But say, look-a here, you've gotta git out an' hustle. I ain't goin' t' support yeh, or I'll go broke b'fore night. I ain't no millionaire.'

'I take me oath, Willie,' said the assassin earnestly, 'th' on'y thing I really needs is a ball. Me t'roat feels like a fryin' pan. But as I can't get a ball, why, th' next bes' thing is breakfast, an' if yeh do that for me, b' Gawd, I say yeh was th' whitest lad I ever see.'

They spent a few moments in dexterous exchanges of phrases, in which they each protested that the other was, as the assassin had originally said, 'a respecterble gentlem'n'. And they concluded with mutual assurances that they were the souls of intelligence and virtue. Then they went into the restaurant.

There was a long counter, dimly lighted from hidden sources. Two or three men in soiled white aprons rushed here and there.

The youth bought a bowl of coffee for two cents and a roll for one cent. The assassin purchased the same. The bowls were webbed with brown seams, and the tin spoons wore an air of having emerged from the first pyramid. Upon them were black moss-like encrustations of age, and they were bent and scarred from the attacks of long-forgotten teeth. But over their repast the wanderers waxed warm and mellow. The assassin grew affable as the hot mixture went soothingly down his parched throat, and the young man felt courage flow in his veins.

Memories began to throng in on the assassin, and he brought forth long tales, intricate, incoherent, delivered with a chattering swiftness as from an old woman. ' – great job out 'n Orange. Boss keep yeh hustlin', though, all time. I was there three days, and then I went an' ask 'im t' lend me a dollar. "G–g–go ter the devil," he says, an' I lose me job. South no good. Damn niggers work for twenty-five an' thirty cents a day. Run white man out. Good grub, though. Easy livin'.

'Yas; useter work little in Toledo, raftin' logs. Make two or three dollars er day in the spring. Lived high. Cold as ice, though, in the winter.

'I was raised in northern N'York. O–o–oh, yeh jest ought to live there. No beer ner whisky, though, 'way off in the woods. But all th' good hot grub yeh can eat. B' Gawd, I hung around there long as I could till th' ol' man fired me. "Git t' hell outa here, yeh wuthless skunk, git t' hell outa here, an' go die," he says. "You're a hell of a father," I says, "you are," an' I quit 'im.'

As they were passing from the dim eating-place, they encountered an old man who was trying to steal forth with a tiny package of food, but a tall man with an indomitable moustache stood dragon-fashion, barring the way of escape. They heard the old man raise a plaintive protest. 'Ah, you always want to know what I take out, and you never see that I usually bring a package in here from my place of business.'

As the wanderers trudged slowly along Park Row, the assassin began to expand and grow blithe. 'B' Gawd, we've been livin' like kings,' he said, smacking appreciative lips.

'Look out, or we'll have t' pay fer it t'night,' said the youth with gloomy warning.

But the assassin refused to turn his gaze toward the future. He went with a limping step, into which he injected a suggestion of lamb-like gambols. His mouth was wreathed in a red grin.

In City Hall Park the two wanderers sat down in the little circle of benches sanctified by traditions of their class. They huddled in their old garments, slumbrously conscious of the march of the hours which for them had no meaning.

The people of the street hurrying hither and thither made a blend of black figures, changing, yet frieze-like. They walked in their good clothes as upon important missions, giving no gaze to the two wanderers seated upon the benches. They expressed to the young man his infinite distance from all he valued. Social position, comfort, the pleasures of living were unconquerable kingdoms. He felt a sudden awe.

And in the background a multitude of buildings, of pitiless hues and sternly high, were to him emblematic of a nation forcing its regal head into the clouds, throwing no downward glances; in the sublimity of its aspirations ignoring the wretches who may flounder at its feet. The roar of the city in his ear was to him the confusion of strange tongues, babbling heedlessly; it was the clink of coin, the voice of the city's hopes, which were to him no hopes.

He confessed himself an outcast, and his eyes from under the lowered rim of his hat began to glance guiltily, wearing the criminal expression that comes with certain convictions.

Shame

'Don't come in here botherin' me,' said the cook, intolerantly. 'What with your mother bein' away on a visit, an' your father comin' home soon to lunch, I have enough on my mind – and that without bein' bothered with *you*. The kitchen is no place for little boys, anyhow. Run away, and don't be interferin' with my work.'

She frowned and made a grand pretence of being deep in herculean labours; but Jimmie did not run away.

'Now – they're goin' to have a picnic,' he said, half audibly.

'What?'

'Now – they're goin' to have a picnic.'

'Who's goin' to have a picnic?' demanded the cook, loudly. Her accent could have led one to suppose that if the projectors did not turn out to be the proper parties, she immediately would forbid this picnic.

Jimmie looked at her with more hopefulness. After twenty minutes of futile skirmishing, he had at least succeeded in introducing the subject. To her question he answered, eagerly: 'Oh, everybody! Lots and lots of boys and girls. Everybody.'

'Who's everybody?'

According to custom, Jimmie began to singsong through his nose in a quite indescribable fashion an enumeration of the prospective picnickers: 'Willie Dalzel an' Dan Earl an' Ella Earl an' Wolcott Margate an' Reeves Margate an' Minnie Phelps an' – oh – lots more girls an' – everybody. An' their mothers an' big sisters too.' Then he announced a new bit of information: 'They're goin' to have a picnic.'

'Well, let them,' said the cook, blandly.

Jimmie fidgeted for a time in silence. At last he murmured, 'I – now – I thought maybe you'd let me go.'

The cook turned from her work with an air of irritation and amazement that Jimmie should still be in the kitchen. 'Who's stoppin' you?' she asked, sharply. 'I ain't stoppin' you, am I?'

'No,' admitted Jimmie, in a low voice.

'Well, why don't you go, then? Nobody's stoppin' you.'

'But,' said Jimmie, 'I – you – now – each feller has got to take somethin' to eat with 'm.'

'Oh ho!' cried the cook, triumphantly. 'So that's it, is it? So that's what you've been shyin' round here fer, eh? Well, you may as well take yourself off without more words. What with your mother bein' away on a visit, an' your father comin' home soon to his lunch, I have enough on my mind – an' that without being bothered with *you*.'

Jimmie made no reply, but moved in grief toward the door. The cook continued: 'Some people in this house seem to think there's 'bout a thousand cooks in this kitchen. Where I used to work b'fore, there was some reason in 'em. I ain't a horse. A picnic!'

Jimmie said nothing, but he loitered.

'Seems as if I had enough to do, without havin' *you* come round talkin' about picnics. Nobody ever seems to think of the work I have to do. Nobody ever seems to think of it. Then they come and talk to me about picnics! What do I care about picnics?'

Jimmie loitered.

'Where I used to work b'fore, there was some reason in 'em. I never heard tell of no picnics right on top of your mother bein' away on a visit an' your father comin' home soon to his lunch. It's all foolishness.'

Little Jimmie leaned his head flat against the wall and began to weep. She stared at him scornfully. 'Cryin', eh? Cryin'? What are you cryin' fer?'

'N–n–nothin',' sobbed Jimmie.

There was a silence, save for Jimmie's convulsive breathing. At length the cook said: 'Stop that blubberin', now. Stop it! This kitchen ain't no place fer it. Stop it! . . . Very well! If you don't stop, I won't give you nothin' to go to the picnic with – there!'

For the moment he could not end his tears. 'You never said,' he sputtered – 'you never said you'd give me anything.'

'An' why would I?' she cried, angrily. 'Why would I – with you in here a-cryin' an' a-blubberin' an' a-bleatin' round? Enough to drive a woman crazy! I don't see how you could expect me to! The idea!'

Suddenly Jimmie announced: 'I've stopped cryin'. I ain't goin' to cry no more 'tall.'

'Well, then,' grumbled the cook – 'well, then, stop it. I've got enough on my mind.' It chanced that she was making for luncheon some salmon croquettes. A tin still half full of pinky prepared fish was beside her on the table. Still grumbling, she seized a loaf of bread and, wielding a knife, she cut from this loaf four slices, each of which was as big as a six-shilling novel. She profligately spread them with butter, and jabbing the point of her knife into the salmon-tin, she brought up bits of salmon, which she flung and flattened upon the bread. Then she crashed the pieces of bread together in pairs, much as one would clash cymbals. There was no doubt in her own mind but that she had created two sandwiches.

'There,' she cried. 'That'll do you all right. Lemme see. What'll I put 'em in? There – I've got it.' She thrust the sandwiches into a small pail and jammed on the lid. Jimmie was ready for the picnic. 'Oh, thank you, Mary!' he cried, joyfully, and in a moment he was off, running swiftly.

The picnickers had started nearly half an hour earlier, owing to his inability to attack and subdue the cook quickly, but he knew that the rendezvous was in the grove of tall, pillar-like hemlocks and pines that grew on a rocky knoll at the lake shore. His heart was very light as he sped, swinging his pail. But a few minutes previously his soul had been gloomed in despair; now he was happy. He was going to the picnic, where privilege of participation was to be bought by the contents of the little tin pail.

When he arrived in the outskirts of the grove he heard a merry clamour, and when he reached the top of the knoll he looked down the slope upon a scene which almost made his little breast burst with joy. They actually had two camp fires! Two camp fires! At one of them Mrs Earl was making something – chocolate, no doubt – and at the other a young lady in white duck and a sailor hat was dropping eggs into boiling water. Other grown-up people had spread a white cloth and were laying upon it things from baskets. In the deep cool shadow of the trees the children scurried, laughing. Jimmie hastened forward to join his friends.

Homer Phelps caught first sight of him. 'Ho!' he shouted; 'here comes Jimmie Trescott! Come on, Jimmie; you be on our side!' The children had divided themselves into two bands for some purpose of play. The others of Homer Phelps's party loudly endorsed his plan. 'Yes, Jimmie, you be on *our* side.' Then arose the usual dispute. 'Well, we got the weakest side.'

' 'Tain't any weaker'n ours.'

Homer Phelps suddenly started, and looking hard, said, 'What you got in the pail, Jim?'

Jimmie answered somewhat uneasily, 'Got m' lunch in it.'

Instantly that brat of a Minnie Phelps simply tore down the sky with her shrieks of derision. 'Got his *lunch* in it! In a *pail!*' She ran screaming to her mother. 'Oh, mamma! Oh, mamma! Jimmie Trescott's got his picnic in a pail!'

Now there was nothing in the nature of this fact particularly to move the others – notably the boys, who were not competent to care if he had brought his luncheon in a coal-bin; but such is the instinct of childish society that they all immediately moved away from him. In a moment he had been made a social leper. All old intimacies were flung into the lake, so to speak. They dared not compromise themselves. At safe distances the boys shouted, scornfully: 'Huh! Got his picnic in a pail!' Never again during that picnic did the little girls speak of him as Jimmie Trescott. His name now was Him.

His mind was dark with pain as he stood, the hang-dog, kicking the gravel, and muttering as defiantly as he was able, 'Well, I can have it in a pail if I want to.' This statement of freedom was of no importance, and he knew it, but it was the only idea in his head.

He had been baited at school for being detected in writing a letter to little

Cora, the angel child, and he had known how to defend himself, but this situation was in no way similar. This was a social affair, with grown people on all sides. It would be sweet to catch the Margate twins, for instance, and hammer them into a state of bleating respect for his pail; but that was a matter for the jungles of childhood, where grown folk seldom penetrated. He could only glower.

The amiable voice of Mrs Earl suddenly called: 'Come, children! Everything's ready!' They scampered away, glancing back for one last gloat at Jimmie standing there with his pail.

He did not know what to do. He knew that the grown folk expected him at the spread, but if he approached he would be greeted by a shameful chorus from the children – more especially from some of those damnable little girls. Still, luxuries beyond all dreaming were heaped on that cloth. One could not forget them. Perhaps if he crept up modestly, and was very gentle and very nice to the little girls, they would allow him peace. Of course it had been dreadful to come with a pail to such a grand picnic, but they might forgive him.

Oh no, they would not! He knew them better. And then suddenly he remembered with what delightful expectations he had raced to this grove, and self-pity overwhelmed him, and he thought he wanted to die and make everyone feel sorry.

The young lady in white duck and a sailor hat looked at him, and then spoke to her sister, Mrs Earl. 'Who's that hovering in the distance, Emily?'

Mrs Earl peered. 'Why, it's Jimmie Trescott! Jimmie, come to the picnic! Why don't you come to the picnic, Jimmie?'

He began to sidle toward the cloth.

But at Mrs Earl's call there was another outburst from many of the children. 'He's got his picnic in a pail! *In a pail!* Got it in a pail!'

Minnie Phelps was a shrill fiend. 'Oh, mamma, he's got it in that pail! See! Isn't it funny? Isn't it dreadful funny?'

'What ghastly prigs children are, Emily!' said the young lady. 'They are spoiling that boy's whole day, breaking his heart, the little cats! I think I'll go over and talk to him.'

'Maybe you had better not,' answered Mrs Earl, dubiously. 'Somehow these things arrange themselves. If you interfere, you are likely to prolong everything.'

'Well, I'll try, at least,' said the young lady.

At the second outburst against him Jimmie had crouched down by a tree, half hiding behind it, half pretending that he was not hiding behind it. He turned his sad gaze toward the lake. The bit of water seen through the shadows seemed perpendicular, a slate-coloured wall. He heard a noise near him, and turning, he perceived the young lady looking down at him. In her hands she held plates. 'May I sit near you?' she asked, coolly.

Jimmie could hardly believe his ears. After disposing herself and the plates upon the pine needles, she made brief explanation. 'They're rather crowded, you see, over there. I don't like to be crowded at a picnic, so I thought I'd come here. I hope you don't mind.'

Jimmie made haste to find his tongue. 'Oh, I don't mind! I like to have you here.' The ingenuous emphasis made it appear that the fact of his liking to have her there was in the nature of a law-dispelling phenomenon, but she did not smile.

'How large is that lake?' she asked.

Jimmie, falling into the snare, at once began to talk in the manner of a proprietor of the lake. 'Oh, it's almost twenty miles long, an' in one place it's almost four miles wide! an' it's deep, too – awful deep – an' it's got real steamboats on it, an' – oh – lots of other boats, an' – an' – an' – '

'Do you go out on it sometimes?'

'Oh, lots of times! My father's got a boat,' he said, eyeing her to note the effect of his words.

She was correctly pleased and struck with wonder. 'Oh, has he?' she cried, as if she never before had heard of a man owning a boat.

Jimmie continued: 'Yes, an' it's a grea' big boat, too, with sails, real sails; an' sometimes he takes me out in her, too; an' once he took me fishin', an' we had sandwiches, plenty of 'em, an' my father he drank beer right out of the bottle – *right out of the bottle!*'

The young lady was properly overwhelmed by this amazing intelligence. Jimmie saw the impression he had created, and enthusiastically resumed his narrative: 'An' after, he let me throw the bottles in the water, and I throwed 'em 'way, 'way, 'way out. An' they sank, an' – never comed up,' he concluded, dramatically.

His face was glorified; he had forgotten all about the pail; he was absorbed in this communion with a beautiful lady who was so interested in what he had to say.

She indicated one of the plates, and said, indifferently: 'Perhaps you would like some of those sandwiches. I made them. Do you like olives? And there's a devilled egg. I made that also.'

'Did you really?' said Jimmie, politely. His face gloomed for a moment because the pail was recalled to his mind, but he timidly possessed himself of a sandwich.

'Hope you are not going to scorn my devilled egg,' said his goddess. 'I am very proud of it.' He did not; he scorned little that was on the plate.

Their gentle intimacy was ineffable to the boy. He thought he had a friend, a beautiful lady, who liked him more than she did anybody at the picnic, to say the least. This was proved by the fact that she had flung aside the luxuries of the spread cloth to sit with him, the exile. Thus early did he fall a victim to woman's wiles.

'Where do you live?' he asked, suddenly.

'Oh, a long way from here! In New York.'

His next question was put very bluntly. 'Are you married?'

'Oh, no!' she answered, gravely.

Jimmie was silent for a time, during which he glanced shyly and furtively up at her face. It was evident that he was somewhat embarrassed. Finally he said, 'When I grow up to be a man – '

'Oh, that is some time yet!' said the beautiful lady.

'But when I *do*, I – I should like to marry you.'

'Well, I will remember it,' she answered; 'but don't talk of it now, because it's such a long time, and – I wouldn't wish you to consider yourself bound.' She smiled at him.

He began to brag. 'When I grow up to be a man, I'm goin' to have lots an' lots of money, an' I'm goin' to have a grea' big house an' a horse an' a shotgun, an' lots an' lots of books 'bout elephants an' tigers, an' lots an' lots of ice-cream an' pie an' – caramels.' As before, she was impressed; he could see it. 'An' I'm goin' to have lots an' lots of children – 'bout three hundred, I guess – an' there won't none of 'em be girls. They'll all be boys – like me.'

'Oh, my!' she said.

His garment of shame was gone from him. The pail was dead and well buried. It seemed to him that months elapsed as he dwelt in happiness near the beautiful lady and trumpeted his vanity.

At last there was a shout. 'Come on! we're going home.' The picnickers trooped out of the grove. The children wished to resume their jeering, for Jimmie still gripped his pail, but they were restrained by the circumstances. He was walking at the side of the beautiful lady.

During this journey he abandoned many of his habits. For instance, he never travelled without skipping gracefully from crack to crack between the stones, or without pretending that he was a train of cars, or without some mumming device of childhood. But now he behaved with dignity. He made no more noise than a little mouse. He escorted the beautiful lady to the gate of the Earl home, where he awkwardly, solemnly, and wistfully shook hands in goodbye. He watched her go up the walk; the door clanged.

On his way home he dreamed. One of these dreams was fascinating. Supposing the beautiful lady was his teacher in school! Oh, my! wouldn't he be a good boy, sitting like a statuette all day long, and knowing every lesson to perfection, and – everything. And then supposing that a boy should sass her. Jimmie painted himself waylaying that boy on the homeward road, and the fate of the boy was a thing to make strong men cover their eyes with their hands. And she would like him more and more – more and more. And he – he would be a little god.

But as he was entering his father's grounds an appalling recollection came to him. He was returning with the bread and butter and salmon untouched in the pail! He could imagine the cook, nine feet tall, waving her fist. 'An' so that's what I took trouble for, is it? So's you could bring it back? So's you could bring it back?' He skulked toward the house like a marauding bush-ranger. When he neared the kitchen door he made a desperate rush past it, aiming to gain the stables and there secrete his guilt. He was nearing them, when a thunderous voice hailed him from the rear: 'Jimmie Trescott, where you goin' with that pail?'

It was the cook. He made no reply, but plunged into the shelter of the stables. He whirled the lid from the pail and dashed its contents beneath a heap of blankets. Then he stood panting, his eyes on the door. The cook did not pursue, but she was bawling, 'Jimmie Trescott, what you doin' with that pail?'

He came forth, swinging it. 'Nothin',' he said, in virtuous protest.

'I know better,' she said, sharply, as she relieved him of his curse.

In the morning Jimmie was playing near the stable, when he heard a shout from Peter Washington, who attended Dr Trescott's horses: 'Jim! Oh, Jim!'

'What?'

'Come yah.'

Jimmie went reluctantly to the door of the stable, and Peter Washington asked, 'Wut's dish yere fish an' brade doin' unner dese yer blankups?'

'I don't know. I didn't have nothin' to do with it,' answered Jimmie, indignantly.

'Don' tell *me*!' cried Peter Washington as he flung it all away – 'don' tell *me*! When I fin' fish an' brade unner dese yer blankups, I don' go an' think dese yer ho'ses er yer pop's put 'em dar. I *know*. An' if I caitch enny more dish yer fish an' brade in dish yer stable, *I'll* tell yer pop.'

A Dark-Brown Dog

A child was standing on a street-corner. He leaned with one shoulder against a high board fence and swayed the other to and fro, the while kicking carelessly at the gravel.

Sunshine beat upon the cobbles, and a lazy summer wind raised yellow dust which trailed in clouds down the avenue. Clattering trucks moved with indistinctness through it. The child stood dreamily gazing.

After a time, a little dark-brown dog came trotting with an intent air down the sidewalk. A short rope was dragging from his neck. Occasionally he trod upon the end of it and stumbled.

He stopped opposite the child, and the two regarded each other. The dog hesitated for a moment, but presently he made some little advances with his tail. The child put out his hand and called him. In an apologetic manner the dog came close, and the two had an interchange of friendly pattings and waggles. The dog became more enthusiastic with each moment of the interview, until with his gleeful caperings he threatened to overturn the child. Whereupon the child lifted his hand and struck the dog a blow upon the head.

This thing seemed to overpower and astonish the little dark-brown dog, and wounded him to the heart. He sank down in despair at the child's feet. When the blow was repeated, together with an admonition in childish sentences, he turned over upon his back, and held his paws in a peculiar manner. At the same time with his ears and his eyes he offered a small prayer to the child.

He looked so comical on his back, and holding his paws peculiarly, that the child was greatly amused and gave him little taps repeatedly, to keep him so. But the little dark-brown dog took this chastisement in the most serious way and no doubt considered that he had committed some grave crime, for he wriggled contritely and showed his repentance in every way that was in his power. He pleaded with the child and petitioned him, and offered more prayers.

At last the child grew weary of this amusement and turned toward home. The dog was praying at the time. He lay on his back and turned his eyes upon the retreating form.

Presently he struggled to his feet and started after the child. The latter wandered in a perfunctory way toward his home, stopping at times to investigate various matters. During one of these pauses he discovered the little dark-brown dog who was following him with the air of a footpad.

The child beat his pursuer with a small stick he had found. The dog lay down and prayed until the child had finished and resumed his journey. Then he scrambled erect and took up the pursuit again.

On the way to his home the child turned many times and beat the dog, proclaiming with childish gestures that he held him in contempt as an unimportant dog, with no value save for a moment. For being this quality of animal the dog apologised and eloquently expressed regret, but he continued stealthily to follow the child. His manner grew so very guilty that he slunk like an assassin.

When the child reached his doorstep, the dog was industriously ambling a few yards in the rear. He became so agitated with shame when he again confronted the child that he forgot the dragging rope. He tripped upon it and fell forward.

The child sat down on the step and the two had another interview. During it the dog greatly exerted himself to please the child. He performed a few gambols with such abandon that the child suddenly saw him to be a valuable thing. He made a swift, avaricious charge and seized the rope.

He dragged his captive into a hall and up many long stairways in a dark tenement. The dog made willing efforts, but he could not hobble very skilfully up the stairs because he was very small and soft, and at last the pace of the engrossed child grew so energetic that the dog became panic-stricken. In his mind he was being dragged toward a grim unknown. His eyes grew wild with the terror of it. He began to wiggle his head frantically and to brace his legs.

The child redoubled his exertions. They had a battle on the stairs. The child was victorious because he was completely absorbed in his purpose, and because the dog was very small. He dragged his acquirement to the door of his home, and finally with triumph across the threshold.

No one was in. The child sat down on the floor and made overtures to the dog. These the dog instantly accepted. He beamed with affection upon his new friend. In a short time they were firm and abiding comrades.

When the child's family appeared, they made a great row. The dog was examined and commented upon and called names. Scorn was levelled at him from all eyes, so that he became much embarrassed and drooped like a scorched plant. But the child went sturdily to the centre of the floor, and, at the top of his voice, championed the dog. It happened that he was roaring protestations, with his arms clasped about the dog's neck, when the father of the family came in from work.

The parent demanded to know what the blazes they were making the kid howl for. It was explained in many words that the infernal kid wanted to introduce a disreputable dog into the family.

A family council was held. On this depended the dog's fate, but he in no way heeded, being busily engaged in chewing the end of the child's dress.

The affair was quickly ended. The father of the family, it appears, was in a particularly savage temper that evening, and when he perceived that it would amaze and anger everybody if such a dog were allowed to remain, he decided that it should be so. The child, crying softly, took his friend off to a retired part of the room to hob-nob with him, while the father quelled a fierce rebellion of his wife. So it came to pass that the dog was a member of the household.

He and the child were associated together at all times save when the child slept. The child became a guardian and a friend. If the large folk kicked the dog and threw things at him, the child made loud and violent objections. Once when the child had run, protesting loudly, with tears raining down his face and his arms outstretched, to protect his friend, he had been struck in the head with a very large saucepan from the hand of his father, enraged at some seeming lack of courtesy in the dog. Ever after, the family were careful how they threw things at the dog. Moreover, the latter grew very skilful in avoiding missiles and feet. In a small room containing a stove, a table, a bureau and some chairs, he would display strategic ability of a high order, dodging, feinting and scuttling about among the furniture. He could force three or four people armed with brooms, sticks and handfuls of coal, to use all their ingenuity to get in a blow. And even when they did, it was seldom that they could do him a serious injury or leave any imprint.

But when the child was present these scenes did not occur. It came to be recognised that if the dog was molested, the child would burst into sobs, and as the child, when started, was very riotous and practically unquenchable, the dog had therein a safeguard.

However, the child could not always be near. At night, when he was asleep, his dark-brown friend would raise from some black corner a wild, wailful cry, a song of infinite loneliness and despair, that would go shuddering and sobbing among the buildings of the block and cause people to swear. At these times the singer would often be chased all over the kitchen and hit with a great variety of articles.

Sometimes, too, the child himself used to beat the dog, although it is not known that he ever had what truly could be called a just cause. The dog always accepted these thrashings with an air of admitted guilt. He was too much of a dog to try to look to be a martyr or to plot revenge. He received the blows with deep humility, and furthermore he forgave his friend the moment the child had finished, and was ready to caress the child's hand with his little red tongue.

When misfortune came upon the child, and his troubles overwhelmed him, he would often crawl under the table and lay his small distressed head on the dog's back. The dog was ever sympathetic. It is not to be supposed that at such times he took occasion to refer to the unjust beatings his friend, when provoked, had administered to him.

He did not achieve any notable degree of intimacy with the other members of the family. He had no confidence in them, and the fear that he would express at their casual approach often exasperated them exceedingly. They used to gain a certain satisfaction in underfeeding him, but finally his friend the child grew to watch the matter with some care, and when he forgot it, the dog was often successful in secret for himself.

So the dog prospered. He developed a large bark, which came wondrously from such a small rug of a dog. He ceased to howl persistently at night. Sometimes, indeed, in his sleep, he would utter little yells, as from pain, but that occurred, no doubt, when in his dreams he encountered huge flaming dogs who threatened him direfully.

His devotion to the child grew until it was a sublime thing. He wagged at his approach; he sank down in despair at his departure. He could detect the sound of the child's step among all the noises of the neighbourhood. It was like a calling voice to him.

The scene of their companionship was a kingdom governed by this terrible potentate, the child; but neither criticism nor rebellion ever lived for an instant in the heart of the one subject. Down in the mystic, hidden fields of his little dog-soul bloomed flowers of love and fidelity and perfect faith.

The child was in the habit of going on many expeditions to observe strange things in the vicinity. On these occasions his friend usually jogged aimfully along behind. Perhaps, though, he went ahead. This necessitated his turning around every quarter-minute to make sure the child was coming. He was filled with a large idea of the importance of these journeys. He would carry himself with such an air! He was proud to be the retainer of so great a monarch.

One day, however, the father of the family got quite exceptionally drunk. He came home and held carnival with the cooking utensils, the furniture and his wife. He was in the midst of this recreation when the child, followed by the dark-brown dog, entered the room. They were returning from their voyages.

The child's practised eye instantly noted his father's state. He dived under the table, where experience had taught him was a rather safe place. The dog, lacking skill in such matters, was, of course, unaware of the true condition of affairs. He looked with interested eyes at his friend's sudden dive. He interpreted it to mean: joyous gambol. He started to patter across the floor to join him. He was the picture of a little dark-brown dog *en route* to a friend.

The head of the family saw him at this moment. He gave a huge howl of joy, and knocked the dog down with a heavy coffeepot. The dog, yelling in supreme astonishment and fear, writhed to his feet and ran for cover. The man kicked out with a ponderous foot. It caused the dog to swerve as if caught in a tide. A second blow of the coffeepot laid him upon the floor.

Here the child, uttering loud cries, came valiantly forth like a knight. The father of the family paid no attention to these calls of the child, but advanced with glee upon the dog. Upon being knocked down twice in swift succession, the latter apparently gave up all hope of escape. He rolled over on his back and held his paws in a peculiar manner. At the same time with his eyes and his ears he offered up a small prayer.

But the father was in a mood for having fun, and it occurred to him that it would be a fine thing to throw the dog out of the window. So he reached down and, grabbing the animal by a leg, lifted him, squirming, up. He swung him two or three times hilariously about his head, and then flung him with great accuracy through the window.

The soaring dog created a surprise in the block. A woman watering plants in an opposite window gave an involuntary shout and dropped a flowerpot. A man in another window leaned perilously out to watch the flight of the dog. A woman who had been hanging out clothes in a yard began to caper wildly. Her mouth was filled with clothes-pins, but her arms gave vent to a sort of exclamation. In appearance she was like a gagged prisoner. Children ran whooping.

The dark-brown body crashed in a heap on the roof of a shed five stories below. From thence it rolled to the pavement of an alleyway.

The child in the room far above burst into a long, dirge-like cry, and toddled hastily out of the room. It took him a long time to reach the alley, because his size compelled him to go downstairs backward, one step at a time, and holding with both hands to the step above.

When they came for him later, they found him seated by the body of his dark-brown friend.

Upturned Face

'What will we do now?' said the adjutant, troubled and excited.

'Bury him,' said Timothy Lean.

The two officers looked down close to their toes where lay the body of their comrade. The face was chalk-blue; gleaming eyes stared at the sky. Over the two upright figures was a windy sound of bullets, and on the top of the hill Lean's prostrate company of Spitzbergen infantry was firing measured volleys.

'Don't you think it would be better – ' began the adjutant. 'We might leave him until tomorrow.'

'No,' said Lean. 'I can't hold that post an hour longer. I've got to fall back, and we've got to bury old Bill.'

'Of course,' said the adjutant, at once. 'Your men got entrenching tools?'

Lean shouted back to his little line, and two men came slowly, one with a pick, one with a shovel. They started in the direction of the Rostina sharp-shooters. Bullets cracked near their ears. 'Dig here,' said Lean gruffly. The men, thus caused to lower their glances to the turf, became hurried and frightened merely because they could not look to see whence the bullets came. The dull beat of the pick striking the earth sounded amid the swift snap of close bullets. Presently the other private began to shovel.

'I suppose,' said the adjutant, slowly, 'we'd better search his clothes for – things.'

Lean nodded. Together in curious abstraction they looked at the body. Then Lean stirred his shoulders suddenly, arousing himself.

'Yes,' he said, 'we'd better see what he's got.' He dropped to his knees, and his hands approached the body of the dead officer. But his hands wavered over the buttons of the tunic. The first button was brick-red with drying blood, and he did not seem to dare touch it.

'Go on,' said the adjutant, hoarsely.

Lean stretched his wooden hand, and his fingers fumbled the blood-stained buttons. At last he rose with ghastly face. He had gathered a watch, a whistle, a pipe, a tobacco pouch, a handkerchief, a little case of cards and papers. He looked at the adjutant. There was a silence. The adjutant was feeling that he had been a coward to make Lean do all the grisly business.

'Well,' said Lean, 'that's all, I think. You have his sword and revolver?'

'Yes,' said the adjutant, his face working, and then he burst out in a sudden strange fury at the two privates. 'Why don't you hurry up with that grave? What are you doing, anyhow? Hurry, do you hear? I never saw such stupid – '

Even as he cried out in his passion the two men were labouring for their lives. Ever overhead the bullets were spitting.

The grave was finished. It was not a masterpiece – a poor little shallow thing. Lean and the adjutant again looked at each other in a curious silent communication.

Suddenly the adjutant croaked out a weird laugh. It was a terrible laugh, which had its origin in that part of the mind which is first moved by the singing of the nerves. 'Well,' he said, humorously to Lean, 'I suppose we had best tumble him in.'

'Yes,' said Lean. The two privates stood waiting, bent over their implements. 'I suppose,' said Lean, 'it would be better if we laid him in ourselves.'

'Yes,' said the adjutant. Then apparently remembering that he had made Lean search the body, he stooped with great fortitude and took hold of the dead officer's clothing. Lean joined him. Both were particular that their fingers should not feel the corpse. They tugged away; the corpse lifted, heaved, toppled, flopped into the grave, and the two officers, straightening, looked again at each other – they were always looking at each other. They sighed with relief.

The adjutant said, 'I suppose we should – we should say something. Do you know the service, Tim?'

'They don't read the service until the grave is filled in,' said Lean, pressing his lips to an academic expression.

'Don't they?' said the adjutant, shocked that he had made the mistake.

'Oh, well,' he cried, suddenly, 'let us – let us say something – while he can hear us.'

'All right,' said Lean. 'Do you know the service?'

'I can't remember a line of it,' said the adjutant.

Lean was extremely dubious. 'I can repeat two lines, but – '

'Well, do it,' said the adjutant. 'Go as far as you can. That's better than nothing. And the beasts have got our range exactly.'

Lean looked at his two men. 'Attention,' he barked. The privates came to attention with a click, looking much aggrieved. The adjutant lowered his helmet to his knee. Lean, bareheaded, he stood over the grave. The Rostina sharpshooters fired briskly.

'Oh, Father, our friend has sunk in the deep waters of death, but his spirit has leaped toward Thee as the bubble arises from the lips of the drowning. Perceive, we beseech, O Father, the little flying bubble, and – '

Lean, although husky and ashamed, had suffered no hesitation up to this point, but he stopped with a hopeless feeling and looked at the corpse.

The adjutant moved uneasily. 'And from Thy superb heights – ' he began, and then he too came to an end.

'And from Thy superb heights,' said Lean.

The adjutant suddenly remembered a phrase in the back part of the Spitzbergen burial service, and he exploited it with the triumphant manner of a man who has recalled everything, and can go on.

'Oh, God, have mercy –'

'Oh, God, have mercy – said Lean.

'Mercy,' repeated the adjutant, in quick failure.

'Mercy,' said Lean. And then he was moved by some violence of feeling, for he turned suddenly upon his two men and tigerishly said, 'Throw the dirt in.'

The fire of the Rostina sharpshooters was accurate and continuous.

*   *   *

One of the aggrieved privates came forward with his shovel. He lifted his first shovel-load of earth, and for a moment of inexplicable hesitation it was held poised above this corpse, which from its chalk-blue face looked keenly out from the grave. Then the soldier emptied his shovel on – on the feet.

Timothy Lean felt as if tons had been swiftly lifted from off his forehead. He had felt that perhaps the private might empty the shovel on – on the face. It had been emptied on the feet. There was a great point gained there – ha, ha! – the first shovelful had been emptied on the feet. How satisfactory!

The adjutant began to babble. 'Well, of course – a man we've messed with all these years – impossible – you can't, you know, leave your intimate friends rotting on the field. Go on, for God's sake, and shovel, you!'

The man with the shovel suddenly ducked, grabbed his left arm with his right hand, and looked at his officer for orders. Lean picked the shovel from the ground. 'Go to the rear,' he said to the wounded man. He also addressed the other private. 'You get under cover, too; I'll finish this business.'

The wounded man scrambled hard still for the top of the ridge without devoting any glances to the direction whence the bullets came, and the other man followed at an equal pace; but he was different, in that he looked back anxiously three times.

This is merely the way – often – of the hit and unhit.

Timothy Lean filled the shovel, hesitated, and then in a movement which was like a gesture of abhorrence he flung the dirt into the grave, and as it landed it made a sound – plop! Lean suddenly stopped and mopped his brow – a tired labourer.

'Perhaps we have been wrong,' said the adjutant. His glance wavered stupidly. 'It might have been better if we hadn't buried him just at this time. Of course, if we advance tomorrow the body would have been –'

'Damn you,' said Lean, 'shut your mouth!' He was not the senior officer.

He again filled the shovel and flung the earth. Always the earth made that sound – plop! For a space Lean worked frantically, like a man digging himself out of danger.

Soon there was nothing to be seen but the chalk-blue face. Lean filled the shovel. 'Good God,' he cried to the adjutant. 'Why didn't you turn him somehow when you put him in? This – ' Then Lean began to stutter.

The adjutant understood. He was pale to the lips. 'Go on, man,' he cried, beseechingly, almost in a shout. Lean swung back the shovel. It went forward in a pendulum curve. When the earth landed it made a sound – plop!

ELLA D'ARCY

Ella D'Arcy was born in London in 1851 to Irish parents and educated in Germany and France. Initially, D'Arcy studied to become a visual artist but problems with her eyesight led her to turn to fiction writing as an alternative. Her fiction style won acclaim from Henry Harland and *The Yellow Book* circle. She worked with Harland as assistant editor for the periodical's three-year run. D'Arcy was also a longtime friend of the writer Charlotte Mew, a *Yellow Book* contributor herself, who was in love with D'Arcy. Both D'Arcy's style and subject matter were ground-breaking, challenging traditional morality as much as convent–ional narrative styles. Her writing also questioned the standard representations of women. In 1895, D'Arcy saw the publication of her first collection of short stories, *Monochromes*. This was followed in 1898 by another entitled *Modern Instances*. She published the novel *The Bishop's Dilemma* that same year. D'Arcy also translated André Maurois's biography of Percy Bysshe Shelley, *Ariel*, into English. D'Arcy died in 1939.

Irremediable

A young man strolled along a country road one August evening after a long delicious day – a day of that blessed idleness the man of leisure never knows: one must be a bank clerk forty-nine weeks out of the fifty-two before one can really appreciate the exquisite enjoyment of doing nothing for twelve hours at a stretch. Willoughby had spent the morning lounging about a sunny rickyard; then, when the heat grew unbearable, he had retreated to an orchard, where, lying on his back in the long cool grass, he had traced the pattern of the apple-leaves diapered above him upon the summer sky; now that the heat of the day was over he had come to roam whither sweet fancy led him, to lean over gates, view the prospect, and meditate upon the pleasures of a well-spent day. Five such days had already passed over his head, fifteen more remained to him. Then farewell to freedom and clean country air! Back again to London and another year's toil.

He came to a gate on the right of the road. Behind it a footpath meandered up over a grassy slope. The sheep nibbling on its summit cast long shadows down the hill almost to his feet. Road and fieldpath were equally new to him, but the latter offered greener attractions; he vaulted lightly over the gate and had so little idea he was taking thus the first step towards ruin that he began to whistle 'White Wings' from pure joy of life.

The sheep stopped feeding and raised their heads to stare at him from pale-lashed eyes; first one and then another broke into a startled run, until there was a sudden woolly stampede of the entire flock. When Willoughby gained the ridge from which they had just scattered, he came in sight of a woman sitting on a stile at the farther end of the field. As he advanced towards her he saw that she was young, and that she was not what is called 'a lady' – of which he was glad: an earlier episode in his career having indissolubly associated in his mind ideas of feminine refinement with those of feminine treachery.

He thought it probable this girl would be willing to dispense with the formalities of an introduction, and that he might venture with her on some pleasant foolish chat.

As she made no movement to let him pass he stood still, and, looking at her, began to smile.

She returned his gaze from unabashed dark eyes, and then laughed, showing teeth white, sound, and smooth as split hazelnuts.

'Do you wanter get over?' she remarked familiarly.

'I'm afraid I can't without disturbing you.'

'Dontcher think you're much better where you are?' said the girl, on which Willoughby hazarded: 'You mean to say looking at you? Well, perhaps I am!'

The girl at this laughed again, but nevertheless dropped herself down into the farther field; then, leaning her arms upon the crossbar, she informed the young man: 'No, I don't wanter spoil your walk. You were goin' p'raps ter Beacon Point? It's very pretty that wye.'

'I was going nowhere in particular,' he replied; 'just exploring, so to speak. I'm a stranger in these parts.'

'How funny! Imer stranger here too. I only come down larse Friday to stye with a naunter mine in Horton. Are you stying in Horton?'

Willoughby told her he was not in Orton, but at Povey Cross Farm out in the other direction.

'Oh, Mrs Payne's, ain't it? I've heard aunt speak ovver. She takes summer boarders, don't chee? I egspeck you come from London, heh?'

'And I expect you come from London too?' said Willoughby, recognising the familiar accent.

'You're as sharp as a needle,' cried the girl with her unrestrained laugh; 'so I do. I'm here for a hollerday 'cos I was so done up with the work and the hot weather. I don't look as though I'd bin ill, do I? But I was, though: for it was just stiflin' hot up in our workrooms all larse month, an' tailorin's awful hard work at the bester times.'

Willoughby felt a sudden accession of interest in her. Like many intelligent young men, he had dabbled a little in Socialism, and at one time had wandered among the dispossessed; what's more, since then, he had caught up and held loosely the new doctrine – it is a good and fitting thing that woman also should earn her bread by the sweat of her brow. Always in reference to the woman who, fifteen months before, had treated him ill, he had said to himself that even the breaking of stones in the road should be considered a more feminine employment than the breaking of hearts.

He gave way therefore to a movement of friendliness for this working daughter of the people, and joined her on the other side of the stile in token of his approval. She, twisting round to face him, leaned now with her back against the bar, and the sunset fires lent a fleeting glory to her face. Perhaps she guessed how becoming the light was, for she took off her hat and let it touch to gold the ends and fringes of her rough abundant hair. Thus and at this moment she made an agreeable picture, to which stood as background all the beautiful, wooded Southshire view.

'You don't really mean to say you are a tailoress?' said Willoughby, with a sort of eager compassion.

'I do, though! An' I've bin one ever since I was fourteen. Look at my fingers if you don't b'lieve me.'

She put out her right hand, and he took hold of it, as he was expected to do. The finger-ends were frayed and blackened by needle-pricks, but the hand itself was plump, moist, and not unshapely. She meanwhile examined Willoughby's fingers enclosing hers.

'It's easy ter see you've never done no work!' she said, half admiring, half envious. 'I s'pose you're a tip-top swell, ain't you?'

'Oh, yes! I'm a tremendous swell indeed!' said Willoughby, ironically. He thought of his hundred and thirty pounds' salary; and he mentioned his position in the British and Colonial Bank, without shedding much illumination on her mind, for she insisted: 'Well, anyhow, you're a gentleman. I've often wished I was a lady. It must be so nice ter wear fine clo'es an' never have ter do any work all day long.'

Willoughby thought it innocent of the girl to say this; it reminded him of his own notion as a child – that kings and queens put on their crowns the first thing on rising in the morning. His cordiality rose another degree.

'If being a gentleman means having nothing to do,' said he, smiling, 'I can certainly lay no claim to the title. Life isn't all beer and skittles with me, any more than it is with you. Which is the better reason for enjoying the present moment, don't you think? Suppose, now, like a kind little girl, you were to show me the way to Beacon Point, which you say is so pretty?'

She required no further persuasion. As he walked beside her through the upland fields where the dusk was beginning to fall and the white evening moths to emerge from their daytime hiding-places, she asked him many personal questions, most of which he thought fit to parry. Taking no offence thereat, she told him, instead, much concerning herself and her family. Thus he learned her name was Esther Stables, that she and her people lived Whitechapel way; that her father was seldom sober, and her mother always ill; and that the aunt with whom she was staying kept the post-office and general shop in Orton village. He learned, too, that Esther was discontented with life in general; that, though she hated being at home, she found the country dreadfully dull; and that, consequently, she was extremely glad to have made his acquaintance. But what he chiefly realised when they parted was that he had spent a couple of pleasant hours talking nonsense with a girl who was natural, simple-minded, and entirely free from that repellently protective atmosphere with which a woman of the 'classes' so carefully surrounds herself. He and Esther had 'made friends' with the ease and rapidity of children before they have learned the dread meaning of 'etiquette', and they said good-night, not without some talk of meeting each other again.

Obliged to breakfast at a quarter to eight in town, Willoughby was always luxuriously late when in the country, where he took his meals also in leisurely fashion, often reading from a book propped up on the table before him. But the morning after his meeting with Esther Stables found him less disposed to read than usual. Her image obtruded itself upon the printed page, and at length grew so importunate he came to the conclusion the only way to lay it was to confront it with the girl herself.

Wanting some tobacco, he saw a good reason for going into Orton. Esther had told him he could get tobacco and everything else at her aunt's. He found the post-office to be one of the first houses in the widely spaced village street. In front of the cottage was a small garden ablaze with old-fashioned flowers; and in a large garden at one side were apple-trees, raspberry and currant bushes, and six thatched beehives on a bench. The bowed windows of the little shop were partly screened by sunblinds; nevertheless the lower panes still displayed a heterogeneous collection of goods – lemons, hanks of yarn, white linen buttons upon blue cards, sugar cones, churchwarden pipes and tobacco jars. A letter-box opened its narrow mouth low down in one wall, and over the door swung the sign, 'Stamps and money-order office', in black letters on white enamelled iron.

The interior of the shop was cool and dark. A second glass-door at the back permitted Willoughby to see into a small sitting-room, and out again through a low and square-paned window to the sunny landscape beyond. Silhouetted against the light were the heads of two women; the rough young head of yesterday's Esther, the lean outline and bugled cap of Esther's aunt.

It was the latter who at the jingling of the doorbell rose from her work and came forward to serve the customer; but the girl, with much mute meaning in her eyes, and a finger laid upon her smiling mouth, followed behind. Her aunt heard her footfall. 'What do you want here, Esther?' she said with thin disapproval; 'get back to your sewing.'

Esther gave the young man a signal seen only by him and slipped out into the side-garden, where he found her when his purchases were made. She leaned over the privet-hedge to intercept him as he passed.

'Aunt's an awful ole maid,' she remarked apologetically; 'I b'lieve she'd never let me say a word to ennyone if she could help it.'

'So you got home all right last night?' Willoughby enquired; 'what did your aunt say to you?'

'Oh, she arst me where I'd been, and I tolder a lotter lies.' Then, with a woman's intuition, perceiving that this speech jarred, Esther made haste to add, 'She's so dreadful hard on me. I dursn't tell her I'd been with a gentleman or she'd never have let me out alone again.'

'And at present I suppose you'll be found somewhere about that same stile every evening?' said Willoughby foolishly, for he really did not much care whether he met her again or not. Now he was actually in her company, he was surprised at himself for having given her a whole morning's thought; yet the eagerness of her answer flattered him, too.

'Tonight I can't come, worse luck! It's Thursday, and the shops here close of a Thursday at five. I'll havter keep aunt company. But tomorrer? I can be there tomorrer. You'll come, say?'

'Esther!' cried a vexed voice, and the precise, right-minded aunt emerged through a row of raspberry bushes; 'whatever are you thinking about, delayin' the gentleman in this fashion?' She was full of rustic and official civility for 'the gentleman', but indignant with her niece. 'I don't want none of your London manners down here,' Willoughby heard her say as she marched the girl off.

He himself was not sorry to be released from Esther's too friendly eyes, and he spent an agreeable evening over a book, and this time managed to forget her completely.

Though he remembered her first thing next morning, it was to smile wisely and determine he would not meet her again. Yet by dinner-time the day seemed long; why, after all, should he not meet her? By tea-time prudence triumphed anew – no, he would not go. Then he drank his tea hastily and set off for the stile.

Esther was waiting for him. Expectation had given an additional colour to her cheeks, and her red-brown hair showed here and there a beautiful glint of gold. He could not help admiring the vigorous way in which it waved and twisted, or the little curls which grew at the nape of her neck, tight and close as those of a young lamb's fleece. Her neck here was admirable, too, in its smooth creaminess; and when her eyes lighted up with such evident pleasure at his coming, how avoid the conviction she was a good and nice girl after all?

He proposed they should go down into the little copse on the right, where they would be less disturbed by the occasional passer-by. Here, seated on a felled tree-trunk, Willoughby began that bantering, silly, meaningless form of conversation known among the 'classes' as flirting. He had but the wish to make himself agreeable, and to while away the time. Esther, however, misunderstood him.

Willoughby's hand lay palm downwards on his knee, and she, noticing a ring which he wore on his little finger, took hold of it.

'What a funny ring!' she said; 'let's look?'

To disembarrass himself of her touch, he pulled the ring off and gave it her to examine.

'What's that ugly dark green stone?' she asked.

'It's called a sardonyx.'

'What's it for?' she said, turning it about.

'It's a signet ring, to seal letters with.'

'An' there's a sorter king's head scratched on it, an' some writin' too, only I carnt make it out.'

'It isn't the head of a king, although it wears a crown,' Willoughby explained, 'but the head and bust of a Saracen against whom my ancestor of many hundred years ago went to fight in the Holy Land. And the words cut round it are our motto, "Vertue vauncet", which means virtue prevails.'

Willoughby may have displayed some accession of dignity in giving this bit of family history, for Esther fell into uncontrolled laughter, at which he was much displeased. And when the girl made as though she would put the ring on her own finger, asking, 'Shall I keep it?' he coloured up with sudden annoyance.

'It was only my fun!' said Esther hastily, and gave him the ring back, but his cordiality was gone. He felt no inclination to renew the idle-word pastime, said it was time to go, and, swinging his cane vexedly, struck off the heads of the flowers and the weeds as he went. Esther walked by his side in complete silence, a phenomenon of which he presently became conscious. He felt rather ashamed of having shown temper.

'Well, here's your way home,' said he with an effort at friendliness. 'Goodbye; we've had a nice evening anyhow. It was pleasant down there in the woods, eh?'

He was astonished to see her eyes soften with tears, and to hear the real emotion in her voice as she answered, 'It was just heaven down there with you until you turned so funny-like. What had I done to make you cross? Say you forgive me, do!'

'Silly child!' said Willoughby, completely mollified, 'I'm not the least angry. There, goodbye!' and like a fool he kissed her.

He anathematised his folly in the white light of next morning, and, remembering the kiss he had given her, repented it very sincerely. He had an uncomfortable suspicion she had not received it in the same spirit in which it had been bestowed, but, attaching more serious meaning to it, would build expectations thereon which must be left unfulfilled. It was best indeed not to meet her again; for he acknowledged to himself that, though he only half liked, and even slightly feared her, there was a certain attraction about her – was it in her dark unflinching eyes or in her very red lips? – which might lead him into greater follies still.

Thus it came about that for two successive evenings Esther waited for him in vain, and on the third evening he said to himself, with a grudging relief, that by this time she had probably transferred her affections to someone else.

It was Saturday, the second Saturday since he left town. He spent the day about the farm, contemplated the pigs, inspected the feeding of the stock and assisted at the afternoon milking. Then at evening, with a refilled pipe, he went for a long lean over the west gate, while he traced fantastic pictures and wove romances in the glories of the sunset.

He had watched the colours glow from gold to scarlet and change to crimson and sink at last to sad purple reefs and isles, when the sudden consciousness of someone being near him made him turn round. There stood Esther, and her eyes were full of eagerness and anger.

'Why have you never been to the stile again?' she asked him. 'You promised to come faithful, and you never came. Why have you not kep' your promise? Why? Why?' she persisted, stamping her foot because Willoughby remained silent.

What could he say? Tell her she had no business to follow him like this; or own, what was, unfortunately, the truth, he was just a little glad to see her?

'P'raps you don't care for me any more?' she said. 'Well, why did you kiss me, then?'

Why, indeed! thought Willoughby, marvelling at his own idiocy, and yet – such is the inconsistency of man – not wholly without the desire to kiss her again. And while he looked at her she suddenly flung herself down on the hedge-bank at his feet and burst into tears. She did not cover up her face, but simply pressed one cheek down upon the grass while the water poured from her eyes with astonishing abundance. Willoughby saw the dry earth turn dark and moist as it drank the tears in. This, his first experience of Esther's powers of weeping, distressed him horribly; never in his life before had he seen anyone weep like that – he should not have believed such a thing possible; he was alarmed, too, lest she should be noticed from the house. He opened the gate; 'Esther!' he begged, 'don't cry. Come out here, like a dear girl, and let us talk sensibly.'

Because she stumbled, unable to see her way through wet eyes, he gave her his hand, and they found themselves in a field of corn, walking along the narrow grass-path that skirted it, in the shadow of the hedgerow.

'What is there to cry about because you have not seen me for two days?' he began; 'why, Esther, we are only strangers, after all. When we have been at home a week or two we shall scarcely remember each other's names.'

Esther sobbed at intervals, but her tears had ceased. 'It's fine for you to talk of home,' she said to this. 'You've got something that is a home, I s'pose? But me! my home's like hell, with nothing but quarrellin' and cursin', and a father who beats us whether sober or drunk. Yes!' she repeated shrewdly, seeing the lively disgust on Willoughby's face, 'he beat me, all ill as I was, jus' before I come away. I could show you the bruises on my arms still. And now to go back there after knowin' you! It'll be worse than ever. I can't endure it, and I won't! I'll put an end to it or myself somehow, I swear!'

'But my poor Esther, how can I help it? what can I do?' said Willoughby. He was greatly moved, full of wrath with her father, with all the world which makes women suffer. He had suffered himself at the hands of a woman and severely, but this, instead of hardening his heart, had only rendered it the more supple. And yet he had a vivid perception of the peril in which he stood. An interior voice urged him to break away, to seek safety in flight even at the cost of appearing cruel or ridiculous; so, coming to a point in the field where an elm-bole jutted out across the path, he saw with relief he could now withdraw his hand from the girl's, since they must walk singly to skirt round it.

Esther took a step in advance, stopped and suddenly turned to face him; she held out her two hands and her face was very near his own.

'Don't you care for me one little bit?' she said wistfully, and surely sudden madness fell upon him. For he kissed her again, he kissed her many times, he took her in his arms, and pushed all thoughts of the consequences far from him.

But when, an hour later, he and Esther stood by the last gate on the road to Orton, some of these consequences were already calling loudly to him.

'You know I have only a hundred and thirty a year?' he told her; 'it's no very brilliant prospect for you to marry me on that.'

For he had actually offered her marriage, although to the mediocre man such a proceeding must appear incredible, uncalled for. But to Willoughby, overwhelmed with sadness and remorse, it seemed the only atonement possible.

Sudden exultation leaped at Esther's heart.

'Oh! I'm used to managing,' she told him confidently, and mentally resolved to buy herself, so soon as she was married, a black-feather boa, such as she had coveted last winter.

Willoughby spent the remaining days of his holiday in thinking out and planning with Esther the details of his return to London and her own, the secrecy to be observed, the necessary legal steps to be taken, and the quiet suburb in which they would set up housekeeping. And, so successfully did he carry out his arrangements, that within five weeks from the day on which he had first met Esther Stables, he and she came out one morning from a church in Highbury, husband and wife. It was a mellow September day, the streets were filled with sunshine, and Willoughby, in reckless high spirits, imagined he saw a reflection of his own gaiety on the indifferent faces of the passers-by. There being no one else to perform the office, he congratulated himself very warmly, and Esther's frequent laughter filled in the pauses of the day.

*   *   *

Three months later Willoughby was dining with a friend, and the hour-hand of the clock nearing ten, the host no longer resisted the guest's growing anxiety to be gone. He arose and exchanged with him good wishes and goodbyes.

'Marriage is evidently a most successful institution,' said he, half-jesting, half-sincere; 'you almost make me inclined to go and get married myself. Confess now your thoughts have been at home the whole evening.'

Willoughby thus addressed turned red to the roots of his hair, but did not deny it.

The other laughed. 'And very commendable they should be,' he continued, 'since you are scarcely, so to speak, out of your honeymoon.'

With a social smile on his lips, Willoughby calculated a moment before replying, 'I have been married exactly three months and three days.' Then, after a few words respecting their next meeting, the two shook hands and parted – the young host to finish the evening with books and pipe, the young husband to set out on a twenty minutes' walk to his home.

It was a cold, clear December night following a day of rain. A touch of frost in the air had dried the pavements, and Willoughby's footfall ringing upon the stones re-echoed down the empty suburban street. Above his head was a dark, remote sky thickly powdered with stars, and as he turned westward Alpherat hung for a moment 'comme le point sur un *i* ', over the slender spire of St John's. But he was insensible to the worlds about him; he was absorbed in his own thoughts, and these, as his friend had surmised, were entirely with his wife. For Esther's face was always before his eyes, her voice was always in his ears, she filled the universe for him; yet only four months ago he had never seen her, had never heard her name. This was the curious part of it – here in December he found himself the husband of a girl who was completely dependent upon him not only for food, clothes and lodging, but for her present happiness, her whole future life; and last July he had been scarcely more than a boy himself, with no greater care on his mind than the pleasant difficulty of deciding where he should spend his annual three weeks' holiday.

But it is events, not months or years, which age. Willoughby, who was only twenty-six, remembered his youth as a sometime companion irrevocably lost to him; its vague, delightful hopes were now crystallised into definite ties, and its happy irresponsibilities displaced by a sense of care, inseparable perhaps from the most fortunate of marriages.

As he reached the street in which he lodged his pace involuntarily slackened. While still some distance off, his eye sought out and distinguished the windows of the room in which Esther awaited him. Through the broken slats of the Venetian blinds he could see the yellow gaslight within. The parlour beneath was in darkness; his landlady had evidently gone to bed, there being no light over the hall-door either. In some apprehension he consulted his watch under the last street-lamp he passed, to find comfort in assuring himself it was only ten minutes after ten. He let himself in with his latch-key, hung up his hat and overcoat by the sense of touch, and, groping his way upstairs, opened the door of the first-floor sitting-room.

At the table in the centre of the room sat his wife, leaning upon her elbows, her two hands thrust up into her ruffled hair; spread out before her was a crumpled yesterday's newspaper, and so interested was she to all appearance in its contents that she neither spoke nor looked up as Willoughby entered. Around her were the still uncleared tokens of her last meal: tea-slops, breadcrumbs and an egg-shell crushed to fragments upon a plate, which was one of those trifles that set Willoughby's teeth on edge –

whenever his wife ate an egg she persisted in turning the egg-cup upside down upon the tablecloth, and pounding the shell to pieces in her plate with her spoon.

The room was repulsive in its disorder. The one lighted burner of the gaselier, turned too high, hissed up into a long tongue of flame. The fire smoked feebly under a newly administered shovelful of 'slack', and a heap of ashes and cinders littered the grate. A pair of walking boots, caked in dry mud, lay on the hearth-rug just where they had been thrown off. On the mantelpiece, amidst a dozen other articles which had no business there, was a bedroom-candlestick; and every single article of furniture stood crookedly out of its place.

Willoughby took in the whole intolerable picture, and yet spoke with kindliness. 'Well, Esther! I'm not so late, after all. I hope you did not find the time dull by yourself?' Then he explained the reason of his absence. He had met a friend he had not seen for a couple of years, who had insisted on taking him home to dine.

His wife gave no sign of having heard him; she kept her eyes riveted on the paper before her.

'You received my wire, of course,' Willoughby went on, 'and did not wait?'

Now she crushed the newspaper up with a passionate movement, and threw it from her. She raised her head, showing cheeks blazing with anger, and dark, sullen, unflinching eyes.

'I did wyte then!' she cried. 'I wyted till near eight before I got your old telegraph! I s'pose that's what you call the manners of a "gentleman", to keep your wife mewed up here, while you go gallivantin' off with your fine friends?'

Whenever Esther was angry, which was often, she taunted Willoughby with being 'a gentleman', although this was the precise point about him which at other times found most favour in her eyes. But tonight she was envenomed by the idea he had been enjoying himself without her, stung by fear lest he should have been in company with some other woman.

Willoughby, hearing the taunt, resigned himself to the inevitable. Nothing that he could do might now avert the breaking storm; all his words would only be twisted into fresh griefs. But sad experience had taught him that to take refuge in silence was more fatal still. When Esther was in such a mood as this it was best to supply the fire with fuel, that, through the very violence of the conflagration, it might the sooner burn itself out.

So he said what soothing things he could, and Esther caught them up, disfigured them, and flung them back at him with scorn. She reproached him with no longer caring for her; she vituperated the conduct of his family in never taking the smallest notice of her marriage; and she detailed the insolence of the landlady who had told her that morning she pitied 'poor Mr

Willoughby', and had refused to go out and buy herrings for Esther's early dinner.

Every affront or grievance, real or imaginary, since the day she and Willoughby had first met, she poured forth with a fluency due to frequent repetition, for, with the exception of today's added injuries, Willoughby had heard the whole litany many times before.

While she raged and he looked at her, he remembered he had once thought her pretty. He had seen beauty in her rough brown hair, her strong colouring, her full red mouth. He fell into musing . . . a woman may lack beauty, he told himself, and yet be loved . . .

Meanwhile Esther reached white heats of passion, and the strain could no longer be sustained. She broke into sobs and began to shed tears with the facility peculiar to her. In a moment her face was all wet with the big drops which rolled down her cheeks faster and faster, and fell with audible splashes on to the table, on to her lap, on to the floor. To this tearful abundance, formerly a surprising spectacle, Willoughby was now acclimatised; but the remnant of chivalrous feeling not yet extinguished in his bosom forbade him to sit stolidly by while a woman wept, without seeking to console her. As on previous occasions, his peace-overtures were eventually accepted. Esther's tears gradually ceased to flow, she began to exhibit a sort of compunction, she wished to be forgiven, and, with the kiss of reconciliation, passed into a phase of demonstrative affection perhaps more trying to Willoughby's patience than all that had preceded it. 'You don't love me?' she questioned, 'I'm sure you don't love me?' she reiterated; and he asseverated that he loved her until he despised himself. Then at last, only half satisfied, but wearied out with vexation – possibly, too, with a movement of pity at the sight of his haggard face – she consented to leave him. Only, what was he going to do? she asked suspiciously – write those rubbishing stories of his? Well, he must promise not to stay up more than half an hour at the latest – only until he had smoked one pipe.

Willoughby promised, as he would have promised anything on earth to secure to himself a half-hour's peace and solitude. Esther groped for her slippers, which were kicked off under the table; scratched four or five matches along the box and threw them away before she succeeded in lighting her candle; set it down again to contemplate her tear-swollen reflection in the chimney-glass, and burst out laughing.

'What a fright I do look, to be sure!' she remarked complacently, and again thrust her two hands up through her disordered curls. Then, holding the candle at such an angle that the grease ran over on to the carpet, she gave Willoughby another vehement kiss and trailed out of the room with an ineffectual attempt to close the door behind her.

Willoughby got up to shut it himself, and wondered why it was that Esther never did any one mortal thing efficiently or well. Good God! how irritable he felt. It was impossible to write. He must find an outlet for his impatience, rend or mend something. He began to straighten the room, but a wave of disgust came over him before the task was fairly commenced. What was the use? Tomorrow all would be bad as before. What was the use of doing anything? He sat down by the table and leaned his head upon his hands.

*   *   *

The past came back to him in pictures: his boyhood's past first of all. He saw again the old home, every inch of which was familiar to him as his own name; he reconstructed in his thought all the old well-known furniture, and replaced it precisely as it had stood long ago. He passed again a childish finger over the rough surface of the faded Utrecht velvet chairs, and smelled again the strong fragrance of the white lilac tree, blowing in through the open parlour-window. He savoured anew the pleasant mental atmosphere produced by the dainty neatness of cultured women, the companionship of a few good pictures, of a few good books. Yet this home had been broken up years ago, the dear familiar things had been scattered far and wide, never to find themselves under the same roof again; and from those near relatives who still remained to him he lived now hopelessly estranged.

Then came the past of his first love-dream, when he worshipped at the feet of Nora Beresford, and, with the whole-heartedness of the true fanatic, clothed his idol with every imaginable attribute of virtue and tenderness. To this day there remained a secret shrine in his heart wherein the lady of his young ideal was still enthroned, although it was long since he had come to perceive she had nothing whatever in common with the Nora of reality. For the real Nora he had no longer any sentiment, she had passed altogether out of his life and thoughts; and yet, so permanent is all influence, whether good or evil, that the effect she wrought upon his character remained. He recognised tonight that her treatment of him in the past did not count for nothing among the various factors which had determined his fate.

Now, the past of only last year returned, and, strangely enough, this seemed farther removed from him than all the rest. He had been particularly strong, well and happy this time last year. Nora was dismissed from his mind, and he had thrown all his energies into his work. His tastes were sane and simple, and his dingy, furnished rooms had become through habit very pleasant to him. In being his own, they were invested with a greater charm than another man's castle. Here he had smoked and studied, here he had made many a glorious voyage into the land of books. Many a homecoming, too, rose up before him out of the dark ungenial streets, to a clear blazing fire, a neatly laid cloth, an evening of ideal enjoyment; many a summer twilight when he mused at the open window, plunging his gaze deep into the recesses of his neighbour's lime tree, where the unseen sparrows chattered with such unflagging gaiety.

He had always been given to much daydreaming, and it was in the silence of his rooms of an evening that he turned his phantasmal adventures into stories for the magazines; here had come to him many an editorial refusal, but here, too, he had received the news of his first unexpected success. All his happiest memories were embalmed in those shabby, badly furnished rooms.

Now all was changed. Now might there be no longer any soft indulgence of the hour's mood. His rooms and everything he owned belonged now to Esther, too. She had objected to most of his photographs, and had removed them. She hated books, and were he ever so ill-advised as to open one in her presence, she immediately began to talk, no matter how silent or how sullen her previous mood had been. If he read aloud to her she either yawned despairingly, or was tickled into laughter where there was no reasonable cause. At first Willoughby had tried to educate her, and had gone hopefully to the task. It is so natural to think you may make what you will of the woman who loves you. But Esther had no wish to improve. She evinced all the self-satisfaction of an illiterate mind. To her husband's gentle admonitions she replied with brevity that she thought her way quite as good as his; or, if he didn't approve of her pronunciation, he might do the other thing, she was too old to go to school again. He gave up the attempt, and, with humiliation at his previous fatuity, perceived that it was folly to expect that a few weeks of his companionship could alter or pull up the impressions of years, or rather of generations.

Yet here he paused to admit a curious thing: it was not only Esther's bad habits which vexed him, but habits quite unblameworthy in themselves which he never would have noticed in another, irritated him in her. He disliked her manner of standing, of walking, of sitting in a chair, of folding her hands. Like a lover, he was conscious of her proximity without seeing her. Like a lover, too, his eyes followed her every movement, his ear noted every change in her voice. But then, instead of being charmed by everything as the lover is, everything jarred upon him.

What was the meaning of this? Tonight the anomaly pressed upon him: he reviewed his position. Here was he, quite a young man, just twenty-six years of age, married to Esther, and bound to live with her so long as life should last – twenty, forty, perhaps fifty years more. Every day of those years to be spent in her society; he and she face to face, soul to soul; they two alone amid all the whirling, busy, indifferent world. So near together in semblance; in truth, so far apart as regards all that makes life dear.

Willoughby groaned. From the woman he did not love, whom he had never loved, he might not again go free; so much he recognised. The feeling he had once entertained for Esther, strange compound of mistaken chivalry and flattered vanity, was long since extinct; but what, then, was the sentiment with which she inspired him? For he was not indifferent to her – no, never for one instant could he persuade himself he was indifferent, never for one instant could he banish her from his thoughts. His mind's eye followed her during his hours of absence as pertinaciously as his bodily eye dwelt upon her actual presence. She was the principal object of the universe to him, the centre around which his wheel of life revolved with an appalling fidelity.

What did it mean? What could it mean? he asked himself with anguish.

And the sweat broke out upon his forehead and his hands grew cold, for on a sudden the truth lay there like a written word upon the tablecloth before him. This woman, whom he had taken to himself for better, for worse, inspired him with a passion, intense indeed, all-masterful, soul-subduing as Love itself . . . But when he understood the terror of his Hatred, he laid his head upon his arms and wept, not facile tears like Esther's, but tears wrung out from his agonising, unavailing regret.

AMELIA B. EDWARDS

Amelia Ann Blandford Edwards, the daughter of one of Wellington's officers, was born in London on 7 June 1831. At a very early age she displayed considerable literary and artistic talent. She became a contributor to various magazines and newspapers, and besides many miscellaneous works she wrote eight novels, the most successful of which were *Debenham's Vow* (1870) and *Lord Brackenbury* (1880). In the winter of 1873–4 she visited Egypt and was profoundly impressed by the new openings for archaeological research. She learnt the hieroglyphic characters and made a considerable collection of Egyptian antiquities. In 1877 she published *A Thousand Miles up the Nile*, with illustrations by herself, and in 1882 was largely instrumental in founding the Egypt Exploration Fund. It was at this point that she abandoned her other literary work, writing only on Egyptology. She died at Weston-super-Mare, Somerset, on 15 April 1892, bequeathing her valuable collection of Egyptian antiquities to University College, London, together with a sum to found a chair of Egyptology.

The Four-Fifteen Express

The events which I am about to relate took place between nine and ten years ago. Sebastopol had fallen in the early spring, the Peace of Paris had been concluded since March, our commercial relations with the Russian empire were but recently renewed; and I, returning home after my first northward journey since the war, was well pleased with the prospect of spending the month of December under the hospitable and thoroughly English roof of my excellent friend, Jonathan Jelf, Esquire, of Dumbleton Manor, Clayborough, East Anglia. Travelling in the interests of the well-known firm in which it is my lot to be a junior partner, I had been called upon to visit not only the capitals of Russia and Poland, but had found it also necessary to pass some weeks among the trading ports of the Baltic; whence it came that the year was already far spent before I again set foot on English soil, and that, instead of shooting pheasants with him, as I had hoped, in October, I came to be my friend's guest during the more genial Christmastide.

My voyage over, and a few days given up to business in Liverpool and London, I hastened down to Clayborough with all the delight of a school-boy whose holidays are at hand. My way lay by the Great East Anglian line as far as Clayborough station, where I was to be met by one of the Dumbleton carriages and conveyed across the remaining nine miles of country. It was a foggy afternoon, singularly warm for the 4th of December, and I had arranged to leave London by the 4:15 express. The early darkness of winter had already closed in; the lamps were lighted in the carriages; a clinging damp dimmed the windows, adhered to the door-handles, and pervaded all the atmosphere; while the gas-jets at the neighbouring book-stand diffused a luminous haze that only served to make the gloom of the terminus more visible. Having arrived some seven minutes before the starting of the train, and, by the connivance of the guard, taken sole possession of an empty compartment, I lighted my travelling-lamp, made myself particularly snug, and settled down to the undisturbed enjoyment of a book and a cigar. Great, therefore, was my disappointment when, at the last moment, a gentle-man came hurrying along the platform, glanced into my carriage, opened the locked door with a private key, and stepped in.

It struck me at the first glance that I had seen him before – a tall, spare man, thin-lipped, light-eyed, with an ungraceful stoop in the shoulders and scant grey hair worn somewhat long upon the collar. He carried a light waterproof coat, an umbrella, and a large brown japanned deed-box, which last he placed under the seat. This done, he felt carefully in his breast-pocket, as if to make certain of the safety of his purse or pocket-book, laid his umbrella in the netting overhead, spread the waterproof across his knees, and exchanged his hat for a travelling-cap of some Scotch material. By this time the train was moving out of the station and into the faint grey of the wintry twilight beyond.

I now recognised my companion. I recognised him from the moment when he removed his hat and uncovered the lofty, furrowed and somewhat narrow brow beneath. I had met him, as I distinctly remembered, some three years before, at the very house for which, in all probability, he was now bound, like myself. His name was Dwerrihouse, he was a lawyer by profession, and, if I was not greatly mistaken, was first cousin to the wife of my host. I knew also that he was a man eminently 'well-to-do', both as regarded his professional and private means. The Jelfs entertained him with that sort of observant courtesy which falls to the lot of the rich relation, the children made much of him, and the old butler, albeit somewhat surly 'to the general', treated him with deference. I thought, observing him by the vague mixture of lamplight and twilight, that Mrs Jelf's cousin looked all the worse for the three years' wear and tear which had gone over his head since our last meeting. He was very pale, and had a restless light in his eye that I did not remember to have observed before. The anxious lines, too, about his mouth were deepened, and there was a cavernous, hollow look about his cheeks and temples which seemed to speak of sickness or sorrow. He had glanced at me as he came in, but without any gleam of recognition in his face. Now he glanced again, as I fancied, somewhat doubtfully. When he did so for the third or fourth time I ventured to address him.

'Mr John Dwerrihouse, I think?'

'That is my name,' he replied.

'I had the pleasure of meeting you at Dumbleton about three years ago.'

Mr Dwerrihouse bowed. 'I thought I knew your face,' he said; 'but your name, I regret to say – '

'Langford – William Langford. I have known Jonathan Jelf since we were boys together at Merchant Taylors', and I generally spend a few weeks at Dumbleton in the shooting season. I suppose we are bound for the same destination?'

'Not if you are on your way to the manor,' he replied. 'I am travelling upon business – rather troublesome business too – while you, doubtless, have only pleasure in view.'

'Just so. I am in the habit of looking forward to this visit as to the brightest three weeks in all the year.'

'It is a pleasant house,' said Mr Dwerrihouse.

'The pleasantest I know.'

'And Jelf is thoroughly hospitable.'

'The best and kindest fellow in the world!'

'They have invited me to spend Christmas week with them,' pursued Mr Dwerrihouse, after a moment's pause.

'And you are coming?'

'I cannot tell. It must depend on the issue of this business which I have in hand. You have heard perhaps that we are about to construct a branch line from Blackwater to Stockbridge.'

I explained that I had been for some months away from England, and had therefore heard nothing of the contemplated improvement. Mr Dwerrihouse smiled complacently.

'It *will* be an improvement,' he said, 'a great improvement. Stockbridge is a flourishing town, and needs but a more direct railway communication with the metropolis to become an important centre of commerce. This branch was my own idea. I brought the project before the board, and have myself superintended the execution of it up to the present time.'

'You are an East Anglian director, I presume?'

'My interest in the company,' replied Mr Dwerrihouse, 'is threefold. I am a director, I am a considerable shareholder, and, as head of the firm of Dwerrihouse, Dwerrihouse & Craik, I am the company's principal solicitor.'

Loquacious, self-important, full of his pet project, and apparently unable to talk on any other subject, Mr Dwerrihouse then went on to tell of the opposition he had encountered and the obstacles he had overcome in the cause of the Stockbridge branch. I was entertained with a multitude of local details and local grievances. The rapacity of one squire, the impracticability of another, the indignation of the rector whose glebe was threatened, the culpable indifference of the Stockbridge townspeople, who could *not* be brought to see that their most vital interests hinged upon a junction with the Great East Anglian line; the spite of the local newspaper, and the unheard-of difficulties attending the Common question, were each and all laid before me with a circumstantiality that possessed the deepest interest for my excellent fellow-traveller, but none whatever for myself. From these, to my despair, he went on to more intricate matters: to the approximate expenses of construction per mile; to the estimates sent in by different contractors; to the probable traffic returns of the new line; to the provisional clauses of the new act as enumerated in Schedule D of the company's last half-yearly report; and so on and on and on, till my head ached and my attention flagged and my eyes kept closing in spite of every effort that I made to keep them open. At length I was roused by these words: 'Seventy-five thousand pounds, cash down.'

'Seventy-five thousand pounds, cash down,' I repeated, in the liveliest tone I could assume. 'That is a heavy sum.'

'A heavy sum to carry here,' replied Mr Dwerrihouse, pointing significantly to his breastpocket, 'but a mere fraction of what we shall ultimately have to pay.'

'You do not mean to say that you have seventy-five thousand pounds at this moment upon your person?' I exclaimed.

'My good sir, have I not been telling you so for the last half-hour?' said Mr Dwerrihouse, testily. 'That money has to be paid over at half-past eight o'clock this evening, at the office of Sir Thomas's solicitors, on completion of the deed of sale.'

'But how will you get across by night from Blackwater to Stockbridge with seventy-five thousand pounds in your pocket?'

'To Stockbridge!' echoed the lawyer. 'I find I have made myself very imperfectly understood. I thought I had explained how this sum only carries us as far as Mallingford – the first stage, as it were, of our journey – and how our route from Blackwater to Mallingford lies entirely through Sir Thomas Liddell's property.'

'I beg your pardon,' I stammered. 'I fear my thoughts were wandering. So you only go as far as Mallingford tonight?'

'Precisely. I shall get a conveyance from the Blackwater Arms. And you?'

'Oh, Jelf sends a trap to meet me at Clayborough! Can I be the bearer of any message from you?'

'You may say, if you please, Mr Langford, that I wished I could have been your companion all the way, and that I will come over, if possible, before Christmas.'

'Nothing more?'

Mr Dwerrihouse smiled grimly. 'Well,' he said, 'you may tell my cousin that she need not burn the hall down in my honour this time, and that I shall be obliged if she will order the blue-room chimney to be swept before I arrive.'

'That sounds tragic. Had you a conflagration on the occasion of your last visit to Dumbleton?'

'Something like it. There had been no fire lighted in my bedroom since the spring, the flue was foul, and the rooks had built in it; so when I went up to dress for dinner I found the room full of smoke and the chimney on fire. Are we already at Blackwater?'

The train had gradually come to a pause while Mr Dwerrihouse was speaking, and, on putting my head out of the window, I could see the station some few hundred yards ahead. There was another train before us blocking the way, and the guard was making use of the delay to collect the Blackwater tickets. I had scarcely ascertained our position when the ruddy-faced official appeared at our carriage door.

'Tickets, sir!' said he.

'I am for Clayborough,' I replied, holding out the tiny pink card.

He took it, glanced at it by the light of his little lantern, gave it back, looked, as I fancied, somewhat sharply at my fellow-traveller, and disappeared.

'He did not ask for yours,' I said, with some surprise.

'They never do,' replied Mr Dwerrihouse; 'they all know me, and of course I travel free.'

'Blackwater! Blackwater!' cried the porter, running along the platform beside us as we glided into the station.

Mr Dwerrihouse pulled out his deed-box, put his travelling-cap in his pocket, resumed his hat, took down his umbrella, and prepared to be gone.

'Many thanks, Mr Langford, for your society,' he said, with old-fashioned courtesy. 'I wish you a good-evening.'

'Good-evening,' I replied, putting out my hand.

But he either did not see it or did not choose to see it, and, slightly lifting his hat, stepped out upon the platform. Having done this, he moved slowly away and mingled with the departing crowd.

Leaning forward to watch him out of sight, I trod upon something which proved to be a cigar-case. It had fallen, no doubt, from the pocket of his waterproof coat, and was made of dark morocco leather, with a silver monogram upon the side. I sprang out of the carriage just as the guard came up to lock me in.

'Is there one minute to spare?' I asked, eagerly. 'The gentleman who travelled down with me from town has dropped his cigar-case; he is not yet out of the station.'

'Just a minute and a half, sir,' replied the guard. 'You must be quick.'

I dashed along the platform as fast as my feet could carry me. It was a large station, and Mr Dwerrihouse had by this time got more than halfway to the farther end.

I, however, saw him distinctly, moving slowly with the stream. Then, as I drew nearer, I saw that he had met some friend, that they were talking as they walked, that they presently fell back somewhat from the crowd and stood aside in earnest conversation. I made straight for the spot where they were waiting. There was a vivid gas-jet just above their heads, and the light fell full upon their faces. I saw both distinctly – the face of Mr Dwerrihouse and the face of his companion. Running, breathless, eager as I was, getting in the way of porters and passengers, and fearful every instant lest I should see the train going on without me, I yet observed that the newcomer was considerably younger and shorter than the director, that he was sandy-haired, mustachioed, small-featured, and dressed in a close-cut suit of Scotch tweed. I was now within a few yards of them. I ran against a stout gentleman, I was nearly knocked down by a luggage-truck, I stumbled over a carpet-bag; I gained the spot just as the driver's whistle warned me to return.

To my utter stupefaction, they were no longer there. I had seen them but two seconds before – and they were gone! I stood still; I looked to right and left; I saw no sign of them in any direction. It was as if the platform had gaped and swallowed them.

'There were two gentlemen standing here a moment ago,' I said to a porter at my elbow; 'which way can they have gone?'

'I saw no gentlemen, sir,' replied the man. The whistle shrilled out again. The guard, far up the platform, held up his arm, and shouted to me to 'come on!'

'If you're going on by this train, sir,' said the porter, 'you must run for it.'

I did run for it, just gained the carriage as the train began to move, was shoved in by the guard, and left, breathless and bewildered, with Mr Dwerri-house's cigar-case still in my hand.

It was the strangest disappearance in the world; it was like a trans-formation trick in a pantomime. They were there one moment – palpably there, with the gaslight full upon their faces – and the next moment they were gone. There was no door near, no window, no staircase; it was a mere slip of barren platform, tapestried with big advertisements. Could anything be more mysterious?

It was not worth thinking about, and yet, for my life, I could not help pondering upon it – pondering, wondering, conjecturing, turning it over and over in my mind, and beating my brains for a solution of the enigma. I thought of it all the way from Blackwater to Clayborough. I thought of it all the way from Clayborough to Dumbleton, as I rattled along the smooth highway in a trim dog-cart, drawn by a splendid black mare and driven by the silentest and dapperest of East Anglian grooms.

We did the nine miles in something less than an hour, and pulled up before the lodge-gates just as the church clock was striking half-past seven. A couple of minutes more, and the warm glow of the lighted hall was flooding out upon the gravel, a hearty grasp was on my hand, and a clear jovial voice was bidding me 'welcome to Dumbleton'.

'And now, my dear fellow,' said my host, when the first greeting was over, 'you have no time to spare. We dine at eight, and there are people coming to meet you, so you must just get the dressing business over as quickly as may be. By the way, you will meet some acquaintances: the Biddulphs are coming, and Prendergast (Prendergast of the Skirmishers) is staying in the house. Adieu! Mrs Jelf will be expecting you in the drawing-room.'

I was ushered to my room – not the blue room, of which Mr Dwerrihouse had made disagreeable experience, but a pretty little bachelor's chamber, hung with a delicate chintz and made cheerful by a blazing fire. I unlocked my portmanteau. I tried to be expeditious, but the memory of my railway adventure haunted me. I could not get free of it; I could not shake it off. It impeded me, worried me, it tripped me up, it caused me to mislay my studs, to mistie my cravat, to wrench the buttons off my gloves. Worst of all, it made me so late that the party had all assembled before I reached the drawing-room. I had scarcely paid my respects to Mrs Jelf when dinner was announced, and we paired off, some eight or ten couples strong, into the dining-room.

I am not going to describe either the guests or the dinner. All provincial parties bear the strictest family resemblance, and I am not aware that an East Anglian banquet offers any exception to the rule. There was the usual country baronet and his wife; there were the usual country parsons and their wives; there was the sempiternal turkey and haunch of venison. *Vanitas vanitatum.* There is nothing new under the sun.

I was placed about midway down the table. I had taken one rector's wife down to dinner, and I had another at my left hand. They talked across me, and their talk was about babies; it was dreadfully dull. At length there came a pause. The entrées had just been removed, and the turkey had come upon the scene. The conversation had all along been of the languidest, but at this moment it happened to have stagnated altogether. Jelf was carving the turkey; Mrs Jelf looked as if she was trying to think of something to say; everybody else was silent. Moved by an unlucky impulse, I thought I would relate my adventure.

'By the way, Jelf,' I began, 'I came down part of the way today with a friend of yours.'

'Indeed!' said the master of the feast, slicing scientifically into the breast of the turkey. 'With whom, pray?'

'With one who bade me tell you that he should, if possible, pay you a visit before Christmas.'

'I cannot think who that could be,' said my friend, smiling.

'It must be Major Thorp,' suggested Mrs Jelf.

I shook my head. 'It was not Major Thorp,' I replied; 'it was a near relation of your own, Mrs Jelf.'

'Then I am more puzzled than ever,' replied my hostess. 'Pray tell me who it was.'

'It was no less a person than your cousin, Mr John Dwerrihouse.'

Jonathan Jelf laid down his knife and fork. Mrs Jelf looked at me in a strange, startled way, and said never a word.

'And he desired me to tell you, my dear madam, that you need not take the trouble to burn the hall down in his honour this time, but only to have the chimney of the blue room swept before his arrival.'

Before I had reached the end of my sentence I became aware of something ominous in the faces of the guests. I felt I had said something which I had better have left unsaid, and that for some unexplained reason my words had evoked a general consternation. I sat confounded, not daring to utter another syllable, and for at least two whole minutes there was dead silence round the table. Then Captain Prendergast came to the rescue.

'You have been abroad for some months, have you not, Mr Langford?' he said, with the desperation of one who flings himself into the breach.

'I heard you had been to Russia. Surely you have something to tell us of the state and temper of the country after the war?'

I was heartily grateful to the gallant Skirmisher for this diversion in my favour. I answered him, I fear, somewhat lamely; but he kept the conversation up, and presently one or two others joined in and so the difficulty, whatever it might have been, was bridged over – bridged over, but not repaired. A something, an awkwardness, a visible constraint remained. The guests hitherto had been simply dull, but now they were evidently uncomfortable and embarrassed.

The dessert had scarcely been placed upon the table when the ladies left the room. I seized the opportunity to select a vacant chair next Captain Prendergast.

'In heaven's name,' I whispered, 'what was the matter just now? What had I said?'

'You mentioned the name of John Dwerrihouse.'

'What of that? I had seen him not two hours before.'

'It is a most astounding circumstance that you should have seen him,' said Captain Prendergast. 'Are you sure it was he?'

'As sure as of my own identity. We were talking all the way between London and Blackwater. But why does that surprise you?'

'*Because*,' replied Captain Prendergast, dropping his voice to the lowest whisper – '*because John Dwerrihouse absconded three months ago with seventy-five thousand pounds of the company's money, and has never been heard of since.*'

John Dwerrihouse had absconded three months ago – and I had seen him only a few hours back! John Dwerrihouse had embezzled seventy-five thousand pounds of the company's money, yet told me that he carried that sum upon his person! Were ever facts so strangely incongruous, so difficult to reconcile? How should he have ventured again into the light of day? How dared he show himself along the line? Above all, what had he been doing throughout those mysterious three months of disappearance?

Perplexing questions these – questions which at once suggested themselves to the minds of all concerned, but which admitted of no easy solution. I could find no reply to them. Captain Prendergast had not even a suggestion to offer. Jonathan Jelf, who seized the first opportunity of drawing me aside and learning all that I had to tell, was more amazed and bewildered than either of us. He came to my room that night, when all the guests were gone, and we talked the thing over from every point of view; without, it must be confessed, arriving at any kind of conclusion.

'I do not ask you,' he said, 'whether you can have mistaken your man. That is impossible.'

'As impossible as that I should mistake some stranger for yourself.'

'It is not a question of looks or voice, but of facts. That he should have alluded to the fire in the blue room is proof enough of John Dwerrihouse's identity. How did he look?'

'Older, I thought; considerably older, paler, and more anxious.'

'He has had enough to make him look anxious, anyhow,' said my friend, gloomily, 'be he innocent or guilty.'

'I am inclined to believe that he is innocent,' I replied. 'He showed no embarrassment when I addressed him, and no uneasiness when the guard came round. His conversation was open to a fault. I might almost say that he talked too freely of the business which he had in hand.'

'That is strange, for I know no one more reticent on such subjects. He actually told you that he had the seventy-five thousand pounds in his pocket?'

'He did.'

'Humph! My wife has an idea about it, and she may be right – '

'What idea?'

'Well, she fancies – women are so clever, you know, at putting themselves inside people's motives – she fancies that he was tempted, that he did actually take the money, and that he has been concealing himself these three months in some wild part of the country, struggling possibly with his conscience all the time, and daring neither to abscond with his booty nor to come back and restore it.'

'But now that he has come back?'

'That is the point. She conceives that he has probably thrown himself upon the company's mercy, made restitution of the money, and, being forgiven, is permitted to carry the business through as if nothing whatever had happened.'

'The last,' I replied, 'is an impossible case. Mrs Jelf thinks like a generous and delicate-minded woman, but not in the least like a board of railway directors. They would never carry forgiveness so far.'

'I fear not; and yet it is the only conjecture that bears a semblance of likelihood. However we can run over to Clayborough tomorrow and see if anything is to be learned. By the way Prendergast tells me you picked up his cigar-case.'

'I did so, and here it is.'

Jelf took the cigar-case, examined it by the light of the lamp, and said at once that it was beyond doubt Mr Dwerrihouse's property, and that he remembered to have seen him use it.

'Here, too, is his monogram on the side,' he added – 'a big J transfixing a capital D. He used to carry the same on his note-paper.'

'It offers, at all events, a proof that I was not dreaming.'

'Ay, but it is time you were asleep and dreaming now. I am ashamed to have kept you up so long. Good-night.'

'Good-night, and remember that I am more than ready to go with you to Clayborough or Blackwater or London or anywhere, if I can be of the least service.'

'Thanks! I know you mean it, old friend, and it may be that I shall put you to the test. Once more, good-night.'

So we parted for that night, and met again in the breakfast-room at half-past eight next morning. It was a hurried, silent, uncomfortable meal; none of us had slept well, and all were thinking of the same subject. Mrs Jelf had evidently been crying. Jelf was impatient to be off, and both Captain Prendergast and myself felt ourselves to be in the painful position of outsiders who are involuntarily brought into a domestic trouble. Within twenty minutes after we had left the breakfast-table the dog-cart was brought round and my friend and I were on the road to Clayborough.

'Tell you what it is, Langford,' he said, as we sped along between the wintry hedges, 'I do not much fancy to bring up Dwerrihouse's name at Clayborough. All the officials know that he is my wife's relation, and the subject just now is hardly a pleasant one. If you don't much mind, we will make the 11:10 to Blackwater. It's an important station, and we shall stand a far better chance of picking up information there than at Clayborough.'

So we took the 11:10, which happened to be an express, and, arriving at Blackwater about a quarter before twelve, proceeded at once to prosecute our enquiry.

We began by asking for the station-master, a big, blunt, businesslike person, who at once averred that he knew Mr John Dwerrihouse perfectly well, and that there was no director on the line whom he had seen and spoken to so frequently.

'He used to be down here two or three times a week about three months ago,' said he, 'when the new line was first set afoot; but since then, you know, gentlemen – '

He paused significantly.

Jelf flushed scarlet.

'Yes, yes,' he said, hurriedly; 'we know all about that. The point now to be ascertained is whether anything has been seen or heard of him lately.'

'Not to my knowledge,' replied the station-master.

'He is not known to have been down the line any time yesterday, for instance?'

The station-master shook his head. 'The East Anglian, sir,' said he, 'is about the last place where he would dare to show himself. Why, there isn't a station-master, there isn't a guard, there isn't a porter, who doesn't know Mr Dwerrihouse by sight as well as he knows his own face in the looking-glass, or who wouldn't telegraph for the police as soon as he had set eyes on him at any point along the line. Bless you, sir! there's been a standing order out against him ever since the 25th of September last.'

'And yet,' pursued my friend, 'a gentleman who travelled down yesterday from London to Clayborough by the afternoon express testifies that he saw Mr Dwerrihouse in the train, and that Mr Dwerrihouse alighted at Blackwater station.'

'Quite impossible, sir,' replied the station-master promptly.

'Why impossible?'

'Because there is no station along the line where he is so well known or where he would run so great a risk. It would be just running his head into the lion's mouth; he would have been mad to come nigh Blackwater station; and if he had come he would have been arrested before he left the platform.'

'Can you tell me who took the Blackwater tickets of that train?'

'I can, sir. It was the guard, Benjamin Somers.'

'And where can I find him?'

'You can find him, sir, by staying here, if you please, till one o'clock. He will be coming through with the up express from Crampton, which stays in Blackwater for ten minutes.'

We waited for the up express, beguiling the time as best we could by strolling along the Blackwater road till we came almost to the outskirts of the town, from which the station was distant nearly a couple of miles. By one o'clock we were back again upon the platform and waiting for the train. It came punctually, and I at once recognised the ruddy-faced guard who had gone down with my train the evening before.

'The gentlemen want to ask you something about Mr Dwerrihouse, Somers,' said the station-master, by way of introduction.

The guard flashed a keen glance from my face to Jelf's and back again to mine. 'Mr John Dwerrihouse, the late director?' said he, interrogatively.

'The same,' replied my friend. 'Should you know him if you saw him?'

'Anywhere, sir.'

'Do you know if he was in the 4:15 express yesterday afternoon?'

'He was not, sir.'

'How can you answer so positively?'

'Because I looked into every carriage and saw every face in that train, and I could take my oath that Mr Dwerrihouse was not in it. This gentleman was,' he added, turning sharply upon me. 'I don't know that I ever saw him before in my life, but I remember *his* face perfectly. You nearly missed taking your seat in time at this station, sir, and you got out at Clayborough.'

'Quite true, guard,' I replied; 'but do you not remember the face of the gentleman who travelled down in the same carriage with me as far as here?'

'It was my impression, sir, that you travelled down alone,' said Somers, with a look of some surprise.

'By no means. I had a fellow-traveller as far as Blackwater, and it was in trying to restore him the cigar-case which he had dropped in the carriage that I so nearly let you go on without me.'

'I remember your saying something about a cigar-case, certainly,' replied the guard; 'but – '

'You asked for my ticket just before we entered the station.'

'I did, sir.'

'Then you must have seen him. He sat in the corner next the very door to which you came.'

'No, indeed; I saw no one.'

I looked at Jelf. I began to think the guard was in the ex-director's confidence, and paid for his silence.

'If I had seen another traveller I should have asked for his ticket,' added Somers. 'Did you see me ask for his ticket, sir?'

'I observed that you did not ask for it, but he explained that by saying – ' I hesitated. I feared I might be telling too much, and so broke off abruptly.

The guard and the station-master exchanged glances. The former looked impatiently at his watch.

'I am obliged to go on in four minutes more, sir,' he said.

'One last question, then,' interposed Jelf, with a sort of desperation. 'If this gentleman's fellow traveller had been Mr John Dwerrihouse, and he had been sitting in the corner next the door in which you took the tickets, could you have failed to see and recognise him?'

'No, sir; it would have been quite impossible!'

'And you are certain you did *not* see him?'

'As I said before, sir, I could take my oath, I did not see him. And if it wasn't that I don't like to contradict a gentleman, I would say I could also take my oath that this gentlemen was quite alone in the carriage the whole way from London to Clayborough. Why, sir,' he added dropping his voice so as to be inaudible to the station-master, who had been called away to speak to some person close by, 'you expressly asked me to give you a compartment to yourself, and I did so. I locked you in, and you were so good as to give me something for myself.'

'Yes; but Mr Dwerrihouse had a key of his own.'

'I never saw him, sir; I saw no one in that compartment but yourself. Beg pardon, sir; my time's up.'

And with this the ruddy guard touched his cap and was gone. In another minute the heavy panting of the engine began afresh, and the train glided slowly out of the station.

We looked at each other for some moments in silence. I was the first to speak. 'Mr Benjamin Somers knows more than he chooses to tell,' I said.

'Humph! do you think so?'

'It must be. He could not have come to the door without seeing him; it's impossible.'

'There is one thing not impossible, my dear fellow.'

'What is that?'

'That you may have fallen asleep and dreamed the whole thing.'

'Could I dream of a branch line that I had never heard of? Could I dream of a hundred and one business details that had no kind of interest for me? Could I dream of the seventy-five thousand pounds?'

'Perhaps you might have seen or heard some vague account of the affair while you were abroad. It might have made no impression upon you at the time, and might have come back to you in your dreams, recalled perhaps by the mere names of the stations on the line.'

'What about the fire in the chimney of the blue room – should I have heard of that during my journey?'

'Well, no; I admit there is a difficulty about that point.'

'And what about the cigar-case?'

'Ay, by Jove! there is the cigar-case. That *is* a stubborn fact. Well, it's a mysterious affair, and it will need a better detective than myself, I fancy, to clear it up. I suppose we may as well go home.'

*　　*　　*

A week had not gone by when I received a letter from the secretary of the East Anglian Railway Company, requesting the favour of my attendance at a special board meeting not then many days distant. No reasons were alleged and no apologies offered for this demand upon my time, but they had heard, it was clear, of my enquiries anent the missing director, and had a mind to put me through some sort of official examination upon the subject. Being still a guest at Dumbleton Hall, I had to go up to London for the purpose and Jonathan Jelf accompanied me. I found the direction of the Great East Anglian line represented by a party of some twelve or fourteen gentlemen seated in solemn conclave round a huge green-baize table, in a gloomy boardroom adjoining the London terminus.

Being courteously received by the chairman (who at once began by saying that certain statements of mine respecting Mr John Dwerrihouse had come to the knowledge of the direction, and that they in consequence desired to confer with me on those points), we were placed at the table and the inquiry proceeded in due form.

I was first asked if I knew Mr John Dwerrihouse, how long I had been acquainted with him, and whether I could identify him at sight. I was then asked when I had seen him last. To which I replied, 'On the 4th of this present month, December, 1856.' Then came the enquiry of where I had seen him on that fourth day of December; to which I replied that I met him in a first-class compartment of the 4:15 down express, that he got in just as the train was leaving the London terminus, and that he alighted at Black-water station. The chairman then enquired whether I had held any communication with my fellow-traveller; whereupon I related, as nearly as I could remember it, the whole bulk and substance of Mr John Dwerrihouse's diffuse information respecting the new branch line.

To all this the board listened with profound attention, while the chairman presided and the secretary took notes. I then produced the cigar-case. It was passed from hand to hand, and recognised by all. There was not a man

present who did not remember that plain cigar-case with its silver monogram, or to whom it seemed anything less than entirely corroborative of my
evidence. When at length I had told all that I had to tell, the chairman
whispered something to the secretary; the secretary touched a silver handbell, and the guard, Benjamin Somers, was ushered into the room. He was
then examined as carefully as myself. He declared that he knew Mr John
Dwerrihouse perfectly well, that he could not be mistaken in him, that he
remembered going down with the 4:15 express on the afternoon in question,
that he remembered me, and that, there being one or two empty first-class
compartments on that especial afternoon, he had, in compliance with my
request, placed me in a carriage by myself. He was positive that I remained
alone in that compartment all the way from London to Clayborough. He
was ready to take his oath that Dwerrihouse was neither in that carriage with
me nor in any other compartment of that train. He remembered distinctly to
have examined my ticket to Blackwater; was certain that there was no one
else at that time in the carriage; could not have failed to observe a second
person, if there had been one; had that second person been Mr John
Dwerrihouse, should have quietly double-locked the door of the carriage
and have at once given information to the Blackwater station-master. So
clear, so decisive, so ready, was Somers with this testimony, that the board
looked fairly puzzled.

'You hear this person's statement, Mr Langford,' said the chairman. 'It
contradicts yours in every particular. What have you to say in reply?'

'I can only repeat what I said before. I am quite as positive of the truth of
my own assertions as Mr Somers can be of the truth of his.'

'You say that Mr Dwerrihouse alighted in Blackwater, and that he was in
possession of a private key. Are you sure that he had not alighted by means
of that key before the guard came round for the tickets?'

'I am quite positive that he did not leave the carriage till the train had
fairly entered the station, and the other Blackwater passengers alighted. I
even saw that he was met there by a friend.'

'Indeed! Did you see that person distinctly?'

'Quite distinctly.'

'Can you describe his appearance?'

'I think so. He was short and very slight, sandy-haired, with a bushy
moustache and beard, and he wore a closely fitting suit of grey tweed. His
age I should take to be about thirty-eight or forty.'

'Did Mr Dwerrihouse leave the station in this person's company?'

'I cannot tell. I saw them walking together down the platform, and then I
saw them standing inside under a gas-jet, talking earnestly. After that I lost
sight of them quite suddenly, and just then my train went on, and I with it.'

The chairman and secretary conferred together in an undertone. The
directors whispered to one another. One or two looked suspiciously at the

guard. I could see that my evidence remained unshaken, and that, like myself, they suspected some complicity between the guard and the defaulter.

'How far did you conduct that 4:15 express on the day in question, Somers?' asked the chairman.

'All through, sir,' replied the guard, 'from London to Crampton.'

'How was it that you were not relieved at Clayborough? I thought there was always a change of guards at Clayborough.'

'There used to be, sir, till the new regulations came in force last midsummer, since when the guards in charge of express trains go the whole way through.'

The chairman turned to the secretary.

'I think it would be as well,' he said, 'if we had the day-book to refer to upon this point.'

Again the secretary touched the silver handbell, and desired the porter in attendance to summon Mr Raikes. From a word or two dropped by another of the directors I gathered that Mr Raikes was one of the under-secretaries.

He came, a small, slight, sandy-haired, keen-eyed man, with an eager, nervous manner, and a forest of light beard and moustache. He just showed himself at the door of the boardroom, and, being requested to bring a certain day-book from a certain shelf in a certain room, bowed and vanished.

He was there such a moment, and the surprise of seeing him was so great and sudden, that it was not till the door had closed upon him that I found voice to speak. He was no sooner gone, however, than I sprang to my feet.

'That person,' I said, 'is the same who met Mr Dwerrihouse upon the platform at Blackwater!'

There was a general movement of surprise. The chairman looked grave and somewhat agitated.

'Take care, Mr Langford,' he said; 'take care what you say.'

'I am as positive of his identity as of my own.'

'Do you consider the consequences of your words? Do you consider that you are bringing a charge of the gravest character against one of the company's servants?'

'I am willing to be put upon my oath, if necessary. The man who came to that door a minute since is the same whom I saw talking with Mr Dwerrihouse on the Blackwater platform. Were he twenty times the company's servant, I could say neither more nor less.'

The chairman turned again to the guard.

'Did you see Mr Raikes in the train or on the platform?' he asked.

Somers shook his head. 'I am confident Mr Raikes was not in the train,' he said, 'and I certainly did not see him on the platform.'

The chairman turned next to the secretary.

'Mr Raikes is in your office, Mr Hunter,' he said. 'Can you remember if he was absent on the 4th instant?'

'I do not think he was,' replied the secretary, 'but I am not prepared to speak positively. I have been away most afternoons myself lately, and Mr Raikes might easily have absented himself if he had been disposed.'

At this moment the under-secretary returned with the day-book under his arm.

'Be pleased to refer, Mr Raikes,' said the chairman, 'to the entries of the 4th instant, and see what Benjamin Somers's duties were on that day.'

Mr Raikes threw open the cumbrous volume, and ran a practised eye and finger down some three or four successive columns of entries. Stopping suddenly at the foot of a page, he then read aloud that Benjamin Somers had on that day conducted the 4:15 express from London to Crampton.

The chairman leaned forward in his seat, looked the under-secretary full in the face, and said, quite sharply and suddenly: 'Where were you, Mr Raikes, on the same afternoon?'

'*I*, sir?'

'You, Mr Raikes. Where were you on the afternoon and evening of the 4th of the present month?'

'Here, sir, in Mr Hunter's office. Where else should I be?'

There was a dash of trepidation in the under-secretary's voice as he said this, but his look of surprise was natural enough.

'We have some reason for believing, Mr Raikes, that you were absent that afternoon without leave. Was this the case?'

'Certainly not, sir. I have not had a day's holiday since September. Mr Hunter will bear me out in this.'

Mr Hunter repeated what he had previously said on the subject, but added that the clerks in the adjoining office would be certain to know. Whereupon the senior clerk, a grave, middle-aged person in green glasses, was summoned and interrogated.

His testimony cleared the under-secretary at once. He declared that Mr Raikes had in no instance, to his knowledge, been absent during office hours since his return from his annual holiday in September.

I was confounded. The chairman turned to me with a smile, in which a shade of covert annoyance was scarcely apparent.

'You hear, Mr Langford?' he said.

'I hear, sir; but my conviction remains unshaken.'

'I fear, Mr Langford, that your convictions are very insufficiently based,' replied the chairman, with a doubtful cough. 'I fear that you "dream dreams", and mistake them for actual occurrences. It is a dangerous habit of mind, and might lead to dangerous results. Mr Raikes here would have found himself in an unpleasant position had he not proved so satisfactory an alibi.'

I was about to reply, but he gave me no time.

'I think, gentlemen,' he went on to say, addressing the board, 'that we should be wasting time to push this inquiry further. Mr Langford's evidence would seem to be of an equal value throughout. The testimony of Benjamin Somers disproves his first statement, and the testimony of the last witness disproves his second. I think we may conclude that Mr Langford fell asleep in the train on the occasion of his journey to Clayborough, and dreamed an unusually vivid and circumstantial dream, of which, however, we have now heard quite enough.'

There are few things more annoying than to find one's positive convictions met with incredulity. I could not help feeling impatience at the turn that affairs had taken. I was not proof against the civil sarcasm of the chairman's manner. Most intolerable of all, however, was the quiet smile lurking about the corners of Benjamin Somers's mouth, and the half-triumphant, half-malicious gleam in the eyes of the under-secretary. The man was evidently puzzled and somewhat alarmed. His looks seemed furtively to interrogate me. Who was I? What did I want? Why had I come there to do him an ill turn with his employers? What was it to me whether or no he was absent without leave?

Seeing all this, and perhaps more irritated by it than the thing deserved, I begged leave to detain the attention of the board for a moment longer. Jelf plucked me impatiently by the sleeve.

'Better let the thing drop,' he whispered. 'The chairman's right enough; you dreamed it, and the less said now the better.'

I was not to be silenced, however, in this fashion. I had yet something to say, and I would say it. It was to this effect: that dreams were not usually productive of tangible results, and that I requested to know in what way the chairman conceived I had evolved from my dream so substantial and well-made a delusion as the cigar-case which I had had the honour to place before him at the commencement of our interview.

'The cigar-case, I admit, Mr Langford,' the chairman replied, 'is a very strong point in your evidence. It is your *only* strong point, however, and there is just a possibility that we may all be misled by a mere accidental resemblance. Will you permit me to see the case again?'

'It is unlikely,' I said, as I handed it to him, 'that any other should bear precisely this monogram, and also be in all other particulars exactly similar.'

The chairman examined it for a moment in silence, and then passed it to Mr Hunter. Mr Hunter turned it over and over, and shook his head.

'This is no mere resemblance,' he said. 'It is John Dwerrihouse's cigar-case to a certainty. I remember it perfectly; I have seen it a hundred times.'

'I believe I may say the same,' added the chairman; 'yet how account for the way in which Mr Langford asserts that it came into his possession?'

'I can only repeat,' I replied, 'that I found it on the floor of the carriage after Mr Dwerrihouse had alighted. It was in leaning out to look after him that I trod upon it, and it was in running after him for the purpose of restoring it that I saw, or believed I saw, Mr Raikes standing aside with him in earnest conversation.'

Again I felt Jonathan Jelf plucking at my sleeve.

'Look at Raikes,' he whispered; 'look at Raikes!'

I turned to where the under-secretary had been standing a moment before, and saw him, white as death, with lips trembling and livid, stealing toward the door.

To conceive a sudden, strange, and indefinite suspicion, to fling myself in his way, to take him by the shoulders as if he were a child, and turn his craven face, perforce, towards the board, were with me the work of an instant.

'Look at him!' I exclaimed. 'Look at his face! I ask no better witness to the truth of my words.'

The chairman's brow darkened.

'Mr Raikes,' he said, sternly, 'if you know anything you had better speak.'

Vainly trying to wrench himself from my grasp, the under-secretary stammered out an incoherent denial.

'Let me go,' he said. 'I know nothing – you have no right to detain me – let me go!'

'Did you, or did you not, meet Mr John Dwerrihouse at Blackwater station? The charge brought against you is either true or false. If true, you will do well to throw yourself upon the mercy of the board and make full confession of all that you know.'

The under-secretary wrung his hands in an agony of helpless terror.

'I was away!' he cried. 'I was two hundred miles away at the time! I know nothing about it – I have nothing to confess – I am innocent – I call God to witness I am innocent!'

'Two hundred miles away!' echoed the chairman. 'What do you mean?'

'I was in Devonshire. I had three weeks' leave of absence – I appeal to Mr Hunter – Mr Hunter knows I had three weeks' leave of absence! I was in Devonshire all the time; I can prove I was in Devonshire!'

Seeing him so abject, so incoherent, so wild with apprehension, the directors began to whisper gravely among themselves, while one got quietly up and called the porter to guard the door.

'What has your being in Devonshire to do with the matter?' said the chairman. 'When were you in Devonshire?'

'Mr Raikes took his leave in September,' said the secretary, 'about the time when Mr Dwerrihouse disappeared.'

'I never even heard that he had disappeared till I came back!'

'That must remain to be proved,' said the chairman. 'I shall at once put this matter in the hands of the police. In the meanwhile, Mr Raikes, being myself a magistrate and used to dealing with these cases, I advise you to offer no resistance but to confess while confession may yet do you service. As for your accomplice –'

The frightened wretch fell upon his knees.

'I had no accomplice!' he cried. 'Only have mercy upon me – only spare my life, and I will confess all! I didn't mean to harm him! I didn't mean to hurt a hair of his head! Only have mercy upon me, and let me go!'

The chairman rose in his place, pale and agitated.

'Good heavens!' he exclaimed, 'what horrible mystery is this? What does it mean?'

'As sure as there is a God in heaven,' said Jonathan Jelf, 'it means that murder has been done.'

'No! no! no!' shrieked Raikes, still upon his knees, and cowering like a beaten hound, 'not murder! No jury that ever sat could bring it in murder. I thought I had only stunned him – I never meant to do more than stun him! Manslaughter – manslaughter – not murder!'

Overcome by the horror of this unexpected revelation, the chairman covered his face with his hand and for a moment or two remained silent.

'Miserable man,' he said at length, 'you have betrayed yourself.'

'You bade me confess! You urged me to throw myself upon the mercy of the board!'

'You have confessed to a crime which no one suspected you of having committed,' replied the chairman, 'and which this board has no power either to punish or forgive. All that I can do for you is to advise you to submit to the law, to plead guilty, and to conceal nothing. When did you do this deed?'

The guilty man rose to his feet, and leaned heavily against the table. His answer came reluctantly, like the speech of one dreaming.

'On the 22d of September!'

On the 22d of September! I looked in Jonathan Jelf's face, and he in mine. I felt my own smiling with a strange sense of wonder and dread. I saw his blanch suddenly, even to the lips.

'Merciful Heaven!' he whispered. *'What was it, then, that you saw in the train?'*

What was it that I saw in the train? That question remains unanswered to this day. I have never been able to reply to it. I only know that it bore the living likeness of the murdered man, whose body had then been lying some ten weeks under a rough pile of branches and brambles and rotting leaves, at the bottom of a deserted chalk-pit about halfway between Blackwater and Mallingford. I know that it spoke and moved and looked as that man spoke and moved and looked in life; that I heard, or seemed to hear, things revealed which I could never otherwise have learned; that I was guided, as it were, by that vision on the platform to the identification of the murderer; and that, a passive instrument myself, I was destined, by means of these mysterious teachings to bring about the ends of justice. For these things I have never been able to account.

As for that matter of the cigar-case, it proved, on enquiry, that the carriage in which I travelled down that afternoon to Clayborough had not been in use for several weeks, and was, in point of fact, the same in which poor John Dwerrihouse had performed his last journey. The case had doubtless been dropped by him, and had lain unnoticed till I found it.

Upon the details of the murder I have no need to dwell. Those who desire more ample particulars may find them, and the written confession of Augustus Raikes, in the files of *The Times* for 1856. Enough that the under-secretary, knowing the history of the new line, and following the negotiation step by step through all its stages, determined to waylay Mr Dwerrihouse, rob him of the seventy-five thousand pounds, and escape to America with his booty.

In order to effect these ends he obtained leave of absence a few days before the time appointed for the payment of the money, secured his passage across the Atlantic in a steamer advertised to start on the 23rd, provided himself with a heavily loaded 'life-preserver', and went down to Blackwater to await the arrival of his victim. How he met him on the platform with a pretended message from the board, how he offered to conduct him by a short cut across the fields to Mallingford, how, having brought him to a lonely place, he struck him down with the life-preserver, and so killed him, and how, finding what he had done, he dragged the body to the verge of an out-of-the-way chalk-pit, and there flung it in and piled it over with branches and brambles, are facts still fresh in the memories of those who, like the connoisseurs in De Quincey's famous essay, regard murder as a fine art. Strangely enough, the murderer having done his work, was afraid to leave the country. He declared that he had not intended to take the director's life, but only to stun and rob him and that, finding the blow had killed, he dared not fly for fear of drawing down suspicion upon his head. As a mere robber he would have been safe in the States, but as a murderer he would inevitably have been pursued and given up to justice. So he forfeited his passage, returned to the office as usual at the end of his leave, and locked up his ill-gotten thousands till a more convenient opportunity. In the meanwhile he had the satisfaction of finding that Mr Dwerrihouse was universally believed to have absconded with the money, no one knew how or whither.

Whether he meant murder or not, however, Mr Augustus Raikes paid the full penalty of his crime, and was hanged at the Old Bailey in the second week in January, 1857. Those who desire to make his further acquaintance may see him any day (admirably done in wax) in the Chamber of Horrors at Madame Tussaud's exhibition in Baker Street. He is there to be found in the midst of a select society of ladies and gentlemen of atrocious memory, dressed in the close-cut tweed suit which he wore on the evening of the murder, and holding in his hand the identical life-preserver with which he committed it.

GEORGE EGERTON

Mary Chavelita Dunne (George Egerton) was born in Australia in 1859. During her childhood she lived in New Zealand, Chile, Wales, Ireland and Germany. After the death of her mother in 1875, she helped raise her younger siblings, living in Dublin, London and New York. After running away to Norway with one of her father's friends, Henry Higginson, she returned to England and married George Egerton Clairmonte, whose name she took as her pseudonym. During three years in Norway (1887–90) Egerton became inspired by Henrik Ibsen, August Strindberg and Knut Hamson. Her writing career began with the 1893 publication of *Keynotes* by Elkin Matthews and John Lane. The book proved extremely popular both in Europe and North America. It exemplified for many the fiction of the 'New Woman', while Aubrey Beardsley's cover design marked it as modern and daring. *Keynotes* and the subsequent collection *Discords* (1894) were also published by Lane. The genre of the short story accommodated Egerton's approach to exploring women's psychology; in Elaine Showalter's words, Egerton set out 'to invent a new literary form for the feminine unconscious'. She married for a second time in 1901. Her later writing did not live up to her early promise and she faded from view. She died in 1945.

A Little Grey Glove

*The Book of Life begins with a man and a woman in a
garden. It ends with Revelations.*

OSCAR WILDE

Yes, most fellows' book of life may be said to begin at the chapter where
woman comes in; mine did. She came in years ago, when I was a raw
undergraduate. With the sober thought of retrospective analysis, I may say
she was not all my fancy painted her; indeed now that I come to think of it
there was no fancy about the vermeil of her cheeks, rather an artificial
reality; she had her bower in the bar of the Golden Boar, and I was madly in
love with her, seriously intent on lawful wedlock. Luckily for me she threw
me over for a neighbouring pork butcher, but at the time I took it hardly,
and it made me sex-shy. I was a very poor man in those days. One feels one's
griefs more keenly then, one hasn't the wherewithal to buy distraction.
Besides, ladies snubbed me rather, on the rare occasions I met them. Later I
fell in for a legacy, the forerunner of several; indeed, I may say I am beastly
rich. My tastes are simple too, and I haven't any poor relations. I believe they
are of great assistance in getting rid of superfluous capital – wish I had some!
It was after the legacy that women discovered my attractions. They found
that there was something superb in my plainness (before, they said ugliness),
something after the style of the late Victor Emanuel, something infinitely
more striking than mere ordinary beauty. At least so Harding told me his
sister said, and she had the reputation of being a clever girl. Being an only
child, I never had the opportunity other fellows had of studying the undress
side of women through familiar intercourse, say with sisters. Their most
ordinary belongings were sacred to me. I had, I used to be told, ridiculous
high-flown notions about them (by the way I modified those considerably
on closer acquaintance). I ought to study them, nothing like a woman for
developing a fellow. So I laid in a stock of books in different languages,
mostly novels, in which women played title roles, in order to get up some
definite data before venturing amongst them. I can't say I derived much
benefit from this course. There seemed to be as great a diversity of opinion
about the female species as, let us say, about the Salmonidae.

My friend Ponsonby Smith, who is one of the oldest fly-fishers in the
three kingdoms, said to me once: 'Take my word for it, there are only four
true *Salmo*: the *salar*, the *trutta*, the *fario*, the *ferox*; all the rest are just
varieties, subgenuses of the above; stick to that.' Some writing fellow divided

all the women into good-uns and bad-uns. But as a conscientious stickler for truth, I must say that in women as in trout, I have found myself faced with most puzzling varieties that were a tantalising blending of several qualities. I then resolved to study them on my own account. I pursued the Eternal Feminine in a spirit of purely scientific investigation. I knew you'd laugh sceptically at that, but it's a fact. I was impartial in my selection of subjects for observation – French, German, Spanish, as well as the home product. Nothing in petticoats escaped me. I devoted myself to the freshest *ingénue* as well as the experienced widow of three departed; and I may as well confess that the more I saw of her, the less I understood her. But I think they understood me. They refused to take me *au serieux*. When they weren't fleecing me, they were interested in the state of my soul (I preferred the former), but all humbugged me equally, so I gave them up. I took to rod and gun instead, *pro salute animae*; it's decidedly safer. I have scoured every country in the globe; indeed I can say that I have shot and fished in woods and waters where no other white man, perhaps, ever dropped a beast or played a fish before. There is no life like the life of a free wanderer, and no lore like the lore one gleans in the great book of nature. But one must have freed one's spirit from the taint of the town before one can even read the alphabet of its mystic meaning.

What has this to do with the glove? True, not much, and yet it has a connection – it accounts for me.

Well, for twelve years I have followed the impulses of the wandering spirit that dwells in me. I have seen the sun rise in Finland and gild the Devil's Knuckles as it sank behind the Drachensberg. I have caught the barba and the gamer yellow fish in the Vaal River, taken muskelunge and black-bass in Canada, thrown a fly over *guapote* and *cavallo* in Central American lakes, and choked the monster eels of the Mauritius with a cunningly faked-up duckling. But I have been shy as a chub at the shadow of a woman.

Well, it happened last year. I came back on business – another confounded legacy; end of June too, just as I was off to Finland. But Messrs. Thimble and Rigg, the highly respectable firm who look after my affairs, represented that I owed it to others, whom I kept out of their share of the legacy, to stay near town till affairs were wound up. They told me, with a view to reconcile me perhaps, of a trout stream with a decent inn near it; an unknown stream in Kent. It seems a junior member of the firm is an angler, at least he sometimes catches pike or perch in the Medway some way from the stream where the trout rise in audacious security from artificial lures. I stipulated for a clerk to come down with any papers to be signed, and started at once for Victoria. I decline to tell the name of my find, firstly because the trout are the gamest little fish that ever rose to fly and run to a good two pounds. Secondly, I have paid for all the rooms in the inn for the next year, and I want it to myself. The glove is lying on the table next me as I write. If it isn't in my breast-pocket or under my pillow, it is in some place where I can see it. It has a delicate grey body (suede, I think they call it) with a whipping of silver round the top, and a darker grey silk tag to fasten it. It is marked $5\frac{3}{4}$ inside, and has a delicious scent about it, to keep off moths, I suppose; naphthaline is better. It reminds me of a 'silver-sedge' tied on a ten hook. I startled the good landlady of the little inn (there is no village fortunately) when I arrived with the only porter of the tiny station laden with traps. She hesitated about a private sitting-room, but eventually we compromised matters, as I was willing to share it with the other visitor. I got into knicker-bockers at once, collared a boy to get me worms and minnow for the morrow, and as I felt too lazy to unpack tackle, just sat in the shiny armchair (made comfortable by the successive sitting of former occupants) at the open window and looked out.

The river, not the trout stream, winds to the right, and the trees cast trembling shadows into its clear depths. The red tiles of a farm roof show between the beeches, and break the monotony of blue sky background. A dusty waggoner is slaking his thirst with a tankard of ale. I am conscious of the strange lonely feeling that a visit to England always gives me. Away in strange lands, even in solitary places, one doesn't feel it somehow. One is filled with the hunter's lust, bent on a 'kill', but at home in the quiet country, with the smoke curling up from some fireside, the mowers busy laying the hay in swaths, the children tumbling under the trees in the orchards, and a girl singing as she spreads the clothes on the sweetbriar hedge, amidst a scene quick with home sights and sounds, a strange lack creeps in and makes itself felt in a dull, aching way. Oddly enough, too, I had a sense of uneasiness, a 'something going to happen'. I had often experienced it when out alone in a great forest, or on an unknown lake, and it always meant 'beware danger' of some kind. But why should I feel it here? Yet I did, and I couldn't shake it off. I took to examining the room. It was a commonplace one of the usual type. But there was a work-basket on the table, a dainty thing, lined with blue satin. There was a bit of lace stretched over shiny blue linen, with the needle sticking in it – such fairy work, like cobwebs seen from below, spun from a branch against a background of sky. A gold thimble, too, with initials, not the landlady's, I know. What pretty things, too, in the basket! A scissors, a capital shape for fly-making; a little file, and some floss silk and tinsel, the identical colour I want for a new fly I have in my head, one that will be a demon to kill. The northern devil I mean to call him. Someone looks in behind me, and a light step passes upstairs. I drop the basket, I don't know why. There are some reviews near it. I take up one, and am soon buried in an article on Tasmanian fauna. It is strange, but whenever I do know anything about a subject, I always find these writing fellows either entirely ignorant or damned wrong.

After supper, I took a stroll to see the river. It was a silver-grey evening, with just the last lemon and pink streaks of the sunset staining the sky. There had been a shower, and somehow the smell of the dust after rain mingled with the mignonette in the garden brought back vanished scenes of small-boyhood, when I caught minnows in a bottle, and dreamt of a shilling rod as happiness unattainable. I turned aside from the road in accordance with directions, and walked towards the stream. Halloa! someone before me, what a bore! The angler is hidden by an elder bush, but I can see the fly drop delicately, artistically on the water. Fishing upstream, too! There is a bit of broken water there, and the midges dance in myriads; a silver gleam, and the line spins out, and the fly falls just in the right place. It is growing dusk, but the fellow is an adept at quick, fine casting – I wonder what fly he has on – why, he's going to try downstream now! I hurry forward, and as I near him, I swerve to the left out of the way. S–s–s–s! a sudden sting in the lobe of my ear. Hey! I cry as I find I am caught; the tail fly is fast in it. A slight, grey-clad woman holding the rod lays it carefully down and comes towards me through the gathering dusk. My first impulse is to snap the gut and take to my heels, but I am held by something less tangible but far more powerful than the grip of the Limerick hook in my ear.

'I am very sorry!' she says in a voice that matched the evening, it was so quiet and soft; 'but it was exceedingly stupid of you to come behind like that.'

'I didn't think you threw such a long line; I thought I was safe,' I stammered.

'Hold this!' she says, giving me a diminutive fly-book, out of which she has taken a scissors. I obey meekly. She snips the gut. 'Have you a sharp knife? If I strip the hook you can push it through; it is lucky it isn't in the cartilage.'

I suppose I am an awful idiot, but I only handed her the knife, and she proceeded as calmly as if stripping a hook in a man's ear were an everyday occurrence. Her gown is of some soft grey stuff, and her grey leather belt is silver clasped. Her hands are soft and cool and steady, but there is a rarely disturbing thrill in their gentle touch. The thought flashed through my mind that I had just missed that, a woman's voluntary tender touch, not a paid caress, all my life.

'Now you can push it through yourself. I hope it won't hurt much.' Taking the hook, I push it through, and a drop of blood follows it. 'Oh!' she cries, but I assure her it is nothing, and stick the hook surreptitiously in my coat sleeve. Then we both laugh, and I look at her for the first time. She has a very white forehead, with little tendrils of hair blowing round it under her grey cap, her eyes are grey. I didn't see that then, I only saw they were steady, smiling eyes that matched her mouth. Such a mouth, the most maddening mouth a man ever longed to kiss, above a too-pointed chin, soft as a child's; indeed, the whole face looks soft in the misty light.

'I am sorry I spoilt your sport!' I say.

'Oh, that don't matter, it's time to stop. I got two brace, one a beauty.'

She is winding in her line, and I look in her basket; they *are* beauties, one two-pounder, the rest running from a half to a pound.

'What fly?'

'Yellow dun took that one, but your assailant was a partridge spider.' I sling her basket over my shoulder; she takes it as a matter of course, and we retrace our steps. I feel curiously happy as we walk towards the road; there is a novel delight in her nearness; the feel of woman works subtly and strangely in me; the rustle of her skirt as it brushes the black-heads in the meadow-grass, and the delicate perfume, partly violets, partly herself, that comes to me with each of her movements is a rare pleasure. I am hardly surprised when she turns into the garden of the inn, I think I knew from the first that she would.

'Better bathe that ear of yours, and put a few drops of carbolic in the water.' She takes the basket as she says it, and goes into the kitchen. I hurry over this, and go into the little sitting-room. There is a tray with a glass of milk and some oaten cakes upon the table. I am too disturbed to sit down; I stand at the window and watch the bats flitter in the gathering moonlight, and listen with quivering nerves for her step – perhaps she will send for the tray, and not come after all. What a fool I am to be disturbed by a grey-clad witch with a tantalising mouth! That comes of loafing about doing nothing. I mentally darn the old fool who saved her money instead of spending it. Why the devil should I be bothered? I don't want it anyhow. She comes in as I fume, and I forget everything at her entrance. I push the armchair towards the table, and she sinks quietly into it, pulling the tray nearer. She has a wedding ring on, but somehow it never strikes me to wonder if she is married or a widow or who she may be. I am content to watch her break her biscuits. She has the prettiest hands, and a trick of separating her last fingers when she takes hold of anything. They remind me of white orchids I saw somewhere. She led me to talk: about Africa, I think. I liked to watch her eyes glow deeply in the shadow and then catch light as she bent forward to say something in her quick responsive way.

'Long ago when I was a girl,' she said once.

'Long ago?' I echo incredulously, 'surely not?'

'Ah, but yes, you haven't seen me in the daylight,' with a soft little laugh. 'Do you know what the gypsies say? "Never judge a woman or a ribbon by candlelight." They might have said moonlight equally well.'

She rises as she speaks, and I feel an overpowering wish to have her put out her hand. But she does not, she only takes the work-basket and a book, and says good-night with an inclination of her little head.

I go over and stand next to her chair; I don't like to sit in it, but I like to put my hand where her head leant, and fancy, if she were there, how she would look up.

I woke next morning with a curious sense of pleasurable excitement. I whistled from very lightness of heart as I dressed. When I got down I found the landlady clearing away her breakfast things. I felt disappointed and resolved to be down earlier in future. I didn't feel inclined to try the minnow. I put them in a tub in the yard and tried to read and listen for her step. I dined alone. The day dragged terribly. I did not like to ask about her, I had a notion she might not like it. I spent the evening on the river. I might have filled a good basket, but I let the beggars rest. After all, I had caught fish enough to stock all the rivers in Great Britain. There are other things than trout in the world. I sit and smoke a pipe where she caught me last night. If I half close my eyes I can see hers, and her mouth, in the smoke. That is one of the curious charms of baccy, it helps to reproduce brain pictures. After a bit, I think 'perhaps she has left'. I get quite feverish at the thought and hasten back. I must ask. I look up at the window as I pass; there is surely a gleam of white. I throw down my traps and hasten up. She is leaning with her arms on the window-ledge staring out into the gloom. I could swear I caught a suppressed sob as I entered. I cough, and she turns quickly and bows slightly. A bonnet and gloves and lace affair and a lot of papers are lying on the table. I am awfully afraid she is going. I say –

'Please don't let me drive you away, it is so early yet. I half expected to see you on the river.'

'Nothing so pleasant; I have been up in town' (the tears have certainly got into her voice) 'all day; it was so hot and dusty, I am tired out.'

The little servant brings in the lamp and a tray with a bottle of lemonade.

'Mistress hasn't any lemons, 'm, will this do?'

'Yes,' she says wearily, she is shading her eyes with her hand; 'anything; I am fearfully thirsty.'

'Let me concoct you a drink instead. I have lemons and ice and things. My man sent me down supplies today; I leave him in town. I am rather a dab at drinks; I learnt it from the Yankees; about the only thing I did learn from them I care to remember. Susan!' The little maid helps me to get the materials, and *she* watches me quietly. When I give it to her she takes it with a smile (she *has* been crying). That is an ample thank you. She looks quite old. Something more than tiredness called up those lines in her face.

* * *

Well, ten days passed; sometimes we met at breakfast, sometimes at supper, sometimes we fished together or sat in the straggling orchard and talked; she neither avoided me nor sought me. She is the most charming mixture of child and woman I ever met. She is a dual creature. Now I never met that in a man. When she is here without getting a letter in the morning or going to town, she seems like a girl. She runs about in her grey gown and little cap and laughs, and seems to throw off all thought like an irresponsible child.

She is eager to fish, or pick gooseberries and eat them daintily, or sit under the trees and talk. But when she goes to town – I notice she always goes when she gets a lawyer's letter, there is no mistaking the envelope – she comes home tired and haggard-looking, an old woman of thirty-five. I wonder why. It takes her, even with her elasticity of temperament, nearly a day to get young again. I hate her to go to town; it is extraordinary how I miss her; I can't recall, when she is absent, her saying anything very wonderful, but she converses all the time. She has a gracious way of filling the place with herself, there is an entertaining quality in her very presence. We had one rainy afternoon; she tied me some flies (I shan't use any of them); I watched the lights in her hair as she moved, it is quite golden in some places, and she has a tiny mole near her left ear and another on her left wrist. On the eleventh day she got a letter but she didn't go to town, she stayed up in her room all day; twenty times I felt inclined to send her a line, but I had no excuse. I heard the landlady say as I passed the kitchen window: 'Poor dear! I'm sorry to lose her!' Lose her? I should think not. It has come to this with me that I don't care to face any future without her; and yet I know nothing about her, not even if she is a free woman. I shall find that out the next time I see her. In the evening I catch a glimpse of her gown in the orchard, and I follow her. We sit down near the river. Her left hand is lying gloveless next to me in the grass.

'Do you think from what you have seen of me that I would ask a question out of any mere impertinent curiosity?'

She starts. 'No, I do not!'

I take up her hand and touch the ring. 'Tell me, does this bind you to anyone?'

I am conscious of a buzzing in my ears and a dancing blurr of water and sky and trees, as I wait (it seems to me an hour) for her reply. I felt the same sensation once before, when I got drawn into some rapids and had an awfully narrow shave, but of that another time.

The voice is shaking.

'I am not legally bound to anyone, at least; but why do you ask?' she looks me square in the face as she speaks, with a touch of haughtiness I never saw in her before.

Perhaps the great relief I feel, the sense of joy at knowing she is free, speaks out of my face, for hers flushes and she drops her eyes, her lips tremble. I don't look at her again, but I can see her all the same. After a while she says – 'I half intended to tell you something about myself this evening, now I *must*. Let us go in. I shall come down to the sitting-room after your supper.' She takes a long look at the river and the inn, as if fixing the place in her memory; it strikes me with a chill that there is a goodbye in her gaze. Her eyes rest on me a moment as they come back, there is a sad look in their grey clearness. She swings her little grey gloves in her hand as we walk back. I can hear her walking up and down overhead; how tired she will be, and how slowly the time goes. I am standing at one side of the window when she enters; she stands at the other, leaning her head against the shutter with her hands clasped before her. I can hear my own heart beating and, I fancy, hers through the stillness. The suspense is fearful. At length she says – 'You have been a long time out of England; you don't read the papers?'

'No.' A pause. I believe my heart is beating inside my head.

'You asked me if I was a free woman. I don't pretend to misunderstand why you asked me. I am not a beautiful woman, I never was. But there must be something about me, there is in some women, "essential femininity" perhaps, that appeals to all men. What I read in your eyes I have seen in many men's before, but before God I never tried to rouse it. Today' (with a sob), 'I can say I am free, yesterday morning I could not. Yesterday my husband gained his case and divorced me!' she closes her eyes and draws in her under-lip to stop its quivering. I want to take her in my arms, but I am afraid to.

'I did not ask you any more than if you were free!'

'No, but I am afraid you don't quite take in the meaning. I did not divorce my husband, he divorced *me*, he got a decree *nisi*; do you understand now?' she is speaking with difficulty, 'do you know what that implies?'

I can't stand her face any longer. I take her hands, they are icy cold, and hold them tightly. 'Yes, I know what it implies, that is, I know the legal and social conclusion to be drawn from it – if that is what you mean. But I never asked you for that information. I have nothing to do with your past. You did not exist for me before the day we met on the river. I take you from that day and I ask you to marry me.'

I feel her tremble and her hands get suddenly warm. She turns her head and looks at me long and searchingly, then she says – 'Sit down, I want to say something!'

I obey, and she comes and stands next the chair. I can't help it, I reach up my arm, but she puts it gently down.

'No, you must listen without touching me or I shall go back to the window. I don't want to influence you a bit by any personal magnetism I possess. I want you to listen – I have told you he divorced me, the co-respondent was an old friend, a friend of my childhood, of my girlhood. He died just after the first application was made, luckily for me. He would have considered my honour before my happiness. *I* did not defend the case, it wasn't likely – ah, if you knew all! He proved his case; given clever counsel, willing witnesses to whom you make it worth while, and no defence, divorce is always attainable even in England. But remember: I figure as an adulteress in every English-speaking paper. If you buy last week's evening papers – do you remember the day I was in town?' – I nod – 'you will see a sketch of me in that day's; someone, perhaps he, must have given it; it was from an old photograph. I bought one at Victoria as I came out; it is funny' (with an hysterical laugh) 'to buy a caricature of one's own poor face at a news-stall.

Yet in spite of that I have felt glad. The point for you is that I made no defence to the world, and' (with a lifting of her head) 'I will make no apology, no explanation, no denial to you, now or ever. I am very desolate and your attention came very warm to me, but I don't love you. Perhaps I could learn to' (with a rush of colour), 'for what you have said tonight, and it is because of that I tell you to weigh what this means. Later, when your care for me will grow into habit, you may chafe at my past. It is from that I would save you.'

I hold out my hands and she comes and puts them aside and takes me by the beard and turns up my face and scans it earnestly. She must have been deceived a good deal. I let her do as she pleases, it is the wisest way with women, and it is good to have her touch me in that way. She seems satisfied. She stands leaning against the arm of the chair and says – 'I must learn first to think of myself as a free woman again, it almost seems wrong today to talk like this; can you understand that feeling?'

I nod assent.

'Next time I must be sure, and you must be sure,' she lays her fingers on my mouth as I am about to protest, 'S–sh! You shall have a year to think. If you repeat then what you have said today, I shall give you your answer. You must not try to find me. I have money. If I am living, I will come here to you. If I am dead, you will be told of it. In the year between I shall look upon myself as belonging to you, and render an account if you wish of every hour. You will not be influenced by me in any way, and you will be able to reason it out calmly. If you think better of it, don't come.'

I feel there would be no use trying to move her, I simply kiss her hands and say: 'As you will, dear woman; I shall be here.'

We don't say any more; she sits down on a footstool with her head against my knee, and I just smooth it. When the clocks strike ten through the house, she rises and I stand up. I see that she has been crying quietly, poor lonely little soul. I lift her off her feet and kiss her, and stammer out my sorrow at losing her, and she is gone.

Next morning the little maid brought me an envelope from the lady, who left by the first train. It held a little grey glove; that is why I carry it always, and why I haunt the inn and never leave it for longer than a week; why I sit and dream in the old chair that has a ghost of her presence always; dream of the spring to come with the mayfly on the wing, and the young summer when midges dance, and the trout are growing fastidious; when she will come to me across the meadow grass, through the silver haze, as she did before; come with her grey eyes shining to exchange herself for her little grey glove.

MARY ELEANOR WILKINS FREEMAN

Mary Eleanor Wilkins Freeman was born in Randolph, Massachusetts on 31 October 1852. She passed the greater part of her life in Massachusetts and Vermont and for many years was the private secretary of Oliver Wendell Holmes. Freeman began writing stories and verse for children while still a teenager to help support her family and was quickly successful. Her best known work was written in the 1880s and 1890s while she lived in Randolph. She produced more than two dozen volumes of published short stories and novels. She is best known for two collections of stories, *A Humble Romance and Other Stories* (1887) and *A New England Nun and Other Stories* (1891), which deal mostly with New England life and are among the best of their kind. Freeman is also remembered for her novel *Pembroke* (1894), and she contributed a notable chapter to the collaborative novel *The Whole Family* (1908). In 1902 she married Dr Charles M. Freeman of Metuchen, New Jersey. In April 1926, Freeman became the first recipient of the William Dean Howells Medal for Distinction in Fiction from the American Academy of Arts and Letters. She died on 13 March 1930 and was interred in Hillside Cemetery in Scotch Plains, New Jersey.

The Copy-Cat

That affair of Jim Simmons's cats never became known. Two little boys and a little girl can keep a secret – that is, sometimes. The two little boys had the advantage of the little girl because they could talk over the affair together, and the little girl, Lily Jennings, had no intimate girl friend to tempt her to confidence. She had only little Amelia Wheeler, commonly called by the pupils of Madame's school 'The Copy-Cat'.

Amelia was an odd little girl – that is, everybody called her odd. She was that rather unusual creature, a child with a definite ideal; and that ideal was Lily Jennings. However, nobody knew that. If Amelia's mother, who was a woman of strong character, had suspected, she would have taken strenuous measures to prevent such a peculiar state of affairs; the more so because she herself did not in the least approve of Lily Jennings. Mrs Diantha Wheeler (Amelia's father had died when she was a baby) often remarked to her own mother, Mrs Stark, and to her mother-in-law, Mrs Samuel Wheeler, that she did not feel that Mrs Jennings was bringing up Lily exactly as she should. 'That child thinks entirely too much of her looks,' said Mrs Diantha. 'When she walks past here she switches those ridiculous frilled frocks of hers as if she were entering a ballroom, and she tosses her head and looks about to see if anybody is watching her. If I were to see Amelia doing such things I should be very firm with her.'

'Lily Jennings is a very pretty child,' said Mother-in-law Wheeler, with an under-meaning, and Mrs Diantha flushed. Amelia did not in the least resemble the Wheelers, who were a handsome set. She looked remarkably like her mother, who was a plain woman, only little Amelia did not have a square chin. Her chin was pretty and round, with a little dimple in it. In fact, Amelia's chin was the prettiest feature she had. Her hair was phenomenally straight. It would not even yield to hot curling-irons, which her grandmother Wheeler had tried surreptitiously several times when there was a little girls' party. 'I never saw such hair as that poor child has in all my life,' she told the other grandmother, Mrs Stark. 'Have the Starks always had such very straight hair?'

Mrs Stark stiffened her chin. Her own hair was very straight. 'I don't know,' said she, 'that the Starks have had any straighter hair than other people. If Amelia does not have anything worse to contend with than straight hair I rather think she will get along in the world as well as most people.'

'It's thin, too,' said Grandmother Wheeler, with a sigh, 'and it hasn't a mite of colour. Oh, well, Amelia is a good child, and beauty isn't everything.'

Grandmother Wheeler said that as if beauty were a great deal, and Grandmother Stark arose and shook out her black silk skirts. She had money, and loved to dress in rich black silks and laces.

'It is very little, very little indeed,' said she, and she eyed Grandmother Wheeler's lovely old face, like a wrinkled old rose as to colour, faultless as to feature, and swept about by the loveliest waves of shining silver hair.

Then she went out of the room, and Grandmother Wheeler, left alone, smiled. She knew the worth of beauty for those who possess it and those who do not. She had never been quite reconciled to her son's marrying such a plain girl as Diantha Stark, although she had money. She considered beauty on the whole as a more valuable asset than mere gold. She regretted always that poor little Amelia, her only grandchild, was so very plain-looking. She always knew that Amelia was very plain, and yet sometimes the child puzzled her. She seemed to see reflections of beauty, if not beauty itself, in the little colourless face, in the figure, with its too-large joints and utter absence of curves. She sometimes even wondered privately if some subtle resemblance to the handsome Wheelers might not be in the child and yet appear. But she was mistaken. What she saw was pure mimicry of a beautiful ideal.

Little Amelia tried to stand like Lily Jennings; she tried to walk like her; she tried to smile like her; she made endeavours, very often futile, to dress like her. Mrs Wheeler did not in the least approve of furbelows for children. Poor little Amelia went clad in severe simplicity; durable woollen frocks in winter, and washable, unfadeable, and non-soil-showing frocks in summer. She, although her mother had perhaps more money wherewith to dress her than had any of the other mothers, was the plainest-clad little girl in school. Amelia, moreover, never tore a frock, and, as she did not grow rapidly, one lasted several seasons. Lily Jennings was destructive, although dainty. Her pretty clothes were renewed every year. Amelia was helpless before that problem. For a little girl burning with aspirations to be and look like another little girl who was beautiful and wore beautiful clothes to be obliged to set forth for Madame's on a lovely spring morning, when thin attire was in evidence, dressed in dark-blue-and-white-checked gingham, which she had worn for three summers, and with sleeves which, even to childish eyes, were anachronisms, was a trial. Then to see Lily flutter in a frock like a perfectly new white flower was torture; not because of jealousy – Amelia was not jealous; but she so admired the other little girl, and so loved her, and so wanted to be like her.

As for Lily, she hardly ever noticed Amelia. She was not aware that she herself was an object of adoration; for she was a little girl who searched for admiration in the eyes of little boys rather than little girls, although very innocently. She always glanced slyly at Johnny Trumbull when she wore a pretty new frock, to see if he noticed. He never did, and she was sharp enough to know it. She was also child enough not to care a bit, but to take a queer pleasure in the sensation of scorn which she felt in consequence. She would eye Johnny from head to foot, his boy's clothing somewhat spotted, his bulging pockets, his always dusty shoes, and when he twisted uneasily, not understanding why, she had a thrill of purely feminine delight. It was on one such occasion that she first noticed Amelia Wheeler particularly.

It was a lovely warm morning in May, and Lily was a darling to behold – in a big hat with a wreath of blue flowers, her hair tied with enormous blue silk bows, her short skirts frilled with eyelet embroidery, her slender silk legs, her little white sandals. Madame's maid had not yet struck the Japanese gong, and all the pupils were out on the lawn, Amelia, in her clean, ugly gingham and her serviceable brown sailor hat, hovering near Lily, as usual, like a common, very plain butterfly near a particularly resplendent blossom. Lily really noticed her. She spoke to her confidentially; she recognised her fully as another of her own sex, and presumably of similar opinions.

'Ain't boys ugly, anyway?' enquired Lily of Amelia, and a wonderful change came over Amelia. Her sallow cheeks bloomed; her eyes showed blue glitters; her little skinny figure became instinct with nervous life. She smiled charmingly, with such eagerness that it smote with pathos and bewitched.

'Oh yes, oh yes,' she agreed, in a voice like a quick flute obbligato. 'Boys are ugly.'

'Such clothes!' said Lily.

'Yes, such clothes!' said Amelia.

'Always spotted,' said Lily.

'Always covered all over with spots,' said Amelia.

'And their pockets always full of horrid things,' said Lily.

'Yes,' said Amelia.

Amelia glanced openly at Johnny Trumbull; Lily with a sidewise effect.

Johnny had heard every word. Suddenly he arose to action and knocked down Lee Westminster, and sat on him.

'Lemme up!' said Lee.

Johnny had no quarrel whatever with Lee. He grinned, but he sat still. Lee, the sat-upon, was a sharp little boy. 'Showing off before the gals!' he said, in a thin whisper.

'Hush up!' returned Johnny.

'Will you give me a writing-pad – I lost mine, and mother said I couldn't have another for a week if I did – if I don't holler?' enquired Lee.

'Yes. Hush up!'

Lee lay still, and Johnny continued to sit upon his prostrate form. Both were out of sight of Madame's windows, behind a clump of the cedars which graced her lawn.

'Always fighting,' said Lily, with a fine crescendo of scorn. She lifted her chin high, and also her nose.

'Always fighting,' said Amelia, and also lifted her chin and nose. Amelia was a born mimic. She actually looked like Lily, and she spoke like her.

Then Lily did a wonderful thing. She doubled her soft little arm into an inviting loop for Amelia's little claw of a hand.

'Come along, Amelia Wheeler,' said she. 'We don't want to stay near horrid, fighting boys. We will go by ourselves.'

And they went. Madame had a headache that morning, and the Japanese gong did not ring for fifteen minutes longer. During that time Lily and Amelia sat together on a little rustic bench under a twinkling poplar, and they talked, and a sort of miniature sun-and-satellite relation was established between them, although neither was aware of it. Lily, being on the whole a very normal little girl, and not disposed to even a full estimate of herself as compared with others of her own sex, did not dream of Amelia's adoration, and Amelia, being rarely destitute of self-consciousness, did not understand the whole scope of her own sentiments. It was quite sufficient that she was seated close to this wonderful Lily, and agreeing with her to the verge of immolation.

'Of course,' said Lily, 'girls are pretty, and boys are just as ugly as they can be.'

'Oh yes,' said Amelia, fervently.

'But,' said Lily, thoughtfully, 'it is queer how Johnny Trumbull always comes out ahead in a fight, and he is not so very large, either.'

'Yes,' said Amelia, but she realised a pang of jealousy. 'Girls could fight, I suppose,' said she.

'Oh yes, and get their clothes all torn and messy,' said Lily.

'I shouldn't care,' said Amelia. Then she added, with a little toss, 'I almost know I could fight.' The thought even floated through her wicked little mind that fighting might be a method of wearing out obnoxious and durable clothes.

'You!' said Lily, and the scorn in her voice wilted Amelia.

'Maybe I couldn't,' said she.

'Of course you couldn't, and if you could, what a sight you'd be. Of course it wouldn't hurt your clothes as much as some, because your mother dresses you in strong things, but you'd be sure to get black and blue, and what would be the use, anyway? You couldn't be a boy, if you did fight.'

'No. I know I couldn't.'

'Then what is the use? We are a good deal prettier than boys, and cleaner, and have nicer manners, and we must be satisfied.'

'You are prettier,' said Amelia, with a look of worshipful admiration at Lily's sweet little face.

'You are prettier,' said Lily. Then she added, equivocally, 'Even the very homeliest girl is prettier than a boy.'

Poor Amelia, it was a good deal for her to be called prettier than a very dusty boy in a fight. She fairly dimpled with delight, and again she smiled charmingly. Lily eyed her critically.

'You aren't so very homely, after all, Amelia,' she said. 'You needn't think you are.'

Amelia smiled again.

'When you look like you do now you are real pretty,' said Lily, not knowing or even suspecting the truth, that she was regarding in the face of this little ardent soul her own, as in a mirror.

However, it was after that episode that Amelia Wheeler was called 'Copy-Cat'. The two little girls entered Madame's select school arm in arm, when the musical gong sounded, and behind them came Lee Westminster and Johnny Trumbull, surreptitiously dusting their garments, and ever after the fact of Amelia's adoration and imitation of Lily Jennings was evident to all. Even Madame became aware of it, and held conferences with two of the under-teachers.

'It is not at all healthy for one child to model herself so entirely upon the pattern of another,' said Miss Parmalee.

'Most certainly it is not,' agreed Miss Acton, the music-teacher. 'Why, that poor little Amelia Wheeler had the rudiments of a fairly good contralto. I had begun to wonder if the poor child might not be able at least to sing a little, and so make up for – other things; and now she tries to sing high like Lily Jennings, and I simply cannot prevent it. She has heard Lily play, too, and has lost her own touch, and now it is neither one thing nor the other.'

'I might speak to her mother,' said Madame, thoughtfully. Madame was American born, but she had married a French gentleman, long since deceased, and his name sounded well on her circulars. She and her two under-teachers were drinking tea in her library.

Miss Parmalee, who was a true lover of her pupils, gasped at Madame's proposition. 'Whatever you do, please do not tell that poor child's mother,' said she.

'I do not think it would be quite wise, if I may venture to express an opinion,' said Miss Acton, who was a timid soul, and always inclined to shy at her own ideas.

'But why?' asked Madame.

'Her mother,' said Miss Parmalee, 'is a quite remarkable woman, with great strength of character, but she would utterly fail to grasp the situation.'

'I must confess,' said Madame, sipping her tea, 'that I fail to understand it. Why any child not an absolute idiot should so lose her own identity in another's absolutely bewilders me. I never heard of such a case.'

Miss Parmalee, who had a sense of humour, laughed a little. 'It is bewildering,' she admitted. 'And now the other children see how it is, and call her "Copy-Cat" to her face, but she does not mind. I doubt if she understands, and neither does Lily, for that matter. Lily Jennings is full of mischief, but she moves in straight lines; she is not conceited or self-conscious, and she really likes Amelia, without knowing why.'

'I fear Lily will lead Amelia into mischief,' said Madame, 'and Amelia has always been such a good child.'

'Lily will never *mean* to lead Amelia into mischief,' said loyal Miss Parmalee.

'But she will,' said Madame.

'If Lily goes, I cannot answer for Amelia's not following,' admitted Miss Parmalee.

'I regret it all very much indeed,' sighed Madame, 'but it does seem to me still that Amelia's mother – '

'Amelia's mother would not even believe it, in the first place,' said Miss Parmalee.

'Well, there is something in that,' admitted Madame. 'I myself could not even imagine such a situation. I would not know of it now if you and Miss Acton had not told me.'

'There is not the slightest use in telling Amelia not to imitate Lily, because she does not know that she is imitating her,' said Miss Parmalee. 'If she were to be punished for it, she could never comprehend the reason.'

'That is true,' said Miss Acton. 'I realise that when the poor child squeaks instead of singing. All I could think of this morning was a little mouse caught in a trap which she could not see. She does actually squeak! – and some of her low notes, although, of course, she is only a child, and has never attempted much, promised to be very good.'

'She will have to squeak, for all I can see,' said Miss Parmalee. 'It looks to me like one of those situations that no human being can change for better or worse.'

'I suppose you are right,' said Madame, 'but it is most unfortunate, and Mrs Wheeler is such a superior woman, and Amelia is her only child, and this is such a very subtle and regrettable affair. Well, we have to leave a great deal to providence.'

'If,' said Miss Parmalee, 'she could only get angry when she is called "Copy-Cat".' Miss Parmalee laughed, and so did Miss Acton. Then all the ladies had their cups refilled, and left providence to look out for poor little Amelia Wheeler, in her mad pursuit of her ideal in the shape of another little girl possessed of the exterior graces which she had not.

Meantime the little 'Copy-Cat' had never been so happy. She began to improve in her looks also. Her grandmother Wheeler noticed it first, and spoke of it to Grandmother Stark. 'That child may not be so plain, after all,' said she. 'I looked at her this morning when she started for school, and I thought for the first time that there was a little resemblance to the Wheelers.'

Grandmother Stark sniffed, but she looked gratified. 'I have been noticing it for some time,' said she, 'but as for looking like the Wheelers, I thought this morning for a minute that I actually saw my poor dear husband looking at me out of that blessed child's eyes.'

Grandmother Wheeler smiled her little, aggravating, curved, pink smile.

But even Mrs Diantha began to notice the change for the better in Amelia. She, however, attributed it to an increase of appetite and a system of deep breathing which she had herself taken up and enjoined Amelia to follow. Amelia was following Lily Jennings instead, but that her mother did not know. Still, she was gratified to see Amelia's little sallow cheeks taking on pretty curves and a soft bloom, and she was more inclined to listen when Grandmother Wheeler ventured to approach the subject of Amelia's attire.

'Amelia would not be so bad-looking if she were better dressed, Diantha,' said she.

Diantha lifted her chin, but she paid heed. 'Why, does not Amelia dress perfectly well, mother?' she enquired.

'She dresses well enough, but she needs more ribbons and ruffles.'

'I do not approve of so many ribbons and ruffles,' said Mrs Diantha. 'Amelia has perfectly neat, fresh black or brown ribbons for her hair, and ruffles are not sanitary.'

'Ruffles are pretty,' said Grandmother Wheeler, 'and blue and pink are pretty colours. Now, that Jennings girl looks like a little picture.'

But that last speech of Grandmother Wheeler's undid all the previous good. Mrs Diantha had an unacknowledged – even to herself – disapproval of Mrs Jennings which dated far back in the past, for a reason which was quite unworthy of her and of her strong mind. When she and Lily's mother had been girls, she had seen Mrs Jennings look like a picture, and had been perfectly well aware that she herself fell far short of an artist's ideal. Perhaps if Mrs Stark had believed in ruffles and ribbons, her daughter might have had a different mind when Grandmother Wheeler had finished her little speech.

As it was, Mrs Diantha surveyed her small, pretty mother-in-law with dignified serenity, which savoured only delicately of a snub. 'I do not myself approve of the way in which Mrs Jennings dresses her daughter,' said she, 'and I do not consider that the child presents to a practical observer as good an appearance as my Amelia.'

Grandmother Wheeler had a temper. It was a childish temper and soon over – still, a temper. 'Lord,' said she, 'if you mean to say that you think your poor little snipe of a daughter, dressed like a little maid-of-all-work, can compare with that lovely little Lily Jennings, who is dressed like a doll! – '

'I do not wish that my daughter should be dressed like a doll,' said Mrs Diantha, coolly.

'Well, she certainly isn't,' said Grandmother Wheeler. 'Nobody would ever take her for a doll as far as looks or dress are concerned. She may be *good* enough. I don't deny that Amelia is a good little girl, but her looks could be improved on.'

'Looks matter very little,' said Mrs Diantha.

'They matter very much,' said Grandmother Wheeler, pugnaciously, her blue eyes taking on a peculiar opaque glint, as always when she lost her temper, 'very much indeed. But looks can't be helped. If poor little Amelia wasn't born with pretty looks, she wasn't. But she wasn't born with such ugly clothes. She might be better dressed.'

'I dress my daughter as I consider best,' said Mrs Diantha. Then she left the room.

Grandmother Wheeler sat for a few minutes, her blue eyes opaque, her little pink lips a straight line; then suddenly her eyes lit, and she smiled. 'Poor Diantha,' said she, 'I remember how Henry used to like Lily Jennings's mother before he married Diantha. Sour grapes hang high.' But Grandmother Wheeler's beautiful old face was quite soft and gentle. From her heart she pitied the reacher after those high-hanging sour grapes, for Mrs Diantha had been very good to her.

Then Grandmother Wheeler, who had a mild persistency not evident to a casual observer, began to make plans and lay plots. She was resolved, Diantha or not, that her granddaughter, her son's child, should have some fine feathers. The little conference had taken place in her own room, a large, sunny one, with a little storeroom opening from it. Presently Grandmother Wheeler rose, entered the storeroom, and began rummaging in some old trunks. Then followed days of secret work. Grandmother Wheeler had been noted as a fine needlewoman, and her hand had not yet lost its cunning. She had one of Amelia's ugly little ginghams, purloined from a closet, for size, and she worked two or three dainty wonders. She took Grandmother Stark into her confidence. Sometimes the two ladies, by reason of their age, found it possible to combine with good results.

'Your daughter Diantha is one woman in a thousand,' said Grandmother Wheeler, diplomatically, one day, 'but she never did care much for clothes.'

'Diantha,' returned Grandmother Stark, with a suspicious glance, 'always realised that clothes were not the things that mattered.'

'And, of course, she is right,' said Grandmother Wheeler, piously. 'Your Diantha is one woman in a thousand. If she cared as much for fine clothes as some women, I don't know where we should all be. It would spoil poor little Amelia.'

'Yes, it would,' assented Grandmother Stark. 'Nothing spoils a little girl more than always to be thinking about her clothes.'

'Yes, I was looking at Amelia the other day, and thinking how much more sensible she appeared in her plain gingham than Lily Jennings in all her ruffles and ribbons. Even if people were all noticing Lily, and praising her, thinks I to myself, "How little difference such things really make. Even if our dear Amelia does stand to one side, and nobody notices her, what real matter is it?" ' Grandmother Wheeler was inwardly chuckling as she spoke.

Grandmother Stark was at once alert. 'Do you mean to say that Amelia is really not taken so much notice of because she dresses plainly?' said she.

'You don't mean that you don't know it, as observant as you are?' replied Grandmother Wheeler.

'Diantha ought not to let it go as far as that,' said Grandmother Stark.

Grandmother Wheeler looked at her queerly.

'Why do you look at me like that?'

'Well, I did something I feared I ought not to have done. And I didn't know what to do, but your speaking so makes me wonder – '

'Wonder what?'

Then Grandmother Wheeler went to her little storeroom and emerged bearing a box. She displayed the contents – three charming little white frocks fluffy with lace and embroidery.

'Did you make them?'

'Yes, I did. I couldn't help it. I thought if the dear child never wore them, it would be some comfort to know they were in the house.'

'That one needs a broad blue sash,' said Grandmother Stark.

Grandmother Wheeler laughed. She took her impecuniosity easily. 'I had to use what I had,' said she.

'I will get a blue sash for that one,' said Grandmother Stark, 'and a pink sash for that, and a flowered one for that.'

'Of course they will make all the difference,' said Grandmother Wheeler. 'Those beautiful sashes will really make the dresses.'

'I will get them,' said Grandmother Stark, with decision. 'I will go right down to Mann Brothers' store now and get them.'

'Then I will make the bows, and sew them on,' replied Grandmother Wheeler, happily.

It thus happened that little Amelia Wheeler was possessed of three beautiful dresses, although she did not know it.

For a long time neither of the two conspiring grandmothers dared divulge the secret. Mrs Diantha was a very determined woman, and even her own mother stood somewhat in awe of her. Therefore, little Amelia went to school during the spring term soberly clad as ever, and even on the festive last day wore nothing better than a new blue gingham, made too long, to allow for shrinkage, and new blue hair-ribbons. The two grandmothers almost wept in secret conclave over the lovely frocks which were not worn.

'I respect Diantha,' said Grandmother Wheeler. 'You know that. She is one woman in a thousand, but I do hate to have that poor child go to school today with so many to look at her, and she dressed so unlike all the other little girls.'

'Diantha has got so much sense, it makes her blind and deaf,' declared Grandmother Stark. 'I call it a shame, if she is my daughter.'

'Then you don't venture – '

Grandmother Stark reddened. She did not like to own to awe of her daughter. 'I *venture*, if that is all,' said she, tartly. 'You don't suppose I am afraid of Diantha? – but she would not let Amelia wear one of the dresses, anyway, and I don't want the child made any unhappier than she is.'

'Well, I will admit,' replied Grandmother Wheeler, 'if poor Amelia knew she had these beautiful dresses and could not wear them she might feel worse about wearing that homely gingham.'

'Gingham!' fairly snorted Grandmother Stark. 'I cannot see why Diantha thinks so much of gingham. It shrinks, anyway.'

Poor little Amelia did undoubtedly suffer on that last day, when she sat among the others gaily clad, and looked down at her own common little skirts. She was very glad, however, that she had not been chosen to do any of the special things which would have necessitated her appearance upon the little flower-decorated platform. She did not know of the conversation between Madame and her two assistants.

'I would have Amelia recite a little verse or two,' said Madame, 'but how can I?' Madame adored dress, and had a lovely new one of sheer dull-blue stuff, with touches of silver, for the last day.

'Yes,' agreed Miss Parmalee, 'that poor child is sensitive, and for her to stand on the platform in one of those plain ginghams would be too cruel.'

'Then, too,' said Miss Acton, 'she would recite her verses exactly like Lily Jennings. She can make her voice exactly like Lily's now. Then everybody would laugh, and Amelia would not know why. She would think they were laughing at her dress, and that would be dreadful.'

If Amelia's mother could have heard that conversation everything would have been different, although it is puzzling to decide in what way.

It was on the last of the summer vacation in early September, just before school began, that a climax came to Amelia's idolatry and imitation of Lily. The Jenningses had not gone away that summer, so the two little girls had been thrown together a good deal. Mrs Diantha never went away during a summer. She considered it her duty to remain at home, and she was quite pitiless to herself when it came to a matter of duty.

However, as a result she was quite ill during the last of August and the first of September. The season had been unusually hot, and Mrs Diantha had not spared herself from her duty on account of the heat. She would have scorned herself if she had done so. But she could not, strong-minded as she was, avert something like a heat prostration after a long walk under a burning sun, nor weeks of confinement and idleness in her room afterward.

When September came, and a night or two of comparative coolness, she felt stronger; still she was compelled by most unusual weakness to refrain from her energetic trot in her duty-path; and then it was that something happened.

One afternoon Lily fluttered over to Amelia's, and Amelia, ever on the watch, spied her.

'May I go out and see Lily?' she asked Grandmother Stark.

'Yes, but don't talk under the windows; your mother is asleep.'

Amelia ran out.

'I declare,' said Grandmother Stark to Grandmother Wheeler, 'I was half a mind to tell that child to wait a minute and slip on one of those pretty dresses. I hate to have her go on the street in that old gingham, with that Jennings girl dressed up like a wax doll.'

'I know it.'

'And now poor Diantha is so weak – and asleep – it would not have annoyed her.'

'I know it.'

Grandmother Stark looked at Grandmother Wheeler. Of the two she possessed a greater share of original sin compared with the size of her soul. Moreover, she felt herself at liberty to circumvent her own daughter. Whispering, she unfolded a daring scheme to the other grandmother, who stared at her aghast a second out of her lovely blue eyes, then laughed softly.

'Very well,' said she, 'if you dare.'

'I rather think I dare!' said Grandmother Stark. 'Isn't Diantha Wheeler my own daughter?' Grandmother Stark had grown much bolder since Mrs Diantha had been ill.

Meantime Lily and Amelia walked down the street until they came to a certain vacant lot intersected by a footpath between tall, feathery grasses and goldenrod and asters and milkweed. They entered the footpath, and swarms of little butterflies rose around them, and once in a while a protesting bumblebee.

'I am afraid we will be stung by the bees,' said Amelia.

'Bumblebees never sting,' said Lily; and Amelia believed her.

When the footpath ended, there was the river-bank. The two little girls sat down under a clump of brook willows and talked, while the river, full of green and blue and golden lights, slipped past them and never stopped.

Then Lily proceeded to unfold a plan, which was not philosophical, but naughtily ingenious. By this time Lily knew very well that Amelia admired her, and imitated her as successfully as possible, considering the drawback of dress and looks.

When she had finished Amelia was quite pale. 'I am afraid, I am afraid, Lily,' said she.

'What of?'

'My mother will find out; besides, I am afraid it isn't right.'

'Whoever told you it was wrong?'

'Nobody ever did,' admitted Amelia.

'Well, then you haven't any reason to think it is,' said Lily, triumphantly. 'And how is your mother ever going to find it out?'

'I don't know.'

'Isn't she ill in her room? And does she ever come to kiss you good-night, the way my mother does, when she is well?'

'No,' admitted Amelia.

'And neither of your grandmothers?'

'Grandmother Stark would think it was silly, like mother, and Grandmother Wheeler can't go up and down stairs very well.'

'I can't see but you are perfectly safe. I am the only one that runs any risk at all. I run a great deal of risk, but I am willing to take it,' said Lily with a virtuous air. Lily had a small but rather involved scheme simply for her own ends, which did not seem to call for much virtue, but rather the contrary.

Lily had overheard Arnold Carruth and Johnny Trumbull and Lee Westminster and another boy, Jim Patterson, planning a most delightful affair, which even in the case of the boys was fraught with danger, secrecy and doubtful rectitude. Not one of the four boys had had a vacation from the village that summer, and their young minds had become charged, as it were, with the seeds of revolution and rebellion. Jim Patterson, the son of the rector, and of them all the most venturesome, had planned to take – he called it 'take'; he meant to pay for it, anyway, he said, as soon as he could shake enough money out of his nickel savings-bank – one of his father's Plymouth Rock chickens and have a chicken-roast in the woods back of Dr Trumbull's. He had planned for Johnny to take some ears of corn suitable for roasting from his father's garden; for Lee to take some cookies out of a stone jar in his mother's pantry; and for Arnold to take some potatoes. Then they four would steal forth under cover of night, build a campfire, roast their spoils, and feast.

Lily had resolved to be of the party. She resorted to no open methods; the stones of the fighting suffragettes were not for her, little honey-sweet, curled, and ruffled darling; rather the timeworn, if not time-sanctified, weapons of her sex, little instruments of wiles, and tiny dodges, and tiny subterfuges, which would serve her best.

'You know,' she said to Amelia, 'you don't look like me. Of course you know that, and that can't be helped; but you do walk like me, and talk like me, you know that, because they call you "Copy-Cat".'

'Yes, I know,' said poor Amelia.

'I don't mind if they do call you "Copy-Cat",' said Lily, magnanimously. 'I don't mind a bit. But, you see, my mother always comes upstairs to kiss me good night after I have gone to bed, and tomorrow night she has a dinner-party, and she will surely be a little late, and I can't manage unless you help me. I will get one of my white dresses for you, and all you have to do is to climb out of your window into that cedar tree – you know you can climb down that, because you are so afraid of burglars climbing up – and you can slip on my dress; you had better throw it out of the window and not try to climb in it, because my dresses tear awful easy, and we might get caught that way. Then you just sneak down to our house, and I shall be outdoors; and when you go upstairs, if the doors should be open, and anybody should call, you can answer just like me; and I have found that light curly wig Aunt Laura wore when she had her head shaved after she had a fever, and you just put that on and go to bed, and mother will never know when she kisses you good night. Then after the roast I will go to your house, and climb up that tree, and go to bed in your room. And I will have one of your gingham dresses to wear, and very early in the morning I will get up, and you get up, and we both of us can get down the back stairs without being seen, and run home.'

Amelia was almost weeping. It was her worshipped Lily's plan, but she was horribly scared. 'I don't know,' she faltered.

'Don't know! You've got to! You don't love me one single bit or you wouldn't stop to think about whether you didn't know.' It was the world-old argument which floors love. Amelia succumbed.

The next evening a frightened little girl clad in one of Lily Jennings's white embroidered frocks was racing to the Jenningses' house, and another little girl, not at all frightened, but enjoying the stimulus of mischief and unwontedness, was racing to the wood behind Dr Trumbull's house, and that little girl was clad in one of Amelia Wheeler's ginghams. But the plan went all awry.

Lily waited, snuggled up behind an alder bush, and the boys came, one by one, and she heard this whispered, although there was no necessity for whispering, 'Jim Patterson, where's that hen?'

'Couldn't get her. Grabbed her, and all her tail-feathers came out in a bunch right in my hand, and she squawked so, father heard. He was in his study writing his sermon, and he came out, and if I hadn't hid behind the chicken-coop and then run I couldn't have got here. But I can't see as you've got any corn, Johnny Trumbull.'

'Couldn't. Every single ear was cooked for dinner.'

'I couldn't bring any cookies, either,' said Lee Westminster; 'there weren't any cookies in the jar.'

'And I couldn't bring the potatoes, because the outside cellar door was locked,' said Arnold Carruth. 'I had to go down the back-stairs and out the south door, and the inside cellar door opens out of our dining-room, and I daren't go in there.'

'Then we might as well go home,' said Johnny Trumbull. 'If I had been you, Jim Patterson, I would have brought that old hen if her tail-feathers *had* come out. Seems to me you scare awful easy.'

'Guess if you had heard her squawk!' said Jim, resentfully. 'If you want to try to lick me, come on, Johnny Trumbull. Guess you don't darse call me scared again.'

Johnny eyed him standing there in the gloom. Jim was not large, but very wiry, and the ground was not suited for combat. Johnny, although a victor, would probably go home considerably the worse in appearance; and he could anticipate the consequences were his father to encounter him.

'Shucks!' said Johnny Trumbull, of the fine old Trumbull family and Madame's exclusive school. 'Shucks! who wants your old hen? We had chicken for dinner, anyway.'

'So did we,' said Arnold Carruth.

'We did, and corn,' said Lee.

'We did,' said Jim.

Lily stepped forth from the alder bush. 'If,' said she, 'I were a boy, and had started to have a chicken-roast, I would have *had* a chicken-roast.'

But every boy, even the valiant Johnny Trumbull, was gone in a mad scutter. This sudden apparition of a girl was too much for their nerves. They never even knew who the girl was, although little Arnold Carruth said she had looked to him like 'Copy-Cat', but the others scouted the idea.

Lily Jennings made the best of her way out of the wood across lots to the road. She was not in a particularly enviable case. Amelia Wheeler was presumably in her bed, and she saw nothing for it but to take the difficult way to Amelia's.

Lily tore a great rent in the gingham going up the cedar tree, but that was nothing to what followed. She entered, through Amelia's window, her prim little room, to find herself confronted by Amelia's mother in a wrapper, and her two grandmothers. Grandmother Stark had over her arm a beautiful white embroidered dress. The two old ladies had entered the room in order to lay the white dress on a chair and take away Amelia's gingham, and there was no Amelia. Mrs Diantha had heard the commotion, and had risen, thrown on her wrapper, and come. Her mother had turned upon her.

'It is all your fault, Diantha,' she had declared.

'My fault?' echoed Mrs Diantha, bewildered. 'Where is Amelia?'

'We don't know,' said Grandmother Stark, 'but you have probably driven her away from home by your cruelty.'

'Cruelty?'

'Yes, cruelty. What right had you to make that poor child look like a fright, so people laughed at her? We have made her some dresses that look decent, and had come here to take away those old gingham things that look as if she lived in the almshouse and leave these, so she would either have to wear them or go without, when we found she had gone.'

It was at that crucial moment that Lily entered by way of the window.

'Here she is now,' shrieked Grandmother Stark. 'Amelia, where – ' Then she stopped short.

Everybody stared at Lily's beautiful face suddenly gone white. For once Lily was frightened. She lost all self-control. She began to sob. She could scarcely tell the absurd story for sobs, but she told, every word.

Then, with a sudden boldness, she too turned on Mrs Diantha. 'They call poor Amelia "Copy-Cat",' said she, 'and I don't believe she would ever have tried so hard to look like me only my mother dresses me so I look nice, and you send Amelia to school looking awfully.' Then Lily sobbed again.

'My Amelia is at your house, as I understand?' said Mrs Diantha, in an awful voice.

'Ye–es, ma–am.'

'Let me go,' said Mrs Diantha, violently, to Grandmother Stark, who tried to restrain her. Mrs Diantha dressed herself and marched down the street, dragging Lily after her. The little girl had to trot to keep up with the tall woman's strides, and all the way she wept.

It was to Lily's mother's everlasting discredit, in Mrs Diantha's opinion, but to Lily's wonderful relief, that when she heard the story, standing in the hall in her lovely dinner dress, with the strains of music floating from the drawing-room, and cigar smoke floating from the dining-room, she laughed. When Lily said, 'And there wasn't even any chicken-roast, mother,' she nearly had hysterics.

'If you think this is a laughing matter, Mrs Jennings, I do not,' said Mrs Diantha, and again her dislike and sorrow at the sight of that sweet, mirthful face was over her. It was a face to be loved, and hers was not.

'Why, I went upstairs and kissed the child good-night, and never suspected,' laughed Lily's mother.

'I got Aunt Laura's curly, light wig for her,' explained Lily, and Mrs Jennings laughed again.

It was not long before Amelia, in her gingham, went home, led by her mother – her mother, who was trembling with weakness now. Mrs Diantha did not scold. She did not speak, but Amelia felt with wonder her little hand held very tenderly by her mother's long fingers.

When at last she was undressed and in bed, Mrs Diantha, looking very pale, kissed her, and so did both grandmothers.

Amelia, being very young and very tired, went to sleep. She did not know that that night was to mark a sharp turn in her whole life. Thereafter she went to school 'dressed like the best', and her mother petted her as nobody had ever known her mother could pet.

It was not so very long afterward that Amelia, out of her own improvement in appearance, developed a little stamp of individuality.

One day Lily wore a white frock with blue ribbons, and Amelia wore one with coral pink. It was a particular day in school; there was company, and tea was served.

'I told you I was going to wear blue ribbons,' Lily whispered to Amelia.

Amelia smiled lovingly back at her. 'Yes, I know, but I thought I would wear pink.'

The Amethyst Comb

Miss Jane Carew was at the railroad station waiting for the New York train. She was about to visit her friend, Mrs Viola Longstreet. With Miss Carew was her maid, Margaret, a middle-aged New England woman, attired in the stiffest and most correct of maid-uniforms. She carried an old, large sole-leather bag, and also a rather large sole-leather jewel-case. The jewel-case, carried openly, was rather an unusual sight at a New England railroad station, but few knew what it was. They concluded it to be Margaret's special handbag. Margaret was a very tall, thin woman, unbending as to carriage and expression. The one thing out of absolute plumb about Margaret was her little black bonnet. That was askew. Time had bereft the woman of so much hair that she could fasten no headgear with security, especially when the wind blew, and that morning there was a stiff gale. Margaret's bonnet was cocked over one eye.

Miss Carew noticed it. 'Margaret, your bonnet is crooked,' she said.

Margaret straightened her bonnet, but immediately the bonnet veered again to the side, weighted by a stiff jet aigrette. Miss Carew observed the careen of the bonnet, realised that it was inevitable, and did not mention it again. Inwardly she resolved upon the removal of the jet aigrette later on. Miss Carew was slightly older than Margaret, and dressed in a style some-what beyond her age. Jane Carew had been alert upon the situation of departing youth. She had eschewed gay colours and extreme cuts, and had her bonnets made to order, because there were no longer anything but hats in the millinery shop. The milliner in Wheaton, where Miss Carew lived, had objected, for Jane Carew inspired reverence.

'A bonnet is too old for you. Miss Carew,' she said. 'Women much older than you wear hats.'

'I trust that I know what is becoming to a woman of my years, thank you. Miss Waters,' Jane had replied, and the milliner had meekly taken her order.

After Miss Carew had left, the milliner told her girls that she had never seen a woman so perfectly crazy to look her age as Miss Carew. 'And she a pretty woman, too,' said the milliner; 'as straight as an arrer, and slim, and with all that hair, scarcely turned at all.'

Miss Carew, with all her haste to assume years, remained a pretty woman, softly slim, with an abundance of dark hair, showing little grey. Sometimes Jane reflected, uneasily, that it ought at her time of life to be entirely grey. She hoped nobody would suspect her of dyeing it. She wore it parted in the middle, folded back smoothly, and braided in a compact mass on the top of her head. The style of her clothes was slightly behind the fashion, just enough to suggest conservatism and age. She carried a little silver-bound bag in one nicely gloved hand; with the other she held daintily out of the dust of the platform her dress-skirt. A glimpse of a silk frilled petticoat, of slender feet, and ankles delicately slim, was visible before the onslaught of the wind. Jane Carew made no futile effort to keep her skirts down before the wind-gusts. She was so much of the gentlewoman that she could be gravely oblivious to the exposure of her ankles. She looked as if she had never heard of ankles when her black silk skirts lashed about them. She rose superbly above the situation. For some abstruse reason Margaret's skirts were not affected by the wind. They might have been weighted with buckram, although it was no longer in general use. She stood, except for her veering bonnet, as stiffly immovable as a wooden doll.

Miss Carew seldom left Wheaton. This visit to New York was an innovation. Quite a crowd gathered about Jane's sole-leather trunk when it was dumped on the platform by the local expressman. 'Miss Carew is going to New York,' one said to another, with much the same tone as if he had said, 'The great elm on the common is going to move into Dr Jones's front yard.'

When the train arrived, Miss Carew, followed by Margaret, stepped aboard with a majestic disregard of ankles. She sat beside a window, and Margaret placed the bag on the floor and held the jewel-case in her lap. The case contained the Carew jewels. They were not especially valuable, although they were rather numerous. There were cameos in brooches and heavy gold bracelets; corals which Miss Carew had not worn since her young girlhood. There were a set of garnets, some badly cut diamonds in earrings and rings, some seed-pearl ornaments, and a really beautiful set of amethysts. There were a necklace, two brooches – a bar and a circle – earrings, a ring and a comb. Each piece was charming, set in filigree gold with seed-pearls, but perhaps of them all the comb was the best. It was a very large comb. There was one great amethyst in the centre of the top; on either side was an intricate pattern of plums in small amethysts, and seed-pearl grapes, with leaves and stems of gold. Margaret in charge of the jewel-case was imposing. When they arrived in New York she confronted everybody whom she met with a stony stare, which was almost accusative and convictive of guilt, in spite of entire innocence on the part of the person stared at. It was inconceivable that any mortal would have dared lay violent hands upon that jewel-case under that stare. It would have seemed to partake of the nature of grand larceny from providence.

When the two reached the up-town residence of Viola Longstreet, Viola gave a little scream at the sight of the case.

'My dear Jane Carew, here you are with Margaret carrying that jewel-case out in plain sight. How dare you do such a thing? I really wonder you have not been held up a dozen times.'

Miss Carew smiled her gentle but almost stern smile – the Carew smile, which consisted in a widening and slightly upward curving of tightly closed lips.

'I do not think,' said she, 'that anybody would be apt to interfere with Margaret.'

Viola Longstreet laughed, the ringing peal of a child, although she was as old as Miss Carew. 'I think you are right, Jane,' said she. 'I don't believe a crook in New York would dare face that maid of yours. He would as soon encounter Plymouth Rock. I am glad you have brought your delightful old jewels, although you never wear anything except those lovely old pearl sprays and dull diamonds.'

'Now,' stated Jane, with a little toss of pride, 'I have Aunt Felicia's amethysts.'

'Oh, sure enough! I remember you did write me last summer that she had died and you had the amethysts at last. She must have been very old.'

'Ninety-one.'

'She might have given you the amethysts before. You, of course, will wear them; and I – am going to borrow the corals!'

Jane Carew gasped.

'You do not object, do you, dear? I have a new dinner-gown which clamours for corals, and my bank-account is strained, and I could buy none equal to those of yours, anyway.'

'Oh, I do not object,' said Jane Carew; still she looked aghast.

Viola Longstreet shrieked with laughter. 'Oh, I know. You think the corals too young for me. You have not worn them since you left off dotted muslin. My dear, you insisted upon growing old – I insisted upon remaining young. I had two new dotted muslins last summer. As for corals, I would wear them in the face of an opposing army! Do not judge me by yourself, dear. You laid hold of Age and held him, although you had your complexion and your shape and hair. As for me, I had my complexion and kept it. I also had my hair and kept it. My shape has been a struggle, but it was worth while. I, my dear, have held Youth so tight that he has almost choked to death, but held him I have. You cannot deny it. Look at me, Jane Carew, and tell me if, judging by my looks, you can reasonably state that I have no longer the right to wear corals.'

Jane Carew looked. She smiled the Carew smile. 'You *do* look very young, Viola,' said Jane, 'but you are not.'

'Jane Carew,' said Viola, 'I am young. May I wear your corals at my dinner tomorrow night?'

'Why, of course, if you think – '

'If I think them suitable. My dear, if there were on this earth ornaments more suitable to extreme youth than corals, I would borrow them if you owned them, but, failing that, the corals will answer. Wait until you see me in that taupe dinner-gown and the corals!'

Jane waited. She visited with Viola, whom she loved, although they had little in common, partly because of leading widely different lives, partly because of constitutional variations. She was dressed for dinner fully an hour before it was necessary, and she sat in the library reading when Viola swept in.

Viola was really entrancing. It was a pity that Jane Carew had such an unswerving eye for the essential truth that it could not be appeased by actual effect. Viola had doubtless, as she had said, struggled to keep her slim shape, but she had kept it, and, what was more, kept it without evidence of struggle. If she was in the least hampered by tight lacing and length of undergarment, she gave no evidence of it as she curled herself up in a big chair and (Jane wondered how she could bring herself to do it) crossed her legs, revealing one delicate foot and ankle, silk-stockinged with taupe, and shod with a coral satin slipper with a silver heel and a great silver buckle. On Viola's fair round neck the Carew corals lay bloomingly; her beautiful arms were clasped with them; a great coral brooch with wonderful carving confined a graceful fold of the taupe over one hip, a coral comb surmounted the shining waves of Viola's hair. Viola was an ash-blonde, her complexion was as roses, and the corals were ideal for her. As Jane regarded her friend's beauty, however, the fact that Viola was not young, that she was as old as herself, hid it and overshadowed it.

'Well, Jane, don't you think I look well in the corals, after all?' asked Viola, and there was something pitiful in her voice.

When a man or a woman holds fast to youth, even if successfully, there is something of the pitiful and the tragic involved. It is the everlasting struggle of the soul to retain the joy of earth, whose fleeting distinguishes it from heaven, and whose retention is not accomplished without an inner knowledge of its futility.

'I suppose you do, Viola,' replied Jane Carew, with the inflexibility of fate, 'but I really think that only very young girls ought to wear corals.'

Viola laughed, but the laugh had a minor cadence. 'But I *am* a young girl, Jane,' she said. 'I *must* be a young girl. I never had any girlhood when I should have had. You know that.'

Viola had married, when very young, a man old enough to be her father, and her wedded life had been a sad affair, to which, however, she seldom alluded. Viola had much pride with regard to the inevitable past.

'Yes,' agreed Jane. Then she added, feeling that more might be expected, 'Of course I suppose that marrying so very young does make a difference.'

'Yes,' said Viola, 'it does. In fact, it makes of one's girlhood an anticlimax, of which many dispute the wisdom, as you do. But have it I will. Jane, your amethysts are beautiful.'

Jane regarded the clear purple gleam of a stone on her arm. 'Yes,' she agreed, 'Aunt Felicia's amethysts have always been considered very beautiful.'

'And such a full set,' said Viola.

'Yes,' said Jane. She coloured a little, but Viola did not know why. At the last moment Jane had decided not to wear the amethyst comb, because it seemed to her altogether too decorative for a woman of her age, and she was afraid to mention it to Viola. She was sure that Viola would laugh at her and insist upon her wearing it.

'The earrings are lovely,' said Viola. 'My dear, I don't see how you ever consented to have your ears pierced.'

'I was very young, and my mother wished me to,' replied Jane, blushing.

The doorbell rang. Viola had been covertly listening for it all the time. Soon a very beautiful young man came with a curious dancing step into the room. Harold Lind always gave the effect of dancing when he walked. He always, moreover, gave the effect of extreme youth and of the utmost joy and mirth in life itself. He regarded everything and everybody with a smile as of humorous appreciation, and yet the appreciation was so good-natured that it offended nobody.

'Look at me – I am absurd and happy; look at yourself, also absurd and happy; look at everybody else likewise; look at life – a jest so delicious that it is quite worth one's while dying to be made acquainted with it.' That is what Harold Lind seemed to say. Viola Longstreet became even more youthful under his gaze; even Jane Carew regretted that she had not worn her amethyst comb and began to doubt its unsuitability. Viola very soon called the young man's attention to Jane's amethysts, and Jane always wondered why she did not then mention the comb. She removed a brooch and a bracelet for him to inspect.

'They are really wonderful,' he declared. 'I have never seen greater depth of colour in amethysts.'

'Mr Lind is an authority on jewels,' declared Viola. The young man shot a curious glance at her, which Jane remembered long afterward. It was one of those glances which are as keystones to situations.

Harold looked at the purple stones with the expression of a child with a toy. There was much of the child in the young man's whole appearance, but of a mischievous and beautiful child, of whom his mother might observe, with adoration and ill-concealed boastfulness, 'I can never tell what that child will do next!'

Harold returned the bracelet and brooch to Jane, and smiled at her as if amethysts were a lovely purple joke between her and himself, uniting them by a peculiar bond of fine understanding. 'Exquisite, Miss Carew,' he said. Then he looked at Viola. 'Those corals suit you wonderfully, Mrs Long-street,' he observed, 'but amethysts would also suit you.'

'Not with this gown,' replied Viola, rather pitifully. There was something in the young man's gaze and tone which she did not understand, but which she vaguely quivered before.

Harold certainly thought the corals were too young for Viola. Jane understood, and felt an unworthy triumph. Harold, who was young enough in actual years to be Viola's son, and was younger still by reason of his disposition, was amused by the sight of her in corals, although he did not intend to betray his amusement. He considered Viola in corals as too rude a jest to share with her. Had poor Viola once grasped Harold Lind's estimation of her she would have as soon gazed upon herself in her coffin. Harold's comprehension of the essentials was beyond Jane Carew's. It was fairly ghastly, partaking of the nature of X-rays, but it never disturbed Harold Lind. He went along his dance-track undisturbed, his blue eyes never losing their high lights of glee, his lips never losing their inscrutable smile at some happy understanding between life and himself. Harold had fair hair, which was very smooth and glossy. His skin was like a girl's. He was so beautiful that he showed cleverness in an affectation of carelessness in dress. He did not like to wear evening clothes, because they had necessarily to be immaculate. That evening Jane regarded him with an inward criticism that he was too handsome for a man. She told Viola so when the dinner was over and he and the other guests had gone.

'He is very handsome,' she said, 'but I never like to see a man quite so handsome.'

'You will change your mind when you see him in tweeds,' returned Viola. 'He loathes evening clothes.'

Jane regarded her anxiously. There was something in Viola's tone which disturbed and shocked her. It was inconceivable that Viola should be in love with that youth, and yet – 'He looks very young,' said Jane in a prim voice.

'He *is* young,' admitted Viola; 'still, not quite so young as he looks. Sometimes I tell him he will look like a boy if he lives to be eighty.'

'Well, he must be very young,' persisted Jane.

'Yes,' said Viola, but she did not say how young. Viola herself, now that the excitement was over, did not look so young as at the beginning of the evening. She removed the corals, and Jane considered that she looked much better without them.

'Thank you for your corals, dear,' said Viola. 'Where is Margaret?'

Margaret answered for herself by a tap on the door. She and Viola's maid, Louisa, had been sitting on an upper landing, out of sight, watching the guests downstairs. Margaret took the corals and placed them in their nest in the jewel-case, also the amethysts, after Viola had gone. The jewel-case was a curious old affair with many compartments. The amethysts required two. The comb was so large that it had one for itself. That was the reason why Margaret did not discover that evening that it was gone. Nobody discovered it for three days, when Viola had a little card-party. There was a whist-table for Jane, who had never given up the reserved and stately game. There were six tables in Viola's pretty living-room, with a little conservatory at one end and a leaping hearth fire at the other. Jane's partner was a stout old gentleman whose wife was shrieking with merriment at an auction-bridge table. The other whist-players were a stupid, very small young man who was aimlessly willing to play anything, and an amiable young woman who believed in self-denial. Jane played conscientiously. She returned trump leads, and played second hand low, and third high, and it was not until the third rubber was over that she saw. It had been in full evidence from the first. Jane would have seen it before the guests arrived, but Viola had not put it in her hair until the last moment. Viola was wild with delight, yet shamefaced and a trifle uneasy. In a soft, white gown, with violets at her waist, she was playing with Harold Lind, and in her ash-blond hair was Jane Carew's amethyst comb. Jane gasped and paled. The amiable young woman who was her opponent stared at her. Finally she spoke in a low voice.

'Aren't you well, Miss Carew?' she asked.

The men, in their turn, stared. The stout one rose fussily. 'Let me get a glass of water,' he said. The stupid small man stood up and waved his hands with nervousness.

'Aren't you well?' asked the amiable young lady again.

Then Jane Carew recovered her poise. It was seldom that she lost it. 'I am quite well, thank you, Miss Murdock,' she replied. 'I believe diamonds are trumps.'

They all settled again to the play, but the young lady and the two men continued glancing at Miss Carew. She had recovered her dignity of manner, but not her colour. Moreover, she had a bewildered expression. Resolutely she abstained from glancing again at her amethyst comb in Viola Longstreet's ash-blond hair, and gradually, by a course of subconscious reasoning as she carefully played her cards, she arrived at a conclusion which caused her colour to return and the bewildered expression to disappear.

When refreshments were served, the amiable young lady said, kindly: 'You look quite yourself, now, dear Miss Carew, but at one time while we were playing I was really alarmed. You were very pale.'

'I did not feel in the least ill,' replied Jane Carew. She smiled her Carew smile at the young lady. Jane had settled it with herself that of course Viola had borrowed that amethyst comb, appealing to Margaret. Viola ought not to have done that; she should have asked her, Miss Carew; and Jane wondered, because Viola was very well bred; but of course that was what had happened. Jane had come down before Viola, leaving Margaret in her room, and Viola had asked her. Jane did not then remember that Viola had not even been told that there was an amethyst comb in existence. She remembered when Margaret, whose face was as pale and bewildered as her own, mentioned it, when she was brushing her hair.

'I saw it, first thing. Miss Jane,' said Margaret. 'Louisa and I were on the landing, and I looked down and saw your amethyst comb in Mrs Long-street's hair.'

'She had asked you for it, because I had gone downstairs?' asked Jane, feebly.

'No, Miss Jane. I had not seen her. I went out right after you did. Louisa had finished Mrs Longstreet, and she and I went down to the mail-box to post a letter, and then we sat on the landing, and – I saw your comb.'

'Have you,' asked Jane, 'looked in the jewel-case?'

'Yes, Miss Jane.'

'And it is not there?'

'It is not there, Miss Jane.' Margaret spoke with a sort of solemn intoning. She recognised what the situation implied, and she, who fitted squarely and entirely into her humble state, was aghast before a hitherto unimagined occurrence. She could not, even with the evidence of her senses against a lady and her mistress's old friend, believe in them. Had Jane told her firmly that she had not seen that comb in that ash-blond hair she might have been hypnotised into agreement. But Jane simply stared at her, and the Carew dignity was more shaken than she had ever seen it.

'Bring the jewel-case here, Margaret,' ordered Jane in a gasp.

Margaret brought the jewel-case, and everything was taken out; all the compartments were opened, but the amethyst comb was not there. Jane could not sleep that night. At dawn she herself doubted the evidence of her senses. The jewel-case was thoroughly overlooked again, and still Jane was incredulous that she would ever see her comb in Viola's hair again. But that evening, although there were no guests except Harold Lind, who dined at the house, Viola appeared in a pink-tinted gown, with a knot of violets at her waist, and – she wore the amethyst comb. She said not one word concerning it; nobody did. Harold Lind was in wild spirits. The conviction grew upon Jane that the irresponsible, beautiful youth was covertly amusing himself at her, at Viola's, at everybody's expense. Perhaps he included himself. He talked incessantly, not in reality brilliantly, but with an effect of sparkling effervescence which was fairly dazzling. Viola's servants restrained with difficulty their laughter at his sallies. Viola regarded Harold with ill-concealed tenderness and admiration. She herself looked even younger than usual, as if the innate youth in her leaped to meet this charming comrade.

Jane felt sickened by it all. She could not understand her friend. Not for one minute did she dream that there could be any serious outcome of the situation: that Viola would marry this mad youth, who, she knew, was making such covert fun at her expense; but she was bewildered and indignant. She wished that she had not come. That evening when she went to her room she directed Margaret to pack, as she intended to return home the next day. Margaret began folding gowns with alacrity. She was as conservative as her mistress and she severely disapproved of many things. However, the matter of the amethyst comb was uppermost in her mind. She was wild with curiosity. She hardly dared enquire, but finally she did.

'About the amethyst comb, ma'am?' she said, with a delicate cough.

'What about it, Margaret?' returned Jane, severely.

'I thought perhaps Mrs Longstreet had told you how she happened to have it.'

Poor Jane Carew had nobody in whom to confide. For once she spoke her mind to her maid. 'She has not said one word. And, oh, Margaret, I don't know what to think of it.'

Margaret pursed her lips.

'What do *you* think, Margaret?'

'I don't know, Miss Jane.'

'I don't.'

'I did not mention it to Louisa,' said Margaret.

'Oh, I hope not!' cried Jane.

'But she did to me,' said Margaret. 'She asked had I seen Miss Viola's new comb, and then she laughed, and I thought from the way she acted that – ' Margaret hesitated.

'That what?'

'That she meant Mr Lind had given Miss Viola the comb.'

Jane started violently. 'Absolutely impossible!' she cried. 'That, of course, is nonsense. There must be some explanation. Probably Mrs Longstreet will explain before we go.'

Mrs Longstreet did not explain. She wondered and expostulated when Jane announced her firm determination to leave, but she seemed utterly at a loss for the reason. She did not mention the comb.

When Jane Carew took leave of her old friend she was entirely sure in her own mind that she would never visit her again – might never even see her again.

Jane was unutterably thankful to be back in her own peaceful home, over which no shadow of absurd mystery brooded; only a calm afternoon light of life, which disclosed gently but did not conceal or betray. Jane settled back into her pleasant life, and the days passed, and the weeks, and the months, and the years. She heard nothing whatever from or about Viola Longstreet for three years. Then, one day, Margaret returned from the city, and she had met Viola's old maid Louisa in a department store, and she had news. Jane wished for strength to refuse to listen, but she could not muster it. She listened while Margaret brushed her hair.

'Louisa has not been with Miss Viola for a long time,' said Margaret. 'She is living with somebody else. Miss Viola lost her money, and had to give up her house and her servants, and Louisa said she cried when she said goodbye.'

Jane made an effort. 'What became of – ' she began.

Margaret answered the unfinished sentence. She was excited by gossip as by a stimulant. Her thin cheeks burned, her eyes blazed. 'Mr Lind,' said Margaret, 'Louisa told me, had turned out to be real bad. He got into some money trouble, and then' – Margaret lowered her voice – 'he was arrested for taking a lot of money which didn't belong to him. Louisa said he had been in some business where he handled a lot of other folks' money, and he cheated the men who were in the business with him, and he was tried, and Miss Viola, Louisa thinks, hid away somewhere so they wouldn't call her to testify, and then he had to go to prison; but – ' Margaret hesitated.

'What is it?' asked Jane.

'Louisa thinks he died about a year and a half ago. She heard the lady where she lives now talking about it. The lady used to know Miss Viola, and she heard the lady say Mr Lind had died in prison, that he couldn't stand the hard life, and that Miss Viola had lost all her money through him, and then' – Margaret hesitated again, and her mistress prodded sharply – 'Louisa said that she heard the lady say that she had thought Miss Viola would marry him, but she hadn't, and she had more sense than she had thought.'

'Mrs Longstreet would never for one moment have entertained the thought of marrying Mr Lind; he was young enough to be her grandson,' said Jane, severely.

'Yes, ma'am,' said Margaret.

It so happened that Jane went to New York that day week, and at a jewellery counter in one of the shops she discovered the amethyst comb. There were on sale a number of bits of antique jewellery, the precious flotsam and jetsam of old and wealthy families which had drifted, nobody knew before what currents of adversity, into that harbour of sale for all the world to see. Jane made no enquiries; the saleswoman volunteered simply the information that the comb was a real antique, and the stones were real amethysts and pearls, and the setting was solid gold, and the price was thirty dollars; and Jane bought it. She carried her old amethyst comb home, but she did not show it to anybody. She replaced it in its old compartment in her jewel-case and thought of it with wonder, with a hint of joy at regaining it, and with much sadness. She was still fond of Viola Longstreet. Jane did not easily part with her loves. She did not know where Viola was. Margaret had enquired of Louisa, who did not know. Poor Viola had probably drifted into some obscure harbour of life wherein she was hiding until life was over.

And then Jane met Viola one spring day on Fifth Avenue.

'It is a very long time since I have seen you,' said Jane with a reproachful accent, but her eyes were tenderly enquiring.

'Yes,' agreed Viola. Then she added, 'I have seen nobody. Do you know what a change has come in my life?' she asked.

'Yes, dear,' replied Jane, gently. 'My Margaret met Louisa once and she told her.'

'Oh yes – Louisa,' said Viola. 'I had to discharge her. My money is about gone. I have only just enough to keep the wolf from entering the door of a hall bedroom in a respectable boarding-house. However, I often hear him howl, but I do not mind at all. In fact, the howling has become company for me. I rather like it. It is queer what things one can learn to like. There are a few left yet, like the awful heat in summer, and the food, which I do not fancy, but that is simply a matter of time.'

Viola's laugh was like a bird's song – a part of her – and nothing except death could silence it for long.

'Then,' said Jane, 'you stay in New York all summer?'

Viola laughed again. 'My dear,' she replied, 'of course. It is all very simple. If I left New York, and paid board anywhere, I would never have enough money to buy my return fare, and certainly not to keep that wolf from my hall-bedroom door.'

'Then,' said Jane, 'you are going home with me.'

'I cannot consent to accept charity, Jane,' said Viola. 'Don't ask me.'

Then, for the first time in her life, Viola Longstreet saw Jane Carew's eyes blaze with anger. 'You dare to call it charity coming from me to you?' she said, and Viola gave in.

When Jane saw the little room where Viola lived, she marvelled, with the exceedingly great marvelling of a woman to whom love of a man has never come, at a woman who could give so much and with no return.

Little enough to pack had Viola. Jane understood with a shudder of horror that it was almost destitution, not poverty, to which her old friend was reduced.

'You shall have that north-east room which you always liked,' she told Viola when they were on the train.

'The one with the old-fashioned peacock paper, and the pine tree growing close to one window?' said Viola, happily.

Jane and Viola settled down to life together, and Viola, despite the tragedy which she had known, realised a peace and happiness beyond her imagination. In reality, although she still looked so youthful, she was old enough to enjoy the pleasures of later life. Enjoy them she did to the utmost. She and Jane made calls together, entertained friends at small and stately dinners, and gave little teas. They drove about in the old Carew carriage. Viola had some new clothes. She played very well on Jane's old piano. She embroidered, she gardened. She lived the sweet, placid life of an older lady in a little village, and loved it. She never mentioned Harold Lind.

Not among the vicious of the earth was poor Harold Lind; rather among those of such beauty and charm that the earth spoils them, making them, in their own estimation, free guests at all its tables of bounty. Moreover, the young man had, deeply rooted in his character, the traits of a mischievous child, rejoicing in his mischief more from a sense of humour so keen that it verged on cruelty than from any intention to harm others. Over that affair of the amethyst comb, for instance, his irresponsible, selfish, childish soul had fairly revelled in glee. He had not been fond of Viola, but he liked her fondness for himself. He had made sport of her, but only for his own entertainment – never for the entertainment of others. He was a beautiful creature, seeking out paths of pleasure and folly for himself alone, which ended as do all paths of earthly pleasure and folly. Harold had admired Viola, but from the same point of view as Jane Carew's. Viola had, when she looked her youngest and best, always seemed so old as to be venerable to him. He had at times compunctions, as if he were making a jest of his grandmother. Viola never knew the truth about the amethyst comb. He had considered that one of the best frolics of his life. He had simply purloined it and presented it to Viola, and merrily left matters to settle themselves.

Viola and Jane had lived together a month before the comb was mentioned. Then one day Viola was in Jane's room and the jewel-case was out, and she began examining its contents. When she found the amethyst comb she gave a little cry. Jane, who had been seated at her desk and had not seen what was going on, turned around.

Viola stood holding the comb, and her cheeks were burning. She fondled the trinket as if it had been a baby. Jane watched her. She began to understand the bare facts of the mystery of the disappearance of her amethyst comb, but the subtlety of it was for ever beyond her. Had the other woman explained what was in her mind, in her heart – how that reckless young man whom she had loved had given her the treasure because he had heard her admire Jane's amethysts, and she, all unconscious of any wrongdoing, had ever regarded it as the one evidence of his thoughtful tenderness, it being the one gift she had ever received from him; how she parted with it, as she had parted with her other jewels, in order to obtain money to purchase comforts for him while he was in prison – Jane could not have understood. The fact of an older woman being fond of a young man, almost a boy, was beyond her mental grasp. She had no imagination with which to comprehend that innocent, pathetic, almost terrible love of one who has trodden the earth long for one who has just set dancing feet upon it. It was noble of Jane Carew that, lacking all such imagination, she acted as she did: that, although she did not, could not, formulate it to herself, she would no more have deprived the other woman and the dead man of that one little unscathed bond of tender goodness than she would have robbed his grave of flowers.

Viola looked at her. 'I cannot tell you all about it; you would laugh at me,' she whispered; 'but this was mine once.'

'It is yours now, dear,' said Jane.

ELIZABETH GASKELL

Elizabeth Cleghorn Gaskell was born in Chelsea on 29 September 1810. Her mother was a Holland of Sandlebridge in Cheshire, her father from Berwick. Successively a Unitarian minister, a tutor in classics, a farmer and a contributor to major reviews, he became in 1806 Keeper of the Papers at the Treasury in London. His wife died a year after Elizabeth's birth. A son John, born on 27 November 1798, became a mate in the merchant marine. Elizabeth was brought up by her mother's sister, Hannah Lumb, a widow living at Knutsford. In 1821 she sent Elizabeth for five years to a first-class private school for girls in Warwickshire. In 1832 she married William Gaskell, junior minister of a very important Unitarian chapel at Cross Street in Manchester. They had seven children between 1833 and 1846. Four girls only survived, the greatest loss being that of a son who almost reached his first birthday. Both William and Elizabeth wrote verse, but it was Elizabeth Gaskell who became known after 1847 for accomplished novels, stories and articles. Her circle of acquaintance widened dramatically. In 1850 she made friends with Charlotte Brontë, of whom after her unexpected death she swiftly wrote a major biography, *The Life of Charlotte Brontë* (1857). The revival of Elizabeth Gaskell's reputation in the last few decades has meant that works like *Mary Barton* (1848), *Ruth* (1853), *North and South* (1855), *Sylvia's Lovers* (1863) and *Cousin Phillis* (1864) can now be found in a number of editions, together with selections from her short stories and a collected edition of her brilliant letters (1966, 1997). *Wives and Daughters*, which many regard as her masterpiece, was not quite finished at her death on 12 November 1865.

The Crooked Branch

Not many years after the beginning of this century, a worthy couple of the name of Huntroyd occupied a small farm in the North Riding of Yorkshire. They had married late in life, although they were very young when they first began to 'keep company' with each other. Nathan Huntroyd had been farm-servant to Hester Rose's father, and had made up to her at a time when her parents thought she might do better; and so, without much consultation of her feelings, they had dismissed Nathan in somewhat cavalier fashion. He had drifted far away from his former connections, when an uncle of his died, leaving Nathan – by this time upwards of forty years of age – enough money to stock a small farm, and yet have something over to put in the bank against bad times. One of the consequences of this bequest was that Nathan was looking out for a wife and housekeeper, in a kind of discreet and leisurely way, when one day he heard that his old love, Hester, was not married and flourishing, as he had always supposed her to be, but a poor maid-of-all-work, in the town of Ripon. For her father had had a succession of misfortunes, which had brought him in his old age to the workhouse; her mother was dead; her only brother struggling to bring up a large family; and Hester herself a hard-working, homely-looking (at thirty-seven) servant. Nathan had a kind of growling satisfaction (which only lasted a minute or two, however) in hearing of these turns of fortune's wheel. He did not make many intelligible remarks to his informant, and to no one else did he say a word. But, a few days afterwards, he presented himself, dressed in his Sunday best, at Mrs Thompson's back-door in Ripon.

Hester stood there, in answer to the good sound knock his good sound oak-stick made: she, with the light full upon her, he in shadow. For a moment there was silence. He was scanning the face and figure of his old love, for twenty years unseen. The comely beauty of youth had faded away entirely; she was, as I have said, homely-looking, plain-featured, but with a clean skin, and pleasant frank eyes. Her figure was no longer round, but tidily draped in a blue and white bed-gown, tied round her waist by her white apron-strings, and her short red linsey petticoat showed her tidy feet and ankles. Her former lover fell into no ecstasies. He simply said to himself, 'She'll do'; and forthwith began upon his business.

'Hester, thou dost not mind me. I am Nathan, as thy father turned off at a minute's notice, for thinking of thee for a wife, twenty year come Michaelmas next. I have not thought much upon matrimony since. But Uncle Ben has died leaving me a small matter in the bank; and I have taken

Nab-End Farm, and put in a bit of stock, and shall want a missus to see after it. Wilt like to come? I'll not mislead thee. It's dairy, and it might have been arable. But arable takes more horses nor it suited me to buy, and I'd the offer of a tidy lot of kine. That's all. If thou'll have me, I'll come for thee as soon as the hay is gotten in.'

Hester only said, 'Come in, and sit thee down.'

He came in, and sat down. For a time, she took no more notice of him than of his stick, bustling about to get dinner ready for the family whom she served. He meanwhile watched her brisk sharp movements, and repeated to himself, 'She'll do!' After about twenty minutes of silence thus employed, he got up, saying, 'Well, Hester, I'm going. When shall I come back again?'

'Please thysel', and thou'll please me,' said Hester, in a tone that she tried to make light and indifferent; but he saw that her colour came and went, and that she trembled while she moved about. In another moment Hester was soundly kissed; but, when she looked round to scold the middle-aged farmer, he appeared so entirely composed that she hesitated.

He said: 'I have pleased mysel', and thee too, I hope. Is it a month's wage, and a month's warning? Today is the eighth. July eighth is our wedding-day. I have no time to spend a-wooing before then, and wedding must na take long. Two days is enough to throw away, at our time o' life.'

It was like a dream; but Hester resolved not to think more about it till her work was done. And when all was cleaned up for the evening, she went and gave her mistress warning, telling her all the history of her life in a very few words. That day month she was married from Mrs Thompson's house.

The issue of the marriage was one boy, Benjamin. A few years after his birth, Hester's brother died at Leeds, leaving ten or twelve children. Hester sorrowed bitterly over this loss; and Nathan showed her much quiet sympathy, although he could not but remember that Jack Rose had added insult to the bitterness of his youth. He helped his wife to make ready to go by the waggon to Leeds. He made light of the household difficulties, which came thronging into her mind after all was fixed for her departure. He filled her purse, that she might have wherewithal to alleviate the immediate wants of her brother's family. And, as she was leaving, he ran after the waggon. 'Stop, stop!' he cried. 'Hetty, if thou wilt – if it wunnot be too much for thee – bring back one of Jack's wenches for company, like. We've enough and to spare; and a lass will make the house winsome, as a man may say.'

The waggon moved on; while Hester had such a silent swelling of gratitude in her heart, as was both thanks to her husband and thanksgiving to God.

And that was the way that little Bessy Rose came to be an inmate of Nab-End Farm.

Virtue met with its own reward in this instance, and in a clear and tangible shape, too; which need not delude people in general into thinking that such is the usual nature of virtue's rewards! Bessy grew up a bright, affectionate, active girl; a daily comfort to her uncle and aunt. She was so much a darling in the household that they even thought her worthy of their only son Benjamin, who was perfection in their eyes. It is not often the case that two plain, homely people have a child of uncommon beauty; but it is so sometimes, and Benjamin Huntroyd was one of these exceptional cases. The hard-working, labour-and-care-marked farmer, and the mother, who could never have been more than tolerably comely in her best days, produced a boy who might have been an earl's son for grace and beauty. Even the hunting squires of the neighbourhood reined up their horses to admire him, as he opened the gates for them. He had no shyness, he was so accustomed from his earliest years to admiration from strangers and adoration from his parents. As for Bessy Rose, he ruled imperiously over her heart from the time she first set eyes on him. And, as she grew older, she grew on in loving, persuading herself that what her uncle and aunt loved so dearly it was her duty to love dearest of all. At every unconscious symptom of the young girl's love for her cousin, his parents smiled and winked: all was going on as they wished; no need to go far afield for Benjamin's wife. The household could go on as it was now; Nathan and Hester sinking into the rest of years, and relinquishing care and authority to those dear ones, who, in the process of time, might bring other dear ones to share their love.

But Benjamin took it all very coolly. He had been sent to a day-school in the neighbouring town – a grammar-school in the high state of neglect in which the majority of such schools were thirty years ago. Neither his father nor his mother knew much of learning. All they knew (and that directed their choice of a school) was that they could not, by any possibility, part with their darling to a boarding-school; that some schooling he must have; and that Squire Pollard's son went to Highminster Grammar School. Squire Pollard's son, and many another son destined to make his parents' hearts ache, went to this school. If it had not been so utterly a bad place of education, the simple farmer and his wife might have found it out sooner. But not only did the pupils there learn vice, they also learnt deceit. Benjamin was naturally too clever to remain a dunce; or else, if he had chosen so to be, there was nothing in Highminster Grammar School to hinder his being a dunce of the first water. But, to all appearance, he grew clever and gentlemanlike. His father and mother were even proud of his airs and graces, when he came home for the holidays, taking them for proofs of his refinement, although the practical effect of such refinement was to make him express his contempt for his parents' homely ways and simple ignorance. By the time he was eighteen, an articled clerk in an attorney's office at Highminster – for he had quite declined becoming a 'mere clod-hopper', that is to say, a hard-working, honest farmer like his father – Bessy Rose was the only person who was dissatisfied with him. The little girl of fourteen instinctively felt there was something wrong about him. Alas! two years more, and the girl of sixteen worshipped his very shadow, and would not see that aught could be wrong with one so soft-spoken, so handsome, so kind as Cousin Benjamin. For Benjamin had discovered that the way to cajole his parents out of money for every indulgence he fancied, was to pretend to forward their innocent scheme, and make love to his pretty cousin, Bessy Rose. He cared just enough for her to make this work of necessity not disagreeable at the time he was performing it. But he found it tiresome to remember her little claims upon him, when she was no longer present. The letters he had promised her during his weekly absence at Highminster, the trifling commissions she had asked him to do for her, were all considered in the light of troubles; and, even when he was with her, he resented the enquiries she made as to his mode of passing his time, or what female acquaintances he had in Highminster.

When his apprenticeship was ended, nothing would serve him but that he must go up to London for a year or two. Poor Farmer Huntroyd was beginning to repent of his ambition of making his son Benjamin a gentleman. But it was too late to repine now. Both father and mother felt this; and, however sorrowful they might be, they were silent, neither demurring nor assenting to Benjamin's proposition when first he made it. But Bessy, through her tears, noticed that both her uncle and aunt seemed unusually tired that night, and sat hand-in-hand on the fireside settle, idly gazing into the bright flame, as if they saw in it pictures of what they had once hoped their lives would have been. Bessy rattled about among the supper things, as she put them away after Benjamin's departure, making more noise than usual – as if noise and bustle was what she needed to keep her from bursting out crying – and, having at one keen glance taken in the position and looks of Nathan and Hester, she avoided looking in that direction again, for fear the sight of their wistful faces should make her own tears overflow.

'Sit thee down, lass – sit thee down! Bring the creepie-stool to the fireside, and let's have a bit of talk over the lad's plans,' said Nathan, at last rousing himself to speak. Bessy came and sat down in front of the fire, and threw her apron over her face, as she rested her head on both hands. Nathan felt as if it was a chance which of the two women burst out crying first. So he thought he would speak, in hopes of keeping off the infection of tears.

'Didst ever hear of this mad plan afore, Bessy?'

'No, never!' Her voice came muffled and changed from under her apron. Hester felt as if the tone, both of question and answer, implied blame; and this she could not bear.

'We should ha' looked to it when we bound him; for of necessity it would ha' come to this. There's examins, and catechises, and I dunno what all for him to be put through in London. It's not his fault.'

'Which on us said it were?' asked Nathan, rather put out. 'Tho', for that matter, a few weeks would carry him over the mire, and make him as good a lawyer as any judge among 'em. Oud Lawson the attorney told me that, in a talk I had wi' him a bit sin. Na, na! it's the lad's own hankering after London that makes him want for to stay there for a year, let alone two.'

Nathan shook his head.

'And if it be his own hankering,' said Bessy, putting down her apron, her face all flame, and her eyes swollen up, 'I dunnot see harm in it. Lads aren't like lasses, to be teed to their own fireside like th' crook yonder. It's fitting for a young man to go abroad and see the world, afore he settles down.'

Hester's hand sought Bessy's; and the two women sat in sympathetic defiance of any blame that should be thrown on the beloved absent. Nathan only said: 'Nay, wench, dunnot wax up so; whatten's done's done; and worse, it's my doing. I mun needs make my bairn a gentleman; and we mun pay for it.'

'Dear uncle! he wunna spend much, I'll answer for it; and I'll scrimp and save i' the house, to make it good.'

'Wench!' said Nathan solemnly, 'it were not paying in cash I were speaking on: it were paying in heart's care, and heaviness of soul. Lunnon is a place where the devil keeps court as well as King George; and my poor chap has more nor once welly fallen into his clutches here. I dunno what he'll do, when he gets close within sniff of him.'

'Don't let him go, father!' said Hester, for the first time taking this view. Hitherto she had only thought of her own grief at parting with him. 'Father, if you think so, keep him here, safe under your own eye!'

'Nay!' said Nathan, 'he's past time o' life for that. Why, there's not one on us knows where he is at this present time, and he not gone out of our sight an hour. He's too big to be put back i' th' go-cart, mother, or to keep within doors, with the chair turned bottom-upwards.'

'I wish he were a wee bairn lying in my arms again! It were a sore day when I weaned him; and I think life's been gettin' sorer and sorer at every turn he's ta'en towards manhood.'

'Coom, lass; that's noan the way to be talking. Be thankful to marcy that thou'st getten a man for thy son as stands five foot eleven in's stockings, and neer a sick piece about him. We wunnot grudge him his fling, will we, Bess, my wench? He'll be coming back in a year, or, may be, a bit more, and be a' for settling in a quiet town like, wi' a wife that's noan so fur fra' me at this very minute. An' we oud folk, as we get into years, must gi' up farm, and tak a bit on a house near Lawyer Benjamin.'

And so the good Nathan, his own heart heavy enough, tried to soothe his womenkind. But, of the three, his eyes were longest in closing, his apprehensions the deepest founded.

'I misdoubt me I hanna done well by th' lad. I misdoubt me sore,' was the thought that kept him awake till day began to dawn. 'Summat's wrong about him, or folk would na look at me wi' such piteous-like een, when they speak on him. I can see th' meaning of it, tho' I'm too proud to let on. And Lawson, too, he holds his tongue more nor he should do, when I ax him how my lad's getting on, and whatten sort of a lawyer he'll mak. God be marciful to Hester an' me, if th' lad's gone away! God be marciful! But, may be, it's this lying waking a' the night through, that maks me so fearfu'. Why, when I were his age, I daur be bound I should ha' spent money fast enoof, i' I could ha' come by iy. But I had to arn it; that maks a great differ'. Well! It were hard to thwart th' child of our old age, and we waitin' so long for to have 'un!' Next morning, Nathan rode Moggy, the cart-horse, into Highminster to see Mr Lawson. Anybody who saw him ride out of his own yard would have been struck with the change in him which was visible when he returned: a change greater than a day's unusual exercise should have made in a man of his years. He scarcely held the reins at all. One jerk of Moggy's head would have plucked them out of his hands. His head was bent forward, his eyes looking on some unseen thing, with long, unwinking gaze. But, as he drew near home on his return, he made an effort to recover himself.

'No need fretting them,' he said; 'lads will be lads. But I didna think he had it in him to be so thowtless, young as he is. Well, well! he'll maybe get more wisdom i' Lunnon. Anyways, it's best to cut him off fra such evil lads as Will Hawker, and suchlike. It's they as have led my boy astray. He were a good chap till he knowed them – a good chap till he knowed them.' But he put all his cares in the background, when he came into the house-place, where both Bessy and his wife met him at the door, and both would fain lend a hand to take off his greatcoat.

'Theer, wenches, theer! ye might let a man alone for to get out on's clothes! Why, I might ha' struck thee, lass.' And he went on talking, trying to keep them off for a time from the subject that all had at heart. But there was no putting them off for ever; and, by dint of repeated questioning on his wife's part, more was got out than he had ever meant to tell – enough to grieve both his hearers sorely; and yet the brave old man still kept the worst in his own breast.

The next day, Benjamin came home for a week or two, before making his great start to London. His father kept him at a distance, and was solemn and quiet in his manner to the young man. Bessy, who had shown anger enough at first, and had uttered many a sharp speech, began to relent, and then to feel hurt and displeased that her uncle should persevere so long in his cold, reserved manner – and Benjamin just going to leave them! Her aunt went, tremblingly busy, about the clothes-presses and drawers, as if afraid of letting herself think either of the past or the future; only once or twice, coming behind her son, she suddenly stooped over his sitting figure, and kissed his cheek, and stroked his hair. Bessy remembered afterwards – long years afterwards – how he had tossed his head away with nervous irritability on one of these occasions, and had muttered – her aunt did not hear it, but Bessy did: 'Can't you leave a man alone?'

Towards Bessy herself he was pretty gracious. No other words express his manner . . . it was not warm, nor tender, nor cousinly, but there was an assumption of underbred politeness towards her as a young, pretty woman; which politeness was neglected in his authoritative or grumbling manner towards his mother, or his sullen silence before his father. He once or twice ventured on a compliment to Bessy on her personal appearance. She stood still, and looked at him with astonishment.

'Have my eyes changed sin' last thou saw'st them,' she asked, 'that thou must be telling me about 'em i' that fashion? I'd rayther by a deal see thee helping thy mother, when she's dropped her knitting-needle and canna see i' th' dusk for to pick it up.'

But Bessy thought of his pretty speech about her eyes, long after he had forgotten making it, and when he would have been puzzled to tell the colour of them. Many a day, after he was gone, did she look earnestly in the little oblong looking-glass, which hung up against the wall of her little sleeping-chamber, but which she used to take down in order to examine the eyes he had praised, murmuring to herself, 'Pretty, soft grey eyes! Pretty, soft grey eyes!' until she would hang up the glass again, with a sudden laugh and a rosy blush.

In the days when he had gone away to the vague distance and vaguer place – the city called London – Bessy tried to forget all that had gone against her feeling of the affection and duty that a son owed to his parents; and she had many things to forget of this kind that would keep surging up into her mind. For instance, she wished that he had not objected to the home-spun, home-made shirts which his mother and she had had such pleasure in getting ready for him. He might not know, it was true – and so her love urged – how carefully and evenly the thread had been spun: how, not content with bleaching the yarn in the sunniest meadow, the linen, on its return from the weaver's, had been spread out afresh on the sweet summer grass, and watered carefully, night after night, when there was no dew to perform the kindly office. He did not know – for no one but Bessy herself did – how many false or large stitches, made large and false by her aunt's failing eyes (who yet liked to do the choicest part of the stitching all by herself), Bessy had unpicked at night in her own room, and with dainty fingers had re-stitched; sewing eagerly in the dead of night. All this he did not know; or he could never have complained of the coarse texture, the old-fashioned make of these shirts, and urged on his mother to give him part of her little store of egg- and butter-money, in order to buy newer-fashioned linen in Highminster.

When once that little precious store of his mother's was discovered, it was well for Bessy's peace of mind that she did not know how loosely her aunt counted up the coins, mistaking guineas for shillings, or just the other way, so that the amount was seldom the same in the old black spoutless teapot. Yet this son, this hope, this love, had still a strange power of fascination over the household. The evening before he left, he sat between his parents, a hand in theirs on either side, and Bessy on the old creepie-stool, her head lying on her aunt's knee, and looking up at him from time to time, as if to learn his face off by heart; till his glances, meeting hers, made her drop her eyes, and only sigh.

He stopped up late that night with his father, long after the women had gone to bed. But not to sleep; for I will answer for it the grey-haired mother never slept a wink till the late dawn of the autumn day; and Bessy heard her uncle come upstairs with heavy, deliberate footsteps, and go to the old stocking which served him for bank, and count out the golden guineas; once he stopped, but again he went on afresh, as if resolved to crown his gift with liberality. Another long pause – in which she could but indistinctly hear continued words, it might have been advice, it might be a prayer, for it was in her uncle's voice – and then father and son came up to bed. Bessy's room was but parted from her cousin's by a thin wooden partition; and the last sound she distinctly heard, before her eyes, tired out with crying, closed themselves in sleep, was the guineas clinking down upon each other at regular intervals, as if Benjamin were playing at pitch and toss with his father's present.

After he was gone, Bessy wished so he had asked her to walk part of the way with him into Highminster. She was all ready, her things laid out on the bed; but she could not accompany him without invitation.

The little household tried to close over the gap as best they might. They seemed to set themselves to their daily work with unusual vigour; but somehow, when evening came there had been little done. Heavy hearts never make light work, and there was no telling how much care and anxiety each had had to bear in secret in the field, at the wheel, or in the dairy. Formerly, he was looked for every Saturday – looked for, though he might not come; or, if he came, there were things to be spoken about that made his visit anything but a pleasure: still, he might come, and all things might go right; and then what sunshine, what gladness to those humble people! But now he was away, and dreary winter was come on; old folks' sight fails, and the evenings were long and sad, in spite of all Bessy could do or say. And he did not write so often as he might – so each one thought; though each one would have been ready to defend him from either of the others who had expressed such a thought aloud. 'Surely,' said Bessy to herself, when the first primroses peeped out in a sheltered and sunny hedge-bank, and she gathered them as she passed home from afternoon church – 'surely, there never will be such a dreary, miserable winter again as this has been.' There had been a great change in Nathan and Hester Huntroyd during this last year. The spring before, when Benjamin was yet the subject of more hopes than fears, his father and mother looked what I may call an elderly middle-aged couple: people who had a good deal of hearty work in them yet. Now – it was not his absence alone that caused the change – they looked frail and old, as if each day's natural trouble was a burden more than they could bear. For Nathan had heard sad reports about his only child, and had told them solemnly to his wife – as things too bad to be believed, and yet, 'God help us if he is indeed such a lad as this!' Their eyes were become too dry and hollow for many tears; they sat together, hand in hand; and shivered, and sighed, and did not speak many words, or dare to look at each other: and then Hester had said: 'We mauna tell th' lass. Young folks' hearts break wi' a little, and she'd be apt to fancy it were true.' Here the old woman's voice broke into a kind of piping cry; but she struggled, and her next words were all right. 'We mauna tell her: he's bound to be fond on her, and, may be, if she thinks well on him, and loves him, it will bring him straight!'

'God grant it !' said Nathan.

'God shall grant it!' said Hester, passionately moaning out her words; and then repeating them, alas! with a vain repetition.

'It's a bad place for lying, is Highminster,' said she at length, as if impatient of the silence. 'I never knowed such a place for getting up stories. But Bessy knows nought on 'em and nother you nor me belie'es 'em, that's one blessing.'

But, if they did not in their hearts believe them, how came they to look so sad and worn, beyond what mere age could make them?

Then came round another year, another winter, yet more miserable than the last. This year, with the primroses, came Benjamin; a bad, hard, flippant young man, with yet enough of specious manners and handsome countenance to make his appearance striking at first to those to whom the aspect of a London fast young man of the lowest order is strange and new. Just at first, as he sauntered in with a swagger and an air of indifference, which was partly assumed, partly real, his old parents felt a simple kind of awe of him, as if he were not their son, but a real gentleman; but they had too much fine instinct in their homely natures not to know, after a very few minutes had passed, that this was not a true prince.

'Whatten ever does he mean,' said Hester to her niece, as soon as they were alone, 'by a' them maks and wear-locks? And he minces his words, as if his tongue were clipped short, or split like a magpie's. Hech! London is as bad as a hot day i' August for spoiling good flesh; for he were a good-looking lad when he went up; and now, look at him, with his skin gone into lines and flourishes, just like the first page on a copybook.'

'I think he looks a good deal better, aunt, for them new-fashioned whiskers!' said Bessy, blushing still at the remembrance of the kiss he had given her on first seeing her – a pledge, she thought, poor girl, that, in spite of his long silence in letter-writing, he still looked upon her as his troth-plight wife. There were things about him which none of them liked, although they never spoke of them; yet there was also something to gratify them in the way in which he remained quiet at Nab-End, instead of seeking variety, as he had formerly done, by constantly stealing off to the neighbouring town. His father had paid all the debts that he knew of, soon after Benjamin had gone up to London; so there were no duns that his parents knew of to alarm him, and keep him at home. And he went out in the morning with the old man, his father, and lounged by his side, as Nathan went round his fields, with busy yet infirm gait; having heart, as he would have expressed it, in all that was going on, because at length his son seemed to take an interest in the farming affairs, and stood patiently by his side, while he compared his own small galloways with the great shorthorns looming over his neighbour's hedge.

'It's a slovenly way, thou seest, that of selling th' milk; folk don't care whether its good or not, so that they get their pint-measure of stuff that's watered afore it leaves th' beast, instead o' honest cheating by the help o' th' pump. But look at Bessy's butter, what skill it shows! part her own manner o' making, and part good choice o' cattle. It's a pleasure to see her basket, a' packed ready to go to market; and it's noan o' a pleasure for to see the buckets fu' of their blue starch-water as yon beasts give. I'm thinking they crossed th' breed wi' a pump not long sin'. Hech! but our Bessy's a clever canny wench! I sometimes think thou'lt be for gie'ing up th' law, and taking to th' oud trade, when thou wedst wi' her!' This was intended to be a skilful way of ascertaining whether there was any ground for the old farmer's wish and prayer, that Benjamin might give up the law and return to the primitive occupation of his father. Nathan dared to hope it now, since his son had never made much by his profession, owing, as he had said, to his want of a connection; and the farm, and the stock, and the clean wife, too, were ready to his hand; and Nathan could safely rely on himself never, in his most unguarded moments, to reproach his son with the hardly-earned hundreds that had been spent on his education. So the old man listened with painful interest to the answer which his son was evidently struggling to make, coughing a little and blowing his nose before he spoke.

'Well, you see, father, law is a precarious livelihood; a man, as I may express myself, has no chance in the profession unless he is known – known to the judges, and tip-top barristers, and that sort of thing. Now, you see, my mother and you have no acquaintance that you may call exactly in that line. But luckily I have met with a man, a friend, as I may say, who is really a first-rate fellow, knowing everybody, from the Lord Chancellor downwards; and he has offered me a share in his business – a partnership, in short' – He hesitated a little.

'I'm sure that's uncommon kind of the gentleman,' said Nathan. 'I should like for to thank him mysen; for it's not many as would pick up a young chap out o' th' dirt, as it were, and say, "Here's hauf my good fortune for you, sir, and your very good health!" Most on 'em when they're gettin' a bit o' luck, run off wi' it to keep it a' to themselves, and gobble it down in a corner. What may be his name? for I should like to know it.'

'You don't quite apprehend me, father. A great deal of what you've said is true to the letter. People don't like to share their good luck, as you say.'

'The more credit to them as does,' broke in Nathan.

'Ay, but, you see, even such a fine fellow as my friend Cavendish does not like to give away half his good practice for nothing. He expects an equivalent.'

' "An equivalent?" ' said Nathan; his voice had dropped down an octave. 'And what may that be? There's always some meaning in grand words, I take it; though I am not book-larned enough to find it out.'

'Why, in this case, the equivalent he demands for taking me into partnership, and afterwards relinquishing the whole business to me, is three hundred pounds down.'

Benjamin looked sideways from under his eyes, to see how his father took the proposition. His father struck his stick deep down in the ground; and, leaning one hand upon it, faced round at him.

'Then thy fine friend may go and be hanged. Three hunder pounds! I'll be darned an' danged too, if I know where to get 'em, if I'd be making a fool o' thee an' mysen too.'

He was out of breath by this time. His son took his father's first words in dogged silence; it was but the burst of surprise he had led himself to expect, and did not daunt him for long.

'I should think, sir – '

' "Sir" – whatten for dost thou "sir" me? Is them your manners? I'm plain Nathan Huntroyd, who never took on to be a gentleman; but I have paid my way up to this time, which I shannot do much longer, if I'm to have a son coming an' asking me for three hundred pound, just meet same as if I were a cow, and had nothing to do but let down my milk to the first person as strokes me.'

'Well, father,' said Benjamin, with an affectation of frankness; 'then there's nothing for me but to do as I have often planned before – go and emigrate.'

'And what?' said his father, looking sharply and steadily at him.

'Emigrate. Go to America, or India, or some colony where there would be an opening for a young man of spirit.'

Benjamin had reserved this proposition for his trump card, expecting by means of it to carry all before him. But, to his surprise, his father plucked his stick out of the hole he had made when he so vehemently thrust it into the ground, and walked on four or five steps in advance; there he stood still again, and there was a dead silence for a few minutes.

'It 'ud, maybe, be the best thing thou couldst do,' the father began. Benjamin set his teeth hard to keep in curses. It was well for poor Nathan he did not look round then, and see the look his son gave him. 'But it would come hard like upon us, upon Hester and me; for, whether thou'rt a good 'un or not, thou'rt our flesh and blood, our only bairn; and, if thou'rt not all as a man could wish, it's, maybe, been the fault on our pride i' the – It 'ud kill the missus, if he went off to Amerikay, and Bess, too, the lass as thinks so much on him!' The speech, originally addressed to his son, had wandered off into a monologue – as keenly listened to by Benjamin, however, as if it had all been spoken to him. After a pause of consideration, his father turned round: 'Yon man – I wunnot call him a friend o' yourn, to think of asking you for such a mint o' money – is not th' only one, I'll be bound, as could give ye a start i' the law? Other folks 'ud, maybe, do it for less?'

'Not one of 'em; to give me equal advantages,' said Benjamin, thinking he perceived signs of relenting.

'Well, then, thou may'st tell him that it's nother he nor thee as'll see th' sight o' three hundred pound o' my money. I'll not deny as I've a bit laid up again' a rainy day; it's not so much as thatten, though; and a part on it is for Bessy, as has been like a daughter to us.'

'But Bessy is to be your real daughter some day, when I've a home to take her to,' said Benjamin; for he played very fast and loose, even in his own mind, with his engagement to Bessy. Present with her, when she was looking her brightest and best, he behaved to her as if they were engaged lovers; absent from her, he looked upon her rather as a good wedge, to be driven into his parents' favour on his behalf. Now, however, he was not exactly untrue in speaking as if he meant to make her his wife; for the thought was in his mind, though he made use of it to work upon his father.

'It will be a dree day for us, then,' said the old man. 'But God'll have us in His keeping, and'll, may-happen, be taking more care on us i' heaven by that time than Bess, good lass as she is, has had on us at Nab-End. Her heart is set on thee, too. But, lad, I hanna gotten the three hunder; I keeps my cash i' th' stocking, thou know'st, till it reaches fifty pound, and then I takes it to Ripon Bank. Now the last scratch they'n gi'en me made it just two-hunder, and I hanna but on to fifteen pound yet i' the stockin', and I meant one hunder an' the red cow's calf to be for Bess, she's ta'en such pleasure like i' rearing it.'

Benjamin gave a sharp glance at his father, to see if he was telling the truth; and that a suspicion of the old man, his father, had entered into the son's head, tells enough of his own character.

'I canna do it, I canna do it, for sure; although I shall like to think as I had helped on the wedding. There's the black heifer to be sold yet, and she'll fetch a matter of ten pound; but a deal on't will be needed for seed-corn, for the arable did but bad last year, and I thought I would try – I'll tell thee what, lad! I'll make it as though Bess lent thee her hunder, only thou must give her a writ of hand for it; and thou shalt have a' the money i' Ripon Bank, and see if the lawyer wunnot let thee have a share of what he offered thee at three hunder for two. I dunnot mean for to wrong him; but thou must get a fair share for the money. At times, I think thou'rt done by folk; now I wadna have you cheat a bairn of a brass farthing; same time, I wadna have thee so soft as to be cheated.'

To explain this, it should be told that some of the bills, which Benjamin had received money from his father to pay, had been altered so as to cover other and less creditable expenses which the young man had incurred; and the simple old farmer, who had still much faith left in him for his boy, was acute enough to perceive that he had paid above the usual price for the articles he had purchased.

After some hesitation, Benjamin agreed to receive the two hundred, and promised to employ it to the best advantage in setting himself up in business. He had, nevertheless, a strange hankering after the additional fifteen pounds that was left to accumulate in the stocking. It was his, he thought, as heir to his father; and he soon lost some of his usual complaisance for Bessy that evening, as he dwelt on the idea that there was money being laid by for her, and grudged it to her even in imagination. He thought more of this fifteen pounds that he was not to have than of all the hardly-earned and humbly-saved two hundred that he was to come into possession of. Meanwhile, Nathan was in unusual spirits that evening. He was so generous and affectionate at heart that he had an unconscious satisfaction in having helped two people on the road to happiness by the sacrifice of the greater part of his property. The very fact of having trusted his son so largely seemed to make Benjamin more worthy of trust in his father's estimation. The sole idea he tried to banish was that, if all came to pass as he hoped, both Benjamin and Bessy would be settled far away from Nab-End; but then he had a child-like reliance that 'God would take care of him and his missus, somehow or anodder. It wur o' no use looking too far ahead.'

Bessy had to hear many unintelligible jokes from her uncle that night, for he made no doubt that Benjamin had told her all that had passed; whereas the truth was, his son had said never a word to his cousin on the subject.

When the old couple were in bed, Nathan told his wife of the promise he had made to his son, and the plan in life which the advance of the two hundred was to promote. Poor Hester was a little startled at the sudden change in the destination of the sum, which she had long thought of with secret pride as 'money i' th' bank'. But she was willing enough to part with it, if necessary, for Benjamin. Only, how such a sum could be necessary, was the puzzle. But even the perplexity was jostled out of her mind by the over-whelming idea, not only of 'our Ben' settling in London, but of Bessy going there too as his wife. This great trouble swallowed up all care about money, and Hester shivered and sighed all the night through with distress.

In the morning, as Bessy was kneading the bread, her aunt, who had been sitting by the fire in an unusual manner for one of her active habits, said, 'I reckon we maun go to th' shop for our bread; an' that's a thing I never thought to come to so long as I lived.'

Bessy looked up from her kneading, surprised.

'I'm sure, I'm noan going to eat their nasty stuff. What for do ye want to get baker's bread, aunt? This dough will rise as high as a kite in a south wind.'

'I'm not up to kneading as I could do once; it welly breaks my back; and, when tou'rt off in London, I reckon we maun buy our bread, first time in my life.'

'I'm not a-goin to London,' said Bessy, kneading away with fresh resolution, and growing very red, either with the idea or the exertion.

'But our Ben is going partner wi' a great London lawyer; and thou know'st he'll not tarry long but what he'll fetch thee.'

'Now, aunt,' said Bessy, stripping her arms of the dough, but still not looking up, 'if that's all, don't fret yourself. Ben will have twenty minds in his head, afore he settles, eyther in business or in wedlock. I sometimes wonder,' she said, with increasing vehemence, 'why I go on thinking on him; for I dunnot think he thinks on me, when I'm out o' sight. I've a month's mind to try and forget him this time, when he leaves us – that I have!'

'For shame, wench! and he to be planning and purposing, all for thy sake! It wur only yesterday as he wur talking to thy uncle, and mapping it out so clever; only, thou seest, wench, it'll be dree work for us when both thee and him is gone.'

The old woman began to cry the kind of tearless cry of the aged. Bessy hastened to comfort her; and the two talked, and grieved, and hoped, and planned for the days that now were to be, till they ended, the one in being consoled, the other in being secretly happy.

Nathan and his son came back from Highminster that evening with their business transacted in the roundabout way which was most satisfactory to the old man. If he had thought it necessary to take half as much pains in ascertaining the truth of the plausible details by which his son bore out the story of the offered partnership, as he did in trying to get his money conveyed to London in the most secure manner, it would have been well for him. But he knew nothing of all this, and acted in the way which satisfied his anxiety best. He came home tired, but content; not in such high spirits as on the night before, but as easy in his mind as he could be on the eve of his son's departure. Bessy, pleasantly agitated by her aunt's tale of the morning of her cousin's true love for her ('what ardently we wish we long believe') and the plan which was to end in their marriage – end to her, the woman, at least – looked almost pretty in her bright, blushing comeliness, and more than once, as she moved about from kitchen to dairy, Benjamin pulled her towards him, and gave her a kiss. To all such proceedings the old couple were wilfully blind; and, as night drew on, everyone became sadder and quieter, thinking of the parting that was to be on the morrow. As the hours slipped away, Bessy too became subdued; and, by and by, her simple cunning was exerted to get Benjamin to sit down next his mother, whose very heart was yearning after him, as Bessy saw. When once her child was placed by her side, and she had got possession of his hand, the old woman kept stroking it, and murmuring long unused words of endearment, such as she had spoken to him while he was yet a little child. But all this was wearisome to him. As long as he might play with, and plague, and caress Bessy, he had not been sleepy; but now he yawned loudly. Bessy could have boxed his ears for not curbing this gaping; at any rate, he need not have done it so openly – so almost ostentatiously. His mother was more pitiful.

'Thou'rt tired, my lad!' said she, putting her hand fondly on his shoulder; but it fell off, as he stood up suddenly, and said: 'Yes, deuced tired! I'm off to bed.' And with a rough, careless kiss all round, even to Bessy, as if he was 'deuced tired' of playing the lover, he was gone; leaving the three to gather up their thoughts slowly, and follow him upstairs.

He seemed almost impatient at them for rising betimes to see him off the next morning, and made no more of a goodbye than some such speech as this: 'Well, good folk, when next I see you, I hope you'll have merrier faces than you have today. Why, you might be going to a funeral; it's enough to scare a man from the place; you look quite ugly to what you did last night, Bess.'

He was gone; and they turned into the house, and settled to the long day's work without many words about their loss. They had no time for unnecessary talking, indeed; for much had been left undone, during his short visit, that ought to have been done, and they had now to work double tides. Hard work was their comfort for many a long day.

For some time Benjamin's letters, if not frequent, were full of exultant accounts of his well-doing. It is true that the details of his prosperity were somewhat vague; but the fact was broadly and unmistakenly stated. Then came longer pauses; shorter letters, altered in tone. About a year after he had left them, Nathan received a letter which bewildered and irritated him exceedingly. Something had gone wrong – what, Benjamin did not say – but the letter ended with a request that was almost a demand for the remainder of his father's savings, whether in the stocking or in the bank. Now, the year had not been prosperous with Nathan; there had been an epidemic among cattle, and he had suffered along with his neighbours; and, moreover, the price of cows, when he had bought some to repair his wasted stock, was higher than he had ever remembered it before. The fifteen pounds in the stocking, which Benjamin left, had diminished to little more than three; and to have that required of him in so peremptory a manner! Before Nathan imparted the contents of this letter to anyone (Bessy and her aunt had gone to market in a neighbour's cart that day), he got pen and ink and paper, and wrote back an ill-spelt, but very explicit and stern negative. Benjamin had had his portion; and if he could not make it do, so much the worse for him; his father had no more to give him. That was the substance of the letter.

The letter was written, directed, and sealed, and given to the country postman, returning to Highminster after his day's distribution and collection of letters, before Hester and Bessy came back from market. It had been a pleasant day of neighbourly meeting and sociable gossip; prices had been high, and they were in good spirits – only agreeably tired, and full of small pieces of news. It was some time before they found out how flatly all their talk fell on the ears of the stay-at-home listener. But, when they saw that his depression was caused by something beyond their powers of accounting for by any little everyday cause, they urged him to tell them what was the matter. His anger had not gone off. It had rather increased by dwelling upon it, and he spoke it out in good, resolute terms; and, long ere he had ended, the two women were as sad, if not as angry, as himself. Indeed, it was many days before either feeling wore away in the minds of those who entertained them. Bessy was the soonest comforted, because she found a vent for her sorrow in action: action that was half as a kind of compensation for many a sharp word that she had spoken when her cousin had done anything to displease her on his last visit, and half because she believed that he never could have written such a letter to his father unless his want of money had been very pressing and real; though how he could ever have wanted money so soon, after such a heap of it had been given to him, was more than she could justly say. Bessy got out all her savings of little presents of sixpences and shillings, ever since she had been a child – of all the money she had gained for the eggs of two hens, called her own; she put the whole together, and it was above two pounds – two pounds five and sevenpence, to speak accurately – and, leaving out the penny as a nest-egg for her future savings, she made up the rest in a little parcel, and sent it, with a note, to Benjamin's address in London:

From a well-wisher

DEAR BENJAMIN – Unkle has lost 2 cows and a vast of monney. He is a good deal Angored, but more Troubled. So no more at present. Hopeing this will finding you well As it leaves us. Tho' lost to Site, To Memory Dear. Repayment not kneeded.

Your effectonet cousin,

ELIZABETH ROSE

When this packet was once fairly sent off, Bessy began to sing again over her work. She never expected the mere form of acknowledgement; indeed, she had such faith in the carrier (who took parcels to York, whence they were forwarded to London by coach), that she felt sure he would go on purpose to London to deliver anything entrusted to him, if he had not full confidence in the person, persons, coach and horses, to whom he committed it. Therefore she was not anxious that she did not hear of its arrival. 'Giving a thing to a man as one knows,' said she to herself, 'is a vast different to poking a thing through a hole into a box, th' inside of which one has never clapped eyes on; and yet letters get safe, some ways or another.' (The belief in the infallibility of the post was destined to a shock before long.) But she had a secret yearning for Benjamin's thanks, and some of the old words of love that she had been without so long. Nay, she even thought – when, day after day, week after week, passed by without a line – that he might be winding up his affairs in that weary, wasteful London, and coming back to Nab-End to thank her in person.

One day – her aunt was upstairs, inspecting the summer's make of cheeses, her uncle out in the fields – the postman brought a letter into the kitchen to Bessy. A country postman, even now, is not much pressed for time; and in those days there were but few letters to distribute, and they were only sent out from Highminster once a week into the district in which Nab-End was situated; and, on those occasions, the letter-carrier usually paid morning calls on the various people for whom he had letters. So, half-standing by the dresser, half-sitting on it, he began to rummage out his bag.

'It's a queer-like thing I've got for Nathan this time. I am afraid it will bear ill news in it; for there's 'Dead Letter Office' stamped on the top of it.'

'Lord save us!' said Bessy, and sat down on the nearest chair, as white as a sheet. In an instant, however, she was up; and, snatching the ominous letter out of the man's hands, she pushed him before her out of the house, and said, 'Be off wi' thee, afore aunt comes down'; and ran past him as hard as she could, till she reached the field where she expected to find her uncle.

'Uncle,' said she, breathless, 'what is it? Oh, uncle, speak! Is he dead?'

Nathan's hands trembled, and his eyes dazzled, 'Take it,' he said, 'and tell me what it is.'

'It's a letter – it's from you to Benjamin, it is – and there's words written on it, "Not known at the address given"; so they've sent it back to the writer – that's you, uncle. Oh, it gave me such a start, with them nasty words written outside!'

Nathan had taken the letter back into his own hands, and was turning it over, while he strove to understand what the quick-witted Bessy had picked up at a glance. But he arrived at a different conclusion.

'He's dead!' said he. 'The lad is dead, and he never knowed how as I were sorry I wrote to 'un so sharp. My lad! my lad!' Nathan sat down on the ground where he stood, and covered his face with his old, withered hands. The letter returned to him was one which he had written, with infinite pains and at various times, to tell his child, in kinder words and at greater length than he had done before, the reasons why he could not send him the money demanded. And now Benjamin was dead; nay, the old man immediately jumped to the conclusion that his child had been starved to death, without money, in a wild, wide, strange place.

All he could say at first was, 'My heart, Bess – my heart is broken!' And he put his hand to his side, still keeping his shut eyes covered with the other, as though he never wished to see the light of day again.

Bessy was down by his side in an instant, holding him in her arms, chafing and kissing him. 'It's noan so bad, uncle; he's not dead; the letter does not say that, dunnot think it. He's flitted from that lodging, and the lazy tykes dunna know where to find him; and so they just send y' back th' letter, instead of trying fra' house to house, as Mark Benson would. I've always heerd tell on south-country folk for laziness. He's noan dead, uncle; he's just flitted; and he'll let us know afore long where he's gotten to. Maybe it's a cheaper place; for that lawyer has cheated him, ye reck'lect, and he'll be trying to live for as little as he can, that's all, uncle. Dunnot take on so; for it doesna say he's dead.'

By this time Bessy was crying with agitation, although she firmly believed in her own view of the case, and had felt the opening of the ill-favoured letter as a great relief. Presently she began to urge, both with word and action, upon her uncle, that he should sit no longer on the damp grass, She pulled him up; for he was very stiff, and, as he said, 'all shaken to dithers'. She made him walk about, repeating over and over again her solution of the case, always in the same words, beginning again and again, 'He's noan dead; it's just been a flitting,' and so on. Nathan shook his head, and tried to be convinced; but it was a steady belief in his own heart for all that. He looked so deathly ill on his return home with Bessy (for she would not let him go on with his day's work) that his wife made sure he had taken cold; and he, weary and indifferent to life, was glad to subside into bed and the rest from exertion which his real bodily illness gave him. Neither Bessy nor he spoke of the letter again, even to each other, for many days; and she found means to stop Mark Benson's tongue and satisfy his kindly curiosity, by giving him the rosy side of her own view of the case.

Nathan got up again an older man in looks and constitution by ten years for that week of bed. His wife gave him many a scolding on his imprudence for sitting down in the wet field, if ever so tired. But now she, too, was beginning to be uneasy at Benjamin's long-continued silence. She could not write herself; but she urged her husband many a time to send a letter to ask for news of her lad. He said nothing in reply for some time; at length, he told her he would write next Sunday afternoon. Sunday was his general day for writing, and this Sunday he meant to go to church for the first time since his illness. On Saturday he was very persistent, against his wife's wishes (backed by Bessy as hard as she could), in resolving to go into Highminster to market. The change would do him good, he said. But he came home tired, and a little mysterious in his ways. When he went to the shippon the last thing at night, he asked Bessy to go with him, and hold the lantern, while he looked at an ailing cow; and, when they were fairly out of the ear-shot of the house, he pulled a little shop-parcel from his pocket and said, 'Thou'lt put that on ma Sunday hat, wilt 'on, lass? It'll be a bit on a comfort to me; for I know my lad's dead and gone, though I dunna speak on it, for fear o' grieving th' old woman and ye.'

'I'll put it on, uncle, if – But he's noan dead.' (Bessy was sobbing.)

'I know – I know, lass. I dunnot wish other folk to hold my opinion; but I'd like to wear a bit o' crape out o' respect to my boy. It 'ud have done me good for to have ordered a black coat; but she'd see if I had na' on my wedding-coat, Sundays, for a' she's losing her eyesight, poor old wench! But she'll ne'er take notice o' a bit o' crape. Thou'lt put it on all canny and tidy.'

So Nathan went to church with a strip of crape, as narrow as Bessy durst venture to make it, round his hat. Such is the contradictoriness of human nature that, though he was most anxious his wife should not hear of his conviction that their son was dead, he was half-hurt that none of his neighbours noticed his sign of mourning so far as to ask him for whom he wore it.

But after a while, when they never heard a word from or about Benjamin, the household wonder as to what had become of him grew so painful and strong, that Nathan no longer kept the idea to himself. Poor Hester, however, rejected it with her whole will, heart, and soul. She could and would not believe – nothing should make her believe – that her only child Benjamin had died without some sign of love or farewell to her. No arguments could shake her in this. She believed that, if all natural means of communication between her and him had been cut off at the last supreme moment – if death had come upon him in an instant, sudden and unexpected – her intense love would have been supernaturally made conscious of the blank. Nathan at times tried to feel glad that she should still hope to see the lad again; but at other moments he wanted her sympathy in his grief, his self-reproach, his weary wonder as to how and what they had done wrong in the treatment of their son that he had been such a care and sorrow to his parents. Bessy was convinced, first by her aunt, and then by her uncle – honestly convinced – on both sides of the argument, and so, for the time, able to sympathise with each. But she lost her youth in a very few months: she looked set and middle-aged, long before she ought to have done, and rarely smiled and never sang again.

All sorts of new arrangements were required by the blow which told so miserably upon the energies of all the household at Nab-End. Nathan could no longer go about and direct his two men, taking a good turn at the work himself at busy times. Hester lost her interest in the dairy; for which, indeed, her increasing loss of sight unfitted her. Bessy would either do field-work, or attend to the cows and the shippon, or churn, or make cheese; she did all well, no longer merrily, but with something of stern cleverness. But she was not sorry when her uncle, one evening, told her aunt and her that a neighbouring farmer, Job Kirkby, had made him an offer to take so much of his land off his hands as would leave him only pasture enough for two cows, and no arable to attend to; while Farmer Kirkby did not wish to interfere with anything in the house, only would be glad to use some of the out-buildings for fattening his cattle.

'We can do wi' Hawky and Daisy; it'll leave us eight or ten pound o' butter to take to market i' summer time, and keep us fra' thinking too much, which is what I'm dreading on as I get into years.'

'Ay,' said his wife. 'Thou'll not have to go so far afield, if it's only the Aster-Toft as is on thy hands. And Bess will have to gie up her pride i' cheese, and tak' to making cream-butter. I'd allays a fancy for trying at cream-butter; but th' whey had to be used; else, where I come fra', they'd never ha' looked near whey-butter.'

When Hester was left alone with Bessy, she said, in allusion to this change of plan, 'I'm thankful to the Lord that it is as it is; for I were allays afeared Nathan would have to gie up the house and farm altogether, and then the lad would na know where to find us when he came back fra' Merikay. He's gone there for to make his fortune, I'll be bound. Keep up thy heart, lass, he'll be home some day; and have sown his wild oats. Eh! but thatten's a pretty story i' the Gospel about the Prodigal, who'd to eat the pigs' vittle at one time, but ended i' clover in his father's house. And I'm sure our Nathan'll be ready to forgive him, and love him, and make much of him – maybe a deal more nor me, who never gave in to 's death. It'll be liken to a resurrection to our Nathan.'

Farmer Kirkby, then, took by far the greater part of the land belonging to Nab-End Farm; and the work about the rest, and about the two remaining cows, was easily done by three pairs of willing hands, with a little occasional assistance. The Kirkby family were pleasant enough to have to deal with. There was a son, a stiff, grave bachelor, who was very particular and methodical about his work, and rarely spoke to anyone. But Nathan took it into his head that John Kirkby was looking after Bessy, and was a good deal troubled in his mind in consequence; for it was the first time he had to face the effects of his belief in his son's death; and he discovered, to his own surprise, that he had not that implicit faith which would make it easy for him to look upon Bessy as the wife of another man than the one to whom she had been betrothed in her youth. As, however, John Kirkby seemed in no hurry to make his intentions (if indeed he had any) clear to Bessy, it was only now and then that his jealousy on behalf of his lost son seized upon Nathan.

But people, old, and in deep hopeless sorrow, grow irritable at times, however they may repent and struggle against their irritability. There were days when Bessy had to bear a good deal from her uncle; but she loved him so dearly and respected him so much, that, high as her temper was to all other people, she never returned him a rough or impatient word. And she had a reward in the conviction of his deep, true affection for her, and her aunt's entire and most sweet dependence upon her.

One day, however – it was near the end of November – Bessy had had a good deal to bear, that seemed more than usually unreasonable, on the part of her uncle. The truth was, that one of Kirkby's cows was ill, and John Kirkby was a good deal about in the farmyard; Bessy was interested about the animal, and had helped in preparing a mash over their own fire, that had to be given warm to the sick creature. If John had been out of the way, there would have been no one more anxious about the affair than Nathan: both because he was naturally kind-hearted and neighbourly, and also because he was rather proud of his reputation for knowledge in the diseases of cattle. But because John was about, and Bessy helping a little in what had to be done, Nathan would do nothing, and chose to assume that 'nothing to think on ailed th' beast; but lads and lasses were allays fain to be feared on something'. Now John was upwards of forty, and Bessy nearly eight-and-twenty; so the terms lads and lasses did not exactly apply to their case.

When Bessy brought the milk in from their own cows, towards half-past five o'clock, Nathan bade her make the doors, and not be running out i' the dark and cold about other folks' business; and, though Bessy was a little surprised and a good deal annoyed at his tone, she sat down to her supper without making a remonstrance. It had long been Nathan's custom to look out the last thing at night, to see 'what mak' o' weather it wur'; and when, towards half-past eight, he got his stick and went out – two or three steps from the door, which opened into the house-place where they were sitting – Hester put her hand on her niece's shoulder and said: 'He's gotten a touch o' rheumatics, as twinges him and makes him speak so sharp. I didna like to ask thee afore him, but how's yon poor beast?'

'Very ailing, belike. John Kirkby wur off for th' cow-doctor when I cam in. I reckon they'll have to stop up wi' t a' night.'

Since their sorrows, her uncle had taken to reading a chapter in the Bible aloud, the last thing at night. He could not read fluently, and often hesitated long over a word, which he miscalled at length; but the very fact of opening the book seemed to soothe those old bereaved parents; for it made them feel quiet and safe in the presence of God, and took them out of the cares and troubles of this world into that futurity which, however dim and vague, was to their faithful hearts as a sure and certain rest. This little quiet time – Nathan sitting with his horn spectacles, the tallow candle between him and the Bible throwing a strong light on his reverent, earnest face; Hester sitting on the other side of the fire, her head bowed in attentive listening; now and then shaking it, and moaning a little, but when a promise came, or any good tidings of great joy, saying 'Amen' with fervour; Bessy by her aunt, perhaps her mind a little wandering to some household cares, or it might be on thoughts of those who were absent – this little quiet pause, I say, was grateful and soothing to this household, as a lullaby to a tired child. But this night, Bessy, sitting opposite to the long, low window, only shaded by a few geraniums that grew in the sill, and to the door alongside that window through which her uncle had passed not a quarter of an hour before, saw the wooden latch of the door gently and almost noiselessly lifted up, as if some-one were trying it from the outside.

She was startled, and watched again, intently; but it was perfectly still now. She thought it must have been that it had not fallen into its proper place when her uncle had come in and locked the door. It was just enough to make her uncomfortable, no more; and she almost persuaded herself it must have been fancy. Before going upstairs, however, she went to the window, to look out into the darkness; but all was still. Nothing to be seen; nothing to be heard. So the three went quietly upstairs to bed.

The house was little better than a cottage. The front door opened on a house-place, over which was the old couple's bedroom. To the left, as you entered this pleasant house-place, and at close right angles with the entrance, was a door that led into the small parlour, which was Hester's and Bessy's pride, although not half as comfortable as the house-place, and never on any occasion used as a sitting-room. There were shells and bunches of honesty in the fireplace; the best chest of drawers, and a company set of gaudy-coloured china, and a bright common carpet on the floor; but all failed to give it the aspect of the homely comfort and delicate cleanliness of the house-place. Over this parlour was the bedroom which Benjamin had slept in when a boy, when at home. It was kept, still, in a kind of readiness for him. The bed was yet there, in which none had slept since he had last done, eight or nine years ago; and every now and then a warming-pan was taken quietly and silently up by his old mother, and the bed thoroughly aired. But this she did in her husband's absence, and without saying a word to anyone; nor did Bessy offer to help her, though her eyes often filled with tears as she saw her aunt still going through the hopeless service. But the room had become a receptacle for all unused things; and there was always a corner of it appropriated to the winter's store of apples. To the left of the house-place, as you stood facing the fire, on the side opposite to the window and outer door, were two other doors; the one on the right led into a kind of back kitchen, which had a lean-to roof, and a door opening on to the farmyard and back-premises; the left-hand door gave on the stairs, underneath which was a closet, in which various household treasures were kept; and beyond that was the dairy, over which Bessy slept, her little chamber window opening just above the sloping roof of the back-kitchen. There were neither blinds nor shutters to any of the windows, either upstairs or down; the house was built of stone; and there was heavy framework of the same material around the little casement windows, and the long, low window of the house-place was divided by what, in grander dwellings, would be called mullions.

By nine o'clock this night of which I am speaking, all had gone upstairs to bed; it was even later than usual, for the burning of candles was regarded so much in the light of an extravagance that the household kept early hours even for country-folk. But, somehow, this evening, Bessy could not sleep; although in general she was in deep slumber five minutes after her head touched the pillow. Her thoughts ran on the chances for John Kirkby's cow, and a little fear lest the disorder might be epidemic and spread to their own cattle. Across all these homely cares came a vivid, uncomfortable recollection of the way in which the door-latch went up and down, without any sufficient agency to account for it. She felt more sure now than she had done downstairs that it was a real movement, and no effect of her imagination. She wished that it had not happened just when her uncle was reading, that she might at once have gone quick to the door, and convinced herself of the cause. As it was, her thoughts ran uneasily on the supernatural; and thence to Benjamin, her dear cousin and playfellow, her early lover. She had long given him up as lost for ever to her, if not actually dead; but this very giving him up for ever involved a free, full forgiveness of all his wrongs to her. She thought tenderly of him, as of one who might have been led astray in his later years, but who existed rather in her recollection as the innocent child, the spirited lad, the handsome, dashing young man. If John Kirkby's quiet attentions had ever betrayed his wishes to Bessy – if indeed he ever had any wishes on the subject – her first feeling would have been to compare his weather-beaten, middle-aged face and figure with the face and figure she remembered well, but never more expected to see in this life. So thinking, she became very restless, and weary of bed, but, after long tossing and turning, ending in a belief that she should never get to sleep at all that night, she went off soundly and suddenly.

As suddenly she was wide awake, sitting up in bed, listening to some noise that must have awakened her, but which was not repeated for some time. Surely it was in her uncle's room – her uncle was up; but, for a minute or two, there was no further sound. Then she heard him open his door, and go downstairs, with hurried, stumbling steps. She now thought that her aunt must be ill, and hastily sprang out of bed, and was putting on her petticoat with hurried, trembling hands, and had just opened her chamber door, when she heard the front door undone, and a scuffle, as of the feet of several people, and many rude, passionate words, spoken hoarsely below the breath. Quick as thought she understood it all – the house was lonely – her uncle had the reputation of being well-to-do – they had pretended to be belated, and had asked their way or something. What a blessing that John Kirkby's cow was sick, for there were several men watching with him! She went back, opened her window, squeezed herself out, slid down the lean-to roof, and ran bare-foot and breathless to the shippon: 'John, John, for the love of God, come quick; there's robbers in the house, and uncle and aunt'll be murdered!' she whispered, in terrified accents, through the closed and barred shippon door. In a moment it was undone, and John and the cow-doctor stood there, ready to act, if they but understood her rightly. Again she repeated her words, with broken, half-unintelligible explanations of what she as yet did not rightly understand.

'Front door is open, say'st thou?' said John, arming himself with a pitchfork, while the cow-doctor took some other implement. 'Then I reckon we'd best make for that way o' getting into th' house, and catch 'em all in a trap.'

'Run! run!' was all Bessy could say, taking hold of John Kirkby's arm, and pulling him along with her. Swiftly did the three run to the house, round the corner, and in at the open front-door. The men carried the horn lantern they had been using in the shippon; and, by the sudden oblong light that it threw, Bessy saw the principal object of her anxiety, her uncle, lying stunned and helpless on the kitchen-floor. Her first thought was for him; for she had no idea that her aunt was in any immediate danger, although she heard the noise of feet, and fierce, subdued voices upstairs.

'Make th' door fast behind us, lass. We'll not let 'em escape!' said brave John Kirkby, dauntless in a good cause, though he knew not how many there might be above. The cow-doctor fastened and locked the door, saying, 'There!' in a defiant tone, as he put the key in his pocket. It was to be a struggle for life or death, or, at any rate, for effectual capture or desperate escape. Bessy kneeled down by her uncle, who did not speak or give any sign of consciousness. Bessy raised his head by drawing a pillow off the settle, and putting it under him; she longed to go for water into the back kitchen, but the sound of a violent struggle, and of heavy blows, and of low, hard curses spoken through closed teeth, and muttered passion, as though breath were too much needed for action to be wasted in speech, kept her still and quiet by her uncle's side in the kitchen, where the darkness might almost be felt, so thick and deep was it. Once – in a pause of her own heart's beating – a sudden terror came over her; she perceived, in that strange way in which the presence of a living creature forces itself on our consciousness in the darkest room, that someone was near her, keeping as still as she. It was not the poor old man's breathing that she heard, nor the radiation of his presence that she felt; someone else was in the kitchen; another robber, perhaps, left to guard the old man, with murderous intent if his consciousness returned. Now Bessy was fully aware that self-preservation would keep her terrible companion quiet, as there was no motive for his betraying himself stronger than the desire of escape; any effort for which he, the unseen witness, must know would be rendered abortive by the fact of the door being locked.

Yet, with the knowledge that he was there, close to her still, silent as the grave – with fearful, it might be deadly, unspoken thoughts in his heart – possibly even with keener and stronger sight than hers, as longer accustomed to the darkness, able to discern her figure and posture, and glaring at her like some wild beast – Bessy could not fail to shrink from the vision that her fancy presented! And still the struggle went on upstairs; feet slipping, blows sounding, and the wrench of intentioned aims, the strong gasps for breath, as the wrestlers paused for an instant. In one of these pauses, Bessy felt conscious of a creeping movement close to her, which ceased when the noise of the strife above died away, and was resumed when it again began. She was aware of it by some subtle vibration of the air, rather than by touch or sound. She was sure that he who had been close to her one minute as she knelt was, the next, passing stealthily towards the inner door which led to the staircase. She thought he was going to join and strengthen his accomplices, and, with a great cry, she sprang after him; but just as she came to the doorway, through which some dim portion of light from the upper chambers came, she saw one man thrown downstairs, with such violence that he fell almost at her very feet, while the dark, creeping figure glided suddenly away to the left, and as suddenly entered the closet beneath the stairs. Bessy had no time to wonder as to his purpose in so doing, whether he had at first designed to aid his accomplices in their desperate fight or not. He was an enemy, a robber, that was all she knew, and she sprang to the door of the closet, and in a trice had locked it on the outside. And then she stood frightened, panting in that dark corner, sick with terror lest the man who lay before her was either John Kirkby or the cow-doctor. If it were either of those friendly two, what would become of the other – of her uncle, her aunt, herself? But, in a very few minutes, this wonder was ended; her two defenders came slowly and heavily down the stairs, dragging with them a man, fierce, sullen, despairing – disabled with terrible blows, which had made his face one bloody, swollen mass. As for that, neither John nor the cow-doctor was much more presentable. One of them bore the lantern in his teeth; for all their strength was taken up by the weight of the fellow they were bearing.

'Take care,' said Bessy, from her corner; 'there's a chap just beneath your feet. I dunno know if he's dead or alive; and uncle lies on the floor just beyond.'

They stood still on the stairs for a moment; just then the robber they had thrown downstairs stirred and moaned.

'Bessy,' said John, 'run off to th' stable and fetch ropes and gearing for us to bind 'em; and we'll rid the house on 'em, and thou can'st go see after th' oud folks, who need it sadly.'

Bessy was back in a very few minutes. When she came in, there was more light in the house-place, for someone had stirred up the raked fire.

'That felly makes as though his leg were broken,' said John, nodding towards the man still lying on the ground. Bessy felt almost sorry for him as they handled him – not over-gently – and bound him, only half-conscious, as hardly and tightly as they had done his fierce, surly companion. She even felt so sorry for his evident agony, as they turned him over and over, that she ran to get him a cup of water to moisten his lips.

'I'm loth to leave yo' with him alone,' said John, 'though I'm thinking his leg is broken for sartin, and he can't stir, even if he comes to hissel, to do yo' any harm. But we'll just take off this chap, and mak sure of him, and then one on us'll come back to yo', and we can, maybe, find a gate or so for yo' to get shut on him o' th' house. This felly's made safe enough, I'll be bound,' said he, looking at the burglar, who stood, bloody and black, with fell hatred on his sullen face. His eye caught Bessy's, as hers fell on him with dread so evident that it made him smile; and the look and the smile prevented the words from being spoken which were on Bessy's lips.

She dared not tell, before him, that an able-bodied accomplice still remained in the house; lest, somehow, the door which kept him a prisoner should be broken open and the fight renewed. So she only said to John, as he was leaving the house: 'Thou'll not be long away, for I'm afeared of being left wi' this man.'

'He'll noan do thee harm,' said John.

'No! but I'm feared lest he should die. And there's uncle and aunt. Come back soon, John!'

'Ay, ay!' said he, half-pleased; 'I'll be back, never fear me.'

So Bessy shut the door after them, but did not lock it, for fear of mis-chances in the house, and went once more to her uncle, whose breathing, by this time, was easier than when she had first returned into the house-place with John and the doctor. By the light of the fire, too, she could now see that he had received a blow on the head, which was probably the occasion of his stupor. Round this wound, which was bleeding pretty freely, Bessy put cloths dipped in cold water; and then, leaving him for a time, she lighted a candle, and was about to go upstairs to her aunt, when, just as she was passing the bound and disabled robber, she heard her name softly, urgently called: 'Bessy, Bessy!' At first the voice sounded so close that she thought it must be the unconscious wretch at her feet. But, once again, that voice thrilled through her: 'Bessy, Bessy! for God's sake, let me out!'

She went to the stair-closet door, and tried to speak, but could not, her heart beat so terribly. Again, close to her ear: 'Bessy, Bessy! they'll be back directly; let me out, I say! For God's sake, let me out!' And he began to kick violently against the panels.

'Hush! hush!' she said, sick with a terrible dread, yet with a will strongly resisting her conviction. 'Who are you?' But she knew – knew quite well.

'Benjamin.' An oath. 'Let me out, I say, and I'll be off, and out of England by tomorrow night, never to come back, and you'll have all my father's money.'

'D'ye think I care for that?' said Bessy vehemently, feeling with trembling hands for the lock; 'I wish there was noan such a thing as money i' the world, afore yo'd come to this. There, yo're free, and I charge yo' never to let me see your face again. I'd ne'er ha' let yo' loose but for fear o' breaking their hearts, if yo' hanna killed him already.' But, before she had ended her speech, he was gone – off into the black darkness, leaving the door open wide. With a new terror in her mind, Bessy shut it afresh – shut it and bolted it this time. Then she sat down on the first chair, and relieved her soul by giving a great and exceeding bitter cry. But she knew it was no time for giving way; and, lifting herself up with as much effort as if each of her limbs was a heavy weight, she went into the back kitchen, and took a drink of cold water. To her surprise, she heard her uncle's voice saying feebly: 'Carry me up, and lay me by her.'

But Bessy could not carry him; she could only help his faint exertions to walk upstairs; and, by the time he was there, sitting panting on the first chair she could find, John Kirkby and Atkinson returned. John came up now to her aid. Her aunt lay across the bed in a fainting-fit, and her uncle sat in so utterly broken-down a state that Bessy feared immediate death for both. But John cheered her up, and lifted the old man into his bed again; and, while Bessy tried to compose poor Hester's limbs into a position of rest, John went down to hunt about for the little store of gin which was always kept in a corner cupboard against emergencies.

'They've had a sore fright,' said he, shaking his head, as he poured a little gin and hot water into their mouths with a teaspoon, while Bessy chafed their cold feet; 'and it and the cold have been welly too much for 'em, poor old folk!'

He looked tenderly at them, and Bessy blessed him in her heart for that look.

'I maun be off. I sent Atkinson up to th' farm for to bring down Bob, and Jack came wi' him back to th' shippon, for to look after t'other man. He began blackguarding us all round, so Bob and Jack were gagging him wi' bridles when I left.'

'Ne'er give heed to what he says,' cried poor Bessy, a new panic besetting her. 'Folks o' his sort are allays for dragging other folk into their mischief. I'm right glad he were well gagged.'

'Well! but what I were saying were this: Atkinson and me will take t'other chap, who seems quiet enough, to th' shippon, and it'll be one piece o' work for to mind them and the cow; and I'll saddle t' old bay mare and ride for constables and doctor fra' Highminster. I'll bring Dr Preston up to see Nathan and Hester first; and then, I reckon, th' broken-legged chap down below must have his turn for all as he's met wi' his misfortunes in a wrong line o' life.'

'Ay!' said Bessy. 'We maun ha' the doctor sure enough, for look at them how they lie – like two stone statues on a church monument, so sad and solemn!'

'There's a look o' sense come back into their faces though, sin' they supped that gin-and-water. I'd keep on a-bathing his head and giving them a sup on't fra' time to time, if I was you, Bessy.'

Bessy followed him downstairs, and lighted the men out of the house. She dared not light them carrying their burden until they passed round the corner of the house, so strong was her fearful conviction that Benjamin was lurking near, seeking again to enter. She rushed back into the kitchen, bolted and barred the door, and pushed the end of the dresser against it, shutting her eyes as she passed the uncurtained window, for fear of catching a glimpse of a white face pressed against the glass, and gazing at her. The poor old couple lay quiet and speechless, although Hester's position had slightly altered: she had turned a little on her side towards her husband, and had laid one shrivelled arm around his neck. But he was just as Bessy had left him, with the wet cloths around his head, his eyes not wanting in a certain intelligence, but solemn, and unconscious to all that was passing around as the eyes of death.

His wife spoke a little from time to time – said a word of thanks, perhaps, or so; but he, never. All the rest of that terrible night, Bessy tended the poor old couple with constant care, her own heart so stunned and bruised in its feelings that she went about her pious duties almost like one in a dream. The November morning was long in coming; nor did she perceive any change, either for the worse or the better, before the doctor came, about eight o'clock. John Kirkby brought him; and was full of the capture of the two burglars.

As far as Bessy could make out, the participation of that unnatural third was unknown. It was a relief almost sickening in the revulsion it gave her from her terrible fear, which now she felt had haunted and held possession of her all night long, and had, in fact, paralysed her from thinking. Now she felt and thought with acute and feverish vividness, owing, no doubt, in part, to the sleepless night she had passed. She felt almost sure that her uncle (possibly her aunt, too) had recognised Benjamin; but there was a faint chance that they had not done so, and wild horses should never tear the secret from her, nor should any inadvertent word betray the fact that there had been a third person concerned. As to Nathan, he had never uttered a word. It was her aunt's silence that made Bessy fear lest Hester knew, somehow, that her son was concerned.

The doctor examined them both closely; looked hard at the wound on Nathan's head; asked questions which Hester answered shortly and unwillingly, and Nathan not at all – shutting his eyes, as if even the sight of a stranger was pain to him. Bessy replied, in their stead, to all that she could answer respecting their state, and followed the doctor downstairs with a beating heart. When they came into the house-place, they found John had opened the outer door to let in some fresh air, had brushed the hearth and made up the fire, and put the chairs and table in their right places. He reddened a little as Bessy's eye fell upon his swollen and battered face, but tried to smile it off in a dry kind of way: 'Yo' see, I'm an ould bachelor, and I just thought as I'd redd up things a bit. How dun yo' find 'em, doctor?'

'Well, the poor old couple have had a terrible shock. I shall send them some soothing medicine to bring down the pulse, and a lotion for the old man's head. It is very well it bled so much; there might have been a good deal of inflammation.' And so he went on, giving directions to Bessy for keeping them quietly in bed through the day. From these directions she gathered that they were not, as she had feared all night long, near to death. The doctor expected them to recover, though they would require care. She almost wished it had been otherwise, and that they, and she too, might have just lain down to their rest in the churchyard – so cruel did life seem to her; so dreadful the recollection of that subdued voice of the hidden robber smiting her with recognition.

All this time, John was getting things ready for breakfast, with something of the handiness of a woman. Bessy half-resented his officiousness in pressing Dr Preston to have a cup of tea, she did so want him to be gone and leave her alone with her thoughts. She did not know that all was done for love of her; that the hard-featured, short-spoken John was thinking all the time how ill and miserable she looked, and trying with tender artifices to make it incumbent upon her sense of hospitality to share Dr Preston's meal.

'I've seen as the cows is milked,' said he, 'yourn and all; and Atkinson's brought ours round fine. Whatten a marcy it were as she were sick this very night! Yon two chaps 'ud ha' made short work on't, if yo' hadna fetched us in; and, as it were, we had a sore tussle. One on 'em'll bear the marks on't to his dying day, wunnot he, doctor?'

'He'll barely have his leg well enough to stand his trial at York Assizes; they're coming off in a fortnight from now.'

'Ay, and that reminds me, Bessy, yo'll have to go witness before Justice Royds. Constables bade me tell yo' and gie yo' this summons. Dunnot be feared: it will not be a long job, though I'm not saying as it'll be a pleasant one. Yo'll have to answer questions as to how, and all about it; and Jane' (his sister) 'will come and stop wi' th' oud folks; and I'll drive yo' in the shandry.'

No one knew why Bessy's colour blenched, and her eye clouded. No one knew how she apprehended lest she should have to say that Benjamin had been of the gang; if indeed, in some way, the law had not followed on his heels quick enough to catch him.

But that trial was spared her; she was warned by John to answer questions, and say no more than was necessary, for fear of making her story less clear; and, as she was known, by character at least, to Justice Royds and his clerk, they made the examination as little formidable as possible.

When all was over, and John was driving her back again, he expressed his rejoicing that there would be evidence enough to convict the men without summoning Nathan and Hester to identify them. Bessy was so tired that she hardly understood what an escape it was; how far greater than even her companion understood.

Jane Kirkby stayed with her for a week or more, and was an unspeakable comfort. Otherwise she sometimes thought she should have gone mad, with the face of her uncle always reminding her, in its stony expression of agony, of that fearful night. Her aunt was softer in her sorrow, as became one of her faithful and pious nature; but it was easy to see how her heart bled inwardly. She recovered her strength sooner than her husband; but, as she recovered, the doctor perceived the rapid approach of total blindness. Every day, nay, every hour of the day, that Bessy dared, without fear of exciting their suspicions of her knowledge, she told them, as she had anxiously told them at first, that only two men, and those perfect strangers, had been discovered as being concerned in the burglary. Her uncle would never have asked a question about it, even if she had withheld all information respecting the affair; but she noticed the quick, watching, waiting glance of his eye, when-ever she returned from any person or place where she might have been supposed to gain intelligence if Benjamin were suspected or caught: and she hastened to relieve the old man's anxiety, by always telling all that she had heard; thankful that, as the days passed on, the danger she sickened to think of grew less and less.

Day by day, Bessy had ground for thinking that her aunt knew more than she had apprehended at first. There was something so very humble and touching in Hester's blind way of feeling about for her husband – stern, woebegone Nathan – and mutely striving to console him in the deep agony of which Bessy learnt, from this loving, piteous manner, that her aunt was conscious. Her aunt's face looked blankly up into his, tears slowly running down from her sightless eyes; while from time to time, when she thought herself unheard by any save him, she would repeat such texts as she had heard at church in happier days, and which she thought, in her true, simple piety, might tend to console him. Yet, day by day, her aunt grew more and more sad.

Three or four days before assize-time, two summonses to attend the trial at York were sent to the old people. Neither Bessy, nor John, nor Jane, could understand this: for their own notices had come long before, and they had been told that their evidence would be enough to convict.

But, alas! the fact was that the lawyer employed to defend the prisoners had heard from them that there was a third person engaged, and had heard who that third person was; and it was this advocate's business to diminish, if possible, the guilt of his clients, by proving that they were but tools in the hands of one who had, from his superior knowledge of the premises and the daily customs of the inhabitants, been the originator and planner of the whole affair. To do this, it was necessary to have the evidence of the parents, who, as the prisoners had said, must have recognised the voice of the young man, their son. For no one knew that Bessy, too, could have borne witness to his having been present; and, as it was supposed that Benjamin had escaped out of England, there was no exact betrayal of him on the part of his accomplices.

Wondering, bewildered, and weary, the old couple reached York, in company with John and Bessy, on the eve of the day of the trial. Nathan was still so self-contained that Bessy could never guess what had been passing in his mind. He was almost passive under his old wife's trembling caresses. He seemed hardly conscious of them, so rigid was his demeanour.

She, Bessy feared at times, was becoming childish; for she had evidently so great and anxious a love for her husband that her memory seemed going in her endeavours to melt the stoniness of his aspect and manners; she appeared occasionally to have forgotten why he was so changed, in her piteous little attempts to bring him back to his former self.

'They'll, for sure, never torture them, when they see what old folks they are!' cried Bessy, on the morning of the trial, a dim fear looming over her mind. 'They'll never be so cruel, for sure?'

But 'for sure' it was so. The barrister looked up at the judge, almost apologetically, as he saw how hoary-headed and woeful an old man was put into the witness-box when the defence came on and Nathan Huntroyd was called on for his evidence.

'It is necessary, on behalf of my clients, my lord, that I should pursue a course which, for all other reasons, I deplore.'

'Go on!' said the judge. 'What is right and legal must be done.' But, an old man himself, he covered his quivering mouth with his hand as Nathan, with grey, unmoved face, and solemn, hollow eyes, placing his two hands on each side of the witness-box, prepared to give his answers to questions, the nature of which he was beginning to foresee, but would not shrink from replying to truthfully; 'the very stones' (as he said to himself, with a kind of dulled sense of the Eternal justice) 'rise up against such a sinner'.

'Your name is Nathan Huntroyd, I believe?'

'It is.'

'You live at Nab-End Farm?'

'I do.'

'Do you remember the night of November the twelfth?'

'Yes.'

'You were awakened that night by some noise, I believe. What was it?'

The old man's eyes fixed themselves upon his questioner with the look of a creature brought to bay. That look the barrister never forgets. It will haunt him till his dying day.

'It was a throwing-up of stones against our window.'

'Did you hear it at first?'

'No.'

'What awakened you, then?'

'She did.'

'And then you both heard the stones. Did you hear anything else?'

A long pause. Then a low, clear, 'Yes.'

'What?'

'Our Benjamin asking us for to let him in. She said as it were him, leastways.'

'And you thought it was him, did you not?'

'I told her' (this time in a louder voice) 'for to get to sleep, and not be thinking that every drunken chap as passed by were our Benjamin, for that he were dead and gone.'

'And she?'

'She said as that she'd heerd our Benjamin, afore she were welly awake, axing for to be let in. But I bade her ne'er heed her dreams, but turn on her other side and get to sleep again.'

'And did she?'

A long pause – judge, jury, bar, audience, all held their breath. At length Nathan said, 'No!'

'What did you do then? (My lord, I am compelled to ask these painful questions.)'

'I saw she wadna be quiet: she had allays thought he would come back to us, like the Prodigal i' th' Gospels.' (His voice choked a little; but he tried to make it steady, succeeded, and went on.) 'She said, if I wadna get up, she would; and just then I heerd a voice. I'm not quite mysel', gentlemen – I've been ill and i' bed, an' it makes me trembling-like. Someone said, "Father, mother, I'm here, starving i' the cold – wunnot yo' get up and let me in?"'

'And that voice was – ?'

'It were like our Benjamin's. I see whatten yo're driving at, sir, and I'll tell yo' truth, though it kills me to speak it. I dunnot say it were our Benjamin as spoke, mind yo' – I only say it were like – '

'That's all I want, my good fellow. And on the strength of that entreaty, spoken in your son's voice, you went down and opened the door to these two prisoners at the bar, and to a third man?'

Nathan nodded assent, and even that counsel was too merciful to force him to put more into words.

'Call Hester Huntroyd.'

An old woman, with a face of which the eyes were evidently blind, with a sweet, gentle, careworn face, came into the witness-box, and meekly curtseyed to the presence of those whom she had been taught to respect – a presence she could not see.

There was something in her humble, blind aspect, as she stood waiting to have something done to her – what her poor troubled mind hardly knew – that touched all who saw her, inexpressibly. Again the counsel apologised, but the judge could not reply in words; his face was quivering all over, and the jury looked uneasily at the prisoners' counsel. That gentleman saw that he might go too far, and send their sympathies off on the other side; but one or two questions he must ask. So, hastily recapitulating much that he had learned from Nathan, he said, 'You believed it was your son's voice asking to be let in?'

'Ay! Our Benjamin came home, I'm sure; choose where he is gone.'

She turned her head about, as if listening for the voice of her child, in the hushed silence of the court.

'Yes; he came home that night – and your husband went down to let him in?'

'Well! I believe he did. There was a great noise of folk downstair.'

'And you heard your son Benjamin's voice among the others?'

'Is it to do him harm, sir?' asked she, her face growing more intelligent and intent on the business in hand.

'That is not my object in questioning you. I believe he has left England; so nothing you can say will do him any harm. You heard your son's voice, I say?'

'Yes, sir. For sure I did.'

'And some men came upstairs into your room? What did they say?'

'They axed where Nathan kept his stocking.'

'And you – did you tell them?'

'No, sir, for I knew Nathan would not like me to.'

'What did you do then?'

A shade of reluctance came over her face, as if she began to perceive causes and consequences.

'I just screamed on Bessy – that's my niece, sir.'

'And you heard someone shout out from the bottom of the stairs?'

She looked piteously at him, but did not answer.

'Gentlemen of the jury, I wish to call your particular attention to this fact; she acknowledges she heard someone shout – some third person, you observe – shout out to the two above. What did he say? That is the last question I shall trouble you with. What did the third person, left behind, downstairs, say?'

Her face worked – her mouth opened two or three times as if to speak – she stretched out her arms imploringly; but no word came, and she fell back into the arms of those nearest to her.

Nathan forced himself forward into the witness-box: 'My Lord Judge, a woman bore ye, as I reckon; it's a cruel shame to serve a mother so. It wur my son, my only child, as called out for us t' open door, and who shouted out for to hold th' oud woman's throat if she did na stop her noise, when she'd fain ha' cried for her niece to help. And now yo've truth, and a' th' truth, and I'll leave yo' to th' judgement o' God for th' way yo've getten at it.'

Before night the mother was stricken with paralysis, and lay on her death-bed. But the broken-hearted go Home, to be comforted of God.

Right at Last

Dr Brown was poor, and had to make his way in the world. He had gone to study his profession in Edinburgh, and his energy, ability, and good conduct had entitled him to some notice on the part of the professors. Once introduced to the ladies of their families, his prepossessing appearance and pleasing manners made him a universal favourite; and perhaps no other student received so many invitations to dancing- and evening-parties, or was so often singled out to fill up an odd vacancy at the last moment at the dinner-table. No one knew particularly who he was, or where he sprang from; but then he had no near relations, as he had once or twice observed; so he was evidently not hampered with low-born or low-bred connections. He had been in mourning for his mother when he first came to college.

All this much was summoned to the recollection of Professor Frazer by his niece Margaret, as she stood before him one morning in his study; telling him, in a low, but resolute voice that, the night before, Dr James Brown had offered her marriage – that she had accepted him – and that he was intending to call on Professor Frazer (her uncle and natural guardian) that very morning, to obtain his consent to their engagement. Professor Frazer was perfectly aware, from Margaret's manner, that his consent was regarded by her as a mere form, for that her mind was made up: and he had more than once had occasion to find out how inflexible she could be. Yet he, too, was of the same blood, and held to his own opinions in the same obdurate manner. The consequence of which frequently was that uncle and niece had argued themselves into mutual bitterness of feeling, without altering each other's opinions one jot. But Professor Frazer could not restrain himself on this occasion, of all others.

'Then, Margaret, you will just quietly settle down to be a beggar, for that lad Brown has little or no money to think of marrying upon: you that might be my Lady Kennedy, if you would!'

'I could not, uncle.'

'Nonsense, child! Sir Alexander is a personable and agreeable man – middle-aged, if you will – well, a wilful woman maun have her way; but, if I had had a notion that this youngster was sneaking into my house to cajole you into fancying him, I would have seen him far enough before I had ever let your aunt invite him to dinner. Ay! you may mutter; but I say, no gentleman would ever have come into my house to seduce my niece's affections, without first informing me of his intentions, and asking my leave.'

'Dr Brown is a gentleman, Uncle Frazer, whatever you may think of him.'

'So you think – so you think. But who cares for the opinion of a love-sick girl? He is a handsome, plausible young fellow, of good address. And I don't mean to deny his ability. But there is something about him I never did like, and now it's accounted for. And Sir Alexander – Well, well! your aunt will be disappointed in you, Margaret. But you were always a headstrong girl. Has this Jamie Brown ever told you who or what his parents were, or where he comes from? I don't ask about his forebears, for he does not look like a lad who has ever had ancestors; and you a Frazer of Lovat! Fie, for shame, Margaret ! Who is this Jamie Brown?'

'He is James Brown, Doctor of Medicine of the University of Edinburgh: a good, clever young man, whom I love with my whole heart,' replied Margaret, reddening.

'Hoot! is that the way for a maiden to speak? Where does he come from? Who are his kinsfolk? Unless he can give a pretty good account of his family and prospects, I shall just bid him begone, Margaret; and that I tell you fairly.'

'Uncle' (her eyes were filling with hot indignant tears), 'I am of age; you know he is good and clever; else why have you had him so often to your house? I marry him, and not his kinsfolk. He is an orphan. I doubt if he has any relations that he keeps up with. He has no brothers nor sisters. I don't care where he comes from.'

'What was his father?' asked Professor Frazer coldly.

'I don't know. Why should I go prying into every particular of his family, and asking who his father was, and what was the maiden name of his mother, and when his grandmother was married?'

'Yet I think I have heard Margaret Frazer speak up pretty strongly in favour of a long line of unspotted ancestry.'

'I had forgotten our own, I suppose, when I spoke so. Simon, Lord Lovat, is a creditable great-uncle to the Frazers! If all tales be true, he ought to have been hanged for a felon, instead of beheaded like a loyal gentleman.'

'Oh! if you're determined to foul your own nest, I have done. Let James Brown come in; I will make him my bow, and thank him for condescending to marry a Frazer.'

'Uncle,' said Margaret, now fairly crying, 'don't let us part in anger! We love each other in our hearts. You have been good to me, and so has my aunt. But I have given my word to Dr Brown, and I must keep it. I should love him, if he was the son of a ploughman. We don't expect to be rich; but he has a few hundreds to start with, and I have my own hundred a year – '

'Well, well, child, don't cry! You have settled it all for yourself, it seems; so I wash my hands of it. I shake off all responsibility. You will tell your aunt what arrangements you make with Dr Brown about your marriage; and I will do what you wish in the matter. But don't send the young man in to me to ask my consent! I neither give it nor withhold it. It would have been different if it had been Sir Alexander.'

'Oh! Uncle Frazer, don't speak so. See Dr Brown, and at any rate – for my sake – tell him you consent! Let me belong to you that much! It seems so desolate at such a time to have to dispose of myself, as if nobody owned or cared for me.'

The door was thrown open, and Dr James Brown was announced. Margaret hastened away; and, before he was aware, the Professor had given a sort of consent, without asking a question of the happy young man; who hurried away to seek his betrothed, leaving her uncle muttering to himself.

Both Dr and Mrs Frazer were so strongly opposed to Margaret's engagement, in reality, that they could not help showing it by manner and implication; although they had the grace to keep silent. But Margaret felt even more keenly than her lover that he was not welcome in the house. Her pleasure in seeing him was destroyed by her sense of the coldness with which he was received, and she willingly yielded to his desire of a short engagement; which was contrary to their original plan of waiting until he should be settled in practice in London, and should see his way clear to such an income as would render their marriage a prudent step. Dr and Mrs Frazer neither objected nor approved. Margaret would rather have had the most vehement opposition than this icy coldness. But it made her turn with redoubled affection to her warm-hearted and sympathising lover. Not that she had ever discussed her uncle and aunt's behaviour with him. As long as he was apparently unaware of it, she would not awaken him to a sense of it. Besides, they had stood to her so long in the relation of parents, that she felt she had no right to bring in a stranger to sit in judgement upon them.

So it was rather with a heavy heart that she arranged their future *ménage* with Dr Brown, unable to profit by her aunt's experience and wisdom. But Margaret herself was a prudent and sensible girl. Although accustomed to a degree of comfort in her uncle's house that almost amounted to luxury, she could resolutely dispense with it, when occasion required. When Dr Brown started for London, to seek and prepare their new home, she enjoined him not to make any but the most necessary preparations for her reception. She would herself superintend all that was wanting when she came. He had some old furniture, stored up in a warehouse, which had been his mother's. He proposed selling it, and buying new in its place. Margaret persuaded him not to do this, but to make it go as far as it could. The household of the newly-married couple was to consist of a Scotchwoman long connected with the Frazer family, who was to be the sole female servant, and of a man whom Dr Brown picked up in London, soon after he had fixed on a house – a man named Crawford, who had lived for many years with a gentleman now gone abroad who gave him the most excellent character in reply to Dr Brown's enquiries. This gentleman had employed Crawford in a number of ways, so that in fact he was a kind of Jack-of-all-trades; and Dr Brown, in every letter to Margaret, had some new accomplishment of his servant's to relate. This he did with the more fullness and zest because Margaret had slightly questioned the wisdom of starting in life with a manservant, but had yielded to Dr Brown's arguments on the necessity of keeping up a respectable appearance, making a decent show, etc., to anyone who might be inclined to consult him but be daunted by the appearance of old Christie out of the kitchen, and unwilling to leave a message with one who spoke such unintelligible English. Crawford was so good a carpenter that he could put up shelves, adjust faulty hinges, mend locks, and even went the length of constructing a box of some old boards that had once formed a packing-case. Crawford, one day, when his master was too busy to go out for his dinner, improvised an omelette as good as any Dr Brown had ever tasted in Paris, when he was studying there. In short, Crawford was a kind of Admirable Crichton in his way, and Margaret was quite convinced that Dr Brown was right in his decision that they must have a manservant – even before she was respectfully greeted by Crawford, as he opened the door to the newly-married couple, when they came to their new home after their short wedding tour.

Dr Brown was rather afraid lest Margaret should think the house bare and cheerless in its half-furnished state; for he had obeyed her injunctions and bought as little furniture as might be, in addition to the few things he had inherited from his mother. His consulting-room (how grand it sounded!) was completely arranged, ready for stray patients; and it was well calculated to make a good impression on them. There was a Turkey-carpet on the floor, that had been his mother's, and was just sufficiently worn to give it the air of respectability which handsome pieces of furniture have when they look as if they had not just been purchased for the occasion, but are in some degree hereditary. The same appearance pervaded the room: the library-table (bought second-hand, it must be confessed), the bureau – that had been his mother's – the leather chairs (as hereditary as the library-table), the shelves Crawford had put up for Dr Brown's medical books, a good engraving on the wall, gave altogether so pleasant an aspect to the apartment that both Dr and Mrs Brown thought, for that evening at any rate, that poverty was just as comfortable a thing as riches. Crawford had ventured to take the liberty of placing a few flowers about the room, as his humble way of welcoming his mistress – late autumn-flowers, blending the idea of summer with that of winter, suggested by the bright little fire in the grate. Christie sent up delicious scones for tea; and Mrs Frazer had made up for her want of geniality, as well as she could, by a store of marmalade and mutton hams. Dr Brown could not be easy in his comfort, until he had shown Margaret, almost with a groan, how many rooms were as yet unfurnished – how much remained to be done. But she laughed at his alarm lest she should be disappointed in her new home; declared that she should like nothing better than planning and contriving; that, what with her own talent for upholstery and Crawford's for joinery, the rooms would be furnished as if by magic, and no bills – the usual consequences of comfort – be forthcoming. But, with the morning and daylight, Dr Brown's anxiety returned. He saw and felt every crack in the ceiling, every spot on the paper, not for himself, but for Margaret. He was constantly in his own mind, as it seemed, comparing the home he had brought her to with the one she had left. He seemed constantly afraid lest she had repented, or would repent having married him. This morbid restlessness was the only drawback to their great happiness; and, to do away with it, Margaret was led into expenses much beyond her original intention. She bought this article in preference to that, because her husband, if he went shopping with her, seemed so miserable if he suspected that she denied herself the slightest wish on the score of economy. She learnt to avoid taking him out with her when she went to make her purchases as it was a very simple thing to her to choose the least expensive thing, even though it were the ugliest, when she was by herself, but not a simple painless thing to harden her heart to his look of mortification when she quietly said to the shopman that she could not afford this or that. On coming out of a shop after one of these occasions, he had said, 'Oh, Margaret, I ought not to have married you. You must forgive me – I have so loved you.'

'Forgive you, James?' said she. 'For making me so happy? What should make you think I care so much for rep in preference to moreen? Don't speak so again, please!'

'Oh, Margaret! but don't forget how I ask you to forgive me.'

Crawford was everything that he had promised to be, and more than could be desired. He was Margaret's right hand in all her little household plans, in a way which irritated Christie not a little. This feud between Christie and Crawford was indeed the greatest discomfort in the household. Crawford was silently triumphant in his superior knowledge of London, in her favour upstairs, in this power of assisting his mistress, and in the consequent privilege of being frequently consulted. Christie was for ever regretting Scotland, and hinting at Margaret's neglect of one who had followed her fortunes into a strange country to make a favourite of a stranger, and one who was none so good as he ought to be, as she would sometimes affirm. But, as she never brought any proof of her vague accusations, Margaret did not choose to question her, but set them down to a jealousy of her fellow-servant, which the mistress did all in her power to heal. On the whole, however, the four people forming this family lived together in tolerable harmony. Dr Brown was more than satisfied with his house, his servants, his professional prospects, and most of all with his little energetic wife. Margaret, from time to time, was taken aback by certain moods of her husband's; but the tendency of these moods was not to weaken her affection, rather to call out a feeling of pity for what appeared to her morbid sufferings and suspicions – a pity ready to be turned into sympathy, as soon as she could discover any definite cause for his occasional depression of spirits. Christie did not pretend to like Crawford; but, as Margaret quietly declined to listen to her grumblings and discontent on this head, and as Crawford himself was almost painfully solicitous to gain the good opinion of the old Scotchwoman, there was no rupture between them. On the whole, the popular, successful Dr Brown was apparently the most anxious person in his family. There could be no great cause for this as regarded his money affairs. By one of those lucky accidents which sometimes lift a man up out of his struggles, and carry him on to smooth, unencumbered ground, he made a great step in his professional progress; and their income from this source was likely to be fully as much as Margaret and he had ever anticipated in their most sanguine moments, with the likelihood, too, of steady increase, as the years went on.

I must explain myself more fully on this head.

Margaret herself had rather more than a hundred a year; sometimes, indeed, her dividends had amounted to a hundred and thirty or forty pounds; but on that she dared not rely. Dr Brown had seventeen hundred remaining of the three thousand left him by his mother; and out of this he had to pay for some of the furniture, the bills for which had not been sent in at the time, in spite of all Margaret's entreaties that such might be the case. They came in about a week before the time when the events I am going to narrate took place. Of course they amounted to more than even the prudent Margaret had expected; and she was a little dispirited to find how much money it would take to liquidate them. But, curiously and contradictorily enough – as she had often noticed before – any real cause for anxiety or disappointment did not seem to affect her husband's cheerfulness. He laughed at her dismay over her accounts, jingled the proceeds of that day's work in his pockets, counted it out to her, and calculated the year's probable income from that day's gains. Margaret took the guineas, and carried them upstairs to her own *secretaire* in silence, having learnt the difficult art of trying to swallow down her household cares in the presence of her husband. When she came back, she was cheerful, if grave. He had taken up the bills in her absence, and had been adding them together.

'Two hundred and thirty-six pounds,' he said, putting the accounts away, to clear the table for tea, as Crawford brought in the things. 'Why, I don't call that much. I believe I reckoned on their coming to a great deal more. I'll go into the City tomorrow, and sell out some shares, and set your little heart at ease. Now don't go and put a spoonful less tea in tonight to help to pay these bills. Earning is better than saving, and I am earning at a famous rate. Give me good tea, Maggie, for I have done a good day's work.'

They were sitting in the doctor's consulting-room, for the better economy of fire. To add to Margaret's discomfort, the chimney smoked this evening. She had held her tongue from any repining words; for she remembered the old proverb about a smoky chimney and a scolding wife; but she was more irritated by the puffs of smoke coming over her pretty white work than she cared to show; and it was in a sharper tone than usual that she spoke, in bidding Crawford take care and have the chimney swept. The next morning all had cleared brightly off. Her husband had convinced her that their money matters were going on well; the fire burned briskly at breakfast time; and the unwonted sun shone in at the windows. Margaret was surprised when Crawford told her that he had not been able to meet with a chimney-sweeper that morning; but that he had tried to arrange the coals in the grate, so that, for this one morning at least, his mistress should not be annoyed, and, by the next, he would take care to secure a sweep. Margaret thanked him, and acquiesced in all plans about giving a general cleaning to the room; the more readily, because she felt that she had spoken sharply the night before. She decided to go and pay all her bills, and make some distant calls on the next morning; and her husband promised to go into the City and provide her with the money.

This he did. He showed her the notes that evening, locked them up for the night in his bureau; and, lo, in the morning they were gone! They had breakfasted in the back parlour, or half-furnished dining-room. A char-woman was in the front room, cleaning after the sweep. Dr Brown went to his bureau, singing an old Scotch tune as he left the dining-room. It was so long before he came back that Margaret went to look for him. He was sitting in the chair nearest to the bureau, leaning his head upon it, in an attitude of the deepest despondency. He did not seem to hear Margaret's step as she made her way among rolled-up carpets and chairs piled on each other. She had to touch him on the shoulder before she could rouse him.

'James, James!' she said in alarm.

He looked up at her almost as if he did not know her.

'Oh, Margaret!' he said, and took hold of her hands, and hid his face in her neck.

'Dearest love, what is it?' she asked, thinking he was suddenly taken ill.

'Someone has been to my bureau since last night,' he groaned, without either looking up or moving.

'And taken the money,' said Margaret, in an instant understanding how it stood. It was a great blow; a great loss, far greater than the few extra pounds by which the bills had exceeded her calculations: yet it seemed as if she could bear it better. 'Oh dear!' she said, 'that is bad; but after all – do you know,' she said, trying to raise his face, so that she might look into it, and give him the encouragement of her honest loving eyes, 'at first I thought you were deadly ill, and all sorts of dreadful possibilities rushed through my mind – it is such a relief, to find that it is only money – '

'Only money!' he echoed sadly, avoiding her look, as if he could not bear to show her how much he felt it.

'And after all,' she said with spirit, 'it can't be gone far. Only last night, it was here. The chimney-sweep – we must send Crawford for the police directly. You did not take the numbers of the notes?' ringing the bell as she spoke.

'No; they were only to be in our possession one night,' he said.

'No, to be sure not.'

The charwoman now appeared at the door with her pail of hot water. Margaret looked into her face, as if to read guilt or innocence. She was a *protégée* of Christie's, who was not apt to accord her favour easily, or without good grounds; an honest, decent widow, with a large family to maintain by her labour – that was the character in which Margaret had engaged her; and she looked it. Grimy in her dress – because she could not spare the money or time to be clean – her skin looked healthy and cared for; she had a straight-forward, businesslike appearance about her, and seemed in no ways daunted nor surprised to see Dr and Mrs Brown standing in the middle of the room in displeased perplexity and distress. She went about her business without taking any particular notice of them. Margaret's suspicions settled down yet more distinctly upon the chimney-sweeper; but he could not have gone far; the notes could hardly have got into circulation. Such a sum could not have been spent by such a man in so short a time; and the restoration of the money was her first, her only object. She had scarcely a thought for subsequent duties, such as prosecution of the offender, and the like consequences of crime. While her whole energies were bent on the speedy recovery of the money, and she was rapidly going over the necessary steps to be taken, her husband 'sat all poured out into his chair', as the Germans say; no force in him to keep his limbs in any attitude requiring the slightest exertion; his face sunk, miserable, and with that foreshadowing of the lines of age which sudden distress is apt to call out on the youngest and smoothest faces.

'What can Crawford be about?' said Margaret, pulling the bell again with vehemence. 'Oh, Crawford!' as the man at that instant appeared at the door.

'Is anything the matter?' he said, interrupting her, as if alarmed into an unusual discomposure by her violent ringing. 'I had just gone round the corner with the letter master gave me last night for the post; and when I came back Christie told me you had rung for me, ma'am. I beg your pardon, but I have hurried so,' and, indeed, his breath did come quickly, and his face was full of penitent anxiety.

'Oh, Crawford! I am afraid the sweep has got into your master's bureau, and taken all the money he put there last night. It is gone, at any rate. Did you ever leave him in the room alone?'

'I can't say, ma'am; perhaps I did. Yes; I believe I did. I remember now – I had my work to do; and I thought the charwoman was come, and I went to my pantry; and some time after Christie came to me, complaining that Mrs Roberts was so late; and then I knew that he must have been alone in the room. But, dear me, ma'am, who would have thought there had been so much wickedness in him?'

'How was it that he got into the bureau?' said Margaret, turning to her husband. 'Was the lock broken?'

He roused himself up, like one who wakens from sleep.

'Yes! No! I suppose I had turned the key without locking it last night. The bureau was closed, not locked, when I went to it this morning, and the bolt was shot.' He relapsed into inactive, thoughtful silence.

'At any rate, it is no use losing time in wondering now. Go, Crawford, as fast as you can, for a policeman. You know the name of the chimney-sweeper, of course,' she added, as Crawford was preparing to leave the room.

'Indeed, ma'am, I'm very sorry, but I just agreed with the first who was passing along the street. If I could have known – '

But Margaret had turned away with an impatient gesture of despair. Crawford went, without another word, to seek a policeman.

In vain did his wife try and persuade Dr Brown to taste any breakfast; a cup of tea was all he would try to swallow; and that was taken in hasty gulps, to clear his dry throat, as he heard Crawford's voice talking to the policeman whom he was ushering in.

The policeman heard all and said little. Then the inspector came. Dr Brown seemed to leave all the talking to Crawford, who apparently liked nothing better. Margaret was infinitely distressed and dismayed by the effect the robbery seemed to have had on her husband's energies. The probable loss of such a sum was bad enough; but there was something so weak and poor in character in letting it affect him so strongly as to deaden all energy and destroy all hopeful spring, that, although Margaret did not dare to define her feeling, nor the cause of it, to herself she had the fact before her perpetually that, if she were to judge of her husband from this morning only, she must learn to rely on herself alone in all cases of emergency. The inspector repeatedly turned from Crawford to Dr and Mrs Brown for answers to his enquiries. It was Margaret who replied, with terse, short sentences, very different from Crawford's long, involved explanations.

At length the inspector asked to speak to her alone. She followed him out of the room, past the affronted Crawford and her despondent husband. The inspector gave one sharp look at the charwoman, who was going on with her scouring with stolid indifference, turned her out, and then asked Margaret where Crawford came from – how long he had lived with them, and various other questions, all showing the direction his suspicions had taken. This shocked Margaret extremely; but she quickly answered every enquiry, and, at the end, watched the inspector's face closely, and waited for the avowal of the suspicion.

He led the way back to the other room without a word, however. Crawford had left, and Dr Brown was trying to read the morning's letters (which had just been delivered); but his hands shook so much that he could not see a line.

'Dr Brown,' said the inspector, 'I have little doubt that your manservant has committed this robbery. I judge so from his whole manner; and from his anxiety to tell the story, and his way of trying to throw suspicion on the chimney-sweeper, neither whose name nor whose dwelling he can give; at least he says not. Your wife tells us he has already been out of the house this morning, even before he went to summon a policeman; so there is little doubt that he has found means for concealing or disposing of the notes; and you say you do not know the numbers. However, that can probably be ascertained.'

At this moment Christie knocked at the door, and, in a state of great agitation, demanded to speak to Margaret. She brought up an additional store of suspicious circumstances, none of them much in themselves, but all tending to criminate her fellow-servant. She had expected to find herself blamed for starting the idea of Crawford's guilt, and was rather surprised to find herself listened to with attention by the inspector. This led her to tell many other little things, all bearing against Crawford, which a dread of being thought jealous and quarrelsome had led her to conceal before from her master and mistress. At the end of her story the inspector said: 'There can be no doubt of the course to be taken. You, sir, must give your man-servant in charge. He will be taken before the sitting magistrate directly; and there is already evidence enough to make him be remanded for a week, during which time we may trace the notes, and complete the chain.'

'Must I prosecute?' said Dr Brown, almost lividly pale. 'It is, I own, a serious loss of money to me; but there will be the further expenses of the prosecution – the loss of time – the – '

He stopped. He saw his wife's indignant eyes fixed upon him, and shrank from their look of unconscious reproach.

'Yes, inspector,' he said; 'I give him in charge. Do what you will. Do what is right. Of course I take the consequences. We take the consequences. Don't we, Margaret?' He spoke in a kind of wild, low voice, of which Margaret thought it best to take no notice.

'Tell us exactly what to do,' she said very coldly and quietly, addressing herself to the policeman.

He gave her the necessary directions as to their attending at the police office, and bringing Christie as a witness, and then went away to take measures for securing Crawford.

Margaret was surprised to find how little hurry or violence needed to be used in Crawford's arrest. She had expected to hear sounds of commotion in the house, if indeed Crawford himself had not taken the alarm and escaped. But, when she had suggested the latter apprehension to the inspector, he smiled, and told her that, when he had first heard of the charge from the policeman on the beat, he had stationed a detective officer within sight of the house, to watch all ingress or egress; so that Crawford's whereabouts would soon have been discovered, if he had attempted to escape.

Margaret's attention was now directed to her husband. He was making hurried preparations for setting off on his round of visits, and evidently did not wish to have any conversation with her on the subject of the morning's event. He promised to be back by eleven o'clock; before which time, the inspector assured them, their presence would not be needed. Once or twice, Dr Brown said, as if to himself, 'It is a miserable business.' Indeed, Margaret felt it to be so; and, now that the necessity for immediate speech and action was over, she began to fancy that she must be very hard-hearted – very deficient in common feeling; inasmuch as she had not suffered like her husband at the discovery that the servant – whom they had been learning to consider as a friend, and to look upon as having their interests so warmly at heart – was, in all probability, a treacherous thief. She remembered all his pretty marks of attention to her, from the day when he had welcomed her arrival at her new home by his humble present of flowers, until only the day before, when, seeing her fatigued, he had, unasked, made her a cup of coffee – coffee such as none but he could make. How often had he thought of warm dry clothes for her husband; how wakeful had he been at nights; how diligent in the mornings! It was no wonder that her husband felt this discovery of domestic treason acutely. It was she who was hard and selfish, thinking more of the recovery of the money than of the terrible disappointment in character, if the charge against Crawford were true.

At eleven o'clock her husband returned with a cab. Christie had thought the occasion of appearing at a police office worthy of her Sunday clothes, and was as smart as her possessions could make her. But Margaret and her husband looked as pale and sorrow-stricken as if they had been the accused, and not the accusers.

Dr Brown shrank from meeting Crawford's eye, as the one took his place in the witness-box, the other in the dock. Yet Crawford was trying – Margaret was sure of this – to catch his master's attention. Failing that, he looked at Margaret with an expression she could not fathom. Indeed, the whole character of his face was changed. Instead of the calm, smooth look of attentive obedience, he had assumed an insolent, threatening expression of defiance; smiling occasionally in a most unpleasant manner, as Dr Brown spoke of the bureau and its contents. He was remanded for a week; but, the evidence as yet being far from conclusive, bail for his appearance was taken. This bail was offered by his brother, a respectable tradesman, well known in his neighbourhood and to whom Crawford had sent on his arrest.

So Crawford was at large again, much to Christie's dismay; who took off her Sunday clothes, on her return home, with a heavy heart, hoping, rather than trusting, that they should not all be murdered in their beds before the week was out. It must be confessed, Margaret herself was not entirely free from fears of Crawford's vengeance; his eyes had looked so maliciously and vindictively at her and at her husband as they gave their evidence.

But his absence in the household gave Margaret enough to do to prevent her dwelling on foolish fears. His being away made a terrible blank in their daily comfort, which neither Margaret nor Christie – exert themselves as they would – could fill up; and it was the more necessary that all should go on smoothly, as Dr Brown's nerves had received such a shock at the discovery of the guilt of his favourite, trusted servant, that Margaret was led at times to apprehend a serious illness. He would pace about the room at night, when he thought she was asleep, moaning to himself – and in the morning he would require the utmost persuasion to induce him to go out and see his patients. He was worse than ever, after consulting the lawyer whom he had employed to conduct the prosecution. There was, as Margaret was brought unwillingly to perceive, some mystery in the case; for he eagerly took his letters from the post, going to the door as soon as he heard the knock, and concealing their directions from her. As the week passed away, his nervous misery still increased.

One evening – the candles were not lighted – when he was sitting over the fire in a listless attitude, resting his head on his hand, and that supported on his knee, Margaret determined to try an experiment to see if she could not probe, and find out the nature of the sore that he hid with such constant care. She took a stool and sat down at his feet, taking his hand in hers.

'Listen, dearest James, to an old story I once heard. It may interest you. There were two orphans, boy and girl in their hearts, though they were a young man and young woman in years. They were not brother and sister, and by and by they fell in love; just in the same fond silly way you and I did, you remember. Well, the girl was amongst her own people; but the boy was far away from his – if indeed he had any alive. But the girl loved him so dearly for himself, that sometimes she thought she was glad that he had no one to care for him but just her alone. Her friends did not like him as much as she did; for, perhaps, they were wise, grave, cold people, and she, I dare say, was very foolish. And they did not like her marrying the boy; which was just stupidity in them, for they had not a word to say against him. But, about a week before the marriage-day was fixed, they thought they had found out something – my darling love, don't take away your hand – don't tremble so, only just listen! Her aunt came to her and said: "Child, you must give up your lover: his father was tempted, and sinned; and, if he is now alive, he is a transported convict. The marriage cannot take place." But the girl stood up and said: "If he has known this great sorrow and shame, he needs my love all the more. I will not leave him, nor forsake him, but love him all the better. And I charge you, aunt, as you hope to receive a blessing for doing as you would be done by, that you tell no one!" I really think that girl awed her aunt, in some strange way, into secrecy. But, when she was left alone, she cried long and sadly to think what a shadow rested on the heart she loved so dearly; and she meant to strive to lighten his life, and to conceal for ever that she had heard of its burden; but now she thinks – Oh, my husband! how you must have suffered' – as he bent down his head on her shoulder and cried terrible man's tears.

'God be thanked!' he said at length. 'You know all, and you do not shrink from me. Oh, what a miserable, deceitful coward I have been! Suffered! Yes – suffered enough to drive me mad; and, if I had but been brave, I might have been spared all this long twelve months of agony. But it is right I should have been punished. And you knew it even before we were married, when you might have been drawn back!'

'I could not; you would not have broken off your engagement with me, would you, under the like circumstances, if our cases had been reversed?'

'I do not know. Perhaps I might; for I am not so brave, so good, so strong as you, my Margaret. How could I be? Let me tell you more. We wandered about, my mother and I, thankful that our name was such a common one, but shrinking from every allusion – in a way which no one can understand, who has not been conscious of an inward sore. Living in an assize town was torture; a commercial one was nearly as bad. My father was the son of a dignified clergyman, well known to his brethren: a cathedral town was to be avoided, because there the circumstance of the Dean of St Botolph's son having been transported was sure to be known. I had to be educated; therefore we had to live in a town; for my mother could not bear to part from me, and I was sent to a day-school. We were very poor for our station – no! we had no station; we were the wife and child of a convict – poor for my mother's early habits, I should have said. But, when I was about fourteen, my father died in his exile, leaving, as convicts in those days sometimes did, a large fortune. It all came to us. My mother shut herself up, and cried and prayed for a whole day. Then she called me in, and took me into her counsel. We solemnly pledged ourselves to give the money to some charity, as soon as I was legally of age. Till then the interest was laid by, every penny of it, though sometimes we were in sore distress for money, my education cost so much. But how could we tell in what way the money had been accumulated?' Here he dropped his voice. 'Soon after I was one-and-twenty, the papers rang with admiration of the unknown munificent donor of certain sums. I loathed their praises. I shrank from all recollection of my father. I remembered him dimly, but always as angry and violent with my mother. My poor, gentle mother! Margaret, she loved my father; and, for her sake, I have tried, since her death, to feel kindly towards his memory. Soon after my mother's death, I came to know you, my jewel, my treasure!'

After a while, he began again. 'But, oh, Margaret! even now you do not know the worst. After my mother's death, I found a bundle of law papers – of newspaper reports about my father's trial. Poor soul! why she had kept them, I cannot say. They were covered over with notes in her handwriting; and, for that reason, I kept them. It was so touching to read her record of the days spent by her in her solitary innocence, while he was embroiling himself deeper and deeper in crime. I kept this bundle (as I thought so safely!) in a secret drawer of my bureau; but that wretch Crawford has got hold of it. I missed the papers that very morning. The loss of them was infinitely worse than the loss of the money; and now Crawford threatens to bring out the one terrible fact, in open court, if he can; and his lawyer may do it, I believe. At any rate, to have it blazoned out to the world – I who have spent my life in fearing this hour! But most of all for you, Margaret! Still – if only it could be avoided! Who will employ the son of Brown, the noted forger? I shall lose all my practice. Men will look askance at me as I enter their doors. They will drive me into crime. I sometimes fear that crime is hereditary! Oh, Margaret! what am I to do?'

'What can you do?' she asked.

'I can refuse to prosecute.'

'Let Crawford go free, you knowing him to be guilty?'

'I know him to be guilty.'

'Then, simply, you cannot do this thing. You let loose a criminal upon the public.'

'But, if I do not, we shall come to shame and poverty. It is for you I mind it, not for myself. I ought never to have married.'

'Listen to me. I don't care for poverty; and, as to shame, I should feel it twenty times more grievously if you and I consented to screen the guilty, from any fear or for any selfish motives of our own. I don't pretend that I shall not feel it, when first the truth is known. But my shame will turn into pride, as I watch you live it down. You have been rendered morbid, dear husband, by having something all your life to conceal. Let the world know the truth, and say the worst. You will go forth a free, honest, honourable man, able to do your future work without fear.'

'That scoundrel Crawford has sent for an answer to his impudent note,' said Christie, putting in her head at the door.

'Stay! May *I* write it?' said Margaret.

She wrote:

Whatever you may do or say, there is but one course open to us. No threats can deter your master from doing his duty. Margaret Brown.

'There!' she said, passing it to her husband; 'he will see that I know all; and I suspect he has reckoned something on your tenderness for me.'

Margaret's note only enraged, it did not daunt, Crawford. Before a week was out, everyone who cared knew that Dr Brown, the rising young physician, was son of the notorious Brown, the forger. All the consequences took place which he had anticipated. Crawford had to suffer a severe sentence; and Dr Brown and his wife had to leave their house and go to a smaller one; they had to pinch and to screw, aided in all most zealously by the faithful Christie. But Dr Brown was lighter-hearted than he had ever been before in his conscious lifetime. His foot was now firmly planted on the ground, and every step he rose was a sure gain. People did say that Margaret had been seen, in those worst times, on her hands and knees cleaning her own doorstep. But I don't believe it, for Christie would never have let her do that. And, as far as my own evidence goes, I can only say that, the last time I was in London, I saw a brass-plate, with 'Dr James Brown' upon it, on the door of a handsome house in a handsome square. And as I looked, I saw a brougham drive up to the door, and a lady get out, and go into that house, who was certainly the Margaret Frazer of old days – graver; more portly; more stern, I had almost said. But, as I watched and thought, I saw her come to the dining-room window with a baby in her arms, and her whole face melted into a smile of infinite sweetness.

The Manchester Marriage

Mr and Mrs Openshaw came from Manchester to settle in London. He had been, what is called in Lancashire, a 'salesman' for a large manufacturing firm, who were extending their business, and opening a warehouse in the city, where Mr Openshaw was now to superintend their affairs. He rather enjoyed the change, having a kind of curiosity about London, which he had never yet been able to gratify in his brief visits to the metropolis. At the same time, he had an odd, shrewd, contempt for the inhabitants, whom he always pictured to himself as fine, lazy people; caring nothing but for fashion and aristocracy, and lounging away their days in Bond Street, and such places; ruining good English, and ready in their turn to despise him as a provincial. The hours that the men of business kept in the city scandalised him too, accustomed as he was to the early dinners of Manchester folk and the consequently far longer evenings. Still, he was pleased to go to London; though he would not for the world have confessed it, even to himself, and always spoke of the step to his friends as one demanded of him by the interests of his employers, and sweetened to him by a considerable increase of salary. This, indeed, was so liberal that he might have been justified in taking a much larger house than the one he did, had he not thought himself bound to set an example to Londoners of how little a Manchester man of business cared for show. Inside, however, he furnished it with an unusual degree of comfort, and, in the wintertime, he insisted on keeping up as large fires as the grates would allow, in every room where the temperature was in the least chilly. Moreover, his northern sense of hospitality was such, that, if he were at home, he could hardly suffer a visitor to leave the house without forcing meat and drink upon him. Every servant in the house was well warmed, well fed, and kindly treated; for their master scorned all petty saving in aught that conduced to comfort; while he amused himself by following out all his accustomed habits and individual ways, in defiance of what any of his new neighbours might think.

His wife was a pretty, gentle woman, of suitable age and character. He was forty-two, she thirty-five. He was loud and decided; she soft and yielding. They had two children; or rather, I should say, she had two; for the elder, a girl of eleven, was Mrs Openshaw's child by Frank Wilson, her first husband. The younger was a little boy, Edwin, who could just prattle, and to whom his father delighted to speak in the broadest and most unintelligible Lancashire dialect, in order to keep up what he called the true Saxon accent.

Mrs Openshaw's Christian name was Alice, and her first husband had been her own cousin. She was the orphan niece of a sea-captain in Liverpool; a quiet, grave little creature, of great personal attraction when she was fifteen or sixteen, with regular features and a blooming complexion. But she was very shy, and believed herself to be very stupid and awkward; and was frequently scolded by her aunt, her own uncle's second wife. So when her cousin, Frank Wilson, came home from a long absence at sea, and first was kind and protective to her, secondly, attentive, and thirdly, desperately in love with her, she hardly knew how to be grateful enough to him. It is true, she would have preferred his remaining in the first or second stages of behaviour; for his violent love puzzled and frightened her. Her uncle neither helped nor hindered the love affair; though it was going on under his own eyes. Frank's stepmother had such a variable temper that there was no knowing whether what she liked one day she would like the next, or not. At length she went to such extremes of crossness, that Alice was only too glad to shut her eyes and rush blindly at the chance of escape from domestic tyranny offered her by a marriage with her cousin; and, liking him better than any one in the world, except her uncle (who was at this time at sea), she went off one morning and was married to him; her only bridesmaid being the housemaid at her aunt's. The consequence was that Frank and his wife went into lodgings, and Mrs Wilson refused to see them, and turned away Norah, the warm-hearted housemaid, whom they accordingly took into their service. When Captain Wilson returned from his voyage, he was very cordial with the young couple, and spent many an evening at their lodgings, smoking his pipe, and sipping his grog; but he told them that, for quietness' sake, he could not ask them to his own house; for his wife was bitter against them. They were not, however, very unhappy about this.

The seed of future unhappiness lay rather in Frank's vehement, passionate disposition; which led him to resent his wife's shyness and want of demonstrativeness as failures in conjugal duty. He was already tormenting himself, and her too, in a slighter degree, by apprehensions and imaginations of what might befall her during his approaching absence at sea. At last, he went to his father and urged him to insist upon Alice's being once more received under his roof; the more especially as there was now a prospect of her confinement while her husband was away on his voyage. Captain Wilson was, as he himself expressed it, 'breaking up', and unwilling to undergo the excitement of a scene; yet he felt that what his son said was true. So he went to his wife. And before Frank set sail, he had the comfort of seeing his wife installed in her old little garret in his father's house. To have placed her in the one best spare room, was a step beyond Mrs Wilson's powers of submission or generosity. The worst part about it, however, was that the faithful Norah had to be dismissed. Her place as housemaid had been filled up; and, even if it had not, she had forfeited Mrs Wilson's good opinion for ever. She comforted her young master and mistress by pleasant prophecies of the time when they would have a household of their own; of which, whatever service she might be in meanwhile, she should be sure to form a part. Almost the last action Frank did, before setting sail, was going with Alice to see Norah once more at her mother's house; and then he went away.

Alice's father-in-law grew more and more feeble as winter advanced. She was of great use to her stepmother in nursing and amusing him; and, although there was anxiety enough in the household, there was, perhaps, more of peace than there had been for years; for Mrs Wilson had not a bad heart, and was softened by the visible approach of death to one whom she loved, and also touched by the lonely condition of the young creature, expecting her first confinement in her husband's absence. To this relenting mood Norah owed the permission to come and nurse Alice when her baby was born, and to remain to attend on Captain Wilson.

Before one letter had been received from Frank (who had sailed for the East Indies and China), his father died. Alice was always glad to remember that he had held her baby in his arms, and kissed and blessed it before his death. After that, and the consequent examination into the state of his affairs, it was found that he had left far less property than people had been led by his style of living to expect; and what money there was, was all settled upon his wife, and at her disposal after her death. This did not signify much to Alice, as Frank was now first mate of his ship, and, in another voyage or two, would be captain. Meanwhile he had left her rather more than two hundred pounds (all his savings) in the bank.

It became time for Alice to hear from her husband. One letter from the Cape she had already received. The next was to announce his arrival in India. As week after week passed over, and no intelligence of the ship having got there reached the office of the owners, and the captain's wife was in the same state of ignorant suspense as Alice herself, her fears grew most oppressive. At length the day came when, in reply to her enquiry at the Shipping Office, they told her that the owners had given up hope of ever hearing more of the *Betsy-Jane*, and had sent in their claim upon the underwriters. Now that he was gone for ever, she first felt a yearning, longing love for the kind cousin, the dear friend, the sympathising protector, whom she should never see again – first felt a passionate desire to show him his child, whom she had hitherto rather craved to have all to herself – her own sole possession. Her grief was, however, noiseless, and quiet – rather to the scandal of Mrs Wilson, who bewailed her stepson as if he and she had always lived together in perfect harmony, and who evidently thought it her duty to burst into fresh tears at every strange face she saw; dwelling on his poor young widow's desolate state, and the helplessness of the fatherless child, with an unction, as if she liked the excitement of the sorrowful story.

So passed away the first days of Alice's widowhood. By and by things subsided into their natural and tranquil course. But, as if this young creature was always to be in some heavy trouble, her ewe-lamb began to be ailing, pining, and sickly. The child's mysterious illness turned out to be some affection of the spine, likely to affect health, but not to shorten life – at least, so the doctors said. But the long, dreary suffering of one whom a mother loves as Alice loved her only child, is hard to look forward to. Only Norah guessed what Alice suffered; no one but God knew.

And so it fell out that when Mrs Wilson, the elder, came to her one day, in violent distress, occasioned by a very material diminution in the value of the property that her husband had left her – a diminution which made her income barely enough to support herself, much less Alice – the latter could hardly understand how anything which did not touch health or life could cause such grief, and she received the intelligence with irritating composure. But when, that afternoon, the little sick child was brought in, and the grandmother – who after all loved it well – began a fresh moan over her losses to its unconscious ears – saying how she had planned to consult this or that doctor, and to give it this or that comfort or luxury in after years, but that now all chance of this had passed away – Alice's heart was touched, and she drew near to Mrs Wilson with unwonted caresses, and, in a spirit not unlike to that of Ruth, entreated that, come what would, they might remain together. After much discussion in succeeding days, it was arranged that Mrs Wilson should take a house in Manchester, furnishing it partly with what furniture she had, and providing the rest with Alice's remaining two hundred pounds. Mrs Wilson was herself a Manchester woman, and naturally longed to return to her native town; some connections of her own, too, at that time required lodgings, for which they were willing to pay pretty handsomely. Alice undertook the active superintendence and superior work of the household; Norah, willing, faithful Norah, offered to cook, scour, do anything in short, so that she might but remain with them.

The plan succeeded. For some years, their first lodgers remained with them, and all went smoothly – with the one sad exception of the little girl's increasing deformity. How that mother loved that child, it is not for words to tell!

Then came a break of misfortune. Their lodgers left, and no one succeeded to them. After some months, it became necessary to remove to a smaller house; and Alice's tender conscience was torn by the idea that she ought not to be a burden to her mother-in-law, but to go out and seek her own maintenance. And leave her child! The thought came like the sweeping boom of a funeral bell over her heart.

By and by, Mr Openshaw came to lodge with them. He had started in life as the errand-boy and sweeper-out of a warehouse; had struggled up through all the grades of employment in it, fighting his way through the hard striving Manchester life with strong, pushing energy of character. Every spare moment of time had been sternly given up to self-teaching. He was a capital accountant, a good French and German scholar, a keen, far-seeing tradesman – understanding markets, and the bearing of events, both near and distant, on trade: and yet, with such vivid attention to present details, that I do not think he ever saw a group of flowers in the fields without thinking whether their colours would, or would not, form harmonious contrasts in the coming spring muslins and prints. He went to debating societies, and threw himself with all his heart and soul into politics – esteeming, it must be owned, every man a fool or a knave who differed from him, and overthrowing his opponents rather by the loud strength of his language than the calm strength of his logic. There was something of the Yankee in all this. Indeed, his theory ran parallel to the famous Yankee motto, 'England flogs creation, and Manchester flogs England.' Such a man, as may be fancied, had had no time for falling in love, or any such nonsense. At the age when most young men go through their courting and matrimony, he had not the means of keeping a wife, and was far too practical to think of having one. And now that he was in easy circumstances, a rising man, he considered women almost as incumbrances to the world, with whom a man had better have as little to do as possible. His first impression of Alice was indistinct, and he did not care enough about her to make it distinct. 'A pretty yea-nay kind of woman', would have been his description of her, if he had been pushed into a corner. He was rather afraid, in the beginning, that her quiet ways arose from a listlessness and laziness of character, which would have been exceedingly discordant to his active, energetic nature. But, when he found out the punctuality with which his wishes were attended to, and her work was done; when he was called in the morning at the very stroke of the clock, his shaving-water scalding hot, his fire bright, his coffee made exactly as his peculiar fancy dictated (for he was a man who had his theory about everything based upon what he knew of science, and often perfectly original) – then he began to think: not that Alice had any peculiar merit, but that he had got into remarkably good lodgings; his restlessness wore away, and he began to consider himself as almost settled for life in them.

Mr Openshaw had been too busy, all his days, to be introspective. He did not know that he had any tenderness in his nature; and if he had become conscious of its abstract existence, he would have considered it as a manifestation of disease in some part of him. But he was decoyed into pity unawares; and pity led on to tenderness. That little helpless child – always carried about by one of the three busy women of the house, or else patiently threading coloured beads in the chair from which, by no effort of its own, could it ever move – the great grave blue eyes, full of serious, not uncheerful, expression, giving to the small delicate face a look beyond its years – the soft plaintive voice dropping out but few words, so unlike the continual prattle of a child – caught Mr Openshaw's attention in spite of himself. One day – he half scorned himself for doing so – he cut short his dinner-hour to go in search of some toy, which should take the place of those eternal beads. I forget what he bought; but, when he gave the present (which he took care to do in a short, abrupt manner, and when no one was by to see him), he was almost thrilled by the flash of delight that came over that child's face, and he could not help, all through that afternoon, going over and over again the picture left on his memory, by the bright effect of unexpected joy on the little girl's face. When he returned home, he found his slippers placed by his sitting-room fire; and even more careful attention paid to his fancies than was habitual in those model lodgings. When Alice had taken the last of his tea-things away – she had been silent as usual till then – she stood for an instant with the door in her hand. Mr Openshaw looked as if he were deep in his book, though in fact he did not see a line but was heartily wishing the woman would go, and not make any palaver of gratitude. But she only said: 'I am very much obliged to you, sir. Thank you very much,' and – was gone, even before he could send her away with a 'There, my good woman, that's enough!'

For some time longer he took no apparent notice of the child. He even hardened his heart into disregarding her sudden flush of colour and little timid smile of recognition, when he saw her by chance. But, after all, this could not last for ever; and, having a second time given way to tenderness, there was no relapse. The insidious enemy having thus entered his heart, in the guise of compassion to the child, soon assumed the more dangerous form of interest in the mother. He was aware of this change of feeling – despised himself for it – struggled with it; nay, internally yielded to it and cherished it, long before he suffered the slightest expression of it, by word, action, or look to escape him. He watched Alice's docile, obedient ways to her stepmother; the love which she had inspired in the rough Norah (roughened by the wear and tear of sorrow and years); but, above all, he saw the wild, deep, passionate affection existing between her and her child. They spoke little to anyone else, or when anyone else was by; but, when alone together, they talked, and murmured, and cooed, and chattered so continually that Mr Openshaw first wondered what they could find to say to each other, and next became irritated because they were always so grave and silent with him. All this time, he was perpetually devising small new pleasures for the child. His thoughts ran, in a pertinacious way, upon the desolate life before her; and often he came back from his day's work loaded with the very thing Alice had been longing for, but had not been able to procure. One time, it was a little chair for drawing the little sufferer along the streets; and, many an evening, following her along himself, regardless of the remarks of his acquaintances. One day in autumn, he put down his newspaper as Alice came in with the breakfast and said, in as indifferent a voice as he could assume, 'Mrs Frank, is there any reason why we two should not put up our horses together?'

Alice stood still in perplexed wonder. What did he mean? He had resumed the reading of his newspaper, as if he did not expect any answer; so she found silence her safest course, and went on quietly arranging his breakfast, without another word passing between them. Just as he was leaving the house, to go to the warehouse as usual, he turned back and put his head into the bright, neat, tidy kitchen, where all the women breakfasted in the morning: 'You'll think of what I said, Mrs Frank' (this was her name with the lodgers), 'and let me have your opinion upon it tonight.'

Alice was thankful that her mother and Norah were too busy talking together to attend much to this speech. She determined not to think about it at all through the day; and, of course, the effort not to think, made her think all the more. At night she sent up Norah with his tea. But Mr Openshaw almost knocked Norah down as she was going out at the door, by pushing past her and calling out, 'Mrs Frank!' in an impatient voice, at the top of the stairs.

Alice went up, rather than seem to have affixed too much meaning to his words.

'Well, Mrs Frank,' he said, 'what answer? Don't make it too long; for I have lots of office work to get through tonight.'

'I hardly know what you meant, sir,' said truthful Alice.

'Well! I should have thought you might have guessed. You're not new at this sort of work, and I am. However, I'll make it plain this time. Will you have me to be thy wedded husband, and serve me, and love me, and honour me, and all that sort of thing? Because, if you will, I will do as much by you, and be a father to your child – and that's more than is put in the Prayer-book. Now, I'm a man of my word; and what I say, I feel; and what I promise, I'll do. Now, for your answer!'

Alice was silent. He began to make the tea, as if her reply was a matter of perfect indifference to him; but, as soon as that was done, he became impatient.

'Well?' said he.

'How long, sir, may I have to think over it?'

'Three minutes!' (looking at his watch). 'You've had two already – that makes five. Be a sensible woman, say Yes, and sit down to tea with me, and we'll talk it over together; for, after tea, I shall be busy; say No' (he hesitated a moment to try and keep his voice in the same tone), 'and I shan't say another word about it, but pay up a year's rent for my rooms tomorrow, and be off. Time's up! Yes or no?'

'If you please, sir – you have been so good to little Ailsie – '

'There, sit down comfortably by me on the sofa, and let us have our tea together. I am glad to find you are as good and sensible as I took you for.'

And this was Alice Wilson's second wooing.

Mr Openshaw's will was too strong, and his circumstances too good, for him not to carry all before him. He settled Mrs Wilson in a comfortable house of her own, and made her quite independent of lodgers. The little that Alice said with regard to future plans was in Norah's behalf.

'No,' said Mr Openshaw. 'Norah shall take care of the old lady as long as she lives; and, after that, she shall either come and live with us, or, if she likes it better, she shall have a provision for life – for your sake, missus. No one who has been good to you or the child shall go unrewarded. But even the little one will be better for some fresh stuff about her. Get her a bright, sensible girl as a nurse: one who won't go rubbing her with calf's-foot jelly as Norah does; wasting good stuff outside that ought to go in, but will follow doctors' directions; which, as you must see pretty clearly by this time, Norah won't; because they give the poor little wench pain. Now, I'm not above being nesh for other folks myself. I can stand a good blow, and never change colour; but, set me in the operating-room in the Infirmary, and I turn as sick as a girl. Yet, if need were, I would hold the little wench on my knees while she screeched with pain, if it were to do her poor back good. Nay, nay, wench! keep your white looks for the time when it comes – I don't say it ever will. But this I know, Norah will spare the child and cheat the doctor, if she can. Now, I say, give the bairn a year or two's chance, and then, when the pack of doctors have done their best – and, maybe, the old lady has gone – we'll have Norah back, or do better for her.'

The pack of doctors could do no good to little Ailsie. She was beyond their power. But her father (for so he insisted on being called, and also on Alice's no longer retaining the appellation of Mamma, but becoming henceforward Mother), by his healthy cheerfulness of manner, his clear decision of purpose, his odd turns and quirks of humour, added to his real strong love for the helpless little girl, infused a new element of brightness and confidence into her life; and, though her back remained the same, her general health was strengthened, and Alice – never going beyond a smile herself – had the pleasure of seeing her child taught to laugh.

As for Alice's own life, it was happier than it had ever been before. Mr Openshaw required no demonstration, no expressions of affection from her. Indeed, these would rather have disgusted him. Alice could love deeply, but could not talk about it. The perpetual requirement of loving words, looks, and caresses, and misconstruing their absence into absence of love, had been the great trial of her former married life. Now, all went on clear and straight, under the guidance of her husband's strong sense, warm heart, and powerful will. Year by year, their worldly prosperity increased. At Mrs Wilson's death, Norah came back to them, as nurse to the newly-born little Edwin; into which post she was not installed without a pretty strong oration on the part of the proud and happy father; who declared that if he found out that Norah ever tried to screen the boy by a falsehood, or to make him nesh either in body or mind, she should go that very day. Norah and Mr

Openshaw were not on the most thoroughly cordial terms; neither of them fully recognising or appreciating the other's best qualities.

This was the previous history of the Lancashire family who had now removed to London.

They had been there about a year, when Mr Openshaw suddenly informed his wife that he had determined to heal long-standing feuds, and had asked his uncle and aunt Chadwick to come and pay them a visit and see London. Mrs Openshaw had never seen this uncle and aunt of her husband's. Years before she had married him, there had been a quarrel. All she knew was that Mr Chadwick was a small manufacturer in a country town in South Lancashire. She was extremely pleased that the breach was to be healed, and began making preparations to render their visit pleasant.

They arrived at last. Going to see London was such an event to them that Mrs Chadwick had made all new linen fresh for the occasion – from night-caps downwards; and as for gowns, ribbons, and collars, she might have been going into the wilds of Canada where never a shop is, so large was her stock. A fortnight before the day of her departure for London, she had formally called to take leave of all her acquaintance; saying she should need every bit of the intermediate time for packing up. It was like a second wedding in her imagination; and, to complete the resemblance which an entirely new ward-robe made between the two events, her husband brought her back from Manchester, on the last market-day before they set off, a gorgeous pearl-and-amethyst brooch, saying, 'Lunnon should see that Lancashire folks knew a handsome thing when they saw it.'

For some time after Mr and Mrs Chadwick arrived at the Openshaws' there was no opportunity for wearing this brooch; but at length they obtained an order to see Buckingham Palace, and the spirit of loyalty demanded that Mrs Chadwick should wear her best clothes in visiting the abode of her sovereign. On her return, she hastily changed her dress; for Mr Openshaw had planned that they should go to Richmond, drink tea, and return by moonlight. Accordingly, about five o'clock, Mr and Mrs Openshaw and Mr and Mrs Chadwick set off.

The housemaid and cook sat below, Norah hardly knew where. She was always engrossed in the nursery, in tending her two children, and in sitting by the restless, excitable Ailsie till she fell asleep. By and by, the housemaid Bessy tapped gently at the door. Norah went to her, and they spoke in whispers.

'Nurse! there's someone downstairs wants you.'

'Wants me! Who is it?'

'A gentleman – '

'A gentleman? Nonsense!'

'Well! a man, then, and he asks for you, and he rang at the front-door bell, and has walked into the dining-room.'

'You should never have let him,' exclaimed Norah, 'master and missus out – '

'I did not want him to come in; but, when he heard you lived here, he walked past me, and sat down on the first chair, and said, "Tell her to come and speak to me." There is no gaslighted in the room, and supper is all set out.'

'He'll be off with the spoons!' exclaimed Norah, putting the housemaid's fear into words, and preparing to leave the room, first, however, giving a look to Ailsie, sleeping soundly and calmly.

Downstairs she went, uneasy fears stirring in her bosom. Before she entered the dining-room she provided herself with a candle, and, with it in her hand, she went in, looking around her in the darkness for her visitor.

He was standing up, holding by the table. Norah and he looked at each other, gradual recognition coming into their eyes.

'Norah?' at length he asked.

'Who are you?' asked Norah, with the sharp tones of alarm and incredulity. 'I don't know you,' trying, by futile words of disbelief, to do away with the terrible fact before her.

'Am I so changed?' he said, pathetically. 'I dare say I am. But, Norah, tell me!' he breathed hard, 'where is my wife? Is she – is she alive?'

He came nearer to Norah, and would have taken her hand; but she backed away from him; looking at him all the time with staring eyes, as if he were some horrible object. Yet he was a handsome, bronzed, good-looking fellow, with beard and moustache, giving him a foreign-looking aspect; but his eyes! there was no mistaking those eager, beautiful eyes – the very same that Norah had watched not half an hour ago, till sleep stole softly over them.

'Tell me, Norah – I can bear it – I have feared it so often. Is she dead?' Norah still kept silence. 'She is dead!' He hung on Norah's words and looks, as if for confirmation or contradiction.

'What shall I do?' groaned Norah. 'Oh, sir! why did you come? how did you find me out? where have you been? We thought you dead, we did indeed!' She poured out words and questions to gain time, as if time would help her.

'Norah! answer me this question straight, by yes or no – Is my wife dead?'

'No, she is not!' said Norah, slowly and heavily.

'Oh, what a relief! Did she receive my letters? But perhaps you don't know. Why did you leave her? Where is she? Oh, Norah, tell me all quickly!'

'Mr Frank!' said Norah at last, almost driven to bay by her terror lest her mistress should return at any moment, and find him there – unable to consider what was best to be done or said – rushing at something decisive, because she could not endure her present state: 'Mr Frank! we never heard a line from you, and the ship-owners said you had gone down, you and everyone else. We thought you were dead, if ever man was, and poor Miss Alice and her little sick, helpless child! Oh, sir, you must guess it,' cried the poor creature at last, bursting out into a passionate fit of crying, 'for indeed I cannot tell it. But it was no one's fault. God help us all this night!'

Norah had sat down. She trembled too much to stand. He took her hands in his. He squeezed them hard, as if, by physical pressure, the truth could be wrung out.

'Norah.' This time his tone was calm, stagnant as despair. 'She has married again!'

Norah shook her head sadly. The grasp slowly relaxed. The man had fainted.

There was brandy in the room. Norah forced some drops into Mr Frank's mouth, chafed his hands, and – when mere animal life returned, before the mind poured in its flood of memories and thoughts – she lifted him up, and rested his head against her knees. Then she put a few crumbs of bread taken from the supper-table, soaked in brandy, into his mouth. Suddenly he sprang to his feet.

'Where is she? Tell me this instant.' He looked so wild, so mad, so desperate, that Norah felt herself to be in bodily danger; but her time of dread had gone by. She had been afraid to tell him the truth, and then she had been a coward. Now, her wits were sharpened by the sense of his desperate state. He must leave the house. She would pity him afterwards; but now she must rather command and upbraid; for he must leave the house before her mistress came home. That one necessity stood clear before her.

'She is not here: that is enough for you to know. Nor can I say exactly where she is' (which was true to the letter if not to the spirit). 'Go away, and tell me where to find you tomorrow, and I will tell you all. My master and mistress may come back at any minute, and then what would become of me, with a strange man in the house?'

Such an argument was too petty to touch his excited mind.

'I don't care for your master and mistress. If your master is a man, he must feel for me – poor shipwrecked sailor that I am – kept for years a prisoner amongst savages, always, always, always thinking of my wife and my home – dreaming of her by night, talking to her, though she could not hear, by day. I loved her more than all heaven and earth put together. Tell me where she is, this instant, you wretched woman!'

The clock struck ten. Desperate positions require desperate measures.

'If you will leave the house now, I will come to you tomorrow and tell you all. What is more, you shall see your child now. She lies sleeping upstairs. Oh, sir, you have a child, you do not know that as yet – a little weakly girl – with just a heart and soul beyond her years. We have reared her up with such care! We watched her, for we thought for many a year she might die any day, and we tended her, and no hard thing has come near her, and no rough word has ever been said to her. And now you come and will take her life into your hand, and will crush it. Strangers to her have been kind to her; but her own father – Mr Frank, I am her nurse, and I love her, and I tend her, and I would do anything for her that I could. Her mother's heart beats as hers beats; and, if she suffers a pain, her mother trembles all over. If she is happy, it is her mother that smiles and is glad. If she is growing stronger, her mother is healthy: if she dwindles, her mother languishes. If she dies – well, I don't know: it is not everyone can lie down and die when they wish it. Come upstairs, Mr Frank, and see your child. Seeing her will do good to your poor heart. Then go away, in God's name, just this one night; tomorrow, if need be, you can do anything – kill us all if you will, or show yourself a great, grand man, whom God will bless for ever and ever. Come, Mr Frank, the look of a sleeping child is sure to give peace.'

She led him upstairs, at first almost helping his steps, till they came near the nursery door. She had well-nigh forgotten the existence of little Edwin. It struck upon her with affright as the shaded light fell over the other cot; but she skilfully threw that corner of the room into darkness, and let the light fall on the sleeping Ailsie. The child had thrown down the coverings, and her deformity, as she lay with her back to them, was plainly visible through her slight nightgown. Her little face, deprived of the lustre of her eyes, looked wan and pinched, and had a pathetic expression in it, even as she slept. The poor father looked and looked with hungry, wistful eyes, into which the big tears came swelling up slowly and dropped heavily down, as he stood trembling and shaking all over. Norah was angry with herself for growing impatient of the length of time that long lingering gaze lasted. She thought that she waited for full half an hour before Frank stirred. And then – instead of going away – he sank down on his knees by the bedside, and buried his face in the clothes. Little Ailsie stirred uneasily. Norah pulled him up in terror. She could afford no more time, even for prayer, in her extremity of fear; for surely the next moment would bring her mistress home. She took him forcibly by the arm; but, as he was going, his eye lighted on the other bed: he stopped. Intelligence came back into his face. His hands clenched.

'His child?' he asked.

'Her child,' replied Norah. 'God watches over him,' said she instinctively; for Frank's looks excited her fears, and she needed to remind herself of the Protector of the helpless.

'God has not watched over me,' he said, in despair; his thoughts apparently recoiling on his own desolate, deserted state. But Norah had no time for pity. Tomorrow she would be as compassionate as her heart prompted. At length she guided him downstairs, and shut the outer door, and bolted it – as if by bolts to keep out facts.

Then she went back into the dining-room, and effaced all traces of his presence, as far as she could. She went upstairs to the nursery and sat there, her head on her hand, thinking what was to come of all this misery. It seemed to her very long before her master and mistress returned; yet it was hardly eleven o'clock. She heard the loud, hearty Lancashire voices on the stairs and, for the first time, she understood the contrast of the desolation of the poor man who had so lately gone forth in lonely despair.

It almost put her out of patience to see Mrs Openshaw come in, calmly smiling, handsomely dressed, happy, easy, to enquire after her children.

'Did Ailsie go to sleep comfortably?' she whispered to Norah.

'Yes.'

Her mother bent over her, looking at her slumbers with the soft eyes of love. How little she dreamed who had looked on her last! Then she went to Edwin, with perhaps less wistful anxiety in her countenance, but more of pride. She took off her things, to go down to supper. Norah saw her no more that night.

Beside having a door into the passage, the sleeping-nursery opened out of Mr and Mrs Openshaw's room, in order that they might have the children more immediately under their own eyes. Early the next summer morning, Mrs Openshaw was awakened by Ailsie's startled call of 'Mother! mother!' She sprang up, put on her dressing-gown, and went to her child. Ailsie was only half awake, and in a not unusual state of terror.

'Who was he mother? Tell me!'

'Who, my darling? No one is here. You have been dreaming, love. Waken up quite. See, it is broad daylight.'

'Yes,' said Ailsie, looking round her; then clinging to her mother, 'but a man was here in the night, mother.'

'Nonsense, little goose. No man has ever come near you!'

'Yes, he did. He stood there. Just by Norah. A man with hair and a beard. And he knelt down and said his prayers. Norah knows he was here, mother' (half angrily, as Mrs Openshaw shook her head in smiling incredulity).

'Well! we will ask Norah when she comes,' said Mrs Openshaw, soothingly. 'But we won't talk any more about him now. It is not five o'clock; it is too early for you to get up. Shall I fetch you a book and read to you?'

'Don't leave me, mother,' said the child, clinging to her. So Mrs Openshaw sat on the bedside talking to Ailsie, and telling her of what they had done at Richmond the evening before, until the little girl's eyes slowly closed and she once more fell asleep.

'What was the matter?' asked Mr Openshaw, as his wife returned robed.

'Ailsie wakened up in a fright, with some story of a man having been in the room to say his prayers – a dream, I suppose.' And no more was said at the time.

Mrs Openshaw had almost forgotten the whole affair when she got up about seven o'clock. But, by and by, she heard a sharp altercation going on in the nursery – Norah speaking angrily to Ailsie, a most unusual thing. Both Mr and Mrs Openshaw listened in astonishment.

'Hold your tongue, Ailsie! let me hear none of your dreams; never let me hear you tell that story again!'

Ailsie began to cry.

Mr Openshaw opened the door of communication, before his wife could say a word.

'Norah, come here!'

The nurse stood at the door, defiant. She perceived she had been heard, but she was desperate.

'Don't let me hear you speak in that manner to Ailsie again,' he said sternly, and shut the door.

Norah was infinitely relieved for she had dreaded some questioning; and a little blame for sharp speaking was what she could well bear, if cross examination was let alone.

Downstairs they went, Mr Openshaw carrying Ailsie; the sturdy Edwin coming step by step, right foot foremost, always holding his mother's hand. Each child was placed in a chair by the breakfast-table, and then Mr and Mrs Openshaw stood together at the window, awaiting their visitors' appearance and making plans for the day.

There was a pause. Suddenly Mr Openshaw turned to Ailsie, and said, 'What a little goosey somebody is with her dreams, wakening up poor, tired mother in the middle of the night, with a story of a man being in the room.'

'Father! I'm sure I saw him,' said Ailsie, half crying. 'I don't want to make Norah angry; but I was not asleep, for all she says I was. I had been asleep – and I wakened up quite wide awake, though I was so frightened. I kept my eyes nearly shut, and I saw the man quite plain. A great brown man with a beard. He said his prayers. And then he looked at Edwin. And then Norah took him by the arm and led him away, after they had whispered a bit together.'

'Now, my little woman must be reasonable,' said Mr Openshaw, who was always patient with Ailsie. 'There was no man in the house last night at all. No man comes into the house, as you know, if you think; much less goes up into the nursery. But sometimes we dream something has happened, and the dream is so like reality that you are nor the first person, little woman, who has stood out that the thing has really happened.'

'But, indeed it was not a dream!' said Ailsie, beginning to cry.

Just then Mr and Mrs Chadwick came down, looking grave and discomposed. All during breakfast time, they were silent and uncomfortable. As soon as the breakfast things were taken away, and the children had been carried upstairs, Mr Chadwick began, in an evidently preconcerted manner, to enquire if his nephew was certain that all his servants were honest; for Mrs Chadwick had that morning missed a very valuable brooch, which she had worn the day before. She remembered taking it off when she came home from Buckingham Palace. Mr Openshaw's face contracted into hard lines: grew like what it was before he had known his wife and her child. He rang the bell, even before his uncle had done speaking. It was answered by the housemaid.

'Mary, was anyone here last night, while we were away?'

'A man, sir, came to speak to Norah.'

'To speak to Norah! Who was he? How long did he stay?'

'I'm sure I can't tell, sir. He came – perhaps about nine. I went up to tell Norah in the nursery, and she came down to speak to him. She let him out, sir. She will know who he was, and how long he stayed.'

She waited a moment to be asked any more questions, but she was not, so she went away.

A minute afterwards, Mr Openshaw made as though he were going out of the room; but his wife laid her hand on his arm: 'Do not speak to her before the children,' she said, in her low, quiet voice. 'I will go up and question her.'

'No! I must speak to her. You must know,' said he, turning to his uncle and aunt, 'my missus has an old servant, as faithful as ever woman was, I do believe, as far as love goes – but at the same time, who does not always speak truth, as even the missus must allow. Now, my notion is that this Norah of ours has been come over by some good-for-nothing chap (for she's at the time o' life when they say women pray for husbands – "any, good Lord, any") and has let him into our house, and the chap has made off with your brooch, and m'appen many another thing beside. It's only saying that Norah is soft-hearted, and doesn't stick at a white lie – that's all, missus.'

It was curious to notice how his tone, his eyes, his whole face was changed, as he spoke to his wife; but he was the resolute man through all. She knew better than to oppose him; so she went upstairs, and told Norah her master wanted to speak to her, and that she would take care of the children in the meanwhile.

Norah rose to go, without a word. Her thoughts were these: 'If they tear me to pieces, they shall never know through me. He may come – and then, just Lord have mercy upon us all! for some of us are dead folk to a certainty. But he shall do it; not me.'

You may fancy, now, her look of determination, as she faced her master alone in the dining-room; Mr and Mrs Chadwick having left the affair in their nephew's hands, seeing that he took it up with such vehemence.

'Norah! Who was that man that came to my house last night?'

'Man, sir!' As if infinitely surprised; but it was only to gain time.

'Yes; the man that Mary let in; that she went upstairs to the nursery to tell you about; that you came down to speak to; the same chap, I make no doubt, that you took into the nursery to have your talk out with; the one Ailsie saw, and afterwards dreamed about, thinking, poor wench! she saw him say his prayers, when nothing, I'll be bound, was further from his thoughts; the one that took Mrs Chadwick's brooch, value ten pounds. Now, Norah! Don't go off. I'm as sure, as my name's Thomas Openshaw, that you knew nothing of this robbery. But I do think you've been imposed on, and that's the truth. Some good-for-nothing chap has been making up to you, and you've been just like all other women, and have turned a soft place in your heart to him; and he came last night a-lovering, and you had him up in the nursery, and he made use of his opportunities, and made off with a few things on his way down! Come, now, Norah: it's no blame to you, only you must not be such a fool again! Tell us,' he continued, 'what name he gave you, Norah. I'll be bound, it was not the right one; but it will be a clue for the police.'

Norah drew herself up. 'You may ask that question, and taunt me with my being single, and with my credulity, as you will, Master Openshaw. You'll get no answer from me. As for the brooch, and the story of theft and burglary; if any friend ever came to see me (which I defy you to prove, and deny), he'd be just as much above doing such a thing as you yourself, Mr Openshaw – and more so too; for I'm not at all sure as everything you have is rightly come by, or would be yours long, if every man had his own.' She meant, of course, his wife; but he understood her to refer to his property in goods and chattels.

'Now, my good woman,' said he, 'I'll just tell you truly, I never trusted you out and out; but my wife liked you, and I thought you had many a good point about you. If you once begin to sauce me, I'll have the police to you, and get out the truth in a court of justice, if you'll not tell it me quietly and civilly here. Now, the best thing you can do is quietly to tell me who the fellow is. Look here! a man comes to my house; asks for you; you take him upstairs; a valuable brooch is missing next day; we know that you, and Mary, and cook, are honest; but you refuse to tell us who the man is . Indeed, you've told one lie already about him, saying no one was here last night. Now, I just put it to you, what do you think a policeman would say to this, or a magistrate? A magistrate would soon make you tell the truth, my good woman.'

'There's never the creature born that should get it out of me,' said Norah. 'Not unless I choose to tell.'

'I've a great mind to see,' said Mr Openshaw, growing angry at the defiance. Then, checking himself, he thought before he spoke again: 'Norah, for your missus's sake I don't want to go to extremities. Be a sensible woman, if you can. It's no great disgrace, after all, to have been taken in. I ask you once more – as a friend – who was this man that you let into my house last night?'

No answer. He repeated the question in an impatient tone. Still no answer. Norah's lips were set in determination not to speak.

'Then there is but one thing to be done. I shall send for a policeman.'

'You will not,' said Norah, starting forward. 'You shall not, sir! No policeman shall touch me. I know nothing of the brooch, but I know this: ever since I was four-and-twenty, I have thought more of your wife than of myself; ever since I saw her, a poor motherless girl, put upon in her uncle's house, I have thought more of serving her than of serving myself. I have cared for her and her child, as nobody ever cared for me. I don't cast blame on you, sir, but I say it's ill giving up one's life to anyone; for, at the end, they will turn round upon you, and forsake you. Why does not my missus come herself to suspect me? Maybe, she is gone for the police? But I don't stay here, either for police, or magistrate, or master. You're an unlucky lot. I believe there's a curse on you. I'll leave you this very day. Yes! I'll leave that poor Ailsie, too. I will! No good will ever come to you!'

Mr Openshaw was utterly astonished at this speech; most of which was completely unintelligible to him, as may easily be supposed. Before he could make up his mind what to say, or what to do, Norah had left the room. I do not think he had ever really intended to send for the police to this old servant of his wife's; for he had never for a moment doubted her perfect honesty. But he had intended to compel her to tell him who the man was, and in this he was baffled. He was, consequently, much irritated. He returned to his uncle and aunt in a state of great annoyance and perplexity, and told them he could get nothing out of the woman; that some man had been in the house the night before; but that she refused to tell who he was. At this moment his wife came in, greatly agitated, and asked what had happened to Norah; for she had put on her things in passionate haste, and left the house.

'This looks suspicious,' said Mr Chadwick. 'It is not the way in which an honest person would have acted.'

Mr Openshaw kept silence. He was sorely perplexed. But Mrs Openshaw turned round on Mr Chadwick, with a sudden fierceness no one ever saw in her before. 'You don't know Norah, uncle! She is gone because she is deeply hurt at being suspected. Oh, I wish I had seen her – that I had spoken to her myself. She would have told me anything.' Alice wrung her hands.

'I must confess,' continued Mr Chadwick to his nephew, in a lower voice, 'I can't make you out. You used to be a word and a blow, and oftenest the blow first; and now, when there is every cause for suspicion, you just do nought. Your missus is a very good woman, I grant; but she may have been put upon as well as other folk, I suppose. If you don't send for the police, I shall.'

'Very well,' replied Mr Openshaw, surlily. 'I can't clear Norah. She won't clear herself, as I believe she might if she would. Only I wash my hands of it; for I am sure the woman herself is honest, and she's lived a long time with my wife, and I don't like her to come to shame.'

'But she will then be forced to clear herself. That, at any rate, will be a good thing.'

'Very well, very well! I am heart-sick of the whole business. Come, Alice, come up to the babies; they'll be in a sore way. I tell you, uncle,' he said, turning round once more to Mr Chadwick, suddenly and sharply, after his eye had fallen on Alice's wan, tearful, anxious face; 'I'll have no sending for the police, after all. I'll buy my aunt twice as handsome a brooch this very day; but I'll not have Norah suspected, and my missus plagued. There's for you!'

He and his wife left the room. Mr Chadwick quietly waited till he was out of hearing, and then said to his wife, 'For all Tom's heroics, I'm just quietly going for a detective, wench. Thou need'st know nought about it.'

He went to the police station, and made a statement of the case. He was gratified by the impression which the evidence against Norah seemed to make. The men all agreed in his opinion, and steps were to be immediately taken to find out where she was. Most probably, as they suggested, she had gone at once to the man, who, to all appearance, was her lover. When Mr Chadwick asked how they would find her out, they smiled, shook their heads, and spoke of mysterious but infallible ways and means. He returned to his nephew's house with a very comfortable opinion of his own sagacity. He was met by his wife with a penitent face:

'Oh master, I've found my brooch! It was just sticking by its pin in the flounce of my brown silk, that I wore yesterday. I took it off in a hurry, and it must have caught in it: and I hung up my gown in the closet. Just now, when I was going to fold it up, there was the brooch! I'm very vexed, but I never dreamt but what it was lost!'

Her husband muttering something very like, 'Confound thee and thy brooch too! I wish I'd never given it thee,' snatched up his hat, and rushed back to the station, hoping to be in time to stop the police from searching for Norah. But a detective was already gone off on the errand.

Where was Norah? Half mad with the strain of the fearful secret, she had hardly slept through the night for thinking what must be done. Upon this terrible state of mind had come Ailsie's questions, showing that she had seen the Man, as the unconscious child called her father. Lastly came the suspicion of her honesty. She was little less than crazy as she ran upstairs and dashed on her bonnet and shawl, leaving all else, even her purse, behind her. In that house she would not stay. That was all she knew or was clear about. She would not even see the children again, for fear it should weaken her. She dreaded above everything Mr Frank's return to claim his wife. She could not tell what remedy there was for a sorrow so tremendous, for her to stay to witness. The desire of escaping from the coming event was a stronger motive for her departure than her soreness about the suspicions directed against her; although this last had been the final goad to the course she took. She walked away almost at headlong speed; sobbing as she went, as she had not dared to do during the past night for fear of exciting wonder in those who might hear her. Then she stopped. An idea came into her mind that she would leave London altogether, and betake herself to her native town of

Liverpool. She felt in her pocket for her purse as she drew near the Euston Square station with this intention. She had left it at home. Her poor head aching, her eyes swollen with crying, she had to stand still, and think, as well as she could, where next she should bend her steps. Suddenly the thought flashed into her mind that she would go and find poor Mr Frank. She had been hardly kind to him the night before, though her heart had bled for him ever since. She remembered his telling her, when she enquired for his address, almost as she had pushed him out of the door, of some hotel in a street not far distant from Euston Square. Thither she went: with what intention she scarcely knew, but to assuage her conscience by telling him how much she pitied him. In her present state she felt herself unfit to counsel, or restrain, or assist, or do aught else but sympathise and weep. The people of the inn said such a person had been there; had arrived only the day before; had gone out soon after his arrival, leaving his luggage in their care; but had never come back. Norah asked for leave to sit down, and await the gentleman's return. The landlady – pretty secure in the deposit of luggage against any probable injury – showed her into a room, and quietly locked the door on the outside. Norah was utterly worn out, and fell asleep – a shivering, starting, uneasy slumber, which lasted for hours.

The detective, meanwhile, had come up with her some time before she entered the hotel, into which he followed her. Asking the landlady to detain her for an hour or so, without giving any reason beyond showing his authority (which made the landlady applaud herself a good deal for having locked her in), he went back to the police station to report his proceedings. He could have taken her directly; but his object was, if possible, to trace out the man who was supposed to have committed the robbery. Then he heard of the discovery of the brooch; and consequently did not care to return.

Norah slept till even the summer evening began to close in. Then started up. Someone was at the door. It would be Mr Frank; and she dizzily pushed back her ruffled grey hair, which had fallen over her eyes, and stood looking to see him. Instead, there came in Mr Openshaw and a policeman.

'This is Norah Kennedy,' said Mr Openshaw.

'Oh, sir,' said Norah, 'I did not touch the brooch; indeed I did not. Oh, sir, I cannot live to be thought so badly of;' and very sick and faint, she suddenly sank down on the ground. To her surprise, Mr Openshaw raised her up very tenderly. Even the policeman helped to lay her on the sofa; and, at Mr Openshaw's desire, he went for some wine and sandwiches; for the poor gaunt woman lay there almost as if dead with weariness and exhaustion.

'Norah,' said Mr Openshaw, in his kindest voice, 'the brooch is found. It was hanging to Mrs Chadwick's gown. I beg your pardon. Most truly I beg your pardon, for having troubled you about it. My wife is almost broken-hearted. Dear, Norah – or, stay, first drink this glass of wine,' said he, lifting her head, and pouring a little down her throat.

As she drank, she remembered where she was, and whom she was waiting for. She suddenly pushed Mr Openshaw away, saying, 'Oh, sir, you must go. You must not stop a minute. If he comes back, he will kill you.'

'Alas, Norah! I do not know who "he" is. But someone is gone away who will never come back: someone who knew you, and whom I am afraid you cared for.'

'I don't understand you, sir,' said Norah, her master's kind and sorrowful manner bewildering her yet more than his words. The policeman had left the room at Mr Openshaw's desire, and they two were alone.

'You know what I mean, when I say someone is gone who will never come back. I mean that he is dead!'

'Who?' said Norah, trembling all over.

'A poor man has been found in the Thames this morning – drowned.'

'Did he drown himself?' asked Norah, solemnly.

'God only knows,' replied Mr Openshaw, in the same tone. 'Your name and address at our house were found in his pocket: that, and his purse, were the only things that were found upon him. I am sorry to say it, my poor Norah; but you are required to go and identify him.'

'To what?' asked Norah.

'To say who it is. It is always done, in order that some reason may be discovered for the suicide – if suicide it was. – I make no doubt, he was the man who came to see you at our house last night. – It is very sad, I know.' He made pauses between each little clause, in order to try and bring back her senses, which he feared were wandering – so wild and sad was her look.

'Master Openshaw,' said she, at last, 'I've a dreadful secret to tell you – only you must never breathe it to anyone, and you and I must hide it away for ever. I thought to have done it all by myself, but I see I cannot. Yon poor man – yes! the dead, drowned creature – is, I fear, Mr Frank, my mistress's first husband!'

Mr Openshaw sat down, as if shot. He did not speak; but, after a while, he signed to Norah to go on.

'He came to me last night – when – God be thanked! you were all away at Richmond. He asked me if his wife was dead or alive. I was a brute, and thought more of your all coming home than of his sore trial: I spoke out sharp, and said she was married again, and very content and happy; I all but turned him away: and now he lies dead and cold.'

'God forgive me!' said Mr Openshaw.

'God forgive us all!' said Norah. 'Yon poor man needs forgiveness, perhaps, less than anyone among us. He had been among the savages – shipwrecked – I know not what – and he had written letters which had never reached my poor missus.'

'He saw his child!'

'He saw her – yes! I took him up, to give his thoughts another start; for I believed he was going mad on my hands. I came to seek him here, as I more than half promised. My mind misgave me when I heard he never came in. Oh, sir! it must be him!'

Mr Openshaw rang the bell. Norah was almost too much stunned to wonder at what he did. He asked for writing materials, wrote a letter, and then said to Norah: 'I am writing to Alice to say I shall be unavoidably absent for a few days; that I have found you; that you are well, and send her your love, and will come home tomorrow. You must go with me to the Police Court; you must identify the body; I will pay high to keep names and details out of the papers.'

'But where are you going, sir?'

He did not answer her directly. Then he said: 'Norah! I must go with you, and look on the face of the man whom I have so injured – unwittingly, it is true; but it seems to me as if I had killed him. I will lay his head in the grave, as if he were my only brother: and how he must have hated me! I cannot go home to my wife till all that I can do for him is done. Then I go with a dreadful secret on my mind. I shall never speak of it again, after these days are over. I know you will not, either.' He shook hands with her: and they never named the subject again, the one to the other.

Norah went home to Alice the next day. Not a word was said on the cause of her abrupt departure a day or two before. Alice had been charged by her husband, in his letter, not to allude to the supposed theft of the brooch; so she, implicitly obedient to those whom she loved both by nature and habit, was entirely silent on the subject, only treated Norah with the most tender respect, as if to make up for unjust suspicion.

Nor did Alice enquire into the reason why Mr Openshaw had been absent during his uncle and aunt's visit, after he had once said that it was unavoidable. He came back grave and quiet; and from that time forth was curiously changed. More thoughtful, and perhaps less active; quite as decided in conduct, but with new and different rules for the guidance of that conduct. Towards Alice he could hardly be more kind than he had always been; but he now seemed to look upon her as someone sacred, and to be treated with reverence, as well as tenderness. He throve in business, and made a large fortune, one half of which was settled upon her.

Long years after these events – a few months after her mother died – Ailsie and her 'father' (as she always called Mr Openshaw) drove to a cemetery a little way out of town, and she was carried to a certain mound by her maid, who was then sent back to the carriage. There was a headstone, with F. W. and a date upon it. That was all. Sitting by the grave, Mr Openshaw told her the story; and for the sad fate of that poor father whom she had never known, he shed the only tears she ever saw fall from his eyes.

WILLIAM SCHWENCK GILBERT

W. S. Gilbert was born in London on 18 November 1836. He studied at King's College and became a clerk in the Privy-Council Office from 1857 to 1862. He was called to the bar in 1864 but he failed to attract lucrative briefs and made his living writing humorous contributions to magazines like *Punch*. Under his boyhood nickname 'Bab', he wrote and illustrated a series of highly popular comic verses, primarily for the magazine *Fun*, known as the 'Bab Ballads'. But it is as the librettist of Sir Arthur Sullivan's light operas that he is best remembered. He died in Harrow Weald, Middlesex, on 29 May 1911.

An Inverted Love Story

I am a poor paralysed fellow who, for many years past, has been confined to a bed or a sofa. For the last six years I have occupied a small room, giving on to one of the side canals of Venice, and having no one about me but a deaf old woman, who makes my bed and attends to my food; and there I eke out a poor income of about thirty pounds a year by making watercolour drawings of flowers and fruit (they are the cheapest models in Venice), and these I send to a friend in London, who sells them to a dealer for small sums. But, on the whole, I am happy and content.

It is necessary that I should describe the position of my room rather minutely. Its only window is about five feet above the water of the canal, and above it the house projects some six feet, and overhangs the water, the projecting portion being supported by stout piles driven into the bed of the canal. This arrangement has the disadvantage (among others) of so limiting my upward view that I am unable to see more than about ten feet of the height of the house immediately opposite to me, although, by reaching as far out of the window as my infirmity will permit, I can see for a considerable distance up and down the canal, which does not exceed fifteen feet in width. But, although I can see but little of the material house opposite, I can see its reflection upside down in the canal, and I take a good deal of inverted interest in such of its inhabitants as show themselves from time to time (always upside down) on its balconies and at its windows.

When I first occupied my room, about six years ago, my attention was directed to the reflection of a little girl of thirteen or so (as nearly as I could judge), who passed every day on a balcony just above the upward range of my limited field of view. She had a glass of flowers and a crucifix on a little table by her side; and as she sat there, in fine weather, from early morning until dark, working assiduously all the time, I concluded that she earned her living by needlework. She was certainly an industrious little girl, and, as far as I could judge from her upside-down reflection, neat in her dress and pretty. She had an old mother, an invalid, who, on warm days, would sit on the balcony with her, and it interested me to see the little maid wrap the old lady in shawls, and bring pillows for her chair, and a stool for her feet, and every now and again lay down her work and kiss and fondle the old lady for half a minute, and then take up her work again.

Time went by, and as the little maid grew up, her reflection grew down, and at last she was quite a little woman of, I suppose, sixteen or seventeen. I can only work for a couple of hours or so in the brightest part of the day, so

I had plenty of time on my hands in which to watch her movements, and sufficient imagination to weave a little romance about her, and to endow her with a beauty which, to a great extent, I had to take for granted. I saw – or fancied that I could see – that she began to take an interest in *my* reflection (which, of course, she could see as I could see hers); and one day, when it appeared to me that she was looking right at it – that is to say when her reflection appeared to be looking right at me – I tried the desperate experiment of nodding to her, and to my intense delight her reflection nodded in reply. And so our two reflections became known to one another.

It did not take me very long to fall in love with her, but a long time passed before I could make up my mind to do more than nod to her every morning, when the old woman moved me from my bed to the sofa at the window, and again in the evening, when the little maid left the balcony for that day. One day, however, when I saw her reflection looking at mine, I nodded to her, and threw a flower into the canal. She nodded several times in return, and I saw her direct her mother's attention to the incident. Then every morning I threw a flower into the water for 'good-morning', and another in the evening for 'good-night', and I soon discovered that I had not altogether thrown them in vain, for one day she threw a flower to join mine, and she laughed and clapped her hands when she saw the two flowers join forces and float away together. And then every morning and every evening she threw her flower when I threw mine, and when the two flowers met she clapped her hands, and so did I; but when they were separated, as they sometimes were, owing to one of them having met an obstruction which did not catch the other, she threw up her hands in a pretty affectation of despair, which I tried to imitate but in an English and unsuccessful fashion. And when they were rudely run down by a passing gondola (which happened not unfrequently) she pretended to cry, and I did the same. Then, in pretty pantomime, she would point downwards to the sky to tell me that it was destiny that had caused the shipwreck of our flowers, and I, in pantomime, not nearly so pretty, would try to convey to her that destiny would be kinder next time, and that perhaps tomorrow our flowers would be more fortunate – and so the innocent courtship went on. One day she showed me her crucifix and kissed it, and thereupon I took a little silver crucifix that always stood by me, and kissed that, and so she knew that we were one in religion.

One day the little maid did not appear on her balcony, and for several days I saw nothing of her; and although I threw my flowers as usual, no flower came to keep it company. However, after a time, she reappeared, dressed in black, and crying often, and then I knew that the poor child's mother was dead, and, as far as I knew, she was alone in the world. The flowers came no more for many days, nor did she show any sign of recognition, but kept her eyes on her work, except when she placed her handkerchief to them. And opposite to her was the old lady's chair, and I could see that, from time to time, she would lay down her work and gaze at it, and then a flood of tears would come to her relief. But at last one day she roused herself to nod to me, and then her flower came, day by day, and my flower went forth to join it, and with varying fortunes the two flowers sailed away as of yore.

But the darkest day of all to me was when a good-looking young gondolier, standing right end uppermost in his gondola (for I could see *him* in the flesh), worked his craft alongside the house, and stood talking to her as she sat on the balcony. They seemed to speak as old friends – indeed, as well as I could make out, he held her by the hand during the whole of their interview which lasted quite half an hour. Eventually he pushed off, and left my heart heavy within me. But I soon took heart of grace, for as soon as he was out of sight, the little maid threw two flowers growing on the same stem – an allegory of which I could make nothing, until it broke upon me that she meant to convey to me that he and she were brother and sister, and that I had no cause to be sad. And thereupon I nodded to her cheerily, and she nodded to me, and laughed aloud, and I laughed in return, and all went on again as before.

Then came a dark and dreary time, for it became necessary that I should undergo treatment that confined me absolutely to my bed for many days, and I worried and fretted to think that the little maid and I should see each other no longer, and worse still, that she would think that I had gone away without even hinting to her that I was going. And I lay awake at night wondering how I could let her know the truth, and fifty plans flitted through my brain, all appearing to be feasible enough at night, but absolutely wild and impracticable in the morning. One day – and it was a bright day indeed for me – the old woman who tended me told me that a gondolier had enquired whether the English signor had gone away or had died; and so I learnt that the little maid had been anxious about me, and that she had sent her brother to enquire, and the brother had no doubt taken to her the reason of my protracted absence from the window.

From that day, and ever after during my three weeks of bed-keeping, a flower was found every morning on the ledge of my window, which was within easy reach of anyone in a boat; and when at last a day came when I could be moved, I took my accustomed place on my sofa at the window, and the little maid saw me, and stood on her head (so to speak) and clapped her hands upside down with a delight that was as eloquent as my right-end-up delight could be. And so the first time the gondolier passed my window I beckoned to him, and he pushed alongside, and told me, with many bright smiles, that he was glad indeed to see me well again. Then I thanked him and his sister for their many kind thoughts about me during my retreat, and I then learnt from him that her name was Angela, and that she was the best and purest maiden in all Venice, and that anyone might think himself happy indeed who could call her sister, but that he was happier even than her brother, for he was to be married to her, and indeed they were to be married the next day.

Thereupon my heart seemed to swell to bursting, and the blood rushed through my veins so that I could hear it and nothing else for a while. I managed at last to stammer forth some words of awkward congratulation, and he left me, singing merrily, after asking permission to bring his bride to see me on the morrow as they returned from church.

'For,' said he, 'my Angela has known you very long – ever since she was a child, and she has often spoken to me of the poor Englishman who was a good Catholic, and who lay all day long for years and years on a sofa at a window, and she had said over and over again how dearly she wished she could speak to him and comfort him; and one day, when you threw a flower into the canal, she asked me whether she might throw another, and I told her yes, for he would understand that it meant sympathy for one sorely afflicted.'

And so I learned that it was pity, and not love, except indeed such love as is akin to pity, that prompted her to interest herself in my welfare, and there was an end of it all.

For the two flowers that I thought were on one stem were two flowers tied together (but I could not tell that), and they were meant to indicate that she and the gondolier were affianced lovers, and my expressed pleasure at this symbol delighted her, for she took it to mean that I rejoiced in her happiness.

And the next day the gondolier came with a train of other gondoliers, all decked in their holiday garb, and on his gondola sat Angela, happy, and blushing at her happiness. Then he and she entered the house in which I dwelt, and came into my room (and it was strange indeed, after so many years of inversion, to see her with her head above her feet!), and then she wished me happiness and a speedy restoration to good health (which could never be); and I, in broken words and with tears in my eyes, gave her the little silver crucifix that had stood by my bed or my table for so many years. And Angela took it reverently, and crossed herself, and kissed it, and so departed with her delighted husband.

And as I heard the song of the gondoliers as they went their way – the song dying away in the distance as the shadows of the sundown closed around me – I felt that they were singing the requiem of the only love that had ever entered my heart.

GEORGE GISSING

George Robert Gissing was born on 22 November 1857 in Wake-field, Yorkshire. His father, who died when he was thirteen, was a chemist from a family of Suffolk shoemakers. Gissing won a scholarship to Owens College (now the University of Manchester), and in 1874 he took his BA exam at the University of London where he was placed first in England for both English and Latin. In 1875 he fell in love with a woman of ill-repute, Marianne Helen Harrison, 'Nell'. Trying to support her financially, he was caught stealing money from other students. The sentence for him was one month's hard labour at Bellevue Prison in Manchester. Gissing's mother sent him to the United States to start anew. It was a difficult period of adjustment, full of the hard work and misery so often reflected in his novels. In Chicago, Gissing was barely able to support himself with his writing. His first fiction, *The Sins of the Fathers*, was published in the *Chicago Tribune* in 1877. The same year Gissing returned to England and again met Nell whom he married on 27 October 1879; in February 1888 she died in a Lambeth slum. Soon after this Gissing travelled to Italy, then France, Naples and Greece. On 25 February 1891 he married another uneducated young woman, Edith Alice Underwood, who was committed to an insane asylum in 1902. Estranged from her, Gissing had moved to France in 1898 with a young French writer, Gabrielle Fleury. Gissing's literary output was prodigious in spite of his many vicissitudes. He is best remembered as the author of *New Grub Street* (1891). He died in France on 3 December 1903.

In Honour Bound

At the top of a dim-windowed house near Gray's Inn Road, in two rooms of his own furnishing, lived a silent, solitary man. He was not old (six-and-thirty at most), and the gentle melancholy of his countenance suggested no quarrel with the world, but rather a placid absorption in congenial studies. His name was Filmer; he had occupied this lodging for seven or eight years; only at long intervals did a letter reach him, and the sole person who visited his retreat was Mrs Mayhew, the charwoman. Mrs Mayhew came at ten o'clock in the morning, and busied herself about the rooms for an hour or so. Sometimes the lodger remained at home, sitting at his big table heaped with books, and exchanging a friendly word with his attendant; sometimes he had gone out before her arrival, and in that case he would have been found at the British Museum. Filmer abjured the society of men for that of words; he was a philological explorer, tracking slowly and patiently the capricious river of human speech. He published nothing, but saw the approaching possibility of a great work, which should do honour to his name.

Proud amid poverty, and shrinking with a nervous sensitiveness from the commerce of mankind, he often passed weeks at a time without addressing a familiar word to any mortal save Mrs Mayhew. He had made friends with his charwoman, though not till the experience of years taught him to regard her with entire confidence and no little respect. To her he even spoke of his studies, half soliloquising, indeed, but feeling it not impossible that she might gather some general conception of what he meant. In turn, Mrs Mayhew confided to him some details of her own history, which threw light upon the fact that she neither looked nor spoke like an ordinary charwoman. She was a meagre but trim-bodied little person of about the same age as her employer, clean, neat, and brisk, her face sharply outlined, with large good-humoured eyes, and a round mouth. A widow, she said, for ten years and more; childless; pretty much alone in the world, though she had relatives not badly off. Shamefaced hints made known to Filmer that she blamed only herself for her poor condition, and one day she confessed to him that her weakness had been drink. When first he engaged her services she was struggling painfully out of the mire, battling with old temptations, facing toil and hunger. 'And now, sir,' she said, with her modest, childish laugh, 'I feel almost a respectable woman; I do, indeed!' Whereat Filmer smiled pensively and nodded.

No life could be less eventful than his. He enjoyed an income of seventy pounds, and looked not for increase. Of his costume he took no thought, his diet was the simplest conceivable. He wanted no holidays. Leisure to work in his own way, blessed independence – this sufficed him.

On a morning of December (the year was 1869) Mrs Mayhew came to the house as usual, went upstairs and tapped at Filmer's door. On entering she was surprised to see a fireless grate, and on the table no trace of breakfast. Filmer stood by the window; she bade him good-morning, and looked about the room in surprise.

'I'm going out,' said the student, in a voice unlike his own. 'I didn't trouble to light the fire.'

She observed his face.

'But won't you have breakfast, sir? I'll get some in a minute.'

'No, thank you. I shall get some – somewhere – '

He went into the bedroom, was absent a few minutes, and returned with his overcoat.

'I wanted to speak to you, sir,' said Mrs Mayhew, diffidently. 'But if you are in a hurry – '

'No, no. Certainly not. I have plenty of time.'

'I am very sorry to tell you, sir, that, after next week, I shan't be able to come. But,' she hastened to add, 'I can recommend someone who'll do the work just as well.'

Filmer listened without appearance of concern; he seemed to have a difficulty in fixing his thoughts on the matter.

'I am going to take a little shop,' pursued the other, 'a little general shop. It's part of the house where I've been living. The woman that's had it hasn't done well: but it was her own fault; she didn't attend to business, and she – but there's no need to trouble you with such things, sir. Someone advised me to see what I could do in that way, and I thought it over. The landlord will let me have the shop, and a room behind it, and another room upstairs, for twenty-eight pounds a year, if I pay a quarter in advance. That's seven pounds, you see, sir; and I ought to have about twenty pounds altogether to start with. I've got a little more than ten, and I know someone who'll lend me another ten, I think.' She spoke quickly, a glow of excitement in her cheeks. 'And I feel sure I can make the business pay. I've seen a good deal of it, from living in the house. There's lots of people round about who would deal with me, and of course I could begin with a small stock, and – '

Her breath failed; she broke off with a pant and a laugh. Filmer, after standing for a moment as if in uncertainty, said that he was very glad to hear all this, and that he would talk with her about it on the morrow. At present he must go out – on business – special and disagreeable business. But he would talk tomorrow. And so, without further remark, he went his way.

The next morning Mrs Mayhew saw that her employer was still in a most unusual frame of mind. He had a fire, but was sitting by it in gloomy idleness. To her 'Good-morning' he merely nodded, and only when she had finished putting the bedroom to rights did he show a disposition to speak.

'Well, Mrs Mayhew,' he said at length, 'I also have news to tell. I have lost all my money, and have nothing to live upon.'

Her large eyes gazed at him with astonishment and compassion.

'Oh, Mr Filmer! What a dreadful thing!'

'Bad; there's no disguising it.' He struggled to speak without dolefulness; his limbs moved nervously, and he stared away from his companion. 'No hope, now, of writing my book. All over with me. I must earn my living – I don't know how. It's twelve years since I ever thought of such a thing; I felt safe for my whole life. All gone at a blow; you can read about it in the newspaper.'

'But – but you can't surely have lost everything, sir?'

'I have a few pounds. About thirty pounds, I think. What's the use of that? I don't want very much, but' – he tried to jest – 'I can't live on ten shillings a year.'

'But with all your learning, Mr Filmer –'

'Yes, I must find something. Go and teach in a school, or something of the kind. But I'm afraid you can't understand what it means to me.'

He became silent. Mrs Mayhew looked up and down, moved uneasily, played with the corners of her apron, and at last found resolution to speak.

'Mr Filmer' – her eyes were very bright and eager – 'you couldn't live in one room, I'm afraid, sir?'

'One room?' He glanced vacantly at her. 'Why not? Of course I could. I spend nearly all my time at the Museum. But –'

'I hardly like to say it, sir, but there's something – if you thought – I told you I was going to have a room behind the shop, and one upstairs. I meant to let the one upstairs.'

He interrupted, rather coldly.

'Oh, I would take it at once if I had the least prospect of being able to live. But what is the use of settling down anywhere with thirty pounds? To write my book I need at least two years, and a quiet mind –'

'But I was going to say something else, sir, if you'll excuse the liberty. I told you I shall have to borrow some money, and – and I'm not quite sure after all that I can get it. Will *you* lend it me, sir?' This came out with a jerk, on an impulse of great daring. 'If you would lend me ten pounds, I could afford to let you have the room, and – and to supply you with meals, and in that way pay it back. I'm quite sure I could.' She grew excited again. 'If I miss getting the shop, somebody else will step in, and make money out of it. I *know* I could very soon make two or three pounds a week out of that business!'

She stopped suddenly, awed by the listener's face. Filmer, for the first time since her knowledge of him, looked coldly distant, even offended.

'I beg your pardon, sir. I oughtn't to have said such a thing.'

He stood up.

'It was a kind thought, Mrs Mayhew; but – I really don't know – ' His face was changing. 'I should very much like to let you have the money. A few days ago I would gladly have done so. But – '

His tongue faltered. He looked at the woman, and saw how her countenance had fallen.

'Ten pounds,' he said abruptly, 'couldn't last – for my support – more than a few weeks.'

'Not by itself, sir,' replied the other, eagerly; 'but money grows so when it's put into trade. I do believe it would bring in a pound a week. Or, at all events, I'm quite sure it would bring enough – '

She glanced, involuntarily, at the breakfast table, which seldom showed anything but bread and butter.

'In that case,' said Filmer, laughing, 'I should be a partner in the business.'

Mrs Mayhew smiled, and made no answer.

That day they could not arrive at a decision; but after nightfall Filmer walked along the street in which he knew Mrs Mayhew lived, and looked for the shop. That which answered to her description was a miserable little hole, where seemingly business was still being carried on; the glimmer of one gas-jet rather suggested than revealed objects in the window – a loaf, some candles, a bundle of firewood, and so on. He hurried past, and got into another street as quickly as possible.

Later, he was prowling in the same locality, and again he went past the shop. This time he observed it more deliberately. After all, the place itself was not so squalid as it had seemed; by daylight it might look tolerable. And the street could not be called a slum. Other considerations apart he could contemplate having his abode here; for he knew nobody, and never had to fear a visit. Besides the little chandler's there were only two shops; no public-house, and hardly any traffic of a noisy kind.

In his great need, his horror of going forth among strangers (for of course his lodgings were now too expensive to be kept a day longer than he could help), Filmer compromised with himself. By lending Mrs Mayhew ten pounds he might justly accept from her a lodging and the plainest sustenance for, say, ten weeks, and in that time he would of necessity have taken some steps towards earning a livelihood. Some of his books and furniture he must sell, thus adding to the petty reserve which stood between him and starvation. If it would really be helping the good woman, as well as benefiting himself, common sense bade him disregard the fastidiousness which at first had been shocked by such a proposal. 'Beggars cannot be choosers,' said the old adage; he must swallow his pride.

Waking at the dead hour of night, and facing once more the whole terrible significance of what had befallen him, not easily grasped in daytime, he resolved to meet the charwoman next morning in a humble and grateful spirit. His immediate trouble thus overcome, he could again sleep.

And so it came about that, in some few days, Filmer found himself a tenant of the front room above the chandler's shop. As he still had the familiar furniture about him, he suffered less uneasiness – his removal once over – than might have been anticipated. True, he moaned the loss of beloved volumes; but, on the other hand, his purse had gained by it. As soon as possible he repaired to the Museum, and there, in the seat he had occupied for years, and with books open before him, he tried to think calmly.

Mrs Mayhew, meanwhile, had entered exultantly into possession of her business premises; the little shop was stocked much better than for a long time, and customers followed each other throughout the day. In his utter ignorance of such transactions, the philologist accepted what she had at first told him as a sufficient explanation of the worthy woman's establishment in shop-keeping. To a practical eye, it would have seemed not a little mysterious that some twenty pounds had sufficed for all the preparations; but Filmer merely glanced with satisfaction at the shop front as he came and went, and listened trustfully when Mrs Mayhew informed him that the first week's profits enabled her to purchase some new fittings, as well as provide for all current expenditure.

Under these circumstances, it was not wonderful that the student experienced a diminution of personal anxiety. Saying to himself every day that he must take some step, he yet took none save that literal step which brought him daily to the Museum. A fortnight, and he had actually resumed work; three weeks, and he was busy with the initial chapter of his great book; a month, and he scarcely troubled himself to remember that his income had vanished. For Mrs Mayhew did not let a day pass without assuring him that his ten pounds – his share in the partnership – produced more than enough to represent the cost of his board and lodging. He lived better than in the old days, had an excellent supper on coming home from the Museum, a warm breakfast before setting out. And these things caused him no astonishment. The literary recluse sees no limit to the potentialities of 'trade'.

At length he remembered that ten weeks had gone by, and on a Sunday morning he summoned his partner to a conference. The quondam char-woman looked a very presentable person as she entered in her Sunday gown. Though she still did a good deal of rough work, her hands were becoming softer and more shapely. In shop and house she had the assistance of a young girl, the daughter of the people who occupied the upper rooms, and it was this girl – Amanda Wilkes by name, and known to her friends as 'Manda – who generally waited upon Filmer.

'Mrs Mayhew,' he began gravely, 'I begin to feel that I have no right to continue living in this way. You have long since paid me back the small sum I lent you –'

'Oh, but I have explained to you, sir,' broke in the other, who bated nothing of her accustomed respect, 'that money is always making more –

indeed it is. It makes enough for you to live upon, as long – oh, as long as you like.'

The philologist drew a silent breath, and stared at the floor.

'Now *don't* trouble yourself, sir!' begged Mrs Mayhew, 'please don't! If you can be content to live here – until – '

'I am more than content so far as personal comfort goes. But – well, let me explain to you. At last, I have really made a beginning with my book. If my misfortune hadn't happened I might have put it off for years; so, in one way, perhaps that loss was a good thing. I am working very hard – '

'Oh, I *know* you are, Mr Filmer. I can't think how you do with so little sleep, sir. I'm sure I wonder your health doesn't break down.'

'No, no; I do well enough: I'm used to it. But the point is that I may be a year or two on this book – a year or two, and how can I possibly go on presuming upon your great kindness to me – '

Mrs Mayhew laughed, and for the hundredth time put before him the commercial view of the matter. Once again he suffered himself to be reassured, though with much nervous twitching of head and limbs; and after this he seldom recurred to his scruple.

Two years went by, and in the early months of the third Filmer's treatise lay finished. As he sat one evening by his fireside, smoking a delicious pipe, he flattered himself that he had made a solid contribution to the science of Comparative Philology. He was thirty-eight years old; young enough still to enjoy any honour or reward the learned world might choose to offer him. What he now had to do was to discover a publisher who would think this book worth the expense of printing. Long ago he had made up his mind that, if profit there were, Mrs Mayhew must share in it. Though his ten pounds had kept him alive all this time, yet clearly it would not have done so but for Mrs Mayhew's skill and labour; he felt himself vastly indebted to her, and earnestly hoped that he might be able to show his gratitude in some substantial form.

Fortune favoured him. His manuscript came into the hands of a generous scholar, a man after his own heart, who not only recommended it to the publisher in terms of enthusiasm, but expressed an earnest desire to make the acquaintance of the author. Filmer, no longer ashamed before his fellows, went forth from the hermitage above the chandler's shop, and was seen of men. He still had money enough to provide himself with decent clothing, and on a certain day his appearance so astonished Mrs Mayhew that she exclaimed tremulously: 'Are you going, Mr Filmer? Are you going to leave us?'

'I can't say,' was his nervous answer. 'I don't know yet whether I shall make any money by my book.'

He told her how things were tending.

'Oh,' she answered, 'then I'm sure you will soon get back to your proper position. After all, sir, you know, you oughtn't to be living in this poor way. You are a learned gentleman.'

Her voice was agitated, and her thoughts seemed to wander. The philologist examined her for a moment, but she turned away with a hurried excuse that she was wanted downstairs.

That day Filmer brooded.

In another month it was known that his book would be published; whether he profited thereby must depend upon its success. In the meantime, one or two fragments of the work were to appear in the *Journal of Comparative Philology*; moreover, the author himself was to read a paper before an erudite society. Overcoming false delicacy, he had made known his position (without detail) to the philological friend who took so much interest in him, and before long a practical suggestion was made, which, if it could be carried out, would assure him at all events a modest livelihood.

Amid all this promise of prosperity, Filmer was beset by graver trouble than he had known since that disastrous day, now two years and a half ago. He could no longer doubt that the prospect of his departure affected Mrs Mayhew very painfully. She kept out of his way, and when meeting was inevitable spoke the fewest possible words. More, he had once, on entering his room unexpectedly, surprised her there in a tearful condition; yes, unmistakably weeping; and she hurried out of his sight.

What could it mean? Her business throve; all appeared well with her. Could the mere thought of losing his companionship cause her such acute distress? If so –

He took long walks, musing anxiously over the situation. At home he shrank into himself, moved without sound, tried, if such a thing were possible, to dwell in the house and yet not be there. He stayed out late at night, fearing to meet Mrs Mayhew as he entered. Ludicrous as it sounded to a man who had long since forgotten the softer dreams of youth, Mrs Mayhew might perchance have conceived an attachment for him. They had now known each other for many years, and long ago the simple-minded woman used to talk with him in a way that betrayed kindly feeling. She, it must be remembered, did not strictly belong to the class in which he found her; she was the daughter of a man of business, had gone to school, had been married to a solicitor's clerk. Probably her life contained a darker incident than anything she had disclosed; perhaps she had left her husband, or been repudiated by him. But a strong character ultimately saved her; she was now beyond reproach. And if he were about to inflict a great sorrow upon her, his own suffering would be scarcely less severe.

As he crept softly into the house one night, he came face to face with a tall man whom he remembered to have seen here on several former occasions; decently dressed, like a clerk or shopman, forty years old or so, and not ill-looking. Filmer, with a glance at him, gave good-evening, but, to his surprise, the stranger made no reply; nay, it seemed to him that he was regarded with a distinctly unamiable stare. This troubled him for the moment, sensitive as he was, but he concluded that the ill-conditioned fellow was a friend of the family upstairs, and soon forgot the occurrence.

A day or two later, as the girl 'Manda served his breakfast, she looked at him oddly, and seemed desirous of saying something. This young person was now about seventeen, and rather given to friskiness, though Mrs Mayhew called her an excellent girl, and treated her like a sister.

'If you please, Mr Filmer,' she began, in an unusually diffident tone.

'Yes?'

'Is it true that you're going to leave us, sir?'

She smirked a little, and altogether behaved strangely.

'Who told you I was going to?' asked Filmer.

'Oh! – Mrs Mayhew said as it was likely, sir.' Again she dropped her eyes, and fidgeted.

The philologist, much disturbed, spoke on an impulse. 'Yes,' he said, 'I am going – very soon. I may have to leave any day.'

'Oh!' was the reply, and to his ears it sounded like an expression of relief. But why 'Manda should be glad of his departure he could not imagine.

However, his resolve was taken. He had no right to remain here. Prospects or no prospects, he would engage a room in a quite different part of the town, and make his few pounds last as long as possible.

And on this resolve he had the strength to act. Dreadful to him in anticipation, the parting with Mrs Mayhew came about in the simplest and easiest way. When he had made known his purpose – with nervous solemnity which tried to mask as genial friendliness – the listener kept a brief silence. Then she asked, in a low voice, whether he was quite sure that he had means enough to live upon. Oh yes; he felt no uneasiness, things were shaping themselves satisfactorily.

'Of course, Mrs Mayhew, we are not saying goodbye.' He laughed, as if in mockery of the idea. 'We shall see each other from time to time – often! Such old friends – '

Her dubious look and incomplete phrase of assent – her eyes cast down – troubled him profoundly. But the dreaded interview was over. In a few days he removed his furniture. Happily the leave-taking was not in private; 'Manda and her mother both shared in it; yet poor Mrs Mayhew's eyes had a sorrowful dimness, and her attempted gaiety weighed upon his spirits.

He lived now in the south-west of London, and refrained even from visits to the British Museum. The breaking-up of his life-long habits, the idleness into which he had fallen, encouraged a morbid activity of conscience; under grey autumnal skies he walked about the roads and the parks, by the riverside, and sometimes beyond the limits of town, but there was no escape from a remorseful memory. When two or three weeks had passed, his unrest began to be complicated with fears of destitution. But, of a sudden, the half promise that had been made to him was fulfilled: the erudite society offered him a post which, in his modest computation, represented all that a man could desire of worldly prosperity. He could now establish himself beneath some reputable roof, repurchase his books, look forward to a life of congenial duty and intellectual devotion. But –

His wandering steps brought him to the Chelsea Embankment, where he leaned upon the parapet, and gazed at the sullen river.

To whom – to whom did he owe all this? Who was it that had saved him at that black time when he thought of death as his only friend? Who had toiled for him, cared for him, whilst he wrote his book? Now at length he was able to evince gratitude otherwise than in mere words, and like a dastard he slunk away. He had deserted the woman who loved him.

And why? She was not his equal; yet certainly not so far his inferior that, even in the sight of the world, he need be ashamed of her. The merest cowardice, the plainest selfishness, withheld him from returning to Mrs Mayhew and making her that offer which he was in honour bound to make.

Yes, in honour bound. Thus far had his delicate sensibilities, his philosophical magnanimity, impelled the lonely scholar. Love of woman he knew not, but a generous warmth of heart enabled him to contemplate the wooing and wedding of his benefactress without repugnance. In a sense it would be loss of liberty; but might he not find compensation in domestic comfort, in the tender care that would be lavished upon him? But the higher view – a duty discharged, a heart solaced –

The next day was Sunday. In the morning there fell heavy rain: after noon the clouds swept eastward, and rays of sunlight glistened on the wet streets. Filmer had sat totally unoccupied. He made a pretence of eating the dinner that was brought to him, and then, having attired himself as though he had not a minute to lose, left home. Travelling by omnibus, he reached the neighbourhood hitherto so carefully shunned; he walked rapidly to the familiar street, and, with heart throbbing painfully, he stood before the little chandler's shop, which of course was closed.

A knock at the door. It was answered by 'Manda, who stared and smiled, and seemed neither glad nor sorry to see him, but somehow in perturbation.

'Is Mrs Mayhew in?' whispered, rather than spoke, the philologist.

'No, sir. She went out not long ago – with Mr Marshall. And she won't be back just yet – p'raps not till supper.'

'With – with Mr Marshall?'

'Yes, sir,' 'Manda grinned. 'They're going to be married next Saturday, sir.'

Filmer straightened himself and stood like a soldier at attention.

'To be married? – Mrs Mayhew?'

The girl laughed, nodded, seemed greatly amused.

'I should like to come in, and – and speak to you for a moment.'

'Oh yes, sir,' she smirked. 'There's nobody in. Would you mind coming into the shop?'

He followed. The well-remembered odour of Mrs Mayhew's merchandise enveloped him about, and helped still further to confuse his thoughts in a medley of past and present. Over the shop window hung a dirty yellow blind, through which the sunshine struggled dimly. Filmer hesitated for a moment.

'Who is Mr Marshall, 'Manda?' he was able to ask at length.

'Don't you know, sir?' She stood before him in a perky attitude, her fingers interlaced. 'You've seen him. A tall man – dark-looking – '

'Ah! Yes, I remember. I have seen him. How long has Mrs Mayhew known him?'

'Oh, a long, long time. He lent her a lot of money when she started the shop. They'd have been married before, only Mr Marshall's wife was alive – in a 'sylum.'

'In an asylum?'

'Brought on by drink, they say. There's all sorts of tales about her.'

The philologist eased himself by moving a few paces. He looked from the pile of firewood bundles before the counter to a row of canisters on the topmost shelf.

'I'm glad to hear this,' at length fell from his lips. 'Just say I called; and that I – I'll call again some day.'

'Manda's odd expression arrested his eyes. He turned away, however, and stepped out into the passage, where little if any daylight penetrated. Behind him, 'Manda spoke.

'I don't think I'd come again, sir.'

'Why not?'

He tried to see her face, but she kept in shadow.

'Mr Marshall mightn't like it, sir. Nor Mrs Mayhew – Mrs Marshall as *will* be.'

'Not like it ?'

'You won't say anything, if I tell you?' said the girl, in a low and hurried yet laughing tone. 'It made a little trouble – because you was here. Mr Marshall thought – ' a giggle filled the lacuna. 'And Mrs Mayhew didn't like to say anything to you. She's that kind to everybody – '

Filmer stretched his hand to the door, fumbled at the latch, and at length got out. It took some hours before his shamefaced misery yielded to the blissful sense of relief and of freedom.

An Old Maid's Triumph

To this day's event Miss Hurst had looked anxiously forward for no less than thirty years. It was just thirty years since time and fate had made her dependent for a living upon her own exertions, without the least hope of aid from love or duty. Till then – that is, up to her twenty-eighth year – she had supported herself, but with frequent hospitality of kinsfolk to make the efforts lighter. Now, at eight-and-fifty, she had received from her pupils' parents, with all possible kindness of wording, the anticipated notice that after next quarter her services would be no more in request. So it had come at last, and fervently she thanked heaven for the courage which enabled her to face it with so much composure. That there was no possibility of another engagement she took for granted; perhaps it was only out of delicate consideration that these good friends had kept her so long. She did not feel very old; was not conscious of mental decay; but probably others had observed some sign of it. At such an age as this who could expect to be retained as governess to young people? Doubtless it would be an injustice to her pupils. Moreover, she was ready for the change; again, heaven be thanked!

'What will the poor old thing do?' asked Mrs Fletcher of her husband. 'Impossible, I fear, that she can have saved anything.'

'Don't see how the deuce she can have done,' Mr Fletcher replied. 'There are – institutions, I believe. I wish we could do something; but you know the state of things. Of course, a rather larger cheque – say double the quarter's salary; but I'm afraid that's all I can pretend to do.'

However, Miss Hurst *had* found it possible to save, though what the fact signified was known only to herself. Tonight she made up her account with life, and it stood thus. At eight-and-twenty she had owned a sum of nearly thirty pounds, which ever since had remained intact. For the thirty years that followed her average earnings had been twenty-nine pounds per annum, and out of this she had put aside what amounted to fifteen pounds a year – sometimes more, sometimes less. Very seldom, indeed, had she suffered from ill-health; only once had she spent six months unemployed. Accumulation of petty interest – the Bank and Government security were all she had ever dared to confide in – by this time made a sensible increment. With tremulous calculation she grasped the joyous certainty that a life of independence was assured to her. It must be by purchase of an annuity. She had never consulted anyone on her financial affairs: common sense, and a strictly reticent habit, had guided her safely thus far. For the last and all-important pecuniary transaction she felt thoroughly prepared, so long had she reflected upon it, and with such sedulous exactitude.

Beauty was never hers, nor much natural grace: nowadays she looked a very homely, but a very nice old lady, with something of austerity in her countenance which imposed respect. She spoke with a gentle firmness, smiling only when there was occasion for it. In education she knew herself much behind the teachers of today; her mental powers were not more than ordinary; but nature had given her that spirit of refinement which is not otherwise to be acquired. Generally able to win the regard of well-conditioned children, she had always been looked upon as an excellent disciplinarian, which accounted in large measure for her professional success.

Her success! Never had she received the wages of a middling cook; yet the importance of her trust through life was such as cannot be exaggerated, and the duties laid upon her had been discharged with a competence, a conscientiousness, which no money could repay. Her success! At the age of fifty-eight she tremblingly calculated her hope of being able to live out the rest of her life with *not less* than twenty shillings a week.

And the life history which explained this great achievement. Miss Hurst could not have written it; she possessed neither the faculty nor the self-esteem needful for such a work; but assuredly it deserved to be written. Reflect upon the simple assertion that, from her twenty-eighth to her fifty-eighth year this woman had never unavoidably spent one shilling-piece. She, with the instincts and desires of the educated class, had never allowed herself one single indulgence which cost more than a copper or so. Ah! the story of those holiday times which she was obliged to spend at her own cost, of the brief seasons when she was out of employment! Being a woman she, of course, found it easier to practise this excessive parsimony than any man would have done; yet she was not, like so many women, naturally penurious. She longed for the delight of travel, she often hungered for books which a very slight outlay would have procured her, she reproached herself for limiting her charity to a mite at church collections. Mean lodgings were horrible to her, yet again and again she had occupied all but the meanest. And all this out of sheer dread of some day finding herself destitute, helpless, at the mercy of a world which never spares its brutality to those who perforce require its compassion. What a life! Yet it had not embittered her; her gentle courage, sustained by old-fashioned piety, had never failed. And now she saw herself justified of her faith in providence.

Having regard to her sound constitution, she might live another twenty years. Her capital, merely put out to interest, would not afford sustenance. But the purchase of an annuity might assure at once her bodily comfort and her self-respect. Carefully had she studied the tables, the comparative advantages offered by many companies. The fact that a hundred pounds will yield a woman less than a man had often troubled her; she understood the reason, but could not quite reconcile herself to the result. As a man, she would have saved vastly more; as a woman, the longer-lived, she must be content to receive less for her smaller opportunities.

Throughout this last quarter her behaviour differed in no outward respect from that of years past; she worked with the same admirable honesty of purpose, and kept the same countenance of sober cheerfulness. In her heart she was ever so little troubled. At the end of her engagement there would be due to her a payment of seven pounds ten, and the total of her possessions would then fall *slightly* short of a sum needed to purchase the annuity on which she had fixed her hopes. She desired a clear fifty-two pounds per annum, twenty shillings a week: surely no excessive demand. Yet it seemed as if she must content herself with a smaller income. It might, however, prove possible to earn the extra sum – a mere trifle. Yes, it might be possible; she would hope.

On the last day, when her pupils were preparing to leave home for the seaside, Mrs Fletcher called her apart, and spoke with confidential sweetness.

'Miss Hurst, need I say how very sorry we all are to part with you? I do so wish that circumstances allowed of my asking you to come back again after the holidays. But – really there is no harm in my telling you that we are obliged to – to make certain changes in our establishment.'

The governess listened with grave sympathy.

'Have you heard of any other engagement?' pursued the lady, with doubtful voice and eyes drooping.

'Not yet, Mrs Fletcher,' was the cheerful reply. 'I should like to find one, if it were only for a short time.'

'I will do my utmost in the way of making enquiries. And – let me give you the cheque, Miss Hurst. My husband begs you will accept from us, as a mark of our great – our very great – esteem, something more than the sum strictly due. I am sure we shall never be out of our debt to you.'

In her own room Miss Hurst eagerly inspected the little slip of paper – it was a cheque for twice her quarter's salary. There was a great leap of her heart, a rush of tears to her eyes. She held the security of independent life. The long fight was over, and she had triumphed.

The Scrupulous Father

It was market day in the little town; at one o'clock a rustic company besieged the table of the Greyhound, lured by savoury odours and the frothing of amber ale. Apart from three frequenters of the ordinary, in a small room prepared for overflow sat two persons of a different stamp – a middle-aged man, bald, meagre, unimpressive, but wholly respectable in bearing and apparel, and a girl, evidently his daughter, who had the look of the latter twenties, her plain dress harmonising with a subdued charm of features and a timidity of manner not ungraceful. Whilst waiting for their meal they conversed in an undertone; their brief remarks and ejaculations told of a long morning's ramble from the seaside resort some miles away; in their quiet fashion they seemed to have enjoyed themselves, and dinner at an inn evidently struck them as something of an escapade. Rather awkwardly the girl arranged a handful of wild flowers which she had gathered, and put them for refreshment into a tumbler of water; when a woman entered with viands, silence fell upon the two; after hesitations and mutual glances, they began to eat with nervous appetite.

Scarcely was their modest confidence restored when in the doorway sounded a virile voice, gaily humming, and they became aware of a tall young man, red-headed, anything but handsome, flushed and perspiring from the sunny road; his open jacket showed a blue cotton shirt without waistcoat, in his hand was a shabby straw hat, and thick dust covered his boots. One would have judged him a tourist of the noisier class, and his rather loud 'Good-morning!' as he entered the room seemed a serious menace to privacy; on the other hand, the rapid buttoning of his coat, and the quiet choice of a seat as far as possible from the two guests whom his arrival disturbed, indicated a certain tact. His greeting had met with the merest murmur of reply; their eyes on their plates, father and daughter resolutely disregarded him; yet he ventured to speak again.

'They're busy here today. Not a seat to be had in the other room.'

It was apologetic in intention, and not rudely spoken. After a moment's delay the bald, respectable man made a curt response.

'This room is public, I believe.'

The intruder held his peace. But more than once he glanced at the girl, and after each furtive scrutiny his plain visage manifested some disturbance, a troubled thoughtfulness. His one look at the mute parent was from beneath contemptuous eyebrows.

Very soon another guest appeared, a massive agricultural man, who descended upon a creaking chair and growled a remark about the hot weather. With him the red-haired pedestrian struck into talk. Their topic was beer. Uncommonly good, they agreed, the local brew, and each called for a second pint. What, they asked in concert, would England be without her ale? Shame on the base traffickers who enfeebled or poisoned this noble liquor! And how cool it was – ah! The right sort of cellar! He of the red hair hinted at a third pewter.

These two were still but midway in their stout attack on meat and drink, when father and daughter, having exchanged a few whispers, rose to depart. After leaving the room, the girl remembered that she had left her flowers behind; she durst not return for them, and, knowing her father would dislike to do so, said nothing about the matter.

'A pity!' exclaimed Mr Whiston (that was his respectable name) as they strolled away. 'It looked at first as if we should have such a nice quiet dinner.'

'I enjoyed it all the same,' replied his companion, whose name was Rose.

'That abominable habit of drinking!' added Mr Whiston austerely. He himself had quaffed water, as always. 'Their ale, indeed! See the coarse, gross creatures it produces!'

He shuddered. Rose, however, seemed less consentient than usual. Her eyes were on the ground; her lips were closed with a certain firmness. When she spoke, it was on quite another subject.

They were Londoners. Mr Whiston held the position of draughtsman in the office of a geographical publisher; though his income was small, he had always practised a rigid economy, and the possession of a modest private capital put him beyond fear of reverses. Profoundly conscious of social limits, he felt it a subject for gratitude that there was nothing to be ashamed of in his calling, which he might fairly regard as a profession, and he nursed this sense of respectability as much on his daughter's behalf as on his own. Rose was an only child; her mother had been dead for years; her kinsfolk on both sides laid claim to the title of gentlefolk, but supported it on the narrowest margin of independence. The girl had grown up in an atmosphere unfavourable to mental development, but she had received a fairly good education, and nature had dowered her with intelligence. A sense of her father's conscientiousness and of his true affection forbade her to criticise openly the principles on which he had directed her life; hence a habit of solitary meditation, which half fostered, yet half opposed, the gentle diffidence of Rose's character.

Mr Whiston shrank from society, ceaselessly afraid of receiving less than his due; privately, meanwhile, he deplored the narrowness of the social opportunities granted to his daughter, and was for ever forming schemes for her advantage – schemes which never passed beyond the stage of nervous speculation. They inhabited a little house in a western suburb, a house illumined with every domestic virtue; but scarcely a dozen persons crossed the threshold within a twelvemonth. Rose's two or three friends were, like herself, mistrustful of the world. One of them had lately married after a very long engagement, and Rose still trembled from the excitement of that occasion, still debated fearfully with herself on the bride's chances of happiness. Her own marriage was an event so inconceivable that merely to glance at the thought appeared half immodest and wholly irrational.

Every winter Mr Whiston talked of new places which he and Rose would visit when the holidays came round; every summer he shrank from the thought of adventurous novelty, and ended by proposing a return to the same western seaside-town, to the familiar lodgings. The climate suited neither him nor his daughter, who both needed physical as well as moral bracing; but they only thought of this on finding themselves at home again, with another long year of monotony before them. And it was so good to feel welcome, respected; to receive the smiling reverences of tradesfolk; to talk with just a little well-bred condescension, sure that it would be appreciated. Mr Whiston savoured these things, and Rose in this respect was not wholly unlike him.

Today was the last of their vacation. The weather had been magnificent throughout; Rose's cheeks were more than touched by the sun, greatly to the advantage of her unpretending comeliness. She was a typical English maiden, rather tall, shapely rather than graceful, her head generally bent, her movements always betraying the diffidence of solitary habit. The lips were her finest feature, their perfect outline indicating sweetness without feebleness of character. Such a girl is at her best towards the stroke of thirty. Rose had begun to know herself; she needed only opportunity to act upon her knowledge.

A train would take them back to the seaside. At the railway station Rose seated herself on a shaded part of the platform, whilst her father, who was exceedingly short of sight, peered over publications on the bookstall. Rather tired after her walk, the girl was dreamily tracing a pattern with the point of her parasol, when someone advanced and stood immediately in front of her. Startled, she looked up, and recognised the red-haired stranger of the inn.

'You left these flowers in a glass of water on the table. I hope I'm not doing a rude thing in asking whether they were left by accident.'

He had the flowers in his hand, their stems carefully protected by a piece of paper. For a moment Rose was incapable of replying; she looked at the speaker; she felt her cheeks burn; in utter embarrassment she said she knew not what.

'Oh! – thank you! I forgot them. It's very kind.'

Her hand touched his as she took the bouquet from him. Without another word the man turned and strode away.

Mr Whiston had seen nothing of this. When he approached, Rose held up the flowers with a laugh.

'Wasn't it kind? I forgot them, you know, and someone from the inn came looking for me.'

'Very good of them, very,' replied her father graciously. 'A very nice inn, that. We'll go again – some day. One likes to encourage such civility; it's rare nowadays.'

He of the red hair travelled by the same train, though not in the same carriage. Rose caught sight of him at the seaside station. She was vexed with herself for having so scantily acknowledged his kindness; it seemed to her that she had not really thanked him at all; how absurd, at her age, to be incapable of common self-command! At the same time she kept thinking of her father's phrase, 'coarse, gross creatures', and it vexed her even more than her own ill behaviour. The stranger was certainly not coarse, far from gross. Even his talk about beer (she remembered every word of it) had been amusing rather than offensive. Was he a 'gentleman'? The question agitated her; it involved so technical a definition, and she felt so doubtful as to the reply. Beyond doubt he had acted in a gentlemanly way; but his voice lacked something. Coarse? Gross? No, no, no! Really, her father was very severe, not to say uncharitable. But perhaps he was thinking of the heavy agricultural man; oh, he must have been!

Of a sudden she felt very weary. At the lodgings she sat down in her bedroom, and gazed through the open window at the sea. A sense of discouragement, hitherto almost unknown, had fallen upon her; it spoilt the blue sky and the soft horizon. She thought rather drearily of the townward journey tomorrow, of her home in the suburbs, of the endless monotony that awaited her. The flowers lay on her lap; she smelt them, dreamed over them. And then – strange incongruity – she thought of beer!

Between tea and supper she and her father rested on the beach. Mr Whiston was reading. Rose pretended to turn the leaves of a book. Of a sudden, as unexpectedly to herself as to her companion, she broke silence.

'Don't you think, father, that we are too much afraid of talking with strangers?'

'Too much afraid?'

Mr Whiston was puzzled. He had forgotten all about the incident at the dinner-table.

'I mean – what harm is there in having a little conversation when one is away from home? At the inn today, you know, I can't help thinking we were rather – perhaps a little too silent.'

'My dear Rose, did you want to talk about beer?'

She reddened, but answered all the more emphatically.

'Of course not. But, when the first gentleman came in, wouldn't it have been natural to exchange a few friendly words? I'm sure he wouldn't have talked of beer to *us*.

'The *gentleman*? I saw no gentleman, my dear. I suppose he was a small clerk, or something of the sort, and he had no business whatever to address us.'

'Oh, but he only said good-morning, and apologised for sitting at our table. He needn't have apologised at all.'

'Precisely. That is just what I mean,' said Mr Whiston with self-satisfaction. 'My dear Rose, if I had been alone, I might perhaps have talked a little, but with you it was impossible. One cannot be too careful. A man like that will take all sorts of liberties. One has to keep such people at a distance.'

A moment's pause, then Rose spoke with unusual decision – 'I feel quite sure, father, that he would not have taken liberties. It seems to me that he knew quite well how to behave himself.'

Mr Whiston grew still more puzzled. He closed his book to meditate this new problem.

'One has to lay down rules,' fell from him at length, sententiously. 'Our position, Rose, as I have often explained, is a delicate one. A lady in circumstances such as yours cannot exercise too much caution. Your natural associates are in the world of wealth; unhappily, I cannot make you wealthy. We have to guard our self-respect, my dear child. Really, it is not *safe* to talk with strangers – least of all at an inn. And you have only to remember that disgusting conversation about beer!'

Rose said no more. Her father pondered a little, felt that he had delivered his soul, and resumed the book.

The next morning they were early at the station to secure good places for the long journey to London. Up to almost the last moment it seemed that they would have a carriage to themselves. Then the door suddenly opened, a bag was flung on to the seat, and after it came a hot, panting man, a red-haired man, recognised immediately by both the travellers.

'I thought I'd missed it!' ejaculated the intruder merrily.

Mr Whiston turned his head away, disgust transforming his countenance. Rose sat motionless, her eyes cast down. And the stranger mopped his forehead in silence.

He glanced at her; he glanced again and again; and Rose was aware of every look. It did not occur to her to feel offended. On the contrary, she fell into a mood of tremulous pleasure, enhanced by every turn of the stranger's eyes in her direction. At him she did not look, yet she saw him. Was it a coarse face? she asked herself. Plain, perhaps, but decidedly not vulgar. The red hair, she thought, was not disagreeably red; she didn't dislike that shade of colour. He was humming a tune; it seemed to be his habit, and it argued healthy cheerfulness. Meanwhile Mr Whiston sat stiffly in his corner, staring at the landscape, a model of respectable muteness.

At the first stop another man entered. This time, unmistakably, a commercial traveller. At once a dialogue sprang up between him and Rufus. The traveller complained that all the smoking compartments were full.

'Why,' exclaimed Rufus, with a laugh, 'that reminds me that I wanted a smoke. I never thought about it till now; jumped in here in a hurry.'

The traveller's 'line' was tobacco; they talked tobacco – Rufus with much gusto. Presently the conversation took a wider scope.

'I envy you,' cried Rufus, 'always travelling about. I'm in a beastly office, and get only a fortnight off once a year. I enjoy it, I can tell you! Time's up today, worse luck! I've a good mind to emigrate. Can you give me a tip about the colonies?'

He talked of how he had spent his holiday. Rose missed not a word, and her blood pulsed in sympathy with the joy of freedom which he expressed. She did not mind his occasional slang; the tone was manly and right-hearted; it evinced a certain simplicity of feeling by no means common in men, whether gentle or other. At a certain moment the girl was impelled to steal a glimpse of his face. After all, was it really so plain? The features seemed to her to have a certain refinement which she had not noticed before.

'I'm going to try for a smoker,' said the man of commerce, as the train slackened into a busy station.

Rufus hesitated. His eye wandered.

'I think I shall stay where I am,' he ended by saying.

In that same moment, for the first time, Rose met his glance. She saw that his eyes did not at once avert themselves; they had a singular expression, a smile which pleaded pardon for its audacity. And Rose, even whilst turning away, smiled in response.

The train stopped. The commercial traveller alighted. Rose, leaning towards her father, whispered that she was thirsty; would he get her a glass of milk or of lemonade? Though little disposed to rush on such errands, Mr Whiston had no choice but to comply; he sped at once for the refreshment-room.

And Rose knew what would happen; she knew perfectly. Sitting rigid, her eyes on vacancy, she felt the approach of the young man, who for the moment was alone with her. She saw him at her side: she heard his voice.

'I can't help it. I want to speak to you. May I?'

Rose faltered a reply.

'It was so kind to bring the flowers. I didn't thank you properly.'

'It's now or never,' pursued the young man in rapid, excited tones. 'Will you let me tell you my name? Will you tell me yours?'

Rose's silence consented. The daring Rufus rent a page from a pocket-book, scribbled his name and address, gave it to Rose. He rent out another page, offered it to Rose with the pencil, and in a moment had secured the precious scrap of paper in his pocket. Scarce was the transaction completed when a stranger jumped in. The young man bounded to his own corner, just in time to see the return of Mr Whiston, glass in hand.

During the rest of the journey Rose was in the strangest state of mind. She did not feel in the least ashamed of herself. It seemed to her that what had happened was wholly natural and simple. The extraordinary thing was that she must sit silent and with cold countenance at the distance of a few feet from a person with whom she ardently desired to converse. Sudden illumination had wholly changed the aspect of life. She seemed to be playing a part in a grotesque comedy rather than living in a world of grave realities. Her father's dignified silence struck her as intolerably absurd. She could have burst into laughter; at moments she was indignant, irritated, tremulous with the spirit of revolt. She detected a glance of frigid superiority with which Mr Whiston chanced to survey the other occupants of the compartment. It amazed her. Never had she seen her father in such an alien light. He bent forward and addressed to her some commonplace remark; she barely deigned a reply. Her views of conduct, of character, had undergone an abrupt and extraordinary change. Having justified without shadow of argument her own incredible proceeding, she judged everything and everybody by some new standard, mysteriously attained. She was no longer the Rose Whiston of yesterday. Her old self seemed an object of compassion. She felt an unspeakable happiness, and at the same time an encroaching fear.

The fear predominated; when she grew aware of the streets of London looming on either hand it became a torment, an anguish. Small-folded, crushed within her palm, the piece of paper with its still unread inscription seemed to burn her. Once, twice, thrice she met the look of her friend. He smiled cheerily, bravely, with evident purpose of encouragement. She knew his face better than that of any oldest acquaintance; she saw in it a manly beauty. Only by a great effort of self-control could she refrain from turning aside to unfold and read what he had written. The train slackened speed, stopped. Yes, it was London. She must arise and go. Once more their eyes met. Then, without recollection of any interval, she was on the Metropolitan Railway, moving towards her suburban home.

A severe headache sent her early to bed. Beneath her pillow lay a scrap of paper with a name and address she was not likely to forget. And through the night of broken slumbers Rose suffered a martyrdom. No more self-glorification! All her courage gone, all her new vitality! She saw herself with the old eyes, and was shame-stricken to the very heart.

Whose the fault? Towards dawn she argued it with the bitterness of misery. What a life was hers in this little world of choking respectabilities! Forbidden this, forbidden that; permitted – the pride of ladyhood. And she was not a lady, after all. What lady would have permitted herself to exchange names and addresses with a strange man in a railway carriage – furtively, too, escaping her father's observation? If not a lady, what *was* she? It meant the utter failure of her breeding and education. The sole end for which she had lived was frustrate. A common, vulgar young woman – well mated, doubtless, with an impudent clerk, whose noisy talk was of beer and tobacco!

This arrested her. Stung to the defence of her friend, who, clerk though he might be, was neither impudent nor vulgar, she found herself driven back upon self-respect. The battle went on for hours; it exhausted her; it undid all the good effects of sun and sea, and left her flaccid, pale.

'I'm afraid the journey yesterday was too much for you,' remarked Mr Whiston, after observing her as she sat mute the next evening.

'I shall soon recover,' Rose answered coldly.

The father meditated with some uneasiness. He had not forgotten Rose's singular expression of opinion after their dinner at the inn. His affection made him sensitive to changes in the girl's demeanour. Next summer they must really find a more bracing resort. Yes, yes; clearly Rose needed bracing. But she was always better when the cool days came round.

On the morrow it was his daughter's turn to feel anxious. Mr Whiston all at once wore a face of indignant severity. He was absent-minded; he sat at table with scarce a word; he had little nervous movements, and subdued mutterings as of wrath. This continued on a second day, and Rose began to suffer an intolerable agitation. She could not help connecting her father's strange behaviour with the secret which tormented her heart.

Had something happened? Had her friend seen Mr Whiston, or written to him?

She had awaited with tremors every arrival of the post. It was probable – more than probable – that *he* would write to her; but as yet no letter came. A week passed, and no letter came. Her father was himself again; plainly she had mistaken the cause of his perturbation. Ten days, and no letter came.

It was Saturday afternoon. Mr Whiston reached home at teatime. The first glance showed his daughter that trouble and anger once more beset him. She trembled, and all but wept, for suspense had overwrought her nerves.

'I find myself obliged to speak to you on a very disagreeable subject' – thus began Mr Whiston over the tea-cups – 'a very unpleasant subject indeed. My one consolation is that it will probably settle a little argument we had down at the seaside.'

As his habit was when expressing grave opinions (and Mr Whiston seldom expressed any other), he made a long pause and ran his fingers through his thin beard. The delay irritated Rose to the last point of endurance.

'The fact is,' he proceeded at length, 'a week ago I received a most extraordinary letter – the most impudent letter I ever read in my life. It came from that noisy, beer-drinking man who intruded upon us at the inn – you remember. He began by explaining who he was, and – if you can believe it – had the impertinence to say that he wished to make my acquaintance! An amazing letter! Naturally, I left it unanswered – the only dignified thing to do. But the fellow wrote again, asking if I had received his proposal. I now replied, briefly and severely, asking him how he came to know my name; secondly, what reason I had given him for supposing that I desired to meet him again. His answer to this was even more outrageous than the first offence. He bluntly informed me that in order to discover my name and address he had followed us home that day from Paddington Station! As if this was not bad enough, he went on to – really, Rose, I feel I must apologise to you, but the fact is I seem to have no choice but to tell you what he said. The fellow tells me, really, that he wants to know *me* only that he may come to know *you*! My first idea was to go with this letter to the police. I am not sure that I shan't do so even yet; most certainly I shall if he writes again. The man may be crazy – he may be dangerous. Who knows but he may come lurking about the house? I felt obliged to warn you of this unpleasant possibility.'

Rose was stirring her tea; also she was smiling. She continued to stir and to smile, without consciousness of either performance.

'You make light of it?' exclaimed her father solemnly.

'Oh father, of course I am sorry you have had this annoyance.'

So little was there of manifest sorrow in the girl's tone and countenance that Mr Whiston gazed at her rather indignantly. His pregnant pause gave birth to one of those admonitory axioms which had hitherto ruled his daughter's life.

'My dear, I advise you never to trifle with questions of propriety. Could there possibly be a better illustration of what I have so often said – that in self-defence we are bound to keep strangers at a distance?'

'Father –'

Rose began firmly, but her voice failed.

'You were going to say, Rose?' She took her courage in both hands.

'Will you allow me to see the letters?'

'Certainly. There can be no objection to that.' He drew from his pocket the envelopes and held them out to his daughter.

With shaking hand Rose unfolded the first letter; it was written in clear commercial character, and was signed 'Charles James Burroughs'. When she had read all, the girl said quietly, 'Are you quite sure, father, that these letters are impertinent?'

Mr Whiston stopped in the act of finger-combing his beard. 'What doubt can there be of it?'

'They seem to me,' proceeded Rose nervously, 'to be very respectful and very honest.'

'My dear, you astound me! Is it respectful to force one's acquaintance upon an unwilling stranger? I really don't understand you. Where is your sense of propriety, Rose? A vulgar, noisy fellow, who talks of beer and tobacco – a petty clerk! And he has the audacity to write to me that he wants to – to make friends with my daughter! Respectful? Honest? Really!'

When Mr Whiston became sufficiently agitated to lose his decorous gravity, he began to splutter, and at such moments he was not impressive. Rose kept her eyes cast down. She felt her strength once more, the strength of a wholly reasonable and half-passionate revolt against that tyrannous propriety which Mr Whiston worshipped.

'Father – '

'Well, my dear?'

'There is only one thing I dislike in these letters – and that is a falsehood.'

'I don't understand.'

Rose was flushing. Her nerves grew tense; she had wrought herself to a simple audacity which overcame small embarrassments.

'Mr Burroughs says that he followed us home from Paddington to discover our address. That is not true. He asked me for my name and address in the train, and gave me his.'

The father gasped.

'He *asked* – ? You *gave* – ?'

'It was whilst you were away in the refreshment-room,' proceeded the girl, with singular self-control, in a voice almost matter-of-fact. 'I ought to tell you, at the same time, that it was Mr Burroughs who brought me the flowers from the inn, when I forgot them. You didn't see him give them to me in the station.'

The father stared.

'But, Rose, what does all this mean? You – you overwhelm me! Go on, please. What next?'

'Nothing, father.'

And of a sudden the girl was so beset with confusing emotions that she hurriedly quitted her chair and vanished from the room.

Before Mr Whiston returned to his geographical drawing on Monday morning, he had held long conversations with Rose, and still longer with himself. Not easily could he perceive the justice of his daughter's quarrel with propriety; many days were to pass, indeed, before he would consent to do more than make enquiries about Charles James Burroughs, and to permit that aggressive young man to give a fuller account of himself in writing. It was by silence that Rose prevailed. Having defended herself against the charge of immodesty, she declined to urge her own inclination or the rights of Mr Burroughs; her mute patience did not lack its effect with the scrupulous but tender parent.

'I am willing to admit, my dear,' said Mr Whiston one evening, *à propos* of nothing at all, 'that the falsehood in that young man's letter gave proof of a certain delicacy.'

'Thank you, father,' replied Rose, very quietly and simply.

It was next morning that the father posted a formal, proper, self-respecting note of invitation, which bore results.

A Victim of Circumstances

In the summer of 1869, an artist, whose wanderings had led him far into rural England, rambled one sunny morning about the town of Glastonbury. Like all but a very few Englishmen, he cared little for the ancient history of his land: Avalon was a myth that did not speak to his imagination, and the name of Dunstan echoed but faintly for him out of old school books. His delight was in the rare quaint beauty of the noiseless streets, in the ruined abbey with its overgrowth, its great elms, its smooth sward where sheep were nibbling, and in the exquisite bits of homely landscape discoverable at every turn. He would have liked to remain here for several days, but in the evening he must needs journey on.

After a midday meal at the inn which was built for the use of pilgrims four hundred years ago, he turned his steps towards a spot it still behoved him to visit, though its associations awoke in him but a languid curiosity. This was Wirrall Hill, a little grassy ascent just outside the town – famous for ages throughout Christendom as the place of the Holy Thorn, the budding staff set by Joseph of Arimathea when he landed from his voyage. A thorn is still preserved on the summit: having considered it with a smile, the artist threw himself upon the grass, and gazed at what interested him much more, the scene spread before his eyes.

Opposite lay Glastonbury, its red-roofed houses (above them the fine old towers of St John and St Benedict) clustered about the foot of that high conical hill called the Tor, which with its ruined church beacons over so many miles of plain. Northward the view was bounded by the green Mendips, lovely in changing lights and shadows.

In the west, far upon a flat horizon, glimmered the Severn Sea. White lines of road marked the landscape in every direction; the willow-bordered rhines – great trenches to save the fields from flood – wound among crops or cattled pasturage; and patches of rich brown showed where peat was stacked. A scene perfect in its kind, so ancient, peaceful, dream-inspiring.

He was awakened from reverie by the sound of voices. At a short distance stood two children, a little boy and a still smaller girl, doubtless brother and sister: they had just caught sight of the stranger, and were looking at him with frank, wide eyes, their talk suspended by his presence. Our friend (he was a bachelor of fifty) did not care much for very young people, but this small couple were more than usually interesting; he thought he had never seen such pretty children. They were dressed very simply, but with a taste which proved that they did not belong to working folk; their faces, too, had nothing in common with those of little rustics, but were delicately featured, remarkably intelligent, toned in softest cream colour. The boy (perhaps seven years old) wore a tunic and knickerbockers, and carried a wand higher than himself; the girl, a year younger, who had golden curly locks, and a red sash about her waist, held in her arms the tiniest of terrier pups.

'How do you do?' cried the artist, in the friendliest voice he could command, nodding to them. 'Here's a comfortable place; come and sit down.'

They hesitated, but only for a moment. Then the boy advanced, and the girl followed more timidly. After a few rather awkward attempts the artist drew them into conversation. Their wits corresponded to their faces; when he spoke of the hill on which they were sitting, he found that the boy knew all about its history.

'Joseph of Arimathea,' said the youngster, with perfect pronunciation of the long word, 'had eleven companions. Father is painting them.'

'Painting them? What! your father is a painter?'

'Yes,' the boy answered proudly. 'Like Michelangelo and Raphael.'

'Now that's a curious thing. I am a painter too!'

They examined him keenly, the little girl allowing her puppy to escape, so that in a few moments she had to run away after it.

'Are you an historical painter?' enquired the boy with much earnestness.

'No. Landscape only.'

'Oh!'

The tone was of disappointment.

'What is your father's name? Perhaps I have heard of him.'

'Horace Miles Castledine,' was the reply, again uttered proudly.

The artist averted his face and kept silence for a moment.

'Mine is Godfrey Banks,' he said at length; 'not such a nice name as your father's.'

'No, not so nice. But it isn't a bad name. I like Godfrey. And are you famous?'

'Some people like my pictures.'

'But are you really famous – like my father is going to be?'

'I am afraid not.'

'But you are very old, you know,' said the lad. 'Father is only thirty – quite young for an artist. When he gets as old as you, he'll be famous all through the world – like Michelangelo.'

'I'm very glad to hear that. Where does your father live?'

'Just down there – not far. Shall I take you to see him and tell him you're a painter?'

'That would be very kind, yes, I would like to go.'

The artist had made up his mind that he must not leave Glastonbury without visiting this most notable of its inhabitants, a man who, in the year 1869, was engaged on an historical painting – subject, 'The Landing of Joseph of Arimathea in Britain' – and who plainly had the habit of declaring before his offspring that in a few years his fame would circle the earth.

Addressing his companion as 'Murie' – which probably meant Muriel – the youngster announced that they would return home forthwith, and with many signs of delight he led the way. Banks held his hand to the little girl, who accepted it very sweetly; with her other arm she enfolded the puppy. And thus they moved forward.

In less than a quarter of an hour the guide pointed to his father's dwelling. It was one of a row of simple cottages, old and prettily built; in the small garden were hollyhocks, sunflowers, tall lilies, and other familiar flowers blooming luxuriantly, and over the front of the house trailed a vine. A delightful abode in certain moods, no doubt; but where could be the studio?

The artist took from his pocket a visiting card.

'I will stay here,' he said, 'until you have given that to your father and asked if I may be allowed to see him.'

Two or three minutes elapsed; and when the boy reappeared, it was in the company of a singular looking man. This person (one would have judged him less than thirty) had a short, slim figure, and a large head with long, beautiful hair, almost as golden as that of his younger child. He wore a dressing-gown, which had once been magnificent, of blue satin richly worked; time had faded its glories, and it showed a patch here and there. On his feet were slippers, erst of corresponding splendour; but they, too, had felt the touch of the destroyer, and seemed ready to fall to pieces. His neck was bare. The features of the man lacked distinction; one felt that they were grievously out of keeping with such original attire, that they suggested the most respectable of everyday garments. A small perky nose, lips and chin of irreproachable form and the kindliest expression, blue eyes which widened themselves in a perpetual endeavour to look inspired – that was all one cared to notice, save, perhaps, the rare delicacy of his complexion.

He came quickly forward, smiling with vast gratification.

'Mr Banks, you do me a great honour! Pray come in! My wife is unfortunately from home; she would have been overjoyed!'

His voice was quite frank and pleasant; the listener had prepared himself for some intolerable form of euphemism, and felt an agreeable surprise.

They entered, and went first of all into a tiny sitting-room, gracefully furnished. Castledine could not conceal his excitement; for here was one of is the first artists of the day, a man really to be reverenced, coming – if only by chance – to inspect his work and utter words of encouragement! He kept up a dancing movement round three sides of the table whilst his visitor spoke ordinary civilities.

'My studio,' he explained at length, 'is upstairs. I have very little convenience, but for the present it must do. The picture I am engaged upon I should like to have undertaken on a larger scale; but that couldn't be managed.'

'My little friend here,' replied the artist, 'has told me what the subject is.'

'Yes – yes!' said Castledine, breathlessly. 'But of course he couldn't explain the principles on which I work. I must tell you, first of all, Mr Banks, that I have had no academic instruction. I trust you don't think that is fatal?'

'Fatal? Surely not.'

'I was married – I am happy to say – very early; at two and twenty, in fact.' He blushed a little. 'At that time I lived in Lincolnshire; I was in business. But from boyhood I had studied drawing – quite seriously, I assure you; so much so, that I passed the South Kensington examinations.' He pointed to a framed certificate on the wall. 'I even went in for anatomy – seriously you know. In anatomy I feel pretty sound. At my marriage I was able to get a little more leisure; we went to Paris and to the Netherlands, and it was then I determined to become a painter. I didn't feel altogether justified – as a married man – in abandoning business, but I managed to give a good half of each day to serious work – really serious. Then we decided to go to London for a year or two, and I studied independently at the National Gallery. The figure was to be my forte; I had understood that from the first; I worked very seriously from the life – made quite a vast number of the most thorough studies. I haven't wholly neglected landscape, but I should be ashamed to speak to you of what I have done in that direction. All the time, I still gave attention to – to my business; but at last it was clear to me that I must take a bold step – the step inevitable to every serious artist – and give myself entirely to painting. So, two years ago, we came to live here, and I began my studies for what I hope may be a – a work one needn't feel ashamed of.'

'You chose the place because of its quietness?'

'I must explain to you.' He still moved dancingly about the table, forgetting even to ask his visitor to be seated. 'From boyhood I have felt very strongly that artists have never paid sufficient attention to the early history of England. It seemed to me that this was a great field for any man with true enthusiasm. My wife – who sympathises with me in most things – encourages this idea. She has a great delight in the history of the English Church, and on one of our holidays we came down here to see Wells and Glastonbury. Then it was that I conceived the thought I am now trying to work out on canvas. I felt that I couldn't do better than work on the very spot – in this atmosphere of antiquity.'

'I understand.'

'But I must explain. It will occur to you – what about costumes and that kind of thing? Here my principle comes in. It seems to me that our modern painters attach far too much importance to these accessories. Now we know that the great men cared very little about them – that is to say, about antiquarian details. They painted boldly, intent upon the subject – the human interest – the human figure. I am trying to follow them. Of course I avoid grotesque improprieties, but otherwise I allow my imagination free play. No one really knows how Joseph of Arimathea and his companions were dressed; I have devised costumes which seem to me appropriate.'

He spoke hurriedly, watching the listener's face as if he dreaded a sign of disapproval. But Godfrey Banks was all courteous attention.

'Of course, I use models. There is one man who sits for me often – a very fine fellow. And I – but perhaps you will come upstairs.'

'Gladly.'

Castledine intimated to his children that they were to remain below; then he led the way to the upper storey, and into a back room – lighted from the north indeed, but with obstruction of trees, and through a small window. Fastened upon the wall opposite this window was a canvas of about eight feet by five, covered with figures in various stages of advancement, some little more than outlined. Impossible for the painter to get more than two good paces away from his picture. A deal table and two chairs were the only furniture, but every free bit of wall was covered with small canvases and drawings on paper.

'Not much convenience, as I said,' remarked Castledine, with nervous glances, his whole frame breathing tremulous eagerness. 'But men have done serious things, you know, under difficulties. I hope before long to get a skylight; that would be a vast improvement.'

'Yes,' murmured the other, absently.

He was regarding the great picture. One glance had sufficed to confirm his worst fears; the thing had neither execution nor promise. It was simply an example of pretentious amateurism: no drawing, no composition, no colour, not even a hint of the imaginative faculty. In grouping the figures about Joseph (who watched the instantaneous budding of his pilgrim's staff) Castledine seemed to have been influenced by a recollection of Raphael's 'Feed my Sheep' cartoon; the drapery, at all events, was Raphaelesque. What remark could be made that would spare the painter's feelings, and yet not be stultifying to the critic?

'It ought really to be seen from farther off,' panted Castledine, whose heart was already sinking as he read the countenance of his judge.

'Yes. And wouldn't it perhaps have been wiser to take a smaller canvas – under the circumstances? You have set yourself a task of extreme difficulty.'

'The difficulty inspires me,' said the other, but this time with feigned animation. He had fully expected an admiring utterance of some kind as soon as ever his companion's eyes fell on the picture; but the silence was not caused by awe, and could mean nothing but dissatisfaction.

As Banks's look strayed in embarrassment, it chanced to light upon the little table by the window. There lay a watercolour drawing, still fixed on the board but seemingly finished, the colour box open beside it. He moved a step nearer, for the drawing struck him as of interest. It was a bit of local landscape, a rendering of just such a delightful motif as had held his attention again and again, through the day. For quite two minutes he examined it gravely, Castledine, with an air of mortified abstraction, glancing from him to the canvas.

'And yet,' exclaimed the artist suddenly, turning round, 'you spoke slightingly of your endeavours in landscape!'

Castledine seemed not to understand the remark; his delicate cheek grew warm; his eyes fell for a moment, then turned absently to the drawing.

'You think – ' he began, stammeringly.

'Can you show me anything else of this kind?' Banks enquired, with a smile.

It was no novelty in his experience that a man of marked aptitude for one line of work should hold with obstinate blindness to another, in which he could do nothing effectual; but here seemed to be a very curious instance of such perversity. Again he scrutinised the watercolour. And whilst he did so Castledine took from a portfolio that was leaning against the wall some half-dozen similar drawings. In silence he handed these to the artist, who regarded them one after another with unmistakable pleasure.

'You think they're worth something, Mr Banks?'

'They seem to me really very good,' replied the critic, as one who weighs his words.

It was on his lips to add: 'Did you really do these?' but Castledine's silence seemed to make the question as needless as it would have been uncivil.

'If I may venture to offer counsel,' he continued, 'I should say, go in for this kind of thing with all your energy.'

'You – you don't care for my picture – I'm afraid – '

'I feel that it would be very unjust to speak unfavourably of it. In so small a studio it's simply impossible to face the demands of such a work – hard enough under any conditions. But these watercolours – my dear sir, how can you have been so doubtful of their merit? Have you never shown them to any one?'

'Never.'

'Will you give me one of them in exchange for a thing of my own, which I would send you?'

'With great pleasure; choose which you like.'

'It shall be this, then.'

Castledine was so plainly chagrined by the slighting of his great work that the artist sought to console him with more effusive praise of the drawings than he would otherwise have felt justified in offering. Imperfections were obvious enough to his practised eye. The things would not stand beside a David Cox or a Copley Fielding, but there was a promise of uncommon excellence. No ordinary amateur could by any degree of perseverance have obtained the happy effects which characterised this pencil. After all, Castledine's artistic fervour meant something. He had gone shockingly astray, but it was not too late to hope that he would cultivate his true faculty with fine results.

They conversed for half an hour, then Banks made known the necessity he was under of quitting Glastonbury early that evening, and with much friendliness prepared to take his leave. Downstairs he was met by the children; he tapped the girl's glossy head with the rolled drawing and said to her father: 'It was a happy chance that brought these little people to me up on the hill. No one had ever more appropriate guides to an artist's house.'

Castledine beamed with sincere pleasure.

'They are healthy,' he said, catching up the child in his arms, 'that's a great thing.'

So the visitor went his way, musing and wondering.

2

'What's that in his hand?' asked the boy, as he stood watching at the door. 'Have you given him something, father?'

'Yes. A little drawing he wished to take. Come, we must get tea.'

There was no servant in the cottage. A neighbour's daughter came to do occasional rough work, but all else was seen to by Mrs Castledine. That lady had gone this morning to Wells, on no very agreeable errand; the circumstances of the family were straitened, and a pressing need for ready money obliged her to sell a gold watch which was lying by. Her husband seemed the natural person to do business of this kind, but his time was too valuable. Mrs Castledine had insisted on going herself, and she would not be back for another hour or two.

With his children Castledine was usually a model father, full of joke and song and grotesque playfulness: tender as a woman, yet not foolishly indulgent. But the visit of the distinguished artist had a grievous effect upon him; whilst boiling the kettle and laying the tea things he grew silent and gloomy. His nerves were disordered; he broke a cup, and fretted over the accident. Presently the little ones could not get from him a word or a smile. He drank some tea, bade the boy guard his sister, and went upstairs.

To reappear again in a few minutes. He could not remain in one place. The sight of his picture caused him acute misery, gradually changing to resentment, and when he came in sight of the watercolour by the window, he turned sharply away.

A well-dressed lad of sixteen knocked at the front-door.

'You weren't able to come for my drawing-lesson, Mr Castledine?' he said, when the long-haired man presented himself.

'Upon my word! I entirely forgot it!' was the despondent reply. 'Someone just called at the time.'

The excuse was invalid, for Castledine ought to have gone for the lesson half an hour before Banks's arrival. But he had in truth forgotten all about his engagement. With a promise to come on the morrow, he dismissed his pupil, and strayed about the house more dismally than ever.

At length Mrs Castledine returned.

She was not handsome, but had a face of far nobler stamp than her husband's – a warm, animated face, with kind eyes and the lips of mother-hood, infinitely patient. In entering she looked both tired and excited. The first thought was for her children; she caught them both in her arms, kneeling down to them, and bathed her face in their curls. Then –

'Where's father? Upstairs?'

'Yes,' replied the boy; 'and he won't play with us because he's got a headache, and a landscape painter has been to see him – not a very famous painter – Godfrey Banks.'

'What are you talking about, darling? Godfrey Banks has been here? Sit down quietly, and I'll go and see father.'

She hurried up the crazy little staircase, and threw open the door of the studio.

'Horace! have you a headache, dear? What's this that the children tell me? Has Godfrey Banks really been to see you?'

'Yes.'

'But what's the matter? Did he – ?'

She checked herself, glancing uneasily at the great picture.

'Well, you see, I don't think he knows much about historical painting. I suspect he was put out by the originality of the thing, if the truth were told.'

'Perhaps so,' murmured his wife, in a tone which betrayed anxiety, but no sceptical disposition regarding the work discussed. She asked for particulars of the visit; and when this was talked over, Castledine enquired what success she had had at Wells. At once her face changed to a sly good-humour; she opened her little handbag, searched in it mysteriously for a moment, then laid upon the table a sovereign.

'You don't mean to say that's all?' cried her husband.

Smiling, she brought forth a second sovereign, a third, a fourth – and so on till she had displayed the sum of ten guineas. Finally, there appeared the gold watch, which she held triumphantly aloft. Castledine was amazed, and demanded what it all meant.

'Listen, and you shall hear. You remember our reading in the paper the other day about Mr Merriman of Wells, and his fine collection of pictures?'

Castledine nodded, gazing at her in painful suspense.

'Thinking and thinking,' she continued, 'of all sorts of ways of getting money, I made up my mind to try something which was perhaps hopeless, yet it seemed to me worth trying. I resolved to go to this Mr Merriman and show him two of my watercolours.'

She broke off, alarmed by her husband's look.

'You think I did wrong, Horace?'

'No, no. Go on! What happened?'

'I went to his house, and he was very kind indeed – a most courtly gentleman. And I showed him the sketches – saying they were by a friend of mine. I didn't dare to say I had done them myself, lest he should think them worthless before he had really looked at them.'

Her modesty was exquisite; she spoke with perfect good faith and simplicity.

'And what do you think? He liked them so much that he offered to give me five guineas for each, at once. And he said he would take more, if my friend had any to dispose of!'

'Then you told him they were yours?' asked Castledine in an uncertain voice.

'No, not even then. I had a pleasure, then, in keeping the secret. He was discretion itself; didn't ask a single troublesome question, not even my name. And I have been thinking all the way home how good it would be for you to know him! Don't you think so? If we told him the truth about the water-colours, and then got him to look at your picture, mightn't it be of great advantage to you?'

Castledine smiled in a sickly way, murmuring assent.

The children's voices calling impatiently put an end to the talk. Castledine said that he would have a walk before dark, to see if he could get rid of his headache; and having made himself rather more like a man of this world, he went forth.

He was in sore perplexity and travail of spirit. What in the name of common sense had possessed him to tell that silent lie to Godfrey Banks? For the present, perchance, no harm would come of it; but sooner or later what he had done must almost certainly be discovered by his wife, if not by other people.

For, in their serious need, how was it possible to neglect a promising source of income? Here were two men, both excellent judges, who declared the watercolours of value. Yet he had never suspected it. The fact was, his wife's work had been growing better and better by gradual stages, the result of her great patience; this progress he ignored, taking it for granted that she was still at the same point in art as at the time of their marriage, when she drew and coloured not much better than the schoolgirl with a pretty taste in that kind of thing. She spoke too humbly of her attempts, and assented so cheerfully to all his views of what was worth doing in art. But for a strong vein of artistic faculty in her composition, she must long ago have been discouraged and have given up even amusing herself with sketching from nature. Castledine was quite incompetent to direct her, or to estimate what she did. Convinced that his own genius would display itself in grand subjects on big canvases, he had got into the habit of slighting all work of modest aim and dimensions. Now and then, asked to look at some drawing which his wife had finished, he said: 'Pretty – very pretty'; and she, who was the real artist, bowed her head to the dictum of the pretender, in whose future, by force of love, she firmly believed.

Evil promptings came into his mind. He felt a preposterous jealousy. Yes, that was why he had allowed Banks to think him the artist of the water-colours; he could not bear to become altogether insignificant, subordinate even to his wife. Had the great picture received a modicum of praise, he could have told the truth about the little drawings. But self-esteem held his tongue, and minute after minute went by – and the lie was irrevocable, or seemed so.

He wandered some distance into the country, and did not return home till an hour after sunset.

His wife was waiting anxiously. Long ago the children lay in bed. She was alone, and troubled because of the strange way in which her joyful news had been received. Being a woman of clear enough judgement in most things, she divined the astonishing truth that her husband was a little envious of the success that had come to her, whilst he laboured year after year without a gleam of encouragement. How was such feeling compatible with the love she always recognised in him? But men were singular beings, especially those blest or cursed with genius.

Castledine entered silently, fatigued and miserable. Wisely, his wife did not constrain him to talk. She set his accustomed supper of warm bread and milk before him, and waited patiently. When he had eaten, he allowed his hand to be taken and caressed; and of a sudden remorseful tenderness subdued him.

'Hilda, I have behaved like a blackguard – '

'Nonsense, dear!'

'Oh, but wait! I'm going to tell you something disgraceful. I can't look you in the face, but I must tell you.'

He began to unburden his conscience. With red cheeks, burning ears, and eyes like those of a dog conscious of wrong-doing, he half explained how he had been led into deceit. Yet did not tell the whole truth; could not, though aware that what he concealed was the better part of his excuse. He found it impossible to avow that Banks had not a word of commendation for the big picture. Partly to relieve his confusion, and in part because she was really anxious, before discussing the other matter, to know the judgement of such a man as Banks on the work with which all their hopes were connected, Hilda asked: 'But what did he say that so discouraged you?'

'Oh, he didn't discourage me,' replied her husband, with nervous impatience. 'He talked about the difficulties I must be finding – in such a little studio, you know. I could see that he didn't quite trust himself to speak decidedly about figure painting. He has never done anything but landscape, and so it was natural. He didn't discourage me in the least!'

'Did he like the attitude of Joseph?'

'Yes, he liked that. I saw he was impressed by that,' stammered Castledine; 'and the grouping in general, and the scheme of colour. Don't think for a moment, Hilda, that he discouraged me. But what a blackguard you must think me to go and – '

She kept silence.

'I shall write to Banks,' he continued, 'and make a clean breast of it. I can't help what he thinks. He shall know that I deceived him.'

'But, Horace, you say you didn't actually tell him that the drawings were your work – ?'

'No. I only allowed him to suppose it.'

'Then why need you do anything at all?'

He glanced at her, and Hilda's eyes fell, a slight colour mantling in her cheeks.

In the first moment she had felt ashamed of what he had done, and very uneasy about the position in which it placed them. The shame still troubled her, but she deemed it so impossible for Horace to go through the humiliation of confessing a lie – the consequence of which might even be of lasting detriment to him – that in a flash her mind had contrived how to cloak the deception by continuing it. What woman has the courage to bid her husband face a mortifying ordeal in the cause of truth, especially when the result of such ordeal will be to glorify herself at his expense? Of a sudden her countenance changed; she laughed, and began to speak as if the matter were trifling.

'Now, what a good thing that I didn't tell Mr Merriman! Let the drawings go without a name. No, no; better still! They shall be signed "H. Castledine"; that's my name, and yours as well!'

Hope began to brighten the listener's face, but for very decency he made a show of resistance.

'I can't allow it, Hilda! I've suffered too much already for cheating you of your praise. And think, we shall be only too glad to sell as many drawings as you can make. How is it possible to keep up such a deception for ever?'

'For ever?' she laughed with mirthful mockery. 'As if we should be long in difficulties! Why, you will have finished your picture in a few months, and then we shall have no more trouble. You don't imagine that these little sketches are really important enough to be talked about? Let us sell as many as we can; they won't please for very long, and in a year or two no one will remember them.'

'But it's a monstrous shame – '

'Nonsense! Now go on steadily with your work, and let me draw away whilst the summer lasts. We'll send some of the sketches to London, and see if dealers will buy them. And, you know, Mr Merriman has promised to take more of them. As if it mattered, Horace! Husband and wife are one, I hope!'

And so, in spite of her conscience, Hilda settled the question. On the morrow, Castledine forced himself to resume painting with a semblance of confident zeal. The ten guineas would go a long way, and with their help he was soon able to believe that Godfrey Banks knew less than nothing about the higher walks of art.

He prided himself upon the slowness with which he worked. 'All great works of art,' he was wont to say, 'take a long time.' It often happened that he sat through a whole morning merely gazing at his canvas; Leonardo, he reminded Hilda, had the same habit. This mental labour exhausted him, and, for a day or two after, he found it necessary to read novels, or wander with his children about the fields. Of late he had been earning a little money as a teacher of drawing; but this employment was degrading; it always made him incapable of handling a brush for the next twenty-four hours.

About a week after the visit of the landscape painter, there arrived the drawing promised in exchange for that he took away. Of course it was a delightful bit of work. Castledine remarked, 'Pretty – very pretty,' and paid no more attention; but Hilda kept it before her for days, studying and profiting by its masterly characteristics.

The watercolours sent up to London were readily sold. With this resource before her, Hilda was relieved from any necessity of applying again to Mr Merriman. Conducting business by correspondence, Horace could sign himself simply 'H. Castledine', and needed not to state that he was the artist. But one day towards the end of October a carriage stopped before the house, and Hilda, at the window, was alarmed by seeing the connoisseur from Wells alight and approach. She rushed upstairs to her husband, spoke a few words of agitated surprise, and ran down again to answer the knock at the door.

Mr Merriman was past middle age, lean, tall, grave of aspect. On seeing Hilda, he for an instant looked puzzled; it was plain that he remembered her. But without reference to their former meeting, he explained, in very pleasant tones, that he wished to see Mr Castledine, of whom he had recently heard in a conversation with Mr Godfrey Banks the painter. Leaving him in the parlour, Hilda again hurried upstairs.

'You must come!' she whispered, trying her best to look as if she enjoyed the joke. 'Mr Banks has sent him here. He knew me again. You must say that I took the watercolours to sell without your knowledge.'

'But how can I – ?'

'Of course you can, for it's the truth. Say you had thought very little of them – were absorbed in your great picture, and that we were dreadfully short of money just then. Do, do be careful!'

Mr Merriman stayed for more than an hour. Less conscious than Banks, he did not allow himself to be struck dumb by the sight of 'Joseph of Arimathea', but found something to say which, though it meant little enough, was balm to Castledine's feelings. Naturally, however, he kept conversation as much as possible to the subject of watercolours. Horace had little difficulty in following his wife's instructions; when he told the story of Hilda's visit to Wells, the connoisseur showed himself relieved from an embarrassment.

'I had made up my mind,' he said, 'that the lady was herself the artist, though it was difficult to account for her not being willing to admit it. When Banks happened to bring out the drawing you gave him, I recognised the workmanship at once, but something of the mystery still remained. I'm not sure,' he added, laughing, 'that I didn't begin to think of larceny.'

Horace joined in the laugh with great heartiness, and thereupon Mrs Castledine was summoned up to the studio. Mr Merriman repeated his laudation of the watercolours, and appeared so taken up with them that only at the moment of leaving was he obliged to invent a few more phrases for Joseph and the Holy Thorn. To these words Hilda listened eagerly, and they sufficed to inspirit her. When the visitor was gone, she talked exultantly about the painting, and, with her husband's help, avoided a syllable of reference to the imposture which had again been successfully practised.

3

In one sense Hilda Castledine did not underestimate her work; for the last year she had been conscious of great improvements, and at times it disappointed her that Horace seemed not to recognise this advance. She had explained his indifference by humbly admitting to herself that after all she remained an amateur – the kind of person especially distasteful to artists of strong individuality. But this excuse was no longer valid; her work had a market value, and that owing to no sensational qualities, to no passing fancy of the public, but in virtue of simple merits which make their claim felt wherever men are capable of recognising true art. When it was necessary to speak of the matter with her husband, she still used a slighting tone; but her eyes were opened, and she saw, among other things, that Horace had either been insincere with her or was lacking in judgement. This consciousness became a fixed trouble, and blended with the self-reproach due to the falsehood she had undertaken to support.

That perfect harmony which had reigned in the little household was gravely disturbed. Castledine could no longer work; when he shut himself into the studio it was only because he grew ashamed of open idling. He knew that Mr Merriman's encouragement meant nothing; Banks's silent criticism sank deeper into his mind. A process of disillusion was hastened by the moral imbroglio into which he had slipped. In spite of conceit, he was anything but a man of lax principles; prior to that hapless day of Banks's visit he had never been guilty of grave untruth. But, as generally happens, harassment of material cares had weakened his character and prepared him for yielding to temptation. Already he had begun to regard his picture with secret uneasiness, to weary of the great task; left to himself he would probably have abandoned Joseph of Arimathea and, in face of financial trials, either have seriously taken up the profession of drawing-master, or have returned to his old business. Now he could neither renounce his labour nor pursue it. A sense of shame constantly haunted him – shame at being supported by his wife, shame at taking the credit due to her, shame at his own futility. Even the hours spent with his children were spoilt; he no longer had that pure joy in their affection which used to be the best element of his life.

It was significant that Hilda had ceased to sit with him in the studio. When working at home, she retired to her bedroom – not venturing to use the parlour lest her occupation should be observed. Even from the children she began to conceal, as far as possible, her artistic pursuits; they might speak to strangers, and, worse still, they might in future years conceive suspicions affecting their father's honesty. Every day she said to herself that the life of falsehood to which she was committed must not last long.

That she was living thus resulted from her own lack of firmness; it was she who had withheld Horace from an avowal of his fault. She admitted it, lamented it, and understood the disastrous results for which she was responsible. At the same time she blamed Horace – even though her heart loathed and utterly rejected the idea of doing so.

Her faith in him had suffered a blow from which it would not recover. This, too, she did her best to deny; but no effort enabled her to talk with him of his work as formerly. She saw that on his side there existed a corresponding unwillingness; this relieved her from a painful endeavour, but otherwise only intensified the moral disease she had contracted.

One natural result of her artistic success was the development of an ambition which hitherto had taken only the lowliest forms. Formerly she cared for no approval but her husband's, and when even this was denied she could recompense herself with happiness of home. Now it cost her a continual struggle to repress the impulses which signified that she was something more than wife and mother. Her gifts had ripened; a long, patient apprenticeship was over, and but for unfriendly circumstances she would have hastened to enlarge her experience amid nobler scenes. The simple lowland landscape no longer satisfied her. Of this, however, she must not speak, must not even think. Had she not doomed her art to eventual sterility? Impossible to continue for a lifetime secretly producing work which admirers and purchasers would attribute to Horace. Even if her nature were equal to the strain, it was obvious that discovery and disgrace must sooner or later befall the perpetrators of so singular a fraud.

In seeking to defend Horace from the results for puerile falsehood, she had sacrificed a future rich in the happiest possibilities for herself, her husband and her children.

Mr Merriman invited them to spend a day with him at Wells, that they might see his pictures. The children would accompany them. All arrangements were made, and a fine morning summoned them to set forth early; but at the last moment Hilda declared that she did not feel well enough to go.

For several days she had been troubled with a cold caught in damp fields; it seemed better, but a sleepless night had dispirited her, and she could not endure the thought of practising deceit in return for their friend's kindness.

'My head is too bad,' she professed, when Horace went to speak with her in private.

'That's a pretence,' was his impatient answer. 'Why couldn't you say before that you had rather not go?'

'You will be far more at ease without me, Horace.'

He turned away, with difficulty refraining from an outburst of anger. It was very rarely indeed that they spoke to each other in any voice but that of affection; at present, both felt irritable, and desired to be apart. Horace moved towards the door, but perverse feeling got the upper hand with him.

'If this is how you are going to behave,' he exclaimed suddenly, 'why did you prevent me from having done with lies when I wished to?'

They could not face each other. Hilda trembled from head to foot, and her tongue retorted in spite of her will: 'Why did you make it necessary for me to save you from shame?'

He hastened out of the room and out of the house. Hearing the front door close, Hilda all but sprang forward to recall him. The children, running in with anxious questions, helped her to resist the impulse.

'Mother isn't well enough to go, my darlings,' she said, taking them in her arms. 'Father must go alone, and you shall stay to keep me company.'

She shed a few tears, but presently commanded herself, and turned to the common duties of the house. Evidently Horace had gone. There was a fear in her mind lest he should resolve on some act of expiation – such as confessing his fault to Mr Merriman: but it seemed unlikely; he had not enough force of character. The depreciatory thought afflicted her; she spent a day of struggle with her emotions, and determined that this first scene of discord should also be the last. Rather than the peace of their home should be marred, she would support every trial. On his return, Horace should find her with the old face of tender welcome. It was she who had done the worse wrong; she must atone for it by self-denial, by cheerful devotion, and hope that some escape from the consequences of their weakness might soon be discoverable.

Castledine was back again at four in the afternoon. He came in anxious and shamefaced, not ill-tempered. The reception that awaited him, though not unlooked for, brought tears to his eyes.

'A letter has come for you,' said Hilda, when they had exchanged words of forgiveness.

'Who's this from, I wonder?'

It proved to be an offer of the post of drawing-master at a boarding-school in the neighbourhood. This was no surprise, for the father of Horace's pupil had already suggested the possibility of his filling a position left vacant at the summer holidays. The demand upon his time would be only two hours a week, and the payment of corresponding slightness.

'I shall take it,' he announced with an air of resignation. 'Curious that this should come today; I have a promise of two other private pupils. On the way home I met Mr Brownson, and he recommended me to call on a friend of his who has two little girls to be taught drawing. I shall take that too.'

And with a sigh he stared at the ceiling.

The Mr Brownson in question was their only acquaintance at Glastonbury. They had known him for a month or two. People of education who choose (or are compelled) to live in a peasant's cottage, will never have any difficulty in avoiding intercourse with the better class folk of their neighbourhood; an anomalous position is a safeguard against the attentions of country society. But for this isolation, Hilda could hardly have entertained the thought of passing off her own drawings as her husband's. It looked now as if their connections were likely to extend; and herefrom might result new anxieties.

'I have something else to tell you,' said Castledine, presently, in a tone that suggested grave deliberation. 'For the present – just for the present only – I think I shall put the "Joseph" aside.'

Hilda listened breathlessly; she could find nothing to say, and after a short silence her husband proceeded –

'The fact of the matter is, I have attempted something – not beyond my strength, but impossible in my situation. There's no finishing a picture of that size in such a studio. Merriman thinks I have done wonders – all things considered. But miracles are not in my power. I must wait till we have a larger house.'

'I am sure that is wise,' Hilda murmured, consolingly.

'If you really think so, that settles it. For the present, "Joseph" must stand aside. I shall get a small canvas, and begin at the "King Alfred". Won't that be better? I mentioned the thing to Merriman, and he seemed to be much interested. But I tell you what, Hilda: it's not only a larger studio that I need; I'm afraid I'm rusting in this out-of-the-world place.'

'Yes – I too have had that fear,' she assented with much readiness. 'I am sure it would be better for you to be in a town – if we could only manage it!'

'We must plan it somehow. Yes, I am decidedly rusting; that's the explanation of the dull, tired feeling I have had for a long time. The fact of the matter is, if I can't live by my painting, I must be content to give up a part of each day to lessons. It's a wretched necessity, but then it's better than having to give up art altogether – isn't it? If I had to do that, it would be all over with me, you know.'

He looked at her very gravely, a pathetic wrinkle on his brow.

Hilda made up her mind that the project of leaving Glastonbury should be carried out, and before very long. But for what had befallen, the lanes and fields and watercourses in their autumnal colouring would have afforded her calm delight, and have supplied infinite material for her pencil. But that was all over; she feared the thoughts that were suggested by every favourite nook or view. The renunciation on which she had resolved, if possible at all, would only be so amid strange surroundings – all the better if remote from natural beauty. In a town she might perhaps forget the misery of frustrated impulses.

Horace procured the small canvas, and transferred to it the outlines of a drawing which he had prepared and laid aside more than a year ago. But he got no further than this. Distaste for the subject speedily assailed him; he mooned about his little room or slipped away in truancy, or else declared that the skies were too gloomy for painting, and amused himself with his children. Hilda had entirely ceased her watercolour work, and no remark on the subject ever passed between them. Meanwhile, she was corresponding with a married sister who lived in the north, trying to discover if Horace could hope for employment as teacher in that town. The undertaking seemed feasible. She succeeded, moreover, in borrowing a sum of money to meet the expenses of removal and settlement. Thereupon it was decided that they should quit Glastonbury at Christmas.

Castledine brightened wonderfully at the prospect of change. He began to talk as in the old days, of great achievements that lay before him. Again he assured his little boy and girl that someday their father's name would be rumoured to the ends of the earth – 'Like those of Michelangelo and Raphael'. He resumed the satin dressing-gown, of late discarded, and began to make what he called anatomical studies, in charcoal, on huge sheets of paper. The packing of his 'Joseph of Arimathea' occupied him for many days; so precious a canvas must not be exposed to risk in the removal.

And as for his wife, she seemed to have recovered the sweet and placid patience which was always her characteristic. No one divined what lay beneath her tender smile, with its touch of sadness – least of all Horace himself. No one knew of the long sleepless nights when she wept silently over a glorious hope that had come only to vanish. She had her moments of rebellion, but subdued herself by remembering that her own weakness was to blame for these sorrows. An artist no longer, however her artistic soul might revolt, the duties of wife and mother must suffice for all her energies, and supply all her happiness.

Then she packed away her colours and sketchbooks – it was once for all. She never drew again and never again looked at the accumulated work which was her preparation for a futile success.

4

In the bar parlour of one of those comfortable little inns (not hotels, and still less gin-shops) which are yet discoverable if you seek far enough from London, destroyer of all simple ease, three men were sitting. It was New Year's Eve. At this hour, past ten o'clock, the streets of the market town had fallen into stillness; the house itself was very quiet, only an occasional laugh, or a voice raised in seasonable greeting, came from the bar. For more than five minutes the three men had kept silence. Two sat by the fire, with long clay pipes in hand, and glasses reachable on the mantelpiece; they were middle-aged, and by their dress seemed to be well-doing tradesmen. The third leaned back in a corner, his arms crossed, his head bent; he too wore broadcloth, but it had seen more than fair service. His plain and not very intelligent face declared an uneasy mind, and thin straggling hair of unusual length heightened the woebegone effect of his general appearance.

One of his companions turned to look at him, and said in a friendly voice: 'Rather quiet tonight, Mr Castledine?'

He nodded and sighed, but made no other answer.

'Let's hope that 1890 will treat us better than 1889 has done,' continued the other, cheeringly. 'Won't do, you know, to begin the New Year in low spirits. Never meet trouble halfway.'

Castledine let his arms fall, looked into his empty glass, and said in a husky voice: 'I've had a shock today.'

'Sorry to hear that. How was it?'

The third man had turned his head in curiosity. For a moment Castledine glanced from one to the other, seeming to hesitate; then he changed his position, stroked his stubbly chin, coughed, and began to speak with an air of impressiveness.

'I went to call upon Sir William Barnard.' A pause invited the hearers to look surprised or respectful. 'I have no personal acquaintance with him, but I had my reasons for thinking that he might be disposed to recommend me a pupil or two. It isn't my habit, you know, to trouble people with this kind of application, but just at present I have to stir myself. Things are dull in my profession.'

'Like in every other,' remarked the man hitherto silent.

'I fear so. Well, Sir William was at home, and he received me without a minute's delay. I explained to him who I was and what I wanted. He looked at me with a good deal of interest and said, "Mr Castledine, your name is familiar to me. Are you a landscape painter?" I answered that in days gone by

I had done a little work of that kind, and he looked still more interested. "I see from your card," he said, "that your first initial is H. Now I have two little watercolours, bits of Somerset landscape, which I prize very highly, and they are both signed H. Castledine. Are they your work, I wonder?" "Yes, Sir William," I answered, "I have no doubt they are." At that he was really delighted, and asked me at once to come into Lady Barnard's boudoir and look at the drawings. And there they hung, my work of just twenty years ago!'

His voice sank mournfully. He shook his head, sighed, and watched the faces of the listeners, who knew not what to say.

'I'm a victim of circumstances,' he continued in a moment, 'if ever man was. It puzzles you, no doubt, that I should once have done great things, and yet at my age, only fifty, be nothing but an obscure drawing-master. You don't understand the artist's nature. You can't imagine how completely an artist is at the mercy of circumstances.'

Assuredly the worthy men had but slight understanding of these things. They exchanged a glance, muttered 'Ah!' and still listened.

'I told my story to Sir William, and he was deeply moved – deeply moved. He said he would exert himself to be of use to me.'

'Well, that means a good deal, I should think,' said one of the hearers. 'It ought to have cheered you up.'

'Perhaps so; but you don't know what it meant is to be reminded of power and reputation that are gone for ever. When I did those two little water-colours, anyone would have said that I had a brighter future than most artists then living. Landscape wasn't really my strong point. I was an historical painter. I lived at Glastonbury, in Somerset; an out-of-the-way place, if you like; but even there I was sought out by great artists. The late Godfrey Banks – you have heard of him, I hope? – one of the greatest men in the English school, called upon me one day, just to see a picture I was engaged upon. He was astonished at finding me in a little cottage, with nothing but a tiny back bedroom for a studio. "How's this, Mr Castledine?" he said; "how can you work under such conditions as these?" "You may well ask, Mr Banks," I replied. "Circumstances, circumstances. Can't afford anything better at present." He was shocked and angry. You must understand that an artist's reputation doesn't always mean money. My little watercolours sold for just enough to keep me and my family alive; but my great work had to be done very slowly – very slowly. Banks was delighted with what I showed him – a great picture, filling all one side of the room; but it almost brought tears to his eyes to think I should be labouring against such terrible odds.'

'Didn't he help you?' was asked.

'Help me, my dear sir? How could he? An artist cannot go round with a hat soliciting alms. He could only hope that my great picture might soon be finished, and sold for a satisfactory price. But it was never to be finished!'

'Why not?'

'It's very difficult to explain an artist's obstacles. But, from the first, circumstances were against me. I married at two-and-twenty – a rash, indeed a fatal, step. I encumbered myself with a wife and family (though the best wife and the sweetest children that man ever had) at an age when I ought, above everything, to have been independent – free to travel, to study. Already I had overtaxed my health in working at art when circumstances compelled me to earn a living in other ways. And whilst at Glastonbury my strength and spirits were so completely shattered that – well, well, I don't like to speak of it. Would you believe that my poor wife had to go and sell her watch to provide us with food? That,' he added, quickly, 'was before I had found out that my watercolours would sell. I thought so little of them. And now two of them are hanging in Lady Barnard's boudoir, together with a Millet and a Turner and other masterpieces! Yes, a victim of circumstances, if ever man was!'

His companions kept a sympathetic silence.

'We left Glastonbury; but ill-luck followed us. I had to toil as a drawing-master, and before long my artistic faculty deserted me – crushed out by hard circumstances. Four years later my wife died – of a fever she caught in dirty lodgings at the seaside. The noblest wife that ever man had!' A tear ran down his cheek. 'I was left with the two children – a boy and a girl. My son would have been a great painter. At twelve years old he had done astonishing things. But he died at fourteen, after a dreadful illness – poor, dear little lad! And my poor, dear little girl married a blackguard – a blackguard, who took her off to the colonies, and makes her life so miserable that I dread to have a letter from her, though she does her best to put a good face on things, poor child! All of us, victims of circumstances.'

He stood up, turned aside to blow his nose and wipe his cheeks, and began to move towards the door. Before going forth, he faced his companions again, and said hoarsely: 'Gentlemen, I wish you a Happy New Year!'

The Elixir

In 1886, I chanced to be spending a few weeks in a manufacturing town in the Midlands. I was engrossed in business which allowed me little leisure, and which brought me into contact with only two or three of the townsfolk; of local story and gossip I knew next to nothing. One evening, as I took the air in a ramble along the main streets, my eye was caught by a movement of people towards a public building. I discovered that a political meeting was about to be held, and idle curiosity took me into the hall. Home Rule was the topic of the day; Mr Gladstone's Home Rule Bill had set the town in a ferment, and Conservative feeling was eager to utter itself from a crowded platform. Speeches neither good nor bad consumed as much time as I cared to give to this kind of entertainment; I wished to get away, and was calculating the chances of doing so without annoyance to myself or others when an excited murmur among the assembly caused me to look with interest at the new speaker who was just rising. A tall, handsome, middle-aged man, dark-eyed, dark-bearded, his face flushed, and a fine energy in his attitude as he began to speak – a very different type from those I had been observing. The first notes of his voice affected me oddly; I seemed to know the man, to have heard him talk, and yet I could not altogether attach any memory to his features.

'Who is that?' I whispered to my neighbour.

'Mr Orgreave – don't you know?'

'Manufacturer?'

'Yes. Stood for the Radicals at last election and got beaten.'

Mr Orgreave was making a remarkably good speech, and that in spite of the groans, hisses, angry outcries, which punctuated his periods. He had evidently come to beard the Conservative lion in its den; he enjoyed the tumult his oratory aroused; his eyes flashed with the joy of battle, and his voice rose triumphant over the noisy wrath of the meeting. No political speech I ever heard gave me so much pleasure. The man was on fire with his conviction, and flung out his defiances right gloriously. All the time, I kept wondering who it was that – in voice at all events – he so much resembled. The result of his harangue was uproar, ending in mere chaos. Somewhere about midnight I struggled out of the howling and hustling crowd, and found my way home. And the next day I kept bursting into laughter over the recollection of that speech and its consequences.

I was very busy. Mr Orgreave passed out of my mind.

Shortly after my return to London, chance brought me into the company of an interesting man whom I had lost sight of for a good many years. His name was Holland; we had known each other slightly, in our salad days, and coming together with new causes for interest in each other's lives, we talked much of old times and old acquaintances.

'I wonder,' said Holland once, after a fit of musing, 'what became of Shacklewell. You knew Shacklewell? Yes, of course you did.'

'Shacklewell! It's long since I thought of him. You probably knew him much better than I did.'

'At one time we were very thick. Dead long since, no doubt. Probably dead in a hospital. The kind of fellow bound to go under.'

I pondered my memories, and there arose before me a man of four-and-twenty, handsome, well built, meant for healthy and long life, but ruined by his passions. A clever fellow, furiously ambitious, but never likely to do anything, so little had he of patience or self-management. Of his circumstances I remembered nothing.

'Poor, wasn't he?'

'Chronically hard up,' replied Holland. 'If he's alive, he owes me a good many sovereigns. I found him one day in bed, scarcely able to move for want of food. "Why didn't you let me know?" I asked. And he said that he had come to a decision; he would go to bed, and lie there, and if nobody came with help, he would just quietly starve to death. He was capable of it, too. Tremendous force of will in that fellow, but the kind of will that was no use to him. Yet I always felt that it only needed the right circumstances to make him as good and capable a man as any living.'

I shook my head.

'Did you ever know a case of redemption by change of circumstances? – I mean, of a man like Shacklewell, an out-and-outer.'

'Perhaps not. And then, it wasn't only money he wanted. He was mad about women.'

'Vice? or romance?'

'Why, I think the latter,' Holland replied. 'I can't be quite sure, and at that time of life one doesn't distinguish very carefully, but I never thought of him as vicious. Of course he took what was offered, and I remember one or two nasty scrapes; I believe he got into the divorce court among other things. But no; I think he had the ideal before him, the romantic ideal. Did you ever hear him read love-poetry? It was rather fine: I've often thought of it. If he could have married the right woman – but there was no chance of that, no chance.'

We brooded.

'Who were his people?'

'Oh, very obscure, I imagine; he never spoke of them. I don't know where he came from, or where he had got his education. Shouldn't wonder if he was somebody's illegitimate son, cut adrift with a little money, to go to the devil. Poor chap, he's there, no doubt.'

'You never heard of him after you left England?'

'Never. I remember our last meeting. Shacklewell was drunk, poor old boy, and talked wildly. He asked me, among other suggestive questions, whether a man mightn't turn pirate somewhere in the Pacific, and so get enough to begin life with! And he talked about some woman – somebody else's wife, of course – who had offered him a thousand pounds, which, of course, he refused. I never knew what to believe of those stories, but I think he was capable of refusing even a thousand pounds; I never saw a trace of the cad in him! Well, we said goodbye, and promised to write to each other. I did write, after a year, but the letter came back through the office. And no one has ever been able to give me news of Shacklewell.'

I think it must have been nearly three months after this conversation that Holland and I found ourselves dining together at the National Liberal Club, guests of a friend of ours whom it is needless to name, an excellent fellow – politician, poet and many another thing – who was never so happy as when he played host at a sumptuous board. The party happened to be rather a large one, a score at least; it celebrated some forgotten occasion. Arriving early, I was at once presented to a man whom I really felt glad to meet, no other than my eloquent defender of Home Rule, Mr Orgreave. He looked at me, I thought, with peculiar intentness, and pressed my hand very cordially. Encouraged by this behaviour, I told him that, in a way, I had already made his acquaintance: the story amused him vastly, and he laughed as hearty a laugh as ever I heard. After five minutes' talk, my interest in the man grew to a strong liking. He, on his side, seemed to have a corresponding feeling, and when he merrily suggested that I should run down to the borough he yet hoped to represent, and support him on the platform at another noisy meeting, I answered that I would certainly do so.

Holland was one of the last to arrive; a minute or two afterwards we had taken our seats at table, where I was glad to find that I had Orgreave for a neighbour. Just opposite was Holland. He, I soon noticed, seemed to be paying particular attention to my new friend, listening to all he said, and often gazing fixedly at him. Once or twice our eyes met, and in Holland's I saw such a strange look, such an expression of puzzlement and uneasiness, that I wondered what was the matter with him. No sooner did we rise after dinner than I stepped towards him; he, I found, was making still more eagerly for me; he caught my arm and drew me aside.

'Who was that on your left hand?' he asked, abruptly and earnestly.

'A man called Orgreave; wealthy manufacturer down at —, a delightful fellow.'

'Good God! I would have sworn it was Shacklewell.'

As the words fell from his lips, I experienced the strangest sensation. At once I knew of whose voice it was that Orgeave's reminded me; of course it was the voice of that half-forgotten fellow, Shacklewell. And the laugh – yes, that, too, was Shacklewell's. All this I imparted to Holland, who, whilst we talked, still kept his eyes on Orgreave.

'It's the most extraordinary resemblance I ever knew,' he murmured. 'The beard, of course, makes a difference, but if one could imagine Shacklewell with ten years of prosperity behind him. And, do you know what?' He lowered his voice. 'That man keeps eyeing us in a very queer way; indeed he does. Hanged if I don't ask Ned to introduce me, and have a talk with him.'

This he did; with the result that, when I parted from him that night, he could think and speak of but one subject: the astounding resemblance, blended with curious differences, of Orgreave and the lost Shacklewell.

'I didn't like to ask if he had a relative of that name. It might be a sore point. But I shall certainly be driven to do it if I meet him again.'

Two days later I had a note from Holland. It ran somehow thus:

Dear G——, it is Shacklewell, no other than Shacklewell, the very Shacklewell we used to know. If it hadn't been I should have puzzled myself into Bedlam. I met him last night, at another dinner, and afterwards, with a queer look, he asked me if I would go and have a smoke with him at his hotel. An astounding story! You shall hear all I know of it when we meet.

That event happened speedily, and I learnt the outlines of Shacklewell's adventures. But better was when I heard the story from his own lips, six months afterwards. The old acquaintance and the new friendship had by that time blended; I was staying at the man's house, knew his wife and children, and felt thoroughly at home with him. Over our pipes by the fireside, he unbosomed himself.

'By the by,' was his first remark tending thitherwards, 'I don't think I owe you any money, do I?'

'Money?'

'From fifteen years ago, I mean.' His smile did me good. 'I owed Holland a few pounds, and I've paid them. But I don't think I ever had the impudence to borrow from you.'

I reassured him.

'I never cadged and sponged, thank heaven.' He spread his hands over the fire. 'Holland, and one or two other fellows, could afford to keep a poor devil going. You can't think how difficult I find it to revive that part of my life. I mean that it's gone so misty and remote. Yet I force myself to think it back now and then, just because gratitude is a good thing. On the day when I forget to feel grateful to my wife, I shall be pretty near the end of all things.'

I knew that he could never mention his wife without a softening of the voice. There was an odd glistening in his eyes as he spoke of her now.

'You marvel at the change in me, don't you? The change in me myself, apart from circumstances. The elixir, my dear fellow – the elixir!'

'What do you mean?'

'I mean happiness. That's what transformed me, gave me a new life, a clean soul! In my case there was no other salvation. My ideal woman, and a solid income. Pretty large demands, I'm aware; but it was my destiny, you see. I'm the one man in a million who gets what he wants, and, having got it, I had drunk the elixir of life. I don't maintain that it's a fine type of character, but it's mine. On the one hand, death blaspheming in a gutter; on the other, a life of health and splendid happiness, with philosophy enough to face the end. No third possibility in my case. And here you see me.'

I looked at him well, and I confess I envied him.

'One ought to believe in God, I suppose. The truth is, I do, in a way. Only I can't see why I was so guided. What led me half across England in those days of despair, fifteen years ago? My wife believes in the good old providence, and I shall end by thinking the same.'

'Come, tell me about it. You were tramping?'

'It was a morning of summer, not long after Holland went to India. I got up, and asked myself how I was going to eat that day. A bedroom at a shilling a night, paid for in advance; my luggage – a comb, a toothbrush, and a little bundle of underclothing. I owned nothing else in the world, and hadn't a farthing in my pockets.

'I went out, and walked along the streets. It was me, I suppose, but I can't realise it. I was close on madness. It had to be death, I thought, and I couldn't decide on the manner of it; I had arguments with myself. The river was best; I walked eastward, aiming at the docks.

'Somewhere, in a decent street, a faintness came over me, and I had to sit down on a doorstep. Presently the door opened, and a woman came out, a young, pretty woman. "What's the matter?" she asked. "Hunger," I said – in fact I hadn't eaten much for two or three days. As soon as she heard that, she took out her purse, and offered me sixpence; and I accepted it, thanking her. What's more, I bought food.

'After eating, I strolled on, doubtful about the river. I believe it was that woman's good and pretty face that did it – made me think of all I was going to lose. I must have said to myself, "By heaven! I'll have another try." I stopped at a stationer's shop with the idea of asking if they knew of any employment. But in the window was an open number of the *Illustrated London News* – open at a picture called 'The Tramp'. A picture of a jolly, ragged fellow, eating bread and cheese on the grass, in a lovely bit of lane – at that moment the most alluring picture I ever saw. And I said to myself, "Go on the tramp! Go out into the fields and lanes and beg a crust, and sleep under the hedge, and, after a day or two, see how life looks." And I started straight away – right off into open Essex, and somehow feeling better than for a long time. Yes, I can get back that feeling – the wonderful hope that shot up in me. I do believe in providence; I can't help!'

He looked at me with wide eyes, marvelling at his own story; and I felt the thrill which is sometimes communicated by a passionate speaker.

'I tramped, and I begged, and I was alive a week after. Alive and well. I felt as if I was making for some point – some definite goal. Yet I never thought of the road; I just went straight forward, and, queer thing, many a time I was in great spirits, enjoying the glorious country, picking flowers, singing songs. It happened to be superb weather. I had a bathe now and then, and felt it did me good. I remember once, when I was stripped, looking at my strong, shapely limbs, and saying to myself that I couldn't have been made to die like a scrofulous East-end cripple. Every day I had more faith in life. When I begged at a cottage door, I must have looked and spoken as if I were doing the people a favour by asking them for bread. I grew arrogant in a sense of liberty and hopefulness! Wasn't it all strange?

'I got a long way north; as far as – well, as far as a village not a mile from here. That day I hadn't been able to beg much food; towards night I felt very hungry. Wandering through fields, I came to a little gate that opened into an orchard; beyond I could see the roof of a house, not large, but something more than a cottage. Apples tempted me; I thought I would risk it, and take one or two which no one would ever miss. The place seemed quiet enough, no one was likely to come into the orchard at that moment. I opened the wicket, I plucked three apples, I turned back; and there on the outer side of the gate, a girl was standing – a lady.

' "Do you want someone?" she asked.

' "No, I have been stealing apples."

'Those were the very words. I answered them without thought. I had to say just those words and no others.

'She looked at me in astonishment. Of course there was an incongruity between my accent and my appearance. She looked at me and I at her. I didn't think her beautiful – until she smiled. She was about three-and-twenty, nicely dressed. Just the hair, just the complexion I loved in a woman. And when she smiled, I had something come over me.

' "Why do you steal apples?" she asked – an exquisite voice.

' "Because I'm hungry! I've tried to beg food, but have had no luck today."

' "You don't speak like a beggar."

' "No, I wasn't born to it."

'I could see she wanted to go past me, and I came out into the field, and moved a little away. When she was on the orchard side of the gate she spoke again.

' "If you are in want, go round to the front door of this house and ask to see Mr Littlestone."

'I watched her away through the trees, and then I did what she had told me. A servant showed me into a dining-room, and there came a pleasant old fellow, with cheeks like the apples I had in my pocket, and began to question me. Will you believe that, ten minutes after, we were sitting in his library debating the doctrine of Determinism! I had said something which touched a sensitive point in him; he stood for the freedom of the will, and took me into his study to read me a passage from Coleridge! I didn't give way, and my independence seemed to please him.

' "Well," he said, at length; "and where does the law of causation indicate that you shall sleep tonight?"

'My hearty laugh flattered him, I suppose, and he held out some money – half a sovereign.

' "There! go to the inn and make yourself a bit more presentable, and – if it has been so fore-ordained – come tomorrow morning at ten and ask to see me."

'Next day I told him everything. The story bewildered him a little, and now and then he didn't look very pleased. But in the end he said that if I really wanted to support myself he thought he could get me something to do in the neighbouring town. My whole mind was so changed that I eagerly accepted his offer, anything, I said, any sort of work that gave a man a chance in the world. So he sent me into the town to call on a friend of his, a manufacturer. And in a day or two I was sitting on a stool doing the kind of work I had been accustomed to years before, and which I thought I would die rather than begin again.'

At this point, he gave me a sketch of his life before I had ever known him. Needless to repeat the details, but they filled a gap in my understanding of his history, and made what followed somewhat more credible.

'Just a year after – the very anniversary of the day on which I stole the apples – I was married. I can't say that I ever felt a surprise at what had happened to me. The second time I went to Mr Littlestone's (to tell him that I had got a place) I saw again the girl who had met me in the orchard, and I said to myself, "There is my wife." To anyone else the thought would have seemed lunacy; but I knew. One thing I couldn't foresee,' he added, laughing, 'was that I should begin the new life with a new name.'

'Miss Orgreave had no male relatives?' I remarked.

'Nor female either. Old Littlestone, when I staggered him with the news that she had consented to be my wife, told me of the provision in her father's will that whoever married her should take the name of Orgreave. It mattered nothing to me; in fact, I was glad of it – glad to shake off the last bit of my old self. When I heard how wealthy I was going to be, I smiled carelessly – never was such a philosopher! Having won the ideal woman, a huge host of money seemed only a natural appendage, the kind of thing one might have expected to follow.'

I mused a little, then said: 'I won't, of course, ask you how you won your wife. But perhaps you wouldn't mind telling me whether your position had improved at all before the wooing began.'

Shacklewell (or Orgreave) gave one of his joyous laughs.

'Devil a bit! I earned twenty-five shillings a week all through the year. As a matter of fact – there's no reason why I shouldn't tell you – all my love-making was done through the post. Like my impudence, wasn't it? I wrote to Miss Orgreave ten days after I got my place as clerk. No answer. I wrote a second time. Answer: Three lines. I wrote every week – every three days – every day! I shouldn't wonder if they were the best love-letters a man ever composed. Someday I shall ask my wife to let me see them again. I remember saying in one of them something like this: "Now if I were a girl in your position, I should be tempted by the chance of working a sort of miracle. Here's a man, crazy with love of you, one of the few men to whom a woman's love is the crown of all things. He has been down into hell – and narrowly escaped staying there. He has known all along that his only hope lay in the wild possibility of his attaining happiness. Leave him in his poverty and his misery, and he would sink, choked at last in mud. Lift him out of it, and he would become a man, clean, strong and joyous. Doesn't the thought tempt you? You have the elixir of life; won't you give me a draught of it, and watch the miracle that follows?" Well, it might have been bunkum, you know, but it wasn't; I meant it from my soul, and she knew that I meant it, and she had faith in her power. And here you see me!'

Yes, I saw him, and admired him, and thought him the one favourite of fortune I had ever known. He lived with such gusto that to come near him was to imbibe something of his joy in life. He imparted vigour to all with whom he talked. Of the woman to whom he owed everything (save the inborn capacity for happiness), I shall only say that one divined in her his fit companion; before others she was reserved and a trifle shy, but her few soft words always carried excellent sense, and her beautiful eyes had, at moments, a glow which fascinated. That she was more than proud of her husband, one saw whenever they were together; all his aims were hers, and hers all his gallant enthusiasms.

They had three children at that time – I am writing of springtime, 1887. Much has happened since then. When I called on Mrs Orgreave a year ago, her daughter walked with me to the churchyard, where two boys and their father lie in the same grave.

'My mother is sad sometimes,' she said, 'but never gloomy, never embittered by her sorrows. She has a wonderful belief in happiness, and lives only to procure it for as many as she can. She often says: "Let people know happiness if it is only for one day." And my father used to say the same'.

'He had reason for his faith.'

'I know. Not long ago I read the story of his life, which he wrote in the last year.'

'I heard it once from his own lips,' I said.

The Prize Lodger

The ordinary West-End Londoner – who is a citizen of no city at all, but dwells amid a mere conglomerate of houses at a certain distance from Charing Cross – has known a fleeting surprise when, by rare chance, his eye has fallen upon the name of some such newspaper as the *Battersea Times*, the *Camberwell Mercury* or the *Islington Gazette*. To him, these and the like districts are nothing more than compass points of the huge metropolis. He may be in practice acquainted with them; if historically inclined, he may think of them as old-time villages swallowed up by insatiable London; but he has never grasped the fact that in Battersea, Camberwell, Islington, there are people living who name these places as their home; who are born, subsist and die there as though in a distinct town, and practically without consciousness of its obliteration in the map of a world capital.

The stable element of this population consists of more or less old-fashioned people. Round about them is the ceaseless coming and going of nomads who keep abreast with the time, who take their lodgings by the week, their houses by the month; who camp indifferently in regions old and new, learning their geography in train and tram-car. Abiding parishioners are wont to be either very poor or established in a moderate prosperity; they lack enterprise, either for good or ill: if comfortably off, they owe it, as a rule, to some predecessor's exertion. And for the most part, though little enough endowed with the civic spirit, they abundantly pride themselves on their local permanence.

Representative of this class was Mr Archibald Jordan, a native of Islington, and, at the age of five-and-forty, still faithful to the streets which he had trodden as a child. His father started a small grocery business in Upper Street; Archibald succeeded to the shop, advanced soberly, and at length admitted a partner, by whose capital and energy the business was much increased. After his thirtieth year Mr Jordan ceased to stand behind the counter. Of no very active disposition, and but moderately set on gain, he found it pleasant to spend a few hours daily over the books and the correspondence, and for the rest of his time to enjoy a gossipy leisure, straying among the acquaintances of a lifetime, or making new in the decorous bar-parlours, billiard-rooms, and other such retreats which allured his bachelor liberty. His dress and bearing were unpretentious, but impressively respectable; he never allowed his garments (made by an Islington tailor, an old schoolfellow) to exhibit the least sign of wear, but fashion affected their style as little as possible. Of middle height, and tending to portliness, he walked at an unvarying pace, as a man who had never known undignified hurry; in his familiar thoroughfares he glanced about him with a good-humoured air of proprietorship, or with a look of thoughtful criticism for any changes that might be going forward. No one had ever spoken flatteringly of his visage; he knew himself a very homely-featured man, and accepted the fact, as something that had neither favoured nor hindered him in life. But it was his conviction that no man's eye had a greater power of solemn and overwhelming rebuke, and this gift he took a pleasure in exercising, however trivial the occasion.

For five-and-twenty years he had lived in lodgings; always within the narrow range of Islington respectability, yet never for more than a twelve-month under the same roof. This peculiar feature of Mr Jordan's life had made him a subject of continual interest to local landladies, among whom were several lifelong residents, on friendly terms of old time with the Jordan family. To them it seemed an astonishing thing that a man in such circum-stances had not yet married; granting this eccentricity, they could not imagine what made him change his abode so often. Not a landlady in Islington but would welcome Mr Jordan in her rooms, and, having got him, do her utmost to prolong the connection. He had been known to quit a house on the paltriest excuse, removing to another in which he could not expect equally good treatment. There was no accounting for it: it must be taken as an ultimate mystery of life, and made the most of as a perennial topic of neighbourly conversation.

As to the desirability of having Mr Jordan for a lodger there could be no difference of opinion among rational womankind. Mrs Wiggins, indeed, had taken his sudden departure from her house so ill that she always spoke of him abusively; but who heeded Mrs Wiggins? Even in the sadness of hope deferred, those ladies who had entertained him once, and speculated on his possible return, declared Mr Jordan a 'thorough gentleman'. Lodgers, as a class, do not recommend themselves in Islington; Mr Jordan shone against the dusky background with almost dazzling splendour. To speak of lodgers as of cattle, he was a prize creature. A certain degree of comfort he firmly exacted; he might be a trifle fastidious about cooking; he stood upon his dignity; but no one could say that he grudged reward for service rendered. It was his practice to pay more than the landlady asked. Twenty-five shillings a week, you say? I shall give you twenty-eight. *But* – ' and with raised forefinger he went through the catalogue of his demands. Everything must be done precisely as he directed; even in the laying of his table he insisted upon certain minute peculiarities, and to forget one of them was to earn that gaze of awful reprimand which Mr Jordan found (or thought) more efficacious than any spoken word. Against this precision might be set his strange indulgence in the matter of bills; he merely regarded the total, was never known to dispute an item. Only twice in his long experience had he quitted a lodging because of exorbitant charges, and on these occasions he sternly refused to discuss the matter. 'Mrs Hawker, I am paying your account with the addition of one week's rent. Your rooms will be vacant at eleven o'clock tomorrow morning.' And until the hour of departure no entreaty, no prostration, could induce him to utter a syllable.

It was on the 1st of June 1889, his forty-fifth birthday, that Mr Jordan removed from quarters he had occupied for ten months, and became a lodger in the house of Mrs Elderfield.

Mrs Elderfield, a widow aged three-and-thirty with one little girl, was but a casual resident in Islington; she knew nothing of Mr Jordan, and made no enquiries about him. Strongly impressed, as every woman must needs be, by his air and tone of mild authority, she congratulated herself on the arrival of such an inmate; but no subservience appeared in her demeanour; she behaved with studious civility, nothing more. Her words were few and well chosen. Always neatly dressed, yet always busy, she moved about the house with quick, silent step, and cleanliness marked her path. The meals were well cooked, well served. Mr Jordan being her only lodger, she could devote to him an undivided attention. At the end of his first week the critical gentleman felt greater satisfaction than he had ever known.

The bill lay upon his table at breakfast-time. He perused the items, and, much against his habit, reflected upon them. Having breakfasted, he rang the bell.

'Mrs Elderfield –'

He paused, and looked gravely at the widow. She had a plain, honest, healthy face, with resolute lips, and an eye that brightened when she spoke; her well-knit figure, motionless in its respectful attitude, declared a thoroughly sound condition of the nerves.

'Mrs Elderfield, your bill is so very moderate that I think you must have forgotten something.'

'Have you looked it over, sir?'

'I never trouble with the details. Please examine it.'

'There is no need, sir. I never make a mistake.'

'I said, Mrs Elderfield, please *examine* it.'

She seemed to hesitate, but obeyed.

'The bill is quite correct, sir.'

'Thank you.'

He paid it at once and said no more.

The weeks went on. To Mr Jordan's surprise, his landlady's zeal and efficiency showed no diminution, a thing unprecedented in his long and varied experience. After the first day or two he had found nothing to correct; every smallest instruction was faithfully carried out. Moreover, he knew for the first time in his life the comfort of absolutely clean rooms. The best of his landladies hitherto had not risen above that conception of cleanliness which is relative to London soot and fog. His palate, too, was receiving an education. Probably he had never eaten of a joint rightly cooked, or tasted a potato boiled as it should be; more often than not, the food set before him had undergone a process which left it masticable indeed, but void of savour and nourishment. Many little attentions of which he had never dreamed kept him in a wondering cheerfulness. And at length he said to himself: 'Here I shall stay.'

Not that his constant removals had been solely due to discomfort and a hope of better things. The secret – perhaps not entirely revealed even to himself – lay in Mr Jordan's sense of his own importance, and his uneasiness whenever he felt that, in the eyes of a landlady, he was becoming a mere everyday person – an ordinary lodger. No sooner did he detect a sign of this than he made up his mind to move. It gave him the keenest pleasure of which he was capable when, on abruptly announcing his immediate departure, he perceived the landlady's profound mortification. To make the blow heavier he had even resorted to artifice, seeming to express a most lively contentment during the very days when he had decided to leave and was asking himself where he should next abide. One of his delights was to return to a house which he had quitted years ago, to behold the excitement and bustle occasioned by his appearance, and play the good-natured autocrat over grovelling dependents. In every case, save the two already mentioned, he had parted with his landlady on terms of friendliness, never vouchsafing a reason for his going away, genially eluding every attempt to obtain an explanation, and at the last abounding in graceful recognition of all that had been done for him. Mr Jordan shrank from dispute, hated every sort of contention; this characteristic gave a certain refinement to his otherwise commonplace existence. Vulgar vanity would have displayed itself in precisely the acts and words from which his self-esteem nervously shrank. And of late he had been thinking over the list of landladies, with a half-formed desire to settle down, to make himself a permanent home. Doubtless as a result of this state of mind, he betook himself to a strange house, where, as from neutral ground, he might reflect upon the lodgings he knew, and judge between their merits. He could not foresee what awaited him under Mrs Elderfield's roof; the event impressed him as providential; he felt, with singular emotion, that choice was taken out of his hands. Lodgings could not be more than perfect, but such he had found.

It was not his habit to chat with landladies. At times he held forth to them on some topic of interest, suavely, instructively; if he gave in to their ordinary talk, it was with a half-absent smile of condescension. Mrs Elderfield seeming as little disposed to gossip as himself, a month elapsed before he knew anything of her history; but one evening the reserve on both sides was broken. His landlady modestly enquired whether she was giving satisfaction, and Mr Jordan replied with altogether unwonted fervour. In the dialogue that ensued, they exchanged personal confidences. The widow had lost her husband four years ago; she came from the Midlands, but had long dwelt in London. Then fell from her lips a casual remark which made the hearer uneasy.

'I don't think I shall always stay here. The neighbourhood is too crowded. I should like to have a house somewhere farther out.'

Mr Jordan did not comment on this, but it kept a place in his daily thoughts, and became at length so much of an anxiety that he invited a renewal of the subject.

'You have no intention of moving just yet, Mrs Elderfield?'

'I was going to tell you, sir,' replied the landlady, with her respectful calm, 'that I have decided to make a change next spring. Some friends of mine have gone to live at Wood Green, and I shall look for a house in the same neighbourhood.'

Mr Jordan was, in private, gravely disturbed. He who had flitted from house to house for many years, distressing the souls of landladies, now lamented the prospect of a forced removal. It was open to him to accompany Mrs Elderfield, but he shrank from the thought of living in so remote a district. Wood Green! The very name appalled him, for he had never been able to endure the country. He betook himself one dreary autumn afternoon to that northern suburb, and what he saw did not at all reassure him. On his way back he began once more to review the list of old lodgings.

But from that day his conversations with Mrs Elderfield grew more frequent, more intimate. In the evening he occasionally made an excuse for knocking at her parlour door, and lingered for a talk which ended only at supper time. He spoke of his own affairs, and grew more ready to do so as his hearer manifested a genuine interest, without impertinent curiosity. Little by little he imparted to Mrs Elderfield a complete knowledge of his commercial history, of his pecuniary standing – matters of which he had never before spoken to a mere acquaintance. A change was coming over him; the foundations of habit crumbled beneath his feet; he lost his look of complacence, his self-confident and superior tone. Bar-parlours and billiard-rooms saw him but rarely and flittingly. He seemed to have lost his pleasure in the streets of Islington, and spent all his spare time by the fireside, perpetually musing.

On a day in March one of his old landladies, Mrs Higdon, sped to the house of another, Mrs Evans, panting under a burden of strange news. Could it be believed! Mr Jordan was going to marry – to marry that woman in whose house he was living! Mrs Higdon had it on the very best authority – that of Mr Jordan's partner, who spoke of the affair without reserve. A new house had already been taken – at Wood Green. Well! After all these years, after so many excellent opportunities, to marry a mere stranger and forsake Islington! In a moment Mr Jordan's character was gone; had he figured in the police court under some disgraceful charge, these landladies could hardly have felt more shocked and professed themselves more disgusted. The intelligence spread. Women went out of their way to have a sight of Mrs Elderfield's house; they hung about for a glimpse of that sinister person herself. She had robbed them, every one, of a possible share in Islington's prize lodger. Had it been one of themselves they could have borne the chagrin; but a woman whom not one of them knew, an alien! What base arts had she practised? Ah, it was better not to enquire too closely into the secrets of that lodging-house.

Though every effort was made to learn the time and place of the ceremony, Mr Jordan's landladies had the mortification to hear of his wedding only when it was over. Of course, this showed that he felt the disgracefulness of his behaviour; he was not utterly lost to shame. It could only be hoped that he would not know the bitterness of repentance.

Not till he found himself actually living in the house at Wood Green did Mr Jordan realise how little his own will had had to do with the recent course of events. Certainly, he had made love to the widow, and had asked her to marry him; but from that point onward he seemed to have put himself entirely in Mrs Elderfield's hands, granting every request, meeting halfway every suggestion she offered, becoming, in short, quite a different kind of man from his former self. He had not been sensible of a moment's reluctance; he enjoyed the novel sense of yielding himself to affectionate guidance. His wits had gone wool-gathering; they returned to him only after the short honeymoon at Brighton, when he stood upon his own hearth-rug, and looked round at the new furniture and ornaments which symbolised a new beginning of life.

The admirable landlady had shown herself energetic, clear-headed, and full of resource; it was she who chose the house, and transacted all the business in connection with it; Mr Jordan had merely run about in her company from place to place, smiling approval and signing cheques. No one could have gone to work more prudently, or obtained what she wanted at smaller outlay; for all that, Mr Jordan, having recovered something like his normal frame of mind, viewed the results with consternation. Left to himself, he would have taken a very small house, and furnished it much in the style of Islington lodgings; as it was, he occupied a ten-roomed 'villa', with appointments which seemed to him luxurious, aristocratic. True, the expenditure was of no moment to a man in his position, and there was no fear that Mrs Jordan would involve him in dangerous extravagance; but he had always lived with such excessive economy that the sudden change to a life correspondent with his income could not but make him uncomfortable.

Mrs Jordan had, of course, seen to it that her personal appearance harmonised with the new surroundings. She dressed herself and her young daughter with careful appropriateness. There was no display, no purchase of gewgaws – merely garments of good quality, such as became people in easy circumstances. She impressed upon her husband that this was nothing more than a return to the habits of her earlier life. Her first marriage had been a sad mistake; it had brought her down in the world. Now she felt restored to her natural position.

After a week of restlessness, Mr Jordan resumed his daily visits to the shop in Upper Street, where he sat as usual among the books and the correspondence, and tried to assure himself that all would henceforth be well with him. No more changing from house to house; a really comfortable home in which to spend the rest of his days; a kind and most capable wife to look after all his needs, to humour all his little habits. He could not have taken a wiser step.

For all that, he had lost something, though he did not yet understand what it was. The first perception of a change not for the better flashed upon him one evening in the second week, when he came home an hour later than his wont. Mrs Jordan, who always stood waiting for him at the window, had no smile as he entered.

'Why are you late?' she asked, in her clear, restrained voice.

'Oh – something or other kept me.'

This would not do. Mrs Jordan quietly insisted on a full explanation of the delay, and it seemed to her unsatisfactory.

'I hope you won't be irregular in your habits, Archibald,' said his wife, with gentle admonition. 'What I always liked in you was your methodical way of living. I shall be very uncomfortable if I never know when to expect you.'

'Yes, my dear, but – business, you see – '

'But you have explained that you *could* have been back at the usual time.'

'Yes – that's true – but – '

'Well, well, you won't let it happen again. Oh really, Archibald!' she suddenly exclaimed. 'The idea of you coming into the room with muddy boots! Why, look! There's a patch of mud on the carpet – '

'It was my hurry to speak to you,' murmured Mr Jordan, in confusion.

'Please go at once and take your boots off. And you left your slippers in the bedroom this morning. You must always bring them down, and put them in the dining-room cupboard; then they're ready for you when you come into the house.'

Mr Jordan had but a moderate appetite for his dinner, and he did not talk so pleasantly as usual. This was but the beginning of troubles such as he had not for a moment foreseen. His wife, having since their engagement taken the upper hand, began to show her determination to keep it, and day by day her rule grew more galling to the ex-bachelor. He himself, in the old days, had plagued his landladies by insisting upon method and routine, by his faddish attention to domestic minutiae; he now learnt what it was to be subjected to the same kind of despotism, exercised with much more exasperating persistence. Whereas Mrs Elderfield had scrupulously obeyed every direction given by her lodger, Mrs Jordan was evidently resolved that her husband should live, move, and have his being in the strictest accordance with her own ideal. Not in any spirit of nagging, or ill-tempered unreasonableness; it was merely that she had her favourite way of doing every conceivable thing, and felt so sure it was the best of all possible ways that she could not endure any other. The first serious disagreement between them had reference to conduct at the breakfast-table. After a broken night, feeling headachy and worried, Mr Jordan took up his newspaper, folded it conveniently, and set it against the bread so that he could read while eating. Without a word, his wife gently removed it, and laid it aside on a chair.

'What are you doing?' he asked gruffly.

'You mustn't read at meals, Archibald. It's bad manners, and bad for your digestion.'

'I've read the news at breakfast all my life, and I shall do so still,' exclaimed the husband, starting up and recovering his paper.

'Then you will have breakfast by yourself. Nelly, we must go into the other room till papa has finished.'

Mr Jordan ate mechanically, and stared at the newspaper with just as little consciousness. Prompted by the underlying weakness of his character to yield for the sake of peace, wrath made him dogged, and the more steadily he regarded his position, the more was he appalled by the outlook. Why, this meant downright slavery! He had married a woman so horribly like himself in several points that his only hope lay in overcoming her by sheer violence. A thoroughly good and well-meaning woman, an excellent housekeeper, the kind of wife to do him credit and improve his social position; but self-willed, pertinacious, and probably thinking herself his superior in every respect. He had nothing to fear but subjection – the one thing he had never anticipated, the one thing he could never endure.

He went off to business without seeing his wife again, and passed a lamentable day. At his ordinary hour of return, instead of setting off homeward, he strayed about the by-streets of Islington and Pentonville. Not till this moment had he felt how dear they were to him, the familiar streets; their very odours fell sweet upon his nostrils. Never again could he go hither and thither, among the old friends, the old places, to his heart's content. What had possessed him to abandon this precious liberty! The thought of Wood Green revolted him; live there as long as he might, he would never be at home. He thought of his wife (now waiting for him) with fear, and then with a reaction of rage. Let her wait! He – Archibald Jordan – before whom women had bowed and trembled for five-and-twenty years – was *he* to come and go at a wife's bidding? And at length the thought seemed so utterly preposterous that he sped northward as fast as possible, determined to right himself this very evening.

Mrs Jordan sat alone. He marched into the room with muddy boots, flung his hat and overcoat into a chair, and poked the fire violently. His wife's eye was fixed on him, and she first spoke – in the quiet voice that he dreaded.

'What do you mean by carrying on like this, Archibald?'

'I shall carry on as I like in my own house – hear that?'

'I do hear it, and I'm very sorry too. It gives me a very bad opinion of you. You will *not* do as you like in your own house. Rage as you please. You will *not* do as you like in your own house.'

There was a contemptuous anger in her eye which the man could not face. He lost all control of himself, uttered coarse oaths, and stood quivering. Then the woman began to lecture him; she talked steadily, acrimoniously, for more than an hour, regardless of his interruptions. Nervously exhausted, he fled at length from the room. A couple of hours later they met again in the nuptial chamber, and again Mrs Jordan began to talk. Her point, as before, was that he had begun married life about as badly as possible. Why had he married her at all? What fault had she committed to incur such outrageous usage? But, thank goodness, she had a will of her own, and a proper self-respect; behave as he might, she would still persevere in the path of womanly duty. If he thought to make her life unbearable he would find his mistake; she simply should not heed him; perhaps he would return to his senses before long – and in this vein Mrs Jordan continued until night was at odds with morning, only becoming silent when her partner had sunk into the oblivion of uttermost fatigue.

The next day Mr Jordan's demeanour showed him, for the moment at all events, defeated. He made no attempt to read at breakfast; he moved about very quietly. And in the afternoon he came home at the regulation hour.

Mrs Jordan had friends in the neighbourhood, but she saw little of them. She was not a woman of ordinary tastes. Everything proved that, to her mind, the possession of a nice house, with the prospects of a comfortable life, was an end in itself; she had no desire to exhibit her well-furnished rooms, or to gad about talking of her advantages. Every moment of her day was taken up in the superintendence of servants, the discharge of an infinitude of housewifely tasks. She had no assistance from her daughter; the girl went to school, and was encouraged to study with the utmost application. The husband's presence in the house seemed a mere accident – save in the still nocturnal season, when Mrs Jordan bestowed upon him her counsel and her admonitions.

After the lapse of a few days Mr Jordan again offered combat, and threw himself into it with a frenzy.

'Look here!' he shouted at length, 'either you or I are going to leave this house. I can't live with you – understand? I hate the sight of you!'

'Go on!' retorted the other, with mild bitterness. 'Abuse me as much as you like, I can bear it. I shall continue to do my duty, and unless you have recourse to personal violence, here I remain. If you go too far, of course the law must defend me!'

This was precisely what Mr Jordan knew and dreaded; the law was on his wife's side, and by applying at a police court for protection she could overwhelm him with shame and ridicule, which would make life intolerable. Impossible to argue with this woman. Say what he might, the fault always seemed his. His wife was simply doing her duty – in a spirit of admirable thoroughness; he, in the eyes of a third person, would appear an unreasonable and violent curmudgeon. Had it not all sprung out of his obstinacy with regard to reading at breakfast? How explain to anyone what he suffered in his nerves, in his pride, in the outraged habitudes of a lifetime?

That evening he did not return to Wood Green. Afraid of questions if he showed himself in the old resorts, he spent some hours in a billiard-room near King's Cross, and towards midnight took a bedroom under the same roof. On going to business next day, he awaited with tremors either a telegram or a visit from his wife; but the whole day passed, and he heard nothing. After dark he walked once more about the beloved streets, pausing now and then to look up at the windows of this or that well-remembered house. Ah, if he durst but enter and engage a lodging! Impossible – for ever impossible!

He slept in the same place as on the night before. And again a day passed without any sort of enquiry from Wood Green. When evening came he went home.

Mrs Jordan behaved as though he had returned from business in the usual way. 'Is it raining?' she asked, with a half-smile. And her husband replied, in as matter-of-fact a tone as he could command, 'No, it isn't.' There was no mention between them of his absence. That night, Mrs Jordan talked for an hour or two of his bad habit of stepping on the paint when he went up and down stairs, then fell calmly asleep.

But Mr Jordan did not sleep for a long time. What! was he, after all, to be allowed his liberty *out* of doors, provided he relinquished it within? Was it really the case that his wife, satisfied with her house and furniture and income, did not care a jot whether he stayed away or came home? There, indeed, gleamed a hope. When Mr Jordan slept, he dreamed that he was back again in lodgings at Islington, tasting an extraordinary bliss. Day dissipated the vision, but still Mrs Jordan spoke not a word of his absence, and with trembling still he hoped.

THOMAS HARDY

Thomas Hardy was born in Higher Bockhampton, Dorset, in 1840. He attended local schools and was apprenticed to an architect, working in the profession from 1856 to 1872. In 1871 his novel *Desperate Remedies* was accepted for publication, but it was the commercial success of his third novel, *Far from the Madding Crowd* (1874), that made him financially secure enough to marry Emma Gifford. Hardy continued writing novels until the unfavourable reception of *Jude the Obscure* (1895); he then concentrated on poetry, which he had been writing since his youth. Emma Hardy died in 1912, and in 1914 he married Florence Emily Dugdale. He died in 1928.

The Three Strangers

Among the few features of agricultural England which retain an appearance but little modified by the lapse of centuries may be reckoned the high, grassy, and furzy downs, coombs, or eweleases, as they are indifferently called, that fill a large area of certain counties in the south and south-west. If any mark of human occupation is met with hereon it usually takes the form of the solitary cottage of some shepherd.

Fifty years ago such a lonely cottage stood on such a down, and may possibly be standing there now. In spite of its loneliness, however, the spot, by actual measurement, was not more than five miles from a county town. Yet what of that? Five miles of irregular upland, during the long, inimical seasons, with their sleets, snows, rains and mists, afford withdrawing space enough to isolate a Timon or a Nebuchadnezzar; much less, in fair weather, to please that less repellent tribe, the poets, philosophers, artists, and others who 'conceive and meditate of pleasant things'.

Some old earthen camp or barrow, some clump of trees, at least some starved fragment of ancient hedge, is usually taken advantage of in the execution of these forlorn dwellings; but in the present case such a kind of shelter had been disregarded. Higher Crowstairs, as the house was called, stood quite detached and undefended. The only reason for its precise situation seemed to be the crossing of two footpaths at right angles hard by, which may have crossed there and thus for a good five hundred years. The house was thus exposed to the elements on all sides. But, though the wind up here blew unmistakably when it did blow, and the rain hit hard whenever it fell, the various weathers of the winter season were not quite so formidable on the coomb as they were imagined to be by dwellers on low ground. The raw rimes were not so pernicious as in the hollows, and the frosts were scarcely so severe. When the shepherd and his family who tenanted the house were pitied for their sufferings from the exposure, they said that upon the whole they were less inconvenienced by 'wuzzes and flames' (hoarses and phlegms) than when they had lived by the stream of a snug neighbouring valley.

The night of March 28, 182—, was precisely one of the nights that were wont to call forth these expressions of commiseration. The level rain-storm smote walls, slopes and hedges like the cloth-yard shafts of Senlac and Crecy. Such sheep and outdoor animals as had no shelter stood with their buttocks to the wind, while the tails of little birds trying to roost on some scraggy thorn were blown inside out like umbrellas. The gable end of the cottage was stained with wet, and the eaves-droppings flapped against the wall. Yet never was commiseration for the shepherd more misplaced. For that cheerful rustic was entertaining a large party in glorification of the christening of his second girl.

The guests had arrived before the rain began to fall, and they were all now assembled in the chief- or living-room of the dwelling. A glance into the apartment at eight o'clock on this eventful evening would have resulted in the opinion that it was as cosy and comfortable a nook as could be wished for in boisterous weather. The calling of its inhabitant was proclaimed by a number of highly polished sheep-crooks, without stems, that were hung ornamentally over the fireplace, the curl of each shining crook varying from the antiquated type engraved in the patriarchal pictures of old family Bibles to the most approved fashion of the last local sheep fair. The room was lighted by half a dozen candles, having wicks only a trifle smaller than the grease which enveloped them, in sticks that were never used but at high-days, holy days and family feasts. The lights were scattered about the room, two of them standing on the chimney-piece. This position of candles was in itself significant. Candles on the chimney-piece always meant a party.

On the hearth, in front of a back brand to give substance, blazed a fire of thorns, that crackled 'like the laughter of the fool'.

Nineteen persons were gathered here. Of these, five women, wearing gowns of various bright hues, sat in chairs along the wall; girls shy and not shy filled the window-bench; four men, including Charley Jake, the hedge-carpenter, Elijah New, the parish clerk, and John Pitcher, a neighbouring dairyman, the shepherd's father-in-law, lolled in the settle; a young man and maid, who were blushing over tentative *pourparlers* on a life-companionship, sat beneath the corner cupboard; and an elderly engaged man of fifty or upward moved restlessly about from spots where his betrothed was not to the spot where she was. Enjoyment was pretty general, and so much the more prevailed in being unhampered by conventional restrictions. Absolute confidence in one another's good opinion begat perfect ease, while the finishing stroke of manner, amounting to a truly princely serenity, was lent to the majority by the absence of any expression or trait denoting that they wished to get on in the world, enlarge their minds, or do any eclipsing thing whatever, which nowadays so generally nips the bloom and *bonhomie* of all except the two extremes of the social scale.

Shepherd Fennel had married well, his wife being a dairyman's daughter from the valley below, who brought fifty guineas in her pocket – and kept them there till they should be required for ministering to the needs of a coming family. This frugal woman had been somewhat exercised as to the character that should be given to the gathering. A sit-still party had its advantages; but an undisturbed position of ease in chairs and settles was apt to lead on the men to such an unconscionable deal of toping that they would sometimes fairly drink the house dry. A dancing-party was the alternative;

but this, while avoiding the foregoing objection on the score of good drink, had a counterbalancing disadvantage in the matter of good victuals, the ravenous appetites engendered by the exercise causing immense havoc in the buttery. Shepherdess Fennel fell back upon the intermediate plan of mingling short dances with short periods of talk and singing, so as to hinder any ungovernable rage in either. But this scheme was entirely confined to her own gentle mind; the shepherd himself was in the mood to exhibit the most reckless phases of hospitality.

The fiddler was a boy of those parts, about twelve years of age, who had a wonderful dexterity in jigs and reels, though his fingers were so small and short as to necessitate a constant shifting for the high notes, from which he scrambled back to the first position with sounds not of unmixed purity of tone. At seven the shrill 'tweedledee' of this youngster had begun, accompanied by a booming ground bass from Elijah New, the parish clerk, who had thoughtfully brought with him his favourite musical instrument, the serpent. Dancing was instantaneous, Mrs Fennel privately enjoining the players on no account to let the dance exceed the length of a quarter of an hour.

But Elijah and the boy, in the excitement of their position, quite forgot the injunction. Moreover, Oliver Giles, a man of seventeen, one of the dancers, who was enamoured of his partner, a fair girl of thirty-three rolling years, had recklessly handed a new crown-piece to the musicians as a bribe to keep going as long as they had muscle and wind. Mrs Fennel, seeing the steam begin to generate on the countenances of her guests, crossed over and touched the fiddler's elbow and put her hand on the serpent's mouth. But they took no notice, and, fearing she might lose her character of genial hostess if she were to interfere too markedly, she retired and sat down helpless. And so the dance whizzed on with cumulative fury, the performers moving in their planet-like courses, direct and retrograde, from apogee to perigee, till the hand of the well-kicked clock at the bottom of the room had travelled over the circumference of an hour.

While these cheerful events were in course of enactment within Fennel's pastoral dwelling, an incident having considerable bearing on the party had occurred in the gloomy night without. Mrs Fennel's concern about the growing fierceness of the dance corresponded in point of time with the ascent of a human figure to the solitary hill of Higher Crowstairs from the direction of the distant town. This personage strode on through the rain without a pause, following the little worn path which, farther on in its course, skirted the shepherd's cottage.

It was nearly the time of full moon, and on this account, though the sky was lined with a uniform sheet of dripping cloud, ordinary objects out of doors were readily visible. The sad, wan light revealed the lonely pedestrian to be a man of supple frame; his gait suggested that he had somewhat passed the period of perfect and instinctive agility, though not so far as to be otherwise than rapid of motion when occasion required. In point of fact, he might have been about forty years of age. He appeared tall; but a recruiting sergeant, or other person accustomed to the judging of men's heights by the eye, would have discerned that this was chiefly owing to his gauntness, and that he was not more than five feet eight or nine.

Notwithstanding the regularity of his tread, there was caution in it, as in that of one who mentally feels his way; and, despite the fact that it was not a black coat nor a dark garment of any sort that he wore, there was something about him which suggested that he naturally belonged to the black-coated tribes of men. His clothes were of fustian and his boots hobnailed, yet in his progress he showed not the mud-accustomed bearing of hobnailed and fustianed peasantry.

By the time that he had arrived abreast of the shepherd's premises, the rain came down, or rather came along, with yet more determined violence. The outskirts of the little homestead partially broke the force of wind and rain, and this induced him to stand still. The most salient of the shepherd's domestic erections was an empty sty at the forward corner of his hedgeless garden, for in these latitudes the principle of masking the homelier features of your establishment by a conventional frontage was unknown. The traveller's eye was attracted to this small building by the pallid shine of the wet slates that covered it. He turned aside, and, finding it empty, stood under the pent-roof for shelter.

While he stood, the boom of the serpent within and the lesser strains of the fiddler reached the spot, as an accompaniment to the surging hiss of the flying rain on the sod, its louder beating on the cabbage-leaves of the garden, on the eight or ten beehives just discernible by the path, and its dripping from the eaves into a row of buckets and pans that had been placed under the walls of the cottage; for at Higher Crowstairs, as at all such elevated domiciles, the grand difficulty of housekeeping was an insufficiency of water, and a casual rainfall was utilised by turning out as catchers every utensil that the house contained. Some queer stories might be told of the contrivances for economy in suds and dish-waters that are absolutely necessitated in upland habitations during the droughts of summer. But at this season there were no such exigencies; a mere acceptance of what the skies bestowed was sufficient for an abundant store.

At last the notes of the serpent ceased and the house was silent. This cessation of activity aroused the solitary pedestrian from the reverie into which he had lapsed, and, emerging from the shed, with an apparently new intention, he walked up the path to the house door. Arrived here, his first act was to kneel down on a large stone beside the row of vessels and to drink a copious draught from one of them. Having quenched his thirst, he rose and lifted his hand to knock, but paused with his eye upon the panel. Since the dark surface of the wood revealed absolutely nothing, it was evident that he must be mentally looking through the door, as if he wished to measure thereby all the possibilities that a house of this sort might include, and how they might bear upon the question of his entry.

In his indecision he turned and surveyed the scene around. Not a soul was anywhere visible. The garden path stretched downward from his feet, gleaming like the track of a snail; the roof of the little well (mostly dry), the well-cover, the top rail of the garden gate, were varnished with the same dull liquid glaze; while, far away in the vale, a faint whiteness of more than usual extent showed that the rivers were high in the meads. Beyond all this winked a few bleared lamplights through the beating drops, lights that denoted the situation of the county town from which he had appeared to come. The absence of all notes of life in that direction seemed to clinch his intentions, and he knocked at the door.

Within a desultory chat had taken the place of movement and musical sound. The hedge-carpenter was suggesting a song to the company, which nobody just then was inclined to undertake, so that the knock afforded a not unwelcome diversion.

'Walk in!' said the shepherd, promptly.

The latch clicked upward, and out of the night our pedestrian appeared upon the doormat. The shepherd arose, snuffed two of the nearest candles and turned to look at him.

Their light disclosed that the stranger was dark in complexion and not unprepossessing as to feature. His hat, which for a moment he did not remove, hung low over his eyes, without concealing that they were large, open and determined, moving with a flash rather than a glance round the room. He seemed pleased with the survey, and, baring his shaggy head, said, in a rich, deep voice, 'The rain is so heavy, friends, that I ask leave to come in and rest awhile.'

'To be sure, stranger,' said the shepherd. 'And, faith, you've been lucky in choosing your time, for we are having a bit of a fling for a glad cause – though, to be sure, a man could hardly wish that glad cause to happen more than once a year.'

'Nor less,' spoke up a woman; 'for 'tis best to get your family over and done with as soon as you can, so as to be all the earlier out of the fag o't.'

'And what may be this glad cause?' asked the stranger.

'A birth and christening,' said the shepherd.

The stranger hoped his host might not be made unhappy either by too many or too few of such episodes, and, being invited by a gesture to a pull at the mug, he readily acquiesced. His manner, which before entering had been so dubious, was now altogether that of a careless and candid man.

'Late to be traipsing athwart this coomb – hey?' said the engaged man of fifty.

'Late it is, master, as you say. I'll take a seat in the chimney-corner if you have nothing to urge against it, ma'am, for I am a little moist on the side that was next the rain.'

Mrs Shepherd Fennel assented, and made room for the self-invited comer, who, having got completely inside the chimney-corner, stretched out his legs and his arms with the expansiveness of a person quite at home.

'Yes, I am rather thin in the vamp,' he said, freely, seeing that the eyes of the shepherd's wife fell upon his boots, 'and I am not well fitted, either. I have had some rough times lately, and have been forced to pick up what I can get in the way of wearing; but I must find a suit better fit for working-days when I reach home.'

'One of hereabouts?' she enquired.

'Not quite that – farther up the country.'

'I thought so. And so am I; and by your tongue you come from my neighbourhood.'

'But you would hardly have heard of me,' he said, quickly. 'My time would be long before yours, ma'am, you see.'

This testimony to the youthfulness of his hostess had the effect of stopping her cross-examination.

'There is only one thing more wanted to make me happy,' continued the newcomer; 'and that is a little 'baccy, which I am sorry to say I am out of.'

'I'll fill your pipe,' said the shepherd.

'I must ask you to lend me a pipe likewise.'

'A smoker, and no pipe about ye?'

'I have dropped it somewhere on the road.'

The shepherd filled and handed him a new clay pipe, saying as he did so, 'Hand me your 'baccy-box; I'll fill that too, now I am about it.'

The man went through the movement of searching his pockets.

'Lost that too?' said his entertainer, with some surprise.

'I am afraid so,' said the man, with some confusion. 'Give it to me in a screw of paper.'

Lighting his pipe at the candle with a suction that drew the whole flame into the bowl, he resettled himself in the corner, and bent his looks upon the faint steam from his damp legs as if he wished to say no more.

Meanwhile the general body of guests had been taking little notice of this visitor by reason of an absorbing discussion in which they were engaged with the band about a tune for the next dance. The matter being settled, they were about to stand up, when an interruption came in the shape of another knock at the door.

At sound of the same the man in the chimney-corner took up the poker and began stirring the fire as if doing it thoroughly were the one aim of his existence, and a second time the shepherd said, 'Walk in!' In a moment another man stood upon the straw-woven doormat. He too was a stranger.

This individual was one of a type radically different from the first. There was more of the commonplace in his manner, and a certain jovial cosmopolitanism sat upon his features. He was several years older than the first arrival, his hair being slightly frosted, his eyebrows bristly, and his whiskers cut back from his cheeks. His face was rather full and flabby, and yet it was not altogether a face without power. A few grog-blossoms marked the neighbourhood of his nose. He flung back his long drab greatcoat, revealing that beneath it he wore a suit of cinder-grey shade throughout, large, heavy seals, of some metal or other that would take a polish, dangling from his fob as his only personal ornament. Shaking the water-drops from his low-crowned, glazed hat, he said, 'I must ask for a few minutes' shelter, comrades, or I shall be wetted to my skin before I get to Casterbridge.'

'Make yerself at home, master,' said the shepherd, perhaps a trifle less heartily than on the first occasion. Not that Fennel had the least tinge of niggardliness in his composition, but the room was far from large, spare chairs were not numerous, and damp companions were not altogether comfortable at close quarters for the women and girls in their bright-coloured gowns.

However, the second comer, after taking off his greatcoat and hanging his hat on a nail in one of the ceiling beams as if he had been specially invited to put it there, advanced, and sat down at the table. This had been pushed so closely into the chimney-corner, to give all available room to the dancers, that its inner edge grazed the elbow of the man who had ensconced himself by the fire, and thus the two strangers were brought into close companionship. They nodded to each other by way of breaking the ice of unacquaintance, and the first stranger handed his neighbour the large mug – a huge vessel of brown ware, having its upper edge worn away, like a threshold, by the rub of whole genealogies of thirsty lips that had gone the way of all flesh, and bearing the following inscription burned upon its rotund side in yellow letters:

THERE IS NO FUN UNTILL I CUM.

The other man, nothing loath, raised the mug to his lips, and drank on and on and on, till a curious blueness overspread the countenance of the shepherd's wife, who had regarded with no little surprise the first stranger's free offer to the second of what did not belong to him to dispense.

'I knew it!' said the toper to the shepherd, with much satisfaction. 'When I walked up your garden afore coming in, and saw the hives all of a row, I said to myself, "Where there's bees there's honey, and where there's honey there's mead." But mead of such a truly comfortable sort as this I really didn't expect to meet in my older days.' He took yet another pull at the mug, till it assumed an ominous horizontality.

'Glad you enjoy it!' said the shepherd, warmly.

'It is goodish mead,' assented Mrs Fennel, with an absence of enthusiasm which seemed to say that it was possible to buy praise for one's cellar at too heavy a price. 'It is trouble enough to make – and really I hardly think we shall make any more. For honey sells well, and we can make shift with a drop o' small mead and metheglin for common use from the comb washings.'

'Oh, but you'll never have the heart!' reproachfully cried the stranger in cinder grey, after taking up the mug a third time and setting it down empty. 'I love mead, when 'tis old like this, as I love to go to church o' Sundays or to relieve the needy any day of the week.'

'Ha, ha, ha!' said the man in the chimney-corner, who, in spite of the taciturnity induced by the pipe of tobacco, could not or would not refrain from this slight testimony to his comrade's humour.

Now the old mead of those days, brewed of the purest first-year or maiden honey, four pounds to the gallon – with its due complement of whites of eggs, cinnamon, ginger, cloves, mace, rosemary, yeast, and processes of working, bottling and cellaring – tasted remarkably strong; but it did not taste so strong as it actually was. Hence, presently the stranger in cinder grey at the table, moved by its creeping influence, unbuttoned his waistcoat, threw himself back in his chair, spread his legs, and made his presence felt in various ways.

'Well, well, as I say,' he resumed, 'I am going to Casterbridge, and to Casterbridge I must go. I should have been almost there by this time; but the rain drove me in to ye, and I'm not sorry for it.'

'You don't live in Casterbridge?' said the shepherd.

'Not as yet, though I shortly mean to move there.'

'Going to set up in trade, perhaps?'

'No, no,' said the shepherd's wife; 'it is easy to see that the gentleman is rich and don't want to work at anything.'

The cinder-grey stranger paused, as if to consider whether he would accept that definition of himself. He presently rejected it by answering, 'Rich is not quite the word for me, dame. I do work, and I must work. And even if I only get to Casterbridge by midnight I must begin work there at eight tomorrow morning. Yes, hot or wet, blow or snow, famine or sword, my day's work tomorrow must be done.'

'Poor man! Then, in spite o' seeming, you be worse off than we?' replied the shepherd's wife.

' 'Tis the nature of my trade, men and maidens. 'Tis the nature of my trade more than my poverty. But really and truly, I must up and off, or I shan't get a lodging in the town.'

However, the speaker did not move, and directly added, 'There's time for one more draught of friendship before I go, and I'd perform it at once if the mug were not dry.'

'Here's a mug o' small,' said Mrs Fennel. 'Small, we call it, though, to be sure, 'tis only the first wash o' the combs.'

'No,' said the stranger, disdainfully; 'I won't spoil your first kindness by partaking o' your second.'

'Certainly not,' broke in Fennel. 'We don't increase and multiply every day, and I'll fill the mug again.' He went away to the dark place under the stairs where the barrel stood. The shepherdess followed him.

'Why should you do this?' she said, reproachfully, as soon as they were alone. 'He's emptied it once, though it held enough for ten people; and now he's not contented wi' the small, but must needs call for more o' the strong! And a stranger unbeknown to any of us! For my part, I don't like the look o' the man at all.'

'But he's in the house, my honey, and 'tis a wet night, and a christening. Daze it, what's a cup of mead more or less? There'll be plenty more next bee-burning.'

'Very well – this time, then,' she answered, looking wistfully at the barrel. 'But what is the man's calling, and where is he one of, that he should come in and join us like this?'

'I don't know. I'll ask him again.'

The catastrophe of having the mug drained dry at one pull by the stranger in cinder grey was effectually guarded against this time by Mrs Fennel. She poured out his allowance in a small cup, keeping the large one at a discreet distance from him. When he had tossed off his portion the shepherd renewed his enquiry about the stranger's occupation.

The latter did not immediately reply, and the man in the chimney-corner, with sudden demonstrativeness, said, 'Anybody may know my trade – I'm a wheelwright.'

'A very good trade for these parts,' said the shepherd.

'And anybody may know mine – if they've the sense to find it out,' said the stranger in cinder grey.

'You may generally tell what a man is by his claws,' observed the hedge-carpenter, looking at his hands. 'My fingers be as full of thorns as an old pincushion is of pins.'

The hands of the man in the chimney-corner instinctively sought the shade, and he gazed into the fire as he resumed his pipe. The man at the table took up the hedge-carpenter's remark, and added smartly, 'True; but the oddity of my trade is that, instead of setting a mark upon me, it sets a mark upon my customers.'

No observation being offered by anybody in elucidation of this enigma, the shepherd's wife once more called for a song. The same obstacles presented themselves as at the former time: one had no voice, another had forgotten the first verse. The stranger at the table, whose soul had now risen to a good working temperature, relieved the difficulty by exclaiming that to start the company he would sing himself. Thrusting one thumb into the armhole of his waistcoat, he waved the other hand in the air, and, with an extemporising gaze at the shining sheep-crooks above the mantelpiece, began:

> 'Oh, my trade it is the rarest one,
> Simple shepherds all,
> My trade is a sight to see;
> For my customers I tie, and take them up on high,
> And waft 'em to a far countree.'

The room was silent when he had finished the verse, with one exception, that of the man in the chimney-corner, who, at the singer's word, 'Chorus!' joined him in a deep bass voice of musical relish:

> 'And waft 'em to a far countree.'

Oliver Giles, John Pitcher the dairyman, the parish clerk, the engaged man of fifty, the row of young women against the wall, seemed lost in thought not of the gayest kind. The shepherd looked meditatively on the ground; the shepherdess gazed keenly at the singer, and with some suspicion; she was doubting whether this stranger was merely singing an old song from recollection, or composing one there and then for the occasion. All were as perplexed at the obscure revelation as the guests at Belshazzar's feast, except the man in the chimney-corner, who quietly said, 'Second verse, stranger,' and smoked on.

The singer thoroughly moistened himself from his lips inward, and went on with the next stanza, as requested:

> 'My tools are but common ones,
> Simple shepherds all,
> My tools are no sight to see:
> A little hempen string, and a post whereon to swing,
> Are implements enough for me.'

Shepherd Fennel glanced round. There was no longer any doubt that the stranger was answering his question rhythmically. The guests one and all started back with suppressed exclamations. The young woman engaged to the man of fifty fainted halfway, and would have proceeded, but, finding him wanting in alacrity for catching her, she sat down trembling.

'Oh, he's the – ' whispered the people in the background, mentioning the name of an ominous public officer. 'He's come to do it. 'Tis to be at Casterbridge gaol tomorrow – the man for sheep-stealing – the poor clock-maker we heard of, who used to live away at Anglebury and had no work to do – Timothy Sommers, whose family were a-starving, and so he went out of Anglebury by the highroad, and took a sheep in open daylight, defying the farmer and the farmer's wife and the farmer's man and every man Jack among 'em. He' (and they nodded toward the stranger of the terrible trade) 'is come from up the country to do it because there's not enough to do in his own county town, and he's got the place here, now our own county man's dead; he's going to live in the same cottage under the prison wall.'

The stranger in cinder grey took no notice of this whispered string of observations, but again wetted his lips. Seeing that his friend in the chimney-corner was the only one who reciprocated his joviality in any way, he held out his cup toward that appreciative comrade, who also held out his own. They clinked together, the eyes of the rest of the room hanging upon the singer's actions. He parted his lips for the third verse, but at that moment another knock was audible upon the door. This time the knock was faint and hesitating.

The company seemed scared; the shepherd looked with consternation towards the entrance, and it was with some effort that he resisted his alarmed wife's deprecatory glance, and uttered for the third time the welcoming words, 'Walk in!'

The door was gently opened, and another man stood upon the mat. He, like those who had preceded him, was a stranger. This time it was a short, small personage, of fair complexion, and dressed in a decent suit of dark clothes.

'Can you tell me the way to – ' he began; when, gazing round the room to observe the nature of the company among whom he had fallen, his eyes lighted on the stranger in cinder grey. It was just at the instant when the latter, who had thrown his mind into his song with such a will that he scarcely heeded the interruption, silenced all whispers and enquiries by bursting into his third verse:

> 'Tomorrow is my working-day,
> Simple shepherds all,
> Tomorrow is a working-day for me;
> For the farmer's sheep is slain, and the lad who did it ta'en,
> And on his soul may God ha' merc–y!'

The stranger in the chimney-corner, waving his cup with the singer so heartily that his mead splashed over on the hearth, repeated in his bass voice as before:

> 'And on his soul may God ha' mercy!'

All this time the third stranger had been standing in the doorway. Finding now that he did not come forward or go on speaking, the guests particularly regarded him. They noticed, to their surprise, that he stood before them the picture of abject terror-his knees trembling, his hand shaking so violently that the door-latch, by which he supported himself, rattled audibly; his white lips were parted, and his eyes fixed on the merry officer of justice in the middle of the room. A moment more, and he had turned, closed the door, and fled.

'What a man can it be?' said the shepherd.

The rest, between the awfulness of their late discovery and the odd conduct of this third visitor, looked as if they knew not what to think, and said nothing. Instinctively they withdrew farther and farther from the grim gentleman in their midst, whom some of them seemed to take for the prince of darkness himself, till they formed a remote circle, an empty space of floor being left between them and him – *Circulus, cuius centrum diabolus.*

The room was so silent – though there were more than twenty people in it – that nothing could be heard but the patter of the rain against the window-shutters, accompanied by the occasional hiss of a stray drop that fell down the chimney into the fire, and the steady puffing of the man in the corner, who had now resumed his pipe of long clay.

The stillness was unexpectedly broken. The distant sound of a gun reverberated through the air, apparently from the direction of the county town.

'Be jiggered!' cried the stranger who had sung the song, jumping up.

'What does that mean?' asked several.

'A prisoner escaped from the gaol – that's what it means.'

All listened. The sound was repeated, and none of them spoke but the man in the chimney-corner, who said quietly, 'I've often been told that in this county they fire a gun at such times, but I never heard it till now.'

'I wonder if it is *my* man?' murmured the personage in cinder grey.

'Surely it is!' said the shepherd, involuntarily. 'And surely we've seen him! That little man who looked in at the door by now, and quivered like a leaf when he seed ye and heard your song.'

'His teeth chattered, and the breath went out of his body,' said the dairyman.

'And his heart seemed to sink within him like a stone,' said Oliver Giles.

'And he bolted as if he'd been shot at,' said the hedge-carpenter.

'True – his teeth chattered, and his heart seemed to sink, and he bolted as if he'd been shot at,' slowly summed up the man in the chimney-corner.

'I didn't notice it,' remarked the grim songster.

'We were all a-wondering what made him run off in such a fright,' faltered one of the women against the wall, 'and now 'tis explained.'

The firing of the alarm-gun went on at intervals, low and sullenly, and their suspicions became a certainty. The sinister gentleman in cinder grey roused himself. 'Is there a constable here?' he asked, in thick tones. 'If so, let him step forward.'

The engaged man of fifty stepped quavering out of the corner, his betrothed beginning to sob on the back of the chair.

'You are a sworn constable?'

'I be, sir.'

'Then pursue the criminal at once, with assistance, and bring him back here. He can't have gone far.'

'I will, sir, I will – when I've got my staff. I'll home and get it, and come sharp here, and start in a body.'

'Staff! never mind your staff – the man'll be gone!'

'But I can't do nothing without my staff – can I, William, and John, and Charles Jake? No; for there's the king's royal crown a-painted on en in yaller and gold, and the lion and the unicorn, so as when I raise en up and hit my prisoner 'tis made a lawful blow thereby. I wouldn't 'tempt to take up a man without my staff – no, not I. If I hadn't the law to gie me courage, why, instead o' my taking him up he might take up me!'

'Now, I'm a king's man myself, and can give you authority enough for this,' said the formidable person in cinder grey. 'Now then, all of ye, be ready. Have ye any lanterns?'

'Yes; have ye any lanterns? I demand it,' said the constable.

'And the rest of you able-bodied – '

'Able-bodied men – yes – the rest of ye,' said the constable.

'Have you some good stout staves and pitchforks – '

'Staves and pitchforks – in the name o' the law. And take 'em in yer hands and go in quest, and do as we in authority tell ye.'

Thus aroused, the men prepared to give chase. The evidence was, indeed, though circumstantial, so convincing that but little argument was needed to show the shepherd's guests that, after what they had seen, it would look very much like connivance if they did not instantly pursue the unhappy third stranger, who could not as yet have gone more than a few hundred yards over such uneven country.

A shepherd is always well provided with lanterns; and, lighting these hastily, and with hurdle-staves in their hands, they poured out of the door, taking a direction along the crest of the hill, away from the town, the rain having fortunately a little abated.

Disturbed by the noise, or possibly by unpleasant dreams of her baptism, the child who had been christened began to cry heartbrokenly in the room overhead. These notes of grief came down through the chinks of the floor to the ears of the women below, who jumped up, one by one, and seemed glad of the excuse to ascend and comfort the baby; for the incidents of the last half-hour greatly oppressed them. Thus in the space of two or three minutes the room on the ground floor was deserted quite.

But it was not for long. Hardly had the sound of footsteps died away when a man returned round the corner of the house from the direction the pursuers had taken. Peeping in at the door, and seeing nobody there, he entered leisurely. It was the stranger of the chimney-corner, who had gone out with the rest. The motive of his return was shown by his helping himself to a cut piece of skimmer-cake that lay on a ledge beside where he had sat, and which he had apparently forgotten to take with him. He also poured out half a cup more mead from the quantity that remained, ravenously eating and drinking these as he stood. He had not finished when another figure came in just as quietly – the stranger in cinder grey.

'Oh, you here?' said the latter, smiling. 'I thought you had gone to help in the capture.' And this speaker also revealed the object of his return by looking solicitously round for the fascinating mug of old mead.

'And I thought you had gone,' said the other, continuing his skimmer-cake with some effort.

'Well, on second thoughts, I felt there were enough without me,' said the first, confidentially, 'and such a night as it is, too. Besides, 'tis the business o' the government to take care of its criminals, not mine.'

'True, so it is; and I felt as you did – there were enough without me.'

'I don't want to break my limbs running over the humps and hollows of this wild country.'

'Nor I, either, between you and me.'

'These shepherd people are used to it – simple-minded souls, you know, stirred up to anything in a moment. They'll have him ready for me before the morning, and no trouble to me at all.'

'They'll have him, and we shall have saved ourselves all labour in the matter.'

'True, true. Well, my way is to Casterbridge, and 'tis as much as my legs will do to take me that far. Going the same way?'

'No, I am sorry to say. I have to get home over there' (he nodded indefinitely to the right), 'and I feel as you do – that it is quite enough for my legs to do before bedtime.'

The other had by this time finished the mead in the mug, after which, shaking hands at the door and wishing each other well, they went their several ways.

In the meantime the company of pursuers had reached the end of the hog's-back elevation which dominated this part of the coomb. They had decided on no particular plan of action, and, finding that the man of the baleful trade was no longer in their company, they seemed quite unable to form any such plan now. They descended in all directions down the hill, and straightway several of the parties fell into the snare set by nature for all misguided midnight ramblers over the lower cretaceous formation. The 'lynchets', or flint slopes, which belted the escarpment at intervals of a dozen yards, took the less cautious ones unawares, and, losing their footing on the rubbly steep, they slid sharply downward, the lanterns rolling from their hands to the bottom, and there lying on their sides till the horn was scorched through.

When they had again gathered themselves together, the shepherd, as the man who knew the country best, took the lead, and guided them round these treacherous inclines. The lanterns, which seemed rather to dazzle their eyes and warn the fugitive than to assist them in the exploration, were extinguished, due silence was observed, and in this more rational order they plunged into the vale. It was a grassy, briery, moist channel, affording some shelter to any person who had sought it; but the party perambulated it in vain, and ascended on the other side. Here they wandered apart, and after an interval closed together again to report progress. At the second time of closing in they found themselves near a lonely oak, the single tree on this part of the upland, probably sown there by a passing bird some hundred years before; and here, standing a little to one side of the trunk, as motionless as the trunk itself, appeared the man they were in quest of, his outline being well defined against the sky beyond. The band noiselessly drew up and faced him.

'Your money or your life!' said the constable, sternly, to the still figure.

'No, no,' whispered John Pitcher. ' 'Tisn't our side ought to say that. That's the doctrine of vagabonds like him, and we be on the side of the law.'

'Well, well,' replied the constable, impatiently, 'I must say something, mustn't I? And if you had all the weight o' this undertaking upon your mind, perhaps you'd say the wrong thing too. Prisoner at the bar, surrender, in the name of the Fath – the crown, I mane!'

The man under the tree seemed now to notice them for the first time, and, giving them no opportunity whatever for exhibiting their courage, he strolled slowly towards them. He was, indeed, the little man, the third stranger, but his trepidation had in a great measure gone.

'Well, travellers,' he said, 'did I hear ye speak to me?'

'You did; you've got to come and be our prisoner at once,' said the constable. 'We arrest ye on the charge of not biding in Casterbridge gaol in a decent, proper manner, to be hung tomorrow morning. Neighbours, do your duty, and seize the culpet!'

On hearing the charge, the man seemed enlightened, and, saying not another word, resigned himself with preternatural civility to the search-party, who, with their staves in their hands, surrounded him on all sides, and marched him back towards the shepherd's cottage.

It was eleven o'clock by the time they arrived. The light shining from the open door, a sound of men's voices within, proclaimed to them, as they approached the house, that some new events had arisen in their absence. On entering they discovered the shepherd's living-room to be invaded by officers from Casterbridge gaol and a well-known magistrate who lived at the nearest country-seat, intelligence of the escape having become generally circulated.

'Gentlemen,' said the constable, 'I have brought back your man – not without risk and danger, but everyone must do his duty. He is inside this circle of able-bodied persons, who have lent me useful aid, considering their ignorance of crown work. Men, bring forward your prisoner.' And the third stranger was led to the light.

'Who is this?' said one of the officials.

'The man,' said the constable.

'Certainly not,' said the other turnkey, and the first corroborated his statement.

'But how can it be otherwise?' asked the constable. 'Or why was he so terrified at sight o' the singing instrument of the law?' Here he related the strange behaviour of the third stranger on entering the house.

'Can't understand it,' said the officer, coolly. All I know is that it is not the condemned man. He's quite a different character from this one; a gauntish fellow, with dark hair and eyes, rather good-looking, and with a musical bass voice that, if you heard it once, you'd never mistake as long as you lived.'

'Why, souls, 'twas the man in the chimney-corner!'

'Hey – what?' said the magistrate, coming forward after enquiring particulars from the shepherd in the background. 'Haven't you got the man, after all?'

'Well, sir,' said the constable, 'he's the man we were in search of, that's true; and yet he's not the man we were in search of. For the man we were in search of was not the man we wanted, sir, if you understand my every-day way; for 'twas the man in the chimney-corner.'

'A pretty kettle of fish altogether!' said the magistrate. 'You had better start for the other man at once.'

The prisoner now spoke for the first time. The mention of the man in the chimney-corner seemed to have moved him as nothing else could do. 'Sir,' he said, stepping forward to the magistrate, 'take no more trouble about me. The time is come when I may as well speak. I have done nothing; my crime is that the condemned man is my brother. Early this afternoon I left home at Anglebury to tramp it all the way to Casterbridge gaol to bid him farewell. I was benighted, and called here to rest and ask the way. When I opened the door I saw before me the very man, my brother, that I thought to see in the condemned cell at Casterbridge. He was in this chimney-corner; and, jammed close to him, so that he could not have got out if he had tried, was the executioner who'd come to take his life, singing a song about it, and not knowing that it was his victim who was close by, joining in to save appearances. My brother looked a glance of agony at me, and I knew he meant, "Don't reveal what you see; my life depends on it." I was so terror-struck that I could hardly stand, and, not knowing what I did, I turned and hurried away.'

The narrator's manner and tone had the stamp of truth, and his story made a great impression on all around.

'And do you know where your brother is at the present time?' asked the magistrate.

'I do not. I have never seen him since I closed this door.'

'I can testify to that, for we've been between ye ever since,' said the constable.

Where does he think to fly to? What is his occupation?'

'He's a watch- and clock-maker, sir.'

' 'A said 'a was a wheelwright – a wicked rogue,' said the constable.

'The wheels o' clocks and watches he meant, no doubt,' said Shepherd Fennel. 'I thought his hands were palish for's trade.'

'Well, it appears to me that nothing can be gained by retaining this poor man in custody,' said the magistrate; 'your business lies with the other unquestionably.'

And so the little man was released offhand; but he looked nothing the less sad on that account, it being beyond the power of magistrate or constable to rase out the written troubles in his brain, for they concerned another, whom he regarded with more solicitude than himself. When this was done, and the man had gone his way, the night was found to be so far advanced that it was deemed useless to renew the search before the next morning.

Next day, accordingly, the quest for the clever sheep-stealer became general and keen – to all appearance, at least. But the intended punishment was cruelly disproportioned to the transgression, and the sympathy of a great many country folk in that district was strongly on the side of the fugitive. Moreover, his marvellous coolness and daring under the unprecedented circumstances of the shepherd's party won their admiration. So that it may be questioned if all those who ostensibly made themselves so busy in exploring woods and fields and lanes were quite so thorough when it came to the private examination of their own lofts and outhouses. Stories were afloat of a mysterious figure being occasionally seen in some old overgrown trackway or other, remote from turnpike roads; but when a search was instituted in any of these suspected quarters nobody was found. Thus the days and weeks passed without tidings.

In brief, the bass-voiced man of the chimney-corner was never recaptured. Some said that he went across the sea, others that he did not, but buried himself in the depths of a populous city.

At any rate, the gentleman in cinder grey never did his morning's work at Casterbridge, nor met anywhere at all for business purposes the comrade with whom he had passed an hour of relaxation in the lonely house on the coomb.

The grass has long been green on the graves of Shepherd Fennel and his frugal wife; the guests who made up the christening-party have mainly followed their entertainers to the tomb; the baby in whose honour they all had met is a matron in the sear and yellow leaf; but the arrival of the three strangers at the shepherd's that night, and the details connected therewith, is a story as well known as ever in the country about Higher Crowstairs.

The Waiting Supper

I

Whoever had perceived the yeoman standing on Squire Everard's lawn in the dusk of that October evening fifty years ago might have said at first sight that he was loitering there from idle curiosity. For a large five-light window of the manor-house in front of him was unshuttered and uncurtained, so that the illuminated room within could be scanned almost to its four corners. Obviously nobody was ever expected to be in this part of the grounds after nightfall.

The apartment thus swept by an eye from without was occupied by two persons; they were sitting over dessert, the tablecloth having been removed in the old-fashioned way. The fruits were local, consisting of apples, pears, nuts, and such other products of the summer as might be presumed to grow on the estate. There was strong ale and rum on the table, and but little wine. Moreover, the appointments of the dining-room were simple and homely even for the date, betokening a countrified household of the smaller gentry, without much wealth or ambition – formerly a numerous class, but now in great part ousted by the territorial landlords.

One of the two sitters was a young lady in white muslin, who listened somewhat impatiently to the remarks of her companion, an elderly, rubicund personage, whom the merest stranger could have pronounced to be her father. The watcher evinced no signs of moving, and it became evident that affairs were not so simple as they first had seemed. The tall farmer was in fact no accidental spectator, and he stood by premeditation close to the trunk of a tree, so that had any traveller passed along the road without the park gate, or even round the lawn to the door, that person would scarce have noticed the other, notwithstanding that the gate was quite near at hand, and the park little larger than a paddock. There was still light enough in the western heaven to brighten faintly one side of the man's face, and to show against the trunk of the tree behind the admirable cut of his profile; also to reveal that the front of the manor-house, small though it seemed, was solidly built of stone in that never-to-be-surpassed style for the English country residence – the mullioned and transomed Elizabethan.

The lawn, although neglected, was still as level as a bowling-green – which indeed it might once have served for; and the blades of grass before the window were raked by the candle-shine, which stretched over them so far as to touch the yeoman's face in front.

Within the dining-room there were also, with one of the twain, the same signs of a hidden purpose that marked the farmer. The young lady's mind was straying as clearly into the shadows as that of the loiterer was fixed upon the room – nay, it could be said that she was quite conscious of his presence outside. Impatience caused her foot to beat silently on the carpet, and she more than once rose to leave the table. This proceeding was checked by her father, who would put his hand upon her shoulder and unceremoniously press her down into her chair till he should have concluded his observations. Her replies were brief enough, and there was factitiousness in her smiles of assent to his views. A small iron casement between two of the mullions was open, and some occasional words of the dialogue were audible without.

'As for drains – how can I put in drains? The pipes don't cost much, that's true; but the labour in sinking the trenches is ruination. And then the gates – they should be hung to stone posts, otherwise there's no keeping them up through harvest.' The squire's voice was strongly toned with the local accent, so that he said 'drains' and 'geats' like the rustics on his estate.

The landscape without grew darker, and the young man's figure seemed to be absorbed into the trunk of the tree. The small stars filled in between the larger, the nebulae between the small stars, the trees quite lost their voice; and if there was still a sound, it was from the cascade of a stream which stretched along under the trees that bounded the lawn on its northern side.

At last the young girl did get to her feet and secure her retreat. 'I have something to do, papa,' she said. 'I shall not be in the drawing-room just yet.'

'Very well,' replied he. 'Then I won't hurry.' And closing the door behind her, he drew his decanters together and settled down in his chair.

Three minutes after that a woman's shape emerged from the drawing-room window, and passing through a wall-door to the entrance front, came across the grass. She kept well clear of the dining-room window, but enough of its light fell on her to show, escaping from the dark-hooded cloak that she wore, stray verges of the same light dress which had figured but recently at the dinner-table. The hood was contracted tight about her face with a drawing-string, making her countenance small and baby-like, and lovelier even than before.

Without hesitation she brushed across the grass to the tree under which the young man stood concealed. The moment she had reached him he enclosed her form with his arm. The meeting and embrace, though by no means formal, were yet not passionate; the whole proceeding was that of persons who had repeated the act so often as to be unconscious of its performance. She turned within his arm, and faced in the same direction with himself, which was towards the window; and thus they stood without speaking, the back of her head leaning against his shoulder. For a while each seemed to be thinking his and her diverse thoughts.

'You have kept me waiting a long time, dear Christine,' he said at last. 'I wanted to speak to you particularly, or I should not have stayed. How came you to be dining at this time o' night?'

'Father has been out all day, and dinner was put back till six. I know I have kept you; but Nicholas, how can I help it sometimes, if I am not to run any risk? My poor father insists upon my listening to all he has to say; since my brother left he has had nobody else to listen to him; and tonight he was particularly tedious on his usual topics – draining, and tenant-farmers, and the village people. I must take daddy to London; he gets so narrow always staying here.'

'And what did you say to it all?'

'Well, I took the part of the tenant-farmers, of course, as the beloved of one should in duty do.' There followed a little break or gasp, implying a strangled sigh.

'You are sorry you have encouraged that beloving one?'

'Oh no, Nicholas . . . What is it you want to see me for particularly?'

'I know you are sorry, as time goes on, and everything is at a deadlock, with no prospect of change, and your rural swain loses his freshness! Only think, this secret understanding between us has lasted near three year, ever since you was a little over sixteen.'

'Yes; it has been a long time.'

'And I an untamed, uncultivated man, who has never seen London, and knows nothing about society at all.'

'Not uncultivated, dear Nicholas. Untravelled, socially unpractised, if you will,' she said, smiling. 'Well, I did sigh; but not because I regret being your promised one. What I do sometimes regret is that the scheme, which my meetings with you are but a part of, has not been carried out completely. You said, Nicholas, that if I consented to swear to keep faith with you, you would go away and travel, and see nations, and peoples, and cities, and take a professor with you, and study books and art, simultaneously with your study of men and manners; and then come back at the end of two years, when I should find that my father would by no means be indisposed to accept you as a son-in-law. You said your reason for wishing to get my promise before starting was that your mind would then be more at rest when you were far away, and so could give itself more completely to knowledge than if you went as my unaccepted lover only, fuming with anxiety as to how I should be when you came back. I saw how reasonable that was; and solemnly swore myself to you in consequence. But instead of going to see the world you stay on and on here to see me.'

'And you don't want me to see you?'

'Yes – no – it is not that. It is that I have latterly felt frightened at what I am doing when not in your actual presence. It seems so wicked not to tell my father that I have a lover close at hand, within touch and view of both of us; whereas if you were absent my conduct would not seem quite so treacherous.

The realities would not stare at one so. You would be a pleasant dream to me, which I should be free to indulge in without reproach of my conscience; I should live in hopeful expectation of your returning fully qualified to claim me boldly of my father. There, I have been terribly frank, I know.'

He in his turn had lapsed into gloomy breathings now. 'I did plan it as you state,' he answered. 'I did mean to go away the moment I had your promise. But, dear Christine, I did not foresee two or three things. I did not know what a lot of pain it would cost to tear myself from you. And I did not know that my stingy uncle – heaven forgive me for calling him so! – would so flatly refuse to advance me money for my purpose – the scheme of travelling with a first-rate tutor costing a formidable sum o' money. You have no idea what it would cost!'

'But I have said that I'll find the money.'

'Ah, there,' he returned, 'you have hit a sore place. To speak truly, dear, I would rather stay unpolished a hundred years than take your money.'

'But why? Men continually use the money of the women they marry.'

'Yes; but not till afterwards. No man would like to touch your money at present, and I should feel very mean if I were to do so in present circumstances. That brings me to what I was going to propose. But no – upon the whole I will not propose it now.'

'Ah! I would guarantee expenses, and you won't let me! The money is my personal possession: it comes to me from my late grandfather, and not from my father at all.'

He laughed forcedly and pressed her hand. 'There are more reasons why I cannot tear myself away,' he added. 'What would become of my uncle's farming? Six hundred acres in this parish, and five hundred in the next – a constant traipsing from one farm to the other; he can't be in two places at once. Still, that might be got over if it were not for the other matters. Besides, dear, I still should be a little uneasy, even though I have your promise, lest somebody should snap you up away from me.'

'Ah, you should have thought of that before. Otherwise I have committed myself for nothing.'

'I should have thought of it,' he answered gravely. 'But I did not. There lies my fault, I admit it freely. Ah, if you would only commit yourself a little more, I might at least get over that difficulty! But I won't ask you. You have no idea how much you are to me still; you could not argue so coolly if you had. What property belongs to you I hate the very sound of; it is you I care for. I wish you hadn't a farthing in the world but what I could earn for you!'

'I don't altogether wish that,' she murmured.

'I wish it, because it would have made what I was going to propose much easier to do than it is now. Indeed I will not propose it, although I came on purpose, after what you have said in your frankness.'

'Nonsense, Nic. Come, tell me. How can you be so touchy?'

'Look at this then, Christine dear.' He drew from his breast-pocket a sheet of paper and unfolded it, when it was observable that a seal dangled from the bottom.

'What is it?' She held the paper sideways, so that what there was of window-light fell on its surface. 'I can only read the Old English letters – why – our names! Surely it is not a marriage-licence?'

'It is.'

She trembled. 'Oh Nic! how could you do this – and without telling me!'

'Why should I have thought I must tell you? You had not spoken "frankly" then as you have now. We have been all to each other more than these two years, and I thought I would propose that we marry privately, and that I then leave you on the instant. I would have taken my travelling-bag to church, and you would have gone home alone. I should not have started on my adventures in the brilliant manner of our original plan, but should have roughed it a little at first; my great gain would have been that the absolute possession of you would have enabled me to work with spirit and purpose, such as nothing else could do. But I dare not ask you now – so frank as you have been.'

She did not answer. The document he had produced gave such unexpected substantiality to the venture with which she had so long toyed as a vague dream merely, that she was, in truth, frightened a little. 'I – don't know about it!' she said.

'Perhaps not. Ah, my little lady, you are wearying of me!'

'No, Nic,' responded she, creeping closer. 'I am not. Upon my word, and truth, and honour, I am not, Nic.'

'A mere tiller of the soil, as I should be called,' he continued, without heeding her. 'And you – well, a daughter of one of the – I won't say oldest families, because that's absurd, all families are the same age – one of the longest chronicled families about here, whose name is actually the name of the place.'

'That's not much, I am sorry to say! My poor brother – but I won't speak of that . . . Well,' she murmured mischievously, after a pause, 'you certainly would not need to be uneasy if I were to do this that you want me to do. You would have me safe enough in your trap then; I couldn't get away!'

'That's just it!' he said vehemently. 'It is a trap – you feel it so, and that though you wouldn't be able to get away from me you might particularly wish to! Ah, if I had asked you two years ago you would have agreed instantly. But I thought I was bound to wait for the proposal to come from you as the superior!'

'Now you are angry, and take seriously what I meant purely in fun. You don't know me even yet! To show you that you have not been mistaken in me, I do propose to carry out this licence. I'll marry you, dear Nicholas, tomorrow morning.'

'Ah, Christine! I am afraid I have stung you on to this, so that I cannot –'

'No, no, no!' she hastily rejoined; and there was something in her tone which suggested that she had been put upon her mettle and would not flinch. 'Take me whilst I am in the humour. What church is the licence for?'

'That I've not looked to see – why our parish church here, of course. Ah, then we cannot use it! We dare not be married here.'

'We do dare,' said she. 'And we will too, if you'll be there.'

'If I'll be there!'

They speedily came to an agreement that he should be in the church-porch at ten minutes to eight on the following morning, awaiting her; and that, immediately after the conclusion of the service which would make them one, Nicholas should set out on his long-deferred educational tour, towards the cost of which she was resolving to bring a substantial sub-scription with her to church. Then, slipping from him, she went indoors by the way she had come, and Nicholas bent his steps homewards.

2

Instead of leaving the spot by the gate, he flung himself over the fence, and pursued a direction towards the river under the trees. And it was now, in his lonely progress, that he showed for the first time outwardly that he was not altogether unworthy of her. He wore long water-boots reaching above his knees, and, instead of making a circuit to find a bridge by which he might cross the Froom – the river aforesaid – he made straight for the point whence proceeded the low roar that was at this hour the only evidence of the stream's existence. He speedily stood on the verge of the waterfall which caused the noise, and stepping into the water at the top of the fall, waded through with the sure tread of one who knew every inch of his footing, even though the canopy of trees rendered the darkness almost absolute, and a false step would have precipitated him into the pool beneath. Soon reaching the boundary of the grounds, he continued in the same direct line to traverse the alluvial valley, full of brooks and tributaries to the main stream – in former times quite impassable, and impassable in winter now. Sometimes he would cross a deep gully on a plank not wider than the hand; at another time he ploughed his way through beds of spear-grass, where at a few feet to the right or left he might have been sucked down into a morass. At last he reached firm land on the other side of this watery tract, and came to his house on the rise behind – Elsenford – an ordinary farmstead, from the back of which rose indistinct breathings, belchings and snortings, the rattle of halters, and other familiar features of an agriculturist's home.

While Nicholas Long was packing his bag in an upper room of this dwelling, Miss Christine Everard sat at a desk in her own chamber at Froom-Everard manor-house, looking with pale fixed countenance at the candles.

'I ought – I must now!' she whispered to herself. 'I should not have begun it if I had not meant to carry it through! It runs in the blood of us, I suppose.' She alluded to a fact unknown to her lover, the clandestine marriage of an aunt under circumstances somewhat similar to the present. In a few minutes she had penned the following note:

October 13, 183 —

DEAR MR BEALAND – Can you make it convenient to yourself to meet me at the church tomorrow morning at eight? I name the early hour because it would suit me better than later on in the day. You will find me in the chancel, if you can come. An answer yes or no by the bearer of this will be sufficient.

CHRISTINE EVERARD

She sent the note to the rector immediately, waiting at a small side-door of the house till she heard the servant's footsteps returning along the lane, when she went round and met him in the passage. The rector had taken the trouble to write a line, and answered that he would meet her with pleasure.

A dripping fog which ushered in the next morning was highly favourable to the scheme of the pair. At that time of the century Froom–Everard House had not been altered and enlarged; the public lane passed close under its walls; and there was a door opening directly from one of the old parlours – the south parlour, as it was called – into the lane which led to the village. Christine came out this way, and after following the lane for a short distance entered upon a path within a belt of plantation, by which the church could be reached privately. She even avoided the churchyard gate, walking along to a place where the turf without the low wall rose into a mound, enabling her to mount upon the coping and spring down inside. She crossed the wet graves, and so glided round to the door. He was there, with his bag in his hand. He kissed her with a sort of surprise, as if he had expected that at the last moment her heart would fail her.

Though it had not failed her, there was, nevertheless, no great ardour in Christine's bearing – merely the momentum of an antecedent impulse. They went up the aisle together, the bottle-green glass of the old lead quarries admitting but little light at that hour, and under such an atmosphere. They stood by the altar-rail in silence, Christine's skirt visibly quivering at each beat of her heart.

Presently a quick step ground upon the gravel, and Mr Bealand came round by the front. He was a quiet bachelor, courteous towards Christine, and not at first recognising in Nicholas a neighbouring yeoman (for he lived aloofly in the next parish), advanced to her without revealing any surprise at her unusual request. But in truth he was surprised, the keen interest taken by many country young women at the present day in church decoration and festivals being then unknown.

'Good morning,' he said; and repeated the same words to Nicholas more mechanically.

'Good morning,' she replied gravely. 'Mr Bealand, I have a serious reason for asking you to meet me – us, I may say. We wish you to marry us.'

The rector's gaze hardened to fixity, rather between than upon either of them, and he neither moved nor replied for some time.

'Ah!' he said at last.

'And we are quite ready.'

'I had no idea – '

'It has been kept rather private,' she said calmly.

'Where are your witnesses?'

'They are outside in the meadow, sir. I can call them in a moment,' said Nicholas.

'Oh – I see it is – Mr Nicholas Long,' said Mr Bealand, and turning again to Christine, 'Does your father know of this?'

'Is it necessary that I should answer that question, Mr Bealand?'

'I am afraid it is – highly necessary.'

Christine began to look concerned.

'Where is the licence?' the rector asked; 'since there have been no banns.'

Nicholas produced it, Mr Bealand read it, an operation which occupied him several minutes – or at least he made it appear so; till Christine said impatiently, 'We are quite ready, Mr Bealand. Will you proceed? Mr Long has to take a journey of a great many miles today.'

'And you?'

'No. I remain.'

Mr Bealand assumed firmness. 'There is something wrong in this,' he said. 'I cannot marry you without your father's presence.'

'But have you a right to refuse us?' interposed Nicholas. 'I believe we are in a position to demand your fulfilment of our request.'

'No, you are not! Is Miss Everard of age? I think not. I think she is months from being so. Eh, Miss Everard?'

'Am I bound to tell that?'

'Certainly. At any rate you are bound to write it. Meanwhile I refuse to solemnise the service. And let me entreat you two young people to do nothing so rash as this, even if by going to some strange church, you may do so without discovery. The tragedy of marriage – '

'Tragedy?'

'Certainly. It is full of crises and catastrophes, and ends with the death of one of the actors. The tragedy of marriage, as I was saying, is one I shall not be a party to your beginning with such light hearts, and I shall feel bound to put your father on his guard, Miss Everard. Think better of it, I entreat you! Remember the proverb, "Marry in haste and repent at leisure."'

Christine, spurred by opposition, almost stormed at him. Nicholas implored; but nothing would turn that obstinate rector. She sat down and reflected. By and by she confronted Mr Bealand.

'Our marriage is not to be this morning, I see,' she said. 'Now grant me one favour, and in return I'll promise you to do nothing rashly. Do not tell my father a word of what has happened here.'

'I agree – if you undertake not to elope.'

She looked at Nicholas, and he looked at her. 'Do you wish me to elope, Nic?' she asked.

'No,' he said.

So the compact was made, and they left the church singly, Nicholas remaining till the last, and closing the door. On his way home, carrying the well-packed bag which was just now to go no farther, the two men who were mending water-carriers in the meadows approached the hedge, as if they had been on the alert all the time.

'You said you mid want us for zummat, sir?'

'All right – never mind,' he answered through the hedge. 'I did not require you after all.'

3

At a manor not far away there lived a queer and primitive couple who had lately been blessed with a son and heir. The christening took place during the week under notice, and this was followed by a feast for the parishioners. Christine's father, one of the same generation and kind, had been asked to drive over and assist in the entertainment, and Christine, as a matter of course, accompanied him.

When they reached Athelhall, as the house was called, they found the usually quiet nook a lively spectacle. Tables had been spread in the apartment which lent its name to the whole building – the hall proper, which was covered with a fine open-timbered roof, whose braces, purlins, and rafters made a brown thicket of oak overhead. Here tenantry of all ages sat with their wives and families, and the servants were assisted in their ministrations by the sons and daughters of the owner's friends and neighbours. Christine lent a hand among the rest.

She was holding a plate in each hand towards a huge brown platter of baked rice-pudding, from which a footman was scooping a large spoonful, when a voice reached her ear over her shoulder: 'Allow me to hold them for you.'

Christine turned, and recognised in the speaker the nephew of the entertainer, a young man from London, whom she had already met on two or three occasions.

She accepted the proffered help, and from that moment, whenever he passed her in their marchings to and fro during the remainder of the serving, he smiled acquaintance. When their work was done, he improved the few words into a conversation. He plainly had been attracted by her fairness.

Bellston was a self-assured young man, not particularly good-looking, with more colour in his skin than even Nicholas had. He had flushed a little in attracting her notice, though the flush had nothing of nervousness in it – the air with which it was accompanied making it curiously suggestive of a flush of anger; and even when he laughed it was difficult to banish that fancy.

The late autumn sunlight streamed in through the window panes upon the heads and shoulders of the venerable patriarchs of the hamlet, and upon the middle-aged, and upon the young; upon men and women who had played out, or were to play, tragedies or tragi-comedies in that nook of civilisation not less great, essentially, than those which, enacted on more central arenas, fix the attention of the world. One of the party was a cousin of Nicholas Long's, who sat with her husband and children.

To make himself as locally harmonious as possible, Mr Bellston remarked to his companion on the scene – 'It does one's heart good,' he said, 'to see these simple peasants enjoying themselves.'

'Oh Mr Bellston!' exclaimed Christine; 'don't be too sure about that word "simple"! You little think what they see and meditate! Their reasonings and emotions are as complicated as ours.'

She spoke with a vehemence which would have been hardly present in her words but for her own relation to Nicholas. The sense of that produced in her a nameless depression thenceforward. The young man, however, still followed her up.

'I am glad to hear you say it,' he returned warmly. 'I was merely attuning myself to your mood, as I thought. The real truth is that I know more of the Parthians, and Medes, and dwellers in Mesopotamia – almost of any people, indeed – than of the English rustics. Travel and exploration are my profession, not the study of the British peasantry.'

Travel. There was sufficient coincidence between his declaration and the course she had urged upon her lover, to lend Bellston's account of himself a certain interest in Christine's ears. He might perhaps be able to tell her something that would be useful to Nicholas, if their dream were carried out. A door opened from the hall into the garden, and she somehow found herself outside, chatting with Mr Bellston on this topic, till she thought that upon the whole she liked the young man. The garden being his uncle's, he took her round it with an air of proprietorship; and they went on amongst the Michaelmas daisies and chrysanthemums, and through a door to the fruit-garden. A greenhouse was open, and he went in and cut her a bunch of grapes.

'How daring of you! They are your uncle's.'

'Oh, he don't mind – I do anything here. A rough old buffer, isn't he?'

She was thinking of her Nic, and felt that, by comparison with her present acquaintance, the farmer more than held his own as a fine and intelligent fellow; but the harmony with her own existence in little things, which she found here, imparted an alien tinge to Nicholas just now. The latter, idealised by moonlight, or a thousand miles of distance, was altogether a more romantic object for a woman's dream than this smart new-lacquered man; but in the sun of afternoon, and amid a surrounding company, Mr Bellston was a very tolerable companion.

When they re-entered the hall, Bellston entreated her to come with him up a spiral stair, in the thickness of the wall, leading to a passage and gallery whence they could look down upon the scene below. The people had finished their feast, the newly-christened baby had been exhibited, and a few words having been spoken to them they began, amid a racketing of forms, to make for the greensward without, Nicholas's cousin and cousin's husband and cousin's children among the rest. While they were filing out, a voice was heard calling – 'Hallo! – here, Jim; where are you?' said Bellston's uncle. The young man descended, Christine following at leisure.

'Now will ye be a good fellow,' the squire continued, 'and set them going outside in some dance or other that they know? I'm dog-tired, and I want to have a yew words with Mr Everard before we join 'em – hey, Everard? They are shy till somebody starts 'em; afterwards they'll keep gwine brisk enough.'

'Ay, that they wool,' said Squire Everard.

They followed to the lawn; and here it proved that James Bellston was as shy, or rather as averse, as any of the tenantry themselves to acting the part of fugleman. Only the parish people had been at the feast, but outlying neighbours had now strolled in for a dance.

'They want "Speed the Plough",' said Bellston, coming up breathless. 'It must be a country dance, I suppose? Now, Miss Everard, do have pity upon me. I am supposed to lead off; but really I know no more about speeding the plough than a child just born! Would you take one of the villagers? – just to start them, my uncle says. Suppose you take that handsome young farmer over there – I don't know his name, but I dare say you do – and I'll come on with one of the dairyman's daughters as a second couple.'

Christine turned in the direction signified, and changed colour – though in the shade nobody noticed it, 'Oh, yes – I know him,' she said coolly. 'He is from near our own place – Mr Nicholas Long.'

'That's capital – then you can easily make him stand as first couple with you. Now I must pick up mine.'

'I – I think I'll dance with you, Mr Bellston,' she said with some trepidation. 'Because, you see,' she explained eagerly, 'I know the figure and you don't – so that I can help you; while Nicholas Long, I know, is familiar with the figure, and that will make two couples who know it – which is necessary, at least.'

Bellston showed his gratification by one of his angry-pleasant flushes – he had hardly dared to ask for what she proffered freely; and having requested

Nicholas to take the dairyman's daughter, led Christine to her place, Long promptly stepping up second with his charge. There were grim silent depths in Nic's character; a small deedy spark in his eye, as it caught Christine's, was all that showed his consciousness of her. Then the fiddlers began – the celebrated Mellstock fiddlers who, given free stripping, could play from sunset to dawn without turning a hair. The couples wheeled and swung, Nicholas taking Christine's hand in the course of business with the figure, when she waited for him to give it a little squeeze; but he did not.

Christine had the greatest difficulty in steering her partner through the maze, on account of his self-will, and when at last they reached the bottom of the long line, she was breathless with her hard labour. Resting here, she watched Nic and his lady; and, though she had decidedly cooled off in these later months, began to admire him anew. Nobody knew these dances like him, after all, or could do anything of this sort so well. His performance with the dairyman's daughter so won upon her that when 'Speed the Plough' was over she contrived to speak to him.

'Nic, you are to dance with me next time.'

He said he would, and presently asked her in a formal public manner, lifting his hat gallantly. She showed a little backwardness, which he quite understood, and allowed him to lead her to the top, a row of enormous length appearing below them as if by magic as soon as they had taken their places. Truly the squire was right when he said that they only wanted starting.

'What is it to be?' whispered Nicholas.

She turned to the band. 'The Honeymoon,' she said.

And then they trod the delightful last-century measure of that name, which if it had been ever danced better, was never danced with more zest. The perfect responsiveness which their tender acquaintance threw into the motions of Nicholas and his partner lent to their gyrations the fine adjustment of two interacting parts of a single machine. The excitement of the movement carried Christine back to the time – the unreflecting, passionate time, about two years before – when she and Nic had been incipient lovers only; and it made her forget the carking anxieties, the vision of social breakers ahead, that had begun to take the gilding off her position now. Nicholas, on his part, had never ceased to be a lover; no personal worries had as yet made him conscious of any staleness, flatness or unprofitableness in his admiration of Christine.

'Not quite so wildly, Nic,' she whispered. 'I don't object personally; but they'll notice us. How came you here?'

'I heard that you had driven over; and I set out – on purpose for this.'

'What – you have walked?'

'Yes. If I had waited for one of uncle's horses I should have been too late.'

'Five miles here and five back – ten miles on foot – merely to dance!'

'With you. What made you think of this old "Honeymoon" thing?'

'O! it came into my head when I saw you, as what would have been a reality with us if you had not been stupid about that licence, and had got it for a distant church.'

'Shall we try again?'

'No – I don't know. I'll think it over.'

The villagers admired their grace and skill, as the dancers themselves perceived; but they did not know what accompanied that admiration in one spot, at least.

'People who wonder they can foot it so featly together should know what some others think,' a waterman was saying to his neighbour. 'Then their wonder would be less.'

His comrade asked for information.

'Well – really I hardly believe it – but 'tis said they be man and wife. Yes, sure – went to church and did the job a'most afore 'twas light one morning. But mind, not a word of this; for 'twould be the loss of a winter's work to me if I had spread such a report and it were not true.'

When the dance had ended she rejoined her own section of the company. Her father and Mr Bellston the elder had now come out from the house, and were smoking in the background. Presently she found that her father was at her elbow.

'Christine, don't dance too often with young Long – as a mere matter of prudence, I mean, as volk might think it odd, he being one of our own neighbouring farmers. I should not mention this to 'ee if he were an ordinary young fellow; but being superior to the rest it behoves you to be careful.'

'Exactly, papa,' said Christine.

But the revived sense that she was deceiving him threw a damp over her spirits. 'But, after all,' she said to herself, 'he is a young man of Elsenford, handsome, able, and the soul of honour; and I am a young woman of the adjoining parish, who have been constantly thrown into communication with him. Is it not, by nature's rule, the most proper thing in the world that I should marry him, and is it not an absurd conventional regulation which says that such a union would be wrong?'

It may be concluded that the strength of Christine's large-minded argument was rather an evidence of weakness than of strength in the passion it concerned, which had required neither argument nor reasoning of any kind for its maintenance when full and flush in its early days.

When driving home in the dark with her father she sank into pensive silence. She was thinking of Nicholas having to trudge on foot all those miles back after his exertions on the sward. Mr Everard, arousing himself from a nap, said suddenly, 'I have something to mention to 'ee, by George – so I have, Chris! You probably know what it is?'

She expressed ignorance, wondering if her father had discovered anything of her secret.

'Well, according to him you know it. But I will tell 'ee. Perhaps you noticed young Jim Bellston walking me off down the lawn with him? – whether or no, we walked together a good while; and he informed me that he wanted to pay his addresses to 'ee. I naturally said that it depended upon yourself; and he replied that you were willing enough; you had given him particular encouragement – showing your preference for him by specially choosing him for your partner – hey? "In that case," says I, "go on and conquer – settle it with her – I have no objection." The poor fellow was very grateful, and in short, there we left the matter. He'll propose tomorrow.'

She saw now to her dismay what James Bellston had read as encouragement. 'He has mistaken me altogether,' she said. 'I had no idea of such a thing.'

'What, you won't have him?'

'Indeed, I cannot!'

'Chrissy,' said Mr Everard with emphasis, 'there's noobody whom I should so like you to marry as that young man. He's a thoroughly clever fellow, and fairly well provided for. He's travelled all over the temperate zone; but he says that directly he marries he's going to give up all that, and be a regular stay-at-home. You would be nowhere safer than in his hands.'

'It is true,' she answered. 'He is a highly desirable match, and I should be well provided for, and probably very safe in his hands.'

'Then don't be skittish, and stand-to.'

She had spoken from her conscience and understanding, and not to please her father. As a reflecting woman she believed that such a marriage would be a wise one. In great things Nicholas was closest to her nature; in little things Bellston seemed immeasurably nearer than Nic; and life was made up of little things.

Altogether the firmament looked black for Nicholas Long, notwithstanding her half-hour's ardour for him when she saw him dancing with the dairyman's daughter. Most great passions, movements and beliefs – individual and national – burst during their decline into a temporary irradiation, which rivals their original splendour; and then they speedily become extinct. Perhaps the dance had given the last flare-up to Christine's love. It seemed to have improvidently consumed for its immediate purpose all her ardour forwards, so that for the future there was nothing left but frigidity.

Nicholas had certainly been very foolish about that licence!

4

This laxity of emotional tone was further increased by an incident, when, two days later, she kept an appointment with Nicholas in the Sallows. The Sallows was an extension of shrubberies and plantations along the banks of the Froom, accessible from the lawn of Froom-Everard House only, except by wading through the river at the waterfall or elsewhere. Near the brink was a thicket of box in which a trunk lay prostrate; this had been once or twice their trysting-place, though it was by no means a safe one; and it was here she sat awaiting him now.

The noise of the stream muffled any sound of footsteps, and it was before she was aware of his approach that she looked up and saw him wading across at the top of the waterfall.

Noontide lights and dwarfed shadows always banished the romantic aspect of her love for Nicholas. Moreover, something new had occurred to disturb her; and if ever she had regretted giving way to a tenderness for him – which perhaps she had not done with any distinctness – she regretted it now. Yet in the bottom of their hearts those two were excellently paired, the very twin halves of a perfect whole; and their love was pure. But at this hour surfaces showed garishly, and obscured the depths. Probably her regret appeared in her face.

He walked up to her without speaking, the water running from his boots; and, taking one of her hands in each of his own, looked narrowly into her eyes.

'Have you thought it over?'

'What?'

'Whether we shall try again; you remember saying you would at the dance?'

'Oh, I had forgotten that!'

'You are sorry we tried at all!' he said accusingly.

'I am not so sorry for the fact as for the rumours,' she said.

'Ah! rumours?'

'They say we are already married.'

'Who?'

'I cannot tell exactly. I heard some whispering to that effect. Somebody in the village told one of the servants, I believe. This man said that he was crossing the churchyard early on that unfortunate foggy morning, and heard voices in the chancel, and peeped through the window as well as the dim panes would let him; and there he saw you and me and Mr Bealand, and so on; but thinking his surmises would be dangerous knowledge, he hastened on. And so the story got afloat. Then your aunt, too – '

'Good Lord! – what has she done?'

The story was told her, and she said proudly, "O yes, it is true enough. I have seen the licence. But it is not to be known yet."'

'Seen the licence? How the – '

'Accidentally, I believe, when your coat was hanging somewhere.'

The information, coupled with the infelicitous word 'proudly', caused Nicholas to flush with mortification. He knew that it was in his aunt's nature to make a brag of that sort; but worse than the brag was the fact that this was the first occasion on which Christine had deigned to show her consciousness that such a marriage would be a source of pride to his relatives – the only two he had in the world.

'You are sorry, then, even to be thought my wife, much less to be it.' He dropped her hand, which fell lifelessly.

'It is not sorry exactly, dear Nic. But I feel uncomfortable and vexed that after screwing up my courage, my fidelity, to the point of going to church, you should have so muddled – managed the matter that it has ended in neither one thing nor the other. How can I meet acquaintances, when I don't know what they are thinking of me?'

'Then, dear Christine, let us mend the muddle. I'll go away for a few days and get another licence, and you can come to me.'

She shrank from this perceptibly. 'I cannot screw myself up to it a second time,' she said. 'I am sure I cannot! Besides, I promised Mr Bealand. And yet how can I continue to see you after such a rumour? We shall be watched now, for certain.'

'Then don't see me.'

'I fear I must not for the present. Altogether – '

'What?'

'I am very depressed.'

These views were not very inspiriting to Nicholas, as he construed them. It may indeed have been possible that he construed them wrongly, and should have insisted upon her making the rumour true. Unfortunately, too, he had come to her in a hurry through brambles and briars, water and weed, and the shaggy wildness which hung about his appearance at this fine and correct time of day lent an impracticability to the look of him.

'You blame me – you repent your courses – you repent that you ever, ever owned anything to me!'

'No, Nicholas, I do not repent that,' she returned gently, though with firmness. 'But I think that you ought not to have got that licence without asking me first; and I also think that you ought to have known how it would be if you lived on here in your present position, and made no effort to better it. I can bear whatever comes, for social ruin is not personal ruin or even personal disgrace. But as a sensible, new-risen poet says, whom I have been reading this morning:

> The world and its ways have a certain worth:
> And to press a point while these oppose
> Were simple policy. Better wait.

As soon as you had got my promise, Nic, you should have gone away – yes – and made a name, and come back to claim me. That was my silly girlish dream about my hero.'

'Perhaps I can do as much yet! And would you have indeed liked better to live away from me for family reasons, than to run a risk in seeing me for affection's sake? Oh what a cold heart it has grown! If I had been a prince, and you a dairymaid, I'd have stood by you in the face of the world!'

She shook her head. 'Ah – you don't know what society is – you don't know.'

'Perhaps not. Who was that strange gentleman of about seven-and-twenty I saw at Mr Bellston's christening feast?'

'Oh – that was his nephew James. Now he is a man who has seen an unusual extent of the world for his age. He is a great traveller, you know.'

'Indeed.'

'In fact an explorer. He is very entertaining.'

'No doubt.'

Nicholas received no shock of jealousy from her announcement. He knew her so well that he could see she was not in the least in love with Bellston. But he asked if Bellston were going to continue his explorations.

'Not if he settles in life. Otherwise he will, I suppose.'

'Perhaps I could be a great explorer, too, if I tried.'

'You could, I am sure.'

They sat apart, and not together; each looking afar off at vague objects, and not in each other's eyes. Thus the sad autumn afternoon waned, while the waterfall hissed sarcastically of the inevitableness of the unpleasant. Very different this from the time when they had first met there.

The nook was most picturesque; but it looked horridly common and stupid now. Their sentiment had set a colour hardly less visible than a material one on surrounding objects, as sentiment must where life is but thought. Nicholas was as devoted as ever to the fair Christine; but unhappily he too had moods and humours, and the division between them was not closed.

She had no sooner got indoors and sat down to her work-table than her father entered the drawing-room.

She handed him his newspaper; he took it without a word, went and stood on the hearthrug, and flung the paper on the floor.

'Christine, what's the meaning of this terrible story? I was just on my way to look at the register.'

She looked at him without speech.

'You have married – Nicholas Long?'

'No, father.'

'No? Can you say no in the face of such facts as I have been put in possession of?'

'Yes.'

'But – the note you wrote to the rector – and the going to church?'

She briefly explained that their attempt had failed.

'Ah! Then this is what that dancing meant, was it? By —, it makes me – How long has this been going on, may I ask?'

'This what?'

'What, indeed! Why, making him your beau. Now listen to me. All's well that ends well; from this day, madam, this moment, he is to be nothing more to you. You are not to see him. Cut him adrift instantly! I only wish his volk were on my farm – out they should go, or I would know the reason why. However, you are to write him a letter to this effect at once.'

'How can I cut him adrift?'

'Why not? You must, my good maid!'

'Well, though I have not actually married him, I have solemnly sworn to be his wife when he comes home from abroad to claim me. It would be gross perjury not to fulfil my promise. Besides, no woman can go to church with a man to deliberately solemnise matrimony, and refuse him afterwards, if he does nothing wrong meanwhile.'

The uttered sound of her strong conviction seemed to kindle in Christine a livelier perception of all its bearings than she had known while it had lain unformulated in her mind. For when she had done speaking she fell down on her knees before her father, covered her face, and said, 'Please, please forgive me, papa! How could I do it without letting you know! I don't know, I don't know!'

When she looked up she found that, in the turmoil of his mind, her father was moving about the room. 'You are within an ace of ruining yourself, ruining me, ruining us all!' he said. 'You are nearly as bad as your brother, begad!'

'Perhaps I am – yes – perhaps I am!'

'That I should father such a harum-scarum brood!'

'It is very bad; but Nicholas – '

'He's a scoundrel!'

'He is not a scoundrel!' cried she, turning quickly. 'He's as good and worthy as you or I, or anybody bearing our name, or any nobleman in the kingdom, if you come to that! Only – only' – she could not continue the argument on those lines. 'Now, father, listen!' she sobbed; 'if you taunt me, I'll go off and join him at his farm this very day, and marry him tomorrow, that's what I'll do!'

'I don't taant ye!'

'I wish to avoid unseemliness as much as you.'

She went away. When she came back a quarter of an hour later, thinking to find the room empty, he was standing there as before, never having apparently moved. His manner had quite changed. He seemed to take a resigned and entirely different view of circumstances.

'Christine, here's a paragraph in the paper hinting at a secret wedding, and I'm blazed if it don't point to you. Well, since this was to happen, I'll bear it, and not complain. All volk have crosses, and this is one of mine. Now, this is what I've got to say – I feel that you must carry out this attempt at marrying Nicholas Long. Faith, you must! The rumour will become a scandal if you don't – that's my view. I have tried to look at the brightest side of the case. Nicholas Long is a young man superior to most of his class, and fairly presentable. And he's not poor – at least his uncle is not. I believe the old muddler could buy me up any day. However, a farmer's wife you must be, as far as I can see. As you've made your bed, so ye must lie. Parents propose, and ungrateful children dispose. You shall marry him, and immediately.'

Christine hardly knew what to make of this. 'He is quite willing to wait, and so am I. We can wait for two or three years, and then he will be as worthy as – '

'You must marry him. And the sooner the better, if 'tis to be done at all . . . And yet I did wish you could have been Jim Bellston's wife. I did wish it! But no.'

'I, too, wished it and do still, in one sense,' she returned gently. His moderation had won her out of her defiant mood, and she was willing to reason with him.

'You do?' he said surprised.

'I see that in a worldly sense my conduct with Mr Long may be considered a mistake.'

'H'm – I am glad to hear that – after my death you may see it more clearly still; and you won't have long to wait, to my reckoning.'

She fell into bitter repentance, and kissed him in her anguish. 'Don't say that!' she cried. 'Tell me what to do?'

'If you'll leave me for an hour or two I'll think. Drive to the market and back – the carriage is at the door – and I'll try to collect my senses. Dinner can be put back till you return.'

In a few minutes she was dressed, and the carriage bore her up the hill which divided the village and manor from the market-town.

5

A quarter of an hour brought her into the High Street, and for want of a more important errand she called at the harness-maker's for a dog-collar that she required.

It happened to be market-day, and Nicholas, having postponed the engagements which called him thither to keep the appointment with her in the Sallows, rushed off at the end of the afternoon to attend to them as well as he could. Arriving thus in a great hurry on account of the lateness of the hour, he still retained the wild, amphibious appearance which had marked him when he came up from the meadows to her side – an exceptional condition of things which had scarcely ever before occurred. When she crossed the pavement from the shop door, the shopman bowing and escorting her to the carriage, Nicholas chanced to be standing at the road-waggon office, talking to the master of the waggons. There were a good many people about, and those near paused and looked at her transit, in the full stroke of the level October sun, which went under the brims of their hats, and pierced through their button-holes. From the group she heard murmured the words: 'Mrs Nicholas Long.'

The unexpected remark, not without distinct satire in its tone, took her so greatly by surprise that she was confounded. Nicholas was by this time nearer, though coming against the sun he had not yet perceived her. Influenced by her father's lecture, she felt angry with him for being there and causing this awkwardness. Her notice of him was therefore slight, supercilious perhaps, slurred over; and her vexation at his presence showed distinctly in her face as she sat down in her seat. Instead of catching his waiting eye, she positively turned her head away.

A moment after she was sorry she had treated him so; but he was gone.

Reaching home she found on her dressing-table a note from her father. The statement was brief:

I have considered and am of the same opinion. You must marry him. He can leave home at once and travel as proposed. I have written to him to this effect. I don't want any victuals, so don't wait dinner for me.

Nicholas was the wrong kind of man to be blind to his Christine's mortification, though he did not know its entire cause. He had lately fore-seen something of this sort as possible.

'It serves me right,' he thought, as he trotted homeward. 'It was absurd – wicked of me to lead her on so. The sacrifice would have been too great – too cruel!' And yet, though he thus took her part, he flushed with indignation every time he said to himself, 'She is ashamed of me!'

On the ridge which overlooked Froom-Everard he met a neighbour of his – a stock-dealer – in his gig, and they drew rein and exchanged a few words. A part of the dealer's conversation had much meaning for Nicholas.

'I've had occasion to call on Squire Everard,' the former said; 'but he couldn't see me on account of being quite knocked up at some bad news he has heard.'

Nicholas rode on past Froom-Everard to Elsenford Farm, pondering. He had new and startling matter for thought as soon as he got there. The squire's note had arrived. At first he could not credit its import; then he saw further, took in the tone of the letter, saw the writer's contempt behind the words, and understood that the letter was written as by a man hemmed into a corner. Christine was defiantly – insultingly – hurled at his head. He was accepted because he was so despised.

And yet with what respect he had treated her and hers! Now he was reminded of what an agricultural friend had said years ago, seeing the eyes of Nicholas fixed on Christine as on an angel when she passed: 'Better a little fire to warm 'ee than a great one to burn 'ee. No good can come of throwing your heart there.' He went into the mead, sat down, and asked himself four questions:

1 How could she live near her acquaintance as his wife, even in his absence, without suffering martyrdom from the stings of their contempt?
2 Would not this entail total estrangement between Christine and her family also, and her own consequent misery?
3 Must not such isolation extinguish her affection for him?
4 Supposing that her father rigged them out as colonists and sent them off to America, was not the effect of such exile upon one of her gentle nurture likely to be as the last?

In short, whatever they should embark in together would be cruelty to her, and his death would be a relief. It would, indeed, in one aspect be a relief to her now, if she were so ashamed of him as she had appeared to be that day. Were he dead, this little episode with him would fade away like a dream.

Mr Everard was a good-hearted man at bottom, but to take his enraged offer seriously was impossible. Obviously it was hotly made in his first bitterness at what he had heard. The least thing that he could do would be to go away and never trouble her more. To travel and learn and come back in two years, as mapped out in their first sanguine scheme, required a staunch heart on her side, if the necessary expenditure of time and money were to be afterwards justified; and it were folly to calculate on that when he had seen today that her heart was failing her already. To travel and disappear and not be heard of for many years would be a far more independent stroke, and it would leave her entirely unfettered. Perhaps he might rival in this kind the accomplished Mr Bellston, of whose journeyings he had heard so much.

He sat and sat, and the fog rose out of the river, enveloping him like a fleece; first his feet and knees, then his arms and body, and finally submerging his head. When he had come to a decision he went up again into the homestead. He would be independent, if he died for it, and he would free Christine. Exile was the only course. The first step was to inform his uncle of his determination.

Two days later Nicholas was on the same spot in the mead, at almost the same hour of eve. But there was no fog now; a blusterous autumn wind had ousted the still, golden days and misty nights; and he was going, full of purpose, in the opposite direction. When he had last entered the mead he was an inhabitant of the Froom valley; in forty-eight hours he had severed himself from that spot as completely as if he had never belonged to it. All that appertained to him in the Froom valley now was circumscribed by the portmanteau in his hand.

In making his preparations for departure he had unconsciously held a faint, foolish hope that she would communicate with him and make up their estrangement in some soft womanly way. But she had given no signal, and it was too evident to him that her latest mood had grown to be her fixed one, proving how well founded had been his impulse to set her free.

He entered the Sallows, found his way in the dark to the garden-door of the house, slipped under it a note to tell her of his departure, and explaining its true reason to be a consciousness of her growing feeling that he was an encumbrance and a humiliation. Of the direction of his journey and of the date of his return he said nothing.

His course now took him into the high road, which he pursued for some miles in a north-easterly direction, still spinning the thread of sad inferences, and asking himself why he should ever return. At daybreak he stood on the hill above Shottsford-Forum, and awaited a coach which passed about this time along that highway towards Melchester and London.

6

Some fifteen years after the date of the foregoing incidents, a man who had dwelt in far countries, and viewed many cities, arrived at Roy-Town, a roadside hamlet on the old western turnpike road, not five miles from Froom-Everard, and put up at the Buck's Head, an isolated inn at that spot. He was still barely of middle age, but it could be seen that a haze of grey was settling upon the locks of his hair, and that his face had lost colour and curve, as if by exposure to bleaching climates and strange atmospheres, or from ailments incidental thereto. He seemed to observe little around him, by reason of the intrusion of his musings upon the scene. In truth Nicholas Long was just now the creature of old hopes and fears consequent upon his arrival – this man who once had not cared if his name were blotted out from that district. The evening light showed wistful lines which he could not smooth away by the worldling's gloss of nonchalance that he had learnt to fling over his face.

The Buck's Head was a somewhat unusual place for a man of this sort to choose as a house of sojourn in preference to some Casterbridge inn four miles farther on. Before he left home it had been a lively old tavern at which High-flyers and Heralds and Tally-hoes had changed horses on their stages up and down the country; but now the house was rather cavernous and chilly, the stable-roofs were hollow-backed, the landlord was asthmatic, and the traffic gone.

He arrived in the afternoon, and when he had sent back the fly and was having a nondescript meal, he put a question to the waiting-maid with a mien of indifference.

'Squire Everard, of Froom-Everard Manor, has been dead some years, I believe?'

She replied in the affirmative.

'And are any of the family left there still?'

'Oh no, bless you, sir! They sold the place years ago – Squire Everard's son did – and went away. I've never heard where they went to. They came quite to nothing.'

'Never heard anything of the young lady – the squire's daughter?'

'No. You see 'twas before I came to these parts.'

When the waitress left the room, Nicholas pushed aside his plate and gazed out of the window. He was not going over into the Froom Valley altogether on Christine's account, but she had greatly animated his motive in coming that way. Anyhow he would push on there now that he was so near, and not ask questions here where he was liable to be wrongly informed. The fundamental enquiry he had not ventured to make – whether Christine had married before the family went away. He had abstained because of an absurd dread of extinguishing hopeful surmise. That the Everards had left their old home was bad enough intelligence for one day.

Rising from the table he put on his hat and went out, ascending towards the upland which divided this district from his native vale. The first familiar feature that met his eye was a little spot on the distant sky – a clump of trees standing on a barrow which surmounted a yet more remote upland – a point where, in his childhood, he had believed people could stand and see America. He reached the farther verge of the plateau on which he had entered. Ah, there was the valley – a greenish-grey stretch of colour – still looking placid and serene, as though it had not much missed him. If Christine was no longer there, why should he pause over it this evening? His uncle and aunt were dead, and tomorrow would be soon enough to enquire for remoter relatives. Thus, disinclined to go farther, he turned to retrace his way to the inn.

In the backward path he now perceived the figure of a woman, who had been walking at a distance behind him; and as she drew nearer he began to be startled. Surely, despite the variations introduced into that figure by changing years, its ground-lines were those of Christine?

Nicholas had been sentimental enough to write to Christine immediately on landing at Southampton a day or two before this, addressing his letter at a venture to the old house, and merely telling her that he planned to reach the Roy-Town inn on the present afternoon. The news of the scattering of the Everards had dissipated his hope of hearing of her; but here she was.

So they met – there, alone, on the open down by a pond, just as if the meeting had been carefully arranged.

She threw up her veil. She was still beautiful, though the years had touched her; a little more matronly – much more homely. Or was it only that he was much less homely now – a man of the world – the sense of homeliness being relative? Her face had grown to be pre-eminently of the sort that would be called interesting. Her habiliments were of a demure and sober cast, though she was one who had used to dress so airily and so gaily. Years had laid on a few shadows too in this.

'I received your letter,' she said, when the momentary embarrassment of their first approach had passed. 'And I thought I would walk across the hills today, as it was fine. I have just called at the inn, and they told me you were out. I was now on my way homeward.'

He hardly listened to this, though he intently gazed at her. 'Christine,' he said, 'one word. Are you free?'

'I – I am in a certain sense,' she replied, colouring.

The announcement had a magical effect. The intervening time between past and present closed up for him, and moved by an impulse which he had combated for fifteen years, he seized her two hands and drew her towards him.

She started back, and became almost a mere acquaintance. 'I have to tell you,' she gasped, 'that I have – been married.'

Nicholas's rose-coloured dream was immediately toned down to a greyish tinge.

'I did not marry till many years after you had left,' she continued in the humble tones of one confessing to a crime. 'Oh Nic,' she cried reproachfully, 'how could you stay away so long?'

'Whom did you marry?'

'Mr Bellston.'

'I – ought to have expected it.' He was going to add, 'And is he dead?' but he checked himself. Her dress unmistakably suggested widowhood; and she had said she was free.

'I must now hasten home,' said she. 'I felt that, considering my short-comings at our parting so many years ago, I owed you the initiative now.'

'There is some of your old generosity in that. I'll walk with you, if I may. Where are you living, Christine?'

'In the same house, but not on the old conditions. I have part of it on lease; the farmer now tenanting the premises found the whole more than he wanted, and the owner allowed me to keep what rooms I chose. I am poor now, you know, Nicholas, and almost friendless. My brother sold the Froom-Everard estate when it came to him, and the person who bought it turned our home into a farmhouse. Till my father's death my husband and I lived in the manor-house with him, so that I have never lived away from the spot.'

She was poor. That, and the change of name, sufficiently accounted for the inn-servant's ignorance of her continued existence within the walls of her old home.

It was growing dusk, and he still walked with her. A woman's head arose from the declivity before them, and as she drew nearer, Christine asked him to go back.

'This is the wife of the farmer who shares the house,' she said. 'She is accustomed to come out and meet me whenever I walk far and am benighted. I am obliged to walk everywhere now.'

The farmer's wife, seeing that Christine was not alone, paused in her advance, and Nicholas said, 'Dear Christine, if you are obliged to do these things, I am not, and what wealth I can command you may command likewise. They say rolling stones gather no moss; but they gather dross sometimes. I was one of the pioneers to the gold-fields, you know, and made a sufficient fortune there for my wants. What is more, I kept it. When I had done this I was coming home, but hearing of my uncle's death I changed my plan, travelled, speculated and increased my fortune. Now, before we part: you remember you stood with me at the altar once, and therefore I speak with less preparation than I should otherwise use. Before we part, then, I ask shall another again intrude between us? Or shall we complete the union we began?'

She trembled – just as she had done at that very minute of standing with him in the church, to which he had recalled her mind. 'I will not enter into that now, dear Nicholas,' she replied. 'There will be more to talk of and consider first – more to explain, which it would have spoiled this meeting to have entered into now.'

'Yes, yes; but – '

'Further than the brief answer I first gave, Nic, don't press me tonight. I still have the old affection for you, or I should not have sought you. Let that suffice for the moment.'

'Very well, dear one. And when shall I call to see you?'

'I will write and fix an hour. I will tell you everything of my history then.'

And thus they parted, Nicholas feeling that he had not come here fruitlessly. When she and her companion were out of sight he retraced his steps to Roy-Town, where he made himself as comfortable as he could in the deserted old inn of his boyhood's days. He missed her companionship this evening more than he had done at any time during the whole fifteen years; and it was as though instead of separation there had been constant communion with her throughout that period. The tones of her voice had stirred his heart in a nook which had lain stagnant ever since he last heard them. They recalled the woman to whom he had once lifted his eyes as to a goddess. Her announcement that she had been another's came as a little shock to him, and he did not now lift his eyes to her in precisely the same way as he had lifted them at first. But he forgave her for marrying Bellston; what could he expect after fifteen years?

He slept at Roy-Town that night, and in the morning there was a short note from her, repeating more emphatically her statement of the previous evening – that she wished to inform him clearly of her circumstances, and to calmly consider with him the position in which she was placed. Would he call upon her on Sunday afternoon, when she was sure to be alone?

'Nic,' she wrote on, 'what a cosmopolite you are! I expected to find my old yeoman still; but I was quite awed in the presence of such a citizen of the world. Did I seem rusty and unpractised? Ah – you seemed so once to me!'

Tender playful words; the old Christine was in them. She said Sunday afternoon, and it was now only Saturday morning. He wished she had said today; that short revival of her image had vitalised to sudden heat feelings that had almost been stilled. Whatever she might have to explain as to her position – and it was awkwardly narrowed, no doubt – he could not give her up. Miss Everard or Mrs Bellston, what mattered it? – she was the same Christine.

He did not go outside the inn all Saturday. He had no wish to see or do anything but to await the coming interview. So he smoked, and read the local newspaper of the previous week, and stowed himself in the chimney-corner. In the evening he felt that he could remain indoors no longer, and the moon being near the full, he started from the inn on foot in the same direction as that of yesterday, with the view of contemplating the old village and its precincts, and hovering round her house under the cloak of night.

With a stout stick in his hand he climbed over the five miles of upland in a comparatively short space of time. Nicholas had seen many strange lands and trodden many strange ways since he last walked that path, but as he trudged he seemed wonderfully like his old self, and had not the slightest difficulty in finding the way. In descending to the meads the streams perplexed him a little, some of the old footbridges having been removed; but he ultimately got across the larger water-courses, and pushed on to the village, avoiding her residence for the moment, lest she should encounter him, and think he had not respected the time of her appointment.

He found his way to the churchyard, and first ascertained where lay the two relations he had left alive at his departure; then he observed the grave-stones of other inhabitants with whom he had been well acquainted, till by degrees he seemed to be in the society of all the elder Froom-Everard population, as he had known the place. Side by side as they had lived in his day here were they now. They had moved house in mass.

But no tomb of Mr Bellston was visible, though, as he had lived at the manor-house, it would have been natural to find it here. In truth Nicholas was more anxious to discover that than anything, being curious to know how long he had been dead. Seeing from the glimmer of a light in the church that somebody was there cleaning for Sunday he entered, and looked round upon the walls as well as he could. But there was no monument to her husband, though one had been erected to the squire.

Nicholas addressed the young man who was sweeping. 'I don't see any monument or tomb to the late Mr Bellston?'

'Oh no, sir; you won't see that,' said the young man drily.

'Why, pray?'

'Because he's not buried here. He's not Christian-buried anywhere, as far as we know. In short, perhaps he's not buried at all; and between ourselves, perhaps he's alive.'

Nicholas sank an inch shorter. 'Ah,' he answered.

'Then you don't know the peculiar circumstances, sir?'

'I am a stranger here – as to late years.'

'Mr Bellston was a traveller – an explorer – it was his calling; you may have heard his name as such?'

'I remember.' Nicholas recalled the fact that this very bent of Mr Bellston's was the incentive to his own roaming.

'Well, when he married he came and lived here with his wife and his wife's father, and said he would travel no more. But after a time he got weary of biding quiet here, and weary of her – he was not a good husband to the young lady by any means – and he betook himself again to his old trick of roving – with her money. Away he went, quite out of the realm of human foot, into the bowels of Asia, and never was heard of more. He was murdered, it is said, but nobody knows; though as that was nine years ago he's dead enough in principle, if not in corporation. His widow lives quite humble, for between her husband and her brother she's left in very lean pasturage.'

Nicholas went back to the Buck's Head without hovering round her dwelling. This then was the explanation which she had wanted to make. Not dead, but missing. How could he have expected that the first fair promise of happiness held out to him would remain untarnished? She had said that she was free; and legally she was free, no doubt. Moreover, from her tone and manner he felt himself justified in concluding that she would be willing to run the risk of a union with him, in the improbability of her husband's existence. Even if that husband lived, his return was not a likely event, to judge from his character. A man who could spend her money on his own personal adventures would not be anxious to disturb her poverty after such a lapse of time.

Well, the prospect was not so unclouded as it had seemed. But could he, even now, give up Christine?

7

Two months more brought the year nearly to a close, and found Nicholas Long tenant of a spacious house in the market-town nearest to Froom-Everard. A man of means, genial character, and a bachelor, he was an object of great interest to his neighbours, and to his neighbours' wives and daughters. But he took little note of this, and had made it his business to go twice a week, no matter what the weather, to the now farmhouse at Froom-Everard, a wing of which had been retained as the refuge of Christine. He always walked, to give no trouble in putting up a horse to a housekeeper whose staff was limited.

The two had put their heads together on the situation, had gone to a solicitor, had balanced possibilities, and had resolved to make the plunge of matrimony. 'Nothing venture, nothing have,' Christine had said, with some of her old audacity.

With almost gratuitous honesty they had let their intentions be widely known. Christine, it is true, had rather shrunk from publicity at first; but Nicholas argued that their boldness in this respect would have good results. With his friends he held that there was not the slightest probability of her being other than a widow, and a challenge to the missing man now, followed by no response, would stultify any unpleasant remarks which might be thrown at her after their union. To this end a paragraph was inserted in the Wessex papers, announcing that their marriage was proposed to be celebrated on such and such a day in December.

His periodic walks along the south side of the valley to visit her were among the happiest experiences of his life. The yellow leaves falling around him in the foreground, the well-watered meads on the left hand, and the woman he loved awaiting him at the back of the scene, promised a future of much serenity, as far as human judgement could foresee. On arriving, he would sit with her in the 'parlour' of the wing she retained, her general sitting-room, where the only relics of her early surroundings were an old clock from the other end of the house, and her own piano. Before it was quite dark they would stand, hand in hand, looking out of the window across the flat turf to the dark clump of trees which hid further view from their eyes.

'Do you wish you were still mistress here, dear?' he once said.

'Not at all,' said she cheerfully. 'I have a good enough room, and a good enough fire, and a good enough friend. Besides, my latter days as mistress of the house were not happy ones, and they spoilt the place for me. It was a punishment for my faithlessness. Nic, you do forgive me? Really you do?'

The twenty-third of December, the eve of the wedding-day, had arrived at last in the train of such uneventful ones as these. Nicholas had arranged to visit her that day a little later than usual, and see that everything was ready with her for the morrow's event and her removal to his house; for he had begun to look after her domestic affairs, and to lighten as much as possible the duties of her housekeeping.

He was to come to an early supper, which she had arranged to take the place of a wedding-breakfast next day – the latter not being feasible in her present situation. An hour or so after dark the wife of the farmer who lived in the other part of the house entered Christine's parlour to lay the cloth.

'What with getting the ham skinned, and the black-puddings hotted up,' she said, 'it will take me all my time before he's here, if I begin this minute.'

'I'll lay the table myself,' said Christine, jumping up. 'Do you attend to the cooking.'

'Thank you, ma'am. And perhaps 'tis no matter, seeing that it is the last night you'll have to do such work. I knew this sort of life wouldn't last long for 'ee, being born to better things.'

'It has lasted rather long, Mrs Wake. And if he had not found me out it would have lasted all my days.'

'But he did find you out.'

'He did. And I'll lay the cloth immediately.'

Mrs Wake went back to the kitchen, and Christine began to bustle about. She greatly enjoyed preparing this table for Nicholas and herself with her own hands. She took artistic pleasure in adjusting each article to its position, as if half an inch error were a point of high importance. Finally she placed the two candles where they were to stand, and sat down by the fire.

Mrs Wake re-entered and regarded the effect. 'Why not have another candle or two, ma'am?' she said. ' 'Twould make it livelier. Say four.'

'Very well,' said Christine, and four candles were lighted. 'Really,' she added, surveying them, 'I have been now so long accustomed to little economies that they look quite extravagant.'

'Ah, you'll soon think nothing of forty in his grand new house! Shall I bring in supper directly he comes, ma'am?'

'No, not for half an hour; and, Mrs Wake, you and Betsy are busy in the kitchen, I know; so when he knocks don't disturb yourselves; I can let him in.'

She was again left alone, and, as it still wanted some time to Nicholas's appointment, she stood by the fire, looking at herself in the glass over the mantel. Reflectively raising a lock of her hair just above her temple she uncovered a small scar. That scar had a history. The terrible temper of her late husband – those sudden moods of irascibility which had made even his friendly excitements look like anger – had once caused him to set that mark upon her with the bezel of a ring he wore. He declared that the whole thing was an accident. She was a woman, and kept her own opinion.

Christine then turned her back to the glass and scanned the table and the candles, shining one at each corner like types of the four Evangelists, and thought they looked too assuming – too confident. She glanced up at the clock, which stood also in this room, there not being space enough for it in the passage. It was nearly seven, and she expected Nicholas at half-past. She liked the company of this venerable article in her lonely life: its tickings and whizzings were a sort of conversation. It now began to strike the hour. At the end something grated slightly. Then, without any warning, the clock slowly inclined forward and fell at full length upon the floor.

The crash brought the farmer's wife rushing into the room. Christine had well-nigh sprung out of her shoes. Mrs Wake's enquiry what had happened was answered by the evidence of her own eyes.

'How did it occur?' she said.

'I cannot say; it was not firmly fixed, I suppose. Dear me, how sorry I am! My dear father's hall-clock! And now I suppose it is ruined.'

Assisted by Mrs Wake, she lifted the clock. Every inch of glass was, of course, shattered, but very little harm besides appeared to be done. They propped it up temporarily, though it would not go again.

Christine had soon recovered her composure, but she saw that Mrs Wake was gloomy. 'What does it mean, Mrs Wake?' she said. 'Is it ominous?'

'It is a sign of a violent death in the family.'

'Don't talk of it. I don't believe such things; and don't mention it to Mr Long when he comes. He's not in the family yet, you know.'

'Oh no, it cannot refer to him,' said Mrs Wake musingly.

'Some remote cousin, perhaps,' observed Christine, no less willing to humour her than to get rid of a shapeless dread which the incident had caused in her own mind. 'And – supper is almost ready, Mrs Wake?'

'In three-quarters of an hour.'

Mrs Wake left the room, and Christine sat on. Though it still wanted fifteen minutes to the hour at which Nicholas had promised to be there, she began to grow impatient. After the accustomed ticking the dead silence was oppressive. But she had not to wait so long as she had expected; steps were heard approaching the door, and there was a knock.

Christine was already there to open it. The entrance had no lamp, but it was not particularly dark out of doors. She could see the outline of a man, and cried cheerfully, 'You are early; it is very good of you.'

'I beg pardon. It is not Mr Bellston himself – only a messenger with his bag and greatcoat. But he will be here soon.'

The voice was not the voice of Nicholas, and the intelligence was strange. 'I – I don't understand. Mr Bellston?' she faintly replied.

'Yes, ma'am. A gentleman – a stranger to me – gave me these things at Casterbridge station to bring on here, and told me to say that Mr Bellston had arrived there, and is detained for half an hour, but will be here in the course of the evening.'

She sank into a chair. The porter put a small battered portmanteau on the floor, the coat on a chair, and looking into the room at the spread table said, 'If you are disappointed, ma'am, that your husband (as I s'pose he is) is not come, I can assure you he'll soon be here. He's stopped to get a shave, to my thinking, seeing he wanted it. What he said was that I could tell you he had heard the news in Ireland, and would have come sooner, his hand being forced; but was hindered crossing by the weather, having took passage in a sailing vessel. What news he meant he didn't say.'

'Ah, yes,' she faltered. It was plain that the man knew nothing of her intended remarriage.

Mechanically rising and giving him a shilling, she answered to his 'good-night' and he withdrew, the beat of his footsteps lessening in the distance. She was alone; but in what a solitude.

Christine stood in the middle of the hall, just as the man had left her, in the gloomy silence of the stopped clock within the adjoining room, till she aroused herself, and turning to the portmanteau and greatcoat brought them to the light of the candles, and examined them. The portmanteau bore painted upon it the initials 'J. B.' in white letters – the well-known initials of her husband.

She examined the greatcoat. In the breast-pocket was an empty spirit flask, which she firmly fancied she recognised as the one she had filled many times for him when he was living at home with her.

She turned desultorily hither and thither, until she heard another tread without, and there came a second knocking at the door. She did not respond to it; and Nicholas – for it was he – thinking that he was not heard by reason of a concentration on tomorrow's proceedings, opened the door softly, and came on to the door of her room, which stood unclosed, just as it had been left by the Casterbridge porter.

Nicholas uttered a blithe greeting and cast his eye round the parlour, which with its tall candles, blazing fire, snow-white cloth and prettily spread table formed a cheerful spectacle enough for a man who had been walking in the dark for an hour.

'My bride – almost, at last!' he cried, encircling her with his arms.

Instead of responding, her figure became limp, frigid, heavy; her head fell back, and he found that she had fainted.

It was natural, he thought. She had had many little worrying matters to attend to, and but slight assistance. He ought to have seen more effectually to her affairs; the closeness of the event had over-excited her. Nicholas kissed her unconscious face – more than once, little thinking what news it was that had changed its aspect. Loth to call Mrs Wake, he carried Christine to a couch and laid her down. This had the effect of reviving her. Nicholas bent and whispered in her ear, 'Lie quiet, dearest, no hurry; and dream, dream, dream of happy days. It is only I. You will soon be better.' He held her by the hand.

'No, no, no!' she said, with a stare. 'Oh, how can this be?'

Nicholas was alarmed and perplexed, but the disclosure was not long delayed. When she had sat up, and by degrees made the stunning event known to him, he stood as if transfixed.

'Ah – is it so?' said he. Then, becoming quite meek, 'And why was he so cruel as to – delay his return till now?'

She dutifully recited the explanation her husband had given her through the messenger; but her mechanical manner of telling it showed how much she doubted its truth. It was too unlikely that his arrival at such a dramatic moment should not be a contrived surprise, quite of a piece with his previous dealings towards her.

'But perhaps it may be true – and he may have become kind now – not as he used to be,' she faltered. 'Yes, perhaps, Nicholas, he is an altered man – we'll hope he is. I suppose I ought not to have listened to my legal advisers, and assumed his death so surely! Anyhow, I am roughly received back into – the right way!'

Nicholas burst out bitterly: 'Oh what too, too honest fools we were! – to so court daylight upon our intention by putting that announcement in the papers! Why could we not have married privately, and gone away, so that he would never have known what had become of you, even if he had returned? Christine, he has done it to . . . But I'll say no more. Of course we – might fly now.'

'No, no; we might not,' said she hastily.

'Very well. But this is hard to bear! "When I looked for good then evil came unto me, and when I waited for light there came darkness." So once said a sorely tried man in the land of Uz, and so say I now! . . . I wonder if he is almost here at this moment?'

She told him she supposed Bellston was approaching by the path across the fields, having sent on his greatcoat, which he would not want walking.

'And is this meal laid for him, or for me?'

'It was laid for you.'

'And it will be eaten by him?'

'Yes.'

'Christine, are you sure that he is come, or have you been sleeping over the fire and dreaming it?'

She pointed anew to the portmanteau with the initials 'J. B.', and to the coat beside it.

'Well, goodbye – goodbye! Curse that parson for not marrying us fifteen years ago!'

It is unnecessary to dwell further upon that parting. There are scenes wherein the words spoken do not even approximate to the level of the mental communion between the actors. Suffice it to say that part they did, and quickly; and Nicholas, more dead than alive, went out of the house homewards.

Why had he ever come back? During his absence he had not cared for Christine as he cared now. If he had been younger he might have felt tempted to descend into the meads instead of keeping along their edge. The Froom was down there, and he knew of quiet pools in that stream to which death would come easily. But he was too old to put an end to himself for such a reason as love; and another thought, too, kept him from seriously contemplating any desperate act. His affection for her was strongly protective, and in the event of her requiring a friend's support in future troubles there was none but himself left in the world to afford it. So he walked on.

Meanwhile Christine had resigned herself to circumstances. A resolve to continue worthy of her history and of her family lent her heroism and dignity. She called Mrs Wake, and explained to that worthy woman as much of what had occurred as she deemed necessary. Mrs Wake was too amazed to reply; she retreated slowly, her lips parted; till at the door she said with a dry mouth, 'And the beautiful supper, ma'am?'

'Serve it when he comes.'

'When Mr Bellston – yes, ma'am, I will.' She still stood gazing, as if she could hardly take in the order.

'That will do, Mrs Wake. I am much obliged to you for all your kindness.' And Christine was left alone again, and then she wept.

She sat down and waited. That awful silence of the stopped clock began anew, but she did not mind it now. She was listening for a footfall in a state of mental tensity which almost took away from her the power of motion. It seemed to her that the natural interval for her husband's journey thither must have expired; but she was not sure, and waited on.

Mrs Wake again came in. 'You have not rung for supper – '

'He is not yet come, Mrs Wake. If you want to go to bed, bring in the supper and set it on the table. It will be nearly as good cold. Leave the door unbarred.'

Mrs Wake did as was suggested, made up the fire, and went away. Shortly afterwards Christine heard her retire to her chamber. But Christine still sat on, and still her husband postponed his entry.

She aroused herself once or twice to freshen the fire, but was ignorant how the night was going. Her watch was upstairs and she did not make the effort to go up to consult it. In her seat she continued; and still the supper waited, and still he did not come.

At length she was so nearly persuaded that the arrival of his things must have been a dream after all, that she again went over to them, felt them, and examined them. His they unquestionably were; and their forwarding by the porter had been quite natural. She sighed and sat down again.

Presently she fell into a doze, and when she again became conscious she found that the four candles had burnt into their sockets and gone out. The fire still emitted a feeble shine. Christine did not take the trouble to get more candles, but stirred the fire and sat on.

After a long period she heard a creaking of the chamber floor and stairs at the other end of the house, and knew that the farmer's family were getting up. By and by Mrs Wake entered the room, candle in hand, bouncing open the door in her morning manner, obviously without any expectation of finding a person there.

'Lord-a-mercy! What, sitting here again, ma'am?'

'Yes, I am sitting here still.'

'You've been there ever since last night?'

'Yes.'

'Then – '

'He's not come.'

'Well, he won't come at this time o' morning,' said the farmer's wife. 'Do 'ee get on to bed, ma'am. You must be shrammed to death!'

It occurred to Christine now that possibly her husband had thought better of obtruding himself upon her company within an hour of revealing his existence to her, and had decided to pay a more formal visit next day. She therefore adopted Mrs Wake's suggestion and retired.

8

Nicholas had gone straight home, neither speaking to nor seeing a soul. From that hour a change seemed to come over him. He had ever possessed a full share of self-consciousness; he had been readily piqued, had shown an unusual dread of being personally obtrusive. But now his sense of self, as an individual provoking opinion, appeared to leave him. When, therefore, after a day or two of seclusion, he came forth again, and the few acquaintances he had formed in the town condoled with him on what had happened, and pitied his haggard looks, he did not shrink from their regard as he would have done formerly, but took their sympathy as it would have been accepted by a child.

It reached his ears that Bellston had not appeared on the evening of his arrival at any hotel in the town or neighbourhood, or entered his wife's house at all. 'That's a part of his cruelty,' thought Nicholas. And when two or three days had passed, and still no account came to him of Bellston having joined her, he ventured to set out for Froom-Everard.

Christine was so shaken that she was obliged to receive him as she lay on a sofa, beside the square table which was to have borne their evening feast. She fixed her eyes wistfully upon him, and smiled a sad smile.

'He has not come?' said Nicholas under his breath.

'He has not.'

Then Nicholas sat beside her, and they talked on general topics merely like saddened old friends. But they could not keep away the subject of Bellston, their voices dropping as it forced its way in. Christine, no less than Nicholas, knowing her husband's character, inferred that, having stopped her game, as he would have phrased it, he was taking things leisurely, and, finding nothing very attractive in her limited mode of living, was meaning to return to her only when he had nothing better to do.

The bolt which laid low their hopes had struck so recently that they could hardly look each other in the face when speaking that day. But when a week or two had passed, and all the horizon still remained as vacant of Bellston as before, Nicholas and she could talk of the event with calm wonderment. Why had he come, to go again like this?

And then there set in a period of resigned surmise, during which so like, so very like, was day to day, that to tell of one of them is to tell of all. Nicholas would arrive between three and four in the afternoon, a faint trepidation influencing his walk as he neared her door. He would knock; she would always reply in person, having watched for him from the window. Then he would whisper – 'He has not come?'

'He has not,' she would say.

Nicholas would enter then, and she being ready bonneted, they would walk into the Sallows together as far as to the spot which they had frequently made their place of appointment in their youthful days. A plank bridge, which Bellston had caused to be thrown over the stream during his residence with her in the manor-house, was now again removed, and all was just the same as in Nicholas's time, when he had been accustomed to wade across on the edge of the cascade and come up to her like a merman from the deep. Here on the felled trunk, which still lay rotting in its old place, they would now sit, gazing at the descending sheet of water, with its never-ending sarcastic hiss at their baffled attempts to make themselves one flesh. Returning to the house they would sit down together to tea, after which, and the confidential chat that accompanied it, he walked home by the declining light. This proceeding became as periodic as an astronomical recurrence. Twice a week he came – all through that winter, all through the spring following, through the summer, through the autumn, the next winter, the next year, and the next, till an appreciable span of human life had passed by. Bellston still tarried.

Years and years Nic walked that way, at this interval of three days, from his house in the neighbouring town; and in every instance the aforesaid order of things was customary; and still on his arrival the form of words went on – 'He has not come?'

'He has not.'

So they grew older. The dim shape of that third one stood continually between them; they could not displace it; neither, on the other hand, could it effectually part them. They were in close communion, yet not indissolubly united; lovers, yet never growing cured of love. By the time that the fifth year of Nic's visiting had arrived, on about the five-hundredth occasion of his presence at her tea-table, he noticed that the bleaching process which had begun upon his own locks was also spreading to hers. He told her so, and they laughed. Yet she was in good health: a condition of suspense, which would have half-killed a man, had been endured by her without complaint, and even with composure.

One day, when these years of abeyance had numbered seven, they had strolled as usual as far as the waterfall, whose faint roar formed a sort of calling voice sufficient in the circumstances to direct their listlessness. Pausing there, he looked up at her face and said, 'Why should we not try again, Christine? We are legally at liberty to do so now. Nothing venture nothing have.'

But she would not. Perhaps a little primness of idea was by this time ousting the native daring of Christine. 'What he has done once he can do twice,' she said. 'He is not dead, and if we were to marry he would say we had "forced his hand", as he said before, and duly reappear.'

Some years after, when Christine was about fifty, and Nicholas fifty-three, a new trouble of a minor kind arrived. He found an inconvenience in traversing the distance between their two houses, particularly in damp weather, the years he had spent in trying climates abroad having sown the seeds of rheumatism, which made a journey undesirable on inclement days, even in a carriage. He told her of this new difficulty, as he did of everything.

'If you could live nearer,' suggested she.

Unluckily there was no house near. But Nicholas, though not a millionaire, was a man of means; he obtained a small piece of ground on lease at the nearest spot to her home that it could be so obtained, which was on the opposite brink of the Froom, this river forming the boundary of the Froom-Everard manor; and here he built a cottage large enough for his wants. This took time, and when he got into it he found its situation a great comfort to him. He was not more than five hundred yards from her now, and gained a new pleasure in feeling that all sounds which greeted his ears, in the day or in the night, also fell upon hers – the caw of a particular rook, the voice of a neighbouring nightingale, the whistle of a local breeze, or the purl of the fall in the meadows, whose rush was a material rendering of time's ceaseless scour over themselves, wearing them away without uniting them.

Christine's missing husband was taking shape as a myth among the surrounding residents; but he was still believed in as corporeally imminent by Christine herself, and also, in a milder degree, by Nicholas. For a curious unconsciousness of the long lapse of time since his revelation of himself seemed to affect the pair. There had been no passing events to serve as chronological milestones, and the evening on which she had kept supper waiting for him still loomed out with startling nearness in their retrospects.

In the seventeenth pensive year of this their parallel march towards the common bourne, a labourer came in a hurry one day to Nicholas's house and brought strange tidings. The present owner of Froom-Everard – a non-resident – had been improving his property in sundry ways, and one of these was by dredging the stream which, in the course of years, had become choked with mud and weeds in its passage through the Sallows. The process necessitated a reconstruction of the waterfall. When the river had been pumped dry for this purpose, the skeleton of a man had been found jammed among the piles supporting the edge of the fall. Every particle of his flesh and clothing had been eaten by fishes or abraded to nothing by the water, but the relics of a gold watch remained, and on the inside of the case was engraved the name of the maker of her husband's watch, which she well remembered.

Nicholas, deeply agitated, hastened down to the place and examined the remains attentively, afterwards going across to Christine, and breaking the discovery to her. She would not come to view the skeleton, which lay extended on the grass, not a finger or toe-bone missing, so neatly had the aquatic operators done their work. Conjecture was directed to the question how Bellston had got there; and conjecture alone could give an explanation.

It was supposed that, on his way to call upon her, he had taken a short cut through the grounds, with which he was naturally very familiar, and coming to the fall under the trees had expected to find there the plank which, during his occupancy of the premises with Christine and her father, he had placed there for crossing into the meads on the other side instead of wading across as Nicholas had done. Before discovering its removal he had probably over-balanced himself, and was thus precipitated into the cascade, the piles beneath the descending current wedging him between them like the prongs of a pitchfork, and effectually preventing the rising of his body, over which the weeds grew. Such was the reasonable supposition concerning the discovery; but proof was never forthcoming.

'To think,' said Nicholas, when the remains had been decently interred, and he was again sitting with Christine – though not beside the waterfall – 'to think how we visited him! How we sat over him, hours and hours, gazing at him, bewailing our fate, when all the time he was ironically hissing at us from the spot, in an unknown tongue, that we could marry if we chose!'

She echoed the sentiment with a sigh.

'I have strange fancies,' she said. 'I suppose it must have been my husband who came back, and not some other man.'

Nicholas felt that there was little doubt. 'Besides – the skeleton,' he said.

'Yes . . . If it could have been another person's – but no, of course it was he.'

'You might have married me on the day we had fixed, and there would have been no impediment. You would now have been seventeen years my wife, and we might have had tall sons and daughters.'

'It might have been so,' she murmured.

'Well – is it still better late than never?'

The question was one which had become complicated by the increasing years of each. Their wills were somewhat enfeebled now, their hearts sickened of tender enterprise by hope too long deferred. Having postponed the consideration of their course till a year after the interment of Bellston, each seemed less disposed than formerly to take it up again.

'Is it worth while, after so many years?' she said to him. 'We are fairly happy as we are – perhaps happier than we should be in any other relation, seeing what old people we have grown. The weight is gone from our lives;

the shadow no longer divides us: then let us be joyful together as we are, dearest Nic, in the days of our vanity; and with mirth and laughter let old wrinkles come.'

He fell in with these views of hers to some extent. But occasionally he ventured to urge her to reconsider the case, though he spoke not with the fervour of his earlier years.

A Changed Man

I

The person who, next to the actors themselves, chanced to know most of their story lived just below Top o' Town (as the spot was called) in an old substantially-built house, distinguished among its neighbours by having an oriel window on the first floor, whence could be obtained a raking view of the High Street, west and east, the former including Laura's dwelling, the end of the Town Avenue hard by (in which were played the odd pranks hereafter to be mentioned), the Port Bredy road rising westwards and the turning that led to the cavalry barracks where the captain was quartered. Looking eastward down the town from the same favoured gazebo, the long perspective of houses declined and dwindled till they merged in the highway across the moor. The white riband of road disappeared over Grey's Bridge a quarter of a mile off, to plunge into innumerable rustic windings, shy shades and solitary undulations up hill and down dale for one hundred and twenty miles till it exhibited itself at Hyde Park Corner as a smooth bland surface in touch with a busy and fashionable world.

To the barracks aforesaid had recently arrived the —th Hussars, a regiment new to the locality. Almost before any acquaintance with its members had been made by the townspeople, a report spread that they were a 'crack' body of men, and had brought a splendid band. For some reason or other the town had not been used as the headquarters of cavalry for many years, the various troops stationed there having consisted of casual detachments only; so that it was with a sense of honour that everybody – even the small furniture-broker from whom the married troopers hired tables and chairs – received the news of their crack quality.

In those days the Hussar regiments still wore over the left shoulder that attractive attachment, or frilled half-coat, hanging loosely behind like the wounded wing of a bird, which was called the pelisse, though it was known among the troopers themselves as a 'sling-jacket'. It added amazingly to their picturesqueness in women's eyes, and, indeed, in the eyes of men also.

The burgher who lived in the house with the oriel window sat during a great many hours of the day in that projection, for he was an invalid, and time hung heavily on his hands unless he maintained a constant interest in proceedings without. Not more than a week after the arrival of the Hussars his ears were assailed by the shout of one schoolboy to another in the street below.

'Have 'ee heard this about the Hussars? They are haunted! Yes – a ghost troubles 'em; he has followed 'em about the world for years.'

A haunted regiment: that was a new idea for either invalid or stalwart. The listener in the oriel came to the conclusion that there were some lively characters among the —th Hussars.

He made Captain Maumbry's acquaintance in an informal manner at an afternoon tea to which he went in a wheeled chair – one of the very rare outings that the state of his health permitted. Maumbry showed himself to be a handsome man of twenty-eight or thirty, with an attractive hint of wickedness in his manner that was sure to make him adorable with good young women. The large dark eyes that lit his pale face expressed this wickedness strongly, though such was the adaptability of their rays that one could think they might have expressed sadness or seriousness just as readily, if he had had a mind for such.

An old and deaf lady who was present asked Captain Maumbry bluntly: 'What's this we hear about you? They say your regiment is haunted.'

The captain's face assumed an aspect of grave, even sad, concern. 'Yes,' he replied, 'it is too true.'

Some younger ladies smiled till they saw how serious he looked, when they looked serious likewise.

'Really?' said the old lady.

'Yes. We naturally don't wish to say much about it.'

'No, no; of course not. But – how haunted?'

'Well; the – thing, as I'll call it, follows us. In country quarters or town, abroad or at home, it's just the same.'

'How do you account for it?'

'H'm.' Maumbry lowered his voice. 'Some crime committed by certain of our regiment in past years, we suppose.'

'Dear me . . . How very horrid, and singular!'

'But, as I said, we don't speak of it much.'

'No . . . no.'

When the Hussar was gone, a young lady, disclosing a long-suppressed interest, asked if the ghost had been seen by any of the town.

The lawyer's son, who always had the latest borough news, said that, though it was seldom seen by anyone but the Hussars themselves, more than one townsman and woman had already set eyes on it, to his or her terror. The phantom mostly appeared very late at night, under the dense trees of the Town Avenue nearest the barracks. It was about ten feet high; its teeth chattered with a dry naked sound, as if they were those of a skeleton; and its hip-bones could be heard grating in their sockets.

During the darkest weeks of winter several timid persons were seriously frightened by the object answering to this cheerful description, and the police began to look into the matter. Whereupon the appearances grew less frequent, and some of the boys of the regiment thankfully stated that they had not been so free from ghostly visitation for years as they had become since their arrival in Casterbridge.

This playing at ghosts was the most innocent of the amusements indulged in by the choice young spirits who inhabited the lichened, red-brick building at the top of the town bearing W.D. and a broad arrow on its quoins. Far more serious escapades – levities relating to love, wine, cards, betting – were talked of, with no doubt more or less of exaggeration. That the Hussars, Captain Maumbry included, were the cause of bitter tears to several young women of the town and country is unquestionably true, despite the fact that the gaieties of the young men wore a more staring colour in this old-fashioned place than they would have done in a large and modern city.

2

Regularly once a week they rode out in marching order.

Returning up the town on one of these occasions, the romantic pelisse flapping behind each horseman's shoulder in the soft south-west wind, Captain Maumbry glanced up at the oriel. A mutual nod was exchanged between him and the person who sat there reading. The reader and a friend in the room with him followed the troop with their eyes all the way up the street, till, when the soldiers were opposite the house in which Laura lived, that young lady became discernible in the balcony.

'They are engaged to be married, I hear,' said the friend.

'Who – Maumbry and Laura? Never – so soon?'

'Yes.'

'He'll never marry. Several girls have been mentioned in connection with his name. I am sorry for Laura.'

'Oh, but you needn't be. They are excellently matched.'

'She's only one more.'

'She's one more, and more still. She has regularly caught him. She is a born player of the game of hearts, and she knew how to beat him in his own practices. If there is one woman in the town who has any chance of holding her own and marrying him, she is that woman.'

This was true, as it turned out. By natural proclivity Laura had from the first entered heart and soul into military romance as exhibited in the plots and characters of those living exponents of it who came under her notice. From her earliest young womanhood civilians, however promising, had no chance of winning her interest if the meanest warrior were within the horizon. It may be that the position of her uncle's house (which was her home) at the corner of West Street nearest the barracks, the daily passing of the troops, the constant blowing of trumpet-calls a furlong from her windows, coupled with the fact that she knew nothing of the inner realities of military life, and hence idealised it, had also helped her mind's original bias for thinking men-at-arms the only ones worthy of a woman's heart.

Captain Maumbry was a typical prize; one whom all surrounding maidens had coveted, ached for, angled for, wept for, had by her judicious management become subdued to her purpose; and in addition to the pleasure of marrying the man she loved, Laura had the joy of feeling herself hated by the mothers of all the marriageable girls of the neighbourhood.

The man in the oriel went to the wedding; not as a guest, for at this time he was but slightly acquainted with the parties; but mainly because the church was close to his house; partly, too, for a reason which moved many others to be spectators of the ceremony: a subconsciousness that, though the couple might be happy in their experiences, there was sufficient possibility of their being otherwise to colour the musings of an onlooker with a pleasing pathos of conjecture. He could on occasion do a pretty stroke of rhyming in those days, and he beguiled the time of waiting by pencilling on a blank page of his prayer-book a few lines which, though kept private then, may be given here:

At a Hasty Wedding
(Triolet)

If hours be years the twain are blest,
For now they solace swift desire
By lifelong ties that tether zest
If hours be years. The twain are blest
Do eastern suns slope never west,
Nor pallid ashes follow fire.
If hours be years the twain are blest
For now they solace swift desire.

As if, however, to falsify all prophecies, the couple seemed to find in marriage the secret of perpetuating the intoxication of a courtship which, on Maumbry's side at least, had opened without serious intent. During the winter following they were the most popular pair in and about Casterbridge – nay in South Wessex itself. No smart dinner in the country houses of the younger and gayer families within driving distance of the borough was complete without their lively presence; Mrs Maumbry was the blithest of the whirling figures at the county ball; and when followed that inevitable incident of garrison-town life, an amateur dramatic entertainment, it was just the same. The acting was for the benefit of such and such an excellent charity – nobody cared what, provided the play were played – and both Captain Maumbry and his wife were in the piece, having been in fact, by mutual consent, the originators of the performance. And so with laughter, and thoughtlessness, and movement, all went merrily. There was a little backwardness in the bill-paying of the couple; but in justice to them it must be added that sooner or later all owings were paid.

3

At the chapel-of-ease attended by the troops there arose above the edge of the pulpit one Sunday an unknown face. This was the face of a new curate. He placed upon the desk, not the familiar sermon book, but merely a Bible. The person who tells these things was not present at that service, but he soon learnt that the young curate was nothing less than a great surprise to his congregation: a mixed one always, for though the Hussars occupied the body of the building, its nooks and corners were crammed with civilians, whom, up to the present, even the least uncharitable would have described as being attracted thither less by the services than by the soldiery.

Now there arose a second reason for squeezing into an already over-crowded church. The persuasive and gentle eloquence of Mr Sainway operated like a charm upon those accustomed only to the higher and dryer styles of preaching, and for a time the other churches of the town were thinned of their sitters.

At this point in the nineteenth century the sermon was the sole reason for churchgoing amongst a vast body of religious people. The liturgy was a formal preliminary, which, like the royal proclamation in a court of assize, had to be got through before the real interest began; and on reaching home the question was simply: Who preached, and how did he handle his subject? Even had an archbishop officiated in the service proper nobody would have cared much about what was said or sung. People who had formerly attended in the morning only began to go in the evening, and even to the special addresses in the afternoon.

One day when Captain Maumbry entered his wife's drawing-room, filled with hired furniture, she thought he was somebody else, for he had not come upstairs humming the most catching air afloat in musical circles or in his usual careless way.

'What's the matter, Jack?' she said without looking up from a note she was writing.

'Well – not much, that I know.'

'Oh, but there is,' she murmured as she wrote.

'Why – this cursed new lath in a sheet – I mean the new parson! He wants us to stop the band-playing on Sunday afternoons.'

Laura looked up aghast.

'Why, it is the one thing that enables the few rational beings hereabouts to keep alive from Saturday to Monday!'

'He says all the town flock to the music and don't come to the service, and that the pieces played are profane, or mundane, or inane, or something – not what ought to be played on Sunday. Of course 'tis Lautmann who settles those things.'

Lautmann was the bandmaster.

The barrack-green on Sunday afternoons had, indeed, become the promenade of a great many townspeople cheerfully inclined, many even of those who attended in the morning at Mr Sainway's service; and little boys who ought to have been listening to the curate's afternoon lecture were too often seen rolling upon the grass and making faces behind the more dignified listeners.

Laura heard no more about the matter, however, for two or three weeks, when suddenly remembering it she asked her husband if any further objections had been raised.

'Oh – Mr Sainway. I forgot to tell you. I've made his acquaintance. He is not a bad sort of man.'

Laura asked if either Maumbry or some others of the officers did not give the presumptuous curate a good setting down for his interference.

'Oh well – we've forgotten that. He's a stunning preacher, they tell me.'

The acquaintance developed apparently, for the captain said to her a little later on, 'There's a good deal in Sainway's argument about having no band on Sunday afternoons. After all, it is close to his church. But he doesn't press his objections unduly.'

'I am surprised to hear you defend him!'

'It was only a passing thought of mine. We naturally don't wish to offend the inhabitants of the town if they don't like it.'

'But they do.'

The invalid in the oriel never clearly gathered the details of progress in this conflict of lay and clerical opinion; but so it was that, to the disappointment of musicians, the grief of out-walking lovers, and the regret of the junior population of the town and country round, the band-playing on Sunday afternoons ceased in Casterbridge barrack-square.

By this time the Maumbrys had frequently listened to the preaching of the gentle if narrow-minded curate; for these light-natured, hit-or-miss, rackety people went to church like others for respectability's sake. None so orthodox as your unmitigated worldling. A more remarkable event to the man in the window was the sight of Captain Maumbry and Mr Sainway walking down the High Street in earnest conversation. On his mentioning this fact to a caller he was assured that it was a matter of common talk that they were always together.

The observer would soon have learnt this with his own eyes if he had not been told. They began to pass together nearly every day. Hitherto Mrs Maumbry, in fashionable walking clothes, had usually been her husband's companion; but this was less frequent now. The close and singular friendship between the two men went on for nearly a year, when Mr Sainway was presented to a living in a densely populated town in the midland counties. He bade the parishioners of his old place a reluctant farewell and departed, the touching sermon he preached on the occasion being published by the local printer. Everybody was sorry to lose him; and it was with genuine grief that his Casterbridge congregation learnt later on that soon after his induction to his benefice, during some bitter weather, he had fallen seriously ill of inflammation of the lungs, of which he eventually died.

We now get below the surface of things. Of all who had known the dead curate, none grieved for him like the man who on his first arrival had called him a 'lath in a sheet'. Mrs Maumbry had never greatly sympathised with the impressive parson; indeed, she had been secretly glad that he had gone away to better himself. He had considerably diminished the pleasures of a woman by whom the joys of earth and good company had been appreciated to the full. Sorry for her husband in his loss of a friend who had been none of hers, she was yet quite unprepared for the sequel.

'There is something that I have wanted to tell you lately, dear,' he said one morning at breakfast with hesitation. 'Have you guessed what it is?'

She had guessed nothing.

'That I think of retiring from the army.'

'What!'

'I have thought more and more of Sainway since his death, and of what he used to say to me so earnestly. And I feel certain I shall be right in obeying a call within me to give up this fighting trade and enter the Church.'

'What – be a parson?'

'Yes.'

'But what should I do?'

'Be a parson's wife.'

'Never!' she affirmed.

'But how can you help it?'

'I'll run away rather!' she said vehemently;

'No, you mustn't,' Maumbry replied, in the tone he used when his mind was made up. 'You'll get accustomed to the idea, for I am constrained to carry it out, though it is against my worldly interests. I am forced on by a Hand outside me to tread in the steps of Sainway.'

'Jack,' she asked, with calm pallor and round eyes; 'do you mean to say seriously that you are arranging to be a curate instead of a soldier?'

'I might say a curate is a soldier – of the Church Militant; but I don't want to offend you with doctrine. I distinctly say, yes.'

Late one evening, a little time onward, he caught her sitting by the dim firelight in her room. She did not know he had entered; and he found her weeping. 'What are you crying about, poor dearest?' he said.

She started. 'Because of what you have told me!' The captain grew very unhappy; but he was undeterred.

In due time the town learnt, to its intense surprise, that Captain Maumbry had retired from the —th Hussars and gone to Fountall Theological College to prepare for the ministry.

4

'Oh, the pity of it! Such a dashing soldier – so popular – such an acquisition to the town – the soul of social life here! And now! . . . One should not speak ill of the dead, but that dreadful Mr Sainway – it was too cruel of him!'

This is a summary of what was said when Captain, now the Reverend, John Maumbry was enabled by circumstances to indulge his heart's desire of returning to the scene of his former exploits in the capacity of a minister of the Gospel. A low-lying district of the town, which at that date was crowded with impoverished cottagers, was crying for a curate, and Mr Maumbry generously offered himself as one willing to undertake labours that were certain to produce little result, and no thanks, credit, or emolument.

Let the truth be told about him as a clergyman – he proved to be anything but a brilliant success. Painstaking, single-minded, deeply in earnest as all could see, his delivery was laboured, his sermons were dull to listen to, and alas, too, too long. Even the dispassionate judges who sat by the hour in the bar-parlour of the White Hart – an inn standing at the dividing line between the poor quarter aforesaid and the fashionable quarter of Maumbry's former triumphs, and hence affording a position of strict impartiality – agreed in substance with the young ladies to the westward, though their views were somewhat more tersely expressed: 'Surely, God A'mighty spwiled a good sojer to make a bad pa'son when He shifted Cap'n Ma'mbry into a sarpless!'

The latter knew that such things were said, but he pursued his daily labours in and out of the hovels with serene unconcern.

It was about this time that the invalid in the oriel became more than a mere bowing acquaintance of Mrs Maumbry's. She had returned to the town with her husband, and was living with him in a little house in the centre of his circle of ministration, when by some means she became one of the invalid's visitors. After a general conversation while sitting in his room with a friend of both, an incident led up to the matter that still rankled deeply in her soul. Her face was now paler and thinner than it had been; even more attractive, her disappointments having inscribed themselves as meek thoughtfulness on a look that was once a little frivolous. The two ladies had called to be allowed to use the window for observing the departure of the Hussars, who were leaving for barracks much nearer to London.

The troopers turned the corner of Barrack Road into the top of High Street, headed by their band playing 'The Girl I Left Behind Me' (which was formerly always the tune for such times, though it is now nearly disused). They came and passed the oriel, where an officer or two, looking up and discovering Mrs Maumbry, saluted her, whose eyes filled with tears as the notes of the band waned away. Before the little group had recovered from that sense of the romantic which such spectacles impart, Mr Maumbry came along the pavement. He probably had bidden his former brethren-in-arms a farewell at the top of the street, for he walked from that direction in his rather shabby clerical clothes, and with a basket on his arm which seemed to hold some purchases he had been making for his poorer parishioners. Unlike the soldiers he went along quite unconscious of his appearance or of the scene around.

The contrast was too much for Laura. With lips that now quivered, she asked the invalid what he thought of the change that had come to her.

It was difficult to answer, and with a wilfulness that was too strong in her she repeated the question.

'Do you think,' she added, 'that a woman's husband has a right to do such a thing, even if he does feel a certain call to it?'

Her listener sympathised too largely with both of them to be anything but unsatisfactory in his reply. Laura gazed longingly out of the window towards the thin dusty line of Hussars, now smalling towards the Mellstock Ridge. 'I,' she said, 'who should have been in their van on the way to London, am doomed to fester in a hole in Durnover Lane!'

Many events had passed and many rumours had been current concerning her before the invalid saw her again after her leave-taking that day.

5

Casterbridge had known many military and civil episodes; many happy times, and times less happy; and now came the time of her visitation. The scourge of cholera had been laid on the suffering country, and the low-lying purlieus of this ancient borough had more than their share of the infliction. Mixen Lane, in the Durnover quarter, and in Maumbry's parish, was where the blow fell most heavily. Yet there was a certain mercy in its choice of a date, for Maumbry was the man for such an hour.

The spread of the epidemic was so rapid that many left the town and took lodgings in the villages and farms. Mr Maumbry's house was close to the most infected street, and he himself was occupied morn, noon and night in endeavours to stamp out the plague and in alleviating the sufferings of the victims. So, as a matter of ordinary precaution, he decided to isolate his wife somewhere away from him for a while.

She suggested a village by the sea, near Budmouth Regis, and lodgings were obtained for her at Creston, a spot divided from the Casterbridge valley by a high ridge that gave it quite another atmosphere, though it lay no more than six miles off.

Thither she went. While she was rusticating in this place of safety, and her husband was slaving in the slums, she struck up an acquaintance with a lieutenant in the —st Foot, a Mr Vannicock, who was stationed with his regiment at the Budmouth infantry barracks. As Laura frequently sat on the shelving beach, watching each thin wave slide up to her, and hearing, without heeding, its gnaw at the pebbles in its retreat, he often took a walk that way.

The acquaintance grew and ripened. Her situation, her history, her beauty, her age – a year or two above his own – all tended to make an impression on the young man's heart, and a reckless flirtation was soon in blithe progress upon that lonely shore.

It was said by her detractors afterwards that she had chosen her lodging to be near this gentleman, but there is reason to believe that she had never seen him till her arrival there. Just now Casterbridge was so deeply occupied with its own sad affairs – a daily burying of the dead and destruction of contaminated clothes and bedding – that it had little inclination to promulgate such gossip as may have reached its ears on the pair. Nobody long considered Laura in the tragic cloud which overhung all.

Meanwhile, on the Budmouth side of the hill the very mood of men was in contrast. The visitation there had been slight and much earlier, and normal occupations and pastimes had been resumed. Mr Maumbry had arranged to see Laura twice a week in the open air, that she might run no risk from him; and, having heard nothing of the faint rumour, he met her as usual one dry and windy afternoon on the summit of the dividing hill, near where the high road from town to town crosses the old ridgeway at right angles.

He waved his hand, and smiled as she approached, shouting to her: 'We will keep this wall between us, dear.' (Walls formed the field-fences here.) 'You mustn't be endangered. It won't be for long, with God's help!'

'I will do as you tell me, Jack. But you are running too much risk yourself, aren't you? I get little news of you; but I fancy you are.'

'Not more than others.'

Thus somewhat formally they talked, an insulating wind beating the wall between them like a mill-weir.

'But you wanted to ask me something?' he added.

'Yes. You know we are trying in Budmouth to raise some money for your sufferers; and the way we have thought of is by a dramatic performance. They want me to take a part.'

His face saddened. 'I have known so much of that sort of thing, and all that accompanies it! I wish you had thought of some other way.'

She said lightly that she was afraid it was all settled. 'You object to my taking a part, then? Of course – '

He told her that he did not like to say he positively objected. He wished they had chosen an oratorio, or lecture, or anything more in keeping with the necessity it was to relieve.

'But,' said she impatiently, 'people won't come to oratorios or lectures! They will crowd to comedies and farces.'

'Well, I cannot dictate to Budmouth how it shall earn the money it is going to give us. Who is getting up this performance?'

'The boys of the —st.'

'Ah, yes; our old game!' replied Mr Maumbry. 'The grief of Casterbridge is the excuse for their frivolity. Candidly, dear Laura, I wish you wouldn't play in it. But I don't forbid you to. I leave the whole to your judgement.'

The interview ended, and they went their ways northward and south-ward. Time disclosed to all concerned that Mrs Maumbry played in the comedy as the heroine, the lover's part being taken by Mr Vannicock.

6

Thus was helped on an event which the conduct of the mutually attracted ones had been generating for some time.

It is unnecessary to give details. The —st Foot left for Bristol, and this precipitated their action. After a week of hesitation she agreed to leave her home at Creston and meet Vannicock on the ridge hard by, and to accompany him to Bath, where he had secured lodgings for her, so that she would be only about a dozen miles from his quarters.

Accordingly, on the evening chosen, she laid on her dressing-table a note for her husband running thus:

> DEAR JACK – I am unable to endure this life any longer, and I have resolved to put an end to it. I told you I should run away if you persisted in being a clergyman, and now I am doing it. One cannot help one's nature. I have resolved to throw in my lot with Mr Vannicock, and I hope rather than expect you will forgive me. L.

Then, with hardly a scrap of luggage, she went, ascending to the ridge in the dusk of early evening. Almost on the very spot where her husband had stood at their last tryst she beheld the outline of Vannicock, who had come all the way from Bristol to fetch her.

'I don't like meeting here – it is so unlucky!' she cried to him. 'For God's sake let us have a place of our own. Go back to the milestone, and I'll come on.'

He went back to the milestone that stands on the north slope of the ridge, where the old and new roads diverge, and she joined him there.

She was taciturn and sorrowful when he asked her why she would not meet him on the top. At last she enquired how they were going to travel.

He explained that he proposed to walk to Mellstock Hill, on the other side of Casterbridge, where a fly was waiting to take them by a cross-cut into the Ivell Road, and onward to that town. The Bristol railway was open to Ivell.

This plan they followed, and walked briskly through the dull gloom till they neared Casterbridge, which place they avoided by turning to the right at the Roman Amphitheatre and bearing round to Durnover Cross. Thence the way was solitary and open across the moor to the hill whereon the Ivell fly awaited them.

'I have noticed for some time,' she said, 'a lurid glare over the Durnover end of the town. It seems to come from somewhere about Mixen Lane.'

'The lamps,' he suggested.

'There's not a lamp as big as a rushlight in the whole lane. It is where the cholera is worst.'

By Standfast Corner, a little beyond the Cross, they suddenly obtained an end view of the lane. Large bonfires were burning in the middle of the way, with a view to purifying the air; and from the wretched tenements with which the lane was lined in those days persons were bringing out bedding and clothing. Some was thrown into the fires, the rest placed in wheel-barrows and wheeled into the moor directly in the track of the fugitives.

They followed on, and came up to where a vast copper was set in the open air. Here the linen was boiled and disinfected. By the light of the lanterns Laura discovered that her husband was standing by the copper, and that it was he who unloaded the barrow and immersed its contents. The night was so calm and muggy that the conversation by the copper reached her ears.

'Are there many more loads tonight?'

'There's the clothes o' they that died this afternoon, sir. But they might bide till tomorrow, for you must be tired out.'

'We'll do it at once, for I can't ask anybody else to undertake it. Overturn that load on the grass and fetch the rest.'

The man did so and went off with the barrow. Maumbry paused for a moment to wipe his face, and resumed his homely drudgery amid this squalid and reeking scene, pressing down and stirring the contents of the copper with what looked like an old rolling-pin. The steam therefrom, laden with death, travelled in a low trail across the meadow.

Laura spoke suddenly: 'I won't go tonight after all. He is so tired, and I must help him. I didn't know things were so bad as this!'

Vannicock's arm dropped from her waist, where it had been resting as they walked.

'Will you leave?' she asked.

'I will if you say I must. But I'd rather help too.' There was no expostulation in his tone.

Laura had gone forward. 'Jack,' she said, 'I am come to help!'

The weary curate turned and held up the lantern. 'Oh – what, is it you, Laura?' he asked in surprise. 'Why did you come into this? You had better go back – the risk is great.'

'But I want to help you, Jack. Please let me help! I didn't come by myself –

Mr Vannicock kept me company. He will make himself useful too, if he's not gone on. Mr Vannicock!'

The young lieutenant came forward reluctantly. Mr Maumbry spoke formally to him, adding as he resumed his labour, 'I thought the —st Foot had gone to Bristol.'

'We have. But I have run down again for a few things.'

The two newcomers began to assist, Vannicock placing on the ground the small bag containing Laura's toilet articles that he had been carrying. The barrowman soon returned with another load, and all continued work for nearly a half-hour, when a coachman came out from the shadows to the north.

'Beg pardon, sir,' he whispered to Vannicock, 'but I've waited so long on Mellstock hill that at last I drove down to the turnpike; and seeing the light here, I ran on to find out what had happened.'

Lieutenant Vannicock told him to wait a few minutes, and the last barrow-load was got through. Mr Maumbry stretched himself and breathed heavily, saying, 'There; we can do no more.'

As if from the relaxation of effort he seemed to be seized with violent pain. He pressed his hands to his sides and bent forward.

'Ah! I think it has got hold of me at last,' he said with difficulty. 'I must try to get home. Let Mr Vannicock take you back, Laura.'

He walked a few steps, they helping him, but was obliged to sink down on the grass.

'I am – afraid – you'll have to send for a hurdle, or shutter, or something,' he went on feebly, 'or try to get me into the barrow.'

But Vannicock had called to the driver of the fly, and they waited until it was brought on from the turnpike hard by. Mr Maumbry was placed therein. Laura entered with him, and they drove to his humble residence near the Cross, where he was got upstairs.

Vannicock stood outside by the empty fly awhile, but Laura did not reappear. He thereupon entered the fly and told the driver to take him back to Ivell.

7

Mr Maumbry had over-exerted himself in the relief of the suffering poor, and fell a victim – one of the last – to the pestilence which had carried off so many. Two days later he lay in his coffin.

Laura was in the room below. A servant brought in some letters, and she glanced them over. One was the note from herself to Maumbry, informing him that she was unable to endure life with him any longer and was about to elope with Vannicock. Having read the letter she took it upstairs to where the dead man was, and slipped it into his coffin. The next day she buried him.

She was now free.

She shut up his house at Durnover Cross and returned to her lodgings at Creston. Soon she had a letter from Vannicock, and six weeks after her husband's death her lover came to see her.

'I forgot to give you back this – that night,' he said presently, handing her the little bag she had taken as her whole luggage when leaving.

Laura received it and absently shook it out. There fell upon the carpet her brush, comb, slippers, nightdress, and other simple necessaries for a journey. They had an intolerably ghastly look now, and she tried to cover them.

'I can now,' he said, 'ask you to belong to me legally – when a proper interval has gone – instead of as we meant.'

There was languor in his utterance, hinting at a possibility that it was perfunctorily made. Laura picked up her articles, answering that he certainly could so ask her – she was free. Yet not her expression either could be called an ardent response. Then she blinked more and more quickly and put her handkerchief to her face. She was weeping violently.

He did not move or try to comfort her in any way. What had come between them? No living person. They had been lovers. There was now no material obstacle whatever to their union. But there was the insistent shadow of that unconscious one: the thin figure of him, moving to and fro in front of the ghastly furnace in the gloom of Durnover Moor.

Yet Vannicock called upon Laura when he was in the neighbourhood, which was not often; but in two years, as if on purpose to further the marriage which everybody was expecting, the —st Foot returned to Budmouth Regis.

Thereupon the two could not help encountering each other at times. But whether because the obstacle had been the source of the love, or from a sense of error, and because Mrs Maumbry bore a less attractive look as a widow than before, their feelings seemed to decline from their former incandescence to a mere tepid civility. What domestic issues supervened in Vannicock's further story the man in the oriel never knew; but Mrs Maumbry lived and died a widow.

Alicia's Diary

I

She Misses Her Sister

JULY 7   I wander about the house in a mood of unutterable sadness, for my dear sister Caroline has left home today with my mother, and I shall not see them again for several weeks. They have accepted a long-standing invitation to visit some old friends of ours, the Marlets, who live at Versailles for cheapness – my mother thinking that it will be for the good of Caroline to see a little of France and Paris. But I don't quite like her going. I fear she may lose some of that childlike simplicity and gentleness which so characterise her, and have been nourished by the seclusion of our life here. Her solicitude about her pony before starting was quite touching, and she made me promise to visit it daily, and see that it came to no harm.

Caroline gone abroad, and I left here! It is the reverse of an ordinary situation, for good or ill-luck has mostly ordained that I should be the absent one. Mother will be quite tired out by the young enthusiasm of Caroline. She will demand to be taken everywhere – to Paris continually, of course; to all the stock shrines of history's devotees: to palaces and prisons; to kings' tombs and queens' tombs; to cemeteries and picture-galleries, and royal hunting forests. My poor mother, having gone over most of this ground many times before, will perhaps not find the perambulation so exhilarating as will Caroline herself. I wish I could have gone with them. I would not have minded having my legs walked off to please Caroline. But this regret is absurd: I could not, of course, leave my father with not a soul in the house to attend to the calls of the parishioners or to pour out his tea.

JULY 15   A letter from Caroline today. It is very strange that she tells me nothing which I expected her to tell – only trivial details. She seems dazzled by the brilliancy of Paris – which no doubt appears still more brilliant to her from the fact of her only being able to obtain occasional glimpses of it. She would see that Paris, too, has a seamy side if you live there. I was not aware that the Marlets knew so many people. If, as mother has said, they went to reside at Versailles for reasons of economy, they will not effect much in that direction while they make a practice of entertaining all the acquaintances who happen to be in their neighbourhood. They do not confine their hospitalities to English people, either. I wonder who this M. de la Feste is, in whom Caroline says my mother is so much interested.

JULY 18   Another letter from Caroline. I have learnt from this epistle that M. Charles de la Feste is 'only one of the many friends of the Marlets'; that though a Frenchman by birth, and now again temporarily at Versailles, he has lived in England many many years; that he is a talented landscape and marine painter, and has exhibited at the Salon, and I think in London. His style and subjects are considered somewhat peculiar in Paris – rather English than Continental. I have not as yet learnt his age, or his condition, married or single. From the tone and nature of her remarks about him he sometimes seems to be a middle-aged family man, sometimes quite the reverse. From his nomadic habits I should say the latter is the most likely. He has travelled and seen a great deal, she tells me, and knows more about English literature than she knows herself.

JULY 21   Letter from Caroline. Query: Is 'a friend of ours and the Marlets', of whom she now anonymously and mysteriously speaks, the same personage as the 'M. de la Feste' of her former letters? He must be the same, I think, from his pursuits. If so, whence this sudden change of tone? . . . I have been lost in thought for at least a quarter of an hour since writing the preceding sentence. Suppose my dear sister is falling in love with this young man – there is no longer any doubt about his age; what a very awkward, risky thing for her! I do hope that my mother has an eye on these proceedings. But, then, poor mother never sees the drift of anything: she is in truth less of a mother to Caroline than I am. If I were there, how jealously I would watch him, and ascertain his designs!

  I am of a stronger nature than Caroline. How I have supported her in the past through her little troubles and great griefs! Is she agitated at the presence of this, to her, new and strange feeling? But I am assuming her to be desperately in love, when I have no proof of anything of the kind. He may be merely a casual friend, of whom I shall hear no more.

JULY 24   Then he is a bachelor, as I suspected. 'If M. de la Feste ever marries he will', etc. So she writes. They are getting into close quarters, obviously. Also, 'Something to keep my hair smooth, which M. de la Feste told me he had found useful for the tips of his moustache.' Very naïvely related this; and with how much unconsciousness of the intimacy between them that the remark reveals! But my mother – what can she be doing? Does she know of this? And if so, why does she not allude to it in her letters to my father? . . . I have been to look at Caroline's pony, in obedience to her reiterated request that I would not miss a day in seeing that she was well cared for. Anxious as Caroline was about this pony of hers before starting, she now never mentioned the poor animal once in her letters. The image of her pet suffers from displacement.

AUGUST 3   Caroline's forgetfulness of her pony has naturally enough extended to me, her sister. It is ten days since she last wrote, and but for a note from my mother I should not know if she were dead or alive.

2

News Interesting and Serious

AUGUST 5   A cloud of letters. A letter from Caroline, another from mother; also one from each to my father.

The probability to which all the intelligence from my sister has pointed of late turns out to be a fact. There is an engagement, or almost an engagement, announced between my dear Caroline and M. de la Feste – to Caroline's sublime happiness, and my mother's entire satisfaction; as well as to that of the Marlets. They and my mother seem to know all about the young man – which is more than I do, though a little extended information about him, considering that I am Caroline's elder sister, would not have been amiss. I half feel with my father, who is much surprised, and, I am sure, not altogether satisfied, that he should not have been consulted at all before matters reached such a definite stage, though he is too amiable to say so openly. I don't quite say that a good thing should have been hindered for the sake of our opinion, if it is a good thing; but the announcement comes very suddenly. It must have been foreseen by my mother for some time that this upshot was probable, and Caroline might have told me more distinctly that M. de la Feste was her lover, instead of alluding so mysteriously to him as only a friend of the Marlets, and lately dropping his name altogether. My father, without exactly objecting to him as a Frenchman, 'wishes he were of English or some other reasonable nationality for one's son-in-law', but I tell him that the demarcations of races, kingdoms and creeds are wearing down every day, that patriotism is a sort of vice, and that the character of the individual is all we need think about in this case. I wonder if, in the event of their marriage, he will continue to live at Versailles, or if he will come to England.

AUGUST 7   A supplemental letter from Caroline, answering, by anticipation, some of the aforesaid queries. She tells me that 'Charles', though he makes Versailles his present home, is by no means bound by his profession to continue there; that he will live just where she wishes, provided it be not too far from some centre of thought, art and civilisation. My mother and herself both think that the marriage should not take place till next year. He exhibits landscapes and canal scenery every year, she says; so I suppose he is popular, and that his income is sufficient to keep them in comfort. If not, I do not see why my father could not settle something more on them than he had intended, and diminish by a little what he had proposed for me, whilst it was imagined that I should be the first to stand in need of such.

'Of engaging manner, attractive appearance and virtuous character' is the reply I receive from her in answer to my request for a personal description. That is vague enough, and I would rather have had one definite fact of complexion, voice, deed or opinion. But of course she has no eye now for material qualities; she cannot see him as he is. She sees him irradiated with glories such as never appertained and never will appertain to any man, foreign, English or colonial. To think that Caroline, two years my junior, and so childlike as to be five years my junior in nature, should be engaged to be married before me. But that is what happens in families more often than we are apt to remember.

AUGUST 16   Interesting news today. Charles, she says, has pleaded that their marriage may just as well be this year as next; and he seems to have nearly converted my mother to the same way of thinking. I do not myself see any reason for delay, beyond the standing one of my father having as yet had no opportunity of forming an opinion upon the man, the time, or anything. However, he takes his lot very quietly, and they are coming home to talk the question over with us; Caroline having decided not to make any positive arrangements for this change of state till she has seen me. Subject to my own and my father's approval, she says, they are inclined to settle the date of the wedding for November, three months from the present time, that it shall take place here in the village, that I, of course, shall be bridesmaid, and many other particulars. She draws an artless picture of the probable effect upon the minds of the villagers of this romantic performance in the chancel of our old church, in which she is to be chief actor – the foreign gentleman dropping down like a god from the skies, picking her up, and triumphantly carrying her off. Her only grief will be separation from me, but this is to be assuaged by my going and staying with her for long months at a time. This simple prattle is very sweet to me, my dear sister, but I cannot help feeling sad at the occasion of it. In the nature of things it is obvious that I shall never be to you again what I hitherto have been: your guide, counsellor and most familiar friend.

M. de la Feste does certainly seem to be all that one could desire as protector to a sensitive fragile child like Caroline, and for that I am thankful. Still, I must remember that I see him as yet only through her eyes. For her sake I am intensely anxious to meet him, and scrutinise him through and through, and learn what the man is really made of who is to have such a treasure in his keeping. The engagement has certainly been formed a little precipitately; I quite agree with my father in that: still, good and happy marriages have been made in a hurry before now, and mother seems well satisfied.

AUGUST 20   A terrible announcement came this morning; and we are in deep trouble. I have been quite unable to steady my thoughts on anything today till now – half-past eleven at night – and I only attempt writing these notes because I am too restless to remain idle, and there is nothing but waiting and waiting left for me to do. Mother has been taken dangerously ill at Versailles: they were within a day or two of starting; but all thought of leaving must now be postponed, for she cannot possibly be moved in her present state. I don't like the sound of haemorrhage at all in a woman of her full habit, and Caroline and the Marlets have not exaggerated their accounts I am certain. On the receipt of the letter my father instantly decided to go to her, and I have been occupied all day in getting him off, for as he calculates on being absent several days, there have been many matters for him to arrange before setting out – the chief being to find someone who will do duty for him next Sunday – a quest of no small difficulty at such short notice; but at last poor old feeble Mr Dugdale has agreed to attempt it, with Mr Highman, the scripture reader, to assist him in the lessons.

I fain would have gone with my father to escape the irksome anxiety of awaiting her; but somebody had to stay, and I could best be spared. George has driven him to the station to meet the last train by which he will catch the midnight boat, and reach Havre some time in the morning. He hates the sea, and a night passage in particular. I hope he will get there without mishap of any kind; but I feel anxious for him, stay-at-home as he is, and unable to cope with any difficulty. Such an errand, too; the journey will be sad enough at best. I almost think I ought to have been the one to go to her.

August 21   I nearly fell asleep of heaviness of spirit last night over my writing. My father must have reached Paris by this time; and now here comes a letter . . .

Later   The letter was to express an earnest hope that my father had set out. My poor mother is sinking, they fear. What will become of Caroline? O, how I wish I could see mother; why could not we both have gone?

Later   I get up from my chair, and walk from window to window, and then come and write a line. I cannot even divine how poor Caroline's marriage is to be carried out if mother dies. I pray that father may have got there in time to talk to her and receive some directions from her about Caroline and M. de la Feste – a man whom neither my father nor I have seen. I, who might be useful in this emergency, am doomed to stay here, waiting in suspense.

August 23   A letter from my father containing the sad news that my mother's spirit has flown. Poor little Caroline is heartbroken – she was always more my mother's pet than I was. It is some comfort to know that my father arrived in time to hear from her own lips her strongly expressed wish that Caroline's marriage should be solemnised as soon as possible. M. de la Feste seems to have been a great favourite of my dear mother's; and I suppose it now becomes almost a sacred duty of my father to accept him as a son-in-law without criticism.

Her Gloom Lightens a Little

SEPTEMBER 10   I have inserted nothing in my diary for more than a fortnight. Events have been altogether too sad for me to have the spirit to put them on paper. And yet there comes a time when the act of recording one's trouble is recognised as a welcome method of dwelling upon it . . .

My dear mother has been brought home and buried here in the parish. It was not so much her own wish that this should be done as my father's, who particularly desired that she should lie in the family vault beside his first wife. I saw them side by side before the vault was closed – two women beloved by one man. As I stood, and Caroline by my side, I fell into a sort of dream, and had an odd fancy that Caroline and I might be also beloved of one, and lie like these together – an impossibility, of course, being sisters. When I awoke from my reverie Caroline took my hand and said it was time to leave.

SEPTEMBER 14   The wedding is indefinitely postponed. Caroline is like a girl awakening in the middle of a somnambulistic experience, and does not realise where she is, or how she stands. She walks about silently, and I cannot tell her thoughts, as I used to do. It was her own doing to write to M. de la Feste and tell him that the wedding could not possibly take place this autumn as originally planned. There is something depressing in this long postponement if she is to marry him at all; and yet I do not see how it could be avoided.

OCTOBER 20   I have had so much to occupy me in consoling Caroline that I have been continually overlooking my diary. Her life was much nearer to my mother's than mine was. She has never, as I, lived away from home long enough to become self-dependent, and hence in her first loss, and all that it involved, she drooped like a rain-beaten lily. But she is of a nature whose wounds soon heal, even though they may be deep, and the supreme poignancy of her sorrow has already passed.

My father is of opinion that the wedding should not be delayed too long. While at Versailles he made the acquaintance of M. de la Feste, and though they had but a short and hurried communion with each other, he was much impressed by M. de la Feste's disposition and conduct, and is strongly in favour of his suit. It is odd that Caroline's betrothed should influence in his favour all who come near him. His portrait, which dear Caroline has shown me, exhibits him to be of a physique that partly accounts for this: but there must be something more than mere appearance, and it is probably some sort of glamour or fascinating power – the quality which prevented Caroline from describing him to me with any accuracy of detail. At the same time, I see from the photograph that his face and head are remarkably well formed;

and though the contours of his mouth are hidden by his moustache, his arched brows show well the romantic disposition of a true lover and painter of nature. I think that the owner of such a face as this must be tender and sympathetic and true.

OCTOBER 30 As my sister's grief for her mother becomes more and more calmed, her love for M. de la Feste begins to reassume its former absorbing command of her. She thinks of him incessantly, and writes whole treatises to him by way of letters. Her blank disappointment at his announcement of his inability to pay us a visit quite so soon as he had promised was quite tragic. I, too, am disappointed, for I wanted to see and estimate him. But having arranged to go to Holland to seize some aerial effects for his pictures, which are only to be obtained at this time of the autumn, he is obliged to postpone his journey this way, which is now to be made early in the new year. I think myself that he ought to have come at all sacrifices, considering Caroline's recent loss, the sad postponement of what she was looking forward to, and her single-minded affection for him. Still, who knows; his professional success is important. Moreover, she is cheerful, and hopeful, and the delay will soon be overpast.

4

She Beholds the Attractive Stranger

FEBRUARY 16 We have had such a dull life here all the winter that I have found nothing important enough to set down, and broke off my journal accordingly. I resume it now to make an entry on the subject of dear Caroline's future. It seems that she was too grieved, immediately after the loss of our mother, to answer definitely the question of M. de la Feste how long the postponement was to be; then, afterwards, it was agreed that the matter should be discussed on his autumn visit; but as he did not come, it has remained in abeyance till this week, when Caroline, with the greatest simplicity and confidence, has written to him without any further pressure on his part, and told him that she is quite ready to fix the time, and will do so as soon as he arrives to see her. She is a little frightened now, lest it should seem forward in her to have revived the subject of her own accord; but she may assume that his question has been waiting on for an answer ever since, and that she has, therefore, acted only within her promise. In truth, the secret at the bottom of it all is that she is somewhat saddened because he has not latterly reminded her of the pause in their affairs – that, in short, his original impatience to possess her is not now found to animate him so obviously. I suppose that he loves her as much as ever; indeed, I am sure he must do so, seeing how lovable she is. It is mostly thus with all men when women are out of their sight; they grow negligent. Caroline must have patience, and remember that a man of his genius has many and important calls upon his time. In justice to her I must add that she does remember it fairly well, and has as much patience as any girl ever had in the circumstances. He hopes to come at the beginning of April at latest. Well, when he comes we shall see him.

APRIL 5   I think that what M. de la Feste writes is reasonable enough, though Caroline looks heart-sick about it. It is hardly worth while for him to cross all the way to England and back just now, while the sea is so turbulent, seeing that he will be obliged, in any event, to come in May, when he has to be in London for professional purposes, at which time he can take us easily on his way both coming and going. When Caroline becomes his wife she will be more practical, no doubt; but she is such a child as yet that there is no contenting her with reasons. However, the time will pass quickly, there being so much to do in preparing a trousseau for her, which must now be put in hand in order that we may have plenty of leisure to get it ready. On no account must Caroline be married in half-mourning; I am sure that mother, could she know, would not wish it, and it is odd that Caroline should be so intractably persistent on this point, when she is usually so yielding.

APRIL 30   This month has flown on swallow's wings. We are in a great state of excitement – I as much as she – I cannot quite tell why. He is really coming in ten days, he says.

MAY 9, *4 p.m.*   I am so agitated I can scarcely write, and yet am particularly impelled to do so before leaving my room. It is the unexpected shape of an expected event which has caused my absurd excitement, which proves me almost as much a schoolgirl as Caroline.

   M. de la Feste was not, as we understood, to have come till tomorrow; but he is here – just arrived. All household directions have devolved upon me, for my father, not thinking M. de la Feste would appear before us for another four-and-twenty hours, left home before post time to attend a distant consecration; and hence Caroline and I were in no small excitement when Charles's letter was opened, and we read that he had been unexpectedly favoured in the dispatch of his studio work, and would follow his letter in a few hours. We sent the covered carriage to meet the train indicated, and waited like two newly strung harps for the first sound of the returning wheels. At last we heard them on the gravel; and the question arose who was to receive him. It was, strictly speaking, my duty; but I felt timid; I could not help shirking it, and insisted that Caroline should go down. She did not, however, go near the door as she usually does when anybody is expected, but waited palpitating in the drawing-room. He little thought when he saw the silent hall, and the apparently deserted house, how that house was at the very same moment alive and throbbing with interest under the surface. I stood at the back of the upper landing, where nobody could see me from downstairs, and heard him walk across the hall – a lighter step than my father's – and heard him then go into the drawing-room, and the servant shut the door behind him and go away.

What a pretty lovers' meeting they must have had in there all to themselves! Caroline's sweet face looking up from her black gown – how it must have touched him. I know she wept very much, for I heard her; and her eyes will be red afterwards, and no wonder, poor dear, though she is no doubt happy. I can imagine what she is telling him while I write this – her fears lest anything should have happened to prevent his coming after all – gentle, smiling reproaches for his long delay; and things of that sort. His two portmanteaus are at this moment crossing the landing on the way to his room. I wonder if I ought to go down.

A little later I have seen him! It was not at all in the way that I intended to encounter him, and I am vexed. Just after his portmanteaus were brought up I went out from my room to descend, when, at the moment of stepping towards the first stair, my eyes were caught by an object in the hall below, and I paused for an instant, till I saw that it was a bundle of canvas and sticks, composing a sketching tent and easel. At the same nick of time the drawing-room door opened and the affianced pair came out. They were saying they would go into the garden; and he waited a moment while she put on her hat. My idea was to let them pass on without seeing me, since they seemed not to want my company, but I had got too far on the landing to retreat; he looked up, and stood staring at me – engrossed to a dream-like fixity. Thereupon I, too, instead of advancing as I ought to have done, stood moonstruck and awkward, and before I could gather my weak senses sufficiently to descend, she had called him, and they went out by the garden door together. I then thought of following them, but have changed my mind, and come here to jot down these few lines. It is all I am fit for . . .

He is even more handsome than I expected. I was right in feeling he must have an attraction beyond that of form: it appeared even in that momentary glance. How happy Caroline ought to be. But I must, of course, go down to be ready with tea in the drawing-room by the time they come indoors.

11 p.m. I have made the acquaintance of M. de la Feste; and I seem to be another woman from the effect of it. I cannot describe why this should be so, but conversation with him seems to expand the view, and open the heart, and raise one as upon stilts to wider prospects. He has a good intellectual forehead, perfect eyebrows, dark hair and eyes, an animated manner, and a persuasive voice. His voice is soft in quality – too soft for a man, perhaps; and yet on second thoughts I would not have it less so. We have been talking of his art: I had no notion that art demanded such sacrifices or such tender devotion; or that there were two roads for choice within its precincts, the road of vulgar money-making and the road of high aims and consequent inappreciation for many long years by the public. That he has adopted the latter need not be said to those who understand him. It is a blessing for Caroline that she has been chosen by such a man, and she ought not to lament at postponements and delays, since they have arisen unavoidably. Whether he finds hers a sufficiently rich nature, intellectually and emotionally, for his own, I know not, but he seems occasionally to be disappointed at her simple views of things. Does he really feel such love for her at this moment as he no doubt believes himself to be feeling, and as he no doubt hopes to feel for the remainder of his life towards her?

It was a curious thing he told me when we were left for a few minutes alone; that Caroline had alluded so slightly to me in her conversation and letters that he had not realised my presence in the house here at all. But, of course, it was only natural that she should write and talk most about herself. I suppose it was on account of the fact of his being taken in some measure unawares that I caught him on two or three occasions regarding me fixedly in a way that disquieted me somewhat, having been lately in so little society; till my glance aroused him from his reverie, and he looked elsewhere in some confusion. It was fortunate that he did so, and thus failed to notice my own. It shows that he, too, is not particularly a society person.

MAY 10   Have had another interesting conversation with M. de la Feste on schools of landscape painting in the drawing-room after dinner this evening – my father having fallen asleep, and left nobody but Caroline and myself for Charles to talk to. I did not mean to say so much to him, and had taken a volume of *Modern Painters* from the bookcase to occupy myself with, while leaving the two lovers to themselves; but he would include me in his audience, and I was obliged to lay the book aside. However, I insisted on keeping Caroline in the conversation, though her views on pictorial art were only too charmingly crude and primitive.

Tomorrow, if fine, we are all three going to Wherryborne Wood, where Charles will give us practical illustrations of the principles of colouring that he has enumerated tonight. I am determined not to occupy his attention to the exclusion of Caroline, and my plan is that when we are in the dense part of the wood I will lag behind, and slip away, and leave them to return by themselves. I suppose the reason of his attentiveness to me lies in his simply wishing to win the good opinion of one who is so closely united to Caroline, and so likely to influence her good opinion of him.

MAY 11, *late*   I cannot sleep, and in desperation have lit my candle and taken up my pen. My restlessness is occasioned by what has occurred today, which at first I did not mean to write down, or trust to any heart but my own. We went to Wherryborne Wood – Caroline, Charles and I, as we had intended – and walked all three along the green track through the midst, Charles in the middle between Caroline and myself. Presently I found that, as usual, he and I were the only talkers, Caroline amusing herself by observing birds and squirrels as she walked docilely alongside her betrothed. Having noticed this I dropped behind at the first opportunity and slipped among the trees, in a direction in which I knew I should find another path that would take me home. Upon this track I by and by emerged, and walked along it in silent thought till, at a bend, I suddenly encountered M. de la Feste standing stock still and smiling thoughtfully at me.

'Where is Caroline?' said I.

'Only a little way off,' says he. 'When we missed you from behind us we thought you might have mistaken the direction we had followed, so she has gone one way to find you and I have come this way.'

We then went back to find Caroline, but could not discover her anywhere, and the upshot was that he and I were wandering about the woods alone for more than an hour. On reaching home we found she had given us up after searching a little while, and arrived there some time before. I should not be so disturbed by the incident if I had not perceived that, during her absence from us, he did not make any earnest effort to rediscover her; and in answer to my repeated expressions of wonder as to whither she could have wandered he only said, 'Oh, she's quite safe; she told me she knew the way home from any part of this wood. Let us go on with our talk. I assure you I value this privilege of being with one I so much admire more than you imagine;' and other things of that kind. I was so foolish as to show a little perturbation – I cannot tell why I did not control myself; and I think he noticed that I was not cool. Caroline has, with her simple good faith, thought nothing of the occurrence; yet altogether I am not satisfied.

5

Her Situation is a Trying One

MAY 15   The more I think of it day after day, the more convinced I am that my suspicions are true. He is too interested in me – well, in plain words, loves me; or, not to degrade that phrase, has a wild passion for me; and his affection for Caroline is that towards a sister only. That is the distressing truth; how it has come about I cannot tell, and it wears upon me.

A hundred little circumstances have revealed this to me, and the longer I dwell upon it the more agitating does the consideration become. Heaven only can help me out of the terrible difficulty in which this places me. I have done nothing to encourage him to be faithless to her. I have studiously kept out of his way; have persistently refused to be a third in their interviews. Yet all to no purpose. Some fatality has seemed to rule, ever since he came to the house, that this disastrous inversion of things should arise. If I had only foreseen the possibility of it before he arrived, how gladly would I have departed on some visit or other to the meanest friend to hinder such an apparent treachery. But I blindly welcomed him – indeed, made myself particularly agreeable to him for her sake.

There is no possibility of my suspicions being wrong; not until they have reached absolute certainty have I dared even to admit the truth to myself. His conduct today would have proved them true had I entertained no previous apprehensions. Some photographs of myself came for me by post, and they were handed round at the breakfast table and criticised. I put them temporarily on a side table, and did not remember them until an hour afterwards when I was in my own room. On going to fetch them I discovered him standing at the table with his back towards the door bending over the photographs, one of which he raised to his lips.

The witnessing this act so frightened me that I crept away to escape observation. It was the climax to a series of slight and significant actions all tending to the same conclusion. The question for me now is, what am I to do? To go away is what first occurs to me, but what reason can I give Caroline and my father for such a step? Besides, it might precipitate some sort of catastrophe by driving Charles to desperation. For the present, therefore, I have decided that I can only wait, though his contiguity is strangely disturbing to me now, and I hardly retain strength of mind to encounter him. How will the distressing complication end?

MAY 19   And so it has come! My mere avoidance of him has precipitated the worst issue – a declaration. I had occasion to go into the kitchen garden to gather some of the double ragged-robins which grew in a corner there. Almost as soon as I had entered I heard footsteps without. The door opened and shut, and I turned to behold him just inside it. As the garden is closed by four walls and the gardener was absent, the spot ensured absolute privacy. He came along the path by the asparagus-bed, and overtook me.

'You know why I come, Alicia?' said he, in a tremulous voice.

I said nothing, and hung my head, for by his tone I did know.

'Yes,' he went on, 'it is you I love; my sentiment towards your sister is one of affection too, but protective, tutelary affection – no more. Say what you will I cannot help it. I mistook my feeling for her, and I know how much I am to blame for my want of self-knowledge. I have fought against this discovery night and day; but it cannot be concealed. Why did I ever see you, since I could not see you till I had committed myself? At the moment my eyes beheld you on that day of my arrival, I said, "This is the woman for whom my manhood has waited." Ever since an unaccountable fascination has riveted my heart to you. Answer one word!'

'Oh, M. de la Feste!' I burst out. What I said more I cannot remember, but I suppose that the misery I was in showed pretty plainly, for he said, 'Something must be done to let her know; perhaps I have mistaken her affection, too; but all depends upon what you feel.'

'I cannot tell what I feel,' said I, 'except that this seems terrible treachery; and every moment that I stay with you here makes it worse! . . . Try to keep faith with her – her young heart is tender; believe me there is no mistake in the quality of her love for you. Would there were! This would kill her if she knew it!'

He sighed heavily. 'She ought never to be my wife,' he said. 'Leaving my own happiness out of the question, it would be a cruelty to her to unite her to me.'

I said I could not hear such words from him, and begged him in tears to go away; he obeyed, and I heard the garden door shut behind him. What is to be the end of the announcement, and the fate of Caroline?

MAY 20   I put a good deal on paper yesterday, and yet not all. I was, in truth, hoping against hope, against conviction, against too conscious self-judgement. I scarcely dare own the truth now, yet it relieves my aching heart to set it down. Yes, I love him – that is the dreadful fact, and I can no longer parry, evade, or deny it to myself though to the rest of the world it can never be owned. I love Caroline's betrothed, and he loves me. It is no yesterday's passion, cultivated by our converse; it came at first sight, independently of my will; and my talk with him yesterday made rather against it than for it, but, alas, did not quench it. God forgive us both for this terrible treachery.

MAY 25   All is vague; our courses shapeless. He comes and goes, being occupied, ostensibly at least, with sketching in his tent in the wood. Whether he and she see each other privately I cannot tell, but I rather think they do not; that she sadly awaits him, and he does not appear. Not a sign from him that my repulse has done him any good, or that he will endeavour to keep faith with her. Oh, if I only had the compulsion of a god, and the self-sacrifice of a martyr!

MAY 31   It has all ended – or rather this act of the sad drama has ended – in nothing. He has left us. No day for the fulfilment of the engagement with Caroline is named, my father not being the man to press anyone on such a matter, or, indeed, to interfere in any way. We two girls are, in fact, quite defenceless in a case of this kind; lovers may come when they choose, and desert when they choose; poor father is too urbane to utter a word of remonstrance or enquiry. Moreover, as the approved of my dead mother, M. de la Feste has a sort of autocratic power with my father, who holds it unkind to her memory to have an opinion about him. I, feeling it my duty, asked M. de la Feste at the last moment about the engagement, in a voice I could not keep firm.

'Since the death of your mother all has been indefinite – all!' he said gloomily. That was the whole. Possibly, Wherryborne Rectory may see him no more.

JUNE 7   M. de la Feste has written – one letter to her, one to me. Hers could not have been very warm, for she did not brighten on reading it. Mine was an ordinary note of friendship, filling an ordinary sheet of paper, which I handed over to Caroline when I had finished looking it through. But there was a scrap of paper in the bottom of the envelope, which I dared not show anyone. This scrap is his real letter: I scanned it alone in my room, trembling, hot and cold by turns. He tells me he is very wretched; that he deplores what has happened, but was helpless. Why did I let him see me, if only to make him faithless. Alas, alas!

JUNE 21   My dear Caroline has lost appetite, spirits, health. Hope deferred maketh the heart sick. His letters to her grow colder – if indeed he has written more than one. He has refrained from writing again to me – he knows it is no use. Altogether the situation that he and she and I are in is melancholy in the extreme. Why are human hearts so perverse?

6

Her Ingenuity Instigates Her

SEPTEMBER 19   Three months of anxious care – till at length I have taken the extreme step of writing to him. Our chief distress has been caused by the state of poor Caroline, who, after sinking by degrees into such extreme weakness as to make it doubtful if she can ever recover full vigour, has today been taken much worse. Her position is very critical. The doctor says plainly that she is dying of a broken heart – and that even the removal of the cause may not now restore her. Ought I to have written to Charles sooner? But how could I when she forbade me? It was her pride only which instigated her, and I should not have obeyed.

SEPTEMBER 26   Charles has arrived and has seen her. He is shocked, conscience-stricken, remorseful. I have told him that he can do no good beyond cheering her by his presence. I do not know what he thinks of proposing to her if she gets better, but he says little to her at present; indeed he dares not: his words agitate her dangerously.

SEPTEMBER 28   After a struggle between duty and selfishness, such as I pray to heaven I may never have to undergo again, I have asked him for pity's sake to make her his wife, here and now, as she lies. I said to him that the poor child would not trouble him long; and such a solemnisation would soothe her last hours as nothing else could do. He said that he would willingly do so, and had thought of it himself, but for one forbidding reason: in the event of her death as his wife he can never marry me, her sister, according to our laws. I started at his words. He went on: 'On the other hand, if I were sure that immediate marriage with me would save her life, I would not refuse, for possibly I might after a while, and out of sight of you, make myself fairly content with one of so sweet a disposition as hers; but if, as is probable, neither my marrying her nor any other act can avail to save her life, by so doing I lose both her and you.' I could not answer him.

SEPTEMBER 29   He continued firm in his reasons for refusal till this morning, and then I became possessed with an idea, which I at once propounded to him. It was that he should at least consent to a form of marriage with Caroline, in consideration of her love; a form which need not be a legal union, but one which would satisfy her sick and enfeebled soul. Such things have been done, and the sentiment of feeling herself his would inexpressibly comfort her mind, I am sure. Then, if she is taken from us, I should not have lost the power of becoming his lawful wife at some future day, if it indeed should be deemed expedient; if, on the other hand, she lives, he can on her recovery inform her of the incompleteness of their marriage contract, the ceremony can be repeated, and I can, and I am sure willingly would, avoid troubling them with my presence till grey hairs and wrinkles make his unfortunate passion for me a thing of the past. I put all this before him; but he demurred.

SEPTEMBER 30   I have urged him again. He says he will consider. It is no time to mince matters, and as a further inducement I have offered to enter into a solemn engagement to marry him myself a year after her death.

Later   An agitating interview. He says he will agree to whatever I propose, the three possibilities and our contingent acts being recorded as follows: First, in the event of dear Caroline being taken from us, I marry him on the expiration of a year; Second, in the forlorn chance of her recovery I take upon myself the responsibility of explaining to Caroline the true nature of the ceremony he has gone through with her, that it was done at my suggestion to make her happy at once, before a special licence could be obtained, and that a public ceremony at church is awaiting her; Third, in the unlikely event of her cooling, and refusing to repeat the ceremony with him, I leave England, join him abroad, and there wed him, agreeing not to live in England again till Caroline has either married another or regards her attachment to Charles as a bygone matter. I have thought over these conditions, and have agreed to them all as they stand.

11 p.m.   I do not much like this scheme, after all. For one thing, I have just sounded my father on it before parting with him for the night, my impression having been that he would see no objection. But he says he could on no account countenance any such unreal proceeding; however good our intentions, and even though the poor girl were dying, it would not be right. So I sadly seek my pillow.

OCTOBER 1   I am sure my father is wrong in his view. Why is it not right, if it would be balm to Caroline's wounded soul, and if a real ceremony is absolutely refused by Charles – moreover is hardly practicable in the difficulty of getting a special licence, even if he agreed? My father does not know, or will not believe, that Caroline's attachment has been the cause of her hopeless condition. But that it is so, and that the form of words would give her inexpressible happiness, I know well; for I whispered tentatively in her ear on such marriages, and the effect was great. Henceforth my father cannot be taken into confidence on the subject of Caroline. He does not understand her.

12 o'clock noon   I have taken advantage of my father's absence today to confide my secret notion to a thoughtful young man, who called here this morning to speak to my father. He is the Mr Theophilus Higham, of whom I have already had occasion to speak – a scripture reader in the next town, and is soon going to be ordained. I told him the pitiable case, and my remedy. He says ardently that he will assist me – would do anything for me (he is, in truth, an admirer of mine); he sees no wrong in such an act of charity. He is coming again to the house this afternoon before my father returns, to carry out the idea. I have spoken to Charles, who promises to be ready. I must now break the news to Caroline.

11 o'clock p.m.   I have been in too much excitement till now to set down the result. We have accomplished our plan; and though I feel like a guilty sinner, I am glad. My father, of course, is not to be informed as yet. Caroline has had a seraphic expression upon her wasted, transparent face ever since. I should hardly be surprised if it really saved her life even now, and rendered a legitimate union necessary between them. In that case my father can be informed of the whole proceeding, and in the face of such wonderful success cannot disapprove. Meanwhile poor Charles has not lost the possibility of taking unworthy me to fill her place should she – But I cannot contemplate that alternative unmoved, and will not write it. Charles left for the south of Europe immediately after the ceremony. He was in a high-strung, throbbing, almost wild state of mind at first, but grew calmer under my exhortations. I had to pay the penalty of receiving a farewell kiss from him, which I much regret, considering its meaning; but he took me so unexpectedly, and in a moment was gone.

OCTOBER 6   She certainly is better, and even when she found that Charles had been suddenly obliged to leave, she received the news quite cheerfully. The doctor says that her apparent improvement may be delusive; but I think our impressing upon her the necessity of keeping what has occurred a secret from papa, and everybody, helps to give her a zest for life.

OCTOBER 8   She is still mending. I am glad to have saved her – my only sister – if I have done so; though I shall now never become Charles's wife.

A Surprise Awaits Her

FEBRUARY 5   Writing has been absolutely impossible for a long while; but I now reach a stage at which it seems possible to jot down a line. Caroline's recovery, extending over four months, has been very engrossing; at first slow, latterly rapid. But a fearful complication of affairs attends it!

> O what a tangled web we weave
> When first we practise to deceive!

Charles has written reproachfully to me from Venice, where he is. He says how can he fulfil in the real what he has enacted in the counterfeit, while he still loves me? Yet how, on the other hand, can he leave it unfulfilled? All this time I have not told her, and up to this minute she believes that he has indeed taken her for better, for worse, till death them do part. It is a harassing position for me, and all three. In the awful approach of death, one's judgement loses its balance, and we do anything to meet the exigencies of the moment, with a single eye to the one who excites our sympathy, and from whom we seem on the brink of being separated for ever.

Had he really married her at that time all would be settled now. But he took too much thought; she might have died, and then he had his reason. If indeed it had turned out so, I should now be perhaps a sad woman; but not a tempest-tossed one . . . The possibility of his claiming me after all is what lies at the root of my agitation. Everything hangs by a thread. Suppose I tell her the marriage was a mockery; suppose she is indignant with me and with him for the deception – and then? Otherwise, suppose she is not indignant but forgives all; he is bound to marry her; and honour constrains me to urge him thereto, in spite of what he protests, and to smooth the way to this issue by my method of informing her. I have meant to tell her the last month – ever since she has been strong enough to bear such tidings; but I have been without the power – the moral force. Surely I must write, and get him to come and assist me.

MARCH 14   She continually wonders why he does not come, the five months of his enforced absence having expired; and still more she wonders why he does not write oftener. His last letter was cold, she says, and she fears he regrets his marriage, which he may only have celebrated with her for pity's sake, thinking she was sure to die. It makes one's heart bleed to hear her hovering thus so near the truth, and yet never discerning its actual shape.

A minor trouble besets me, too, in the person of the young scripture reader, whose conscience pricks him for the part he played. Surely I am punished, if ever woman were, for a too ingenious perversion of her better judgement!

APRIL 2   She is practically well. The faint pink revives in her cheek, though it is not quite so full as heretofore. But she still wonders what she can have done to offend 'her dear husband', and I have been obliged to tell the smallest part of the truth – an unimportant fragment of the whole, in fact. I said that I feared for the moment he might regret the precipitancy of the act, which her illness caused, his affairs not having been quite sufficiently advanced for marriage just then, though he will doubtless come to her as soon as he has a home ready. Meanwhile I have written to him, peremptorily, to come and relieve me in this awful dilemma. He will find no note of love in that.

APRIL 10   To my alarm the letter I lately addressed to him at Venice, where he is staying, as well as the last one she sent him, have received no reply. She thinks he is ill. I do not quite think that, but I wish we could hear from him. Perhaps the peremptoriness of my words had offended him; it grieves me to think it possible. I offend him! But too much of this. I must tell her the truth, or she may in her ignorance commit herself to some course or other that may be ruinously compromising. She said plaintively just now that if he could see her, and know how occupied with him and him alone is her every waking hour, she is sure he would forgive her the wicked presumption of becoming his wife. Very sweet all that, and touching. I could not conceal my tears.

APRIL 15   The house is in confusion; my father is angry and distressed, and I am distracted. Caroline has disappeared – gone away secretly. I cannot help thinking that I know where she is gone to. How guilty I seem, and how innocent she! Oh that I had told her before now!

1 o'clock   No trace of her as yet. We find also that the little waiting-maid we have here in training has disappeared with Caroline, and there is not much doubt that Caroline, fearing to travel alone, has induced this girl to go with her as companion. I am almost sure she has started in desperation to find him, and that Venice is her goal. Why should she run away, if not to join her husband, as she thinks him? Now that I consider, there have been indications of this wish in her for days, as in birds of passage there lurk signs of their incipient intention; and yet I did not think she would have taken such an extreme step, unaided, and without consulting me. I can only jot down the bare facts – I have no time for reflections. But fancy Caroline travelling across the continent of Europe with a chit of a girl, who will be more of a charge than an assistance! They will be a mark for every marauder who encounters them.

Evening, 8 o'clock   Yes, it is as I surmised. She has gone to join him. A note posted by her in Budmouth Regis at daybreak has reached me this afternoon – thanks to the fortunate chance of one of the servants calling for letters in town today, or I should not have got it until tomorrow. She merely asserts her determination of going to him, and has started privately, that nothing may hinder her; stating nothing about her route. That such a gentle thing should suddenly become so calmly resolute quite surprises me. Alas, he may have left Venice – she may not find him for weeks – may not at all.

My father, on learning the facts, bade me at once have everything ready by nine this evening, in time to drive to the train that meets the night steamboat. This I have done, and there being an hour to spare before we start, I relieve the suspense of waiting by taking up my pen. He says overtake her we must, and calls Charles the hardest of names. He believes, of course, that she is merely an infatuated girl rushing off to meet her lover; and how can the wretched I tell him that she is more, and in a sense better than that – yet not sufficiently more and better to make this flight to Charles anything but a still greater danger to her than a mere lover's impulse. We shall go by way of Paris, and we think we may overtake her there. I hear my father walking restlessly up and down the hall, and can write no more.

8

She Travels in Pursuit

APRIL 16, *evening, Paris, Hôtel —*   There is no overtaking her at this place; but she has been here, as I thought, no other hotel in Paris being known to her. We go on tomorrow morning.

APRIL 18 – *Venice*   A morning of adventures and emotions which leave me sick and weary, and yet unable to sleep, though I have lain down on the sofa of my room for more than an hour in the attempt. I therefore make up my diary to date in a hurried fashion, for the sake of the riddance it affords to ideas which otherwise remain suspended hotly in the brain.

We arrived here this morning in broad sunlight, which lit up the sea-girt buildings as we approached so that they seemed like a city of cork floating raft-like on the smooth, blue deep. But I only glanced from the carriage window at the lovely scene, and we were soon across the intervening water and inside the railway station. When we got to the front steps the row of black gondolas and the shouts of the gondoliers so bewildered my father that he was understood to require two gondolas instead of one with two oars, and so I found him in one and myself in another. We got this righted after a while, and were rowed at once to the hotel on the Riva degli Schiavoni where M. de la Feste had been staying when we last heard from him, the way being down the Grand Canal for some distance, under the Rialto, and then by narrow canals which eventually brought us under the Bridge of Sighs – harmonious to our moods! – and out again into open water. The scene was purity itself as to colour, but it was cruel that I should behold it for the first time under such circumstances.

As soon as I entered the hotel, which is an old-fashioned place, like most places here, where people are taken *en pension* as well as the ordinary way, I rushed to the framed list of visitors hanging in the hall, and in a moment I saw Charles's name upon it among the rest. But she was our chief thought. I turned to the hall porter, and – knowing that she would have travelled as 'Madame de la Feste' – I asked for her under that name, without my father hearing. (He, poor soul, was making confused enquiries outside the door about 'an English lady', as if there were not a score of English ladies at hand.)

'She has just come,' said the porter. 'Madame came by the very early train this morning, when monsieur was asleep, and she requested us not to disturb him. She is now in her room.'

Whether Caroline had seen us from the window, or overheard me, I do not know, but at that moment I heard footsteps on the bare marble stairs, and she appeared in person descending.

'Caroline!' I exclaimed, 'why have you done this?' and rushed up to her.

She did not answer; but looked down to hide her emotion, which she conquered after the lapse of a few seconds, putting on a practical tone that belied her.

'I am just going to my husband,' she said. 'I have not yet seen him. I have not been here long.' She condescended to give no further reason for her movements, and made as if to move on. I implored her to come into a private room where I could speak to her in confidence, but she objected. However, the dining-room, close at hand, was quite empty at this hour, and I got her inside and closed the door. I do not know how I began my explanation, or how I ended it, but I told her briefly and brokenly enough that the marriage was not real.

'Not real?' she said vacantly.

'It is not,' said I. 'You will find that it is all as I say.'

She could not believe my meaning even then. 'Not his wife?' she cried. 'It is impossible. What am I, then?'

I added more details, and reiterated the reason for my conduct as well as I could; but heaven knows how very difficult I found it to feel a jot more justification for it in my own mind than she did in hers.

The revulsion of feeling, as soon as she really comprehended all, was most distressing. After her grief had in some measure spent itself she turned against both him and me.

'Why should I have been deceived like this?' she demanded, with a bitter haughtiness of which I had not deemed such a tractable creature capable. 'Do you suppose that anything could justify such an imposition? What, oh what a snare you have spread for me!'

I murmured, 'Your life seemed to require it,' but she did not hear me. She sank down in a chair, covered her face, and then my father came in. 'Oh, here you are!' he said. 'I could not find you. And Caroline!'

'And were you, papa, a party to this strange deed of kindness?'

'To what?' said he.

Then out it all came, and for the first time he was made acquainted with the fact that the scheme for soothing her illness, which I had sounded him upon, had been really carried out. In a moment he sided with Caroline. My repeated assurance that my motive was good availed less than nothing. In a minute or two Caroline arose and went abruptly out of the room, and my father followed her, leaving me alone to my reflections.

I was so bent upon finding Charles immediately that I did not notice whither they went. The servants told me that M. de la Feste was just outside smoking, and one of them went to look for him, I following; but before we had gone many steps he came out of the hotel behind me. I expected him to be amazed; but he showed no surprise at seeing me, though he showed another kind of feeling to an extent which dismayed me. I may have revealed something similar; but I struggled hard against all emotion, and as soon as I could I told him she had come. He simply said 'Yes' in a low voice.

'You know it, Charles?' said I.

'I have just learnt it,' he said.

'Oh, Charles,' I went on, 'having delayed completing your marriage with her till now, I fear it has become a serious position for us. Why did you not reply to our letters?'

'I was purposing to reply in person: I did not know how to address her on the point – how to address you. But what has become of her?'

'She has gone off with my father,' said I; 'indignant with you, and scorning me.'

He was silent: and I suggested that we should follow them, pointing out the direction which I fancied their gondola had taken. As the one we got into was doubly manned we soon came in view of their two figures ahead of us, while they were not likely to observe us, our boat having the *felze* on, while theirs was uncovered. They shot into a narrow canal just beyond the Giardino Reale, and by the time we were floating up between its slimy walls we saw them getting out of their gondola at the steps which lead up near the end of the Via 22 Marzo. When we reached the same spot they were walking up and down the Via in consultation. Getting out he stood on the lower steps watching them. I watched him. He seemed to fall into a reverie.

'Will you not go and speak to her?' said I at length.

He assented, and went forward. Still he did not hasten to join them, but, screened by a projecting window, observed their musing converse. At last he looked back at me; whereupon I pointed forward, and he in obedience stepped out, and met them face to face. Caroline flushed hot, bowed haughtily to him, turned away, and taking my father's arm violently, led him off before he had had time to use his own judgement. They disappeared into a narrow *calle*, or alley, leading to the back of the buildings on the Grand Canal.

M. de la Feste came slowly back; as he stepped in beside me I realised my position so vividly that my heart might almost have been heard to beat. The third condition had arisen – the least expected by either of us. She had refused him; he was free to claim me.

We returned in the boat together. He seemed quite absorbed till we had turned the angle into the Grand Canal, when he broke the silence. 'She spoke very bitterly to you in the *salle à manger*,' he said. 'I do not think she was quite warranted in speaking so to you, who had nursed her so tenderly.'

'Oh, but I think she was,' I answered. 'It was there I told her what had been done; she did not know till then.'

'She was very dignified – very striking,' he murmured. 'You were more.'

'But how do you know what passed between us,' said I. He then told me that he had seen and heard all. The dining-room was divided by folding-doors from an inner portion, and he had been sitting in the latter part when we entered the outer, so that our words were distinctly audible.

'But, dear Alicia,' he went on, 'I was more impressed by the affection of your apology to her than by anything else. And do you know that now the conditions have arisen which give me liberty to consider you my affianced?' I had been expecting this, but yet was not prepared. I stammered out that we would not discuss it then.

'Why not?' said he. 'Do you know that we may marry here and now? She has cast off both you and me.'

'It cannot be,' said I, firmly. 'She has not been fairly asked to be your wife in fact – to repeat the service lawfully; and until that has been done it would be grievous sin in me to accept you.'

I had not noticed where the gondoliers were rowing us. I suppose he had given them some direction unheard by me, for as I resigned myself in despairing indolence to the motion of the gondola, I perceived that it was taking us up the Canal and, turning into a side opening near the Palazzo Grimani, drawing up at some steps near the end of a large church.

'Where are we?' said I.

'It is the Church of the Frari,' he replied. 'We might be married there. At any rate, let us go inside, and grow calm, and decide what to do.'

When we had entered I found that whether a place to marry in or not, it was one to depress. The word which Venice speaks most constantly – decay – was in a sense accentuated here. The whole large fabric itself seemed sinking into an earth which was not solid enough to bear it. Cobwebbed cracks zigzagged the walls, and similar webs clouded the window-panes. A sickly-sweet smell pervaded the aisles. After walking about with him a little while in embarrassing silences, divided only by his cursory explanations of the monuments and other objects, and almost fearing he might produce a marriage licence, I went to a door in the south transept which opened into the sacristy.

I glanced through it, towards the small altar at the upper end. The place was empty save for one figure, and she was kneeling here in front of the beautiful altarpiece by Bellini. Beautiful though it was she seemed not to see it. She was weeping and praying as though her heart was broken. She was my sister Caroline. I beckoned to Charles, and he came to my side, and looked through the door with me.

'Speak to her,' said I. 'She will forgive you.'

I gently pushed him through the doorway, and went back into the transept, down the nave, and onward to the west door. There I saw my father, to whom I spoke. He answered severely that, having first obtained comfortable quarters in a pension on the Grand Canal, he had gone back to the hotel on the Riva degli Schiavoni to find me; but that I was not there. He was now waiting for Caroline, to accompany her back to the pension, at which she had requested to be left to herself as much as possible till she could regain some composure.

I told him that it was useless to dwell on what was past, that I no doubt had erred, that the remedy lay in the future and their marriage. In this he quite agreed with me, and on my informing him that M. de la Feste was at that moment with Caroline in the sacristy, he assented to my proposal that we should leave them to themselves, and return together to await them at the pension, where he had also engaged a room for me. This we did, and going up to the chamber he had chosen for me, which overlooked the Canal, I leant from the window to watch for the gondola that should contain Charles and my sister.

They were not long in coming. I recognised them by the colour of her sunshade as soon as they turned the bend on my right hand. They were side by side of necessity, but there was no conversation between them, and I thought that she looked flushed and he pale. When they were rowed in to the steps of our house he handed her up. I fancied she might have refused his assistance, but she did not. Soon I heard her pass my door, and wishing to know the result of their interview I went downstairs, seeing that the gondola had not put off with him. He was turning from the door, but not towards the water, intending apparently to walk home by way of the *calle* which led into the Via 22 Marzo.

'Has she forgiven you?' said I.

'I have not asked her,' he said.

'But you are bound to do so,' I told him.

He paused, and then said, 'Alicia, let us understand each other. Do you mean to tell me, once for all, that if your sister is willing to become my wife you absolutely make way for her, and will not entertain any thought of what I suggested to you any more?'

'I do tell you so,' said I with dry lips. 'You belong to her – how can I do otherwise?'

'Yes; it is so; it is purely a question of honour,' he returned. 'Very well then, honour shall be my word, and not my love. I will put the question to her frankly; if she says yes, the marriage shall be. But not here. It shall be at your own house in England.'

'When?' said I.

'I will accompany her there,' he replied, 'and it shall be within a week of her return. I have nothing to gain by delay. But I will not answer for the consequences.'

'What do you mean?' said I. He made no reply, went away, and I came back to my room.

9

She Witnesses the End

APRIL 20, *10.30 p.m.*   Milan – We are thus far on our way homeward. I, being decidedly *de trop*, travel apart from the rest as much as I can. Having dined at the hotel here, I went out by myself; regardless of the proprieties, for I could not stay in. I walked at a leisurely pace along the Via Allesandro Manzoni till my eye was caught by the grand Galleria Vittorio Emanuele, and I entered under the high glass arcades till I reached the central octagon, where I sat down on one of a group of chairs placed there. Becoming accustomed to the stream of promenaders, I soon observed, seated on the chairs opposite, Caroline and Charles. This was the first occasion on which I had seen them en *tête-à-tête* since my conversation with him. She soon caught sight of me; averted her eyes; then, apparently abandoning herself to an impulse, she jumped up from her seat and came across to me. We had not spoken to each other since the meeting in Venice.

'Alicia,' she said, sitting down by my side, 'Charles asks me to forgive you, and I do forgive you.'

I pressed her hand, with tears in my eyes, and said, 'And do you forgive him?'

'Yes,' said she, shyly.

'And what's the result?' said I.

'We are to be married directly we reach home.'

This was almost the whole of our conversation; she walked home with me, Charles following a little way behind, though she kept turning her head, as if anxious that he should overtake us. 'Honour and not love' seemed to ring in my ears. So matters stand. Caroline is again happy.

APRIL 25   We have reached home, Charles with us. Events are now moving in silent speed, almost with velocity, indeed; and I sometimes feel oppressed by the strange and preternatural ease which seems to accompany their flow. Charles is staying at the neighbouring town; he is only waiting for the marriage licence; when obtained he is to come here, be quietly married to her, and carry her off. It is rather resignation than content which sits on his face; but he has not spoken a word more to me on the burning subject, or deviated one hair's breadth from the course he laid down. They may be happy in time to come: I hope so. But I cannot shake off depression.

MAY 6   Eve of the wedding. Caroline is serenely happy, though not blithe. But there is nothing to excite anxiety about her. I wish I could say the same of him. He comes and goes like a ghost, and yet nobody seems to observe this strangeness in his mien.

I could not help being here for the ceremony; but my absence would have resulted in less disquiet on his part, I believe. However, I may be wrong in attributing causes; my father simply says that Charles and Caroline have as good a chance of being happy as other people. Well, tomorrow settles all.

MAY 7   They are married: we have just returned from church. Charles looked so pale this morning that my father asked him if he was ill. He said, 'No: only a slight headache;' and we started for the church.

There was no hitch or hindrance; and the thing is done.

4 p.m.   They ought to have set out on their journey by this time; but there is an unaccountable delay. Charles went out half an hour ago, and has not yet returned. Caroline is waiting in the hall; but I am dreadfully afraid they will miss the train. I suppose the trifling hindrance is of no account; and yet I am full of misgivings . . .

SEPTEMBER 14   Four months have passed; only four months! It seems like years. Can it be that only seventeen weeks ago I set on this paper the fact of their marriage? I am now an aged woman by comparison!

On that never to be forgotten day we waited and waited, and Charles did not return. At six o'clock, when poor little Caroline had gone back to her room in a state of suspense impossible to describe, a man who worked in the water-meadows came to the house and asked for my father. He had an interview with him in the study. My father then rang his bell, and sent for me. I went down; and I then learnt the fatal news. Charles was no more. The waterman had been going to shut down the hatches of a weir in the meads when he saw a hat on the edge of the pool below, floating round and round in the eddy, and looking into the pool saw something strange at the bottom. He knew what it meant, and lowering the hatches so that the water was still, could distinctly see the body. It is needless to write particulars that were in the newspapers at the time. Charles was brought to the house, but he was dead.

We all feared for Caroline; and she suffered much; but strange to say, her suffering was purely of the nature of deep grief which found relief in sobbing and tears. It came out at the inquest that Charles had been accustomed to cross the meads to give an occasional half-crown to an old man who lived on the opposite hill, who had once been a landscape painter in a humble way till he lost his eyesight; and it was assumed that he had gone thither for the same purpose today, and to bid him farewell. On this information the coroner's jury found that his death had been caused by misadventure; and everybody believes to this hour that he was drowned while crossing the weir to relieve the old man. Except one: she believes in no accident. After the stunning effect of the first news, I thought it strange that he should have chosen to go on such an errand at the last moment, and to go personally, when there was so little time to spare, since any gift could have been so easily sent by another hand. Further reflection has convinced me that this step out of life was as much a part of the day's plan as was the wedding in the church hard by. They were the two halves of his complete intention when he gave me on the Grand Canal that assurance which I shall never forget: 'Very well, then; honour shall be my word, not love. If she says yes, the marriage shall be.'

I do not know why I should have made this entry at this particular time; but it has occurred to me to do it – to complete, in a measure, that part of my desultory chronicle which relates to the love-story of my sister and Charles. She lives on meekly in her grief; and will probably outlive it; while I – but never mind me.

10

She Adds a Note Long After

Five-years later   I have lighted upon this old diary, which it has interested me to look over, containing, as it does, records of the time when life shone more warmly in my eye than it does now. I am impelled to add one sentence to round off its record of the past. About a year ago my sister Caroline, after a persistent wooing, accepted the hand and heart of Theophilus Higham, once the blushing young scripture reader who assisted at the substitute for a marriage I planned, and now the fully ordained curate of the next parish. His penitence for the part he played ended in love. We have all now made atonement for our sins against her: may she be deceived no more.

The Grave by the Handpost

I never pass through Chalk-Newton without turning to regard the neighbouring upland, at a point where a lane crosses the lone straight highway dividing this from the next parish, a sight which does not fail to recall the event that once happened there; and, though it may seem superfluous, at this date, to disinter more memories of village history, the whispers of that spot may claim to be preserved.

It was on a dark, yet mild and exceptionally dry evening at Christmas-time (according to the testimony of William Dewy of Mellstock, Michael Mail, and others) that the choir of Chalk-Newton – a large parish situate about halfway between the towns of Ivel and Casterbridge, and now a railway station – left their homes just before midnight to repeat their annual harmonies under the windows of the local population. The band of instrumentalists and singers was one of the largest in the county; and, unlike the smaller and finer Mellstock string-band, which eschewed all but the catgut, it included brass and reed performers at full Sunday services, and reached all across the west gallery.

On this night there were two or three violins, two 'cellos, a tenor viol, double bass, hautboy, clarionets, serpent, and seven singers. It was, however, not the choir's labours but what its members chanced to witness that particularly marked the occasion.

They had pursued their rounds for many years without meeting with any incident of an unusual kind, but tonight, according to the assertions of several, there prevailed, to begin with, an exceptionally solemn and thoughtful mood among two or three of the oldest in the band, as if they were thinking they might be joined by the phantoms of dead friends who had been of their number in earlier years, and now were mute in the churchyard under flattening mounds – friends who had shown greater zest for melody in their time than was shown in this; or that some past voice of a semi-transparent figure might quaver from some bedroom-window its acknowledgement of their nocturnal greeting, instead of a familiar living neighbour. Whether this were fact or fancy, the younger members of the choir met together with their customary thoughtlessness and buoyancy. When they had gathered by the stone stump of the cross in the middle of the village, near the White Horse Inn, which they made their starting point, someone observed that they were full early, that it was not yet twelve o'clock. The local waits of those days mostly refrained from sounding a note before Christmas morning had astronomically arrived, and not caring to return to their beer, they decided to begin with some outlying cottages in Sidlinch Lane, where the people had no clocks, and would not know whether it were night or morning. In that direction they accordingly went; and as they ascended to higher ground their attention was attracted by a light beyond the houses, quite at the top of the lane.

The road from Chalk-Newton to Broad Sidlinch is about two miles long and in the middle of its course, where it passes over the ridge dividing the two villages, it crosses at right angles, as has been stated, the lonely monotonous old highway known as Long Ash Lane, which runs, straight as a surveyor's line, many miles north and south of this spot, on the foundation of a Roman road, and has often been mentioned in these narratives. Though now quite deserted and grass-grown, at the beginning of the century it was well kept and frequented by traffic. The glimmering light appeared to come from the precise point where the roads intersected.

'I think I know what that mid mean!' one of the group remarked.

They stood a few moments, discussing the probability of the light having origin in an event of which rumours had reached them, and resolved to go up the hill.

Approaching the high land their conjectures were strengthened. Long Ash Lane cut athwart them, right and left; and they saw that at the junction of the four ways, under the handpost, a grave was dug, into which, as the choir drew nigh, a corpse had just been thrown by the four Sidlinch men employed for the purpose. The cart and horse which had brought the body thither stood silently by.

The singers and musicians from Chalk-Newton halted, and looked on while the gravediggers shovelled in and trod down the earth, till, the hole being filled, the latter threw their spades into the cart, and prepared to depart.

'Who mid ye be a-burying there?' asked Lot Swanhills in a raised voice. 'Not the sergeant?'

The Sidlinch men had been so deeply engrossed in their task that they had not noticed the lanterns of the Chalk-Newton choir till now.

'What – be you the Newton carol-singers?' returned the representatives of Sidlinch.

'Ay, sure. Can it be that it is old Sergeant Holway you've a-buried there?'

' 'Tis so. You've heard about it, then?'

The choir knew no particulars – only that he had shot himself in his apple-closet on the previous Sunday. 'Nobody seem'th to know what 'a did it for, 'a b'lieve? Leastwise, we don't know at Chalk-Newton,' continued Lot.

'Oh yes. It all came out at the inquest.'

The singers drew close, and the Sidlinch men, pausing to rest after their labours, told the story. 'It was all owing to that son of his, poor old man. It broke his heart.'

'But the son is a soldier, surely; now with his regiment in the East Indies?'

'Ay. And it have been rough with the army over there lately. 'Twas a pity his father persuaded him to go. But Luke shouldn't have twyted the sergeant o't, since 'a did it for the best.'

The circumstances, in brief, were these: The sergeant who had come to this lamentable end, father of the young soldier who had gone with his regiment to the East, had been singularly comfortable in his military experiences, these having ended long before the outbreak of the great war with France. On his discharge, after duly serving his time, he had returned to his native village, and married, and taken kindly to domestic life. But the war in which England next involved herself had cost him many frettings that age and infirmity prevented him from being ever again an active unit of the army. When his only son grew to young manhood, and the question arose of his going out in life, the lad expressed his wish to be a mechanic. But his father advised enthusiastically for the army.

'Trade is coming to nothing in these days,' he said. 'And if the war with the French lasts, as it will, trade will be still worse. The army, Luke – that's the thing for 'ee. 'Twas the making of me, and 'twill be the making of you. I hadn't half such a chance as you'll have in these splendid hotter times.'

Luke demurred, for he was a home-keeping, peace-loving youth. But, putting respectful trust in his father's judgement, he at length gave way, and enlisted in the —rd Foot. In the course of a few weeks he was sent out to India to his regiment, which had distinguished itself in the East under General Wellesley.

But Luke was unlucky. News came home indirectly that he lay sick out there; and then on one recent day when his father was out walking, the old man had received tidings that a letter awaited him at Casterbridge. The sergeant sent a special messenger the whole nine miles, and the letter was paid for and brought home; but though, as he had guessed, it came from Luke, its contents were of an unexpected tenor.

The letter had been written during a time of deep depression. Luke said that his life was a burden and a slavery, and bitterly reproached his father for advising him to embark on a career for which he felt unsuited. He found himself suffering fatigues and illnesses without gaining glory, and engaged in a cause which he did not understand or appreciate. If it had not been for his father's bad advice he, Luke, would now have been working comfortably at a trade in the village that he had never wished to leave.

After reading the letter the sergeant advanced a few steps till he was quite out of sight of everybody, and then sat down on the bank by the wayside.

When he arose half an hour later he looked withered and broken, and from that day his natural spirits left him. Wounded to the quick by his son's sarcastic stings, he indulged in liquor more and more frequently. His wife had died some years before this date, and the sergeant lived alone in the house which had been hers. One morning in the December under notice the report of a gun had been heard on his premises, and on entering the neighbours found him in a dying state. He had shot himself with an old firelock that he used for scaring birds; and from what he had said the day before, and the arrangements he had made for his decease, there was no doubt that his end had been deliberately planned, as a consequence of the despondency into which he had been thrown by his son's letter. The coroner's jury returned a verdict of *felo de se*.

'Here's his son's letter,' said one of the Sidlinch men. ' 'Twas found in his father's pocket. You can see by the state o't how many times he read it over. Howsomever, the Lord's will be done, since it must, whether or no.'

The grave was filled up and levelled, no mound being shaped over it. The Sidlinch men then bade the Chalk-Newton choir good-night, and departed with the cart in which they had brought the sergeant's body to the hill. When their tread had died away from the ear, and the wind swept over the isolated grave with its customary siffle of indifference, Lot Swanhills turned and spoke to old Richard Toller, the hautboy player.

' 'Tis hard upon a man, and he a wold sojer, to serve en so, Richard. Not that the sergeant was ever in a battle bigger than would go into a half-acre paddock, that's true. Still, his soul ought to hae as good a chance as another man's, all the same, hey?'

Richard replied that he was quite of the same opinion. 'What d'ye say to lifting up a carrel over his grave, as 'tis Christmas, and no hurry to begin down in parish, and 'twouldn't take up ten minutes, and not a soul up here to say us nay, or know anything about it?'

Lot nodded assent. 'The man ought to hae his chances,' he repeated.

'Ye may as well spet upon his grave, for all the good we shall do en by what we lift up, now he's got so far,' said Notton, the clarionet man and professed sceptic of the choir. 'But I'm agreed if the rest be.'

They thereupon placed themselves in a semicircle by the newly stirred earth, and roused the dull air with the well-known Number Sixteen of their collection, which Lot gave out as being the one he thought best suited to the occasion and the mood

> He comes the pri—soners to re—lease,
> In Sa—tan's bon—dage held.

'Jown it – we've never played to a dead man afore,' said Ezra Cattstock, when, having concluded the last verse, they stood reflecting for a breath or two. 'But it do seem more merciful than to go away and leave en, as they t'other fellers have done.'

'Now backalong to Newton, and by the time we get overright the pa'son's 'twill be half after twelve,' said the leader.

They had not, however, done more than gather up their instruments when the wind brought to their notice the noise of a vehicle rapidly driven up the same lane from Sidlinch which the gravediggers had lately retraced. To avoid being run over when moving on, they waited till the benighted traveller, whoever he might be, should pass them where they stood in the wider area of the cross.

In half a minute the light of the lanterns fell upon a hired fly, drawn by a steaming and jaded horse. It reached the handpost, when a voice from the inside cried, 'Stop here!' The driver pulled rein. The carriage door was opened from within, and there leapt out a private soldier in the uniform of some line regiment. He looked around, and was apparently surprised to see the musicians standing there.

'Have you buried a man here?' he asked.

'No. We bain't Sidlinch folk, thank God; we be Newton choir. Though a man is just buried here, that's true; and we've raised a carrel over the poor mortal's natomy. What – do my eyes see before me young Luke Holway, that went wi' his regiment to the East Indies, or do I see his spirit straight from the battlefield? Be you the son that wrote the letter – '

'Don't – don't ask me. The funeral is over, then?'

'There wer no funeral, in a Christen manner of speaking. But's buried, sure enough. You must have met the men going back in the empty cart.'

'Like a dog in a ditch, and all through me!'

He remained silent, looking at the grave, and they could not help pitying him. 'My friends,' he said, 'I understand better now. You have, I suppose, in neighbourly charity, sung peace to his soul? I thank you, from my heart, for your kind pity. Yes; I am Sergeant Holway's miserable son – I'm the son who has brought about his father's death, as truly as if I had done it with my own hand!'

'No, no. Don't ye take on so, young man. He'd been naturally low for a good while, off and on, so we hear.'

'We were out in the East when I wrote to him. Everything had seemed to go wrong with me. Just after my letter had gone we were ordered home. That's how it is you see me here. As soon as we got into barracks at Casterbridge I heard o' this . . . Damn me! I'll dare to follow my father, and make away with myself, too. It is the only thing left to do!'

'Don't ye be rash, Luke Holway, I say again; but try to make amends by your future life. And maybe your father will smile a smile down from heaven upon 'ee for 't.'

He shook his head. 'I don't know about that!' he answered bitterly.

'Try and be worthy of your father at his best. 'Tis not too late.'

'D'ye think not? I fancy it is! . . . Well, I'll turn it over. Thank you for your good counsel. I'll live for one thing, at any rate. I'll move father's body to a decent Christian churchyard, if I do it with my own hands. I can't save his life, but I can give him an honourable grave. He shan't lie in this accursed place!'

'Ay, as our pa'son says, 'tis a barbarous custom they keep up at Sidlinch, and ought to be done away wi'. The man a' old soldier, too. You see, our pa'son is not like yours at Sidlinch.'

'He says it is barbarous, does he? So it is!' cried the soldier. 'Now hearken, my friends.' Then he proceeded to enquire if they would increase his indebtedness to them by undertaking the removal, privately, of the body of the suicide to the churchyard, not of Sidlinch, a parish he now hated, but of Chalk-Newton. He would give them all he possessed to do it.

Lot asked Ezra Cattstock what he thought of it.

Cattstock, the 'cello player, who was also the sexton, demurred, and advised the young soldier to sound the rector about it first. 'Mid be he would object, and yet 'a mid'nt. The pa'son o' Sidlinch is a hard man, I own ye, and 'a said if folk will kill theirselves in hot blood they must take the consequences. But ours don't think like that at all, and might allow it.'

'What's his name?'

'The honourable and reverent Mr Oldham, brother to Lord Wessex. But you needn't be afeard o' en on that account. He'll talk to 'ee like a common man, if so be you haven't had enough drink to gie 'ee bad breath.'

'Oh, the same as formerly. I'll ask him. Thank you. And that duty done – '

'What then?'

'There's war in Spain. I hear our next move is there. I'll try to show myself to be what my father wished me. I don't suppose I shall – but I'll try in my feeble way. That much I swear – here over his body. So help me God.'

Luke smacked his palm against the white handpost with such force that it shook. 'Yes, there's war in Spain; and another chance for me to be worthy of father.'

So the matter ended that night. That the private acted in one thing as he had vowed to do soon became apparent, for during the Christmas week the rector came into the churchyard when Cattstock was there, and asked him to find a spot that would be suitable for the purpose of such an interment, adding that he had slightly known the late sergeant, and was not aware of any law which forbade him to assent to the removal, the letter of the rule having been observed. But as he did not wish to seem moved by opposition to his neighbour at Sidlinch, he had stipulated that the act of charity should be carried out at night, and as privately as possible, and that the grave should be in an obscure part of the enclosure. 'You had better see the young man about it at once,' added the rector.

But before Ezra had done anything Luke came down to his house. His furlough had been cut short, owing to new developments in the war in the Peninsula, and being obliged to go back to his regiment immediately, he was compelled to leave the exhumation and reinterment to his friends. Everything was paid for, and he implored them all to see it carried out forthwith.

With this the soldier left. The next day Ezra, on thinking the matter over, again went across to the rectory, struck with sudden misgiving. He had remembered that the sergeant had been buried without a coffin, and he was not sure that a stake had not been driven through him. The business would be more troublesome than they had at first supposed.

'Yes, indeed!' murmured the rector. 'I am afraid it is not feasible after all.'

The next event was the arrival of a headstone by carrier from the nearest town; to be left at Mr Ezra Cattstock's; all expenses paid. The sexton and the carrier deposited the stone in the former's outhouse; and Ezra, left alone, put on his spectacles and read the brief and simple inscription:

HERE LYETH THE BODY OF
SAMUEL HOLWAY
LATE SERGEANT IN HIS MAJESTY'S
—RD REGIMENT OF FOOT
WHO DEPARTED THIS LIFE
DECEMBER 20TH 180—
ERECTED BY L. H.

I am not worthy to be called thy son.

Ezra again called at the riverside rectory. 'The stone is come, sir. But I'm afeard we can't do it nohow.'

'I should like to oblige him,' said the gentlemanly old incumbent. 'And I would forgo all fees willingly. Still, if you and the others don't think you can carry it out, I am in doubt what to say.'

Well, sir; I've made enquiry of a Sidlinch woman as to his burial, and what I thought seems true. They buried en wi' a new six-foot hurdle-saul drough's body, from the sheep-pen up in North Ewelease, though they won't own to it now. And the question is, is the moving worthwhile, considering the awkwardness?'

'Have you heard anything more of the young man?'

Ezra had only heard that he had embarked that week for Spain with the rest of the regiment. 'And if he's as desperate as 'a seemed, we shall never see him here in England again.'

'It is an awkward case,' said the rector.

Ezra talked it over with the choir; one of whom suggested that the stone might be erected at the crossroads. This was regarded as impracticable. Another said that it might be set up in the churchyard without removing the body; but this was seen to be dishonest. So nothing was done.

The headstone remained in Ezra's outhouse till, growing tired of seeing it there, he put it away among the bushes at the bottom of his garden. The subject was sometimes revived among them, but it always ended with: 'Considering how 'a was buried, we can hardly make a job o't.'

There was always the consciousness that Luke would never come back, an impression strengthened by the disasters which were rumoured to have befallen the army in Spain. This tended to make their inertness permanent. The headstone grew green as it lay on its back under Ezra's bushes; then a tree by the river was blown down, and, falling across the stone, cracked it in three pieces. Ultimately the pieces became buried in the leaves and mould.

Luke had not been born a Chalk-Newton man, and he had no relations left in Sidlinch, so that no tidings of him reached either village throughout the war. But after Waterloo and the fall of Napoleon there arrived at Sidlinch one day an English sergeant-major covered with stripes and, as it turned out, rich in glory. Foreign service had so totally changed Luke Holway that it was not until he told his name that the inhabitants recognised him as the sergeant's only son.

He had served with unswerving effectiveness through the Peninsular campaigns under Wellington; had fought at Busaco, Fuentes d'Onore, Ciudad Rodrigo, Badajoz, Salamanca, Vittoria, Quatre Bras and Waterloo; and had now returned to enjoy a more than earned pension and repose in his native district.

He hardly stayed in Sidlinch longer than to take a meal on his arrival. The same evening he started on foot over the hill to Chalk-Newton, passing the handpost, and saying as he glanced at the spot, 'Thank God: he's not there!' Nightfall was approaching when he reached the latter village; but he made straight for the churchyard. On his entering it there remained light enough to discern the headstones by, and these he narrowly scanned. But though he searched the front part by the road, and the back part by the river, what he sought he could not find – the grave of Sergeant Holway, and a memorial bearing the inscription: *I am not worthy to be called thy son.*

He left the churchyard and made enquiries. The honourable and reverend old rector was dead, and so were many of the choir; but by degrees the sergeant-major learnt that his father still lay at the crossroads in Long Ash Lane.

Luke pursued his way moodily homewards, to do which, in the natural course, he would be compelled to repass the spot, there being no other road between the two villages. But he could not now go by that place, vociferous with reproaches in his father's tones; and he got over the hedge and wandered deviously through the ploughed fields to avoid the scene. Through many a fight and fatigue Luke had been sustained by the thought that he was restoring the family honour and making noble amends. Yet his father lay still in degradation. It was rather a sentiment than a fact that his father's body had been made to suffer for his own misdeeds; but to his super-sensitiveness it seemed that his efforts to retrieve his character and to propitiate the shade of the insulted one had ended in failure.

He endeavoured, however, to shake off his lethargy, and, not liking the associations of Sidlinch, hired a small cottage at Chalk-Newton which had long been empty. Here he lived alone, becoming quite a hermit, and allowing no woman to enter the house.

The Christmas after taking up his abode herein he was sitting in the chimney corner by himself, when he heard faint notes in the distance, and soon a melody burst forth immediately outside his own window; it came from the carol-singers, as usual; and though many of the old hands, Ezra and Lot included, had gone to their rest, the same old carols were still played out of the same old books. There resounded through the sergeant-major's window-shutters the familiar lines that the deceased choir had rendered over his father's grave:

> He comes the pri–soners to re–lease,
> In Sa–tan's bon–dage held.

When they had finished they went on to another house, leaving him to silence and loneliness as before.

The candle wanted snuffing, but he did not snuff it, and he sat on till it had burnt down into the socket and made waves of shadow on the ceiling.

The Christmas cheerfulness of next morning was broken at breakfast-time by tragic intelligence which went down the village like wind. Sergeant-Major Holway had been found shot through the head by his own hand at the cross-roads in Long Ash Lane where his father lay buried.

On the table in the cottage he had left a piece of paper, on which he had written his wish that he might be buried at the Cross beside his father. But the paper was accidentally swept to the floor, and overlooked till after his funeral, which took place in the ordinary way in the churchyard.

A Mere Interlude

I

The traveller in school-books, who vouched in dryest tones for the fidelity to fact of the following narrative, used to add a ring of truth to it by opening with a nicety of criticism on the heroine's personality. People were wrong, he declared, when they surmised that Baptista Trewthen was a young woman with scarcely emotions or character. There was nothing in her to love, and nothing to hate – so ran the general opinion. That she showed few positive qualities was true. The colours and tones which changing events paint on the faces of active womankind were looked for in vain upon hers. But still waters run deep; and no crisis had come in the years of her early maidenhood to demonstrate what lay hidden within her, like metal in a mine.

She was the daughter of a small farmer in St Maria's, one of the Isles of Lyonesse beyond Off-Wessex, who had spent a large sum, as there understood, on her education, by sending her to the mainland for two years. At nineteen she was entered at the Training College for Teachers, and at twenty-one nominated to a school in the country, near Tor-upon-Sea, whither she proceeded after the Christmas examination and holidays.

The months passed by from winter to spring and summer, and Baptista applied herself to her new duties as best she could, till an uneventful year had elapsed. Then an air of abstraction pervaded her bearing as she walked to and fro, twice a day, and she showed the traits of a person who had something on her mind. A widow, by name Mrs Wace, in whose house Baptista Trewthen had been provided with a sitting-room and bedroom till the school-house should be built, noticed this change in her youthful tenant's manner, and at last ventured to press her with a few questions.

'It has nothing to do with the place, nor with you,' said Miss Trewthen.

'Then it is the salary?'

'No, nor the salary.'

'Then it is something you have heard from home, my dear.'

Baptista was silent for a few moments. 'It is Mr Heddegan,' she murmured. 'Him they used to call David Heddegan before he got his money.'

'And who is the Mr Heddegan they used to call David?'

'An old bachelor at Giant's Town, St Maria's, with no relations whatever, who lives about a stone's throw from father's. When I was a child he used to take me on his knee and say he'd marry me someday. Now I am a woman the jest has turned earnest, and he is anxious to do it. And father and mother says I can't do better than have him.'

'He's well off?'

'Yes – he's the richest man we know – as a friend and neighbour.'

'How much older did you say he was than yourself?'

'I didn't say. Twenty years at least.'

'And an unpleasant man in the bargain perhaps?'

'No – he's not unpleasant.'

'Well, child, all I can say is that I'd resist any such engagement if it's not palatable to 'ee. You are comfortable here, in my little house, I hope. All the parish like 'ee: and I've never been so cheerful, since my poor husband left me to wear his wings, as I've been with 'ee as my lodger.'

The schoolmistress assured her landlady that she could return the sentiment. 'But here comes my perplexity,' she said. 'I don't like keeping school. Ah, you are surprised – you didn't suspect it. That's because I've concealed my feeling. Well, I simply hate school. I don't care for children – they are unpleasant, troublesome little things, whom nothing would delight so much as to hear that you had fallen down dead. Yet I would even put up with them if it was not for the inspector. For three months before his visit I didn't sleep soundly. And the Committee of Council are always changing the code, so that you don't know what to teach, and what to leave untaught. I think father and mother are right. They say I shall never excel as a schoolmistress if I dislike the work so, and that therefore I ought to get settled by marrying Mr Heddegan. Between us two, I like him better than school; but I don't like him quite so much as to wish to marry him.'

These conversations, once begun, were continued from day to day; till at length the young girl's elderly friend and landlady threw in her opinion on the side of Miss Trewthen's parents. All things considered, she declared, the uncertainty of the school, the labour, Baptista's natural dislike for teaching, it would be as well to take what fate offered, and make the best of matters by wedding her father's old neighbour and prosperous friend.

The Easter holidays came round, and Baptista went to spend them as usual in her native isle, going by train into Off-Wessex and crossing by packet from Pen-zephyr. When she returned in the middle of April her face wore a more settled aspect.

'Well?' said the expectant Mrs Wace.

'I have agreed to have him as my husband,' said Baptista, in an off-hand way. 'Heaven knows if it will be for the best or not. But I have agreed to do it, and so the matter is settled.'

Mrs Wace commended her; but Baptista did not care to dwell on the subject, so that allusion to it was very infrequent between them. Nevertheless, among other things, she repeated to the widow from time to time in monosyllabic remarks that the wedding was really impending; that it was arranged for the summer, and that she had given notice of leaving the school at the August holidays. Later on she announced more specifically that her marriage was to take place immediately after her return home at the beginning of the month aforesaid.

She now corresponded regularly with Mr Heddegan. Her letters from him were seen, at least on the outside, and in part within, by Mrs Wace. Had she read more of their interiors than the occasional sentences shown her by Baptista she would have perceived that the scratchy, rusty handwriting of Miss Trewthen's betrothed conveyed little more matter than details of their future housekeeping, and his preparations for the same, with innumerable 'my dears' sprinkled in disconnectedly, to show the depth of his affection without the inconveniences of syntax.

2

It was the end of July – dry, too dry, even for the season, the delicate green herbs and vegetables that grew in this favoured end of the kingdom tasting rather of the watering-pot than of the pure fresh moisture from the skies. Baptista's boxes were packed, and one Saturday morning she departed by a waggonette to the station, and thence by train to Pen-zephyr, from which port she was, as usual, to cross the water immediately to her home, and become Mr Heddegan's wife on the Wednesday of the week following.

She might have returned a week sooner. But though the wedding day had loomed so near, and the banns were out, she delayed her departure till this last moment, saying it was not necessary for her to be at home long beforehand. As Mr Heddegan was older than herself, she said, she was to be married in her ordinary summer bonnet and grey silk frock, and there were no preparations to make that had not been amply made by her parents and intended husband.

In due time, after a hot and tedious journey, she reached Pen-zephyr. She here obtained some refreshment, and then went towards the pier, where she learnt to her surprise that the little steamboat plying between the town and the islands had left at eleven o'clock; the usual hour of departure in the afternoon having been forestalled in consequence of the fogs which had for a few days prevailed towards evening, making twilight navigation dangerous.

This being Saturday, there was now no other boat till Tuesday, and it became obvious that here she would have to remain for the three days, unless her friends should think fit to rig out one of the island's sailing-boats and come to fetch her – a not very likely contingency, the sea distance being nearly forty miles.

Baptista, however, had been detained in Pen-zephyr on more than one occasion before, either on account of bad weather or some such reason as the present, and she was therefore not in any personal alarm. But, as she was to be married on the following Wednesday, the delay was certainly inconvenient to a more than ordinary degree, since it would leave less than a day's interval between her arrival and the wedding ceremony.

Apart from this awkwardness she did not much mind the accident. It was indeed curious to see how little she minded. Perhaps it would not be too much to say that, although she was going to do the critical deed of her life quite willingly, she experienced an indefinable relief at the postponement of her meeting with Heddegan. But her manner after making discovery of the hindrance was quiet and subdued, even to passivity itself; as was instanced by her having, at the moment of receiving information that the steamer had sailed, replied, 'Oh,' so coolly to the porter with her luggage, that he was almost disappointed at her lack of disappointment.

The question now was, should she return again to Mrs Wace, in the village of Lower Wessex, or wait in the town at which she had arrived. She would have preferred to go back, but the distance was too great; moreover, having left the place for good, and somewhat dramatically, to become a bride, a return, even for so short a space, would have been a trifle humiliating.

Leaving, then, her boxes at the station, her next anxiety was to secure a respectable, or rather genteel, lodging in the popular seaside resort confronting her. To this end she looked about the town, in which, though she had passed through it half a dozen times, she was practically a stranger.

Baptista found a room to suit her over a fruiterer's shop; where she made herself at home, and set herself in order after her journey. An early cup of tea having revived her spirits she walked out to reconnoitre.

Being a schoolmistress she avoided looking at the schools, and having a sort of trade connection with books, she avoided looking at the booksellers; but wearying of the other shops she inspected the churches; not that for her own part she cared much about ecclesiastical edifices; but tourists looked at them, and so would she – a proceeding for which no one would have credited her with any great originality, such, for instance, as that she subsequently showed herself to possess. The churches soon oppressed her. She tried the museum, but came out because it seemed lonely and tedious.

Yet the town and the walks in this land of strawberries, these headquarters of early English flowers and fruit, were then, as always, attractive. From the more picturesque streets she went to the town gardens, and the pier, and the harbour, and looked at the men at work there, loading and unloading as in the time of the Phoenicians.

'Not Baptista? Yes, Baptista it is!'

The words were uttered behind her. Turning round she gave a start, and became confused, even agitated, for a moment. Then she said in her usual undemonstrative manner, 'Oh – is it really you, Charles?'

Without speaking again at once, and with a half-smile, the newcomer glanced her over. There was much criticism, and some resentment – even temper – in his eye.

'I am going home,' continued she. 'But I have missed the boat.'

He scarcely seemed to take in the meaning of this explanation, in the intensity of his critical survey. 'Teaching still? What a fine schoolmistress you make, Baptista, I warrant!' he said with a slight flavour of sarcasm, which was not lost upon her.

'I know I am nothing to brag of,' she replied. 'That's why I have given up.'

'Oh – given up? You astonish me.'

'I hate the profession.'

'Perhaps that's because I am in it.'

'Oh no, it isn't. But I am going to enter on another life altogether. I am going to be married next week to Mr David Heddegan.'

The young man – fortified as he was by a natural cynical pride and passionateness – winced at this unexpected reply, notwithstanding.

'Who is Mr David Heddegan?' he asked, as indifferently as lay in his power.

She informed him the bearer of the name was a general merchant of Giant's Town, St Maria's Island – her father's nearest neighbour and oldest friend.

'Then we shan't see anything more of you on the mainland?' enquired the schoolmaster.

'Oh, I don't know about that,' said Miss Trewthen.

'Here endeth the career of the belle of the boarding-school your father was foolish enough to send you to. A "general merchant's" wife in the Lyonesse Isles. Will you sell pounds of soap and pennyworths of tin tacks, or whole bars of saponaceous matter and great tenpenny nails?'

'He's not in such a small way as that!' she almost pleaded. 'He owns ships, though they are rather little ones!'

'Oh, well, it is much the same. Come, let us walk on; it is tedious to stand still. I thought you would be a failure in education,' he continued, when she obeyed him and strolled ahead. 'You never showed power that way. You remind me much of some of those women who think they are sure to be great actresses if they go on the stage, because they have a pretty face, and forget that what we require is acting. But you found your mistake, didn't you?'

'Don't taunt me, Charles.' It was noticeable that the young schoolmaster's tone caused her no anger or retaliatory passion; far otherwise: there was a tear in her eye. 'How is it you are at Pen-zephyr?' she enquired.

'I don't taunt you. I speak the truth, purely in a friendly way, as I should to anyone I wished well. Though for that matter I might have some excuse even for taunting you. Such a terrible hurry as you've been in. I hate a woman who is in such a hurry.'

'How do you mean that?'

'Why – to be somebody's wife or other – anything's wife rather than nobody's. You couldn't wait for me, oh no. Well, thank God, I'm cured of all that!'

'How merciless you are!' she said bitterly. 'Wait for you? What does that mean, Charley? You never showed – anything to wait for – anything special towards me.'

'Oh come, Baptista dear; come!'

'What I mean is, nothing definite,' she expostulated. 'I suppose you liked me a little; but it seemed to me to be only a pastime on your part, and that you never meant to make an honourable engagement of it.'

'There, that's just it! You girls expect a man to mean business at the first look. No man when he first becomes interested in a woman has any definite scheme of engagement to marry her in his mind, unless he is meaning a vulgar mercenary marriage. However, I did at last mean an honourable engagement, as you call it, come to that.'

'But you never said so, and an indefinite courtship soon injures a woman's position and credit, sooner than you think.'

'Baptista, I solemnly declare that in six months I should have asked you to marry me.'

She walked along in silence, looking on the ground, and appearing very uncomfortable.

Presently he said, 'Would you have waited for me if you had known?'

To this she whispered in a sorrowful whisper, 'Yes!'

They went still farther in silence – passing along one of the beautiful walks on the outskirts of the town, yet not observant of scene or situation. Her shoulder and his were close together, and he clasped his fingers round the small of her arm – quite lightly, and without any attempt at impetus; yet the act seemed to say, 'Now I hold you, and my will must be yours.'

Recurring to a previous question of hers he said, 'I have merely run down here for a day or two from school near Trufal, before going off to the north for the rest of my holiday. I have seen my relations at Redrutin quite lately, so I am not going there this time. How little I thought of meeting you! How very different the circumstances would have been if, instead of parting again as we must in half an hour or so, possibly for ever, you had been now just going off with me, as my wife, on our honeymoon trip. Ha – ha – well – so humorous is life!'

She stopped suddenly. 'I must go back now – this is altogether too painful, Charley! It is not at all a kind mood you are in today.'

'I don't want to pain you – you know I do not,' he said more gently. 'Only it just exasperates me – this you are going to do. I wish you would not.'

'What?'

'Marry him. There, now I have showed you my true sentiments.'

'I must do it now,' said she.

'Why?' he asked, dropping the off-hand masterful tone he had hitherto spoken in, and becoming earnest; still holding her arm, however, as if she were his chattel to be taken up or put down at will. 'It is never too late to break off a marriage that's distasteful to you. Now I'll say one thing, and it is truth: I wish you would marry me instead of him, even now, at the last moment, though you have served me so badly.'

'Oh, it is not possible to think of that!' she answered hastily, shaking her head. 'When I get home all will be prepared – it is ready even now – the things for the party, the furniture, Mr Heddegan's new suit, and everything. I should require the courage of a tropical lion to go home there and say I wouldn't carry out my promise!'

'Then go, in heaven's name! But there would be no necessity for you to go home and face them in that way. If we were to marry, it would have to be at once, instantly; or not at all. I should think your affection not worth the having unless you agreed to come back with me to Trufal this evening, where we could be married by licence on Monday morning. And then no Mr David Heddegan or anybody else could get you away from me.'

'I must go home by the Tuesday boat,' she faltered. 'What would they think if I did not come?'

'You could go home by that boat just the same. All the difference would be that I should go with you. You could leave me on the quay, where I'd have a smoke, while you went and saw your father and mother privately; you could then tell them what you had done, and that I was waiting not far off; that I was a schoolmaster in a fairly good position, and a young man you had known when you were at the Training College. Then I would come boldly forward; and they would see that it could not be altered, and so you wouldn't suffer a lifelong misery by being the wife of a wretched old gaffer you don't like at all. Now, honestly; you do like me best, don't you, Baptista?'

'Yes.'

'Then we will do as I say.'

She did not pronounce a clear affirmative. But that she consented to the novel proposition at some moment or other of that walk was apparent by what occurred a little later.

3

An enterprise of such pith required, indeed, less talking than consideration. The first thing they did in carrying it out was to return to the railway station, where Baptista took from her luggage a small trunk of immediate necessaries which she would in any case have required after missing the boat. That same afternoon they travelled up the line to Trufal.

Charles Stow (as his name was), despite his disdainful indifference to things, was very careful of appearances, and made the journey independently of her though in the same train. He told her where she could get board and lodgings in the city; and with merely a distant nod to her of a provisional kind, went off to his own quarters, and to see about the licence.

On Sunday she saw him in the morning across the nave of the pro-cathedral. In the afternoon they walked together in the fields, where he told her that the licence would be ready next day, and would be available the day after, when the ceremony could be performed as early after eight o'clock as they should choose.

His courtship, thus renewed after an interval of two years, was as impetuous, violent even, as it was short. The next day came and passed, and the final arrangements were made. Their agreement was to get the ceremony over as soon as they possibly could the next morning, so as to go on to Pen-zephyr at once, and reach that place in time for the boat's departure the same day. It was in obedience to Baptista's earnest request that Stow consented thus to make the whole journey to Lyonesse by land and water at one heat, and not break it at Pen-zephyr; she seemed to be oppressed with a dread of lingering anywhere, this great first act of disobedience to her parents once accomplished, with the weight on her mind that her home had to be con-vulsed by the disclosure of it. To face her difficulties over the water immediately she had created them was, however, a course more desired by Baptista than by her lover; though for once he gave way.

The next morning was bright and warm as those which had preceded it. By six o'clock it seemed nearly noon, as is often the case in that part of England in the summer season. By nine they were husband and wife. They packed up and departed by the earliest train after the service; and on the way discussed at length what she should say on meeting her parents, Charley dictating the turn of each phrase. In her anxiety they had travelled so early that when they reached Pen-zephyr they found there were nearly two hours on their hands before the steamer's time of sailing.

Baptista was extremely reluctant to be seen promenading the streets of the watering-place with her husband till, as above stated, the household at Giant's Town should know the unexpected course of events from her own lips; and it was just possible, if not likely, that some Lyonessian might be prowling about there, or even have come across the sea to look for her. To meet anyone to whom she was known, and to have to reply to awkward questions about the strange young man at her side before her well-framed announcement had been delivered at proper time and place, was a thing she could not contemplate with equanimity. So, instead of looking at the shops and harbour, they went along the coast a little way.

The heat of the morning was by this time intense. They clambered up on some cliffs, and while sitting there, looking around at St Michael's Mount and other objects, Charles said to her that he thought he would run down to the beach at their feet, and take just one plunge into the sea.

Baptista did not much like the idea of being left alone; it was gloomy, she said. But he assured her he would not be gone more than a quarter of an hour at the outside, and she passively assented.

Down he went, disappeared, appeared again, and looked back. Then he again proceeded, and vanished, till, as a small waxen object, she saw him emerge from the nook that had screened him, cross the white fringe of foam, and walk into the undulating mass of blue. Once in the water he seemed less inclined to hurry than before; he remained a long time; and, unable either to appreciate his skill or criticise his want of it at that distance, she withdrew her eyes from the spot, and gazed at the still outline of St Michael's – now beautifully toned in grey.

Her anxiety for the hour of departure, and to cope at once with the approaching incidents that she would have to manipulate as best she could, sent her into a reverie. It was now Tuesday; she would reach home in the evening – a very late time they would say; but, as the delay was a pure accident, they would deem her marriage to Mr Heddegan tomorrow still practicable. Then Charles would have to be produced from the background. It was a terrible undertaking to think of, and she almost regretted her temerity in wedding so hastily that morning. The rage of her father would be so crushing; the reproaches of her mother so bitter; and perhaps Charles would answer hotly, and perhaps cause estrangement till death. There had obviously been no alarm about her at St Maria's, or somebody would have sailed across to enquire for her. She had, in a letter written at the beginning of the week, spoken of the hour at which she intended to leave her country schoolhouse; and from this her friends had probably perceived that by such timing she would run a risk of losing the Saturday boat. She had missed it, and as a consequence sat here on the shore as Mrs Charles Stow.

This brought her to the present, and she turned from the outline of St Michael's Mount to look about for her husband's form. He was, as far as she could discover, no longer in the sea. Then he was dressing. By moving a few steps she could see where his clothes lay. But Charles was not beside them.

Baptista looked back again at the water in bewilderment, as if her senses were the victim of some sleight of hand. Not a speck or spot resembling a man's head or face showed anywhere. By this time she was alarmed, and her alarm intensified when she perceived a little beyond the scene of her husband's bathing a small area of water, the quality of whose surface differed from that of the surrounding expanse as the coarse vegetation of some foul patch in a mead differs from the fine green of the remainder. Elsewhere it looked flexuous, here it looked vermiculated and lumpy, and her marine experiences suggested to her in a moment that two currents met and caused a turmoil at this place.

She descended as hastily as her trembling limbs would allow. The way down was terribly long, and before reaching the heap of clothes it occurred to her that, after all, it would be best to run first for help. Hastening along in a lateral direction she proceeded inland till she met a man, and soon afterwards two others. To them she exclaimed, 'I think a gentleman who was bathing is in some danger. I cannot see him as I could. Will you please run and help him, at once, if you will be so kind?'

She did not think of turning to show them the exact spot, indicating it vaguely by the direction of her hand, and still going on her way with the idea of gaining more assistance. When she deemed, in her faintness, that she had carried the alarm far enough, she faced about and dragged herself back again. Before reaching the now dreaded spot she met one of the men.

'We can see nothing at all, miss,' he declared.

Having gained the beach, she found the tide in, and no sign of Charley's clothes. The other men whom she had besought to come had disappeared, it must have been in some other direction, for she had not met them going away. They, finding nothing, had probably thought her alarm a mere conjecture, and given up the quest.

Baptista sank down upon the stones near at hand. Where Charley had undressed was now sea. There could not be the least doubt that he was drowned, and his body sucked under by the current; while his clothes, lying within high-water mark, had probably been carried away by the rising tide.

She remained in a stupor for some minutes, till a strange sensation succeeded the aforesaid perceptions, mystifying her intelligence, and leaving her physically almost inert. With his personal disappearance, the last three days of her life with him seemed to be swallowed up, also his image, in her mind's eye, waned curiously, receded far away, grew stranger and stranger, less and less real. Their meeting and marriage had been so sudden, unpremeditated, adventurous, that she could hardly believe that she had played her part in such a reckless drama. Of all the few hours of her life with Charles, the portion that most insisted in coming back to memory was their fortuitous encounter on the previous Saturday, and those bitter reprimands with which he had begun the attack, as it might be called, which had piqued her to an unexpected consummation.

A sort of cruelty, an imperiousness, even in his warmth, had characterised Charles Stow. As a lover he had ever been a bit of a tyrant; and it might pretty truly have been said that he had stung her into marriage with him at last. Still more alien from her life did these reflections operate to make him; and then they would be chased away by an interval of passionate weeping and mad regret. Finally, there returned upon the confused mind of the young wife the recollection that she was on her way homeward, and that the packet would sail in three-quarters of an hour.

Except the parasol in her hand, all she possessed was at the station awaiting her onward journey.

She looked in that direction; and, entering one of those undemonstrative phases so common with her, walked quietly on.

At first she made straight for the railway; but suddenly turning she went to a shop and wrote an anonymous line announcing his death by drowning to the only person she had ever heard Charles mention as a relative. Posting this stealthily, and with a fearful look around her, she seemed to acquire a terror of the late events, pursuing her way to the station as if followed by a spectre.

When she got to the office she asked for the luggage that she had left there on the Saturday as well as the trunk left on the morning just lapsed. All were put in the boat, and she herself followed. Quickly as these things had been done, the whole proceeding, nevertheless, had been almost automatic on Baptista's part, ere she had come to any definite conclusion on her course.

Just before the bell rang she heard a conversation on the pier which removed the last shade of doubt from her mind, if any had existed, that she was Charles Stow's widow. The sentences were but fragmentary, but she could easily piece them out.

'A man drowned – swam out too far – was a stranger to the place – people in boat – saw him go down – couldn't get there in time.'

The news was little more definite than this as yet; though it may as well be stated once for all that the statement was true. Charley, with the over-confidence of his nature, had ventured out too far for his strength, and succumbed in the absence of assistance, his lifeless body being at that moment suspended in the transparent mid-depths of the bay. His clothes, however, had merely been gently lifted by the rising tide, and floated into a nook hard by, where they lay out of sight of the passers-by till a day or two after.

4

In ten minutes they were steaming out of the harbour for their voyage of four or five hours, at whose ending she would have to tell her strange story.

As Pen-zephyr and all its environing scenes disappeared behind Mousehole and St Clement's Isle, Baptista's ephemeral, meteor-like husband impressed her yet more as a fantasy. She was still in such a trance-like state that she had been an hour on the little packet-boat before she became aware of the agitating fact that Mr Heddegan was on board with her. Involuntarily she slipped from her left hand the symbol of her wifehood.

'Hee-hee! Well, the truth is, I wouldn't interrupt 'ee. "I reckon she don't see me, or won't see me," I said, "and what's the hurry? She'll see enough o' me soon!" I hope ye be well, mee deer?'

He was a hale, well-conditioned man of about five and fifty, of the complexion common to those whose lives are passed on the bluffs and beaches of an ocean isle. He extended the four quarters of his face in a genial smile, and his hand for a grasp of the same magnitude. She gave her own in surprised docility, and he continued: 'I couldn't help coming across to meet 'ee. What an unfortunate thing you missing the boat and not coming Saturday! They meant to have warned 'ee that the time was changed, but forgot it at the last moment. The truth is that I should have informed 'ee myself; but I was that busy finishing up a job last week, so as to have this week free, that I trusted to your father for attending to these little things. However, so plain and quiet as it is all to be, it really do not matter so much as it might otherwise have done, and I hope ye haven't been greatly put out. Now, if you'd sooner that I should not be seen talking to 'ee – if 'ee feel shy at all before strangers – just say. I'll leave 'ee to yourself till we get home.'

'Thank you much. I am indeed a little tired, Mr Heddegan.'

He nodded urbane acquiescence, strolled away immediately, and minutely inspected the surface of the funnel, till some female passengers of Giant's Town tittered at what they must have thought a rebuff – for the approaching wedding was known to many on St Maria's Island, though to nobody else-where. Baptista coloured at their satire, and called him back, and forced herself to commune with him in at least a mechanically friendly manner.

The opening event had been thus different from her expectation, and she had adumbrated no act to meet it. Taken aback she passively allowed circumstances to pilot her along; and so the voyage was made.

It was near dusk when they touched the pier of Giant's Town, where several friends and neighbours stood awaiting them. Her father had a lantern in his hand. Her mother, too, was there, reproachfully glad that the delay had at last ended so simply. Mrs Trewthen and her daughter went together along the Giant's Walk, or promenade, to the house, rather in advance of her husband and Mr Heddegan, who talked in loud tones which reached the women over their shoulders.

Some would have called Mrs Trewthen a good mother; but though well meaning she was maladroit, and her intentions missed their mark. This might have been partly attributable to the slight deafness from which she suffered. Now, as usual, the chief utterances came from her lips.

'Ah, yes, I'm so glad, my child, that you've got over safe. It is all ready, and everything so well arranged, that nothing but misfortune could hinder you settling as, with God's grace, becomes 'ee. Close to your mother's door a'most, 'twill be a great blessing, I'm sure; and I was very glad to find from your letters that you'd held your word sacred. That's right – make your word your bond always. Mrs Wace seems to be a sensible woman. I hope the Lord will do for her as he's doing for you no long time hence. And how did 'ee get over the terrible journey from Tor-upon-Sea to Pen-zephyr? Once you'd done with the railway, of course, you seemed quite at home. Well, Baptista, conduct yourself seemly, and all will be well.'

Thus admonished, Baptista entered the house, her father and Mr Hedde-gan immediately at her back. Her mother had been so didactic that she had felt herself absolutely unable to broach the subjects in the centre of her mind.

The familiar room, with the dark ceiling, the well-spread table, the old chairs, had never before spoken so eloquently of the times ere she knew or had heard of Charley Stow. She went upstairs to take off her things, her mother remaining below to complete the disposition of the supper, and attend to the preparation of tomorrow's meal, altogether composing such an array of pies, from pies of fish to pies of turnips, as was never heard of outside the Western Duchy. Baptista, once alone, sat down and did nothing; and was called before she had taken off her bonnet.

'I'm coming,' she cried, jumping up, and speedily disapparelling herself, brushed her hair with a few touches and went down.

Two or three of Mr Heddegan's and her father's friends had dropped in, and expressed their sympathy for the delay she had been subjected to. The meal was a most merry one except to Baptista. She had desired privacy, and there was none; and to break the news was already a greater difficulty than it had been at first. Everything around her, animate and inanimate, great and small, insisted that she had come home to be married; and she could not get a chance to say nay.

One or two people sang songs, as overtures to the melody of the morrow, till at length bedtime came, and they all withdrew, her mother having retired a little earlier. When Baptista found herself again alone in her bedroom the case stood as before: she had come home with much to say, and she had said nothing.

It was now growing clear even to herself that Charles being dead, she had not determination sufficient within her to break tidings which, had he been alive, would have imperatively announced themselves. And thus with the stroke of midnight came the turning of the scale; her story should remain untold. It was not that upon the whole she thought it best not to attempt to tell it; but that she could not undertake so explosive a matter. To stop the wedding now would cause a convulsion in Giant's Town little short of volcanic. Weakened, tired, and terrified as she had been by the day's adventures, she could not make herself the author of such a catastrophe. But how refuse Heddegan without telling? It really seemed to her as if her marriage with Mr Heddegan were about to take place as if nothing had intervened.

Morning came. The events of the previous days were cut off from her present existence by scene and sentiment more completely than ever. Charles Stow had grown to be a special being of whom, owing to his character, she entertained rather fearful than loving memory. Baptista could hear when she awoke that her parents were already moving about downstairs. But she did not rise till her mother's rather rough voice resounded up the staircase as it had done on the preceding evening.

'Baptista! Come, time to be stirring! The man will be here, by heaven's blessing, in three-quarters of an hour. He has looked in already for a minute or two – and says he's going to the church to see if things be well forward.'

Baptista arose, looked out of the window, and took the easy course. When she emerged from the regions above she was arrayed in her new silk frock and best stockings, wearing a linen jacket over the former for breakfasting, and her common slippers over the latter, not to spoil the new ones on the rough precincts of the dwelling.

It is unnecessary to dwell at any great length on this part of the morning's proceedings. She revealed nothing; and married Heddegan, as she had given her word to do, on that appointed August day.

5

Mr Heddegan forgave the coldness of his bride's manner during and after the wedding ceremony, full well aware that there had been considerable reluctance on her part to acquiesce in this neighbourly arrangement, and, as a philosopher of long standing, holding that whatever Baptista's attitude now, the conditions would probably be much the same six months hence as those which ruled among other married couples.

An absolutely unexpected shock was given to Baptista's listless mind about an hour after the wedding service. They had nearly finished the midday dinner when the now husband said to her father, 'We think of starting about two. And the breeze being so fair we shall bring up inside Pen-zephyr new pier about six at least.'

'What – are we going to Pen-zephyr?' said Baptista. 'I don't know anything of it.'

'Didn't you tell her?' asked her father of Heddegan.

It transpired that, owing to the delay in her arrival, this proposal too, among other things, had in the hurry not been mentioned to her, except some time ago as a general suggestion that they would go somewhere. Heddegan had imagined that any trip would be pleasant, and one to the mainland the pleasantest of all.

She looked so distressed at the announcement that her husband willingly offered to give it up, though he had not had a holiday off the island for a whole year. Then she pondered on the inconvenience of staying at Giant's Town, where all the inhabitants were bonded, by the circumstances of their situation, into a sort of family party, which permitted and encouraged on such occasions as these oral criticism that was apt to disturb the equanimity of newly married girls, and would especially worry Baptista in her strange situation. Hence, unexpectedly, she agreed not to disorganise her husband's plans for the wedding jaunt, and it was settled that, as originally intended, they should proceed in a neighbour's sailing boat to the metropolis of the district.

In this way they arrived at Pen-zephyr without difficulty or mishap. Bidding adieu to Jenkin and his man, who had sailed them over, they strolled arm in arm off the pier, Baptista silent, cold and obedient. Heddegan had arranged to take her as far as Plymouth before their return, but to go no farther than where they had landed that day. Their first business was to find an inn; and in this they had unexpected difficulty, since for some reason or other – possibly the fine weather – many of the nearest at hand were full of tourists and commercial travellers. He led her on till he reached a tavern which, though comparatively unpretending, stood in as attractive a spot as any in the town; and this, somewhat to their surprise after their previous experience, they found apparently empty. The considerate old man, thinking that Baptista was educated to artistic notions, though he himself was deficient in them, had decided that it was most desirable to have, on such an occasion as the present, an apartment with 'a good view' (the expression being one he had often heard in use among tourists); and he therefore asked for a favourite room on the first floor, from which a bow-window protruded, for the express purpose of affording such an outlook.

The landlady, after some hesitation, said she was sorry that particular apartment was engaged; the next one, however, or any other in the house, was unoccupied.

'The gentleman who has the best one will give it up tomorrow, and then you can change into it,' she added, as Mr Heddegan hesitated about taking the adjoining and less commanding one.

'We shall be gone tomorrow, and shan't want it,' he said.

Wishing not to lose customers, the landlady earnestly continued that since he was bent on having the best room, perhaps the other gentleman would not object to move at once into the one they despised, since, though nothing could be seen from the window, the room was equally large.

'Well, if he doesn't care for a view,' said Mr Heddegan, with the air of a highly artistic man who did.

'Oh no – I am sure he doesn't,' she said. 'I can promise that you shall have the room you want. If you would not object to go for a walk for half an hour, I could have it ready, and your things in it, and a nice tea laid in the bow-window by the time you come back?'

This proposal was deemed satisfactory by the fussy old tradesman, and they went out. Baptista nervously conducted him in an opposite direction to her walk of the former day in other company, showing on her wan face, had he observed it, how much she was beginning to regret her sacrificial step for mending matters that morning.

She took advantage of a moment when her husband's back was turned to enquire casually in a shop if anything had been heard of the gentleman who was sucked down in the eddy while bathing.

The shopman said, 'Yes, his body has been washed ashore,' and had just handed Baptista a newspaper on which she discerned the heading, A SCHOOLMASTER DROWNED WHILE BATHING, when her husband turned to join her. She might have pursued the subject without raising suspicion; but it was more than flesh and blood could do, and completing a small purchase she almost ran out of the shop.

'What is your terrible hurry, mee deer?' said Heddegan, hastening after.

'I don't know – I don't want to stay in shops,' she gasped.

'And we won't,' he said. 'They are suffocating this weather. Let's go back and have some tay!'

They found the much desired apartment awaiting their entry. It was a sort of combination bed- and sitting-room, and the table was prettily spread with high tea in the bow-window, a bunch of flowers in the midst, and a best-parlour chair on each side. Here they shared the meal by the ruddy light of the vanishing sun. But though the view had been engaged, regardless of expense, exclusively for Baptista's pleasure, she did not direct any keen attention out of the window. Her gaze as often fell on the floor and walls of the room as elsewhere, and on the table as much as on either, beholding nothing at all.

But there was a change. Opposite her seat was the door, upon which her eyes presently became riveted like those of a little bird upon a snake. For, on a peg at the back of the door, there hung a hat; such a hat – surely, from its peculiar make, the actual hat – that had been worn by Charles. Conviction grew to certainty when she saw a railway ticket sticking up from the band. Charles had put the ticket there – she had noticed the act.

Her teeth almost chattered; she murmured something incoherent. Her husband jumped up and said, 'You are not well! What is it? What shall I get 'ee?'

'Smelling salts!' she said, quickly and desperately; 'at that chemist's shop you were in just now.'

He jumped up like the anxious old man that he was, caught up his own hat from a back table, and without observing the other hastened out and down-stairs.

Left alone she gazed and gazed at the back of the door, then spasmodically rang the bell. An honest-looking country maidservant appeared in response.

'A hat!' murmured Baptista, pointing with her finger. 'It does not belong to us.'

'Oh yes, I'll take it away,' said the young woman with some hurry. 'It belongs to the other gentleman.'

She spoke with a certain awkwardness, and took the hat out of the room. Baptista had recovered her outward composure. 'The other gentleman?' she said. 'Where is the other gentleman?'

'He's in the next room, ma'am. He removed out of this to oblige 'ee.'

'How can you say so? I should hear him if he were there,' said Baptista, sufficiently recovered to argue down an apparent untruth.

'He's there,' said the girl, hardily.

'Then it is strange that he makes no noise,' said Mrs Heddegan, convicting the girl of falsity by a look.

'He makes no noise; but it is not strange,' said the servant.

All at once a dread took possession of the bride's heart, like a cold hand laid thereon; for it flashed upon her that there was a possibility of reconciling the girl's statement with her own knowledge of facts.

'Why does he make no noise?' she weakly said.

The waiting-maid was silent, and looked at her questioner. 'If I tell you, ma'am, you won't tell missis?' she whispered.

Baptista promised.

'Because he's a-lying dead!' said the girl. 'He's the schoolmaster that was drownded yesterday.'

'Oh!' said the bride, covering her eyes. 'Then he was in this room till just now?'

'Yes,' said the maid, thinking the young lady's agitation natural enough. 'And I told missis that I thought she oughtn't to have done it, because I don't hold it right to keep visitors so much in the dark where death's concerned; but she said the gentleman didn't die of anything infectious; she was a poor, honest, innkeeper's wife, she says, who had to get her living by making hay while the sun sheened. And owing to the drownded gentleman being brought here, she said, it kept so many people away that we were empty, though all the other houses were full. So when your good man set his mind upon the room, and she would have lost good paying folk if he'd not had it, it wasn't to be supposed, she said, that she'd let anything stand in the way. Ye won't say that I've told ye, please, m'm? All the linen has been changed, and as the inquest won't be till tomorrow, after you are gone, she thought you wouldn't know a word of it, being strangers here.'

The returning footsteps of her husband broke off further narration. Baptista waved her hand, for she could not speak. The waiting-maid quickly withdrew, and Mr Heddegan entered with the smelling salts and other nostrums.

'Any better?' he questioned.

'I don't like the hotel,' she exclaimed, almost simultaneously. 'I can't bear it – it doesn't suit me!'

'Is that all that's the matter?' he returned pettishly (this being the first time of his showing such a mood). 'Upon my heart and life such trifling is trying to any man's temper, Baptista! Sending me about from here to yond, and then when I come back saying 'ee don't like the place that I have sunk so much money and words to get for 'ee. 'Od dang it all, 'tis enough to – But I won't say any more at present, mee deer, though it is just too much to expect to turn out of the house now. We shan't get another quiet place at this time of the evening – every other inn in the town is bustling with rackety folk of one sort and t'other, while here 'tis as quiet as the grave – the country, I would say. So bide still, d'ye hear, and tomorrow we shall be out of the town altogether – as early as you like.'

The obstinacy of age had, in short, overmastered its complaisance, and the young woman said no more. The simple course of telling him that in the adjoining room lay a corpse which had lately occupied their own might, it would have seemed, have been an effectual one without further disclosure, but to allude to that subject, however it was disguised, was more than Heddegan's young wife had strength for. Horror broke her down. In the contingency one thing only presented itself to her paralysed regard – that here she was doomed to abide, in a hideous contiguity to the dead husband and the living, and her conjecture did, in fact, bear itself out. That night she lay between the two men she had married – Heddegan on the one hand, and on the other through the partition against which the bed stood, Charles Stow.

6

Kindly time had withdrawn the foregoing event three days from the present of Baptista Heddegan. It was ten o'clock in the morning; she had been ill, not in an ordinary or definite sense, but in a state of cold stupefaction, from which it was difficult to arouse her so much as to say a few sentences. When questioned she had replied that she was pretty well.

Their trip, as such, had been something of a failure. They had gone on as far as Falmouth, but here he had given way to her entreaties to return home. This they could not very well do without repassing through Pen-zephyr, at which place they had now again arrived.

In the train she had seen a weekly local paper, and read there a paragraph detailing the inquest on Charles. It was added that the funeral was to take place at his native town of Redrutin on Friday.

After reading this she had shown no reluctance to enter the fatal neighbourhood of the tragedy, only stipulating that they should take their rest at a different lodging from the first; and now comparatively braced up and calm – indeed a cooler creature altogether than when last in the town, she said to David that she wanted to walk out for a while, as they had plenty of time on their hands.

'To a shop as usual, I suppose, mee deer?'

'Partly for shopping,' she said. 'And it will be best for you, dear, to stay in after trotting about so much, and have a good rest while I am gone.'

He assented; and Baptista sallied forth. As she had stated, her first visit was made to a shop, a draper's. Without the exercise of much choice she purchased a black bonnet and veil, also a black stuff gown; a black mantle she already wore. These articles were made up into a parcel which, in spite of the saleswoman's offers, her customer said she would take with her. Bearing it on her arm she turned to the railway, and at the station got a ticket for Redrutin.

Thus it appeared that, on her recovery from the paralysed mood of the former day, while she had resolved not to blast utterly the happiness of her present husband by revealing the history of the departed one, she had also determined to indulge a certain odd, inconsequent, feminine sentiment of decency, to the small extent to which it could do no harm to any person. At Redrutin she emerged from the railway carriage in the black attire purchased at the shop, having during the transit made the change in the empty compartment she had chosen. The other clothes were now in the bandbox and parcel. Leaving these at the cloakroom she proceeded onward, and after a wary survey reached the side of a hill whence a view of the burial ground could be obtained.

It was now a little before two o'clock. While Baptista waited a funeral procession ascended the road. Baptista hastened across, and by the time the procession entered the cemetery gates she had unobtrusively joined it.

In addition to the schoolmaster's own relatives (not a few), the paragraph in the newspapers of his death by drowning had drawn together many neighbours, acquaintances and onlookers. Among them she passed unnoticed, and with a quiet step pursued the winding path to the chapel, and afterwards thence to the grave. When all was over, and the relatives and idlers had withdrawn, she stepped to the edge of the chasm. From beneath her mantle she drew a little bunch of forget-me-nots, and dropped them in upon the coffin. In a few minutes she also turned and went away from the cemetery. By five o'clock she was again in Pen-zephyr.

'You have been a mortal long time!' said her husband, crossly. 'I allowed you an hour at most, mee deer.'

'It occupied me longer,' said she.

'Well – I reckon it is wasting words to complain. Hang it, ye look so tired and wisht that I can't find heart to say what I would!'

'I am – weary and wisht, David; I am. We can get home tomorrow for certain, I hope?'

'We can. And please God we will!' said Mr Heddegan heartily, as if he too were weary of his brief honeymoon. 'I must be into business again on Monday morning at latest.'

They left by the next-morning steamer, and in the afternoon took up their residence in their own house at Giant's Town.

The hour that she reached the island it was as if a material weight had been removed from Baptista's shoulders. Her husband attributed the change to the influence of the local breezes after the hot-house atmosphere of the mainland. However that might be, settled here, a few doors from her mother's dwelling, she recovered in no very long time much of her customary bearing, which was never very demonstrative. She accepted her position calmly, and faintly smiled when her neighbours learned to call her Mrs Heddegan, and said she seemed likely to become the leader of fashion in Giant's Town.

Her husband was a man who had made considerably more money by trade than her father had done, and perhaps the greater profusion of surroundings at her command than she had heretofore been mistress of was not without an effect upon her. One week, two weeks, three weeks passed; and, being pre-eminently a young woman who allowed things to drift, she did nothing whatever either to disclose or conceal traces of her first marriage; or to learn if there existed possibilities – which there undoubtedly did – by which that hasty contract might become revealed to those about her at any unexpected moment.

While yet within the first month of her marriage, and on an evening just before sunset, Baptista was standing within her garden adjoining the house when she saw passing along the road a personage clad in a greasy black coat and battered tall hat, which, common enough in the slums of a city, had an odd appearance in St Maria's. The tramp, as he seemed to be, marked her at once – bonnetless and unwrapped as she was her features were plainly recognisable – and with an air of friendly surprise came and leant over the wall.

'What! don't you know me?' said he.

She had some dim recollection of his face, but said that she was not acquainted with him.

'Why, your witness to be sure, ma'am. Don't you mind the man that was mending the church-window when you and your intended husband walked up to be made one; and the clerk called me down from the ladder, and I came and did my part by writing my name and occupation?'

Baptista glanced quickly around; her husband was out of earshot. That would have been of less importance but for the fact that the wedding witnessed by this personage had not been the wedding with Mr Heddegan, but the one on the day previous.

'I've had a misfortune since then, that's pulled me under,' continued her friend. 'But don't let me damp yer wedded joy by naming the particulars. Yes, I've seen changes since; though 'tis but a short time ago – let me see, only a month next week, I think; for 'twere the first or second day in August.'

'Yes – that's when it was,' said another man, a sailor, who had come up with a pipe in his mouth, and felt it necessary to join in (Baptista having receded to escape further speech). 'For that was the first time I set foot in Giant's Town; and her husband took her to him the same day.'

A dialogue then proceeded between the two men outside the wall, which Baptista could not help hearing.

'Ay, I signed the book that made her one flesh,' repeated the decayed glazier. 'Where's her goodman?'

'About the premises somewhere; but you don't see 'em together much,' replied the sailor in an undertone. 'You see, he's older than she.'

'Older? I should never have thought it from my own observation,' said the glazier. 'He was a remarkably handsome man.'

'Handsome? Well, there he is – we can see for ourselves.'

David Heddegan had, indeed, just shown himself at the upper end of the garden; and the glazier, looking in bewilderment from the husband to the wife, saw the latter turn pale.

Now that decayed glazier was a far-seeing and cunning man – too far-seeing and cunning to allow himself to thrive by simple and straightforward means – and he held his peace, till he could read more plainly the meaning of this riddle, merely adding carelessly, 'Well – marriage do alter a man, 'tis true. I should never ha' knowed him!'

He then stared oddly at the disconcerted Baptista, and moving on to where he could again address her, asked her to do him a good turn, since he once had done the same for her. Understanding that he meant money, she handed him some, at which he thanked her, and instantly went away.

7

She had escaped exposure on this occasion; but the incident had been an awkward one, and should have suggested to Baptista that sooner or later the secret must leak out. As it was, she suspected that at any rate she had not heard the last of the glazier.

In a day or two, when her husband had gone to the old town on the other side of the island, there came a gentle tap at the door, and the worthy witness of her first marriage made his appearance a second time.

'It took me hours to get to the bottom of the mystery – hours!' he said with a gaze of deep confederacy which offended her pride very deeply. 'But thanks to a good intellect I've done it. Now, ma'am, I'm not a man to tell tales, even when a tale would be so good as this. But I'm going back to the mainland again, and a little assistance would be as rain on thirsty ground.'

'I helped you two days ago,' began Baptista.

'Yes – but what was that, my good lady? Not enough to pay my passage to Pen-zephyr. I came over on your account, for I thought there was a mystery somewhere. Now I must go back on my own. Mind this – 'twould be very awkward for you if your old man were to know. He's a queer temper, though he may be fond.'

She knew as well as her visitor how awkward it would be; and the hush-money she paid was heavy that day. She had, however, the satisfaction of watching the man to the steamer, and seeing him diminish out of sight. But Baptista perceived that the system into which she had been led of purchasing silence thus was one fatal to her peace of mind, particularly if it had to be continued.

Hearing no more from the glazier she hoped the difficulty was past. But another week only had gone by, when, as she was pacing the Giant's Walk (the name given to the promenade), she met the same personage in the company of a fat woman carrying a bundle.

'This is the lady, my dear,' he said to his companion. 'This, ma'am, is my wife. We've come to settle in the town for a time, if so be we can find room.'

'That you won't do,' said she. 'Nobody can live here who is not privileged.'

'I am privileged,' said the glazier, 'by my trade.'

Baptista went on, but in the afternoon she received a visit from the man's wife. This honest woman began to depict, in forcible colours, the necessity for keeping up the concealment.

'I will intercede with my husband, ma'am,' she said. 'He's a true man if rightly managed; and I'll beg him to consider your position. 'Tis a very nice house you've got here,' she added, glancing round, 'and well worth a little sacrifice to keep it.'

The unlucky Baptista staved off the danger on this third occasion as she had done on the previous two. But she formed a resolve that if the attack were once more to be repeated she would face a revelation – worse though that must now be than before she had attempted to purchase silence by bribes. Her tormentors, never believing her capable of acting upon such an intention, came again; but she shut the door in their faces. They retreated, muttering something; but she went to the back of the house, where David Heddegan was.

She looked at him, unconscious of all. The case was serious; she knew that well; and all the more serious in that she liked him better now than she had done at first. Yet, as she herself began to see, the secret was one that was sure to disclose itself. Her name and Charles's stood indelibly written in the registers; and though a month only had passed as yet it was a wonder that his clandestine union with her had not already been discovered by his friends. Thus spurring herself to the inevitable, she spoke to Heddegan.

'David, come indoors. I have something to tell you.'

He hardly regarded her at first. She had discerned that during the last week or two he had seemed preoccupied, as if some private business harassed him. She repeated her request. He replied with a sigh, 'Yes, certainly, mee deer.'

When they had reached the sitting-room and shut the door, she repeated, faintly, 'David, I have something to tell you – a sort of tragedy I have concealed. You will hate me for having so far deceived you; but perhaps my telling you voluntarily will make you think a little better of me than you would do otherwise.'

'Tragedy?' he said, awakening to interest. 'Much you can know about tragedies, mee deer, that have been in the world so short a time!'

She saw that he suspected nothing, and it made her task the harder. But on she went steadily. 'It is about something that happened before we were married,' she said.

'Indeed!'

'Not a very long time before – a short time. And it is about a lover,' she faltered.

'I don't much mind that,' he said mildly. 'In truth, I was in hopes 'twas more.'

'In hopes!'

'Well, yes.'

This screwed her up to the necessary effort. 'I met my old sweetheart. He scorned me, chid me, dared me, and I went and married him. We were coming straight here to tell you all what we had done; but he was drowned; and I thought I would say nothing about him: and I married you, David, for the sake of peace and quietness. I've tried to keep it from you, but have found I cannot. There – that's the substance of it, and you can never, never forgive me, I am sure!'

She spoke desperately. But the old man, instead of turning black or blue, or slaying her in his indignation, jumped up from his chair and began to caper around the room in quite an ecstatic emotion.

'Oh, happy thing! How well it falls out!' he exclaimed, snapping his fingers over his head. 'Ha-ha – the knot is cut – I see a way out of my trouble – ha-ha!'

She looked at him without uttering a sound, till, as he still continued smiling joyfully, she said, 'Oh – what do you mean! Is it done to torment me?'

'No – no! Oh, mee deer, your story helps me out of the most heart-aching quandary a poor man ever found himself in! You see, it is this – I've got a tragedy, too; and unless you had had one to tell, I could never have seen my way to tell mine!'

'What is yours – what is it?' she asked, with altogether a new view of things.

'Well – it is a bouncer; mine is a bouncer!' said he, looking on the ground and wiping his eyes.

'Not worse than mine?'

'Well – that depends upon how you look at it. Yours had to do with the past alone; and I don't mind it. You see, we've been married a month, and it don't jar upon me as it would if we'd only been married a day or two. Now mine refers to past, present and future; so that – '

'Past, present and future!' she murmured. 'It never occurred to me that you had a tragedy, too.'

'But I have!' he said, shaking his head. 'In fact, four.'

'Then tell 'em!' cried the young woman.

'I will – I will. But be considerate, I beg 'ee, mee deer. Well – I wasn't a bachelor when I married 'ee, any more than you were a spinster. Just as you was a widow-woman, I was a widow-man.'

'Ah!' said she, with some surprise. 'But is that all? – then we are nicely balanced,' she added, relieved.

'No – it is not all. There's the point. I am not only a widower.'

'Oh, David!'

'I am a widower with four tragedies – that is to say, four strapping girls – the eldest taller than you. Don't 'ee look so struck – dumb-like! It fell out in this way. I knew the poor woman, their mother, in Pen-zephyr for some years; and – to cut a long story short – I privately married her at last, just before she died. I kept the matter secret, but it is getting known among the people here by degrees. I've long felt for the children – that it is my duty to have them here, and do something for them. I have not had courage to break it to 'ee, but I've seen lately that it would soon come to your ears, and that hev worried me.'

'Are they educated?' said the ex-schoolmistress.

'No. I am sorry to say they have been much neglected; in truth, they can hardly read. And so I thought that by marrying a young schoolmistress I should get someone in the house who could teach 'em, and bring 'em into genteel condition, all for nothing. You see, they are growed up too tall to be sent to school.'

'Oh, mercy!' she almost moaned. 'Four great girls to teach the rudiments to, and have always in the house with me spelling over their books; and I hate teaching, it kills me. I am bitterly punished – I am, I am!'

'You'll get used to 'em, mee deer, and the balance of secrets – mine against yours – will comfort your heart with a sense of justice. I could send for 'em this week very well – and I will! In faith, I could send this very day. Baptista, you have relieved me of all my difficulty!'

Thus the interview ended, so far as this matter was concerned. Baptista was too stupefied to say more, and when she went away to her room she wept from very mortification at Mr Heddegan's duplicity. Education, the one thing she abhorred; the shame of it to delude a young wife so!

The next meal came round. As they sat, Baptista would not suffer her eyes to turn towards him. He did not attempt to intrude upon her reserve, but every now and then looked under the table and chuckled with satisfaction at the aspect of affairs. 'How very well matched we be!' he said, comfortably.

Next day, when the steamer came in, Baptista saw her husband rush down to meet it; and soon after there appeared at her door four tall, hipless, shoulderless girls, dwindling in height and size from the eldest to the youngest, like a row of Pan pipes; at the head of them standing Heddegan. He smiled pleasantly through the grey fringe of his whiskers and beard, and turning to the girls said, 'Now come forrard, and shake hands properly with your stepmother.'

Thus she made their acquaintance, and he went out, leaving them together. On examination the poor girls turned out to be not only plain-looking, which she could have forgiven, but to have such a lamentably meagre intellectual equipment as to be hopelessly inadequate as companions. Even the eldest, almost her own age, could only read with difficulty words of two syllables; and taste in dress was beyond their comprehension. In the long vista of future years she saw nothing but dreary drudgery at her detested old trade without prospect of reward.

She went about quite despairing during the next few days – an unpromising, unfortunate mood for a woman who had not been married six weeks. From her parents she concealed everything. They had been amongst the few acquaintances of Heddegan who knew nothing of his secret, and were indignant enough when they saw such a ready-made household foisted upon their only child. But she would not support them in their remonstrances.

'No, you don't yet know all,' she said.

Thus Baptista had sense enough to see the retributive fairness of this issue. For some time, whenever conversation arose between her and Heddegan, which was not often, she always said, 'I am miserable, and you know it. Yet I don't wish things to be otherwise.'

But one day when he asked, 'How do you like 'em now?' her answer was unexpected. 'Much better than I did,' she said, quietly. 'I may like them very much some day.'

This was the beginning of a serener season for the chastened spirit of Baptista Heddegan. She had, in truth, discovered, underneath the crust of uncouthness and meagre articulation which was due to their troglodytean existence, that her unwelcomed daughters had natures that were unselfish almost to sublimity. The harsh discipline accorded to their young lives, before their mother's wrong had been righted, had operated less to crush them than to lift them above all personal ambition. They considered the world and its contents in a purely objective way, and their own lot seemed only to affect them as that of certain human beings among the rest, whose troubles they knew rather than suffered.

This was such an entirely new way of regarding life to a woman of Baptista's nature, that her attention, from being first arrested by it, became deeply interested. By imperceptible pulses her heart expanded in sympathy with theirs. The sentences of her tragi-comedy, her life, confused till now, became clearer daily. That in humanity, as exemplified by these girls, there was nothing to dislike, but infinitely much to pity, she learnt with the lapse of each week in their company. She grew to like the girls of unpromising exterior, and from liking she got to love them; till they formed an unexpected point of junction between her own and her husband's interests, generating a sterling friendship at least, between a pair in whose existence there had threatened to be neither friendship nor love.

W. W. JACOBS

William Wymark Jacobs was born in Wapping in 1863, the son of an East London dock worker. He left school when he was sixteen to join the civil service as a clerk in the Post Office Savings Bank. Never really happy in his work, he began writing short stories, mostly concerned with the sea and nautical culture. In 1896, he published his first collection of short stories, *Many Cargoes*, which was well received. An excellent humourist, Jacobs became one of the most popular English writers of that genre in the early twentieth century. Today he is best remembered for his macabre story *The Monkey's Paw* (1902), which appeared first in *Harper's Monthly* and which was reprinted in his third collection of short stories, *The Lady of the Barge*, that same year. His other works include *More Cargoes* (1898), *Little Freights* (1901), *At Sunwich Port* (1902), *A Master of Craft* (1903), *Dialstone Lane* (1904), *Short Cruises* (1907), *Sailor's Knots* (1909), *Ship's Company* (1911), *Night Watches* (1914), *Castaways* (1916), *Deep Waters* (1919), *Sea Whispers* (1926) and *Snug Harbour* (1931). He died in 1943.

The Well

Two men stood in the billiard-room of an old country house, talking. Play, which had been of a half-hearted nature, was over, and they were at the window looking over the park stretching away beneath them, conversing idly.

'Your time's nearly up, Jem,' said one at length, 'this time six weeks you'll be yawning out the honeymoon and cursing the man – woman I mean – who invented them.'

Jem Benson stretched his long limbs in the chair and grunted in dissent.

'I've never understood it,' continued Wilfred Carr. 'It's not in my line at all; I never had enough money for my own wants, let alone for two. Perhaps if I were as rich as you or Croesus I might regard it differently.'

There was just sufficient meaning in the latter part of the remark for his cousin to forbear to reply to it. He continued to gaze out of the window and to smoke slowly.

'Not being as rich as Croesus – or you,' resumed Carr, regarding him from beneath lowered lids, 'I paddle my own canoe down the stream of Time, and tying it to my friends' door-posts, go in to eat their dinners.'

'Quite Venetian,' said Jem Benson, still looking out of the window. 'It's not a bad thing for you, Wilfred, that you have the doorposts and dinners – and friends.'

Carr grunted in his turn. 'Seriously though, Jem,' he said, slowly, 'you're a lucky fellow, a very lucky fellow. If there is a better girl above ground than Olive, I should like to see her.'

'Yes,' said the other, quietly.

'She's such an exceptional girl,' continued Carr, staring out of the window. 'She's so good and gentle. She thinks you are a bundle of all the virtues.'

He laughed frankly and joyously, but the other man did not join him. 'Strong sense – of right and wrong, though,' continued Carr, musingly. 'Do you know, I believe that if she found out that you were not – '

'Not what?' demanded Benson, turning upon him fiercely, 'Not what?'

'Everything that you are,' returned his cousin, with a grin that belied his words, 'I believe she'd drop you.'

'Talk about something else,' said Benson, slowly; 'your pleasantries are not always in the best taste.'

Wilfred Carr rose and taking a cue from the rack, bent over the board and practised one or two favourite shots. 'The only other subject I can talk about just at present is my own financial affairs,' he said slowly, as he walked round the table.

'Talk about something else,' said Benson again, bluntly.

'And the two things are connected,' said Carr, and dropping his cue he half sat on the table and eyed his cousin.

There was a long silence. Benson pitched the end of his cigar out of the window, and leaning back closed his eyes.

'Do you follow me?' enquired Carr at length.

Benson opened his eyes and nodded at the window.

'Do you want to follow my cigar?' he demanded.

'I should prefer to depart by the usual way for your sake,' returned the other, unabashed. 'If I left by the window all sorts of questions would be asked, and you know what a talkative chap I am.'

'So long as you don't talk about my affairs,' returned the other, restraining himself by an obvious effort, 'you can talk yourself hoarse.'

'I'm in a mess,' said Carr, slowly, 'a devil of a mess. If I don't raise fifteen hundred by this day fortnight, I may be getting my board and lodging free.'

'Would that be any change?' questioned Benson.

'The quality would,' retorted the other. 'The address also would not be good. Seriously, Jem, will you let me have the fifteen hundred?'

'No,' said the other, simply.

Carr went white. 'It's to save me from ruin,' he said, thickly.

'I've helped you till I'm tired,' said Benson, turning and regarding him, 'and it is all to no good. If you've got into a mess, get out of it. You should not be so fond of giving autographs away.'

'It's foolish, I admit,' said Carr, deliberately. 'I won't do so any more. By the way, I've got some to sell. You needn't sneer. They're not my own.'

'Whose are they?' enquired the other.

'Yours.'

Benson got up from his chair and crossed over to him. 'What is this?' he asked, quietly. 'Blackmail?'

'Call it what you like,' said Carr. 'I've got some letters for sale, price fifteen hundred. And I know a man who would buy them at that price for the mere chance of getting Olive from you. I'll give you first offer.'

'If you have got any letters bearing my signature, you will be good enough to give them to me,' said Benson, very slowly.

'They're mine,' said Carr, lightly; 'given to me by the lady you wrote them to. I must say that they are not all in the best possible taste.'

His cousin reached forward suddenly, and catching him by the collar of his coat pinned him down on the table.

'Give me those letters,' he breathed, sticking his face close to Carr's.

'They're not here,' said Carr, struggling. 'I'm not a fool. Let me go, or I'll raise the price.'

The other man raised him from the table in his powerful hands, apparently with the intention of dashing his head against it. Then suddenly his hold relaxed as an astonished-looking maidservant entered the room with letters. Carr sat up hastily.

'That's how it was done,' said Benson, for the girl's benefit as he took the letters.

'I don't wonder at the other man making him pay for it, then,' said Carr, blandly.

'You will give me those letters?' said Benson, suggestively, as the girl left the room.

'At the price I mentioned, yes,' said Carr; 'but so sure as I am a living man, if you lay your clumsy hands on me again, I'll double it. Now, I'll leave you for a time while you think it over.'

He took a cigar from the box and lighting it carefully quitted the room. His cousin waited until the door had closed behind him, and then turning to the window sat there in a fit of fury as silent as it was terrible.

The air was fresh and sweet from the park, heavy with the scent of new-mown grass. The fragrance of a cigar was now added to it, and glancing out he saw his cousin pacing slowly by. He rose and went to the door, and then, apparently altering his mind, he returned to the window and watched the figure of his cousin as it moved slowly away into the moonlight. Then he rose again, and, for a long time, the room was empty.

*   *   *

It was empty when Mrs Benson came in some time later to say good-night to her son on her way to bed. She walked slowly round the table, and pausing at the window gazed from it in idle thought, until she saw the figure of her son advancing with rapid strides towards the house. He looked up at the window.

'Good-night,' said she.

'Good-night,' said Benson, in a deep voice.

'Where is Wilfred?'

'Oh, he has gone,' said Benson.

'Gone?'

'We had a few words; he was wanting money again, and I gave him a piece of my mind. I don't think we shall see him again.'

'Poor Wilfred!' sighed Mrs Benson. 'He is always in trouble of some sort. I hope that you were not too hard upon him.'

'No more than he deserved,' said her son, sternly. 'Good-night.'

2

The well, which had long ago fallen into disuse, was almost hidden by the thick tangle of undergrowth which ran riot at that corner of the old park. It was partly covered by the shrunken half of a lid, above which a rusty windlass creaked in company with the music of the pines when the wind blew strongly.

The full light of the sun never reached it, and the ground surrounding it was moist and green when other parts of the park were gasping with the heat.

Two people walking slowly round the park in the fragrant stillness of a summer evening strayed in the direction of the well.

'No use going through this wilderness, Olive,' said Benson, pausing on the outskirts of the pines and eyeing with some disfavour the gloom beyond.

'Best part of the park,' said the girl briskly; 'you know it's my favourite spot.'

'I know you're very fond of sitting on the coping,' said the man slowly, 'and I wish you wouldn't. One day you will lean back too far and fall in.'

'And make the acquaintance of Truth,' said Olive lightly. 'Come along.'

She ran from him and was lost in the shadow of the pines, the bracken crackling beneath her feet as she ran. Her companion followed slowly, and emerging from the gloom saw her poised daintily on the edge of the well with her feet hidden in the rank grass and nettles which surrounded it. She motioned her companion to take a seat by her side, and smiled softly as she felt a strong arm passed about her waist.

'I like this place,' said she, breaking a long silence, 'it is so dismal – so uncanny. Do you know I wouldn't dare to sit here alone, Jem. I should imagine that all sorts of dreadful things were hidden behind the bushes and trees, waiting to spring out on me. Ugh!'

'You'd better let me take you in,' said her companion tenderly; 'the well isn't always wholesome, especially in the hot weather. Let's make a move.'

The girl gave an obstinate little shake, and settled herself more securely on her seat.

'Smoke your cigar in peace,' she said quietly. 'I am settled here for a quiet talk. Has anything been heard of Wilfred yet?'

'Nothing.'

'Quite a dramatic disappearance, isn't it?' she continued. 'Another scrape, I suppose, and another letter for you in the same old strain; "Dear Jem, help me out." '

Jem Benson blew a cloud of fragrant smoke into the air, and holding his cigar between his teeth brushed away the ash from his coat sleeves.

'I wonder what he would have done without you,' said the girl, pressing his arm affectionately. 'Gone under long ago, I suppose. When we are married, Jem, I shall presume upon the relationship to lecture him. He is very wild, but he has his good points, poor fellow.'

'I never saw them,' said Benson, with startling bitterness. 'God knows I never saw them.'

'He is nobody's enemy but his own,' said the girl, startled by this outburst.

'You don't know much about him,' said the other, sharply. 'He was not above blackmail; not above ruining the life of a friend to do himself a benefit. A loafer, a cur, and a liar!'

The girl looked up at him soberly but timidly and took his arm without a word, and they both sat silent while evening deepened into night and the beams of the moon, filtering through the branches, surrounded them with a silver network. Her head sank upon his shoulder, till suddenly with a sharp cry she sprang to her feet.

'What was that?' she cried breathlessly.

'What was what?' demanded Benson, springing up and clutching her fast by the arm.

She caught her breath and tried to laugh.

'You're hurting me, Jem.'

His hold relaxed.

'What is the matter?' he asked gently. 'What was it startled you?'

'I was startled,' she said, slowly, putting her hands on his shoulder. 'I suppose the words I used just now are ringing in my ears, but I fancied that somebody behind us whispered, "Jem, help me out." '

'Fancy,' repeated Benson, and his voice shook; 'but these fancies are not good for you. You – are frightened – at the dark and the gloom of these trees. Let me take you back to the house.'

'No, I'm not frightened,' said the girl, reseating herself. 'I should never be really frightened of anything when you were with me, Jem. I'm surprised at myself for being so silly.'

The man made no reply but stood, a strong, dark figure, a yard or two from the well, as though waiting for her to join him.

'Come and sit down, sir,' cried Olive, patting the brickwork with her small, white hand, 'one would think that you did not like your company.'

He obeyed slowly and took a seat by her side, drawing so hard at his cigar that the light of it shone upon his face at every breath. He passed his arm, firm and rigid as steel, behind her, with his hand resting on the brickwork beyond.

'Are you warm enough?' he asked tenderly, as she made a little movement. 'Pretty fair,' she shivered; 'one oughtn't to be cold at this time of the year, but there's a cold, damp air comes up from the well.'

As she spoke a faint splash sounded from the depths below, and for the second time that evening, she sprang from the well with a little cry of dismay.

'What is it now?' he asked in a fearful voice. He stood by her side and gazed at the well, as though half expecting to see the cause of her alarm emerge from it.

'Oh, my bracelet,' she cried in distress, 'my poor mother's bracelet. I've dropped it down the well.'

'Your bracelet!' repeated Benson, dully. 'Your bracelet? The diamond one?'

'The one that was my mother's,' said Olive. 'Oh, we can get it back surely. We must have the water drained off.'

'Your bracelet!' repeated Benson, stupidly.

'Jem,' said the girl in terrified tones, 'dear Jem, what is the matter?'

For the man she loved was standing regarding her with horror. The moon which touched it was not responsible for all the whiteness of the distorted face, and she shrank back in fear to the edge of the well. He saw her fear and by a mighty effort regained his composure and took her hand.

'Poor little girl,' he murmured, 'you frightened me. I was not looking when you cried, and I thought that you were slipping from my arms, down – down – '

His voice broke, and the girl throwing herself into his arms clung to him convulsively.

'There, there,' said Benson, fondly, 'don't cry, don't cry.'

'Tomorrow,' said Olive, half-laughing, half-crying, 'we will all come round the well with hook and line and fish for it. It will be quite a new sport.'

'No, we must try some other way,' said Benson. 'You shall have it back.'

'How?' asked the girl.

'You shall see,' said Benson. 'Tomorrow morning at latest you shall have it back. Till then promise me that you will not mention your loss to anyone. Promise.'

'I promise,' said Olive, wonderingly. 'But why not?'

'It is of great value, for one thing, and – But there – there are many reasons. For one thing it is my duty to get it for you.'

'Wouldn't you like to jump down for it?' she asked mischievously. 'Listen.'

She stooped for a stone and dropped it down.

'Fancy being where that is now,' she said, peering into the blackness; 'fancy going round and round like a mouse in a pail, clutching at the slimy sides, with the water filling your mouth, and looking up to the little patch of sky above.'

'You had better come in,' said Benson, very quietly. 'You are developing a taste for the morbid and horrible.'

The girl turned, and taking his arm walked slowly in the direction of the house; Mrs Benson, who was sitting in the porch, rose to receive them.

'You shouldn't have kept her out so long,' she said chidingly. 'Where have you been?'

'Sitting on the well,' said Olive, smiling, 'discussing our future.'

'I don't believe that place is healthy,' said Mrs Benson, emphatically. 'I really think it might be filled in, Jem.'

'All right,' said her son, slowly. 'Pity it wasn't filled in long ago.'

He took the chair vacated by his mother as she entered the house with Olive, and with his hands hanging limply over the sides sat in deep thought. After a time he rose, and going upstairs to a room which was set apart for sporting requisites, selected a sea-fishing line and some hooks and stole softly downstairs again. He walked swiftly across the park in the direction of the well, turning before he entered the shadow of the trees to look back at the lighted windows of the house. Then having arranged his line he sat on the edge of the well and cautiously lowered it.

He sat with his lips compressed, occasionally looking about him in a startled fashion, as though he half expected to see something peering at him from the belt of trees. Time after time he lowered his line until at length in pulling it up he heard a little metallic tinkle against the side of the well.

He held his breath then, and forgetting his fears drew the line in inch by inch, so as not to lose its precious burden. His pulse beat rapidly, and his eyes were bright. As the line came slowly in he saw the catch hanging to the hook, and with a steady hand drew the last few feet in. Then he saw that instead of the bracelet he had hooked a bunch of keys.

With a faint cry he shook them from the hook into the water below, and stood breathing heavily. Not a sound broke the stillness of the night. He walked up and down a bit and stretched his great muscles; then he came back to the well and resumed his task.

For an hour or more the line was lowered without result. In his eagerness he forgot his fears, and with eyes bent down the well fished slowly and carefully. Twice the hook became entangled in something, and was with difficulty released. It caught a third time, and all his efforts failed to free it. Then he dropped the line down the well, and with head bent walked towards the house.

He went first to the stables at the rear, and then retiring to his room for some time paced restlessly up and down. Then without removing his clothes he flung himself upon the bed and fell into a troubled sleep.

3

Long before anybody else was astir he arose and stole softly downstairs. The sunlight was stealing in at every crevice, and flashing in long streaks across the darkened rooms. The dining-room into which he looked struck chill and cheerless in the dark yellow light which came through the lowered blinds. He remembered that it had the same appearance when his father lay dead in the house; now, as then, everything seemed ghastly and unreal; the very chairs standing as their occupants had left them the night before seemed to be indulging in some dark communication of ideas.

Slowly and noiselessly he opened the hall door and passed into the fragrant air beyond. The sun was shining on the drenched grass and trees, and a slowly vanishing white mist rolled like smoke about the grounds. For a moment he stood, breathing deeply the sweet air of the morning, and then walked in the direction of the stables.

The rusty creaking of a pump-handle and a spatter of water upon the red-tiled courtyard showed that somebody else was astir, and a few steps farther he beheld a brawny, sandy-haired man gasping wildly under severe self-infliction at the pump.

'Everything ready, George?' he asked quietly.

'Yes, sir,' said the man, straightening up suddenly and touching his forehead. 'Bob's just finishing the arrangements inside. It's a lovely morning for a dip. The water in that well must be just icy.'

'Be as quick as you can,' said Benson, impatiently.

'Very good, sir,' said George, burnishing his face harshly with a very small towel which had been hanging over the top of the pump. 'Hurry up, Bob.'

In answer to his summons a man appeared at the door of the stable with a coil of stout rope over his arm and a large metal candlestick in his hand.

'Just to try the air, sir,' said George, following his master's glance, 'a well gets rather foul sometimes, but if a candle can live down it, a man can.'

His master nodded, and the man, hastily pulling up the neck of his shirt and thrusting his arms into his coat, followed him as he led the way slowly to the well.

'Beg pardon, sir,' said George, drawing up to his side, 'but you are not looking over and above well this morning. If you'll let me go down I'd enjoy the bath.'

'No, no,' said Benson, peremptorily.

'You ain't fit to go down, sir,' persisted his follower. 'I've never seen you look so before. Now if – '

'Mind your business,' said his master curtly.

George became silent and the three walked with swinging strides through the long wet grass to the well. Bob flung the rope on the ground and at a sign from his master handed him the candlestick.

'Here's the line for it, sir,' said Bob, fumbling in his pockets.

Benson took it from him and tied it to the candlestick. Then he placed it on the edge of the well, and striking a match, lit the candle and began slowly to lower it.

'Hold hard, sir,' said George, quickly, laying his hand on his arm, 'you must tilt it or the string'll burn through.'

Even as he spoke the string parted and the candlestick fell into the water below.

Benson swore quietly.

'I'll soon get another,' said George, starting up.

'Never mind, the well's all right,' said Benson.

'It won't take a moment, sir,' said the other over his shoulder.

'Are you master here, or am I?' said Benson hoarsely.

George came back slowly, a glance at his master's face stopping the protest upon his tongue, and he stood by watching him sulkily as he sat on the well and removed his outer garments. Both men watched him curiously, as having completed his preparations he stood grim and silent with his hands by his sides.

'I wish you'd let me go, sir,' said George, plucking up courage to address him. 'You ain't fit to go, you've got a chill or something. I shouldn't wonder it's the typhoid. They've got it in the village bad.'

For a moment Benson looked at him angrily, then his gaze softened. 'Not this time, George,' he said, quietly. He took the looped end of the rope and placed it under his arms, and sitting down threw one leg over the side of the well.

'How are you going about it, sir?' queried George, laying hold of the rope and signing to Bob to do the same.

'I'll call out when I reach the water,' said Benson; 'then pay out three yards more quickly so that I can get to the bottom.'

'Very good, sir,' answered both.

Their master threw the other leg over the coping and sat motionless. His back was turned towards the men as he sat with head bent, looking down the shaft. He sat for so long that George became uneasy.

'All right, sir?' he enquired.

'Yes,' said Benson, slowly. 'If I tug at the rope, George, pull up at once. Lower away.'

The rope passed steadily through their hands until a hollow cry from the darkness below and a faint splashing warned them that he had reached the water. They gave him three yards more and stood with relaxed grasp and strained ears, waiting.

'He's gone under,' said Bob in a low voice.

The other nodded, and moistening his huge palms took a firmer grip of the rope.

Fully a minute passed, and the men began to exchange uneasy glances. Then a sudden tremendous jerk followed by a series of feebler ones nearly tore the rope from their grasp.

'Pull!' shouted George, placing one foot on the side and hauling desperately. 'Pull! pull! He's stuck fast; he's not coming; PULL!'

In response to their terrific exertions the rope came slowly in, inch by inch, until at length a violent splashing was heard, and at the same moment a scream of unutterable horror came echoing up the shaft.

'What a weight he is!' panted Bob. 'He's stuck fast or something. Keep still, sir; for heaven's sake, keep still.'

For the taut rope was being jerked violently by the struggles of the weight at the end of it. Both men with grunts and sighs hauled it in foot by foot.

'All right, sir,' cried George, cheerfully.

He had one foot against the well, and was pulling manfully; the burden was nearing the top. A long pull and a strong pull, and the face of a dead man with mud in the eyes and nostrils came peering over the edge. Behind it was the ghastly face of his master; but this he saw too late, for with a great cry he let go his hold of the rope and stepped back. The suddenness overthrew his assistant, and the rope tore through his hands. There was a frightful splash.

'You fool!' stammered Bob, and ran to the well helplessly.

'Run!' cried George. 'Run for another line.'

He bent over the coping and called eagerly down as his assistant sped back to the stables shouting wildly. His voice re-echoed down the shaft, but all else was silence.

An Elaborate Elopement

I have always had a slight suspicion that the following narrative is not quite true. It was related to me by an old seaman who, among other incidents of a somewhat adventurous career, claimed to have received Napoleon's sword at the Battle of Trafalgar, and a wound in the back at Waterloo. I prefer to tell it in my own way, his being so garnished with nautical terms and expletives as to be half unintelligible and somewhat horrifying. Our talk had been of love and courtship, and after making me a present of several tips, invented by himself, and considered invaluable by his friends, he related this story of the courtship of a chum of his as illustrating the great lengths to which young bloods were prepared to go in his days to attain their ends.

It was a fine clear day in June when Hezekiah Lewis, captain and part-owner of the schooner *Thames*, bound from London to Aberdeen, anchored off the little out-of-the-way town of Orford in Suffolk. Among other antiquities, the town possessed Hezekiah's widowed mother, and when there was no very great hurry – the world went slower in those days – the dutiful son used to go ashore in the ship's boat, and after a filial tap at his mother's window, which often startled the old woman considerably, pass on his way to see a young lady to whom he had already proposed five times without effect.

The mate and crew of the schooner, seven all told, drew up in a little knot as the skipper, in his shore-going clothes, appeared on deck, and regarded him with an air of grinning, mysterious interest.

'Now you all know what you have got to do?' queried the skipper.

'Ay, ay,' replied the crew, grinning still more deeply.

Hezekiah regarded them closely, and then, ordering the boat to be lowered, scrambled over the side and was pulled swiftly towards the shore.

A sharp scream, and a breathless 'Lawk-a-mussy me!' as he tapped at his mother's window, assured him that the old lady was alive and well, and he continued on his way until he brought up at a small but pretty house in the next road.

'Morning, Mr Rumbolt,' said he heartily to a stout, red-faced man, who sat smoking in the doorway.

'Morning, cap'n, morning,' said the red-faced man.

'Is the rheumatism any better?' enquired Hezekiah anxiously, as he grasped the other's huge hand.

'So, so,' said the other. 'But it ain't the rheumatism so much what troubles me,' he resumed, lowering his voice, and looking round cautiously. 'It's Kate.'

'What?' said the skipper.

'You've heard of a man being henpecked?' continued Mr Rumbolt, in tones of husky confidence.

The captain nodded.

'I'm *chick-pecked*,' murmured the other.

'What?' enquired the astonished mariner again.

'Chick-pecked,' repeated Mr Rumbolt firmly. '*Chick-pecked*. D'ye understand me?'

The captain said that he did, and stood silent awhile, with the air of a man who wants to say something, but is half afraid to. At last, with a desperate appearance of resolution, he bent down to the old man's ear.

'That's the deaf 'un,' said Mr Rumbolt promptly.

Hezekiah changed ears, speaking at first slowly and awkwardly, but becoming more fluent as he warmed with his subject, while the expression of his listener's face gradually changed from incredulous bewilderment to one of uncontrollable mirth. He became so uproarious that he was fain to push the captain away from him, and lean back in his chair and choke and laugh until he nearly lost his breath, at which crisis a remarkably pretty girl appeared from the back of the house, and patted him with hearty goodwill.

'That'll do, my dear,' said the choking Mr Rumbolt. 'Here's Captain Lewis.'

'I can see him,' said his daughter calmly. 'What's he standing on one leg for?'

The skipper, who really was standing in a somewhat constrained attitude, coloured violently, and planted both feet firmly on the ground.

'Being as I was passing close in, Miss Rumbolt,' said he, 'and coming ashore to see mother – '

To the captain's discomfort, manifestations of a further attack on the part of Mr Rumbolt appeared, but were promptly quelled by the daughter.

'Mother?' she repeated encouragingly,

'I thought I'd come on and ask you just to pay a sort o' flying visit to the *Thames*.'

'Thank you, I'm comfortable enough where I am,' said the girl.

'I've got a couple of monkeys and a bear aboard, which I'm taking to a menagerie in Aberdeen,' continued the captain, 'and the thought struck me you might possibly like to see 'em.'

'Well, I don't know,' said the damsel in a flutter. 'Is it a big bear?'

'Have you ever seen an elephant?' enquired Hezekiah cautiously.

'Only in pictures,' replied the girl.

'Well, it's as big as that, nearly,' said he.

The temptation was irresistible, and Miss Rumbolt, telling her father that she should not be long, disappeared into the house in search of her hat and jacket, and ten minutes later the brawny rowers were gazing their fill into her deep blue eyes as she sat in the stern of the boat and told Lewis to behave himself.

It was but a short pull out to the schooner, and Miss Rumbolt was soon on the deck, lavishing endearments on the monkey, and energetically prodding the bear with a handspike to make him growl. The noise of the offended animal as he strove to get through the bars of his cage was terrific, and the girl was in the full enjoyment of it, when she became aware of a louder noise still, and turning round, saw the seamen at the windlass.

'Why, what are they doing?' she demanded, 'getting up anchor?'

'Ahoy, there!' shouted Hezekiah sternly. 'What are you doing with that windlass?'

As he spoke, the anchor peeped over the edge of the bows, and one of the seamen running past them took the helm.

'Now then,' shouted the fellow, 'stand by. Look lively there with them sails.'

Obeying a light touch of the helm, the schooner's bowsprit slowly swung round from the land, and the crew, hauling lustily on the ropes, began to hoist the sails.

'What the devil are you up to?' thundered the skipper. 'Have you all gone mad? What does it all mean?'

'It means,' said one of the seamen, whose fat, amiable face was marred by a fearful scowl, 'that we've got a new skipper.'

'Good heavens, a mutiny!' exclaimed the skipper, starting melodramatically against the cage, and drawing hastily away again. 'Where's the mate?'

'He's with us,' said another seaman, brandishing his sheath knife, and scowling fearfully. 'He's our new captain.'

In confirmation of this the mate now appeared from below with an axe in his hand, and approaching his captain, roughly ordered him below.

'I'll defend this lady with my life,' cried Hezekiah, taking the handspike from Kate, and raising it above his head.

'Nobody'll hurt a hair of her beautiful head,' said the mate, with a tender smile.

'Then I yield,' said the skipper, drawing himself up, and delivering the handspike with the air of a defeated admiral tendering his sword.

'Good,' said the mate briefly, as one of the men took it.

'What!' demanded Miss Rumbolt excitedly, 'aren't you going to fight them? Here, give me the handspike.'

Before the mate could interfere, the sailor, with thoughtless obedience, handed it over, and Miss Rumbolt at once tried to knock him over the head. Being thwarted in this design by the man taking flight, she lost her temper entirely, and bore down like a hurricane on the remaining members of the crew who were just approaching.

They scattered at once, and ran up the rigging like cats, and for a few moments the girl held the deck; then the mate crept up behind her, and with the air of a man whose job exactly suited him, clasped her tightly round the waist, while one of the seamen disarmed her.

'You must both go below till we've settled what to do with you,' said the mate, reluctantly releasing her.

With a wistful glance at the handspike, the girl walked to the cabin, followed slowly by the skipper.

'This is a bad business,' said the latter, shaking his head solemnly, as the indignant Miss Rumbolt seated herself.

'Don't talk to me, you coward!' said the girl energetically.

The skipper started.

'*I* made three of 'em run,' said Miss Rumbolt, 'and you did nothing. You just stood still, and let them take the ship. I'm ashamed of you.'

The skipper's defence was interrupted by a hoarse voice shouting to them to come on deck, where they found the mutinous crew gathered aft round the mate. The girl cast a look at the shore, which was now dim and indistinct, and turned somewhat pale as the serious nature of her position forced itself upon her.

'Lewis,' said the mate.

'Well,' growled the skipper.

'This ship's going in the lace and brandy trade, and if so be as you're sensible you can go with it as mate, d'ye hear?'

'An' s'pose I do; what about the lady?' enquired the captain.

'You and the lady'll have to get spliced,' said the mate sternly. 'Then there'll be no tales told. A Scotch marriage is as good as any, and we'll just lay off and put you ashore, and you can get tied up as right as ninepence.'

'Marry a coward like that?' demanded Miss Rumbolt, with spirit; 'not if I know it. Why, I'd sooner marry that old man at the helm.'

'Old Bill's got three wives a'ready to my sartin knowledge,' spoke up one of the sailors. 'The lady's got to marry Cap'n Lewis, so don't let's have no fuss about it.'

'I won't,' said the lady, stamping violently.

The mutineers appeared to be in a dilemma, and, following the example of the mate, scratched their heads thoughtfully.

'We thought you liked him,' said the mate, at last, feebly.

'You had no business to think,' said Miss Rumbolt. 'You are bad men, and you'll all be hung, every one of you; I shall come and see it.'

'The cap'n's welcome to her for me,' murmured the helmsman in a husky whisper to the man next to him. 'The vixen!'

'Very good,' said the mate. 'If you won't, you won't. This end of the ship'll belong to you after eight o'clock of a night. Lewis, you must go for'ard with the men.'

'And what are you going to do with me after?' enquired the fair prisoner.

The seven men shrugged their shoulders helplessly, and Hezekiah, looking depressed, lit his pipe, and went and leaned over the side.

The day passed quietly. The orders were given by the mate, and Hezekiah lounged moodily about, a prisoner at large. At eight o'clock Miss Rumbolt was given the key of the state-room, and the men who were not in the watch went below.

The morning broke fine and clear with a light breeze, which, towards midday, dropped entirely, and the schooner lay rocking lazily on a sea of glassy smoothness. The sun beat fiercely down, bringing the fresh paint on the taffrail up in blisters, and sorely trying the tempers of the men who were doing odd jobs on deck.

The cabin, where the two victims of a mutinous crew had retired for coolness, got more and more stuffy, until at length even the scorching deck seemed preferable, and the girl, with a faint hope of finding a shady corner, went languidly up the companion-ladder.

For some time the skipper sat alone, pondering gloomily over the state of affairs as he smoked his short pipe. He was aroused at length from his apathy by the sound of the companion being noisily closed, while loud frightened cries and hurrying footsteps on deck announced that something extra-ordinary was happening. As he rose to his feet he was confronted by Kate Rumbolt, who, panting and excited, waved a big key before him.

'I've done it,' she cried, her eyes sparkling.

'Done what?' shouted the mystified skipper.

'Let the bear loose,' said the girl. 'Ha, ha! you should have seen them run. You should have seen the fat sailor!'

'Let the – phew – let the – Good heavens! here's a pretty kettle of fish!' he choked.

'Listen to them shouting,' cried the exultant Kate, clapping her hands. 'Just listen.'

'Those shouts are from aloft,' said Hezekiah sternly, 'where you and I ought to be.'

'I've closed the companion,' said the girl reassuringly.

'Closed the companion!' repeated Hezekiah, as he drew his knife. 'He can smash it like cardboard, if the fit takes him. Go in here.'

He opened the door of his state-room.

'Shan't!' said Miss Rumbolt politely.

'Go in at once!' cried the skipper. 'Quick with you.'

'Sha –' began Miss Rumbolt again. Then she caught his eye, and went in like a lamb. 'You come too,' she said prettily.

'I've got to look after my ship and my men,' said the skipper. 'I suppose you thought the ship would steer itself, didn't you?'

'Mutineers deserve to be eaten,' whimpered Miss Rumbolt piously, some-what taken aback by the skipper's demeanour.

Hezekiah looked at her.

'They're not mutineers, Kate,' he said quietly. 'It was just a piece of mad folly of mine. They're as honest a set of old sea dogs as ever breathed, and I only hope they are all safe up aloft. I'm going to lock you in; but don't be frightened, it shan't hurt you.'

He slammed the door on her protests, and locked it, and, slipping the key of the cage in his pocket, took a firm grip of his knife, and, running up the steps, gained the deck. Then his breath came more freely, for the mate, who was standing a little way up the fore rigging, after tempting the bear with his foot, had succeeded in dropping a noose over its head. The brute made a furious attempt to extricate itself, but the men hurried down with other lines, and in a short space of time the bear presented much the same appearance as the lion in Aesop's *Fables*, and was dragged and pushed, a heated and indignant mass of fur, back to its cage.

Having locked up one prisoner the skipper went below and released the other, who passed quickly from a somewhat hysterical condition to one of such haughty disdain that the captain was thoroughly cowed, and stood humbly aside to let her pass.

The fat seaman was standing in front of the cage as she reached it, and regarding the bear with much satisfaction until Kate sidled up to him, and begged him, as a personal favour, to go in the cage and undo it.

'Undo it! Why he'd kill me!' gasped the fat seaman, aghast at such simplicity.

'I don't think he would,' said his tormenter, with a bewitching smile; 'and I'll wear a lock of your hair all my life if you do. But you'd better give it to me before you go in.'

'I ain't going in,' said the fat sailor shortly.

'Not for me?' queried Kate archly,

'Not for fifty like you,' replied the old man firmly. 'He nearly had me when he was loose. I can't think how he got out.'

'Why, I let him out,' said Miss Rumbolt airily. 'Just for a little run. How would you like to be shut up all day?'

The sailor was just going to tell her with more fluency than politeness when he was interrupted. 'That'll do,' said the skipper, who had come behind them. 'Go for'ard, you. There's been enough of this fooling; the lady thought you had taken the ship. Thompson, I'll take the helm; there's a little wind coming. Stand by there.'

He walked aft and relieved the steersman, awkwardly conscious that the men were becoming more and more interested in the situation, and also that Kate could hear some of their remarks. As he pondered over the subject, and tried to think of a way out of it, the cause of all the trouble came and stood by him.

'Did my father know of this?' she enquired.

'I don't know that he did exactly,' said the skipper uneasily. 'I just told him not to expect you back that night.'

'And what did he say?' said she.

'Said he wouldn't sit up,' said the skipper, grinning, despite himself.

Kate drew a breath the length of which boded no good to her parent, and looked over the side.

'I was afraid of that traveller chap from Ipswich,' said Hezekiah, after a pause. 'Your father told me he was hanging round you again, so I thought I – well, I was a blamed fool anyway.'

'See how ridiculous you have made me look before all these men,' said the girl angrily.

'They've been with me for years,' said Hezekiah apologetically, 'and the mate said it was a magnificent idea. He quite raved about it, he did. I wouldn't have done it with some crews, but we've had some dirty times together, and they've stood by me well. But of course that's nothing to do with you. It's been an adventure I'm very sorry for, very.'

'A pretty safe adventure for *you*,' said the girl scornfully. '*you* didn't risk much. Look here, I like brave men. If you go in the cage and undo that bear, I'll marry you. That's what *I* call an adventure.'

'Smith,' called the skipper quietly, 'come and take the helm a bit.'

The seaman obeyed, and Lewis, accompanied by the girl, walked forward.

At the bear's cage he stopped, and, fumbling in his pocket for the key, steadily regarded the brute as it lay gnashing its teeth, and trying in vain to bite the ropes which bound it.

'You're afraid,' said the girl tauntingly; 'you're quite white.'

The captain made no reply, but eyed her so steadily that her gaze fell. He drew the key from his pocket and inserted it in the huge lock, and was just turning it, when a soft arm was drawn through his, and a soft voice murmured sweetly in his ear, 'Never mind about the old bear.'

And he did not mind.

Three at Table

The talk in the coffee-room had been of ghosts and apparitions, and nearly everybody present had contributed his mite to the stock of information upon a hazy and somewhat threadbare subject. Opinions ranged from rank incredulity to childlike faith, one believer going so far as to denounce unbelief as impious, with a reference to the Witch of Endor, which was somewhat marred by being complicated in an inexplicable fashion with the story of Jonah.

'Talking of Jonah,' he said solemnly, with a happy disregard of the fact that he had declined to answer several eager questions put to him on the subject, 'look at the strange tales sailors tell us.'

'I wouldn't advise you to believe all those,' said a bluff, clean-shaven man, who had been listening without speaking much. 'You see when a sailor gets ashore he's expected to have something to tell, and his friends would be rather disappointed if he had not.'

'It's a well-known fact,' interrupted the first speaker firmly, 'that sailors are very prone to see visions.'

'They are,' said the other dryly, 'they generally see them in pairs, and the shock to the nervous system frequently causes headache next morning.'

'You never saw anything yourself?' suggested an unbeliever.

'Man and boy,' said the other, 'I've been at sea thirty years, and the only unpleasant incident of that kind occurred in the quiet English countryside.'

'And that?' said another man.

'I was a young man at the time,' said the narrator, drawing at his pipe and glancing good-humouredly at the company. 'I had just come back from China, and my own people being away I went down into the country to invite myself to stay with an uncle. When I got down to the place I found it closed and the family in the South of France; but as they were due back in a couple of days I decided to put up at the Royal George, a very decent inn, and await their return.

'The first day I passed well enough; but in the evening the dullness of the rambling old place, in which I was the only visitor, began to weigh upon my spirits, and the next morning after a late breakfast I set out with the intention of having a brisk day's walk.

'I started off in excellent spirits, for the day was bright and frosty, with a powdering of snow on the iron-bound roads and nipped hedges, and the country had to me all the charm of novelty. It was certainly flat, but with plenty of timber, and the villages through which I passed were old and picturesque.

'I lunched luxuriously on bread and cheese and beer in the bar of a small inn, and resolved to go a little farther before turning back. When at length I found I had gone far enough, I turned up a lane at right angles to the road I was passing, and resolved to find my way back by another route. It is a long lane that has no turning, but this had several, each of which had turnings of its own, which generally led, as I found by trying two or three of them, into the open marshes. Then, tired of lanes, I resolved to rely upon the small compass which hung from my watch-chain and go home across country.

'I had got well into the marshes when a white fog, which had been for some time hovering round the edge of the ditches, began gradually to spread. There was no escaping it, but by aid of my compass I was saved from making a circular tour and fell instead into frozen ditches or stumbled over roots in the grass. I kept my course, however, until at four o'clock, when night was coming rapidly up to lend a hand to the fog, I was fain to confess myself lost.

'The compass was now no good to me, and I wandered about miserably, occasionally giving a shout on the chance of being heard by some passing shepherd or farmhand. At length by great good luck I found my feet on a rough road driven through the marshes, and by walking slowly and tapping with my stick managed to keep to it. I had followed it for some distance when I heard footsteps approaching me.

'We stopped as we met, and the new arrival, a sturdy-looking countryman, hearing of my plight, walked back with me for nearly a mile, and putting me on to a road gave me minute instructions how to reach a village some three miles distant.

'I was so tired that three miles sounded like ten, and besides that, a little way off from the road I saw dimly a lighted window. I pointed it out, but my companion shuddered and looked round him uneasily.

' "You won't get no good there," he said, hastily.

' "Why not?" I asked.

' "There's a something there, sir," he replied, "what 'tis I dunno, but the little 'un belonging to a gamekeeper as used to live in these parts see it, and it was never much good afterwards. Some say as it's a poor mad thing, others says as it's a kind of animal; but whatever it is, it ain't good to see."

' "Well, I'll keep on, then," I said. "Good-night."

'He went back whistling cheerily until his footsteps died away in the distance, and I followed the road he had indicated until it divided into three, any one of which to a stranger might be said to lead straight on. I was now cold and tired, and having half made up my mind walked slowly back towards the house.

'At first all I could see of it was the little patch of light at the window. I made for that until it disappeared suddenly, and I found myself walking into a tall hedge. I felt my way round this until I came to a small gate, and opening it cautiously, walked, not without some little nervousness, up a long path which led to the door. There was no light and no sound from within. Half repenting of my temerity I shortened my stick and knocked lightly upon the door.

'I waited a couple of minutes and then knocked again, and my stick was still beating the door when it opened suddenly and a tall bony old woman, holding a candle, confronted me.

' "What do you want?" she demanded gruffly.

' "I've lost my way," I said, civilly; "I want to get to Ashville."

' "Don't know it," said the old woman.

'She was about to close the door when a man emerged from a room at the side of the hall and came towards us. An old man of great height and breadth of shoulder.

' "Ashville is fifteen miles distant," he said slowly.

' "If you will direct me to the nearest village, I shall be grateful," I remarked.

'He made no reply, but exchanged a quick, furtive glance with the woman. She made a gesture of dissent.

' "The nearest place is three miles off," he said, turning to me and apparently trying to soften a naturally harsh voice; "if you will give me the pleasure of your company, I will make you as comfortable as I can."

'I hesitated. They were certainly a queer-looking couple, and the gloomy hall with the shadows thrown by the candle looked hardly more inviting than the darkness outside.

' "You are very kind," I murmured, irresolutely, "but – "

' "Come in," he said quickly; "shut the door, Anne."

'Almost before I knew it I was standing inside and the old woman, muttering to herself, had closed the door behind me. With a queer sensation of being trapped I followed my host into the room, and taking the proffered chair warmed my frozen fingers at the fire.

' "Dinner will soon be ready," said the old man, regarding me closely. "If you will excuse me."

'I bowed and he left the room. A minute afterward I heard voices: his and the old woman's, and, I fancied, a third. Before I had finished my inspection of the room he returned, and regarded me with the same strange look I had noticed before.

' "There will be three of us at dinner," he said, at length. "We two and my son."

'I bowed again, and secretly hoped that that look didn't run in the family.

' "I suppose you don't mind dining in the dark," he said, abruptly.

' "Not at all," I replied, hiding my surprise as well as I could, "but really I'm afraid I'm intruding. If you'll allow me – "

'He waved his huge gaunt hands. "We're not going to lose you now we've got you," he said, with a dry laugh. "It's seldom we have company, and now we've got you we'll keep you. My son's eyes are bad, and he can't stand the light. Ah, here is Anne."

'As he spoke the old woman entered, and, eyeing me stealthily, began to lay the cloth, while my host, taking a chair the other side of the hearth, sat looking silently into the fire. The table set, the old woman brought in a pair of fowls ready carved in a dish, and placing three chairs, left the room. The old man hesitated a moment, and then, rising from his chair, placed a large screen in front of the fire and slowly extinguished the candles.

' "Blind man's holiday," he said, with clumsy jocosity, and groping his way to the door opened it. Somebody came back into the room with him, and in a slow, uncertain fashion took a seat at the table, and the strangest voice I have ever heard broke a silence which was fast becoming oppressive.

' "A cold night," it said slowly.

'I replied in the affirmative, and light or no light, fell to with an appetite which had only been sharpened by the snack in the middle of the day. It was somewhat difficult eating in the dark, and it was evident from the behaviour of my invisible companions that they were as unused to dining under such circumstances as I was. We ate in silence until the old woman blundered into the room with some sweets and put them with a crash upon the table.

' "Are you a stranger about here?" enquired the curious voice again.

'I replied in the affirmative, and murmured something about my luck in stumbling upon such a good dinner.

' "Stumbling is a very good word for it," said the voice grimly. "You have forgotten the port, father."

' "So I have," said the old man, rising. "It's a bottle of the 'Celebrated' today; I will get it myself."

'He felt his way to the door, and closing it behind him, left me alone with my unseen neighbour. There was something so strange about the whole business that I must confess to more than a slight feeling of uneasiness.

'My host seemed to be absent a long time. I heard the man opposite lay down his fork and spoon, and half fancied I could see a pair of wild eyes shining through the gloom like a cat's.

'With a growing sense of uneasiness I pushed my chair back. It caught the hearthrug, and in my efforts to disentangle it the screen fell over with a crash and in the flickering light of the fire I saw the face of the creature opposite. With a sharp catch of my breath I left my chair and stood with clenched fists beside it. Man or beast, which was it? The flame leaped up and then went out, and in the mere red glow of the fire it looked more devilish than before.

'For a few moments we regarded each other in silence; then the door opened and the old man returned. He stood aghast as he saw the warm firelight, and then approaching the table mechanically put down a couple of bottles.

' "I beg your pardon," said I, reassured by his presence, "but I have accidentally overturned the screen. Allow me to replace it."

' "No," said the old man, gently, "let it be. We have had enough of the dark. I'll give you a light."

'He struck a match and slowly lit the candles. Then – I saw that the man opposite had but the remnant of a face, a gaunt wolfish face in which one unquenched eye, the sole remaining feature, still glittered. I was greatly moved, some suspicion of the truth occurring to me.

' "My son was injured some years ago in a burning house," said the old man. "Since then we have lived a very retired life. When you came to the door we – " his voice trembled, "that is – my son – "

' "I thought," said the son simply, "that it would be better for me not to come to the dinner-table. But it happens to be my birthday, and my father would not hear of my dining alone, so we hit upon this foolish plan of dining in the dark. I'm sorry I startled you."

' "I am sorry," said I, as I reached across the table and gripped his hand, "that I am such a fool; but it was only in the dark that you startled me."

'From a faint tinge in the old man's cheek and a certain pleasant softening of the poor solitary eye in front of me I secretly congratulated myself upon this last remark.

' "We never see a friend," said the old man, apologetically, "and the temptation to have company was too much for us. Besides, I don't know what else you could have done."

' "Nothing else half so good, I'm sure," said I.

' "Come," said my host, with almost a sprightly air. "Now we know each other, draw our chairs to the fire and let's keep this birthday in a proper fashion."

'He drew a small table to the fire for the glasses and produced a box of cigars, and placing a chair for the old servant, sternly bade her to sit down and drink. If the talk was not sparkling, it did not lack for vivacity, and we were soon as merry a party as I have ever seen. The night wore on so rapidly that we could hardly believe our ears when in a lull in the conversation a clock in the hall struck twelve.

' "A last toast before we retire," said my host, pitching the end of his cigar into the fire and turning to the small table.

'We had drunk several before this, but there was something impressive in the old man's manner as he rose and took up his glass. His tall figure seemed to get taller, and his voice rang as he gazed proudly at his disfigured son.

' "The health of the children my boy saved!" he said, and drained his glass at a draught.'

After the Inquest

It was a still fair evening in late summer in the parish of Wapping. The hands had long since left, and the night watchman having abandoned his trust in favour of a neighbouring bar, the wharf was deserted.

An elderly seaman came to the gate and paused irresolute, then, seeing all was quiet, stole cautiously on to the jetty, and stood for some time gazing curiously down on to the deck of the billy-boy *Psyche* lying alongside.

With the exception of the mate, who, since the lamented disappearance of its late master and owner, was acting as captain, the deck was as deserted as the wharf. He was smoking an evening pipe in all the pride of a first command, his eye roving fondly from the blunt bows and untidy deck of his craft to her clumsy stern, when a slight cough from the man above attracted his attention.

'How do, George?' said the man on the jetty, somewhat sheepishly, as the other looked up.

The mate opened his mouth, and his pipe fell from it and smashed to pieces unnoticed.

'Got much stuff in her this trip?' continued the man, with an obvious attempt to appear at ease.

The mate, still looking up, backed slowly to the other side of the deck, but made no reply.

'What's the matter, man?' said the other testily. 'You don't seem over-pleased to see me.'

He leaned over as he spoke, and laying hold of the rigging, descended to the deck, while the mate took his breath in short, exhilarating gasps.

'Here I am, George,' said the intruder, 'turned up like a bad penny, an' glad to see your handsome face again, I can tell you.'

In response to this flattering remark George gurgled.

'Why,' said the other, with an uneasy laugh, 'did you think I was dead, George? Ha, ha! Feel that!'

He fetched the horrified man a thump in the back, which stopped even his gurgles.

'That feel like a dead man?' asked the smiter, raising his hand again. 'Feel' –

The mate moved back hastily. 'That'll do,' said he fiercely; 'ghost or no ghost, don't you hit me like that again.'

'A' right, George,' said the other, as he meditatively felt the stiff grey whiskers which framed his red face. 'What's the news?'

'The news,' said George, who was of slow habits and speech, 'is that you was found last Tuesday week off St Katherine's Stairs, you was sat on Friday week at the Town o' Ramsgate public-house, and buried on Monday afternoon at Lowestoft.'

'Buried?' gasped the other, 'sat on? You've been drinking, George.'

'An' a pretty penny your funeral cost, I can tell you,' continued the mate. 'There's a headstone being made now – "Lived lamented and died respected",' I think it is, with "Not lost, but gone before", at the bottom.'

'Lived respected and died lamented, you mean,' growled the old man; 'well, a nice muddle you have made of it between you. Things always go wrong when I'm not here to look after them.'

'You ain't dead, then?' said the mate, taking no notice of this unreasonable remark. 'Where've you been all this long time?'

'No more than you're master o' this 'ere ship,' replied Mr Harbolt grimly. 'I – I've been a bit queer in the stomach, an' I took a little drink to correct it. Foolish like, I took the wrong drink, and it must have got into my head.'

'That's the worst of not being used to it,' said the mate, without moving a muscle.

The skipper eyed him solemnly, but the mate stood firm.

'Arter that,' continued the skipper, still watching him suspiciously, 'I remember no more distinctly until this morning, when I found myself sitting on a step down Poplar way and shiverin', with the morning newspaper and a crowd round me.'

'Morning newspaper!' repeated the mystified mate. 'What was that for?'

'Decency. I was wrapped up in it,' replied the skipper. 'Where I came from or how I got there I don't know more than Adam. I s'pose I must have been ill; I seem to remember taking something out of a bottle pretty often. Some old gentleman in the crowd took me into a shop and bought me these clothes, an' here I am. My own clo'es and thirty pounds o' freight money I had in my pocket is all gone.'

'Well, I'm hearty glad to see you back,' said the mate. 'It's quite a homecoming for you, too. Your missis is down aft.'

'My missis? What the devil's she aboard for?' growled the skipper, successfully controlling his natural gratification at the news.

'She's been with us these last two trips,' replied the mate. 'She's had business to settle in London, and she's been going through your lockers to clear up, like.'

'My lockers!' groaned the skipper. 'Good heavens! there's things in them lockers I wouldn't have her see for the world; women are so fussy an' so fond o' making something out o' nothing. There's a pore female, touched a bit in the upper storey, what's been writing love letters to me, George.'

'Three pore females,' said the precise mate; 'the missis has got all the letters tied up with blue ribbon. Very far gone they was, too, poor creeters.'

'George,' said the skipper in a broken voice, 'I'm a ruined man. I'll never hear the end o' this. I guess I'll go an' sleep for'ard this voyage, and lie low. Be keerful you don't let on I'm aboard, an' after she's home I'll take the ship again, and let the thing leak out gradual. Come to life bit by bit, so to speak. It wouldn't do to scare her, George, an' in the meantime I'll try an' think o' some explanation to tell her. You might be thinking too.'

'I'll do what I can,' said the mate.

'Crack me up to the old girl all you can; tell her I used to write to all sorts o' people when I got a drop of drink in me; say how thoughtful I always was of her. You might tell her about that gold locket I bought for her an' got robbed of.'

'Gold locket?' said the mate in tones of great surprise. 'What gold locket? Fust I've heard of it.'

'Any gold locket,' said the skipper irritably; 'anything you can think of; you needn't be pertikler. Arter that you can drop little hints about people being buried in mistake for others, so as to prepare her a bit – I don't want to scare her.'

'Leave it to me,' said the mate.

'I'll go an' turn in now, I'm dead tired,' said the skipper. 'I s'pose Joe and the boy's asleep?'

George nodded, and meditatively watched the other as he pushed back the fore-scuttle and drew it after him as he descended. Then a thought struck the mate, and he ran hastily forward and threw his weight on the scuttle just in time to frustrate the efforts of Joe and the boy, who were coming on deck to tell him a new ghost story. The confusion below was frightful, the skipper's cry of, 'It's only me, Joe,' not possessing the soothing effect which he intended. They calmed down at length, after their visitor had convinced them that he really was flesh and blood and fists, and the boy's attention being directed to a small rug in the corner of the fo'c'sle, the skipper took his bunk and was soon fast asleep.

He slept so soundly that the noise of the vessel getting under way failed to rouse him, and she was well out in the open river when he awoke, and after cautiously protruding his head through the scuttle, ventured on deck. For some time he stood eagerly sniffing the cool, sweet air, and then, after a look round, gingerly approached the mate, who was at the helm.

'Give me a hold on her,' said he.

'You had better get below again, if you don't want the missis to see you,' said the mate. 'She's gettin' up – nasty temper she's in too.'

The skipper went forward grumbling. 'Send down a good breakfast, George,' said he.

To his great discomfort the mate suddenly gave a low whistle, and regarded him with a look of blank dismay. 'Good gracious!' he cried, 'I forgot all about it. Here's a pretty kettle of fish – well, well.'

'Forgot about what?' asked the skipper uneasily.

'The crew take their meals in the cabin now,' replied the mate, ' 'cos the missis says it's more cheerful for 'em, and she's l'arning 'em to eat their wittles properly.'

The skipper looked at him aghast. 'You'll have to smuggle me up some grub,' he said at length. 'I'm not going to starve for nobody.'

'Easier said than done,' said the mate. 'The missis has got eyes like needles; still, I'll do the best I can for you. Look out! Here she comes.'

The skipper fled hastily, and, safe down below, explained to the crew how they were to secrete portions of their breakfast for his benefit. The amount of explanation required for so simple a matter was remarkable, the crew manifesting a denseness which irritated him almost beyond endurance. They promised, however, to do the best they could for him, and returned in triumph after a hearty meal, and presented their enraged commander with a few greasy crumbs and the tail of a bloater.

For the next two days the wind was against them, and they made but little progress. Mrs Harbolt spent most of her time on deck, thereby confining her husband to his evil-smelling quarters below. Matters were not improved for him by the crew, who, resenting his rough treatment of them, were doing their best to starve him into civility. Most of the time he kept in his bunk – or rather Jemmy's bunk – a prey to despondency and hunger of an acute type, venturing on deck only at night to prowl uneasily about and bemoan his condition.

On the third night Mrs Harbolt was later in retiring than usual, and it was nearly midnight before the skipper, who had been indignantly waiting for her to go, was able to get on deck and hold counsel with the mate.

'I've done what I could for you,' said the latter, fishing a crust from his pocket, which Harbolt took thankfully. 'I've told her all the yarns I could think of about people turning up after they was buried and the like.'

'What'd she say?' queried the skipper eagerly, between his bites.

'Told me not to talk like that,' said the mate; 'said it showed a want o' trust in providence to hint at such things. Then I told her what you asked me about the locket, only I made it a bracelet worth ten pounds.'

'That pleased her?' suggested the other hopefully.

The mate shook his head. 'She said I was a born fool to believe you'd been robbed of it,' he replied. 'She said what you'd done was to give it to one o' them pore females. She's been going on frightful about it all the afternoon – won't talk o' nothing else.'

'I don't know what's to be done,' groaned the skipper despondently. 'I shall be dead afore we get to port if this wind holds. Go down and get me something to eat George; I'm starving.'

'Everything's locked up, as I told you afore,' said the mate.

'As the master of this ship,' said the skipper, drawing himself up, 'I order you to go down and get me something to eat. You can tell the missus it's for you if she says anything.'

'I'm hanged if I will,' said the mate sturdily. 'Why don't you go down and have it out with her like a man? She can't eat you.'

'I'm not going to,' said the other shortly. 'I'm a determined man, and when I say a thing I mean it. It's going to be broken to her gradual, as I said; I don't want her to be scared, poor thing.'

'I know who'd be scared the most,' murmured the mate.

The skipper looked at him fiercely, and then sat down wearily on the hatches with his hands between his knees, rising, after a time, to get the dipper and drink copiously from the water-cask. Then, replacing it with a sigh, he bade the mate a surly good-night and went below.

To his dismay he found when he awoke in the morning that what little wind there was had dropped in the night, and the billy-boy was just rising and falling lazily on the water in a fashion most objectionable to an empty stomach. It was the last straw, and he made things so uncomfortable below that the crew were glad to escape on deck, where they squatted down in the bows, and proceeded to review a situation which was rapidly becoming unbearable.

'I've 'ad enough of it, Joe,' grumbled the boy. 'I'm sore all over with sleeping on the floor, and the old man's temper gets wuss and wuss. I'm going to be ill.'

'Whaffor?' queried Joe dully.

'You tell the missus I'm down below ill. Say you think I'm dying,' responded the infant Machiavelli; 'then you'll see somethink if you keep your eyes open.'

He went below again, not without a little nervousness, and, clambering into Joe's bunk, rolled over on his back and gave a deep groan.

'What's the matter with *you*!' growled the skipper, who was lying in the other bunk staving off the pangs of hunger with a pipe.

'I'm very ill – dying,' said Jemmy, with another groan.

'You'd better stay in bed and have your breakfast brought down here, then,' said the skipper kindly.

'I don't want no breakfast,' said Jem faintly.

'That's no reason why you shouldn't have it sent down, you unfeeling little brute,' said the skipper indignantly. 'You tell Joe to bring you down a great plate o' cold meat and pickles, and some coffee; that's what you want.'

'All right, sir,' said Jemmy. 'I hope they won't let the missus come down here, in case it's something catching. I wouldn't like her to be took bad.'

'Eh?' said the skipper, in alarm. 'Certainly not. Here, you go up and die on deck. Hurry up with you.'

'I can't; I'm too weak,' said Jemmy.

'You get up on deck at once; d'ye hear me?' hissed the skipper, in alarm.

'I c–c–c–can't help it,' sobbed Jemmy, who was enjoying the situation amazingly. 'I b'lieve it's sleeping on the hard floor's snapped something inside me.'

'If you don't go, I'll take you,' said the skipper, and he was about to rise to put his threat into execution when a shadow fell across the opening, and a voice, which thrilled him to the core, said softly, 'Jemmy!'

'Yes 'm?' said Jemmy languidly, as the skipper flattened himself in his bunk and drew the clothes over him.

'How do you feel?' enquired Mrs Harbolt.

'Bad all over,' said Jemmy. 'Oh, don't come down, mum – please don't.'

'Rubbish!' said Mrs Harbolt tartly, as she came slowly and carefully down backwards. 'What a dark hole this is, Jemmy. No wonder you're ill. Put your tongue out.'

Jemmy complied.

'I can't see properly here,' murmured the lady, 'but it looks very large. S'pose you go in the other bunk, Jemmy. It's a good bit higher than this, and you'd get more air and be more comfortable altogether.'

'Joe wouldn't like it, mum,' said the boy anxiously. The last glimpse he had had of the skipper's face did not make him yearn to share his bed with him.

'Stuff an' nonsense!' said Mrs Harbolt hotly. 'Who's Joe, I'd like to know? Out you come.'

'I can't move, mum,' said Jemmy firmly.

'Nonsense!' said the lady. 'I'll just put it straight for you first, then in it you go.'

'No, don't, mum,' shouted Jemmy, now thoroughly alarmed at the success of his plot. 'There, there's a gentleman in that bunk. A gentleman we brought from London for a change of sea air.'

'My goodness gracious!' ejaculated the surprised Mrs Harbolt. 'I never did. Why, what's he had to eat?'

'He – he – didn't want nothing to eat,' said Jemmy, with a woeful disregard for facts.

'What's the matter with him?' enquired Mrs Harbolt, eyeing the bunk curiously. 'What's his name? Who is he?'

'He's been lost a long time,' said Jemmy, 'and he's forgotten who he is – he's a oldish man with a red face an' a little white whisker all round it – a very nice-looking man, I mean,' he interposed hurriedly. 'I don't think he's quite right in his head, 'cos he says he ought to have been buried instead of someone else. Oh!'

The last word was almost a scream, for Mrs Harbolt, staggering back, pinched him convulsively.

'Jemmy!' she gasped, in a trembling voice, as she suddenly remembered certain mysterious hints thrown out by the mate. 'Who is it?'

'The *captain!*' said Jemmy, and, breaking from her clasp, slipped from his bed and darted hastily on deck, just as the pallid face of his commander broke through the blankets and beamed anxiously on his wife.

* * *

Five minutes later, as the crew gathered aft were curiously eyeing the fo'c'sle, Mrs Harbolt and the skipper came on deck. To the great astonishment of the mate, the eyes of the redoubtable woman were slightly wet, and, regardless of the presence of the men, she clung fondly to her husband as they walked slowly to the cabin. Ere they went below, however, she called the grinning Jemmy to her, and, to his private grief and public shame, tucked his head under her arm and kissed him fondly.

In the Library

The fire had burnt low in the library, for the night was wet and warm. It was now little more than a grey shell, and looked desolate. Trayton Burleigh, still hot, rose from his armchair, and turning out one of the gas-jets, took a cigar from a box on a side-table and resumed his seat again.

The apartment, which was on the third floor at the back of the house, was a combination of library, study and smoke-room, and was the daily despair of the old housekeeper who, with the assistance of one servant, managed the house. It was a bachelor establishment, and had been left to Trayton Burleigh and James Fletcher by a distant connection of both men some ten years before.

Trayton Burleigh sat back in his chair watching the smoke of his cigar through half-closed eyes. Occasionally he opened them a little wider and glanced round the comfortable, well-furnished room, or stared with a cold gleam of hatred at Fletcher as he sat sucking stolidly at his brier pipe. It was a comfortable room and a valuable house, half of which belonged to Trayton Burleigh; and yet he was to leave it in the morning and become a rogue and a wanderer over the face of the earth. James Fletcher had said so. James Fletcher, with the pipe still between his teeth and speaking from one corner of his mouth only, had pronounced his sentence.

'It hasn't occurred to you, I suppose,' said Burleigh, speaking suddenly, 'that I might refuse your terms.'

'No,' said Fletcher, simply.

Burleigh took a great mouthful of smoke and let it roll slowly out.

'I am to go out and leave you in possession?' he continued. 'You will stay here sole proprietor of the house; you will stay at the office sole owner and representative of the firm? You are a good hand at a deal, James Fletcher.'

'I am an honest man,' said Fletcher, 'and to raise sufficient money to make your defalcations good will not by any means leave me the gainer, as you very well know.'

'There is no necessity to borrow,' began Burleigh, eagerly. 'We can pay the interest easily, and in course of time make the principal good without a soul being the wiser.'

'That you suggested before,' said Fletcher, 'and my answer is the same. I will be no man's confederate in dishonesty; I will raise every penny at all costs, and save the name of the firm – and yours with it – but I will never have you darken the office again, or sit in this house after tonight.'

'You won't,' cried Burleigh, starting up in a frenzy of rage.

'I won't,' said Fletcher. 'You can choose the alternative: disgrace and penal servitude. Don't stand over me; you won't frighten me, I can assure you. Sit down.'

'You have arranged so many things in your kindness,' said Burleigh, slowly, resuming his seat again, 'have you arranged how I am to live?'

'You have two strong hands, and health,' replied Fletcher. 'I will give you the two hundred pounds I mentioned, and after that you must look out for yourself. You can take it now.'

He took a leather case from his breast pocket, and drew out a roll of notes. Burleigh, watching him calmly, stretched out his hand and took them from the table. Then he gave way to a sudden access of rage, and crumpling them in his hand, threw them into a corner of the room. Fletcher smoked on.

'Mrs Marl is out?' said Burleigh, suddenly.

Fletcher nodded. 'She will be away the night,' he said, slowly; 'and Jane too; they have gone together somewhere, but they will be back at half-past eight in the morning.'

'You are going to let me have one more breakfast in the old place, then,' said Burleigh. 'Half-past eight, half-past – '

He rose from his chair again. This time Fletcher took his pipe from his mouth and watched him closely. Burleigh stooped, and picking up the notes, placed them in his pocket.

'If I am to be turned adrift, it shall not be to leave you here,' he said, in a thick voice.

He crossed over and shut the door; as he turned back Fletcher rose from his chair and stood confronting him. Burleigh put his hand to the wall, and drawing a small Japanese sword from its sheath of carved ivory, stepped slowly towards him.

'I give you one chance, Fletcher,' he said, grimly. 'You are a man of your word. Hush this up and let things be as they were before, and you are safe.'

'Put that down,' said Fletcher, sharply.

'I warn you, I mean what I say!' cried the other.

'I mean what I said!' answered Fletcher.

He looked round at the last moment for a weapon, then he turned back at a sharp sudden pain, and saw Burleigh's clenched fist nearly touching his breast-bone. The hand came away from his breast again, and something with it. It went a long way off. Trayton Burleigh suddenly went to a great distance and the room darkened. It got quite dark, and Fletcher, with an attempt to raise his hands, let them fall to his sides instead, and fell in a heap to the floor.

He was so still that Burleigh could hardly realise that it was all over, and stood stupidly waiting for him to rise again. Then he took out his hand-kerchief as though to wipe the sword, but thinking better of it, put it back into his pocket again, and threw the weapon on to the floor.

The body of Fletcher lay where it had fallen, the white face turned up to the gas. In life he had been a commonplace-looking man, not to say vulgar; now Burleigh, with a feeling of nausea, drew back towards the door, until the body was hidden by the table, and relieved from the sight, he could think more clearly. He looked down carefully and examined his clothes and his boots. Then he crossed the room again, and with his face averted, turned out the gas. Something seemed to stir in the darkness, and with a faint cry he blundered towards the door before he had realised that it was the clock. It struck twelve.

He stood at the head of the stairs trying to recover himself; trying to think. The gas on the landing below, the stairs and the furniture, all looked so prosaic and familiar that he could not realise what had occurred. He walked slowly down and turned the light out. The darkness of the upper part of the house was now almost appalling, and in a sudden panic he ran downstairs into the lighted hall, and snatching a hat from the stand, went to the door and walked down to the gate.

Except for one window the neighbouring houses were in darkness, and the lamps shone on a silent street. There was a little rain in the air, and the muddy road was full of pebbles. He stood at the gate trying to screw up his courage to enter the house again. Then he noticed a figure coming slowly up the road and keeping close to the palings.

The full realisation of what he had done broke in upon him when he found himself turning to fly from the approach of the constable. The wet cape glistening in the lamplight, the slow, heavy step, made him tremble. Suppose the thing upstairs was not quite dead and should cry out? Suppose the constable should think it strange for him to be standing there and follow him in? He assumed a careless attitude, which did not feel careless, and as the man passed bade him good-night, and made a remark as to the weather.

Ere the sound of the other's footsteps had gone quite out of hearing, he turned and entered the house again before the sense of companionship should have quite departed. The first flight of stairs was lighted by the gas in the hall, and he went up slowly. Then he struck a match and went up steadily, past the library door, and with firm fingers turned on the gas in his bedroom and lit it. He opened the window a little way, and sitting down on his bed, tried to think.

He had got eight hours. Eight hours and two hundred pounds in small notes. He opened his safe and took out all the loose cash it contained, and walking about the room, gathered up and placed in his pockets such articles of jewellery as he possessed.

The first horror had now to some extent passed, and was succeeded by the fear of death.

With this fear on him he sat down again and tried to think out the first moves in that game of skill of which his life was the stake. He had often read of people of hasty temper, evading the police for a time, and eventually falling into their hands for lack of the most elementary common sense. He had heard it said that they always made some stupid blunder, left behind them some damning clue. He took his revolver from a drawer and saw that it was loaded. If the worst came to the worst, he would die quickly.

Eight hours' start; two hundred odd pounds. He would take lodgings at first in some populous district, and let the hair on his face grow. When the hue-and-cry had ceased, he would go abroad and start life again. He would go out of a night and post letters to himself, or better still, postcards, which his landlady would read. Postcards from cheery friends, from a sister, from a brother. During the day he would stay in and write, as became a man who described himself as a journalist.

Or suppose he went to the sea? Who would look for him in flannels, bathing and boating with ordinary happy mortals? He sat and pondered. One might mean life, and the other death. Which?

His face burned as he thought of the responsibility of the choice. So many people went to the sea at that time of year that he would surely pass unnoticed. But at the sea one might meet acquaintances. He got up and nervously paced the room again. It was not so simple, now that it meant so much, as he had thought.

The sharp little clock on the mantelpiece rang out 'one', followed immediately by the deeper note of that in the library. He thought of the clock, it seemed the only live thing in that room, and shuddered. He wondered whether the thing lying by the far side of the table heard it. He wondered –

He started and held his breath with fear. Somewhere downstairs a board creaked loudly, then another. He went to the door, and opening it a little way, but without looking out, listened. The house was so still that he could hear the ticking of the old clock in the kitchen below. He opened the door a little wider and peeped out. As he did so there was a sudden sharp outcry on the stairs, and he drew back into the room and stood trembling before he had quite realised that the noise had been made by the cat. The cry was unmistakable; but what had disturbed it?

There was silence again, and he drew near the door once more. He became certain that something was moving stealthily on the stairs. He heard the boards creak again, and once the rails of the balustrade rattled. The silence and suspense were frightful. Suppose that the something which had been Fletcher waited for him in the darkness outside?

He fought his fears down, and opening the door, determined to see what was beyond. The light from his room streamed out on to the landing, and he peered about fearfully. Was it fancy, or did the door of Fletcher's room opposite close as he looked? Was it fancy, or did the handle of the door really turn?

In perfect silence, and watching the door as he moved, to see that nothing came out and followed him, he proceeded slowly down the dark stairs. Then his jaw fell, and he turned sick and faint again. The library door, which he distinctly remembered closing, and which, moreover, he had seen was closed when he went upstairs to his room, now stood open some four or five inches. He fancied that there was a rustling inside, but his brain refused to be certain. Then plainly and unmistakably he heard a chair pushed against the wall.

He crept to the door, hoping to pass it before the thing inside became aware of his presence. Something crept stealthily about the room. With a sudden impulse he caught the handle of the door and, closing it violently, turned the key in the lock, then he ran madly down the stairs.

A fearful cry sounded from the room, and a heavy hand beat upon the panels of the door. The house rang with the blows, but above them sounded the loud hoarse cries of human fear. Burleigh, halfway down to the hall, stopped with his hand on the balustrade and listened. The beating ceased, and a man's voice cried out loudly for God's sake to let him out.

At once Burleigh saw what had happened and what it might mean for him. He had left the hall door open after his visit to the front, and some wandering bird of the night had entered the house. No need for him to go now. No need to hide either from the hangman's rope or the felon's cell. The fool above had saved him. He turned and ran upstairs again just as the prisoner in his furious efforts to escape wrenched the handle from the door.

'Who's there?' he cried, loudly.

'Let me out!' cried a frantic voice. 'For God's sake, open the door! There's something here.'

'Stay where you are!' shouted Burleigh, sternly. 'Stay where you are! If you come out, I'll shoot you like a dog!'

The only response was a smashing blow on the lock of the door. Burleigh raised his pistol, and aiming at the height of a man's chest, fired through the panel.

The report and the crashing of the wood made one noise, succeeded by an unearthly stillness, then the noise of a window hastily opened. Burleigh fled down the stairs, and flinging wide the hall door, shouted loudly for assistance.

It happened that a sergeant and the constable on the beat had just met in the road. They came towards the house at a run. Burleigh, with incoherent explanations, ran upstairs before them, and halted outside the library door. The prisoner was still inside, still trying to demolish the lock of the sturdy oaken door. Burleigh tried to turn the key, but the lock was too damaged to admit of its moving. The sergeant drew back and, shoulder foremost, hurled himself at the door and burst it open.

He stumbled into the room, followed by the constable, and two shafts of light from the lanterns at their belts danced round the room. A man lurking behind the door made a dash for it, and the next instant the three men were locked together.

Burleigh, standing in the doorway, looked on coldly, reserving himself for the scene which was to follow. Except for the stumbling of the men and the sharp catch of the prisoner's breath, there was no noise. A helmet fell off and bounced and rolled along the floor. The men fell; there was a sobbing snarl and a sharp click. A tall figure rose from the floor; the other, on his knees, still held the man down. The standing figure felt in his pocket, and, striking a match, lit the gas.

The light fell on the flushed face and fair beard of the sergeant. He was bare-headed and his hair dishevelled. Burleigh entered the room and gazed eagerly at the half-insensible man on the floor – a short, thick-set fellow with a white, dirty face and a black moustache. His lip was cut and bled down his neck. Burleigh glanced furtively at the table. The cloth had come off in the struggle and was now in the place where he had left Fletcher.

'Hot work, sir,' said the sergeant, with a smile. 'It's fortunate we were handy.'

The prisoner raised a heavy head and looked up with unmistakable terror in his eyes. 'All right, sir,' he said, trembling, as the constable increased the pressure of his knee. 'I 'ain't been in the house ten minutes altogether. I swear, I've not.'

The sergeant regarded him curiously.

'It don't signify,' he said, slowly; 'ten minutes or ten seconds won't make any difference.'

The man shook and began to whimper.

'It was 'ere when I come,' he said, eagerly; 'take that down, sir. I've only just come, and it was 'ere when I come. I tried to get away then, but I was locked in.'

'What was?' demanded the sergeant.

'That,' he said, desperately.

The sergeant, following the direction of the terror-stricken black eyes, stooped by the table. Then, with a sharp exclamation, he dragged away the cloth. Burleigh, with a sharp cry of horror, reeled back against the wall.

'All right, sir,' said the sergeant, catching him; 'all right. Turn your head away.'

He pushed him into a chair, and crossing the room, poured out a glass of whiskey and brought it to him. The glass rattled against his teeth, but he drank it greedily, and then groaned faintly. The sergeant waited patiently. There was no hurry.

'Who is it, sir?' he asked at length.

'My friend – Fletcher,' said Burleigh, with an effort. 'We lived together.' He turned to the prisoner.

'You damned villain!'

'He was dead when I come in the room, gentlemen,' said the prisoner, strenuously. 'He was on the floor dead, and when I see 'im, I tried to get out. S' 'elp me he was. You heard me call out, sir. I shouldn't ha' called out if I'd killed him.'

'All right,' said the sergeant, gruffly; 'you'd better hold your tongue, you know.'

'You keep quiet,' urged the constable.

The sergeant knelt down and raised the dead man's head.

'I 'ad nothing to do with it,' repeated the man on the floor. 'I 'ad nothing to do with it. I never thought of such a thing. I've only been in the place ten minutes; put that down, sir.'

The sergeant groped with his left hand, and picking up the Japanese sword, held it at him.

'I've never seen it before,' said the prisoner, struggling.

'It used to hang on the wall,' said Burleigh. 'He must have snatched it down. It was on the wall when I left Fletcher a little while ago.'

'How long?' enquired the sergeant.

'Perhaps an hour, perhaps half an hour,' was the reply. 'I went to my bedroom.'

The man on the floor twisted his head and regarded him narrowly.

'You done it!' he cried, fiercely. 'You done it, and you want me to swing for it.'

'That'll do,' said the indignant constable.

The sergeant let his burden gently to the floor again.

'You hold your tongue, you devil!' he said, menacingly.

He crossed to the table and poured a little spirit into a glass and took it in his hand. Then he put it down again and crossed to Burleigh.

'Feeling better, sir?' he asked.

The other nodded faintly.

'You won't want this thing any more,' said the sergeant.

He pointed to the pistol which the other still held, and taking it from him gently, put it into his pocket.

'You've hurt your wrist, sir,' he said, anxiously.

Burleigh raised one hand sharply, and then the other.

'This one, I think,' said the sergeant. 'I saw it just now.'

He took the other's wrists in his hand, and suddenly holding them in the grip of a vice, whipped out something from his pocket – something hard and cold, which snapped suddenly on Burleigh's wrists, and held them fast.

'That's right,' said the sergeant; 'keep quiet.'

The constable turned round in amaze; Burleigh sprang towards him furiously.

'Take these things off!' he choked. 'Have you gone mad? Take them off!'

'All in good time,' said the sergeant.

'Take them off!' cried Burleigh again.

For answer the sergeant took him in a powerful grip, and staring steadily at his white face and gleaming eyes, forced him to the other end of the room and pushed him into a chair.

'Collins,' he said, sharply.

'Sir?' said the astonished subordinate.

'Run to the doctor at the corner hard as you can run!' said the other. 'This man is not dead!'

As the man left the room the sergeant took up the glass of spirits he had poured out, and kneeling down by Fletcher again, raised his head and tried to pour a little down his throat. Burleigh, sitting in his corner, watched like one in a trance. He saw the constable return with the breathless surgeon, saw the three men bending over Fletcher, and then saw the eyes of the dying man open and the lips of the dying man move. He was conscious that the sergeant made some notes in a pocket-book, and that all three men eyed him closely. The sergeant stepped towards him and placed his hand on his shoulder, and obedient to the touch, he arose and went with him out into the night.

A Case of Desertion

The sun was just rising as the small tub-like steamer, or, to be more correct, steam-barge, the *Bulldog*, steamed past the sleeping town of Gravesend at a good six knots per hour.

There had been a little discussion on the way between her crew and the engineer, who, down in his grimy little engine-room, did his own stoking and everything else necessary. The crew, consisting of captain, mate and boy, who were doing their first trip on a steamer, had been transferred at the last moment from their sailing-barge the *Witch*, and found to their discomfort that the engineer, who had not expected to sail so soon, was terribly and abusively drunk. Every moment he could spare from his engines he thrust the upper part of his body through the small hatchway, and rowed with his commander.

'Ahoy, bargee!' he shouted, popping up like a jack-in-the-box, after a brief cessation of hostilities.

'Don't take no notice of 'im,' said the mate. ' 'E's got a bottle of brandy down there, an' he's 'alf mad.'

'If I knew anything o' them blessed engines,' growled the skipper, 'I'd go and hit 'im over the head.'

'But you don't,' said the mate, 'and neither do I, so you'd better keep quiet.'

'You think you're a fine feller,' continued the engineer, 'standing up there an' playing with that little wheel. You think you're doing all the work. What's the boy doing? Send him down to stoke.'

'Go down,' said the skipper, grinning with fury, and the boy reluctantly obeyed.

'You think,' said the engineer pathetically, after he had cuffed the boy's head and dropped him down below by the scruff of his neck, 'you think because I've got a black face I'm not a man. There's many a hoily face 'ides a good 'art.'

'I don't think nothing about it,' grunted the skipper; 'you do your work, and I'll do mine.'

'Don't you give me none of your back answers,' bellowed the engineer, ' 'cos I won't have 'em.'

The skipper shrugged his shoulders and exchanged glances with his sympathetic mate. 'Wait till I get 'im ashore,' he murmured.

'The biler is wore out,' said the engineer, reappearing after a hasty dive below. 'It may bust at any moment.'

As though to confirm his words fearful sounds were heard proceeding from below.

'It's only the boy,' said the mate, 'he's scared – natural.'

'I thought it was the biler,' said the skipper, with a sigh of relief. 'It was loud enough.'

As he spoke the boy got his head out of the hatchway, and, rendered desperate with fear, fairly fought his way past the engineer and gained the deck.

'Very good,' said the engineer, as he followed him on deck and staggered to the side. 'I've had enough o' you lot.'

'Hadn't you better go down to them engines?' shouted the skipper.

'Am I your *slave*?' demanded the engineer tearfully. 'Tell me that. Am I your slave?'

'Go down and do your work like a sensible man,' was the reply.

At these words the engineer took umbrage at once, and, scowling fiercely, removed his greasy jacket and flung his cap on the deck. He then finished the brandy which he had brought up with him, and gazed owlishly at the Kentish shore. 'I'm going to have a wash,' he said loudly, and, sitting down, removed his boots.

'Go down to the engines first,' said the skipper, 'and I'll send the boy to you with a bucket and some soap.'

'Bucket!' replied the engineer scornfully, as he moved to the side. 'I'm going to have a proper wash.'

'Hold him!' roared the skipper suddenly. 'Hold him!'

The mate, realising the situation, rushed to seize him, but the engineer, with a mad laugh, put his hands on the side and vaulted into the water. When he rose the steamer was twenty yards ahead.

'Go astern!' yelled the mate.

'How can I go astern when there's nobody at the engines?' shouted the skipper, as he hung on to the wheel and brought the boat's head sharply round. 'Git a line ready.'

The mate, with a coil of rope in his hand, rushed to the side, but his benevolent efforts were frustrated by the engineer, who, seeing the boat's head making straight for him, saved his life by an opportune dive. The steamer rushed by.

'Turn 'er agin!' screamed the mate.

The captain was already doing so, and in a remarkably short space of time the boat, which had described a complete circle, was making again for the engineer.

'Look out for the line!' shouted the mate warningly.

'I don't want your line,' yelled the engineer. 'I'm going ashore.'

'Come aboard!' shouted the captain imploringly, as they swept past again. 'We can't manage the engines.'

'Put her round again,' said the mate. 'I'll go for him with the boat. Haul her in, boy.'

The boat, which was dragging astern, was hauled close, and the mate tumbled into her, followed by the boy, just as the captain was in the middle of another circle – to the intense indignation of a crowd of shipping, large and small, which was trying to get by.

'Ahoy!' yelled the master of a tug which was towing a large ship. 'Take that steam roundabout out of the way. What the thunder are you doing?'

'Picking up my engineer,' replied the captain, as he steamed right across the other's bows, and nearly ran down a sailing-barge, the skipper of which, a Salvation Army man, was nobly fighting with his feelings.

'Why don't you stop?' he yelled.

' 'Cos I can't,' wailed the skipper of the *Bulldog*, as he threaded his way between a huge steamer and a schooner, who, in avoiding him, were getting up a little collision on their own account.

'Ahoy, *Bulldog*! Ahoy!' called the mate. 'Stand by to pick us up. We've got him.'

The skipper smiled in an agonised fashion as he shot past, hotly pursued by his boat. The feeling on board the other craft as they got out of the way of the *Bulldog*, and nearly ran down her boat, and then, in avoiding that, nearly ran down something else, cannot be put into plain English, but several captains ventured into the domains of the ornamental with marked success.

'Shut off steam!' yelled the engineer, as the *Bulldog* went by again. 'Draw the fires, then.'

'Who's going to steer while I do it?' bellowed the skipper, as he left the wheel for a few seconds to try and get a line to throw them.

By this time the commotion in the river was frightful, and the captain's steering, as he went on his round again, something marvellous to behold. A strange lack of sympathy on the part of brother captains added to his troubles. Every craft he passed had something to say to him, busy as they were, and the remarks were as monotonous as they were insulting. At last, just as he was resolving to run his boat straight down the river until he came to a halt for want of steam, the mate caught the rope he flung, and the *Bulldog* went down the river with her boat made fast to her stern.

'Come aboard, you – you lunatic!' he shouted.

'Not afore I knows 'ow I stand,' said the engineer, who was now beautifully sober, and in full possession of a somewhat acute intellect.

'What do you mean?' demanded the skipper.

'I don't come aboard,' shouted the engineer, 'until you and the mate and the bye all swear as you won't say nothing about this little game.'

'I'll report you the moment I get ashore,' roared the skipper. 'I'll give you in charge for desertion. I'll – '

With a supreme gesture the engineer prepared to dive, but the watchful mate fell on his neck and tripped him over a seat.

'Come aboard!' cried the skipper, aghast at such determination. 'Come aboard, and I'll give you a licking when we get ashore instead.'

'Honour bright?' enquired the engineer.

'Honour bright,' chorused the three.

The engineer, with all the honours of war, came on board, and, after remarking that he felt chilly bathing on an empty stomach, went down below and began to stoke. In the course of the voyage he said that it was worth while making such a fool of himself if only to see the skipper's beautiful steering, warmly asseverating that there was not another man on the river that could have done it. Before this insidious flattery the skipper's wrath melted like snow before the sun, and by the time they reached port he would as soon have thought of hitting his own father as his smooth-tongued engineer.

Cupboard Love

In the comfortable living-room at Negget's farm, half-parlour and half-kitchen, three people sat at tea in the waning light of a November afternoon. Conversation, which had been brisk, had languished somewhat, owing to Mrs Negget glancing at frequent intervals toward the door, behind which she was convinced the servant was listening, and checking the finest periods and the most startling suggestions with a warning *ssh!*

'Go on, uncle,' she said, after one of these interruptions.

'I forget where I was,' said Mr Martin Bodfish, shortly.

'Under our bed,' Mr Negget reminded him.

'Yes, watching,' said Mrs Negget, eagerly.

It was an odd place for an ex-policeman, especially as a small legacy added to his pension had considerably improved his social position, but Mr Bodfish had himself suggested it in the professional hope that the person who had taken Mrs Negget's gold brooch might try for further loot. He had, indeed, suggested baiting the dressing-table with the farmer's watch, an idea which Mr Negget had promptly vetoed.

'I can't help thinking that Mrs Pottle knows something about it,' said Mrs Negget, with an indignant glance at her husband.

'Mrs Pottle,' said the farmer, rising slowly and taking a seat on the oak settle built in the fireplace, 'has been away from the village for near a fortnit.'

'I didn't say she took it,' snapped his wife. 'I said I believe she knows something about it, and so I do. She's a horrid woman. Look at the way she encouraged her girl Looey to run after that young traveller from Smithson's. The whole fact of the matter is, it isn't your brooch, so you don't care.'

'I said – ' began Mr Negget.

'I know what you said,' retorted his wife, sharply, 'and I wish you'd be quiet and not interrupt uncle. Here's my uncle been in the police twenty-five years, and you won't let him put a word in edgeways.'

'My way o' looking at it,' said the ex-policeman, slowly, 'is different to that o' the law; my idea is, an' always has been, that everybody is guilty until they've proved their innocence.'

'It's a wonderful thing to me,' said Mr Negget in a low voice to his pipe, 'as they should come to a house with a retired policeman living in it. Looks to me like somebody that ain't got much respect for the police.'

The ex-policeman got up from the table, and taking a seat on the settle opposite the speaker, slowly filled a long clay and took a spill from the fireplace. His pipe lit, he turned to his niece, and slowly bade her go over the account of her loss once more.

'I missed it this morning,' said Mrs Negget, rapidly, 'at ten minutes past twelve o'clock by the clock, and half-past five by my watch which wants looking to. I'd just put the batch of bread into the oven, and gone upstairs and opened the box that stands on my drawers to get a lozenge, and I missed the brooch.'

'Do you keep it in that box?' asked the ex-policeman, slowly.

'Always,' replied his niece. 'I at once came downstairs and told Emma that the brooch had been stolen. I said that I named no names, and didn't wish to think bad of anybody, and that if I found the brooch back in the box when I went up stairs again, I should forgive whoever took it.'

'And what did Emma say?' enquired Mr Bodfish.

'Emma said a lot o' things,' replied Mrs Negget, angrily. 'I'm sure by the lot she had to say you'd ha' thought she was the missis and me the servant. I gave her a month's notice at once, and she went straight upstairs and sat on her box and cried.'

'Sat on her box?' repeated the ex-constable, impressively. 'Oh!'

'That's what I thought,' said his niece, 'but it wasn't, because I got her off at last and searched it through and through. I never saw anything like her clothes in all my life. There was hardly a button or a tape on; and as for her stockings – '

'She don't get much time,' said Mr Negget, slowly.

'That's right; I thought you'd speak up for her,' cried his wife, shrilly.

'Look here – ' began Mr Negget, laying his pipe on the seat by his side and rising slowly.

'Keep to the case in hand,' said the ex-constable, waving him back to his seat again. 'Now, Lizzie.'

'I searched her box through and through,' said his niece, 'but it wasn't there; then I came down again and had a rare good cry all to myself.'

'That's the best way for you to have it,' remarked Mr Negget, feelingly.

Mrs Negget's uncle instinctively motioned his niece to silence, and holding his chin in his hand, scowled frightfully in the intensity of thought.

'See a cloo?' enquired Mr Negget, affably.

'You ought to be ashamed of yourself, George,' said his wife, angrily; 'speaking to uncle when he's looking like that.'

Mr Bodfish said nothing; it is doubtful whether he even heard these remarks; but he drew a huge notebook from his pocket, and after vainly trying to point his pencil by suction, took a knife from the table and hastily sharpened it.

'Was the brooch there last night?' he enquired.

'It were,' said Mr Negget, promptly. 'Lizzie made me get up just as the owd clock were striking twelve to get her a lozenge.'

'It seems pretty certain that the brooch went since then,' mused Mr Bodfish.

'It would seem like it to a plain man,' said Mr Negget, guardedly.

'I should like to see the box,' said Mr Bodfish.

Mrs Negget went up and fetched it and stood eyeing him eagerly as he raised the lid and inspected the contents. It contained only a few lozenges and some bone studs. Mr Negget helped himself to a lozenge, and going back to his seat, breathed peppermint.

'Properly speaking, that ought not to have been touched,' said the ex-constable, regarding him with some severity.

'Eh!' said the startled farmer, putting his finger to his lips.

'Never mind,' said the other, shaking his head. 'It's too late now.'

'He doesn't care a bit,' said Mrs Negget, somewhat sadly. 'He used to keep buttons in that box with the lozenges until one night he gave me one by mistake. Yes, you may laugh – I'm glad you *can* laugh.'

Mr Negget, feeling that his mirth was certainly ill-timed, shook for some time in a noble effort to control himself, and despairing at length, went into the back place to recover. Sounds of blows indicative of Emma slapping him on the back did not add to Mrs Negget's serenity.

'The point is,' said the ex-constable, 'could anybody have come into your room while you was asleep and taken it?'

'No,' said Mrs Negget, decisively. 'I'm a very poor sleeper, and I'd have woke at once, but if a flock of elephants was to come in the room they wouldn't wake George. He'd sleep through anything.'

'Except her feeling under my piller for her handkerchief,' corroborated Mr Negget, returning to the sitting-room.

Mr Bodfish waved them to silence, and again gave way to deep thought. Three times he took up his pencil, and laying it down again, sat and drummed on the table with his fingers. Then he arose, and with bent head walked slowly round and round the room until he stumbled over a stool.

'Nobody came to the house this morning, I suppose?' he said at length, resuming his seat.

'Only Mrs Driver,' said his niece.

'What time did she come?' enquired Mr Bodfish.

'Here! look here!' interposed Mr Negget. 'I've known Mrs Driver thirty year a'most.'

'What time did she come?' repeated the ex-constable, pitilessly.

His niece shook her head. 'It might have been eleven, and again it might have been earlier,' she replied. 'I was out when she came.'

'Out!' almost shouted the other.

Mrs Negget nodded. 'She was sitting in here when I came back.'

Her uncle looked up and glanced at the door behind which a small staircase led to the room above.

'What was to prevent Mrs Driver going up there while you were away?' he demanded.

'I shouldn't like to think that of Mrs Driver,' said his niece, shaking her head; 'but then in these days one never knows what might happen. Never. I've given up thinking about it. However, when I came back, Mrs Driver was here, sitting in that very chair you are sitting in now.'

Mr Bodfish pursed up his lips and made another note. Then he took a spill from the fireplace, and lighting a candle, went slowly and carefully up the stairs. He found nothing on them but two caked rims of mud, and being too busy to notice Mr Negget's frantic signalling, called his niece's attention to them.

'What do you think of that?' he demanded, triumphantly.

'Somebody's been up there,' said his niece. 'It isn't Emma, because she hasn't been outside the house all day; and it can't be George, because he promised me faithful he'd never go up there in his dirty boots.'

Mr Negget coughed, and approaching the stairs, gazed with the eye of a stranger at the relics as Mr Bodfish hotly rebuked a suggestion of his niece's to sweep them up.

'Seems to me,' said the conscience-stricken Mr Negget, feebly, 'as they're rather large for a woman.'

'Mud cakes,' said Mr Bodfish, with his most professional manner; 'a small boot would pick up a lot this weather.'

'So it would,' said Mr Negget, and with brazen effrontery not only met his wife's eye without quailing, but actually glanced down at her boots.

Mr Bodfish came back to his chair and ruminated. Then he looked up and spoke.

'It was missed this morning at ten minutes past twelve,' he said, slowly; 'it was there last night. At eleven o'clock you came in and found Mrs Driver sitting in that chair.'

'No, the one you're in,' interrupted his niece.

'It don't signify,' said her uncle. 'Nobody else has been near the place, and Emma's box has been searched.

'Thoroughly searched,' testified Mrs Negget.

'Now the point is, what did Mrs Driver come for this morning?' resumed the ex-constable. 'Did she come – '

He broke off and eyed with dignified surprise a fine piece of wireless telegraphy between husband and wife. It appeared that Mr Negget sent off a humorous message with his left eye, the right being for some reason closed, to which Mrs Negget replied with a series of frowns and staccato shakes of the head, which her husband found easily translatable. Under the austere stare of Mr Bodfish their faces at once regained their wonted calm, and the ex-constable in a somewhat offended manner resumed his enquiries.

'Mrs Driver has been here a good bit lately,' he remarked, slowly.

Mr Negget's eyes watered, and his mouth worked piteously.

'If you can't behave yourself, George – ' began his wife, fiercely.

'What is the matter?' demanded Mr Bodfish. 'I'm not aware that I've said anything to be laughed at.'

'No more you have, uncle,' retorted his niece; 'only George is such a stupid. He's got an idea in his silly head that Mrs Driver – But it's all nonsense, of course.'

'I've merely got a bit of an idea that it's a wedding-ring, not a brooch, Mrs Driver is after,' said the farmer to the perplexed constable.

Mr Bodfish looked from one to the other. 'But you always keep yours on, Lizzie, don't you?' he asked.

'Yes, of course,' replied his niece, hurriedly; 'but George has always got such strange ideas. Don't take no notice of him.'

Her uncle sat back in his chair, his face still wrinkled perplexedly; then the wrinkles vanished suddenly, chased away by a huge glow, and he rose wrathfully and towered over the matchmaking Mr Negget. 'How dare you?' he gasped.

Mr Negget made no reply, but in a cowardly fashion jerked his thumb towards his wife.

'Oh! George! How can you say so?' said the latter.

'I should never ha' thought of it by myself,' said the farmer; 'but I think they'd make a very nice couple, and I'm sure Mrs Driver thinks so.'

The ex-constable sat down in wrathful confusion, and taking up his notebook again, watched over the top of it the silent charges and counter-charges of his niece and her husband.

'If I put my finger on the culprit,' he asked at length, turning to his niece, 'what do you wish done to her?'

Mrs Negget regarded him with an expression which contained all the Christian virtues rolled into one.

'Nothing,' she said, softly. 'I only want my brooch back.'

The ex-constable shook his head at this leniency.

'Well, do as you please,' he said, slowly. 'In the first place, I want you to ask Mrs Driver here to tea tomorrow – oh, I don't mind Negget's ridiculous ideas – pity he hasn't got something better to think of; if she's guilty, I'll soon find it out. I'll play with her like a cat with a mouse. I'll make her convict herself.'

'Look here!' said Mr Negget, with sudden vigour. 'I won't have it. I won't have no woman asked here to tea to be got at like that. There's only my friends comes here to tea, and if any friend stole anything o' mine, I'd be one o' the first to hush it up.'

'If they were all like you, George,' said his wife, angrily, 'where would the law be?'

'Or the police?' demanded Mr Bodfish, staring at him.

'I won't have it!' repeated the farmer, loudly. 'I'm the law here, and I'm the police here. That little tiny bit o' dirt was off my boots, I dare say. I don't care if it was.'

'Very good,' said Mr Bodfish, turning to his indignant niece; 'if he likes to look at it that way, there's nothing more to be said. I only wanted to get your brooch back for you, that's all; but if he's against it – '

'I'm against your asking Mrs Driver here to my house to be got at,' said the farmer.

'O' course if you can find out who took the brooch, and get it back again anyway, that's another matter.'

Mr Bodfish leaned over the table towards his niece.

'If I get an opportunity, I'll search her cottage,' he said, in a low voice. 'Strictly speaking, it ain't quite a legal thing to do, o' course, but many o' the finest pieces of detective work have been done by breaking the law. If she's a kleptomaniac, it's very likely lying about somewhere in the house.'

He eyed Mr Negget closely, as though half expecting another outburst, but none being forthcoming, sat back in his chair again and smoked in silence, while Mrs Negget, with a carpet-brush which almost spoke, swept the pieces of dried mud from the stairs.

Mr Negget was the last to go to bed that night, and finishing his pipe over the dying fire, sat for some time in deep thought. He had from the first raised objections to the presence of Mr Bodfish at the farm, but family affection, coupled with an idea of testamentary benefits, had so wrought with his wife that he had allowed her to have her own way. Now he half fancied that he saw a chance of getting rid of him. If he could only enable the widow to catch him searching her house, it was highly probable that the ex-constable would find the village somewhat too hot to hold him. He gave his right leg a congratulatory slap as he thought of it, and knocking the ashes from his pipe, went slowly up to bed.

He was so amiable next morning that Mr Bodfish, who was trying to explain to Mrs Negget the difference between theft and kleptomania, spoke before him freely. The ex-constable defined kleptomania as a sort of amiable weakness found chiefly among the upper circles, and cited the case of a lady of title whose love of diamonds, combined with great hospitality, was a source of much embarrassment to her guests.

For the whole of that day Mr Bodfish hung about in the neighbourhood of the widow's cottage, but in vain, and it would be hard to say whether he or Mr Negget, who had been discreetly shadowing him, felt the disappointment most. On the day following, however, the ex-constable from a distant hedge saw a friend of the widow's enter the cottage, and a little later both ladies emerged and walked up the road.

He watched them turn the corner, and then, with a cautious glance round, which failed, however, to discover Mr Negget, the ex-constable strolled casually in the direction of the cottage, and approaching it from the rear, turned the handle of the door and slipped in.

He searched the parlour hastily, and then, after a glance from the window, ventured upstairs. And he was in the thick of his self-imposed task when his graceless nephew by marriage, who had met Mrs Driver and referred pathetically to a raging thirst which he had hoped to have quenched with some of her home-brewed, brought the ladies back again.

'I'll go round the back way,' said the wily Negget as they approached the cottage. 'I just want to have a look at that pig of yours.'

He reached the back door at the same time as Mr Bodfish, and placing his legs apart, held it firmly against the frantic efforts of the ex-constable. The struggle ceased suddenly, and the door opened easily just as Mrs Driver and her friend appeared in the front room, and the farmer, with a keen glance at the door of the larder which had just closed, took a chair while his hostess drew a glass of beer from the barrel in the kitchen.

Mr Negget drank gratefully and praised the brew. From beer the conversation turned naturally to the police, and from the police to the listening Mr Bodfish, who was economising space by sitting on the bread-pan, and trembling with agitation.

'He's a lonely man,' said Negget, shaking his head and glancing from the corner of his eye at the door of the larder. In his wildest dreams he had not imagined so choice a position, and he resolved to give full play to an idea which suddenly occurred to him.

'I dare say,' said Mrs Driver, carelessly, conscious that her friend was watching her.

'And the heart of a little child,' said Negget; 'you wouldn't believe how simple he is.'

Mrs Clowes said that it did him credit, but, speaking for herself, she hadn't noticed it.

'He was talking about you night before last,' said Negget, turning to his hostess; 'not that that's anything fresh. He always is talking about you nowadays.'

The widow coughed confusedly and told him not to be foolish.

'Ask my wife,' said the farmer, impressively; 'they were talking about you for hours. He's a very shy man is my wife's uncle, but you should see his face change when your name's mentioned.'

As a matter of fact, Mr Bodfish's face was at that very moment taking on a deeper shade of crimson.

'Everything you do seems to interest him,' continued the farmer, disregarding Mrs Driver's manifest distress; 'he was asking Lizzie about your calling on Monday; how long you stayed, and where you sat; and after she'd told him, I'm blest if he didn't go and sit in the same chair!'

This romantic setting to a perfectly casual action on the part of Mr

Bodfish affected the widow visibly, but its effect on the ex-constable nearly upset the bread-pan.

'But here,' continued Mr Negget, with another glance at the larder, 'he might go on like that for years. He's a wunnerful shy man – big, and gentle, and shy. He wanted Lizzie to ask you to tea yesterday.'

'Now, Mr Negget,' said the blushing widow. 'Do be quiet.'

'Fact,' replied the farmer; 'solemn fact, I assure you. And he asked her whether you were fond of jewellery.'

'I met him twice in the road near here yesterday,' said Mrs Clowes, suddenly. 'Perhaps he was waiting for you to come out.'

'I dare say,' replied the farmer. 'I shouldn't wonder but what he's hanging about somewhere near now, unable to tear himself away.'

Mr Bodfish wrung his hands, and his thoughts reverted instinctively to instances in his memory in which charges of murder had been altered by the direction of a sensible judge to manslaughter. He held his breath for the next words.

Mr Negget drank a little more ale and looked at Mrs Driver.

'I wonder whether you've got a morsel of bread and cheese?' he said, slowly. 'I've come over that hungry – '

The widow and Mr Bodfish rose simultaneously. It required not the brain of a trained detective to know that the cheese was in the larder. The unconscious Mrs Driver opened the door, and then with a wild scream fell back before the emerging form of Mr Bodfish into the arms of Mrs Clowes. The glass of Mr Negget smashed on the floor, and the farmer himself, with every appearance of astonishment, stared at the apparition open-mouthed.

'Mr – Bodfish!' he said at length, slowly.

Mr Bodfish, incapable of speech, glared at him ferociously.

'Leave him alone,' said Mrs Clowes, who was ministering to her friend. 'Can't you see the man's upset at frightening her? She's coming round, Mr Bodfish; don't be alarmed.'

'Very good,' said the farmer, who found his injured relative's gaze somewhat trying. 'I'll go, and leave him to explain to Mrs Driver why he was hidden in her larder. It don't seem a proper thing to me.'

'Why, you silly man,' said Mrs Clowes, gleefully, as she paused at the door, 'that don't want any explanation. Now, Mr Bodfish, we're giving you your chance. Mind you make the most of it, and don't be too shy.'

She walked excitedly up the road with the farmer, and bidding him good-bye at the corner, went off hastily to spread the news. Mr Negget walked home soberly, and hardly staying long enough to listen to his wife's account of the finding of the brooch between the chest of drawers and the wall, went off to spend the evening with a friend, and ended by making a night of it.

HENRY JAMES

Henry James was born on 15 April 1843 in New York City into a wealthy family. His father was one of the best-known intellectuals in mid-nineteenth-century America. In his youth James travelled back and forth between Europe and America. At the age of nineteen he briefly attended Harvard Law School, but preferred reading literature to studying law. From an early age James had read the classics of English, American, French and German literature and the Russian classics in translation. After living in Paris, where he was contributor to the *New York Tribune*, James moved to England, living first in London and then in Rye, Sussex. During his first years in Europe James wrote novels that portrayed Americans living abroad. In 1905 James visited America for the first time in twenty-five years, and wrote 'Jolly Corner'. Among James's masterpieces are *Daisy Miller* (1879), *The Portrait of a Lady* (1881), *The Bostonians* (1886), *What Maisie Knew* (1897), *The Wings of a Dove* (1902) and *The Ambassadors* (1903). James's most famous short story must be 'The Turn of the Screw', a ghost story in which the question of childhood corruption obsesses a governess.

The outbreak of World War 1 was a shock for James and in 1915 he became a British citizen as a declaration of loyalty to his adopted country and in protest against the US's refusal to enter the war. James suffered a stroke on 2 December 1915. He died three months later in Rye on 28 February 1916.

Paste

'I've found a lot more things,' her cousin said to her the day after the second funeral; 'they're up in her room – but they're things I wish *you'd* look at.'

The pair of mourners, sufficiently stricken, were in the garden of the vicarage together, before luncheon, waiting to be summoned to that meal, and Arthur Prime had still in his face the intention, she was moved to call it rather than the expression, of feeling something or other. Some such appearance was in itself of course natural within a week of his stepmother's death, within three of his father's; but what was most present to the girl, herself sensitive and shrewd, was that he seemed somehow to brood without sorrow, to suffer without what she in her own case would have called pain. He turned away from her after this last speech – it was a good deal his habit to drop an observation and leave her to pick it up without assistance. If the vicar's widow, now in her turn finally translated, had not really belonged to him it was not for want of her giving herself, so far as he ever would take her; and she had lain for three days all alone at the end of the passage, in the great cold chamber of hospitality, the dampish greenish room where visitors slept and where several of the ladies of the parish had, without effect, offered, in pairs and successions, piously to watch with her. His personal connection with the parish was now slighter than ever, and he had really not waited for this opportunity to show the ladies what he thought of them. She felt that she herself had, during her doleful month's leave from Bleet, where she was governess, rather taken her place in the same snubbed order; but it was presently, none the less, with a better little hope of coming in for some remembrance, some relic, that she went up to look at the things he had spoken of, the identity of which, as a confused cluster of bright objects on a table in the darkened room, shimmered at her as soon as she had opened the door.

They met her eyes for the first time, but in a moment, before touching them, she knew them as things of the theatre, as very much too fine to have been with any verisimilitude things of the vicarage. They were too dreadfully good to be true, for her aunt had had no jewels to speak of, and these were coronets and girdles, diamonds, rubies and sapphires. Flagrant tinsel and glass, they looked strangely vulgar, but if after the first queer shock of them she found herself taking them up it was for the very proof, never yet so distinct to her, of a far-off faded story. An honest widowed cleric with a small son and a large sense of Shakespeare had, on a brave latitude of habit as well as of taste – since it implied his having in very fact dropped deep into the 'pit' – conceived for an obscure actress several years older than himself an admiration of which the prompt offer of his reverend name and hortatory hand was the sufficiently candid sign. The response had perhaps in those dim years, so far as eccentricity was concerned, even bettered the proposal, and Charlotte, turning the tale over, had long since drawn from it a measure of the career renounced by the undistinguished comedienne – doubtless also tragic, or perhaps pantomimic, at a pinch – of her late uncle's dreams. This career couldn't have been eminent and must much more probably have been comfortless.

'You see what it is – old stuff of the time she never liked to mention.'

Our young woman gave a start; her companion had after all rejoined her and had apparently watched a moment her slightly scared recognition. 'So I said to myself,' she replied. Then to show intelligence, yet keep clear of twaddle: 'How peculiar they look!'

'They look awful,' said Arthur Prime. 'Cheap gilt, diamonds as big as potatoes. These are trappings of a ruder age than ours. Actors do themselves better now.'

'Oh now,' said Charlotte, not to be less knowing, 'actresses have real diamonds.'

'Some of them.' Arthur spoke dryly.

'I mean the bad ones – the nobodies too.'

'Oh some of the nobodies have the biggest. But mamma wasn't of that sort.'

'A nobody?' Charlotte risked.

'Not a nobody to whom somebody – well, not a nobody with diamonds. It isn't all worth, this trash, five pounds.'

There was something in the old gewgaws that spoke to her, and she continued to turn them over. 'They're relics. I think they have their melancholy and even their dignity.'

Arthur observed another pause. 'Do you care for them?' he then asked. 'I mean,' he promptly added, 'as a souvenir.'

'Of you?' Charlotte threw off.

'Of me? What have I to do with it? Of your poor dead aunt who was so kind to you,' he said with virtuous sternness.

'Well, I'd rather have them than nothing.'

'Then please take them,' he returned in a tone of relief which expressed somehow more of the eager than of the gracious.

'Thank you.' Charlotte lifted two or three objects up and set them down again. Though they were lighter than the materials they imitated they were so much more extravagant that they struck her in truth as rather an awkward heritage, to which she might have preferred even a matchbox or a penwiper. They were indeed shameless pinchbeck. 'Had you any idea she had kept them?'

'I don't at all believe she *had* kept them or knew they were there, and I'm very sure my father didn't. They had quite equally worked off any tenderness for the connection. These odds and ends, which she thought had been given away or destroyed, had simply got thrust into a dark corner and been forgotten.'

Charlotte wondered. 'Where then did you find them?'

'In that old tin box' – and the young man pointed to the receptacle from which he had dislodged them and which stood on a neighbouring chair. 'It's rather a good box still, but I'm afraid I can't give you *that*.'

The girl took no heed of the box; she continued only to look at the trinkets. 'What corner had she found?'

'She hadn't "found" it,' her companion sharply insisted; 'she had simply lost it. The whole thing had passed from her mind. The box was on the top shelf of the old schoolroom closet, which, until one put one's head into it from a step-ladder, looked, from below, quite cleared out. The door's narrow and the part of the closet to the left goes well into the wall. The box had stuck there for years.'

Charlotte was conscious of a mind divided and a vision vaguely troubled, and once more she took up two or three of the subjects of this revelation; a big bracelet in the form of a gilt serpent with many twists and beady eyes, a brazen belt studded with emeralds and rubies, a chain, of flamboyant architecture, to which, at the Theatre Royal, Little Peddlington, Hamlet's mother must have been concerned to attach the portrait of the successor to Hamlet's father. 'Are you very sure they're not really worth something? Their mere weight alone – !' she vaguely observed, balancing a moment a royal diadem that might have crowned one of the creations of the famous Mrs Jarley.

But Arthur Prime, it was clear, had already thought the question over and found the answer easy. 'If they had been worth anything to speak of she would long ago have sold them. My father and she had unfortunately never been in a position to keep any considerable value locked up.' And while his companion took in the obvious force of this he went on with a flourish just marked enough not to escape her: 'If they're worth anything at all – why you're only the more welcome to them.'

Charlotte had now in her hand a small bag of faded figured silk – one of those antique conveniences that speak to us, in terms of evaporated camphor and lavender, of the part they have played in some personal history; but though she had for the first time drawn the string she looked much more at the young man than at the questionable treasure it appeared to contain. 'I shall like them. They're all I have.'

'All you have – ?'

'That belonged to her.'

He swelled a little, then looked about him as if to appeal – as against her avidity – to the whole poor place. 'Well, what else do you want?'

'Nothing. Thank you very much.' With which she bent her eyes on the article wrapped, and now only exposed, in her superannuated satchel – a string of large pearls, such a shining circle as might once have graced the neck of a provincial Ophelia and borne company to a flaxen wig. 'This perhaps *is* worth something. Feel it.' And she passed him the necklace, the weight of which she had gathered for a moment into her hand.

He measured it in the same way with his own, but remained quite detached. 'Worth at most thirty shillings.'

'Not more?'

'Surely not if it's paste?'

'But *is* it paste?'

He gave a small sniff of impatience. 'Pearls nearly as big as filberts?'

'But they're heavy,' Charlotte declared.

'No heavier than anything else.' And he gave them back with an allowance for her simplicity. 'Do you imagine for a moment they're real?'

She studied them a little, feeling them, turning them round. 'Mightn't they possibly be?'

'Of that size – stuck away with that trash?'

'I admit it isn't likely,' Charlotte presently said. 'And pearls are so easily imitated.'

'That's just what – to a person who knows – they're not. These have no lustre, no play.'

'No – they *are* dull. They're opaque.'

'Besides,' he lucidly enquired, 'how could she ever have come by them?'

'Mightn't they have been a present?'

Arthur stared at the question as if it were almost improper. 'Because actresses are exposed – ?' He pulled up, however, not saying to what, and before she could supply the deficiency had, with the sharp ejaculation of 'No, they mightn't!' turned his back on her and walked away. His manner made her feel she had probably been wanting in tact, and before he returned to the subject, the last thing that evening, she had satisfied herself of the ground of his resentment. They had been talking of her departure the next morning, the hour of her train and the fly that would come for her, and it was precisely these things that gave him his effective chance. 'I really can't allow you to leave the house under the impression that my stepmother was at *any* time of her life the sort of person to allow herself to be approached – '

'With pearl necklaces and that sort of thing?' Arthur had made for her somehow the difficulty that she couldn't show him she understood him without seeming pert.

It at any rate only added to his own gravity. 'That sort of thing, exactly.'

'I didn't think when I spoke this morning – but I see what you mean.'

'I mean that she was beyond reproach,' said Arthur Prime.

'A hundred times yes.'

'Therefore if she couldn't, out of her slender gains, ever have paid for a row of pearls – '

'She couldn't, in that atmosphere, ever properly have had one? Of course she couldn't. I've seen perfectly since our talk,' Charlotte went on, 'that that string of beads isn't even as an imitation very good. The little clasp itself doesn't seem even gold. With false pearls, I suppose,' the girl mused, 'it naturally wouldn't be.'

'The whole thing's rotten paste,' her companion returned as if to have done with it. 'If it were *not*, and she had kept it all these years hidden – '

'Yes?' Charlotte sounded as he paused.

'Why I shouldn't know what to think!'

'Oh I see.' She had met him with a certain blankness, but adequately enough, it seemed, for him to regard the subject as dismissed; and there was no reversion to it between them before, on the morrow, when she had with difficulty made a place for them in her trunk, she carried off these florid survivals.

At Bleet she found small occasion to revert to them and, in an air charged with such quite other references, even felt, after she had laid them away, much enshrouded, beneath various piles of clothing, that they formed a collection not wholly without its note of the ridiculous. Yet she was never, for the joke, tempted to show them to her pupils, though Gwendolen and Blanche in particular always wanted, on her return, to know what she had brought back; so that without an accident by which the case was quite changed they might have appeared to enter on a new phase of interment. The essence of the accident was the sudden illness, at the last moment, of Lady Bobby, whose advent had been so much counted on to spice the five days' feast laid out for the coming of age of the eldest son of the house; and its equally marked effect was the dispatch of a pressing message, in quite another direction, to Mrs Guy, who, could she by a miracle be secured – she was always engaged ten parties deep – might be trusted to supply, it was believed, an element of exuberance scarcely less potent. Mrs Guy was already known to several of the visitors already on the scene, but she wasn't yet known to our young lady, who found her, after many wires and counter-wires had at last determined the triumph of her arrival, a strange charming little red-haired black-dressed woman, a person with the face of a baby and the authority of a commodore. She took on the spot the discreet, the exceptional young governess into the confidence of her designs and, still more, of her doubts; intimating that it was a policy she almost always promptly pursued.

'Tomorrow and Thursday are all right,' she said frankly to Charlotte on the second day, 'but I'm not half-satisfied with Friday.'

'What improvement then do you suggest?'

'Well, my strong point, you know, is *tableaux vivants*.'

'Charming. And what is your favourite character?'

'Boss!' said Mrs Guy with decision; and it was very markedly under that ensign that she had, within a few hours, completely planned her campaign and recruited her troop. Every word she uttered was to the point, but none more so than, after a general survey of their equipment, her final enquiry of Charlotte. She had been looking about, but half-appeased, at the muster of decoration and drapery. 'We shall be dull. We shall want more colour. You've nothing else?'

Charlotte had a thought. 'No – I've *some* things.'

'Then why don't you bring them?'

The girl weighed it. 'Would you come to my room?'

'No,' said Mrs Guy – 'bring them tonight to mine.'

So Charlotte, at the evening's end, after candlesticks had flickered through brown old passages bedward, arrived at her friend's door with the burden of her aunt's relics. But she promptly expressed a fear. 'Are they too garish?'

When she had poured them out on the sofa Mrs Guy was but a minute, before the glass, in clapping on the diadem. 'Awfully jolly – we can do *Ivanhoe*!'

'But they're only glass and tin.'

'Larger than life they are, *rather*! – which is exactly what's wanted for tableaux. *Our* jewels, for historic scenes, don't tell – the real thing falls short. Rowena must have rubies as big as eggs. Leave them with me,' Mrs Guy continued – 'they'll inspire me. Good-night.'

The next morning she was in fact – yet very strangely – inspired. 'Yes, *I'll* do Rowena. But I don't, my dear, understand.'

'Understand what?'

Mrs Guy gave a very lighted stare. 'How you come to have such things.'

Poor Charlotte smiled. 'By inheritance.'

'Family jewels?'

'They belonged to my aunt, who died some months ago. She was on the stage a few years in early life, and these are a part of her trappings.'

'She left them to you?'

'No; my cousin, her stepson, who naturally has no use for them, gave them to me for remembrance of her. She was a dear kind thing, always so nice to me, and I was fond of her.'

Mrs Guy had listened with frank interest. 'But it's *he* who must be a dear kind thing!'

Charlotte wondered. 'You think so?'

'Is *he*,' her friend went on, 'also "always so nice" to you?'

The girl, at this, face to face there with the brilliant visitor in the deserted breakfast-room, took a deeper sounding. 'What is it?'

'Don't you know?'

Something came over her. 'The pearls – ?' But the question fainted on her lips.

'Doesn't *he* know?'

Charlotte found herself flushing. 'They're *not* paste?'

'Haven't you looked at them?'

She was conscious of two kinds of embarrassment. '*You* have?'

'Very carefully.'

'And they're real?'

Mrs Guy became slightly mystifying and returned for all answer: 'Come again, when you've done with the children, to my room.'

Our young woman found she had done with the children that morning so promptly as to reveal to them a new joy, and when she reappeared before Mrs Guy this lady had already encircled a plump white throat with the only ornament, surely, in all the late Mrs Prime's – the effaced Miss Bradshaw's – collection, in the least qualified to raise a question. If Charlotte had never yet once, before the glass, tied the string of pearls about her own neck, this was because she had been capable of no such stoop to approved 'imitation'; but she had now only to look at Mrs Guy to see that, so disposed, the ambiguous objects might have passed for frank originals. 'What in the world have you done to them?'

'Only handled them, understood them, admired them and put them on. That's what pearls want; they want to be worn – it wakes them up. They're alive, don't you see? How *have* these been treated? They must have been buried, ignored, despised. They were half-dead. Don't you *know* about pearls?' Mrs Guy threw off as she fondly fingered the necklace.

'How *should* I? Do *you*?'

'Everything. These were simply asleep, and from the moment I really touched them – well,' said their wearer lovingly, 'it only took one's eye!'

'It took more than mine – though I did just wonder; and than Arthur's,' Charlotte brooded. She found herself almost panting. 'Then their value – ?'

'Oh their value's excellent.'

The girl, for a deep contemplative moment, took another plunge into the wonder, the beauty and the mystery. 'Are you *sure*?'

Her companion wheeled round for impatience. 'Sure? For what kind of an idiot, my dear, do you take me?'

It was beyond Charlotte Prime to say. 'For the same kind as Arthur – and as myself,' she could only suggest. 'But my cousin didn't know. He thinks they're worthless.'

'Because of the rest of the lot? Then your cousin's an ass. But what – if, as I understood you, he gave them to you – has he to do with it?'

'Why if he gave them to me as worthless and they turn out precious – !'

'You must give them back? I don't see that – if he was such a noodle. He took the risk.'

Charlotte fed, in fancy, on the pearls, which decidedly were exquisite, but which at the present moment somehow presented themselves much more as

Mrs Guy's than either as Arthur's or as her own. 'Yes – he did take it; even after I had distinctly hinted to him that they looked to me different from the other pieces.'

'Well then!' said Mrs Guy with something more than triumph – with a positive odd relief.

But it had the effect of making our young woman think with more intensity. 'Ah you see he thought they couldn't be different, because – so peculiarly – they shouldn't be.'

'Shouldn't? I don't understand.'

'Why how would she have got them?' – so Charlotte candidly put it.

'She? Who?' There was a capacity in Mrs Guy's tone for a sinking of persons – !

'Why the person I told you of: his stepmother, my uncle's wife – among whose poor old things, extraordinarily thrust away and out of sight, he happened to find them.'

Mrs Guy came a step nearer to the effaced Miss Bradshaw. 'Do you mean she may have stolen them?'

'No. But she had been an actress.'

'Oh well then,' cried Mrs Guy, 'wouldn't that be just how?'

'Yes, except that she wasn't at all a brilliant one, nor in receipt of large pay.' The girl even threw off a nervous joke. 'I'm afraid she couldn't have been our Rowena.'

Mrs Guy took it up. 'Was she very ugly?'

'No. She may very well, when young, have looked rather nice.'

'Well then!' was Mrs Guy's sharp comment and fresh triumph.

'You mean it was a present? That's just what he so dislikes the idea of her having received – a present from an admirer capable of going such lengths.'

'Because she wouldn't have taken it for nothing? *Speriamo* – that she wasn't a brute. The "length" her admirer went was the length of a whole row. Let us hope she was just a little kind!'

'Well,' Charlotte went on, 'that she was "kind" might seem to be shown by the fact that neither her husband, nor his son, nor I, his niece, knew or dreamed of her possessing anything so precious; by her having kept the gift all the rest of her life beyond discovery – out of sight and protected from suspicion.'

'As if, you mean' – Mrs Guy was quick – 'she had been wedded to it and yet was ashamed of it? Fancy,' she laughed while she manipulated the rare beads, 'being ashamed of *these*!'

'But you see she had married a clergyman.'

'Yes, she must have been "rum". But at any rate he had married *her*. What did he suppose?'

'Why that she had never been of the sort by whom such offerings are encouraged.'

'Ah my dear, the sort by whom they're *not* – !' But Mrs Guy caught herself up. 'And her stepson thought the same?'

'Overwhelmingly.'

'Was he then, if only her stepson – '

'So fond of her as that comes to? Yes; he had never known, consciously, his real mother, and, without children of her own, she was very patient and nice with him. And I liked her so,' the girl pursued, 'that at the end of ten years, in so strange a manner, to "give her away" – '

'Is impossible to you? Then don't!' said Mrs Guy with decision.

'Ah, but if they're real I can't keep them!' Charlotte, with her eyes on them, moaned in her impatience. 'It's too difficult.'

'Where's the difficulty, if he has such sentiments that he'd rather sacrifice the necklace than admit it, with the presumption it carries with it, to be genuine? You've only to be silent.'

'And keep it? How can I ever wear it?'

'You'd have to hide it, like your aunt?' Mrs Guy was amused. 'You can easily sell it.'

Her companion walked round her for a look at the affair from behind. The clasp was certainly, doubtless intentionally, misleading, but everything else was indeed lovely. 'Well, I must think. Why didn't *she* sell them?' Charlotte broke out in her trouble.

Mrs Guy had an instant answer. 'Doesn't that prove what they secretly recalled to her? You've only to be silent!' she ardently repeated.

'I must think – I must think!'

Mrs Guy stood with her hands attached but motionless. 'Then you want them back?'

As if with the dread of touching them Charlotte retreated to the door. 'I'll tell you tonight.'

'But may I wear them?'

'Meanwhile?'

'This evening – at dinner.'

It was the sharp selfish pressure of this that really, on the spot, determined the girl; but for the moment, before closing the door on the question, she only said: 'As you like!'

They were busy much of the day with preparation and rehearsal, and at dinner that evening the concourse of guests was such that a place among them for Miss Prime failed to find itself marked. At the time the company rose she was therefore alone in the schoolroom, where, towards eleven o'clock, she received a visit from Mrs Guy. This lady's white shoulders heaved, under the pearls, with an emotion that the very red lips which formed, as if for the full effect, the happiest opposition of colour, were not slow to translate. 'My dear, you should have seen the sensation – they've had a success!'

Charlotte, dumb a moment, took it all in. 'It *is* as if they knew it – they're more and more alive. But so much the worse for both of us! I can't,' she brought out with an effort, 'be silent.'

'You mean to return them?'

'If I don't I'm a thief.'

Mrs Guy gave her a long hard look: what was decidedly not of the baby in Mrs Guy's face was a certain air of established habit in the eyes. Then, with a sharp little jerk of her head and a backward reach of her bare beautiful arms, she undid the clasp and, taking off the necklace, laid it on the table. 'If you do, you're a goose.'

'Well, of the two – !' said our young lady, gathering it up with a sigh. And as if to get it, for the pang it gave, out of sight as soon as possible, she shut it up, clicking the lock, in the drawer of her own little table; after which, when she turned again, her companion looked naked and plain without it. 'But what will you say?' it then occurred to her to demand.

'Downstairs – to explain?' Mrs Guy was after all trying at least to keep her temper. 'Oh I'll put on something else and say the clasp's broken. And you won't of course name *me* to him,' she added.

'As having undeceived me? No – I'll say that, looking at the thing more carefully, it's my own private idea.'

'And does he know how little you really know?'

'As an expert – surely. And he has always much the conceit of his own opinion.'

'Then he won't believe you – as he so hates to. He'll stick to his judgement and maintain his gift, and we shall have the darlings back!' With which reviving assurance Mrs Guy kissed her young friend for good-night.

She was not, however, to be gratified or justified by any prompt event, for, whether or no paste entered into the composition of the ornament in question, Charlotte shrank from the temerity of dispatching it to town by post. Mrs Guy was thus disappointed of the hope of seeing the business settled – 'by return', she had seemed to expect – before the end of the revels. The revels, moreover, rising to a frantic pitch, pressed for all her attention, and it was at last only in the general confusion of leave-taking that she made, parenthetically, a dash at the person in the whole company with whom her contact had been most interesting.

'Come, what will you take for them?'

'The pearls? Ah, you'll have to treat with my cousin.'

Mrs Guy, with quick intensity, lent herself. 'Where then does he live?'

'In chambers in the Temple. You can find him.'

'But what's the use, if *you* do neither one thing nor the other?'

'Oh I *shall* do the "other",' Charlotte said: 'I'm only waiting till I go up. You want them so awfully?' She curiously, solemnly again, sounded her.

'I'm dying for them. There's a special charm in them – I don't know what it is: they tell so their history.'

'But what do you know of that?'

'Just what they themselves say. It's all *in* them – and it comes out. They breathe a tenderness – they have the white glow of it. My dear,' hissed Mrs Guy in supreme confidence and as she buttoned her glove – 'they're things of love!'

'Oh!' our young woman vaguely exclaimed.

'They're things of passion!'

'Mercy!' she gasped, turning short off. But these words remained, though indeed their help was scarce needed, Charlotte being in private face to face with a new light, as she by this time felt she must call it, on the dear dead kind colourless lady whose career had turned so sharp a corner in the middle. The pearls had quite taken their place as a revelation. She might have received them for nothing – admit that; but she couldn't have kept them so long and so unprofitably hidden, couldn't have enjoyed them only in secret, for nothing; and she had mixed them in her reliquary with false things in order to put curiosity and detection off the scent. Over this strange fact poor Charlotte interminably mused: it became more touching, more attaching for her than she could now confide to any ear. How bad or how happy – in the sophisticated sense of Mrs Guy and the young man at the Temple – the effaced Miss Bradshaw must have been to have had to be so mute! The little governess at Bleet put on the necklace now in secret sessions; she wore it sometimes under her dress; she came to feel verily a haunting passion for it. Yet in her penniless state she would have parted with it for money; she gave herself also to dreams of what in this direction it would do for her. The sophistry of her so often saying to herself that Arthur had after all definitely pronounced her welcome to any gain from his gift that might accrue – this trick remained innocent, as she perfectly knew it for what it was. Then there was always the possibility of his – as she could only picture it – rising to the occasion. Mightn't he have a grand magnanimous moment? – mightn't he just say, 'Oh I couldn't of course have afforded to let you have it if I had known; but since you *have* got it, and have made out the truth by your own wit, I really can't screw myself down to the shabbiness of taking it back'?

She had, as it proved, to wait a long time – to wait till, at the end of several months, the great house of Bleet had, with due deliberation, for the season, transferred itself to town; after which, however, she fairly snatched at her first freedom to knock, dressed in her best and armed with her disclosure, at the door of her doubting kinsman. It was still with doubt and not quite with the face she had hoped that he listened to her story. He had turned pale, she thought, as she produced the necklace, and he appeared above all disagreeably affected. Well, perhaps there was reason, she more than ever remembered; but what on earth was one, in close touch with the fact, to do? She had laid the pearls on his table, where, without his having at first put so much as a finger to them, they met his hard cold stare.

'I don't believe in them,' he simply said at last.

'That's exactly then,' she returned with some spirit, 'what I wanted to hear!'

She fancied that at this his colour changed; it was indeed vivid to her afterwards – for she was to have a long recall of the scene – that she had made him quite angrily flush. 'It's a beastly unpleasant imputation, you know!' – and he walked away from her as he had always walked at the vicarage.

'It's none of *my* making, I'm sure,' said Charlotte Prime. 'If you're afraid to believe they're real – '

'Well?' – and he turned, across the room, sharp round at her.

'Why it's not my fault.'

He said nothing more, for a moment, on this; he only came back to the table. 'They're what I originally said they were. They're rotten paste.'

'Then I may keep them?'

'No. I want a better opinion.'

'Than your own?'

'Than *your* own.' He dropped on the pearls another queer stare; then, after a moment, bringing himself to touch them, did exactly what she had herself done in the presence of Mrs Guy at Bleet – gathered them together, marched off with them to a drawer, put them in and clicked the key. 'You say I'm afraid,' he went on as he again met her; 'but I shan't be afraid to take them to Bond Street.'

'And if the people say they're real – ?'

He had a pause and then his strangest manner. 'They won't say it! They shan't!'

There was something in the way he brought it out that deprived poor Charlotte, as she was perfectly aware, of any manner at all. 'Oh!' she simply sounded, as she had sounded for her last word to Mrs Guy; and within a minute, without more conversation, she had taken her departure.

A fortnight later she received a communication from him, and toward the end of the season one of the entertainments in Eaton Square was graced by the presence of Mrs Guy. Charlotte was not at dinner, but she came down afterwards, and this guest, on seeing her, abandoned a very beautiful young man on purpose to cross and speak to her. The guest displayed a lovely necklace and had apparently not lost her habit of overflowing with the pride of such ornaments.

'Do you see?' She was in high joy.

They were indeed splendid pearls – so far as poor Charlotte could feel that she knew, after what had come and gone, about such mysteries. The poor girl had a sickly smile. 'They're almost as fine as Arthur's.'

'Almost? Where, my dear, are your eyes? They *are* "Arthur's"!' After which, to meet the flood of crimson that accompanied her young friend's start: 'I tracked them – after your folly, and, by miraculous luck, recognised them in the Bond Street window to which he had disposed of them.'

'*Disposed* of them?' Charlotte gasped. 'He wrote me that I had insulted his mother and that the people had shown him he was right – had pronounced them utter paste.'

Mrs Guy gave a stare. 'Ah I told you he wouldn't bear it! No. But I had, I assure you,' she wound up, 'to drive my bargain!'

Charlotte scarce heard or saw; she was full of her private wrong. 'He wrote me,' she panted, 'that he had smashed them.'

Mrs Guy could only wonder and pity. 'He's really morbid!' But it wasn't quite clear which of the pair she pitied; though the young person employed in Eaton Square felt really morbid too after they had separated and she found herself full of thought. She even went the length of asking herself what sort of a bargain Mrs Guy had driven and whether the marvel of the recognition in Bond Street had been a veracious account of the matter. Hadn't she perhaps in truth dealt with Arthur directly? It came back to Charlotte almost luridly that she had had his address.

The Beast in the Jungle

I

What determined the speech that startled him in the course of their encounter scarcely matters, being probably but some words spoken by himself quite without intention – spoken as they lingered and slowly moved together after their renewal of acquaintance. He had been conveyed by friends an hour or two before to the house at which she was staying; the party of visitors at the other house, of whom he was one, and thanks to whom it was his theory, as always, that he was lost in the crowd, had been invited over to luncheon. There had been after luncheon much dispersal, all in the interest of the original motive, a view of Weatherend itself and the fine things, intrinsic features, pictures, heirlooms, treasures of all the arts, that made the place almost famous; and the great rooms were so numerous that guests could wander at their will, hang back from the principal group and in cases where they took such matters with the last seriousness give themselves up to mysterious appreciations and measurements. There were persons to be observed, singly or in couples, bending toward objects in out-of-the-way corners with their hands on their knees and their heads nodding quite as with the emphasis of an excited sense of smell. When they were two they either mingled their sounds of ecstasy or melted into silences of even deeper import, so that there were aspects of the occasion that gave it for Marcher much the air of the 'look round', previous to a sale highly advertised, that excites or quenches, as may be, the dream of acquisition. The dream of acquisition at Weatherend would have had to be wild indeed, and John Marcher found himself, among such suggestions, disconcerted almost equally by the presence of those who knew too much and by that of those who knew nothing. The great rooms caused so much poetry and history to press upon him that he needed some straying apart to feel in a proper relation with them, though this impulse was not, as happened, like the gloating of some of his companions, to be compared to the movements of a dog sniffing a cupboard. It had an issue promptly enough in a direction that was not to have been calculated.

It led, briefly, in the course of the October afternoon, to his closer meeting with May Bartram, whose face, a reminder, yet not quite a remembrance, as they sat much separated at a very long table, had begun merely by troubling him rather pleasantly. It affected him as the sequel of something of which he had lost the beginning. He knew it, and for the time quite welcomed it, as a continuation, but didn't know what it continued, which was an interest or an amusement the greater as he was also somehow aware – yet without a direct sign from her – that the young woman herself hadn't lost the thread. She hadn't lost it, but she wouldn't give it back to him, he saw, without some putting forth of his hand for it; and he not only saw that, but saw several things more, things odd enough in the light of the fact that at the moment some accident of grouping brought them face to face he was still merely fumbling with the idea that any contact between them in the past would have had no importance. If it had had no importance he scarcely knew why his actual impression of her should so seem to have so much; the answer to which, however, was that in such a life as they all appeared to be leading for the moment one could but take things as they came. He was satisfied, without in the least being able to say why, that this young lady might roughly have ranked in the house as a poor relation; satisfied also that she was not there on a brief visit, but was more or less a part of the establishment – almost a working, a remunerated part. Didn't she enjoy at periods a protection that she paid for by helping, among other services, to show the place and explain it, deal with the tiresome people, answer questions about the dates of the building, the styles of the furniture, the authorship of the pictures, the favourite haunts of the ghost? It wasn't that she looked as if you could have given her shillings – it was impossible to look less so. Yet when she finally drifted toward him, distinctly handsome, though ever so much older – older than when he had seen her before – it might have been as an effect of her guessing that he had, within the couple of hours, devoted more imagination to her than to all the others put together, and had thereby penetrated to a kind of truth that the others were too stupid for. She *was* there on harder terms than anyone; she was there as a consequence of things suffered, one way and another, in the interval of years; and she remembered him very much as she was remembered – only a good deal better.

By the time they at last thus came to speech they were alone in one of the rooms – remarkable for a fine portrait over the chimney-place – out of which their friends had passed, and the charm of it was that even before they had spoken they had practically arranged with each other to stay behind for talk. The charm, happily, was in other things too – partly in there being scarce a spot at Weatherend without something to stay behind for. It was in the way the autumn day looked into the high windows as it waned; the way the red light, breaking at the close from under a low sombre sky, reached out in a long shaft and played over old wainscots, old tapestry, old gold, old colour. It was most of all perhaps in the way she came to him as if, since she had been turned on to deal with the simpler sort, he might, should he choose to keep the whole thing down, just take her mild attention for a part of her general business. As soon as he heard her voice, however, the gap was filled up and the missing link supplied; the slight irony he divined in her attitude lost its advantage. He almost jumped at it to get there before her. 'I met you years and years ago in Rome. I remember all about it.' She confessed to disappointment – she had been so sure he didn't; and to prove how well he did he began to pour forth the particular recollections that popped up as he called for them. Her face and her voice, all at his service now, worked the miracle – the impression operating like the torch of a lamplighter who touches into flame, one by one, a long row of gas-jets. Marcher flattered himself the illumination was brilliant, yet he was really still more pleased on her showing him, with amusement, that in his haste to make everything right he had got most things rather wrong. It hadn't been at Rome – it had been at Naples; and it hadn't been eight years before – it had been more nearly ten. She hadn't been, either, with her uncle and aunt, but with her mother and brother; in addition to which it was not with the Pembles *he* had been, but with the Boyers, coming down in their company from Rome – a point on which she insisted, a little to his confusion, and as to which she had her evidence in hand. The Boyers she had known, but didn't know the Pembles, though she had heard of them, and it was the people he was with who had made them acquainted. The incident of the thunderstorm that had raged round them with such violence as to drive them for refuge into an excavation – this incident had not occurred at the Palace of the Caesars, but at Pompeii, on an occasion when they had been present there at an important find.

He accepted her amendments, he enjoyed her corrections, though the moral of them was, she pointed out, that he *really* didn't remember the least thing about her; and he only felt it as a drawback that when all was made strictly historic there didn't appear much of anything left. They lingered together still, she neglecting her office – for from the moment he was so clever she had no proper right to him – and both neglecting the house, just waiting as to see if a memory or two more wouldn't again breathe on them. It hadn't taken them many minutes, after all, to put down on the table, like the cards of a pack, those that constituted their respective hands; only what came out was that the pack was unfortunately not perfect – that the past, invoked, invited, encouraged, could give them, naturally, no more than it had. It had made them anciently meet – her at twenty, him at twenty-five; but nothing was so strange, they seemed to say to each other, as that, while so occupied, it hadn't done a little more for them. They looked at each other as with the feeling of an occasion missed; the present would have been so much better if the other, in the far distance, in the foreign land, hadn't been so stupidly meagre. There weren't, apparently, all counted, more than a dozen little old things that had succeeded in coming to pass between them; trivialities of youth, simplicities of freshness, stupidities of ignorance, small possible germs, but too deeply buried – too deeply (didn't it seem?) to sprout after so many years. Marcher could only feel he ought to have rendered her some service – saved her from a capsized boat in the bay or at least recovered her dressing-bag, filched from her cab in the streets of Naples by a *lazzarone* with a stiletto. Or it would have been nice if he could have been taken with fever all alone at his hotel, and she could have come to look after him, to write to his people, to drive him out in convalescence. *Then* they would be in possession of the something or other that their actual show seemed to lack. It yet somehow presented itself, this show, as too good to be spoiled; so that they were reduced for a few minutes more to wondering a little helplessly why – since they seemed to know a certain number of the same people – their reunion had been so long averted. They didn't use that name for it, but their delay from minute to minute to join the others was a kind of confession that they didn't quite want it to be a failure. Their attempted supposition of reasons for their not having met but showed how little they knew of each other. There came in fact a moment when Marcher felt a positive pang. It was vain to pretend she was an old friend, for all the communities were wanting, in spite of which it was as an old friend that he saw she would have suited him. He had new ones enough – was surrounded with them for instance on the stage of the other house; as a new one he probably wouldn't have so much as noticed her. He would have liked to invent something, get her to make-believe with him that some passage of a romantic or critical kind *had* originally occurred. He was really almost reaching out in imagination – as against time – for something that would do, and saying to himself that if it didn't come this sketch of a fresh start would show for quite awkwardly bungled. They would separate, and now for no second or no third chance. They would have tried and not succeeded. Then it was, just at the turn, as he afterwards made it out to himself, that, everything else failing, she herself decided to take up the case and, as it were, save the situation. He felt as soon as she spoke that she had been consciously keeping back what she said and hoping to get on without it; a scruple in her that immensely touched him when, by the end of three or four minutes more, he was able to measure it. What she brought out, at any rate, quite cleared the air and supplied the link – the link it was so odd he should frivolously have managed to lose.

'You know you told me something I've never forgotten and that again and again has made me think of you since; it was that tremendously hot day when we went to Sorrento, across the bay, for the breeze. What I allude to was what you said to me, on the way back, as we sat under the awning of the boat enjoying the cool. Have you forgotten?'

He had forgotten, and was even more surprised than ashamed. But the great thing was that he saw in this no vulgar reminder of any 'sweet' speech. The vanity of women had long memories, but she was making no claim on him of a compliment or a mistake. With another woman, a totally different one, he might have feared the recall possibly even of some imbecile 'offer'. So, in having to say that he had indeed forgotten, he was conscious rather of a loss than of a gain; he already saw an interest in the matter of her mention. 'I try to think – but I give it up. Yet I remember the Sorrento day.'

'I'm not very sure you do,' May Bartram after a moment said; 'and I'm not very sure I ought to want you to. It's dreadful to bring a person back at any time to what he was ten years before. If you've lived away from it,' she smiled, 'so much the better.'

'Ah if *you* haven't why should I?' he asked.

'Lived away, you mean, from what I myself was?'

'From what I was. I was of course an ass,' Marcher went on; 'but I would rather know from you just the sort of ass I was than – from the moment you have something in your mind – not know anything.'

Still, however, she hesitated. 'But if you've completely ceased to be that sort – ?'

'Why I can then all the more bear to know. Besides, perhaps I haven't.'

'Perhaps. Yet if you haven't,' she added, 'I should suppose you'd remember. Not indeed that I in the least connect with my impression the invidious name you use. If I had only thought you foolish,' she explained, 'the thing I speak of wouldn't so have remained with me. It was about yourself.' She waited as if it might come to him; but as, only meeting her eyes in wonder, he gave no sign, she burnt her ships. 'Has it ever happened?'

Then it was that, while he continued to stare, a light broke for him and the blood slowly came to his face, which began to burn with recognition.

'Do you mean I told you – ?' But he faltered, lest what came to him shouldn't be right, lest he should only give himself away.

'It was something about yourself that it was natural one shouldn't forget – that is if one remembered you at all. That's why I ask you,' she smiled, 'if the thing you then spoke of has ever come to pass?'

Oh then he saw, but he was lost in wonder and found himself embarrassed. This, he also saw, made her sorry for him, as if her allusion had been a mistake. It took him but a moment, however, to feel it hadn't been, much as it had been a surprise. After the first little shock of it her knowledge on the contrary began, even if rather strangely, to taste sweet to him. She was the only other person in the world then who would have it, and she had had it all these years, while the fact of his having so breathed his secret had unaccountably faded from him. No wonder they couldn't have met as if nothing had happened. 'I judge,' he finally said, 'that I know what you mean. Only I had strangely enough lost any sense of having taken you so far into my confidence.'

'Is it because you've taken so many others as well?'

'I've taken nobody. Not a creature since then.'

'So that I'm the only person who knows?'

'The only person in the world.'

'Well,' she quickly replied, 'I myself have never spoken. I've never, never repeated of you what you told me.' She looked at him so that he perfectly believed her. Their eyes met over it in such a way that he was without a doubt. 'And I never will.'

She spoke with an earnestness that, as if almost excessive, put him at ease about her possible derision. Somehow the whole question was a new luxury to him – that is from the moment she was in possession. If she didn't take the sarcastic view she clearly took the sympathetic, and that was what he had had, in all the long time, from no one whomsoever. What he felt was that he couldn't at present have begun to tell her, and yet could profit perhaps exquisitely by the accident of having done so of old. 'Please don't then. We're just right as it is.'

'Oh I am,' she laughed, 'if you are!' To which she added: 'Then you do still feel in the same way?'

It was impossible he shouldn't take to himself that she was really interested, though it all kept coining as a perfect surprise. He had thought of himself so long as abominably alone, and lo he wasn't alone a bit. He hadn't been, it appeared, for an hour – since those moments on the Sorrento boat. It was she who had been, he seemed to see as he looked at her – she who had been made so by the graceless fact of his lapse of fidelity. To tell her what he had told her – what had it been but to ask something of her? something that she had given, in her charity, without his having, by a remembrance, by a return of the spirit, failing another encounter, so much as thanked her. What he had asked of her had been simply at first not to laugh at him. She had beautifully not done so for ten years, and she was not doing so now. So he had endless gratitude to make up. Only for that he must see just how he had figured to her. 'What, exactly, was the account I gave – ?'

'Of the way you did feel? Well, it was very simple. You said you had had from your earliest time, as the deepest thing within you, the sense of being kept for something rare and strange, possibly prodigious and terrible, that was sooner or later to happen to you, that you had in your bones the foreboding and the conviction of, and that would perhaps overwhelm you.'

'Do you call that very simple?' John Marcher asked.

She thought a moment. 'It was perhaps because I seemed, as you spoke, to understand it.'

'You do understand it?' he eagerly asked.

Again she kept her kind eyes on him. 'You still have the belief?'

'Oh!' he exclaimed helplessly. There was too much to say.

'Whatever it's to be,' she clearly made out, 'it hasn't yet come.'

He shook his head in complete surrender now. 'It hasn't yet come. Only, you know, it isn't anything I'm to do, to achieve in the world, to be distinguished or admired for. I'm not such an ass as *that*. It would be much better, no doubt, if I were.'

'It's to be something you're merely to suffer?'

'Well, say to wait for – to have to meet, to face, to see suddenly break out in my life; possibly destroying all further consciousness, possibly annihilating me; possibly, on the other hand, only altering everything, striking at the root of all my world and leaving me to the consequences, however they shape themselves.'

She took this in, but the light in her eyes continued for him not to be that of mockery. 'Isn't what you describe perhaps but the expectation – or at any rate the sense of danger, familiar to so many people – of falling in love?'

John Marcher thought. 'Did you ask me that before?'

'No – I wasn't so free-and-easy then. But it's what strikes me now.'

'Of course,' he said after a moment, 'it strikes you. Of course it strikes *me*. Of course what's in store for me may be no more than that. The only thing is,' he went on, 'that I think if it had been that I should by this time know.'

'Do you mean because you've *been* in love?' And then as he but looked at her in silence: 'You've been in love, and it hasn't meant such a cataclysm, hasn't proved the great affair?'

'Here I am, you see. It hasn't been overwhelming.'

'Then it hasn't been love,' said May Bartram.

'Well, I at least thought it was. I took it for that – I've taken it till now. It was agreeable, it was delightful, it was miserable,' he explained. 'But it wasn't strange. It wasn't what my affair's to be.'

'You want something all to yourself – something that nobody else knows or *has* known?'

'It isn't a question of what I "want" – God knows I don't want anything. It's only a question of the apprehension that haunts me – that I live with day by day.'

He said this so lucidly and consistently that he could see it further impose itself. If she hadn't been interested before she'd have been interested now.

'Is it a sense of coming violence?'

Evidently now too again he liked to talk of it. 'I don't think of it as – when it does come – necessarily violent. I only think of it as natural and as of course above all unmistakable. I think of it simply as *the* thing. *The* thing will of itself appear natural.'

'Then how will it appear strange?'

Marcher bethought himself. 'It won't – to *me*.'

'To whom then?'

'Well,' he replied, smiling at last, 'say to you.'

'Oh then I'm to be present?'

'Why you are present – since you know.'

'I see.' She turned it over. 'But I mean at the catastrophe.'

At this, for a minute, their lightness gave way to their gravity; it was as if the long look they exchanged held them together. 'It will only depend on yourself – if you'll watch with me.'

'Are you afraid?' she asked.

'Don't leave me now,' he went on.

'Are you afraid?' she repeated.

'Do you think me simply out of my mind?' he pursued instead of answering. 'Do I merely strike you as a harmless lunatic?'

'No,' said May Bartram. 'I understand you. I believe you.'

'You mean you feel how my obsession – poor old thing – may correspond to some possible reality?'

'To some possible reality.'

'Then you *will* watch with me?'

She hesitated, then for the third time put her question. 'Are you afraid?'

'Did I tell you I was – at Naples?'

'No, you said nothing about it.'

'Then I don't know. And I should like to know,' said John Marcher. 'You'll tell me yourself whether you think so. If you'll watch with me you'll see.'

'Very good then.' They had been moving by this time across the room, and at the door, before passing out, they paused as for the full wind-up of their understanding. 'I'll watch with you,' said May Bartram.

2

The fact that she 'knew' – knew and yet neither chaffed him nor betrayed him – had in a short time begun to constitute between them a goodly bond, which became more marked when, within the year that followed their afternoon at Weatherend, the opportunities for meeting multiplied. The event that thus promoted these occasions was the death of the ancient lady her great-aunt, under whose wing, since losing her mother, she had to such an extent found shelter, and who, though but the widowed mother of the new successor to the property, had succeeded – thanks to a high tone and a high temper – in not forfeiting the supreme position at the great house. The deposition of this personage arrived but with her death, which, followed by many changes, made in particular a difference for the young woman in whom Marcher's expert attention had recognised from the first a dependant with a pride that might ache though it didn't bristle. Nothing for a long time had made him easier than the thought that the aching must have been much soothed by Miss Bartram's now finding herself able to set up a small home in London. She had acquired property, to an amount that made that luxury just possible, under her aunt's extremely complicated will, and when the whole matter began to be straightened out, which indeed took time, she let him know that the happy issue was at last in view. He had seen her again before that day, both because she had more than once accompanied the ancient lady to town and because he had paid another visit to the friends who so conveniently made of Weatherend one of the charms of their own hospitality. These friends had taken him back there; he had achieved there again with Miss Bartram some quiet detachment; and he had in London succeeded in persuading her to more than one brief absence from her aunt. They went together, on these latter occasions, to the National Gallery and the South Kensington Museum, where, among vivid reminders, they talked of Italy at large – not now attempting to recover, as at first, the taste of their youth and their ignorance. That recovery, the first day at Weatherend, had served its purpose well, had given them quite enough; so that they were, to Marcher's sense, no longer hovering about the head-waters of their stream, but had felt their boat pushed sharply off and down the current.

They were literally afloat together; for our gentleman this was marked, quite as marked as that the fortunate cause of it was just the buried treasure of her knowledge. He had with his own hands dug up this little hoard, brought to light – that is to within reach of the dim day constituted by their discretions and privacies – the object of value the hiding-place of which he had, after putting it into the ground himself, so strangely, so long forgotten. The rare luck of his having again just stumbled on the spot made him indifferent to any other question; he would doubtless have devoted more time to the odd accident of his lapse of memory if he hadn't been moved to devote so much to the sweetness, the comfort, as he felt, for the future, that this accident itself had helped to keep fresh. It had never entered into his plan that anyone should 'know', and mainly for the reason that it wasn't in him to tell anyone. That would have been impossible, for nothing but the amusement of a cold world would have waited on it. Since, however, a mysterious fate had opened his mouth betimes, in spite of him, he would count that a compensation and profit by it to the utmost. That the right person *should* know tempered the asperity of his secret more even than his shyness had permitted him to imagine; and May Bartram was clearly right, because – well, because there she was. Her knowledge simply settled it; he would have been sure enough by this time had she been wrong. There was that in his situation, no doubt, that disposed him too much to see her as a mere confidant, taking all her light for him from the fact – the fact only – of her interest in his predicament; from her mercy, sympathy, seriousness, her consent not to regard him as the funniest of the funny. Aware, in fine, that her price for him was just in her giving him this constant sense of his being admirably spared, he was careful to remember that she had also a life of her own, with things that might happen to *her*, things that in friendship one should likewise take account of. Something fairly remarkable came to pass with him, for that matter, in this connection – something represented by a certain passage of his consciousness, in the suddenest way, from one extreme to the other.

He had thought himself, so long as nobody knew, the most disinterested person in the world, carrying his concentrated burden, his perpetual suspense, ever so quietly, holding his tongue about it, giving others no glimpse of it nor of its effect upon his life, asking of them no allowance and only making on his side all those that were asked. He hadn't disturbed people with the queerness of their having to know a haunted man, though he had had moments of rather special temptation on hearing them say they were forsooth 'unsettled'. If they were as unsettled as he was – he who had never been settled for an hour in his life – they would know what it meant. Yet it wasn't, all the same, for him to make them, and he listened to them civilly enough. This was why he had such good – though possibly such rather colourless – manners; this was why, above all, he could regard himself, in a greedy world, as decently – as in fact perhaps even a little sublimely – unselfish. Our point is accordingly that he valued this character quite sufficiently to measure his present danger of letting it lapse, against which he promised himself to be much on his guard. He was quite ready, none the less, to be selfish just a little, since surely no more charming occasion for it had come to him. 'Just a little', in a word, was just as much as Miss Bartram, taking one day with another, would let him. He never would be in the least coercive, and would keep well before him the lines on which consideration for her – the very highest – ought to proceed. He would thoroughly establish the heads under which her affairs, her requirements, her peculiarities – he went so far as to give them the latitude of that name – would come into their intercourse. All this naturally was a sign of how much he took the intercourse itself for granted. There was nothing more to be done about that. It simply existed; had sprung into being with her first penetrating question to him in the autumn light there at Weatherend. The real form it should have taken on the basis that stood out large was the form of their marrying. But the devil in this was that the very basis itself put marrying out of the question. His conviction, his apprehension, his obsession, in short, wasn't a privilege he could invite a woman to share; and that consequence of it was precisely what was the matter with him. Something or other lay in wait for him, amid the twists and the turns of the months and the years, like a crouching beast in the jungle. It signified little whether the crouching beast were destined to slay him or to be slain. The definite point was the inevitable spring of the creature; and the definite lesson from that was that a man of feeling didn't cause himself to be accompanied by a lady on a tiger-hunt. Such was the image under which he had ended by figuring his life.

They had at first, none the less, in the scattered hours spent together, made no allusion to that view of it; which was a sign he was handsomely alert to give that he didn't expect, that he in fact didn't care, always to be talking about it. Such a feature in one's outlook was really like a hump on one's back. The difference it made every minute of the day existed quite independently of discussion. One discussed of course *like* a hunchback, for there was always, if nothing else, the hunchback face. That remained, and she was watching him; but people watched best, as a general thing, in silence, so that such would be predominantly the manner of their vigil. Yet he didn't want, at the same time, to be tense and solemn; tense and solemn was what he imagined he too much tended to be with other people. The thing to be, with the one person who knew, was easy and natural – to make the reference rather than be seeming to avoid it, to avoid it rather than be seeming to make it, and to keep it, in any case, familiar, facetious even, rather than pedantic and portentous. Some such consideration as the latter was doubtless in his mind for instance when he wrote pleasantly to Miss Bartram that perhaps the great thing he had so long felt as in the lap of the gods was no more than this circumstance, which touched him so nearly, of her acquiring a house in London. It was the first allusion they had yet again made, needing any other hitherto so little; but when she replied, after having given him the news, that she was by no means satisfied with such a trifle as the climax to so special a suspense, she almost set him wondering if she hadn't even a larger conception of singularity for him than he had for himself. He was at all events destined to become aware little by little, as time went by, that she was all the while looking at his life, judging it, measuring it, in the light of the thing she knew, which grew to be at last, with the consecration of the years, never mentioned between them save as 'the real truth' about him. That had always been his own form of reference to it, but she adopted the form so quietly that, looking back at the end of a period, he knew there was no moment at which it was traceable that she had, as he might say, got inside his idea, or exchanged the attitude of beautifully indulging for that of still more beautifully believing him.

It was always open to him to accuse her of seeing him but as the most harmless of maniacs, and this, in the long run – since it covered so much ground – was his easiest description of their friendship. He had a screw loose for her but she liked him in spite of it and was practically, against the rest of the world, his kind wise keeper, unremunerated but fairly amused and, in the absence of other near ties, not disreputably occupied. The rest of the world of course thought him queer, but she, she only, knew how, and above all why, queer; which was precisely what enabled her to dispose the concealing veil in the right folds. She took his gaiety from him – since it had to pass with them for gaiety – as she took everything else; but she certainly so far justified by her unerring touch his finer sense of the degree to which he had ended by convincing her. *She* at least never spoke of the secret of his life except as 'the real truth about you', and she had in fact a wonderful way of making it seem, as such, the secret of her own life too. That was in fine how he so constantly felt her as allowing for him; he couldn't on the whole call it anything else. He allowed for himself, but she, exactly, allowed still more; partly because, better placed for a sight of the matter, she traced his unhappy perversion through reaches of its course into which he could scarce follow it. He knew how he felt, but, besides knowing that, she knew how he looked as well; he knew each of the things of importance he was insidiously kept from doing, but she could add up the amount they made, understand how much, with a lighter weight on his spirit, he might have done, and thereby establish how, clever as he was, he fell short. Above all she was in the secret of the difference between the forms he went through – those of his little office under Government, those of caring for his modest patrimony, for his library, for his garden in the country, for the people in London whose invitations he accepted and repaid – and the detachment that reigned beneath them and that made of all behaviour, all that could in the least be called behaviour, a long act of dissimulation. What it had come to was that he wore a mask painted with the social simper, out of the eye-holes of which there looked eyes of an expression not in the least matching the other features. This the stupid world, even after years, had never more than half discovered. It was only May Bartram who had, and she achieved, by an art indescribable, the feat of at once – or perhaps it was only alternately – meeting the eyes from in front and mingling her own vision, as from over his shoulder, with their peep through the apertures.

So while they grew older together she did watch with him, and so she let this association give shape and colour to her own existence. Beneath *her* forms as well detachment had learned to sit, and behaviour had become for her, in the social sense, a false account of herself. There was but one account of her that would have been true all the while and that she could give straight to nobody, least of all to John Marcher. Her whole attitude was a virtual statement, but the perception of that only seemed called to take its place for him as one of the many things necessarily crowded out of his consciousness. If she had moreover, like himself, to make sacrifices to their real truth, it was to be granted that her compensation might have affected her as more prompt and more natural. They had long periods, in this London time, during which, when they were together, a stranger might have listened to them without in the least pricking up his ears; on the other hand the real truth was equally liable at any moment to rise to the surface, and the auditor would then have wondered indeed what they were talking about. They had from an early hour made up their mind that society was, luckily, unintelligent, and the margin allowed them by this had fairly become one of their commonplaces. Yet there were still moments when the situation turned almost fresh – usually under the effect of some expression drawn from herself. Her expressions doubtless repeated themselves, but her intervals were generous. 'What saves us, you know, is that we answer so completely to so usual an appearance: that of the man and woman whose friendship has become such a daily habit – or almost – as to be at last indispensable.' That for instance was a remark she had frequently enough had occasion to make, though she had given it at different times different developments. What we are especially concerned with is the turn it happened to take from her one afternoon when he had come to see her in honour of her birthday. This anniversary had fallen on a Sunday, at a season of thick fog and general outward gloom; but he had brought her his customary offering, having known her now long enough to have established a hundred small traditions. It was one of his proofs to himself, the present he made her on her birthday, that he hadn't sunk into real selfishness. It was mostly nothing more than a small trinket, but it was always fine of its kind, and he was regularly careful to pay for it more than he thought he could afford. 'Our habit saves you, at least, don't you see?, because it makes you, after all, for the vulgar, indistinguishable from other men. What's the most inveterate mark of men in general? Why the capacity to spend endless time with dull women – to spend it I won't say without being bored, but without minding that they are, without being driven off at a tangent by it; which comes to the same thing. I'm your dull woman, a part of the daily bread for which you pray at church. That covers your tracks more than anything.'

'And what covers yours?' asked Marcher, whom his dull woman could mostly to this extent amuse. 'I see of course what you mean by your saving me, in this way and that, so far as other people are concerned – I've seen it all along. Only what is it that saves *you*? I often think, you know, of that.'

She looked as if she sometimes thought of that too, but rather in a different way. 'Where other people, you mean, are concerned?'

'Well, you're really so in with me, you know – as a sort of result of my being so in with yourself. I mean of my having such an immense regard for you, being so tremendously mindful of all you've done for me. I sometimes ask myself if it's quite fair. Fair I mean to have so involved and – since one may say it – interested you. I almost feel as if you hadn't really had time to do anything else.'

'Anything else but be interested?' she asked. 'Ah what else does one ever want to be? If I've been "watching" with you, as we long ago agreed I was to do, watching's always in itself an absorption.'

'Oh certainly,' John Marcher said, 'if you hadn't had your curiosity – ! Only doesn't it sometimes come to you as time goes on that your curiosity isn't being particularly repaid?'

May Bartram had a pause. 'Do you ask that, by any chance, because you feel at all that yours isn't? I mean because you have to wait so long.'

Oh he understood what she meant! 'For the thing to happen that never does happen? For the beast to jump out? No, I'm just where I was about it. It isn't a matter as to which I can *choose*, I can decide for a change. It isn't one as to which there *can* be a change. It's in the lap of the gods. One's in the hands of one's law – there one is. As to the form the law will take, the way it will operate, that's its own affair.'

'Yes,' Miss Bartram replied; 'of course one's fate's coming, of course it *has* come in its own form and its own way, all the while. Only, you know, the form and the way in your case were to have been – well, something so exceptional and, as one may say, so particularly *your* own.'

Something in this made him look at her with suspicion. 'You say "were to *have* been", as if in your heart you had begun to doubt.'

'Oh!' she vaguely protested.

'As if you believed,' he went on, 'that nothing will now take place.'

She shook her head slowly but rather inscrutably. 'You're far from my thought.'

He continued to look at her. 'What then is the matter with you?'

'Well,' she said after another wait, 'the matter with me is simply that I'm more sure than ever my curiosity, as you call it, will be but too well repaid.'

They were frankly grave now; he had got up from his seat, had turned once more about the little drawing-room to which, year after year, he brought his inevitable topic; in which he had, as he might have said, tasted their intimate community with every sauce, where every object was as familiar to him as the things of his own house and the very carpets were worn with his fitful walk very much as the desks in old counting-houses are worn by the elbows of generations of clerks. The generations of his nervous moods had been at work there, and the place was the written history of his whole middle life. Under the impression of what his friend had just said he knew himself, for some reason, more aware of these things; which made him, after a moment, stop again before her. 'Is it possibly that you've grown afraid?'

'Afraid?' He thought, as she repeated the word, that his question had made her, a little, change colour; so that, lest he should have touched on a truth, he explained very kindly: 'You remember that that was what you asked *me* long ago – that first day at Weatherend.'

'Oh yes, and you told me you didn't know – that I was to see for myself. We've said little about it since, even in so long a time.'

'Precisely,' Marcher interposed – 'quite as if it were too delicate a matter for us to make free with. Quite as if we might find, on pressure, that I *am* afraid. For then,' he said, 'we shouldn't, should we? quite know what to do.'

She had for the time no answer to this question. 'There have been days when I thought you were. Only, of course,' she added, 'there have been days when we have thought almost anything.'

'Everything. Oh!' Marcher softly groaned, as with a gasp, half spent, at the face, more uncovered just then than it had been for a long while, of the imagination always with them. It had always had it's incalculable moments of glaring out, quite as with the very eyes of the very beast, and, used as he was to them, they could still draw from him the tribute of a sigh that rose from the depths of his being. All they had thought, first and last, rolled over him; the past seemed to have been reduced to mere barren speculation. This in fact was what the place had just struck him as so full of – the simplification of everything but the state of suspense. That remained only by seeming to hang in the void surrounding it. Even his original fear, if fear it had been, had lost itself in the desert. 'I judge, however,' he continued, 'that you see I'm not afraid now.'

'What I see, as I make it out, is that you've achieved something almost unprecedented in the way of getting used to danger. Living with it so long and so closely you've lost your sense of it; you know it's there, but you're indifferent, and you cease even, as of old, to have to whistle in the dark. Considering what the danger is,' May Bartram wound up, 'I'm bound to say I don't think your attitude could well be surpassed.'

John Marcher faintly smiled. 'It's heroic?'

'Certainly – call it that.'

It was what he would have liked indeed to call it. 'I *am* then a man of courage?'

'That's what you were to show me.'

He still, however, wondered. 'But doesn't the man of courage know what he's afraid of – or not afraid of? I don't know *that*, you see. I don't focus it. I can't name it. I only know I'm exposed.'

'Yes, but exposed – how shall I say? – so directly. So intimately. That's surely enough.'

'Enough to make you feel then – as what we may call the end and the upshot of our watch – that I'm not afraid?'

'You're not afraid. But it isn't,' she said, 'the end of our watch. That is, it isn't the end of yours. You've everything still to see.'

'Then why haven't you?' he asked. He had had, all along, today, the sense of her keeping something back, and he still had it. As this was his first impression of that it quite made a date. The case was the more marked as she didn't at first answer; which in turn made him go on. 'You know something I don't.' Then his voice, for that of a man of courage, trembled a little. 'You know what's to happen.' Her silence, with the face she showed, was almost a confession – it made him sure. 'You know, and you're afraid to tell me. It's so bad that you're afraid I'll find out.'

All this might be true, for she did look as if, unexpectedly to her, he had crossed some mystic line that she had secretly drawn round her. Yet she might, after all, not have worried; and the real climax was that he himself, at all events, needn't. 'You'll never find out.'

3

It was all to have made, none the less, as I have said, a date; which came out in the fact that again and again, even after long intervals, other things that passed between them were in relation to this hour but the character of recalls and results. Its immediate effect had been indeed rather to lighten insistence

– almost to provoke a reaction; as if their topic had dropped by its own weight and as if moreover, for that matter, Marcher had been visited by one of his occasional warnings against egotism. He had kept up, he felt, and very decently on the whole, his consciousness of the importance of not being selfish, and it was true that he had never sinned in that direction without promptly enough trying to press the scales the other way. He often repaired his fault, the season permitting, by inviting his friend to accompany him to the opera; and it not infrequently thus happened that, to show he didn't wish her to have but one sort of food for her mind, he was the cause of her appearing there with him a dozen nights in the month. It even happened that, seeing her home at such times, he occasionally went in with her to finish, as he called it, the evening, and, the better to make his point, sat down to the frugal but always careful little supper that awaited his pleasure. His point was made, he thought, by his not eternally insisting with her on himself; made for instance, at such hours, when it befell that, her piano at hand and each of them familiar with it, they went over passages of the opera together. It chanced to be on one of these occasions, however, that he reminded her of her not having answered a certain question he had put to her during the talk that had taken place between them on her last birthday. 'What is it that saves *you*?' – saved her, he meant, from that appearance of variation from the usual human type. If he had practically escaped remark, as she pretended, by doing, in the most important particular, what most men do – find the answer to life in patching up an alliance of a sort with a woman no better than himself – how had she escaped it, and how could the alliance, such as it was, since they must suppose it had been more or less noticed, have failed to make her rather positively talked about?

'I never said,' May Bartram replied, 'that it hadn't made me a good deal talked about.'

'Ah well then you're not "saved".'

'It hasn't been a question for me. If you've had your woman I've had,' she said, 'my man.'

'And you mean that makes you all right?'

Oh it was always as if there were so much to say!

'I don't know why it shouldn't make me – humanly, which is what we're speaking of – as right as it makes you.'

'I see,' Marcher returned. ' "Humanly", no doubt, as showing that you're living for something. Not, that is, just for me and my secret.'

May Bartram smiled. 'I don't pretend it exactly shows that I'm not living for you. It's my intimacy with you that's in question.'

He laughed as he saw what she meant. 'Yes, but since, as you say, I'm only, so far as people make out, ordinary, you're – aren't you? no more than ordinary either. You help me to pass for a man like another. So if I *am*, as I understand you, you're not compromised. Is that it?'

She had another of her waits, but she spoke clearly enough. 'That's it. It's all that concerns me – to help you to pass for a man like another.'

He was careful to acknowledge the remark handsomely. 'How kind, how beautiful, you are to me! How shall I ever repay you?'

She had her last grave pause, as if there might be a choice of ways. But she chose. 'By going on as you are.'

It was into this going on as he was that they relapsed, and really for so long a time that the day inevitably came for a further sounding of their depths. These depths, constantly bridged over by a structure firm enough in spite of its lightness and of its occasional oscillation in the somewhat vertiginous air, invited on occasion, in the interest of their nerves, a dropping of the plummet and a measurement of the abyss. A difference had been made moreover, once for all, by the fact that she had all the while not appeared to feel the need of rebutting his charge of an idea within her that she didn't dare to express – a charge uttered just before one of the fullest of their later discussions ended. It had come up for him then that she 'knew' something and that what she knew was bad – too bad to tell him. When he had spoken of it as visibly so bad that she was afraid he might find it out, her reply had left the matter too equivocal to be let alone and yet, for Marcher's special sensibility, almost too formidable again to touch. He circled about it at a distance that alternately narrowed and widened and that still wasn't much affected by the consciousness in him that there was nothing she could 'know', after all, any better than he did. She had no source of knowledge he hadn't equally – except of course that she might have finer nerves. That was what women had where they were interested; they made out things, where people were concerned, that the people often couldn't have made out for themselves. Their nerves, their sensibility, their imagination, were conductors and revealers, and the beauty of May Bartram was in particular that she had given herself so to his case. He felt in these days what, oddly enough, he had never felt before, the growth of a dread of losing her by some catastrophe – some catastrophe that yet wouldn't at all be *the* catastrophe: partly because she had almost of a sudden begun to strike him as more useful to him than ever yet, and partly by reason of an appearance of uncertainty in her health, coincident and equally new. It was characteristic of the inner detachment he had hitherto so successfully cultivated and to which our whole account of him is a reference, it was characteristic that his complications, such as they were, had never yet seemed so as at this crisis to thicken about him, even to the point of making him ask himself if he were, by any chance, of a truth, within sight or sound, within touch or reach, within the immediate jurisdiction, of the thing that waited.

When the day came, as come it had to, that his friend confessed to him her fear of a deep disorder in her blood, he felt somehow the shadow of a change and the chill of a shock. He immediately began to imagine aggravations and disasters, and above all to think of her peril as the direct menace for himself of personal privation. This indeed gave him one of those partial recoveries of equanimity that were agreeable to him – it showed him that what was still first in his mind was the loss she herself might suffer. 'What if she should have to die before knowing, before seeing – ?' It would have been brutal, in the early stages of her trouble, to put that question to her; but it had immediately sounded for him to his own concern, and the possibility was what most made him sorry for her. If she did 'know', moreover, in the sense of her having had some – what should he think? – mystical irresistible light, this would make the matter not better, but worse, inasmuch as her original adoption of his own curiosity had quite become the basis of her life. She had been living to see what would *be* to be seen, and it would quite lacerate her to have to give up before the accomplishment of the vision. These reflections, as I say, quickened his generosity; yet, make them as he might, he saw himself, with the lapse of the period, more and more disconcerted. It lapsed for him with a strange steady sweep, and the oddest oddity was that it gave him, independently of the threat of much inconvenience, almost the only positive surprise his career, if career it could be called, had yet offered him. She kept the house as she had never done; he had to go to her to see her – she could meet him nowhere now, though there was scarce a corner of their loved old London in which she hadn't in the past, at one time or another, done so; and he found her always seated by her fire in the deep old-fashioned chair she was less and less able to leave. He had been struck one day, after an absence exceeding his usual measure, with her suddenly looking much older to him than he had ever thought of her being; then he recognised that the suddenness was all on his side – he had just simply and suddenly noticed. She looked older because inevitably, after so many years, she *was* old, or almost; which was of course true in still greater measure of her companion. If she was old, or almost, John Marcher assuredly was, and yet it was her showing of the lesson, not his own, that brought the truth home to him. His surprises began here; when once they had begun they multiplied; they came rather with a rush: it was as if, in the oddest way in the world, they had all been kept back, sown in a thick cluster, for the late afternoon of life, the time at which for people in general the unexpected has died out.

One of them was that he should have caught himself – for he *had* so done – *really* wondering if the great accident would take form now as nothing more than his being condemned to see this charming woman, this admirable friend, pass away from him. He had never so unreservedly qualified her as while confronted in thought with such a possibility; in spite of which there was small doubt for him that as an answer to his long riddle the mere effacement of even so fine a feature of his situation would be an abject anticlimax. It would represent, as connected with his past attitude, a drop of dignity under the shadow of which his existence could only become the most grotesques of failures. He had been far from holding it a failure – long as he had waited for the appearance that was to make it a success. He had waited for quite another thing, not for such a thing as that. The breath of his good faith came short, however, as he recognised how long he had waited, or how long at least his companion had. That she, at all events, might be recorded as having waited in vain – this affected him sharply, and all the more because of his at first having done little more than amuse himself with the idea. It grew more grave as the gravity of her condition grew, and the state of mind it produced in him, which he himself ended by watching as if it had been some definite disfigurement of his outer person, may pass for another of his surprises. This conjoined itself still with another, the really stupefying consciousness of a question that he would have allowed to shape itself had he dared. What did everything mean – what, that is, did *she* mean, she and her vain waiting and her probable death and the soundless admonition of it all – unless that, at this time of day, it was simply, it was overwhelmingly too late? He had never at any stage of his queer consciousness admitted the whisper of such a correction; he had never till within these last few months been so false to his conviction as not to hold that what was to come to him had time, whether *he* struck himself as having it or not. That at last, at last, he certainly hadn't it, to speak of, or had it but in the scantiest measure – such, soon enough, as things went with him, became the inference with which his old obsession had to reckon: and this it was not helped to do by the more and more confirmed appearance that the great vagueness casting the long shadow in which he had lived had, to attest itself, almost no margin left. Since it was in time that he was to have met his fate, so it was in time that his fate was to have acted; and as he waked up to the sense of no longer being young, which was exactly the sense of being stale, just as that, in turn, was the sense of being weak, he waked up to another matter beside. It all hung together; they were subject, he and the great vagueness, to an equal and indivisible law. When the possibilities themselves had accordingly turned stale, when the secret of the gods had grown faint, had perhaps even quite evaporated, that, and that only, was failure. It wouldn't have been failure to be bankrupt, dishonoured, pilloried, hanged; it was failure not to be anything. And so, in the dark valley into which his path had taken its unlooked-for twist, he wondered not a little as he groped. He didn't care what awful crash might overtake him, with what ignominy or what monstrosity he might yet be associated – since he wasn't after all too utterly old to suffer – if it would only be decently proportionate to the posture he had kept, all his life, in the threatened presence of it. He had but one desire left – that he shouldn't have been 'sold'.

Then it was that, one afternoon, while the spring of the year was young and new she met all in her own way his frankest betrayal of these alarms. He had gone in late to see her, but evening hadn't settled and she was presented to him in that long fresh light of waning April days which affects us often with a sadness sharper than the greyest hours of autumn. The week had been warm, the spring was supposed to have begun early, and May Bartram sat, for the first time in the year, without a fire; a fact that, to Marcher's sense, gave the scene of which she formed part a smooth and ultimate look, an air of knowing, in its immaculate order and cold meaningless cheer, that it would never see a fire again. Her own aspect – he could scarce have said why – intensified this note. Almost as white as wax, with the marks and signs in her face as numerous and as fine as if they had been etched by a needle, with soft white draperies relieved by a faded green scarf on the delicate tone of which the years had further refined, she was the picture of a serene and exquisite but impenetrable sphinx, whose head, or indeed all whose person, might have been powdered with silver. She was a sphinx, yet with her white petals and green fronds she might have been a lily too – only an artificial lily, wonderfully imitated and constantly kept, without dust or stain, though not exempt from a slight droop and a complexity of faint creases, under some clear glass bell. The perfection of household care, of high polish and finish, always reigned in her rooms, but they now looked most as if everything had been wound up, tucked in, put away, so that she might sit with folded hands and with nothing more to do. She was 'out of it', to Marcher's vision; her work was over; she communicated with him as across some gulf or from some island of rest that she had already reached, and it made him feel strangely abandoned. Was it – or rather wasn't it – that if for so long she had been watching with him the answer to their question must have swum into her ken and taken on its name, so that her occupation was verily gone? He had as much as charged her with this in saying to her, many months before, that she even then knew something she was keeping from him. It was a point he had never since ventured to press, vaguely fearing as he did that it might become a difference, perhaps a disagreement, between them. He had in this later time turned nervous, which was what he in all the other years had never been; and the oddity was that his nervousness should have waited till he had begun to doubt, should have held off so long as he was sure. There was something, it seemed to him, that the wrong word would bring down on his head, something that would so at least ease off his tension. But he wanted not to speak the wrong word; that would make everything ugly. He wanted the knowledge he lacked to drop on him, if drop it could, by its own august weight. If she was to forsake him it was surely for her to take leave. This was why he didn't directly ask her again what she knew; but it was also why, approaching the matter from another side, he said to her in the course of his visit: 'What do you regard as the very worst that at this time of day *can* happen to me?'

He had asked her that in the past often enough; they had, with the odd irregular rhythm of their intensities and avoidances, exchanged ideas about it and then had seen the ideas washed away by cool intervals, washed like figures traced in sea-sand. It had ever been the mark of their talk that the oldest allusions in it required but a little dismissal and reaction to come out again, sounding for the hour as new. She could thus at present meet his enquiry quite freshly and patiently. 'Oh yes, I've repeatedly thought, only it always seemed to me of old that I couldn't quite make up my mind. I thought of dreadful things, between which it was difficult to choose; and so must you have done.'

'Rather! I feel now as if I had scarce done anything else. I appear to myself to have spent my life in thinking of nothing but dreadful things. A great many of them I've at different times named to you, but there were others I couldn't name.'

'They were too, too dreadful?'

'Too, too dreadful – some of them.'

She looked at him a minute, and there came to him as he met it, an inconsequent sense that her eyes, when one got their full clearness, were still as beautiful as they had been in youth, only beautiful with a strange cold light – a light that somehow was a part of the effect, if it wasn't rather a part of the cause, of the pale hard sweetness of the season and the hour. 'And yet,' she said at last, 'there are horrors we've mentioned.'

It deepened the strangeness to see her, as such a figure in such a picture, talk of 'horrors', but she was to do in a few minutes something stranger yet – though even of this he was to take the full measure but afterwards – and the note of it already trembled. It was, for the matter of that, one of the signs that her eyes were having again the high flicker of their prime. He had to admit, however, what she said. 'Oh yes, there were times when we did go far.' He caught himself in the act of speaking as if it all were over. Well, he wished it were; and the consummation depended for him clearly more and more on his friend.

But she had now a soft smile. 'Oh far – !'

It was oddly ironic. 'Do you mean you're prepared to go further?'

She was frail and ancient and charming as she continued to look at him, yet it was rather as if she had lost the thread. 'Do you consider that we went far?'

'Why I thought it the point you were just making – that we *had* looked most things in the face.'

'Including each other?' She still smiled. 'But you're quite right. We've had together great imaginations, often great fears; but some of them have been unspoken.'

'Then the worst – we haven't faced that. I *could* face it, I believe, if I knew what you think it. I feel,' he explained, 'as if I had lost my power to conceive such things.' And he wondered if he looked as blank as he sounded. 'It's spent.'

'Then why do you assume,' she asked, 'that mine isn't?'

'Because you've given me signs to the contrary. It isn't a question for you of conceiving, imagining, comparing. It isn't a question now of choosing.' At last he came out with it. 'You know something I don't. You've shown me that before.'

These last words had affected her, he made out in a moment, exceedingly, and she spoke with firmness. 'I've shown you, my dear, nothing.'

He shook his head. 'You can't hide it.'

'Oh, oh!' May Bartram sounded over what she couldn't hide. It was almost a smothered groan.

'You admitted it months ago, when I spoke of it to you as of something you were afraid I should find out. Your answer was that I couldn't, that I wouldn't, and I don't pretend I have. But you had something therefore in mind, and I see now how it must have been, how it still is, the possibility that, of all possibilities, has settled itself for you as the worst. This,' he went on, 'is why I appeal to you. I'm only afraid of ignorance today – I'm not afraid of knowledge.' And then as for a while she said nothing: 'What makes me sure is that I see in your face and feel here, in this air and amid these appearances, that you're out of it. You've done. You've had your experience. You leave me to my fate.'

Well, she listened, motionless and white in her chair, as on a decision to be made, so that her manner was fairly an avowal, though still, with a small fine inner stiffness, an imperfect surrender. 'It *would* be the worst,' she finally let herself say. 'I mean the thing I've never said.'

It hushed him a moment. 'More monstrous than all the monstrosities we've named?'

'More monstrous. Isn't that what you sufficiently express,' she asked, 'in calling it the worst?'

Marcher thought. 'Assuredly – if you mean, as I do, something that includes all the loss and all the shame that are thinkable.'

'It would if it *should* happen,' said May Bartram. 'What we're speaking of, remember, is only my idea.'

'It's your belief,' Marcher returned. 'That's enough for me. I feel your beliefs are right. Therefore if, having this one, you give me no more light on it, you abandon me.'

'No, no!' she repeated. 'I'm with you – don't you see? – still.' And as to make it more vivid to him she rose from her chair – a movement she seldom risked in these days – and showed herself, all draped and all soft, in her fairness and slimness. 'I haven't forsaken you.'

It was really, in its effort against weakness, a generous assurance, and had the success of the impulse not, happily, been great, it would have touched him to pain more than to pleasure. But the cold charm in her eyes had spread, as she hovered before him, to all the rest of her person, so that it was for the minute almost a recovery of youth. He couldn't pity her for that; he could only take her as she showed – as capable even yet of helping him. It was as if, at the same time, her light might at any instant go out; wherefore he must make the most of it. There passed before him with intensity the three or four things he wanted most to know; but the question that came of itself to his lips really covered the others. 'Then tell me if I shall consciously suffer.'

She promptly shook her head. 'Never!'

It confirmed the authority he imputed to her, and it produced on him an extraordinary effect. 'Well, what's better than that? Do you call that the worst?'

'You think nothing is better?' she asked.

She seemed to mean something so special that he again sharply wondered, though still with the dawn of a prospect of relief. 'Why not, if one doesn't *know*?' After which, as their eyes, over his question, met in a silence, the dawn deepened, and something to his purpose came prodigiously out of her very face. His own, as he took it in, suddenly flushed to the forehead, and he gasped with the force of a perception to which, on the instant, everything fitted. The sound of his gasp filled the air; then he became articulate. 'I see – if I don't suffer!'

In her own look, however, was doubt. 'You see what?'

'Why what you mean – what you've always meant.'

She again shook her head. 'What I mean isn't what I've always meant. It's different.'

'It's something new?'

She hung back from it a little. 'Something new. It's not what you think. I see what you think.'

His divination drew breath then; only her correction might be wrong. 'It isn't that I *am* a blockhead?' he asked between faintness and grimness. 'It isn't that it's all a mistake?'

'A mistake?' she pityingly echoed. *That* possibility, for her, he saw, would be monstrous; and if she guaranteed him the immunity from pain it would accordingly not be what she had in mind. 'Oh no,' she declared; 'it's nothing of that sort. You've been right.'

Yet he couldn't help asking himself if she weren't, thus pressed, speaking but to save him. It seemed to him he should be most in a hole if his history should prove all a platitude. 'Are you telling me the truth, so that I shan't have been a bigger idiot than I can bear to know? I *haven't* lived with a vain imagination, in the most besotted illusion? I haven't waited but to see the door shut in my face?'

She shook her head again. 'However the case stands *that* isn't the truth. Whatever the reality, it *is* a reality. The door isn't shut. The door's open,' said May Bartram.

'Then something's to come?'

She waited once again, always with her cold sweet eyes on him. 'It's never too late.' She had, with her gliding step, diminished the distance between them, and she stood nearer to him, close to him, a minute, as if still charged with the unspoken. Her movement might have been for some finer emphasis of what she was at once hesitating and deciding to say. He had been standing by the chimney-piece, fireless and sparely adorned, a small perfect old French clock and two morsels of rosy Dresden constituting all its furniture; and her hand grasped the shelf while she kept him waiting, grasped it a little as for support and encouragement. She only kept him waiting, however; that is he only waited. It had become suddenly, from her movement and attitude, beautiful and vivid to him that she had something more to give him; her wasted face delicately shone with it – it glittered almost as with the white lustre of silver in her expression. She was right, incontestably, for what he saw in her face was the truth, and strangely, without consequence, while their talk of it as dreadful was still in the air, she appeared to present it as inordinately soft. This, prompting bewilderment, made him but gape the more gratefully for her revelation, so that they continued for some minutes silent, her face shining at him, her contact imponderably pressing, and his stare all kind but all expectant. The end, none the less, was that what he had expected failed to come to him. Something else took place instead, which seemed to consist at first in the mere closing of her eyes. She gave way at the same instant to a slow fine shudder, and though he remained staring – though he stared in fact but the harder – turned off and regained her chair. It was the end of what she had been intending, but it left him thinking only of that.

'Well, you don't say – ?'

She had touched in her passage a bell near the chimney and had sunk back strangely pale. 'I'm afraid I'm too ill.'

'Too ill to tell me?' it sprang up sharp to him, and almost to his lips, the fear she might die without giving him light. He checked himself in time from so expressing his question, but she answered as if she had heard the words.

'Don't you know – now?'

' "Now" – ?' She had spoken as if some difference had been made within the moment. But her maid, quickly obedient to her bell, was already with them. 'I know nothing.' And he was afterwards to say to himself that he must have spoken with odious impatience, such an impatience as to show that, supremely disconcerted, he washed his hands of the whole question.

'Oh!' said May Bartram.

'Are you in pain?' he asked as the woman went to her.

'No,' said May Bartram.

Her maid, who had put an arm round her as if to take her to her room, fixed on him eyes that appealingly contradicted her; in spite of which, however, he showed once more his mystification.

'What then has happened?'

She was once more, with her companion's help, on her feet, and, feeling withdrawal imposed on him, he had blankly found his hat and gloves and had reached the door. Yet he waited for her answer.

'What *was* to,' she said.

5

He came back the next day, but she was then unable to see him, and as it was literally the first time this had occurred in the long stretch of their acquaintance he turned away, defeated and sore, almost angry – or feeling at least that such a break in their custom was really the beginning of the end – and wandered alone with his thoughts, especially with the one he was least able to keep down. She was dying and he would lose her; she was dying and his life would end. He stopped in the park, into which he had passed, and stared before him at his recurrent doubt. Away from her the doubt pressed again; in her presence he had believed her, but as he felt his forlornness he threw himself into the explanation that, nearest at hand, had most of a miserable warmth for him and least of a cold torment. She had deceived him to save him – to put him off with something in which he should be able to rest. What could the thing that was to happen to him be, after all, but just this thing that had began to happen? Her dying, her death, his consequent solitude – that was what he had figured as the beast in the jungle, that was what had been in the lap of the gods. He had had her word for it as he left her – what else on earth could she have meant? It wasn't a thing of a monstrous order; not a fate rare and distinguished; not a stroke of fortune that overwhelmed and immortalised; it had only the stamp of the common doom. But poor Marcher at this hour judged the common doom sufficient. It would serve his turn, and even as the consummation of infinite waiting he would bend his pride to accept it. He sat down on a bench in the twilight. He hadn't been a fool. Something had *been*, as she had said, to come. Before he rose indeed it had quite struck him that the final fact really matched with the long avenue through which he had had to reach it. As sharing his suspense and as giving herself all, giving her life, to bring it to an end, she had come with him every step of the way. He had lived by her aid, and to leave her behind would be cruelly, damnably to miss her. What could be more overwhelming than that?

Well, he was to know within the week; for though she kept him a while at bay, left him restless and wretched during a series of days on each of which he asked about her only again to have to turn away, she ended his trial by receiving him where she had always received him. Yet she had been brought out at some hazard into the presence of so many of the things that were, consciously, vainly, half their past, and there was scant service left in the gentleness of her mere desire, all too visible, to check his obsession and wind up his long trouble. That was clearly what she wanted; the one thing more for her own peace while she could still put out her hand. He was so affected by her state that, once seated by her chair, he was moved to let everything go; it was she herself therefore who brought him back, took up again, before she dismissed him, her last word of the other time. She showed how she wished to leave their business in order. 'I'm not sure you understood. You've nothing to wait for more. It *has* come.'

Oh, how he looked at her! 'Really?'

'Really.'

'The thing that, as you said, *was* to?'

'The thing that we began in our youth to watch for.'

Face to face with her once more he believed her; it was a claim to which he had so abjectly little to oppose. 'You mean that it has come as a positive definite occurrence, with a name and a date?'

'Positive. Definite. I don't know about the "name", but, oh with a date!'

He found himself again too helplessly at sea. 'But come in the night – come and passed me by?'

May Bartram had her strange faint smile. 'Oh no, it hasn't passed you by!'

'But if I haven't been aware of it and it hasn't touched me – ?'

'Ah, your not being aware of it' – and she seemed to hesitate an instant to deal with this – 'your not being aware of it is the strangeness in the strangeness. It's the wonder *of* the wonder.' She spoke as with the softness almost of a sick child, yet now at last, at the end of all, with the perfect straightness of a sibyl. She visibly knew that she knew, and the effect on him was of something co-ordinate, in its high character, with the law that had ruled him. It was the true voice of the law; so on her lips would the law itself have sounded. 'It *has* touched you,' she went on. 'It has done its office. It has made you all its own.'

'So utterly without my knowing it?'

'So utterly without your knowing it.' His hand, as he leaned to her, was on the arm of her chair, and, dimly smiling always now, she placed her own on it. 'It's enough if I know it.'

'Oh!' he confusedly breathed, as she herself of late so often had done.

'What I long ago said is true. You'll never know now, and I think you ought to be content. You've *had* it,' said May Bartram.

'But had what?'

'Why what was to have marked you out. The proof of your law. It has acted. I'm too glad,' she then bravely added, 'to have been able to see what it's *not*.'

He continued to attach his eyes to her, and with the sense that it was all beyond him, and that *she* was too, he would still have sharply challenged her hadn't he so felt it an abuse of her weakness to do more than take devoutly what she gave him, take it hushed as to a revelation. If he did speak, it was out of the foreknowledge of his loneliness to come. 'If you're glad of what it's "not" it might then have been worse?'

She turned her eyes away, she looked straight before her; with which after a moment: 'Well, you know our fears.'

He wondered. 'It's something then we never feared?'

On this slowly she turned to him. 'Did we ever dream, with all our dreams, that we should sit and talk of it thus?'

He tried for a little to make out that they had; but it was as if their dreams, numberless enough, were in solution in some thick cold mist through which thought lost itself. 'It might have been that we couldn't talk.'

'Well' – she did her best for him – 'not from this side. This, you see,' she said, 'is the *other* side.'

'I think,' poor Marcher returned, 'that all sides are the same to me.' Then, however, as she gently shook her head in correction: 'We mightn't, as it were, have got across – ?'

'To where we are – no. We're *here*' – she made her weak emphasis.

'And much good does it do us!' was her friend's frank comment.

'It does us the good it can. It does us the good that *it* isn't here. It's past. It's behind,' said May Bartram. 'Before – ' but her voice dropped.

He had got up, not to tire her, but it was hard to combat his yearning. She after all told him nothing but that his light had failed – which he knew well enough without her. 'Before – ?' he blankly echoed.

'Before you see, it was always to *come*. That kept it present.'

'Oh I don't care what comes now! Besides,' Marcher added, 'it seems to me I liked it better present, as you say, than I can like it absent with *your* absence.'

'Oh mine!' – and her pale hands made light of it.

'With the absence of everything.' He had a dreadful sense of standing there before her for – so far as anything but this proved, this bottomless drop was concerned – the last time of their life. It rested on him with a weight he felt he could scarce bear, and this weight it apparently was that still pressed out what remained in him of speakable protest. 'I believe you; but I can't begin to pretend I understand. *Nothing*, for me, is past; nothing *will* pass till I pass myself, which I pray my stars may be as soon as possible. Say, however,' he added, 'that I've eaten my cake, as you contend, to the last crumb – how can the thing I've never felt at all be the thing I was marked out to feel?'

She met him perhaps less directly, but she met him unperturbed. 'You take your "feelings" for granted. You were to suffer your fate. That was not necessarily to know it.'

'How in the world – when what is such knowledge but suffering?'

She looked up at him a while in silence. 'No – you don't understand.'

'I suffer,' said John Marcher.

'Don't, don't!'

'How can I help at least *that*?'

'*Don't*!' May Bartram repeated.

She spoke it in a tone so special, in spite of her weakness, that he stared an instant – stared as if some light, hitherto hidden, had shimmered across his vision. Darkness again closed over it, but the gleam had already become for him an idea. 'Because I haven't the right – ?'

'Don't *know* – when you needn't,' she mercifully urged. 'You needn't – for we shouldn't.'

'Shouldn't?' If he could but know what she meant!

'No – it's too much.'

'Too much?' he still asked but with a mystification that was the next moment of a sudden to give way. Her words, if they meant something, affected him in this light – the light also of her wasted face – as meaning *all*, and the sense of what knowledge had been for herself came over him with a rush which broke through into a question. 'Is it of that then you're dying?'

She but watched him, gravely at first, as to see, with this, where he was, and she might have seen something or feared something that moved her sympathy. 'I would live for you still – if I could.' Her eyes closed for a little, as if, withdrawn into herself, she were for a last time trying. 'But I can't!' she said as she raised them again to take leave of him.

She couldn't indeed, as but too promptly and sharply appeared, and he had no vision of her after this that was anything but darkness and doom. They had parted for ever in that strange talk; access to her chamber of pain, rigidly guarded, was almost wholly forbidden him; he was feeling now moreover, in the face of doctors, nurses, the two or three relatives attracted doubtless by the presumption of what she had to 'leave', how few were the rights, as they were called in such cases, that he had to put forward, and how odd it might even seem that their intimacy shouldn't have given him more of them. The stupidest fourth cousin had more, even though she had been nothing in such a person's life. She had been a feature of features in *his*, for what else was it to have been so indispensable? Strange beyond saying were the ways of existence, baffling for him the anomaly of his lack, as he felt it to be, of producible claim. A woman might have been, as it were, everything to him, and it might yet present him in no connection that anyone seemed held to recognise. If this was the case in these closing weeks it was the case more sharply on the occasion of the last offices rendered, in the great grey London cemetery, to what had been mortal, to what had been precious, in his friend. The concourse at her grave was not numerous, but he saw himself treated as scarce more nearly concerned with it than if there had been a thousand others. He was in short from this moment face to face with the fact that he was to profit extraordinarily little by the interest May Bartram had taken in him. He couldn't quite have said what he expected, but he hadn't surely expected this approach to a double privation. Not only had her interest failed him, but he seemed to feel himself unattended – and for a reason he couldn't seize – by the distinction, the dignity, the propriety, if nothing else, of the man markedly bereaved. It was as if, in the view of society he had not *been* markedly bereaved, as if there still failed some sign or proof of it, and as if none the less his character could never be affirmed nor the deficiency ever made up. There were moments as the weeks went by when he would have liked, by some almost aggressive act, to take his stand on the intimacy of his loss, in order that it *might* be questioned and his retort, to the relief of his spirit, so recorded; but the moments of an irritation more helpless followed fast on these, the moments during which, turning things over with a good conscience but with a bare horizon, he found himself wondering if he oughtn't to have begun, so to speak, further back.

He found himself wondering indeed at many things, and this last speculation had others to keep it company. What could he have done, after all, in her lifetime, without giving them both, as it were, away? He couldn't have made known she was watching him, for that would have published the superstition of the beast. This was what closed his mouth now – now that the jungle had been thrashed to vacancy and that the beast had stolen away. It sounded too foolish and too flat; the difference for him in this particular, the extinction in his life of the element of suspense, was such as in fact to surprise him. He could scarce have said what the effect resembled; the abrupt cessation, the positive prohibition, of music perhaps, more than anything else, in some place all adjusted and all accustomed to sonority and to attention. If he could at any rate have conceived lifting the veil from his image at some moment of the past (what had he done, after all, if not lift it to *her*?), so to do this today, to talk to people at large of the jungle cleared and confide to them that he now felt it as safe, would have been not only to see them listen as to a goodwife's tale, but really to hear himself tell one. What it presently came to in truth was that poor Marcher waded through his beaten grass, where no life stirred, where no breath sounded, where no evil eye seemed to gleam from a possible lair, very much as if vaguely looking for the beast, and still more as if acutely missing it. He walked about in an existence that had grown strangely more spacious, and, stopping fitfully in places where the undergrowth of life struck him as closer, asked himself yearningly, wondered secretly and sorely, if it would have lurked here or there. It would have at all events *sprung*; what was at least complete was his belief in the truth itself of the assurance given him. The change from his old sense to his new was absolute and final: what was to happen had so absolutely and finally happened that he was as little able to know a fear for his future as to know a hope; so absent in short was any question of anything still to come. He was to live entirely with the other question, that of his unidentified past, that of his having to see his fortune impenetrably muffled and masked.

The torment of this vision became then his occupation; he couldn't perhaps have consented to live but for the possibility of guessing. She had told him, his friend, not to guess; she had forbidden him, so far as he might, to know, and she had even in a sort denied the power in him to learn: which were so many things, precisely, to deprive him of rest. It wasn't that he wanted, he argued for fairness, that anything past and done should repeat itself; it was only that he shouldn't, as an anticlimax, have been taken sleeping so sound as not to be able to win back by an effort of thought the lost stuff of consciousness. He declared to himself at moments that he would either win it back or have done with consciousness for ever; he made this idea his one motive in fine, made it so much his passion that none other, to compare with it, seemed ever to have touched him. The lost stuff of consciousness became thus for him as a strayed or stolen child to an unappeasable father; he hunted it up and down very much as if he were knocking at doors and enquiring of the police. This was the spirit in which, inevitably, he set himself to travel; he started on a journey that was to be as long as he could make it; it danced before him that, as the other side of the globe couldn't possibly have less to say to him, it might, by a possibility of suggestion, have more. Before he quitted London, however, he made a pilgrimage to May Bartram's grave, took his way to it through the endless avenues of the grim suburban necropolis, sought it out in the wilderness of tombs, and, though he had come but for the renewal of the act of farewell, found himself, when he had at last stood by it, beguiled into long intensities. He stood for an hour, powerless to turn away and yet powerless to penetrate the darkness of death; fixing with his eyes her inscribed name and date, beating his forehead against the fact of the secret they kept, drawing his breath, while he waited, as if some sense would in pity of him rise from the stones. He kneeled on the stones, however, in vain; they kept what they concealed; and if the face of the tomb did become a face for him it was because her two names became a pair of eyes that didn't know him. He gave them a last long look, but no palest light broke.

6

He stayed away, after this, for a year; he visited the depths of Asia, spending himself on scenes of romantic interest, of superlative sanctity; but what was present to him everywhere was that for a man who had known what *he* had known the world was vulgar and vain. The state of mind in which he had lived for so many years shone out to him, in reflection, as a light that coloured and refined, a light beside which the glow of the East was garish cheap and thin. The terrible truth was that he had lost – with everything else – a distinction as well; the things he saw couldn't help being common when he had become common to look at them. He was simply now one of them himself – he was in the dust, without a peg for the sense of difference; and there were hours when, before the temples of gods and the sepulchres of kings, his spirit turned for nobleness of association to the barely discriminated slab in the London suburb. That had become for him, and more intensely with time and distance, his one witness of a past glory. It was all that was left to him for proof or pride, yet the past glories of pharaohs were nothing to him as he thought of it. Small wonder then that he came back to it on the morrow of his return. He was drawn there this time as irresistibly as the other, yet with a confidence, almost, that was doubtless the effect of the many months that had elapsed. He had lived, in spite of himself, into his change of feeling, and in wandering over the earth had wandered, as might be said, from the circumference to the centre of his desert. He had settled to his safety and accepted perforce his extinction; figuring to himself, with some colour, in the likeness of certain little old men he remembered to have seen, of whom, all meagre and wizened as they might look, it was related that they had in their time fought twenty duels or been loved by ten princesses. They indeed had been wondrous for others while he was but wondrous for himself; which, however, was exactly the cause of his haste to renew the wonder by getting back, as he might put it, into his own presence. That had quickened his steps and checked his delay. If his visit was prompt it was because he had been separated so long from the part of himself that alone he now valued.

It's accordingly not false to say that he reached his goal with a certain elation and stood there again with a certain assurance. The creature beneath the sod knew of his rare experience, so that, strangely now, the place had lost for him its mere blankness of expression. It met him in mildness – not, as before, in mockery; it wore for him the air of conscious greeting that we find, after absence, in things that have closely belonged to us and which seem to confess of themselves to the connection. The plot of ground, the graven tablet, the tended flowers affected him so as belonging to him that he resembled for the hour a contented landlord reviewing a piece of property. Whatever had happened – well, had happened. He had not come back this time with the vanity of that question, his former worrying 'What, *what*?' now practically so spent. Yet he would none the less never again so cut himself off from the spot; he would come back to it every month, for if he did nothing else by its aid he at least held up his head. It thus grew for him, in the oddest way, a positive resource; he carried out his idea of periodical returns, which took their place at last among the most inveterate of his habits. What it all amounted to, oddly enough, was that in his finally so simplified world this garden of death gave him the few square feet of earth on which he could still most live. It was as if, being nothing anywhere else for anyone, nothing even for himself, he were just everything here, and if not for a crowd of witnesses or indeed for any witness but John Marcher, then by clear right of the register that he could scan like an open page. The open page was the tomb of his friend, and *there* were the facts of the past, there the truth of his life, there the backward reaches in which he could lose himself. He did this from time to time with such effect that he seemed to wander through the old years with his hand in the arm of a companion who was, in the most extraordinary manner, his other, his younger self; and to wander, which was more extraordinary yet, round and round a third presence – not wandering she, but stationary, still, whose eyes, turning with his revolution, never ceased to follow him, and whose seat was his point, so to speak, of orientation. Thus in short he settled to live – feeding only on the sense that he once *had* lived, and dependent on it not alone for a support but for an identity.

It sufficed him in its way for months and the year elapsed; it would doubtless even have carried him further but for an accident, superficially slight, which moved him, quite in another direction, with a force beyond any of his impressions of Egypt or of India. It was a thing of the merest chance – the turn, as he afterwards felt, of a hair, though he was indeed to live to believe that if light hadn't come to him in this particular fashion it would still have come in another. He was to live to believe this, I say, though he was not to live, I may not less definitely mention, to do much else. We allow him at any rate the benefit of the conviction, struggling up for him at the end, that, whatever might have happened or not happened, he would have come round of himself to the light. The incident of an autumn day had put the match to the train laid from of old by his misery. With the light before him he knew that even of late his ache had only been smothered. It was strangely drugged, but it throbbed; at the touch it began to bleed. And the touch, in the event, was the face of a fellow-mortal. This face, one grey afternoon when the leaves were thick in the alleys, looked into Marcher's own, at the cemetery, with an expression like the cut of a blade. He felt it, that is, so deep down that he winced at the steady thrust. The person who so mutely assaulted him was a figure he had noticed, on reaching his own goal, absorbed by a grave a short distance away, a grave apparently fresh, so that the emotion of the visitor would probably match it for frankness. This fact alone forbade further attention, though during the time he stayed he remained vaguely conscious of his neighbour, a middle-aged man apparently, in mourning, whose bowed back, among the clustered monuments and mortuary yews, was constantly presented. Marcher's theory that these were elements in contact with which he himself revived, had suffered, on this occasion, it may be granted, a marked, an excessive check. The autumn day was dire for him as none had recently been, and he rested with a heaviness he had not yet known on the low stone table that bore May Bartram's name. He rested without power to move, as if some spring in him, some spell vouchsafed, had suddenly been broken for ever. If he could have done that moment as he wanted he would simply have stretched himself on the slab that was ready to take him, treating it as a place prepared to receive his last sleep. What in all the wide world had he now to keep awake for? He stared before him with the question, and it was then that, as one of the cemetery walks passed near him, he caught the shock of the face.

His neighbour at the other grave had withdrawn, as he himself, with force enough in him, would have done by now, and was advancing along the path on his way to one of the gates. This brought him close, and his pace was slow, so that – and all the more as there was a kind of hunger in his look – the two men were for a minute directly confronted. Marcher knew him at once for one of the deeply stricken – a perception so sharp that nothing else in the picture comparatively lived, neither his dress, his age, nor his presumable character and class; nothing lived but the deep ravage of the features that he showed. He *showed* them – that was the point; he was moved, as he passed, by some impulse that was either a signal for sympathy or, more possibly, a challenge to an opposed sorrow. He might already have been aware of our friend, might at some previous hour have noticed in him the smooth habit of the scene, with which the state of his own senses so scantly consorted, and might thereby have been stirred as by an overt discord. What Marcher was at all events conscious of was in the first place that the image of scarred passion presented to him was conscious too – of something that profaned the air; and, in the second, that roused, startled, shocked, he was yet the next moment looking after it, as it went, with envy. The most extraordinary thing that had happened to him – though he had given that name to other matters as well – took place, after his immediate vague stare, as a consequence of this impression. The stranger passed, but the raw glare of his grief remained, making our friend wonder in pity what wrong, what wound it expressed, what injury not to be healed. What had the man *had* to make him, by the loss of it, so bleed and yet live?

Something – and this reached him with a pang – that *he*, John Marcher, hadn't; the proof of which was precisely John Marcher's arid end. No passion had ever touched him, for this was what passion meant; he had survived and maundered and pined, but where had been *his* deep ravage? The extraordinary thing we speak of was the sudden rush of the result of this question. The sight that had just met his eyes named to him, as in letters of quick flame, something he had utterly, insanely missed, and what he had missed made these things a train of fire, made them mark themselves in an anguish of inward throbs. He had seen *outside* of his life, not learned it within, the way a woman was mourned when she had been loved for herself: such was the force of his conviction of the meaning of the stranger's face, which still flared for him as a smoky torch. It hadn't come to him, the knowledge, on the wings of experience; it had brushed him, jostled him, upset him, with the disrespect of chance, the insolence of accident. Now that the illumination had begun, however, it blazed to the zenith, and what he presently stood there gazing at was the sounded void of his life. He gazed, he drew breath, in pain; he turned in his dismay, and, turning, he had before him in sharper incision than ever the open page of his story. The name on the table smote him as the passage of his neighbour had done, and what it said to him, full in the face, was that she was what he had missed. This was the awful thought, the answer to all the past, the vision at the dread clearness of which he turned as cold as the stone beneath him. Everything fell together, confessed, explained, overwhelmed; leaving him most of all stupefied at the blindness he had cherished. The fate he had been marked for he had met with a vengeance – he had emptied the cup to the lees; he had been the man of his time, *the* man, to whom nothing on earth was to have happened. That was the rare stroke – that was his visitation. So he saw it, as we say, in pale horror, while the pieces fitted and fitted. So *she* had seen it while he didn't, and so she served at this hour to drive the truth home. It was the truth, vivid and monstrous, that all the while he had waited the wait was itself his portion. This the companion of his vigil had at a given moment perceived, and she had then offered him the chance to baffle his doom. One's doom, however, was never baffled, and on the day she told him his own had come down she had seen him but stupidly stare at the escape she offered him.

The escape would have been to love her; then, *then* he would have lived. *She* had lived – who could say now with what passion? – since she had loved him for himself; whereas he had never thought of her (ah, how it hugely glared at him!) but in the chill of his egotism and the light of her use. Her spoken words came back to him – the chain stretched and stretched. The beast had lurked indeed, and the beast, at its hour, had sprung; it had sprung in that twilight of the cold April when, pale, ill, wasted, but all beautiful, and perhaps even then recoverable, she had risen from her chair to stand before him and let him imaginably guess. It had sprung as he didn't guess; it had sprung as she hopelessly turned from him, and the mark, by the time he left her, had fallen where it *was* to fall. He had justified his fear and achieved his fate; he had failed, with the last exactitude, of all he was to fail of; and a moan now rose to his lips as he remembered she had prayed he mightn't know. This horror of waking – *this* was knowledge, knowledge under the breath of which the very tears in his eyes seemed to freeze. Through them, none the less, he tried to fix it and hold it; he kept it there before him so that he might feel the pain. That at least, belated and bitter, had something of the taste of life. But the bitterness suddenly sickened him, and it was as if, horribly, he saw, in the truth, in the cruelty of his image, what had been appointed and done. He saw the jungle of his life and saw the lurking beast; then, while he looked, perceived it, as by a stir of the air, rise, huge and hideous, for the leap that was to settle him. His eyes darkened – it was close; and, instinctively turning, in his hallucination, to avoid it, he flung himself, face down, on the tomb.

The Real Thing

I

When the porter's wife (she used to answer the house-bell), announced 'A gentleman – with a lady, sir,' I had, as I often had in those days, for the wish was father to the thought, an immediate vision of sitters. Sitters my visitors in this case proved to be; but not in the sense I should have preferred. However, there was nothing at first to indicate that they might not have come for a portrait. The gentleman, a man of fifty, very high and very straight, with a moustache slightly grizzled and a dark grey walking-coat admirably fitted, both of which I noted professionally – I don't mean as a barber or yet as a tailor – would have struck me as a celebrity if celebrities often were striking. It was a truth of which I had for some time been conscious that a figure with a good deal of frontage was, as one might say, almost never a public institution. A glance at the lady helped to remind me of this paradoxical law: she also looked too distinguished to be a 'personality'. Moreover one would scarcely come across two variations together.

Neither of the pair spoke immediately – they only prolonged the preliminary gaze which suggested that each wished to give the other a chance. They were visibly shy; they stood there letting me take them in – which, as I afterwards perceived, was the most practical thing they could have done. In this way their embarrassment served their cause. I had seen people painfully reluctant to mention that they desired anything so gross as to be represented on canvas; but the scruples of my new friends appeared almost insurmountable. Yet the gentleman might have said, 'I should like a portrait of my wife,' and the lady might have said, 'I should like a portrait of my husband.' Perhaps they were not husband and wife – this naturally would make the matter more delicate. Perhaps they wished to be done together – in which case they ought to have brought a third person to break the news.

'We come from Mr Rivet,' the lady said at last, with a dim smile which had the effect of a moist sponge passed over a 'sunk' piece of painting, as well as of a vague allusion to vanished beauty. She was as tall and straight, in her degree, as her companion, and with ten years less to carry. She looked as sad as a woman could look whose face was not charged with expression; that is her tinted oval mask showed friction as an exposed surface shows it. The hand of time had played over her freely, but only to simplify. She was slim and stiff, and so well dressed, in dark blue cloth, with lappets and pockets and buttons, that it was clear she employed the same tailor as her husband.

The couple had an indefinable air of prosperous thrift – they evidently got a good deal of luxury for their money. If I was to be one of their luxuries it would behove me to consider my terms.

'Ah, Claude Rivet recommended me?' I enquired; and I added that it was very kind of him, though I could reflect that, as he only painted landscape, this was not a sacrifice.

The lady looked very hard at the gentleman, and the gentleman looked round the room. Then staring at the floor a moment and stroking his moustache, he rested his pleasant eyes on me with the remark: 'He said you were the right one.'

'I try to be, when people want to sit.'

'Yes, we should like to,' said the lady anxiously.

'Do you mean together?'

My visitors exchanged a glance. 'If you could do anything with *me*, I suppose it would be double,' the gentleman stammered.

'Oh yes, there's naturally a higher charge for two figures than for one.'

'We should like to make it pay,' the husband confessed.

'That's very good of you,' I returned, appreciating so unwonted a sympathy – for I supposed he meant pay the artist.

A sense of strangeness seemed to dawn on the lady. 'We mean for the illustrations – Mr Rivet said you might put one in.'

'Put one in – an illustration?' I was equally confused.

'Sketch her off, you know,' said the gentleman, colouring.

It was only then that I understood the service Claude Rivet had rendered me; he had told them that I worked in black and white, for magazines, for story-books, for sketches of contemporary life, and consequently had frequent employment for models. These things were true, but it was not less true (I may confess it now – whether because the aspiration was to lead to everything or to nothing I leave the reader to guess) that I couldn't get the honours, to say nothing of the emoluments, of a great painter of portraits out of my head. My 'illustrations' were my pot-boilers; I looked to a different branch of art (far and away the most interesting it had always seemed to me) to perpetuate my fame. There was no shame in looking to it also to make my fortune; but that fortune was by so much further from being made from the moment my visitors wished to be 'done' for nothing. I was disappointed; for in the pictorial sense I had immediately *seen* them. I had seized their type – I had already settled what I would do with it. Something that wouldn't absolutely have pleased them, I afterwards reflected.

'Ah, you're – you're – a – ?' I began, as soon as I had mastered my surprise. I couldn't bring out the dingy word 'models'; it seemed to fit the case so little.

'We haven't had much practice,' said the lady.

'We've got to *do* something, and we've thought that an artist in your line might perhaps make something of us,' her husband threw off. He further mentioned that they didn't know many artists and that they had gone first, on the off-chance (he painted views of course, but sometimes put in figures – perhaps I remembered), to Mr Rivet, whom they had met a few years before at a place in Norfolk where he was sketching.

'We used to sketch a little ourselves,' the lady hinted.

'It's very awkward, but we absolutely *must* do something,' her husband went on.

'Of course, we're not so *very* young,' she admitted, with a wan smile.

With the remark that I might as well know something more about them, the husband had handed me a card extracted from a neat new pocket-book (their appurtenances were all of the freshest) and inscribed with the words 'Major Monarch'. Impressive as these words were they didn't carry my knowledge much further; but my visitor presently added: 'I've left the army, and we've had the misfortune to lose our money. In fact our means are dreadfully small.'

'It's an awful bore,' said Mrs Monarch.

They evidently wished to be discreet – to take care not to swagger because they were gentlefolks. I perceived they would have been willing to recognise this as something of a drawback, at the same time that I guessed at an underlying sense – their consolation in adversity – that they *had* their points. They certainly had; but these advantages struck me as preponderantly social; such for instance as would help to make a drawing-room look well. However, a drawing-room was always, or ought to be, a picture.

In consequence of his wife's allusion to their age Major Monarch observed: 'Naturally, it's more for the figure that we thought of going in. We can still hold ourselves up.' On the instant I saw that the figure was indeed their strong point. His 'naturally' didn't sound vain, but it lighted up the question. '*She* has got the best,' he continued, nodding at his wife, with a pleasant after-dinner absence of circumlocution. I could only reply, as if we were in fact sitting over our wine, that this didn't prevent his own from being very good; which led him in turn to rejoin: 'We thought that if you ever have to do people like us, we might be something like it. *She*, particularly – for a lady in a book, you know.'

I was so amused by them that, to get more of it, I did my best to take their point of view; and though it was an embarrassment to find myself appraising physically, as if they were animals on hire or useful blacks, a pair whom I should have expected to meet only in one of the relations in which criticism is tacit, I looked at Mrs Monarch judicially enough to be able to exclaim, after a moment, with conviction: 'Oh yes, a lady in a book!' She was singularly like a bad illustration.

'We'll stand up, if you like,' said the major; and he raised himself before me with a really grand air.

I could take his measure at a glance – he was six feet two and a perfect gentleman. It would have paid any club in process of formation and in want of a stamp to engage him at a salary to stand in the principal window. What struck me immediately was that in coming to me they had rather missed their vocation; they could surely have been turned to better account for advertising purposes. I couldn't of course see the thing in detail, but I could see them make someone's fortune – I don't mean their own. There was something in them for a waistcoat-maker, a hotel-keeper or a soap-vendor. I could imagine 'We always use it' pinned on their bosoms with the greatest effect; I had a vision of the promptitude with which they would launch a table d'hôte.

Mrs Monarch sat still, not from pride but from shyness, and presently her husband said to her: 'Get up, my dear, and show how smart you are.' She obeyed, but she had no need to get up to show it. She walked to the end of the studio, and then she came back blushing, with her fluttered eyes on her husband. I was reminded of an incident I had accidentally had a glimpse of in Paris – being with a friend there, a dramatist about to produce a play – when an actress came to him to ask to be entrusted with a part. She went through her paces before him, walked up and down as Mrs Monarch was doing. Mrs Monarch did it quite as well, but I abstained from applauding. It was very odd to see such people apply for such poor pay. She looked as if she had ten thousand a year. Her husband had used the word that described her: she was, in the London current jargon, essentially and typically 'smart'. Her figure was, in the same order of ideas, conspicuously and irreproachably 'good'. For a woman of her age her waist was surprisingly small; her elbow moreover had the orthodox crook. She held her head at the conventional angle; but why did she come to *me*? She ought to have tried on jackets at a big shop. I feared my visitors were not only destitute, but 'artistic' – which would be a great complication. When she sat down again I thanked her, observing that what a draughtsman most valued in his model was the faculty of keeping quiet.

'Oh, *she* can keep quiet,' said Major Monarch. Then he added, jocosely: 'I've always kept her quiet.'

'I'm not a nasty fidget, am I?' Mrs Monarch appealed to her husband.

He addressed his answer to me. 'Perhaps it isn't out of place to mention – because we ought to be quite businesslike, oughtn't we? – that when I married her she was known as the Beautiful Statue.'

'Oh dear!' said Mrs Monarch, ruefully.

'Of course I should want a certain amount of expression,' I rejoined.

'Of *course*!' they both exclaimed.

'And then I suppose you know that you'll get awfully tired.'

'Oh, we *never* get tired!' they eagerly cried.

'Have you had any kind of practice?'

They hesitated – they looked at each other. 'We've been photographed, *immensely*,' said Mrs Monarch.

'She means the fellows have asked us,' added the major.

'I see – because you're so good-looking.'

'I don't know what they thought, but they were always after us.'

'We always got our photographs for nothing,' smiled Mrs Monarch.

'We might have brought some, my dear,' her husband remarked.

'I'm not sure we have any left. We've given quantities away,' she explained to me.

'With our autographs and that sort of thing,' said the major.

'Are they to be got in the shops?' I enquired, as a harmless pleasantry.

'Oh, yes; hers – they used to be.'

'Not now,' said Mrs Monarch, with her eyes on the floor.

2

I could fancy the 'sort of thing' they put on the presentation-copies of their photographs, and I was sure they wrote a beautiful hand. It was odd how quickly I was sure of everything that concerned them. If they were now so poor as to have to earn shillings and pence, they never had had much of a margin. Their good looks had been their capital, and they had good-humouredly made the most of the career that this resource marked out for them. It was in their faces, the blankness, the deep intellectual repose of the twenty years of country-house visiting which had given them pleasant intonations. I could see the sunny drawing-rooms, sprinkled with periodicals she didn't read, in which Mrs Monarch had continuously sat; I could see the wet shrubberies in which she had walked, equipped to admiration for either exercise. I could see the rich covers the major had helped to shoot and the wonderful garments in which, late at night, he repaired to the smoking-room to talk about them. I could imagine their leggings and waterproofs, their knowing tweeds and rugs, their rolls of sticks and cases of tackle and neat umbrellas; and I could evoke the exact appearance of their servants and the compact variety of their luggage on the platforms of country stations.

They gave small tips, but they were liked; they didn't do anything them-selves, but they were welcome. They looked so well everywhere; they gratified the general relish for stature, complexion and 'form'. They knew it without fatuity or vulgarity, and they respected themselves in consequence. They were not superficial; they were thorough and kept themselves up – it had been their line. People with such a taste for activity had to have some line. I could feel how, even in a dull house, they could have been counted upon for cheerfulness. At present something had happened – it didn't matter what, their little income had grown less, it had grown least – and they had to do something for pocket-money. Their friends liked them, but didn't like to support them. There was something about them that represented credit – their clothes, their manners, their type; but if credit is a large empty pocket in which an occasional chink reverberates, the chink at least must be audible. What they wanted of me was to help to make it so. Fortunately they had no children – I soon divined that. They would also perhaps wish our relations to be kept secret: this was why it was 'for the figure' – the reproduction of the face would betray them.

I liked them – they were so simple; and I had no objection to them if they would suit. But, somehow, with all their perfections I didn't easily believe in them. After all they were amateurs, and the ruling passion of my life was the detestation of the amateur. Combined with this was another perversity – an innate preference for the represented subject over the real one: the defect of the real one was so apt to be a lack of representation. I liked things that appeared; then one was sure. Whether they *were* or not was a subordinate and almost always a profitless question. There were other considerations, the first of which was that I already had two or three people in use, notably a young person with big feet, in alpaca, from Kilburn, who for a couple of years had come to me regularly for my illustrations and with whom I was still – perhaps ignobly – satisfied. I frankly explained to my visitors how the case stood; but they had taken more precautions than I supposed. They had reasoned out their opportunity, for Claude Rivet had told them of the projected *édition de luxe* of one of the writers of our day – the rarest of the novelists – who, long neglected by the multitudinous vulgar and dearly prized by the attentive (need I mention Philip Vincent?) had had the happy fortune of seeing, late in life, the dawn and then the full light of a higher criticism – an estimate in which, on the part of the public, there was something really of expiation. The edition in question, planned by a publisher of taste, was practically an act of high reparation; the wood-cuts with which it was to be enriched were the homage of English art to one of the most independent representatives of English letters. Major and Mrs Monarch confessed to me that they had hoped I might be able to work *them* into my share of the enterprise. They knew I was to do the first of the books, *Rutland Ramsay*, but I had to make clear to them that my participation in the rest of the affair – this first book was to be a test – was to depend on the satisfaction I should give. If this should be limited my employers would drop me without a scruple. It was therefore a crisis for me, and naturally I was making special preparations, looking about for new people, if they should be necessary, and securing the best types. I admitted however that I should like to settle down to two or three good models who would do for everything.

'Should we have often to – a – put on special clothes?' Mrs Monarch timidly demanded.

'Dear, yes – that's half the business.'

'And should we be expected to supply our own costumes?'

'Oh, no; I've got a lot of things. A painter's models put on – or put off – anything he likes.'

'And do you mean – a – the same?'

'The same?'

Mrs Monarch looked at her husband again.

'Oh, she was just wondering,' he explained, 'if the costumes are in *general* use.' I had to confess that they were, and I mentioned further that some of them (I had a lot of genuine, greasy last-century things) had served their time, a hundred years ago, on living, world-stained men and women. 'We'll put on anything that fits,' said the major.

'Oh, I arrange that – they fit in the pictures.'

'I'm afraid I should do better for the modern books. I would come as you like,' said Mrs Monarch.

'She has got a lot of clothes at home: they might do for contemporary life,' her husband continued.

'Oh, I can fancy scenes in which you'd be quite natural.' And indeed I could see the slipshod rearrangements of stale properties – the stories I tried to produce pictures for without the exasperation of reading them – whose sandy tracts the good lady might help to people. But I had to return to the fact that for this sort of work – the daily mechanical grind – I was already equipped; the people I was working with were fully adequate.

'We only thought we might be more like *some* characters,' said Mrs Monarch mildly, getting up.

Her husband also rose; he stood looking at me with a dim wistfulness that was touching in so fine a man. 'Wouldn't it be rather a pull sometimes to have – a – to have – ?' He hung fire; he wanted me to help him by phrasing what he meant. But I couldn't – I didn't know. So he brought it out, awkwardly: 'The *real* thing: a gentleman, you know, or a lady.' I was quite ready to give a general assent – I admitted that there was a great deal in that. This encouraged Major Monarch to say, following up his appeal with an unacted gulp: 'It's awfully hard – we've tried everything.' The gulp was communicative; it proved too much for his wife. Before I knew it Mrs Monarch had dropped again upon a divan and burst into tears. Her husband sat down beside her, holding one of her hands; whereupon she quickly dried her eyes with the other, while I felt embarrassed as she looked up at me. 'There isn't a confounded job I haven't applied for – waited for – prayed for. You can fancy we'd be pretty bad first. Secretaryships and that sort of thing? You might as well ask for a peerage. I'd be *anything* – I'm strong; a messenger or a coalheaver. I'd put on a gold-laced cap and open carriage-doors in front of the haberdasher's; I'd hang about a station, to carry portmanteaus; I'd be a postman. But they won't *look* at you; there are thousands, as good as yourself, already on the ground. *Gentlemen*, poor beggars, who have drunk their wine, who have kept their hunters!'

I was as reassuring as I knew how to be, and my visitors were presently on their feet again while, for the experiment, we agreed on an hour. We were discussing it when the door opened and Miss Churm came in with a wet umbrella. Miss Churm had to take the omnibus to Maida Vale and then walk half a mile. She looked a trifle blowsy and slightly splashed. I scarcely ever saw her come in without thinking afresh how odd it was that, being so little in herself, she should yet be so much in others. She was a meagre little Miss Churm, but she was an ample heroine of romance. She was only a freckled cockney, but she could represent everything from a fine lady to a shepherdess; she had the faculty, as she might have had a fine voice or long hair. She couldn't spell, and she loved beer, but she had two or three 'points', and practice, and a knack, and mother-wit, and a kind of whimsical sensibility, and a love of the theatre, and seven sisters, and not an ounce of respect, especially for the *h*. The first thing my visitors saw was that her umbrella was wet, and in their spotless perfection they visibly winced at it. The rain had come on since their arrival.

'I'm all in a soak; there *was* a mess of people in the bus. I wish you lived near a stytion,' said Miss Churm. I requested her to get ready as quickly as possible, and she passed into the room in which she always changed her dress. But before going out she asked me what she was to get into this time.

'It's the Russian princess, don't you know?' I answered; 'the one with the "golden eyes", in black velvet, for the long thing in the *Cheapside*.'

'Golden eyes? I *say*!' cried Miss Churm, while my companions watched her with intensity as she withdrew. She always arranged herself, when she was late, before I could turn round; and I kept my visitors a little, on purpose, so that they might get an idea, from seeing her, what would be expected of themselves. I mentioned that she was quite my notion of an excellent model – she was really very clever.

'Do you think she looks like a Russian princess?' Major Monarch asked, with lurking alarm.

'When I make her, yes.'

'Oh, if you have to *make* her – !' he reasoned, acutely.

'That's the most you can ask. There are so many that are not makeable.'

'Well now, *here's* a lady' – and with a persuasive smile he passed his arm into his wife's – 'who's already made!'

'Oh, I'm not a Russian princess,' Mrs Monarch protested, a little coldly. I could see that she had known some and didn't like them. There, immediately, was a complication of a kind that I never had to fear with Miss Churm.

This young lady came back in black velvet – the gown was rather rusty and very low on her lean shoulders – and with a Japanese fan in her red hands. I reminded her that in the scene I was doing she had to look over someone's head. 'I forget whose it is; but it doesn't matter. Just look over a head.'

'I'd rather look over a stove,' said Miss Churm; and she took her station near the fire. She fell into position, settled herself into a tall attitude, gave a certain backward inclination to her head and a certain forward droop to her fan, and looked, at least to my prejudiced sense, distinguished and charming, foreign and dangerous. We left her looking so, while I went downstairs with Major and Mrs Monarch.

'I think I could come about as near it as that,' said Mrs Monarch.

'Oh, you think she's shabby, but you must allow for the alchemy of art.'

However, they went off with an evident increase of comfort, founded on their demonstrable advantage in being the real thing. I could fancy them shuddering over Miss Churm. She was very droll about them when I went back, for I told her what they wanted.

'Well, if *she* can sit I'll tyke to bookkeeping,' said my model.

'She's very ladylike,' I replied, as an innocent form of aggravation.

'So much the worse for *you*. That means she can't turn round.'

'She'll do for the fashionable novels.'

'Oh yes, she'll *do* for them!' my model humorously declared. 'Ain't they bad enough without her?' I had often sociably denounced them to Miss Churm.

3

It was for the elucidation of a mystery in one of these works that I first tried Mrs Monarch. Her husband came with her, to be useful if necessary – it was sufficiently clear that as a general thing he would prefer to come with her. At first I wondered if this were for 'propriety's' sake – if he were going to be jealous and meddling. The idea was too tiresome, and if it had been confirmed it would speedily have brought our acquaintance to a close. But I soon saw there was nothing in it and that if he accompanied Mrs Monarch it was (in addition to the chance of being wanted) simply because he had nothing else to do. When she was away from him his occupation was gone – she never *had* been away from him. I judged, rightly, that in their awkward situation their close union was their main comfort and that this union had no weak spot. It was a real marriage, an encouragement to the hesitating, a nut for pessimists to crack. Their address was humble (I remember afterwards thinking it had been the only thing about them that was really professional), and I could fancy the lamentable lodgings in which the major would have been left alone. He could bear them with his wife – he couldn't bear them without her.

He had too much tact to try and make himself agreeable when he couldn't be useful; so he simply sat and waited when I was too absorbed in my work to talk. But I liked to make him talk – it made my work, when it didn't interrupt it, less sordid, less special. To listen to him was to combine the excitement of going out with the economy of staying at home. There was only one hindrance: that I seemed not to know any of the people he and his wife had known. I think he wondered extremely, during the term of our intercourse, whom the deuce I *did* know. He hadn't a stray sixpence of an idea to fumble for; so we didn't spin it very fine – we confined ourselves to questions of leather and even of liquor (saddlers and breeches-makers and how to get good claret cheap), and matters like 'good trains' and the habits of small game. His lore on these last subjects was astonishing, he managed to inter-weave the station-master with the ornithologist. When he couldn't talk about greater things he could talk cheerfully about smaller, and since I couldn't accompany him into reminiscences of the fashionable world he could lower the conversation without a visible effort to my level.

So earnest a desire to please was touching in a man who could so easily have knocked one down. He looked after the fire and had an opinion on the draught of the stove, without my asking him, and I could see that he thought many of my arrangements not half clever enough. I remember telling him that if I were only rich I would offer him a salary to come and teach me how to live. Sometimes he gave a random sigh, of which the essence was: 'Give me even such a bare old barrack as *this*, and I'd do something with it!' When I wanted to use him he came alone; which was an illustration of the superior courage of women. His wife could bear her solitary second floor, and she was in general more discreet; showing by various small reserves that she was alive to the propriety of keeping our relations markedly professional – not letting them slide into sociability. She wished it to remain clear that she and the major were employed, not cultivated, and if she approved of me as a superior, who could be kept in his place, she never thought me quite good enough for an equal.

She sat with great intensity, giving the whole of her mind to it, and was capable of remaining for an hour almost as motionless as if she were before a photographer's lens. I could see she had been photographed often, but somehow the very habit that made her good for that purpose unfitted her for mine. At first I was extremely pleased with her ladylike air, and it was a satisfaction, on coming to follow her lines, to see how good they were and how far they could lead the pencil. But after a few times I began to find her too insurmountably stiff; do what I would with it my drawing looked like a photograph or a copy of a photograph. Her figure had no variety of expression – she herself had no sense of variety. You may say that this was my business, was only a question of placing her. I placed her in every conceivable position, but she managed to obliterate their differences. She was always a lady certainly, and into the bargain was always the same lady. She was the real thing, but always the same thing. There were moments when I was oppressed by the serenity of her confidence that she *was* the real thing. All her dealings with me and all her husband's were an implication that this was lucky for *me*. Meanwhile I found myself trying to invent types that approached her own, instead of making her own transform itself – in the clever way that was not impossible, for instance, to poor Miss Churm. Arrange as I would and take the precautions I would, she always, in my pictures, came out too tall – landing me in the dilemma of having represented a fascinating woman as seven feet high, which, out of respect perhaps to my own very much scantier inches, was far from my idea of such a personage.

The case was worse with the major – nothing I could do would keep *him* down, so that he became useful only for the representation of brawny giants. I adored variety and range, I cherished human accidents, the illustrative note; I wanted to characterise closely, and the thing in the world I most hated was the danger of being ridden by a type. I had quarrelled with some of my friends about it – I had parted company with them for maintaining that one *had* to be, and that if the type was beautiful (witness Raphael and Leonardo), the servitude was only a gain. I was neither Leonardo nor Raphael; I might only be a presumptuous young modern searcher, but I held that everything was to be sacrificed sooner than character. When they averred that the haunting type in question could easily *be* character, I retorted, perhaps superficially: 'Whose?' It couldn't be everybody's – it might end in being nobody's.

After I had drawn Mrs Monarch a dozen times I perceived more clearly than before that the value of such a model as Miss Churm resided precisely in the fact that she had no positive stamp, combined of course with the other fact that what she did have was a curious and inexplicable talent for imitation. Her usual appearance was like a curtain which she could draw up at request for a capital performance. This performance was simply suggestive; but it was a word to the wise – it was vivid and pretty. Sometimes, even, I thought it, though she was plain herself, too insipidly pretty; I made it a reproach to her that the figures drawn from her were monotonously (*bêtement*, as we used to say) graceful. Nothing made her more angry: it was so much her pride to feel that she could sit for characters that had nothing in common with each other. She would accuse me at such moments of taking away her 'reputytion'.

It suffered a certain shrinkage, this queer quantity, from the repeated visits of my new friends. Miss Churm was greatly in demand, never in want of employment, so I had no scruple in putting her off occasionally, to try them more at my ease. It was certainly amusing at first to do the real thing – it was amusing to do Major Monarch's trousers. They *were* the real thing, even if he did come out colossal. It was amusing to do his wife's back hair (it was so mathematically neat) and the particular 'smart' tension of her tight stays. She lent herself especially to positions in which the face was somewhat averted or blurred; she abounded in ladylike back views and *profils perdus*. When she stood erect she took naturally one of the attitudes in which court-painters represent queens and princesses; so that I found myself wondering whether, to draw out this accomplishment, I couldn't get the editor of the *Cheapside* to publish a really royal romance, 'A Tale of Buckingham Palace'. Sometimes, however, the real thing and the make-believe came into contact;

by which I mean that Miss Churm, keeping an appointment or coming to make one on days when I had much work in hand, encountered her invidious rivals. The encounter was not on their part, for they noticed her no more than if she had been the housemaid; not from intentional loftiness, but simply because, as yet, professionally, they didn't know how to fraternise, as I could guess that they would have liked – or at least that the Major would. They couldn't talk about the omnibus – they always walked; and they didn't know what else to try – she wasn't interested in good trains or cheap claret. Besides, they must have felt – in the air – that she was amused at them, secretly derisive of their ever knowing how. She was not a person to conceal her scepticism if she had had a chance to show it. On the other hand Mrs Monarch didn't think her tidy; for why else did she take pains to say to me (it was going out of the way, for Mrs Monarch), that she didn't like dirty women?

One day when my young lady happened to be present with my other sitters (she even dropped in, when it was convenient, for a chat), I asked her to be so good as to lend a hand in getting tea – a service with which she was familiar and which was one of a class that, living as I did in a small way, with slender domestic resources, I often appealed to my models to render. They liked to lay hands on my property, to break the sitting, and sometimes the china – I made them feel Bohemian. The next time I saw Miss Churm after this incident she surprised me greatly by making a scene about it – she accused me of having wished to humiliate her. She had not resented the outrage at the time, but had seemed obliging and amused, enjoying the comedy of asking Mrs Monarch, who sat vague and silent, whether she would have cream and sugar, and putting an exaggerated simper into the question. She had tried intonations – as if she too wished to pass for the real thing; till I was afraid my other visitors would take offence.

Oh, *they* were determined not to do this; and their touching patience was the measure of their great need. They would sit by the hour, uncomplaining, till I was ready to use them; they would come back on the chance of being wanted and would walk away cheerfully if they were not. I used to go to the door with them to see in what magnificent order they retreated. I tried to find other employment for them – I introduced them to several artists. But they didn't 'take', for reasons I could appreciate, and I became conscious, rather anxiously, that after such disappointments they fell back upon me with a heavier weight. They did me the honour to think that it was I who was most *their* form. They were not picturesque enough for the painters, and in those days there were not so many serious workers in black and white. Besides, they had an eye to the great job I had mentioned to them – they had secretly set their hearts on supplying the right essence for my pictorial vindication of our fine novelist. They knew that for this undertaking I should want no costume-effects, none of the frippery of past ages – that it was a case in which everything would be contemporary and satirical and, presumably, genteel. If I could work them into it their future would be assured, for the labour would of course be long and the occupation steady.

One day Mrs Monarch came without her husband – she explained his absence by his having had to go to the City. While she sat there in her usual anxious stiffness there came, at the door, a knock which I immediately recognised as the subdued appeal of a model out of work. It was followed by the entrance of a young man whom I easily perceived to be a foreigner and who proved in fact an Italian acquainted with no English word but my name, which he uttered in a way that made it seem to include all others. I had not then visited his country, nor was I proficient in his tongue; but as he was not so meanly constituted – what Italian is? – as to depend only on that member for expression he conveyed to me, in familiar but graceful mimicry, that he was in search of exactly the employment in which the lady before me was engaged. I was not struck with him at first, and while I continued to draw I emitted rough sounds of discouragement and dismissal. He stood his ground, however, not importunately, but with a dumb, dog-like fidelity in his eyes which amounted to innocent impudence – the manner of a devoted servant (he might have been in the house for years), unjustly suspected. Suddenly I saw that this very attitude and expression made a picture, whereupon I told him to sit down and wait till I should be free. There was another picture in the way he obeyed me, and I observed as I worked that there were others still in the way he looked wonderingly, with his head thrown back, about the high studio. He might have been crossing himself in St Peter's. Before I finished I said to myself: 'The fellow's a bankrupt orange-monger, but he's a treasure.'

When Mrs Monarch withdrew he passed across the room like a flash to open the door for her, standing there with the rapt, pure gaze of the young Dante spellbound by the young Beatrice. As I never insisted, in such situations, on the blankness of the British domestic, I reflected that he had the making of a servant (and I needed one, but couldn't pay him to be only that), as well as of a model; in short I made up my mind to adopt my bright adventurer if he would agree to officiate in the double capacity. He jumped at my offer, and in the event my rashness (for I had known nothing about him) was not brought home to me. He proved a sympathetic though a desultory ministrant, and had in a wonderful degree the *sentiment de la pose*. It was uncultivated, instinctive; a part of the happy instinct which had guided him to my door and helped him to spell out my name on the card nailed to it. He had had no other introduction to me than a guess, from the shape of my high north window, seen outside, that my place was a studio and that as a studio it would contain an artist. He had wandered to England in search of fortune, like other itinerants, and had embarked, with a partner and a small green handcart, on the sale of penny ices. The ices had melted away and the partner had dissolved in their train. My young man wore tight yellow trousers with reddish stripes and his name was Oronte. He was sallow but fair, and when I put him into some old clothes of my own he looked like an Englishman. He was as good as Miss Churm, who could look, when required, like an Italian.

4

I thought Mrs Monarch's face slightly convulsed when, on her coming back with her husband, she found Oronte installed. It was strange to have to recognise in a scrap of a *lazzarone* a competitor to her magnificent major. It was she who scented danger first, for the major was anecdotically unconscious. But Oronte gave us tea, with a hundred eager confusions (he had never seen such a queer process), and I think she thought better of me for having at last an 'establishment'. They saw a couple of drawings that I had made of the establishment, and Mrs Monarch hinted that it never would have struck her that he had sat for them. 'Now the drawings you make from *us*, they look exactly like us,' she reminded me, smiling in triumph; and I recognised that this was indeed just their defect. When I drew the Monarchs I couldn't, somehow, get away from them – get into the character I wanted to represent; and I had not the least desire my model should be discoverable in my picture. Miss Churm never was, and Mrs Monarch thought I hid her, very properly, because she was vulgar; whereas if she was lost it was only as the dead who go to heaven are lost – in the gain of an angel the more.

By this time I had got a certain start with *Rutland Ramsay*, the first novel in the great projected series; that is I had produced a dozen drawings, several with the help of the major and his wife, and I had sent them in for approval. My understanding with the publishers, as I have already hinted, had been that I was to be left to do my work, in this particular case, as I liked, with the whole book committed to me; but my connection with the rest of the series was only contingent. There were moments when, frankly, it *was* a comfort to have the real thing under one's hand; for there were characters in *Rutland Ramsay* that were very much like it. There were people presumably as straight as the major and women of as good a fashion as Mrs Monarch. There was a great deal of country-house life – treated, it is true, in a fine, fanciful, ironical, generalised way – and there was a considerable implication of knickerbockers and kilts. There were certain things I had to settle at the outset; such things for instance as the exact appearance of the hero, the particular bloom of the heroine. The author of course gave me a lead, but there was a margin for interpretation. I took the Monarchs into my confidence, I told them frankly what I was about, I mentioned my embarrassments and alternatives. 'Oh, take *him*!' Mrs Monarch murmured sweetly, looking at her husband; and 'What could you want better than my wife?' the major enquired, with the comfortable candour that now prevailed between us.

I was not obliged to answer these remarks – I was only obliged to place my sitters. I was not easy in mind, and I postponed, a little timidly perhaps, the solution of the question. The book was a large canvas, the other figures were numerous, and I worked off at first some of the episodes in which the hero and the heroine were not concerned. When once I had set *them* up I should have to stick to them – I couldn't make my young man seven feet high in one place and five feet nine in another. I inclined on the whole to the latter measurement, though the major more than once reminded me that *he* looked about as young as anyone. It was indeed quite possible to arrange him, for the figure, so that it would have been difficult to detect his age. After the spontaneous Oronte had been with me a month, and after I had given him to understand several different times that his native exuberance would presently constitute an insurmountable barrier to our further intercourse, I waked to a sense of his heroic capacity. He was only five feet seven, but the remaining inches were latent. I tried him almost secretly at first, for I was really rather afraid of the judgement my other models would pass on such a choice. If they regarded Miss Churm as little better than a snare, what would they think of the representation by a person so little the real thing as an Italian street-vendor of a protagonist formed by a public school?

If I went a little in fear of them it was not because they bullied me, because they had got an oppressive foothold, but because in their really pathetic decorum and mysteriously permanent newness they counted on me so intensely. I was therefore very glad when Jack Hawley came home: he was always of such good counsel. He painted badly himself, but there was no one like him for putting his finger on the place. He had been absent from England for a year; he had been somewhere – I don't remember where – to get a fresh eye. I was in a good deal of dread of any such organ, but we were old friends; he had been away for months and a sense of emptiness was creeping into my life. I hadn't dodged a missile for a year.

He came back with a fresh eye, but with the same old black velvet blouse, and the first evening he spent in my studio we smoked cigarettes till the small hours. He had done no work himself, he had only got the eye; so the field was clear for the production of my little things. He wanted to see what I had done for the *Cheapside*, but he was disappointed in the exhibition. That at least seemed the meaning of two or three comprehensive groans which, as he lounged on my big divan, on a folded leg, looking at my latest drawings, issued from his lips with the smoke of the cigarette.

'What's the matter with you?' I asked.

'What's the matter with *you*?'

'Nothing save that I'm mystified.'

'You are indeed. You're quite off the hinge. What's the meaning of this new fad?' And he tossed me, with visible irreverence, a drawing in which I happened to have depicted both my majestic models. I asked if he didn't think it good, and he replied that it struck him as execrable, given the sort of thing I had always represented myself to him as wishing to arrive at; but I let that pass, I was so anxious to see exactly what he meant. The two figures in the picture looked colossal, but I supposed this was *not* what he meant, inasmuch as, for aught he knew to the contrary, I might have been trying for that. I maintained that I was working exactly in the same way as when he last had done me the honour to commend me. 'Well, there's a big hole some-where,' he answered; 'wait a bit and I'll discover it.' I depended upon him to do so: where else was the fresh eye? But he produced at last nothing more luminous than 'I don't know – I don't like your types.' This was lame, for a critic who had never consented to discuss with me anything but the question of execution, the direction of strokes and the mystery of values.

'In the drawings you've been looking at I think my types are very handsome.'

'Oh, they won't do!'

'I've had a couple of new models.'

'I see you have. *They* won't do.'

'Are you very sure of that?'

'Absolutely – they're stupid.'

'You mean *I* am – for I ought to get round that.'

'You *can't* – with such people. Who are they?'

I told him, as far as was necessary, and he declared, heartlessly: 'Ce sont des gens qu'il faut mettre à la porte.'

'You've never seen them; they're awfully good,' I compassionately objected.

'Not seen them? Why, all this recent work of yours drops to pieces with them. It's all I want to see of them.'

'No one else has said anything against it – the *Cheapside* people are pleased.'

'Everyone else is an ass, and the *Cheapside* people the biggest asses of all. Come, don't pretend, at this time of day, to have pretty illusions about the public, especially about publishers and editors. It's not for *such* animals you work – it's for those who know, *coloro che sanno*; so keep straight for *me* if you can't keep straight for yourself. There's a certain sort of thing you tried for from the first – and a very good thing it is. But this twaddle isn't *in* it.' When I talked with Hawley later about *Rutland Ramsay* and its possible successors he declared that I must get back into my boat again or I would go to the bottom. His voice in short was the voice of warning.

I noted the warning, but I didn't turn my friends out of doors. They bored me a good deal; but the very fact that they bored me admonished me not to sacrifice them – if there was anything to be done with them – simply to irritation. As I look back at this phase they seem to me to have pervaded my life not a little. I have a vision of them as most of the time in my studio, seated, against the wall, on an old velvet bench to be out of the way, and looking like a pair of patient courtiers in a royal ante-chamber. I am convinced that during the coldest weeks of the winter they held their ground because it saved them fire. Their newness was losing its gloss, and it was impossible not to feel that they were objects of charity. Whenever Miss Churm arrived they went away, and after I was fairly launched in *Rutland Ramsay* Miss Churm arrived pretty often. They managed to express to me tacitly that they supposed I wanted her for the low life of the book, and I let them suppose it, since they had attempted to study the work – it was lying about the studio – without discovering that it dealt only with the highest circles. They had dipped into the most brilliant of our novelists without deciphering many passages. I still took an hour from them, now and again, in spite of Jack Hawley's warning: it would be time enough to dismiss them, if dismissal should be necessary, when the rigour of the season was over. Hawley had made their acquaintance – he had met them at my fireside – and thought them a ridiculous pair. Learning that he was a painter they tried to approach him, to show him too that they were the real thing; but he looked at them, across the big room, as if they were miles away: they were a compendium of everything that he most objected to in the social system of his country. Such people as that, all convention and patent-leather, with ejaculations that stopped conversation, had no business in a studio. A studio was a place to learn to see, and how could you see through a pair of feather beds?

The main inconvenience I suffered at their hands was that, at first, I was shy of letting them discover how my artful little servant had begun to sit to me for *Rutland Ramsay*. They knew that I had been odd enough (they were prepared by this time to allow oddity to artists) to pick a foreign vagabond out of the streets, when I might have had a person with whiskers and credentials; but it was some time before they learned how high I rated his accomplishments. They found him in an attitude more than once, but they never doubted I was doing him as an organ-grinder. There were several things they never guessed, and one of them was that for a striking scene in the novel, in which a footman briefly figured, it occurred to me to make use of Major Monarch as the menial. I kept putting this off, I didn't like to ask him to don the livery – besides the difficulty of finding a livery to fit him. At last, one day late in the winter, when I was at work on the despised Oronte (he caught one's idea in an instant), and was in the glow of feeling that I was going very straight, they came in, the major and his wife, with their society laugh about nothing (there was less and less to laugh at), like country-callers – they always reminded me of that – who have walked across the park after church and are presently persuaded to stay to luncheon. Luncheon was over, but they could stay to tea – I knew they wanted it. The fit was on me, however, and I couldn't let my ardour cool and my work wait, with the fading daylight, while my model prepared it. So I asked Mrs Monarch if she would mind laying it out – a request which, for an instant, brought all the blood to her face. Her eyes were on her husband's for a second, and some mute telegraphy passed between them. Their folly was over the next instant; his cheerful shrewdness put an end to it. So far from pitying their wounded pride, I must add, I was moved to give it as complete a lesson as I could. They bustled about together and got out the cups and saucers and made the kettle boil. I know they felt as if they were waiting on my servant, and when the tea was prepared I said: 'He'll have a cup, please – he's tired.' Mrs Monarch brought him one where he stood, and he took it from her as if he had been a gentleman at a party, squeezing a crush-hat with an elbow.

Then it came over me that she had made a great effort for me – made it with a kind of nobleness – and that I owed her a compensation. Each time I saw her after this I wondered what the compensation could be. I couldn't go on doing the wrong thing to oblige them. Oh, it *was* the wrong thing, the stamp of the work for which they sat – Hawley was not the only person to say it now. I sent in a large number of the drawings I had made for *Rutland Ramsay*, and I received a warning that was more to the point than Hawley's. The artistic adviser of the house for which I was working was of opinion that many of my illustrations were not what had been looked for. Most of these illustrations were the subjects in which the Monarchs had figured. Without going into the question of what *had* been looked for, I saw at this rate I shouldn't get the other books to do. I hurled myself in despair upon Miss Churm, I put her through all her paces. I not only adopted Oronte publicly as my hero, but one morning when the major looked in to see if I didn't require him to finish a figure for the *Cheapside*, for which he had begun to sit the week before, I told him that I had changed my mind – I would do the drawing from my man. At this my visitor turned pale and stood looking at me. 'Is *he* your idea of an English gentleman?' he asked.

I was disappointed, I was nervous, I wanted to get on with my work; so I replied with irritation: 'Oh, my dear major – I can't be ruined for *you*!'

He stood another moment; then, without a word, he quitted the studio. I drew a long breath when he was gone, for I said to myself that I shouldn't see him again. I had not told him definitely that I was in danger of having my work rejected, but I was vexed at his not having felt the catastrophe in the air, read with me the moral of our fruitless collaboration, the lesson that, in the deceptive atmosphere of art, even the highest respectability may fail of being plastic.

I didn't owe my friends money, but I did see them again. They re-appeared together, three days later, and under the circumstances there was something tragic in the fact. It was a proof to me that they could find nothing else in life to do. They had threshed the matter out in a dismal conference – they had digested the bad news that they were not in for the series. If they were not useful to me even for the *Cheapside* their function seemed difficult to determine, and I could only judge at first that they had come, forgivingly, decorously, to take a last leave. This made me rejoice in secret that I had little leisure for a scene; for I had placed both my other models in position together and I was pegging away at a drawing from which I hoped to derive glory. It had been suggested by the passage in which Rutland Ramsay, drawing up a chair to Artemisia's piano-stool, says extraordinary things to her while she ostensibly fingers out a difficult piece of music. I had done Miss Churm at the piano before – it was an attitude in which she knew how to take on an absolutely poetic grace. I wished the two figures to 'compose' together, intensely, and my little Italian had entered perfectly into my conception. The pair were vividly before me, the piano had been pulled out; it was a charming picture of blended youth and murmured love, which I had only to catch and keep. My visitors stood and looked at it, and I was friendly to them over my shoulder.

They made no response, but I was used to silent company and went on with my work, only a little disconcerted (even though exhilarated by the sense that *this* was at least the ideal thing) at not having got rid of them after all. Presently I heard Mrs Monarch's sweet voice beside, or rather above me: 'I wish her hair was a little better done.' I looked up and she was staring with a strange fixedness at Miss Churm, whose back was turned to her. 'Do you mind my just touching it?' she went on – a question which made me spring up for an instant, as with the instinctive fear that she might do the young lady a harm. But she quieted me with a glance I shall never forget – I confess I should like to have been able to paint *that* – and went for a moment to my model. She spoke to her softly, laying a hand upon her shoulder and bending over her; and as the girl, understanding, gratefully assented, she disposed her rough curls, with a few quick passes, in such a way as to make Miss Churm's head twice as charming. It was one of the most heroic personal services I have ever seen rendered. Then Mrs Monarch turned away with a low sigh and, looking about her as if for something to do, stooped to the floor with a noble humility and picked up a dirty rag that had dropped out of my paint-box.

The major meanwhile had also been looking for something to do and, wandering to the other end of the studio, saw before him my breakfast things, neglected, unremoved. 'I say, can't I be useful *here*?' he called out to me with an irrepressible quaver. I assented with a laugh that I fear was awkward and for the next ten minutes, while I worked, I heard the light clatter of china and the tinkle of spoons and glass. Mrs Monarch assisted her husband – they washed up my crockery, they put it away. They wandered off into my little scullery, and I afterwards found that they had cleaned my knives and that my slender stock of plate had an unprecedented surface. When it came over me, the latent eloquence of what they were doing, I confess that my drawing was blurred for a moment – the picture swam. They had accepted their failure, but they couldn't accept their fate. They had bowed their heads in bewilderment to the perverse and cruel law in virtue of which the real thing could be so much less precious than the unreal; but they didn't want to starve. If my servants were my models, my models might be my servants. They would reverse the parts – the others would sit for the ladies and gentlemen, and *they* would do the work. They would still be in the studio – it was an intense dumb appeal to me not to turn them out. 'Take us on,' they wanted to say – 'we'll do *anything*.'

When all this hung before me the *afflatus* vanished – my pencil dropped from my hand. My sitting was spoiled and I got rid of my sitters, who were also evidently rather mystified and awestruck. Then, alone with the major and his wife, I had a most uncomfortable moment. He put their prayer into a single sentence: 'I say, you know – just let *us* do for you, can't you?' I couldn't – it was dreadful to see them emptying my slops; but I pretended I could, to oblige them, for about a week. Then I gave them a sum of money to go away; and I never saw them again. I obtained the remaining books, but my friend Hawley repeats that Major and Mrs Monarch did me a permanent harm, got me into a second-rate trick. If it be true I am content to have paid the price – for the memory.

The Pupil

I

The poor young man hesitated and procrastinated: it cost him such an effort to broach the subject of terms, to speak of money to a person who spoke only of feelings and, as it were, of the aristocracy. Yet he was unwilling to take leave, treating his engagement as settled, without some more conventional glance in that direction than he could find an opening for in the manner of the large affable lady who sat there drawing a pair of soiled *gants de Suède* through a fat jewelled hand and, at once pressing and gliding, repeated over and over everything but the thing he would have liked to hear. He would have liked to hear the figure of his salary; but just as he was nervously about to sound that note the little boy came back – the little boy Mrs Moreen had sent out of the room to fetch her fan. He came back without the fan, only with the casual observation that he couldn't find it. As he dropped this cynical confession he looked straight and hard at the candidate for the honour of taking his education in hand. This personage reflected somewhat grimly that the thing he should have to teach his little charge would be to appear to address himself to his mother when he spoke to her – especially not to make her such an improper answer as that.

When Mrs Moreen bethought herself of this pretext for getting rid of their companion, Pemberton supposed it was precisely to approach the delicate subject of his remuneration. But it had been only to say some things about her son that it was better a boy of eleven shouldn't catch. They were extravagantly to his advantage save when she lowered her voice to sigh, tapping her left side familiarly, 'And all overclouded by *this*, you know; all at the mercy of a weakness – !' Pemberton gathered that the weakness was in the region of the heart. He had known the poor child was not robust: this was the basis on which he had been invited to treat, through an English lady, an Oxford acquaintance, then at Nice, who happened to know both his needs and those of the amiable American family looking out for something really superior in the way of a resident tutor.

The young man's impression of his prospective pupil, who had come into the room as if to see for himself the moment Pemberton was admitted, was not quite the soft solicitation the visitor had taken for granted. Morgan Moreen was somehow sickly without being 'delicate', and that he looked intelligent – it is true Pemberton wouldn't have enjoyed his being stupid – only added to the suggestion that, as with his big mouth and big ears he really couldn't be called pretty, he might too utterly fail to please. Pemberton was modest, was even timid; and the chance that his small scholar might prove cleverer than himself had quite figured, to his anxiety, among the dangers of an untried experiment. He reflected, however, that these were risks one had to run when one accepted a position, as it was called, in a private family; when as yet one's university honours had, pecuniarily speaking, remained barren. At any rate when Mrs Moreen got up as to intimate that, since it was understood he would enter upon his duties within the week, she would let him off now, he succeeded, in spite of the presence of the child, in squeezing out a phrase about the rate of payment. It was not the fault of the conscious smile which seemed a reference to the lady's expensive identity, it was not the fault of this demonstration, which had, in a sort, both vagueness and point, if the allusion didn't sound rather vulgar. This was exactly because she became still more gracious to reply: 'Oh! I can assure you that all that will be quite regular.'

Pemberton only wondered, while he took up his hat, what 'all that' was to amount to – people had such different ideas. Mrs Moreen's words, however, seemed to commit the family to a pledge definite enough to elicit from the child a strange little comment in the shape of the mocking foreign ejaculation 'Oh là-là!'

Pemberton, in some confusion, glanced at him as he walked slowly to the window with his back turned, his hands in his pockets and the air in his elderly shoulders of a boy who didn't play. The young man wondered if he should be able to teach him to play, though his mother had said it would never do and that this was why school was impossible. Mrs Moreen exhibited no discomfiture; she only continued blandly: 'Mr Moreen will be delighted to meet your wishes. As I told you, he has been called to London for a week. As soon as he comes back you shall have it out with him.'

This was so frank and friendly that the young man could only reply, laughing as his hostess laughed: 'Oh I don't imagine we shall have much of a battle.'

'They'll give you anything you like,' the boy remarked unexpectedly, returning from the window. 'We don't mind what anything costs – we live awfully well.'

'My darling, you're too quaint!' his mother exclaimed, putting out to caress him a practised but ineffectual hand. He slipped out of it, but looked with intelligent innocent eyes at Pemberton, who had already had time to notice that from one moment to the other his small satiric face seemed to change its time of life. At this moment it was infantine, yet it appeared also to be under the influence of curious intuitions and knowledges. Pemberton rather disliked precocity and was disappointed to find gleams of it in a disciple not yet in his teens. Nevertheless he divined on the spot that Morgan wouldn't prove a bore. He would prove on the contrary a source of agitation. This idea held the young man, in spite of a certain repulsion.

'You pompous little person! We're not extravagant!' Mrs Moreen gaily protested, making another unsuccessful attempt to draw the boy to her side. 'You must know what to expect,' she went on to Pemberton.

'The less you expect the better!' her companion interposed. 'But we *are* people of fashion.'

'Only so far as *you* make us so!' Mrs Moreen tenderly mocked. 'Well then, on Friday – don't tell me you're superstitious – and mind you don't fail us. Then you'll see us all. I'm so sorry the girls are out. I guess you'll like the girls. And, you know, I've another son, quite different from this one.'

'He tries to imitate me,' Morgan said to their friend.

'He tries? Why he's twenty years old!' cried Mrs Moreen.

'You're very witty,' Pemberton remarked to the child – a proposition his mother echoed with enthusiasm, declaring Morgan's sallies to be the delight of the house.

The boy paid no heed to this; he only enquired abruptly of the visitor, who was surprised afterwards that he hadn't struck him as offensively forward: 'Do you *want* very much to come?'

'Can you doubt it after such a description of what I shall hear?' Pemberton replied. Yet he didn't want to come at all; he was coming because he had to go somewhere, thanks to the collapse of his fortune at the end of a year abroad spent on the system of putting his scant patrimony into a single full wave of experience. He had had his full wave but couldn't pay the score at his inn. Moreover he had caught in the boy's eyes the glimpse of a far-off appeal.

'Well, I'll do the best I can for you,' said Morgan; with which he turned away again. He passed out of one of the long windows; Pemberton saw him go and lean on the parapet of the terrace. He remained there while the young man took leave of his mother, who, on Pemberton's looking as if he expected a farewell from him, interposed with: 'Leave him, leave him; he's so strange!' Pemberton supposed her to fear something he might say. 'He's a genius – you'll love him,' she added. 'He's much the most interesting person in the family.' And before he could invent some civility to oppose to this she wound up with: 'But we're all good, you know!'

'He's a genius – you'll love him!' were words that recurred to our aspirant before the Friday, suggesting among many things that geniuses were not invariably loveable. However, it was all the better if there was an element that would make tutorship absorbing: he had perhaps taken too much for granted it would only disgust him. As he left the villa after his interview he looked up at the balcony and saw the child leaning over it. 'We shall have great larks!' he called up.

Morgan hung fire a moment and then gaily returned: 'By the time you come back I shall have thought of something witty!'

This made Pemberton say to himself: 'After all he's rather nice.'

On the Friday he saw them all, as Mrs Moreen had promised, for her husband had come back and the girls and the other son were at home. Mr Moreen had a white moustache, a confiding manner and, in his buttonhole, the ribbon of a foreign order – bestowed, as Pemberton eventually learned, for services. For what services he never clearly ascertained: this was a point – one of a large number – that Mr Moreen's manner never confided. What it emphatically did confide was that he was even more a man of the world than you might first make out. Ulick, the firstborn, was in visible training for the same profession – under the disadvantage as yet, however, of a buttonhole but feebly floral and a moustache with no pretensions to type. The girls had hair and figures and manners and small fat feet, but had never been out alone. As for Mrs Moreen, Pemberton saw on a nearer view that her elegance was intermittent and her parts didn't always match. Her husband, as she had promised, met with enthusiasm Pemberton's ideas in regard to a salary. The young man had endeavoured to keep these stammerings modest, and Mr Moreen made it no secret that *he* found them wanting in 'style'. He further mentioned that he aspired to be intimate with his children, to be their best friend, and that he was always looking out for them. That was what he went off for, to London and other places – to look out; and this vigilance was the theory of life, as well as the real occupation, of the whole family. They all looked out, for they were very frank on the subject of its being necessary. They desired it to be understood that they were earnest people, and also that their fortune, though quite adequate for earnest people, required the most careful administration. Mr Moreen, as the parent bird, sought sustenance for the nest. Ulick invoked support mainly at the club, where Pemberton guessed that it was usually served on green cloth. The girls used to do up their hair and their frocks themselves, and our young man felt appealed to to be glad, in regard to Morgan's education, that, though it must naturally be of the best, it didn't cost too much. After a little he *was* glad, forgetting at times his own needs in the interest inspired by the child's character and culture and the pleasure of making easy terms for him.

During the first weeks of their acquaintance Morgan had been as puzzling as a page in an unknown language – altogether different from the obvious little Anglo-Saxons who had misrepresented childhood to Pemberton. Indeed the whole mystic volume in which the boy had been amateurishly bound demanded some practice in translation. Today, after a considerable interval, there is something phantasmagoric, like a prismatic reflection or a serial novel, in Pemberton's memory of the queerness of the Moreens. If it were not for a few tangible tokens – a lock of Morgan's hair cut by his own hand,

and the half-dozen letters received from him when they were disjoined – the whole episode and the figures peopling it would seem too inconsequent for anything but dreamland. Their supreme quaintness was their success – as it appeared to him for a while at the time – since he had never seen a family so brilliantly equipped for failure. Wasn't it success to have kept him so hatefully long? Wasn't it success to have drawn him in that first morning at *déjeuner*, the Friday he came – it was enough to *make* one superstitious – so that he utterly committed himself, and this not by calculation or on a signal, but from a happy instinct which made them, like a band of gypsies, work so neatly together? They amused him as much as if they had really been a band of gypsies. He was still young and had not seen much of the world – his English years had been properly arid; therefore the reversed conventions of the Moreens – for they had *their* desperate proprieties – struck him as topsy-turvy. He had encountered nothing like them at Oxford; still less had any such note been struck to his younger American ear during the four years at Yale in which he had richly supposed himself to be reacting against a Puritan strain. The reaction of the Moreens, at any rate, went ever so much further. He had thought himself very sharp that first day in hitting them all off in his mind with the 'cosmopolite' label. Later it seemed feeble and colourless – confessedly helplessly provisional.

However when he first applied it to them he felt a glow of joy – for an instructor he was still empirical – rise from the apprehension that living with them would really be to see life. Their sociable strangeness was an intimation of that – their chatter of tongues, their gaiety and good humour, their infinite dawdling (they were always getting themselves up, but it took for ever, and Pemberton had once found Mr Moreen shaving in the drawing-room), their French, their Italian and, cropping up in the foreign fluencies, their cold tough slices of American. They lived on macaroni and coffee – they had these articles prepared in perfection – but they knew recipes for a hundred other dishes. They overflowed with music and song, were always humming and catching each other up, and had a sort of professional acquaintance with Continental cities. They talked of 'good places' as if they had been pick-pockets or strolling players. They had at Nice a villa, a carriage, a piano and a banjo, and they went to official parties. They were a perfect calendar of the 'days' of their friends, which Pemberton knew them, when they were indisposed, to get out of bed to go to, and which made the week larger than life when Mrs Moreen talked of them with Paula and Amy. Their initiations gave their new inmate at first an almost dazzling sense of culture. Mrs Moreen had translated something at some former period – an author whom it made Pemberton feel *borné* never to have heard of. They could imitate Venetian and sing Neapolitan, and when they wanted to say something very particular communicated with each other in an ingenious dialect of their own, an elastic spoken cipher which Pemberton at first took for some patois of one of their countries, but which he 'caught on to' as he would not have grasped provincial development of Spanish or German.

'It's the family language – Ultramoreen,' Morgan explained to him drolly enough; but the boy rarely condescended to use it himself, though he dealt in colloquial Latin as if he had been a little prelate.

Among all the 'days' with which Mrs Moreen's memory was taxed she managed to squeeze in one of her own, which her friends sometimes forgot. But the house drew a frequented air from the number of fine people who were freely named there and from several mysterious men with foreign titles and English clothes whom Morgan called the princes and who, on sofas with the girls, talked French very loud – though sometimes with some oddity of accent – as if to show they were saying nothing improper. Pemberton wondered how the princes could ever propose in that tone and so publicly: he took for granted cynically that this was what was desired of them. Then he recognised that even for the chance of such an advantage Mrs Moreen would never allow Paula and Amy to receive alone. These young ladies were not at all timid, but it was just the safeguards that made them so candidly free. It was a houseful of Bohemians who wanted tremendously to be Philistines.

In one respect, however, certainly they achieved no rigour – they were wonderfully amiable and ecstatic about Morgan. It was a genuine tenderness, an artless admiration, equally strong in each. They even praised his beauty, which was small, and were as afraid of him as if they felt him of finer clay. They spoke of him as a little angel and a prodigy – they touched on his want of health with long vague faces. Pemberton feared at first an extravagance that might make him hate the boy, but before this happened he had become extravagant himself. Later, when he had grown rather to hate the others, it was a bribe to patience for him that they were at any rate nice about Morgan, going on tiptoe if they fancied he was showing symptoms, and even giving up somebody's 'day' to procure him a pleasure. Mixed with this too was the oddest wish to make him independent, as if they had felt themselves not good enough for him. They passed him over to the new members of their circle very much as if wishing to force some charity of adoption on so free an agent and get rid of their own charge. They were delighted when they saw Morgan take so to his kind playfellow, and could think of no higher praise for the young man. It was strange how they contrived to reconcile the appearance, and indeed the essential fact, of adoring the child with their eagerness to wash their hands of him. Did they want to get rid of him before he should find them out? Pemberton was finding them out month by month. The boy's fond family, however this might be, turned their backs with exaggerated delicacy, as if to avoid the reproach of interfering. Seeing in time how little he had in common with them – it was by *them* he first observed it; they proclaimed it with complete humility – his companion was moved to speculate on the mysteries of transmission, the far jumps of heredity. Where his detachment from most of the things they represented had come from was more than an observer could say – it certainly had burrowed under two or three generations.

As for Pemberton's own estimate of his pupil, it was a good while before he got the point of view, so little had he been prepared for it by the smug young barbarians to whom the tradition of tutorship, as hitherto revealed to him, had been adjusted. Morgan was scrappy and surprising, deficient in many properties supposed common to the *genus* and abounding in others that were the portion only of the supernaturally clever. One day Pemberton made a great stride: it cleared up the question to perceive that Morgan *was* supernaturally clever and that, though the formula was temporarily meagre, this would be the only assumption on which one could successfully deal with him. He had the general quality of a child for whom life had not been simplified by school, a kind of homebred sensibility which might have been bad for himself but was charming for others, and a whole range of refinement and perception – little musical vibrations as taking as picked-up airs – begotten by wandering about Europe at the tail of his migratory tribe. This might not have been an education to recommend in advance, but its results with so special a subject were as appreciable as the marks on a piece of fine porcelain. There was at the same time in him a small strain of stoicism, doubtless the fruit of having had to begin early to bear pain, which counted for pluck and made it of less consequence that he might have been thought at school rather a polyglot little beast. Pemberton indeed quickly found himself rejoicing that school was out of the question: in any million of boys it was probably good for all but one, and Morgan was that millionth. It would have made him comparative and superior – it might have made him really require kicking. Pemberton would try to be school himself – a bigger seminary than five hundred grazing donkeys, so that, winning no prizes, the boy would remain unconscious and irresponsible and amusing – amusing, because, though life was already intense in his childish nature, freshness still made there a strong draught for jokes. It turned out that even in the still air of Morgan's various disabilities jokes flourished greatly. He was a pale, lean, acute, undeveloped little cosmopolite, who liked intellectual gymnastics and who also, as regards the behaviour of mankind, had noticed more things than you might suppose, but who nevertheless had his proper playroom of superstitions, where he smashed a dozen toys a day.

3

At Nice once, toward evening, as the pair rested in the open air after a walk, and looked over the sea at the pink western lights, he said suddenly to his comrade: 'Do you like it, you know – being with us all in this intimate way?'

'My dear fellow, why should I stay if I didn't?'

'How do I know you'll stay? I'm almost sure you won't, very long.'

'I hope you don't mean to dismiss me,' said Pemberton.

Morgan debated, looking at the sunset. 'I think if I did right I ought to.'

'Well, I know I'm supposed to instruct you in virtue; but in that case don't do right.'

'You're very young – fortunately,' Morgan went on, turning to him again.

'Oh yes, compared with you!'

'Therefore it won't matter so much if you do lose a lot of time.'

'That's the way to look at it,' said Pemberton accommodatingly.

They were silent a minute; after which the boy asked: 'Do you like my father and my mother very much?'

'Dear me, yes. They're charming people.'

Morgan received this with another silence; then unexpectedly, familiarly, but at the same time affectionately, he remarked: 'You're a jolly old humbug!'

For a particular reason the words made our young man change colour. The boy noticed in an instant that he had turned red, whereupon he turned red himself and pupil and master exchanged a longish glance in which there was a consciousness of many more things than are usually touched upon, even tacitly, in such a relation. It produced for Pemberton an embarrassment; it raised in a shadowy form a question – this was the first glimpse of it – destined to play a singular and, as he imagined, owing to the altogether peculiar conditions, an unprecedented part in his intercourse with his little companion. Later, when he found himself talking with the youngster in a way in which few youngsters could ever have been talked with, he thought of that clumsy moment on the bench at Nice as the dawn of an understanding that had broadened. What had added to the clumsiness then was that he thought it his duty to declare to Morgan that he might abuse him, Pemberton, as much as he liked, but must never abuse his parents. To this Morgan had the easy retort that he hadn't dreamed of abusing them; which appeared to be true: it put Pemberton in the wrong.

'Then why am I a humbug for saying *I* think them charming?' the young man asked, conscious of a certain rashness.

'Well – they're not *your* parents.'

'They love you better than anything in the world – never forget that,' said Pemberton.

'Is that why you like them so much?'

'They're very kind to me,' Pemberton replied evasively.

'You *are* a humbug!' laughed Morgan, passing an arm into his tutor's. He leaned against him looking oft at the sea again and swinging his long thin legs.

'Don't kick my shins,' said Pemberton while he reflected, 'Hang it, I can't complain of them to the child!'

'There's another reason, too,' Morgan went on, keeping his legs still.

'Another reason for what?'

'Besides their not being your parents.'

'I don't understand you,' said Pemberton.

'Well, you will before long. All right!'

He did understand fully before long, but he made a fight even with himself before he confessed it. He thought it the oddest thing to have a struggle with the child about. He wondered he didn't hate the hope of the Moreens for bringing the struggle on. But by the time it began any such sentiment for that scion was closed to him. Morgan was a special case, and to know him was to accept him on his own odd terms. Pemberton had spent his aversion to special cases before arriving at knowledge. When at last he did arrive his quandary was great. Against every interest he had attached himself. They would have to meet things together. Before they went home that evening at Nice the boy had said, clinging to his arm: 'Well, at any rate you'll hang on to the last.'

'To the last?'

'Till you're fairly beaten.'

'*You* ought to be fairly beaten!' cried the young man, drawing him closer.

4

A year after he had come to live with them Mr and Mrs Moreen suddenly gave up the villa at Nice. Pemberton had got used to suddenness, having seen it practised on a considerable scale during two jerky little tours – one in Switzerland the first summer, and the other late in the winter, when they all ran down to Florence and then, at the end of ten days, liking it much less than they had intended, straggled back in mysterious depression. They had returned to Nice 'for ever', as they said; but this didn't prevent their squeezing, one rainy, muggy May night, into a second-class railway carriage – you could never tell by which class they would travel – where Pemberton helped them to stow away a wonderful collection of bundles and bags. The explanation of this manoeuvre was that they had determined to spend the summer 'in some bracing place'; but in Paris they dropped into a small furnished apartment – a fourth floor in a third-rate avenue, where there was a smell on the staircase and the *portier* was hateful – and passed the next four months in blank indigence.

The better part of this baffled sojourn was for the preceptor and his pupil, who, visiting the Invalides and Notre Dame, the Conciergerie and all the museums, took a hundred remunerative rambles. They learned to know their Paris, which was useful, for they came back another year for a longer stay, the general character of which in Pemberton's memory today mixes pitiably and confusedly with that of the first. He sees Morgan's shabby knickerbockers – the everlasting pair that didn't match his blouse and that as he grew longer could only grow faded. He remembers the particular holes in his three or four pairs of coloured stockings.

Morgan was dear to his mother, but he never was better dressed than was absolutely necessary – partly, no doubt, by his own fault, for he was as indifferent to his appearance as a German philosopher. 'My dear fellow, you *are* coming to pieces,' Pemberton would say to him in sceptical remonstrance; to which the child would reply, looking at him serenely up and down: 'My dear fellow, so are you! I don't want to cast you in the shade.' Pemberton could have no rejoinder for this – the assertion so closely represented the fact. If however the deficiencies of his own wardrobe were a chapter by themselves he didn't like his little charge to look too poor. Later he used to say: 'Well, if we're poor, why, after all, shouldn't we look it?' and he consoled himself with thinking there was something rather elderly and gentlemanly in Morgan's disrepair – it differed from the untidiness of the urchin who plays and spoils his things. He could trace perfectly the degrees by which, in proportion as her little son confined himself to his tutor for society, Mrs Moreen shrewdly forbore to renew his garments. She did nothing that didn't show, neglected him because he escaped notice, and then, as he illustrated this clever policy, discouraged at home his public appearances. Her position was logical enough – those members of her family who did show had to be showy.

During this period and several others Pemberton was quite aware of how he and his comrade might strike people; wandering languidly through the Jardin des Plantes as if they had nowhere to go, sitting on the winter days in the galleries of the Louvre, so splendidly ironical to the homeless, as if for the advantage of the *calorifère*. They joked about it sometimes: it was the sort of joke that was perfectly within the boy's compass. They figured themselves as part of the vast vague hand-to-mouth multitude of the enormous city and pretended they were proud of their position in it – it showed them 'such a lot of life' and made them conscious of a democratic brotherhood. If Pemberton couldn't feel a sympathy in destitution with his small companion – for after all Morgan's fond parents would never have let him really suffer – the boy would at least feel it with him, so it came to the same thing. He used sometimes to wonder what people would think they were – to fancy they were looked askance at, as if it might be a suspected case of kidnapping. Morgan wouldn't be taken for a young patrician with a preceptor – he wasn't smart enough; though he might pass for his companion's sickly little brother. Now and then he had a five-franc piece, and except once, when they bought a couple of lovely neckties, one of which he made Pemberton accept, they laid it out scientifically in old books. This was sure to be a great day, always spent on the quays, in a rummage of the dusty boxes that garnish the parapets. Such occasions helped them to live, for their books ran low very soon after the beginning of their acquaintance. Pemberton had a good many in England, but he was obliged to write to a friend and ask him kindly to get some fellow to give him something for them.

If they had to relinquish that summer the advantage of the bracing climate the young man couldn't but suspect this failure of the cup when at their very lips to have been the effect of a rude jostle of his own. This had represented his first blow-out, as he called it, with his patrons; his first successful attempt – though there was little other success about it – to bring them to a consideration of his impossible position. As the ostensible eve of a costly journey the moment had struck him as favourable to an earnest protest, the presentation of an ultimatum. Ridiculous as it sounded, he had never yet been able to compass an uninterrupted private interview with the elder pair or with either of them singly. They were always flanked by their elder children, and poor Pemberton usually had his own little charge at his side. He was conscious of its being a house in which the surface of one's delicacy got rather smudged; nevertheless he had preserved the bloom of his scruple against announcing to Mr and Mrs Moreen with publicity that he shouldn't be able to go on longer without a little money. He was still simple enough to suppose Ulick and Paula and Amy might not know that since his arrival he had only had a hundred and forty francs; and he was magnanimous enough to wish not to compromise their parents in their eyes. Mr Moreen now listened to him, as he listened to everyone and to everything, like a man of the world, and seemed to appeal to him – though not of course too grossly – to try and be a little more of one himself. Pemberton recognised in fact the importance of the character – from the advantage it gave Mr Moreen. He was not even confused or embarrassed, whereas the young man in his service was more so than there was any reason for. Neither was he surprised – at least any more than a gentleman had to be who freely confessed himself a little shocked – though not perhaps strictly at Pemberton.

'We must go into this, mustn't we, dear?' he said to his wife. He assured his young friend that the matter should have his very best attention; and he melted into space as elusively as if, at the door, he were taking an inevitable but deprecatory precedence. When, the next moment, Pemberton found himself alone with Mrs Moreen it was to hear her say: 'I see, I see' – stroking the roundness of her chin and looking as if she were only hesitating between a dozen easy remedies. If they didn't make their push Mr Moreen could at least disappear for several days. During his absence his wife took up the subject again spontaneously, but her contribution to it was merely that she had thought all the while they were getting on so beautifully. Pemberton's reply to this revelation was that unless they immediately put down something on account he would leave them on the spot and for ever. He knew she would wonder how he would get away, and for a moment expected her to enquire. She didn't, for which he was almost grateful to her, so little was he in a position to tell.

'You won't, you *know* you won't – you're too interested,' she said. 'You *are* interested, you know you are, you dear kind man!' She laughed with almost condemnatory archness, as if it were a reproach – though she wouldn't insist; and flirted a soiled pocket-handkerchief at him.

Pemberton's mind was fully made up to take his step the following week. This would give him time to get an answer to a letter he had dispatched to England. If he did in the event nothing of the sort – that is if he stayed another year and then went away only for three months – it was not merely because before the answer to his letter came (most unsatisfactory when it did arrive) Mr Moreen generously counted out to him, and again with the sacrifice to 'form' of a marked man of the world, three hundred francs in elegant ringing gold. He was irritated to find that Mrs Moreen was right, that he couldn't at the pinch bear to leave the child. This stood out clearer for the very reason that, the night of his desperate appeal to his patrons, he had seen fully for the first time where he was. Wasn't it another proof of the success with which those patrons practised their arts that they had managed to avert for so long the illuminating flash? It descended on our friend with a breadth of effect which perhaps would have struck a spectator as comical, after he had returned to his little servile room, which looked into a close court where a bare, dirty opposite wall took, with the sound of shrill clatter, the reflection of lighted back windows. He had simply given himself away to a band of adventurers. The idea, the word itself, wore a romantic horror for him – he had always lived on such safe lines. Later it assumed a more interesting, almost a soothing, sense: it pointed a moral, and Pemberton could enjoy a moral. The Moreens were adventurers not merely because they didn't pay their debts, because they lived on society, but because their whole view of life, dim and confused and instinctive, like that of clever colour-blind animals, was speculative and rapacious and mean. Oh they were 'respectable', and that only made them more *immondes*. The young man's analysis, while he brooded, put it at last very simply – they were adventurers because they were toadies and snobs. That was the completest account of them – it was the law of their being. Even when this truth became vivid to their ingenious inmate he remained unconscious of how much his mind had been prepared for it by the extraordinary little boy who had now become such a complication in his life. Much less could he then calculate on the information he was still to owe the extraordinary little boy.

5

But it was during the ensuing time that the real problem came up – the problem of how far it was excusable to discuss the turpitude of parents with a child of twelve, of thirteen, of fourteen. Absolutely inexcusable and quite impossible it of course at first appeared; and indeed the question didn't press for some time after Pemberton had received his three hundred francs. They produced a temporary lull, a relief from the sharpest pressure. The young man frugally amended his wardrobe and even had a few francs in his pocket. He thought the Moreens looked at him as if he were almost too smart, as if they ought to take care not to spoil him. If Mr Moreen hadn't been such a man of the world he would perhaps have spoken of the freedom of such neckties on the part of a subordinate. But Mr Moreen was always enough a man of the world to let things pass – he had certainly shown that. It was singular how Pemberton guessed that Morgan, though saying nothing about it, knew something had happened. But three hundred francs, especially when one owed money, couldn't last for ever; and when the treasure was gone – the boy knew when it had failed – Morgan did break ground. The party had returned to Nice at the beginning of the winter, but not to the charming villa. They went to a hotel, where they stayed three months, and then moved to another establishment, explaining that they had left the first because, after waiting and waiting, they couldn't get the rooms they wanted. These apartments, the rooms they wanted, were generally very splendid; but fortunately they never *could* get them – fortunately, I mean, for Pemberton, who reflected always that if they had got them there would have been a still scantier educational fund. What Morgan said at last was said suddenly, irrelevantly, when the moment came, in the middle of a lesson, and consisted of the apparently unfeeling words: 'You ought to *filer*, you know – you really ought.'

Pemberton stared. He had learnt enough French slang from Morgan to know that to *filer* meant to up sticks. 'Ah my dear fellow, don't turn me off!'

Morgan pulled a Greek lexicon toward him – he used a Greek–German – to look out a word, instead of asking it of Pemberton. 'You can't go on like this, you know.'

'Like what, my boy?'

'You know they don't pay you up,' said Morgan, blushing and turning his leaves.

'Don't pay me?' Pemberton stared again and feigned amazement. 'What on earth put that into your head?'

'It has been there a long time,' the boy replied rummaging his book.

Pemberton was silent, then he went on: 'I say, what are you hunting for? They pay me beautifully.'

'I'm hunting for the Greek for awful whopper,' Morgan dropped.

'Find that rather for gross impertinence and disabuse your mind. What do I want of money?'

'Oh, that's another question!'

Pemberton wavered – he was drawn in different ways. The severely correct thing would have been to tell the boy that such a matter was none of his business and bid him go on with his lines. But they were really too intimate for that; it was not the way he was in the habit of treating him; there had been no reason it should be. On the other hand Morgan had quite lighted on the truth – he really shouldn't be able to keep it up much longer; therefore why not let him know one's real motive for forsaking him? At the same time it wasn't decent to abuse to one's pupil the family of one's pupil; it was better to misrepresent than to do that. So in reply to his comrade's last exclamation he just declared, to dismiss the subject, that he had received several payments.

'I say – I say!' the boy ejaculated, laughing.

'That's all right,' Pemberton insisted. 'Give me your written rendering.'

Morgan pushed a copybook across the table, and he began to read the page, but with something running in his head that made it no sense. Looking up after a minute or two he found the child's eyes fixed on him and felt in them something strange. Then Morgan said: 'I'm not afraid of the stern reality.'

'I haven't yet seen the thing you *are* afraid of – I'll do you that justice!'

This came out with a jump – it was perfectly true – and evidently gave Morgan pleasure. 'I've thought of it a long time,' he presently resumed.

'Well, don't think of it any more.'

The boy appeared to comply, and they had a comfortable and even an amusing hour. They had a theory that they were very thorough, and yet they seemed always to be in the amusing part of lessons, the intervals between the dull dark tunnels, where there were waysides and jolly views. Yet the morning was brought to a violent end by Morgan's suddenly leaning his arms on the table, burying his head in them and bursting into tears: at which Pemberton was the more startled that, as it then came over him, it was the first time he had ever seen the boy cry and that the impression was consequently quite awful.

The next day, after much thought, he took a decision and, believing it to be just, immediately acted on it. He cornered Mr and Mrs Moreen again and let them know that if on the spot they didn't pay him all they owed him he wouldn't only leave their house but would tell Morgan exactly what had brought him to it.

'Oh you *haven't* told him?' cried Mrs Moreen with a pacifying hand on her well-dressed bosom.

'Without warning you? For what do you take me?' the young man returned.

Mr and Mrs Moreen looked at each other; he could see that they appreciated, as tending to their security, his superstition of delicacy, and yet that there was a certain alarm in their relief. 'My dear fellow,' Mr Moreen demanded, 'what use can you have, leading the quiet life we all do, for such a lot of money?' – a question to which Pemberton made no answer, occupied as he was in noting that what passed in the mind of his patrons was something like: 'Oh then, if we've felt that the child, dear little angel, has judged us and how he regards us, and we haven't been betrayed, he must have guessed – and in short it's *general*!' an inference that rather stirred up Mr and Mrs Moreen, as Pemberton had desired it should. At the same time, if he had supposed his threat would do something towards bringing them round, he was disappointed to find them taking for granted – how vulgar their perception *had* been! – that he had already given them away. There was a mystic uneasiness in their parental breasts, and that had been the inferior sense of it. None the less however, his threat did touch them; for if they had escaped it was only to meet a new danger. Mr Moreen appealed to him, on every precedent, as a man of the world; but his wife had recourse, for the first time since his domestication with them, to a fine *hauteur*, reminding him that a devoted mother, with her child, had arts that protected her against gross misrepresentation.

'I should misrepresent you grossly if I accused you of common honesty!' our friend replied; but as he closed the door behind him sharply, thinking he had not done himself much good, while Mr Moreen lighted another cigarette, he heard his hostess shout after him more touchingly: 'Oh you do, you *do*, put the knife to one's throat!'

The next morning, very early, she came to his room. He recognised her knock, but had no hope she brought him money; as to which he was wrong, for she had fifty francs in her hand. She squeezed forward in her dressing-gown, and he received her in his own, between his bath-tub and his bed. He had been tolerably schooled by this time to the 'foreign ways' of his hosts. Mrs Moreen was ardent, and when she was ardent she didn't care what she did; so she now sat down on his bed, his clothes being on the chairs, and, in her preoccupation, forgot, as she glanced round, to be ashamed of giving him such a horrid room. What Mrs Moreen's ardour now bore upon was the design of persuading him that in the first place she was very good-natured to bring him fifty francs, and that in the second, if he would only see it, he was really too absurd to expect to be *paid*. Wasn't he paid enough without perpetual money – wasn't he paid by the comfortable luxurious home he enjoyed with them all, without a care, an anxiety, a solitary want? Wasn't he sure of his position, and wasn't that everything to a young man like him, quite unknown, with singularly little to show, the ground of whose exorbitant pretensions it had never been easy to discover? Wasn't he paid above all by the sweet relation he had established with Morgan – quite ideal as from master to pupil – and by the simple privilege of knowing and living with so amazingly gifted a child; than whom really (and she meant literally what she said) there was no better company in Europe? Mrs Moreen herself took to appealing to him as a man of the world; she said, 'Voyons, mon cher,' and, 'My dear man, look here now'; and urged him to be reasonable, putting it before him that it was truly a chance for him. She spoke as if, according as he *should* be reasonable, he would prove himself worthy to be her son's tutor and of the extra-ordinary confidence they had placed in him.

After all, Pemberton reflected, it was only a difference of theory and the theory didn't matter much. They had hitherto gone on that of remunerated, as now they would go on that of gratuitous, service; but why should they have so many words about it? Mrs Moreen at all events continued to be convincing; sitting there with her fifty francs she talked and reiterated, as women reiterate, and bored and irritated him, while he leaned against the wall with his hands in the pockets of his wrapper, drawing it together round his legs and looking over the head of his visitor at the grey negations of his window. She wound up with saying: 'You see I bring you a definite proposal.'

'A definite proposal?'

'To make our relations regular, as it were – to put them on a comfortable footing.'

'I see – it's a system,' said Pemberton. 'A kind of organised blackmail.'

Mrs Moreen bounded up, which was exactly what he wanted. 'What do you mean by that?'

'You practise on one's fears – one's fears about the child if one should go away.'

'And pray what would happen to him in that event?' she demanded, with majesty.

'Why he'd be alone with *you*.'

'And pray with whom *should* a child be but with those whom he loves most?'

'If you think that, why don't you dismiss me?'

'Do you pretend he loves you more than he loves *us*?' cried Mrs Moreen.

'I think he ought to. I make sacrifices for him. Though I've heard of those *you* make I don't see them.'

Mrs Moreen stared a moment; then with emotion she grasped her inmate's hand. '*Will* you make it – the sacrifice?'

He burst out laughing. 'I'll see. I'll do what I can. I'll stay a little longer. Your calculation's just – I *do* hate intensely to give him up; I'm fond of him and he thoroughly interests me, in spite of the inconvenience I suffer. You know my situation perfectly. I haven't a penny in the world and, occupied as you see me with Morgan, am unable to earn money.'

Mrs Moreen tapped her undressed arm with her folded bank-note. 'Can't you write articles? Can't you translate as *I* do?'

'I don't know about translating; it's wretchedly paid.'

'I'm glad to earn what I can,' said Mrs Moreen with prodigious virtue.

'You ought to tell me whom you do it for.' Pemberton paused a moment, and she said nothing; so he added: 'I've tried to turn off some little sketches, but the magazines won't have them – they're declined with thanks.'

'You see then you're not such a phoenix,' his visitor pointedly smiled – 'to pretend to abilities you're sacrificing for our sake.'

'I haven't time to do things properly,' he ruefully went on. Then as it came over him that he was almost abjectly good-natured to give these explanations he added: 'If I stay on longer it must be on one condition – that Morgan shall know distinctly on what footing I am.'

Mrs Moreen demurred. 'Surely you don't want to show off to a child?'

'To show *you* off, do you mean?'

Again she cast about, but this time it was to produce a still finer flower. 'And *you* talk of blackmail!'

'You can easily prevent it,' said Pemberton.

'And *you* talk of practising on fears,' she bravely pushed on.

'Yes, there's no doubt I'm a great scoundrel.'

His patroness met his eyes – it was clear she was in straits. Then she thrust out her money at him. 'Mr Moreen desired me to give you this on account.'

'I'm much obliged to Mr Moreen, but we *have* no account.'

'You won't take it?'

'That leaves me more free,' said Pemberton.

'To poison my darling's mind?' groaned Mrs Moreen.

'Oh, your darling's mind!' the young man laughed.

She fixed him a moment, and he thought she was going to break out tormentedly, pleadingly: 'For God's sake, tell me what *is* in it!' But she checked this impulse – another was stronger. She pocketed the money – the crudity of the alternative was comical – and swept out of the room with the desperate concession: 'You may tell him any horror you like!'

6

A couple of days after this, during which he had failed to profit by so free a permission, he had been for a quarter of an hour walking with his charge in silence when the boy became sociable again with the remark: 'I'll tell you how I know it; I know it through Zénobie.'

'Zénobie? Who in the world is *she*?'

'A nurse I used to have – ever so many years ago. A charming woman. I liked her awfully, and she liked me.'

'There's no accounting for tastes. What is it you know through her?'

'Why what their idea is. She went away because they didn't fork out. She did like me awfully, and she stayed two years. She told me all about it – that at last she could never get her wages. As soon as they saw how much she liked me they stopped giving her anything. They thought she'd stay for nothing – just *because*, don't you know?' And Morgan had a queer little conscious, lucid look. 'She did stay ever so long – as long an she could. She was only a poor girl. She used to send money to her mother. At last she couldn't afford it any longer, and went away in a fearful rage one night – I mean of course in a rage against *them*. She cried over me tremendously, she hugged me nearly to death. She told me all about it,' the boy repeated. 'She told me it was their idea. So I guessed, ever so long ago, that they have had the same idea with you.'

'Zénobie was very sharp,' said Pemberton. 'And she made you so.'

'Oh that wasn't Zénobie; that was nature. And experience!' Morgan laughed.

'Well, Zénobie was a part of your experience.'

'Certainly I was a part of hers, poor dear!' the boy wisely sighed. 'And I'm part of yours.'

'A very important part. But I don't see how you know that I've been treated like Zénobie.'

'Do you take me for the biggest dunce you've known?' Morgan asked. 'Haven't I been conscious of what we've been through together?'

'What we've been through?'

'Our privations – our dark days.'

'Oh, our days have been bright enough.'

Morgan went on in silence for a moment. Then he said: 'My dear chap, you're a hero!'

'Well, you're another!' Pemberton retorted.

'No I'm not, but I ain't a baby. I won't stand it any longer. You must get some occupation that pays. I'm ashamed, I'm ashamed!' quavered the boy with a ring of passion, like some high silver note from a small cathedral cloister, that deeply touched his friend.

'We ought to go off and live somewhere together,' the young man said.

'I'll go like a shot if you'll take me.'

'I'd get some work that would keep us both afloat,' Pemberton continued.

'So would I. Why shouldn't I work? I ain't such a beastly little muff as that comes to.'

'The difficulty is that your parents wouldn't hear of it. They'd never part with you; they worship the ground you tread on. Don't you see the proof of it?' Pemberton developed. 'They don't dislike me; they wish me no harm; they're very amiable people; but they're perfectly ready to expose me to any awkwardness in life for your sake.'

The silence in which Morgan received his fond sophistry struck Pemberton somehow as expressive. After a moment the child repeated: 'You are a hero!' Then he added: 'They leave me with you altogether. You've all the responsibility. They put me off on you from morning till night. Why then should they object to my taking up with you completely? I'd help you.'

'They're not particularly keen about my being helped, and they delight in thinking of you as *theirs*. They're tremendously proud of you.'

'I'm not proud of *them*. But you know that,' Morgan returned.

'Except for the little matter we speak of they're charming people,' said Pemberton, not taking up the point made for his intelligence, but wondering greatly at the boy's own, and especially at this fresh reminder of something he had been conscious of from the first – the strangest thing in his friend's large little composition, a temper, a sensibility, even a private ideal, which made him as privately disown the stuff his people were made of. Morgan had in secret a small loftiness which made him acute about betrayed meanness; as well as a critical sense for the manners immediately surrounding him that was quite without precedent in a juvenile nature, especially when one noted that it had not made this nature 'old-fashioned,' as the word is of children – quaint or wizened or offensive. It was as if he had been a little gentleman and had paid the penalty by discovering that he was the only such person in his family. This comparison didn't make him vain, but it could make him melancholy and a trifle austere. While Pemberton guessed at these dim young things, shadows of shadows, he was partly drawn on and partly checked, as for a scruple, by the charm of attempting to sound the little cool shallows that were so quickly growing deeper. When he tried to figure to himself the morning twilight of childhood, so as to deal with it safely, he saw it was never fixed, never arrested, that ignorance, at the instant he touched it, was already flushing faintly into knowledge, that there was nothing that at a given moment you could say an intelligent child didn't know. It seemed to him that he himself knew too much to imagine Morgan's simplicity and too little to disembroil his tangle.

The boy paid no heed to his last remark; he only went on: 'I'd have spoken to them about their idea, as I call it, long ago, if I hadn't been sure what they'd say.'

'And what would they say?'

'Just what they said about what poor Zénobie told me – that it was a horrid, dreadful story, that they had paid her every penny they owed her.'

'Well, perhaps they had,' said Pemberton.

'Perhaps they've paid you!'

'Let us pretend they have, and *n'en parlons plus*.'

'They accused her of lying and cheating' – Morgan stuck to historic truth. 'That's why I don't want to speak to them.'

'Lest they should accuse me, too?' To this Morgan made no answer, and his companion, looking down at him – the boy turned away his eyes, which had filled – saw what he couldn't have trusted himself to utter. 'You're right. Don't worry them,' Pemberton pursued. 'Except for that, they *are* charming people.'

'Except for *their* lying and *their* cheating?'

'I say – I say!' cried Pemberton, imitating a little tone of the lad's which was itself an imitation.

'We must be frank, at the last; we *must* come to an understanding,' said

Morgan with the importance of the small boy who lets himself think he is arranging great affairs – almost playing at shipwreck or at Indians. 'I know all about everything.'

'I dare say your father has his reasons,' Pemberton replied, but too vaguely, as he was aware.

'For lying and cheating?'

'For saving and managing and turning his means to the best account. He has plenty to do with his money. You're an expensive family.'

'Yes, I'm very expensive,' Morgan concurred in a manner that made his preceptor burst out laughing.

'He's saving for *you*,' said Pemberton. 'They think of you in everything they do.'

'He might, while he's about it, save a little – ' The boy paused, and his friend waited to hear what. Then Morgan brought out oddly: 'A little reputation.'

'Oh, there's plenty of that. That's all right!'

'Enough of it for the people they know, no doubt. The people they know are awful.'

'Do you mean the princes? We mustn't abuse the princes.'

'Why not? They haven't married Paula – they haven't married Amy. They only clean out Ulick.'

'You *do* know everything!' Pemberton declared.

'No, I don't, after all. I don't know what they live on, or how they live, or *why* they live! What have they got and how did they get it? Are they rich, are they poor, or have they a *modeste aisance*? Why are they always chiveying about – living one year like ambassadors and the next like paupers? Who are they, anyway, and what are they? I've thought of all that – I've thought of a lot of things. They're so beastly worldly. That's what I hate most – oh, I've *seen* it! All they care about is to make an appearance and to pass for something or other. What the dickens do they want to pass for? What *do* they, Mr Pemberton?'

'You pause for a reply,' said Pemberton, treating the question as a joke, yet wondering too and greatly struck with the boy's intense if imperfect vision. 'I haven't the least idea.'

'And what good does it do? Haven't I seen the way people treat them – the "nice" people, the ones they want to know? They'll take anything from them – they'll lie down and be trampled on. The nice ones hate that – they just sicken them. You're the only really nice person we know.'

'Are you sure? They don't lie down for me!'

'Well, you shan't lie down for them. You've got to go – that's what you've got to do,' said Morgan.

'And what will become of you?'

'Oh, I'm growing up. I shall get off before long. I'll see you later.'

'You had better let me finish you,' Pemberton urged, lending himself to the child's strange superiority.

Morgan stopped in their walk, looking up at him. He had to look up much less than a couple of years before – he had grown, in his loose leanness, so long and high. 'Finish me?' he echoed.

'There are such a lot of jolly things we can do together yet. I want to turn you out – I want you to do me credit.'

Morgan continued to look at him. 'To give you credit – do you mean?'

'My dear fellow, you're too clever to live.'

'That's just what I'm afraid you think. No, no; it isn't fair – I can't endure it. We'll separate next week. The sooner it's over the sooner to sleep.'

'If I hear of anything – any other chance – I promise to go,' Pemberton said.

Morgan consented to consider this. 'But you'll be honest,' he demanded; 'you won't pretend you haven't heard?'

'I'm much more likely to pretend I have.'

'But what can you hear of, this way, stuck in a hole with us? You ought to be on the spot, to go to England – you ought to go to America.'

'One would think you were *my* tutor!' said Pemberton.

Morgan walked on and after a little had begun again: 'Well, now that you know that I know and that we look at the facts and keep nothing back – it's much more comfortable, isn't it?'

'My dear boy, it's so amusing, so interesting, that it will surely be quite impossible for me to forgo such hours as these.'

This made Morgan stop once more. 'You *do* keep something back. Oh you're not straight – *I* am!'

'How am I not straight?'

'Oh you've got your idea!'

'My idea?'

'Why that I probably shan't make old – make older – bones, and that you can stick it out till I'm removed.'

'You *are* too clever to live!' Pemberton repeated.

'I call it a mean idea,' Morgan pursued. 'But I shall punish you by the way I hang on.'

'Look out or I'll poison you!' Pemberton laughed.

'I'm stronger and better every year. Haven't you noticed that there hasn't been a doctor near me since you came?'

'*I'm* your doctor,' said the young man, taking his arm and drawing him tenderly on again.

Morgan proceeded and after a few steps gave a sigh of mingled weariness and relief. 'Ah, now that we look at the facts, it's all right!'

They looked at the facts a good deal after this and one of the first consequences of their doing so was that Pemberton stuck it out, in his friend's parlance, for the purpose. Morgan made the facts so vivid and so droll, and at the same time so bald and so ugly, that there was fascination in talking them over with him, just as there would have been heartlessness in leaving him alone with them. Now that the pair had such perceptions in common it was useless for them to pretend they didn't judge such people; but the very judgement and the exchange of perceptions created another tie. Morgan had never been so interesting as now that he himself was made plainer by the sidelight of these confidences. What came out in it most was the small fine passion of his pride. He had plenty of that, Pemberton felt – so much that one might perhaps wisely wish for it some early bruises. He would have liked his people to have spirit: he had waked up to the sense of their perpetually eating humble-pie. His mother would consume any amount, and his father would consume even more than his mother. He had a theory that Ulick had wriggled out of an 'affair' at Nice: there had once been a flurry at home, a regular panic, after which they all went to bed and took medicine, not to be accounted for on any other supposition. Morgan had a romantic imagination, led by poetry and history, and he would have liked those who 'bore his name' – as he used to say to Pemberton with the humour that made his queer delicacies manly – to carry themselves with an air. But their one idea was to get in with people who didn't want them and to take snubs as if they were honourable scars. Why people didn't want them more he didn't know – that was people's own affair; after all they weren't superficially repulsive, they were a hundred times cleverer than most of the dreary grandees, the 'poor swells' they rushed about Europe to catch up with. 'After all they *are* amusing – they are!' he used to pronounce with the wisdom of the ages. To which Pemberton always replied: 'Amusing – the great Moreen troupe? Why they're altogether delightful; and if it weren't for the hitch that you and I (feeble performers!) make in the *ensemble* they'd carry everything before them.'

What the boy couldn't get over was the fact that this particular blight seemed, in a tradition of self-respect, so undeserved and so arbitrary. No doubt people had a right to take the line they liked; but why should his people have liked the line of pushing and toadying and lying and cheating? What had their forefathers – all decent folk, so far as he knew – done to them, or what had *he* done to them? Who had poisoned their blood with the fifth-rate social ideal, the fixed idea of making smart acquaintances and getting into the *monde chic*, especially when it was foredoomed to failure and exposure? They showed so what they were after; that was what made the people they wanted not want *them*. And never a wince for dignity, never a throb of shame at looking each other in the face, never any independence or resentment or disgust. If his father or his brother would only knock some-one down once or twice a year! Clever as they were they never guessed the impression they made. They were good-natured, yes – as good-natured as Jews at the doors of clothing-shops! But was that the model one wanted one's family to follow? Morgan had dim memories of an old grandfather, the maternal, in New York, whom he had been taken across the ocean at the age of five to see: a gentleman with a high neckcloth and a good deal of pronunciation, who wore a dress-coat in the morning, which made one wonder what he wore in the evening, and had, or was supposed to have 'property' and something to do with the Bible Society. It couldn't have been but that he was a good type. Pemberton himself remembered Mrs Clancy, a widowed sister of Mr Moreen's, who was as irritating as a moral tale and had paid a fortnight's visit to the family at Nice shortly after he came to live with them. She was 'pure and refined', as Amy said over the banjo, and had the air of not knowing what they meant when they talked, and of keeping some-thing rather important back. Pemberton judged that what she kept back was an approval of many of their ways; therefore it was to be supposed that she too was of a good type, and that Mr and Mrs Moreen and Ulick and Paula and Amy might easily have been of a better one if they would.

But that they wouldn't was more and more perceptible from day to day. They continued to 'chivey', as Morgan called it, and in due time became aware of a variety of reasons for proceeding to Venice. They mentioned a great many of them – they were always strikingly frank and had the brightest friendly chatter, at the late foreign breakfast in especial, before the ladies had made up their faces, when they leaned their arms on the table, had something to follow the *demi-tasse*, and, in the heat of familiar discussion as to what they 'really ought' to do, fell inevitably into the languages in which they could *tutoyer*. Even Pemberton liked them then; he could endure even Ulick when he heard him give his little flat voice for the 'sweet sea-city'. That was what made him have a sneaking kindness for them – that they were so out of the workaday world and kept him so out of it. The summer had waned when, with cries of ecstasy, they all passed out on the balcony that overhung the Grand Canal. The sunsets then were splendid and the Dorringtons had arrived. The Dorringtons were the only reason they hadn't talked of at breakfast; but the reasons they didn't talk of at breakfast always came out in the end. The Dorringtons on the other hand came out very little; or else when they did they stayed – as was natural – for hours, during which periods Mrs Moreen and the girls sometimes called at their hotel (to see if they had returned) as many as three times running. The gondola was for the ladies, as in Venice too there were 'days', which Mrs Moreen knew in their order an hour after she arrived. She immediately took one herself, to which the

Dorringtons never came, though on a certain occasion when Pemberton and his pupil were together at St Mark's – where, taking the best walks they had ever had and haunting a hundred churches, they spent a great deal of time – they saw the old lord turn up with Mr Moreen and Ulick, who showed him the dim basilica as if it belonged to them. Pemberton noted how much less, among its curiosities, Lord Dorrington carried himself as a man of the world; wondering too whether, for such services, his companions took a fee from him. The autumn at any rate waned, the Dorringtons departed, and Lord Verschoyle, the eldest son, had proposed neither for Amy nor for Paula.

One sad November day, while the wind roared round the old palace and the rain lashed the lagoon, Pemberton, for exercise and even somewhat for warmth – the Moreens were horribly frugal about fires; it was a cause of suffering to their inmate – walked up and down the big bare *sala* with his pupil. The scagliola floor was cold, the high battered casements shook in the storm, and the stately decay of the place was unrelieved by a particle of furniture. Pemberton's spirits were low, and it came over him that the fortune of the Moreens was now even lower. A blast of desolation, a portent of disgrace and disaster, seemed to draw through the comfortless hall. Mr Moreen and Ulick were in the Piazza, looking out for something, strolling drearily, in mackintoshes, under the arcades; but still, in spite of mackintoshes, unmistakable men of the world. Paula and Amy were in bed – it might have been thought they were staying there to keep warm. Pemberton looked askance at the boy at his side, to see to what extent he was conscious of these dark omens. But Morgan, luckily for him, was now mainly conscious of growing taller and stronger and indeed of being in his fifteenth year. This fact was intensely interesting to him and the basis of a private theory – which, however, he had imparted to his tutor – that in a little while he should stand on his own feet. He considered that the situation would change – that in short he should be 'finished', grown up, producible in the world of affairs and ready to prove himself of sterling ability. Sharply as he was capable at times of analysing, as he called it, his life, there were happy hours when he remained, as he also called it – and as the name, really, of their right ideal – 'jolly' superficial; the proof of which was his fundamental assumption that he should presently go to Oxford, to Pemberton's college, and, aided and abetted by Pemberton, do the most wonderful things. It depressed the young man to see how little in such a project he took account of ways and means: in other connections he mostly kept to the measure. Pemberton tried to imagine the Moreens at Oxford and fortunately failed; yet unless they were to adopt it as a residence there would be no *modus vivendi* for Morgan. How could he live without an allowance, and where was the allowance to come from? He, Pemberton, might live on Morgan; but how could Morgan live on *him*? What was to become of him anyhow? Somehow the fact that he was a big boy now, with better prospects of health, made the question of his future more difficult. So long as he was markedly frail the great consideration he inspired seemed enough of an answer to it. But at the bottom of Pemberton's heart was the recognition of his probably being strong enough to live and not yet strong enough to struggle or to thrive. Morgan himself at any rate was in the first flush of the rosiest consciousness of adolescence, so that the beating of the tempest seemed to him after all but the voice of life and the challenge of fate. He had on his shabby little overcoat, with the collar up, but was enjoying his walk.

It was interrupted at last by the appearance of his mother at the end of the *sala*. She beckoned him to come to her, and while Pemberton saw him, complaisant, pass down the long vista and over the damp false marble, he wondered what was in the air. Mrs Moreen said a word to the boy and made him go into the room she had quitted. Then, having closed the door after him, she directed her steps swiftly to Pemberton. There was something in the air, but his wildest flight of fancy wouldn't have suggested what it proved to be. She signified that she had made a pretext to get Morgan out of the way, and then she enquired – without hesitation – if the young man could favour her with the loan of sixty francs. While, before bursting into a laugh, he stared at her with surprise, she declared that she was awfully pressed for the money; she was desperate for it – it would save her life.

'Dear lady, *c'est trop fort*!' Pemberton laughed in the manner and with the borrowed grace of idiom that marked the best colloquial, the best anecdotic, moments of his friends themselves. 'Where in the world do you suppose I should get sixty francs, *du train dont vous allez*?'

'I thought you worked – wrote things. Don't they pay you?'

'Not a penny.'

'Are you such a fool as to work for nothing?'

'You ought surely to know that.'

Mrs Moreen stared, then she coloured a little. Pemberton saw she had quite forgotten the terms – if 'terms' they could be called – that he had ended by accepting from herself; they had burdened her memory as little as her conscience. 'Oh, yes, I see what you mean – you've been very nice about that; but why drag it in so often?' She had been perfectly urbane with him ever since the rough scene of explanation in his room the morning he made her accept *his* 'terms' – the necessity of his making his case known to Morgan. She had felt no resentment after seeing there was no danger Morgan would take the matter up with her. Indeed, attributing this immunity to the good taste of his influence with the boy, she had once said to Pemberton: 'My dear fellow, it's an immense comfort you're a gentleman.' She repeated this in substance now. 'Of course you're a gentleman – that's a bother the less!' Pemberton reminded her that he had not 'dragged in' anything that wasn't already in as much as his foot was in his shoe; and she also repeated her prayer that, somewhere and somehow, he would find her sixty francs. He took the liberty of hinting that if he could find them it wouldn't be to lend them to *her* – as to which he consciously did himself injustice, knowing that if he had them he would certainly put them at her disposal. He accused himself, at bottom and not unveraciously, of a fantastic, a demoralised sympathy with her. If misery made strange bedfellows it also made strange sympathies. It was moreover a part of the abasement of living with such people that one had to make vulgar retorts, quite out of one's own tradition of good manners. 'Morgan, Morgan, to what pass have I come for you?' he groaned, while Mrs Moreen floated voluminously down the *sala* again to liberate the boy, wailing as she went that everything was too odious.

Before their young friend was liberated there came a thump at the door communicating with the staircase, followed by the apparition of a dripping youth who poked in his head. Pemberton recognised him as the bearer of a telegram and recognised the telegram as addressed to himself. Morgan came back as, after glancing at the signature – that of a relative in London, he was reading the words: 'Found a jolly job for you, engagement to coach opulent youth on own terms. Come at once.' The answer happily was paid and the messenger waited. Morgan, who had drawn near, waited too and looked hard at Pemberton; and Pemberton, after a moment, having met his look, handed him the telegram. It was really by wise looks – they knew each other so well now – that, while the telegraph-boy, in his waterproof cape, made a great puddle on the floor, the thing was settled between them. Pemberton wrote the answer with a pencil against the frescoed wall, and the messenger departed. When he had gone the young man explained himself.

'I'll make a tremendous charge; I'll earn a lot of money in a short time, and we'll live on it.'

'Well, I hope the opulent youth will be a dismal dunce – he probably will – ' Morgan parenthesised – 'and keep you a long time a-hammering of it in.'

'Of course the longer he keeps me the more we shall have for our old age.'

'But suppose *they* don't pay you!' Morgan awfully suggested.

'Oh there are not two such – !' But Pemberton pulled up; he had been on the point of using too invidious a term. Instead of this he said: 'Two such fatalities.'

Morgan flushed – the tears came to his eyes. '*Dites toujours* two such rascally crews!' Then in a different tone he added: 'Happy opulent youth!'

'Not if he's a dismal dunce.'

'Oh, they're happier then. But you can't have everything, can you?' the boy smiled.

Pemberton held him fast, hands on his shoulders – he had never loved him so. 'What will become of you, what will you do?' He thought of Mrs Moreen, desperate for sixty francs.

'I shall become an *homme fait*.' And then, as if he recognised all the bearings of Pemberton's allusion: 'I shall get on with them better when you're not here.'

'Ah, don't say that – it sounds as if I set you against them!'

'You do – the sight of you. It's all right; you know what I mean. I shall be beautiful. I'll take their affairs in hand; I'll marry my sisters.'

'You'll marry yourself!' joked Pemberton; as high, rather tense pleasantry would evidently be the right, or the safest, tone for their separation.

It was, however, not purely in this strain that Morgan suddenly asked: 'But I say – how will you get to your jolly job? You'll have to telegraph to the opulent youth for money to come on.'

Pemberton bethought himself. 'They won't like that, will they?'

'Oh, look out for them!'

Then Pemberton brought out his remedy. 'I'll go to the American Consul; I'll borrow some money of him – just for the few days, on the strength of the telegram.'

Morgan was hilarious. 'Show him the telegram – then collar the money and stay!'

Pemberton entered into the joke sufficiently to reply that for Morgan he was really capable of that; but the boy, growing more serious, and to prove he hadn't meant what he said, not only hurried him off to the consulate – since he was to start that evening, as he had wired to his friend – but made sure of their affair by going with him. They splashed through the tortuous perforations and over the humpbacked bridges, and they passed through the Piazza, where they saw Mr Moreen and Ulick go into a jeweller's shop. The Consul proved accommodating – Pemberton said it wasn't the letter, but Morgan's grand air – and on their way back they went into St Mark's for a hushed ten minutes. Later they took up and kept up the fun of it to the very end; and it seemed to Pemberton a part of that fun that Mrs Moreen, who was very angry when he had announced to her his intention, should charge him, grotesquely and vulgarly and in reference to the loan she had vainly endeavoured to effect, with bolting lest they should 'get something out' of him. On the other hand he had to do Mr Moreen and Ulick the justice to recognise that when on coming in they heard the cruel news they took it like perfect men of the world.

8

When he got at work with the opulent youth, who was to be taken in hand for Balliol, he found himself unable to say if this aspirant had really such poor parts or if the appearance were only begotten of his own long association with an intensely living little mind. From Morgan he heard half a dozen times: the boy wrote charming young letters, a patchwork of tongues, with indulgent postscripts in the family Volapuk and, in little squares and rounds and crannies of the text, the drollest illustrations – letters that he was divided between the impulse to show his present charge as a vain, a wasted incentive, and the sense of something in them that publicity would profane. The opulent youth went up in due course and failed to pass; but it seemed to add to the presumption that brilliancy was not expected of him all at once that his parents, condoning the lapse, which they good-naturedly treated as little as possible as if it were Pemberton's, should have sounded the rally again, begged the young coach to renew the siege.

The young coach was now in a position to lend Mrs Moreen sixty francs, and he sent her a post-office order even for a larger amount. In return for this favour he received a frantic scribbled line from her: 'Implore you to come back instantly – Morgan dreadfully ill.' They were on there rebound, once more in Paris – often as Pemberton had seen them depressed he had never seen them crushed – and communication was therefore rapid. He wrote to the boy to ascertain the state of his health, but awaited the answer in vain. He accordingly, after three days, took an abrupt leave of the opulent youth and, crossing the Channel, alighted at the small hotel, in the quarter of the Champs Elysées, of which Mrs Moreen had given him the address. A deep if dumb dissatisfaction with this lady and her companions bore him company: they couldn't be vulgarly honest, but they could live at hotels, in velvety *entresols*, amid a smell of burnt pastilles, surrounded by the most expensive city in Europe. When he had left them in Venice it was with an irrepressible suspicion that something was going to happen; but the only thing that could have taken place was again their masterly retreat. 'How is he? where is he?' he asked of Mrs Moreen; but before she could speak these questions were answered by the pressure round his neck of a pair of arms, in shrunken sleeves, which still were perfectly capable of an effusive young foreign squeeze.

'Dreadfully ill – I don't see it!' the young man cried. And then to Morgan: 'Why on earth didn't you relieve me? Why didn't you answer my letter?'

Mrs Moreen declared that when she wrote he was very bad, and Pemberton learned at the same time from the boy that he had answered every letter he had received. This led to the clear inference that Pemberton's note had been kept from him so that the game practised should not be interfered with. Mrs Moreen was prepared to see the fact exposed, as Pemberton saw the moment he faced her that she was prepared for a good many other things. She was prepared above all to maintain that she had acted from a sense of duty, that she was enchanted she had got him over, whatever they might say, and that it was useless of him to pretend he didn't know in all his bones that his place at such a time was with Morgan. He had taken the boy away from them and now had no right to abandon him. He had created for himself the gravest responsibilities and must at least abide by what he had done.

'Taken him away from you?' Pemberton exclaimed indignantly.

'Do it – do it for pity's sake; that's just what I want. I can't stand *this* – and such scenes. They're awful frauds – poor dears!' These words broke from Morgan, who had intermitted his embrace, in a key which made Pemberton turn quickly to him and see that he had suddenly seated himself, was breathing in great pain, and was very pale.

'*Now* do you say he's not in a state, my precious pet?' shouted his mother, dropping on her knees before him with clasped hands, but touching him no more than if he had been a gilded idol. 'It will pass – it's only for an instant; but don't say such dreadful things!'

'I'm all right – all right,' Morgan panted to Pemberton, whom he sat looking up at with a strange smile, his hands resting on either side of the sofa.

'Now do you pretend I've been dishonest, that I've deceived?' Mrs Moreen flashed at Pemberton as she got up.

'It isn't *he* says it, it's I!' the boy returned, apparently easier, but sinking back against the wall; while his restored friend, who had sat down beside him, took his hand and bent over him.

'Darling child, one does what one can; there are so many things to consider,' urged Mrs Moreen. 'It's his *place* – his only place. You see *you* think it is now.'

'Take me away – take me away,' Morgan went on, smiling to Pemberton with his white face.

'Where shall I take you, and how – oh, *how*, my boy?' the young man stammered, thinking of the rude way in which his friends in London held that, for his convenience, with no assurance of prompt return, he had thrown them over; of the just resentment with which they would already have called in a successor, and of the scant help to finding fresh employment that resided for him in the grossness of his having failed to pass his pupil.

'Oh, we'll settle that. You used to talk about it,' said Morgan. 'If we can only go, all the rest's a detail.'

'Talk about it as much as you like, but don't think you can attempt it. Mr Moreen would never consent – it would be so *very* hand-to-mouth,' Pemberton's hostess beautifully explained to him. Then to Morgan she made it clearer: 'It would destroy our peace, it would break our hearts. Now that he's back it will be all the same again. You'll have your life, your work and your freedom, and we'll all be happy as we used to be. You'll bloom and grow perfectly well, and we won't have any more silly experiments, will we? They're too absurd. It's Mr Pemberton's place – everyone in his place. You in yours, your papa in his, me in mine – *n'est-ce pas, chéri?* We'll all forget how foolish we've been and have lovely times.'

She continued to talk and to surge vaguely about the little draped stuffy salon while Pemberton sat with the boy, whose colour gradually came back; and she mixed up her reasons, hinting that there were going to be changes, that the other children might scatter (who knew? – Paula had her ideas) and that then it might be fancied how much the poor old parent-birds would want the little nestling. Morgan looked at Pemberton, who wouldn't let him move; and Pemberton knew exactly how he felt at hearing himself called a little nestling. He admitted that he had had one or two bad days, but he protested afresh against the wrong of his mother's having made them the ground of an appeal to poor Pemberton. Poor Pemberton could laugh now, apart from the comicality of Mrs Moreen's mustering so much philosophy for her defence – she seemed to shake it out of her agitated petticoats, which knocked over the light gilt chairs – so little did their young companion, *marked*, unmistakably marked at the best, strike him as qualified to repudiate any advantage.

He himself was in for it at any rate. He should have Morgan on his hands again indefinitely; though indeed he saw the lad had a private theory to produce which would be intended to smooth this down. He was obliged to him for it in advance; but the suggested amendment didn't keep his heart rather from sinking, any more than it prevented him from accepting the prospect on the spot, with some confidence moreover that he should do so even better if he could have a little supper. Mrs Moreen threw out more hints about the changes that were to be looked for, but she was such a mixture of smiles and shudders – she confessed she was very nervous – that he couldn't tell if she were in high feather or only in hysterics. If the family was really at last going to pieces why shouldn't she recognise the necessity of pitching Morgan into some sort of lifeboat? This presumption was fostered by the fact that they were established in luxurious quarters in the capital of pleasure; that was exactly where they naturally *would* be established in view of going to pieces. Moreover didn't she mention that Mr Moreen and the others were enjoying themselves at the opera with Mr Granger, and wasn't *that* also precisely where one would look for them on the eve of a smash? Pemberton gathered that Mr Granger was a rich vacant American – a big bill with a flourishy heading and no items; so that one of Paula's 'ideas' was probably that this time she hadn't missed fire – by which straight shot indeed she would have shattered the general cohesion. And if the cohesion was to crumble what would become of poor Pemberton? He felt quite enough bound up with them to figure to his alarm as a dislodged block in the edifice.

It was Morgan who eventually asked if no supper had been ordered for him; sitting with him below, later, at the dim delayed meal, in the presence of a great deal of corded green plush, a plate of ornamental biscuit and an aloofness marked on the part of the waiter, Mrs Moreen had explained that they had been obliged to secure a room for the visitor out of the house; and Morgan's consolation – he offered it while Pemberton reflected on the nastiness of lukewarm sauces – proved to be, largely, that this circumstance would facilitate their escape. He talked of their escape – recurring to it often afterwards – as if they were making up a 'boy's book' together. But he likewise expressed his sense that there was something in the air, that the Moreens couldn't keep it up much longer. In point of fact, as Pemberton was to see, they kept it up for five or six months. All the while, however, Morgan's contention was designed to cheer him. Mr Moreen and Ulick, whom he had met the day after his return, accepted that return like perfect men of the world. If Paula and Amy treated it even with less formality an allowance was to be made for them, inasmuch as Mr Granger hadn't come to the opera after all. He had only placed his box at their service, with a bouquet for each of the party; there was even one apiece, embittering the thought of his profusion, for Mr Moreen and Ulick. 'They're all like that,' was Morgan's comment; 'at the very last, just when we think we've landed them, they're back in the deep sea!'

Morgan's comments, in these days, were more and more free; they even included a large recognition of the extraordinary tenderness with which he had been treated while Pemberton was away. Oh yes, they couldn't do enough to be nice to him, to show him they had him on their mind and make up for his loss. That was just what made the whole thing so sad and caused him to rejoice after all in Pemberton's return – he had to keep thinking of their affection less, had less sense of obligation. Pemberton laughed out at this last reason, and Morgan blushed and said: 'Well, dash it, you know what I mean.' Pemberton knew perfectly what he meant; but there were a good many things that – dash it too! – it didn't make any clearer. This episode of his second sojourn in Paris stretched itself out wearily, with their resumed readings and wanderings and maunderings, their potterings on the quays, their hauntings of the museums, their occasional lingerings in the Palais Royal, when the first sharp weather came on and there was a comfort in warm emanations, before Chevet's wonderful succulent window. Morgan wanted to hear all about the opulent youth – he took an immense interest in him. Some of the details of his opulence – Pemberton could spare him none of them – evidently fed the boy's appreciation of all his friend had given up to come back to him; but in addition to the greater reciprocity established by that heroism he had always his little brooding theory, in which there was a frivolous gaiety too, that their long probation was drawing to a close. Morgan's conviction that the Moreens couldn't go on much longer kept pace with the unexpended impetus with which, from month to month, they did go on. Three weeks after Pemberton had rejoined them they went on to another hotel, a dingier one than the first; but Morgan rejoiced that his tutor had at least still not sacrificed the advantage of a room outside. He clung to the romantic utility of this when the day, or rather the night, should arrive for their escape.

For the first time, in this complicated connection, our friend felt his collar gall him. It was, as he had said to Mrs Moreen in Venice, *trop fort* – everything was *trop fort*. He could neither really throw off his blighting burden nor find in it the benefit of a pacified conscience or of a rewarded affection. He had spent all the money accruing to him in England, and he saw his youth going and that he was getting nothing back for it. It was all very well of Morgan to count it for reparation that he should now settle on him permanently – there was an irritating flaw in such a view. He saw what the boy had in his mind: the conception that as his friend had had the generosity to come back he must show his gratitude by giving him his life. But the poor friend didn't desire the gift – what could he do with Morgan's dreadful little life? Of course at the same time that Pemberton was irritated he remembered the reason, which was very honourable to Morgan and which dwelt simply in his making one so forget that he was no more than a patched urchin. If one dealt with him on a different basis one's misadventures were one's own fault. So Pemberton waited in a queer confusion of yearning and alarm for the catastrophe which was held to hang over the house of Moreen, of which he certainly at moments felt the symptoms brush his cheek and as to which he wondered much in what form it would find its liveliest effect.

Perhaps it would take the form of sudden dispersal – a frightened *sauve qui peut*, a scuttling into selfish corners. Certainly they were less elastic than of yore; they were evidently looking for something they didn't find. The Dorringtons hadn't reappeared, the princes had scattered; wasn't that the beginning of the end? Mrs Moreen had lost her reckoning of the famous 'days'; her social calendar was blurred – it had turned its face to the wall. Pemberton suspected that the great, the cruel discomfiture had been the unspeakable behaviour of Mr Granger, who seemed not to know what he wanted, or, what was much worse, what *they* wanted. He kept sending flowers, as if to bestrew the path of his retreat, which was never the path of a return. Flowers were all very well, but – Pemberton could complete the proposition. It was now positively conspicuous that in the long run the Moreens were a social failure; so that the young man was almost grateful the run had not been short. Mr Moreen indeed was still occasionally able to get away on business and, what was more surprising, was likewise able to get back. Ulick had no club but you couldn't have discovered it from his appearance, which was as much as ever that of a person looking at life from the window of such an institution; therefore Pemberton was doubly surprised at an answer he once heard him make his mother in the desperate tone of a man familiar with the worst privations. Her question Pemberton had not quite caught; it appeared to be an appeal for a suggestion as to whom they might get to take Amy. 'Let the Devil take her!' Ulick snapped; so that Pemberton could see that they had not only lost their amiability but had ceased to believe in themselves. He could also see that if Mrs Moreen was trying to get people to take her children she might be regarded as closing the hatches for the storm. But Morgan would be the last she would part with.

One winter afternoon – it was a Sunday – he and the boy walked far together in the Bois de Boulogne. The evening was so splendid, the cold lemon-coloured sunset so clear, the stream of carriages and pedestrians so amusing and the fascination of Paris so great, that they stayed out later than usual and became aware that they should have to hurry home to arrive in time for dinner. They hurried accordingly, arm-in-arm, good-humoured and hungry, agreeing that there was nothing like Paris after all and that after everything too that had come and gone they were not yet sated with innocent pleasures. When they reached the hotel they found that, though scandalously late, they were in time for all the dinner they were likely to sit down to. Confusion reigned in the apartments of the Moreens – very shabby ones this time, but the best in the house – and before the interrupted service of the table, with objects displaced almost as if there had been a scuffle and a great wine-stain from an overturned bottle, Pemberton couldn't blink the fact that there had been a scene of the last proprietary firmness. The storm had come – they were all seeking refuge. The hatches were down, Paula and Amy were invisible – they had never tried the most casual art upon Pemberton, but he felt they had enough of an eye to him not to wish to meet him as young ladies whose frocks had been confiscated – and Ulick appeared to have jumped overboard. The host and his staff, in a word, had ceased to 'go on' at the pace of their guests, and the air of embarrassed detention, thanks to a pile of gaping trunks in the passage, was strangely commingled with the air of indignant withdrawal. When Morgan took all this in – and he took it in very quickly – he coloured to the roots of his hair. He had walked from his infancy among difficulties and dangers, but he had never seen a public exposure. Pemberton noticed in a second glance at him that the tears had rushed into his eyes and that they were tears of a new and untasted bitterness. He wondered an instant, for the boy's sake, whether he might successfully pretend not to understand. Not successfully, he felt, as Mr and Mrs Moreen, dinnerless by their extinguished hearth, rose before him in their little dis-honoured *salon*, casting about with glassy eyes for the nearest port in such a storm. They were not prostrate but were horribly white, and Mrs Moreen had evidently been crying. Pemberton quickly learned however that her grief was not for the loss of her dinner, much as she usually enjoyed it, but the fruit of a blow that struck even deeper, as she made all haste to explain. He would see for himself, so far as that went, how the great change had come, the dreadful bolt had fallen, and how they would now all have to turn themselves about. Therefore cruel as it was to them to part with their darling she must look to him to carry a little further the influence he had so fortunately acquired with the boy – to induce his young charge to follow him into some modest retreat. They depended on him – that was the fact – to take their delightful child temporarily under his protection; it would leave Mr Moreen and herself so much more free to give the proper attention (too little, alas! had been given) to the readjustment of their affairs.

'We trust you – we feel we *can*,' said Mrs Moreen, slowly rubbing her plump white hands and looking with compunction hard at Morgan, whose chin, not to take liberties, her husband stroked with a paternal forefinger.

'Oh yes – we feel that we *can*. We trust Mr Pemberton fully, Morgan,' Mr Moreen pursued.

Pemberton wondered again if he might pretend not to understand; but everything good gave way to the intensity of Morgan's understanding. 'Do you mean he may take me to live with him for ever and ever?' cried the boy. 'May take me away, away, anywhere he likes?'

'For ever and ever? *Comme vous-y-allez!*' Mr Moreen laughed indulgently. 'For as long as Mr Pemberton may be so good.'

'We've struggled, we've suffered,' his wife went on; 'but you've made him so your own that we've already been through the worst of the sacrifice.'

Morgan had turned away from his father – he stood looking at Pemberton with a light in his face. His sense of shame for their common humiliated state had dropped; the case had another side – the thing was to clutch at *that*. He had a moment of boyish joy, scarcely mitigated by the reflection that with this unexpected consecration of his hope – too sudden and too violent; the turn taken was away from a *good* boy's book – the 'escape' was left on their hands. The boyish joy was there an instant, and Pemberton was almost scared at the rush of gratitude and affection that broke through his first abasement. When he stammered, 'My dear fellow, what do you say to *that*?' how could one not say something enthusiastic? But there was more need for courage at something else that immediately followed and that made the lad sit down quietly on the nearest chair. He had turned quite livid and had raised his hand to his left side. They were all three looking at him, but Mrs Moreen suddenly bounded forward. 'Ah, his darling little heart!' she broke out; and this time, on her knees before him and without respect for the idol, she caught him ardently in her arms. 'You walked him too far, you hurried him too fast!' she hurled over her shoulder at Pemberton. Her son made no protest, and the next instant, still holding him, she sprang up with her face convulsed and with the terrified cry: 'Help, help! he's going, he's gone!' Pemberton saw with equal horror, by Morgan's own stricken face, that he was beyond their wildest recall. He pulled him half out of his mother's hands, and for a moment, while they held him together, they looked all their dismay into each other's eyes. 'He couldn't stand it with his weak organ,' said Pemberton – 'the shock, the whole scene, the violent emotion.'

'But I thought he *wanted* to go to you!' wailed Mrs Moreen.

'I *told* you he didn't, my dear,' her husband made answer. Mr Moreen was trembling all over and was in his way as deeply affected as his wife. But after the very first he took his bereavement as a man of the world.

The Diary of a Man of Fifty

FLORENCE, April 5th, 1874   They told me I should find Italy greatly changed; and in seven-and-twenty years there is room for changes. But to me everything is so perfectly the same that I seem to be living my youth over again; all the forgotten impressions of that enchanting time come back to me. At the moment they were powerful enough; but they afterwards faded away. What in the world became of them? Whatever becomes of such things, in the long intervals of consciousness? Where do they hide themselves away? in what unvisited cupboards and crannies of our being do they preserve themselves? They are like the lines of a letter written in sympathetic ink; hold the letter to the fire for a while and the grateful warmth brings out the invisible words. It is the warmth of this yellow sun of Florence that has been restoring the text of my own young romance; the thing has been lying before me today as a clear, fresh page. There have been moments during the last ten years when I have felt so portentously old, so fagged and finished, that I should have taken as a very bad joke any intimation that this present sense of juvenility was still in store for me. It won't last, at any rate; so I had better make the best of it. But I confess it surprises me. I have led too serious a life; but that perhaps, after all, preserves one's youth. At all events, I have travelled too far, I have worked too hard, I have lived in brutal climates and associated with tiresome people. When a man has reached his fifty-second year without being, materially, the worse for wear – when he has fair health, a fair fortune, a tidy conscience and a complete exemption from embarrassing relatives – I suppose he is bound, in delicacy, to write himself happy. But I confess I shirk this obligation. I have not been miserable; I won't go so far as to say that – or at least as to write it. But happiness – positive happiness – would have been something different. I don't know that it would have been better, by all measurements – that it would have left me better off at the present time. But it certainly would have made this difference – that I should not have been reduced, in pursuit of pleasant images, to disinter a buried episode of more than a quarter of a century ago. I should have found entertainment more – what shall I call it? – more contemporaneous. I should have had a wife and children, and I should not be in the way of making, as the French say, infidelities to the present. Of course it's a great gain to have had an escape, not to have committed an act of thumping folly; and I suppose that, whatever serious step one might have taken at twenty-five, after a struggle, and with a violent effort, and however one's conduct might appear to be justified by events, there would always remain a certain element of regret; a certain sense of loss lurking in the sense of gain; a tendency to wonder, rather wishfully, what *might* have been. What might have been, in this case, would, without doubt, have been very sad, and what has been has been very cheerful and comfortable; but there are nevertheless two or three questions I might ask myself. Why, for instance, have I never married – why have I never been able to care for any woman as I cared for that one? Ah, why are the mountains blue and why is the sunshine warm? Happiness mitigated by impertinent conjectures – that's about my ticket.

APRIL 6TH   I knew it wouldn't last; it's already passing away. But I have spent a delightful day; I have been strolling all over the place. Everything reminds me of something else, and yet of itself at the same time; my imagination makes a great circuit and comes back to the starting-point. There is that well-remembered odour of spring in the air, and the flowers, as they used to be, are gathered into great sheaves and stacks, all along the rugged base of the Strozzi Palace. I wandered for an hour in the Boboli Gardens; we went there several times together. I remember all those days individually; they seem to me as yesterday. I found the corner where she always chose to sit – the bench of sun-warmed marble, in front of the screen of ilex, with that exuberant statue of Pomona just beside it. The place is exactly the same, except that poor Pomona has lost one of her tapering fingers. I sat there for half an hour, and it was strange how near to me she seemed. The place was perfectly empty – that is, it was filled with *her*. I closed my eyes and listened; I could almost hear the rustle of her dress on the gravel. Why do we make such an ado about death? What is it, after all, but a sort of refinement of life? She died ten years ago, and yet, as I sat there in the sunny stillness, she was a palpable, audible presence. I went afterwards into the gallery of the palace, and wandered for an hour from room to room. The same great pictures hung in the same places, and the same dark frescoes arched above them. Twice, of old, I went there with her; she had a great understanding of art. She understood all sorts of things. Before the Madonna of the Chair I stood a long time. The face is not a particle like hers, and yet reminded me of her. But everything does that. We stood and looked at it together once for half an hour; I remember perfectly what she said.

APRIL 8TH   Yesterday I felt blue – blue and bored; and when I got up this morning I had half a mind to leave Florence. But I went out into the street, beside the Arno, and looked up and down – looked at the yellow river and the violet hills, and then decided to remain – or rather, I decided nothing. I simply stood gazing at the beauty of Florence, and before I had gazed my fill I was in good-humour again, and it was too late to start for Rome. I strolled along the quay, where something presently happened that rewarded me for staying. I stopped in front of a little jeweller's shop, where a great many objects in mosaic were exposed in the window; I stood there for some minutes – I don't know why, for I have no taste for mosaic. In a moment a little girl came and stood beside me – a little girl with a frowsy Italian head, carrying a basket. I turned away, but, as I turned, my eyes happened to fall on her basket. It was covered with a napkin, and on the napkin was pinned a piece of paper, inscribed with an address. This address caught my glance – there was a name on it I knew. It was very legibly written – evidently by a scribe who had made up in zeal what was lacking in skill. *Contessa Salvi-Scarabelli, Via Ghibellina* – so ran the superscription; I looked at it for some moments; it caused me a sudden emotion. Presently the little girl, becoming aware of my attention, glanced up at me, wondering, with a pair of timid brown eyes.

'Are you carrying your basket to the Countess Salvi?' I asked.

The child stared at me. 'To the Countess Scarabelli.'

'Do you know the countess?'

'Know her?' murmured the child, with an air of small dismay.

'I mean, have you seen her?'

'Yes, I have seen her.' And then, in a moment, with a sudden soft smile – '*E bella!*' said the little girl. She was beautiful herself as she said it.

'Precisely; and is she fair or dark?'

The child kept gazing at me. '*Bionda – bionda*,' she answered, looking about into the golden sunshine for a comparison.

'And is she young?'

'She is not young – like me. But she is not old like – like – '

'Like me, eh? And is she married?'

The little girl began to look wise. 'I have never seen the Signor Conte.'

'And she lives in Via Ghibellina?'

'*Sicuro*. In a beautiful palace.'

I had one more question to ask, and I pointed it with certain copper coins. 'Tell me a little – is she good?'

The child inspected a moment the contents of her little brown fist. 'It's you who are good,' she answered.

'Ah, but the countess?' I repeated.

My informant lowered her big brown eyes, with an air of conscientious meditation that was inexpressibly quaint. 'To me she appears so,' she said at last, looking up.

'Ah, then, she must be so,' I said, 'because, for your age, you are very intelligent.' And having delivered myself of this compliment I walked away and left the little girl counting her *soldi*.

I walked back to the hotel, wondering how I could learn something about the Contessa Salvi-Scarabelli. In the doorway I found the innkeeper, and near him stood a young man whom I immediately perceived to be a compatriot, and with whom, apparently, he had been in conversation.

'I wonder whether you can give me a piece of information,' I said to the landlord. 'Do you know anything about the Count Salvi-Scarabelli?'

The landlord looked down at his boots, then slowly raised his shoulders, with a melancholy smile. 'I have many regrets, dear sir – '

'You don't know the name?'

'I know the name, assuredly. But I don't know the gentleman.'

I saw that my question had attracted the attention of the young Englishman, who looked at me with a good deal of earnestness. He was apparently satisfied with what he saw, for he presently decided to speak.

'The Count Scarabelli is dead,' he said, very gravely.

I looked at him a moment; he was a pleasing young fellow. 'And his widow lives,' I observed, 'in Via Ghibellina?'

'I dare say that is the name of the street.' He was a handsome young Englishman, but he was also an awkward one; he wondered who I was and what I wanted, and he did me the honour to perceive that, as regards these points, my appearance was reassuring. But he hesitated, very properly, to talk with a perfect stranger about a lady whom he knew, and he had not the art to conceal his hesitation. I instantly felt it to be singular that though he regarded me as a perfect stranger, I had not the same feeling about him. Whether it was that I had seen him before, or simply that I was struck with his agreeable young face – at any rate, I felt myself, as they say here, in sympathy with him. If I have seen him before I don't remember the occasion, and neither, apparently, does he; I suppose it's only a part of the feeling I have had the last three days about everything. It was this feeling that made me suddenly act as if I had known him a long time.

'Do you know the Countess Salvi?' I asked.

He looked at me a little, and then, without resenting the freedom of my question – 'The Countess Scarabelli, you mean,' he said.

'Yes,' I answered; 'she's the daughter.'

'The daughter is a little girl.'

'She must be grown up now. She must be – let me see – close upon thirty.'

My young Englishman began to smile. 'Of whom are you speaking?'

'I was speaking of the daughter,' I said, understanding his smile. 'But I was thinking of the mother.'

'Of the mother?'

'Of a person I knew twenty-seven years ago – the most charming woman I have ever known. She was the Countess Salvi – she lived in a wonderful old house in Via Ghibellina.'

'A wonderful old house!' my young Englishman repeated.

'She had a little girl,' I went on; 'and the little girl was very fair, like her mother; and the mother and daughter had the same name – Bianca.' I stopped and looked at my companion, and he blushed a little. 'And Bianca Salvi,' I continued, 'was the most charming woman in the world.' He blushed a little more, and I laid my hand on his shoulder. 'Do you know why I tell you this? Because you remind me of what I was when I knew her – when I loved her.' My poor young Englishman gazed at me with a sort of embarrassed and fascinated stare, and still I went on. 'I say that's the reason I told you this – but you'll think it a strange reason. You remind me of my younger self. You needn't resent that – I was a charming young fellow. The Countess Salvi thought so. Her daughter thinks the same of you.'

Instantly, instinctively, he raised his hand to my arm. 'Truly?'

'Ah, you are wonderfully like me!' I said, laughing. 'That was just my state of mind. I wanted tremendously to please her.' He dropped his hand and looked away, smiling, but with an air of ingenuous confusion which quickened my interest in him. 'You don't know what to make of me,' I pursued. 'You don't know why a stranger should suddenly address you in this way and pretend to read your thoughts. Doubtless you think me a little cracked. Perhaps I am eccentric; but it's not so bad as that. I have lived about the world a great deal, following my profession, which is that of a soldier. I have been in India, in Africa, in Canada, and I have lived a good deal alone. That inclines people, I think, to sudden bursts of confidence. A week ago I came into Italy, where I spent six months when I was your age. I came straight to Florence – I was eager to see it again, on account of associations. They have been crowding upon me ever so thickly. I have taken the liberty of giving you a hint of them.' The young man inclined himself a little, in silence, as if he had been struck with a sudden respect. He stood and looked away for a moment at the river and the mountains. 'It's very beautiful,' I said.

'Oh, it's enchanting,' he murmured.

'That's the way I used to talk. But that's nothing to you.'

He glanced at me again. 'On the contrary, I like to hear.'

'Well, then, let us take a walk. If you too are staying at this inn, we are fellow-travellers. We will walk down the Arno to the Cascine. There are several things I should like to ask of you.'

My young Englishman assented with an air of almost filial confidence, and we strolled for an hour beside the river and through the shady alleys of that lovely wilderness. We had a great deal of talk: it's not only myself, it's my whole situation over again.

'Are you very fond of Italy?' I asked.

He hesitated a moment. 'One can't express that.'

'Just so; I couldn't express it. I used to try – I used to write verses. On the subject of Italy I was very ridiculous.'

'So am I ridiculous,' said my companion.

'No, my dear boy,' I answered, 'we are not ridiculous; we are two very reasonable, superior people.'

'The first time one comes – as I have done – it's a revelation.'

'Oh, I remember well; one never forgets it. It's an introduction to beauty.'

'And it must be a great pleasure,' said my young friend, 'to come back.'

'Yes, fortunately the beauty is always here. What form of it,' I asked, 'do you prefer?'

My companion looked a little mystified; and at last he said, 'I am very fond of the pictures.'

'So was I. And among the pictures, which do you like best?'

'Oh, a great many.'

'So did I; but I had certain favourites.'

Again the young man hesitated a little, and then he confessed that the group of painters he preferred, on the whole, to all others, was that of the early Florentines.

I was so struck with this that I stopped short. 'That was exactly my taste!' And then I passed my hand into his arm and we went our way again.

We sat down on an old stone bench in the Cascine, and a solemn blank-eyed Hermes, with wrinkles accentuated by the dust of ages, stood above us and listened to our talk.

'The Countess Salvi died ten years ago,' I said.

My companion admitted that he had heard her daughter say so.

'After I knew her she married again,' I added. 'The Count Salvi died before I knew her – a couple of years after their marriage.'

'Yes, I have heard that.'

'And what else have you heard?'

My companion stared at me; he had evidently heard nothing.

'She was a very interesting woman – there are a great many things to be said about her. Later, perhaps, I will tell you. Has the daughter the same charm?'

'You forget,' said my young man, smiling, 'that I have never seen the mother.'

'Very true. I keep confounding. But the daughter – how long have you known her?'

'Only since I have been here. A very short time.'

'A week?'

For a moment he said nothing. 'A month.'

'That's just the answer I should have made. A week, a month – it was all the same to me.'

'I think it is more than a month,' said the young man.

'It's probably six. How did you make her acquaintance?'

'By a letter – an introduction given me by a friend in England.'

'The analogy is complete,' I said. 'But the friend who gave me my letter to Madame de Salvi died many years ago. He, too, admired her greatly. I don't know why it never came into my mind that her daughter might be living in Florence. Somehow I took for granted it was all over. I never thought of the little girl; I never heard what had become of her. I walked past the palace yesterday and saw that it was occupied; but I took for granted it had changed hands.'

'The Countess Scarabelli,' said my friend, 'brought it to her husband as her marriage-portion.'

'I hope he appreciated it! There is a fountain in the court, and there is a charming old garden beyond it. The countess's sitting-room looks into that garden. The staircase is of white marble, and there is a medallion by Luca della Robbia set into the wall at the place where it makes a bend. Before you come into the drawing-room you stand a moment in a great vaulted place hung round with faded tapestry, paved with bare tiles, and furnished only with three chairs. In the drawing-room, above the fireplace, is a superb Andrea del Sarto. The furniture is covered with pale sea-green.'

My companion listened to all this.

'The Andrea del Sarto is there; it's magnificent. But the furniture is in pale red.'

'Ah, they have changed it, then – in twenty-seven years.'

'And there's a portrait of Madame de Salvi,' continued my friend.

I was silent a moment. 'I should like to see that.'

He too was silent. Then he asked, 'Why don't you go and see it? If you knew the mother so well, why don't you call upon the daughter?'

'From what you tell me I am afraid.'

'What have I told you to make you afraid?'

I looked a little at his ingenuous countenance. 'The mother was a very dangerous woman.'

The young Englishman began to blush again. 'The daughter is not,' he said.

'Are you very sure?'

He didn't say he was sure, but he presently enquired in what way the Countess Salvi had been dangerous.

'You must not ask me that,' I answered 'for after all, I desire to remember only what was good in her.' And as we walked back I begged him to render me the service of mentioning my name to his friend, and of saying that I had known her mother well, and that I asked permission to come and see her.

APRIL 9TH   I have seen that poor boy half a dozen times again, and a most amiable young fellow he is. He continues to represent to me, in the most extraordinary manner, my own young identity; the correspondence is perfect at all points, save that he is a better boy than I. He is evidently acutely interested in his countess, and leads quite the same life with her that I led with Madame de Salvi. He goes to see her every evening and stays half the night; these Florentines keep the most extraordinary hours. I remember, towards 3 a.m., Madame de Salvi used to turn me out. – 'Come, come,' she would say, 'it's time to go. If you were to stay later people might talk.' I don't know at what time he comes home, but I suppose his evening seems as short as mine did. Today he brought me a message from his contessa – a very gracious little speech. She remembered often to have heard her mother speak of me – she called me her English friend. All her mother's friends were dear to her, and she begged I would do her the honour to come and see her. She is always at home of an evening. Poor young Stanmer (he is of the Devonshire Stanmers – a great property) reported this speech verbatim, and of course it can't in the least signify to him that a poor, grizzled, battered soldier, old enough to be his father, should come to call upon his *inammorata*. But I remember how it used to matter to me when other men came; that's a point of difference. However, it's only because I'm so old. At twenty-five I shouldn't have been afraid of myself at fifty-two. Camerino was thirty-four – and then the others! She was always at home in the evening, and they all used to come. They were old Florentine names. But she used to let me stay after them all; she thought an old English name as good. What a transcendent coquette! . . . But *basta cosi* as she used to say. I meant to go tonight to Casa Salvi, but I couldn't bring myself to the point. I don't know what I'm afraid of; I used to be in a hurry enough to go there once. I suppose I am afraid of the very look of the place – of the old rooms, the old walls. I shall go tomorrow night. I am afraid of the very echoes.

APRIL 10TH She has the most extraordinary resemblance to her mother. When I went in I was tremendously startled; I stood starting at her. I have just come home; it is past midnight; I have been all the evening at Casa Salvi. It is very warm – my window is open – I can look out on the river gliding past in the starlight. So, of old, when I came home, I used to stand and look out. There are the same cypresses on the opposite hills.

Poor young Stanmer was there, and three or four other admirers; they all got up when I came in. I think I had been talked about, and there was some curiosity. But why should I have been talked about? They were all youngish men – none of them of my time. She is a wonderful likeness of her mother; I couldn't get over it. Beautiful like her mother, and yet with the same faults in her face; but with her mother's perfect head and brow and sympathetic, almost pitying, eyes. Her face has just that peculiarity of her mother's, which, of all human countenances that I have ever known, was the one that passed most quickly and completely from the expression of gaiety to that of repose. Repose in her face always suggested sadness; and while you were watching it with a kind of awe, and wondering of what tragic secret it was the token, it kindled, on the instant, into a radiant Italian smile. The Countess Scarabelli's smiles tonight, however, were almost uninterrupted. She greeted me – divinely, as her mother used to do; and young Stanmer sat in the corner of the sofa – as I used to do – and watched her while she talked. She is thin and very fair, and was dressed in light, vaporous black that completes the resemblance. The house, the rooms, are almost absolutely the same; there may be changes of detail, but they don't modify the general effect. There are the same precious pictures on the walls of the *salon* – the same great dusky fresco in the concave ceiling. The daughter is not rich, I suppose, any more than the mother. The furniture is worn and faded, and I was admitted by a solitary servant, who carried a twinkling taper before me up the great dark marble staircase.

'I have often heard of you,' said the countess, as I sat down near her; 'my mother often spoke of you.'

'Often?' I answered. 'I am surprised at that.'

'Why are you surprised? Were you not good friends?'

'Yes, for a certain time – very good friends. But I was sure she had forgotten me.'

'She never forgot,' said the countess, looking at me intently and smiling. 'She was not like that.'

'She was not like most other women in any way,' I declared.

'Ah, she was charming,' cried the countess, rattling open her fan. 'I have always been very curious to see you. I have received an impression of you.'

'A good one, I hope.'

She looked at me, laughing, and not answering this: it was just her mother's trick.

' "My Englishman", she used to call you – "*il mio Inglese*".'

'I hope she spoke of me kindly,' I insisted.

The countess, still laughing, gave a little shrug balancing her hand to and fro. 'So–so; I always supposed you had had a quarrel. You don't mind my being frank like this – eh?'

'I delight in it; it reminds me of your mother.'

'Everyone tells me that. But I am not clever like her. You will see for yourself.'

'That speech,' I said, 'completes the resemblance. She was always pretending she was not clever, and in reality – '

'In reality she was an angel, eh? To escape from dangerous comparisons I will admit, then, that I am clever. That will make a difference. But let us talk of you. You are very – how shall I say it? – very eccentric.'

'Is that what your mother told you?'

'To tell the truth, she spoke of you as a great original. But aren't all Englishmen eccentric? All except that one!' and the countess pointed to poor Stanmer, in his corner of the sofa.

'Oh, I know just what he is,' I said.

'He's as quiet as a lamb – he's like all the world,' cried the countess.

'Like all the world – yes. He is in love with you.'

She looked at me with sudden gravity. 'I don't object to your saying that for all the world – but I do for him.'

'Well,' I went on, 'he is peculiar in this: he is rather afraid of you.'

Instantly she began to smile; she turned her face toward Stanmer. He had seen that we were talking about him; he coloured and got up – then came toward us.

'I like men who are afraid of nothing,' said our hostess.

'I know what you want,' I said to Stanmer. 'You want to know what the Signora Contessa says about you.'

Stanmer looked straight into her face, very gravely. 'I don't care a straw what she says.'

'You are almost a match for the Signora Contessa,' I answered. 'She declares she doesn't care a pin's head what you think.'

'I recognise the countess's style!' Stanmer exclaimed, turning away.

'One would think,' said the countess, 'that you were trying to make a quarrel between us.'

I watched him move away to another part of the great saloon; he stood in front of the Andrea del Sarto, looking up at it. But he was not seeing it; he was listening to what we might say. I often stood there in just that way. 'He can't quarrel with you, any more than I could have quarrelled with your mother.'

'Ah, but you did. Something painful passed between you.'

'Yes, it was painful, but it was not a quarrel. I went away one day and never saw her again. That was all.'

The countess looked at me gravely. 'What do you call it when a man does that?'

'It depends upon the case.'

'Sometimes,' said the countess in French, 'it's a *lâcheté*.'

'Yes, and sometimes it's an act of wisdom.'

'And sometimes,' rejoined the countess, 'it's a mistake.'

I shook my head. 'For me it was no mistake.'

She began to laugh again. 'Caro signore, you're a great original. What had my poor mother done to you?'

I looked at our young Englishman, who still had his back turned to us and was staring up at the picture. 'I will tell you some other time,' I said.

'I shall certainly remind you; I am very curious to know.' Then she opened and shut her fan two or three times, still looking at me. What eyes they have! 'Tell me a little,' she went on, 'if I may ask without indiscretion. Are you married?'

'No, Signora Contessa.'

'Isn't that at least a mistake?'

'Do I look very unhappy?'

She dropped her head a little to one side. 'For an Englishman – no!'

'Ah,' said I, laughing, 'you are quite as clever as your mother.'

'And they tell me that you are a great soldier,' she continued; 'you have lived in India. It was very kind of you, so far away, to have remembered our poor dear Italy.'

'One always remembers Italy; the distance makes no difference. I remembered it well the day I heard of your mother's death!'

'Ah, that was a sorrow!' said the countess. 'There's not a day that I don't weep for her. But *che vuole*? She's a saint its paradise.'

'*Sicuro*,' I answered; and I looked some time at the ground. 'But tell me about yourself, dear lady,' I asked at last, raising my eyes. 'You have also had the sorrow of losing your husband.'

'I am a poor widow, as you see. *Che vuole*? My husband died after three years of marriage.'

I waited for her to remark that the late Count Scarabelli was also a saint in paradise, but I waited in vain.

'That was like your distinguished father,' I said.

'Yes, he too died young. I can't be said to have known him; I was but of the age of my own little girl. But I weep for him all the more.'

Again I was silent for a moment.

'It was in India too,' I said presently, 'that I heard of your mother's second marriage.'

The countess raised her eyebrows.

'In India, then, one hears of everything! Did that news please you?'

'Well, since you ask me – no.'

'I understand that,' said the countess, looking at her open fan. 'I shall not marry again like that.'

'That's what your mother said to me,' I ventured to observe.

She was not offended, but she rose from her seat and stood looking at me a moment. Then – 'You should not have gone away!' she exclaimed. I stayed for another hour; it is a very pleasant house.

Two or three of the men who were sitting there seemed very civil and intelligent; one of them was a major of engineers, who offered me a profusion of information upon the new organisation of the Italian army. While he talked, however, I was observing our hostess, who was talking with the others; very little, I noticed, with her young Inglese. She is altogether charming – full of frankness and freedom, of that inimitable *disinvoltura* which in an Englishwoman would be vulgar, and which in her is simply the perfection of apparent spontaneity. But for all her spontaneity she's as subtle as a needle-point, and knows tremendously well what she is about. If she is not a consummate coquette . . . What had she in her head when she said that I should not have gone away? – Poor little Stanmer didn't go away. I left him there at midnight.

APRIL 12TH I found him today sitting in the church of Santa Croce, into which I wandered to escape from the heat of the sun.

In the nave it was cool and dim; he was staring at the blaze of candles on the great altar, and thinking, I am sure, of his incomparable countess. I sat down beside him, and after a while, as if to avoid the appearance of eagerness, he asked me how I had enjoyed my visit to Casa Salvi, and what I thought of the *padrona*.

'I think half a dozen things,' I said, 'but I can only tell you one now. She's an enchantress. You shall hear the rest when we have left the church.'

'An enchantress?' repeated Stanmer, looking at me askance.

He is a very simple youth, but who am I to blame him?

'A charmer,' I said; 'a fascinatress!'

He turned away, staring at the altar candles.

'An artist – an actress,' I went on, rather brutally.

He gave me another glance.

'I think you are telling me all,' he said.

'No, no, there is more.' And we sat a long time in silence.

At last he proposed that we should go out; and we passed into the street, where the shadows had begun to stretch themselves.

'I don't know what you mean by her being an actress,' he said, as we turned homeward.

'I suppose not. Neither should I have known, if anyone had said that to me.'

'You are thinking about the mother,' said Stanmer. 'Why are you always bringing *her* in?'

'My dear boy, the analogy is so great it forces itself upon me.'

He stopped and stood looking at me with his modest, perplexed young face. I thought he was going to exclaim – 'The analogy be hanged!' – but he said after a moment: 'Well, what does it prove?'

'I can't say it proves anything; but it suggests a great many things.'

'Be so good as to mention a few,' he said, as we walked on.

'You are not sure of her yourself,' I began.

'Never mind that – go on with your analogy.'

'That's a part of it. You *are* very much in love with her.'

'That's a part of it too, I suppose?'

'Yes, as I have told you before. You are in love with her, and yet you can't make her out; that's just where I was with regard to Madame de Salvi.'

'And she too was an enchantress, an actress, an artist, and all the rest of it?'

'She was the most perfect coquette I ever knew, and the most dangerous, because the most finished.'

'What you mean, then, is that her daughter is a finished coquette?'

'I rather think so.'

Stanmer walked along for some moments in silence.

'Seeing that you suppose me to be a – a great admirer of the countess,' he said at last, 'I am rather surprised at the freedom with which you speak of her.'

I confessed that I was surprised at it myself. 'But it's on account of the interest I take in you.'

'I am immensely obliged to you!' said the poor boy.

'Ah, of course you don't like it. That is, you like my interest – I don't see how you can help liking that; but you don't like my freedom. That's natural enough; but, my dear young friend, I want only to help you. If a man had said to me – so many years ago – what I am saying to you, I should certainly also, at first, have thought him a great brute. But after a little, I should have been grateful – I should have felt that he was helping me.'

'You seem to have been very well able to help yourself,' said Stanmer. 'You tell me you made your escape.'

'Yes, but it was at the cost of infinite perplexity – of what I may call keen suffering. I should like to save you all that.'

'I can only repeat – it is really very kind of you.'

'Don't repeat it too often, or I shall begin to think you don't mean it.'

'Well,' said Stanmer, 'I think this, at any rate – that you take an extraordinary responsibility in trying to put a man out of conceit of a woman who, as he believes, may make him very happy.'

I grasped his arm, and we stopped, going on with our talk like a couple of Florentines.

'Do you wish to marry her?'

He looked away, without meeting my eyes. 'It's a great responsibility,' he repeated.

'Before heaven,' I said, 'I would have married the mother! You are exactly in my situation.'

'Don't you think you rather overdo the analogy?' asked poor Stanmer.

'A little more, a little less – it doesn't matter. I believe you are in my shoes. But of course, if you prefer it, I will beg a thousand pardons and leave them to carry you where they will.'

He had been looking away, but now he slowly turned his face and met my eyes. 'You have gone too far to retreat; what is it you know about her?'

'About this one – nothing. But about the other – '

'I care nothing about the other!'

'My dear fellow,' I said, 'they are mother and daughter – they are as like as two of Andrea's Madonnas.'

'If they resemble each other, then, you were simply mistaken in the mother.'

I took his arm and we walked on again; there seemed no adequate reply to such a charge. 'Your state of mind brings back my own so completely,' I said presently. 'You admire her – you adore her, and yet, secretly, you mistrust her. You are enchanted with her personal charm, her grace, her wit, her everything; and yet in your private heart you are afraid of her.'

'Afraid of her?'

'Your mistrust keeps rising to the surface; you can't rid yourself of the suspicion that at the bottom of all things she is hard and cruel, and you would be immensely relieved if someone should persuade you that your suspicion is right.'

Stanmer made no direct reply to this; but before we reached the hotel he said – 'What did you ever know about the mother?'

'It's a terrible story,' I answered.

He looked at me askance. 'What did she do?'

'Come to my rooms this evening and I will tell you.'

He declared he would, but he never came. Exactly the way I should have acted!

APRIL 14TH   I went again, last evening, to Casa Salvi, where I found the same little circle, with the addition of a couple of ladies. Stanmer was there, trying hard to talk to one of them, but making, I am sure, a very poor business of it. The countess – well, the countess was admirable. She greeted me like a friend of ten years, toward whom familiarity should not have engendered a want of ceremony; she made me sit near her, and she asked me a dozen questions about my health and my occupations.

'I live in the past,' I said. 'I go into the galleries, into the old palaces and the churches. Today I spent an hour in Michelangelo's chapel at San Lorenzo.'

'Ah yes, that's the past,' said the countess. 'Those things are very old.'

'Twenty-seven years old,' I answered.

'Twenty-seven? *Altro!*'

'I mean my own past,' I said. 'I went to a great many of those places with your mother.'

'Ah, the pictures are beautiful,' murmured the countess, glancing at Stanmer.

'Have you lately looked at any of them?' I asked. 'Have you gone to the galleries with *him*?'

She hesitated a moment, smiling. 'It seems to me that your question is a little impertinent. But I think you are like that.'

'A little impertinent? Never. As I say, your mother did me the honour, more than once, to accompany me to the Uffizzi.'

'My mother must have been very kind to you.'

'So it seemed to me at the time.'

'At the time only?'

'Well, if you prefer, so it seems to me now.'

'Eh,' said the countess, 'she made sacrifices.'

'To what, cara signora? She was perfectly free. Your lamented father was dead – and she had not yet contracted her second marriage.'

'If she was intending to marry again, it was all the more reason she should have been careful.'

I looked at her a moment; she met my eyes gravely, over the top of her fan. 'Are *you* very careful?' I said.

She dropped her fan with a certain violence. 'Ah, yes, you are impertinent!'

'Ah, no,' I said. 'Remember that I am old enough to be your father; that I knew you when you were three years old. I may surely ask such questions. But you are right; one must do your mother justice. She was certainly thinking of her second marriage.'

'You have not forgiven her that!' said the countess, very gravely.

'Have you?' I asked, more lightly.

'I don't judge my mother. That is a mortal sin. My stepfather was very kind to me.'

'I remember him,' I said; 'I saw him a great many times – your mother already received him.'

My hostess sat with lowered eyes, saying nothing; but she presently looked up.

'She was very unhappy with my father.'

'That I can easily believe. And your stepfather – is he still living?'

'He died – before my mother.'

'Did he fight any more duels?'

'He was killed in a duel,' said the countess, discreetly.

It seems almost monstrous, especially as I can give no reason for it – but this announcement, instead of shocking me, caused me to feel a strange exhilaration. Most assuredly, after all these years, I bear the poor man no resentment. Of course I controlled my manner, and simply remarked to the countess that as his fault had been so was his punishment. I think, however, that the feeling of which I speak was at the bottom of my saying to her that I hoped that, unlike her mother's, her own brief married life had been happy.

'If it was not,' she said, 'I have forgotten it now.' – I wonder if the late Count Scarabelli was also killed in a duel, and if his adversary . . . Is it on the books that his adversary, as well, shall perish by the pistol? Which of those gentlemen is he, I wonder? Is it reserved for poor little Stanmer to put a bullet into him? No; poor little Stanmer, I trust, will do as I did. And yet, unfortunately for him, that woman is consummately plausible. She was wonderfully nice last evening; she was really irresistible. Such frankness and freedom, and yet something so soft and womanly; such graceful gaiety, so much of the brightness, without any of the stiffness, of good breeding, and over it all something so picturesquely simple and southern. She is a perfect Italian. But she comes honestly by it. After the talk I have just jotted down she changed her place, and the conversation for half an hour was general. Stanmer indeed said very little; partly, I suppose, because he is shy of talking a foreign tongue. Was I like that – was I so constantly silent? I suspect I was when I was perplexed, and heaven knows that very often my perplexity was extreme. Before I went away I had a few more words tête-à-tête with the Countess.

'I hope you are not leaving Florence yet,' she said; 'you will stay a while longer?'

I answered that I came only for a week, and that my week was over. 'I stay on from day to day, I am so much interested.'

'Eh, it's the beautiful moment. I'm glad our city pleases you!'

'Florence pleases me – and I take a paternal interest to our young friend,' I added, glancing at Stanmer. 'I have become very fond of him.'

'*Bel tipo inglese*,' said my hostess. 'And he is very intelligent; he has a beautiful mind.'

She stood there resting her smile and her clear, expressive eyes upon me.

'I don't like to praise him too much,' I rejoined, 'lest I should appear to praise myself; he reminds me so much of what I was at his age. If your beautiful mother were to come to life for an hour she would see the resemblance.'

She gave me a little amused stare.

'And yet you don't look at all like him!'

'Ah, you didn't know me when I was twenty-five. I was very handsome! And, moreover, it isn't that, it's the mental resemblance. I was ingenuous, candid, trusting, like him.'

'Trusting? I remember my mother once telling me that you were the most suspicious and jealous of men!'

'I fell into a suspicious mood, but I was, fundamentally, not in the least addicted to thinking evil. I couldn't easily imagine any harm of anyone.'

'And so you mean that Mr Stanmer is in a suspicions mood?'

'Well, I mean that his situation is the same as mine.'

The countess gave me one of her serious looks. 'Come,' she said, 'what was it – this famous situation of yours? I have heard you mention it before.'

'Your mother might have told you, since she occasionally did me the honour to speak of me.'

'All my mother ever told me was that you were – a sad puzzle to her.'

At this, of course, I laughed out – I laugh still as I write it.

'Well, then, that was my situation – I was a sad puzzle to a very clever woman.'

'And you mean, therefore, that I am a puzzle to poor Mr Stanmer?'

'He is racking his brains to make you out. Remember it was you who said he was intelligent.'

She looked round at him, and as fortune would have it, his appearance at that moment quite confirmed my assertion. He was lounging back in his chair with an air of indolence rather too marked for a drawing-room, and staring at the ceiling with the expression of a man who has just been asked a conundrum. Madame Scarabelli seemed struck with his attitude.

'Don't you see,' I said, 'he can't read the riddle?'

'You yourself,' she answered, 'said he was incapable of thinking evil. I should be sorry to have him think any evil of *me*.'

And she looked straight at me – seriously, appealingly – with her beautiful candid brow.

I inclined myself, smiling, in a manner which might have meant – 'How could that be possible?'

'I have a great esteem for him,' she went on; 'I want him to think well of me. If I am a puzzle to him, do me a little service. Explain me to him.'

'Explain you, dear lady?'

'You are older and wiser than he. Make him understand me.'

She looked deep into my eyes for a moment, and then she turned away.

APRIL 26TH – I have written nothing for a good many days, but meanwhile I have been half a dozen times to Casa Salvi. I have seen a good deal also of my young friend – had a good many walks and talks with him. I have proposed to him to come with me to Venice for a fortnight, but he won't listen to the idea of leaving Florence. He is very happy in spite of his doubts, and I confess that in the perception of his happiness I have lived over again my own. This is so much the case that when, the other day, he at last made up his mind to ask me to tell him the wrong that Madame de Salvi had done me, I rather checked his curiosity. I told him that if he was bent upon knowing I would satisfy him, but that it seemed a pity, just now, to indulge in painful imagery.

'But I thought you wanted so much to put me out of conceit of our friend.'

'I admit I am inconsistent, but there are various reasons for it. In the first place – it's obvious – I am open to the charge of playing a double game. I profess an admiration for the Countess Scarabelli, for I accept her hospitality, and at the same time I attempt to poison your mind; isn't that the proper expression? I can't exactly make up my mind to that, though my admiration for the countess and my desire to prevent you from taking a foolish step are equally sincere. And then, in the second place, you seem to me, on the whole, so happy! One hesitates to destroy an illusion, no matter how pernicious, that is so delightful while it lasts. These are the rare moments of life. To be young and ardent, in the midst of an Italian spring, and to believe in the moral perfection of a beautiful woman – what an admirable situation! Float with the current; I'll stand on the brink and watch you.'

'Your real reason is that you feel you have no case against the poor lady,' said Stanmer. 'You admire her as much as I do.'

'I just admitted that I admired her. I never said she was a vulgar flirt; her mother was an absolutely scientific one. Heaven knows I admired that! It's a nice point, however, how much one is bound in honour not to warn a young friend against a dangerous woman because one also has relations of civility with the lady.'

'In such a case,' said Stanmer, 'I would break off my relations.'

I looked at him, and I think I laughed.

'Are you jealous of me, by chance?'

He shook his head emphatically.

'Not in the least; I like to see you there, because your conduct contradicts your words.'

'I have always said that the countess is fascinating.'

'Otherwise,' said Stanmer, 'in the case you speak of I would give the lady notice.'

'Give her notice?'

'Mention to her that you regard her with suspicion, and that you propose to do your best to rescue a simple-minded youth from her wiles. That would be more loyal.' And he began to laugh again.

It is not the first time he has laughed at me; but I have never minded it, because I have always understood it.

'Is that what you recommend me to say to the countess?' I asked.

'Recommend you!' he exclaimed, laughing again; 'I recommend nothing. I may be the victim to be rescued, but I am at least not a partner to the conspiracy. Besides,' he added in a moment, 'the countess knows your state of mind.'

'Has she told you so?'

Stanmer hesitated.

'She has begged me to listen to everything you may say against her. She declares that she has a good conscience.'

'Ah,' said I, 'she's an accomplished woman!'

And it is indeed very clever of her to take that tone. Stanmer afterwards assured me explicitly that he has never given her a hint of the liberties I have taken in conversation with – what shall I call it? – with her moral nature; she has guessed them for herself. She must hate me intensely, and yet her manner has always been so charming to me! She is truly an accomplished woman!

MAY 4TH   I have stayed away from Casa Salvi for a week, but I have lingered on in Florence, under a mixture of impulses. I have had it on my conscience not to go near the countess again – and yet from the moment she is aware of the way I feel about her, it is open war. There need be no scruples on either side. She is as free to use every possible art to entangle poor Stanmer more closely as I am to clip her fine-spun meshes. Under the circumstances, however, we naturally shouldn't meet very cordially. But as regards her meshes, why, after all, should I clip them? It would really be very interesting to see Stanmer swallowed up. I should like to see how he would agree with her after she had devoured him – (to what vulgar imagery, by the way, does curiosity reduce a man!) Let him finish the story in his own way, as I finished it in mine. It is the same story; but why, a quarter of a century later, should it have the same *dénouement*? Let him make his own *dénouement*.

MAY 5TH   Hang it, however, I don't want the poor boy to be miserable.

MAY 6TH   Ah, but did my *dénouement* then prove such a happy one?

MAY 7TH   He came to my room late last night; he was much excited. 'What was it she did to you?' he asked.

I answered him first with another question. 'Have you quarrelled with the countess?'

But he only repeated his own. 'What was it she did to you?'

'Sit down and I'll tell you.' And he sat there beside the candle, staring at me. 'There was a man always there – Count Camerino.'

'The man she married?'

'The man she married. I was very much in love with her, and yet I didn't trust her. I was sure that she lied; I believed that she could be cruel. Nevertheless, at moments, she had a charm which made it pure pedantry to be conscious of her faults; and while these moments lasted I would have done anything for her. Unfortunately they didn't last long. But you know what I mean; am I not describing the Scarabelli?'

'The Countess Scarabelli never lied!' cried Stanmer.

'That's just what I would have said to anyone who should have made the insinuation! But I suppose you are not asking me the question you put to me just now from dispassionate curiosity.'

'A man may want to know!' said the innocent fellow.

I couldn't help laughing out. 'This, at any rate, is my story. Camerino was always there; he was a sort of fixture in the house. If I had moments of dislike for the divine Bianca, I had no moments of liking for him. And yet he was a very agreeable fellow, very civil, very intelligent, not in the least disposed to make a quarrel with me. The trouble, of course, was simply that I was jealous of him. I don't know, however, on what ground I could have quarrelled with him, for I had no definite rights. I can't say what I expected – I can't say what, as the matter stood, I was prepared to do. With my name and my prospects, I might perfectly have offered her my hand. I am not sure that she would have accepted it – I am by no means clear that she wanted that. But she wanted, wanted keenly, to attach me to her; she wanted to have me about. I should have been capable of giving up everything – England, my career, my family – simply to devote myself to her, to live near her and see her every day.'

'Why didn't you do it, then?' asked Stanmer.

'Why don't you?'

'To be a proper rejoinder to my question,' he said, rather neatly, 'yours should be asked twenty-five years hence.'

'It remains perfectly true that at a given moment I was capable of doing as I say. That was what she wanted – a rich, susceptible, credulous, convenient young Englishman established near her *en permanence*. And yet,' I added, 'I must do her complete justice. I honestly believe she was fond of me.' At this Stanmer got up and walked to the window; he stood looking out a moment, and then he turned round. 'You know she was older than I,' I went on. 'Madame Scarabelli is older than you. One day in the garden, her mother asked me in an angry tone why I disliked Camerino; for I had been at no pains to conceal my feeling about him, and something had just happened to bring it out. "I dislike him," I said, "because you like him so much." "I assure you I don't like him," she answered. "He has all the appearance of being your lover," I retorted. It was a brutal speech, certainly, but any other man in my place would have made it. She took it very strangely; she turned pale, but she was not indignant. "How can he be my lover after what he has done?" she asked. "What has he done?" She hesitated a good while, then she said: "He killed my husband." "Good heavens!" I cried, "and you receive him!" Do you know what she said? She said, "*Che vuole?*" '

'Is that all?' asked Stanmer.

'No; she went on to say that Camerino had killed Count Salvi in a duel, and she admitted that her husband's jealousy had been the occasion of it. The count, it appeared, was a monster of jealousy – he had led her a dreadful life. He himself, meanwhile, had been anything but irreproachable; he had done a mortal injury to a man of whom he pretended to be a friend, and this affair had become notorious. The gentleman in question had demanded satisfaction for his outraged honour; but for some reason or other (the countess, to do her justice, did not tell me that her husband was a coward), he had not as yet obtained it. The duel with Camerino had come on first; in an access of jealous fury the count had struck Camerino in the face; and this outrage, I know not how justly, was deemed expiable before the other. By an extraordinary arrangement (the Italians have certainly no sense of fair play) the other man was allowed to be Camerino's second. The duel was fought with swords, and the count received a wound of which, though at first it was not expected to be fatal, he died on the following day. The matter was hushed up as much as possible for the sake of the countess's good name, and so successfully that it was presently observed that, among the public, the other gentleman had the credit of having put his blade through M. de Salvi. This gentleman took a fancy not to contradict the impression, and it was allowed to subsist. So long as he consented, it was of course in Camerino's interest not to contradict it, as it left him much more free to keep up his intimacy with the countess.'

Stanmer had listened to all this with extreme attention. 'Why didn't *she* contradict it?'

I shrugged my shoulders. 'I am bound to believe it was for the same reason. I was horrified, at any rate, by the whole story. I was extremely shocked at the countess's want of dignity in continuing to see the man by whose hand her husband had fallen.'

'The husband had been a great brute, and it was not known,' said Stanmer.

'Its not being known made no difference. And as for Salvi having been a brute, that is but a way of saying that his wife, and the man whom his wife subsequently married, didn't like him.'

Stanmer hooked extremely meditative; his eyes were fixed on mine. 'Yes, that marriage is hard to get over. It was not becoming.'

'Ah,' said I, 'what a long breath I drew when I heard of it! I remember the place and the hour. It was at a hill-station in India, seven years after I had left Florence. The post brought me some English papers, and in one of them was a letter from Italy, with a lot of so-called "fashionable intelligence". There, among various scandals in high life, and other delectable items, I read that the Countess Bianca Salvi, famous for some years as the presiding genius of the most agreeable *salon* in Florence, was about to bestow her hand upon Count Camerino, a distinguished Bolognese. Ah, my dear boy, it was a tremendous escape! I had been ready to marry the woman who was capable of that! But my instinct had warned me, and I had trusted my instinct.'

' "Instinct's everything", as Falstaff says!' And Stanmer began to laugh. 'Did you tell Madame de Salvi that your instinct was against her?'

'No; I told her that she frightened me, shocked me, horrified me.'

'That's about the same thing. And what did she say?'

'She asked me what I would have? I called her friendship with Camerino a scandal, and she answered that her husband had been a brute. Besides, no one knew it; therefore it was no scandal. Just *your* argument! I retorted that this was odious reasoning, and that she had no moral sense. We had a passionate argument, and I declared I would never see her again. In the heat of my displeasure I left Florence, and I kept my vow. I never saw her again.'

'You couldn't have been much in love with her,' said Stanmer.

'I was not – three months after.'

'If you had been you would have come back – three days after.'

'So doubtless it seems to you. All I can say is that it was the great effort of my life. Being a military man, I have had on various occasions to face the enemy. But it was not then I needed my resolution; it was when I left Florence in a post-chaise.'

Stanmer turned about the room two or three times, and then he said: 'I don't understand! I don't understand why she should have told you that Camerino had killed her husband. It could only damage her.'

'She was afraid it would damage her more that I should think he was her lover. She wished to say the thing that would most effectually persuade me that he was not her lover – that he could never be. And then she wished to get the credit of being very frank.'

'Good heavens, how you must have analysed her!' cried my companion, staring.

'There is nothing so analytic as disillusionment. But there it is. She married Camerino.'

'Yes, I don't like that,' said Stanmer. He was silent a while, and then he added – 'Perhaps she wouldn't have done so if you had remained.'

He has a little innocent way! 'Very likely she would have dispensed with the ceremony,' I answered, drily.

'Upon my word,' he said, 'you *have* analysed her!'

'You ought to be grateful to me. I have done for you what you seem unable to do for yourself.'

'I don't see any Camerino in my case,' he said.

'Perhaps among those gentlemen I can find one for you.'

'Thank you,' he cried; 'I'll take care of that myself!' And he went away – satisfied, I hope.

MAY 10TH   He's an obstinate little wretch; it irritates me to see him sticking to it. Perhaps he is looking for his Camerino. I shall leave him, at any rate, to his fate; it is growing insupportably hot.

MAY 11TH   I went this evening to bid farewell to the Scarabelli. There was no one there; she was alone in her great dusky drawing-room, which was lighted only by a couple of candles, with the immense windows open over the garden. She was dressed in white; she was deucedly pretty. She asked me, of course, why I had been so long without coming.

'I think you say that only for form,' I answered. 'I imagine you know.'

'*Chè!* what have I done?'

'Nothing at all. You are too wise for that.'

She looked at me a while. 'I think you are a little crazy.'

'Ah no, I am only too sane. I have too much reason rather than too little.'

'You have, at any rate, what we call a fixed idea.'

'There is no harm in that so long as it's a good one.'

'But yours is abominable!' she exclaimed, with a laugh.

'Of course you can't like me or my ideas. All things considered, you have treated me with wonderful kindness, and I thank you and kiss your hands. I leave Florence tomorrow.'

'I won't say I'm sorry!' she said, laughing again. 'But I am very glad to have seen you. I always wondered about you. You are a curiosity.'

'Yes, you must find me so. A man who can resist your charms! The fact is, I can't. This evening you are enchanting; and it is the first time I have been alone with you.'

She gave no heed to this; she turned away. But in a moment she came back, and stood looking at me, and her beautiful solemn eyes seemed to shine in the dimness of the room.

'How *could* you treat my mother so?' she asked.

'Treat her so?'

'How could you desert the most charming woman in the world?'

'It was not a case of desertion; and if it had been it seems to me she was consoled.'

At this moment there was the sound of a step in the ante-chamber, and I saw that the countess perceived it to be Stanmer's.

'That wouldn't have happened,' she murmured. 'My poor mother needed a protector.'

Stanmer came in, interrupting our talk, and looking at me, I thought, with a little air of bravado. He must think me indeed a tiresome, meddlesome bore; and upon my word, turning it all over, I wonder at his docility. After all, he's five-and-twenty – and yet I *must* add, it *does* irritate me – the way he sticks! He was followed in a moment by two or three of the regular Italians, and I made my visit short.

'Goodbye, countess,' I said; and she gave me her hand in silence. 'Do you need a protector?' I added, softly.

She looked at me from head to foot, and then, almost angrily – 'Yes, signore.'

But, to deprecate her anger, I kept her hand an instant, and then bent my venerable head and kissed it. I think I appeased her.

BOLOGNA, MAY 14TH   I left Florence on the 12th, and have been here these three days. Delightful old Italian town – but it lacks the charm of my Florentine secret.

I wrote that last entry five days ago, late at night, after coming back from Casa Salvi. I afterwards fell asleep in my chair; the night was half over when I woke up. Instead of going to bed, I stood a long time at the window, looking out at the river. It was a warm, still night, and the first faint streaks of sunrise were in the sky. Presently I heard a slow footstep beneath my window, and looking down, made out by the aid of a street lamp that Stanmer was but just coming home. I called to him to come to my rooms, and, after an interval, he made his appearance.

'I want to bid you goodbye,' I said; 'I shall depart in the morning. Don't go to the trouble of saying you are sorry. Of course you are not; I must have bullied you immensely.'

He made no attempt to say he was sorry, but he said he was very glad to have made my acquaintance.

'Your conversation,' he said, with his little innocent air, 'has been very suggestive.'

'Have you found Camerino?' I asked, smiling.

'I have given up the search.'

'Well,' I said, 'someday when you find that you have made a great mistake, remember I told you so.'

He looked for a minute as if he were trying to anticipate that day by the exercise of his reason.

'Has it ever occurred to you that *you* may have made a great mistake?'

'Oh yes; everything occurs to one sooner or later.'

That's what I said to him; but I didn't say that the question, pointed by his candid young countenance, had, for the moment, a greater force than it had ever had before.

And then he asked me whether, as things had turned out, I myself had been so especially happy.

PARIS, DECEMBER 17TH A note from young Stanmer, whom I saw in Florence – a remarkable little note, dated Rome, and worth transcribing.

> MY DEAR GENERAL – I have it at heart to tell you that I was married a week ago to the Countess Salvi-Scarabelli. You talked me into a great muddle; but a month after that it was all very clear. Things that involve a risk are like the Christian faith; they must be seen from the inside.
>
> Yours ever,
>
> E.S.
>
> PS – A fig for analogies unless you can find an analogy for my happiness!

His happiness makes him very clever. I hope it will last – I mean his cleverness, not his happiness.

LONDON, APRIL 19TH, 1877 Last night, at Lady H—'s, I met Edmund Stanmer, who married Bianca Salvi's daughter. I heard the other day that they had come to England. A handsome young fellow, with a fresh contented face. He reminded me of Florence, which I didn't pretend to forget; but it was rather awkward, for I remember I used to disparage that woman to him. I had a complete theory about her. But he didn't seem at all stiff; on the contrary, he appeared to enjoy our encounter. I asked him if his wife were there. I had to do that.

'Oh yes, she's in one of the other rooms. Come and make her acquaintance; I want you to know her.'

'You forget that I do know her.'

'Oh no, you don't; you never did.' And he gave a little significant laugh.

I didn't feel like facing the *ci-devant* Scarabelli at that moment; so I said that I was leaving the house, but that I would do myself the honour of calling upon his wife. We talked for a minute of something else, and then, suddenly breaking off and looking at me, he laid his hand on my arm. I must do him the justice to say that he looks felicitous.

'Depend upon it you were wrong!' he said.

'My dear young friend,' I answered, 'imagine the alacrity with which I concede it.'

Something else again was spoken of, but in an instant he repeated his movement.

'Depend upon it you were wrong.'

'I am sure the countess has forgiven me,' I said, 'and in that case you ought to bear no grudge. As I have had the honour to say, I will call upon her immediately.'

'I was not alluding to my wife,' he answered. 'I was thinking of your own story.'

'My own story?'

'So many years ago. Was it not rather a mistake?'

I looked at him a moment; he's positively rosy. 'That's not a question to solve in a London crush.' And I turned away.

APRIL 22ND   I haven't yet called on the *ci-devant*; I am afraid of finding her at home. And that boy's words have been thrumming in my ears – 'Depend upon it you were wrong. Wasn't it rather a mistake?' *Was* I wrong – *was* it a mistake? Was I too cautions – too suspicious – too logical? Was it really a protector she needed – a man who might have helped her? Would it have been for his benefit to believe in her, and was her fault only that I had forsaken her? Was the poor woman very unhappy? God forgive me, how the questions come crowding in! If I marred her happiness, I certainly didn't make my own. And I might have made it – eh? That's a charming discovery for a man of my age!

RUDYARD KIPLING

Rudyard Kipling (1865–1936) was named after the Staffordshire reservoir near Leek beside which his parents became engaged. He was born in India, and spent the first six years of his life there, acquiring Hindustani as a second language and living in a bunga-low like that in *The Jungle Book*. In 1871 he was taken with his sister Alice to England to board at Lorne Lodge in Southsea and there had a miserable time before being sent to the United Services College at Westward Ho! in Devon, the model for *Stalky & Co*. He left school at sixteen to return to India and work on the *Civil and Military Gazette* in Lahore, and his familiarity with all classes of society provided him with material for *Barrack Room Ballads* and *Plain Tales from the Hills*. In 1889 he returned to England and in 1891 published his novel *The Light That Failed*. He married Caroline (Carrie) Balestier the following year and they returned to her home at Brattleboro, Vermont, where Kipling wrote *The Jungle Book*, *The Second Jungle Book* and *Captains Courageous*. In 1896 the family returned to England, where Kipling continued to write prolifically. In 1907 he was the first Englishman to receive the Nobel Prize for Literature. His later years were darkened by the death of his son John at the Battle of Loos in 1915.

The Bronckhorst Divorce-Case

In the daytime, when she moved about me, In the night, when she
was sleeping at my side, – I was wearied, I was wearied of her
presence, Day by day and night by night I grew to hate her – Would
God that she or I had died!

Confessions

There was a man called Bronckhorst – a three-cornered, middle-aged man
in the army – grey as a badger, and, some people said, with a touch of
country-blood in him. That, however, cannot be proved. Mrs Bronckhorst
was not exactly young, though fifteen years younger than her husband. She
was a large, pale, quiet woman, with heavy eyelids over weak eyes, and hair
that turned red or yellow as the lights fell on it.

Bronckhorst was not nice in any way. He had no respect for the pretty
public and private lies that make life a little less nasty than it is. His manner
towards his wife was coarse. There are many things – including actual assault
with the clenched fist – that a wife will endure; but seldom can a wife bear –
as Mrs Bronckhorst bore – with a long course of brutal, hard chaff, making
light of her weaknesses, her headaches, her small fits of gaiety, her dresses,
her queer little attempts to make herself attractive to her husband when she
knows that she is not what she has been, and – worst of all – the love that she
spends on her children. That particular sort of heavy-handed jest was
specially dear to Bronckhorst. I suppose that he had first slipped into it,
meaning no harm, in the honeymoon, when folk find their ordinary stock of
endearments run short, and so go to the other extreme to express their
feelings. A similar impulse makes a man say, '*Hutt*, you old beast!' when a
favourite horse nuzzles his coat-front. Unluckily, when the reaction of
marriage sets in, the form of speech remains, and, the tenderness having
died out, hurts the wife more than she cares to say. But Mrs Bronckhorst was
devoted to her 'Teddy' as she called him. Perhaps that was why he objected
to her. Perhaps – this is only a theory to account for his infamous behaviour
later on – he gave way to the queer, savage feeling that sometimes takes by
the throat a husband twenty years married, when he sees, across the table,
the same, same face of his wedded wife, and knows that, as he has sat facing
it, so must he continue to sit until the day of its death or his own. Most men
and all women know the spasm. It only lasts for three breaths as a rule, must
be a 'throw-back' to times when men and women were rather worse than
they are now, and is too unpleasant to be discussed.

Dinner at the Bronckhorsts' was an infliction few men cared to undergo. Bronckhorst took a pleasure in saying things that made his wife wince. When their little boy came in at dessert Bronckhorst used to give him half a glass of wine, and, naturally enough, the poor little mite got first riotous, next miserable, and was removed screaming. Bronckhorst asked if that was the way Teddy usually behaved, and whether Mrs Bronckhorst could not spare some of her time 'to teach the little beggar decency'. Mrs Bronckhorst, who loved the boy more than her own life, tried not to cry – her spirit seemed to have been broken by her marriage. Lastly, Bronckhorst used to say, 'There! That'll do, that'll do. For God's sake try to behave like a rational woman. Go into the drawing-room.' Mrs Bronckhorst would go, trying to carry it all off with a smile; and the guest of the evening would feel angry and uncomfortable.

After three years of this cheerful life – for Mrs Bronckhorst had no women-friends to talk to – the station was startled by the news that Bronckhorst had instituted proceedings *in the criminal count*, against a man called Biel, who certainly had been rather attentive to Mrs Bronckhorst whenever she had appeared in public. The utter want of reserve with which Bronckhorst treated his own dishonour helped us to know that the evidence against Biel would be entirely circumstantial and native. There were no letters; but Bronckhorst said openly that he would rack heaven and earth until he saw Biel superintending the manufacture of carpets in the Central Jail. Mrs Bronckhorst kept entirely to her house, and let charitable folks say what they pleased. Opinions were divided. Some two-thirds of the station jumped at once to the conclusion that Biel was guilty; but a dozen men who knew and liked him held by him. Biel was furious and surprised. He denied the whole thing, and vowed that he would thrash Bronckhorst within an inch of his life. No jury, we knew, would convict a man on the criminal count on native evidence in a land where you can buy a murder-charge, including the corpse, all complete for fifty-four rupees; but Biel did not care to scrape through by the benefit of a doubt. He wanted the whole thing cleared; but, as he said one night, 'He can prove anything with servants' evidence, and I've only my bare word.' This was almost a month before the case came on; and beyond agreeing with Biel, we could do little. All that we could be sure of was that the native evidence would be bad enough to blast Biel's character for the rest of his service; for when a native begins perjury he perjures himself thoroughly. He does not boggle over details.

Some genius at the end of the table whereat the affair was being talked over, said, 'Look here! I don't believe lawyers are any good. Get a man to wire to Strickland, and beg him to come down and pull us through.'

Strickland was about a hundred and eighty miles up the line. He had not long been married to Miss Youghal, but he scented in the telegram a chance of return to the old detective work that his soul lusted after, and he came down and heard our story. He finished his pipe and said oracularly, 'We must get at the evidence. Oorya bearer, Mussulman *khit* and sweeper *ayah*, I suppose, are the pillars of the charge. I am on in this piece; but I'm afraid I'm getting rusty in my talk.'

He rose and went into Biel's bedroom, where his trunk had been put, and shut the door. An hour later, we heard him say, 'I hadn't the heart to part with my old make-ups when I married. Will this do?' There was a loathly *fakir* salaaming in the doorway.

'Now lend me fifty rupees,' said Strickland, 'and give me your words of honour that you won't tell my wife.'

He got all that he asked for, and left the house while the table drank his health. What he did only he himself knows. A *fakir* hung about Bronckhorst's compound for twelve days. Then a sweeper appeared, and when Biel heard of *him*, he said that Strickland was an angel full-fledged. Whether the sweeper made love to Janki, Mrs Bronckhorst's *ayah*, is a question which concerns Strickland exclusively.

He came back at the end of three weeks, and said quietly, 'You spoke the truth, Biel. The whole business is put up from beginning to end. Jove! It almost astonishes *me*! That Bronckhorst beast isn't fit to live.'

There was uproar and shouting, and Biel said, 'How are you going to prove it? You can't say that you've been trespassing on Bronckhorst's compound in disguise!'

'No,' said Strickland. 'Tell your lawyer-fool, whoever he is, to get up something strong about "inherent improbabilities" and "discrepancies of evidence". He won't have to speak, but it will make him happy, *I'm* going to run this business.'

Biel held his tongue, and the other men waited to see what would happen. They trusted Strickland as men trust quiet men. When the case came off the court was crowded. Strickland hung about in the veranda of the court, till he met the Mohammedan *khitmutgar*. Then he murmured a *fakir*'s blessing in his ear, and asked him how his second wife did. The man spun round, and, as he looked into the eyes of 'Estreekin Sahib', his jaw dropped. You must remember that before Strickland was married, he was, as I have told you already, a power among natives. Strickland whispered a rather coarse vernacular proverb to the effect that he was abreast of all that was going on, and went into the court armed with a gut trainer's-whip.

The Mohammedan was the first witness, and Strickland beamed upon him from the back of the court. The man moistened his lips with his tongue and, in his abject fear of 'Estreekin Sahib' the *fakir*, went back on every detail of his evidence – said he was a poor man, and God was his witness that he had forgotten everything that Bronckhorst Sahib had told him to say. Between his terror of Strickland, the judge, and Bronckhorst he collapsed weeping.

Then began the panic among the witnesses. Janki, the *ayah*, leering chastely behind her veil, turned grey, and the bearer left the court. He said that his mamma was dying, and that it was not wholesome for any man to lie unthriftily in the presence of 'Estreekin Sahib'.

Biel said politely to Bronckhorst, 'Your witnesses don't seem to work. Haven't you any forged letters to produce?' But Bronckhorst was swaying to and fro in his chair, and there was a dead pause after Biel had been called to order.

Bronckhorst's counsel saw the look on his client's face, and without more ado pitched his papers on the little green-baize table, and mumbled something about having been misinformed. The whole court applauded wildly, like soldiers at a theatre, and the judge began to say what he thought.

* * *

Biel came out of the court, and Strickland dropped a gut trainer's-whip in the veranda. Ten minutes later, Biel was cutting Bronckhorst into ribbons behind the old court cells, quietly and without scandal. What was left of Bronckhorst was sent home in a carriage; and his wife wept over it and nursed it into a man again. Later on, after Biel had managed to hush up the counter-charge against Bronckhorst of fabricating false evidence, Mrs Bronckhorst, with her faint, watery smile, said that there had been a mistake, but it wasn't her Teddy's fault altogether. She would wait till her Teddy came back to her. Perhaps he had grown tired of her, or she had tried his patience, and perhaps we wouldn't cut her any more, and perhaps the mothers would let their children play with 'little Teddy' again. He was so lonely. Then the station invited Mrs Bronckhorst everywhere, until Bronckhorst was fit to appear in public, when he went home and took his wife with him. According to latest advices, her Teddy did come back to her, and they are moderately happy. Though, of course, he can never forgive her the thrashing that she was the indirect means of getting for him.

* * *

What Biel wants to know is, 'Why didn't I press home the charge against the Bronckhorst brute, and have him run in?'

What Mrs Strickland wants to know is, 'How *did* my husband bring such a lovely, lovely Waler from your station? I know *all* his money affairs; and I'm *certain* he didn't *buy* it.'

What I want to know is, 'How do women like Mrs Bronckhorst come to marry men like Bronckhorst?'

And my conundrum is the most unanswerable of the three.

Friendly Brook

The valley was so choked with fog that one could scarcely see a cow's length across a field. Every blade, twig, bracken-frond and hoof-print carried water, and the air was filled with the noise of rushing ditches and field-drains, all delivering to the brook below. A week's November rain on water-logged land had gorged her to full flood, and she proclaimed it aloud.

Two men in sackcloth aprons were considering an untrimmed hedge that ran down the hillside and disappeared into mist beside those roarings. They stood back and took stock of the neglected growth, tapped an elbow of hedge-oak here, a mossed beech-stub there, swayed a stooled ash back and forth, and looked at each other.

'I reckon she's about two-rod thick,' said Jabez the younger, 'an' she hasn't felt iron since – when has she, Jesse?'

'Call it twenty-five year, Jabez, an' you won't be far out.'

'Umm!' Jabez rubbed his wet handbill on his wetter coat-sleeve. 'She ain't a hedge. She's all manner o' trees. We'll just about have to – ' He paused, as professional etiquette required.

'Just about have to side her up an' see what she'll bear. But hadn't we best – ?' Jesse paused in his turn, both men being artists and equals.

'Get some kind o' line to go by.' Jabez ranged up and down till he found a thinner place, and with clean snicks of the handbill revealed the original face of the fence. Jesse took over the dripping stuff as it fell forward, and, with a grasp and a kick, made it to lie orderly on the bank till it should be faggoted.

By noon a length of unclean jungle had turned itself into a cattle-proof barrier, tufted here and there with little plumes of the sacred holly which no woodman touches without orders.

'Now we've a witness-board to go by!' said Jesse at last.

'She won't be as easy as this all along,' Jabez answered. 'She'll need plenty stakes and binders when we come to the brook.'

'Well, ain't we plenty?' Jesse pointed to the ragged perspective ahead of them that plunged downhill into the fog. 'I lay there's a cord an' a half o' firewood, let alone faggots, 'fore we get anywheres anigh the brook.'

'The brook's got up a piece since morning,' said Jabez. 'Sounds like's if she was over Wickenden's door-stones.'

Jesse listened, too. There was a growl in the brook's roar as though she worried something hard.

'Yes. She's over Wickenden's door-stones,' he replied. 'Now she'll flood acrost Alder Bay an' that'll ease her.'

'She won't ease Jim Wickenden's hay none if she do,' Jabez grunted. 'I told Jim he'd set that liddle haystack o' his too low down in the medder. I *told* him so when he was drawin' the bottom for it.'

'I told him so, too,' said Jesse. 'I told him 'fore ever you did. I told him when the County Council tarred the roads up along.' He pointed uphill, where unseen automobiles and road-engines droned past continually. 'A tarred road, she shoots every drop o' water into a valley same's a slate roof. 'Tisn't as 'twas in the old days, when the waters soaked in and soaked out in the way o' nature. It rooshes off they tarred roads all of a lump, and naturally every drop is bound to descend into the valley. And there's tar roads both two sides this valley for ten mile. That's what I told Jim Wickenden when they tarred the roads last year. But he's a valley-man. He don't hardly ever journey uphill.'

'What did he say when you told him that?' Jabez demanded, with a little change of voice.

'Why? What did he say to you when *you* told him?' was the answer.

'What he said to you, I reckon, Jesse.'

'Then, you don't need me to say it over again, Jabez.'

'Well, let be how 'twill, what was he gettin' *after* when he said what he said to me?' Jabez insisted.

'I dunno; unless you tell me what manner o' words he said to *you*.'

Jabez drew back from the hedge – all hedges are nests of treachery and eavesdropping – and moved to an open cattle-lodge in the centre of the field.

'No need to go ferretin' around,' said Jesse. 'None can't see us here 'fore we see them.'

'What was Jim Wickenden gettin' at when I said he'd set his stack too near anigh the brook?' Jabez dropped his voice. 'He was in his mind.'

'He ain't never been out of it yet to my knowledge,' Jesse drawled, and uncorked his tea-bottle.

'But then Jim says: "I ain't goin' to shift my stack a yard," he says. "The Brook's been good friends to me, and if she be minded," he says, "to take a snatch at my hay, I ain't settin' out to withstand her." That's what Jim Wickenden says to me last – last June-end 'twas,' said Jabez.

'Nor he hasn't shifted his stack, neither,' Jesse replied. 'An' if there's more rain, the brook she'll shift it for him.'

'No need tell *me*! But I want to know what Jim was gettin' *at*?'

Jabez opened his clasp-knife very deliberately; Jesse as carefully opened his. They unfolded the newspapers that wrapped their dinners, coiled away and pocketed the string that bound the packages, and sat down on the edge of the lodge manger. The rain began to fall again through the fog, and the brook's voice rose.

*　　*　　*

'But I always allowed Mary was his lawful child, like,' said Jabez, after Jesse had spoken for a while.

' 'Tain't so . . . Jim Wickenden's woman she never made nothing. She come out o' Lewes with her stockin's round her heels, an' she never made nor mended aught till she died. *He* had to light fire an' get breakfast every mornin' except Sundays, while she sowed it abed. Then she took an' died, sixteen, seventeen, year back; but she never had no childern.'

'They was valley-folk,' said Jabez apologetically. 'I'd no call to go in among 'em, but I always allowed Mary – '

'No. Mary come out o' one o' those Lunnon Childern Societies. After his woman died, Jim got his mother back from his sister over to Peasmarsh, which she'd gone to house with when Jim married. His mother kept house for Jim after his woman died. They do say 'twas his mother led him on toward adoptin' of Mary – to furnish out the house with a child, like, and to keep him off of gettin' a noo woman. He mostly done what his mother contrived. 'Cardenly, twixt 'em, they asked for a child from one o' those Lunnon Societies – same as it might ha' been these Barnardo children – an' Mary was sent down to 'em, in a candle-box, I've heard.'

'Then Mary is chance-born. I never knowed that,' said Jabez. 'Yet I must ha' heard it some time or other . . . '

'No. She ain't. 'Twould ha' been better for some folk if she had been. She come to Jim in a candle-box with all the proper papers – lawful child o' some couple in Lunnon somewheres – mother dead, father drinkin'. *And* there was that Lunnon society's five shillin's a week for her. Jim's mother she wouldn't despise weekend money, but I never heard Jim was much of a muck-grubber. Let be how 'twill, they two mothered up Mary no bounds, till it looked at last like they'd forgot she wasn't their own flesh an' blood. Yes, I reckon they forgot Mary wasn't their'n by rights.'

'That's no new thing,' said Jabez. 'There's more'n one or two in this parish wouldn't surrender back their Barnarders. You ask Mark Copley an' his woman an' that Barnarder cripple-babe o' theirs.'

'Maybe they need the five shillin',' Jesse suggested.

'It's handy,' said Jabez. 'But the child's more. "Dada" he says, an' "Mumma" he says, with his great rollin' head-piece all hurdled up in that iron collar. *He* won't live long – his backbone's rotten, like. But they Copleys do just about set store by him – five bob or no five bob.'

'Same way with Jim an' his mother,' Jesse went on. 'There was talk betwixt 'em after a few years o' not takin' any more weekend money for Mary; but let alone *she* never passed a farden in the mire 'thout longin's, Jim didn't care, like, to push himself forward into the Society's remembrance. So naun came of it. The weekend money would ha' made no odds to Jim – not after his uncle willed him they four cottages at Eastbourne *an'* money in the bank.'

'That was true, too, then? I heard something in a scadderin' word-o'-mouth way,' said Jabez.

'I'll answer for the house property, because Jim he requested my signed name at the foot o' some papers concernin' it. Regardin' the money in the bank, he nature–ally wouldn't like such things talked about all round the parish, so he took strangers for witnesses.'

'Then 'twill make Mary worth seekin' after?'

'She'll need it. Her Maker ain't done much for her outside nor yet in.'

'That ain't no odds.' Jabez shook his head till the water showered off his hat-brim. 'If Mary has money, she'll be wed before any likely pore maid. She's cause to be grateful to Jim.'

'She hides it middlin' close, then,' said Jesse. 'It don't sometimes look to me as if Mary has her natural rightful feelin's. She don't put on an apron o' Mondays 'thout being druv to it – in the kitchen or the hen-house. She's studyin' to be a schoolteacher. She'll make a beauty! I never knowed her show any sort o' kindness to nobody – not even when Jim's mother was took dumb. No! 'Twadn't no stroke. It stifled the old lady in the throat here. First she couldn't shape her words no shape; then she clucked, like, an' lastly she couldn't more than suck down spoon-meat an' hold her peace. Jim took her to Dr Harding, an' Harding he bundled her off to Brighton Hospital on a ticket, but they couldn't make no stay to her afflictions there; and she was bundled off to Lunnon, an' they lit a great old lamp inside her, and Jim told me they couldn't make out nothing in no sort there; and, along o' one thing an' another, an' all their spyin's and pryin's, she come back a hem sight worse than when she started. Jim said he'd have no more hospitalisin', so he give her a slate, which she tied to her waist-string, and what she was minded to say she writ on it.'

'Now, I never knowed that! But they're valley-folk,' Jabez repeated.

' 'Twadn't particular noticeable, for she wasn't a talkin' woman any time o' her days. Mary had all three's tongue . . . Well, then, two years this summer, come what I'm tellin' you. Mary's Lunnon father, which they'd put clean out o' their minds, arrived down from Lunnon with the law on his side, sayin' he'd take his daughter back to Lunnon, after all. I was working for Mus' Dockett at Pounds Farm that summer, but I was obligin' Jim that evenin' muckin' out his pig-pen. I seed a stranger come traipsin' over the bridge agin' Wickenden's door-stones. 'Twadn't the new County Council bridge with the handrail. They hadn't given it in for a public right o' way then. 'Twas just a bit o' lathy old plank which Jim had throwed acrost the brook for his own conveniences. The man wasn't drunk – only a little concerned in liquor, like – an' his back was a mask where he'd slipped in the muck comin' along. He went up the bricks past Jim's mother, which was feedin' the ducks, an' set himself down at the table inside – Jim was just changin' his socks – an' the man let Jim know all his rights and aims regardin' Mary. Then there just about *was* a hurly-bulloo? Jim's fust mind was to pitch him forth, but he'd done that once in his young days, and got six months up to Lewes jail along o' the man fallin' on his head. So he swallowed his spittle an' let him talk. The law about Mary *was* on the man's side from fust to last, for he showed us all the papers. Then Mary come downstairs – she'd been studyin' for an examination – an' the man tells her who he was, an' she says he had ought to have took proper care of his own flesh and blood while he had it by him, an' not to think he could ree–claim it when it suited. He says somethin' or other, but she looks him up an' down, front an' backwent, an' she just tongues him scadderin' out o' doors, and he went away stuffin' all the papers back into his hat, talkin' most abusefully. Then she come back an' freed her mind against Jim an' his mother for not havin' warned her of her upbringin's, which it come out she hadn't ever been told. They didn't say naun to her. They never did. *I'd* ha' packed her off with any man that would ha' took her – an' God's pity on him!'

'Umm!' said Jabez, and sucked his pipe.

'So then, that was the beginnin'. The man come back again next week or so, an' he catched Jim alone, 'thout his mother this time, an' he fair beazled him with his papers an' his talk – for the law *was* on his side – till Jim went down into his money-purse an' give him ten shillings hush-money – he told me – to withdraw away for a bit an' leave Mary with 'em.'

'But that's no way to get rid o' man or woman,' Jabez said.

'No more 'tis. I told Jim so. "What can I do?" Jim says. "The law's *with* the man. I walk about daytimes thinkin' o' it till I sweats my underclothes wringin', an' I lie abed nights thinkin' o' it till I sweats my sheets all of a sop. 'Tisn't as if I was a young man," he says, "nor yet as if I was a pore man. Maybe he'll drink hisself to death." I e'en a'most told him outright what foolishness he was enterin' into, but he knowed it – he knowed it – because he said next time the man come 'twould be fifteen shillin's. An' next time 'twas. Just fifteen shillin's!'

'An' *was* the man her father?' asked Jabez.

'He had the proofs an' the papers. Jim showed me what that Lunnon Childern's Society had answered when Mary writ up to 'em an' taxed 'em with it. I lay she hadn't been proper polite in her letters to 'em, for they answered middlin' short. They said the matter was out o' their hands, but – let's see if I remember – oh, yes – they ree–gretted there had been an oversight. I reckon they had sent Mary out in the candle-box as a orphan instead o' havin' a father. Terrible awkward! Then, when he'd drinked up the money, the man come again – in his usuals – an' he kept hammerin' on and hammerin' on about his duty to his pore dear wife, an' what he'd do for his dear daughter in Lunnon, till the tears runned down his two dirty cheeks an' he come away with more money. Jim used to slip it into his hand behind the door; but his mother she heard the chink. She didn't hold with hush-money. She'd write out all her feelin's on the slate, an' Jim 'ud be settin' up half the night answerin' back an' showing that the man had the law with him.'

'Hadn't that man no trade nor business, then?'

'He told me he was a printer. I reckon, though, he lived on the rates like the rest of 'em up there in Lunnon.'

'An' how did Mary take it?'

'She said she'd sooner go into service than go with the man. I reckon a mistress 'ud be middlin' put to it for a maid 'fore she put Mary into cap an' gown. She was studyin' to be a schoo–ool–teacher. A beauty she'll make! . . . Well, that was how things went that fall. Mary's Lunnon father kep' comin' an' comin' 'carden as he'd drinked out the money Jim gave him; an' each time he'd put-up his price for not takin' Mary away. Jim's mother, she didn't like partin' with no money, an' bein' obliged to write her feelin's on the slate instead o' givin' 'em vent by mouth, she was just about mad. Just about she *was* mad!

'Come November, I lodged with Jim in the outside room over 'gainst his hen-house. I paid *her* my rent. I was workin' for Dockett at Pounds – gettin' chestnut-bats out o' Perry Shaw. Just such weather as this be – rain atop o' rain after a wet October. (An' I remember it ended in dry frosts right away up to Christmas.) Dockett he'd sent up to Perry Shaw for me – no, he comes puffin' up to me himself – because a big corner-piece o' the bank had slipped into the brook where she makes that elber at the bottom o' the Seventeen Acre, an' all the rubbishy alders an' sallies which he ought to have cut out when he took the farm, they'd slipped with the slip, an' the brook was comin' rooshin' down atop of 'em, an' they'd just about back an' spill the waters over his winter wheat. The water was lyin' in the flats already. "Gor a-mighty, Jesse!" he bellers out at me, "get that rubbish away all manners you can. Don't stop for no fagottin', but give the brook play or my wheat's past salvation. I can't lend you no help," he says, "but work an' I'll pay ye." '

'You had him there,' Jabez chuckled.

'Yes. I reckon I had ought to have drove my bargain, but the brook was backin' up on good bread-corn. So 'cardenly, I laid into the mess of it, workin' off the bank where the trees was drownin' themselves head-down in the roosh – just such weather as this – an' the brook creepin' up on me all the time. 'Long toward noon, Jim comes mowchin' along with his toppin' axe over his shoulder.

' "Be you minded for an extra hand at your job?" he says.

' "Be you minded to turn to?" I ses, an' – no more talk to it – Jim laid in alongside o' me. He's no hunger with a toppin' axe.'

'Maybe, but I've seed him at a job o' throwin' in the woods, an' he didn't seem to make out no shape,' said Jabez. 'He haven't got the shoulders, nor yet the judgement – my opinion – when he's dealin' with full-girt timber. He don't rightly make up his mind where he's goin' to throw her.'

'We wasn't throwin' nothin'. We was cuttin' out they soft alders, an' haulin' 'em up the bank 'fore they could back the waters on the wheat. Jim didn't say much, 'less it was that he'd had a postcard from Mary's Lunnon father, night before, sayin' he was comin' down that mornin'. Jim, he'd sweated all night, an' he didn't reckon hisself equal to the talkin' an' the swearin' an' the cryin', an' his mother blamin' him afterwards on the slate. "It spiled my day to think of it," he ses, when we was eatin' our pieces. "So I've fair cried dunghill an' run. Mother'll have to tackle him by herself. I lay *she* won't give him no hush-money," he ses. "I lay he'll be surprised by the time he's done with *her*," he ses. An' that was e'en a'most all the talk we had concernin' it. But he's no hunger with the toppin' axe.

'The brook she'd crep' up an' up on us, an' she kep' creepin' upon us till we was workin' knee-deep in the shallers, cuttin' an' pookin' an' pullin' what we could get to o' the rubbish. There was a middlin' lot comin' downstream, too – cattle-bars, an' hop-poles, an' odds-ends bats, all poltin' down together; but they rooshed round the elber good shape by the time we'd backed out they drowned trees. Come four o'clock we reckoned we'd done a proper day's work, an' she'd take no harm if we left her. We couldn't puddle about there in the dark an' wet to no more advantage. Jim he was pourin' the water out of his boots – no, I was doin' that. Jim was kneelin' to unlace his'n. "Damn it all, Jesse," he ses, standin' up; "the flood must be over my doorsteps at home, for here comes my old white-top bee-skep!" '

'Yes. I allus heard he paints his bee-skeps,' Jabez put in. 'I dunno paint don't tarrify bees more'n it keeps em' dry.'

' "I'll have a pook at it," he ses, an' he pooks at it as it comes round the elber. The roosh nigh jerked the pooker out of his hand-grips, an' he calls to me, an' I come runnin' barefoot. Then we pulled on the pooker, an' it reared up on eend in the roosh, an' we guessed what 'twas. 'Cardenly we pulled it in into a shaller, an' it rolled a piece, an' a great old stiff man's arm nigh hit me in the face. Then we was sure. "'Tis a man," ses Jim. But the face was all a mask. "I reckon it's Mary's Lunnon father," he ses presently. "Lend me a match and I'll make sure." He never used baccy. We lit three matches one by another, well's we could in the rain, an' he cleaned off some o' the slob with a tussick o' grass. "Yes," he ses. "It's Mary's Lunnon father. He won't tarrify us no more. D'you want him, Jesse?" he ses.

' "No," I ses. "If this was Eastbourne beach like, he'd be half a crown apiece to us 'fore the coroner; but now we'd only lose a day havin' to 'tend the inquest. I lay he fell into the brook."

' "I lay he did," ses Jim. "I wonder if he saw mother." He turns him over, an' opens his coat and puts his fingers in the waistcoat pocket an' starts laughin'. "He's seen mother, right enough," he ses. "An' he's got the best of her, too. *She* won't be able to crow no more over *me* 'bout givin' him money. *I* never give him more than a sovereign. She's give him two!" an' he trousers 'em, laughin' all the time. "An' now we'll pook him back again, for I've done with him," he ses.

'So we pooked him back into the middle of the brook, an' we saw he went round the elber 'thout balkin', an' we walked quite a piece beside of him to set him on his ways. When we couldn't see no more, we went home by the high road, because we knowed the brook 'u'd be out acrost the medders, an' we wasn't goin' to hunt for Jim's little rotten old bridge in that dark – an' rainin' heavens' hard, too. I was middlin' pleased to see light an' vittles again when we got home. Jim he pressed me to come insides for a drink. He don't drink in a generality, but he was rid of all his troubles that evenin', d'ye see? "Mother," he ses so soon as the door ope'd, "have you seen him?" She whips out her slate an' writes down – "No." "Oh, no," ses Jim. "You don't get out of it that way, mother. I lay you *have* seen him, an' I lay he's bested you for all your talk, same as he bested me. Make a clean breast of it, mother," he ses. "He got round you too." She was goin' for the slate again, but he stops her. "It's all right, mother," he ses. "I've seen him sense you have, an' he won't trouble us no more." The old lady looks up quick as a robin, an' she writes, "Did he say so?" "No," ses Jim, laughin'. "He didn't say so. That's how I know. But he bested *you*, mother. You can't have it in at *me* for bein' soft-hearted. You're twice as tender-hearted as what I be. Look!" he ses, an' he shows her the two sovereigns. "Put 'em away where they belong," he ses. "He won't never come for no more; an' now we'll have our drink," he ses, "for we've earned it."

'Nature–ally they weren't goin' to let me see where they kep' their monies. She went upstairs with it – for the whisky.'

'I never knowed Jim was a drinkin' man – in his own house, like,' said Jabez.

'No more he isn't; but what he takes he likes good. He won't tech no publican's hogwash acrost the bar. Four shillin's he paid for that bottle o' whisky. I know, because when the old lady brought it down there wasn't more'n jest a liddle few dreenin's an' dregs in it. Nothin' to set before neighbours, I do assure you.'

' "Why, 'twas half full last week, mother," he ses. "You don't mean," he ses, "you've given him all that as well? It's two shillin's worth," he ses. (That's how I knowed he paid four.) "Well, well, mother, you be too tender-'earted to live. But I don't grudge it to him," he ses. "I don't grudge him nothin' he can keep." So, 'cardenly, we drinked up what little sup was left.'

'An' what become of Mary's Lunnon father?' said Jabez after a full minute's silence.

'I be too tired to go readin' papers of evenin's; but Dockett he told me, that very week, I think, that they'd inquested on a man down at Roberts-bridge which had poked and poked up agin' so many bridges an' banks, like, they couldn't make naun out of him.'

'An' what did Mary say to all these doin's?'

'The old lady bundled her off to the village 'fore her Lunnon father come, to buy weekend stuff (an' she forgot the half o' it). When we come in she was upstairs studyin' to be a schoolteacher. None told her naun about it. 'Twadn't girls' affairs.'

'Reckon *she* knowed?' Jabez went on.

'She? She must have guessed it middlin' close when she saw her money come back. But she never mentioned it in writing so far's I know. She were more worritted that night on account of two-three her chickens bein' drowned, for the flood had skewed their old hen-house round on her postes. I cobbled her up next mornin' when the brook shrinked.'

'An' where did you find the bridge? Some fur downstream, didn't ye?'

'Just where she allus was. She hadn't shifted but very little. The brook had gulled out the bank a piece under one eend o' the plank, so's she was liable to tilt ye sideways if you wasn't careful. But I pooked three-four bricks under her, an' she was all plumb again.'

'Well, I dunno how it *looks* like, but let be how 'twill,' said Jabez, 'he hadn't no business to come down from Lunnon tarrifyin' people, an' threatenin' to take away children which they'd hobbed up for their lawful own – even if 'twas Mary Wickenden.'

'He had the business right enough, an' he had the law with him – no gettin' over that,' said Jesse. 'But he had the drink with him, too, an' that was where he failed, like.'

'Well, well! Let be how 'twill, the brook was a good friend to Jim. I see it now. I allus *did* wonder what he was gettin' at when he said that, when I talked to him about shiftin' the stack. "You dunno everythin'," he ses. "The brook's been a good friend to me," he ses, "an' if she's minded to have a snatch at my hay, *I* ain't settin' out to withstand her."'

'I reckon she's about shifted it, too, by now,' Jesse chuckled. 'Hark! That ain't any slip off the bank which she's got hold of.'

The brook had changed her note again. It sounded as though she were mumbling something soft.

In the Same Boat

'A throbbing vein,' said Dr Gilbert soothingly, 'is the mother of delusion.'

'Then how do you account for my knowing when the thing is due?' Conroy's voice rose almost to a break.

'Of course, but you should have consulted a doctor before using – palliatives.'

'It was driving me mad. And now I can't give them up.'

'Not so bad as that! One doesn't form fatal habits at twenty-five. Think again. Were you ever frightened as a child?'

'I don't remember. It began when I was a boy.'

'With or without the spasm? By the way, do you mind describing the spasm again?'

'Well,' said Conroy, twisting in the chair, 'I'm no musician, but suppose you were a violin-string – vibrating – and someone put his finger on you? As if a finger were put on the naked soul! Awful!'

'So's indigestion – so's nightmare – while it lasts.'

'But the horror afterwards knocks me out for days. And the waiting for it . . . and then this drug habit! It can't go on!' He shook as he spoke, and the chair creaked.

'My dear fellow,' said the doctor, 'when you're older you'll know what burdens the best of us carry. A fox to every Spartan.'

'That doesn't help *me*. I can't! I can't!' cried Conroy, and burst into tears.

'Don't apologise,' said Gilbert, when the paroxysm ended. 'I'm used to people coming a little – unstuck in this room.'

'It's those tablets!' Conroy stamped his foot feebly as he blew his nose. 'They've knocked me out. I used to be fit once. Oh, I've tried exercise and everything. But – if one sits down for a minute when it's due – even at four in the morning – it runs up behind one.'

'Ye–es. Many things come in the quiet of the morning. You always know when the visitation is due?'

'What would I give not to be sure!' he sobbed.

'We'll put that aside for the moment. I'm thinking of a case where what we'll call anaemia of the brain was masked (I don't say cured) by vibration. He couldn't sleep, or thought he couldn't, but a steamer voyage and the thump of the screw – '

'A steamer? After what I've told you!' Conroy almost shrieked. 'I'd sooner . . .'

'Of course *not* a steamer in your case, but a long railway journey the next time you think it will trouble you. It sounds absurd, but – '

'I'd try anything. I nearly have,' Conroy sighed.

'Nonsense! I've given you a tonic that will clear *that* notion from your head. Give the train a chance, and don't begin the journey by bucking yourself up with tablets. Take them along, but hold them in reserve – in reserve.'

'D'you think I've self-control enough, after what you've heard?' said Conroy.

Dr Gilbert smiled. 'Yes. After what I've seen,' he glanced round the room, 'I have no hesitation in saying you have quite as much self-control as many other people. I'll write to you later about your journey. Meantime, the tonic,' and he gave some general directions before Conroy left.

An hour later Dr Gilbert hurried to the links, where the others of his regular weekend game awaited him. It was a rigid round, played as usual at the trot, for the tension of the week lay as heavy on the two King's Counsels and Sir John Chartres as on Gilbert. The lawyers were old enemies of the Admiralty Court, and Sir John of the frosty eyebrows and Abernethy manner was bracketed with, but before, Rutherford Gilbert among nerve-specialists.

At the clubhouse afterwards the lawyers renewed their squabble over a tangled collision case, and the doctors as naturally compared professional matters.

'Lies – all lies,' said Sir John, when Gilbert had told him Conroy's trouble. '*Post hoc, propter hoc*. The man or woman who drugs is *ipso facto* a liar. You've no imagination.'

'Pity you haven't a little – occasionally.'

'I have believed a certain type of patient in my time. It's always the same. For reasons not given in the consulting-room they take to the drug. Certain symptoms follow. They will swear to you, and believe it, that they took the drug to mask the symptoms. What does your man use? Najdolene? I thought so. I had practically the duplicate of your case last Thursday. Same old Najdolene – same old lie.'

'Tell me the symptoms, and I'll draw my own inferences, Johnnie.'

'Symptoms! The girl was rank poisoned with Najdolene. Ramping, stamping possession. Gad, I thought she'd have the chandelier down.'

'Mine came unstuck too, and he has the physique of a bull,' said Gilbert. 'What delusions had yours?'

'Faces – faces with mildew on them. In any other walk of life we'd call it the horrors. She told me, of course, she took the drugs to mask the faces. *Post hoc, propter hoc* again. All liars!'

'What's that?' said the senior KC quickly. 'Sounds professional.'

'Go away! Not for you, Sandy.' Sir John turned a shoulder against him and walked with Gilbert in the chill evening.

To Conroy in his chambers came, one week later, this letter:

DEAR MR CONROY – If your plan of a night's trip on the 17th still holds good, and you have no particular destination in view, you could do me a kindness. A Miss Henschil, in whom I am interested, goes down to the West by the 10.08 from Waterloo (Number 3 platform) on that night. She is not exactly an invalid, but, like so many of us, a little shaken in her nerves. Her maid, of course, accompanies her, but if I knew you were in the same train it would be an additional source of strength. Will you please write and let me know whether the 10.08 from Waterloo, Number 3 platform, on the 17th, suits you, and I will meet you there? Don't forget my caution, and keep up the tonic.

Yours sincerely,

L. RUTHERFORD GILBERT

'He knows I'm scarcely fit to look after myself,' was Conroy's thought. 'And he wants me to look after a woman!'

Yet, at the end of half an hour's irresolution, he accepted.

Now Conroy's trouble, which had lasted for years, was this: on a certain night, while he lay between sleep and wake, he would be overtaken by a long shuddering sigh, which he learned to know was the sign that his brain had once more conceived its horror, and in time – in due time – would bring it forth.

Drugs could so well veil that horror that it shuffled along no worse than as a freezing dream in a procession of disorderly dreams; but over the return of the event drugs had no control. Once that sigh had passed his lips the thing was inevitable, and through the days granted before its rebirth he walked in torment. For the first two years he had striven to fend it off by distractions, but neither exercise nor drink availed. Then he had come to the tablets of the excellent M. Najdol. These guarantee, on the label, 'Refreshing and absolutely natural sleep to the soul-weary.' They are carried in a case with a spring which presses one scented tablet to the end of the tube, whence it can be lipped off in stroking the moustache or adjusting the veil.

Three years of M. Najdol's preparations do not fit a man for many careers. His friends, who knew he did not drink, assumed that Conroy had strained his heart through valiant outdoor exercises, and Conroy had with some care invented an imaginary doctor, symptoms and regimen, which he discussed with them and with his mother in Hereford. She maintained that he would grow out of it, and recommended nux vomica.

When at last Conroy faced a real doctor, it was, he hoped, to be saved from suicide by a strait-waistcoat. Yet Dr Gilbert had but given him more drugs – a tonic, for instance, that would couple railway carriages – and had advised a night in the train. Not alone the horrors of a railway journey (for which a man who dare keep no servant must e'en pack, label and address his own bag), but the necessity for holding himself in hand before a stranger 'a little shaken in her nerves'.

He spent a long forenoon packing, because when he assembled and counted things his mind slid off to the hours that remained of the day before his night, and he found himself counting minutes aloud. At such times the injustice of his fate would drive him to revolts which no servant should witness, but on this evening Dr Gilbert's tonic held him fairly calm while he put up his patent razors.

Waterloo Station shook him into real life. The change for his ticket needed concentration, if only to prevent shillings and pence turning into minutes at the booking-office; and he spoke quickly to a porter about the disposition of his bag. The old 10.08 from Waterloo to the West was an all-night caravan that halted, in the interests of the milk traffic, at almost every station.

Dr Gilbert stood by the door of the one composite corridor-coach, an older and stouter man behind him. 'So glad you're here!' he cried. 'Let me get your ticket.'

'Certainly not,' Conroy answered. 'I got it myself – long ago. My bag's in too,' he added proudly.

'I beg your pardon. Miss Henschil's here. I'll introduce you.'

'But – but,' he stammered – 'think of the state I'm in. If anything happens I shall collapse.'

'Not you. You'd rise to the occasion like a bird. And as for the self-control you were talking of the other day' – Gilbert swung him round – 'look!'

A young man in an ulster over a silk-faced frock-coat stood by the carriage window, weeping shamelessly.

'Oh, but that's only drink,' Conroy said. 'I haven't had one of my – my things since lunch.'

'Excellent!' said Gilbert. 'I knew I could depend on you. Come along. Wait for a minute, Chartres.'

A tall woman, veiled, sat by the far window. She bowed her head as the doctor murmured Conroy knew not what. Then he disappeared and the inspector came for tickets.

'My maid – next compartment,' she said slowly.

Conroy showed his ticket, but in returning it to the sleeve-pocket of his ulster the little silver Najdolene case slipped from his glove and fell to the floor. He snatched it up as the moving train flung him into his seat.

'How nice!' said the woman. She leisurely lifted her veil, unbuttoned the first button of her left glove, and pressed out from its palm a Najdolene-case.

'Don't!' said Conroy, not realising he had spoken.

'I beg your pardon.' The deep voice was measured, even, and low. Conroy knew what made it so.

'I said "don't"! He wouldn't like you to do it!'

'No, he would not.' She held the tube with its ever-presented tablet between finger and thumb. 'But aren't you one of the – ah – "soul-weary" too?'

'That's why. Oh, please don't! Not at first. I – I haven't had one since morning. You – you'll set me off!'

'You? Are you so far gone as that?'

He nodded, pressing his palms together. The train jolted through Vauxhall points, and was welcomed with the clang of empty milk-cans for the West.

After long silence she lifted her great eyes, and, with an innocence that would have deceived any sound man, asked Conroy to call her maid to bring her a forgotten book.

Conroy shook his head. 'No. Our sort can't read. Don't!'

'Were you sent to watch me?' The voice never changed.

'Me? I need a keeper myself much more – *this* night of all!'

'This night? Have you a night, then? They disbelieved *me* when I told them of mine.' She leaned back and laughed, always slowly. 'Aren't doctors stu–upid? They don't know.'

She leaned her elbow on her knee, lifted her veil that had fallen, and, chin in hand, stared at him. He looked at her – till his eyes were blurred with tears.

'Have I been there, think you?' she said.

'Surely – surely,' Conroy answered, for he had well seen the fear and the horror that lived behind the heavy-lidded eyes, the fine tracing on the broad forehead, and the guard set about the desirable mouth.

'Then – suppose we have one – just one apiece? I've gone without since this afternoon.'

He put up his hand, and would have shouted, but his voice broke.

'Don't! Can't you see that it helps me to help you to keep it off? Don't let's both go down together.'

'But I want one. It's a poor heart that never rejoices. Just one. It's my night.'

'It's mine – too. My sixty-fourth, fifth, sixth, seventh.' He shut his lips firmly against the tide of visualised numbers that threatened to carry him along.

'Ah, it's only my thirty-ninth.' She paused as he had done. 'I wonder if I shall last into the sixties . . . Talk to me or I shall go crazy. You're a man. You're the stronger vessel. Tell me when you went to pieces.'

'One, two, three, four, five, six, seven – eight – I beg your pardon.'

'Not in the least. I always pretend I've dropped a stitch of my knitting. I count the days till the last day, then the hours, then the minutes. Do you?'

'I don't think I've done very much else for the last – ' said Conroy, shivering, for the night was cold, with a chill he recognised.

'Oh, how comforting to find someone who can talk sense! It's not always the same date, is it?'

'What difference would that make?' He unbuttoned his ulster with a jerk. 'You're a sane woman. Can't you see the wicked – wicked – wicked' (dust flew from the padded arm-rest as he struck it) unfairness of it? What have I done?'

She laid her large hand on his shoulder very firmly.

'If you begin to think over that,' she said, 'you'll go to pieces and be ashamed. Tell me yours, and I'll tell you mine. Only be quiet – be quiet, lad, or you'll set me off!' She made shift to soothe him, though her chin trembled.

'Well,' said he at last, picking at the arm-rest between them, 'mine's nothing much, of course.'

'Don't be a fool! That's for doctors – and mothers.'

'It's hell,' Conroy muttered. 'It begins on a steamer – on a stifling hot night. I come out of my cabin. I pass through the saloon where the stewards have rolled up the carpets, and the boards are bare and hot and soapy.'

'I've travelled too,' she said.

'Ah! I come on deck. I walk down a covered alleyway. Butcher's meat, bananas, oil, that sort of smell.'

Again she nodded.

'It's a lead-coloured steamer, and the sea's lead-coloured. Perfectly smooth sea – perfectly still ship, except for the engines running, and the waves going off in lines and lines and lines – dull grey. All this time I know something's going to happen.'

'I know. Something is going to happen,' she whispered.

'Then I hear a thud in the engine-room. Then the noise of machinery falling down – like fire-irons – and then two most awful yells. They're more like hoots, and I know – I know while I listen – that it means that two men have died as they hooted. It was their last breath hooting out of them – in most awful pain. Do you understand?'

'I ought to. Go on.'

'That's the first part. Then I hear bare feet running along the alleyway. One of the scalded men comes up behind me and says quite distinctly, "My friend! All is lost!" Then he taps me on the shoulder and I hear him drop down dead.' He panted and wiped his forehead.

'So that is your night?' she said.

'That is my night. It comes every few weeks – so many days after I get what I call sentence. Then I begin to count.'

'Get sentence? D'you mean *this*?' She half closed her eyes, drew a deep breath, and shuddered. ' "Notice" I call it. Sir John thought it was all lies.'

She had unpinned her hat and thrown it on the seat opposite, showing the immense mass of her black hair, rolled low in the nape of the columnar neck and looped over the left ear. But Conroy had no eyes except for her grave eyes.

'Listen now!' said she. 'I walk down a road, a white sandy road near the sea. There are broken fences on either side, and men come and look at me over them.'

'Just men? Do they speak?'

'They try to. Their faces are all mildewy – eaten away,' and she hid her face for an instant with her left hand. 'It's the faces – the faces!'

'Yes. Like my two hoots. I know.'

'Ah! But the place itself – the bareness – and the glitter and the salt smells, and the wind blowing the sand! The men run after me and I run . . . I know what's coming too. One of them touches me.'

'Yes! What comes then? We've both shirked that.'

'One awful shock – not palpitation, but shock, shock, shock!'

'As though your soul were being stopped – as you'd stop a finger-bowl humming?' he said.

'Just that,' she answered. 'One's very soul – the soul that one lives by – stopped. So!'

She drove her thumb deep into the arm-rest. 'And now,' she whined to him, 'now that we've stirred each other up this way, mightn't we have just one?'

'No,' said Conroy, shaking. 'Let's hold on. We're past' – he peered out of the black windows – 'Woking. There's the Necropolis. How long till dawn?'

'Oh, cruel long yet. If one dozes for a minute, it catches one.'

'And how d'you find that this' – he tapped the palm of his glove – 'helps you?'

'It covers up the thing from being too real – if one takes enough – you know. Only – only – one loses everything else. I've been no more than a bogie-girl for two years. What would you give to be real again? This lying's such a nuisance.'

'One must protect oneself – and there's one's mother to think of,' he answered.

'True. I hope allowances are made for us somewhere. Our burden – can you hear? – our burden is heavy enough.'

She rose, towering into the roof of the carriage. Conroy's ungentle grip pulled her back.

'Now *you* are foolish. Sit down,' said he.

'But the cruelty of it! Can't you see it? Don't you feel it? Let's take one now – before I –'

'Sit down!' cried Conroy, and the sweat stood again on his forehead. He had fought through a few nights, and had been defeated on more, and he knew the rebellion that flares beyond control to exhaustion.

She smoothed her hair and dropped back, but for a while her head and throat moved with the sickening motion of a captured wry-neck.

'Once,' she said, spreading out her hands, 'I ripped my counterpane from end to end. That takes strength. I had it then. I've little now. "All dorn," as my little niece says. And you, lad?'

' "All dorn"! Let me keep your case for you till the morning.'

'But the cold feeling is beginning.'

'Lend it me, then.'

'And the drag down my right side. I shan't be able to move in a minute.'

'I can scarcely lift my arm myself,' said Conroy. 'We're in for it.'

'Then why are you so foolish? You know it'll be easier if we have only one – only one apiece.'

She was lifting the case to her mouth. With tremendous effort Conroy caught it. The two moved like jointed dolls, and when their hands met it was as wood on wood.

'You must – not!' said Conroy. His jaws stiffened, and the cold climbed from his feet up.

'Why – must – I – not?' She repeated the words idiotically.

Conroy could only shake his head, while he bore down on the hand and the case in it.

Her speech went from her altogether. The wonderful lips rested half over the even teeth, the breath was in the nostrils only, the eyes dulled, the face set grey, and through the glove the hand struck like ice.

Presently her soul came back and stood behind her eyes – only thing that had life in all that place – stood and looked for Conroy's soul. He too was fettered in every limb, but somewhere at an immense distance he heard his heart going about its work as the engine-room carries on through and beneath the all but overwhelming wave. His one hope, he knew, was not to lose the eyes that clung to his, because there was an evil abroad which would possess him if he looked aside by a hair's-breadth.

The rest was darkness through which some distant planet spun while cymbals clashed. (Beyond Farnborough the 10.08 rolls out many empty milk-cans at every halt.) Then a body came to life with intolerable pricklings. Limb by limb, after agonies of terror, that body returned to him, steeped in most perfect physical weariness such as follows a long day's rowing. He saw the heavy lids droop over her eyes – the watcher behind them departed – and, his soul sinking into assured peace, Conroy slept.

Light on his eyes and a salt breath roused him without shock. Her hand still held his. She slept, forehead down upon it, but the movement of his waking waked her too, and she sneezed like a child.

'I – I think it's morning,' said Conroy.

'And nothing has happened! Did you see your men? I didn't see my faces. Does it mean we've escaped? Did – did you take any after I went to sleep? I'll swear I didn't,' she stammered.

'No, there wasn't any need. We've slept through it.'

'No need! Thank God! There was no need! Oh, look!'

The train was running under red cliffs along a sea-wall washed by waves that were colourless in the early light. Southward the sun rose mistily upon the Channel.

She leaned out of the window and breathed to the bottom of her lungs, while the wind wrenched down her dishevelled hair and blew it below her waist.

'Well!' she said with splendid eyes. 'Aren't you still waiting for something to happen?'

'No. Not till next time. We've been let off,' Conroy answered, breathing as deeply as she.

'Then we ought to say our prayers.'

'What nonsense! Someone will see us.'

'We needn't kneel. Stand up and say "Our Father". We *must*!'

It was the first time since childhood that Conroy had prayed. They laughed hysterically when a curve threw them against an arm-rest.

'Now for breakfast!' she cried. 'My maid – Nurse Blaber – has the basket and things. It'll be ready in twenty minutes. Oh! Look at my hair!' and she went out laughing.

Conroy's first discovery, made without fumbling or counting letters on taps, was that the London and South Western's allowance of washing-water is inadequate. He used every drop, rioting in the cold tingle on neck and arms. To shave in a moving train balked him, but the next halt gave him a chance, which, to his own surprise, he took. As he stared at himself in the mirror he smiled and nodded. There were points about this person with the clear, if sunken, eye and the almost uncompressed mouth. But when he bore his bag back to his compartment, the weight of it on a limp arm humbled that new pride.

'My friend,' he said, half aloud, 'you go into training. You're putty.'

She met him in the spare compartment, where her maid had laid breakfast.

'By Jove!' he said, halting at the doorway, 'I hadn't realised how beautiful you were!'

'The same to you, lad. Sit down. I could eat a horse.'

'I shouldn't,' said the maid quietly. 'The less you eat the better.' She was a small, freckled woman, with light fluffy hair and pale-blue eyes that looked through all veils.

'This is Miss Blaber,' said Miss Henschil. 'He's one of the soul-weary too, Nursey.'

'I know it. But when one has just given it up a full meal doesn't agree. That's why I've only brought you bread and butter.'

She went out quietly, and Conroy reddened.

'We're still children, you see,' said Miss Henschil. 'But I'm well enough to feel some shame of it. D'you take sugar?'

They starved together heroically, and Nurse Blaber was good enough to signify approval when she came to clear away.

'Nursey?' Miss Henschil insinuated, and flushed.

'Do you smoke?' said the nurse coolly to Conroy.

'I haven't in years. Now you mention it, I think I'd like a cigarette – or something.'

'I used to. D'you think it would keep me quiet?' Miss Henschil said.

'Perhaps. Try these.' The nurse handed them her cigarette-case.

'Don't take anything else,' she commanded, and went away with the tea-basket.

'Good!' grunted Conroy, between mouthfuls of tobacco.

'Better than nothing,' said Miss Henschil; but for a while they felt ashamed, yet with the comfort of children punished together.

'Now,' she whispered, 'who were you when you were a man?'

Conroy told her, and in return she gave him her history. It delighted them both to deal once more in worldly concerns – families, names, places and dates – with a person of understanding.

She came, she said, of Lancashire folk – wealthy cotton-spinners, who still kept the broadened *a* and slurred aspirate of the old stock. She lived with an old masterful mother in an opulent world north of Lancaster Gate, where people in society gave parties at a Mecca called the Langham Hotel.

She herself had been launched into society there, and the flowers at the ball had cost eighty-seven pounds; but, being reckoned peculiar, she had made few friends among her own sex. She had attracted many men, for she was a beauty – *the* beauty, in fact, of society, she said.

She spoke utterly without shame or reticence, as a life-prisoner tells his past to a fellow-prisoner; and Conroy nodded across the smoke-rings.

'Do you remember when you got into the carriage?' she asked. '(Oh, I wish I had some knitting!) Did you notice aught, lad?'

Conroy thought back. It was ages since. 'Wasn't there someone outside the door – crying?' he asked.

'He's – he's the little man I was engaged to,' she said. 'But I made him break it off. I told him 'twas no good. But he won't, yo' see.'

'*That* fellow? Why, he doesn't come up to your shoulder.'

'That's naught to do with it. I think all the world of him. I'm a foolish wench' – her speech wandered as she settled herself cosily, one elbow on the arm-rest. 'We'd been engaged – I couldn't help that – and he worships the ground I tread on. But it's no use. I'm not responsible, you see. His two sisters are against it, though I've the money. They're right, but they think it's the dri-ink,' she drawled. 'They're Methody – the Skinners. You see, their grandfather that started the Patton Mills, he died o' the dri–ink.'

'I see,' said Conroy. The grave face before him under the lifted veil was troubled.

'George Skinner.' She breathed it softly. 'I'd make him a good wife, by God's gra–ace – if I could. But it's no use. I'm not responsible. But he'll not take no for an answer. I used to call him "Toots". He's of no consequence, yo' see.'

'That's in Dickens,' said Conroy, quite quickly. 'I haven't thought of Toots for years. He was at Dr Blimber's.'

'And so – that's my trouble,' she concluded, ever so slightly wringing her hands. 'But I – don't you think – there's hope now?'

'Eh?' said Conroy. 'Oh yes! This is the first time I've turned my corner without help. With your help, I should say.'

'It'll come back, though.'

'Then shall we meet it in the same way? Here's my card. Write me your train, and we'll go together.'

'Yes. We must do that. But between times – when we want – ' She looked at her palm, the four fingers working on it. 'It's hard to give 'em up.'

'But think what we have gained already, and let me have the case to keep.'

She shook her head, and threw her cigarette out of the window. 'Not yet.'

'Then let's lend our cases to Nurse Blaber, and we'll get through today on cigarettes. I'll call her while we feel strong.'

She hesitated, but yielded at last, and Nurse Blaber accepted the offerings with a smile.

'*You'll* be all right,' she said to Miss Henschil. 'But if I were *you*' – to Conroy – 'I'd take strong exercise.'

When they reached their destination Conroy set himself to obey Nurse Blaber. He had no remembrance of that day, except one streak of blue sea to his left, gorse-bushes to his right, and, before him, a coast-guard's track marked with white-washed stones that he counted up to the far thousands. As he returned to the little town he saw Miss Henschil on the beach below the cliffs. She kneeled at Nurse Blaber's feet, weeping and pleading.

* * *

Twenty-five days later a telegram came to Conroy's rooms: 'Notice given. Waterloo again. Twenty-fourth.' That same evening he was wakened by the shudder and the sigh that told him his sentence had gone forth. Yet he reflected on his pillow that he had, in spite of lapses, snatched something like three weeks of life, which included several rides on a horse before breakfast – the hour one most craves Najdolene; five consecutive evenings on the river at Hammersmith in a tub where he had well stretched the white arms that passing crews mocked at; a game of rackets at his club; three dinners, one small dance, and one human flirtation with a human woman. More notable still, he had settled his month's accounts, only once confusing petty cash with the days of grace allowed him. Next morning he rode his hired beast in the park victoriously. He saw Miss Henschil on horseback near Lancaster Gate, talking to a young man at the railings.

She wheeled and cantered towards him.

'By Jove! How well you look!' he cried, without salutation. 'I didn't know you rode.'

'I used to once,' she replied. 'I'm all soft now.'

They swept off together down the ride.

'Your beast pulls,' he said.

'Wa–ant him to. Gi–gives me something to think of. How've you been?' she panted. 'I wish chemists' shops hadn't red lights.'

'Have you slipped out and bought some, then?'

'You don't know Nursey. Eh, but it's good to be on a horse again! This chap cost me two hundred.'

'Then you've been swindled,' said Conroy.

'I know it, but it's no odds. I must go back to Toots and send him away. He's neglecting his work for me.'

She swung her heavy-topped animal on his none-too-sound hocks. 'Sentence come, lad?'

'Yes. But I'm not minding it so much this time.'

'Waterloo, then – and God help us!' She thundered back to the little frock-coated figure that waited faithfully near the gate.

Conroy felt the spring sun on his shoulders and trotted home. That evening he went out with a man in a pair oar, and was rowed to a standstill. But the other man owned he could not have kept the pace five minutes longer.

* * *

He carried his bag all down Number 3 platform at Waterloo, and hove it with one hand into the rack.

'Well done!' said Nurse Blaber, in the corridor. 'We've improved too.'

Dr Gilbert and an older man came out of the next compartment.

'Hallo!' said Gilbert. 'Why haven't you been to see me, Mr Conroy? Come under the lamp. Take off your hat. No – no. Sit, you young giant. Very good. Look here a minute, Johnnie.'

A little, round-bellied, hawk-faced person glared at him. 'Gilbert was right about the beauty of the beast,' he muttered. 'D'you keep it in your glove now?' he went on, and punched Conroy in the short ribs.

'No,' said Conroy meekly, but without coughing. 'Nowhere – on my honour! I've chucked it for good.'

'Wait till you are a sound man before you say *that*, Mr Conroy.' Sir John Chartres stumped out, saying to Gilbert in the corridor, 'It's all very fine, but the question is shall I or we "Sir Pandarus of Troy become", eh? We're bound to think of the children.'

'Have you been vetted?' said Miss Henschil, a few minutes after the train started. 'May I sit with you? I – I don't trust myself yet. I can't give up as easily as you can, seemingly.'

'Can't you? I never saw anyone so improved in a month.'

'Look here!' She reached across to the rack, single-handed lifted Conroy's bag, and held it at arm's length. 'I counted ten slowly. And I didn't think of hours or minutes,' she boasted.

'Don't remind me,' he cried.

'Ah! Now I've reminded myself. I wish I hadn't. Do you think it'll be easier for us tonight?'

'Oh, don't.' The smell of the carriage had brought back all his last trip to him, and Conroy moved uneasily.

'I'm sorry. I've brought some games,' she went on. 'Draughts and cards – but they all mean counting. I wish I'd brought chess, but I can't play chess. What can we do? Talk about something.'

'Well, how's Toots, to begin with?' said Conroy.

'Why? Did you see him on the platform?'

'No. Was he there? I didn't notice.'

'Oh yes. He doesn't understand. He's desperately jealous. I told him it doesn't matter. Will you please let me hold your hand? I believe I'm beginning to get the chill.'

'Toots ought to envy me,' said Conroy.

'He does. He paid you a high compliment the other night. He's taken to calling again – in spite of all they say.'

Conroy inclined his head. He felt cold, and knew surely he would be colder.

'He said,' she yawned. '(Beg your pardon.) He said he couldn't see how I could help falling in love with a man like you; and he called himself a damned little rat, and he beat his head on the piano last night.'

'The piano? You play, then?'

'Only to him. He thinks the world of my accomplishments. Then I told him I wouldn't have you if you were the last man on earth instead of only the best-looking – not with a million in each stocking.'

'No, not with a million in each stocking,' said Conroy vehemently. 'Isn't that odd?'

'I suppose so – to anyone who doesn't know. Well, where was I? Oh, George as good as told me I was deceiving him, and he wanted to go away without saying good-night. He hates standing on tiptoe, but he must if I won't sit down.'

Conroy would have smiled, but the chill that foreran the coming of the lier-in-wait was upon him, and his hand closed warningly on hers.

'And – and so – ' she was trying to say, when her hour also overtook her, leaving alive only the fear-dilated eyes that turned to Conroy. Hand froze on hand and the body with it as they waited for the horror in the blackness that heralded it. Yet through the worst Conroy saw, at an uncountable distance, one minute glint of light in his night. Thither would he go and escape his fear; and behold, that light was the light in the watch-tower of her eyes, where her locked soul signalled to his soul: 'Look at me!'

In time, from him and from her, the thing sheered aside, that each soul might step down and resume its own concerns. He thought confusedly of people on the skirts of a thunderstorm, withdrawing from windows where the torn night is to their known and furnished beds. Then he dozed, till in some drowsy turn his hand fell from her warmed hand.

'That's all. The faces haven't come,' he heard her say. 'All – thank God! I don't feel even I need what Nursey promised me. Do you?'

'No.' He rubbed his eyes. 'But don't make too sure.'

'Certainly not. We shall have to try again next month. I'm afraid it will be an awful nuisance for you.'

'Not to me, I assure you,' said Conroy, and they leaned back and laughed at the flatness of the words, after the hells through which they had just risen.

'And now,' she said, strict eyes on Conroy, '*why* wouldn't you take me – not with a million in each stocking?'

'I don't know. That's what I've been puzzling over.'

'So have I. We're as handsome a couple as I've ever seen. Are you well off, lad?'

'They call me so,' said Conroy, smiling.

'That's north-country.' She laughed again. 'Setting aside my good looks and yours, I've four thousand a year of my own, and the rents should make it six. That's a match some old cats would lap tea all night to fettle up.'

'It is. Lucky Toots!' said Conroy.

'Ay,' she answered, 'he'll be the luckiest lad in London if I win through. Who's yours?'

'No – no one, dear. I've been in hell for years. I only want to get out and be alive and – so on. Isn't that reason enough?'

'Maybe, for a man. But I never minded things much till George came. I was all stu–upid like.'

'So was I, but now I think I can live. It ought to be less next month, oughtn't it?' he said.

'I hope so. Ye–es. There's nothing much for a maid except to be married, and I ask no more. Whoever yours is, when you've found her, she shall have a wedding present from Mrs George Skinner that – '

'But she wouldn't understand it any more than Toots.'

'He doesn't matter – except to me. I can't keep my eyes open, thank God! Good-night, lad.'

Conroy followed her with his eyes. Beauty there was, grace there was, strength and enough of the rest to drive better men than George Skinner to beat their heads on piano-tops – but for the new-found life of him Conroy could not feel one flutter of instinct or emotion that turned herward. He put up his feet and fell asleep, dreaming of a joyous, normal world recovered – with interest on arrears. There were many things in it, but no one face of any one woman.

*   *   *

Thrice afterwards they took the same train, and each time their trouble shrank and weakened. Miss Henschil talked of Toots, his multiplied calls, the things he had said to his sisters, the much worse things his sisters had replied; of the late (he seemed very dead to them) M. Najdol's gifts for the soul-weary; of shopping, of house rents, and the cost of really artistic furniture and linen.

Conroy explained the exercises in which he delighted – mighty labours of play undertaken against other mighty men, till he sweated and, having bathed, slept. He had visited his mother, too, in Hereford, and he talked something of her and of the home-life, which his body, cut out of all clean life for five years, innocently and deeply enjoyed. Nurse Blaber was a little interested in Conroy's mother, but, as a rule, she smoked her cigarette and read her paper-backed novels in her own compartment.

On their last trip she volunteered to sit with them, and buried herself in *The Cloister and the Hearth* while they whispered together. On that occasion (it was near Salisbury) at two in the morning, when the lier-in-wait brushed them with his wing, it meant no more than that they should cease talk for the instant, and for the instant hold hands, as even utter strangers on the deep may do when their ship rolls underfoot.

'But still,' said Nurse Blaber, not looking up, 'I think your Mr Skinner might feel jealous of all this.'

'It would be difficult to explain,' said Conroy.

'Then you'd better not be at my wedding,' Miss Henschil laughed.

'After all we've gone through, too. But I suppose you ought to leave me out. Is the day fixed?' he cried.

'Twenty-second of September – in spite of both his sisters. I can risk it now.' Her face was glorious as she flushed.

'My dear chap!' He shook hands unreservedly, and she gave back his grip without flinching. 'I can't tell you how pleased I am!'

'Gracious heavens!' said Nurse Blaber, in a new voice. 'Oh, I beg your pardon. I forgot I wasn't paid to be surprised.'

'What at? Oh, I see!' Miss Henschil explained to Conroy. 'She expected you were going to kiss me, or I was going to kiss you, or something.'

'After all you've gone through, as Mr Conroy said,'

'But I couldn't, could you?' said Miss Henschil, with a disgust as frank as that on Conroy's face. 'It would be horrible – horrible. And yet, of course, you're wonderfully handsome. How d'you account for it, nursey?'

Nurse Blaber shook her head. 'I was hired to cure you of a habit, dear. When you're cured I shall go on to the next case – that senile-decay one at Bournemouth I told you about.'

'And I shall be left alone with George! But suppose it isn't cured,' said Miss Henschil of a sudden. 'Suppose it comes back again. What can I do? I can't send for *him* in this way when I'm a married woman!' She pointed like an infant.

'I'd come, of course,' Conroy answered. 'But, seriously, that *is* a consideration.'

They looked at each other, alarmed and anxious, and then towards Nurse Blaber, who closed her book, marked the place, and turned to face them.

'Have you ever talked to your mother as you have to me?' she said.

'No. I might have spoken to dad – but mother's different. What d'you mean?'

'And you've never talked to your mother either, Mr Conroy?'

'Not till I took Najdolene. Then I told her it was my heart. There's no need to say anything, now that I'm practically over it, is there?'

'Not if it doesn't come back, but – ' She beckoned with a stumpy, triumphant finger that drew their heads close together. 'You know I always go in and read a chapter to mother at tea, child.'

'I know you do. You're an angel,' Miss Henschil patted the blue shoulder next her. 'Mother's Church of England now,' she explained. 'But she'll have her Bible with her pikelets at tea every night like the Skinners.'

'It was Naaman and Gehazi last Tuesday that gave me a clue. I said I'd never seen a case of leprosy, and your mother said she'd seen too many.'

'Where? She never told me,' Miss Henschil began.

'A few months before you were born – on her trip to Australia – at Mola or Molo something or other. It took me three evenings to get it all out.'

'Ay – mother's suspicious of questions,' said Miss Henschil to Conroy. 'She'll lock the door of every room she's in, if it's but for five minutes. She was a Tackberry from Jarrow way, yo' see.'

'She described your men to the life – men with faces all eaten away, staring at her over the fence of a lepers' hospital in this Molo Island. They begged from her, and she ran, she told me, all down the street, back to the pier. One touched her and she nearly fainted. She's ashamed of that still.'

'My men? The sand and the fences?' Miss Henschil muttered.

'Yes. You know how tidy she is and how she hates wind. She remembered that the fences were broken – she remembered the wind blowing. Sand – sun – salt wind – fences – faces – I got it all out of her, bit by bit. You don't know what I know! And it all happened three or four months before you were born. There!' Nurse Blaber slapped her knee with her little hand triumphantly.

'Would that account for it?' Miss Henschil shook from head to foot.

'Absolutely. I don't care whom you ask! You never imagined the thing. It was *laid* on you. It happened on earth to *you*! Quick, Mr Conroy, she's too heavy for me! I'll get the flask.'

Miss Henschil leaned forward and collapsed, as Conroy told her afterwards, like a factory chimney. She came out of her swoon with teeth that chattered on the cup.

'No – no,' she said, gulping. 'It's not hysterics. Yo' see I've no call to hev 'em any more. No call – no reason whatever. God be praised! Can't yo' *feel* I'm a right woman now?'

'Stop hugging me!' said Nurse Blaber. 'You don't know your strength. Finish the brandy and water. It's perfectly reasonable, and I'll lay long odds Mr Conroy's case is something of the same. I've been thinking –'

'I wonder –' said Conroy, and pushed the girl back as she swayed again.

Nurse Blaber smoothed her pale hair. 'Yes. Your trouble, or something like it, happened somewhere on earth or sea to the mother who bore you. Ask her, child. Ask her and be done with it once for all.'

'I will,' said Conroy . . . 'There ought to be –' He opened his bag and hunted breathlessly.

'Bless you! Oh, God bless you, nursey!' Miss Henschil was sobbing. 'You don't know what this means to me. It takes it all off – from the beginning.'

'But doesn't it make any difference to you now?' the nurse asked curiously. 'Now that you're rightfully a woman?'

Conroy, busy with his bag, had not heard. Miss Henschil stared across, and her beauty, freed from the shadow of any fear, blazed up within her. 'I see what you mean,' she said. 'But it hasn't changed anything. I want Toots. *He* has never been out of his mind in his life – except over silly me.'

'It's all right,' said Conroy, stooping under the lamp, *Bradshaw* in hand. 'If I change at Templecombe – for Bristol (Bristol – Hereford – yes) – I can be with mother for breakfast in her room and find out.'

'Quick, then,' said Nurse Blaber. 'We've passed Gillingham quite a while. You'd better take some of our sandwiches.' She went out to get them. Conroy and Miss Henschil would have danced, but there is no room for giants in a South-Western compartment.

'Goodbye, good luck, lad. Eh, but you've changed already – like me. Send a wire to our hotel as soon as you're sure,' said Miss Henschil. 'What should I have done without you?'

'Or I?' said Conroy. 'But it's Nurse Blaber that's saving us really.'

'Then thank her,' said Miss Henschil, looking straight at him. 'Yes, I would. She'd like it.'

When Nurse Blaber came back after the parting at Templecombe her nose and her eyelids were red, but, for all that, her face reflected a great light even while she sniffed over *The Cloister and the Hearth*.

Miss Henschil, deep in a house-furnisher's catalogue, did not speak for twenty minutes. Then she said, between adding totals of best, guest and servants' sheets, 'But why should our times have been the same, nursey?'

'Because a child is born somewhere every second of the clock,' Nurse Blaber answered. 'And besides that, you probably set each other off by talking and thinking about it. You shouldn't, you know.'

'Ay, but you've never been in hell,' said Miss Henschil.

The telegram handed in at Hereford at 12.46 and delivered to Miss Henschil on the beach of a certain village at 2.07 ran thus: *Absolutely confirmed. She says she remembers hearing noise of accident in engine-room returning from India in 'eighty-five.*

'He means the year, not the thermometer,' said Nurse Blaber, throwing pebbles at the cold sea.

'*And two men scalded thus explaining my hoots.* (The idea of telling me that!) *Subsequently silly clergyman passenger ran up behind her calling, for joke, "Friend, all is lost," thus accounting very words.*'

Nurse Blaber purred audibly.

'*She says only remembers being upset minute or two. Unspeakable relief. Best love to nursey, who is jewel. Get out of her what she would like best.* Oh, I oughtn't to have read that,' said Miss Henschil.

'It doesn't matter. I don't want anything,' said Nurse Blaber, 'and if I did I shouldn't get it.'

The Gardener

Everyone in the village knew that Helen Turrell did her duty by all her world, and by none more honourably than by her only brother's unfortunate child. The village knew, too, that George Turrell had tried his family severely since early youth, and were not surprised to be told that, after many fresh starts given and thrown away he, an inspector of Indian Police, had entangled himself with the daughter of a retired non-commissioned officer, and had died of a fall from a horse a few weeks before his child was born.

Mercifully, George's father and mother were both dead, and though Helen, thirty-five and independent, might well have washed her hands of the whole disgraceful affair, she most nobly took charge, though she was, at the time, under threat of lung trouble which had driven her to the South of France. She arranged for the passage of the child and a nurse from Bombay, met them at Marseilles, nursed the baby through an attack of infantile dysentery due the carelessness of the nurse, whom she had had to dismiss, and at last, thin and worn but triumphant, brought the boy late in the autumn, wholly restored, to her Hampshire home.

All these details were public property, for Helen was as open as the day, and held that scandals are only increased by hushing then up. She admitted that George had always been rather a black sheep, but things might have been much worse if the mother had insisted on her right to keep the boy. Luckily, it seemed that people of that class would do almost anything for money, and, as George had always turned to her in his scrapes, she felt herself justified – her friends agreed with her – in cutting the whole non-commissioned officer connection, and giving the child every advantage. A christening, by the rector, under the name of Michael, was the first step. So far as she knew herself, she was not, she said, a child-lover, but, for all his faults, she had been very fond of George, and she pointed out that little Michael had his father's mouth to a line – which made something to build upon.

As a matter of fact, it was the Turrell forehead, broad, low and well shaped, with the widely spaces eyes beneath it, that Michael had most faithfully reproduced. His mouth was somewhat better cut than the family type. But Helen, who would concede nothing good to his mother's side, vowed he was a Turrell all over, and, there being no one to contradict, the likeness was established.

In a few years Michael took his place, as accepted as Helen had always been – fearless, philosophical and fairly good-looking. At six, he wished to know why he could not call her 'mummy', as other boys called their mothers.

She explained that she was only his auntie, and that aunties were not quite the same as mummies, but that, if it gave him pleasure, he might call her 'mummy' at bedtime, for a pet-name between themselves.

Michael kept his secret most loyally, but Helen, as usual, explained the fact to her friends; which when Michael heard, he raged.

'Why did you tell? Why did you tell?' came at the end of the storm.

'Because it's always best to tell the truth,' Helen answered, her arm round him as he shook in his cot.

'All right, but when the troof's ugly I don't think it's nice.'

'Don't you, dear?'

'No, I don't and' – she felt the small body stiffen – 'now you've told, I won't call you 'mummy' any more – not even at bedtimes.'

'But isn't that rather unkind?' said Helen softly.

'I don't care! I don't care! You have hurted me in my insides and I'll hurt you back. I'll hurt you as long as I live!'

'Don't, oh, don't talk like that, dear! You don't know what –'

'I will! And when I'm dead I'll hurt you worse!'

'Thank goodness, I shall be dead long before you, darling.'

'Huh! Emma says, "Never know your luck."' (Michael had been talking to Helen's elderly, flat-faced maid.) 'Lots of little boys die quite soon. So'll I. Then you'll see!'

Helen caught her breath and moved towards the door, but the wail of 'Mummy! Mummy!' drew her back again, and the two wept together.

At ten years old, after two terms at a prep school, something or somebody gave him the idea that his civil status was not quite regular. He attacked Helen on the subject, breaking down her stammered defences with the family directness.

'Don't believe a word of it,' he said, cheerily, at the end. 'People wouldn't have talked like they did if my people had been married. But don't you bother, auntie. I've found out all about my sort in English hist'ry and the Shakespeare bits. There was William the Conqueror to begin with, and – oh, heaps more, and they all got on first-rate. 'Twon't make any difference to you, by being that – will it?'

'As if anything could –' she began.

'All right. We won't talk about it any more if it makes you cry.' He never mentioned the thing again of his own will, but when, two years later, he skilfully managed to have measles in the holidays, as his temperature went up to the appointed one hundred and four he muttered of nothing else, till Helen's voice, piercing at last his delirium, reached him with assurance that nothing on earth or beyond could make any difference between them.

The terms at his public school and the wonderful Christmas, Easter and summer holidays followed each other, variegated and glorious as jewels on a string; and as jewels Helen treasured them. In due time Michael developed his own interests, which ran their courses and gave way to others; but his interest in Helen was constant and increasing throughout. She repaid it with all that she had of affection or could command of counsel and money; and since Michael was no fool, the war took him just before what was like to have been a most promising career.

He was to have gone up to Oxford, with a scholarship, in October. At the end of August he was on the edge of joining the first holocaust of public-school boys who threw themselves into the line; but the captain of his OTC, where he had been sergeant for nearly a year, headed him off and steered him directly to a commission in a battalion so new that half of it still wore the old army red, and the other half was breeding meningitis through living overcrowdedly in damp tents. Helen had been shocked at the idea of direct enlistment.

'But it's in the family,' Michael laughed.

'You don't mean to tell me that you believed that story all this time?' said Helen. (Emma, her maid, had been dead now several years.) 'I gave you my word of honour – and I give it again – that – that it's all right. It is indeed.'

'Oh, that doesn't worry me. It never did,' he replied valiantly. 'What I meant was, I should have got into the show earlier if I'd enlisted – like my grandfather.'

'Don't talk like that! Are you afraid of its ending so soon, then?'

'No such luck. You know what K. says.'

'Yes. But my banker told me last Monday it couldn't possibly last beyond Christmas – for financial reasons.'

'I hope he's right, but our colonel – and he's a regular – say it's going to be a long job.'

Michael's battalion was fortunate in that, by some chance which meant several 'leaves', it was used for coast-defence among shallow trenches on the Norfolk coast; thence sent north to watch the mouth of a Scotch estuary, and, lastly, held for weeks on a baseless rumour of distant service. But, the very day that Michael was to have met Helen for four whole hours at a railway junction up the line, it was hurled out, to help make good the wastage of Loos, and he had only just time to send her a wire of farewell.

In France luck again helped the battalion. It was put down near the salient, where it led a meritorious and unexacting life, while the Somme was being manufactured, and enjoyed the peace of the Armentières and Laventie sectors when that battle began. Finding that it had sound views on protecting its own flanks and could dig, a prudent commander stole it out of its own division, under pretence of helping to lay telegraphs, and used it round Ypres at large.

A month later, and just after Michael had written to Helen that there was nothing special doing and therefore no need to worry, a shell-splinter dropping out of a wet dawn killed him at once. The next shell uprooted and laid down over the body what had been the foundation of a barn wall, so neatly that none but an expert would have guessed that anything unpleasant had happened.

By this time the village was old in experience of war, and, English fashion, had evolved a ritual to meet it. When the postmistress handed her seven-year-old daughter the official telegram to take to Miss Turrell, she observed to the rector's gardener: 'It's Miss Helen's turn now.' He replied, thinking of his own son: 'Well, he's lasted longer than some.' The child herself came to the front-door weeping aloud, because Master Michael had often given her sweets. Helen, presently, found herself pulling down the house-blinds one after one with great care, and saying earnestly to each: 'Missing always means dead.' Then she took her place in the dreary procession that was impelled to go through an inevitable series of unprofitable emotions. The rector, of course, preached hope and prophesied word, very soon, from a prison camp. Several friends, too, told her perfectly truthful tales, but always about other women, to whom, after months and months of silence, their missing had been miraculously restored. Other people urged her to communicate with infallible secretaries of organisations who could communicate with benevolent neutrals, who could extract accurate information from the most secretive of Hun commandants. Helen did and wrote and signed everything that was suggested or put before her.

Once, on one of Michael's leaves, he had taken her over a munition factory, where she saw the progress of a shell from blank-iron to the-all-but finished article. It struck her at the time that the wretched thing was never left alone for a single second; and, 'I'm being manufactured into a bereaved next of kin,' she told herself, as she prepared her documents.

In due course, when all the organisations had deeply or sincerely regretted their inability to trace, etc, something gave way within her and all sensations – save of thankfulness for the release – came to an end in blessed passivity. Michael had died and her world had stood still and she had been one with the full shock of that arrest. Now she was standing still and the world was going forward, but it did not concern her – in no way or relation did it touch her. She knew this by the ease with which she could slip Michael's name into talk and incline her head to the proper angle at the proper murmur of sympathy.

In the blessed realisation of that relief, the Armistice with all its bells broke over her and passed unheeded. At the end of another year she had overcome her physical loathing of the living and returned young, so that she could take them by the hand and almost sincerely wish them well. She had no interest in any aftermath, national or personal, of the war, but, moving at an immense distance, she sat on various relief committees and held strong views – she heard herself delivering them – about the site of the proposed village war memorial.

Then there came to her, as next of kin, an official intimation, backed by a page of a letter to her in indelible pencil, a silver identity-disc and a watch, to the effect that the body of Lieutenant Michael Turrell had been found, identified, and reinterred in Hagenzeele Third Military Cemetery – the letter of the row and the grave's number in that row duly given.

So Helen found herself moved on to another process of the manufacture – to a world full of exultant or broken relatives, now strong in the certainty that there was an altar upon earth where they might lay their love. These soon told her, and by means of timetables made clear, how easy it was and how little it interfered with life's affairs to go and see one's grave.

'So different,' as the rector's wife said, 'if he'd been killed in Mesopotamia, or even Gallipoli.'

The agony of being waked up to some sort of second life drove Helen across the Channel, where, in a new world of abbreviated titles, she learnt that Hagenzeele Third could be comfortably reached by an afternoon train which fitted in with the morning boat, and that there was a comfortable little hotel not three kilometres from Hagenzeele itself, where one could spend quite a comfortable night and see one's grave next morning. All this she had from a Central Authority who lived in a board and tar-paper shed on the skirts of a razed city of whirling lime-dust and blown papers.

'By the way,' said he, 'you know your grave, of course?'

'Yes, thank you,' said Helen, and showed its row and number typed on Michael's own little typewriter. The officer would have checked it, out of one of his many books; but a large Lancashire woman thrust between them and bade him tell her where she might find her son, who had been corporal in the ASC. His proper name, she sobbed, was Anderson, but, coming of respectable folk, he had of course enlisted under the name of Smith; and had been killed at Dickiebush, in early 'fifteen. She had not his number nor did she know which of his two Christian names he might have used with his alias; but her Cook's tourist ticket expired at the end of Easter week, and if by then she could not find her child she should go mad. Whereupon she fell forward on Helen's breast; but the officer's wife came out quickly from a little bedroom behind the office, and the three of them lifted the woman on to the cot.

'They are often like this,' said the officer's wife, loosening the tight bonnet-strings. 'Yesterday she said he'd been killed at Hooge. Are you sure you know your grave? It makes such a difference.'

'Yes, thank you,' said Helen, and hurried out before the woman on the bed should begin to lament again.

Tea in a crowded mauve-and-blue-striped wooden structure, with a false front, carried her still further into the nightmare. She paid her bill beside a stolid, plain-featured Englishwoman, who, hearing her enquire about the train to Hagenzeele, volunteered to come with her.

'I'm going to Hagenzeele myself,' she explained. 'Not to Hagenzeele Third; mine is Sugar Factory, but they call it La Rosière now. It's just south of Hagenzeele Three. Have you got your room at the hotel there?'

'Oh yes, thank you, I've wired.'

'That's better. Sometimes the place is quite full, and at others there's hardly a soul. But they've put bathrooms into the old Lion d'Or – that's the hotel on the west side of Sugar Factory – and it draws off a lot of people, luckily.'

'It's all new to me. This is the first time I've been over.'

'Indeed! This is my ninth time since the Armistice. Not on my own account. I haven't lost anyone, thank God – but, like everyone else, I've a lot of friends at home who have. Coming over as often as I do, I find it helps them to have someone just look at the – place and tell them about it afterwards. And one can take photos for them, too. I get quite a list of commissions to execute.' She laughed nervously and tapped her slung Kodak. 'There are two or three to see at Sugar Factory this time, and plenty of others in the cemeteries all about. My system is to save them up, and arrange them, you know. And when I've got enough commissions for one area to make it worth while, I pop over and execute them. It does comfort people.'

'I suppose so,' Helen answered, shivering as they entered the little train.

'Of course it does. (Isn't it lucky we've got windows-seats?) It must do or they wouldn't ask one to do it, would they? I've a list of quite twelve or fifteen commissions here' – she tapped the Kodak again – 'I must sort them out tonight. Oh, I forgot to ask you. What's yours?'

'My nephew,' said Helen. 'But I was very fond of him.'

'Ah, yes! I sometimes wonder whether they know after death? What do you think?'

'Oh, I don't – I haven't dared to think much about that sort of thing,' said Helen, almost lifting her hands to keep her off.

'Perhaps that's better,' the woman answered. 'The sense of loss must be enough, I expect. Well I won't worry you any more.'

Helen was grateful, but when they reached the hotel Mrs Scarsworth (they had exchanged names) insisted on dining at the same table with her, and after the meal, in the little, hideous salon full of low-voiced relatives, took Helen through her 'commissions' with biographies of the dead, how she happened to know them, and sketches of their next of kin. Helen endured till nearly half-past nine, ere she fled to her room.

Almost at one there was a knock at her door and Mrs Scarsworth entered; her hands, holding the dreadful list, clasped before her.

'Yes – yes – I know,' she began. 'You're sick of me, but I want to tell you something. You – you aren't married, are you? Then perhaps you won't . . . But it doesn't matter. I've got to tell someone. I can't go on any longer like this.'

Mrs Scarsworth had backed against the shut door, and her mouth worked dryly.

In a minute, she said, 'You – you know about these graves of mine I was telling you about downstairs, just now? They really are commissions. At least several of them are.' Here eye wandered round the room. 'What extraordinary wallpapers they have in Belgium, don't you think? . . . Yes. I swear they are commissions. But there's one, d'you see, and – and he was more to me than anything else in the world. Do you understand?'

Helen nodded.

'More than anyone else. And, of course, he oughtn't to have been. He ought to have been nothing to me. But he was. He is. That's why I do the commissions, you see. That's all.'

'But why do you tell me?' Helen asked desperately.

'Because I'm so tired of lying. Tired of lying – always lying – year in and year out. When I don't tell lies I've got to act 'em and I've got to think 'em, always. You don't know what that means. He was everything to me that he oughtn't to have been – the real thing – the only thing that ever happened to me in all my life; and I've had to pretend he wasn't. I've had to watch every word I said, and think out what lie I'd tell next, for years and years!'

'How many years?' Helen asked.

'Six years and four months before, and two and three-quarters after. I've gone to him eight times, since. Tomorrow I'll make the ninth, and – and I can't – I can't go to him again with nobody in the world knowing. I want to be honest with someone before I go. Do you understand? It doesn't matter about me. I was never truthful, even as a girl. But it isn't worthy of him. So – so I – I had to tell you. I can't keep it up any longer. Oh, I can't!'

Next morning Mrs Scarsworth left early on her round of commissions, and Helen walked alone to Hagenzeele Third. The place was still in the making, and stood some five or six feet above the metalled road, which it flanked for hundreds of yards. Culverts across a deep ditch served for entrances through the unfinished boundary wall. She climbed a few wooden-faced earthen steps and then met the entire crowded level of the thing in one held breath. She did not know that Hagenzeele Third counted twenty-one thousand dead already. All she saw was a merciless sea of black crosses, bearing little strips of stamped tin at all angles across their faces. She could distinguish no order or arrangement in their mass; nothing but a waist-high wilderness as of weeds stricken dead, rushing at her. She went forward, moved to the left and the right hopelessly, wondering by what guidance she should ever come to her own. A great distance away there was a line of whiteness. It proved to be a block of some two or three hundred graves whose headstones had already been set, whose flowers were planted out, and whose new-sown grass showed green. Here she could see clear-cut letters at the ends of the rows, and, referring to her slip, realised that it was not here she must look.

A man knelt behind a line of headstones – evidently a gardener, for he was firming a young plant in the soft earth. She went towards him, her paper in her hand. He rose at her approach and without prelude or salutation asked: 'Who are you looking for?'

'Lieutenant Michael Turrell – my nephew', said Helen slowly and word for word, as she had many thousands of times in her life.

The man lifted his eyes and looked at her with infinite compassion before he turned from the fresh-sown grass towards the naked black crosses.

'Come with me,' he said, 'and I will show you where your son lies.'

When Helen left the cemetery she turned for a last look. In the distance she saw the man bending over his young plants; and she went away, supposing him to be the gardener.

D. H. LAWRENCE

David Herbert Lawrence was born on 11 September 1885 in Eastwood, a small mining village in Nottinghamshire in the English Midlands. Despite ill health as a child and a comparatively disadvantaged position in society, he studied at Nottingham University and became a schoolmaster. His first novel, *The White Peacock*, was published in 1911. In 1912 he eloped with Frieda Weekley, the wife of his professor at Nottingham, and from then until his death he wrote feverishly, producing poetry, novels, essays, plays, travel books and short stories, while travelling around the world, settling for periods in Italy, New Mexico and Mexico. Lawrence's greatest novels, *The Rainbow* and *Women in Love*, were completed in 1915 and 1916. His last novel, *Lady Chatterley's Lover*, was banned in 1928 and his paintings confiscated in 1929. He died of tuberculosis in France in 1930.

The Prussian Officer

I

They had marched more than thirty kilometres since dawn, along the white, hot road where occasional thickets of trees threw a moment of shade, then out into the glare again. On either hand, the valley, wide and shallow, glittered with heat; dark-green patches of rye, pale young corn, fallow and meadow and black pine woods spread in a dull, hot diagram under a glistening sky. But right in front the mountains ranged across, pale blue and very still, snow gleaming gently out of the deep atmosphere. And towards the mountains, on and on, the regiment marched between the rye fields and the meadows, between the scraggy fruit trees set regularly on either side the high road. The burnished, dark-green rye threw off a suffocating heat, the mountains drew gradually nearer and more distinct. While the feet of the soldiers grew hotter, sweat ran through their hair under their helmets, and their knapsacks could burn no more in contact with their shoulders, but seemed instead to give off a cold, prickly sensation.

He walked on and on in silence, staring at the mountains ahead, that rose sheer out of the land, and stood fold behind fold, half earth, half heaven, the heaven, the barrier with slits of soft snow, in the pale, bluish peaks.

He could now walk almost without pain. At the start, he had determined not to limp. It had made him sick to take the first steps, and during the first mile or so, he had compressed his breath, and the cold drops of sweat had stood on his forehead. But he had walked it off. What were they after all but bruises! He had looked at them, as he was getting up: deep bruises on the backs of his thighs. And since he had made his first step in the morning, he had been conscious of them, till now he had a tight, hot place in his chest, with suppressing the pain, and holding himself in. There seemed no air when he breathed. But he walked almost lightly.

The captain's hand had trembled at taking his coffee at dawn: his orderly saw it again. And he saw the fine figure of the captain wheeling on horseback at the farmhouse ahead, a handsome figure in pale-blue uniform with facings of scarlet, and the metal gleaming on the black helmet and the sword-scabbard, and dark streaks of sweat coming on the silky bay horse. The orderly felt he was connected with that figure moving so suddenly on horseback: he followed it like a shadow, mute and inevitable and damned by it. And the officer was always aware of the tramp of the company behind, the march of his orderly among the men.

941

The captain was a tall man of about forty, grey at the temples. He had a handsome, finely knit figure, and was one of the best horsemen in the West. His orderly, having to rub him down, admired the amazing riding-muscles of his loins.

For the rest, the orderly scarcely noticed the officer any more than he noticed himself. It was rarely he saw his master's face: he did not look at it. The captain had reddish-brown, stiff hair, that he wore short upon his skull. His moustache was also cut short and bristly over a full, brutal mouth. His face was rather rugged, the cheeks thin. Perhaps the man was the more handsome for the deep lines in his face, the irritable tension of his brow, which gave him the look of a man who fights with life. His fair eyebrows stood bushy over light blue eyes that were always flashing with cold fire.

He was a Prussian aristocrat, haughty and overbearing. But his mother had been a Polish countess. Having made too many gambling debts when he was young, he had ruined his prospects in the army, and remained an infantry captain. He had never married: his position did not allow of it, and no woman had ever moved him to it. His time he spent riding – occasionally he rode one of his own horses at the races – and at the officers' club. Now and then he took himself a mistress. But after such an event, he returned to duty with his brow still more tense, his eyes still more hostile and irritable. With the men, however, he was merely impersonal, though a devil when roused; so that, on the whole, they feared him, but had no great aversion from him. They accepted him as the inevitable.

To his orderly he was at first cold and just and indifferent: he did not fuss over trifles. So that his servant knew practically nothing about him, except just what orders he would give, and how he wanted them obeyed. That was quite simple. Then the change gradually came.

The orderly was a youth of about twenty-two, of medium height, and well built. He had strong, heavy limbs, was swarthy, with a soft, black, young moustache. There was something altogether warm and young about him. He had firmly marked eyebrows over dark, expressionless eyes, that seemed never to have thought, only to have received life direct through his senses, and acted straight from instinct.

Gradually the officer had become aware of his servant's young, vigorous, unconscious presence about him. He could not get away from the sense of the youth's person, while he was in attendance. It was like a warm flame upon the older man's tense, rigid body, that had become almost unliving, fixed. There was something so free and self-contained about him, and something in the young fellow's movement, that made the officer aware of him. And this irritated the Prussian. He did not choose to be touched into life by his servant. He might easily have changed his man, but he did not. He now very rarely looked direct at his orderly, but kept his face averted, as if to avoid seeing him. And yet as the young soldier moved unthinking about the apartment, the elder watched him, and would notice the movement of his strong young shoulders under the blue cloth, the bend of his neck. And it irritated him. To see the soldier's young, brown, shapely peasant's hand grasp the loaf or the wine-bottle sent a flash of hate or of anger through the elder man's blood. It was not that the youth was clumsy: it was rather the blind, instinctive sureness of movement of an unhampered young animal that irritated the officer to such a degree.

Once, when a bottle of wine had gone over, and the red gushed out on to the tablecloth, the officer had started up with an oath, and his eyes, bluey like fire, had held those of the confused youth for a moment. It was a shock for the young soldier. He felt something sink deeper, deeper into his soul, where nothing had ever gone before. It left him rather blank and wondering. Some of his natural completeness in himself was gone, a little uneasiness took its place. And from that time an undiscovered feeling had held between the two men.

Henceforward the orderly was afraid of really meeting his master. His subconsciousness remembered those steely blue eyes and the harsh brows, and did not intend to meet them again. So he always stared past his master, and avoided him. Also, in a little anxiety, he waited for the three months to have gone, when his time would be up. He began to feel a constraint in the captain's presence, and the soldier even more than the officer wanted to be left alone, in his neutrality as servant.

He had served the captain for more than a year, and knew his duty. This he performed easily, as if it were natural to him. The officer and his commands he took for granted, as he took the sun and the rain, and he served as a matter of course. It did not implicate him personally.

But now if he were going to be forced into a personal interchange with his master he would be like a wild thing caught, he felt he must get away.

But the influence of the young soldier's being had penetrated through the officer's stiffened discipline, and perturbed the man in him. He, however, was a gentleman, with long, fine hands and cultivated movements, and was not going to allow such a thing as the stirring of his innate self. He was a man of passionate temper, who had always kept himself suppressed. Occasionally there had been a duel, an outburst before the soldiers. He knew himself to be always on the point of breaking out. But he kept himself hard to the idea of the Service. Whereas the young soldier seemed to live out his warm, full nature, to give it off in his very movements, which had a certain zest, such as wild animals have in free movement. And this irritated the officer more and more.

In spite of himself, the captain could not regain his neutrality of feeling towards his orderly. Nor could he leave the man alone. In spite of himself, he watched him, gave him sharp orders, tried to take up as much of his time as possible. Sometimes he flew into a rage with the young soldier, and bullied him. Then the orderly shut himself off, as it were out of earshot, and waited, with sullen, flushed face, for the end of the noise. The words never pierced to his intelligence, he made himself, protectively, impervious to the feelings of his master.

He had a scar on his left thumb, a deep seam going across the knuckle. The officer had long suffered from it, and wanted to do something to it. Still it was there, ugly and brutal on the young, brown hand. At last the captain's reserve gave way. One day, as the orderly was smoothing out the tablecloth, the officer pinned down his thumb with a pencil, asking: 'How did you come by that?'

The young man winced and drew back at attention.

'A wood axe, Herr Hauptmann,' he answered.

The officer waited for further explanation. None came. The orderly went about his duties. The elder man was sullenly angry. His servant avoided him. And the next day he had to use all his will-power to avoid seeing the scarred thumb. He wanted to get hold of it and – A hot flame ran in his blood.

He knew his servant would soon be free, and would be glad. As yet, the soldier had held himself off from the elder man. The captain grew madly irritable. He could not rest when the soldier was away, and when he was present, he glared at him with tormented eyes. He hated those fine, black brows over the unmeaning, dark eyes, he was infuriated by the free movement of the handsome limbs, which no military discipline could make stiff. And he became harsh and cruelly bullying, using contempt and satire. The young soldier only grew more mute and expressionless.

'What cattle were you bred by that you can't keep straight eyes? Look me in the eyes when I speak to you.'

And the soldier turned his dark eyes to the other's face, but there was no sight in them: he stared with the slightest possible cast, holding back his sight, perceiving the blue of his master's eyes, but receiving no look from them. And the elder man went pale, and his reddish eyebrows twitched. He gave his order, barrenly.

Once he flung a heavy military glove into the young soldier's face. Then he had the satisfaction of seeing the black eyes flare up into his own, like a blaze when straw is thrown on a fire. And he had laughed with a little tremor and a sneer.

But there were only two months more. The youth instinctively tried to keep himself intact: he tried to serve the officer as if the latter were an abstract authority and not a man. All his instinct was to avoid personal contact, even definite hate. But in spite of himself the hate grew, responsive to the officer's passion. However, he put it in the background. When he had left the army he could dare acknowledge it. By nature he was active, and had many friends. He thought what amazing good fellows they were. But, without knowing it, he was alone. Now this solitariness was intensified. It would carry him through his term. But the officer seemed to be going irritably insane, and the youth was deeply frightened.

The soldier had a sweetheart, a girl from the mountains, independent and primitive. The two walked together, rather silently. He went with her, not to talk, but to have his arm round her, and for the physical contact. This eased him, made it easier for him to ignore the captain; for he could rest with her held fast against his chest. And she, in some unspoken fashion, was there for him. They loved each other.

The captain perceived it, and was mad with irritation. He kept the young man engaged all the evenings long, and took pleasure in the dark look that came on his face. Occasionally, the eyes of the two men met, those of the younger sullen and dark, doggedly unalterable, those of the elder sneering with restless contempt.

The officer tried hard not to admit the passion that had got hold of him. He would not know that his feeling for his orderly was anything but that of a man incensed by his stupid, perverse servant. So, keeping quite justified and conventional in his consciousness, he let the other thing run on. His nerves, however, were suffering. At last he slung the end of a belt in his servant's face. When he saw the youth start back, the pain-tears in his eyes and the blood on his mouth, he had felt at once a thrill of deep pleasure and of shame.

But this, he acknowledged to himself, was a thing he had never done before. The fellow was too exasperating. His own nerves must be going to pieces. He went away for some days with a woman.

It was a mockery of pleasure. He simply did not want the woman. But he stayed on for his time. At the end of it, he came back in an agony of irritation, torment, and misery. He rode all the evening, then came straight in to supper. His orderly was out. The officer sat with his long, fine hands lying on the table, perfectly still, and all his blood seemed to be corroding.

At last his servant entered. He watched the strong, easy young figure, the fine eyebrows, the thick black hair. In a week's time the youth had got back his old well-being. The hands of the officer twitched and seemed to be full of mad flame. The young man stood at attention, unmoving, shut off.

The meal went in silence. But the orderly seemed eager. He made a clatter with the dishes.

'Are you in a hurry?' asked the officer, watching the intent, warm face of his servant.

The other did not reply.

'Will you answer my question?' said the captain.

'Yes, sir,' replied the orderly, standing with his pile of deep army plates. The captain waited, looked at him, then asked again: 'Are you in a hurry?'

'Yes, sir,' came the answer that sent a flash through the listener.

'For what?'

'I was going out, sir.'

'I want you this evening.'

There was a moment's hesitation. The officer had a curious stiffness of countenance.

'Yes, sir,' replied the servant, in his throat.

'I want you tomorrow evening also – in fact, you may consider your evenings occupied, unless I give you leave.'

The mouth with the young moustache set close. 'Yes, sir,' answered the orderly, loosening his lips for a moment. He again turned to the door.

'And why have you a piece of pencil in your ear?'

The orderly hesitated, then continued on his way without answering. He set the plates in a pile outside the door, took the stump of pencil from his ear, and put it in his pocket. He had been copying a verse for his sweetheart's birthday card. He returned to finish clearing the table.

The officer's eyes were dancing, he had a little, eager smile. 'Why have you a piece of pencil in your ear?' he asked.

The orderly took his hands full of dishes. His master was standing near the great green stove, a little smile on his face, his chin thrust forward. When the young soldier saw him his heart suddenly ran hot. He felt blind. Instead of answering, he turned dazedly to the door. As he was crouching to set down the dishes, he was pitched forward by a kick from behind. The pots went in a stream down the stairs, he clung to the pillar of the banisters. And as he was rising he was kicked heavily again, and again, so that he clung sickly to the post for some moments. His master had gone swiftly into the room and closed the door. The maidservant downstairs looked up the staircase and made a mocking face at the crockery disaster.

The officer's heart was plunging. He poured himself a glass of wine, part of which he spilled on the floor, and gulped the remainder, leaning against the cool, green stove. He heard his man collecting the dishes from the stairs. Pale, as if intoxicated, he waited. The servant entered again. The captain's heart gave a pang, as of pleasure, seeing the young fellow bewildered and uncertain on his feet, with pain.

'Schöner!' he said.

The soldier was a little slower in coming to attention.

'Yes, sir!'

The youth stood before him, with pathetic young moustache, and fine eyebrows very distinct on his forehead of dark marble.

'I asked you a question.'

'Yes, sir.'

The officer's tone bit like acid.

'Why had you a pencil in your ear?'

Again the servant's heart ran hot, and he could not breathe. With dark, strained eyes, he looked at the officer, as if fascinated. And he stood there sturdily planted, unconscious. The withering smile came into the captain's eyes, and he lifted his foot.

'I – I forgot it – sir,' panted the soldier, his dark eyes fixed on the other man's dancing blue ones.

'What was it doing there?'

He saw the young man's breast heaving as he made an effort for words.

'I had been writing.'

'Writing what?'

Again the soldier looked up and down. The officer could hear him panting. The smile came into the blue eyes. The soldier worked his dry throat, but could not speak. Suddenly the smile lit like a flame on the officer's face, and a kick came heavily against the orderly's thigh. The youth moved a pace sideways. His face went dead, with two black, staring eyes.

'Well?' said the officer.

The orderly's mouth had gone dry, and his tongue rubbed in it as on dry brown-paper. He worked his throat. The officer raised his foot. The servant went stiff.

'Some poetry, sir,' came the crackling, unrecognisable sound of his voice.

'Poetry, what poetry?' asked the captain, with a sickly smile.

Again there was the working in the throat. The captain's heart had suddenly gone down heavily, and he stood sick and tired.

'For my girl, sir,' he heard the dry, inhuman sound.

'Oh!' he said, turning away. 'Clear the table.'

'Click!' went the soldier's throat; then again, 'click!' and then the half-articulate: 'Yes, sir.'

The young soldier was gone, looking old, and walking heavily.

The officer, left alone, held himself rigid, to prevent himself from thinking. His instinct warned him that he must not think. Deep inside him was the intense gratification of his passion, still working powerfully. Then there was a counter-action, a horrible breaking down of something inside him, a whole agony of reaction. He stood there for an hour motionless, a chaos of sensations, but rigid with a will to keep blank his consciousness, to prevent his mind grasping. And he held himself so until the worst of the stress had passed, when he began to drink, drank himself to an intoxication, till he slept obliterated. When he woke in the morning he was shaken to the base of his nature. But he had fought off the realisation of what he had done. He had prevented his mind from taking it in, had suppressed it along with his instincts, and the conscious man had nothing to do with it. He felt only as after a bout of intoxication, weak, but the affair itself all dim and not to be recovered. Of the drunkenness of his passion he successfully refused remembrance. And when his orderly appeared with coffee, the officer assumed the same self he had had the morning before. He refused the event of the past night – denied it had ever been – and was successful in his denial. He had not done any such thing – not he himself. Whatever there might be lay at the door of a stupid, insubordinate servant.

The orderly had gone about in a stupor all the evening. He drank some beer because he was parched, but not much, the alcohol made his feeling come back, and he could not bear it. He was dulled, as if nine-tenths of the ordinary man in him were inert. He crawled about disfigured. Still, when he thought of the kicks, he went sick, and when he thought of the threat of more kicking, in the room afterwards, his heart went hot and faint, and he panted, remembering the one that had come. He had been forced to say, 'For my girl.' He was much too done even to want to cry. His mouth hung slightly open, like an idiot's. He felt vacant, and wasted. So, he wandered at his work, painfully, and very slowly and clumsily, fumbling blindly with the brushes, and finding it difficult, when he sat down, to summon the energy to move again. His limbs, his jaw, were slack and nerveless. But he was very tired. He got to bed at last, and slept inert, relaxed, in a sleep that was rather stupor than slumber, a dead night of stupefaction shot through with gleams of anguish.

In the morning were the manoeuvres. But he woke even before the bugle sounded. The painful ache in his chest, the dryness of his throat, the awful steady feeling of misery made his eyes come awake and dreary at once. He knew, without thinking, what had happened. And he knew that the day had come again, when he must go on with his round. The last bit of darkness was being pushed out of the room. He would have to move his inert body and go on. He was so young, and had known so little trouble, that he was bewildered. He only wished it would stay night, so that he could lie still, covered up by the darkness. And yet nothing would prevent the day from coming, nothing would save him from having to get up and saddle the captain's horse, and make the captain's coffee. It was there, inevitable. And then, he thought, it was impossible. Yet they would not leave him free. He must go and take the coffee to the captain. He was too stunned to understand it. He only knew it was inevitable – inevitable, however long he lay inert.

At last, after heaving at himself, for he seemed to be a mass of inertia, he got up. But he had to force every one of his movements from behind, with his will. He felt lost, and dazed, and helpless. Then he clutched hold of the bed, the pain was so keen. And looking at his thighs, he saw the darker bruises on his swarthy flesh and he knew that, if he pressed one of his fingers on one of the bruises, he should faint. But he did not want to faint – he did not want anybody to know. No one should ever know. It was between him and the captain. There were only the two people in the world now – himself and the captain.

Slowly, economically, he got dressed and forced himself to walk. Everything was obscure, except just what he had his hands on. But he managed to get through his work. The very pain revived his dull senses. The worst remained yet. He took the tray and went up to the captain's room. The officer, pale and heavy, sat at the table. The orderly, as he saluted, felt himself put out of existence. He stood still for a moment submitting to his own nullification – then he gathered himself, seemed to regain himself, and then the captain began to grow vague, unreal, and the younger soldier's heart beat up. He clung to this situation – that the captain did not exist – so that he himself might live. But when he saw his officer's hand tremble as he took the coffee, he felt everything falling shattered. And he went away, feeling as if he himself were coming to pieces, disintegrated. And when the captain was there on horseback, giving orders, while he himself stood, with rifle and knapsack, sick with pain, he felt as if he must shut his eyes – as if he must shut his eyes on everything. It was only the long agony of marching with a parched throat that filled him with one single, sleep-heavy intention: to save himself.

2

He was getting used even to his parched throat. That the snowy peaks were radiant among the sky, that the whity-green glacier-river twisted through its pale shoals, in the valley below, seemed almost supernatural. But he was going mad with fever and thirst. He plodded on uncomplaining. He did not want to speak, not to anybody. There were two gulls, like flakes of water and snow, over the river. The scent of green rye soaked in sunshine came like a sickness. And the march continued, monotonously, almost like a bad sleep.

At the next farmhouse, which stood low and broad near the high road, tubs of water had been put out. The soldiers clustered round to drink. They took off their helmets, and the steam mounted from their wet hair. The captain sat on horseback, watching. He needed to see his orderly. His helmet threw a dark shadow over his light, fierce eyes, but his moustache and mouth and chin were distinct in the sunshine. The orderly must move under the presence of the figure of the horseman. It was not that he was afraid, or cowed. It was as if he was disembowelled, made empty, like an empty shell. He felt himself as nothing, a shadow creeping under the sunshine. And, thirsty as he was, he could scarcely drink, feeling the captain near him. He would not take off his helmet to wipe his wet hair. He wanted to stay in shadow, not to be forced into consciousness. Starting, he saw the light heel of the officer prick the belly of the horse; the captain cantered away, and he himself could relapse into vacancy.

Nothing, however, could give him back his living place in the hot, bright morning. He felt like a gap among it all. Whereas the captain was prouder, overriding. A hot flash went through the young servant's body. The captain was firmer and prouder with life, he himself was empty as a shadow. Again the flash went through him, dazing him out. But his heart ran a little firmer.

The company turned up the hill, to make a loop for the return. Below, from among the trees, the farm-bell clanged. He saw the labourers, mowing barefoot at the thick grass, leave off their work and go downhill, their scythes hanging over their shoulders, like long, bright claws curving down behind them. They seemed like dream-people, as if they had no relation to himself. He felt as in a blackish dream: as if all the other things were there and had form, but he himself was only a consciousness, a gap that could think and perceive.

The soldiers were tramping silently up the glaring hillside. Gradually his head began to revolve, slowly, rhythmically. Sometimes it was dark before his eyes, as if he saw this world through a smoked glass, frail shadows and unreal. It gave him a pain in his head to walk.

The air was too scented, it gave no breath. All the lush greenstuff seemed to be issuing its sap, till the air was deathly, sickly with the smell of greenness. There was the perfume of clover, like pure honey and bees. Then there grew a faint acrid tang – they were near the beeches; and then a queer clattering noise, and a suffocating, hideous smell; they were passing a flock of sheep, a shepherd in a black smock, holding his crook. Why should the sheep huddle together under this fierce sun? He felt that the shepherd would not see him, though he could see the shepherd.

At last there was the halt. They stacked rifles in a conical stack, put down their kit in a scattered circle around it, and dispersed a little, sitting on a small knoll high on the hillside. The chatter began. The soldiers were steaming with heat, but were lively. He sat still, seeing the blue mountains rising upon the land, twenty kilometres away. There was a blue fold in the ranges, then out of that, at the foot, the broad, pale bed of the river, stretches of whity-green water between pinkish-grey shoals among the dark pine woods. There it was, spread out a long way off. And it seemed to come downhill, the river. There was a raft being steered, a mile away. It was a strange country. Nearer, a red-roofed, broad farm with white base and square dots of windows crouched beside the wall of beech foliage on the wood's edge. There were long strips of rye and clover and pale green corn. And just at his feet, below the knoll, was a darkish bog, where globe flowers stood breathless still on their slim stalks. And some of the pale gold bubbles were burst, and a broken fragment hung in the air. He thought he was going to sleep.

Suddenly something moved into this coloured mirage before his eyes. The captain, a small, light-blue and scarlet figure, was trotting evenly between the strips of corn, along the level brow of the hill. And the man making flag-signals was coming on. Proud and sure moved the horseman's figure, the quick, bright thing, in which was concentrated all the light of this morning, which for the rest lay fragile, shining shadow. Submissive, apathetic, the young soldier sat and stared. But as the horse slowed to a walk, coming up the last steep path, the great flash flared over the body and soul of the orderly. He sat waiting. The back of his head felt as if it were weighted with a heavy piece of fire. He did not want to eat. His hands trembled slightly as he moved them. Meanwhile the officer on horseback was approaching slowly and proudly. The tension grew in the orderly's soul. Then again, seeing the captain ease himself on the saddle, the flash blazed through him.

The captain looked at the patch of light blue and scarlet, and dark heads, scattered closely on the hillside. It pleased him. The command pleased him. And he was feeling proud. His orderly was among them in common subjection. The officer rose a little on his stirrups to look. The young soldier sat with averted, dumb face. The captain relaxed on his seat. His slim-legged, beautiful horse, brown as a beech nut, walked proudly uphill. The captain passed into the zone of the company's atmosphere: a hot smell of men, of sweat, of leather. He knew it very well. After a word with the lieutenant, he went a few paces higher, and sat there, a dominant figure, his sweat-marked horse swishing its tail, while he looked down on his men, on his orderly, a nonentity among the crowd.

The young soldier's heart was like fire in his chest, and he breathed with difficulty. The officer, looking downhill, saw three of the young soldiers, two pails of water between them, staggering across a sunny green field. A table had been set up under a tree, and there the slim lieutenant stood, importantly busy. Then the captain summoned himself to an act of courage. He called his orderly.

The flame leapt into the young soldier's throat as he heard the command, and he rose blindly, stifled. He saluted, standing below the officer. He did not look up. But there was the flicker in the captain's voice.

'Go to the inn and fetch me . . .' the officer gave his commands. 'Quick!' he added.

At the last word, the heart of the servant leapt with a flash, and he felt the strength come over his body. But he turned in mechanical obedience, and set off at a heavy run downhill, looking almost like a bear, his trousers bagging over his military boots. And the officer watched this blind, plunging run all the way.

But it was only the outside of the orderly's body that was obeying so humbly and mechanically. Inside had gradually accumulated a core into which all the energy of that young life was compact and concentrated. He executed his commission, and plodded quickly back uphill. There was a pain in his head, as he walked, that made him twist his features unknowingly. But hard there in the centre of his chest was himself, himself, firm, and not to be plucked to pieces.

The captain had gone up into the wood. The orderly plodded through the hot, powerfully smelling zone of the company's atmosphere. He had a curious mass of energy inside him now. The captain was less real than himself. He approached the green entrance to the wood. There, in the half-shade, he saw the horse standing, the sunshine and the flickering shadow of leaves dancing over his brown body. There was a clearing where timber had lately been felled. Here, in the gold-green shade beside the brilliant cup of sunshine, stood two figures, blue and pink, the bits of pink showing out plainly. The captain was talking to his lieutenant.

The orderly stood on the edge of the bright clearing, where great trunks of trees, stripped and glistening, lay stretched like naked, brown-skinned bodies. Chips of wood littered the trampled floor, like splashed light, and the bases of the felled trees stood here and there, with their raw, level tops. Beyond was the brilliant, sunlit green of a beech.

'Then I will ride forward,' the orderly heard his captain say. The lieutenant saluted and strode away. He himself went forward. A hot flash passed through his belly, as he tramped towards his officer.

The captain watched the rather heavy figure of the young soldier stumble forward, and his veins, too, ran hot. This was to be man to man between them. He yielded before the solid, stumbling figure with bent head. The orderly stooped and put the food on a level-sawn tree-base. The captain watched the glistening, sun-inflamed, naked hands. He wanted to speak to the young soldier, but could not. The servant propped a bottle against his thigh, pressed open the cork, and poured out the beer into the mug. He kept his head bent. The captain accepted the mug.

'Hot!' he said, as if amiably.

The flame sprang out of the orderly's heart, nearly suffocating him.

'Yes, sir,' he replied, between shut teeth.

And he heard the sound of the captain's drinking, and he clenched his fists, such a strong torment came into his wrists. Then came the faint clang of the closing pot-lid. He looked up. The captain was watching him. He glanced swiftly away. Then he saw the officer stoop and take a piece of bread from the tree-base. Again the flash of flame went through the young soldier, seeing the stiff body stoop beneath him, and his hands jerked. He looked away. He could feel the officer was nervous. The bread fell as it was being broken. The officer ate the other piece. The two men stood tense and still, the master laboriously chewing his bread, the servant staring with averted face, his fist clenched.

Then the young soldier started. The officer had pressed open the lid of the mug again. The orderly watched the lid of the mug, and the white hand that clenched the handle, as if he were fascinated. It was raised. The youth followed it with his eyes. And then he saw the thin, strong throat of the elder man moving up and down as he drank, the strong jaw working. And the instinct which had been jerking at the young man's wrists suddenly jerked free. He jumped, feeling as if he were rent in two by a strong flame.

The spur of the officer caught in a tree-root, he went down backwards with a crash, the middle of his back thudding sickeningly against a sharp-edged tree-base, the pot flying away. And in a second the orderly, with serious, earnest young face, and underlip between his teeth, had got his knee in the officer's chest and was pressing the chin backward over the farther edge of the tree-stump, pressing, with all his heart behind in a passion of relief, the tension of his wrists exquisite with relief. And with the base of his palms he shoved at the chin, with all his might. And it was pleasant, too, to have that chin, that hard jaw already slightly rough with beard, in his hands. He did not relax one hair's breadth, but, all the force of all his blood exulting in his thrust, he shoved back the head of the other man, till there was a little 'cluck' and a crunching sensation. Then he felt as if his head went to vapour. Heavy convulsions shook the body of the officer, frightening and horrifying the young soldier. Yet it pleased him, too, to repress them. It pleased him to keep his hands pressing back the chin, to feel the chest of the other man yield in expiration to the weight of his strong, young knees, to feel the hard twitchings of the prostrate body jerking his own whole frame, which was pressed down on it.

But it went still. He could look into the nostrils of the other man, the eyes he could scarcely see. How curiously the mouth was pushed out, exaggerating the full lips, and the moustache bristling up from them. Then, with a start, he noticed the nostrils gradually filled with blood. The red brimmed, hesitated, ran over, and went in a thin trickle down the face to the eyes.

It shocked and distressed him. Slowly, he got up. The body twitched and sprawled there, inert. He stood and looked at it in silence. It was a pity *it* was broken. It represented more than the thing which had kicked and bullied him. He was afraid to look at the eyes. They were hideous now, only the whites showing, and the blood running to them. The face of the orderly was drawn with horror at the sight. Well, it was so. In his heart he was satisfied. He had hated the face of the captain. It was extinguished now. There was a heavy relief in the orderly's soul. That was as it should be. But he could not bear to see the long, military body lying broken over the tree-base, the fine fingers crisped. He wanted to hide it away.

Quickly, busily, he gathered it up and pushed it under the felled tree-trunks, which rested their beautiful, smooth length either end on logs. The face was horrible with blood. He covered it with the helmet. Then he pushed the limbs straight and decent, and brushed the dead leaves off the fine cloth of the uniform. So, it lay quite still in the shadow under there. A little strip of sunshine ran along the breast, from a chink between the logs. The orderly sat by it for a few moments. Here his own life also ended.

Then, through his daze, he heard the lieutenant, in a loud voice, explaining to the men outside the wood that they were to suppose the bridge on the river below was held by the enemy. Now they were to march to the attack in such and such a manner. The lieutenant had no gift of expression. The orderly, listening from habit, got muddled. And when the lieutenant began it all again he ceased to hear.

He knew he must go. He stood up. It surprised him that the leaves were glittering in the sun, and the chips of wood reflecting white from the ground. For him a change had come over the world. But for the rest it had not – all seemed the same. Only he had left it. And he could not go back. It was his duty to return with the beer-pot and the bottle. He could not. He had left all that. The lieutenant was still hoarsely explaining. He must go, or they would overtake him. And he could not bear contact with anyone now.

He drew his fingers over his eyes, trying to find out where he was. Then he turned away. He saw the horse standing in the path. He went up to it and mounted. It hurt him to sit in the saddle. The pain of keeping his seat occupied him as they cantered through the wood. He would not have minded anything, but he could not get away from the sense of being divided from the others. The path led out of the trees. On the edge of the wood he pulled up and stood watching. There in the spacious sunshine of the valley soldiers were moving in a little swarm. Every now and then, a man harrowing on a strip of fallow shouted to his oxen, at the turn. The village and the white-towered church was small in the sunshine. And he no longer belonged to it – he sat there, beyond, like a man outside in the dark. He had gone out from everyday life into the unknown, and he could not, he even did not want to go back.

Turning from the sun-blazing valley, he rode deep into the wood. Tree-trunks, like people standing grey and still, took no notice as he went. A doe, herself a moving bit of sunshine and shadow, went running through the flecked shade. There were bright green rents in the foliage. Then it was all pine wood, dark and cool. And he was sick with pain, he had an intolerable great pulse in his head, and he was sick. He had never been ill in his life. He felt lost, quite dazed with all this.

Trying to get down from the horse, he fell, astonished at the pain and his lack of balance. The horse shifted uneasily. He jerked its bridle and sent it cantering jerkily away. It was his last connection with the rest of things.

But he only wanted to lie down and not be disturbed. Stumbling through the trees, he came on a quiet place where beeches and pine trees grew on a slope. Immediately he had lain down and closed his eyes, his consciousness went racing on without him. A big pulse of sickness beat in him as if it throbbed through the whole earth. He was burning with dry heat. But he was too busy, too tearingly active in the incoherent race of delirium to observe.

3

He came to with a start. His mouth was dry and hard, his heart beat heavily, but he had not the energy to get up. His heart beat heavily. Where was he? – the barracks – at home? There was something knocking. And, making an effort, he looked round – trees, and litter of greenery, and reddish, bright, still pieces of sunshine on the floor. He did not believe he was himself, he did not believe what he saw. Something was knocking. He made a struggle towards consciousness, but relapsed. Then he struggled again. And gradually his surroundings fell into relationship with himself. He knew, and a great pang of fear went through his heart. Somebody was knocking. He could see the heavy, black rags of a fir tree overhead. Then everything went black. Yet he did not believe he had closed his eyes. He had not. Out of the blackness sight slowly emerged again. And someone was knocking. Quickly, he saw the blood-disfigured face of his captain, which he hated. And he held himself still with horror. Yet, deep inside him, he knew that it was so, the captain should be dead. But the physical delirium got hold of him. Someone was knocking. He lay perfectly still, as if dead, with fear. And he went unconscious.

When he opened his eyes again, he started, seeing something creeping swiftly up a tree-trunk. It was a little bird. And the bird was whistling overhead. Tap-tap-tap – it was the small, quick bird rapping the tree-trunk with its beak, as if its head were a little round hammer. He watched it curiously. It shifted sharply, in its creeping fashion. Then, like a mouse, it slid down the bare trunk. Its swift creeping sent a flash of revulsion through him. He raised his head. It felt a great weight. Then, the little bird ran out of the shadow across a still patch of sunshine, its little head bobbing swiftly, its white legs twinkling brightly for a moment. How neat it was in its build, so compact, with pieces of white on its wings. There were several of them. They were so pretty – but they crept like swift, erratic mice, running here and there among the beech-mast.

He lay down again exhausted, and his consciousness lapsed. He had a horror of the little creeping birds. All his blood seemed to be darting and creeping in his head. And yet he could not move.

He came to with a further ache of exhaustion. There was the pain in his head, and the horrible sickness, and his inability to move. He had never been ill in his life. He did not know where he was or what he was. Probably he had got sunstroke. Or what else? – he had silenced the captain for ever – some time ago – oh, a long time ago. There had been blood on his face, and his eyes had turned upwards. It was all right, somehow. It was peace. But now he had got beyond himself. He had never been here before. Was it life, or not life? He was by himself. They were in a big, bright place, those others, and he was outside. The town, all the country, a big bright place of light; and he was outside, here, in the darkened open beyond, where each thing existed alone. But they would all have to come out there sometime, those others. Little, and left behind him, they all were. There had been father and mother and sweetheart. What did they all matter? This was the open land.

He sat up. Something scuffled. It was a little, brown squirrel running in lovely, undulating bounds over the floor, its red tail completing the undulation of its body – and then, as it sat up, furling and unfurling. He watched it, pleased. It ran on again, friskily, enjoying itself. It flew wildly at another squirrel, and they were chasing each other, and making little scolding, chattering noises. The soldier wanted to speak to them. But only a hoarse sound came out of his throat. The squirrels burst away – they flew up the trees. And then he saw the one peeping round at him, halfway up a tree-trunk. A start of fear went through him, though, in so far as he was conscious, he was amused. It still stayed, its little, keen face staring at him halfway up the tree-trunk, its little ears pricked up, its clawey little hands clinging to the bark, its white breast reared. He started from it in panic.

Struggling to his feet, he lurched away. He went on walking, walking, looking for something – for a drink. His brain felt hot and inflamed for want of water. He stumbled on. Then he did not know anything. He went unconscious as he walked. Yet he stumbled on, his mouth open.

When, to his dumb wonder, he opened his eyes on the world again, he no longer tried to remember what it was. There was thick, golden light behind golden-green glitterings, and tall, grey-purple shafts, and darknesses farther off, surrounding him, growing deeper. He was conscious of a sense of arrival. He was amid the reality, on the real, dark bottom. But there was the thirst burning in his brain. He felt lighter, not so heavy. He supposed it was newness. The air was muttering with thunder. He thought he was walking wonderfully swiftly and was coming straight to relief – or was it to water?

Suddenly he stood still with fear. There was a tremendous flare of gold, immense – just a few dark trunks like bars between him and it. All the young level wheat was burnished, gold glaring on its silky green. A woman, full-skirted, a black cloth on her head for head-dress, was passing like a block of shadow through the glistening, green corn, into the full glare. There was a farm, too, pale blue in shadow, and the timber black. And there was a church spire, nearly fused away in the gold. The woman moved on, away from him. He had no language with which to speak to her. She was the bright, solid unreality. She would make a noise of words that would confuse him, and her eyes would look at him without seeing him. She was crossing there to the other side. He stood against a tree.

When at last he turned, looking down the long, bare grove whose flat bed was already filling dark, he saw the mountains in a wonder-light, not far away, and radiant. Behind the soft, grey ridge of the nearest range the farther mountains stood golden and pale grey, the snow all radiant like pure, soft gold. So still, gleaming in the sky, fashioned pure out of the ore of the sky, they shone in their silence. He stood and looked at them, his face illuminated. And like the golden, lustrous gleaming of the snow he felt his own thirst bright in him. He stood and gazed, leaning against a tree. And then everything slid away into space.

During the night the lightning fluttered perpetually, making the whole sky white. He must have walked again. The world hung livid round him for moments, fields a level sheen of grey-green light, trees in dark bulk, and the range of clouds black across a white sky. Then the darkness fell like a shutter, and the night was whole. A faint flutter of a half-revealed world, that could not quite leap out of the darkness! – Then there again stood a sweep of pallor for the land, dark shapes looming, a range of clouds hanging over-head. The world was a ghostly shadow, thrown for a moment upon the pure darkness, which returned ever whole and complete.

And the mere delirium of sickness and fever went on inside him – his brain opening and shutting like the night – then sometimes convulsions of terror from something with great eyes that stared round a tree – then the long agony of the march, and the sun decomposing his blood – then the pang of hate for the captain, followed by a pang of tenderness and ease. But everything was distorted, born of an ache and resolving into an ache.

In the morning he came definitely awake. Then his brain flamed with the sole horror of thirstiness! The sun was on his face, the dew was steaming from his wet clothes. Like one possessed, he got up. There, straight in front of him, blue and cool and tender, the mountains ranged across the pale edge of the morning sky. He wanted them – he wanted them alone – he wanted to leave himself and be identified with them. They did not move, they were still soft, with white, gentle markings of snow. He stood still, mad with suffering, his hands crisping and clutching. Then he was twisting in a paroxysm on the grass.

He lay still, in a kind of dream of anguish. His thirst seemed to have separated itself from him, and to stand apart, a single demand. Then the pain he felt was another single self. Then there was the clog of his body, another separate thing. He was divided among all kinds of separate beings. There was some strange, agonised connection between them, but they were drawing farther apart. Then they would all split. The sun, drilling down on him, was drilling through the bond. Then they would all fall, fall through the ever-lasting lapse of space. Then again, his consciousness reasserted itself. He roused on to his elbow and stared at the gleaming mountains. There they ranked, all still and wonderful between earth and heaven. He stared till his eyes went black, and the mountains, as they stood in their beauty, so clean and cool, seemed to have it, that which was lost in him.

4

When the soldiers found him, three hours later, he was lying with his face over his arm, his black hair giving off heat under the sun. But he was still alive. Seeing the open, black mouth the young soldiers dropped him in horror.

He died in the hospital at night, without having seen again.

The doctors saw the bruises on his legs, behind, and were silent.

The bodies of the two men lay together, side by side, in the mortuary, the one white and slender, but laid rigidly at rest, the other looking as if every moment it must rouse into life again, so young and unused, from a slumber.

You Touched Me

The Pottery House was a square, ugly, brick house girt in by the wall that enclosed the whole grounds of the pottery itself. To be sure, a privet hedge partly masked the house and its ground from the pottery-yard and works: but only partly. Through the hedge could be seen the desolate yard, and the many-windowed, factory-like pottery, over the hedge could be seen the chimneys and the outhouses. But inside the hedge, a pleasant garden and lawn sloped down to a willow pool, which had once supplied the works.

The pottery itself was now closed, the great doors of the yard permanently shut. No more the great crates with yellow straw showing through, stood in stacks by the packing shed. No more the drays drawn by great horses rolled down the hill with a high load. No more the pottery-lasses in their clay-coloured overalls, their faces and hair splashed with grey fine mud, shrieked and larked with the men. All that was over.

'We like it much better – oh, much better – quieter,' said Matilda Rockley.

'Oh, yes,' assented Emmie Rockley, her sister.

'I'm sure you do,' agreed the visitor.

But whether the two Rockley girls really liked it better, or whether they only imagined they did, is a question. Certainly their lives were much more grey and dreary now that the grey clay had ceased to spatter its mud and silt its dust over the premises. They did not quite realise how they missed the shrieking, shouting lasses, whom they had known all their lives and disliked so much.

Matilda and Emmie were already old maids. In a thorough industrial district, it is not easy for the girls who have expectations above the common to find husbands. The ugly industrial town was full of men, young men who were ready to marry. But they were all colliers or pottery-hands, mere workmen. The Rockley girls would have about ten thousand pounds each when their father died: ten thousand pounds' worth of profitable house-property. It was not to be sneezed at: they felt so themselves, and refrained from sneezing away such a fortune on any mere member of the proletariat. Consequently, bank-clerks or nonconformist clergymen or even school-teachers having failed to come forward, Matilda had begun to give up all idea of ever leaving the Pottery House.

Matilda was a tall, thin, graceful fair girl, with a rather large nose. She was the Mary to Emmie's Martha: that is, Matilda loved painting and music, and read a good many novels, whilst Emmie looked after the housekeeping. Emmie was shorter, plumper than her sister, and she had no accomplishments. She looked up to Matilda, whose mind was naturally refined and sensible.

In their quiet, melancholy way, the two girls were happy. Their mother was dead. Their father was ill also. He was an intelligent man who had had some education, but preferred to remain as if he were one with the rest of the working people. He had a passion for music and played the violin pretty well. But now he was getting old, he was very ill, dying of a kidney disease. He had been rather a heavy whisky-drinker.

This quiet household, with one servant-maid, lived on year after year in the Pottery House. Friends came in, the girls went out, the father drank himself more and more ill. Outside in the street there was a continual racket of the colliers and their dogs and children. But inside the pottery wall was a deserted quiet.

In all this ointment there was one little fly. Ted Rockley, the father of the girls, had had four daughters, and no son. As his girls grew, he felt angry at finding himself always in a household of women. He went off to London and adopted a boy out of a Charity Institution. Emmie was fourteen years old, and Matilda sixteen, when their father arrived home with his prodigy, the boy of six, Hadrian.

Hadrian was just an ordinary boy from a Charity Home, with ordinary brownish hair and ordinary bluish eyes and of ordinary rather cockney speech. The Rockley girls – there were three at home at the time of his arrival – had resented his being sprung on them. He, with his watchful, charity-institution instinct, knew this at once. Though he was only six years old, Hadrian had a subtle, jeering look on his face when he regarded the three young women. They insisted he should address them as cousin: Cousin Flora, Cousin Matilda, Cousin Emmie. He complied, but there seemed a mockery in his tone.

The girls, however, were kind-hearted by nature. Flora married and left home. Hadrian did very much as he pleased with Matilda and Emmie, though they had certain strictnesses. He grew up in the Pottery House and about the Pottery premises, went to an elementary school, and was invariably called Hadrian Rockley. He regarded Cousin Matilda and Cousin Emmie with a certain laconic indifference, was quiet and reticent in his ways. The girls called him sly, but that was unjust. He was merely cautious, and without frankness. His 'uncle', Ted Rockley, understood him tacitly, their natures were somewhat akin. Hadrian and the elderly man had a real but unemotional regard for one another.

When he was thirteen years old the boy was sent to a high school in the county town. He did not like it. His Cousin Matilda had longed to make a little gentleman of him, but he refused to be made. He would give a little contemptuous curve to his lip, and take on a shy, charity-boy grin, when refinement was thrust upon him. He played truant from the high school, sold his books, his cap with its badge, even his very scarf and pocket-handkerchief, to his school-fellows, and went raking off heaven knows where with the money. So he spent two very unsatisfactory years.

When he was fifteen he announced that he wanted to leave England and go to the colonies. He had kept touch with the Home. The Rockleys knew that, when Hadrian made a declaration, in his quiet, half-jeering manner, it was worse than useless to oppose him. So at last the boy departed, going to Canada under the protection of the institution to which he had belonged. He said goodbye to the Rockleys without a word of thanks, and parted, it seemed, without a pang. Matilda and Emmie wept often to think of how he left them: even on their father's face a queer look came. But Hadrian wrote fairly regularly from Canada. He had entered some electricity works near Montreal, and was doing well.

At last, however, the war came. In his turn, Hadrian joined up and came to Europe. The Rockleys saw nothing of him. They lived on, just the same, in the Pottery House. Ted Rockley was dying of a sort of dropsy, and in his heart he wanted to see the boy. When the armistice was signed, Hadrian had a long leave, and wrote that he was coming home to the Pottery House.

The girls were terribly fluttered. To tell the truth, they were a little afraid of Hadrian. Matilda, tall and thin, was frail in her health, both girls were worn with nursing their father. To have Hadrian, a young man of twenty-one, in the house with them, after he had left them so coldly five years before, was a trying circumstance.

They were in a flutter. Emmie persuaded her father to have his bed made finally in the morning-room downstairs, whilst his room upstairs was prepared for Hadrian. This was done, and preparations were going on for the arrival, when, at ten o'clock in the morning the young man suddenly turned up, quite unexpectedly. Cousin Emmie, with her hair bobbed up in absurd little bobs round her forehead, was busily polishing the stair-rods, while Cousin Matilda was in the kitchen washing the drawing-room ornaments in a lather, her sleeves rolled back on her thin arms, and her head tied up oddly and coquettishly in a duster.

Cousin Matilda blushed deep with mortification when the self-possessed young man walked in with his kit-bag, and put his cap on the sewing machine. He was little and self-confident, with a curious neatness about him that still suggested the Charity Institution. His face was brown, he had a small moustache, he was vigorous enough in his smallness.

'*Well*, is it Hadrian!' exclaimed Cousin Matilda, wringing the lather off her hand. 'We didn't expect you till tomorrow.'

'I got off Monday night,' said Hadrian, glancing round the room.

'Fancy!' said Cousin Matilda. Then, having dried her hands, she went forward, held out her hand, and said: 'How are you?'

'Quite well, thank you,' said Hadrian.

'You're quite a man,' said Cousin Matilda.

Hadrian glanced at her. She did not look her best: so thin, so large-nosed, with that pink-and-white checked duster tied round her head. She felt her disadvantage. But she had had a good deal of suffering and sorrow, she did not mind any more.

The servant entered – one that did not know Hadrian.

'Come and see my father,' said Cousin Matilda.

In the hall they roused Cousin Emmie like a partridge from cover. She was on the stairs pushing the bright stair-rods into place. Instinctively her hand went to the little knobs, her front hair bobbed on her forehead.

'Why!' she exclaimed, crossly. 'What have you come today for?'

'I got off a day earlier,' said Hadrian, and his man's voice so deep and unexpected was like a blow to Cousin Emmie.

'Well, you've caught us in the midst of it,' she said, with resentment. Then all three went into the middle room.

Mr Rockley was dressed – that is, he had on his trousers and socks – but he was resting on the bed, propped up just under the window, from whence he could see his beloved and resplendent garden, where tulips and apple trees were ablaze. He did not look as ill as he was, for the water puffed him up, and his face kept its colour. His stomach was much swollen. He glanced round swiftly, turning his eyes without turning his head. He was the wreck of a handsome, well-built man.

Seeing Hadrian, a queer, unwilling smile went over his face. The young man greeted him sheepishly.

'You wouldn't make a life-guardsman,' he said. 'Do you want something to eat?'

Hadrian looked round – as if for the meal.

'I don't mind,' he said.

'What shall you have – egg and bacon?' asked Emmie shortly.

'Yes, I don't mind,' said Hadrian.

The sisters went down to the kitchen, and sent the servant to finish the stairs.

'Isn't he *altered*?' said Matilda, *sotto voce*.

'Isn't he!' said Cousin Emmie. '*What* a little man!'

They both made a grimace, and laughed nervously.

'Get the frying-pan,' said Emmie to Matilda.

'But he's as cocky as ever,' said Matilda, narrowing her eyes and shaking her head knowingly, as she handed the frying-pan.

'Mannie!' said Emmie sarcastically. Hadrian's new-fledged, cock-sure manliness evidently found no favour in her eyes.

'Oh, he's not bad,' said Matilda. 'You don't want to be prejudiced against him.'

I'm not prejudiced against him, I think he's all right for looks,' said Emmie, 'but there's too much of the little mannie about him.'

'Fancy catching us like this,' said Matilda.

'They've no thought for anything,' said Emmie with contempt. 'You go up and get dressed, our Matilda. I don't care about him. I can see to things, and you can talk to him. I shan't.'

'He'll talk to my father,' said Matilda, meaningful.

'*Sly — !*' exclaimed Emmie, with a grimace.

The sisters believed that Hadrian had come hoping to get something out of their father – hoping for a legacy. And they were not at all sure he would not get it.

Matilda went upstairs to change. She had thought it all out how she would receive Hadrian, and impress him. And he had caught her with her head tied up in a duster, and her thin arms in a basin of lather. But she did not care. She now dressed herself most scrupulously, carefully folded her long, beautiful, blonde hair, touched her pallor with a little rouge, and put her long string of exquisite crystal beads over her soft green dress. Now she looked elegant, like a heroine in a magazine illustration, and almost as unreal.

She found Hadrian and her father talking away. The young man was short of speech as a rule, but he could find his tongue with his 'uncle'. They were both sipping a glass of brandy, and smoking, and chatting like a pair of old cronies. Hadrian was telling about Canada. He was going back there when his leave was up.

'You wouldn't like to stop in England, then?' said Mr Rockley.

'No, I wouldn't stop in England,' said Hadrian.

'How's that? There's plenty of electricians here,' said Mr Rockley.

'Yes. But there's too much difference between the men and the employers over here – too much of that for me,' said Hadrian.

The sick man looked at him narrowly, with oddly smiling eyes.

'That's it, is it?' he replied.

Matilda heard and understood. 'So that's your big idea, is it, my little man,' she said to herself. She had always said of Hadrian that he had no proper *respect* for anybody or anything, that he was sly and *common*. She went down to the kitchen for a *sotto voce* confab with Emmie.

'He thinks a rare lot of himself!' she whispered.

'He's somebody, he is!' said Emmie with contempt.

'He thinks there's too much difference between masters and men, over here,' said Matilda.

'Is it any different in Canada?' asked Emmie.

'Oh, yes – democratic,' replied Matilda, 'He thinks they're all on a level over there.'

'Ay, well he's over here now,' said Emmie dryly, 'so he can keep his place.'

As they talked they saw the young man sauntering down the garden, looking casually at the flowers. He had his hands in his pockets, and his soldier's cap neatly on his head. He looked quite at his ease, as if in possession. The two women, fluttered, watched him through the window.

'We know what he's come for,' said Emmie, churlishly. Matilda looked a long time at the neat khaki figure. It had something of the charity-boy about it still; but now it was a man's figure, laconic, charged with plebeian energy. She thought of the derisive passion in his voice as he had declaimed against the propertied classes, to her father.

'You don't know, Emmie. Perhaps he's not come for that,' she rebuked her sister. They were both thinking of the money.

They were still watching the young soldier. He stood away at the bottom of the garden, with his back to them, his hands in his pockets, looking into the water of the willow pond. Matilda's dark-blue eyes had a strange, full look in them, the lids, with the faint blue veins showing, dropped rather low. She carried her head light and high, but she had a look of pain. The young man at the bottom of the garden turned and looked up the path. Perhaps he saw them through the window. Matilda moved into shadow.

That afternoon their father seemed weak and ill. He was easily exhausted. The doctor came, and told Matilda that the sick man might die suddenly at any moment – but then he might not. They must be prepared.

So the day passed, and the next. Hadrian made himself at home. He went about in the morning in his brownish jersey and his khaki trousers, collarless, his bare neck showing. He explored the pottery premises, as if he had some secret purpose in so doing, he talked with Mr Rockley, when the sick man had strength. The two girls were always angry when the two men sat talking together like cronies. Yet it was chiefly a kind of politics they talked.

On the second day after Hadrian's arrival, Matilda sat with her father in the evening. She was drawing a picture which she wanted to copy. It was very still, Hadrian was gone out somewhere, no one knew where, and Emmie was busy. Mr Rockley reclined on his bed, looking out in silence over his evening-sunny garden.

'If anything happens to me, Matilda,' he said, 'you won't sell this house – you'll stop here – '

Matilda's eyes took their slightly haggard look as she stared at her father.

'Well, we couldn't do anything else,' she said.

'You don't know what you might do,' he said. 'Everything is left to you and Emmie, equally. You do as you like with it – only don't sell this house, don't part with it.'

'No,' she said.

'And give Hadrian my watch and chain, and a hundred pounds out of what's in the bank – and help him if he ever wants helping. I haven't put his name in the will.'

'Your watch and chain, and a hundred pounds – yes. But you'll be here when he goes back to Canada, father.'

'You never know what'll happen,' said her father.

Matilda sat and watched him, with her full, haggard eyes, for a long time, as if tranced. She saw that he knew he must go soon – she saw like a clairvoyant.

Later on she told Emmie what her father had said about the watch and chain and the money.

'What right has *he*' – *he* meaning Hadrian – 'to my father's watch and chain – what has it to do with him? Let him have the money, and get off,' said Emmie. She loved her father.

That night Matilda sat late in her room. Her heart was anxious and breaking, her mind seemed entranced. She was too much entranced even to weep, and all the time she thought of her father, only her father. At last she felt she must go to him.

It was near midnight. She went along the passage and to his room. There was a faint light from the moon outside. She listened at his door. Then she softly opened and entered. The room was faintly dark. She heard a movement on the bed.

'Are you asleep?' she said softly, advancing to the side of the bed.

'Are you asleep?' she repeated gently, as she stood at the side of the bed. And she reached her hand in the darkness to touch his forehead. Delicately, her fingers met the nose and the eyebrows, she laid her fine, delicate hand on his brow. It seemed fresh and smooth – very fresh and smooth. A sort of surprise stirred her, in her entranced state. But it could not waken her. Gently, she leaned over the bed and stirred her fingers over the low-growing hair on his brow.

'Can't you sleep tonight?' she said.

There was a quick stirring in the bed. 'Yes, I can,' a voice answered. It was Hadrian's voice. She started away. Instantly, she was wakened from her late-at-night trance. She remembered that her father was downstairs, that Hadrian had his room. She stood in the darkness as if stung.

'It is you, Hadrian?' she said. 'I thought it was my father.' She was so startled, so shocked, that she could not move. The young man gave an uncomfortable laugh, and turned in his bed.

At last she got out of the room. When she was back in her own room, in the light, and her door was closed, she stood holding up her hand that had touched him, as if it were hurt. She was almost too shocked, she could not endure.

'Well,' said her calm and weary mind, 'it was only a mistake, why take any notice of it.'

But she could not reason her feelings so easily. She suffered, feeling herself in a false position. Her right hand, which she had laid so gently on his face, on his fresh skin, ached now, as if it were really injured. She could not forgive Hadrian for the mistake: it made her dislike him deeply.

Hadrian too slept badly. He had been awakened by the opening of the door, and had not realised what the question meant. But the soft, straying tenderness of her hand on his face startled something out of his soul. He was a charity boy, aloof and more or less at bay. The fragile exquisiteness of her caress startled him most, revealed unknown things to him.

In the morning she could feel the consciousness in his eyes, when she came downstairs. She tried to bear herself as if nothing at all had happened, and she succeeded. She had the calm self-control, self-indifference, of one who has suffered and borne her suffering. She looked at him from her darkish, almost drugged blue eyes, she met the spark of consciousness in his eyes, and quenched it. And with her long, fine hand she put the sugar in his coffee.

But she could not control him as she thought she could. He had a keen memory stinging his mind, a new set of sensations working in his consciousness. Something new was alert in him. At the back of his reticent, guarded mind he kept his secret alive and vivid. She was at his mercy, for he was unscrupulous, his standard was not her standard.

He looked at her curiously. She was not beautiful, her nose was too large, her chin was too small, her neck was too thin. But her skin was clear and fine, she had a high-bred sensitiveness. This queer, brave, high-bred quality she shared with her father. The charity boy could see it in her tapering fingers, which were white and ringed. The same glamour that he knew in the elderly man he now saw in the woman. And he wanted to possess himself of it, he wanted to make himself master of it. As he went about through the old pottery-yard, his secretive mind schemed and worked. To be master of that strange soft delicacy such as he had felt in her hand upon his face – this was what he set himself towards. He was secretly plotting.

He watched Matilda as she went about, and she became aware of his attention, as of some shadow following her. But her pride made her ignore it. When he sauntered near her, his hands in his pockets, she received him with that same commonplace kindliness which mastered him more than any contempt. Her superior breeding seemed to control him. She made herself feel towards him exactly as she had always felt: he was a young boy who lived in the house with them, but was a stranger. Only, she dared not remember his face under her hand. When she remembered that, she was bewildered. Her hand had offended her, she wanted to cut it off. And she wanted, fiercely, to cut off the memory in him. She assumed she had done so.

One day, when he sat talking with his 'uncle', he looked straight into the eyes of the sick man, and said: 'But I shouldn't like to live and die here in Rawsley.'

'No – well – you needn't,' said the sick man.

'Do you think Cousin Matilda likes it?'

'I should think so.'

'I don't call it much of a life,' said the youth. 'How much older is she than me, uncle?'

The sick man looked at the young soldier. 'A good bit,' he said.

'Over thirty?' said Hadrian.

'Well, not so much. She's thirty-two.'

Hadrian considered a while. 'She doesn't look it,' he said.

Again the sick father looked at him.

'Do you think she'd like to leave here?' said Hadrian.

'Nay, I don't know,' replied the father, restive.

Hadrian sat still, having his own thoughts. Then in a small, quiet voice, as if he were speaking from inside himself, he said: 'I'd marry her if you wanted me to.'

The sick man raised his eyes suddenly, and stared. He stared for a long time.

The youth looked inscrutably out of the window.

'*You!*' said the sick man, mocking, with some contempt.

Hadrian turned and met his eyes. The two men had an inexplicable understanding.

'If you wasn't against it,' said Hadrian.

'Nay,' said the father, turning aside, 'I don't think I'm against it. I've never thought of it. But – but Emmie's the youngest.'

He had flushed, and looked suddenly more alive. Secretly he loved the boy.

'You might ask her,' said Hadrian.

The elder man considered. 'Hadn't you better ask her yourself?' he said.

'She'd take more notice of you,' said Hadrian.

They were both silent. Then Emmie came in.

For two days Mr Rockley was excited and thoughtful. Hadrian went about quietly, secretly, unquestioning. At last the father and daughter were alone together. It was very early morning, the father had been in much pain. As the pain abated, he lay still, thinking.

'Matilda!' he said suddenly, looking at his daughter.

'Yes, I'm here,' she said.

'Ay! I want you to do something – '

She rose in anticipation.

'Nay, sit still. I want you to marry Hadrian – '

She thought he was raving. She rose, bewildered and frightened.

'Nay, sit you still, sit you still. You hear what I tell you.'

'But you don't know what you're saying, father.'

'Ay, I know well enough. I want you to marry Hadrian, I tell you.'

She was dumbfounded. He was a man of few words.

'You'll do what I tell you,' he said.

She looked at him slowly. 'What put such an idea in your mind?' she said proudly.

'He did.'

Matilda almost looked her father down, her pride was so offended.

'Why, it's disgraceful,' she said.

'Why?'

She watched him slowly.

'What do you ask me for?' she said. 'It's disgusting.'

'The lad's sound enough,' he replied, testily.

'You'd better tell him to clear out,' she said, coldly.

He turned and looked out of the window. She sat flushed and erect for a long time. At length her father turned to her, looking really malevolent. 'If you won't,' he said, 'you're a fool, and I'll make you pay for your foolishness, do you see?'

Suddenly a cold fear gripped her. She could not believe her senses. She was terrified and bewildered. She stared at her father, believing him to be delirious, or mad, or drunk. What could she do?

'I tell you,' he said. 'I'll send for Whittle tomorrow if you don't. You shall neither of you have anything of mine.'

Whittle was the solicitor. She understood her father well enough: he would send for his solicitor, and make a will leaving all his property to Hadrian: neither she nor Emmie should have anything. It was too much. She rose and went out of the room, up to her own room, where she locked herself in.

She did not come out for some hours. At last, late at night, she confided in Emmie.

'The sliving demon, he wants the money,' said Emmie. 'My father's out of his mind.'

The thought that Hadrian merely wanted the money was another blow to Matilda. She did not love the impossible youth – but she had not yet learned to think of him as a thing of evil. He now became hideous to her mind.

Emmie had a little scene with her father next day.

'You don't mean what you said to our Matilda yesterday, do you, father?' she asked aggressively.

'Yes,' he replied.

'What, that you'll alter your will?'

'Yes.'

'You won't,' said his angry daughter.

But he looked at her with a malevolent little smile.

'Annie!' he shouted. 'Annie!'

He had still power to make his voice carry. The servant maid came in from the kitchen.

'Put your things on, and go down to Whittle's office, and say I want to see Mr Whittle as soon as he can, and will he bring a will-form.'

The sick man lay back a little – he could not lie down. His daughter sat as if she had been struck. Then she left the room.

Hadrian was pottering about in the garden. She went straight down to him.

'Here,' she said. 'You'd better get off. You'd better take your things and go from here, quick.'

Hadrian looked slowly at the infuriated girl.

'Who says so?' he asked.

'*We* say so – get off, you've done enough mischief and damage.'

'Does Uncle say so?'

'Yes, he does.'

'I'll go and ask him.'

But like a fury Emmie barred his way.

'No, you needn't. You needn't ask him nothing at all. We don't want you, so you can go.'

'Uncle's boss here.'

'A man that's dying, and you crawling round and working on him for his money! – you're not fit to live.'

'Oh!' he said. 'Who says I'm working for his money?'

'I say. But my father told our Matilda, and *she* knows what you are. *She* knows what you're after. So you might as well clear out, for all you'll get – guttersnipe!'

He turned his back on her, to think. It had not occurred to him that they would think he was after the money. He *did* want the money – badly. He badly wanted to be an employer himself, not one of the employed. But he knew, in his subtle, calculating way, that it was not for money he wanted Matilda. He wanted both the money and Matilda. But he told himself the two desires were separate, not one. He could not do with Matilda, *without* the money. But he did not want her *for* the money.

When he got this clear in his mind, he sought for an opportunity to tell it her, lurking and watching. But she avoided him. In the evening the lawyer came. Mr Rockley seemed to have a new access of strength – a will was drawn up, making the previous arrangements wholly conditional. The old will held good, if Matilda would consent to marry Hadrian. If she refused then at the end of six months the whole property passed to Hadrian.

Mr Rockley told this to the young man, with malevolent satisfaction. He seemed to have a strange desire, quite unreasonable, for revenge upon the women who had surrounded him for so long, and served him so carefully.

'Tell her in front of me,' said Hadrian.

So Mr Rockley sent for his daughters.

At last they came, pale, mute, stubborn. Matilda seemed to have retired far off, Emmie seemed like a fighter ready to fight to the death. The sick man reclined on the bed, his eyes bright, his puffed hand trembling. But his face had again some of its old, bright handsomeness. Hadrian sat quiet, a little aside: the indomitable, dangerous charity boy.

'There's the will,' said their father, pointing them to the paper.

The two women sat mute and immovable, they took no notice.

'Either you marry Hadrian, or he has everything,' said the father with satisfaction.

'Then let him have everything,' said Matilda boldly.

'He's not! He's not!' cried Emmie fiercely. 'He's not going to have it. The guttersnipe!'

An amused look came on her father's face.

'You hear that, Hadrian,' he said.

'I didn't offer to marry Cousin Matilda for the money,' said Hadrian, flushing and moving on his seat.

Matilda looked at him slowly, with her dark-blue, drugged eyes. He seemed a strange little monster to her.

'Why, you liar, you know you did,' cried Emmie.

The sick man laughed. Matilda continued to gaze strangely at the young man.

'She knows I didn't,' said Hadrian.

He too had his courage, as a rat has indomitable courage in the end. Hadrian had some of the neatness, the reserve, the underground quality of the rat. But he had perhaps the ultimate courage, the most unquenchable courage of all.

Emmie looked at her sister. 'Oh, well,' she said. 'Matilda – don't bother. Let him have everything, we can look after ourselves.'

'I know he'll take everything,' said Matilda, abstractedly.

Hadrian did not answer. He knew in fact that if Matilda refused him he would take everything, and go off with it.

'A clever little mannie – !' said Emmie, with a jeering grimace.

The father laughed noiselessly to himself. But he was tired . . . 'Go on, then,' he said. 'Go on, let me be quiet.'

Emmie turned and looked at him. 'You deserve what you've got,' she said to her father bluntly.

'Go on,' he answered mildly. 'Go on.'

Another night passed – a night nurse sat up with Mr Rockley. Another day came. Hadrian was there as ever, in his woollen jersey and coarse khaki trousers and bare neck. Matilda went about, frail and distant, Emmie black-browed in spite of her blondeness. They were all quiet, for they did not intend the mystified servant to learn anything.

Mr Rockley had very bad attacks of pain, he could not breathe. The end seemed near. They all went about quiet and stoical, all unyielding. Hadrian pondered within himself. If he did not marry Matilda he would go to

Canada with twenty thousand pounds. This was itself a very satisfactory prospect. If Matilda consented he would have nothing – she would have her own money.

Emmie was the one to act. She went off in search of the solicitor and brought him with her. There was an interview, and Whittle tried to frighten the youth into withdrawal – but without avail. The clergyman and relatives were summoned – but Hadrian stared at them and took no notice. It made him angry, however.

He wanted to catch Matilda alone. Many days went by, and he was not successful: she avoided him. At last, lurking, he surprised her one day as she came to pick gooseberries, and he cut off her retreat. He came to the point at once. 'You don't want me, then?' he said, in his subtle, insinuating voice.

'I don't want to speak to you,' she said, averting her face.

'You put your hand on me, though,' he said. 'You shouldn't have done that, and then I should never have thought of it. You shouldn't have touched me.'

'If you were anything decent, you'd know that was a mistake, and forget it,' she said.

'I know it was a mistake – but I shan't forget it. If you wake a man up, he can't go to sleep again because he's told to.'

'If you had any decent feeling in you, you'd have gone away,' she replied.

'I didn't want to,' he replied.

She looked away into the distance. At last she asked: 'What do you persecute me for, if it isn't for the money. I'm old enough to be your mother. In a way I've been your mother.'

'Doesn't matter,' he said. 'You've been no mother to me. Let us marry and go out to Canada – you might as well – you've touched me.'

She was white and trembling. Suddenly she flushed with anger. 'It's so *indecent*,' she said.

'How?' he retorted. 'You touched me.'

But she walked away from him. She felt as if he had trapped her. He was angry and depressed, he felt again despised.

That same evening she went into her father's room.

'Yes,' she said suddenly. 'I'll marry him.'

Her father looked up at her. He was in pain, and very ill.

'You like him now, do you?' he said, with a faint smile.

She looked down into his face, and saw death not far off. She turned and went coldly out of the room.

The solicitor was sent for, preparations were hastily made. In all the interval Matilda did not speak to Hadrian, never answered him if he addressed her. He approached her in the morning.

'You've come round to it, then?' he said, giving her a pleasant look from his twinkling, almost kindly eyes. She looked down at him and turned aside.

She looked down on him both literally and figuratively. Still he persisted, and triumphed.

Emmie raved and wept, the secret flew abroad. But Matilda was silent and unmoved, Hadrian was quiet and satisfied, and nipped with fear also. But he held out against his fear. Mr Rockley was very ill, but unchanged.

On the third day the marriage took place. Matilda and Hadrian drove straight home from the registrar, and went straight into the room of the dying man. His face lit up with a clear twinkling smile.

'Hadrian – you've got her?' he said, a little hoarsely.

'Yes,' said Hadrian, who was pale round the gills.

'Ay, my lad, I'm glad you're mine,' replied the dying man. Then he turned his eyes closely on Matilda.

'Let's look at you, Matilda,' he said. Then his voice went strange and unrecognisable. 'Kiss me,' he said.

She stooped and kissed him. She had never kissed him before, not since she was a tiny child. But she was quiet, very still.

'Kiss him,' the dying man said.

Obediently, Matilda put forward her mouth and kissed the young husband.

'That's right! That's right!' murmured the dying man.

The Blind Man

Isabel Pervin was listening for two sounds – for the sound of wheels on the drive outside and for the noise of her husband's footsteps in the hall. Her dearest and oldest friend, a man who seemed almost indispensable to her living, would drive up in the rainy dusk of the closing November day. The trap had gone to fetch him from the station. And her husband, who had been blinded in Flanders, and who had a disfiguring mark on his brow, would be coming in from the outhouses.

He had been home for a year now. He was totally blind. Yet they had been very happy. The Grange was Maurice's own place. The back was a farmstead, and the Wernhams, who occupied the rear premises, acted as farmers. Isabel lived with her husband in the handsome rooms in front. She and he had been almost entirely alone together since he was wounded. They talked and sang and read together in a wonderful and unspeakable intimacy. Then she reviewed books for a Scottish newspaper, carrying on her old interest, and he occupied himself a good deal with the farm. Sightless, he could still discuss everything with Wernham, and he could also do a good deal of work about the place – menial work, it is true, but it gave him satisfaction. He milked the cows, carried in the pails, turned the separator, attended to the pigs and horses. Life was still very full and strangely serene for the blind man, peaceful with the almost incomprehensible peace of immediate contact in darkness. With his wife he had a whole world, rich and real and invisible.

They were newly and remotely happy. He did not even regret the loss of his sight in these times of dark, palpable joy. A certain exultance swelled his soul.

But as time wore on, sometimes the rich glamour would leave them. Sometimes, after months of this intensity, a sense of burden overcame Isabel, a weariness, a terrible ennui, in that silent house approached between a colonnade of tall-shafted pines. Then she felt she would go mad, for she could not bear it. And sometimes he had devastating fits of depression, which seemed to lay waste his whole being. It was worse than depression – a black misery, when his own life was a torture to him, and when his presence was unbearable to his wife. The dread went down to the roots of her soul as these black days recurred. In a kind of panic she tried to wrap herself up still further in her husband. She forced the old spontaneous cheerfulness and joy to continue. But the effort it cost her was almost too much. She knew she could not keep it up. She felt she would scream with the strain, and would give anything, anything, to escape. She longed to possess her husband utterly; it gave her inordinate joy to have him entirely to herself. And yet, when again he was gone in a black and massive misery, she could not bear him, she could not bear herself; she wished she could be snatched away off the earth altogether, anything rather than live at this cost.

Dazed, she schemed for a way out. She invited friends, she tried to give him some further connection with the outer world. But it was no good. After all their joy and suffering, after their dark, great year of blindness and solitude and unspeakable nearness, other people seemed to them both shallow, prattling, rather impertinent. Shallow prattle seemed presumptuous. He became impatient and irritated, she was wearied. And so they lapsed into their solitude again. For they preferred it.

But now, in a few weeks' time, her second baby would be born. The first had died, an infant, when her husband first went out to France. She looked with joy and relief to the coming of the second. It would be her salvation. But also she felt some anxiety. She was thirty years old, her husband was a year younger. They both wanted the child very much. Yet she could not help feeling afraid. She had her husband on her hands, a terrible joy to her, and a terrifying burden. The child would occupy her love and attention. And then, what of Maurice? What would he do? If only she could feel that he, too, would be at peace and happy when the child came! She did so want to luxuriate in a rich, physical satisfaction of maternity. But the man, what would he do? How could she provide for him, how avert those shattering black moods of his, which destroyed them both?

She sighed with fear. But at this time Bertie Reid wrote to Isabel. He was her old friend, a second or third cousin, a Scotchman, as she was a Scotch-woman. They had been brought up near to one another, and all her life he had been her friend, like a brother, but better than her own brothers. She loved him – though not in the marrying sense. There was a sort of kinship between them, an affinity. They understood one another instinctively. But Isabel would never have thought of marrying Bertie. It would have seemed like marrying in her own family.

Bertie was a barrister and a man of letters, a Scotchman of the intellectual type, quick, ironical, sentimental, and on his knees before the woman he adored but did not want to marry. Maurice Pervin was different. He came of a good old country family – the Grange was not a very great distance from Oxford. He was passionate, sensitive, perhaps over-sensitive, wincing – a big fellow with heavy limbs and a forehead that flushed painfully. For his mind was slow, as if drugged by the strong provincial blood that beat in his veins. He was very sensitive to his own mental slowness, his feelings being quick and acute. So that he was just the opposite to Bertie, whose mind was much quicker than his emotions, which were not so very fine.

From the first the two men did not like each other. Isabel felt that they *ought* to get on together. But they did not. She felt that if only each could have the clue to the other there would be such a rare understanding between them. It did not come off, however. Bertie adopted a slightly ironical attitude, very offensive to Maurice, who returned the Scotch irony with English resentment, a resentment which deepened sometimes into stupid hatred.

This was a little puzzling to Isabel. However, she accepted it in the course of things. Men were made freakish and unreasonable. Therefore, when Maurice was going out to France for the second time, she felt that, for her husband's sake, she must discontinue her friendship with Bertie. She wrote to the barrister to this effect. Bertram Reid simply replied that in this, as in all other matters, he must obey her wishes, if these were indeed her wishes.

For nearly two years nothing had passed between the two friends. Isabel rather gloried in the fact; she had no compunction. She had one great article of faith, which was that husband and wife should be so important to one another that the rest of the world simply did not count. She and Maurice were husband and wife. They loved one another. They would have children. Then let everybody and everything else fade into insignificance outside this connubial felicity. She professed herself quite happy and ready to receive Maurice's friends. She was happy and ready: the happy wife, the ready woman in possession. Without knowing why, the friends retired abashed and came no more. Maurice, of course, took as much satisfaction in this connubial absorption as Isabel did.

He shared in Isabel's literary activities, she cultivated a real interest in agriculture and cattle-raising. For she, being at heart perhaps an emotional enthusiast, always cultivated the practical side of life, and prided herself on her mastery of practical affairs. Thus the husband and wife had spent the five years of their married life. The last had been one of blindness and unspeakable intimacy. And now Isabel felt a great indifference coming over her, a sort of lethargy. She wanted to be allowed to bear her child in peace, to nod by the fire and drift vaguely, physically, from day to day. Maurice was like an ominous thundercloud. She had to keep waking up to remember him.

When a little note came from Bertie, asking if he were to put up a tombstone to their dead friendship, and speaking of the real pain he felt on account of her husband's loss of sight, she felt a pang, a fluttering agitation of reawakening. And she read the letter to Maurice.

'Ask him to come down,' he said.

'Ask Bertie to come here!' she re-echoed.

'Yes – if he wants to.'

Isabel paused for a few moments.

'I know he wants to – he'd only be too glad,' she replied. 'But what about you, Maurice? How would you like it?'

'I should like it.'

'Well – in that case – But I thought you didn't care for him – '

'Oh, I don't know. I might think differently of him now,' the blind man replied. It was rather abstruse to Isabel.

'Well, dear,' she said, 'if you're quite sure – '

'I'm sure enough. Let him come,' said Maurice.

So Bertie was coming, coming this evening, in the November rain and darkness. Isabel was agitated, racked with her old restlessness and indecision. She had always suffered from this pain of doubt, just an agonising sense of uncertainty. It had begun to pass off, in the lethargy of maternity. Now it returned, and she resented it. She struggled as usual to maintain her calm, composed, friendly bearing, a sort of mask she wore over all her body.

A woman had lighted a tall lamp beside the table, and spread the cloth. The long dining-room was dim, with its elegant but rather severe pieces of old furniture. Only the round table glowed softly under the light. It had a rich, beautiful effect. The white cloth glistened and dropped its heavy, pointed lace corners almost to the carpet, the china was old and handsome, creamy-yellow, with a blotched pattern of harsh red and deep blue, the cups large and bell-shaped, the teapot gallant. Isabel looked at it with superficial appreciation.

Her nerves were hurting her. She looked automatically again at the high, uncurtained windows. In the last dusk she could just perceive outside a huge fir-tree swaying its boughs: it was as if she thought it rather than saw it. The rain came flying on the window panes. Ah, why had she no peace? These two men, why did they tear at her? Why did they not come – why was there this suspense?

She sat in a lassitude that was really suspense and irritation. Maurice, at least, might come in – there was nothing to keep him out. She rose to her feet. Catching sight of her reflection in a mirror, she glanced at herself with a slight smile of recognition, as if she were an old friend to herself. Her face was oval and calm, her nose a little arched. Her neck made a beautiful line down to her shoulder. With hair knotted loosely behind, she had something of a warm, maternal look. Thinking this of herself, she arched her eyebrows and her rather heavy eyelids, with a little flicker of a smile, and for a moment her grey eyes looked amused and wicked, a little sardonic, out of her transfigured Madonna face.

Then, resuming her air of womanly patience – she was really fatally self-determined – she went with a little jerk towards the door. Her eyes were slightly reddened.

She passed down the wide hall, and through a door at the end. Then she was in the farm premises. The scent of dairy, and of farm-kitchen, and of farm-yard and of leather almost overcame her: but particularly the scent of dairy. They had been scalding out the pans. The flagged passage in front of her was dark, puddled and wet. Light came out from the open kitchen door.

She went forward and stood in the doorway. The farm-people were at tea, seated at a little distance from her round a long, narrow table, in the centre of which stood a white lamp. Ruddy faces, ruddy hands holding food, red mouths working, heads bent over the tea-cups: men, land-girls, boys: it was tea-time, feeding-time. Some faces caught sight of her. Mrs Wernham, going round behind the chairs with a large black teapot, halting slightly in her walk, was not aware of her for a moment. Then she turned suddenly.

'Oh, is it madam!' she exclaimed. 'Come in, then, come in! We're at tea.' And she dragged forward a chair.

'No, I won't come in,' said Isabel, 'I'm afraid I interrupt your meal.'

'No – no – not likely, madam, not likely.'

'Hasn't Mr Pervin come in, do you know?'

'I'm sure I couldn't say! Missed him, have you, madam?'

'No, I only wanted him to come in,' laughed Isabel, as if shyly.

'Wanted him, did ye? Get you, boy – get up, now – '

Mrs Wernham knocked one of the boys on the shoulder. He began to scrape to his feet, chewing largely.

'I believe he's in top stable,' said another face from the table.

'Ah! No, don't get up. I'm going myself,' said Isabel.

'Don't you go out of a dirty night like this. Let the lad go. Get along wi' ye, boy,' said Mrs Wernham.

'No, no,' said Isabel, with a decision that was always obeyed. 'Go on with your tea, Tom. I'd like to go across to the stable, Mrs Wernham.'

'Did ever you hear tell!' exclaimed the woman.

'Isn't the trap late?' asked Isabel.

'Why, no,' said Mrs Wernham, peering into the distance at the tall, dim clock. 'No, madam – we can give it another quarter or twenty minutes yet, good – yes, every bit of a quarter.'

'Ah! It seems late when darkness falls so early,' said Isabel.

'It do, that it do. Bother the days, that they draw in so,' answered Mrs Wernham. 'Proper miserable!'

'They are,' said Isabel, withdrawing.

She pulled on her overshoes, wrapped a large tartan shawl around her, put on a man's felt hat, and ventured out along the causeways of the first yard. It was very dark. The wind was roaring in the great elms behind the outhouses. When she came to the second yard the darkness seemed deeper. She was unsure of her footing. She wished she had brought a lantern. Rain blew against her. Half she liked it, half she felt unwilling to battle.

She reached at last the just visible door of the stable. There was no sign of a light anywhere. Opening the upper half, she looked in: into a simple well of darkness. The smell of horses, and ammonia, and of warmth was startling to her, in that full night. She listened with all her ears, but could hear nothing save the night, and the stirring of a horse.

'Maurice!' she called, softly and musically, though she was afraid. 'Maurice – are you there?'

Nothing came from the darkness. She knew the rain and wind blew in upon the horses, the hot animal life. Feeling it wrong, she entered the stable, and drew the lower half of the door shut, holding the upper part close. She did not stir, because she was aware of the presence of the dark hindquarters of the horses, though she could not see them, and she was afraid. Something wild stirred in her heart.

She listened intensely. Then she heard a small noise in the distance – far away, it seemed – the chink of a pan, and a man's voice speaking a brief word. It would be Maurice, in the other part of the stable. She stood motionless, waiting for him to come through the partition door. The horses were so terrifyingly near to her, in the invisible.

The loud jarring of the inner door-latch made her start; the door was opened. She could hear and feel her husband entering and invisibly passing among the horses near to her, in darkness as they were, actively inter-mingled. The rather low sound of his voice as he spoke to the horses came velvety to her nerves. How near he was, and how invisible! The darkness seemed to be in a strange swirl of violent life, just upon her. She turned giddy.

Her presence of mind made her call, quietly and musically: 'Maurice! Maurice – dea–ar!'

'Yes,' he answered. 'Isabel?'

She saw nothing, and the sound of his voice seemed to touch her.

'Hello!' she answered cheerfully, straining her eyes to see him. He was still busy, attending to the horses near her, but she saw only darkness. It made her almost desperate. 'Won't you come in, dear?' she said.

'Yes, I'm coming. Just half a minute. *Stand over – now!* Trap's not come, has it?'

'Not yet,' said Isabel.

His voice was pleasant and ordinary, but it had a slight suggestion of the stable to her. She wished he would come away. Whilst he was so utterly invisible she was afraid of him.

'How's the time?' he asked.

'Not yet six,' she replied. She disliked to answer into the dark. Presently he came very near to her, and she retreated out of doors.

'The weather blows in here,' he said, coming steadily forward, feeling for the doors.

She shrank away. At last she could dimly see him.

'Bertie won't have much of a drive,' he said, as he closed the doors.

'He won't indeed!' said Isabel calmly, watching the dark shape at the door.

'Give me your arm, dear,' she said.

She pressed his arm close to her, as she went. But she longed to see him, to look at him. She was nervous. He walked erect, with face rather lifted, but with a curious tentative movement of his powerful, muscular legs. She could feel the clever, careful, strong contact of his feet with the earth, as she balanced against him. For a moment he was a tower of darkness to her, as if he rose out of the earth.

In the house-passage he wavered, and went cautiously, with a curious look of silence about him as he felt for the bench. Then he sat down heavily. He was a man with rather sloping shoulders, but with heavy limbs, powerful legs that seemed to know the earth. His head was small, usually carried high and light. As he bent down to unfasten his gaiters and boots he did not look blind. His hair was brown and crisp, his hands were large, reddish, intelligent, the veins stood out in the wrists; and his thighs and knees seemed massive. When he stood up his face and neck were surcharged with blood, the veins stood out on his temples. She did not look at his blindness.

Isabel was always glad when they had passed through the dividing door into their own regions of repose and beauty. She was a little afraid of him, out there in the animal grossness of the back. His bearing also changed, as he smelt the familiar, indefinable odour that pervaded his wife's surroundings, a delicate, refined scent, very faintly spicy. Perhaps it came from the pot-pourri bowls.

He stood at the foot of the stairs, arrested, listening. She watched him, and her heart sickened. He seemed to be listening to fate.

'He's not here yet,' he said. 'I'll go up and change.'

'Maurice,' she said, 'you're not wishing he wouldn't come, are you?'

'I couldn't quite say,' he answered. 'I feel myself rather on the *qui vive*.'

'I can see you are,' she answered. And she reached up and kissed his cheek. She saw his mouth relax into a slow smile.

'What are you laughing at?' she said roguishly.

'You consoling me,' he answered.

'Nay,' she answered. 'Why should I console you? You know we love each other – you know *how* married we are! What does anything else matter?'

'Nothing at all, my dear.' He felt for her face, and touched it, smiling. '*You're* all right, aren't you?' he asked, anxiously.

'I'm wonderfully all right, love,' she answered. 'It's you I am a little troubled about, at times.'

'Why me?' he said, touching her cheeks delicately with the tips of his fingers. The touch had an almost hypnotising effect on her.

He went away upstairs. She saw him mount into the darkness, unseeing and unchanging. He did not know that the lamps on the upper corridor were unlighted. He went on into the darkness with unchanging step. She heard him in the bathroom.

Pervin moved about almost unconsciously in his familiar surroundings, dark though everything was. He seemed to know the presence of objects before he touched them. It was a pleasure to him to rock thus through a world of things, carried on the flood in a sort of blood-prescience. He did not think much or trouble much. So long as he kept this sheer immediacy of blood-contact with the substantial world he was happy, he wanted no intervention of visual consciousness. In this state there was a certain rich positivity, bordering sometimes on rapture. Life seemed to move in him like a tide lapping, and advancing, enveloping all things darkly. It was a pleasure to stretch forth the hand and meet the unseen object, clasp it, and possess it in pure contact. He did not try to remember, to visualise. He did not want to. The new way of consciousness substituted itself in him.

The rich suffusion of this state generally kept him happy, reaching its culmination in the consuming passion for his wife. But at times the flow would seem to be checked and thrown back. Then it would beat inside him like a tangled sea, and he was tortured in the shattered chaos of his own blood. He grew to dread this arrest, this throw-back, this chaos inside himself, when he seemed merely at the mercy of his own powerful and conflicting elements. How to get some measure of control or surety, this was the question. And when the question rose maddening in him, he would clench his fists as if he would *compel* the whole universe to submit to him. But it was in vain. He could not even compel himself.

Tonight, however, he was still serene, though little tremors of unreasonable exasperation ran through him. He had to handle the razor very carefully, as he shaved, for it was not at one with him, he was afraid of it. His hearing also was too much sharpened. He heard the woman lighting the lamps on the corridor, and attending to the fire in the visitor's room. And then, as he went to his room, he heard the trap arrive. Then came Isabel's voice, lifted and calling, like a bell ringing: 'Is it you, Bertie? Have you come?'

And a man's voice answered out of the wind: 'Hello, Isabel! There you are.'

'Have you had a miserable drive? I'm so sorry we couldn't send a closed carriage. I can't see you at all, you know.'

'I'm coming. No, I liked the drive – it was like Perthshire. Well, how are you? You're looking fit as ever, as far as I can see.'

'Oh, yes,' said Isabel. 'I'm wonderfully well. How are you? Rather thin, I think –'

'Worked to death – everybody's old cry. But I'm all right, Ciss. How's Pervin? – isn't he here?'

'Oh, yes, he's upstairs changing. Yes, he's awfully well. Take off your wet things; I'll send them to be dried.'

'And how are you both, in spirits? He doesn't fret?'

'No – no, not at all. No, on the contrary, really. We've been wonderfully happy, incredibly. It's more than I can understand – so wonderful: the nearness, and the peace –'

'Ah! Well, that's awfully good news – '

They moved away. Pervin heard no more. But a childish sense of desolation had come over him, as he heard their brisk voices. He seemed shut out – like a child that is left out. He was aimless and excluded, he did not know what to do with himself. The helpless desolation came over him. He fumbled nervously as he dressed himself, in a state almost of childishness. He disliked the Scotch accent in Bertie's speech, and the slight response it found on Isabel's tongue. He disliked the slight purr of complacency in the Scottish speech. He disliked intensely the glib way in which Isabel spoke of their happiness and nearness. It made him recoil. He was fretful and beside himself like a child, he had almost a childish nostalgia to be included in the life circle. And at the same time he was a man, dark and powerful and infuriated by his own weakness. By some fatal flaw, he could not be by himself, he had to depend on the support of another. And this very dependence enraged him. He hated Bertie Reid, and at the same time he knew the hatred was nonsense, he knew it was the outcome of his own weakness.

He went downstairs. Isabel was alone in the dining-room. She watched him enter, head erect, his feet tentative. He looked so strong-blooded and healthy, and, at the same time, cancelled. Cancelled – that was the word that flew across her mind. Perhaps it was his scars suggested it.

'You heard Bertie come, Maurice?' she said.

'Yes – isn't he here?'

'He's in his room. He looks very thin and worn.'

'I suppose he works himself to death.'

A woman came in with a tray – and after a few minutes Bertie came down. He was a little dark man, with a very big forehead, thin, wispy hair, and sad, large eyes. His expression was inordinately sad – almost funny. He had odd, short legs.

Isabel watched him hesitate at the door, and glance nervously at her husband. Pervin heard him and turned.

'Here you are, now,' said Isabel. 'Come, let us eat.'

Bertie went across to Maurice. 'How are you, Pervin,' he said, as he advanced.

The blind man stuck his hand out into space, and Bertie took it.

'Very fit. Glad you've come,' said Maurice.

Isabel glanced at them, and glanced away, as if she could not bear to see them.

'Come,' she said. 'Come to table. Aren't you both awfully hungry? I am, tremendously.'

'I'm afraid you waited for me,' said Bertie, as they sat down.

Maurice had a curious monolithic way of sitting in a chair, erect and distant. Isabel's heart always beat when she caught sight of him thus.

'No,' she replied to Bertie. 'We're very little later than usual. We're having a sort of high tea, not dinner. Do you mind? It gives us such a nice long evening, uninterrupted.'

'I like it,' said Bertie.

Maurice was feeling, with curious little movements, almost like a cat kneading her bed, for his place, his knife and fork, his napkin. He was getting the whole geography of his cover into his consciousness. He sat erect and inscrutable, remote-seeming Bertie watched the static figure of the blind man, the delicate tactile discernment of the large, ruddy hands, and the curious mindless silence of the brow, above the scar. With difficulty he looked away, and without knowing what he did, picked up a little crystal bowl of violets from the table, and held them to his nose.

'They are sweet-scented,' he said. 'Where do they come from?'

'From the garden – under the windows,' said Isabel.

'So late in the year – and so fragrant! Do you remember the violets under Aunt Bell's south wall?'

The two friends looked at each other and exchanged a smile, Isabel's eyes lighting up.

'Don't I?' she replied. '*Wasn't* she queer!'

'A curious old girl,' laughed Bertie. 'There's a streak of freakishness in the family, Isabel.'

'Ah – but not in you and me, Bertie,' said Isabel. 'Give them to Maurice, will you?' she added, as Bertie was putting down the flowers. 'Have you smelled the violets, dear? Do! – they are so scented.'

Maurice held out his hand, and Bertie placed the tiny bowl against his large, warm-looking fingers. Maurice's hand closed over the thin white fingers of the barrister. Bertie carefully extricated himself. Then the two watched the blind man smelling the violets. He bent his head and seemed to be thinking. Isabel waited.

'Aren't they sweet, Maurice?' she said at last, anxiously.

'Very,' he said. And he held out the bowl. Bertie took it. Both he and Isabel were a little afraid, and deeply disturbed.

The meal continued. Isabel and Bertie chatted spasmodically. The blind man was silent. He touched his food repeatedly, with quick, delicate touches of his knife-point, then cut irregular bits. He could not bear to be helped. Both Isabel and Bertie suffered: Isabel wondered why. She did not suffer when she was alone with Maurice. Bertie made her conscious of a strangeness.

After the meal the three drew their chairs to the fire, and sat down to talk. The decanters were put on a table near at hand. Isabel knocked the logs on the fire and clouds of brilliant sparks went up the chimney. Bertie noticed a slight weariness in her bearing.

'You will be glad when your child comes now, Isabel?' he said.

She looked up to him with a quick wan smile.

'Yes, I shall be glad,' she answered. 'It begins to seem long. Yes, I shall be very glad. So will you, Maurice, won't you?' she added.

'Yes, I shall,' replied her husband.

'We are both looking forward so much to having it,' she said.

'Yes, of course,' said Bertie.

He was a bachelor, three or four years older than Isabel. He lived in beautiful rooms overlooking the river, guarded by a faithful Scottish man-servant. And he had his friends among the fair sex – not lovers, friends. So long as he could avoid any danger of courtship or marriage, he adored a few good women with constant and unfailing homage, and he was chivalrously fond of quite a number. But if they seemed to encroach on him, he withdrew and detested them.

Isabel knew him very well, knew his beautiful constancy, and kindness, also his incurable weakness, which made him unable ever to enter into close contact of any sort. He was ashamed of himself, because he could not marry, could not approach women physically. He wanted to do so. But he could not. At the centre of him he was afraid, helplessly and even brutally afraid. He had given up hope, had ceased to expect any more that he could escape his own weakness. Hence he was a brilliant and successful barrister, also *littérateur* of high repute, a rich man, and a great social success. At the centre he felt himself neuter, nothing.

Isabel knew him well. She despised him even while she admired him. She looked at his sad face, his little short legs, and felt contempt of him. She looked at his dark grey eyes, with their uncanny, almost childlike intuition, and she loved him. He understood amazingly – but she had no fear of his understanding. As a man she patronised him.

And she turned to the impassive, silent figure of her husband. He sat leaning back, with folded arms, and face a little uptilted. His knees were straight and massive. She sighed, picked up the poker, and again began to prod the fire, to rouse the clouds of soft, brilliant sparks.

'Isabel tells me,' Bertie began suddenly, 'that you have not suffered unbearably from the loss of sight.'

Maurice straightened himself to attend, but kept his arms folded.

'No,' he said, 'not unbearably. Now and again one struggles against it, you know. But there are compensations.'

'They say it is much worse to be stone deaf,' said Isabel.

'I believe it is,' said Bertie. 'Are there compensations?' he added, to Maurice.

'Yes. You cease to bother about a great many things.' Again Maurice stretched his figure, stretched the strong muscles of his back, and leaned backwards, with uplifted face.

'And that is a relief,' said Bertie. 'But what is there in place of the bothering? What replaces the activity?'

There was a pause. At length the blind man replied, as out of a negligent, unattentive thinking: 'Oh, I don't know. There's a good deal when you're not active.'

'Is there?' said Bertie. 'What, exactly? It always seems to me that when there is no thought and no action, there is nothing.'

Again Maurice was slow in replying.

'There is something,' he replied. 'I couldn't tell you what it is.'

And the talk lapsed once more, Isabel and Bertie chatting gossip and reminiscence, the blind man silent.

At length Maurice rose restlessly, a big, obtrusive figure. He felt tight and hampered. He wanted to go away.

'Do you mind,' he said, 'if I go and speak to Wernham?'

'No – go along, dear,' said Isabel.

And he went out. A silence came over the two friends. At length Bertie said: 'Nevertheless, it is a great deprivation, Cissie.'

'It is, Bertie. I know it is.'

'Something lacking all the time,' said Bertie.

'Yes, I know. And yet – and yet – Maurice is right. There is something else, something *there*, which you never knew was there, and which you can't express.'

'What is there?' asked Bertie.

'I don't know – it's awfully hard to define it – but something strong and immediate. There's something strange in Maurice's presence – indefinable – but I couldn't do without it. I agree that it seems to put one's mind to sleep. But when we're alone I miss nothing; it seems awfully rich, almost splendid, you know.'

'I'm afraid I don't follow,' said Bertie.

They talked desultorily. The wind blew loudly outside, rain chattered on the window-panes, making a sharp, drum-sound, because of the closed, mellow-golden shutters inside. The logs burned slowly, with hot, almost invisible small flames. Bertie seemed uneasy, there were dark circles round his eyes. Isabel, rich with her approaching maternity, leaned looking into the fire. Her hair curled in odd, loose strands, very pleasing to the man. But she had a curious feeling of old woe in her heart, old, timeless night-woe.

'I suppose we're all deficient somewhere,' said Bertie.

'I suppose so,' said Isabel wearily.

'Damned, sooner or later.'

'I don't know,' she said, rousing herself. 'I feel quite all right, you know. The child coming seems to make me indifferent to everything, just placid. I can't feel that there's anything to trouble about, you know.'

'A good thing, I should say,' he replied slowly.

'Well, there it is. I suppose it's just nature. If only I felt I needn't trouble about Maurice, I should be perfectly content – '

'But you feel you must trouble about him?'

'Well – I don't know – ' She even resented this much effort.

The evening passed slowly. Isabel looked at the clock. 'I say,' she said. 'It's nearly ten o'clock. Where can Maurice be? I'm sure they're all in bed at the back. Excuse me a moment.'

She went out, returning almost immediately.

'It's all shut up and in darkness,' she said. 'I wonder where he is. He must have gone out to the farm – '

Bertie looked at her.

'I suppose he'll come in,' he said.

'I suppose so,' she said. 'But it's unusual for him to be out now.'

'Would you like me to go out and see?'

'Well – if you wouldn't mind. I'd go, but – ' She did not want to make the physical effort.

Bertie put on an old overcoat and took a lantern. He went out from the side door. He shrank from the wet and roaring night. Such weather had a nervous effect on him: too much moisture everywhere made him feel almost imbecile. Unwilling, he went through it all. A dog barked violently at him. He peered in all the buildings. At last, as he opened the upper door of a sort of intermediate barn, he heard a grinding noise, and looking in, holding up his lantern, saw Maurice, in his shirt-sleeves, standing listening, holding the handle of a turnip-pulper. He had been pulping sweet roots, a pile of which lay dimly heaped in a corner behind him.

'That you, Wernham?' said Maurice, listening.

'No, it's me,' said Bertie.

A large, half-wild grey cat was rubbing at Maurice's leg. The blind man stooped to rub its sides. Bertie watched the scene, then unconsciously entered and shut the door behind him. He was in a high sort of barn-place, from which, right and left, ran off the corridors in front of the stalled cattle. He watched the slow, stooping motion of the other man, as he caressed the great cat.

Maurice straightened himself.

'You came to look for me?' he said.

'Isabel was a little uneasy,' said Bertie.

'I'll come in. I like messing about doing these jobs.'

The cat had reared her sinister, feline length against his leg, clawing at his thigh affectionately. He lifted her claws out of his flesh.

'I hope I'm not in your way at all at the Grange here,' said Bertie, rather shy and stiff.

'My way? No, not a bit. I'm glad Isabel has somebody to talk to. I'm afraid it's I who am in the way. I know I'm not very lively company. Isabel's all right, don't you think? She's not unhappy, is she?'

'I don't think so.'

'What does she say?'

'She says she's very content – only a little troubled about you.'

'Why me?'

'Perhaps afraid that you might brood,' said Bertie, cautiously.

'She needn't be afraid of that.' He continued to caress the flattened grey head of the cat with his fingers. 'What I am a bit afraid of,' he resumed, 'is that she'll find me a dead weight, always alone with me down here.'

'I don't think you need think that,' said Bertie, though this was what he feared himself.

'I don't know,' said Maurice. 'Sometimes I feel it isn't fair that she's saddled with me.' Then he dropped his voice curiously. 'I say,' he asked, secretly struggling, 'is my face much disfigured? Do you mind telling me?'

'There is the scar,' said Bertie, wondering. 'Yes, it is a disfigurement. But more pitiable than shocking.'

'A pretty bad scar, though,' said Maurice.

'Oh, yes.'

There was a pause.

'Sometimes I feel I am horrible,' said Maurice, in a low voice, talking as if to himself. And Bertie actually felt a quiver of horror.

'That's nonsense,' he said.

Maurice again straightened himself, leaving the cat.

'There's no telling,' he said. Then again, in an odd tone, he added: 'I don't really know you, do I?'

'Probably not,' said Bertie.

'Do you mind if I touch you?'

The lawyer shrank away instinctively. And yet, out of very philanthropy, he said, in a small voice: 'Not at all.'

But he suffered as the blind man stretched out a strong, naked hand to him. Maurice accidentally knocked off Bertie's hat.

'I thought you were taller,' he said, starting. Then he laid his hand on Bertie Reid's head, closing the dome of the skull in a soft, firm grasp, gathering it, as it were; then, shifting his grasp and softly closing again, with a fine, close pressure, till he had covered the skull and the face of the smaller man, tracing the brows, and touching the full, closed eyes, touching the small nose and the nostrils, the rough, short moustache, the mouth, the rather strong chin. The hand of the blind man grasped the shoulder, the arm, the hand of the other man. He seemed to take him, in the soft, travelling grasp.

'You seem young,' he said quietly, at last.

The lawyer stood almost annihilated, unable to answer.

'Your head seems tender, as if you were young,' Maurice repeated. 'So do your hands. Touch my eyes, will you? – touch my scar.'

Now Bertie quivered with revulsion. Yet he was under the power of the blind man, as if hypnotised. He lifted his hand, and laid the fingers on the scar, on the scarred eyes. Maurice suddenly covered them with his own hand, pressed the fingers of the other man upon his disfigured eye-sockets, trembling in every fibre, and rocking slightly, slowly, from side to side. He remained thus for a minute or more, whilst Bertie stood as if in a swoon, unconscious, imprisoned.

Then suddenly Maurice removed the hand of the other man from his brow, and stood holding it in his own.

'Oh, my God,' he said, 'we shall know each other now, shan't we? We shall know each other now.'

Bertie could not answer. He gazed mute and terror-struck, overcome by his own weakness. He knew he could not answer. He had an unreasonable fear, lest the other man should suddenly destroy him. Whereas Maurice was actually filled with hot, poignant love, the passion of friendship. Perhaps it was this very passion of friendship which Bertie shrank from most.

'We're all right together now, aren't we?' said Maurice. 'It's all right now, as long as we live, so far as we're concerned?'

'Yes,' said Bertie, trying by any means to escape.

Maurice stood with head lifted, as if listening. The new delicate fulfilment of mortal friendship had come as a revelation and surprise to him, something exquisite and unhoped-for. He seemed to be listening to hear if it were real.

Then he turned for his coat.

'Come,' he said, 'we'll go to Isabel.'

Bertie took the lantern and opened the door. The cat disappeared. The two men went in silence along the causeways. Isabel, as they came, thought their footsteps sounded strange. She looked up pathetically and anxiously for their entrance. There seemed a curious elation about Maurice. Bertie was haggard, with sunken eyes.

'What is it?' she asked.

'We've become friends,' said Maurice, standing with his feet apart, like a strange colossus.

'Friends!' re-echoed Isabel. And she looked again at Bertie. He met her eyes with a furtive, haggard look; his eyes were as if glazed with misery.

'I'm so glad,' she said, in sheer perplexity.

'Yes,' said Maurice.

He was indeed so glad. Isabel took his hand with both hers, and held it fast.

'You'll be happier now, dear,' she said.

But she was watching Bertie. She knew that he had one desire – to escape from this intimacy, this friendship, which had been thrust upon him. He could not bear it that he had been touched by the blind man, his insane reserve broken in. He was like a mollusc whose shell is broken.

The Primrose Path

A young man came out of the Victoria station, looking undecidedly at the taxi-cabs, dark-red and black, pressing against the kerb under the glass-roof. Several men in greatcoats and brass buttons jerked themselves erect to catch his attention, at the same time keeping an eye on the other people as they filtered through the open doorways of the station. Berry, however, was occupied by one of the men, a big, burly fellow whose blue eyes glared back and whose red-brown moustache bristled in defiance.

'Do you *want* a cab, sir?' the man asked, in a half-mocking, challenging voice.

Berry hesitated still.

'Are you Daniel Sutton?' he asked.

'Yes,' replied the other defiantly, with uneasy conscience.

'Then you are my uncle,' said Berry.

They were alike in colouring, and somewhat in features, but the taxi driver was a powerful, well-fleshed man who glared at the world aggressively, being really on the defensive against his own heart. His nephew, of the same height, was thin, well-dressed, quiet and indifferent in his manner. And yet they were obviously kin.

'And who the devil are you?' asked the taxi driver.

'I'm Daniel Berry,' replied the nephew.

'Well, I'm damned – never saw you since you were a kid.'

Rather awkwardly at this late hour the two shook hands.

'How are you, lad?'

'All right. I thought you were in Australia.'

'Been back three months – bought a couple of these damned things' – he kicked the tyre of his taxi-cab in affectionate disgust. There was a moment's silence.

'Oh, but I'm going back out there. I can't stand this cankering, rotten-hearted hell of a country any more; you want to come out to Sydney with me, lad. That's the place for you – beautiful place, oh, you could wish for nothing better. And money in it, too. – How's your mother?'

'She died at Christmas,' said the young man.

'Dead! What! – our Anna!' The big man's eyes stared, and he recoiled in fear. 'God, lad,' he said, 'that's three of 'em gone!'

The two men looked away at the people passing along the pale grey pavements, under the wall of Trinity Church.

'Well, strike me lucky!' said the taxi driver at last, out of breath. 'She wor th' best o' th' bunch of 'em. I see nowt nor hear nowt from any of 'em – they're not worth it, I'll be damned if they are – our sermon-lapping Adela and Maud,' he looked scornfully at his nephew. 'But she was the best of 'em, our Anna was, that's a fact.'

He was talking because he was afraid.

'An' after a hard life like she'd had. How old was she, lad?'

'Fifty-five.'

'Fifty-five . . . ' He hesitated. Then, in a rather hushed voice, he asked the question that frightened him: 'And what was it, then?'

'Cancer.'

'Cancer again, like Julia! I never knew there was cancer in our family. Oh, my good God, our poor Anna, after the life she'd had! – What, lad, do you see any God at the back of that? – I'm damned if I do.'

He was glaring, very blue-eyed and fierce, at his nephew. Berry lifted his shoulders slightly.

'God?' went on the taxi driver, in a curious intense tone, 'You've only to look at the folk in the street to know there's nothing keeps it going but gravitation. Look at 'em. Look at him!' – A mongrel-looking man was nosing past. 'Wouldn't *he* murder you for your watch-chain, but that he's afraid of society. He's got it *in* him . . . Look at 'em.'

Berry watched the townspeople go by, and, sensitively feeling his uncle's antipathy, it seemed he was watching a sort of *danse macabre* of ugly criminals.

'Did you ever see such a God-forsaken crew creeping about! It gives you the very horrors to look at 'em. I sit in this damned car and watch 'em till, I can tell you, I feel like running the cab amuck among 'em, and running myself to kingdom come – '

Berry wondered at this outburst. He knew his uncle was the black sheep, the youngest, the darling of his mother's family. He knew him to be at odds with respectability, mixing with the looser, sporting type, all betting and drinking and showing dogs and birds, and racing. As a critic of life, however, he did not know him. But the young man felt curiously understanding. 'He uses words like I do, he talks nearly as I talk, except that I shouldn't say those things. But I might feel like that, in myself, if I went a certain road.'

'I've got to go to Watmore,' he said. 'Can you take me?'

'When d'you want to go?' asked the uncle fiercely.

'Now.'

'Come on, then. What d'yer stand gassin' on th' causeway for?'

The nephew took his seat beside the driver. The cab began to quiver, then it started forward with a whirr. The uncle, his hands and feet acting mechanically, kept his blue eyes fixed on the highroad into whose traffic the car was insinuating its way. Berry felt curiously as if he were sitting beside an older development of himself. His mind went back to his mother. She had been twenty years older than this brother of hers whom she had loved so dearly. 'He was one of the most affectionate little lads, and such a curly head! I could never have believed he would grow into the great, coarse bully he is – for he's nothing else. My father made a god of him – well, it's a good thing his father is dead. He got in with that sporting gang, that's what did it. Things were made too easy for him, and so he thought of no one but himself, and this is the result.'

Not that 'Joky' Sutton was so very black a sheep. He had lived idly till he was eighteen, then had suddenly married a young, beautiful girl with clear brows and dark grey eyes, a factory girl. Having taken her to live with his parents he, lover of dogs and pigeons, went on to the staff of a sporting paper. But his wife was without uplift or warmth. Though they made money enough, their house was dark and cold and uninviting. He had two or three dogs, and the whole attic was turned into a great pigeon-house. He and his wife lived together roughly, with no warmth, no refinement, no touch of beauty anywhere, except that she was beautiful. He was a blustering, impetuous man, she was rather cold in her soul, did not care about anything very much, was rather capable and close with money. And she had a common accent in her speech. He outdid her a thousand times in coarse language, and yet that cold twang in her voice tortured him with shame that he stamped down in bullying and in becoming more violent in his own speech.

Only his dogs adored him, and to them, and to his pigeons, he talked with rough, yet curiously tender caresses while they leaped and fluttered for joy.

After he and his wife had been married for seven years a little girl was born to them, then later, another. But the husband and wife drew no nearer together. She had an affection for her children almost like a cool governess. He had an emotional man's fear of sentiment, which helped to nip his wife from putting out any shoots. He treated his children roughly, and pretended to think it a good job when one was adopted by a well-to-do maternal aunt. But in his soul he hated his wife that she could give away one of his children. For after her cool fashion, she loved him. With a chaos of a man such as he, she had no chance of being anything but cold and hard, poor thing. For she did love him.

In the end he fell absurdly and violently in love with a rather sentimental young woman who read Browning. He made his wife an allowance and established a new ménage with the young lady, shortly after emigrating with her to Australia. Meanwhile his wife had gone to live with a publican, a widower, with whom she had had one of those curious, tacit understandings of which quiet women are capable, something like an arrangement for provision in the future.

This was as much as the nephew knew. He sat beside his uncle, wondering how things stood at the present. They raced lightly out past the cemetery and along the boulevard, then turned into the rather grimy country. The mud flew out on either side, there was a fine mist of rain which blew in their faces. Berry covered himself up.

In the lanes the high hedges shone black with rain. The silvery grey sky, faintly dappled, spread wide over the low, green land. The elder man glanced fiercely up the road, then turned his red face to his nephew.

'And how're you going on, lad?' he said loudly. Berry noticed that his uncle was slightly uneasy with him. It made him also uncomfortable. The elder man had evidently something pressing on his soul.

'Who are you living with in town?' asked the nephew. 'Have you gone back to Aunt Maud?'

'No,' barked the uncle. 'She wouldn't have me. I offered to – I want to – but she wouldn't.'

'You're alone, then?'

'No, I'm not alone.'

He turned and glared with his fierce blue eyes at his nephew, but said no more for some time. The car ran on through the mud, under the wet wall of the park.

'That other devil tried to poison me,' suddenly shouted the elder man. 'The one I went to Australia with.' At which, in spite of himself, the younger smiled in secret.

'How was that?' he asked.

'Wanted to get rid of me. She got in with another fellow on the ship . . . By Jove, I was bad.'

'Where? – on the ship?'

'No,' bellowed the other. 'No. That was in Wellington, New Zealand. I was bad, and got lower an' lower – couldn't think what was up. I could hardly crawl about. As certain as I'm here, she was poisoning me, to get to th' other chap – I'm certain of it.'

'And what did you do?'

'I cleared out – went to Sydney – '

'And left her?'

'Yes, I thought begod, I'd better clear out if I wanted to live.'

'And you were all right in Sydney?'

'Better in no time – I *know* she was putting poison in my coffee.'

'Hm!'

There was a glum silence. The driver stared at the road ahead, fixedly, managing the car as if it were a live thing. The nephew felt that his uncle was afraid, quite stupefied with fear, fear of life, of death, of himself.

'You're in rooms, then?' asked the nephew.

'No, I'm in a house of my own,' said the uncle defiantly, 'wi' th' best little woman in th' Midlands. She's a marvel. Why don't you come an' see us?'

'I will. Who is she?'

'Oh, she's a good girl – a beautiful little thing. I was clean gone on her first time I saw her. An' she was on me. Her mother lives with us – respectable girl, none o' your . . . '

'And how old is she?'

' – how old is she? – she's twenty-one.'

'Poor thing.'

'*She's* right enough.'

'You'd marry her – getting a divorce – ?'

'I shall marry her.'

There was a little antagonism between the two men.

'Where's Aunt Maud?' asked the younger.

'She's at the Railway Arms – we passed it, just against Rollin's Mill Crossing . . . They sent me a note this morning to go an' see her when I can spare time. She's got consumption.'

'Good Lord! Are you going?'

'Yes – '

But again Berry felt that his uncle was afraid.

The young man got through his commission in the village, had a drink with his uncle at the inn, and the two were returning home. The elder man's subject of conversation was Australia. As they drew near the town they grew silent, thinking both of the public-house. At last they saw the gates of the railway crossing were closed before them.

'Shan't you call?' asked Berry, jerking his head in the direction of the inn, which stood at the corner between two roads, its sign hanging under a bare horse-chestnut tree in front.

'I might as well. Come in an' have a drink,' said the uncle.

It had been raining all the morning, so shallow pools of water lay about. A brewer's wagon, with wet barrels and warm-smelling horses, stood near the door of the inn. Everywhere seemed silent, but for the rattle of trains at the crossing. The two men went uneasily up the steps and into the bar. The place was paddled with wet feet, empty.

As the barman was heard approaching, the uncle asked, his usual bluster slightly hushed by fear: 'What yer goin' ta have, lad? Same as last time?'

A man entered, evidently the proprietor. He was good-looking, with a long, heavy face and quick, dark eyes. His glance at Sutton was swift, a start, a recognition, and a withdrawal, into heavy neutrality.

'How are yer, Dan?' he said, scarcely troubling to speak.

'Are yer, George?' replied Sutton, hanging back. 'My nephew, Dan Berry. Give us Red Seal, George.'

The publican nodded to the younger man, and set the glasses on the bar. He pushed forward the two glasses, then leaned back in the dark corner behind the door, his arms folded, evidently preferring to get back from the watchful eyes of the nephew.

'—'s luck,' said Sutton.

The publican nodded in acknowledgement. Sutton and his nephew drank.

'Why the hell don't you get that road mended in Cinder Hill – ,' said Sutton fiercely, pushing back his driver's cap and showing his short-cut, bristling hair.

'They can't find it in their hearts to pull it up,' replied the publican, laconically.

'Find in their hearts! They want settin' in barrows an' runnin' up an' down it till they cried for mercy.'

Sutton put down his glass. The publican renewed it with a sure hand, at ease in whatsoever he did. Then he leaned back against the bar. He wore no coat. He stood with arms folded, his chin on his chest, his long moustache hanging. His back was round and slack, so that the lower part of his abdomen stuck forward, though he was not stout. His cheek was healthy, brown-red, and he was muscular. Yet there was about him this physical slackness, a reluctance in his slow, sure movements. His eyes were keen under his dark brows, but reluctant also, as if he were gloomily apathetic.

There was a halt. The publican evidently would say nothing. Berry looked at the mahogany bar-counter, slopped with beer, at the whisky-bottles on the shelves. Sutton, his cap pushed back, showing a white brow above a weather-reddened face, rubbed his cropped hair uneasily.

The publican glanced round suddenly. It seemed that only his dark eyes moved.

'Going up?' he asked.

And something, perhaps his eyes, indicated the unseen bedchamber.

'Ay – that's what I came for,' replied Sutton, shifting nervously from one foot to the other. 'She's been asking for me?'

'This morning,' replied the publican, neutral.

Then he put up a flap of the bar, and turned away through the dark doorway behind. Sutton, pulling off his cap, showing a round, short-cropped head which now was ducked forward, followed after him, the buttons holding the strap of his greatcoat behind glittering for a moment.

They climbed the dark stairs, the husband placing his feet carefully, because of his big boots. Then he followed down the passage, trying vaguely to keep a grip on his bowels, which seemed to be melting away, and definitely wishing for a neat brandy. The publican opened a door. Sutton, big and burly in his greatcoat, went past him.

The bedroom seemed light and warm after the passage. There was a red eiderdown on the bed. Then, making an effort, Sutton turned his eyes to see the sick woman. He met her eyes direct, dark, dilated. It was such a shock he almost started away. For a second he remained in torture, as if some invisible flame were playing on him to reduce his bones and fuse him down. Then he saw the sharp white edge of her jaw, and the black hair beside the hollow cheek. With a start he went towards the bed.

'Hello, Maud!' he said. 'Why, what ye been doin'?'

The publican stood at the window with his back to the bed. The husband, like one condemned but on the point of starting away, stood by the bedside staring in horror at his wife, whose dilated grey eyes, nearly all black now, watched him wearily, as if she were looking at something a long way off.

Going exceedingly pale, he jerked up his head and stared at the wall over the pillows. There was a little coloured picture of a bird perched on a bell, and a nest among ivy leaves beneath. It appealed to him, made him wonder, roused a feeling of childish magic in him. They were wonderfully fresh, green ivy leaves, and nobody had seen the nest among them save him.

Then suddenly he looked down again at the face on the bed, to try and recognise it. He knew the white brow and the beautiful clear eyebrows. That was his wife, with whom he had passed his youth, flesh of his flesh, his, himself. Then those tired eyes, which met his again from a long way off, disturbed him until he did not know where he was. Only the sunken cheeks, and the mouth that seemed to protrude now were foreign to him, and filled him with horror. It seemed he lost his identity. He was the young husband of the woman with the clear brows; he was the married man fighting with her whose eyes watched him, a little indifferently, from a long way off; and he was a child in horror of that protruding mouth.

There came the crackling sound of her voice. He knew she had consumption of the throat, and braced himself hard to bear the noise.

'What was it, Maud?' he asked in panic.

Then the broken, crackling voice came again. He was too terrified of the sound of it to hear what was said. There was a pause.

'You'll take Winnie?' the publican's voice interpreted from the window.

'Don't you bother, Maud, I'll take her,' he said, stupefying his mind so as not to understand.

He looked curiously round the room. It was not a bad bedroom, light and warm. There were many medicine bottles aggregated in a corner of the washstand – and a bottle of Three Star brandy, half full. And there were also photographs of strange people on the chest of drawers. It was not a bad room.

Again he started as if he were shot. She was speaking. He bent down, but did not look at her.

'Be good to her,' she whispered.

When he realised her meaning, that he should be good to their child when the mother was gone, a blade went through his flesh.

'I'll be good to her, Maud, don't you bother,' he said, beginning to feel shaky.

He looked again at the picture of the bird. It perched cheerfully under a blue sky, with robust, jolly ivy leaves near. He was gathering his courage to depart. He looked down, but struggled hard not to take in the sight of his wife's face.

'I s'll come again, Maud,' he said. 'I hope you'll go on all right. Is there anything as you want?'

There was an almost imperceptible shake of the head from the sick woman, making his heart melt swiftly again. Then, dragging his limbs, he got out of the room and down the stairs.

The landlord came after him.

'I'll let you know if anything happens,' the publican said, still laconic, but with his eyes dark and swift.

'Ay, a' right,' said Sutton blindly. He looked round for his cap, which he had all the time in his hand. Then he got out of doors.

In a moment the uncle and nephew were in the car jolting on the level crossing. The elder man seemed as if something tight in his brain made him open his eyes wide, and stare. He held the steering wheel firmly. He knew he could steer accurately, to a hair's breadth. Glaring fixedly ahead, he let the car go, till it bounded over the uneven road. There were three coal-carts in a string. In an instant the car grazed past them, almost biting the kerb on the other side. Sutton aimed his car like a projectile, staring ahead. He did not want to know, to think, to realise, he wanted to be only the driver of that quick taxi.

The town drew near, suddenly. There were allotment-gardens with dark-purple twiggy fruit-trees and wet alleys between the hedges. Then suddenly the streets of dwelling-houses whirled close, and the car was climbing the hill, with an angry whirr – up – up – till they rode out on to the crest and could see the tram-cars, dark-red and yellow, threading their way round the corner below, and all the traffic roaring between the shops.

'Got anywhere to go?' asked Sutton of his nephew.

'I was going to see one or two people.'

'Come an' have a bit o' dinner with us,' said the other.

Berry knew that his uncle wanted to be distracted, so that he should not think nor realise. The big man was running hard away from the horror of realisation.

'All right,' Berry agreed.

The car went quickly through the town. It ran up a long street nearly into the country again. Then it pulled up at a house that stood alone, below the road.

'I s'll be back in ten minutes,' said the uncle.

The car went on to the garage. Berry stood curiously at the top of the stone stairs that led from the high road down to the level of the house, an old stone place. The garden was dilapidated. Broken fruit-trees leaned at a sharp angle down the steep bank. Right across the dim grey atmosphere, in a kind of valley on the edge of the town, new suburb-patches showed pinkish on the dark earth. It was a kind of unresolved borderland.

Berry went down the steps. Through the broken black fence of the orchard, long grass showed yellow. The place seemed deserted. He knocked, then knocked again. An elderly woman appeared. She looked like a house-keeper. At first she said suspiciously that Mr Sutton was not in.

'My uncle just put me down. He'll be in in ten minutes,' replied the visitor.

'Oh, are you the Mr Berry who is related to him?' exclaimed the elderly woman. 'Come in – come in.'

She was at once kindly and a little bit servile. The young man entered. It was an old house, rather dark, and sparsely furnished. The elderly woman sat nervously on the edge of one of the chairs in a drawing-room that looked as if it were furnished from dismal relics of dismal homes, and there was a little straggling attempt at conversation. Mrs Greenwell was evidently a working-class woman unused to service or to any formality.

Presently she gathered up courage to invite her visitor into the dining-room. There from the table under the window rose a tall, slim girl with a cat in her arms. She was evidently a little more ladylike than was habitual to her, but she had a gentle, delicate, small nature. Her brown hair almost covered her ears, her dark lashes came down in shy awkwardness over her beautiful blue eyes. She shook hands in a frank way, yet she was shrinking. Evidently she was not sure how her position would affect her visitor. And yet she was assured in herself, shrinking and timid as she was.

'She must be a good deal in love with him,' thought Berry.

Both women glanced shamefacedly at the roughly laid table. Evidently they ate in a rather rough-and-ready fashion.

Elaine – she had this poetic name – fingered her cat timidly, not knowing what to say or to do, unable even to ask her visitor to sit down. He noticed how her skirt hung almost flat on her hips. She was young, scarce developed, a long, slender thing. Her colouring was warm and exquisite.

The elder woman bustled out to the kitchen. Berry fondled the terrier dogs that had come curiously to his heels, and glanced out of the window at the wet, deserted orchard.

This room, too, was not well furnished, and rather dark. But there was a big red fire.

'He always has fox terriers,' he said.

'Yes,' she answered, showing her teeth in a smile.

'Do you like them, too?'

'Yes' – she glanced down at the dogs. 'I like Tam better than Sally –'

Her speech always tailed off into an awkward silence.

'We've been to see Aunt Maud,' said the nephew.

Her eyes, blue and scared and shrinking, met his.

'Dan had a letter,' he explained. 'She's very bad.'

'Isn't it horrible!' she exclaimed, her face crumpling up with fear.

The old woman, evidently a hard-used, rather downtrodden workman's wife, came in with two soup-plates. She glanced anxiously to see how her daughter was progressing with the visitor.

'Mother, Dan's been to see Maud,' said Elaine, in a quiet voice full of fear and trouble.

The old woman looked up anxiously, in question.

'I think she wanted him to take the child. She's very bad, I believe,' explained Berry.

'Oh, we should take Winnie!' cried Elaine. But both women seemed uncertain, wavering in their position. Already Berry could see that his uncle had bullied them, as he bullied everybody. But they were used to unpleasant men, and seemed to keep at a distance.

'Will you have some soup?' asked the mother, humbly.

She evidently did the work. The daughter was to be a lady, more or less, always dressed and nice for when Sutton came in.

They heard him heavily running down the steps outside. The dogs got up. Elaine seemed to forget the visitor. It was as if she came into life. Yet she was nervous and afraid. The mother stood as if ready to exculpate herself.

Sutton burst open the door. Big, blustering, wet in his immense grey coat, he came into the dining-room.

'Hello!' he said to his nephew, 'making yourself at home?'

'Oh, yes,' replied Berry.

'Hello, Jack,' he said to the girl. 'Got owt to grizzle about?'

'What for?' she asked, in a clear, half-challenging voice that had that peculiar twang, almost petulant, so female and so attractive. Yet she was defiant like a boy.

'It's a wonder if you haven't,' growled Sutton. And, with a really intimate movement, he stooped down and fondled his dogs, though paying no attention to them. Then he stood up, and remained with feet apart on the hearthrug, his head ducked forward, watching the girl. He seemed abstracted, as if he could only watch her. His greatcoat hung open, so that she could see his figure, simple and human in the great husk of cloth. She stood nervously with her hands behind her, glancing at him, unable to see anything else. And he was scarcely conscious but of her. His eyes were still strained and staring, and as they followed the girl, when, long-limbed and languid, she moved away, it was as if he saw in her something impersonal, the female, not the woman.

'Had your dinner?' he asked.

'We were just going to have it,' she replied, with the same curious little vibration in her voice, like the twang of a string.

The mother entered, bringing a saucepan from which she ladled soup into three plates.

'Sit down, lad,' said Sutton. 'You sit down, Jack, an' give me mine here.'

'Oh, aren't you coming to table?' she complained.

'No, I tell you,' he snarled, almost pretending to be disagreeable. But she was slightly afraid even of the pretence, which pleased and relieved him. He stood on the hearthrug eating his soup noisily.

'Aren't you going to take your coat off?' she said. 'It's filling the place full of steam.'

He did not answer, but, with his head bent forward over the plate, he ate his soup hastily, to get it done with. When he put down his empty plate, she rose and went to him.

'Do take your coat off, Dan,' she said, and she took hold of the breast of his coat, trying to push it back over his shoulder. But she could not. Only the stare in his eyes changed to a glare as her hand moved over his shoulder. He looked down into her eyes. She became pale, rather frightened-looking, and she turned her face away, and it was drawn slightly with love and fear and misery. She tried again to put off his coat, her thin wrists pulling at it. He stood solidly planted, and did not look at her, but stared straight in front. She was playing with passion, afraid of it, and really wretched because it left her, the person, out of count. Yet she continued. And there came into his bearing, into his eyes, the curious smile of passion, pushing away even the death-horror. It was life stronger than death in him. She stood close to his breast. Their eyes met, and she was carried away.

'Take your coat off, Dan,' she said coaxingly, in a low tone meant for no one but him. And she slid her hands on his shoulder, and he yielded, so that the coat was pushed back. She had flushed, and her eyes had grown very bright. She got hold of the cuff of his coat. Gently, he eased himself, so that she drew it off. Then he stood in a thin suit, which revealed his vigorous, almost mature form.

'What a weight!' she exclaimed, in a peculiar penetrating voice, as she went out hugging the overcoat. In a moment she came back.

He stood still in the same position, a frown over his fiercely staring eyes. The pain, the fear, the horror in his breast were all burning away in the new, fiercest flame of passion.

'Get your dinner,' he said roughly to her.

'I've had all I want,' she said. 'You come an' have yours.'

He looked at the table as if he found it difficult to see things.

'I want no more,' he said.

She stood close to his chest. She wanted to touch him and to comfort him. There was something about him now that fascinated her. Berry felt slightly ashamed that she seemed to ignore the presence of others in the room.

The mother came in. She glanced at Sutton, standing planted on the hearthrug, his head ducked, the heavy frown hiding his eyes. There was a peculiar braced intensity about him that made the elder woman afraid. Suddenly he jerked his head round to his nephew.

'Get on wi' your dinner, lad,' he said, and he went to the door. The dogs, which had continually lain down and got up again, uneasy, now rose and watched. The girl went after him, saying, clearly: 'What did you want, Dan?'

Her slim, quick figure was gone, the door was closed behind her.

There was silence. The mother, still more slave-like in her movement, sat down in a low chair. Berry drank some beer.

'That girl will leave him,' he said to himself. 'She'll hate him like poison. And serve him right. Then she'll go off with somebody else.'

And she did.

The Thorn in the Flesh

I

A wind was running, so that occasionally the poplars whitened as if a flame flew up them. The sky was broken and blue among moving clouds. Patches of sunshine lay on the level fields, and shadows on the rye and the vineyards. In the distance, very blue, the cathedral bristled against the sky, and the houses of the city of Metz clustered vaguely below, like a hill.

Among the fields by the lime trees stood the barracks, upon bare, dry ground, a collection of round-roofed huts of corrugated iron, where the soldiers' nasturtiums climbed brilliantly. There was a tract of vegetable garden at the side, with the soldiers' yellowish lettuces in rows, and at the back the big, hard drilling-yard surrounded by a wire fence.

At this time in the afternoon, the huts were deserted, all the beds pushed up, the soldiers were lounging about under the lime trees waiting for the call to drill. Bachmann sat on a bench in the shade that smelled sickly with blossom. Pale green, wrecked lime flowers were scattered on the ground. He was writing his weekly postcard to his mother. He was a fair, long, limber youth, good looking. He sat very still indeed, trying to write his postcard. His blue uniform, sagging on him as he sat bent over the card, disfigured his youthful shape. His sunburnt hand waited motionless for the words to come. 'Dear mother' – was all he had written. Then he scribbled mechanically: 'Many thanks for your letter with what you sent. Everything is all right with me. We are just off to drill on the fortifications – ' Here he broke off and sat suspended, oblivious of everything, held in some definite suspense. He looked again at the card. But he could write no more. Out of the knot of his consciousness no word would come. He signed himself, and looked up, as a man looks to see if anyone has noticed him in his privacy.

There was a self-conscious strain in his blue eyes, and a pallor about his mouth, where the young, fair moustache glistened. He was almost girlish in his good looks and his grace. But he had something of military consciousness, as if he believed in the discipline for himself, and found satisfaction in delivering himself to his duty. There was also a trace of youthful swagger and dare-devilry about his mouth and his limber body, but this was in suppression now.

He put the postcard in the pocket of his tunic, and went to join a group of his comrades who were lounging in the shade, laughing and talking grossly. Today he was out of it. He only stood near to them for the warmth of the association. In his own consciousness something held him down.

Presently they were summoned to ranks. The sergeant came out to take command. He was a strongly built, rather heavy man of forty. His head was thrust forward, sunk a little between his powerful shoulders, and the strong jaw was pushed out aggressively. But the eyes were smouldering, the face hung slack and sodden with drink.

He gave his orders in brutal, barking shouts, and the little company moved forward, out of the wire-fenced yard to the open road, marching rhythmically, raising the dust. Bachmann, one of the inner file of four deep, marched in the airless ranks, half suffocated with heat and dust and enclosure. Through the moving of his comrades' bodies, he could see the small vines dusty by the roadside, the poppies among the tares fluttering and blown to pieces, the distant spaces of sky and fields all free with air and sunshine. But he was bound in a very dark enclosure of anxiety within himself.

He marched with his usual ease, being healthy and well adjusted. But his body went on by itself. His spirit was clenched apart. And ever the few soldiers drew nearer and nearer to the town, ever the consciousness of the youth became more gripped and separate, his body worked by a kind of mechanical intelligence, a mere presence of mind.

They diverged from the high road and passed in single file down a path among trees. All was silent and green and mysterious, with shadow of foliage and long, green, undisturbed grass. Then they came out in the sunshine on a moat of water, which wound silently between the long, flowery grass, at the foot of the earthworks, that rose in front in terraces walled smooth on the face, but all soft with long grass at the top. Marguerite daisies and lady's-slipper glimmered white and gold in the lush grass, preserved here in the intense peace of the fortifications. Thickets of trees stood round about. Occasionally a puff of mysterious wind made the flowers and the long grass that crested the earthworks above bow and shake as with signals of oncoming alarm.

The group of soldiers stood at the end of the moat, in their light blue and scarlet uniforms, very bright. The sergeant was giving them instructions, and his shout came sharp and alarming in the intense, untouched stillness of the place. They listened, finding it difficult to make the effort of under-standing.

Then it was over, and the men were moving to make preparations. On the other side of the moat the ramparts rose smooth and clear in the sun, sloping slightly back. Along the summit grass grew and tall daisies stood ledged high, like magic, against the dark green of the tree-tops behind. The noise of the town, the running of tram-cars, was heard distinctly, but it seemed not to penetrate this still place.

The water of the moat was motionless. In silence the practice began. One of the soldiers took a scaling ladder, and passing along the narrow ledge at the foot of the earthworks, with the water of the moat just behind him, tried to get a fixture on the slightly sloping wall-face. There he stood, small and isolated, at the foot of the wall, trying to get his ladder settled. At last it held, and the clumsy, groping figure in the baggy blue uniform began to clamber up. The rest of the soldiers stood and watched. Occasionally the sergeant barked a command. Slowly the clumsy blue figure clambered higher up the wall-face. Bachmann stood with his bowels turned to water. The figure of the climbing soldier scrambled out on to the terrace up above, and moved, blue and distinct, among the bright green grass. The officer shouted from below. The soldier tramped along, fixed the ladder in another spot, and carefully lowered himself on to the rungs. Bachmann watched the blind foot groping in space for the ladder, and he felt the world fall away beneath him. The figure of the soldier clung cringing against the face of the wall, cleaving, groping downwards like some unsure insect working its way lower and lower, fearing every movement. At last, sweating and with a strained face, the figure had landed safely and turned to the group of soldiers. But still it had a stiffness and a blank, mechanical look, was something less than human.

Bachmann stood there heavy and condemned, waiting for his own turn and betrayal. Some of the men went up easily enough, and without fear. That only showed it could be done lightly, and made Bachmann's case more bitter. If only he could do it lightly, like that.

His turn came. He knew intuitively that nobody knew his condition. The officer just saw him as a mechanical thing. He tried to keep it up, to carry it through on the face of things. His inside gripped tight, as yet under control, he took the ladder and went along under the wall. He placed his ladder with quick success, and wild, quivering hope possessed him. Then blindly he began to climb. But the ladder was not very firm, and at every hitch a great, sick, melting feeling took hold of him. He clung on fast. If only he could keep that grip on himself, he would get through. He knew this, in agony. What he could not understand was the blind gush of white-hot fear, that came with great force whenever the ladder swerved, and which almost melted his belly and all his joints, and left him powerless. If once it melted all his joints and his belly, he was done. He clung desperately to himself. He knew the fear, he knew what it did when it came, he knew he had only to keep a firm hold. He knew all this. Yet, when the ladder swerved, and his foot missed, there was the great blast of fear blowing on his heart and bowels, and he was melting weaker and weaker, in a horror of fear and lack of control, melting to fall.

Yet he groped slowly higher and higher, always staring upwards with desperate face, and always conscious of the space below. But all of him, body and soul, was growing hot to fusion point. He would have to let go for very relief's sake. Suddenly his heart began to lurch. It gave a great, sickly swoop, rose, and again plunged in a swoop of horror. He lay against the wall inert as if dead, inert, at peace, save for one deep core of anxiety, which knew that it was *not* all over, that he was still high in space against the wall. But the chief effort of will was gone.

There came into his consciousness a small, foreign sensation. He woke up a little. What was it? Then slowly it penetrated him. His water had run down his leg. He lay there, clinging, still with shame, half conscious of the echo of the sergeant's voice thundering from below. He waited, in depths of shame beginning to recover himself. He had been shamed so deeply. Then he could go on, for his fear for himself was conquered. His shame was known and published. He must go on.

Slowly he began to grope for the rung above, when a great shock shook through him. His wrists were grasped from above, he was being hauled out of himself up, up to the safe ground. Like a sack he was dragged over the edge of the earthworks by the large hands, and landed there on his knees, grovelling in the grass to recover command of himself, to rise up on his feet.

Shame, blind, deep shame and ignominy overthrew his spirit and left it writhing. He stood there shrunk over himself, trying to obliterate himself.

Then the presence of the officer who had hauled him up made itself felt upon him. He heard the panting of the elder man, and then the voice came down on his veins like a fierce whip. He shrank in tension of shame.

'Put up your head – eyes front,' shouted the enraged sergeant, and mechanically the soldier obeyed the command, forced to look into the eyes of the sergeant. The brutal, hanging face of the officer violated the youth. He hardened himself with all his might from seeing it. The tearing noise of the sergeant's voice continued to lacerate his body.

Suddenly he set back his head, rigid, and his heart leapt to burst. The face had suddenly thrust itself close, all distorted and showing the teeth, the eyes smouldering into him. The breath of the barking words was on his nose and mouth. He stepped aside in revulsion. With a scream the face was upon him again. He raised his arm, involuntarily, in self-defence. A shock of horror went through him, as he felt his forearm hit the face of the officer a brutal blow. The latter staggered, swerved back, and with a curious cry, reeled backwards over the ramparts, his hands clutching the air. There was a second of silence, then a crash to water.

Bachmann, rigid, looked out of his inner silence upon the scene. Soldiers were running.

'You'd better clear,' said one young, excited voice to him. And with immediate instinctive decision he started to walk away from the spot. He went down the tree-hidden path to the high road where the trams ran to and from the town. In his heart was a sense of vindication, of escape. He was leaving it all, the military world, the shame. He was walking away from it.

Officers on horseback rode sauntering down the street, soldiers passed along the pavement. Coming to the bridge, Bachmann crossed over to the town that heaped before him, rising from the flat, picturesque French houses down below at the water's edge, up a jumble of roofs and chasms of streets, to the lovely dark cathedral with its myriad pinnacles making points at the sky.

He felt for the moment quite at peace, relieved from a great strain. So he turned along by the river to the public gardens. Beautiful were the heaped, purple lilac trees upon the green grass, and wonderful the walls of the horse-chestnut trees, lighted like an altar with white flowers on every ledge. Officers went by, elegant and all coloured, women and girls sauntered in the chequered shade. Beautiful it was, he walked in a vision, free.

2

But where was he going? He began to come out of his trance of delight and liberty. Deep within him he felt the steady burning of shame in the flesh. As yet he could not bear to think of it. But there it was, submerged beneath his attention, the raw, steady-burning shame.

It behoved him to be intelligent. As yet he dared not remember what he had done. He only knew the need to get away, away from everything he had been in contact with.

But how? A great pang of fear went through him. He could not bear his shamed flesh to be put again between the hands of authority. Already the hands had been laid upon him, brutally upon his nakedness, ripping open his shame and making him maimed, crippled in his own control.

Fear became an anguish. Almost blindly he was turning in the direction of the barracks. He could not take the responsibility of himself. He must give himself up to someone. Then his heart, obstinate in hope, became obsessed with the idea of his sweetheart. He would make himself her responsibility.

Blenching as he took courage, he mounted the small, quick-hurrying tram that ran out of the town in the direction of the barracks. He sat motionless and composed, static.

He got out at the terminus and went down the road. A wind was still running. He could hear the faint whisper of the rye, and the stronger swish as a sudden gust was upon it. No one was about. Feeling detached and impersonal, he went down a field-path between the low vines. Many little vine trees rose up in spires, holding out tender pink shoots, waving their tendrils. He saw them distinctly and wondered over them. In a field a little way off, men and women were taking up the hay. The bullock-waggon stood by on the path, the men in their blue shirts, the women with white cloths over their heads carried hay in their arms to the cart, all brilliant and distinct upon the shorn, glowing green acres. He felt himself looking out of darkness on to the glamorous, brilliant beauty of the world around him, outside him.

The baron's house, where Emilie was maidservant, stood square and mellow among trees and garden and fields. It was an old French grange. The barracks was quite near. Bachmann walked, drawn by a single purpose, towards the courtyard. He entered the spacious, shadowy, sun-swept place. The dog, seeing a soldier, only jumped and whined for greeting. The pump stood peacefully in a corner, under a lime tree, in the shade.

The kitchen door was open. He hesitated, then walked in, speaking shyly and smiling involuntarily. The two women started, but with pleasure. Emilie was preparing the tray for afternoon coffee. She stood beyond the table, drawn up, startled, and challenging, and glad. She had the proud, timid eyes of some wild animal, some proud animal. Her black hair was closely banded, her grey eyes watched steadily. She wore a peasant dress of blue cotton sprigged with little red roses, that buttoned tight over her strong maiden breasts.

At the table sat another young woman, the nursery governess, who was picking cherries from a huge heap, and dropping them into a bowl. She was young, pretty, freckled.

'Good day!' she said pleasantly. 'The unexpected.'

Emilie did not speak. The flush came in her dark cheek. She still stood watching, between fear and a desire to escape, and on the other hand joy that kept her in his presence.

'Yes,' he said, bashful and strained, while the eyes of the two women were upon him. 'I've got myself in a mess this time.'

'What?' asked the nursery governess, dropping her hands in her lap. Emilie stood rigid.

Bachmann could not raise his head. He looked sideways at the glistening, ruddy cherries. He could not recover the normal world.

'I knocked Sergeant Huber over the fortifications down into the moat,' he said. 'It was an accident – but – '

And he grasped at the cherries, and began to eat them, unknowing, hearing only Emilie's little exclamation.

'You knocked him over the fortifications!' echoed Fräulein Hesse in horror. 'How?'

Spitting the cherry-stones into his hand, mechanically, absorbedly, he told them.

'Ach!' exclaimed Emilie sharply.

'And how did you get here?' asked Fräulein Hesse.

'I ran off,' he said.

There was a dead silence. He stood, putting himself at the mercy of the women. There came a hissing from the stove, and a stronger smell of coffee. Emilie turned swiftly away. He saw her flat, straight back and her strong loins, as she bent over the stove.

'But what are you going to do?' said Fräulein Hesse, aghast.

'I don't know,' he said, grasping at more cherries. He had come to an end.

'You'd better go to the barracks,' she said. 'We'll get the Herr baron to come and see about it.'

Emilie was swiftly and quietly preparing the tray. She picked it up, and stood with the glittering china and silver before her, impassive, waiting for his reply. Bachmann remained with his head dropped, pale and obstinate. He could not bear to go back.

'I'm going to try to get into France,' he said.

'Yes, but they'll catch you,' said Fräulein Hesse.

Emilie watched with steady, watchful grey eyes.

'I can have a try, if I could hide till tonight,' he said.

Both women knew what he wanted. And they all knew it was no good. Emilie picked up the tray, and went out. Bachmann stood with his head dropped. Within himself he felt the dross of shame and incapacity.

'You'd never get away,' said the governess.

'I can try,' he said.

Today he could not put himself between the hands of the military. Let them do as they liked with him tomorrow, if he escaped today.

They were silent. He ate cherries. The colour flushed bright into the cheek of the young governess.

Emilie returned to prepare another tray

'He could hide in your room,' the governess said to her.

The girl drew herself away. She could not bear the intrusion.

'That is all I can think of that is safe from the children,' said Fräulein Hesse.

Emilie gave no answer. Bachmann stood waiting for the two women. Emilie did not want the close contact with him.

'You could sleep with me,' Fräulein Hesse said to her.

Emilie lifted her eyes and looked at the young man, direct, clear, reserving herself.

'Do you want that?' she asked, her strong virginity proof against him.

'Yes – yes – ' he said uncertainly, destroyed by shame.

She put back her head.

'Yes,' she murmured to herself.

Quickly she filled the tray, and went out.

'But you can't walk over the frontier in a night,' said Fräulein Hesse.

'I can cycle,' he said.

Emilie returned, a restraint, a neutrality, in her bearing.

'I'll see if it's all right,' said the governess.

In a moment or two Bachmann was following Emilie through the square hall, where hung large maps on the walls. He noticed a child's blue coat with brass buttons on the peg, and it reminded him of Emilie walking holding the hand of the youngest child, whilst he watched, sitting under the lime tree. Already this was a long way off. That was a sort of freedom he had lost, changed for a new, immediate anxiety.

They went quickly, fearfully up the stairs and down a long corridor. Emilie opened her door, and he entered, ashamed, into her room.

'I must go down,' she murmured, and she departed, closing the door softly.

It was a small, bare, neat room. There was a little dish for holy-water, a picture of the Sacred Heart, a crucifix, and a prie-Dieu. The small bed lay white and untouched, the wash-hand bowl of red earth stood on a bare table, there was a little mirror and a small chest of drawers. That was all.

Feeling safe, in sanctuary, he went to the window, looking over the courtyard at the shimmering, afternoon country. He was going to leave this land, this life. Already he was in the unknown.

He drew away into the room. The curious simplicity and severity of the little Roman Catholic bedroom was foreign but restoring to him. He looked at the crucifix. It was a long, lean, peasant Christ carved by a peasant in the Black Forest. For the first time in his life, Bachmann saw the figure as a human thing. It represented a man hanging there in helpless torture. He stared at it, closely, as if for new knowledge.

Within his own flesh burned and smouldered the restless shame. He could not gather himself together. There was a gap in his soul. The shame within him seemed to displace his strength and his manhood.

He sat down on his chair. The shame, the roused feeling of exposure acted on his brain, made him heavy, unutterably heavy.

Mechanically, his wits all gone, he took off his boots, his belt, his tunic, put them aside, and lay down, heavy, and fell into a kind of drugged sleep.

Emilie came in a little while, and looked at him. But he was sunk in sleep. She saw him lying there inert, and terribly still, and she was afraid. His shirt was unfastened at the throat. She saw his pure white flesh, very clean and beautiful. And he slept inert. His legs, in the blue uniform trousers, his feet in the coarse stockings, lay foreign on her bed. She went away.

3

She was uneasy, perturbed to her last fibre. She wanted to remain clear, with no touch on her. A wild instinct made her shrink away from any hands which might be laid on her.

She was a foundling, probably of some gypsy race, brought up in a Roman Catholic Rescue Home. A naïve, paganly religious being, she was attached to the baroness, with whom she had served for seven years, since she was fourteen.

She came into contact with no one, unless it were with Ida Hesse, the governess. Ida was a calculating, good-natured, not very straightforward flirt. She was the daughter of a poor country doctor. Having gradually come into connection with Emilie, more an alliance than an attachment, she put no distinction of grade between the two of them. They worked together, sang together, walked together, and went together to the rooms of Franz Brand, Ida's sweetheart. There the three talked and laughed together, or the women listened to Franz, who was a forester, playing on his violin.

In all this alliance there was no personal intimacy between the young women. Emilie was naturally secluded in herself, of a reserved, native race. Ida used her as a kind of weight to balance her own flighty movement. But the quick, shifty governess, occupied always in her dealings with admirers, did all she could to move the violent nature of Emilie towards some connection with men.

But the dark girl, primitive yet sensitive to a high degree, was fiercely virgin. Her blood flamed with rage when the common soldiers made the long, sucking, kissing noise behind her as she passed. She hated them for their almost jeering offers. She was well protected by the baroness.

And her contempt of the common men in general was ineffable. But she loved the baroness, and she revered the baron, and she was at her ease when she was doing something for the service of a gentleman. Her whole nature was at peace in the service of real masters or mistresses. For her, a gentleman had some mystic quality that left her free and proud in service. The common soldiers were brutes, merely nothing. Her desire was to serve.

She held herself aloof. When, on Sunday afternoon, she had looked through the windows of the Reichshalle in passing, and had seen the soldiers dancing with the common girls, a cold revulsion and anger had possessed her. She could not bear to see the soldiers taking off their belts and pulling open their tunics, dancing with their shirts showing through the open, sagging tunic, their movements gross, their faces transfigured and sweaty, their coarse hands holding their coarse girls under the armpits, drawing the female up to their breasts. She hated to see them clutched breast to breast, the legs of the men moving grossly in the dance.

At evening, when she had been in the garden, and heard on the other side of the hedge the sexual inarticulate cries of the girls in the embraces of the soldiers, her anger had been too much for her, and she had cried, loud and cold: 'What are you doing there, in the hedge?'

She would have had them whipped.

But Bachmann was not quite a common soldier. Fräulein Hesse had found out about him, and had drawn him and Emilie together. For he was a handsome, blond youth, erect and walking with a kind of pride, unconscious yet clear. Moreover, he came of a rich farming stock, rich for many generations. His father was dead, his mother controlled the moneys for the time being. But if Bachmann wanted a hundred pounds at any moment, he could have them. By trade he, with one of his brothers, was a waggon-builder. The family had the farming, smithy, and waggon-building of their village. They worked because that was the form of life they knew. If they had chosen, they could have lived independent upon their means.

In this way, he was a gentleman in sensibility, though his intellect was not developed. He could afford to pay freely for things. He had, moreover, his native, fine breeding. Emilie wavered uncertainly before him. So he became her sweetheart, and she hungered after him. But she was virgin, and shy, and needed to be in subjection, because she was primitive and had no grasp on civilised forms of living, nor on civilised purposes.

4

At six o'clock came the enquiry of the soldiers: Had anything been seen of Bachmann?

Fräulein Hesse answered, pleased to be playing a role: 'No, I've not seen him since Sunday – have you, Emilie?'

'No, I haven't seen him,' said Emilie, and her awkwardness was construed as bashfulness.

Ida Hesse, stimulated, asked questions, and played her part. 'But it hasn't killed Sergeant Huber?' she cried in consternation.

'No. He fell into the water. But it gave him a bad shock, and smashed his foot on the side of the moat. He's in hospital. It's a bad lookout for Bachmann.'

Emilie, implicated and captive, stood looking on. She was no longer free, working with all this regulated system which she could not understand and which was almost god-like to her. She was put out of her place. Bachmann was in her room, she was no longer the faithful in service serving with religious surety.

Her situation was intolerable to her. All evening long the burden was upon her, she could not live. The children must be fed and put to sleep. The baron and baroness were going out, she must give them light refreshment. The manservant was coming in to supper after returning with the carriage. And all the while she had the insupportable feeling of being out of the order, self-responsible, bewildered. The control of her life should come from those above her, and she should move within that control. But now she was out of it, uncontrolled and troubled. More than that, the man, the lover, Bachmann, who was he, what was he? He alone of all men contained for her the unknown quantity which terrified her beyond her service. Oh, she had wanted him as a distant sweetheart, not close, like this, casting her out of her world.

When the baron and baroness had departed, and the young manservant had gone out to enjoy himself, she went upstairs to Bachmann. He had wakened up, and sat dimly in the room. Out in the open he heard the soldiers, his comrades, singing the sentimental songs of the nightfall, the drone of the concertina rising in accompaniment.

'Wenn ich zu mei . . . nem Kinde geh' . . .
In seinem Au . . . g die Mutter seh'. . . .'

But he himself was removed from it now. Only the sentimental cry of young, unsatisfied desire in the soldiers' singing penetrated his blood and stirred him subtly. He let his head hang; he had become gradually roused: and he waited in concentration, in another world.

The moment she entered the room where the man sat alone, waiting intensely, the thrill passed through her, she died in terror, and after the death, a great flame gushed up, obliterating her. He sat in trousers and shirt on the side of the bed. He looked up as she came in, and she shrank from his face. She could not bear it. Yet she entered near to him.

'Do you want anything to eat?' she said.

'Yes,' he answered, and as she stood in the twilight of the room with him, he could only hear his heart beat heavily. He saw her apron just level with his face. She stood silent, a little distance off, as if she would be there for ever. He suffered.

As if in a spell she waited, standing motionless and looming there, he sat rather crouching on the side of the bed. A second will in him was powerful and dominating. She drew gradually nearer to him, coming up slowly, as if unconscious. His heart beat up swiftly. He was going to move.

As she came quite close, almost invisibly he lifted his arms and put them round her waist, drawing her with his will and desire. He buried his face into her apron, into the terrible softness of her belly. And he was a flame of passion intense about her. He had forgotten. Shame and memory were gone in a whole, furious flame of passion.

She was quite helpless. Her hands leapt, fluttered, and closed over his head, pressing it deeper into her belly, vibrating as she did so. And his arms tightened on her, his hands spread over her loins, warm as flame on her loveliness. It was intense anguish of bliss for her, and she lost consciousness.

When she recovered, she lay translated in the peace of satisfaction.

It was what she had had no inkling of, never known could be. She was strong with eternal gratitude. And he was there with her. Instinctively with an instinct of reverence and gratitude, her arms tightened in a little embrace upon him who held her thoroughly embraced.

And he was restored and completed, close to her. That little, twitching, momentary clasp of acknowledgment that she gave him in her satisfaction, roused his pride unconquerable. They loved each other, and all was whole. She loved him, he had taken her, she was given to him. It was right. He was given to her, and they were one, complete.

Warm, with a glow in their hearts and faces, they rose again, modest, but transfigured with happiness.

'I will get you something to eat,' she said, and in joy and security of service again, she left him, making a curious little homage of departure. He sat on the side of the bed, escaped, liberated, wondering and happy.

5

Soon she came again with the tray, followed by Fräulein Hesse. The two women watched him eat, watched the pride and wonder of his being, as he sat there blond and naïf again. Emilie felt rich and complete. Ida was a lesser thing than herself.

'And what are you going to do?' asked Fräulein Hesse, jealous.

'I must get away,' he said.

But words had no meaning for him. What did it matter? He had the inner satisfaction and liberty.

'But you'll want a bicycle,' said Ida Hesse.

'Yes,' he said.

Emilie sat silent, removed and yet with him, connected with him in passion. She looked from this talk of bicycles and escape.

They discussed plans. But in two of them was the one will, that Bachmann should stay with Emilie. Ida Hesse was an outsider.

It was arranged, however, that Ida's lover should put out his bicycle, leave it at the hut where he sometimes watched. Bachmann should fetch it in the night, and ride into France. The hearts of all three beat hot in suspense, driven to thought. They sat in a fire of agitation.

Then Bachmann would get away to America, and Emilie would come and join him. They would be in a fine land then. The tale burned up again.

Emilie and Ida had to go round to Franz Brand's lodging. They departed with slight leave-taking. Bachmann sat in the dark, hearing the bugle for retreat sound out of the night. Then he remembered his postcard to his mother. He slipped out after Emilie, gave it her to post. His manner was careless and victorious, hers shining and trustful. He slipped back to shelter.

There he sat on the side of the bed, thinking. Again he went over the events of the afternoon, remembering his own anguish of apprehension because he had known he could not climb the wall without fainting with fear. Still, a flush of shame came alight in him at the memory. But he said to himself: 'What does it matter? – I can't help it, well then I can't. If I go up a height, I get absolutely weak, and can't help myself.' Again memory came over him, and a gush of shame, like fire. But he sat and endured it. It had to be endured, admitted, and accepted. 'I'm not a coward, for all that,' he continued. 'I'm not afraid of danger. If I'm made that way, that heights melt me and make me let go my water' – it was torture for him to pluck at this truth – 'if I'm made like that, I shall have to abide by it, that's all. It isn't all of me.' He thought of Emilie, and was satisfied. 'What I am, I am; and let it be enough,' he thought.

Having accepted his own defect, he sat thinking, waiting for Emilie, to tell her. She came at length, saying that Franz could not arrange about his bicycle this night. It was broken. Bachmann would have to stay over another day.

They were both happy. Emilie, confused before Ida, who was excited and prurient, came again to the young man. She was stiff and dignified with an agony of unusedness. But he took her between his hands, and uncovered her, and enjoyed almost like madness her helpless, virgin body that suffered so strongly, and that took its joy so deeply. While the moisture of torment and modesty was still in her eyes, she clasped him closer, and closer, to the victory and the deep satisfaction of both of them. And they slept together, he in repose still satisfied and peaceful, and she lying close in her static reality.

6

In the morning, when the bugle sounded from the barracks they rose and looked out of the window. She loved his body that was proud and blond and able to take command. And he loved her body that was soft and eternal. They looked at the faint grey vapour of summer steaming off from the greenness and ripeness of the fields. There was no town anywhere, their look ended in the haze of the summer morning. Their bodies rested together, their minds tranquil. Then a little anxiety stirred in both of them from the sound of the bugle. She was called back to her old position, to realise the world of authority she did not understand but had wanted to serve. But this call died away again from her. She had all.

She went downstairs to her work, curiously changed. She was in a new world of her own, that she had never even imagined, and which was the land of promise for all that. In this she moved and had her being. And she extended it to her duties. She was curiously happy and absorbed. She had not to strive out of herself to do her work. The doing came from within her without call or command. It was a delicious outflow, like sunshine, the activity that flowed from her and put her tasks to rights.

Bachmann sat busily thinking. He would have to get all his plans ready. He must write to his mother, and she must send him money to Paris. He would go to Paris, and from thence, quickly, to America. It had to be done. He must make all preparations. The dangerous part was the getting into France. He thrilled in anticipation. During the day he would need a time-table of the trains going to Paris – he would need to think. It gave him delicious pleasure, using all his wits. It seemed such an adventure.

This one day, and he would escape then into freedom. What an agony of need he had for absolute, imperious freedom. He had won to his own being, in himself and Emilie, he had drawn the stigma from his shame, he was beginning to be himself. And now he wanted madly to be free to go on. A home, his work, and absolute freedom to move and to be, in her, with her, this was his passionate desire. He thought in a kind of ecstasy, living an hour of painful intensity.

Suddenly he heard voices, and a tramping of feet. His heart gave a great leap, then went still. He was taken. He had known all along. A complete silence filled his body and soul, a silence like death, a suspension of life and sound. He stood motionless in the bedroom, in perfect suspension.

Emilie was busy passing swiftly about the kitchen preparing the children's breakfasts when she heard the tramp of feet and the voice of the baron. The latter had come in from the garden, and was wearing an old green linen suit. He was a man of middle stature, quick, finely made, and of whimsical charm. His right hand had been shot in the Franco–Prussian War, and now, as always when he was much agitated, he shook it down at his side, as if it hurt. He was talking rapidly to a young, stiff Oberleutnant. Two private soldiers stood bearishly in the doorway.

Emilie, shocked out of herself, stood pale and erect, recoiling.

'Yes, if you think so, we can look,' the baron was hastily and irascibly saying.

'Emilie,' he said, turning to the girl, 'did you put a postcard to the mother of this Bachmann in the box last evening?'

Emilie stood erect and did not answer.

'Yes?' said the baron sharply.

'Yes, Herr baron,' replied Emilie, neutral.

The baron's wounded hand shook rapidly in exasperation. The lieutenant drew himself up still more stiffly. He was right.

'And do you know anything of the fellow?' asked the baron, looking at her with his blazing, greyish-golden eyes. The girl looked back at him steadily, dumb, but her whole soul naked before him. For two seconds he looked at her in silence. Then in silence, ashamed and furious, he turned away.

'Go up!' he said, with his fierce, peremptory command, to the young officer.

The lieutenant gave his order, in military cold confidence, to the soldiers. They all tramped across the hall. Emilie stood motionless, her life suspended.

The baron marched swiftly upstairs and down the corridor, the lieutenant and the common soldiers followed. The baron flung open the door of Emilie's room and looked at Bachmann, who stood watching, standing in shirt and trousers beside the bed, fronting the door. He was perfectly still. His eyes met the furious, blazing look of the baron. The latter shook his wounded hand, and then went still. He looked into the eyes of the soldier, steadily. He saw the same naked soul exposed, as if he looked really into the *man*. And the man was helpless, the more helpless for his singular nakedness.

'Ha!' he exclaimed impatiently, turning to the approaching lieutenant.

The latter appeared in the doorway. Quickly his eyes travelled over the bare-footed youth. He recognised him as his object. He gave the brief command to dress.

Bachmann turned round for his clothes. He was very still, silent in himself. He was in an abstract, motionless world. That the two gentlemen and the two soldiers stood watching him, he scarcely realised. They could not see him.

Soon he was ready. He stood at attention. But only the shell of his body was at attention. A curious silence, a blankness, like something eternal, possessed him. He remained true to himself.

The lieutenant gave the order to march. The little procession went down the stairs with careful, respectful tread, and passed through the hall to the kitchen. There Emilie stood with her face uplifted, motionless and expressionless. Bachmann did not look at her. They knew each other. They were themselves. Then the little file of men passed out into the courtyard.

The baron stood in the doorway watching the four figures in uniform pass through the chequered shadow under the lime trees. Bachmann was walking neutralised, as if he were not there. The lieutenant went brittle and long, the two soldiers lumbered beside. They passed out into the sunny morning, growing smaller, going towards the barracks.

The baron turned into the kitchen. Emilie was cutting bread.

'So he stayed the night here?' he said.

The girl looked at him, scarcely seeing. She was too much herself. The baron saw the dark, naked soul of her body in her unseeing eyes.

'What were you going to do?' he asked.

'He was going to America,' she replied, in a still voice.

'Pah! You should have sent him straight back,' fired the baron.

Emilie stood at his bidding, untouched.

'He's done for now,' he said.

But he could not bear the dark, deep nakedness of her eyes, that scarcely changed under this suffering.

'Nothing but a fool,' he repeated, going away in agitation, and preparing himself for what he could do.

Daughters of the Vicar

I

Mr Lindley was first vicar of Aldecross. The cottages of this tiny hamlet had nestled in peace since their beginning, and the country folk had crossed the lanes and farmlands, two or three miles, to the parish church at Greymeed, on the bright Sunday mornings.

But when the pits were sunk, blank rows of dwellings started up beside the high roads, and a new population, skimmed from the floating scum of workmen, was filled in, the cottages and the country people almost obliterated.

To suit the convenience of these new collier-inhabitants, a church must be built at Aldecross. There was not too much money. And so the little building crouched like a humped stone-and-mortar mouse, with two little turrets at the west corners for ears, in the fields near the cottages and the apple trees, as far as possible from the dwellings down the high road. It had an uncertain, timid look about it. And so they planted big-leaved ivy, to hide its shrinking newness. So that now the little church stands buried in its greenery, stranded and sleeping among the fields, while the brick houses elbow nearer and nearer, threatening to crush it down. It is already obsolete.

The Reverend Ernest Lindley, aged twenty-seven, and newly married, came from his curacy in Suffolk to take charge of his church. He was just an ordinary young man, who had been to Cambridge and taken orders. His wife was a self-assured young woman, daughter of a Cambridgeshire rector. Her father had spent the whole of his thousand a year, so that Mrs Lindley had nothing of her own. Thus the young married people came to Aldecross to live on a stipend of about a hundred and twenty pounds, and to keep up a superior position.

They were not very well received by the new, raw, disaffected population of colliers. Being accustomed to farm labourers, Mr Lindley had considered himself as belonging indisputably to the upper or ordering classes. He had to be humble to the county families, but still, he was of their kind, whilst the common people were something different. He had no doubts of himself.

He found, however, that the collier population refused to accept this arrangement. They had no use for him in their lives, and they told him so, callously. The women merely said they were 'throng', or else, 'Oh, it's no good you coming here, we're Chapel.' The men were quite good-humoured so long as he did not touch them too nigh, they were cheerfully contemptuous of him, with a preconceived contempt he was powerless against.

At last, passing from indignation to silent resentment, even, if he dared have acknowledged it, to conscious hatred of the majority of his flock, and unconscious hatred of himself, he confined his activities to a narrow round of cottages, and he had to submit. He had no particular character, having always depended on his position in society to give him position among men. Now he was so poor, he had no social standing even among the common vulgar tradespeople of the district, and he had not the nature nor the wish to make his society agreeable to them, nor the strength to impose himself where he would have liked to be recognised. He dragged on, pale and miserable and neutral.

At first his wife raged with mortification. She took on airs and used a high hand. But her income was too small, the wrestling with tradesmen's bills was too pitiful, she only met with general, callous ridicule when she tried to be impressive.

Wounded to the quick of her pride, she found herself isolated in an indifferent, callous population. She raged indoors and out. But soon she learned that she must pay too heavily for her outdoor rages, and then she only raged within the walls of the rectory. There her feeling was so strong, that she frightened herself. She saw herself hating her husband, and she knew that, unless she were careful, she would smash her form of life and bring catastrophe upon him and upon herself. So in very fear, she went quiet. She hid, bitter and beaten by fear, behind the only shelter she had in the world, her gloomy, poor parsonage.

Children were born one every year; almost mechanically, she continued to perform her maternal duty, which was forced upon her. Gradually, broken by the suppressing of her violent anger and misery and disgust, she became an invalid and took to her couch.

The children grew up healthy, but unwarmed and rather rigid. Their father and mother educated them at home, made them very proud and very genteel, put them definitely and cruelly in the upper classes, apart from the vulgar around them. So they lived quite isolated. They were good-looking, and had that curiously clean, semi-transparent look of the genteel, isolated poor.

Gradually Mr and Mrs Lindley lost all hold on life, and spent their hours, weeks and years merely haggling to make ends meet, and bitterly repressing and pruning their children into gentility, urging them to ambition, weighting them with duty. On Sunday morning the whole family, except the mother, went down the lane to church, the long-legged girls in skimpy frocks, the boys in black coats and long, grey, unfitting trousers. They passed by their father's parishioners with mute, clear faces, childish mouths closed in pride that was like a doom to them, and childish eyes already unseeing. Miss Mary, the eldest, was the leader. She was a long, slim thing with a fine profile and a proud, pure look of submission to a high fate. Miss Louisa, the second, was short and plump and obstinate-looking. She had more enemies than ideals. She looked after the lesser children, Miss Mary after the elder. The collier children watched this pale, distinguished procession of the vicar's family pass mutely by, and they were impressed by the air of gentility and distance, they made mock of the trousers of the small sons, but they felt inferior in themselves, and hate stirred their hearts.

In her time, Miss Mary received as governess a few little daughters of tradesmen; Miss Louisa managed the house and went among her father's churchgoers, giving lessons on the piano to the colliers' daughters at thirteen shillings for twenty-six lessons.

2

One winter morning, when his daughter Mary was about twenty years old, Mr Lindley, a thin, unobtrusive figure in his black overcoat and his wide-awake, went down into Aldecross with a packet of white papers under his arm. He was delivering the parish almanacs.

A rather pale, neutral man of middle age, he waited while the train thumped over the level-crossing, going up to the pit which rattled busily just along the line. A wooden-legged man hobbled to open the gate, Mr Lindley passed on. Just at his left hand, below the road and the railway, was the red roof of a cottage, showing through the bare twigs of apple trees. Mr Lindley passed round the low wall, and descended the worn steps that led from the highway down to the cottage which crouched darkly and quietly away below the rumble of passing trains and the clank of coal-carts in a quiet little under-world of its own. Snowdrops with tight-shut buds were hanging very still under the bare currant bushes.

The clergyman was just going to knock when he heard a clinking noise, and turning saw through the open door of a black shed just behind him an elderly woman in a black lace cap stooping among reddish big cans, pouring a very bright liquid into a tundish. There was a smell of paraffin. The woman put down her can, took the tundish and laid it on a shelf, then rose with a tin bottle. Her eyes met those of the clergyman.

'Oh, is it you, Mr Lin'ley!' she said, in a complaining tone. 'Go in.'

The minister entered the house. In the hot kitchen sat a big, elderly man with a great grey beard, taking snuff. He grunted in a deep, muttering voice, telling the minister to sit down, and then took no more notice of him, but stared vacantly into the fire. Mr Lindley waited.

The woman came in, the ribbons of her black lace cap, or bonnet, hanging on her shawl. She was of medium stature, everything about her was tidy. She went up a step out of the kitchen, carrying the paraffin tin. Feet were heard entering the room up the step. It was a little haberdashery shop, with parcels on the shelves of the walls, a big, old-fashioned sewing machine with tailor's work lying round it, in the open space. The woman went behind the counter, gave the child who had entered the paraffin bottle, and took from her a jug.

'My mother says shall yer put it down,' said the child, and she was gone. The woman wrote in a book, then came into the kitchen with her jug. The husband, a very large man, rose and brought more coal to the already hot fire. He moved slowly and sluggishly. Already he was going dead; being a tailor, his large form had become an encumbrance to him. In his youth he had been a great dancer and boxer. Now he was taciturn, and inert. The minister had nothing to say, so he sought for his phrases. But John Durant took no notice, existing silent and dull.

Mrs Durant spread the cloth. Her husband poured himself beer into a mug, and began to smoke and drink.

'Shall you have some?' he growled through his beard at the clergyman, looking slowly from the man to the jug, capable of this one idea.

'No, thank you,' replied Mr Lindley, though he would have liked some beer. He must set the example in a drinking parish.

'We need a drop to keep us going,' said Mrs Durant.

She had rather a complaining manner. The clergyman sat on uncomfortably while she laid the table for the half-past ten lunch. Her husband drew up to eat. She remained in her little round armchair by the fire.

She was a woman who would have liked to be easy in her life, but to whose lot had fallen a rough and turbulent family, and a slothful husband who did not care what became of himself or anybody. So, her rather good-looking square face was peevish, she had that air of having been compelled all her life to serve unwillingly, and to control where she did not want to control. There was about her, too, that masterful aplomb of a woman who has brought up and ruled her sons: but even them she had ruled unwillingly. She had enjoyed managing her little haberdashery shop, riding in the carrier's cart to Nottingham, going through the big warehouses to buy her goods. But the fret of managing her sons she did not like. Only she loved her youngest boy, because he was her last, and she saw herself free.

This was one of the houses the clergyman visited occasionally. Mrs Durant, as part of her regulation, had brought up all her sons in the Church. Not that she had any religion. Only, it was what she was used to. Mr Durant was without religion. He read the fervently evangelical *Life of John Wesley* with a curious pleasure, getting from it a satisfaction as from the warmth of the fire, or a glass of brandy. But he cared no more about John Wesley, in fact, than about John Milton, of whom he had never heard.

Mrs Durant took her chair to the table.

'I don't feel like eating,' she sighed.

'Why – aren't you well?' asked the clergyman, patronising.

'It isn't that,' she sighed. She sat with shut, straight mouth. 'I don't know what's going to become of us.'

But the clergyman had ground himself down so long, that he could not easily sympathise.

'Have you any trouble?' he asked.

'Ay, have I any trouble!' cried the elderly woman. 'I shall end my days in the workhouse.'

The minister waited unmoved. What could she know of poverty, in her little house of plenty!

'I hope not,' he said.

'And the one lad as I wanted to keep by me – ' she lamented.

The minister listened without sympathy, quite neutral.

'And the lad as would have been a support to my old age! What is going to become of us?' she said.

The clergyman, justly, did not believe in the cry of poverty, but wondered what had become of the son.

'Has anything happened to Alfred?' he asked.

'We've got word he's gone for a Queen's sailor,' she said sharply.

'He has joined the navy?' exclaimed Mr Lindley. 'I think he could scarcely have done better – to serve his Queen and country on the sea . . .'

'He is wanted to serve *me*,' she cried. 'And I wanted my lad at home.'

Alfred was her baby, her last, whom she had allowed herself the luxury of spoiling.

'You will miss him,' said Mr Lindley, 'that is certain. But this is no regrettable step for him to have taken – on the contrary.'

'That's easy for you to say, Mr Lindley,' she replied tartly. 'Do you think I want my lad climbing ropes at another man's bidding, like a monkey – ?'

'There is no *dishonour*, surely, in serving in the navy?'

'Dishonour this, dishonour that,' cried the angry old woman. 'He goes and makes a slave of himself, and he'll rue it.'

Her angry, scornful impatience nettled the clergyman and silenced him for some moments.

'I do not see,' he retorted at last, white at the gills and inadequate, 'that the Queen's service is any more to be called slavery than working in a mine.'

'At home he was at home, and his own master. *I* know he'll find a difference.'

'It may be the making of him,' said the clergyman. 'It will take him away from bad companionship and drink.'

Some of the Durants' sons were notorious drinkers, and Alfred was not quite steady.

'And why indeed shouldn't he have his glass?' cried the mother. 'He picks no man's pocket to pay for it!'

The clergyman stiffened at what he thought was an allusion to his own profession, and his unpaid bills.

'With all due consideration, I am glad to hear he has joined the navy,' he said.

'Me with my old age coming on, and his father working very little! I'd thank you to be glad about something else besides that, Mr Lindley.'

The woman began to cry. Her husband, quite impassive, finished his lunch of meat-pie, and drank some beer. Then he turned to the fire, as if there were no one in the room but himself.

'I shall respect all men who serve God and their country on the sea, Mrs Durant,' said the clergyman stubbornly.

'That is very well, when they're not your sons who are doing the dirty work. It makes a difference,' she replied tartly.

'I should be proud if one of my sons were to enter the Navy.'

'Ay – well – we're not all of us made alike – '

The minister rose. He put down a large folded paper.

'I've brought the almanac,' he said.

Mrs Durant unfolded it.

'I do like a bit of colour in things,' she said, petulantly.

The clergyman did not reply.

'There's that envelope for the organist's fund – ' said the old woman, and rising, she took the thing from the mantelpiece, went into the shop, and returned sealing it up. 'Which is all I can afford,' she said.

Mr Lindley took his departure, in his pocket the envelope containing Mrs Durant's offering for Miss Louisa's services. He went from door to door delivering the almanacs, in dull routine. Jaded with the monotony of the business, and with the repeated effort of greeting half-known people, he felt barren and rather irritable. At last he returned home.

In the dining-room was a small fire. Mrs Lindley, growing very stout, lay on her couch. The vicar carved the cold mutton; Miss Louisa, short and plump and rather flushed, came in from the kitchen; Miss Mary, dark, with a beautiful white brow and grey eyes, served the vegetables; the children chattered a little, but not exuberantly. The very air seemed starved.

'I went to the Durants,' said the vicar, as he served out small portions of mutton; 'it appears Alfred has run away to join the navy.'

'Do him good,' came the rough voice of the invalid.

Miss Louisa, attending to the youngest child, looked up in protest.

'Why has he done that?' asked Mary's low, musical voice.

'He wanted some excitement, I suppose,' said the vicar. 'Shall we say grace?'

The children were arranged, all bent their heads, grace was pronounced, at the last word every face was being raised to go on with the interesting subject.

'He's just done the right thing, for once,' came the rather deep voice of the mother; 'save him from becoming a drunken sot, like the rest of them.'

'They're not *all* drunken, mama,' said Miss Louisa, stubbornly.

'It's no fault of their upbringing if they're not. Walter Durant is a standing disgrace.'

'As I told Mrs Durant,' said the vicar, eating hungrily, 'it is the best thing he could have done. It will take him away from temptation during the most dangerous years of his life – how old is he – nineteen?'

'Twenty,' said Miss Louisa.

'Twenty!' repeated the vicar. 'It will give him wholesome discipline and set before him some sort of standard of duty and honour – nothing could have been better for him. But – '

'We shall miss him from the choir,' said Miss Louisa, as if taking opposite sides to her parents.

'That is as it may be,' said the vicar. 'I prefer to know he is safe in the navy, than running the risk of getting into bad ways here.'

'Was he getting into bad ways?' asked the stubborn Miss Louisa.

'You know, Louisa, he wasn't quite what he used to be,' said Miss Mary gently and steadily. Miss Louisa shut her rather heavy jaw sulkily. She wanted to deny it, but she knew it was true.

For her he had been a laughing, warm lad, with something kindly and something rich about him. He had made her feel warm. It seemed the days would be colder since he had gone.

'Quite the best thing he could do,' said the mother with emphasis.

'I think so,' said the vicar. 'But his mother was almost abusive because I suggested it.'

He spoke in an injured tone.

'What does she care for her children's welfare?' said the invalid. 'Their wages is all her concern.'

'I suppose she wanted him at home with her,' said Miss Louisa.

'Yes, she did – at the expense of his learning to be a drunkard like the rest of them,' retorted her mother.

'George Durant doesn't drink,' defended her daughter.

'Because he got burned so badly when he was nineteen – in the pit – and that frightened him. The navy is a better remedy than that, at least.'

'Certainly,' said the vicar. 'Certainly.'

And to this Miss Louisa agreed. Yet she could not but feel angry that he had gone away for so many years. She herself was only nineteen.

3

It happened when Miss Mary was twenty-three years old, that Mr Lindley was very ill. The family was exceedingly poor at the time, such a lot of money was needed, so little was forthcoming. Neither Miss Mary nor Miss Louisa had suitors. What chance had they? They met no eligible young men in Aldecross. And what they earned was a mere drop in a void. The girls' hearts were chilled and hardened with fear of this perpetual, cold penury, this narrow struggle, this horrible nothingness of their lives.

A clergyman had to be found for the church work. It so happened the son of an old friend of Mr Lindley's was waiting three months before taking up his duties. He would come and officiate, for nothing. The young clergyman was keenly expected. He was not more than twenty-seven, a Master of Arts of Oxford, had written his thesis on Roman Law. He came of an old Cambridgeshire family, had some private means, was going to take a church in Northamptonshire with a good stipend, and was not married. Mrs Lindley incurred new debts, and scarcely regretted her husband's illness.

But when Mr Massy came, there was a shock of disappointment in the house. They had expected a young man with a pipe and a deep voice, but with better manners than Sidney, the eldest of the Lindleys. There arrived instead a small, *chétif* man, scarcely larger than a boy of twelve, spectacled, timid in the extreme, without a word to utter at first; yet with a certain inhuman self-sureness.

'What a little abortion!' was Mrs Lindley's exclamation to herself on first seeing him, in his buttoned-up clerical coat. And for the first time for many days, she was profoundly thankful to God that all her children were decent specimens.

He had not normal powers of perception. They soon saw that he lacked the full range of human feelings, but had rather a strong, philosophical mind, from which he lived. His body was almost unthinkable, in intellect he was something definite. The conversation at once took a balanced, abstract tone when he participated. There was no spontaneous exclamation, no violent assertion or expression of personal conviction, but all cold, reasonable assertion. This was very hard on Mrs Lindley. The little man would look at her, after one of her pronouncements, and then give, in his thin voice, his own calculated version, so that she felt as if she were tumbling into thin air through a hole in the flimsy floor on which their conversation stood. It was she who felt a fool. Soon she was reduced to a hardy silence.

Still, at the back of her mind, she remembered that he was an unattached gentleman, who would shortly have an income altogether of six or seven hundred a year. What did the man matter, if there were pecuniary ease! The man was a trifle thrown in. After twenty-two years her sentimentality was ground away, and only the millstone of poverty mattered to her. So she supported the little man as a representative of a decent income.

His most irritating habit was that of a sneering little giggle, all on his own, which came when he perceived or related some illogical absurdity on the part of another person. It was the only form of humour he had. Stupidity in thinking seemed to him exquisitely funny. But any novel was unintelligibly meaningless and dull, and to an Irish sort of humour he listened curiously, examining it like mathematics, or else simply not hearing. In normal human relationship he was not there. Quite unable to take part in simple everyday talk, he padded silently round the house, or sat in the dining-room looking nervously from side to side, always apart in a cold, rarefied little world of his own. Sometimes he made an ironic remark, that did not seem humanly relevant, or he gave his little laugh, like a sneer. He had to defend himself and his own insufficiency. And he answered questions grudgingly, with a yes or no, because he did not see their import and was nervous. It seemed to Miss Louisa he scarcely distinguished one person from another, but that he liked to be near her, or to Miss Mary, for some sort of contact which stimulated him unknown.

Apart from all this, he was the most admirable workman. He was unremittingly shy, but perfect in his sense of duty: as far as he could conceive Christianity, he was a perfect Christian. Nothing that he realised he could do for anyone did he leave undone, although he was so incapable of coming into contact with another being, that he could not proffer help. Now he attended assiduously to the sick man, investigated all the affairs of the parish or the church which Mr Lindley had in control, straightened out accounts, made lists of the sick and needy, padded round with help and to see what he could do. He heard of Mrs Lindley's anxiety about her sons, and began to investigate means of sending them to Cambridge. His kindness almost frightened Miss Mary. She honoured it so, and yet she shrank from it. For, in it all Mr Massy seemed to have no sense of any person, any human being whom he was helping: he only realised a kind of mathematical working out, solving of given situations, a calculated well-doing. And it was as if he had accepted the Christian tenets as axioms. His religion consisted in what his scrupulous, abstract mind approved of.

Seeing his acts, Miss Mary must respect and honour him. In consequence she must serve him. To this she had to force herself, shuddering and yet desirous, but he did not perceive it. She accompanied him on his visiting in the parish, and whilst she was cold with admiration for him, often she was touched with pity for the little padding figure with bent shoulders, buttoned up to the chin in his overcoat. She was a handsome, calm girl, tall, with a beautiful repose. Her clothes were poor, and she wore a black silk scarf, having no furs. But she was a lady. As the people saw her walking down Aldecross beside Mr Massy, they said: 'My word, Miss Mary's got a catch. Did ever you see such a sickly little shrimp!'

She knew they were talking so, and it made her heart grow hot against them, and she drew herself as it were protectively towards the little man beside her. At any rate, she could see and give honour to his genuine goodness.

He could not walk fast, or far.

'You have not been well?' she asked, in her dignified way.

'I have an internal trouble.'

He was not aware of her slight shudder. There was silence, whilst she bowed to recover her composure, to resume her gentle manner towards him.

He was fond of Miss Mary. She had made it a rule of hospitality that he should always be escorted by herself or by her sister on his visits in the parish, which were not many. But some mornings she was engaged. Then Miss Louisa took her place. It was no good Miss Louisa's trying to adopt to Mr Massy an attitude of queenly service. She was unable to regard him save with aversion. When she saw him from behind, thin and bent-shouldered, looking like a sickly lad of thirteen, she disliked him exceedingly, and felt a desire to put him out of existence. And yet a deeper justice in Mary made Louisa humble before her sister.

They were going to see Mr Durant, who was paralysed and not expected to live. Miss Louisa was crudely ashamed at being admitted to the cottage in company with the little clergyman.

Mrs Durant was, however, much quieter in the face of her real trouble.

'How is Mr Durant?' asked Louisa.

'He is no different – and we don't expect him to be,' was the reply. The little clergyman stood looking on.

They went upstairs. The three stood for some time looking at the bed, at the grey head of the old man on the pillow, the grey beard over the sheet. Miss Louisa was shocked and afraid.

'It is so dreadful,' she said, with a shudder.

'It is how I always thought it would be,' replied Mrs Durant.

Then Miss Louisa was afraid of her. The two women were uneasy, waiting for Mr Massy to say something. He stood, small and bent, too nervous to speak.

'Has he any understanding?' he asked at length.

'Maybe,' said Mrs Durant. 'Can you hear, John?' she asked loudly. The dull blue eye of the inert man looked at her feebly.

'Yes, he understands,' said Mrs Durant to Mr Massy. Except for the dull look in his eyes, the sick man lay as if dead. The three stood in silence. Miss Louisa was obstinate but heavy-hearted under the load of unlivingness. It was Mr Massy who kept her there in discipline. His non-human will dominated them all.

Then they heard a sound below, a man's footsteps, and a man's voice called subduedly: 'Are you upstairs, mother?'

Mrs Durant started and moved to the door. But already a quick, firm step was running up the stairs.

'I'm a bit early, mother,' a troubled voice said, and on the landing they saw the form of the sailor. His mother came and clung to him. She was suddenly aware that she needed something to hold on to. He put his arms round her, and bent over her, kissing her.

'He's not gone, mother?' he asked anxiously, struggling to control his voice.

Miss Louisa looked away from the mother and son who stood together in the gloom on the landing. She could not bear it that she and Mr Massy should be there. The latter stood nervously, as if ill at ease before the emotion that was running. He was a witness, nervous, unwilling, but dispassionate. To Miss Louisa's hot heart it seemed all, all wrong that they should be there.

Mrs Durant entered the bedroom, her face wet.

'There's Miss Louisa and the vicar,' she said, out of voice and quavering.

Her son, red-faced and slender, drew himself up to salute. But Miss Louisa held out her hand. Then she saw his hazel eyes recognise her for a moment, and his small white teeth showed in a glimpse of the greeting she used to love. She was covered with confusion. He went round to the bed; his boots clicked on the plaster floor, he bowed his head with dignity.

'How are you, dad?' he said, laying his hand on the sheet, faltering. But the old man stared fixedly and unseeing. The son stood perfectly still for a few minutes, then slowly recoiled. Miss Louisa saw the fine outline of his breast, under the sailor's blue blouse, as his chest began to heave.

'He doesn't know me,' he said, turning to his mother. He gradually went white.

'No, my boy!' cried the mother, pitiful, lifting her face. And suddenly she put her face against his shoulder, he was stooping down to her, holding her against him, and she cried aloud for a moment or two. Miss Louisa saw his sides heaving, and heard the sharp hiss of his breath. She turned away, tears streaming down her face. The father lay inert upon the white bed, Mr Massy looked queer and obliterated, so little now that the sailor with his sunburned skin was in the room. He stood waiting. Miss Louisa wanted to die, she wanted to have done. She dared not turn round again to look.

'Shall I offer a prayer?' came the frail voice of the clergyman, and all knelt down.

Miss Louisa was frightened of the inert man upon the bed. Then she felt a flash of fear of Mr Massy, hearing his thin, detached voice. And then, calmed, she looked up. On the far side of the bed were the heads of the mother and son, the one in the black lace cap, with the small white nape of the neck beneath, the other, with brown, sun-scorched hair too close and wiry to allow of a parting, and neck tanned firm, bowed as if unwillingly. The great grey beard of the old man did not move, the prayer continued. Mr Massy prayed with a pure lucidity, that they all might conform to the higher Will. He was like something that dominated the bowed heads, something dispassionate that governed them inexorably. Miss Louisa was afraid of him. And she was bound, during the course of the prayer, to have a little reverence for him. It was like a foretaste of inexorable, cold death, a taste of pure justice.

That evening she talked to Mary of the visit. Her heart, her veins were possessed by the thought of Alfred Durant as he held his mother in his arms; then the break in his voice, as she remembered it again and again, was like a flame through her; and she wanted to see his face more distinctly in her mind, ruddy with the sun, and his golden-brown eyes, kind and careless, strained now with a natural fear, the fine nose tanned hard by the sun, the mouth that could not help smiling at her. And it went through her with pride, to think of his figure, a straight, fine jet of life.

'He is a handsome lad,' said she to Miss Mary, as if he had not been a year older than herself. Underneath was the deeper dread, almost hatred, of the inhuman being of Mr Massy. She felt she must protect herself and Alfred from him.

'When I felt Mr Massy there,' she said, 'I almost hated him. What right had he to be there!'

'Surely he has all right,' said Miss Mary after a pause. 'He is *really* a Christian.'

'He seems to me nearly an imbecile,' said Miss Louisa.

Miss Mary, quiet and beautiful, was silent for a moment:

'Oh, no,' she said. 'Not *imbecile* –'

'Well then – he reminds me of a six months' child – or a five months' child – as if he didn't have time to get developed enough before he was born.'

'Yes,' said Miss Mary, slowly. 'There is something lacking. But there is something wonderful in him: and he is really *good* –'

'Yes,' said Miss Louisa, 'it doesn't seem right that he should be. What right has *that* to be called goodness!'

'But it *is* goodness,' persisted Mary. Then she added, with a laugh: 'And come, you wouldn't deny that as well.'

There was a doggedness in her voice. She went about very quietly. In her soul, she knew what was going to happen. She knew that Mr Massy was stronger than she, and that she must submit to what he was. Her physical self was prouder, stronger than he, her physical self disliked and despised him. But she was in the grip of his moral, mental being. And she felt the days allotted out to her. And her family watched.

4

A few days after, old Mr Durant died. Miss Louisa saw Alfred once more, but he was stiff before her now, treating her not like a person, but as if she were some sort of will in command and he a separate, distinct will waiting in front of her. She had never felt such utter steel-plate separation from anyone. It puzzled her and frightened her. What had become of him? And she hated the military discipline – she was antagonistic to it. Now he was not himself. He was the will which obeys set over against the will which commands. She hesitated over accepting this. He had put himself out of her range. He had ranked himself inferior, subordinate to her. And that was how he would get away from her, that was how he would avoid all connection with her: by fronting her impersonally from the opposite camp, by taking up the abstract position of an inferior.

She went brooding steadily and sullenly over this, brooding and brooding. Her fierce, obstinate heart could not give way. It clung to its own rights. Sometimes she dismissed him. Why should he, inferior, trouble her?

Then she relapsed to him, and almost hated him. It was his way of getting out of it. She felt the cowardice of it, his calmly placing her in a superior class, and placing himself inaccessibly apart, in an inferior, as if she, the sensient woman who was fond of him, did not count. But she was not going to submit. Dogged in her heart she held on to him.

5

In six months' time Miss Mary had married Mr Massy. There had been no love-making, nobody had made any remark. But everybody was tense and callous with expectation. When one day Mr Massy asked for Mary's hand, Mr Lindley started and trembled from the thin, abstract voice of the little man. Mr Massy was very nervous, but so curiously absolute.

'I shall be very glad,' said the vicar, 'but of course the decision lies with Mary herself.' And his still feeble hand shook as he moved a Bible on his desk.

The small man, keeping fixedly to his idea, padded out of the room to find Miss Mary. He sat a long time by her, while she made some conversation, before he had readiness to speak. She was afraid of what was coming, and sat stiff in apprehension. She felt as if her body would rise and fling him aside. But her spirit quivered and waited. Almost in expectation she waited, almost wanting him. And then she knew he would speak.

'I have already asked Mr Lindley,' said the clergyman, while suddenly she looked with aversion at his little knees, 'if he would consent to my proposal.' He was aware of his own disadvantage, but his will was set.

She went cold as she sat, and impervious, almost as if she had become stone.

He waited a moment nervously. He would not persuade her. He himself never even heard persuasion, but pursued his own course. He looked at her, sure of himself, unsure of her, and said: 'Will you become my wife, Mary?'

Still her heart was hard and cold. She sat proudly.

'I should like to speak to mama first,' she said.

'Very well,' replied Mr Massy. And in a moment he padded away.

Mary went to her mother. She was cold and reserved.

'Mr Massy has asked me to marry him, mama,' she said.

Mrs Lindley went on staring at her book. She was cramped in her feeling. 'Well, and what did you say?'

They were both keeping calm and cold.

'I said I would speak to you before answering him.'

This was equivalent to a question. Mrs Lindley did not want to reply to it. She shifted her heavy form irritably on the couch. Miss Mary sat calm and straight, with closed mouth.

'Your father thinks it would not be a bad match,' said the mother, as if casually.

Nothing more was said. Everybody remained cold and shut-off. Miss Mary did not speak to Miss Louisa, the Reverend Ernest Lindley kept out of sight.

At evening Miss Mary accepted Mr Massy.

'Yes, I will marry you,' she said, with even a little movement of tenderness towards him. He was embarrassed, but satisfied. She could see him making some movement towards her, could feel the male in him, something cold and triumphant, asserting itself. She sat rigid, and waited.

When Miss Louisa knew, she was silent with bitter anger against everybody, even against Mary. She felt her faith wounded. Did the real things to her not matter after all? She wanted to get away. She thought of Mr Massy. He had some curious power, some unanswerable right. He was a will that they could not controvert. Suddenly a flush started in her. If he had come to her she would have flipped him out of the room. He was never going to touch *her*. And she was glad. She was glad that her blood would rise and exterminate the little man, if he came too near to her, no matter how her judgement was paralysed by him, no matter how he moved in abstract goodness. She thought she was perverse to be glad, but glad she was. 'I would just flip him out of the room,' she said, and she derived great satisfaction from the open statement. Nevertheless, perhaps she ought still to feel that Mary, on her plane, was a higher being than herself. But then Mary was Mary, and she was Louisa, and that also was inalterable.

Mary, in marrying him, tried to become a pure reason such as he was, without feeling or impulse. She shut herself up, she shut herself rigid against the agonies of shame and the terror of violation which came at first. She *would* not feel, and she *would* not feel. She was a pure will acquiescing to him. She elected a certain kind of fate. She would be good and purely just, she would live in a higher freedom than she had ever known, she would be free of mundane care, she was a pure will towards right. She had sold herself, but she had a new freedom. She had got rid of her body. She had sold a lower thing, her body, for a higher thing, her freedom from material things. She considered that she paid for all she got from her husband. So, in a kind of independence, she moved proud and free. She had paid with her body: that was henceforward out of consideration. She was glad to be rid of it. She had bought her position in the world – that henceforth was taken for granted. There remained only the direction of her activity towards charity and high-minded living.

She could scarcely bear other people to be present with her and her husband. Her private life was her shame. But then, she could keep it hidden. She lived almost isolated in the rectory of the tiny village miles from the railway. She suffered as if it were an insult to her own flesh, seeing the repulsion which some people felt for her husband, or the special manner they had of treating him, as if he were a 'case'. But most people were uneasy before him, which restored her pride.

If she had let herself, she would have hated him, hated his padding round the house, his thin voice devoid of human understanding, his bent little shoulders and rather incomplete face that reminded her of an abortion. But rigorously she kept to her position. She took care of him and was just to him. There was also a deep craven fear of him, something slave-like.

There was not much fault to be found with his behaviour. He was scrupulously just and kind according to his lights. But the male in him was cold and self-complete, and utterly domineering. Weak, insufficient little thing as he was, she had not expected this of him. It was something in the bargain she had not understood. It made her hold her head, to keep still. She knew, vaguely, that she was murdering herself. After all, her body was not quite so easy to get rid of. And this manner of disposing of it – ah, sometimes she felt she must rise and bring about death, lift her hand for utter denial of everything, by a general destruction.

He was almost unaware of the conditions about him. He did not fuss in the domestic way, she did as she liked in the house. Indeed, she was a great deal free of him. He would sit obliterated for hours. He was kind, and almost anxiously considerate. But when he considered he was right, his will was just blindly male, like a cold machine. And on most points he was logically right, or he had with him the right of the creed they both accepted. It was so. There was nothing for her to go against.

Then she found herself with child, and felt for the first time horror, afraid before God and man. This also she had to go through – it was the right. When the child arrived, it was a bonny, healthy lad. Her heart hurt in her body, as she took the baby between her hands. The flesh that was trampled and silent in her must speak again in the boy. After all, she had to live – it was not so simple after all. Nothing was finished completely. She looked and looked at the baby, and almost hated it, and suffered an anguish of love for it. She hated it because it made her live again in the flesh, when she *could* not live in the flesh, she could not. She wanted to trample her flesh down, down, extinct, to live in the mind. And now there was this child. It was too cruel, too racking. For she must love the child. Her purpose was broken in two again. She had to become amorphous, purposeless, without real being. As a mother, she was a fragmentary, ignoble thing.

Mr Massy, blind to everything else in the way of human feeling, became obsessed by the idea of his child. When it arrived, suddenly it filled the whole world of feeling for him. It was his obsession, his terror was for its safety and well-being. It was something new, as if he himself had been born a naked infant, conscious of his own exposure, and full of apprehension. He who had never been aware of anyone else, all his life, now was aware of nothing but the child. Not that he ever played with it, or kissed it, or tended it. He did nothing for it. But it dominated him, it filled, and at the same time emptied his mind. The world was all baby for him.

This his wife must also bear, his question: 'What is the reason that he cries?' – his reminder, at the first sound: 'Mary, that is the child' – his restlessness if the feeding-time were five minutes past. She had bargained for this – now she must stand by her bargain.

6

Miss Louisa, at home in the dingy vicarage, had suffered a great deal over her sister's wedding. Having once begun to cry out against it, during the engagement, she had been silenced by Mary's quiet: 'I don't agree with you about him, Louisa, I *want* to marry him.' Then Miss Louisa had been angry deep in her heart, and therefore silent. This dangerous state started the change in her. Her own revulsion made her recoil from the hitherto undoubted Mary.

'I'd beg the streets barefoot first,' said Miss Louisa, thinking of Mr Massy.

But evidently Mary could perform a different heroism. So she, Louisa the practical, suddenly felt that Mary, her ideal, was questionable after all. How could she be pure – one cannot be dirty in act and spiritual in being. Louisa distrusted Mary's high spirituality. It was no longer genuine for her. And if Mary were spiritual and misguided, why did not her father protect her? Because of the money. He disliked the whole affair, but he backed away, because of the money. And the mother frankly did not care: her daughters could do as they liked. Her mother's pronouncement: 'Whatever happens to *him*, Mary is safe for life,' so evidently and shallowly a calculation, incensed Louisa.

'I'd rather be safe in the workhouse,' she cried.

'Your father will see to that,' replied her mother brutally.

This speech, in its directness, so injured Miss Louisa that she hated her mother deep, deep in her heart, and almost hated herself. It was a long time resolving itself out, this hate. But it worked and worked, and at last the young woman said: 'They are wrong – they are all wrong. They have ground out their souls for what isn't worth anything, and there isn't a grain of love in them anywhere. And I *will* have love. They want us to deny it. They've never found it, so they want to say it doesn't exist. But I *will* have it. I *will* love – it is my birthright. I will love the man I marry – that is all I care about.'

So Miss Louisa stood isolated from everybody. She and Mary had parted over Mr Massy. In Louisa's eyes, Mary was degraded, married to Mr Massy. She could not bear to think of her lofty, spiritual sister degraded in the body like this. Mary was wrong, wrong, wrong: she was not superior, she was flawed, incomplete. The two sisters stood apart. They still loved each other, they would love each other as long as they lived. But they had parted ways. A new solitariness came over the obstinate Louisa, and her heavy jaw set stubbornly. She was going on her own way. But which way? She was quite alone, with a blank world before her. How could she be said to have any way? Yet she had her fixed will to love, to have the man she loved.

7

When her boy was three years old, Mary had another baby, a girl. The three years had gone by monotonously. They might have been an eternity, they might have been brief as a sleep. She did not know. Only, there was always a weight on top of her, something that pressed down her life. The only thing that had happened was that Mr Massy had had an operation. He was always exceedingly fragile. His wife had soon learned to attend to him mechanically, as part of her duty.

But this third year, after the baby girl had been born, Mary felt oppressed and depressed. Christmas drew near: the gloomy, unleavened Christmas of the rectory, where all the days were of the same dark fabric. And Mary was afraid. It was as if the darkness were coming upon her.

'Edward, I should like to go home for Christmas,' she said, and a certain terror filled her as she spoke.

'But you can't leave baby,' said her husband, blinking.

'We can all go.'

He thought, and stared in his collective fashion.

'Why do you wish to go?' he asked.

'Because I need a change. A change would do me good, and it would be good for the milk.'

He heard the will in his wife's voice, and was at a loss. Her language was unintelligible to him. And while she was breeding, either about to have a child, or nursing, he regarded her as a special sort of being.

'Wouldn't it hurt baby to take her by the train?' he said.

'No,' replied the mother, 'why should it?'

They went. When they were in the train, it began to snow. From the window of his first-class carriage the little clergyman watched the big flakes sweep by, like a blind drawn across the country. He was obsessed by thought of the baby, and afraid of the draughts of the carriage.

'Sit right in the corner,' he said to his wife, 'and hold baby close back.'

She moved at his bidding, and stared out of the window. His eternal presence was like an iron weight on her brain. But she was going partially to escape for a few days.

'Sit on the other side, Jack,' said the father. 'It is less draughty. Come to this window.'

He watched the boy in anxiety. But his children were the only beings in the world who took not the slightest notice of him.

'Look, mother, look!' cried the boy. 'They fly right in my face' – he meant the snowflakes.

'Come into this corner,' repeated his father, out of another world.

'He's jumped on this one's back, mother, an' they're riding to the bottom!' cried the boy, jumping with glee.

'Tell him to come on this side,' the little man bade his wife.

'Jack, kneel on this cushion,' said the mother, putting her white hand on the place.

The boy slid over in silence to the place she indicated, waited still for a moment, then almost deliberately, stridently cried: 'Look at all those in the corner, mother, making a heap,' and he pointed to the cluster of snowflakes with finger pressed dramatically on the pane, and he turned to his mother a bit ostentatiously.

'All in a heap!' she said.

He had seen her face, and had her response, and he was somewhat assured. Vaguely uneasy, he was reassured if he could win her attention.

They arrived at the vicarage at half-past two, not having had lunch.

'How are you, Edward?' said Mr Lindley, trying on his side to be fatherly. But he was always in a false position with his son-inlaw, frustrated before him, therefore, as much as possible, he shut his eyes and ears to him. The vicar was looking thin and pale and ill-nourished. He had gone quite grey. He was, however, still haughty; but, since the growing-up of his children, it was a brittle haughtiness that might break at any moment and leave the vicar only an impoverished, pitiable figure. Mrs Lindley took all the notice of her daughter, and of the children. She ignored her son-inlaw. Miss Louisa was clucking and laughing and rejoicing over the baby. Mr Massy stood aside, a bent, persistent little figure.

'Oh a pretty! – a little pretty! oh a cold little pretty come in a railway train!' Miss Louisa was cooing to the infant, crouching on the hearthrug opening the white woollen wraps and exposing the child to the fireglow.

'Mary,' said the little clergyman, 'I think it would be better to give baby a warm bath; she may take a cold.'

'I think it is not necessary,' said the mother, coming and closing her hand judiciously over the rosy feet and hands of the mite. 'She is not chilly.'

'Not a bit,' cried Miss Louisa. 'She's not caught cold.'

'I'll go and bring her flannels,' said Mr Massy, with one idea.

'I can bath her in the kitchen then,' said Mary, in an altered, cold tone.

'You can't, the girl is scrubbing there,' said Miss Louisa. 'Besides, she doesn't want a bath at this time of day.'

'She'd better have one,' said Mary, quietly, out of submission. Miss Louisa's gorge rose, and she was silent.

When the little man padded down with the flannels on his arm, Mrs Lindley asked: 'Hadn't *you* better take a hot bath, Edward?'

But the sarcasm was lost on the little clergyman. He was absorbed in the preparations round the baby.

The room was dull and threadbare, and the snow outside seemed fairy-like by comparison, so white on the lawn and tufted on the bushes. Indoors the heavy pictures hung obscurely on the walls, everything was dingy with gloom.

Except in the fireglow, where they had laid the bath on the hearth. Mrs Massy, her black hair always smoothly coiled and queenly, kneeled by the bath, wearing a rubber apron, and holding the kicking child. Her husband stood holding the towels and the flannels to warm. Louisa, too cross to share in the joy of the baby's bath, was laying the table. The boy was hanging on the door-knob, wrestling with it to get out. His father looked round.

'Come away from the door, Jack,' he said, ineffectually. Jack tugged harder at the knob as if he did not hear. Mr Massy blinked at him.

'He must come away from the door, Mary,' he said. 'There will be a draught if it is opened.'

'Jack, come away from the door, dear,' said the mother, dexterously turning the shiny wet baby on to her towelled knee, then glancing round: 'Go and tell Auntie Louisa about the train.'

Louisa, also afraid to open the door, was watching the scene on the hearth. Mr Massy stood holding the baby's flannel, as if assisting at some ceremonial. If everybody had not been subduedly angry, it would have been ridiculous.

'I want to see out of the window,' Jack said. His father turned hastily.

'Do *you* mind lifting him on to a chair, Louisa,' said Mary hastily. The father was too delicate.

When the baby was flannelled, Mr Massy went upstairs and returned with four pillows, which he set in the fender to warm. Then he stood watching the mother feed her child, obsessed by the idea of his infant.

Louisa went on with her preparations for the meal. She could not have told why she was so sullenly angry. Mrs Lindley, as usual, lay silently watching.

Mary carried her child upstairs, followed by her husband with the pillows. After a while he came down again.

'What is Mary doing? Why doesn't she come down to eat?' asked Mrs Lindley.

'She is staying with baby. The room is rather cold. I will ask the girl to put in a fire.' He was going absorbedly to the door.

'But Mary has had nothing to eat. It is *she* who will catch cold,' said the mother, exasperated.

Mr Massy seemed as if he did not hear. Yet he looked at his mother-in-law, and answered: 'I will take her something.'

He went out. Mrs Lindley shifted on her couch with anger. Miss Louisa glowered. But no one said anything, because of the money that came to the vicarage from Mr Massy.

Louisa went upstairs. Her sister was sitting by the bed, reading a scrap of paper.

'Won't you come down and eat?' the younger asked.

'In a moment or two,' Mary replied, in a quiet, reserved voice that forbade anyone to approach her.

It was this that made Miss Louisa most furious. She went downstairs, and announced to her mother: 'I am going out. I may not be home to tea.'

8

No one remarked on her exit. She put on her fur hat, that the village people knew so well, and the old Norfolk jacket. Louisa was short and plump and plain. She had her mother's heavy jaw, her father's proud brow, and her own grey, brooding eyes that were very beautiful when she smiled. It was true, as the people said, that she looked sulky. Her chief attraction was her glistening, heavy, deep-blonde hair, which shone and gleamed with a richness that was not entirely foreign to her.

'Where am I going?' she said to herself, when she got outside in the snow. She did not hesitate, however, but by mechanical walking found herself descending the hill towards Old Aldecross. In the valley that was black with trees, the colliery breathed in stertorous pants, sending out high conical columns of steam that remained upright, whiter than the snow on the hills, yet shadowy, in the dead air. Louisa would not acknowledge to herself whither she was making her way, till she came to the railway crossing. Then the bunches of snow in the twigs of the apple tree that leaned towards the fence told her she must go and see Mrs Durant. The tree was in Mrs Durant's garden.

Alfred was now at home again, living with his mother in the cottage below the road. From the highway hedge, by the railway crossing, the snowy garden sheered down steeply, like the side of a hole, then dropped straight in a wall. In this depth the house was snug, its chimney just level with the road. Miss Louisa descended the stone stairs, and stood below in the little backyard, in the dimness and the semi-secrecy. A big tree leaned overhead, above the paraffin hut. Louisa felt secure from all the world down there. She knocked at the open door, then looked round. The tongue of garden narrowing in from the quarry bed was white with snow: she thought of the thick fringes of snowdrops it would show beneath the currant bushes in a month's time. The ragged fringe of pinks hanging over the garden brim behind her was whitened now with snow-flakes, that in summer held white blossom to Louisa's face. It was pleasant, she thought, to gather flowers that stooped to one's face from above.

She knocked again. Peeping in, she saw the scarlet glow of the kitchen, red firelight falling on the brick floor and on the bright chintz cushions. It was alive and bright as a peep-show. She crossed the scullery, where still an almanac hung. There was no one about. 'Mrs Durant,' called Louisa softly, 'Mrs Durant.'

She went up the brick step into the front room, that still had its little shop counter and its bundles of goods, and she called from the stair-foot. Then she knew Mrs Durant was out.

She went into the yard to follow the old woman's footsteps up the garden path.

She emerged from the bushes and raspberry canes. There was the whole quarry bed, a wide garden white and dimmed, brindled with dark bushes, lying half submerged. On the left, overhead, the little colliery train rumbled by. Right away at the back was a mass of trees.

Louisa followed the open path, looking from right to left, and then she gave a cry of concern. The old woman was sitting rocking slightly among the ragged snowy cabbages. Louisa ran to her, found her whimpering with little, involuntary cries.

'Whatever have you done?' cried Louisa, kneeling in the snow.

'I've – I've – I was pulling a brussels-sprout stalk – and – oh–h! – something tore inside me. I've had a pain,' the old woman wept from shock and suffering, gasping between her whimpers, 'I've had a pain there – a long time – and now – oh – oh!' She panted, pressed her hand on her side, leaned as if she would faint, looking yellow against the snow. Louisa supported her.

'Do you think you could walk now?' she asked.

'Yes,' gasped the old woman.

Louisa helped her to her feet.

'Get the cabbage – I want it for Alfred's dinner,' panted Mrs Durant.

Louisa picked up the stalk of brussels sprouts, and with difficulty got the old woman indoors. She gave her brandy, laid her on the couch, saying: 'I'm going to send for a doctor – wait just a minute.'

The young woman ran up the steps to the public-house a few yards away. The landlady was astonished to see Miss Louisa.

'Will you send for a doctor at once to Mrs Durant,' she said, with some of her father in her commanding tone.

'Is something the matter?' fluttered the landlady in concern.

Louisa, glancing out up the road, saw the grocer's cart driving to Eastwood. She ran and stopped the man, and told him.

Mrs Durant lay on the sofa, her face turned away, when the young woman came back.

'Let me put you to bed,' Louisa said. Mrs Durant did not resist.

Louisa knew the ways of the working people. In the bottom drawer of the dresser she found dusters and flannels. With the old pit-flannel she snatched out the oven shelves, wrapped them up, and put them in the bed. From the son's bed she took a blanket, and, running down, set it before the fire. Having undressed the little old woman, Louisa carried her upstairs.

'You'll drop me, you'll drop me!' cried Mrs Durant.

Louisa did not answer, but bore her burden quickly. She could not light a fire, because there was no fireplace in the bedroom. And the floor was plaster. So she fetched the lamp, and stood it lighted in one corner.

'It will air the room,' she said.

'Yes,' moaned the old woman.

Louisa ran with more hot flannels, replacing those from the oven shelves. Then she made a bran-bag and laid it on the woman's side. There was a big lump on the side of the abdomen.

'I've felt it coming a long time,' moaned the old lady, when the pain was easier, 'but I've not said anything; I didn't want to upset our Alfred.'

Louisa did not see why 'our Alfred' should be spared.

'What time is it?' came the plaintive voice.

'A quarter to four.'

'Oh!' wailed the old lady, 'he'll be here in half an hour, and no dinner ready for him.'

'Let me do it?' said Louisa, gently.

'There's that cabbage – and you'll find the meat in the pantry – and there's an apple pie you can hot up. But *don't you* do it – !'

'Who will, then?' asked Louisa.

'I don't know,' moaned the sick woman, unable to consider.

Louisa did it. The doctor came and gave serious examination. He looked very grave.

'What is it, doctor?' asked the old lady, looking up at him with old, pathetic eyes in which already hope was dead.

'I think you've torn the skin in which a tumour hangs,' he replied.

'Ay!' she murmured, and she turned away.

'You see, she may die any minute – and it *may* be swaled away,' said the old doctor to Louisa.

The young woman went upstairs again.

'He says the lump may be swaled away, and you may get quite well again,' she said.

'Ay!' murmured the old lady. It did not deceive her. Presently she asked: 'Is there a good fire?'

'I think so,' answered Louisa.

'He'll want a good fire,' the mother said. Louisa attended to it.

Since the death of Durant, the widow had come to church occasionally, and Louisa had been friendly to her. In the girl's heart the purpose was fixed. No man had affected her as Alfred Durant had done, and to that she kept. In her heart, she adhered to him. A natural sympathy existed between her and his rather hard, materialistic mother.

Alfred was the most lovable of the old woman's sons. He had grown up like the rest, however, headstrong and blind to everything but his own will. Like the other boys, he had insisted on going into the pit as soon as he left school, because that was the only way speedily to become a man, level with all the other men. This was a great chagrin to his mother, who would have liked to have this last of her sons a gentleman.

But still he remained constant to her. His feeling for her was deep and unexpressed. He noticed when she was tired, or when she had a new cap. And he bought little things for her occasionally. She was not wise enough to see how much he lived by her.

At the bottom he did not satisfy her, he did not seem manly enough. He liked to read books occasionally, and better still he liked to play the piccolo. It amused her to see his head nod over the instrument as he made an effort to get the right note. It made her fond of him, with tenderness, almost pity, but not with respect. She wanted a man to be fixed, going his own way without knowledge of women. Whereas she knew Alfred depended on her. He sang in the choir because he liked singing. In the summer he worked in the garden, attended to the fowls and pigs. He kept pigeons. He played on Saturday in the cricket or football team. But to her he did not seem the man, the independent man her other boys had been. He was her baby – and whilst she loved him for it, she was a little bit contemptuous of him.

There grew up a little hostility between them. Then he began to drink, as the others had done; but not in their blind, oblivious way. He was a little self-conscious over it. She saw this, and she pitied it in him. She loved him most, but she was not satisfied with him because he was not free of her. He could not quite go his own way.

Then at twenty he ran away and served his time in the navy. This made a man of him. He had hated it bitterly, the service, the subordination. For years he fought with himself under the military discipline, for his own self-respect, struggling through blind anger and shame and a cramping sense of inferiority. Out of humiliation and self-hatred, he rose into a sort of inner freedom. And his love for his mother, whom he idealised, remained the fact of hope and of belief.

He came home again, nearly thirty years old, but naïve and inexperienced as a boy, only with a silence about him that was new: a sort of dumb humility before life, a fear of living. He was almost quite chaste. A strong sensitiveness had kept him from women. Sexual talk was all very well among men, but somehow it had no application to living women. There were two things for him, the *idea* of women, with which he sometimes debauched himself, and real women, before whom he felt a deep uneasiness, and a need to draw away. He shrank and defended himself from the approach of any woman. And then he felt ashamed. In his innermost soul he felt he was not a man, he was less than the normal man. In Genoa he went with an under officer to a drinking house where the cheaper sort of girl came in to look for lovers. He sat there with his glass, the girls looked at him, but they never came to him. He knew that if they did come he could only pay for food and drink for them, because he felt a pity for them, and was anxious lest they lacked good necessities. He could not have gone with one of them: he knew it, and was ashamed, looking with curious envy at the swaggering, easy-passionate Italian, whose body went to a woman by instinctive impersonal attraction. They were men, he was not a man. He sat feeling short, feeling like a leper. And he went away imagining sexual scenes between himself and a woman, walking wrapt in this indulgence. But when the ready woman presented herself, the very fact that she was a palpable woman made it impossible for him to touch her. And this incapacity was like a core of rottenness in him.

So several times he went, drunk, with his companions, to the licensed prostitute-houses abroad. But the sordid insignificance of the experience appalled him. It had not been anything really: it meant nothing. He felt as if he were, not physically, but spiritually impotent: not actually impotent, but intrinsically so.

He came home with this secret, never-changing burden of his unknown, unbestowed self torturing him. His navy training left him in perfect physical condition. He was sensible of, and proud of his body. He bathed and used dumb-bells, and kept himself fit. He played cricket and football. He read books and began to hold fixed ideas which he got from the Fabians. He played his piccolo, and was considered an expert. But at the bottom of his soul was always this canker of shame and incompleteness: he was miserable beneath all his healthy cheerfulness, he was uneasy and felt despicable among all his confidence and superiority of ideas. He would have changed with any mere brute, just to be free of himself, to be free of this shame of self-consciousness. He saw some collier lurching straight forward without misgiving, pursuing his own satisfactions, and he envied him. Anything, he would have given anything for this spontaneity and this blind stupidity which went to its own satisfaction direct.

9

He was not unhappy in the pit. He was admired by the men, and well enough liked. It was only he himself who felt the difference between himself and the others. He seemed to hide his own stigma. But he was never sure that the others did not really despise him for a ninny, as being less a man than they were. Only he pretended to be more manly, and was surprised by the ease with which they were deceived. And, being naturally cheerful, he was happy at his work. He was sure of himself there. Naked to the waist, hot and grimy with labour, they squatted on their heels for a few minutes and talked, seeing each other dimly by the light of the safety lamps, while the black coal rose jutting round them, and the props of wood stood like little pillars in the low, black, very dark temple. Then the pony came and the gang-lad with a message from Number 7, or with a bottle of water from the horse-trough or some news of the world above. The day passed pleasantly enough. There was an ease, a go-as-you-please about the day underground, a delightful camaraderie of men shut off alone from the rest of the world, in a dangerous place, and a variety of labour, holing, loading, timbering, and a glamour of mystery and adventure in the atmosphere, that made the pit not unattractive to him when he had again got over his anguish of desire for the open air and the sea.

This day there was much to do and Durant was not in humour to talk. He went on working in silence through the afternoon.

'Loose-all' came, and they tramped to the bottom. The whitewashed underground office shone brightly. Men were putting out their lamps. They sat in dozens round the bottom of the shaft, down which black, heavy drops of water fell continuously into the sump. The electric lights shone away down the main underground road.

'Is it raining?' asked Durant.

'Snowing,' said an old man, and the younger was pleased. He liked to go up when it was snowing.

'It'll just come right for Christmas,' said the old man.

'Ay,' replied Durant.

'A green Christmas, a fat churchyard,' said the other sententiously.

Durant laughed, showing his small, rather pointed teeth.

The cage came down, a dozen men lined on. Durant noticed tufts of snow on the perforated, arched roof of the chain, and he was pleased.

He wondered how it liked its excursion underground. But already it was getting soppy with black water.

He liked things about him. There was a little smile on his face. But underlying it was the curious consciousness he felt in himself.

The upper world came almost with a flash, because of the glimmer of snow. Hurrying along the bank, giving up his lamp at the office, he smiled to feel the open about him again, all glimmering round him with snow. The hills on either side were pale blue in the dusk, and the hedges looked savage and dark. The snow was trampled between the railway lines. But far ahead, beyond the black figures of miners moving home, it became smooth again, spreading right up to the dark wall of the coppice.

To the west there was a pinkness, and a big star hovered half revealed. Below, the lights of the pit came out crisp and yellow among the darkness of the buildings, and the lights of Old Aldecross twinkled in rows down the bluish twilight.

Durant walked glad with life among the miners, who were all talking animatedly because of the snow. He liked their company, he liked the white dusky world. It gave him a little thrill to stop at the garden gate and see the light of home down below, shining on the silent blue snow.

10

By the big gate of the railway, in the fence, was a little gate, that he kept locked. As he unfastened it, he watched the kitchen light that shone on to the bushes and the snow outside. It was a candle burning till night set in, he thought to himself. He slid down the steep path to the level below. He liked making the first marks in the smooth snow. Then he came through the bushes to the house. The two women heard his heavy boots ring outside on the scraper, and his voice as he opened the door: 'How much worth of oil do you reckon to save by that candle, mother?' He liked a good light from the lamp.

He had just put down his bottle and snap-bag and was hanging his coat behind the scullery door, when Miss Louisa came upon him. He was startled, but he smiled.

His eyes began to laugh – then his face went suddenly straight, and he was afraid.

'Your mother's had an accident,' she said.

'How?' he exclaimed.

'In the garden,' she answered. He hesitated with his coat in his hands. Then he hung it up and turned to the kitchen.

'Is she in bed?' he asked.

'Yes,' said Miss Louisa, who found it hard to deceive him. He was silent. He went into the kitchen, sat down heavily in his father's old chair, and began to pull off his boots. His head was small, rather finely shapen. His brown hair, close and crisp, would look jolly whatever happened. He wore heavy moleskin trousers that gave off the stale, exhausted scent of the pit. Having put on his slippers, he carried his boots into the scullery.

'What is it?' he asked, afraid.

'Something internal,' she replied.

He went upstairs. His mother kept herself calm for his coming. Louisa felt his tread shake the plaster floor of the bedroom above.

'What have you done?' he asked.

'It's nothing, my lad,' said the old woman, rather hard. 'It's nothing. You needn't fret, my boy, it's nothing more the matter with me than I had yesterday, or last week. The doctor said I'd done nothing serious.'

'What were you doing?' asked her son.

'I was pulling up a cabbage, and I suppose I pulled too hard; for, oh – there was such a pain – '

Her son looked at her quickly. She hardened herself.

'But who doesn't have a sudden pain sometimes, my boy. We all do.'

'And what's it done?'

'I don't know,' she said, 'but I don't suppose it's anything.'

The big lamp in the corner was screened with a dark green, so that he could scarcely see her face. He was strung tight with apprehension and many emotions. Then his brow knitted.

'What did you go pulling your inside out at cabbages for,' he asked, 'and the ground frozen? You'd go on dragging and dragging, if you killed yourself.'

'Somebody's got to get them,' she said.

'You needn't do yourself harm.'

But they had reached futility.

Miss Louisa could hear plainly downstairs. Her heart sank. It seemed so hopeless between them.

'Are you sure it's nothing much, mother?' he asked, appealing, after a little silence.

'Ay, it's nothing,' said the old woman, rather bitter.

'I don't want you to – to – to be badly – you know.'

'Go an' get your dinner,' she said. She knew she was going to die: moreover, the pain was torture just then. 'They're only cosseting me up a bit because I'm an old woman. Miss Louisa's *very* good – and she'll have got your dinner ready, so you'd better go and eat it.'

He felt stupid and ashamed. His mother put him off. He had to turn away. The pain burned in his bowels. He went downstairs. The mother was glad he was gone, so that she could moan with pain.

He had resumed the old habit of eating before he washed himself. Miss Louisa served his dinner. It was strange and exciting to her. She was strung up tense, trying to understand him and his mother. She watched him as he sat. He was turned away from his food, looking in the fire. Her soul watched him, trying to see what he was. His black face and arms were uncouth, he was foreign. His face was masked black with coal-dust. She could not see him, she could not even know him. The brown eyebrows, the steady eyes, the coarse, small moustache above the closed mouth – these were the only familiar indications. What was he, as he sat there in his pit-dirt? She could not see him, and it hurt her.

She ran upstairs, presently coming down with the flannels and the bran-bag, to heat them, because the pain was on again.

He was halfway through his dinner. He put down the fork, suddenly nauseated.

'They will soothe the wrench,' she said. He watched, useless and left out.

'Is she bad?' he asked.

'I think she is,' she answered.

It was useless for him to stir or comment. Louisa was busy. She went upstairs. The poor old woman was in a white, cold sweat of pain. Louisa's face was sullen with suffering as she went about to relieve her. Then she sat and waited. The pain passed gradually, the old woman sank into a state of coma. Louisa still sat silent by the bed. She heard the sound of water downstairs. Then came the voice of the old mother, faint but unrelaxing: 'Alfred's washing himself – he'll want his back washing – '

Louisa listened anxiously, wondering what the sick woman wanted.

'He can't bear if his back isn't washed – ' the old woman persisted, in a cruel attention to his needs.

Louisa rose and wiped the sweat from the yellowish brow. 'I will go down,' she said soothingly.

'If you would,' murmured the sick woman.

Louisa waited a moment. Mrs Durant closed her eyes, having discharged her duty. The young woman went downstairs. Herself, or the man, what did they matter? Only the suffering woman must be considered.

Alfred was kneeling on the hearthrug, stripped to the waist, washing himself in a large panchion of earthenware. He did so every evening, when he had eaten his dinner; his brothers had done so before him. But Miss Louisa was strange in the house.

He was mechanically rubbing the white lather on his head, with a repeated, unconscious movement, his hand every now and then passing over his neck. Louisa watched. She had to brace herself to this also. He bent his head into the water, washed it free of soap, and pressed the water out of his eyes.

'Your mother said you would want your back washing,' she said.

Curious how it hurt her to take part in their fixed routine of life! Louisa felt the almost repulsive intimacy being forced upon her. It was all so common, so like herding. She lost her own distinctness.

He ducked his face round, looking up at her in what was a very comical way. She had to harden herself.

'How funny he looks with his face upside down,' she thought. After all, there was a difference between her and the common people. The water in which his arms were plunged was quite black, the soap-froth was darkish. She could scarcely conceive him as human. Mechanically, under the influence of habit, he groped in the black water, fished out soap and flannel, and handed them backward to Louisa. Then he remained rigid and submissive, his two arms thrust straight in the panchion, supporting the weight of his shoulders. His skin was beautifully white and unblemished, of an opaque, solid whiteness. Gradually Louisa saw it: this also was what he was. It fascinated her. Her feeling of separateness passed away: she ceased to draw back from contact with him and his mother. There was this living centre. Her heart ran hot. She had reached some goal in this beautiful, clear, male body. She loved him in a white, impersonal heat. But the sun-burnt, reddish neck and ears: they were more personal, more curious. A tenderness rose in her, she loved even his queer ears. A person – an intimate being he was to her. She put down the towel and went upstairs again, troubled in her heart. She had only seen one human being in her life – and that was Mary. All the rest were strangers. Now her soul was going to open, she was going to see another. She felt strange and pregnant.

'He'll be more comfortable,' murmured the sick woman abstractedly, as Louisa entered the room. The latter did not answer. Her own heart was heavy with its own responsibility. Mrs Durant lay silent awhile, then she murmured plaintively: 'You mustn't mind, Miss Louisa.'

'Why should I?' replied Louisa, deeply moved.

'It's what we're used to,' said the old woman.

And Louisa felt herself excluded again from their life. She sat in pain, with the tears of disappointment distilling her heart. Was that all?

Alfred came upstairs. He was clean, and in his shirt-sleeves. He looked a workman now. Louisa felt that she and he were foreigners, moving in different lives. It dulled her again. Oh, if she could only find some fixed relations, something sure and abiding.

'How do you feel?' he said to his mother.

'It's a bit better,' she replied wearily, impersonally. This strange putting herself aside, this abstracting herself and answering him only what she thought good for him to hear, made the relations between mother and son poignant and cramping to Miss Louisa. It made the man so ineffectual, so nothing. Louisa groped as if she had lost him. The mother was real and positive – he was not very actual. It puzzled and chilled the young woman.

'I'd better fetch Mrs Harrison?' he said, waiting for his mother to decide.

'I suppose we shall have to have somebody,' she replied.

Miss Louisa stood by, afraid to interfere in their business. They did not include her in their lives, they felt she had nothing to do with them, except as a help from outside. She was quite external to them. She felt hurt and powerless against this unconscious difference. But something patient and unyielding in her made her say: 'I will stay and do the nursing: you can't be left.'

The other two were shy, and at a loss for an answer.

'Wes'll manage to get somebody,' said the old woman wearily. She did not care very much what happened, now.

'I will stay until tomorrow, in any case,' said Louisa. 'Then we can see.'

'I'm sure you've no right to trouble yourself,' moaned the old woman. But she must leave herself in any hands.

Miss Louisa felt glad that she was admitted, even in an official capacity. She wanted to share their lives. At home they would need her, now Mary had come. But they must manage without her.

'I must write a note to the vicarage,' she said.

Alfred Durant looked at her enquiringly, for her service. He had always that intelligent readiness to serve, since he had been in the navy. But there was a simple independence in his willingness, which she loved. She felt nevertheless it was hard to get at him. He was so deferential, quick to take the slightest suggestion of an order from her, implicitly, that she could not get at the man in him.

He looked at her very keenly. She noticed his eyes were golden brown, with a very small pupil, the kind of eyes that can see a long way off. He stood alert, at military attention. His face was still rather weather-reddened.

'Do you want pen and paper?' he asked, with deferential suggestion to a superior, which was more difficult for her than reserve.

'Yes, please,' she said.

He turned and went downstairs. He seemed to her so self-contained, so utterly sure in his movement. How was she to approach him? For he would take not one step towards her. He would only put himself entirely and impersonally at her service, glad to serve her, but keeping himself quite removed from her. She could see he felt real joy in doing anything for her, but any recognition would confuse him and hurt him. Strange it was to her, to have a man going about the house in his shirt-sleeves, his waistcoat unbuttoned, his throat bare, waiting on her. He moved well, as if he had plenty of life to spare. She was attracted by his completeness. And yet, when all was ready, and there was nothing more for him to do, she quivered, meeting his questioning look.

As she sat writing, he placed another candle near her. The rather dense light fell in two places on the overfoldings of her hair till it glistened heavy and bright, like a dense golden plumage folded up. Then the nape of her neck was very white, with fine down and pointed wisps of gold. He watched it as it were a vision, losing himself. She was all that was beyond him, of revelation and exquisiteness. All that was ideal and beyond him, she was that – and he was lost to himself in looking at her. She had no connection with him. He did not approach her. She was there like a wonderful distance. But it was a treat, having her in the house. Even with this anguish for his mother tightening about him, he was sensible of the wonder of living this evening. The candles glistened on her hair, and seemed to fascinate him. He felt a little awe of her, and a sense of uplifting, that he and she and his mother should be together for a time, in the strange, unknown atmosphere. And, when he got out of the house, he was afraid. He saw the stars above ringing with fine brightness, the snow beneath just visible, and a new night was gathering round him. He was afraid almost with obliteration. What was this new night ringing about him, and what was he? He could not recognise himself nor any of his surroundings. He was afraid to think of his mother. And yet his chest was conscious of her, and of what was happening to her. He could not escape from her, she carried him with her into an unformed, unknown chaos.

11

He went up the road in an agony, not knowing what it was all about, but feeling as if a red-hot iron were gripped round his chest. Without thinking, he shook two or three tears on to the snow. Yet in his mind he did not believe his mother would die. He was in the grip of some greater consciousness. As he sat in the hall of the vicarage, waiting whilst Mary put things for Louisa into a bag, he wondered why he had been so upset. He felt abashed and humbled by the big house, he felt again as if he were one of the rank and file. When Miss Mary spoke to him, he almost saluted.

'An honest man,' thought Mary. And the patronage was applied as salve to her own sickness. She had station, so she could patronise: it was almost all that was left to her. But she could not have lived without having a certain position. She could never have trusted herself outside a definite place, nor respected herself except as a woman of superior class.

As Alfred came to the latch-gate, he felt the grief at his heart again, and saw the new heavens. He stood a moment looking northward to the Plough climbing up the night, and at the far glimmer of snow in distant fields. Then his grief came on like physical pain. He held tight to the gate, biting his mouth, whispering 'Mother!' It was a fierce, cutting, physical pain of grief, that came on in bouts, as his mother's pain came on in bouts, and was so acute he could scarcely keep erect. He did not know where it came from, the pain, nor why. It had nothing to do with his thoughts. Almost it had nothing to do with him. Only it gripped him and he must submit. The whole tide of his soul, gathering in its unknown towards this expansion into death, carried him with it helplessly, all the fritter of his thought and consciousness caught up as nothing, the heave passing on towards its breaking, taking him farther than he had ever been. When the young man had regained himself, he went indoors, and there he was almost gay. It seemed to excite him. He felt in high spirits: he made whimsical fun of things. He sat on one side of his mother's bed, Louisa on the other, and a certain gaiety seized them all. But the night and the dread was coming on.

Alfred kissed his mother and went to bed. When he was half undressed the knowledge of his mother came upon him, and the suffering seized him in its grip like two hands, in agony. He lay on the bed screwed up tight. It lasted so long, and exhausted him so much, that he fell asleep, without having the energy to get up and finish undressing. He awoke after midnight to find himself stone cold. He undressed and got into bed, and was soon asleep again.

At a quarter to six he woke, and instantly remembered. Having pulled on his trousers and lighted a candle, he went into his mother's room. He put his hand before the candle flame so that no light fell on the bed.

'Mother!' he whispered.

'Yes,' was the reply.

There was a hesitation.

'Should I go to work?'

He waited, his heart was beating heavily.

'I think I'd go, my lad.'

His heart went down in a kind of despair.

'You want me to?'

He let his hand down from the candle flame. The light fell on the bed. There he saw Louisa lying looking up at him. Her eyes were upon him. She quickly shut her eyes and half buried her face in the pillow, her back turned to him. He saw the rough hair like bright vapour about her round head, and the two plaits flung coiled among the bedclothes. It gave him a shock. He stood almost himself, determined. Louisa cowered down. He looked, and met his mother's eyes. Then he gave way again, and ceased to be sure, ceased to be himself.

'Yes, go to work, my boy,' said the mother.

'All right,' replied he, kissing her. His heart was down at despair, and bitter. He went away.

'Alfred!' cried his mother faintly.

He came back with beating heart.

'What, mother?'

'You'll always do what's right, Alfred?' the mother asked, beside herself in terror now he was leaving her. He was too terrified and bewildered to know what she meant.

'Yes,' he said.

She turned her cheek to him. He kissed her, then went away, in bitter despair. He went to work.

12

By midday his mother was dead. The word met him at the pit-mouth. As he had known, inwardly, it was not a shock to him, and yet he trembled. He went home quite calmly, feeling only heavy in his breathing.

Miss Louisa was still at the house. She had seen to everything possible. Very succinctly, she informed him of what he needed to know. But there was one point of anxiety for her.

'You *did* half expect it – it's not come as a blow to you?' she asked, looking up at him. Her eyes were dark and calm and searching. She too felt lost. He was so dark and inchoate.

'I suppose – yes,' he said stupidly. He looked aside, unable to endure her eyes on him.

'I could not bear to think you might not have guessed,' she said.

He did not answer.

He felt it a great strain to have her near him at this time. He wanted to be alone. As soon as the relatives began to arrive, Louisa departed and came no more. While everything was arranging, and a crowd was in the house, whilst he had business to settle, he went well enough, with only those uncontrollable paroxysms of grief. For the rest, he was superficial. By himself, he endured the fierce, almost insane bursts of grief which passed again and left him calm, almost clear, just wondering. He had not known before that everything could break down, that he himself could break down, and all be a great chaos, very vast and wonderful. It seemed as if life in him had burst its bounds, and he was lost in a great, bewildering flood, immense and unpeopled. He himself was broken and spilled out amid it all. He could only breathe panting in silence. Then the anguish came on again.

When all the people had gone from the Quarry Cottage, leaving the young man alone with an elderly housekeeper, then the long trial began. The snow had thawed and frozen, a fresh fall had whitened the grey, this then began to thaw. The world was a place of loose grey slosh. Alfred had nothing to do in the evenings. He was a man whose life had been filled up with small activities. Without knowing it, he had been centralised, polarised in his mother. It was she who had kept him. Even now, when the old housekeeper had left him, he might still have gone on in his old way. But the force and balance of his life was lacking. He sat pretending to read, all the time holding his fists clenched, and holding himself in, enduring he did not know what. He walked the black and sodden miles of field-paths, till he was tired out: but all this was only running away from whence he must return. At work he was all right. If it had been summer he might have escaped by working in the garden till bedtime. But now, there was no escape, no relief, no help. He, perhaps, was made for action rather than for understanding; for doing than for being. He was shocked out of his activities, like a swimmer who forgets to swim.

For a week, he had the force to endure this suffocation and struggle, then he began to get exhausted, and knew it must come out. The instinct of self-preservation became strongest. But there was the question: Where was he to go? The public-house really meant nothing to him, it was no good going there. He began to think of emigration. In another country he would be all right. He wrote to the emigration offices.

On the Sunday after the funeral, when all the Durant people had attended church, Alfred had seen Miss Louisa, impassive and reserved, sitting with Miss Mary, who was proud and very distant, and with the other Lindleys, who were people removed. Alfred saw them as people remote. He did not think about it. They had nothing to do with his life. After service Louisa had come to him and shaken hands.

'My sister would like you to come to supper one evening, if you would be so good.'

He looked at Miss Mary, who bowed. Out of kindness, Mary had proposed this to Louisa, disapproving of herself even as she did so. But she did not examine herself closely.

'Yes,' said Durant awkwardly, 'I'll come if you want me.' But he vaguely felt that it was misplaced.

'You'll come tomorrow evening, then, about half-past six.'

He went. Miss Louisa was very kind to him. There could be no music, because of the babies. He sat with his fists clenched on his thighs, very quiet and unmoved, lapsing, among all those people, into a kind of muse or daze. There was nothing between him and them. They knew it as well as he. But he remained very steady in himself, and the evening passed slowly. Mrs Lindley called him 'young man'.

'Will you sit here, young man?'

He sat there. One name was as good as another. What had they to do with him?

Mr Lindley kept a special tone for him, kind, indulgent, but patronising. Durant took it all without criticism or offence, just submitting. But he did not want to eat – that troubled him, to have to eat in their presence. He knew he was out of place. But it was his duty to stay yet awhile. He answered precisely, in monosyllables.

When he left he winced with confusion. He was glad it was finished. He got away as quickly as possible. And he wanted still more intensely to go right away, to Canada.

Miss Louisa suffered in her soul, indignant with all of them, with him too, but quite unable to say why she was indignant.

13

Two evenings after, Louisa tapped at the door of the Quarry Cottage, at half-past six. He had finished dinner, the woman had washed up and gone away, but still he sat in his pit dirt. He was going later to the New Inn. He had begun to go there because he must go somewhere. The mere contact with other men was necessary to him, the noise, the warmth, the forgetful flight of the hours. But still he did not move. He sat alone in the empty house till it began to grow on him like something unnatural.

He was in his pit dirt when he opened the door.

'I have been wanting to call – I thought I would,' she said, and she went to the sofa. He wondered why she wouldn't use his mother's round armchair. Yet something stirred in him, like anger, when the housekeeper placed herself in it.

'I ought to have been washed by now,' he said, glancing at the clock, which was adorned with butterflies and cherries, and the name of 'T. Brooks, Mansfield'. He laid his black hands along his mottled dirty arms. Louisa looked at him. There was the reserve, and the simple neutrality towards her, which she dreaded in him. It made it impossible for her to approach him.

'I am afraid,' she said, 'that I wasn't kind in asking you to supper.'

'I'm not used to it,' he said, smiling with his mouth, showing the interspaced white teeth. His eyes, however, were steady and unseeing.

'It's not *that*,' she said hastily. Her repose was exquisite and her dark grey eyes rich with understanding. He felt afraid of her as she sat there, as he began to grow conscious of her.

'How do you get on alone?' she asked.

He glanced away to the fire.

'Oh – ' he answered, shifting uneasily, not finishing his answer.

Her face settled heavily.

'How close it is in this room. You have such immense fires. I will take off my coat,' she said.

He watched her take off her hat and coat. She wore a cream cashmir blouse embroidered with gold silk. It seemed to him a very fine garment, fitting her throat and wrists close. It gave him a feeling of pleasure and cleanness and relief from himself.

'What were you thinking about, that you didn't get washed?' she asked, half intimately. He laughed, turning aside his head. The whites of his eyes showed very distinct in his black face.

'Oh,' he said, 'I couldn't tell you.'

There was a pause.

'Are you going to keep this house on?' she asked.

He stirred in his chair, under the question.

'I hardly know,' he said. 'I'm very likely going to Canada.'

Her spirit became very quiet and attentive.

'What for?' she asked.

Again he shifted restlessly on his seat.

'Well' – he said slowly – 'to try the life.'

'But which life?'

'There's various things – farming or lumbering or mining. I don't mind much what it is.'

'And is that what you want?'

He did not think in these terms, so he could not answer.

'I don't know,' he said, 'till I've tried.'

She saw him drawing away from her for ever.

'Aren't you sorry to leave this house and garden?' she asked.

'I don't know,' he answered reluctantly. 'I suppose our Fred would come in – that's what he's wanting.'

'You don't want to settle down?' she asked.

He was leaning forward on the arms of his chair. He turned to her. Her face was pale and set. It looked heavy and impassive, her hair shone richer as she grew white. She was to him something steady and immovable and eternal presented to him. His heart was hot in an anguish of suspense. Sharp twitches of fear and pain were in his limbs. He turned his whole body away from her. The silence was unendurable. He could not bear her to sit there any more. It made his heart go hot and stifled in his breast.

'Were you going out tonight?' she asked.

'Only to the New Inn,' he said.

Again there was silence.

She reached for her hat. Nothing else was suggested to her. She *had* to go. He sat waiting for her to be gone, for relief. And she knew that if she went out of that house as she was, she went out a failure. Yet she continued to pin on her hat; in a moment she would have to go. Something was carrying her.

Then suddenly a sharp pang, like lightning, seared her from head to foot, and she was beyond herself.

'Do you want me to go?' she asked, controlled, yet speaking out of a fiery anguish, as if the words were spoken from her without her intervention.

He went white under his dirt.

'Why?' he asked, turning to her in fear, compelled.

'Do you want me to go?' she repeated.

'Why?' he asked again.

'Because I wanted to stay with you,' she said, suffocated, with her lungs full of fire.

His face worked, he hung forward a little, suspended, staring straight into her eyes, in torment, in an agony of chaos, unable to collect himself. And as if turned to stone, she looked back into his eyes. Their souls were exposed bare for a few moments. It was agony. They could not bear it. He dropped his head, whilst his body jerked with little sharp twitchings.

She turned away for her coat. Her soul had gone dead in her. Her hands trembled, but she could not feel any more. She drew on her coat. There was a cruel suspense in the room. The moment had come for her to go. He lifted his head. His eyes were like agate, expressionless, save for the black points of torture. They held her, she had no will, no life any more. She felt broken.

'Don't you want me?' she said helplessly.

A spasm of torture crossed his eyes, which held her fixed.

'I – I – ' he began, but he could not speak. Something drew him from his chair to her. She stood motionless, spellbound, like a creature given up as prey. He put his hand tentatively, uncertainly, on her arm. The expression of his face was strange and inhuman. She stood utterly motionless. Then clumsily he put his arms round her, and took her, cruelly, blindly, straining her till she nearly lost consciousness, till he himself had almost fallen.

Then, gradually, as he held her gripped, and his brain reeled round, and he felt himself falling, falling from himself, and whilst she, yielded up, swooned to a kind of death of herself, a moment of utter darkness came over him, and they began to wake up again as if from a long sleep. He was himself.

After a while his arms slackened, she loosened herself a little, and put her arms round him, as he held her. So they held each other close, and hid each against the other for assurance, helpless in speech. And it was ever her hands that trembled more closely upon him, drawing him nearer into her, with love.

And at last she drew back her face and looked up at him, her eyes wet, and shining with light. His heart, which saw, was silent with fear. He was with her. She saw his face all sombre and inscrutable, and he seemed eternal to her. And all the echo of pain came back into the rarity of bliss, and all her tears came up.

'I love you,' she said, her lips drawn and sobbing. He put down his head against her, unable to hear her, unable to bear the sudden coming of the peace and passion that almost broke his heart. They stood together in silence whilst the thing moved away a little.

At last she wanted to see him. She looked up. His eyes were strange and glowing, with a tiny black pupil. Strange, they were, and powerful over her. And his mouth came to hers, and slowly her eyelids closed, as his mouth sought hers closer and closer, and took possession of her.

They were silent for a long time, too much mixed up with passion and grief and death to do anything but hold each other in pain and kiss with long, hurting kisses wherein fear was transfused into desire. At last she disengaged herself. He felt as if his heart were hurt, but glad, and he scarcely dared look at her.

'I'm glad,' she said also.

He held her hands in passionate gratitude and desire. He had not yet the presence of mind to say anything. He was dazed with relief.

'I ought to go,' she said.

He looked at her. He could not grasp the thought of her going, he knew he could never be separated from her any more. Yet he dared not assert himself. He held her hands tight.

'Your face is black,' she said.

He laughed.

'Yours is a bit smudged,' he said.

They were afraid of each other, afraid to talk. He could only keep her near to him. After a while she wanted to wash her face. He brought her some warm water, standing by and watching her. There was something he wanted to say, that he dared not. He watched her wiping her face, and making tidy her hair.

'They'll see your blouse is dirty,' he said.

She looked at her sleeves and laughed for joy.

He was sharp with pride.

'What shall you do?' he asked.

'How?' she said.

He was awkward at a reply.

'About me,' he said.

'What do you want me to do?' she laughed.

He put his hand out slowly to her. What did it matter!

'But make yourself clean,' she said.

14

As they went up the hill, the night seemed dense with the unknown. They kept close together, feeling as if the darkness were alive and full of knowledge, all around them. In silence they walked up the hill. At first the street lamps went their way. Several people passed them. He was more shy than she, and would have let her go had she loosened in the least. But she held firm.

Then they came into the true darkness, between the fields. They did not want to speak, feeling closer together in silence. So they arrived at the vicarage gate. They stood under the naked horse-chestnut tree.

'I wish you didn't have to go,' he said.

She laughed a quick little laugh.

'Come tomorrow,' she said, in a low tone, 'and ask father.'

She felt his hand close on hers.

She gave the same sorrowful little laugh of sympathy. Then she kissed him, sending him home.

At home, the old grief came on in another paroxysm, obliterating Louisa, obliterating even his mother for whom the stress was raging like a burst of fever in a wound. But something was sound in his heart.

15

The next evening he dressed to go to the vicarage, feeling it was to be done, not imagining what it would be like. He would not take this seriously. He was sure of Louisa, and this marriage was like fate to him. It filled him also with a blessed feeling of fatality. He was not responsible, neither had her people anything really to do with it.

They ushered him into the little study, which was fireless. By and by the vicar came in. His voice was cold and hostile as he said: 'What can I do for you, young man?'

He knew already, without asking.

Durant looked up at him, again like a sailor before a superior. He had the subordinate manner. Yet his spirit was clear.

'I wanted, Mr Lindley – ' he began respectfully, then all the colour suddenly left his face. It seemed now a violation to say what he had to say. What was he doing there? But he stood on, because it had to be done. He held firmly to his own independence and self-respect. He must not be indecisive. He must put himself aside: the matter was bigger than just his personal self. He must not feel. This was his highest duty.

'You wanted – ' said the vicar.

Durant's mouth was dry, but he answered with steadiness: 'Miss Louisa – Louisa – promised to marry me – '

'You asked Miss Louisa if she would marry you – yes – ' corrected the vicar.

Durant reflected he had not asked her this.

'If she would marry me, sir. I hope you – don't mind.'

He smiled. He was a good-looking man, and the vicar could not help seeing it.

'And my daughter was willing to marry you?' said Mr Lindley.

'Yes,' said Durant seriously. It was pain to him, nevertheless. He felt the natural hostility between himself and the elder man.

'Will you come this way?' said the vicar. He led into the dining-room, where were Mary, Louisa and Mrs Lindley. Mr Massy sat in a corner with a lamp.

'This young man has come on your account, Louisa?' said Mr Lindley.

'Yes,' said Louisa, her eyes on Durant, who stood erect, in discipline. He dared not look at her, but he was aware of her.

'You don't want to marry a collier, you little fool,' cried Mrs Lindley harshly. She lay obese and helpless upon the couch, swathed in a loose, dove-grey gown.

'Oh, hush, mother,' cried Mary, with quiet intensity and pride.

'What means have you to support a wife?' demanded the vicar's wife roughly.

'I!' Durant replied, starting. 'I think I can earn enough.'

'Well, and how much?' came the rough voice.

'Seven and six a day,' replied the young man.

'And will it get to be any more?'

'I hope so.'

'And are you going to live in that poky little house?'

'I think so,' said Durant, 'if it's all right.'

He took small offence, only was upset, because they would not think him good enough. He knew that, in their sense, he was not.

'Then she's a fool, I tell you, if she marries you,' cried the mother roughly, casting her decision.

'After all, mama, it is Louisa's affair,' said Mary distinctly, 'and we must remember – '

'As she makes her bed, she must lie – but she'll repent it,' interrupted Mrs Lindley.

'And after all,' said Mr Lindley, 'Louisa cannot quite hold herself free to act entirely without consideration for her family.'

'What do you want, papa?' asked Louisa sharply.

'I mean that if you marry this man, it will make my position very difficult for me, particularly if you stay in this parish. If you were moving quite away, it would be simpler. But living here in a collier's cottage, under my nose, as it were – it would be almost unseemly. I have my position to maintain, and a position which may not be taken lightly.'

'Come over here, young man,' cried the mother, in her rough voice, 'and let us look at you.'

Durant, flushing, went over and stood – not quite at attention, so that he did not know what to do with his hands. Miss Louisa was angry to see him standing there, obedient and acquiescent. He ought to show himself a man.

'Can't you take her away and live out of sight?' said the mother. 'You'd both of you be better off.'

'Yes, we can go away,' he said.

'Do you want to?' asked Miss Mary clearly.

He faced round. Mary looked very stately and impressive. He flushed.

'I do if it's going to be a trouble to anybody,' he said.

'For yourself, you would rather stay?' said Mary.

'It's my home,' he said, 'and that's the house I was born in.'

'Then' – Mary turned clearly to her parents, 'I really don't see how you can make the conditions, papa. He has his own rights, and if Louisa wants to marry him – '

'Louisa, Louisa!' cried the father impatiently. 'I cannot understand why Louisa should not behave in the normal way. I cannot see why she should only think of herself, and leave her family out of count. The thing is enough in itself, and she ought to try to ameliorate it as much as possible. And if – '

'But I love the man, papa,' said Louisa.

'And I hope you love your parents, and I hope you want to spare them as much of the – the loss of prestige, as possible.'

'We *can* go away to live,' said Louisa, her face breaking to tears. At last she was really hurt.

'Oh, yes, easily,' Durant replied hastily, pale, distressed.

There was dead silence in the room.

'I think it would really be better,' murmured the vicar, mollified.

'Very likely it would,' said the rough-voiced invalid.

'Though I think we ought to apologise for asking such a thing,' said Mary haughtily.

'No,' said Durant. 'It will be best all round.' He was glad there was no more bother. 'And shall we put up the banns here or go to the registrar?' he asked clearly, like a challenge.

'We will go to the registrar,' replied Louisa decidedly.

Again there was a dead silence in the room.

'Well, if you will have your own way, you must go your own way,' said the mother emphatically.

All the time, Mr Massy had sat obscure and unnoticed in a corner of the room. At this juncture he got up, saying: 'There is baby, Mary.'

Mary rose and went out of the room, stately; her little husband padded after her. Durant watched the fragile, small man go, wondering.

'And where,' asked the vicar, almost genial, 'do you think you will go when you are married?'

Durant started.

'I was thinking of emigrating,' he said.

'To Canada? or where?'

'I think to Canada.'

'Yes, that would be very good.'

Again there was a pause.

'We shan't see much of you then, as a son-in-law,' said the mother, roughly but amicably.

'Not much,' he said.

Then he took his leave. Louisa went with him to the gate. She stood before him in distress.

'You won't mind them, will you?' she said humbly.

'I don't mind them, if they don't mind me!' he said. Then he stooped and kissed her.

'Let us be married soon,' she murmured, in tears.

'All right,' he said. 'I'll go tomorrow to Barford.'

Wintry Peacock

There was thin, crisp snow on the ground, the sky was blue, the wind very cold, the air clear. Farmers were just turning out the cows for an hour or so in the midday, and the smell of cow-sheds was unendurable as I entered Tible. I noticed the ash-twigs up in the sky were pale and luminous, passing into the blue. And then I saw the peacocks. There they were in the road before me, three of them – tail-less, brown, speckled birds, with dark-blue necks and ragged crests. They stepped archly over the filigree snow, and their bodies moved with slow motion, like small, light, flat-bottomed boats. I admired them, they were curious. Then a gust of wind caught them, heeled them over as if they were three frail boats, opening their feathers like ragged sails. They hopped and skipped with discomfort, to get out of the draught of the wind. And then, in the lee of the walls, they resumed their arch, wintry motion, light and unballasted now their tails were gone, indifferent. They were indifferent to my presence. I might have touched them. They turned off to the shelter of an open shed.

As I passed the end of the upper house, I saw a young woman just coming out of the back-door. I had spoken to her in the summer. She recognised me at once, and waved to me. She was carrying a pail, wearing a white apron that was longer than her preposterously short skirt, and she had on the cotton bonnet. I took off my hat to her and was going on. But she put down her pail and darted with a swift, furtive movement after me.

'Do you mind waiting a minute?' she said. 'I'll be out in a minute.'

She gave me a slight, odd smile, and ran back. Her face was long and sallow and her nose rather red. But her gloomy black eyes softened caressively to me for a moment, with that momentary humility which makes a man lord of the earth.

I stood in the road, looking at the fluffy, dark-red young cattle that mooed and seemed to bark at me. They seemed happy, frisky cattle, a little impudent, and either determined to go back into the warm shed, or determined not to go back, I could not decide which.

Presently the woman came forward again, her head rather ducked. But she looked up at me and smiled, with that odd, immediate intimacy, something witch-like and impossible.

'Sorry to keep you waiting,' she said. 'Shall we stand in this cart-shed – it will be more out of the wind.'

So we stood among the shafts of the open cart-shed that faced the road. Then she looked down at the ground, a little sideways, and I noticed a small black frown on her brows. She seemed to brood for a moment. Then she looked straight into my eyes, so that I blinked and wanted to turn my face aside. She was searching me for something and her look was too near. The frown was still on her keen, sallow brow.

'Can you speak French?' she asked me abruptly.

'More or less,' I replied.

'I was supposed to learn it at school,' she said. 'But I don't know a word.' She ducked her head and laughed, with a slightly ugly grimace and a rolling of her black eyes.

'No good keeping your mind full of scraps,' I answered.

But she had turned aside her sallow, long face, and did not hear what I said. Suddenly again she looked at me. She was searching. And at the same time she smiled at me, and her eyes looked softly, darkly, with infinite trustful humility into mine. I was being cajoled.

'Would you mind reading a letter for me, in French,' she said, her face immediately black and bitter-looking. She glanced at me, frowning.

'Not at all,' I said.

'It's a letter to my husband,' she said, still scrutinising.

I looked at her, and didn't quite realise. She looked too far into me, my wits were gone. She glanced round. Then she looked at me shrewdly. She drew a letter from her pocket, and handed it to me. It was addressed from France to Lance-Corporal Goyte, at Tible. I took out the letter and began to read it, as mere words. '*Mon cher Alfred*' – it might have been a bit of a torn newspaper. So I followed the script: the trite phrases of a letter from a French-speaking girl to an English soldier. 'I think of you always, always. Do you think sometimes of me?' And then I vaguely realised that I was reading a man's private correspondence. And yet, how could one consider these trivial, facile French phrases private! Nothing more trite and vulgar in the world than such a love-letter – no newspaper more obvious.

Therefore I read with a callous heart the effusions of the Belgian damsel. But then I gathered my attention. For the letter went on:

Notre cher petit bébé – our dear little baby was born a week ago. Almost I died, knowing you were far away, and perhaps forgetting the fruit of our perfect love. But the child comforted me. He has the smiling eyes and virile air of his English father. I pray to the Mother of Jesus to send me the dear father of my child, that I may see him with my child in his arms, and that we may be united in holy family love. Ah, my Alfred, can I tell you how I miss you, how I weep for you. My thoughts are with you always, I think of nothing but you, I live for nothing but you and our dear baby. If you do not come back to me soon, I shall die, and our child will die. But no, you cannot come back to me. But I can come to you, come to England with our child. If you do not wish to present me to your good mother and father, you can meet me in some town, some city, for I shall be so frightened to be alone in England with my child, and no one to take care of us. Yet I must come to you, I must bring my child, my little Alfred to his father, the big, beautiful Alfred that I love so much. Oh, write and tell me where I shall come. I have some money, I am not a penniless creature. I have money for myself and my dear baby –

I read to the end. It was signed: 'Your very happy and still more unhappy Èlise.' I suppose I must have been smiling.

'I can see it makes you laugh,' said Mrs Goyte, sardonically. I looked up at her.

'It's a love-letter, I know that,' she said. 'There's too many "Alfreds" in it.'

'One too many,' I said.

'Oh, yes – And what does she say – Eliza? We know her name's Eliza, that's another thing.' She grimaced a little, looking up at me with a mocking laugh.

'Where did you get this letter?' I said.

'Postman gave it me last week.'

'And is your husband at home?'

'I expect him home tonight. He's been wounded, you know, and we've been applying for him home. He was home about six weeks ago – he's been in Scotland since then. Oh, he was wounded in the leg. Yes, he's all right, a great strapping fellow. But he's lame, he limps a bit. He expects he'll get his discharge – but I don't think he will. We married. We've been married six years – and he joined up the first day of the war. Oh, he thought he'd like the life. He'd been through the South African War. No, he was sick of it, fed up. I'm living with his father and mother – I've no home of my own now. My people had a big farm – over a thousand acres – in Oxfordshire. Not like here – no. Oh, they're very good to me, his father and mother. Oh, yes, they couldn't be better. They think more of me than of their own daughters. But it's not like being in a place of your own, is it? You can't *really* do as you like. No, there's only me and his father and mother at home. Before the war? Oh, he was anything. He's had a good education – but he liked the farming better. Then he was a chauffeur. That's how he knew French. He was driving a gentleman in France for a long time – '

At this point the peacocks came round the corner on a puff of wind.

'Hello, Joey!' she called, and one of the birds came forward, on delicate legs. Its grey speckled back was very elegant, it rolled its full, dark-blue neck as it moved to her. She crouched down. 'Joey, dear,' she said, in an odd, saturnine, caressive voice, 'you're bound to find me, aren't you?' She put her face forward, and the bird rolled his neck, almost touching her face with his beak, as if kissing her.

'He loves you,' I said.

She twisted her face up at me with a laugh.

'Yes,' she said, 'he loves me, Joey does' – then, to the bird – 'and I love Joey, don't I. I *do* love Joey.' And she smoothed his feathers for a moment. Then she rose, saying: 'He's an affectionate bird.'

I smiled at the roll of her 'bir–rrd'.

'Oh, yes, he is,' she protested. 'He came with me from my home seven years ago. Those others are his descendants – but they're not like Joey – *are they, dee–urr?*' Her voice rose at the end with a witch-like cry.

Then she forgot the birds in the cart-shed and turned to business again.

'Won't you read that letter?' she said. 'Read it, so that I know what it says.'

'It's rather behind his back,' I said.

'Oh, never mind him,' she cried. 'He's been behind my back long enough – all these four years. If he never did no worse things behind my back than I do behind his, he wouldn't have cause to grumble. You read me what it says.'

Now I felt a distinct reluctance to do as she bid, and yet I began – " 'My dear Alfred".'

'I guessed that much,' she said. 'Eliza's dear Alfred.' She laughed. 'How do you say it in French? *Eliza?*'

I told her, and she repeated the name with great contempt – '*Élise*'.

'Go on,' she said. 'You're not reading.'

So I began – ' "I have been thinking of you sometimes – have you been thinking of me?" ' –

'Of several others as well, beside her, I'll wager,' said Mrs Goyte.

'Probably not,' said I, and continued. ' "A dear little baby was born here a week ago. Ah, can I tell you my feelings when I take my darling little brother into my arms – " '

'I'll bet it's *his*,' cried Mrs Goyte.

'No,' I said. 'It's her mother's.'

'Don't you believe it,' she cried. 'It's a blind. You mark, it's her own right enough – and his.'

'No,' I said, 'it's her mother's. "He has sweet smiling eyes, but not like your beautiful English eyes – " '

She suddenly struck her hand on her skirt with a wild motion, and bent down, doubled with laughter. Then she rose and covered her face with her hand.

'I'm forced to laugh at the beautiful English eyes,' she said.

'Aren't his eyes beautiful?' I asked.

'Oh, yes – *very*! Go on! – *Joey, dear, dee–urr, Joey!*' – this to the peacock.

'Er – "We miss you very much. We all miss you. We wish you were here to see the darling baby. Ah, Alfred, how happy we were when you stayed with us. We all loved you so much. My mother will call the baby Alfred so that we shall never forget you – " '

'Of course it's his right enough,' cried Mrs Goyte.

'No,' I said. 'It's the mother's. Er – "My mother is very well. My father came home yesterday – on leave. He is delighted with his son, my little brother, and wishes to have him named after you, because you were so good to us all in that terrible time, which I shall never forget. I must weep now when I think of it. Well, you are far away in England, and perhaps I shall never see you again. How did you find your dear mother and father? I am so happy that your wound is better, and that you can nearly walk – " '

'How did he find his dear *wife*!' cried Mrs Goyte. 'He never told her he had one. Think of taking the poor girl in like that!'

' "We are so pleased when you write to us. Yet now you are in England you will forget the family you served so well – " '

'A bit too well – eh, *Joey*!' cried the wife.

' "If it had not been for you we should not be alive now, to grieve and to rejoice in this life, that is so hard for us. But we have recovered some of our losses, and no longer feel the burden of poverty. The little Alfred is a great comfort to me. I hold him to my breast and think of the big, good Alfred, and I weep to think that those times of suffering were perhaps the times of a great happiness that is gone for ever." '

'Oh, but isn't it a shame, to take a poor girl in like that!' cried Mrs Goyte. 'Never to let on that he was married, and raise her hopes – I call it beastly, I do.'

'You don't know,' I said. 'You know how anxious women are to fall in love, wife or no wife. How could he help it, if she was determined to fall in love with him?'

'He could have helped it if he'd wanted.'

'Well,' I said, 'we aren't all heroes.'

'Oh, but that's different! The big, good Alfred! – did ever you hear such tommy-rot in your life! Go on – what does she say at the end?'

'Er – "We shall be pleased to hear of your life in England. We all send many kind regards to your good parents. I wish you all happiness for your future days. Your very affectionate and ever-grateful Èlise." '

There was silence for a moment, during which Mrs Goyte remained with her head dropped, sinister and abstracted. Suddenly she lifted her face, and her eyes flashed.

'Oh, but I call it beastly, I call it mean, to take a girl in like that.'

'Nay,' I said. 'Probably he hasn't taken her in at all. Do you think those French girls are such poor innocent things? I guess she's a great deal more downy than he.'

'Oh, he's one of the biggest fools that ever walked,' she cried.

'There you are!' said I.

'But it's his child right enough,' she said.

'I don't think so,' said I.

'I'm sure of it.'

'Oh, well,' I said, 'if you prefer to think that way.'

'What other reason has she for writing like that –'

I went out into the road and looked at the cattle. 'Who is this driving the cows?' I said.

She too came out. 'It's the boy from the next farm,' she said.

'Oh, well,' said I, 'those Belgian girls! You never know where their letters will end. And, after all, it's his affair – you needn't bother.'

'Oh – !' she cried, with rough scorn – 'it's not *me* that bothers. But it's the nasty meanness of it – me writing him such loving letters' – she put her hand before her face and laughed malevolently – 'and sending him parcels all the time. You bet he fed that gurrl on my parcels – I know he did. It's just like him. I'll bet they laughed together over my letters. I bet anything they did –'.

'Nay,' said I. 'He'd burn your letters for fear they'd give him away.'

There was a black look on her yellow face. Suddenly a voice was heard calling. She poked her head out of the shed, and answered coolly: 'All right!' Then turning to me: 'That's his mother looking after me.'

She laughed into my face, witch-like, and we turned down the road.

*   *   *

When I awoke the morning after this episode, I found the house darkened with deep, soft snow, which had blown against the large west windows, covering them with a screen. I went outside, and saw the valley all white and ghastly below me, the trees beneath black and thin-looking like wire, the rock-faces dark between the glistening shroud, and the sky above sombre, heavy, yellowish-dark, much too heavy for this world below of hollow bluey whiteness figured with black. I felt I was in a valley of the dead. And I sensed I was a prisoner, for the snow was everywhere deep, and drifted in places. So all the morning I remained indoors, looking up the drive at the shrubs so heavily plumed with snow, at the gateposts raised high with a foot or more of extra whiteness. Or I looked down into the white-and-black valley that was utterly motionless and beyond life, a hollow sarcophagus.

Nothing stirred the whole day – no plume fell off the shrubs, the valley was as abstracted as a grove of death. I looked over at the tiny, half-buried farms away on the bare uplands beyond the valley hollow, and I thought of Tible in the snow, of the black witch-like little Mrs Goyte. And the snow seemed to lay me bare to influences I wanted to escape.

In the faint glow of the half-clear light that came about four o'clock in the afternoon, I was roused to see a motion in the snow away below, near where the thorn trees stood very black and dwarfed, like a little savage group, in the dismal white. I watched closely. Yes, there was a flapping and a struggle – a big bird, it must be, labouring in the snow. I wondered. Our biggest birds, in the valley, were the large hawks that often hung flickering opposite my windows, level with me, but high above some prey on the steep valleyside. This was much too big for a hawk – too big for any known bird. I searched in my mind for the largest English wild birds, geese, buzzards.

Still it laboured and strove, then was still, a dark spot, then struggled again. I went out of the house and down the steep slope, at risk of breaking my leg between the rocks. I knew the ground so well – and yet I got well shaken before I drew near the thorn-trees.

Yes, it was a bird. It was Joey. It was the grey-brown peacock with a blue neck. He was snow-wet and spent.

'Joey – Joey, de–urr!' I said, staggering unevenly towards him. He looked so pathetic, rowing and struggling in the snow, too spent to rise, his blue neck stretching out and lying sometimes on the snow, his eye closing and opening quickly, his crest all battered.

'Joey dee–uur! Dee–urr!' I said caressingly to him. And at last he lay still, blinking, in the surged and furrowed snow, whilst I came near and touched him, stroked him, gathered him under my arm. He stretched his long, wetted neck away from me as I held him, none the less he was quiet in my arm, too tired, perhaps, to struggle. Still he held his poor, crested head away from me, and seemed sometimes to droop, to wilt, as if he might suddenly die.

He was not so heavy as I expected, yet it was a struggle to get up to the house with him again. We set him down, not too near the fire, and gently wiped him with cloths. He submitted, only now and then stretched his soft neck away from us, avoiding us helplessly. Then we set warm food by him. I put it to his beak, tried to make him eat. But he ignored it. He seemed to be ignorant of what we were doing, recoiled inside himself inexplicably. So we put him in a basket with cloths, and left him crouching oblivious. His food we put near him. The blinds were drawn, the house was warm, it was night. Sometimes he stirred, but mostly he huddled still, leaning his queer crested head on one side. He touched no food, and took no heed of sounds or movements. We talked of brandy or stimulants. But I realised we had best leave him alone.

In the night, however, we heard him thumping about. I got up anxiously with a candle. He had eaten some food, and scattered more, making a mess. And he was perched on the back of a heavy armchair. So I concluded he was recovered, or recovering.

The next day was clear, and the snow had frozen, so I decided to carry him back to Tible. He consented, after various flappings, to sit in a big fish-bag with his battered head peeping out with wild uneasiness. And so I set off with him, slithering down into the valley, making good progress down in the pale shadow beside the rushing waters, then climbing painfully up the arrested white valleyside, plumed with clusters of young pine trees, into the paler white radiance of the snowy, upper regions, where the wind cut fine. Joey seemed to watch all the time with wide anxious, unseeing eye, brilliant and inscrutable. As I drew near to Tible township he stirred violently in the bag, though I do not know if he had recognised the place. Then, as I came to the sheds, he looked sharply from side to side, and stretched his neck out long. I was a little afraid of him. He gave a loud, vehement yell, opening his sinister beak, and I stood still, looking at him as he struggled in the bag, shaken myself by his struggles, yet not thinking to release him.

Mrs Goyte came darting past the end of the house, her head sticking forward in sharp scrutiny. She saw me, and came forward.

'Have you got Joey?' she cried sharply, as if I were a thief.

I opened the bag, and he flopped out, flapping as if he hated the touch of the snow now. She gathered him up, and put her lips to his beak. She was flushed and handsome, her eyes bright, her hair slack, thick, but more witch-like than ever. She did not speak.

She had been followed by a grey-haired woman with a round, rather sallow face and a slightly hostile bearing.

'Did you bring him with you, then?' she asked sharply. I answered that I had rescued him the previous evening.

From the background slowly approached a slender man with a grey moustache and large patches on his trousers.

'You've got 'im back 'gain, ah see,' he said to his daughter-in-law. His wife explained how I had found Joey.

'Ah,' went on the grey man. 'It wor our Alfred scared him off, back your life. He must'a flyed ower t'valley. Tha ma' thank thy stars as 'e wor fun, Maggie. 'E'd a bin froze. They a bit nesh, you know,' he concluded to me.

'They are,' I answered. 'This isn't their country.'

'No, it isna,' replied Mr Goyte. He spoke very slowly and deliberately, quietly, as if the soft pedal were always down in his voice. He looked at his daughter-in-law as she crouched, flushed and dark, before the peacock, which would lay its long blue neck for a moment along her lap. In spite of his grey moustache and thin grey hair, the elderly man had a face young and almost delicate, like a young man's. His blue eyes twinkled with some inscrutable source of pleasure, his skin was fine and tender, his nose delicately arched. His grey hair being slightly ruffled, he had a debonair look, as of a youth who is in love.

'We mun tell 'im it's come,' he said slowly, and turning he called: 'Alfred – Alfred! Wheer's ter gotten to?'

Then he turned again to the group.

'Get up then, Maggie, lass, get up wi' thee. Tha ma'es too much o' th' bod.'

A young man approached, wearing rough khaki and kneebreeches. He was Danish looking, broad at the loins.

'I's come back then,' said the father to the son; 'leastwise, he's bin browt back, flyed ower the Griff Low.'

The son looked at me. He had a devil-may-care bearing, his cap on one side, his hands stuck in the front pockets of his breeches. But he said nothing.

'Shall you come in a minute, master,' said the elderly woman, to me.

'Ay, come in an' ha'e a cup o' tea or summat. You'll do wi' summat, carrin' that bod. Come on, Maggie wench, let's go in.'

So we went indoors, into the rather stuffy, overcrowded living-room, that was too cosy and too warm. The son followed last, standing in the doorway. The father talked to me.

Maggie put out the tea-cups. The mother went into the dairy again.

'Tha'lt rouse thysen up a bit again, now, Maggie,' the father-in-law said – and then to me: ' 'ers not bin very bright sin' Alfred came whoam, an' the bod flyed awee. 'E come whoam a Wednesday night, Alfred did. But ay, you knowed, didna yer. Ay, 'e comed 'a Wednesday – an' I reckon there wor a bit of a to-do between 'em, worn't there, Maggie?'

He twinkled maliciously to his daughter-in-law, who was flushed, brilliant and handsome.

'Oh, be quiet, father. You're wound up, by the sound of you,' she said to him, as if crossly. But she could never be cross with him.

' 'Ers got 'er colour back this mornin',' continued the father-in-law slowly. 'It's bin heavy weather wi' 'er this last two days. Ay – 'er's bin north-east sin 'er seed you a Wednesday.'

'Father, do stop talking. You'd wear the leg off an iron pot. I can't think where you've found your tongue, all of a sudden,' said Maggie, with caressive sharpness.

'Ah've found it wheer I lost it. Aren't goin' ter come in an' sit thee down, Alfred?'

But Alfred turned and disappeared.

' 'E's got th' monkey on 'is back ower this letter job,' said the father secretly to me. 'Mother, 'er knows nowt about it. Lot o' tomfoolery, isn't it? Ay! What's good o' makkin' a peck o' trouble over what's far enough off, an' ned niver come no nigher. No – not a smite o' use. That's what I tell 'er. 'Er should ta'e no notice on't. Ty, what can y' expect.'

The mother came in again, and the talk became general. Maggie flashed her eyes at me from time to time, complacent and satisfied, moving among the men. I paid her little compliments, which she did not seem to hear. She attended to me with a kind of sinister, witch-like graciousness, her dark head ducked between her shoulders, at once humble and powerful. She was happy as a child attending to her father-in-law and to me. But there was something ominous between her eyebrows, as if a dark moth were settled there – and something ominous in her bent, hulking bearing.

She sat on a low stool by the fire, near her father-in-law. Her head was dropped, she seemed in a state of abstraction. From time to time she would suddenly recover, and look up at us, laughing and chatting. Then she would forget again. Yet in her hulked black forgetting she seemed very near to us.

The door having been opened, the peacock came slowly in, prancing calmly. He went near to her and crouched down, coiling his blue neck. She glanced at him, but almost as if she did not observe him. The bird sat silent, seeming to sleep, and the woman also sat hulked and silent, seemingly oblivious. Then once more there was a heavy step, and Alfred entered. He looked at his wife, and he looked at the peacock crouching by her. He stood large in the doorway, his hands stuck in front of him, in his breeches pockets. Nobody spoke. He turned on his heel and went out again.

I rose also to go. Maggie started as if coming to herself.

'Must you go?' she asked, rising and coming near to me, standing in front of me, twisting her head sideways and looking up at me. 'Can't you stop a bit longer? We can all be cosy today, there's nothing to do outdoors.' And she laughed, showing her teeth oddly. She had a long chin.

I said I must go. The peacock uncoiled and coiled again his long blue neck, as he lay on the hearth. Maggie still stood close in front of me, so that I was acutely aware of my waistcoat buttons.

'Oh, well,' she said, 'you'll come again, won't you? Do come again.'

I promised.

'Come to tea one day – yes, do!'

I promised – one day.

The moment I went out of her presence I ceased utterly to exist for her – as utterly as I ceased to exist for Joey. With her curious abstractedness she forgot me again immediately. I knew it as I left her. Yet she seemed almost in physical contact with me while I was with her.

The sky was all pallid again, yellowish. When I went out there was no sun; the snow was blue and cold. I hurried away down the hill, musing on Maggie. The road made a loop down the sharp face of the slope. As I went crunching over the laborious snow I became aware of a figure striding down the steep scarp to intercept me. It was a man with his hands in front of him, half stuck in his breeches pockets, and his shoulders square – a real farmer of the hills; Alfred, of course. He waited for me by the stone fence.

'Excuse me,' he said as I came up.

I came to a halt in front of him and looked into his sullen blue eyes. He had a certain odd haughtiness on his brows. But his blue eyes stared insolently at me.

'Do you know anything about a letter – in French – that my wife opened – a letter of mine – ?'

'Yes,' said I. 'She asked me to read it to her.'

He looked square at me. He did not know exactly how to feel.

'What was there in it?' he asked.

'Why?' I said. 'Don't you know?'

'She makes out she's burnt it,' he said.

'Without showing it you?' I asked.

He nodded slightly. He seemed to be meditating as to what line of action he should take. He wanted to know the contents of the letter: he must know: and therefore he must ask me, for evidently his wife had taunted him. At the same time, no doubt, he would like to wreak untold vengeance on my unfortunate person. So he eyed me, and I eyed him, and neither of us spoke. He did not want to repeat his request to me. And yet I only looked at him, and considered.

Suddenly he threw back his head and glanced down the valley. Then he changed his position – he was a horse-soldier. Then he looked at me confidentially.

'She burnt the blasted thing before I saw it,' he said.

'Well,' I answered slowly, 'she doesn't know herself what was in it.'

He continued to watch me narrowly. I grinned to myself. 'I didn't like to read her out what there was in it,' I continued.

He suddenly flushed so that the veins in his neck stood out, and he stirred again uncomfortably.

'The Belgian girl said her baby had been born a week ago, and that they were going to call it Alfred,' I told him.

He met my eyes. I was grinning. He began to grin, too.

'Good luck to her,' he said.

'Best of luck,' said I.

'And what did you tell *her*?' he asked.

'That the baby belonged to the old mother – that it was brother to your girl, who was writing to you as a friend of the family.'

He stood smiling, with the long, subtle malice of a farmer.

'And did she take it in?' he asked.

'As much as she took anything else.'

He stood grinning fixedly. Then he broke into a short laugh. 'Good for *her*!' he exclaimed cryptically.

And then he laughed aloud once more, evidently feeling he had won a big move in his contest with his wife.

'What about the other woman?' I asked.

'Who?'

'Èlise.'

'Oh' – he shifted uneasily – 'she was all right – '

'You'll be getting back to her,' I said.

He looked at me. Then he made a grimace with his mouth. 'Not me,' he said. 'Back your life it's a plant.'

'You don't think the *cher petit bébé* is a little Alfred?'

'It might be,' he said.

'Only might?'

'Yes – an' there's lots of mites in a pound of cheese.' He laughed boisterously but uneasily.

'What did she say, exactly?' he asked.

I began to repeat, as well as I could, the phrases of the letter: ' *"Mon cher Alfred – Figure-toi comme je suis désolée –* " '

He listened with some confusion. When I had finished all I could remember, he said: 'They know how to pitch you out a letter, those Belgian lasses.'

'Practice,' said I.

'They get plenty,' he said.

There was a pause.

'Oh, well,' he said. 'I've never got that letter, anyhow.'

The wind blew fine and keen, in the sunshine, across the snow. I blew my nose and prepared to depart.

'And *she* doesn't know anything?' he continued, jerking his head up the hill in the direction of Tible.

'She knows nothing but what I've said – that is, if she really burnt the letter.'

'I believe she burnt it,' he said, 'for spite. She's a little devil, she is. But I shall have it out with her.' His jaw was stubborn and sullen. Then suddenly he turned to me with a new note.

'Why?' he said. 'Why didn't you wring that bloody peacock's neck – that bloody Joey?'

'Why?' I said. 'What for?'

'I hate the brute,' he said. 'I had a shot at him – '

I laughed. He stood and mused.

'Poor little Èlise,' he murmured.

'Was she small – *petite*?' I asked.

He jerked up his head. 'No,' he said. 'Rather tall.'

'Taller than your wife, I suppose.'

Again he looked into my eyes. And then once more he went into a loud burst of laughter that made the still, snow-deserted valley clap again.

'God, it's a knockout!' he said, thoroughly amused. Then he stood at ease, one foot out, his hands in his breeches pockets in front of him, his head thrown back, a handsome figure of a man.

'But I'll do that blasted Joey in – ' he mused.

I ran down the hill, shouting with laughter.

Mother and Daughter

Virginia Bodoin had a good job: she was head of a department in a certain government office, held a responsible position, and earned, to imitate Balzac and be precise about it, seven hundred and fifty pounds a year. That is already something. Rachel Bodoin, her mother, had an income of about six hundred a year, on which she had lived in the capitals of Europe since the effacement of a never very important husband.

Now, after some years of virtual separation and 'freedom', mother and daughter once more thought of settling down. They had become, in course of time, more like a married couple than mother and daughter. They knew one another very well indeed, and each was a little 'nervous' of the other. They had lived together and parted several times. Virginia was now thirty, and she didn't look like marrying. For four years she had been as good as married to Henry Lubbock, a rather spoilt young man who was musical. Then Henry let her down: for two reasons. He couldn't stand her mother. Her mother couldn't stand him. And anybody whom Mrs Bodoin could not stand she managed to sit on, disastrously. So Henry had writhed horribly, feeling his mother-in-law sitting on him tight, and Virginia, after all, in a helpless sort of family loyalty, sitting alongside her mother. Virginia didn't really want to sit on Henry. But when her mother egged her on, she couldn't help it. For ultimately, her mother had power over her; a strange *female* power, nothing to do with parental authority. Virginia had long thrown parental authority to the winds. But her mother had another, much subtler form of domination, female and thrilling, so that when Rachel said: Let's squash him! Virginia had to rush wickedly and gleefully to the sport. And Henry knew quite well when he was being squashed. So that was one of his reasons for going back on Vinny. He called her Vinny, to the superlative disgust of Mrs Bodoin, who always corrected him: My daughter *Virginia* –

The second reason was, again to be Balzacian, that Virginia hadn't a sou of her own. Henry had a sorry two hundred and fifty. Virginia, at the age of twenty-four, was already earning four hundred and fifty. But she was earning them. Whereas Henry managed to earn about twelve pounds per annum, by his precious music. He had realised that he would find it hard to earn more. So that marrying, except with a wife who could keep him, was rather out of the question. Vinny would inherit her mother's money. But then Mrs Bodoin had the health and muscular equipment of the Sphinx. She would live for ever, seeking whom she might devour, and devouring him. Henry lived with Vinny for two years, in the married sense of the words: and Vinny felt they *were* married, minus a mere ceremony. But Vinny had her mother always in the background; often as far back as Paris or Biarritz, but still, within letter reach. And she never realised the funny little grin that came on her own elvish face when her mother, even in a letter, spread her skirts and calmly sat on Henry. She never realised that in spirit she promptly and mischievously sat on him too: she could no more have helped it than the tide can help turning to the moon. And she did not dream that he felt it, and was utterly mortified in his masculine vanity. Women, very often, hypnotise one another, and then, hypnotised, they proceed gently to wring the neck of the man they think they are loving with all their hearts. Then they call it utter perversity on his part that he doesn't like having his neck wrung. They think he is repudiating a heart-felt love. For they are hypnotised. Women hypnotise one another, without knowing it.

In the end, Henry backed out. He saw himself being simply reduced to nothingness by two women, an old witch with muscles like the Sphinx, and a young, spellbound witch, lavish, elvish and weak, who utterly spoilt him but who ate his marrow.

Rachel would write from Paris:

My dear Virginia, as I had a windfall in the way of an investment, I am sharing it with you. You will find enclosed my cheque for twenty pounds. No doubt you will be needing it to buy Henry a suit of clothes, since the spring is apparently come, and the sunlight may be tempted to show him up for what he is worth. I don't want my daughter going around with what is presumably a street-corner musician, but please pay the tailor's bill yourself, or you may have to do it over again later.

Henry got a suit of clothes, but it was as good as a shirt of Nessus, eating him away with subtle poison.

So he backed out. He didn't jump out, or bolt, or carve his way out at the sword's point. He sort of faded out, distributing his departure over a year or more. He was fond of Vinny, and he could hardly do without her, and he was sorry for her. But at length he couldn't see her apart from her mother. She was a young, weak, spendthrift witch, accomplice of her tough-clawed witch of a mother.

Henry made other alliances, got a good hold on elsewhere, and gradually extricated himself. He saved his life, but he had lost, he felt, a good deal of his youth and marrow. He tended now to go fat, a little puffy, somewhat insignificant. And he had been handsome and striking-looking.

The two witches howled when he was lost to them. Poor Virginia was really half crazy, she didn't know what to do with herself. She had a violent recoil from her mother. Mrs Bodoin was filled with furious contempt for her daughter: that she should let such a hooked fish slip out of her hands! that she should allow such a person to turn her down! – 'I don't quite see my daughter seduced and thrown over by a sponging individual such as Henry Lubbock,' she wrote. 'But if it has happened, I suppose it is somebody's fault –'

There was a mutual recoil, which lasted nearly five years. But the spell was not broken. Mrs Bodoin's mind never left her daughter, and Virginia was ceaselessly aware of her mother, somewhere in the universe. They wrote, and met at intervals, but they kept apart in recoil.

The spell, however, was between them, and gradually it worked. They felt more friendly. Mrs Bodoin came to London. She stayed in the same quiet hotel with her daughter: Virginia had had two rooms in an hotel for the past three years. And, at last, they thought of taking an apartment together.

Virginia was now over thirty. She was still thin and odd and elvish, with a very slight and piquant cast in one of her brown eyes, and she still had her odd, twisted smile, and her slow, rather deep-toned voice, that caressed a man like the stroking of subtle fingertips. Her hair was still a natural tangle of curls, a bit dishevelled. She still dressed with a natural elegance which tended to go wrong and a tiny bit sluttish. She still might have a hole in her expensive and perfectly new stockings, and still she might have to take off her shoes in the drawing-room, if she came to tea, and sit there in her stockinged-feet. True, she had elegant feet: she was altogether elegantly shaped. But it wasn't that. It was neither coquetry nor vanity. It was simply that, after having gone to a good shoemaker and paid five guineas for a pair of perfectly simple and natural shoes, made to her feet, the said shoes would hurt her excruciatingly when she had walked half a mile in them, and she would simply have to take them off, even if she sat on the kerb to do it. It was a fatality. There was a touch of the *gamin* in her very feet, a certain sluttishness that wouldn't let them stay properly in nice proper shoes. She practically always wore her mother's old shoes. 'Of course I go through life in mother's old shoes. If she died and left me without a supply, I suppose I should have to go in a bath chair,' she would say, with her odd twisted little grin. She was so elegant, and yet a slut. It was her charm, really.

Just the opposite of her mother. They could wear each other's shoes and each other's clothes, which seemed remarkable, for Mrs Bodoin seemed so much the bigger of the two. But Virginia's shoulders were broad; if she was thin, she had a strong frame, even when she looked a frail rag.

Mrs Bodoin was one of those women of sixty or so, with a terrible inward energy and a violent sort of vitality. But she managed to hide it. She sat with perfect repose, and folded hands. One thought: What a calm woman! Just as one may look at the snowy summit of a quiescent volcano, in the evening light, and think: What peace!

It was a strange *muscular* energy which possessed Mrs Bodoin, as it possesses, curiously enough, many women over fifty, and is usually distasteful in its manifestations. Perhaps it accounts for the lassitude of the young.

But Mrs Bodoin recognised the bad taste in her energetic coevals, so she cultivated repose. Her very way of pronouncing the word, in two syllables: re-pòse, making the second syllable run on into the twilight, showed how much suppressed energy she had. Faced with the problem of iron-grey hair and black eyebrows, she was too clever to try dyeing herself back into youth. She studied her face, her whole figure, and decided that it was *positive*. There was no denying it. There was no wispiness, no hollowness, no limp frail blossom-on-a-bending-stalk about her. Her figure, though not stout, was full, strong and *cambré*. Her face had an aristocratic arched nose, aristocratic who-the-devil-are-you? grey eyes, and cheeks rather long but also rather full. Nothing appealing or youthfully skittish here.

Like an independent woman, she used her wits, and decided most emphatically not to be either youthful or skittish or appealing. She would keep her dignity, for she was fond of it. She was positive. She liked to be positive. She was used to her positivity. So she would just *be* positive.

She turned to the positive period: to the eighteenth century, to Voltaire, to Ninon de l'Enclos and the Pompadour, to Madame la Duchesse and Monsieur le Marquis. She decided that she was not much in the line of la Pompadour or la Duchesse, but almost exactly in the line of Monsieur le Marquis. And she was right. With hair silvering to white, brushed back clean from her positive brow and temples, cut short, but sticking out a little behind, with her rather full, pink face and thin black eyebrows plucked to two fine, superficial crescents, her arching nose and her rather full insolent eyes, she was perfectly eighteenth-century, the early half. That she was Monsieur le Marquis rather than Madame la Marquise made her really modern.

Her appearance was perfect. She wore delicate combinations of grey and pink, maybe with a darkening iron-grey touch, and her jewels were of soft old coloured paste. Her bearing was a sort of alert repose, very calm, but very assured. There was, to use a vulgarism, no getting past her.

She had a couple of thousand pounds she could lay hands on. Virginia, of course, was always in debt. But, after all, Virginia was not to be sniffed at. She made seven hundred and fifty a year.

Virginia was oddly clever, and not clever. She didn't *really* know anything, because anything and everything was interesting to her for the moment, and she picked it up at once. She picked up languages with extraordinary ease, she was fluent in a fortnight. This helped her enormously with her job. She could prattle away with heads of industry, let them come from where they liked. But she didn't *know* any language, not even her own. She picked things up in her sleep, so to speak, without knowing anything about them.

And this made her popular with men. With all her curious facility, they didn't feel small in front of her, because she was like an instrument. She had to be prompted. Some man had to set her in motion, and then she worked, really cleverly. She could collect the most valuable information. She was very useful. She worked with men, spent most of her time with men, her friends were practically all men. She didn't feel easy with women.

Yet she had no lover, nobody seemed eager to marry her, nobody seemed eager to come close to her at all. Mrs Bodoin said: 'I'm afraid Virginia is a one-man woman. I am a one-man woman. So was my mother, and so was my grandmother. Virginia's father was the only man in my life, the only one. And I'm afraid Virginia is the same, tenacious. Unfortunately, the man was what he was, and her life is just left there.'

Henry had said, in the past, that Mrs Bodoin wasn't a one-man woman, she was a no-man woman, and that if she could have had her way, everything male would have been wiped off the face of the earth, and only the female element left.

However, Mrs Bodoin thought that it was now time to make a move. So she and Virginia took a quite handsome apartment in one of the old Blooms-bury Squares, fitted it up and furnished it with extreme care, and with some quite lovely things, got in a very good man, an Austrian, to cook, and they set up married life together, mother and daughter.

At first it was rather thrilling. The two reception-rooms, looking down on the dirty old trees of the square garden, were of splendid proportions, and each with three great windows coming down low, almost to the level of the knees. The chimney-piece was late eighteenth-century. Mrs Bodoin furnished the rooms with a gentle suggestion of Louis-Seize merged with Empire, without keeping to any particular style. But she had, saved from her own home, a really remarkable Aubusson carpet. It looked almost new, as if it had been woven two years ago, and was startling, yet somehow rather splendid, as it spread its rose-red borders and wonderful florid array of silver-grey and gold-grey roses, lilies and gorgeous swans and trumpeting volutes away over the floor. Very aesthetic people found it rather loud, they preferred the worn, dim yellowish Aubusson in the big bedroom. But Mrs Bodoin loved her drawing-room carpet. It was positive, but it was not vulgar. It had a certain grand air in its floridity. She felt it gave her a proper footing. And it behaved very well with her painted cabinets and grey-and-gold brocade chairs and big Chinese vases, which she liked to fill with big flowers: single Chinese peonies, big roses, great tulips, orange lilies. The dim room of London, with all its atmospheric colour, would stand the big, free, fisticuffing flowers.

Virginia, for the first time in her life, had the pleasure of making a home. She was again entirely under her mother's spell, and swept away, thrilled to her marrow. She had had no idea that her mother had got such treasures as the carpets and painted cabinets and brocade chairs up her sleeve: many of them the debris of the Fitzpatrick home in Ireland, Mrs Bodoin being a Fitzpatrick. Almost like a child, like a bride, Virginia threw herself into the business of fixing up the rooms. 'Of course, Virginia, I consider this is *your* apartment,' said Mrs Bodoin. 'I am nothing but your *dame de compagnie*, and shall carry out your wishes entirely, if you will only express them.'

Of course Virginia expressed a few, but not many. She introduced some wild pictures bought from impecunious artists whom she patronised. Mrs Bodoin thought the pictures positive about the wrong things, but as far as possible, she let them stay, looking on them as the necessary element of modern ugliness. But by that element of modern ugliness, wilfully so, it was easy to see the things that Virginia had introduced into the apartment.

Perhaps nothing goes to the head like setting up house. You can get drunk on it. You feel you are creating something. Nowadays it is no longer the 'home', the domestic nest. It is 'my rooms', or 'my house', the great garment which reveals and clothes 'my personality'. Mrs Bodoin, deliberately scheming for Virginia, kept moderately cool over it, but even she was thrilled to the marrow, and of an intensity and ferocity with the decorators and furnishers, astonishing. But Virginia was just all the time tipsy with it, as if she had touched some magic button on the grey wall of life, and with an Open Sesame! her lovely and coloured rooms had begun to assemble out of fairyland. It was far more vivid and wonderful to her than if she had inherited a duchy.

The mother and daughter, the mother in a sort of faded russet crimson and the daughter in silver, began to entertain. They had, of course, mostly men. It filled Mrs Bodoin with a sort of savage impatience to entertain women. Besides, most of Virginia's acquaintances were men. So there were dinners and well-arranged evenings.

It went well, but something was missing. Mrs Bodoin wanted to be gracious, so she held herself rather back. She stayed a little distant, was calm, reposed, eighteenth-century, and determined to be a foil to the clever and slightly elvish Virginia. It was a pose, and alas, it stopped something. She was very nice with the men, no matter what her contempt for them. But the men were uneasy with her: afraid.

What they all felt, all the men guests, was that *for them*, nothing really happened. Everything that happened was between mother and daughter. All the flow was between mother and daughter. A subtle, hypnotic spell encompassed the two women, and try as they might, the men were shut out. More than one young man, a little dazzled, *began* to fall in love with Virginia. But it was impossible. Not only was he shut out, he was, in some way, annihilated. The spontaneity was killed in his bosom. While the two women sat, brilliant and rather wonderful, in magnetic connection at opposite ends of the table, like two witches, a double Circe turning the men not into swine – the men would have liked that well enough – but into lumps.

It was tragic. Because Mrs Bodoin wanted Virginia to fall in love and marry. She really wanted it, and she attributed Virginia's lack of forthcoming to the delinquent Henry. She never realised the hypnotic spell, which of course encompassed her as well as Virginia, and made men just an impossibility to both women, mother and daughter alike.

At this time, Mrs Bodoin hid her humour. She had a really marvellous faculty of humorous imitation. She could imitate the Irish servants from her old home, or the American women who called on her, or the modern lady-like young men, the asphodels, as she called them – 'Of course you know the asphodel is a kind of onion! Oh yes, just an over-bred onion' – who wanted, with their murmuring voices and peeping under their brows, to make her feel very small and very bourgeois. She could imitate them all with a humour that was really touched with genius. But it was devastating. It demolished the objects of her humour so absolutely, smashed them to bits with a ruthless hammer, pounded them to nothing so terribly, that it frightened people, particularly men. It frightened men off.

So she hid it. She hid it. But there it was, up her sleeve, her merciless, hammer-like humour, which just smashed its object on the head and left him brained. She tried to disown it. She tried to pretend, even to Virginia, that she had the gift no more. But in vain; the hammer hidden up her sleeve hovered over the head of every guest, and every guest felt his scalp creep, and Virginia felt her inside creep with a little, mischievous, slightly idiotic grin, as still another fool male was mystically knocked on the head. It was a sort of uncanny sport.

No, the plan was not going to work: the plan of having Virginia fall in love and marry. Of course the men *were* such lumps, such *oeufs farcis*. There was one, at least, that Mrs Bodoin had real hopes of. He was a healthy and normal and very good-looking boy of good family, with no money, alas, but clerking to the House of Lords and very hopeful, and not very clever, but simply in love with Virginia's cleverness. He was just the one Mrs Bodoin would have married for herself. True, he was only twenty-six, to Virginia's thirty-one. But he had rowed in the Oxford eight, and adored horses, talked horses adorably, and was simply infatuated by Virginia's cleverness. To him Virginia had the finest mind on earth. She was as wonderful as Plato, but infinitely more attractive, because she was a woman, and winsome with it. Imagine a winsome Plato with untidy curls and the tiniest little brown-eyed squint and just a hint of woman's pathetic need for a protector, and you may imagine Adrian's feeling for Virginia. He adored her on his knees, but he felt he could protect her.

'Of course he's just a very nice *boy*!' said Mrs Bodoin. 'He's a boy, and that's all you can say. And he always will be a boy. But that's the very nicest kind of man, the only kind you can live with: the eternal boy. Virginia, aren't you attracted to him?'

'Yes, mother! I think he's an awfully nice *boy*, as you say,' replied Virginia, in her rather slow, musical, whimsical voice. But the mocking little curl in the intonation put the lid on Adrian. Virginia was not marrying a nice *boy*! She could be malicious too, against her mother's taste. And Mrs Bodoin let escape her a faint gesture of impatience.

For she had been planning her own retreat, planning to give Virginia the apartment outright, and half of her own income, if she would marry Adrian. Yes, the mother was already scheming how best she could live with dignity on three hundred a year, once Virginia was happily married to that most attractive if slightly brainless *boy*.

A year later, when Virginia was thirty-two, Adrian, who had married a wealthy American girl and been transferred to a job in the legation at Washington in the meantime, faithfully came to see Virginia as soon as he was in London, faithfully knelt at her feet, faithfully thought her the most wonderful spiritual being, and faithfully felt that she, Virginia, could have done wonders with him, which wonders would now never be done, for he had married in the meantime.

Virginia was looking haggard and worn. The scheme of a *ménage à deux* with her mother had not succeeded. And now, work was telling on the younger woman. It is true, she was amazingly facile. But facility wouldn't get her all the way. She had to earn her money, and earn it hard. She had to slog, and she had to concentrate. While she could work by quick intuition and without much responsibility, work thrilled her. But as soon as she had to get down to it, as they say, grip and slog and concentrate, in a really responsible position, it wore her out terribly. She had to do it all off her nerves. She hadn't the same sort of fighting power as a man. Where a man can summon his old Adam in him to fight through his work, a woman has to draw on her nerves, and on her nerves alone. For the old Eve in her will have nothing to do with such work. So that mental responsibility, mental concentration, mental slogging wear out a woman terribly, especially if she is head of a department, and not working *for* somebody.

So poor Virginia was worn out. She was thin as a rail. Her nerves were frayed to bits. And she could never forget her beastly work. She would come home at teatime speechless and done for. Her mother, tortured by the sight of her, longed to say: 'Has anything gone wrong, Virginia? Have you had anything particularly trying at the office today?' But she learned to hold her tongue, and say nothing. The question would be the last straw to Virginia's poor overwrought nerves, and there would be a little scene which, despite Mrs Bodoin's calm and forbearance, offended the elder woman to the quick. She had learned, by bitter experience, to leave her child alone, as one would leave a frail tube of vitriol alone. But of course, she could not keep her *mind* off Virginia. That was impossible. And poor Virginia, under the strain of work and the strain of her mother's awful ceaseless mind, was at the very end of her strength and resources.

Mrs Bodoin had always disliked the fact of Virginia's doing a job. But now she hated it. She hated the whole government office with violent and virulent hate. Not only was it undignified for Virginia to be tied up there, but it was turning her, Mrs Bodoin's daughter, into a thin, nagging, fearsome old maid. Could anything be more utterly English and humiliating to a well-born Irishwoman?

After a long day attending to the apartment, skilfully darning one of the brocade chairs, polishing the Venetian mirrors to her satisfaction, selecting flowers, doing certain shopping and housekeeping, attending perfectly to everything, then receiving callers in the afternoon, with never-ending energy, Mrs Bodoin would go up from the drawing-room after tea and write a few letters, take her bath, dress with great care – she enjoyed attending to her person – and come down to dinner as fresh as a daisy, but far more energetic than that quiet flower. She was ready now for a full evening.

She was conscious, with gnawing anxiety, of Virginia's presence in the house, but she did not see her daughter till dinner was announced. Virginia slipped in, and away to her room unseen, never going into the drawing-room to tea. If Mrs Bodoin heard her daughter's key in the latch, she quickly retired into one of the rooms till Virginia was safely through. It was too much for poor Virginia's nerves even to catch sight of anybody in the house, when she came in from the office. Bad enough to hear the murmur of visitors' voices behind the drawing-room door.

And Mrs Bodoin would wonder: How is she? How is she tonight? I wonder what sort of a day she's had? – And this thought would roam prowling through the house, to where Virginia was lying on her back in her room. But the mother would have to consume her anxiety till dinner-time. And then Virginia would appear, with black lines under her eyes, thin, tense, a young woman out of an office, the stigma upon her: badly dressed, a little acid in humour, with an impaired digestion, not interested in anything, blighted by her work. And Mrs Bodoin, humiliated at the very sight of her, would control herself perfectly, say nothing but the mere smooth nothings of casual speech, and sit in perfect form presiding at a carefully cooked dinner thought out entirely to please Virginia. Then Virginia hardly noticed what she ate.

Mrs Bodoin was pining for an evening with life in it. But Virginia would lie on the couch and put on the loudspeaker. Or she would put a humorous record on the gramophone, and be amused, and hear it again, and be amused, and hear it again, six times, and six times be amused by a mildly funny record that Mrs Bodoin now knew off by heart. 'Why, Virginia, I could repeat that record over to you, if you wished it, without your troubling to wind up that gramophone.' And Virginia, after a pause in which she seemed not to have heard what her mother said, would reply, 'I'm sure you could, mother.' And that simple speech would convey such volumes of contempt for all that Rachel Bodoin was or ever could be or ever had been, contempt for her energy, her vitality, her mind, her body, her very existence, that the elder woman would curl. It seemed as if the ghost of Robert Bodoin spoke out of the mouth of the daughter, in deadly venom. Then Virginia would put on the record for the seventh time.

During the second ghastly year, Mrs Bodoin realised that the game was up. She was a beaten woman, a woman without object or meaning any more. The hammer of her awful female humour, which had knocked so many people on the head, all the people, in fact, that she had come into contact with, had at last flown backwards and hit herself on the head. For her daughter was her other self, her *alter ego*. The secret and the meaning and the power of Mrs Bodoin's whole life lay in the hammer, that hammer of her living humour which knocked everything on the head. That had been her lust and her passion, knocking everybody and everything humorously on the head. She had felt inspired in it: it was a sort of mission. And she had hoped to hand on the hammer to Virginia, her clever, unsolid but still actual daughter, Virginia. Virginia was the continuation of Rachel's own self. Virginia was Rachel's *alter ego*, her other self.

But, alas, it was a half-truth. Virginia had had a father. This fact, which had been utterly ignored by the mother, was gradually brought home to her by the curious recoil of the hammer. Virginia was her father's daughter. Could anything be more unseemly, horrid, more perverse in the natural scheme of things? For Robert Bodoin had been fully and deservedly knocked on the head by Rachel's hammer. Could anything, then, be more disgusting than that he should resurrect again in the person of Mrs Bodoin's own daughter, her own *alter ego* Virginia, and start hitting back with a little spiteful hammer that was David's pebble against Goliath's battle-axe!

But the little pebble was mortal. Mrs Bodoin felt it sink into her brow, her temple, and she was finished. The hammer fell nerveless from her hand.

The two women were now mostly alone. Virginia was too tired to have company in the evening. So there was the gramophone or loudspeaker, or else silence. Both women had come to loathe the apartment. Virginia felt it was the last grand act of bullying on her mother's part, she felt bullied by the assertive Aubusson carpet, by the beastly Venetian mirrors, by the big overcultured flowers. She even felt bullied by the excellent food, and longed again for a Soho restaurant and her two poky shabby rooms in the hotel. She loathed the apartment: she loathed everything. But she had not the energy to move. She had not the energy to do anything. She crawled to her work, and for the rest, she lay flat, gone.

It was Virginia's worn-out inertia that really finished Mrs Bodoin. That was the pebble that broke the bone of her temple: 'To have to attend my daughter's funeral, and accept the sympathy of all her fellow-clerks in her office, no, that is a final humiliation which I must spare myself. No! If Virginia must be a lady-clerk, she must be it henceforth on her own responsibility. I will retire from her existence.'

Mrs Bodoin had tried hard to persuade Virginia to give up her work and come and live with her. She had offered her half her income. In vain. Virginia stuck to her office.

Very well! So be it! The apartment was a fiasco, Mrs Bodoin was longing, longing to tear it to pieces again. One last and final blow of the hammer! 'Virginia, don't you think we'd better get rid of this apartment, and live around as we used to? Don't you think we'll do that?' – 'But all the money you've put into it? And the lease for ten years!' cried Virginia, in a kind of inertia. – 'Never mind! We had the pleasure of making it. And we've had as much pleasure out of living in it as we shall ever have. Now we'd better get rid of it – quickly – don't you think?'

Mrs Bodoin's arms were twitching to snatch the pictures off the walls, roll up the Aubusson carpet, take the china out of the ivory-inlaid cabinet there and then, at that very moment.

'Let us wait till Sunday before we decide,' said Virginia.

'Till Sunday! Four days! As long as that? Haven't we already decided in our own minds?' said Mrs Bodoin.

'We'll wait till Sunday, anyhow,' said Virginia.

The next evening, the Armenian came to dinner. Virginia called him Arnold, with the French pronunciation, Arnault. Mrs Bodoin, who barely tolerated him, and could never get his name, which seemed to have a lot of bouyoums in it, called him either the Armenian, or the Rahat Lakoum, after the name of the sweetmeat, or simply the Turkish Delight.

'Arnault is coming to dinner tonight, mother.'

'Really! The Turkish Delight is coming here to dinner? Shall I provide anything special?' Her voice sounded as if she would suggest snails in aspic.

'I don't think so.'

Virginia had seen a good deal of the Armenian at the office, when she had to negotiate with him on behalf of the Board of Trade. He was a man of about sixty, a merchant, had been a millionaire, was ruined during the war, but was now coming on again, and represented trade in Bulgaria. He wanted to negotiate with the British Government, and the British Government sensibly negotiated with him: at first through the medium of Virginia. Now things were going satisfactorily between Monsieur Arnault, as Virginia called him, and the Board of Trade, so that a sort of friendship had followed the official relations.

The Turkish Delight was sixty, grey-haired and fat. He had numerous grandchildren growing up in Bulgaria, but he was a widower. He had a grey moustache cut like a brush, and glazed brown eyes over which hung heavy lids with white lashes. His manner was humble, but in his bearing there was a certain dogged conceit. One notices the combination sometimes in Jews. He had been very wealthy and kow-towed to, he had been ruined and humiliated, terribly humiliated, and now, doggedly, he was rising up again, his sons backing him, away in Bulgaria. One felt he was not alone. He had his sons, his family, his tribe behind him, away in the Near East.

He spoke bad English, but fairly fluent guttural French. He did not speak much, but he sat. He sat, with his short, fat thighs, as if for eternity, *there*. There was a strange potency in his fat immobile sitting, as if his posterior were connected with the very centre of the earth. And his brain, spinning away at the one point in question, business, was very agile. Business absorbed him. But not in a nervous, personal way. Somehow the family, the tribe was always felt behind him. It was business for the family, the tribe.

With the English he was humble, for the English like such aliens to be humble, and he had had a long schooling from the Turks. And he was always an outsider. Nobody would ever take any notice of him in society. He would just be an outsider, *sitting*.

'I hope, Virginia, you won't ask that Turkish-carpet gentleman when we have other people. I can bear it,' said Mrs Bodoin. 'Some people might mind.'

'Isn't it hard when you can't choose your own company in your own house!' mocked Virginia.

'No! *I* don't care. I can meet anything; and I'm sure, in the way of selling Turkish carpets, your acquaintance is very good. But I don't suppose you look on him as a personal friend – ?'

'I do. I like him quite a lot.'

'Well – ! as you will. But consider your *other* friends.'

Mrs Bodoin was really mortified this time. She looked on the Armenian as one looks on the fat Levantine in a fez who tries to sell one hideous tapestries at Port Said, or on the sea-front at Nice, as being outside the class of human beings and in the class of insects. That he had been a millionaire, and might be a millionaire again, only added venom to her feeling of disgust at being forced into contact with such scum. She could not even squash him, or annihilate him. In scum, there is nothing to squash, for scum is only the unpleasant residue of that which was never anything but squashed.

However, she was not quite just. True, he was fat, and he sat, with short thighs, like a toad, as if seated for a toad's eternity. His colour was of a dirty sort of paste, his brown eyes were glazed under heavy lids. And he never spoke until spoken to, waiting in his toad's silence, like a slave.

But his thick, fine white hair, which stood up on his head like a soft brush, was curiously virile. And his curious small hands, of the same soft dull paste, had a peculiar, fat, soft, masculine breeding of their own. And his dull brown eye could glint with the subtlety of serpents, under the white brush of eyelash. He was tired, but he was not defeated. He had fought, and won, and lost, and was fighting again, always at a disadvantage. He belonged to a defeated race which accepts defeat, but which gets its own back by cunning.

He was the father of sons, the head of a family, one of the heads of a defeated but indestructible tribe. He was not alone, and so you could not lay your finger on him. His whole consciousness was patriarchal and tribal. And somehow, he was humble, but he was indestructible.

At dinner he sat half-effaced, humble, yet with the conceit of the humble. His manners were perfectly good, rather French. Virginia chattered to him in French, and he replied with that peculiar nonchalance of the boulevards, which was the only manner he could command when speaking French. Mrs Bodoin understood, but she was what one would call a heavy-footed linguist, so when she said anything, it was intensely in English. And the Turkish Delight replied in his clumsy English, hastily. It was not his fault that French was being spoken. It was Virginia's.

He was very humble, conciliatory, with Mrs Bodoin. But he cast at her sometimes that rapid glint of a reptilian glance as if to say: 'Yes! I see you! You are a handsome figure. As an *objet de vertu* you are almost perfect.' Thus his connoisseur's, antique-dealer's eye would appraise her. But then his thick white eyebrows would seem to add: 'But what, under holy heaven, are you as a woman? You are neither wife nor mother nor mistress, you have no perfume of sex, you are more dreadful than a Turkish soldier or an English official. No man on earth could embrace you. You are a ghoul, you are a strange genie from the underworld!' And he would secretly invoke the holy names, to shield him.

Yet he was in love with Virginia. He saw, first and foremost, the child in her, as if she were a lost child in the gutter, a waif with a faint, fascinating cast in her brown eyes, waiting till someone would pick her up. A fatherless waif! And he was tribal father, father through all the ages.

Then, on the other hand, he knew her peculiar disinterested cleverness in affairs. That, too, fascinated him: that odd, almost second-sight cleverness about business, and entirely impersonal, entirely in the air. It seemed to him very strange. But it would be an immense help to him in his schemes. He did not really understand the English. He was at sea with them. But with her, he would have a clue to everything. For she was, finally, quite a somebody among these English, these English officials.

He was about sixty. His family was established, in the East, his grandsons were growing up. It was necessary for him to live in London, for some years. This girl would be useful. She had no money, save what she would inherit from her mother. But he would risk that: she would be an investment in his business. And then the apartment. He liked the apartment extremely. He recognised the *cachet*, and the lilies and swans of the Aubusson carpet really did something to him. Virginia said to him: 'Mother gave me the apartment.' So he looked on that as safe. And finally, Virginia was almost a virgin, probably quite a virgin, and, as far as the paternal Oriental male like himself was concerned, entirely virgin. He had a very small idea of the silly puppy-sexuality of the English, so different from the prolonged male voluptuousness of his own pleasures. And last of all, he was physically lonely, getting old and tired.

Virginia of course did not know why she liked being with Arnault. Her cleverness was amazingly stupid when it came to life, to living. She said he was 'quaint'. She said his nonchalant French of the boulevards was 'amusing'. She found his business cunning 'intriguing', and the glint in his dark glazed eyes, under the white, thick lashes, 'sheiky'. She saw him quite often, had tea with him in his hotel, and motored with him one day down to the sea.

When he took her hand in his own soft still hands, there was something so caressing, so possessive in his touch, so strange and positive in his leaning towards her, that though she trembled with fear, she was helpless. – 'But you are so thin, dear little thin thing, you need repose, repose, for the blossom to open, poor little blossom, to become a little fat!' he said in his French.

She quivered, and was helpless. It certainly was quaint! He was so strange and positive, he seemed to have all the power. The moment he realised that she would succumb into his power, he took full charge of the situation, he lost all his hesitation and his humility. He did not want just to make love to her: he wanted to marry her, for all his multifarious reasons. And he must make himself master of her.

He put her hand to his lips, and seemed to draw her life to his in kissing her thin hand. 'The poor child is tired, she needs repose, she needs to be caressed and cared for,' he said in his French. And he drew nearer to her.

She looked up in dread at his glinting, tired dark eyes under the white lashes. But he used all his will, looking back at her heavily and calculating that she must submit. And he brought his body quite near to her, and put his hand softly on her face, and made her lay her face against his breast, as he soothingly stroked her arm with his other hand, 'Dear little thing! dear little thing! Arnault loves her so dearly! Arnault loves her! Perhaps she will marry her Arnault. Dear little girl, Arnault will put flowers in her life, and make her life perfumed with sweetness and content.'

She leaned against his breast and let him caress her. She gave a fleeting, half-poignant, half-vindictive thought to her mother. Then she felt in the air the sense of destiny, destiny. Oh so nice, not to have to struggle. To give way to destiny.

'Will she marry her old Arnault? Eh? Will she marry him?' he asked in a soothing, caressing voice, at the same time compulsive.

She lifted her head and looked at him: the thick white brows, the glinting, tired dark eyes. How queer and comic! How comic to be in his power! And he was looking a little baffled.

'Shall I?' she said, with her mischievous twist of a grin.

'*Mais oui!*' he said, with all the sang-froid of his old eyes. '*Mais oui! Je te contenterai, tu le verras.*'

'*Tu me contenteras!*' she said, with a flickering smile of real amusement at his assurance. 'Will you really content me?'

'But surely! I assure it you. And you will marry me?'

'You must tell mother,' she said, and hid wickedly against his waistcoat again, while the male pride triumphed in him.

Mrs Bodoin had no idea that Virginia was intimate with the Turkish Delight: she did not inquire into her daughter's movements. During the famous dinner, she was calm and a little aloof, but entirely self-possessed. When, after coffee, Virginia left her alone with the Turkish Delight, she made no effort at conversation, only glanced at the rather short, stout man in correct dinner-jacket, and thought how his sort of fatness called for a fez and the full muslin breeches of a bazaar merchant in *The Thief of Baghdad*.

'Do you really prefer to smoke a hookah?' she asked him, with a slow drawl.

'What is a hookah, please?'

'One of those water-pipes. Don't you all smoke them, in the East?'

He only looked mystified and humble, and silence resumed. She little knew what was simmering inside his stillness.

'Madame,' he said, 'I want to ask you something.'

'You do? Then why not ask it?' came her slightly melancholy drawl.

'Yes! It is this. I wish I may have the honour to marry your daughter. She is willing.'

There was a moment's blank pause. Then Mrs Bodoin leaned towards him from her distance, with curious portentousness.

'What was that you said?' she asked. 'Repeat it!'

'I wish I may have the honour to marry your daughter. She is willing to take me.'

His dark, glazed eyes looked at her, then glanced away again. Still leaning forward, she gazed fixedly on him, as if spellbound, turned to stone. She was wearing pink topaz ornaments, but he judged they were paste, moderately good.

'Did I hear you say she is willing to take you?' came the slow, melancholy, remote voice.

'Madame, I think so,' he said, with a bow.

'I think we'll wait till she comes,' she said, leaning back.

There was silence. She stared at the ceiling. He looked closely round the room, at the furniture, at the china in the ivory-inlaid cabinet.

'I can settle five thousand pounds on Mademoiselle Virginia, madame,' came his voice. 'Am I correct to assume that she will bring this apartment and its appointments into the marriage settlement?'

Absolute silence. He might as well have been on the moon. But he was a good sitter. He just sat until Virginia came in.

Mrs Bodoin was still staring at the ceiling. The iron had entered her soul finally and fully.

Virginia glanced at her, but said: 'Have a whisky-and-soda, Arnault?'

He rose and came towards the decanters, and stood beside her: a rather squat, stout man with white head, silent with misgiving. There was the fizz of the syphon: then they came to their chairs.

'Arnault has spoken to you, mother?' said Virginia.

Mrs Bodoin sat up straight, and gazed at Virginia with big, owlish eyes, haggard. Virginia was terrified, yet a little thrilled. Her mother was beaten.

'Is it true, Virginia, that you are *willing* to marry this – Oriental gentle-man?' asked Mrs Bodoin slowly.

'Yes, mother, quite true,' said Virginia, in her teasing soft voice.

Mrs Bodoin looked owlish and dazed.

'May I be excused from having any part in it, or from having anything to do with your future *husband* – I mean having any business to transact with him?' she asked dazedly, in her slow, distinct voice.

'Why, of course!' said Virginia, frightened, smiling oddly.

There was a pause. Then Mrs Bodoin, feeling old and haggard, pulled herself together again.

'Am I to understand that your future husband would like to possess this apartment?' came her voice.

Virginia smiled quickly and crookedly. Arnault just sat, planted on his posterior, and heard. She reposed on him.

'Well – perhaps!' said Virginia. 'Perhaps he would like to know that I possessed it.' She looked at him.

Arnault nodded gravely.

'And do you *wish* to possess it?' came Mrs Bodoin's slow voice. 'Is it your intention to *inhabit* it, with your *husband*?' She put eternities into her long, stressed words.

'Yes, I think it is,' said Virginia. 'You know you *said* the apartment was mine, mother.'

'Very well! It shall be so. I shall send my lawyer to this – Oriental gentleman, if you will leave written instructions on my writing-table. May I ask when you think of getting – *married*?'

'When do you think, Arnault?' said Virginia.

'Shall it be in two weeks?' he said, sitting erect, with his fists on his knees.

'In about a fortnight, mother,' said Virginia.

'I have heard! In two weeks! Very well! In two weeks everything shall be at your disposal. And now, please excuse me.' She rose, made a slight general bow, and moved calmly and dimly from the room. It was killing her that she could not shriek aloud and beat that Levantine out of the house. But she couldn't. She had imposed the restraint on herself.

Arnault stood and looked with glistening eyes round the room. It would be his. When his sons came to England, here he would receive them.

He looked at Virginia. She too was white and haggard, now. And she hung away from him, as if in resentment. She resented the defeat of her mother. She was still capable of dismissing him for ever, and going back to her mother.

'Your mother is a wonderful lady,' he said, going to Virginia and taking her hand. 'But she has no husband to shelter her, she is unfortunate. I am sorry she will be alone. I should be happy if she would like to stay here with us.'

The sly old fox knew what he was about.

'I'm afraid there's no hope of that,' said Virginia, with a return to her old irony.

She sat on the couch, and he caressed her softly and paternally, and the very incongruity of it, there in her mother's drawing-room, amused her. And because he saw that the things in the drawing-room were handsome and valuable, and now they were his, his blood flushed and he caressed the thin girl at his side with passion, because she represented these valuable surroundings, and brought them to his possession. And he said: 'And with me you will be very comfortable, very content, oh, I shall make you content, not like Madame your mother. And you will get fatter, and bloom like the rose. I shall make you bloom like the rose. And shall we say next week, *hein*? Shall it be next week, next Wednesday, that we marry? Wednesday is a good day. Shall it be then?'

'Very well!' said Virginia, caressed again into a luxurious sense of destiny, reposing on fate, having to make no effort, no more effort, all her life.

Mrs Bodoin moved into a hotel next day, and came into the apartment to pack up and extricate herself and her immediate personal belongings only when Virginia was necessarily absent. She and her daughter communicated by letter, as far as was necessary.

And in five days' time Mrs Bodoin was clear. All business that could be settled was settled, all her trunks were removed. She had five trunks, and that was all. Denuded and outcast, she would depart to Paris, to live out the rest of her days.

The last day, she waited in the drawing-room till Virginia should come home. She sat there in her hat and street things, like a stranger.

'I just waited to say goodbye,' she said. 'I leave in the morning for Paris. This is my address. I think everything is settled; if not, let me know and I'll attend to it. Well, goodbye! – and I hope you'll be *very happy*!'

She dragged out the last words sinisterly; which restored Virginia, who was beginning to lose her head.

'Why, I think I may be,' said Virginia, with the twist of a smile.

'I shouldn't wonder,' said Mrs Bodoin pointedly and grimly. 'I think the Armenian grandpapa knows very well what he's about. You're just the harem type, after all.' The words came slowly, dropping, each with a plop! of deep contempt.

'I suppose I am! Rather fun!' said Virginia. 'But I wonder where I got it? Not from you, mother – ' she drawled mischievously.

'I should say *not*.'

'Perhaps daughters go by contraries, like dreams,' mused Virginia wickedly. 'All the harem was left out of you, so perhaps it all had to be put back into me.'

Mrs Bodoin flashed a look at her.

'You have *all* my *pity*!' she said.

'Thank you, dear. You have just a bit of mine.'

ANGELO LEWIS

The Wrong Black Bag

It was the eve of Good Friday. Within the modest parlour of No. 13 Primrose Terrace a little man, wearing a grey felt hat and a red necktie, stood admiring himself in the looking-glass over the mantelpiece. Such a state of things anywhere else would have had no significance whatever; but circumstances proverbially alter cases. At 13 Primrose Terrace it approached the dimensions of a portent.

Not to keep the reader in suspense, the little man was Benjamin Quelch, clerk in the office of Messrs Cobble & Clink, coal merchants, and he was about to carry out a desperate resolution. Most men have some secret ambition; Benjamin's was twofold. For years he had yearned to wear a soft felt hat and to make a trip to Paris, and for years fate, in the person of Mrs Quelch, had stood in the way and prevented the indulgence of his longing. Quelch being, as we have hinted, exceptionally small of stature, had, in accordance with mysterious law of opposites, selected the largest lady of his acquaintance as the partner of his joys. He himself was of a meek and retiring disposition. Mrs Quelch, on the other hand, was a woman of stern and decided temperament, with strong views upon most subjects. She administered Benjamin's finances, regulated his diet and prescribed for him when his health was out of order. Though fond of him in her own way, she ruled him with a rod of iron, and on three points she was inflexible. To make up for his insignificance of stature, she insisted on his wearing the tallest hat that money could procure, to the exclusion of all other head-gear; secondly, on the ground that it looked more 'professional', she would allow him none but black silk neckties; and lastly, she would not let him smoke. She had further an intense repugnance to all things foreign, holding as an article of faith that no good thing, whether in art, cookery or morals, was to be found on other than English soil. When Benjamin once, in a rash moment, suggested a trip to Boulogne by way of summer holiday, the suggestion was received in a manner that took away his appetite for a week afterwards.

The prohibition of smoking Quelch did not much mind; for, having in his salad days made trial of a cheap cigar, the result somehow satisfied him that tobacco was not in his line, and he ceased to yearn for it accordingly. But the tall hat and the black necktie were constant sources of irritation. He had an idea, based on his having once won a drawing prize at school, that nature had intended him for an artist, and he secretly lamented the untoward fate which had thrown him away upon coals. Now the few artists Benjamin had chanced to meet affected a soft and slouchy style of head-gear, and a considerable amount of freedom, generally with a touch of colour, in the region of the neck. Such, therefore, in the fitness of things, should have been the hat and such the neck-gear of Benjamin Quelch, and the veto of his wife only made him yearn for them the more intensely.

In later years he had been seized with a longing to see Paris. It chanced that a clerk in the same office, one Peter Flipp, had made one of a personally conducted party on a visit to the gay city.

The cost of the trip had been but five guineas; but never, surely, were five guineas so magnificently invested. There was a good deal of romance about Flipp, and it may be that his accounts were not entirely trustworthy; but they so fired the imagination of our friend Benjamin that he had at once begun to hoard up surreptitious sixpences, with the hope that someday he too might, by some unforeseen combination of circumstances, be enabled to visit the enchanted city.

And at last that day had come. Mrs Quelch, her three children and her one domestic, had gone to Lowestoft for an Easter outing, Benjamin and a deaf charwoman, Mrs Widger, being left in charge of the family belongings. Benjamin's Easter holidays were limited to Good Friday and Easter Monday, and, as it seemed hardly worth while that he should travel so far as Lowestoft for such short periods, Mrs Quelch had thoughtfully arranged that he should spend the former day at the British Museum and the latter at the Zoological Gardens. Two days after her departure, however, Mr Cobble called Quelch into his private office and told him that if he liked he might for once take holiday from the Friday to the Tuesday inclusive, and join his wife at the seaside.

Quelch accepted the boon with the honest intention of employing it as suggested. Indeed, he had even begun a letter to his wife announcing the pleasing intelligence, and had got as far as 'My dear Penelope', when a wild and wicked thought struck him: why should he not spend his unexpected holiday in Paris?

Laying down his pen, he opened his desk and counted his secret hoard. It amounted to five pounds seventeen, twelve shillings more than Flipp's outlay. There was no difficulty in that direction, and nobody would be any the wiser. His wife would imagine that he was in London, while his employers would believe him to be at Lowestoft. There was a brief struggle in his mind, but the tempter prevailed, and, with a courage worthy of a better cause, he determined to risk it and – *go*.

And thus it came to pass that, on the evening of our story, Benjamin Quelch, having completed his packing – which merely comprised what he was accustomed to call his 'night things', neatly bestowed in a small black hand-bag belonging to Mrs Quelch – stood before the looking-glass and contemplated his guilty splendour – the red necktie and the soft grey felt hat, purchased out of surplus funds. He had expended a couple of guineas in a second-class return ticket, and another two pounds in 'coupons', entitling him to bed, breakfast and dinner for five days at certain specified hotels in Paris. This outlay, with half a crown for a pair of gloves, and a bribe of five shillings to secure the silence of Mrs Widger, left him with little more than a pound in hand, but this small surplus would no doubt amply suffice for his modest needs.

His only regret, as he gazed at himself in the glass, was that he had not had time to grow a moustache, the one thing needed to complete his artistic appearance. But time was fleeting, and he dared not linger over the enticing picture. He stole along the passage, and softly opened the street door. As he did so a sudden panic came over him, and he felt half inclined to abandon his rash design. But as he wavered he caught sight of the detested tall hat hanging up in the passage, and he hesitated no longer. He passed out, and closing the door behind him, started at a brisk pace for Victoria Station.

His plans had been laid with much ingenuity, though at a terrible sacrifice of his usual straightforwardness. He had written a couple of letters to Mrs Quelch, to be posted by Mrs Widger on appropriate days, giving imaginary accounts of his visits to the British Museum and Zoological Gardens, with pointed allusions to the behavior of the elephant, and other circumstantial particulars. To ensure the posting of these in proper order, he had marked the dates in pencil on the envelopes in the corner usually occupied by the postage-stamp, so that when the latter was affixed the figures would be concealed. He explained the arrangement to Mrs Widger, who promised that his instructions should be faithfully carried out.

After a sharp walk he reached the railway station, and in due course found himself steaming across the Channel to Dieppe. The passage was not especially rough, but to poor Quelch, unaccustomed as he was to the sea, it seemed as if the boat must go to the bottom every moment. To the bodily pains of seasickness were added the mental pains of remorse, and between the two he reached Dieppe more dead than alive; indeed, he would almost have welcomed death as a release from his sufferings.

Even when the boat had arrived at the pier he still remained in the berth he had occupied all night, and would probably have continued to lie there had not the steward lifted him by main force to his feet. He seized his black bag with a groan, and staggered on deck. Here he felt a little better, but new terrors seized him at the sight of the gold-laced officials and blue-bloused porters, who lined each side of the gangway, all talking at the top of their voices, and in tones which seemed, to his unaccustomed ear, to convey a thirst for British blood. No sooner had he landed than he was accosted by a ferocious-looking personage (in truth, a harmless custom-house officer), who asked him in French whether he had anything to declare, and made a movement to take his bag in order to mark it as 'passed'. Quelch jumped to the conclusion that the stranger was a brigand bent on depriving him of his property, and he held on to the bag with such tenacity that the *douanier* naturally inferred there was something specially contraband about it. He proceeded to open it, and produced, among sundry other feminine belongings, a lady's frilled and furbelowed nightdress, from which, as he unrolled it, fell a couple of bundles of cigars!

Benjamin's look of astonishment as he saw these unexpected articles produced from his hand-bag was interpreted by the officials as a look of guilt. As a matter of fact, half stupefied by the agonies of the night, he had forgotten the precise spot where he had left his own bag and had picked up in its stead one belonging to the wife of a sporting gentleman on his way to some races at Longchamps. Desiring to smuggle a few 'weeds', and deeming that the presence of such articles would be less likely to be suspected among a lady's belongings, the sporting gentleman had committed them to his companion's keeping. Hand-bags, as a rule, are 'passed' unopened, and such would probably have been the case in the present instance had not Quelch's look of panic excited suspicion. The real owners of the bag had picked up Quelch's, which it precisely resembled, and were close behind him on the gangway. The lady uttered an exclamation of dismay as she saw the contents of her bag spread abroad by the customs officer, but was promptly silenced by her husband. 'Keep your blessed tongue quiet,' he whispered. 'If a bloomin' idiot chooses to sneak our bag, and then to give himself away to the first man that looks at him, he must stand the racket.' Whereupon the sporting gentleman and lady, first taking a quiet peep into Benjamin's bag to make sure that it contained nothing compromising, passed the examiner with a smile of conscious innocence, and, after an interval for refreshment at the buffet, took their seats in the train for Paris.

Meanwhile poor Quelch was taken before a pompous individual with an extra-large moustache and a double allowance of gold lace on his cap and charged not only with defrauding the revenue, but with forcibly resisting an officer in the execution of his duty. The accusation being in French, Quelch did not understand a word of it, and in his ignorance took it for granted that he was accused of stealing the strange bag and its contents. Visions of imprisonment, penal servitude, nay, even capital punishment, floated before his bewildered brain. Finally the official with the large moustache made a speech to him in French, setting forth that for his dishonest attempt to smuggle he must pay a fine of a hundred francs. With regard to the assault on the official, as said official was not much hurt, he graciously agreed to throw that in and make no charge for it. When he had fully explained matters to his own satisfaction he waited to receive the answer of the prisoner; but none was forthcoming, for the best of reasons. It finally dawned on the official that Quelch might not understand French, and he therefore proceeded to address him in what he considered to be his native tongue.

'You smoggle – smoggle seegar. Zen it must zat you pay amende, hundred francs. You me understand? Hundred francs – pay! pay! pay!' At each repetition of the last word he brought down a dirty fist into the palm of the opposite hand immediately under Quelch's nose. 'Hundred francs – Engleesh money, four pound.'

Quelch caught the last words, and was relieved to find that it was merely a money payment that was demanded of him. But he was little better off, for, having but a few shillings in his pocket, to pay four pounds was as much out of his power as if it had been four hundred. He determined to appeal to the mercy of his captors. 'Not got,' he said, apologetically, with a vague idea that by speaking very elementary English he came somehow nearer to French, 'That all,' he continued, producing his little store and holding it out beseechingly to the official. '*Pas assez*, not·enouf,' growled the latter. Quelch tried again in all his pockets, but only succeeded in finding another threepenny piece. The officer shook his head, and, after a brief discussion with his fellows, said, '*Comment-vous appelez-vous, monsieur?* How do you call yourself?'

With a vague idea of keeping his disgrace from his friends, Quelch rashly determined to give a false name. If he had had a few minutes to think it over he would have invented one for the occasion, but his imagination was not accustomed to such sudden calls, and, on the question being repeated, he desperately gave the name of his next-door neighbour, Mr Henry Fladgate. 'Henri Flodgett,' repeated the officer as he wrote it down.

'*Et vous demeurez?* You live where?' And Quelch proceeded to give the address of Mr Fladgate, 11 Primrose Terrace. '*Tres bien*. I send teleg–r–r–amme. *Au violon!*' And poor Benjamin was ignominiously marched to the local police station.

Meanwhile Quelch's arrangements at home were scarcely working as he had intended. The estimable Mrs Widger, partly by reason of her deafness and partly of native stupidity, had only half understood his instructions about the letters. She knew she was to stamp them and she knew she was to post them, but the dates in the corners might have been runic inscriptions for any idea they conveyed to her obfuscated intellect. Accordingly, the first time she visited her usual house of call, which was early on the morning of Good Friday, she proceeded, in her own language, to 'get the dratted things off her mind' by dropping them both into the nearest pillar-box.

On the following day, therefore, Mrs Quelch at Lowestoft was surprised to find on the breakfast-table *two* letters in her Benjamin's handwriting. Her surprise was still greater when, on opening them, she found one to be a graphic account of a visit to the Zoological Gardens on the following Monday. The conclusion was obvious: either Benjamin had turned prophet, and had somehow got ahead of the almanac, or he was 'carrying on' in some very underhand manner. Mrs Quelch decided for the latter alternative, and determined to get to the bottom of the matter at once. She cut a sandwich, put on her bonnet, and, grasping her umbrella in a manner which boded no good to anyone who stayed her progress, started by the next train for Liverpool Street.

On reaching home she extracted from the weeping Widger, who had just been spending the last of Benjamin's five shillings, and was far gone in depression and gin-and-water, that her 'good gentleman' had not been home since Thursday night. This was bad enough, but there was still more conclusive evidence that he was up to no good, in the shape of his tall hat, which hung, silent accuser, on the last peg in the passage.

Having pumped Mrs Widger till there was no more (save tears) to be pumped out of her, Mrs Quelch, still firmly grasping her umbrella, proceeded next door, on the chance that her neighbour, Mrs Fladgate, might be able to give her some information. She found Mrs Fladgate weeping in the parlour with an open telegram before her. Being a woman who did not stand upon ceremony, she read the telegram, which was dated from Dieppe and ran as follows: 'Monsieur Fladgate here detained for to have smuggle cigars. Fine to pay, one hundred franc. Send money and he will be release.'

'Oh, the men, the men!' ejaculated Mrs Quelch, as she dropped into an armchair. 'They're all alike. First Benjamin, and now Fladgate! I shouldn't wonder if they had gone off together.'

'You don't mean to say Mr Quelch has gone too?' sobbed Mrs Fladgate.

'He has taken a shameful advantage of my absence. He has not been home since Thursday evening, and his hat is hanging up in the hall.'

'You don't think he has been m–m–murdered?'

'I'm not afraid of *that*,' replied Mrs Quelch, 'it wouldn't be worth anybody's while. But what has he got on his head? that's what I want to know. Of course, if he's with Mr Fladgate in some foreign den of iniquity, that accounts for it.'

'Don't foreigners wear hats?' enquired Mrs Fladgate, innocently.

'Not the respectable English sort, I'll be bound,' replied Mrs Quelch; 'some outlandish rubbish, I dare say. But I thought Mr Fladgate was on his Scotch journey.' (Mr Fladgate, it should be stated, was a traveller in the oil and colour line.)

'So he is. I mean, so he ought to be. In fact I expected him home today. But now he's in p–p–prison, and I may never see him any m–mo–more.' And Mrs Fladgate wept afresh.

'Stuff and nonsense!' retorted Mrs Quelch. 'You've only to send the money they ask for, and they'll be glad enough to get rid of him. But I wouldn't hurry; I'd let him wait a bit – you'll see him soon enough, never fear.'

The prophecy was fulfilled sooner than the prophet expected. Scarcely were the words out of her mouth when a cab was heard to draw up at the door, and a moment later Fladgate himself, a big, jovial man, wearing a white hat very much on one side, entered the room and threw a bundle of rugs on the sofa.

'Home again, old girl, and glad of it! Mornin', Mrs Quelch,' said the newcomer.

Mrs Fladgate gazed at him doubtfully for a moment, and then flung her arms round his neck, ejaculating, 'Saved, saved!'

'Martha,' said Mrs Quelch, reprovingly, 'have you no self-respect? Is *this* the way you deal with so shameful a deception?' Then, turning to the supposed offender, 'So, Mr Fladgate, you have escaped from your foreign prison.'

'Foreign, how much? Have you both gone dotty, ladies? I've just escaped from a third-class carriage on the London and Northwestern. The space is limited, but I never heard it called a foreign prison.'

'It is useless to endeavour to deceive us,' said Mrs Quelch, sternly. 'Look at that telegram, Mr Fladgate, and deny it if you can. You have been gadding about in some vile foreign place with my misguided husband.'

'Oh, Quelch is in it too, is he? Then it *must* be a bad case. But let's see what we have been up to, for, 'pon my word, I'm quite in the dark at present.'

He held out his hand for the telegram, and read it carefully. 'Somebody's been having a lark with you, old lady,' he said to his wife. 'You know well enough where I've been – my regular northern journey, and nowhere else.'

'I don't believe a word of it,' said Mrs Quelch, 'you men are all alike – deceivers, every one of you.'

'Much obliged for your good opinion, Mrs Quelch. I had no idea Quelch was such a bad lot. But, so far as I am concerned, the thing's easily tested. Here is the bill for my bed last night at Carlisle. Now if I was in Carlisle and larking about at Dieppe at the same time, perhaps you'll kindly explain how I managed it.'

Mrs Quelch was staggered, but not convinced. 'But if – if you were at Carlisle, where is Benjamin, and what does this telegram mean?'

'Not being a wizard, I really can't say; but concerning Quelch, we shall find him, never fear. When did he disappear?'

Mrs Quelch told her story, not forgetting the mysterious letter.

'I think I see daylight,' said Fladgate. 'The party who has got into that mess is Quelch, and, being frightened out of his wits, he has given my name instead of his own. That's about the size of it!'

'But Benjamin doesn't smoke; and how should he come to be at Dieppe?'

'Went for a holiday, I suppose. As for smoking, I shouldn't have thought he was up to it; but with that sat-upon sort of man – begging your pardon, Mrs Quelch – you never know where he may break out. Worms will turn, you know, and sometimes they take a wrong turning.'

'But Benjamin would never dare – '

'That's just it. He daren't do anything when you've got your eye on him.

When you haven't perhaps he may, and perhaps he mayn't. The fact is, you hold up his head too tight, and if he jibs now and then you can't wonder at it.'

'You have a very coarse way of putting things, Mr Fladgate. Mr Quelch is not a horse, that I am aware of.'

'We won't quarrel about the animal, my dear madam, but you may depend upon it, my solution's right. A hardened villain, like myself, say, would never have got into such a scrape, but Quelch don't know enough of the world to keep himself out of mischief. They've got him in quod, that's clear, and the best thing you can do is to send the coin and get him out again.'

'Send money to those swindling Frenchmen? Never! If Benjamin is in prison I will fetch him out myself.'

'You would never risk that dreadful sea passage!' exclaimed Mrs Fladgate. 'And how will you manage the language? You don't understand French.'

'Oh, I shall do very well,' said the heroic woman. 'They won't talk French to *me*!'

That same night a female passenger crossed by the boat from Newhaven to Dieppe. The passage was rough, and the passenger was very seasick; but she still sat grimly upright, never for one moment relaxing her grasp on the handle of her silk umbrella. What she went through on landing, how she finally obtained her husband's release, and what explanations passed between the reunited pair, must be left to the reader's imagination, for Mrs Quelch never told the story. Twenty-four hours later a four-wheeled cab drew up at the Quelchs' door, and from it descended, first a stately female, and then a woebegone little man, in a soft felt hat and a red necktie, both sorely crushed and soiled, with a black bag in his hand. 'Is there a fire in the kitchen?' asked Mrs Quelch the moment she set foot in the house. Being assured that there was, she proceeded down the kitchen stairs, Quelch meekly following her. 'Now,' she said, pointing to the black bag, 'those – things!' Benjamin opened the bag, and tremblingly took out the frilled nightdress and the cigars. His wife pointed to the fire, and he meekly laid them on it. 'Now that necktie.' The necktie followed the cigars. 'And that thing;' and the hat crowned the funeral pile.

The smell was peculiar, and to the ordinary nose disagreeable, but to Mrs Quelch it was as the odour of burnt incense. She watched the heap as it smouldered away, and finally dispersed the embers by a vigorous application of the poker.

'Now, Benjamin,' she said to her trembling spouse, 'I forgive you. But if ever again – '

The warning was left unspoken, but it was not needed. Benjamin's one experience has more than satisfied his yearning for soft raiment and foreign travel, and his hats are taller than ever.

GEORGE MOORE

George Augustus Moore was born on 24 February 1852 in Ballyglass, County Mayo in Ireland. He left his homeland when he was eighteen and went to France to study painting. He came to England in 1882 to begin a writing career and published his first novel, *A Modern Lover*, in 1883, which borrowed much from French literary technique. His best work is *Esther Waters* (1894), which was a commercial success and was followed by *Evelyn Innes* (1898) and *Sister Teresa* (1901). Moore moved to Dublin in 1901 where he assisted in the planning of the Abbey Theatre (Irish National Theatre). He published an excellent collection of short stories, *The Untilled Field*, in 1903. He also produced a number of autobiographical works – *Confessions of a Young Man* (1888), *Memoirs of My Dead Life* (1906) and *Hail and Farewell* (1911). Moore returned to England in 1911 where he produced *The Brook Kerith* (1916), *Heloïse and Abelard* (1921) and *Ulick and Soracha* (1924). He died in London on 21 January 1933.

The Exile

I

Pat Phelan's bullocks were ready for the fair, and so were his pigs; but the two fairs happened to come on the same day, and he thought he would like to sell the pigs himself. His eldest son, James, was staying at home to help Catherine Ford with her churning; Peter, his second son, was not much of a hand at a bargain; it was Pat and James who managed the farm, and when Peter had gone to bed they began to wonder if Peter would be able to sell the bullocks. Pat said Peter had been told the lowest price he could take, James said there was a good demand for cattle, and at last they decided that Peter could not fail to sell the beasts.

Pat was to meet Peter at the crossroads about twelve o'clock in the day. But he had sold his pigs early, and was half an hour in front of him, and sitting on the stile waiting for his son, he thought if Peter got thirteen pounds apiece for the bullocks he would say he had done very well. A good jobber, he thought, would be able to get ten shillings apiece more for them; and he went on thinking of what price Peter would get, until, suddenly looking up the road, whom should he see but Peter coming down the road with the bullocks in front of him. He could hardly believe his eyes, and it was a long story that Peter told him about two men who wanted to buy the bullocks early in the morning. They had offered him eleven pounds ten, and when he would not sell them at that price they had stood laughing at the bullocks and doing all they could to keep off other buyers. Peter was quite certain it was not his fault, and he began to argue. But Pat Phelan was too disappointed to argue with him, and he let him go on talking. At last Peter ceased talking, and this seemed to Pat Phelan a good thing.

The bullocks trotted in front of them. They were seven miles from home, and fifteen miles are hard on fat animals, and he could truly say he was at a loss of three pounds that day if he took into account the animals' keep.

Father and son walked on, and not a word passed between them till they came to Michael Quinn's public-house. 'Did you get three pounds apiece for the pigs, father?'

'I did, and three pounds five.'

'We might have a drink out of that.'

It seemed to Peter that the men inside were laughing at him or at the lemonade he was drinking, and, seeing among them one who had been interfering with him all day, he told him he would put him out of the house, and he would have done it if Mrs Quinn had not told him that no one put a man out of her house without her leave.

'Do you hear that, Peter Phelan?'

'If you can't best them at the fair,' said his father, 'it will be little good for you to put them out of the public-house afterwards.'

And on that Peter swore he would never go to a fair again, and they walked on until they came to the priest's house.

'It was bad for me when I listened to you and James. If I hadn't I might have been in Maynooth now.'

'Now, didn't you come home talking of the polis?'

'Wasn't that after?'

They could not agree as to when his idea of life had changed from the priesthood to the police, nor when it had changed back from the police to the priesthood, and Peter talked on, telling of the authors he had read with Father Tom – Caesar, Virgil, even Quintillian. The priest had said that Quintillian was too difficult for him, and Pat Phelan was in doubt whether the difficulty of Quintillian was a sufficient reason for preferring the police to the priesthood.

'Anyway it isn't a girl that's troubling him,' he said to himself, and he looked at Peter, and wondered how it was that Peter did not want to be married. Peter was a great big fellow, over six feet high, that many a girl would take a fancy to, and Pat Phelan had long had his eye on a girl who would marry him. And his failure to sell the bullocks brought all the advantages of this marriage to Pat Phelan's mind, and he began to talk to his son. Peter listened, and seemed to take an interest in all that was said, expressing now and then a doubt if the girl would marry him; the possibility that she might seemed to turn his thoughts again towards the priesthood.

The bullocks had stopped to graze, and Peter's indecisions threw Pat Phelan fairly out of his humour.

'Well, Peter, I am tired listening to you. If it's a priest you want to be, go in there, and Father Tom will tell you what you must do, and I'll drive the bullocks home myself.' And on that Pat laid his hand on the priest's green gate, and Peter walked through

2

There were trees about the priest's house, and there were two rooms on the right and left of the front door. The parlour was on the left, and when Peter came in the priest was sitting reading in his mahogany armchair. Peter wondered if it were this very mahogany chair that had put the idea of being a priest into his head. Just now, while walking with his father, he had been thinking that they had not even a wooden armchair in their house, though it was the best house in the village – only some stools and some plain wooden chairs.

The priest could see that Peter had come to him for a purpose. But Peter did not speak; he sat raising his pale, perplexed eyes, looking at the priest from time to time, thinking that if he told Father Tom of his failure at the fair, Father Tom might think he only wished to become a priest because he had no taste for farming.

'You said, Father Tom, if I worked hard I should be able to read Quintillian in six months.'

The priest's face always lighted up at the name of a classical author, and Peter said he was sorry he had been taken away from his studies. But he had been thinking the matter over, and his mind was quite made up, and he was sure he would sooner be a priest than anything else.

'My boy, I knew you would never put on the policeman's belt. The bishop will hold an examination for the places that are vacant in Maynooth.' Peter promised to work hard and he already saw himself sitting in an arm-chair, in a mahogany armchair, reading classics, and winning admiration for his learning.

He walked home, thinking that everything was at last decided, when suddenly, without warning, when he was thinking of something else, his heart misgave him. It was as if he heard a voice saying: 'My boy, I don't think you will ever put on the cassock. You will never walk with the biretta on your head.' The priest had said that he did not believe he would ever buckle on the policeman's belt. He was surprised to hear the priest say this, though he had often heard himself thinking the same thing. What surprised and frightened him now was that he heard himself saying he would never put on the cassock and the biretta. It is frightening to hear yourself saying you are not going to do the thing you have just made up your mind you will do.

He had often thought he would like to put the money he would get out of the farm into a shop, but when it came to the point of deciding he had not been able to make up his mind. He had always had a great difficulty in knowing what was the right thing to do. His Uncle William had never thought of anything but the priesthood. James never thought of anything but the farm. A certain friend of his had never thought of doing anything but going to America. Suddenly he heard someone call him.

It was Catherine, and Peter wondered if she were thinking to tell him she was going to marry James. For she always knew what she wanted. Many said that James was not the one she wanted, but Peter did not believe that, and he looked at Catherine and admired her face, and thought what a credit she would be to the family. No one wore such beautifully knitted stockings as Catherine, and no one's boots were so prettily laced.

But not knowing exactly what to say, he asked her if she had come from their house, and he went on talking, telling her that she would find nobody in the parish like James. James was the best farmer in the parish, none such a judge of cattle; and he said all this and a great deal more, until he saw that Catherine did not care to talk about James at all.

'I dare say all you say is right, Peter; but you see he's your brother.'

And then, fearing she had said something hurtful, she told him that she liked James as much as a girl could like a man who was not going to be her husband.

'And you are sure, Catherine, that James is not going to be your husband?'

'Yes,' she said, 'quite sure.'

Their talk had taken them as far as Catherine's door, and Peter went away wondering why he had not told her he was going to Maynooth; for no one would have been able to advise him as well as Catherine, she had such good sense.

3

There was a quarter of a mile between the two houses, and while Peter was talking to Catherine, Pat Phelan was listening to his son James, who was telling his father that Catherine had said she would not marry him.

Pat was over sixty, but he did not give one the impression of an old man. The hair was not grey, there was still a little red in the whiskers. James, who sat opposite to him, holding his hands to the blaze, was not as good-looking a man as his father, the nose was not as fine, nor were the eyes as keen. There was more of the father in Peter than in James.

When Peter opened the half-door, awaking the dozen hens that roosted on the beam, he glanced from one to the other, for he suspected that his father was telling James how he had failed to sell the bullocks. But the tone of his father's voice when he asked him what had detained him on the road told him he was mistaken; and then he remembered that Catherine had said she would not marry James, and he began to pity his brother.

'I met Catherine on the road, and I could do no less than walk as far as her door with her.'

'You could do no less than that, Peter,' said James.

'And what do you mean by that, James?'

'Only this, that it is always the crooked way, Peter; for if it had been you that had asked her she would have had you and jumping.'

'She would have had me!'

'And now don't you think you had better run after her, Peter, and ask her if she'll have you?'

'I'll never do that; and it is hurtful, James, that you should think such a thing of me, that I would go behind your back and try to get a girl from you.'

'I did not mean that, Peter; but if she won't have me, you had better try if you can get her.'

And suddenly Peter felt a resolve come into his heart, and his manner grew exultant.

'I've seen Father Tom, and he said I can pass the examination. I'm going to be a priest.'

And when they were lying down side by side Peter said, 'James, it will be all right.' Knowing there was a great heart-sickness on his brother, he put out his hand. 'As sure as I lie here she will be lying next you before this day twelvemonths. Yes, James, in this very bed, lying here where I am lying now.'

'I don't believe it, Peter.'

Peter loved his brother, and to bring the marriage about he took some money from his father and went to live at Father Tom's, and he worked so hard during the next two months that he passed the bishop's examination. And it was late one night when he went to bid them goodbye at home.

'What makes you so late, Peter?'

'Well, James, I didn't want to meet Catherine on the road.'

'You are a good boy, Peter,' said the father, 'and God will reward you for the love you bear your brother. I don't think there are two better men in the world. God has been good to me to give me two such sons.'

And then the three sat round the fire, and Pat Phelan began to talk family history.

'Well, Peter, you see, there has always been a priest in the family, and it would be a pity if there's not one in this generation. In '48 your grand-uncles joined the rebels, and they had to leave the country. You have an uncle a priest, and you are just like your Uncle William.'

And then James talked, but he did not seem to know very well what he was saying, and his father told him to stop – that Peter was going where God had called him.

'And you will tell her,' Peter said, getting up, 'that I have gone.'

'I haven't the heart for telling her such a thing. She will be finding it out soon enough.'

Outside the house – for he was sleeping at Father Tom's that night – Peter thought there was little luck in James's eyes; inside the house Pat Phelan and James thought that Peter was settled for life.

'He will be a fine man standing on an altar,' James said, 'and perhaps he will be a bishop some day.'

'And you'll see her when you're done reaping, and you won't forget what Peter told you,' said Pat Phelan.

And, after reaping, James put on his coat and walked up the hillside, where he thought he would find Catherine.

'I hear Peter has left you,' she said, as he opened the gate to let the cows through.

'He came last night to bid us goodbye.'

And they followed the cows under the tall hedges.

'I shall be reaping tomorrow,' he said. 'I will see you at the same time.'

And henceforth he was always at hand to help her to drive her cows home; and every night, as he sat with his father by the fire, Pat Phelan expected James to tell him about Catherine. One evening he came back overcome, looking so wretched that his father could see that Catherine had told him she would not marry him.

'She won't have me,' he said.

'A man can always get a girl if he tries long enough,' his father said, hoping to encourage him.

'That would be true enough for another. Catherine knows she will never get Peter. Another man might get her, but I'm always reminding her of Peter.'

She told him the truth one day, that if she did not marry Peter she would marry no one, and James felt like dying. He grew pale and could not speak.

At last he said, 'How is that?'

'I don't know. I don't know, James. But you mustn't talk to me about marriage again.'

And he had to promise her not to speak of marriage again, and he kept his word. At the end of the year she asked him if he had any news of Peter.

'The last news we had of him was about a month ago, and he said he hoped to be admitted into the minor orders.'

And a few days afterwards he heard that Catherine had decided to go into a convent.

'So this is the way it has ended,' he thought. And he seemed no longer fit for work on the farm. He was seen about the road smoking, and sometimes he went down to the ball-alley, and sat watching the games in the evening. It was thought that he would take to drink, but he took to fishing instead, and was out all day in his little boat on the lake, however hard the wind might blow. The fisherman said he had seen him in the part of the lake where the wind blew the hardest, and that he could hardly pull against the waves.

'His mind is away. I don't think he'll do any good in this country,' his father said.

And the old man was very sad, for when James was gone he would have no one, and he did not feel he would be able to work the farm for many years longer. He and James used to sit smoking on either side of the fireplace, and Pat Phelan knew that James was thinking of America all the while. One evening, as they were sitting like this, the door was opened suddenly.

'Peter!' said James. And he jumped up from the fire to welcome his brother.

'It is good for sore eyes to see the sight of you again,' said Pat Phelan. 'Well, tell us the news. If we had known you were coming we would have sent the cart to meet you.'

As Peter did not answer, they began to think that something must have happened. Perhaps Peter was not going to become a priest after all, and would stay at home with his father to learn to work the farm.

'You see, I did not know myself until yesterday. It was only yesterday that –'

'So you are not going to be a priest? We are glad to hear that, Peter.'

'How is that?'

He had thought over what he should say, and without waiting to hear why they were glad, he told them the professor, who overlooked his essays, had refused to recognise their merits – he had condemned the best things in them; and Peter said it was extraordinary that such a man should be appointed to such a place. Then he told that the Church afforded little chances for the talents of young men unless they had a great deal of influence.

And they sat listening to him, hearing how the college might be reformed. He had a gentle, winning way of talking, and his father and brother forgot their own misfortunes thinking how they might help him.

'Well, Peter, you have come back none too soon.'

'And how is that? What have you been doing since I went away? You all wanted to hear about Maynooth.'

'Of course we did, my boy. Tell him, James.'

'Oh! it is nothing particular,' said James. 'It is only this, Peter – I am going to America.'

'And who will work the farm?'

'Well, Peter, we were thinking that you might work it yourself.'

'I work the farm! Going to America, James! But what about Catherine?'

'That's what I'm coming to, Peter. She has gone into a convent. And that's what's happened since you went away. I can't stop here, Peter – I will never do a hand's turn in Ireland – and father is getting too old to go to the fairs. That's what we were thinking when you came in.'

There was a faint tremble in his voice, and Peter saw how heart-sick his brother was.

'I will do my best, James.'

'I knew you would.'

'Yes, I will,' said Peter; and he sat down by the fire.

And his father said: 'You are not smoking, Peter.'

'No,' he said; 'I've given up smoking.'

'Will you drink something?' said James. 'We have got a drain of whiskey in the house.'

'No, I have had to give up spirits. It doesn't agree with me. And I don't take tea in the morning. Have you got any cocoa in the house?'

It was not the cocoa he liked, but he said he would be able to manage.

4

And when the old man came through the doorway in the morning buttoning his braces, he saw Peter stirring his cocoa. There was something absurd as well as something attractive in Peter, and his father had to laugh when he said he couldn't eat American bacon.

'My stomach wouldn't retain it. I require very little, but that little must be the best.'

And when James took him into the farmyard, he noticed that Peter crossed the yard like one who had never been in a farmyard before; he looked less like a farmer than ever, and when he looked at the cows, James wondered if he could be taught to see the difference between an Alderney and a Durham.

'There's Kate,' he said; 'she's a good cow; as good a cow as we have, and we can't get any price for her because of that hump on her back.'

They went to the sties; there were three pigs there and a great sow with twelve little bonhams, and the little ones were white with silky hair, and Peter asked how old they were, and when they would be fit for killing. And James told Peter there were seven acres in the Big Field. 'Last year we had oats in the Holly Field; next year you'll sow potatoes there.' And he explained the rotation of crops. 'And, now,' he said, 'we will go down to Crow's Oak. You have never done any ploughing, Peter; I will show you.'

It was extraordinary how little Peter knew. He could not put the harness on the horse, and he reminded James that he had gone into the post office when he left school. James gave in to him that the old red horse was hard to drive, but James could drive him better than Peter could lead him; and Peter marvelled at the skill with which James raised his hand from the shaft of the plough and struck the horse with the rein whilst he kept the plough steady with the other hand.

'Now, Peter, you must try again.'

At the end of the headland, where the plough turned, Peter always wanted to stop and talk about something; but James said they would have to get on with the work, and Peter walked after the plough, straining after it for three hours, and then he said: 'James, let me drive the horse. I can do no more.'

'You won't feel it so much when you are accustomed to it,' said James.

Anything seemed to him better than a day's ploughing: even getting up at three in the morning to go to a fair.

He went to bed early, as he used to, and they talked of him over the fire, as they used to. But however much they talked, they never seemed to find what they were seeking – his vocation – until one evening an idea suddenly rose out of their talk.

'A good wife is the only thing for Peter,' said Pat.

And they went on thinking.

'A husband would be better for her,' said Pat Phelan, 'than a convent.'

'I cannot say I agree with you there. Think of all the good them nuns are doing.'

'She isn't a nun yet,' said Pat Phelan.

And the men smoked on a while, and they ruminated as they smoked.

'It would be better, James, that Peter got her than that she should stay in a convent.'

'I wouldn't say that,' said James.

'You see,' said his father, 'she did not go into the convent because she had a calling, but because she was crossed in love.'

And after another long while James said, 'It is a bitter dose, I am thinking, father, but you must go and tell her that Peter has left Maynooth.'

'And what would the Reverend Mother be saying to me if I went to her with such a story as that? Isn't your heart broken enough already, James, without wanting me to be breaking it still more? Sure, James, you could never see her married to Peter?'

'If she were to marry Peter I should be able to go to America, and that is the only thing for me.'

'That would be poor consolation for you, James.'

'Well, it is the best I shall get, to see Peter settled, and to know that there will be someone to look after you, father.'

'You are a good son, James.'

They talked on, and as they talked it became clearer to them that some one must go tomorrow to the convent and tell Catherine that Peter had left Maynooth.

'But wouldn't it be a pity,' said Pat Phelan, 'to tell her this if Peter is not going to marry her in the end?'

'I'll have him out of his bed,' said James, 'and he'll tell us before this fire if he will or won't.'

'It's a serious thing you are doing, James, to get a girl out of a convent, I am thinking.'

'It will be on my advice that you will be doing this, father; and now I'll go and get Peter out of his bed.'

And Peter was brought in, asking what they wanted of him at this hour of the night; and when they told him what they had been talking about and the plans they had been making, he said he would be catching his death of cold, and they threw some sods of turf on the fire.

'It is against myself that I am asking a girl to leave the convent, even for you, Peter,' said James. 'But we can think of nothing else.'

'Peter will be able to tell us if it is a sin that we'd be doing.'

'It is only right that Catherine should know the truth before she makes her vows,' Peter said. 'But this is very unexpected, father. I really –'

'Peter, I'd take it as a great kindness. I shall never do a hand's turn in this country. I want to get to America. It will be the saving of me.'

'And now, Peter,' said his father, 'tell us for sure if you will have the girl?'

'Faith I will, though I never thought of marriage, if it be to please James.' Seeing how heart-sick his brother was, he said, 'I can't say I like her as you like her; but if she likes me I will promise to do right by her. James, you're going away; we may never see you again. It is all very sad. And now you'll let me go back to bed.'

'Peter, I knew you would not say no to me; I can't bear this any longer.'

'And now,' said Peter, 'let me go back to bed. I am catching my death.'

And he ran back to his room, and left his brother and father talking by the fire.

5

Pat thought the grey mare would take him in faster than the old red horse; and the old man sat, his legs swinging over the shaft, wondering what he should say to the Reverend Mother, and how she would listen to his story; and when he came to the priest's house a great wish came upon him to ask the priest's advice. The priest was walking up his little lawn reading his breviary, and a great fear came on Pat Phelan, and he thought he must ask the priest what he should do.

The priest heard the story over the little wall, and he was sorry for the old man. It took him a long time to tell the story, and when he was finished the priest said: 'But where are you going, Pat?'

'That's what I stopped to tell you, your reverence. I was thinking I might be going to the convent to tell Catherine that Peter has come back.'

'Well it wasn't yourself that thought of doing such a thing as that, Pat Phelan.'

But at every word the priest said Pat Phelan's face grew more stubborn, and at last he said: 'Well, your reverence, that isn't the advice I expected from you,' and he struck the mare with the ends of the reins and let her trot up the hill. Nor did the mare stop trotting till she had reached the top of the hill, and Pat Phelan had never known her do such a thing before. From the top of the hill there was a view of the bog, and Pat thought of the many fine loads of turf he had had out of that bog, and the many young fellows he had seen there cutting turf. 'But every one is leaving the country,' the old man said to himself, and his chin dropped into his shirt-collar, and he held the reins loosely, letting the mare trot or walk as she liked. And he let many pass him without bidding them the hour of the day, for he was too much overcome by his own grief to notice anyone.

The mare trotted gleefully; soft clouds curled over the low horizon far away, and the sky was blue overhead; and the poor country was very beautiful in the still autumn weather, only it was empty. He passed two or three fine houses that the gentry had left to caretakers long ago. The fences were gone, cattle strayed through the woods, the drains were choked with weeds, the stagnant water was spreading out into the fields, and Pat Phelan noticed these things, for he remembered what this country was forty years ago. The devil a bit of lonesomeness there was in it then.

He asked a girl if they would be thatching the house that autumn; but she answered that the thatch would last out the old people, and she was going to join her sister in America.

'She's right – they're all there now. Why should anyone stop here?' the old man said.

The mare tripped, and he took this to be a sign that he should turn back. But he did not go back. Very soon the town began, in broken pavements and dirty cottages; going up the hill there were some slated roofs, but there was no building of any importance except the church.

At the end of the main street, where the trees began again, the convent stood in the middle of a large garden, and Pat Phelan remembered he had heard that the nuns were doing well with their dairy and their laundry.

He knocked, and a lay-sister peeped through the grating, and then she opened the door a little way, and at first he thought he would have to go back without seeing either Catherine or the Reverend Mother. For he had got no further than, 'Sister Catherine,' when the lay-sister cut him short with the news that Sister Catherine was in retreat, and could see no one. The Reverend Mother was busy.

'But,' said Pat, 'you're not going to let Catherine take vows without hearing me.'

'If it is about Sister Catherine's vows – '

'Yes, it is about them I've come, and I must see the Reverend Mother.'

The lay-sister said Sister Catherine was going to be clothed at the end of the week.

'Well, that is just the reason I've come here.'

On that the lay-sister led him into the parlour, and went in search of the Reverend Mother.

The floor was so thickly beeswaxed that the rug slipped under his feet, and, afraid lest he might fall down, he stood quite still, impressed by the pious pictures on the walls, and by the large books upon the table, and by the poor-box, and by the pious inscriptions. He began to think how much easier was this pious life than the life of the world – the rearing of children, the failure of crops, and the loneliness. Here life slips away without one perceiving it, and it seemed a pity to bring her back to trouble. He stood holding his hat in his old hands, and the time seemed very long. At last the door opened, and a tall woman with sharp, inquisitive eyes came in.

'You have come to speak to me about Sister Catherine?'

'Yes, my lady.'

'And what have you got to tell me about her?'

'Well, my son thought and I thought last night – we were all thinking we had better tell you – last night was the night that my son came back.'

At the word Maynooth a change of expression came into her face, but when he told her that Peter no longer wished to be a priest her manner began to grow hostile again, and she got up from her chair and said: 'But really, Mr Phelan, I have got a great deal of business to attend to.'

'But, my lady, you see that Catherine wanted to marry my son Peter, and it is because he went to Maynooth that she came here. I don't think she'd want to be a nun if she knew that he didn't want to be a priest.'

'I cannot agree with you, Mr Phelan, in that. I have seen a great deal of Sister Catherine – she has been with us now for nearly a year – and if she ever entertained the wishes you speak of, I feel sure she has forgotten them. Her mind is now set on higher things.'

'Of course you may be right, my lady, very likely. It isn't for me to argue with you about such things; but you see I have come a long way, and if I could see Catherine herself – '

'That is impossible. Catherine is in retreat.'

'So the lay-sister told me; but I thought – '

'Sister Catherine is going to be clothed next Saturday, and I can assure you, Mr Phelan, that the wishes you tell me of are forgotten. I know her very well. I can answer for Sister Catherine.'

The rug slipped under the peasant's feet and his eyes wandered round the room; and the Reverend Mother told him how busy she was, she really could not talk to him any more that day.

'You see, it all rests with Sister Catherine herself.'

'That's just it,' said the old man; 'that's just it, my lady. My son Peter, who has come from Maynooth, told us last night that Catherine should know everything that has happened, so that she may not be sorry afterwards, otherwise I wouldn't have come here, my lady. I wouldn't have come to trouble you.'

'I am sorry, Mr Phelan, that your son Peter has left Maynooth. It is sad indeed when one finds that one has not a vocation. But that happens sometimes. I don't think that it will be Catherine's case. And now, Mr Phelan, I must ask you to excuse me,' and the Reverend Mother persuaded the unwilling peasant into the passage, and he followed the lay-sister down the passage to the gate and got into his cart again.

'No wonder,' he thought, 'they don't want to let Catherine out, now that they have got that great farm, and not one among them, I'll be bound, who can manage it except Catherine.'

At the very same moment the same thoughts passed through the Reverend Mother's mind. She had not left the parlour yet, and stood thinking how she should manage if Catherine were to leave them. 'Why,' she asked, 'should he choose to leave Maynooth at such a time? It is indeed unfortunate. There is nothing,' she reflected, 'that gives a woman so much strength as to receive the veil. She always feels stronger after her clothing. She feels that the world is behind her.'

The Reverend Mother reflected that perhaps it would be better for Catherine's sake and for Peter's sake – indeed, for everyone's sake – if she were not to tell Catherine of Pat Phelan's visit until after the clothing. She might tell Catherine three months hence. The disadvantage of this would be that Catherine might hear that Peter had left Maynooth. In a country place news of this kind cannot be kept out of a convent. And if Catherine were going to leave, it were better that she should leave them now than leave them six months hence, after her clothing.

'There are many ways of looking at it,' the Reverend Mother reflected. 'If I don't tell her, she may never hear it. I might tell her later when she has taught one of the nuns how to manage the farm.' She took two steps towards the door and stopped to think again, and she was thinking when a knock came to the door. She answered mechanically, 'Come in,' and Catherine wondered at the Reverend Mother's astonishment.

'I wish to speak to you, dear mother,' she said timidly. But seeing the Reverend Mother's face change expression, she said, 'Perhaps another time will suit you better.'

The Reverend Mother stood looking at her, irresolute; and Catherine, who had never seen the Reverend Mother irresolute before, wondered what was passing in her mind.

'I know you are busy, dear mother, but what I have come to tell you won't take very long.'

'Well, then, tell it to me, my child.'

'It is only this, Reverend Mother. I had better tell you now, for you are expecting the bishop, and my clothing is fixed for the end of the week, and – '

'And,' said the Reverend Mother, 'you feel that you are not certain of your vocation.'

'That is it, dear mother. I thought I had better tell you.' Reading disappointment in the nun's face, Catherine said, 'I hesitated to tell you before. I had hoped that the feeling would pass away; but, dear mother, it isn't my fault; everyone has not a vocation.'

Then Catherine noticed a softening in the Reverend Mother's face, and she asked Catherine to sit down by her; and Catherine told her she had come to the convent because she was crossed in love, and not as the others came, because they wished to give up their wills to God.

'Our will is the most precious thing in us, and that is why the best thing we can do is to give it up to you, for in giving it up to you, dear mother, we are giving it up to God. I know all these things, but – '

'You should have told me of this when you came here, Catherine, and then I would not have advised you to come to live with us.'

'Mother, you must forgive me. My heart was broken, and I could not do otherwise. And you have said yourself that I made the dairy a success.'

'If you had stayed with us, Catherine, you would have made the dairy a success; but we have got no one to take your place. However, since it is the will of God, I suppose we must try to get on as well as we can without you. And now tell me, Catherine, when it was that you changed your mind. It was only the other day you told me you wished to become a nun. You said you were most anxious for your clothing. How is it that you have changed your mind?'

Catherine's eyes brightened, and speaking like one illuminated by some inward light, she said: 'It was the second day of my retreat, mother. I was walking in the garden where the great cross stands amid the rocks. Sister Angela and Sister Mary were with me, and I was listening to what they were saying, when suddenly my thoughts were taken away and I remembered those at home. I remembered Mr Phelan, and James, who wanted to marry me, but whom I would not marry; and it seemed to me that I saw him leaving his father – it seemed to me that I saw him going away to America. I don't know how it was – you will not believe me, dear mother – but I saw the ship lying in the harbour, that is to take him away. And then I thought of the old man sitting at home with no one to look after him, and it was not a seeming, but a certainty, mother. It came over me suddenly that my duty was not here, but there. Of course you can't agree with me, but I cannot resist it, it was a call.'

'But the Evil One, my dear child, calls us too; we must be careful not to mistake the devil's call for God's call.'

'Mother, I dare say.' Tears came to Catherine's eyes, she began to weep. 'I can't argue with you, mother, I only know – ' She could not speak for sobbing, and between her sobs she said, 'I only know that I must go home.'

She recovered herself very soon, and the Reverend Mother took her hand and said: 'Well, my dear child, I shall not stand in your way.'

Even the Reverend Mother could not help thinking that the man who got her would get a charming wife. Her face was rather long and white, and she had long female eyes with dark lashes, and her eyes were full of tenderness. She had spoken out of so deep a conviction that the Reverend Mother had begun to believe that her mission was perhaps to look after this hapless young man; and when she told the Reverend Mother that yesterday she had felt a conviction that Peter was not going to be a priest, the Reverend Mother felt that she must tell her of Pat Phelan's visit.

'I did not tell you at once, my dear child, because I wished to know from yourself how you felt about this matter,' the nun said; and she told Catherine that she was quite right, that Peter had left Maynooth. 'He hopes to marry you, Catherine.'

A quiet glow came into the postulant's eyes, and she seemed engulfed in some deep joy.

'How did he know that I cared for him?' the girl said, half to herself, half to the nun.

'I suppose his father or his brother must have told him,' the nun answered.

And then Catherine, fearing to show too much interest in things that the nun deemed frivolous, said, 'I am sorry to leave before my work is done here. But, mother, so it has all come true; it was extraordinary what I felt that morning in the garden,' she said, returning to her joy. 'Mother, do you believe in visions?'

'The saints, of course, have had visions. We believe in the visions of the saints.'

'But after all, mother, there are many duties besides religious duties.'

'I suppose, Catherine, you feel it to be your duty to look after this young man?'

'Yes, I think that is it. I must go now, mother, and see Sister Angela, and write out for her all I know about the farm, and what she is to do, for if one is not very careful with a farm one loses a great deal of money. There is no such thing as making two ends meet. One either makes money or loses money.'

And then Catherine again seemed to be engulfed in some deep joy, out of which she roused herself with difficulty.

6

When her postulant left the room, the Reverend Mother wrote to Pat Phelan, asking him to come next morning with his cart to fetch Catherine. And next morning, when the lay-sister told Catherine that he was waiting for her, the Reverend Mother said: 'We shall be able to manage, Catherine. You have told Sister Angela everything, and you will not forget to come to see us, I hope.'

'Mr Phelan,' said the lay-sister, 'told me to tell you that one of his sons is going to America today. Sister Catherine will have to go at once if she wishes to see him.'

'I must see James. I must see him before he leaves for America. Oh,' she said, turning to the Reverend Mother, 'do you remember that I told you I had seen the ship? Everything has come true. You can't believe any longer that it is not a call.'

Her box was in the cart, and as Pat turned the mare round he said: 'I hope we won't miss James at the station. That's the reason I came for you so early. I thought you would like to see him.'

'Why did you not come earlier?' she cried. 'All my happiness will be spoilt if I don't see James.'

The convent was already behind her, and her thoughts were now upon poor James, whose heart she had broken. She knew that Peter would never love her as well as James, but this could not be helped. Her vision in the garden consoled her, for she could no longer doubt that she was doing right in going to Peter, that her destiny was with him.

She knew the road well, she knew all the fields, every house and every gap in the walls. Sign after sign went by; at last they were within sight of the station. The signal was still up, and the train had not gone yet; at the end of the platform she saw James and Peter. She let Pat Phelan drive the cart round; she could get to them quicker by running down the steps and crossing the line. The signal went down.

'Peter,' she said, 'we shall have time to talk presently. I want to speak to James now.'

And they walked up to the platform, leaving Peter to talk to his father.

'Paddy Maguire is outside,' Pat said; 'I asked him to stand at the mare's head.'

'James,' said Catherine, 'it is very sad you are going away. We may never see you again, and there is no time to talk, and I've much to say to you.'

'I am going away, Catherine, but maybe I will be coming back someday. I was going to say maybe you would be coming over after me; but the land is good land, and you'll be able to make a living out of it.'

And then they spoke of Peter. James said he was too great a scholar for a farmer, and it was a pity he could not find out what he was fit for – for surely he was fit for something great after all.

And Catherine said: 'I shall be able to make something out of Peter.'

His emotion almost overcame him, and Catherine looked aside so that she should not see his tears.

'This is no time for talking of Peter,' she said. 'You are going away, James, but you will come back. You will find another woman better than I am in America, James. I don't know what to say to you. The train will be here in a minute. I am distracted. But one day you will be coming back, and we shall be very proud of you when you come back. I shall rebuild the house, and we shall be all happy then. Oh! here's the train. Goodbye; you have been very good to me. Oh, James! shall I ever see you again?'

Then the crowd swept them along, and James had to take his father's hand and his brother's hand. There were a great many people in the station – hundreds were going away in the same ship that James was going in. The train was followed by wailing relatives. They ran alongside of the train, waving their hands until they could no longer keep up with the train. James waved a red handkerchief until the train was out of sight. It disappeared in a cutting, and a moment after Catherine and Peter remembered they were standing side by side. They were going to be married in a few days! They started a little, hearing a step beside them. It was old Phelan.

'I think,' he said, 'it is time to be getting home.'

Home Sickness

He told the doctor he was due in the bar-room at eight o'clock in the morning; the bar-room was in a slum in the Bowery; and he had only been able to keep himself in health by getting up at five o'clock and going for long walks in the Central Park.

'A sea voyage is what you want,' said the doctor. 'Why not go to Ireland for two or three months? You will come back a new man.'

'I'd like to see Ireland again.'

And then he began to wonder how the people at home were getting on. The doctor was right. He thanked him, and three weeks afterwards he landed in Cork.

As he sat in the railway carriage he recalled his native village – he could see it and its lake, and then the fields one by one, and the roads. He could see a large piece of rocky land – some three or four hundred acres of headland stretching out into the winding lake. Upon this headland the peasantry had been given permission to build their cabins by former owners of the Georgian house standing on the pleasant green hill. The present owners considered the village a disgrace, but the villagers paid high rents for their plots of ground, and all the manual labour that the Big House required came from the village: the gardeners, the stable helpers, the house- and the kitchen-maids.

He had been thirteen years in America, and when the train stopped at his station, he looked round to sec if there were any changes in it. It was just the same blue limestone station-house as it was thirteen years ago. The platform and the sheds were the same, and there were five miles of road from the station to Duncannon. The sea voyage had done him good, but five miles were too far for him today; the last time he had walked the road, he had walked it in an hour and a half, carrying a heavy bundle on a stick.

He was sorry he did not feel strong enough for the walk; the evening was fine, and he would meet many people coming home from the fair, some of whom he had known in his youth, and they would tell him where he could get a clean lodging. But the carman would be able to tell him that; he called the car that was waiting at the station, and soon he was answering questions about America. But Bryden wanted to hear of those who were still living in the old country, and after hearing the stories of many people he had forgotten, he heard that Mike Scully, who had been away in a situation for many years as a coachman in the King's County, had come back and built a fine house with a concrete floor. Now there was a good loft in Mike Scully's house, and Mike would be pleased to take in a lodger.

Bryden remembered that Mike had been in a situation at the Big House; he had intended to be a jockey, but had suddenly shot up into a fine tall man, and had had to become a coachman instead. Bryden tried to recall the face, but he could only remember a straight nose, and a somewhat dusky complexion. Mike was one of the heroes of his childhood, and his youth floated before him, and he caught glimpses of himself, something that was more than a phantom and less than a reality. Suddenly his reverie was broken: the carman pointed with his whip, and Bryden saw a tall, finely built, middle-aged man coming through the gates, and the driver said: 'There's Mike Scully.'

Mike had forgotten Bryden even more completely than Bryden had forgotten him, and many aunts and uncles were mentioned before he began to understand.

'You've grown into a fine man, James,' he said, looking at Bryden's great width of chest. 'But you are thin in the cheeks, and you're sallow in the cheeks too.'

'I haven't been very well lately – that is one of the reasons I have come back; but I want to see you all again.'

Bryden paid the carman, wished him 'God-speed', and he and Mike divided the luggage between them, Mike carrying the bag and Bryden the bundle, and they walked round the lake, for the townland was at the back of the demesne; and while they walked, James proposed to pay Mike ten shillings a week for his board and lodging.

He remembered the woods thick and well forested; now they were wind-worn, the drains were choked and the bridge leading across the lake inlet was falling away. Their way led between long fields where herds of cattle were grazing; the road was broken – Bryden wondered how the villagers drove their carts over it, and Mike told him that the landlord could not keep it in repair, and he would not allow it to be kept in repair out of the rates, for then it would be a public road, and he did not think there should be a public road through his property.

At the end of many fields they came to the village, and it looked a desolate place, even on this fine evening, and Bryden remarked that the country did not seem to be as much lived in as it used to be. It was at once strange and familiar to see the chickens in the kitchen; and, wishing to re-knit himself to the old habits, he begged of Mrs Scully not to drive them out, saying he did not mind them. Mike told his wife that Bryden was born in Duncannon, and when he mentioned Bryden's name she gave him her hand, after wiping it on her apron, saying he was heartily welcome, only she was afraid he would not care to sleep in a loft.

'Why wouldn't I sleep in a loft, a dry loft! You're thinking a good deal of America over here,' said he, 'but I reckon it isn't all you think it. Here you work when you like and you sit down when you like; but when you have had a touch of blood-poisoning as I had, and when you have seen young people walking with a stick, you think that there is something to be said for old Ireland.'

'Now won't you be taking a sup of milk? You'll be wanting a drink after travelling,' said Mrs Scully.

And when he had drunk the milk Mike asked him if he would like to go inside or if he would like to go for a walk.

'Maybe it is sitting down you would like to be.'

And they went into the cabin, and started to talk about the wages a man could get in America, and the long hours of work.

And after Bryden had told Mike everything about America that he thought would interest him, he asked Mike about Ireland. But Mike did not seem to be able to tell him much that was of interest. They were all very poor – poorer, perhaps, than when he left them.

'I don't think anyone except myself has a five-pound note to his name.'

Bryden hoped he felt sufficiently sorry for Mike. But after all Mike's life and prospects mattered little to him. He had come back in search of health; and he felt better already; the milk had done him good, and the bacon and cabbage in the pot sent forth a savoury odour. The Scullys were very kind, they pressed him to make a good meal; a few weeks of country air and food, they said, would give him back the health he had lost in the Bowery; and when Bryden said he was longing for a smoke, Mike said there was no better sign than that. During his long illness he had never wanted to smoke, and he was a confirmed smoker.

It was comfortable to sit by the mild peat fire watching the smoke of their pipes drifting up the chimney, and all Bryden wanted was to be let alone; he did not want to hear of anyone's misfortunes, but about nine o'clock a number of villagers came in, and their appearance was depressing. Bryden remembered one or two of them – he used to know them very well when he was a boy; their talk was as depressing as their appearance, and he could feel no interest whatever in them. He was not moved when he heard that Higgins the stonemason was dead; he was not affected when he heard that Mary Kelly, who used to go to do the laundry at the Big House, had married; he was only interested when he heard she had gone to America. No, he had not met her there, America is a big place. Then one of the peasants asked him if he remembered Patsy Carabine, who used to do the gardening at the Big House. Yes, he remembered Patsy well. Patsy was in the poor-house. He had not been able to do any work on account of his arm; his house had fallen in; he had given up his holding and gone into the poor-house. All this was very sad, and to avoid hearing any further unpleasantness, Bryden began to tell them about America. And they sat round listening to him; but all the talking was on his side; he wearied of it; and looking round the group he recognised a ragged hunchback with grey hair; twenty years ago he was a young hunchback, and, turning to him, Bryden asked him if he was doing well with his five acres.

'Ah, not much. This has been a bad season. The potatoes failed; they were watery – there is no diet in them.'

These peasants were all agreed that they could make nothing out of their farms. Their regret was that they had not gone to America when they were young; and after striving to take an interest in the fact that O'Connor had lost a mare and foal worth forty pounds, Bryden began to wish himself back in the slum. And when they left the house he wondered if every evening would be like the present one. Mike piled fresh sods on the fire, and he hoped it would show enough light in the loft for Bryden to undress himself by.

The cackling of some geese in the road kept him awake, and the loneliness of the country seemed to penetrate to his bones, and to freeze the marrow in them. There was a bat in the loft – a dog howled in the distance – and then he drew the clothes over his head. Never had he been so unhappy, and the sound of Mike breathing by his wife's side in the kitchen added to his nervous terror. Then he dozed a little; and lying on his back he dreamed he was awake, and the men he had seen sitting round the fireside that evening seemed to him like spectres come out of some unknown region of morass and reedy tarn. He stretched out his hands for his clothes, determined to fly from this house, but remembering the lonely road that led to the station he fell back on his pillow. The geese still cackled, but he was too tired to be kept awake any longer. He seemed to have been asleep only a few minutes when he heard Mike calling him. Mike had come halfway up the ladder and was telling him that breakfast was ready. 'What kind of breakfast will he give me?' Bryden asked himself as he pulled on his clothes. There were tea and hot griddle cakes for breakfast, and there were fresh eggs; there was sunlight in the kitchen and he liked to hear Mike tell of the work he was going to do in the fields. Mike rented a farm of about fifteen acres, at least ten of which were grass; he grew an acre of potatoes and some corn, and some turnips for his sheep. He had a nice bit of meadow, and he took down his scythe, and as he put the whetstone in his belt Bryden noticed a second scythe, and he asked Mike if he should go down with him and help him to finish the field.

'You haven't done any mowing this many a year; I don't think you'd be of much help. You'd better go for a walk by the lake, but you may come in the afternoon if you like and help to turn the grass over.'

Bryden was afraid he would find the lake shore very lonely, but the magic of returning health is sufficient distraction for the convalescent, and the morning passed agreeably. The weather was still and sunny. He could hear the ducks in the reeds. The hours dreamed themselves away, and it became his habit to go to the lake every morning. One morning he met the landlord, and they walked together, talking of the country, of what it had been, and the ruin it was slipping into. James Bryden told him that ill health had brought him back to Ireland; and the landlord lent him his boat, and Bryden rowed about the islands, and resting upon his oars he looked at the old castles, and remembered the prehistoric raiders that the landlord had told him about. He came across the stones to which the lake dwellers had tied their boats, and these signs of ancient Ireland were pleasing to Bryden in his present mood.

As well as the great lake there was a smaller lake in the bog where the villagers cut their turf. This lake was famous for its pike, and the landlord allowed Bryden to fish there, and one evening when he was looking for a frog with which to bait his line he met Margaret Dirken driving home the cows for the milking. Margaret was the herdsman's daughter, and she lived in a cottage near the Big House; but she came up to the village whenever there was a dance, and Bryden had found himself opposite to her in the reels. But until this evening he had had little opportunity of speaking to her, and he was glad to speak to someone, for the evening was lonely, and they stood talking together.

'You're getting your health again,' she said. 'You'll soon be leaving us.'

'I'm in no hurry.'

'You're grand people over there; I hear a man is paid four dollars a day for his work.'

'And how much,' said James, 'has he to pay for his food and for his clothes?'

Her cheeks were bright and her teeth small, white and beautifully even; and a woman's soul looked at Bryden out of her soft Irish eyes. He was troubled and turned aside, and catching sight of a frog looking at him out of a tuft of grass he said: 'I have been looking for a frog to put upon my pike line.'

The frog jumped right and left, and nearly escaped in some bushes, but he caught it and returned with it in his hand.

'It is just the kind of frog a pike will like,' he said. 'Look at its great white belly and its bright yellow back.'

And without more ado he pushed the wire to which the hook was fastened through the frog's fresh body, and dragging it through the mouth he passed the hooks through the hind legs and tied the line to the end of the wire.

'I think,' said Margaret, 'I must be looking after my cows; it's time I got them home.'

'Won't you come down to the lake while I set my line?'

She thought for a moment and said: 'No, I'll see you from here.'

He went down to the reedy tarn, and at his approach several snipe got up, and they flew above his head uttering sharp cries. His fishing-rod was a long hazel stick, and he threw the frog as far as he could into the lake. In doing this he roused some wild ducks; a mallard and two ducks got up, and they flew towards the larger lake. Margaret watched them; they flew in a line with an old castle; and they had not disappeared from view when Bryden came towards her, and he and she drove the cows home together that evening.

They had not met very often when she said, 'James, you had better not come here so often calling to me.'

'Don't you wish me to come?'

'Yes, I wish you to come well enough, but keeping company is not the custom of the country, and I don't want to be talked about.'

'Are you afraid the priest would speak against us from the altar?'

'He has spoken against keeping company, but it is not so much what the priest says, for there is no harm in talking.'

'But if you are going to be married there is no harm in walking out together?'

'Well, not so much, but marriages are made differently in these parts; there is not much courting here.'

And next day it was known in the village that James was going to marry Margaret Dirken.

His desire to excel the boys in dancing had aroused much gaiety in the parish, and for some time past there had been dancing in every house where there was a floor fit to dance upon; and if the cottager had no money to pay for a barrel of beer, James Bryden, who had money, sent him a barrel, so that Margaret might get her dance. She told him that they sometimes crossed over into another parish where the priest was not so averse to dancing, and James wondered. And next morning at mass he wondered at their simple fervour. Some of them held their hands above their heads as they prayed, and all this was very new and very old to James Bryden. But the obedience of these people to their priest surprised him. When he was a lad they had not been so obedient, or he had forgotten their obedience; and he listened in mixed anger and wonderment to the priest who was scolding his parishioners, speaking to them by name, saying that he had heard there was dancing going on in their homes. Worse than that, he said he had seen boys and girls loitering about the roads, and the talk that went on was of one kind – love. He said that newspapers containing love-stories were finding their way into the people's houses, stories about love, in which there was nothing elevating or ennobling. The people listened, accepting the priest's opinion without question. And their submission was pathetic. It was the submission of a primitive people clinging to religious authority, and Bryden contrasted the weakness and incompetence of the people about him with the modern restlessness and cold energy of the people he had left behind him.

One evening, as they were dancing, a knock came to the door, and the piper stopped playing, and the dancers whispered: 'Someone has told on us; it is the priest.'

And the awe-stricken villagers crowded round the cottage fire, afraid to open the door. But the priest said that if they did not open the door he would put his shoulder to it and force it open. Bryden went towards the door, saying he would allow no one to threaten him, priest or no priest, but Margaret caught his arm and told him that if he said anything to the priest, the priest would speak against them from the altar, and they would be shunned by the neighbours. It was Mike Scully who went to the door and let the priest in, and he came in saying they were dancing their souls into hell.

'I've heard of your goings on,' he said – 'of your beer-drinking and dancing. I will not have it in my parish. If you want that sort of thing you had better go to America.'

'If that is intended for me, sir, I will go back tomorrow. Margaret can follow.'

'It isn't the dancing, it's the drinking I'm opposed to,' said the priest, turning to Bryden.

'Well, no one has drunk too much, sir,' said Bryden.

'But you'll sit here drinking all night,' and the priest's eyes went towards the corner where the women had gathered, and Bryden felt that the priest looked on the women as more dangerous than the porter.

'It's after midnight,' he said, taking out his watch. By Bryden's watch it was only half-past eleven, and while they were arguing about the time Mrs Scully offered Bryden's umbrella to the priest, for in his hurry to stop the dancing the priest had gone out without his; and, as if to show Bryden that he bore him no ill-will, the priest accepted the loan of the umbrella, for he was thinking of the big marriage fee that Bryden would pay him.

'I shall be badly off for the umbrella tomorrow,' Bryden said, as soon as the priest was out of the house. He was going with his father-in-law to a fair. His father-in-law was learning him how to buy and sell cattle. And his father-in-law was saying that the country was mending, and that a man might become rich in Ireland if he only had a little capital. Bryden had the capital, and Margaret had an uncle on the other side of the lake who would leave her all he had, that would be fifty pounds, and never in the village of Duncannon had a young couple begun life with so much prospect of success as would James Bryden and Margaret Dirken.

Some time after Christmas was spoken of as the best time for the marriage; James Bryden said that he would not be able to get his money out of America before the spring. The delay seemed to vex him, and he seemed anxious to be married, until one day he received a letter from America, from a man who had served in the bar with him. This friend wrote to ask Bryden if he were coming back. The letter was no more than a passing wish to see Bryden again. Yet Bryden stood looking at it, and everyone wondered what could be in the letter. It seemed momentous, and they hardly believed him when he said it was from a friend who wanted to know if his health were better. He tried to forget the letter, and he looked at the worn fields, divided by walls of loose stones, and a great longing came upon him.

The smell of the Bowery slum had come across the Atlantic, and had found him out in this western headland; and one night he awoke from a dream in which he was hurling some drunken customer through the open doors into the darkness. He had seen his friend in his white duck jacket throwing drink from glass into glass amid the din of voices and strange accents; he had heard the clang of money as it was swept into the till, and his sense sickened for the bar-room. But how should he tell Margaret Dirken that he could not marry her? She had built her life upon this marriage. He could not tell her that he would not marry her . . . yet he must go. He felt as if he were being hunted; the thought that he must tell Margaret that he could not marry her hunted him day after day as a weasel hunts a rabbit. Again and again he went to meet her with the intention of telling her that he did not love her, that their lives were not for one another, that it had all been a mistake, and that happily he had found out it was a mistake soon enough. But Margaret, as if she guessed what he was about to speak of, threw her arms about him and begged him to say he loved her, and that they would be married at once. He agreed that he loved her, and that they would be married at once. But he had not left her many minutes before the feeling came upon him that he could not marry her – that he must go away. The smell of the bar-room hunted him down. Was it for the sake of the money that he might make there that he wished to go back? No, it was not the money. What then? His eyes fell on the bleak country, on the little fields divided by bleak walls; he remembered the pathetic ignorance of the people, and it was these things that he could not endure. It was the priest who came to forbid the dancing. Yes, it was the priest. As he stood looking at the line of the hills the bar-room called to him. He heard the politicians, and the excitement of politics was in his blood again. He must go away from this place – he must get back to the bar-room. Looking up he saw the scanty orchard, and he hated the spare road that led to the village, and he hated the little hill at the top of which the village began, and he hated more than all other places the house where he was to live with Margaret Dirken – if he married her. He could see it from where he stood – by the edge of the lake, with twenty acres of pasture land about it, for the landlord had given up part of his demesne land to them.

He caught sight of Margaret, and he called to her to come through the stile. 'I have just had a letter from America.'

'About the money?' she said.

'Yes, about the money. But I shall have to go over there.'

He stood looking at her, seeking for words; and she guessed from his embarrassment that he would say to her that he must go to America before they were married.

'Do you mean, James, you will have to go at once?'

'Yes,' he said, 'at once. But I shall come back in time to be married in August. It will only mean delaying our marriage a month.'

They walked on a little way talking; every step he took James felt that he was a step nearer the Bowery slum. And when they came to the gate Bryden said: 'I must hasten or I shall miss the train.'

'But,' she said, 'you are not going now – you are not going today?'

'Yes, this morning. It is seven miles. I shall have to hurry not to miss the train.'

And then she asked him if he would ever come back.

'Yes,' he said, 'I am coming back.'

'If you are coming back, James, why not let me go with you?'

'You could not walk fast enough. We should miss the train.'

'One moment, James. Don't make me suffer; tell me the truth. You are not coming back. Your clothes – where shall I send them?'

He hurried away, hoping he would come back. He tried to think that he liked the country he was leaving, that it would be better to have a farmhouse and live there with Margaret Dirken than to serve drinks behind a counter in the Bowery. He did not think he was telling her a lie when he said he was coming back. Her offer to forward his clothes touched his heart, and at the end of the road he stood and asked himself if he should go back to her. He would miss the train if he waited another minute, and he ran on. And he would have missed the train if he had not met a car. Once he was on the car he felt himself safe – the country was already behind him. The train and the boat at Cork were mere formulae; he was already in America.

The moment he landed he felt the thrill of home that he had not found in his native village, and he wondered how it was that the smell of the bar seemed more natural than the smell of the fields, and the roar of crowds more welcome than the silence of the lake's edge. However, he offered up a thanksgiving for his escape, and entered into negotiations for the purchase of the bar-room.

He took a wife, she bore him sons and daughters, the bar-room prospered, property came and went; he grew old, his wife died, he retired from business, and reached the age when a man begins to feel there are not many years in front of him, and that all he has had to do in life has been done. His children married, lonesomeness began to creep about him; in the evening, when he looked into the firelight, a vague, tender reverie floated up, and Margaret's soft eyes and name vivified the dusk. His wife and children passed out of mind, and it seemed to him that that memory was the only real thing he possessed, and the desire to see Margaret again grew intense. But she was an old woman, she had married, maybe she was dead. Well, he would like to be buried in the village where he was born.

There is an unchanging, silent life within every man that none knows but himself, and his unchanging, silent life was his memory of Margaret Dirken. The bar-room was forgotten and all that concerned it, and the things he saw most clearly were the green hillside, and the bog lake and the rushes about it, and the greater lake in the distance, and behind it the blue lines of wandering hills.

Julia Cahill's Curse

In 1895 I was agent of the Irish Industrial Society, and I spent three days with Father O'Hara making arrangements for the establishment of looms for the weaving of homespuns and for acquiring plots of ground whereon to build schools where the village girls could practise lace-making.

The priest was one of the chief supporters of our movement. He was a wise and tactful man, who succeeded not only in living on terms of friendship with one of the worst landlords in Ireland, but in obtaining many concessions from him. When he came to live in Culloch the landlord had said to him that what he would like to do would be to run the ploughshare through the town, and to turn 'Culloch' into Bullock. But before many years had passed Father O'Hara had persuaded this man to use his influence to get a sufficient capital to start a bacon factory. And the town of Culloch possessed no other advantages except an energetic and foreseeing parish priest. It was not a railway terminus, nor was it a seaport.

But, perhaps because of his many admirable qualities, Father O'Hara is not the subject of this story. We find stories in the lives of the weak and the foolish and the improvident, and his name occurs here because he is typical of not a few priests I have met in Ireland.

I left him early one Sunday morning, and he saying that twenty odd miles lay before me, and my first stopping place would be Ballygliesane. I could hear mass there at Father Madden's chapel, and after mass I could call upon him, and that when I had explained the objects of our society I could drive to Rathowen, where there was a great gathering of the clergy. All the priests within ten miles round would be there for the consecration of the new church.

On an outside car one divides one's time in moralising on the state of the country or in chatting with the driver, and as the driver seemed somewhat taciturn I examined the fields as we passed them. They were scanty fields, drifting from thin grass into bog, and from bog into thin grass again, and in the distance there was a rim of melancholy mountains, and the peasants I saw along the road seemed a counterpart of the landscape. 'The land has made them,' I said, 'according to its own image and likeness,' and I tried to find words to define the yearning that I read in their eyes as we drove past. But I could find no words that satisfied me.

'Only music can express their yearning, and they have written it themselves in their folk tunes.'

My driver's eyes were the eyes that one meets everywhere in Ireland, pale, wandering eyes that the land seems to create, and I wondered if his character corresponded to his eyes; and with a view to finding if it did I asked him some questions about Father Madden. He seemed unwilling to talk, but I soon began to see that his silence was the result of shyness rather than dislike of conversation. He was a gentle, shy lad, and I told him that Father O'Hara had said I would see the loneliest parish in Ireland.

'It's true for him,' he answered, and again there was silence. At the end of a mile I asked him if the land in Father Madden's parish was poor, and he said no, it was the best land in the country, and then I was certain that there was some mystery attached to Father Madden.

'The road over there is the mearing.'

And soon after passing this road I noticed that although the land was certainly better than the land about Culloch, there seemed to be very few people on it; and what was more significant than the untilled fields were the ruins, for they were not the cold ruins of twenty, or thirty, or forty years ago, when the people were evicted and their tillage turned into pasture, but the ruins of cabins that had been lately abandoned. Some of the roof trees were still unbroken, and I said that the inhabitants must have left voluntarily.

'Sure they did. Aren't we all going to America?'

'Then it was not the landlord?'

'Ah, it's the landlord who'd have them back if he could.'

'And the priest? How does he get his dues?'

'Those on the other side are always sending their money to their friends and they pay the priest. Sure why should we be staying? Isn't the most of us over there already. It's more like going home than leaving home.'

I told him we hoped to establish new looms in the country, and that Father O'Hara had promised to help us.

'Father O'Hara is a great man,' he said.

'Well, don't you think that with the revival of industries the people might be induced to stay at home?'

'Sorra stay,' said he.

I could see that he was not so convinced about the depopulation of Father O'Hara's parish as he was about Father Madden's, and I tried to induce him to speak his mind.

'Well, your honour, there's many that think there's a curse on the parish.'

'A curse! And who put the curse on the parish?'

'Isn't that the bell ringing for mass, your honour?'

And listening I could head a doleful pealing in the grey sky.

'Does Father Madden know of this curse?'

'Indeed he does; none better.'

'And does he believe in it?'

'There's many who will tell you that he has been saying masses for the last ten years that the curse may be taken off the parish.'

We could now hear the bell tolling quite distinctly, and the driver pointed with his whip, and I could see the cross above the fir trees.

'And there,' he said, 'is Bridget Coyne,' and I saw a blind woman being led along the road. At the moment I supposed he had pointed the woman out because she was blind, though this did not seem a sufficient reason for the note of wonder in his voice; but we were within a few yards of the chapel and there was no time to ask him who Bridget Coyne was. I had to speak to him about finding stabling for the horse. That, he said, was not necessary, he would let the horse graze in the chapel-yard while he himself knelt by the door, so that he could hear mass and keep an eye on his horse. 'I shall want you half an hour after mass is over.' Half an hour, I thought, would suffice to explain the general scope of our movement to Father Madden. I had found that the best way was to explain to each priest in turn the general scope of the movement, and then to pay a second visit a few weeks later. The priest would have considered the ideas that I had put into his head, he would have had time to assimilate them in the interval, and I could generally tell on the second visit if I should find in him a friend, an enemy, or an indifferent.

There was something extraordinary in the appearance of Father Madden's church; a few peasants crouched here and there, and among them I saw the blind woman that the driver had pointed out on the road. She did not move during mass; she knelt or crouched with her shawl drawn over her head, and it was not until the acolyte rang the communion bell that she dared to lift herself up. That day she was the only communicant, and the acolyte did not turn the altar cloth over the rails, he gave her a little bit of the cloth to hold, and, holding it firmly in her fingers, she lifted up her blind face, and when the priest placed the Host on her tongue she sank back overcome.

'This blind woman,' I said to myself, 'will be the priest's last parishioner,' and I saw the priest saying mass in a waste church for the blind woman, everyone else dead or gone.

All her days, I said, are spent by the cabin fire hearing of people going to America, her relations, her brothers and sisters had gone, and every seventh day she is led to hear mass, to receive the Host, and to sink back. Today and tomorrow and the next day will be spent brooding over her happiness, and in the middle of the week she will begin to look forward to the seventh day.

The blind woman seemed strangely symbolical of the parish, the priest too. A short, thick-set man, with a large bald head and a fringe of reddish hair; his hands were fat and short, the nails were bitten, the nose was fleshy and the eyes were small, and when he turned towards the people and said, 'Pax vobiscum,' there was a note of command in his voice. The religion he preached was one of fear. His sermon was filled with flames and gridirons, and ovens and devils with pitchforks, and his parishioners groaned and shook their heads and beat their breasts.

I did not like Father Madden or his sermon. I remembered that there were few young people left in his parish, and it seemed waste of time to appeal to him for help in establishing industries; but it was my business to seek the cooperation of every priest, and I could not permit myself such a licence as the passing over of any priest. What reason could I give? that I did not like his sermon or his bald head? And after mass I went round to see him in the sacristy.

The sacristy was a narrow passage, and there were two acolytes in it, and the priest was taking off his vestments, and people were knocking constantly at the door, and the priest had to tell the acolyte what answer to give. I had only proposed to myself to sketch the objects of our organisation in a general outline to the priest, but it was impossible even to do this, so numerous were the interruptions. When I came to unfold our system of payments, the priest said: 'It is impossible for me to listen to you here. You had better come round with me to my house.'

The invitation was not quite in accordance with the idea I had formed of the man, and while walking across the fields he asked me if I would have a cup of tea with him, and we spoke of the new church at Rathowen. It seemed legitimate to deplore the building of new churches, and I mentioned that while the churches were increasing the people were decreasing, and I ventured to regret that only two ideas seemed to obtain in Ireland, the idea of the religious vocation and the idea of emigration.

'I see,' said Father Madden, 'you are imbued with all the new ideas.'

'But,' I said, 'you don't wish the country to disappear.'

'I do not wish it to disappear,' he said, 'but if it intends to disappear we can do nothing to prevent it from disappearing. Everyone is opposed to emigration now, but I remember when everyone was advocating it. Teach them English and emigrate them was the cure. Now,' he said, 'you wish them to learn Irish and to stay at home. And you are quite certain that this time you have found out the true way. I live very quiet down here, but I hear all the new doctrines. Besides teaching Paddy Durkin to feed his pig, I hear you are going to revive the Gothic. Music and literature are to follow, and among these resurrections there is a good deal of talk about pagan Ireland.'

We entered a comfortable, well-furnished cottage, with a good carpet on the floor, and the walls lined with books, and on either side of the fireplace there were easy chairs, and I thought of the people 'on the other side'.

He took a pot of tea from the hob, and said: 'Now let me pour you out a cup of tea, and you shall tell me about the looms.'

'But,' I said, 'Father Madden, you don't believe much in the future of Ireland, you don't take very kindly to new ideas?'

'New ideas! Every ten years there is a new set. If I had said teach them Irish ten years ago I should have been called a fool, and now if I say teach them English and let them go to America I am called a reactionist. You have come from Father O'Hara' – I could see from the way he said the name that the priests were not friends – 'and he has told you a great many of my people have gone to America. And perhaps you heard him say that they have not gone to America for the sake of better wages but because my rule is too severe, because I put down crossroad dances. Father O'Hara and I think differently, and I have no doubt he thinks he is quite right.'

While we breakfasted Father Madden said some severe things about Father O'Hara, about the church he had built, and the debt that was still upon it. I suppose my face told Father Madden of the interest I took in his opinions, for during breakfast he continued to speak his mind very frankly on all the subjects I wished to hear him speak on, and when breakfast was over I offered him a cigar and proposed that we should go for a walk on his lawn.

'Yes,' he said, 'there are people who think I am a reactionist because I put down the ball-alley.'

'The ball-alley!'

'There used to be a ball-alley by the church, but the boys wouldn't stop playing ball during mass, so I put it down. But you will excuse me a moment.' The priest darted off, and I saw him climb down the wall into the road; he ran a little way along the road calling at the top of his voice, and when I got to the wall I saw him coming back. 'Let me help you,' I said. I pulled him up and we continued our walk; and as soon as he had recovered his breath he told me that he had caught sight of a boy and girl loitering.

'And I hunted them home.'

I asked him why, knowing well the reason, and he said: 'Young people should not loiter along the roads. I don't want bastards in my parish.'

It seemed to me that perhaps bastards were better than no children at all, even from a religious point of view – one can't have religion without life, and bastards may be saints.

'In every country,' I said, 'boys and girls walk together, and the only idealism that comes into the lives of peasants is between the ages of eighteen and twenty, when young people meet in the lanes and linger by the stiles. Afterwards hard work in the fields kills aspiration.'

'The idealism of the Irish people does not go into sex, it goes into religion.'

'But religion does not help to continue the race, and we're anxious to preserve the race, otherwise there will be no religion, or a different religion in Ireland.'

'That is not certain.'

Later on I asked him if the people still believed in fairies. He said that traces of such beliefs survived among the mountain folk.

'There is a great deal of paganism in the language they wish to revive, though it may be as free from Protestantism as Father O'Hara says it is.'

For some reason or other I could see that folklore was distasteful to him, and he mentioned causally that he had put a stop to the telling of fairy-tales round the fire in the evening, and the conversation came to a pause.

'Now I won't detain you much longer, Father Madden. My horse and car are waiting for me. You will think over the establishment of looms. You don't want the country to disappear.'

'No, I don't! And though I do not think the establishment of work-rooms an unmixed blessing I will help you. You must not believe all Father O'Hara says.'

* * *

The horse began to trot, and I to think. He had said that the idealism of the Irish peasant goes into other things than sex.

'If this be true, the peasant is doomed,' I said to myself, and I remembered that Father Madden would not admit that religion is dependent on life, and I pondered. In this country religion is hunting life to the death. In other countries religion has managed to come to terms with life. In the South men and women indulge their flesh and turn the key on religious inquiry; in the North men and women find sufficient interest in the interpretation of the Bible and the founding of new religious sects. One can have faith or morals, both together seem impossible. Remembering how the priest had chased the lovers, I turned to the driver and asked if there was no courting in the country.

'There used to be courting,' he said, 'but now it is not the custom of the country any longer.'

'How do you make up your marriages?'

'The marriages are made by the parents, and I've often seen it that the young couple did not see each other until the evening before the wedding – sometimes not until the very morning of the wedding. Many a marriage I've seen broken off for a half a sovereign – well,' he said, 'if not for half a sovereign, for a sovereign. One party will give forty-nine pounds and the other party wants fifty, and they haggle over that pound, and then the boy's father will say, 'Well, if you won't give the pound you can keep the girl.'

'But do none of you ever want to walk out with a young girl?' I said.

'We're like other people, sir. We would like it well enough, but it isn't the custom of the country, and if we did it we would be talked about.'

I began to like my young carman, and his answer to my question pleased me as much as any answer he had yet given me, and I told him that Father Madden objected to the looms because they entailed meetings, etc., and if he were not present the boys would talk on subjects they should not talk about.

'Now, do you think it is right for a priest to prevent men from meeting to discuss their business?' I said, turning to the driver, determined to force him into an expression of opinion.

'It isn't because he thinks the men would talk about things they should not talk about that he is against an organisation. Didn't he tell your honour that things would have to take their course. That is why he will do nothing, because he knows well enough that everyone in the parish will have to leave it, that every house will have to fall. Only the chapel will remain standing, and the day will come when Father Tom will say mass to the blind woman and to no one else. Did you see the blind woman today at mass, sir, in the right-hand corner, with the shawl over her head?'

'Yes,' I said, 'I saw her. If anyone is a saint, that woman seems to be one.'

'Yes, sir, she is a very pious woman, and her piety is so well known that she is the only one who dared to brave Father Madden; she was the only one who dared to take Julia Cahill to live with her. It was Julia who put the curse on the parish.'

'A curse! But you are joking.'

'No, your honour, there was no joke in it. I was only telling you what must come. She put her curse on the village twenty years ago, and every year a roof has fallen in and a family has gone away.'

'And you believe that all this happens on account of Julia's curse?'

'To be sure I do,' he said. He flicked his horse pensively with the whip, and my disbelief seemed to disincline him for further conversation.

'But,' I said, 'who is Julia Cahill, and how did she get the power to lay a curse upon the village? Was she a young woman or an old one?'

'A young one, sir.'

'How did she get the power?'

'Didn't she go every night into the mountains? She was seen one night over yonder, and the mountains are ten miles off, and whom would she have gone to see except the fairies? And who else could have given her the power to curse the village?'

'But who saw her in the mountains? She would never walk so far in one evening.'

'A shepherd saw her, sir.'

'But he may have been mistaken.'

'He saw her speaking to someone, and nobody for the last two years that she was in this village dared to speak to her but the fairies and the old woman you saw at mass today, sir.'

'Now, tell me about Julia Cahill; what did she do?'

'It is said, sir, she was the finest girl in these parts. I was only a gossoon at the time, about eight or nine, but I remember that she was tall, sir, nearly as tall as you are, and she was as straight as one of those poplar trees,' he said, pointing to three trees that stood against the sky. 'She walked with a little swing in her walk, so that all the boys, I have heard, who were grown up used to look after her, and she had fine black eyes, sir, and she was nearly always laughing. This was the time when Father Madden came to the parish. There was courting in it then, and every young man and every young woman made their own marriages, and their marriages were made at the crossroad dancing, and in the summer evenings under the hedges. There was no dancer like Julia; they used to gather about to see her dance, and whoever walked with her under the hedges in the summer, could never think about another woman. The village was fairly mad about her, many a fight there was over her, so I suppose the priest was right. He had to get rid of her; but I think he might not have been so hard upon her as he was. It is said that he went down to her house one evening – Julia's people were well-to-do people; they kept a shop; you might have seen it as we came along the road, just outside of the village it is. And when he came in there was one of the richest farmers in the country who was trying to get Julia for his wife. Instead of going to Julia, he had gone to the father. There are two counters in the shop, and Julia was at the other, and she had made many a good pound for her parents in that shop; and he said to the father: "Now, what fortune are you going to give with Julia?" And the father said there was many a man who would take her without any, and Julia was listening quietly all the while at the opposite counter. The man who had come to marry her did not know what a spirited girl she was, and he went on till he got the father to say that he would give seventy pounds, and, thinking he had got him so far, he said, "Julia will never cross my doorway unless you give her eighty pounds." Julia said never a word, she just sat there listening, and it was then that the priest came in. He listened for awhile, and then he went over to Julia and said, "Are you not proud to hear that you will have such a fine fortune?" And he said, "I shall be glad to see you married. I would marry you for nothing, for I cannot have any more of your goings-on in my parish. You're the beginning of the dancing and courting here; the ball-alley, too – I am going to put all that down." Julia did not answer a single word to him, and he went over to them that were disputing about the eighty pounds, and he said, "Now, why not make it seventy-five pounds?," and the father agreed to that, since the priest said it, and the three men thought the marriage was settled. And Father Tom thought that he would get not less than ten pounds for the marrying of her. They did not even think to ask her, and little did they think what she was going to say, and what she said was that she would not marry anyone until it pleased herself, and that she would pick a man out of this parish or out of the next that pleased her. Her husband should marry her, and not so many pounds to be paid when they signed the book or when the first baby was born. This is how marriages are settled now. Well, sir, the priest went wild when he heard Julia speak like this; he had only just come to the parish, and did not know how self-minded Julia was. Her father did, though, and he said nothing; he let Julia and the priest fight it out, and he said to the man who had come to marry her, "My good man, you can go your way; you will never get her, I can tell that." And the priest was heard saying, "Do you think I am going to let you go on turning the head of every boy in the parish? Do you think I am going to see fighting and quarrelling for you? Do you think I am going to see you first with one boy and then with the other? Do you think I am going to hear stories like I heard last week about poor Peter Carey, who they say, has gone out of his mind on account of your treatment? No," he said, "I will have no more of you; I will have you out of my parish, or I will have you married." Julia tossed her head, and her father got frightened. He promised the priest that she should walk no more with the young men in the evenings, for he thought he could keep her at home; but he might just as well have promised the priest to tie up the winds. Julia was out the same evening with a young man, and the priest saw her; and next evening she was out with another, and the priest saw her; and not a bit minded was she at the end of the month to marry any of them. It is said that he went down to speak to her a second time, and again a third time; it is said that she laughed at him. After that there was nothing for him to do but to speak against her from the altar. The old people say there were some terrible things in the sermon. I have heard it said that the priest called her the evil spirit that sets men mad. I don't suppose Father Madden intended to say so much, but once he is started the words come pouring out. The people did not understand half of what he said, but they were very much frightened, and I think more frightened at what they did not understand than at what they did. Soon after that the neighbours began to be afraid to go to buy anything in Cahill's shop; even the boys who were most mad after Julia were afraid to speak to her, and her own father put her out. No one in the parish would speak to her; they were all afraid of Father Madden. If it had not been for the blind woman you saw in the chapel today, sir, she would have had to go to the poor-house. The blind woman has a little cabin at the edge of the bog, and there Julia lived. She remained for nearly two years, and had hardly any clothes on her back, but she was beautiful for all that, and the boys, as they came back, sir, from the market used to look towards the little cabin in the hopes of catching sight of her. They only looked when they thought they were not watched, for the priest still spoke against her. He tried to turn the blind woman against Julia, but he could not do that; the blind woman kept her until money came from America. Some say that she went to America; some say that she joined the fairies. But one morning she surely left the parish. One morning Pat Quinn heard somebody knocking at his window, somebody asking if he would lend his cart to take somebody to the railway station. It was five o'clock in the morning, and Pat was a heavy sleeper, and he would not get up, and it is said that she walked barefooted all the way to the station, and that is a good ten miles.'

'But you said something about a curse.'

'Yes, sir, a man who was taking some sheep to the fair saw her: there was a fair that day. He saw her standing at the top of the road. The sun was just above the hill, and looking back she cursed the village, raising both hands, sir, up to the sun, and since that curse was spoken, every year a roof has fallen in.'

There was no doubt that the boy believed what he had told me; I could see that he liked to believe the story, that it was natural and sympathetic to him to believe in it; and for the moment I, too, believed in a dancing girl becoming the evil spirit of a village that would not accept her delight.

'He has sent away Life,' I said to myself, 'and now they are following Life. It is Life they are seeking.'

'It is said, your honour, that she's been seen in America, and I am going there this autumn. You may be sure I will keep a look out for her.'

'But all this is twenty years ago. You will not know her. A woman changes a good deal in twenty years.'

'There will be no change in her, your honour. She has been with the fairies. But, sir, we shall be just in time to see the clergy come out of the cathedral after the consecration,' he said, and he pointed to the town.

It stood in the middle of a flat country, and as we approached it the great wall of the cathedral rose above dirty and broken cottages, and great masses of masonry extended from the cathedral into the town; and these were the nunnery, its schools and laundry; altogether they seemed like one great cloud.

When, I said, will a ray from the antique sun break forth and light up this country again?

The Wedding Gown

It was said, but with what truth I cannot say, that the Roche property had been owned by the O'Dwyers many years ago, several generations past, sometime in the eighteenth century. Only a faint legend of this ownership remained; only once had young Mr Roche heard of it, and it was from his mother he had heard it; among the country people it was forgotten. His mother had told him that his great-great-grandfather, who had made large sums of money abroad, had increased his property by purchase from the O'Dwyers, who then owned, as well as farmed, the hillside on which the Big House stood. The O'Dwyers themselves had forgotten that they were once much greater people than they now were, but the master never spoke to them without remembering it, for though they only thought of themselves as small farmers, dependants on the squire, every one of them, boys and girls alike, retained an air of high birth, which at the first glance distinguished them from the other tenants of the estate. Though they were not aware of it, some sense of their remote origin must have survived in them, and I think that in a still more obscure way some sense of it survived in the countryside, for the villagers did not think worse of the O'Dwyers because they kept themselves aloof from the pleasures of the village and its squabbles. The O'Dwyers kept themselves apart from their fellows without any show of pride, without wounding anyone's feelings.

The head of the family was a man of forty, and he was the trusted servant, almost the friend, of the young master, he was his bailiff and his steward, and he lived in a pretty cottage by the edge of the lake. O'Dwyer's aunts, they were old women, of sixty-eight and seventy, lived in the Big House, the elder had been cook, and the younger housemaid, and both were now past their work, and they lived full of gratitude to the young master, to whom they thought they owed a great deal. He believed the debt to be all on his side, and when he was away he often thought of them, and when he returned home he went to greet them as he might go to the members of his own family. The family of the O'Dwyers' was long lived, and Betty and Mary had a sister far older than themselves, Margaret Kirwin, 'Granny Kirwin', as she was called, and she lived in the cottage by the lake with her nephew, Alec O'Dwyer. She was over eighty, it was said that she was nearly ninety, but her age was not known exactly. Mary O'Dwyer said that Margaret was nearly twenty years older than she, but neither Betty nor Mary remembered the exact date of their sister's birth. They did not know much about her, for though she was their sister, she was almost a stranger to them. She had married when she was sixteen, and had gone away to another part of the country, and they had hardly heard of her for thirty years. It was said that she had been a very pretty girl, and that many men had been in love with her, and it was known for certain that she had gone away with the son of the gamekeeper of the grandfather of the present Mr Roche, so you can understand what a very long while ago it was, and how little of the story of her life had come to the knowledge of those living now.

It was certainly sixty years since she had gone away with this young man; she had lived with him in Meath for some years, nobody knew exactly how many years, maybe some nine or ten years, and then he had died suddenly, and his death, it appears, had taken away from her some part of her reason. It was known for certain that she left Meath after his death, and had remained away many years. She had returned to Meath about twenty years ago, though not to the place she had lived in before. Some said she had experienced misfortunes so great that they had unsettled her mind. She herself had forgotten her story, and one day news had come to Galway – news, but it was sad news, that she was living in some very poor cottage on the edge of Navan town, where her strange behaviour and her strange life had made a scandal of her. The priest had to enquire out her relations, and it took him some time to do this, for the old woman's answers were incoherent, but he at length discovered she came from Galway, and he had written to the O'Dwyers. And immediately on receiving the priest's letter, Alec sent his wife to Navan, and she had come back with the old woman.

'And it was time indeed that I went to fetch her,' she said. 'The boys in the town used to make game of her, and follow her, and throw things at her, and they nearly lost the poor thing the little reason that was left to her. The rain was coming in through the thatch, there was hardly a dry place in the cabin, and she had nothing to eat but a few scraps that the neighbours gave her. Latterly she had forgotten how to make a fire, and she ate the potatoes the neighbours gave her raw, and on her back there were only a few dirty rags. She had no care for anything except for her wedding-gown. She kept that in a box covered over with paper so that no damp should get to it, and she was always folding it and seeing that the moth did not touch it, and she was talking of it when I came in at the door. She thought that I had come to steal it from her. The neighbours told me that that was the way she always was, thinking that someone had come to steal her wedding-gown.'

This was all the news of Margaret Kirwin that Alec O'Dwyer's wife brought back with her. The old woman was given a room in the cottage, and though with food and warmth and kind treatment she became a little less bewildered, a little less like a wild, hunted creature, she never got back her memory sufficiently to tell them all that had happened to her after her husband's death. Nor did she seem as if she wanted to try to remember, she was garrulous only of her early days when the parish bells rang for her wedding, and the furze was in bloom. This was before the Big House on the hill had been built. The hill was then a fine pasture for sheep, and Margaret would often describe the tinkling of the sheep-bells in the valley, and the yellow furze, and the bells that were ringing for her wedding. She always spoke of the bells, though no one could understand where the bells came from. It was not customary to ring the parish bell for weddings, and there was no other bell, so that it was impossible to say how Margaret could have got the idea into her head that bells were ringing for her when she crossed the hill on her way to the church, dressed in the beautiful gown, which the grandmother of the present Mr Roche had dressed her in, for she had always been the favourite, she said, with the old mistress, a much greater favourite than even her two sisters had ever been. Betty and Mary were then little children and hardly remembered the wedding, and could say nothing about the bells.

Margaret Kirwin walked with a short stick, her head lifted hardly higher than the handle and when the family were talking round the kitchen fire she would come among them for a while and say something to them, and then go away, and they felt they had seen someone from another world. She hobbled now and then as far as the garden gate, and she frightened the peasantry, so strange did she seem among the flowers – so old and forlorn, almost cut off from this world, with only one memory to link her to it. It was the spectral look in her eyes that frightened them, for Margaret was not ugly. In spite of all her wrinkles, the form of the face remained, and it was easy, especially when her little grand-niece was by, to see that sixty-five years ago she must have had a long and pleasant face, such as one sees in a fox, and red hair like Molly.

Molly was sixteen, and her grey dress reached only to her ankles. Everyone was fond of the poor old woman; but it was only Molly who had no fear of her at all, and one would often see them standing together beside the pretty paling that separated the steward's garden from the high road. Chestnut trees grew about the house, and china roses over the walls, and in the course of the summer there would be lilies in the garden, and in the autumn hollyhocks and sunflowers. There were a few fruit trees a little farther on, and, lower down, a stream. A little bridge led over the stream into the meadow, and Molly and her grand-aunt used to go as far as the bridge, and everyone wondered what the child and the old woman had to say to each other. Molly was never able to give any clear account of what the old woman said to her during the time they spent by the stream. She had tried once to give Molly an account of one long winter when the lake was frozen from side to side. Then there was something running in her mind about the transport of pillars in front of the Big House – how they had been drawn across the lake by oxen, and how one of the pillars was now lying at the bottom of the lake. That was how Molly took up the story from her, but she understood little of it. Molly's solicitude for the old woman was a subject of admiration, and Molly did not like to take the credit for a kindness and pity which she did not altogether feel. She had never seen anyone dead, and her secret fear was that the old woman might die before she went away to service. Her parents had promised to allow her to go away when she was eighteen, and she lived in the hope that her aunt would live two years longer, and that she would be saved the terror of seeing a dead body. And it was in this intention that she served her aunt, that she carefully minced the old woman's food and insisted on her eating often, and that she darted from her place to fetch the old woman her stick when she rose to go. When Margaret Kirwin was not in the kitchen, Molly was always laughing and talking, and her father and mother often thought it was her voice that brought the old woman out of her room. So the day Molly was grieving because she could not go to the dance the old woman remained in her room, and not seeing her at tea-time they began to be afraid, and Molly was asked to go and fetch her aunt.

'Something may have happened to her, mother. I daren't go.'

And when old Margaret came into the kitchen towards evening she surprised everyone by her question: 'Why is Molly crying?'

No one else had heard Molly sob, if she had sobbed, but everyone knew the reason for her grief; indeed, she had been reproved for it many times that day.

'I will not hear any more about it,' said Mrs O'Dwyer; 'she has been very tiresome all day. Is it my fault if I cannot give her a gown to go to the dance?' And then, forgetting that old Margaret could not understand her, she told her that the servants were having a dance at the Big House, and had asked Molly to come to it. 'But what can I do? She has got no gown to go in. Even if I had the money there would not be time to send for one now, nor to make one. And there are a number of English servants stopping at the house; there are people from all parts of the country, they have brought their servants with them, and I am not going to see my girl worse dressed than the others, so she cannot go. She has heard all this, she knows it . . . I've never seen her so tiresome before.' Mrs O'Dwyer continued to chide her daughter; but her mother's reasons for not allowing her to go to the ball, though unanswerable, did not seem to console Molly, and she sat looking very miserable. 'She has been sitting like that all day,' said Mrs O'Dwyer, 'and I wish that it were tomorrow, for she will not be better until it is all over.'

'But, mother, I am saying nothing; I will go to bed. I don't know why you are blaming me. I am saying nothing. I can't help feeling miserable.'

'No, she don't look a bit cheerful,' the old woman said, 'and I don't like her to be disappointed.' This was the first time that old Margaret had seemed to understand since she came to live with them what was passing about her, and they all looked at her, Mrs O'Dwyer and Alec and Molly. They stood waiting for her to speak again, wondering if the old woman's speech was an accident, or if she had recovered her mind. 'It is a hard thing for a child at her age not to be able to go to the dance at the Big House, now that she has been asked. No wonder Molly is unhappy. I remember the time that I should have been unhappy too, and she is very like me.'

'But, Granny, what can I do? She can't go in the clothes she is wearing, and she has only got one other frock, the one she goes to mass in. I can't allow my daughter – '

But seeing the old woman was about to speak Alec stopped his wife.

'Let us hear what she has to say,' he whispered.

'There is my wedding-gown: that is surely beautiful enough for anyone to wear. It has not been worn since the day I wore it when the bells were ringing, and I went over the hill and was married; and I have taken such care of it that it is the same as it was that day. Molly will look very nice in it; she will look as I looked that day.'

No one spoke; father, mother and daughter stood looking at the old woman. Her offer to lend her wedding-dress had astonished them as much as her recovery of her senses. Everything she once had, and there were tales that she had once been rich, had melted away from her; nothing but this gown remained. How she had watched over it! Since she had come to live with the O'Dwyers she had hardly allowed them to see it. When she took it out of its box to air it and to strew it with camphor she closed her room door. Only once had they seen it, and then only for a few moments. She had brought it out to show it, as a child brings its toy, but the moment they stretched their hands to touch it she had taken it away, and they had heard her locking the box it was in. But now she was going to lend it to Molly. They did not believe she meant what she was saying. They expected her to turn away and to go to her room, forgetful of what she had said. Even if she were to let Molly put the dress on, she would not let her go out of the house with it. She would change her mind at the last minute.

'When does this dancing begin?' she asked, and when they told her she said there would be just time for her to dress Molly, and she asked the girl and her mother to come into her room. Mrs O'Dwyer feared the girl would be put to a bitter disappointment, but if Molly once had the gown on she would not oblige her to take it off.

'In my gown you will be just like what I was when the bells were ringing.'

She took the gown out of its box herself, and the petticoat and the stockings and the shoes; there was everything there.

'The old mistress gave me all these. Molly has got the hair I used to have; she will look exactly like myself. Are they not beautiful shoes?' she said.

'Look at the buckles. They will fit her very well; her feet are the same size as mine were.'

And Molly's feet went into the shoes just as if they had been made for her, and the gown fitted as well as the shoes, and Molly's hair was arranged as nearly as possible according to the old woman's fancy, as she used to wear her hair when it was thick and red like Molly's.

The girl thought that Granny would regret her gift. She expected the old woman would follow her into the kitchen and ask her to take the things off, and that she would not be able to go to the ball after all. She did not feel quite safe until she was a long way from the house, about halfway up the drive. Her mother and father had said that the dance would not be over until maybe six o'clock in the morning, and they offered her the key of the house; but Granny had said that she would sit up for her.

'I will doze a bit upon a chair. If I am tired I will lie down upon my bed. I shall hear Molly; I shall not sleep much. She will not be able to enter the house without my hearing her.'

It was extraordinary to hear her speak like this, and, a little frightened by her sudden sanity, they waited up with her until midnight. Then they tried to persuade her to go to bed, to allow them to lock up the house; but she sat looking into the fire, seeming to see the girl dancing at the ball quite clearly. She seemed so contented that they left her, and for an hour she sat dreaming, seeing Molly young and beautifully dressed in the wedding-gown of more than sixty years ago.

Dream after dream went by, the fire had burned low, the sods were falling into white ashes, and the moonlight began to stream into the room. It was the chilliness that had come into the air that awoke her, and she threw several sods of turf on to the fire. An hour passed, and old Margaret awoke for the last time.

'The bells are ringing, the bells are ringing,' she said, and she went to the kitchen door; she opened it, and stood in the garden under the rays of the moon. The night of her marriage was just such a night as this one, and she had stood in the garden amid the summer flowers, just as she did now.

'The day is beginning,' she said, mistaking the moonlight for the dawn, and, listening, it seemed to her that she heard once more the sound of bells coming across the hill. 'Yes, the bells are ringing,' she said; 'I can hear them quite clearly, and I must hurry and get dressed – I must not keep him waiting.'

And returning to the house, she went to her box, where her gown had lain so many years; and though no gown was there it seemed to her that there was one, and one more beautiful than the gown she had cherished. It was the same gown, only grown more beautiful. It had grown into softer silk, into a more delicate colour; it had become more beautiful, and she held the dream-gown in her hands and she sat with it in the moonlight, thinking how fair he would find her in it. Once her hands went to her hair, and then she dropped them again.

'I must begin to dress myself; I must not keep him waiting.'

The moonlight lay still upon her knees, but little by little the moon moved up the sky, leaving her in the shadow.

It was at this moment, as the shadows grew denser about old Margaret, that the child who was dancing at the ball came to think of her who had given her her gown, and who was waiting for her. It was in the middle of a reel she was dancing, and she was dancing it with Mr Roche, that she felt that something had happened to her aunt.

'Mr Roche,' she said, 'you must let me go away; I cannot dance any more tonight. I am sure that something has happened to my aunt, the old woman, Margaret Kirwin, who lives with us in the Lodge. It was she who lent me this gown. This was her wedding-gown, and for sixty-five years it has never been out of her possession. She has hardly allowed anyone to see it; but she said that I was like her, and she heard me crying because I had no gown to go to the ball, and so she lent me her wedding-gown.'

'You look very nice, Molly, in the wedding-gown, and this is only a fancy.' Seeing the girl was frightened and wanted to go, he said: 'But why do you think that anything has happened to your aunt?'

'She is very old.'

'But she is not much older than she was when you left her.'

'Let me go, Mr Roche; I think I must go. I feel sure that something has happened to her. I never had such a feeling before, and I could not have that feeling if there was no reason for it.'

'Well, if you must go.'

She glanced to where the moon was shining and ran down the drive, leaving Mr Roche looking after her, wondering if after all she might have had a warning of the old woman's death. The night was one of those beautiful nights in May, when the moon soars high in the sky, and all the woods and fields are clothed in the green of spring. But the stillness of the night frightened Molly, and when she stopped to pick up her dress she heard the ducks chattering in the reeds. The world seemed divided into darkness and light. The hawthorn trees threw black shadows that reached into the hollows, and Molly did not dare to go by the path that led through a little wood, lest she should meet Death there. For now it seemed to her that she was running a race with Death, and that she must get to the cottage before him. She did not care to take the short cut, but she ran till her breath failed her. She ran on again, but when she went through the wicket she knew that Death had been before her. She knocked twice; receiving no answer she tried the latch, and was surprised to find the door unlocked. There was a little fire among the ashes, and after blowing the sod for some time she managed to light the candle, and holding it high she looked about the kitchen.

'Auntie, are you asleep? Have the others gone to bed?'

She approached a few steps, and then a strange curiosity came over her, and though she had always feared death she now looked curiously upon death, and she thought that she saw the likeness which her aunt had often noticed.

'Yes,' she said, 'she is like me. I shall be like that some day if I live long enough.'

And then she knocked at the door of the room where her parents were sleeping.

The Way Back

It was a pleasure to meet, even when they had nothing to say, and the two men had stopped to talk.

'Still in London, Rodney.'

'Yes, till the end of the week; and then I go to Italy. And you? You're going to meet Sir Owen Asher at Marseilles.'

'I am going to Ireland,' and, catching sight of a look of astonishment and disapproval on Rodney's face, Harding began to explain why he must return to Ireland.

'The rest of your life is quite clear,' said Rodney. 'You knew from the beginning that Paris was the source of all art, that everyone here who is more distinguished than the others has been to Paris. We go to Paris with baskets on our backs, and sticks in our hands, and bring back what we can pick up. And having lived immersed in art till you're forty, you return to the Catholic Celt! Your biographer will be puzzled to explain this last episode, and, however he may explain it, it will seem a discrepancy.'

'I suppose one should think of one's biographer.'

'It will be more like yourself to get Asher to land you at one of the Italian ports. We will go to Perugia and see Raphael's first frescoes, done when he was sixteen, and the town itself climbing down into ravines. The streets are lonely at midday, but towards evening a breeze blows up from both seas – Italy is very narrow there – and the people begin to come out; and from the battlements one sees the lights of Assisi glimmering through the dusk.'

'I may never see Italy. Go on talking. I like to hear you talk about Italy.'

'There are more beautiful things in Italy than in the rest of the world put together, and there is nothing so beautiful as Italy. Just fancy a man like you never having seen the Campagna. I remember opening my shutters one morning in August at Frascati. The poisonous mists lay like clouds, but the sun came out and shone through them, and the wind drove them before it, and every moment a hill appeared, and the great aqueducts, and the tombs, and the wild grasses at the edge of the tombs waving feverishly; and here and there a pine, or group of pines with tufted heads, like Turner used to draw . . . The plain itself is so shapely. Rome lies like a little dot in the middle of it, and it is littered with ruins. The great tomb of Cecilia Metella is there, built out of blocks of stone as big as an ordinary room. He must have loved her very much to raise such a tomb to her memory, and she must have been a wonderful woman.' Rodney paused a moment and then he said: 'The walls of the tombs are let in with sculpture, and there are seats for wayfarers, and they will last as long as the world – they are everlasting.'

'Of one thing I'm sure,' said Harding. 'I must get out of London. I can't bear its ugliness any longer.'

The two men crossed Piccadilly, and Harding told Rodney Asher's reason for leaving London.

'He says he is subject to nightmares, and lately he has been waking up in the middle of the night thinking that London and Liverpool had joined. Asher is right. No town ought to be more than fifty miles long. I like your description of Perugia. Every town should be walled round, now we trail into endless suburbs.'

'But the Green Park is beautiful, and these evening distances!'

'Never mind the Green Park; come and have a cup of tea. Asher has bought a new picture, I'd like to show it to you. But,' said Harding, 'I forgot to tell you that I met your model.'

'Lucy Delaney? Where?'

'Here, I met her here,' said Harding, and he took Rodney's arm so that he might be able to talk to him more easily. 'One evening, a week ago, I was loitering, just as I was loitering today, and it was at the very door of St James's Hotel that she spoke to me.'

'How did she get to London? and I didn't know that you knew her.'

'A girl came up suddenly and asked me the way to the Gaiety Theatre, and I told her, adding, however, that the Gaiety Theatre was closed. "What shall I do?" I heard her say, and she walked on; I hesitated and then walked after her. "I beg your pardon," I said, "the Gaiety Theatre is closed, but there are other theatres equally good. Shall I direct you?" "Oh, I don't know what I shall do. I have run away from home . . . I have set fire to my school and have come over to London thinking that I might go on the stage." She had set fire to her school! I never saw more winning eyes. But she's a girl men would look after, and not liking to stand talking to her in Piccadilly, I asked her to come down Berkeley Street. I was very curious to know who was this girl who had set fire to her school and had come over to London to go on the stage; and we walked on, she telling me that she had set fire to her school so that she might be able to get away in the confusion. I hoped I should not meet anyone I knew, and let her prattle on until we got to the square. The square shone like a ballroom with a great plume of green branches in the middle and every corner a niche of gaudy window boxes. Past us came the season's stream of carriages, the women resting against the cushions looking like finely cultivated flowers. The beauty of the square that afternoon astonished me. I wondered how it struck Lucy. Very likely she was only thinking of her Gaiety Theatre!'

'But how did you know her name?'

'You remember it was at the corner of Berkeley Square that Evelyn Innes stood when she went to see Owen Asher for the first time, she used to tell me how she stood at the curb watching London passing by her, thinking that one day London would be going to hear her sing. As soon as there was a break in the stream of carriages I took Lucy across. We could talk unobserved in the square, and she continued her story. "I'm nearly seventeen," she said, "and I was sent back to school because I sat for a sculpture."

' "What did you sit for?"

' "For a statue of the Blessed Virgin, and a priest told on me."

' "Then you're Lucy Delaney, and the sculptor you sat for is John Rodney, one of my intimate friends." '

'What an extraordinary coincidence,' said Rodney. 'I never thought that Lucy would stay in Ireland. Go on with your story.'

'When I found out who she was there seemed no great harm in asking her in to have some tea. Asher will forgive you anything if there's a woman in it; you may keep him waiting half an hour if you assure him your appointment is with a married woman. Well, Lucy had arrived that morning in London with threepence in her pocket, so I told the footman to boil a couple of eggs. I should have liked to have offered her a substantial meal, but that would have set the servants talking. Never did a girl eat with a better appetite, and when she had finished a second plateful of buttered toast she began to notice the pictures. I could see that she had been in a studio and had talked about art. It is extraordinary how quick a girl is to acquire the ideas of a man she likes. She admired Manet's picture of Evelyn, and I told her Evelyn's story – knowing it would interest her. "That such a happy fate should be a woman's and that she should reject it,'" her eyes seemed to say. "She is now," I said, "singing Ave Marias at Wimbledon for the pecuniary benefit of the nuns and the possible salvation of her own soul." Her walk tells the length of the limbs and the balance of the body, and my eyes followed her as she moved about the room, and when I told her I had seen the statue and had admired the legs, she turned and said, with a pretty pleased look, that you always said that she had pretty legs. When I asked her if you had made love to her, she said you had not, that you were always too busy with your sculpture.'

'One can't think of two things at the same time. If I had met her in Paris it would have been different.'

'Unfortunately I was dining out that evening. It was hard to know what to do. At last I thought of a lodging-house kept by a praiseworthy person, and took her round there and, cursing my dinner-party, I left her in charge of the landlady.'

'Like a pot of jam left carefully under cover . . . That will be all right till tomorrow,' said Rodney.

'Very likely. It is humiliating to admit it, but it is so; the substance of our lives is woman; all other things are irrelevancies, hypocrisies, subterfuges. We sit talking of sport and politics, and all the while our hearts are filled with memories of women and plans for the capture of women. Consciously or unconsciously we regard every young woman from the one point of view, "Will she do?" You know the little look that passes between men and women as their hansoms cross? Do not the eyes say: "Yes, yes, if we were to meet we might come to an understanding?" We're ashamed that it should be so, but it is the law that is over us. And that night at my dinner-party, while talking to wise mammas and their more or less guileless daughters, I thought of the disgrace if it were found out that I had picked up a girl in the street and put her in charge of the landlady.'

'But one couldn't leave her to the mercy of the street.'

'Quite so; but I'm speaking now of what was in the back of my mind.'

'The pot of jam carefully covered up,' said Rodney, laughing.

'Yes, the pot of jam; and while talking about the responsibilities of Empire, I was thinking that I might send out for a canvas in the morning and sketch something out on it; and when I got home I looked out a photograph of some women bathing. I expected her about twelve, and she found me hard at work.

' "Oh, I didn't know that you were a painter," she said.

' "No more I am; I used to be; and thinking of Rodney's statue and what I can see of you through that dress I thought I'd try and do something like you."

' "I'm thinner than that."

' "You're not thin."

'We argued the point, and I tried to persuade her to give me a sitting. She broke away, saying that it wasn't the same thing, and that she had sat for you because there were no models in Dublin. "You've been very good to me," she said. "I should have had to sleep in the park last night if it had not been for you. Do continue to be good to me and get me on the stage, for if you don't I shall have to go back to Dublin or to America." "America," I said. "Do you want to go to America?" She didn't answer, and when she was pressed for an answer, she said: "Well, all the Irish go to America, I didn't mean anything more; I am too worried to know what I am saying," and then, seeing me turn round to look at my picture, she said, "I will sit to you one of these days, but I am too unhappy and frightened now. I don't like saying no; it is always disagreeable to say no." And seeing it would give her no pleasure to sit, I did not ask her again.'

'I'm sorry you missed seeing something very beautiful.'

'I dare say she'd have sat if I'd have pressed her, but she was under my protection, and it seemed cowardly to press her, for she could not refuse. Suddenly we seemed to have nothing more to say to each other, and I asked her if she'd like to see a manager, and as it seemed a pity she should waste herself on the Gaiety Theatre I took her to see Sir Edward Higgins. The mummer was going out to lunch with a lord and could only think of the people he was going to meet. So we went to Dorking's Theatre, and we found Dorking with his acting manager. The acting manager had been listening for a long while and wasn't sorry for the interruption. But we had not been talking for more than two or three minutes when the call-boy brought in a bundle of newspaper cuttings, and the mummer had not the patience to wait until he was alone – one reads one's cuttings alone – he stuck his knees together and opened the bundle, columns of print flowed over his knees, and after telling us what the critics were saying about him, mention was made of Ibsen, and we wondered if there was any chance of getting the public to come to see a good play. You know the conversation drifts.'

'You couldn't get her an engagement,' said Rodney; 'I should have thought she was suited to the stage.'

'If there had been time I could have done something for her; she's a pretty girl, but you see all these things take a long time, and Lucy wanted an engagement at once. When we left the theatre I began to realise the absurdity of the adventure, and the danger to which I was exposing myself. I, a man of over forty, seeking the seduction of a girl of seventeen – for that is the plain English of it. We walked on side by side, and I asked myself, "What am I to her, what is she to me?" But one may argue with oneself for ever.'

'One may indeed,' said Rodney, laughing, 'one may argue, but the law is over us.'

'Well, the law that is over us compelled me to take her to lunch, and she enjoyed the lunch and the great restaurant. "What a number of butlers," she said. After lunch the same problem confronted me: Was I or was I not going to pursue the adventure? I only knew for certain that I could not walk about the streets with Lucy. She is a pretty girl, but she looked odd enough in her country clothes. Suddenly it struck me that I might take her into the country, to Wimbledon.'

'And you took her there and heard Evelyn Innes sing. And what did Lucy think? A very pretty experiment in experimental psychology.'

'The voice is getting thinner. She sang Stradella's *Chanson D'Eglise*, and Lucy could hardly speak when we came out of church. "Oh, what a wonderful voice," she said, "do you think she regrets?" "Whatever we do, we regret," I answered, not because I thought the observation original, but because it seemed suitable to the occasion; "and we regret still more what we don't do." And I asked myself if I should write to Lucy's people as we walked about the common. But Lucy wanted to hear about Owen Asher and Evelyn, and the operas she had sung, and I told the story of *Tannhäuser* and *Tristan*. She had never heard such stories before, and, as we got up from the warm grass, she said that she could imagine Evelyn standing in the nuns' garden with her eyes fixed on the calm skies, getting courage from them to persevere. Wasn't it clever of her? We dined together in a small restaurant and I spent the evening with her in the lodging-house; the landlady lent us her sitting-room. Lucy is charming, and her happiness is volatile and her melancholy too; she's persuasive and insinuating as a perfume; and when I left the house, it was as if I had come out of a moonlight garden. "Thy green eyes look upon me . . . I love the moonlight of thine eyes." '

'Go on,' said Rodney, 'what happened after that?'

'The most disagreeable thing that ever happened to me in my life. You don't know what it is to be really afraid. I didn't until a fellow came up to me at the club and asked me if I had seen the detectives. Fear is a terrible thing, Rodney; there is nothing so demoralising as fear. You know my staid old club of black mahogany and low ceilings, where half a dozen men sit dining and talking about hunting and two-year-olds. There is a man in that club who has asked me for the last ten years what I am going to do with my two-year-olds. He cannot remember that I never had a two-year-old. But that night he wasn't tipsy, and his sobriety impressed me; he sat down at my table, and after a while he leaned across and asked me if I knew that two detectives had been asking after me. "You had better look to this. These things turn out devilish unpleasantly. Of course there is nothing wrong, but you don't want to appear in the police court," he said.'

'Had she told?'

'She was more frightened than I was when I told her what had happened, but she had done the mischief nevertheless. She had written to her people saying that she had met a friend of Mr Rodney, and that he was looking after her, and that he lived in Berkeley Square; she was quite simple and truthful, and notwithstanding my fear I was sorry for her, for we might have gone away together somewhere, but, of course, that was impossible now; her folly left no course open to me except to go to Dublin and explain everything to her parents.'

'I don't see,' said Rodney, 'that there was anything against you.'

'Yes, but I was judging myself according to inward motives, and for some time I did not see how admirable my conduct would seem to an unintelligent jury. There is nothing to do between London and Holyhead, and I composed the case for the prosecution and the case for the defence and the judge's summing up. I wrote the articles in the newspapers next day and the paragraphs in the evening papers . . . I had met her at the corner of Berkeley Street and she had asked me the way to the Gaiety Theatre; and, being anxious for her safety, I had asked her why she wanted the Gaiety Theatre, for of course if the case came to trial I should not have approved of the Gaiety, and disapproval would have won all the Methodists. The girl had told me that she had set fire to her school, and an excitable girl like that would soon be lost. I don't know what expression the newspapers would use – 'in the labyrinths of London vice', she was just the kind of girl that a little good advice might save from ruin. She had told me that she knew you, I was her only friend, etc. What could I do better than to take her to a lodging-house where I had lodged myself and put her in charge of the landlady? The landlady would be an important witness, and I think it was at Rugby Junction that I began to hear the judge saying I had acted with great discretion and kindness, and left the court without a stain upon my character. Nevertheless, I should have appeared in a police court on a charge of abducting a girl, a seventeen-year-old maiden, and not everyone would be duped by outward appearances; many would have guessed the truth, and, though we're all the same, everyone tries to hide the secret of our common humanity. But I had forgotten to ask Lucy for the address. I only knew the name, and that the Delaneys were cheese-mongers, so I had to call on every cheese-monger called Delaney. My peregrinations were too absurd. "Have you got a daughter? Has she left you and gone to London?" And that all day in one form or another, for it was not until evening that I found the Delaneys I was seeking. The shop was shutting up, but there was a light in the passage, and one of the boys let me in and I went up the narrow stairs.'

'I know them,' said Rodney.

'And the room – '

'I know it,' said Rodney.

'The horsehair chairs full of holes?'

'I know the rails,' said Rodney, 'they catch you about here, across the thighs.'

'The table in the middle of the room; the smell of the petroleum lamp and the great chair – '

'I know,' said Rodney, 'the Buddah seated! An enormous head! The smoking-cap and the tassel hanging out of it!'

'The great cheeks hanging and the little eyes, intelligent eyes, too, under the eyebrows, the only animation in his face. He must be sixteen stone!'

'He is eighteen.'

'The long clay pipe and the fat hands with the nails bitten.'

'I see you have been observing him,' said Rodney.

'The brown waistcoat with the white bone buttons, curving over the belly, and the belly shelving down into the short fat thighs, and the great feet wrapped in woollen slippers!'

'He suffers terribly, and hardly dares to stir out of that chair on account of the stone in the bladder, which he won't have removed.'

'How characteristic the room seemed to me,' said Harding. 'The piano against the wall near the window.'

'I know,' said Rodney. 'Lucy used to sit there playing. She plays beautifully.'

'Yes, she plays very well.'

'Go on,' said Rodney, 'what happened?'

'You know the mother, the thin woman with a pretty figure and the faded hair and the features like Lucy's,'

'Yes.'

'I had just begun my little explanation about the top of Berkeley Square, how a girl came up to me and asked me the way to the Gaiety Theatre, when this little woman rushed forward and, taking hold of both my hands, said: "We are so much obliged to you; and we do not know how much to thank you." A chair was pushed forward – '

'Which chair?' said Rodney. 'I know them all. Was it the one with the hole in the middle, or was the hole in the side?'

' "If it hadn't been for you," said Mrs Delaney, "I don't know what would have happened." "We've much to thank you for," said the big man, and he begged to be excused for not getting up. His wife interrupted him in an explanation regarding his illness, and gradually I began to see that, from their point of view, I was Lucy's saviour, a white knight, a modern Sir Galahad. They hoped I had suffered no inconvenience when the detectives called at the club. They had communicated with Scotland Yard, not because they suspected me of wishing to abduct their daughter, but because they wished to recover their daughter, and it was important that she should be recovered at once, for she was engaged to be married to a mathematical-instrument maker who was on his way from Chicago; he was expected in a few days; he was at that moment on the Atlantic, and if it had not been for my admirable conduct, Mrs Delaney did not know what story she could have told Mr Wainscott.'

'So Lucy is going to marry a mathematical instrument maker in Chicago?'

'Yes,' said Harding, 'and she is probably married to him by now. It went to my heart to tell her that her mother was coming over to fetch her, and that the mathematical-instrument maker would arrive early next week. But I had to tell her these unpleasant things, for I could not take her away in Owen Asher's yacht, her age and the circumstances forbade an agreeable episode among the Greek Islands. She is charming . . . Poor Lucy! She slipped down on the floor very prettily and her hair fell on my knees. "It isn't fair, you're going away on a yacht, and I am going to Chicago." And when I lifted her up she sat upon my knees and wept. "Why don't you take me away?" she said. "My dear Lucy, I'm forty and you're seventeen." Her eyes grew enigmatic. "I shall never live with him," she said.'

'Did you kiss her?'

'We spent the evening together and I was sorry for her.'

'But you don't know for certain that she married Wainscott.'

'Yes. Wainscott wrote me a letter,' and after some searching in his pockets Harding found the letter.

DEAR SIR – Mr and Mrs Delaney have told me of your kindness to Lucy, and Lucy has told me of the trouble you took trying to get her an engagement, and I write to thank you. Lucy did not know at the time that I had become a partner in the firm of Sheldon & Flint, and she thought that she might go on the stage and make money by singing, for she has a pretty voice, to help me to buy a partnership in the business of Sheldon & Flint. It was a kind thought. Lucy's heart is in the right place, and it was kind of you, sir, to take her to different managers. She has given me an exact account of all you did for her.

We are going to be married tomorrow, and next week we sail for the States. I live, sir, in Chicago City, and if you are ever in America Lucy and myself will esteem it an honour if you will come to see us.

Lucy would write to you herself if she were not tired, having had to look after many things.

I am, dear sir,

Very sincerely yours,

JAMES WAINSCOTT

'Lucy wanted life,' said Rodney, 'and she will find her adventure sooner or later. Poor Lucy!'

'Lucy is the stuff that great women are made of and will make a noise in the world yet.'

'It is well she has gone; for it is many years since there was honour in Ireland for a Grania.'

'Maybe you'll meet her in Paris and will do another statue from her.'

'It wouldn't be the same thing. Ah! my statue, my poor statue. Nothing but a lump of clay. I nearly went out of my mind. At first I thought it was the priest who ordered it to be broken. But no, two little boys who heard a priest talking. They tell strange stories in Dublin about that statue. It appears that, after seeing it, Father McCabe went straight to Father Brennan, and the priests sat till midnight, sipping their punch and considering this fine point of theology – if a man may ask a woman to sit naked to him; and then if it would be justifiable to employ a naked woman for a statue of the Virgin. Father Brennan said, "Nakedness is not a sin," and Father McCabe said, "Nakedness may not be in itself a sin, but it leads to sin, and is therefore unjustifiable." At their third tumbler of punch they had reached Raphael, and at the fourth Father McCabe held that bad statues were more likely to excite devotional feelings than good ones, bad statues being further removed from perilous nature.'

'I can see the two priests, I can hear them. If an exception be made in favour of the Virgin, would the sculptor be justified in employing a model to do a statue of a saint?'

'No one supposes that Rubens did not employ a model for his descent from the Cross,' said Rodney.

'A man is different, that's what the priests would say.'

'Yet, that slender body, slipping like a cut flower into women's hands, has inspired more love in women than the Virgin has in men.'

'I can see these two obtuse priests. I can hear them. I should like to write the scene,' said Harding.

The footman brought in the tea, and Harding told him that if Mr Carmady called he was to show him in, and it was not long after that a knock came at the front door.

'You have come in time for a cup of tea, Carmady. You know Rodney?'

'Yes, indeed.'

'Carmady used to come to my studio. Many's the time we've had about the possibility of a neo-pagan Celtic renaissance. But I did not know you were in London. When did you arrive?'

'Yesterday. I'm going to South Africa. There's fighting going on there, and it is a brand new country.'

'Three Irishmen meet,' said Rodney; 'one seeking a country with a future, one seeking a country with a past, and one thinking of going back to a country without past or future.'

'Is Harding going back to Ireland?' said Carmady.

'Yes,' said Rodney. 'You tried to snuff out the Catholic candle, but Harding hopes to trim it.'

'I'm tired of talking about Ireland. I've talked enough.'

'This is the last time, Carmady, you'll be called to talk about Ireland. We'd like to hear you.'

'There is no free thought, and where there is no free thought there is no intellectual life. The priests take their ideas from Rome cut and dried like tobacco and the people take their ideas from the priests cut and dried like tobacco. Ireland is a terrifying example of what becomes of a country when it accepts prejudices and conventions and ceases to enquire out the truth.'

'You don't believe,' said Harding, 'in the possibility of a Celtic renaissance – that with the revival of the languages?'

'I do not believe in Catholics. The Catholic kneels like the camel that burdens may be laid upon him. You know as well as I do, Harding, that the art and literature of the fifteenth and sixteenth centuries were due to a sudden dispersal, a sudden shedding of the prejudices and conventions of the middle ages; the renaissance was a joyous returning to Hellenism, the source of all beauty. There is as little free love in Ireland as there is free thought; men have ceased to care for women and women to care for men. Nothing thrives in Ireland but the celibate, the priest, the nun, and the ox. There is no unfaith, and the violence of the priest is against any sensual transgression. A girl marries at once or becomes a nun – a free girl is a danger. There is no courtship, there is no walking out, and the passion which is the direct inspiration of all the world's music and art is reduced to the mere act of begetting children.'

'Love books his passage in the emigrant ship,' said Rodney. 'You speak truly. There are no bastards in Ireland; and the bastard is the outward sign of inward grace.'

'That which tends to weaken life is the only evil, that which strengthens life the only good, and the result of this puritanical Catholicism will be an empty Ireland.'

'Dead beyond hope of resurrection,' said Rodney.

'I don't say that; a wave of paganism may arise, and only a pagan revival can save Ireland.'

'Ah, the beautiful pagan world!' said Rodney; 'morality is but a dream, an academic discussion, but beauty is a reality.'

'Out of the billions of men that have been born into the world,' said Carmady, 'I am only sure that two would have been better unborn; and the second was but a reincarnation of the first.'

'And who were they?' said Rodney.

'St Paul and Luther. Had it not been for Paul, the whole ghostly theory would have been a failure, and had it not been for Luther the name of Christ would be forgotten now. When the acetic monk, barefooted, ragged, with prayer-haunted eyes, went to Rome, Rome had reverted to her ancient paganism, statues took the place of sacraments, and the cardinals drove about Rome with their mistresses.'

'The Pope, too,' said Rodney.

'Everything was for the best when the pilgrim monk turned in shame and horror from the awakening; the kingdom of the earth was cursed. We certainly owe the last four hundred years of Christianity to Luther.'

'I wonder if that is so,' said Rodney.

After a pause, Carmady continued, 'Belief is declining, but those who disavow the divinity of Christ eagerly insist that they retain his morality – the cowardly morality of the weak who demand a redeemer to redeem them. The morality of the ghetto prevails; Christians are children of the ghetto.'

'It is given to men to choose between sacraments and statues,' said Rodney. 'Beauty is a reality, morality is a myth, and Ireland has always struck me as a place for which God had intended to do something, but He changed his mind and that change of mind happened about a thousand years ago. Quite true that the Gael was hunted as if he were vermin for centuries, and had to think how to save his life. But there is no use thinking what the Gael might have done. It is quite certain he'll never do it now – the time has gone by; everything has been done and gloriously.'

And for a long while Rodney spoke of Italy.

'I'll show you a city,' he said, 'no bigger than Rathmines, and in it Michelangelo, Donatello, Del Sarto and Da Vinci lived, and lived contemporaneously. Now what have these great pagans left the poor Catholic Celt to do? All that he was intended to do he did in the tenth century. Since then he has produced an incredible number of priests and policemen, some fine prize-fighters, and some clever lawyers; but nothing more serious. Ireland is too far north. Sculpture does not get farther north than Paris –

oranges and sculpture! the orange zone and its long cigars, cigars eight inches long, a penny each, and lasting the whole day. They are lighted from a taper that is passed round in the cafés. The fruit that one can buy for three halfpence, enough for a meal! And the eating of the fruit by the edge of the canal – seeing beautiful things all the while. But, Harding, you sit there saying nothing. No, you're not going back to Ireland. Before you came in, Carmady, I was telling Harding that he was not acting fairly towards his biographer. The poor man will not be able to explain this Celtic episode satisfactorily. Nothing short of a Balzac could make it convincing.' Rodney laughed loudly; the idea amused him, and he could imagine a man refraining from any excess that might disturb and perplex or confuse his biographer. 'How did the Celtic idea come to you, Harding? Do you remember?'

'How do ideas come to anyone?' said Harding. 'A thought passes. A sudden feeling comes over you, and you're never the same again. Looking across a park with a view of the mountains in the distance, I perceived a pathetic beauty in the country itself that I had not perceived before; and a year afterwards I was driving about the Dublin mountains, and met two women on the road; there was something pathetic and wistful about them, something dear, something intimate, and I felt drawn towards them. I felt I should like to live among these people again. There is a proverb in Irish which says that no man ever wanders far from his grave sod. We are thrown out, and we circle a while in the air, and return to the feet of the thrower. But what astonished me is the interest that everybody takes in my departure. Everyone seems agreed that nothing could be more foolish, nothing more mad. But if I were to go to meet Asher at Marseilles, and cruise with him in the Greek Islands, and go on to Cairo, and spend the winter talking to wearisome society, everyone would consider my conduct most rational. You, my dear friend, Rodney, you tempt me with Italy and conversations about yellowing marbles; but you won't be angry with me when I tell you that all your interesting utterances about the Italian renaissance would not interest me half so much as what Paddy Durkin and Father Pat will say to me on the roadside.'

ARTHUR MORRISON

Arthur George Morrison was born in London on 1 November 1863. Educated in the East End, Morrison worked as a clerk for a number of years before joining the editorial staff of the *Evening Globe* in 1890. In 1891 he published his first story, *The Street*, which was a critical success. Over the next few years, he produced a number of detective stories and introduced the character Martin Hewitt. In 1896 he published *A Child of the Jago*, undoubtedly his best work and one which graphically describes the living conditions and violence of the East End. He produced a few more novels and stories until 1913, when he effectively retired from writing fiction to concentrate on his collection of Asian prints and paintings. He died on 4 December 1945.

A Poor Stick

Mrs Jennings (or Jinnins, as the neighbours would have it) ruled absolutely at home, when she took so much trouble as to do anything at all there – which was less often than might have been. As for Robert her husband, he was a poor stick, said the neighbours. And yet he was a man with enough of hardihood to remain a non-unionist in the erectors' shop at Maidment's all the years of his service; no mean test of a man's fortitude and resolution, as many a sufferer for independent opinion might testify. The truth was that Bob never grew out of his courtship-blindness. Mrs Jennings governed as she pleased, stayed out or came home as she chose, and cooked a dinner or didn't, as her inclination stood. Thus it was for ten years, during which time there were no children, and Bob bore all things uncomplaining – cooking his own dinner when he found none cooked and sewing on his own buttons. Then of a sudden came children, till in three years there were three; and Bob Jennings had to nurse and to wash them as often as not.

Mrs Jennings at this time was what is called rather a fine woman: a woman of large scale and full development, whose slatternly habits left her coarse black hair to tumble in snake-locks about her face and shoulders half the day; who, clad in half-hooked clothes, bore herself notoriously and unabashed in her fullness; and of whom ill things were said regarding the lodger. The gossips had their excuse. The lodger was an irregular young cabinet-maker, who lost quarters and halves and whole days; who had been seen abroad with his landlady at a time when Bob Jennings was putting the children to bed at home; who on his frequent holidays brought in much beer, which he and the woman shared, while Bob was at work. To carry the tale to Bob would have been a thankless errand, for he would have none of anybody's sympathy, even in regard to miseries plain to his eye. But the thing got about in the workshop, and there his days were made bitter.

At home things grew worse. To return at half-past five, and find the children still undressed, screaming, hungry and dirty, was a matter of habit: to get them food, to wash them, to tend the cuts and bumps sustained through the day of neglect, before lighting a fire and getting tea for himself, were matters of daily duty.

'Ah,' he said to his sister, who came at intervals to say plain things about Mrs Jennings, 'you shouldn't go for to set a man agin 'is wife, Jin. Melier do'n' like work, I know, but that's nach'ral to 'er. She ought to 'a' married a swell 'stead o' me; she might 'a' done easy if she liked, bein' sich a fine gal; but she's good-'arted, is Melier; an' she can't 'elp bein' a bit thoughtless.'

Whereat his sister called him a fool (it was her customary goodbye at such times), and took herself off.

Bob Jennings's intelligence was sufficient for his common needs, but it was never a vast intelligence. Now, under a daily burden of dull misery, it clouded and stooped. The base wit of the workshop he comprehended less, and realised more slowly, than before; and the gaffer cursed him for a sleepy dolt.

Mrs Jennings ceased from any pretence of housewifery, and would some-times sit – perchance not quite sober – while Bob washed the children in the evening, opening her mouth only to express her contempt for him and his establishment, and to make him understand that she was sick of both. Once, exasperated by his quietness, she struck at him, and for a moment he was another man. 'Don't do that, Melier,' he said, 'else I might forget myself.' His manner surprised his wife: and it was such that she never did do that again.

So was Bob Jennings – without a friend in the world, except his sister, who chid him, and the children, who squalled at him – when his wife vanished with the lodger, the clock, a shade of wax flowers, Bob's best boots (which fitted the lodger) and his silver watch. Bob had returned, as usual, to the dirt and the children, and it was only when he struck a light that he found the clock was gone.

'Mummy tooked ve t'ock,' said Milly, the eldest child, who had followed him in from the door, and now gravely observed his movements. 'She tooked ve t'ock an' went ta-ta. An' she tooked ve fyowers.'

Bob lit the paraffin lamp with the green-glass reservoir, and carried it and its evil smell about the house. Some things had been turned over and others had gone, plainly. All Melier's clothes were gone. The lodger was not in, and under his bedroom window, where his box had stood, there was naught but an oblong patch of conspicuously clean wallpaper. In a muddle of doubt and perplexity, Bob found himself at the front door, staring up and down the street. Divers women-neighbours stood at their doors, and eyed him curiously; for Mrs Webster, moralist, opposite, had not watched the day's proceedings (nor those of many other days) for nothing, nor had she kept her story to herself.

He turned back into the house, a vague notion of what had befallen percolating feebly through his bewilderment. 'I dunno – I dunno,' he faltered, rubbing his ear. His mouth was dry, and he moved his lips uneasily, as he gazed with aimless looks about the walls and ceiling. Presently his eyes rested on the child, and, 'Milly,' he said decisively, 'come an 'ave yer face washed.'

He put the children to bed early, and went out. In the morning, when his sister came, because she had heard the news in common with everybody else, he had not returned. Bob Jennings had never lost more than two quarters in his life, but he was not seen at the workshop all this day. His sister stayed in the house, and in the evening, at his regular homing-time, he appeared, haggard and dusty, and began his preparations for washing the children. When he was made to understand that they had been already attended to, he looked doubtful and troubled for a moment. Presently he said: 'I ain't found 'er yet, Jin; I was in 'opes she might 'a' bin back by this. I – I don't expect she'll be very long. She was alwis a bit larky, was Melier; but very good-'arted.'

His sister had prepared a strenuous lecture on the theme of 'I told you so'; but the man was so broken, so meek, and so plainly unhinged in his faculties, that she suppressed it. Instead, she gave him comfortable talk, and made him promise in the end to sleep that night, and take up his customary work in the morning.

He did these things, and could have worked placidly enough had he but been alone; but the tale had reached the workshop, and there was no lack of brutish chaff to disorder him. This the decenter men would have no part in, and even protested against. But the ill-conditioned kept their way, till, at the cry of 'Bell O!' when all were starting for dinner, one of the worst shouted the cruellest gibe of all. Bob Jennings turned on him and knocked him over a scrap-heap.

A shout went up from the hurrying workmen, with a chorus of, 'Serve ye right,' and the fallen joker found himself awkwardly confronted by the shop bruiser. But Bob had turned to a corner, and buried his eyes in the bend of his arm, while his shoulders heaved and shook.

He slunk away home, and stayed there, walking restlessly to and fro, and often peeping down the street from the window. When, at twilight, his sister came again, he had become almost cheerful, and said with some briskness: 'I'm a-goin' to meet 'er, Jin, at seven. I know where she'll be waitin'.'

He went upstairs, and after a little while came down again in his best black coat, carefully smoothing a tall hat of obsolete shape with his pocket-hand-kerchief. 'I ain't wore it for years,' he said. 'I ought to 'a' wore it – it might 'a' pleased 'er. She used to say she wouldn't walk with me in no other – when I used to meet 'er in the evenin', at seven o'clock.' He brushed assiduously, and put the hat on. 'I'd better 'ave a shave round the corner as I go along,' he added, fingering his stubbly chin.

He received as one not comprehending his sister's entreaties to remain at home, but when he went she followed at a little distance. After his penny shave he made for the main road, where company-keeping couples walked up and down all evening. He stopped at a church, and began pacing slowly to and fro before it, eagerly looking out each way as he went.

His sister watched him for nearly half an hour, and then went home. In two hours more she came back with her husband. Bob was still there, walking to and fro.

' 'Ullo, Bob,' said his brother-in-law; 'come along 'ome an' get to bed, there's a good chap. You'll be awright in the mornin'.'

'She ain't turned up,' Bob complained, 'or else I've missed 'er. This is the reg'lar place – where I alwis used to meet 'er. But she'll come tomorrer. She used to leave me in the lurch sometimes, bein' nach'rally larky. But very good-'arted, mindjer; very good-'arted.'

She did not come the next evening, nor the next, nor the evening after, nor the one after that. But Bob Jennings, howbeit depressed and anxious, was always confident. 'Somethink's prevented 'er tonight,' he would say, 'but she'll come tomorrer . . . I'll buy a blue tie tomorrer – she used to like me in a blue tie. I won't miss 'er tomorrer. I'll come a little earlier.'

So it went. The black coat grew ragged in the service, and hobbledehoys, finding him safe sport, smashed the tall hat over his eyes time after time. He wept over the hat, and straightened it as best he might. Was she coming? Night after night, and night and night. But tomorrow . . .

F. W. ROBINSON

Minions of the Moon

Our story is of the time when George III was king, and our scene of action lies only at an old farmhouse six miles or so from Finchley – a quaint, ramshackle, commodious, old-fashioned, thatched farmhouse that we see only in pictures now, and which has long since been improved off the face of the earth.

It was a farm estate that was flourishing bravely in those dear disreputable days when the people paid fivepence a pound for bread, and only dared curse protection in their hearts; when few throve and many starved, and younger sons of gentry, without interest at court or Parliament, either cut the country which served them so badly, or took to business on the king's highway and served the country badly in return.

The Maythorpe Farm belonged to the Pemberthys, and had descended from father to son from days lying too far back to reckon up just now; and a rare, exclusive, conservative, bad-tempered, long-headed race the Pemberthys had always borne the reputation of being, feathering their own nests well, and dying in them fat and prosperous.

There were a good many Pemberthys scattered about the home and midland counties, but it was generally understood in the family that the head of the clan, as it were, lived at Maythorpe Farm, near Finchley, and here the Pemberthys would forgather on any great occasion, such as a marriage, a funeral or a christening, the funeral taking precedence for numbers. There had been a grand funeral at Maythorpe Farm only a few days before our story opens, for Reuben Pemberthy had been consigned to his fathers at the early age of forty-nine. Reuben Pemberthy had left one son behind him, also named Reuben, a stalwart, heavy-browed, good-looking young fellow, who, at two and twenty, was quite as well able to manage the farm and everybody on it as his father had been before him. He had got rid of all his relatives save two six days after his father's funeral; and those two were stopping by general consent, because it was signed, sealed and delivered by those whom it most concerned that the younger woman, his cousin, pretty Sophie Tarne, was to be married before the year was out to the present Reuben Pemberthy, who had wooed her and won her consent when he went down to her mother's house at King's Norton for a few days' trip last summer. Being a steady, handsome fellow, who made love in downright earnest, he impressed Sophie's eighteen years, and was somewhat timidly but graciously accepted as an affianced suitor. It was thought at King's Norton that Mrs Tarne had done a better stroke of business in the first year of her widowhood than her late husband had done – always an unlucky wretch, Timothy – in the whole course of his life. And now Sophie Tarne and her mother were staying for a few days longer at Maythorpe Farm after the funeral.

Mrs Tarne, having been a real Pemberthy before her unfortunate marriage with the improvident draper of King's Norton, was quite one of the family, and seemed more at home at Finchley than was the new widow, Mrs Pemberthy, a poor, unlucky lady, a victim to a chronic state of twittering and jingling and twitching, but one who, despite her shivers, had made the late Reuben a good wife, and was a fair housekeeper even now, although superintending housekeeping in jumps, like a palsy-stricken kangaroo.

So Sophie and her bustling mother were of material assistance to Mrs Pemberthy; and the presence of Sophie in that house of mourning – where the mourning had been speedily got over and business had begun again with commendable celerity – was a considerable source of comfort to young Reuben, when he had leisure after business hours which was not always the case, to resume those tender relations which had borne to him last autumn such happy fruit of promise.

Though there was not much work to do at the farm in the wintertime, when the nights were long and the days short, yet Reuben Pemberthy was generally busy in one way or another; and on the particular day on which our story opens Reuben was away at High Barnet.

It had been a dull, dark day, followed by a dull, dark night. The farm servants had gone to their homes, save the few that were attached to the premises, such as scullery-maids and dairymaids; and Mrs Pemberthy, Mrs Tarne and her daughter Sophie were waiting early supper for Reuben, and wondering what kept him so long from his home and his sweetheart.

Mrs Tarne, accustomed, mayhap, to the roar and bustle of King's Norton, found the farm at Finchley a trifle dull and lonely – not that in a few days after a funeral she could expect any excessive display of life or frivolity – and, oppressed a bit that evening, was a trifle nervous as to the whereabouts of her future son-in-law, who had faithfully promised to be home a clear hour and a half before the present time, and whose word might be always taken to be as good as his bond. Mrs Tarne was the most restless of the three women. Good Mrs Pemberthy, though physically shaken, was not likely to be nervous concerning her son, and, indeed, was at any time only fidgety over her own special complaints – a remarkable trait of character deserving of passing comment here. Sophie was not of a nervous temperament; indeed, for her eighteen years, was apparently a little too cool and methodical; and she was not flurried that evening over the delay in the arrival home of Reuben Pemberthy. She was not imaginative like her mother, and did not associate delay with the dangers of a dark night, though the nights *were* full of danger in the good old times of the third George. She went to the door to look out, after her mother had tripped there for the seventh or eighth time, not for appearances' sake, for she was above that, but to keep her mother company, and to suggest that these frequent excursions to the front door would end in a bad cold.

'I can't help fearing that something has happened to Reu,' said the mother; 'he is always so true to time.'

'There are so many things to keep a man late, mother.'

'Not to keep Reuben. If he said what hour he'd be back – he's like his father, my poor brother – he'd do it to the minute, even if there weren't any reason for his hurry.'

'Which there is,' said Sophie, archly.

'Which there is, Sophie. And why you are so quiet over this I don't know. I am sure when poor Mr Tarne was out late – and he was often very, very late, and the Lord knows where he'd been, either! – I couldn't keep a limb of me still till he came home again. I was as bad as your aunt indoors there till I was sure he was safe and sound.'

'But he always came home safe and sound, mother.'

'Nearly always. I mind the time once, though – bless us and save us, what a gust!' she cried, as the wind came swooping down the hill at them, swirling past them into the dark passage and puffing the lights out in the big pantry beyond, where the maids began to scream. 'I hope he hasn't been blown off his horse.'

'Not very likely that,' said Sophie, 'and Reuben the best horseman in the county. But come in out of the gale, mother; the sleet cuts like a knife too, and he will not come home any the sooner for your letting the wind into the house. And – why, here he comes after all. Hark!'

There was a rattling of horses' hoofs on the frost-bound road; it was a long way in the distance, but it was the unmistakable signal of a well-mounted traveller approaching – of more than one well-mounted traveller, it became quickly apparent, the clattering was so loud and incessant and manifold.

'Soldiers!' said Sophie. 'What can bring them this way?'

'It's the farmers coming the same way as Reuben for protection's sake these winter nights, child.'

'Protection?'

'Haven't you heard of the highwaymen about, and how a single traveller is never safe in these parts? Or a double one either – or – '

'Perhaps these are highwaymen.'

'Oh, good gracious! Let us get indoors and bar up,' cried Mrs Tarne, wholly forgetful of Reuben Pemberthy's safety after this suggestion. 'Yes, it's as likely to be highwaymen as soldiers.'

It was more likely. It was pretty conclusive that the odds were in favour of highwaymen when, five minutes afterwards, eight mounted men rode up to the Maythorpe farmhouse, dismounted with considerable noise and bustle, and commenced at the stout oaken door with the butt-ends of their riding-whips, hammering away incessantly and shouting out much strong language in their vehemence. This, being fortunately bawled forth all at once was incomprehensible to the dwellers within doors, now all scared together and no longer cool and self-possessed.

'Robbers!' said Mrs Tarne.

'We've never been molested before, at least not for twenty years or more,' said Mrs Pemberthy; 'and then I mind – '

'Is it likely to be any of Reuben's friends?' asked Sophie, timidly.

'Oh no; Reuben has no bellowing crowd like that for friends. Ask who is there – somebody.'

But nobody would go to the door save Sophie Tarne herself. The maids were huddled in a heap together in a corner of the dairy, and refused to budge an inch, and Mrs Tarne was shaking more than Mrs Pemberthy.

Sophie, with the colour gone from her face, went boldly back to the door, where the hammering on the panels continued and would have split anything of a less tough fibre than the English oak of which they were constructed.

'Who is there? What do you want?' she gave out in a shrill falsetto; but no one heard her till the questions were repeated about an octave and a half higher.

'Hold hard, Stango; there's a woman calling to us. Stop your row, will you?'

A sudden cessation of the battering ensued, and someone was heard going rapidly backwards over cobblestones amid the laughter of the rest, who had dismounted and were standing outside in the cold, with their hands upon their horses' bridles.

'Who is there?' asked Sophie Tarne again.

'Travellers in need of assistance, and who – ' began a polite and even musical voice, which was interrupted by a hoarse voice: 'Open in the king's name, will you?'

'Open in the fiend's name, won't you?' called out a third and hoarser voice; 'or we'll fire through the windows and burn the place down.'

'What do you want?'

'Silence!' shouted the first one again; 'let me explain, you dogs, before you bark again.'

There was a pause, and the polite gentleman began again in his mellifluous voice: 'We are travellers belated. We require corn for our horses, food for ourselves. There is no occasion for alarm; my friends are noisy, but harmless, I assure you, and the favour of admittance and entertainment here will be duly appreciated. To refuse your hospitality – the hospitality of a Pemberthy – is only to expose yourselves to considerable inconvenience, I fear.'

'Spoken like a book, captain.'

'And, as we intend to come in at all risks,' added a deeper voice, 'it will be better for you not to try and keep us out, d' ye hear? D' ye – captain, if you shake me by the collar again I'll put a bullet through you. I – '

'Silence! Let the worthy folks inside consider the position for five minutes.'

'Not a minute longer, if they don't want the place burned about their ears, mind you,' cried a voice that had not spoken yet.

'Who are you?' asked Sophie, still inclined to parley.

'Travellers, I have told you.'

'Thieves, cutthroats and murderers – eight of us – knights of the road, gentlemen of the highway, and not to be trifled with when half-starved and hard-driven,' cried the hoarse man. 'There, will that satisfy you, wench? Will you let us in or not? It's easy enough for us to smash in the windows and get in that way, isn't it?'

Yes, it was very easy.

'Wait five minutes, please,' said Sophie.

She went back to the parlour and to the two shivering women and the crowd of maids, who had crept from the dairy to the farm parlour, having greater faith in numbers now.

'They had better come in, aunt, especially as we are quite helpless to keep them out. I could fire that gun,' Sophie said, pointing to an unwieldy old blunderbuss slung by straps to the ceiling, 'and I know it's loaded. But I'm afraid it wouldn't be of much use.'

'It might make them angry,' said Mrs Pemberthy.

'It would only kill one at the best,' remarked Mrs Tarne, with a heavy sigh.

'And the rest of the men would kill us, the brutes,' said Mrs Pemberthy. 'Yes, they'd better come in.'

'Lord have mercy upon us,' said Mrs Tarne.

'There's no help for it,' said Mrs Pemberthy. 'Even Reuben would not have dared to keep them out. I mind now their coming like this twenty years agone. It was – '

'I will see to them,' said Sophie, who had become in her young, brave strength quite the mistress of the ceremonies. 'Leave the rest to me.'

'And if you can persuade them to go away – ' began Mrs Tarne; but her daughter had already disappeared, and was parleying through the keyhole with the strangers without.

'Such hospitality as we can offer, gentlemen, shall be at your service, providing always that you treat us with the respect due to gentlewomen and your hosts.'

'Trust to that,' was the reply. 'I will answer for myself and my companions, Mistress Pemberthy.'

'You give me your word of honour?'

'My word of honour,' he repeated; 'our words of honour, speaking for all my good friends present; is it not so, men?'

'Ay, ay – that's right,' chorused the good friends; and then Sophie Tarne, not without an extra plunging of the heart beneath her white crossover, unlocked the stout oaken door and let in her unwelcome visitors.

Seven out of the eight seemed to tumble in all at once, pushing against one another in their eagerness to enter, laughing, shouting and stamping with the heels of their jack-boots on the bright red pantiles of the hall. The eighth intruder followed – a tall, thin man, pale-faced and stern and young, with a heavy horseman's cloak falling from his shoulders, the front of which was gathered up across his arms. A handsome and yet worn face – the face of one who had seen better days and known brighter times – a picturesque kind of vagabond, take him in the candlelight. He raised his hat and bowed low to Sophie Tarne, not offering to shake hands as the rest of them had done who where crowding around her; then he seemed to stand suddenly between them and their salutations, and to brush them unceremoniously aside.

'You see to those horses, Stango and Grapp,' he said, singling out the most obtrusive and the most black-muzzled of his gang. 'Mistress Pemberthy will perhaps kindly trust us for a while with the keys of the stables and corn-bins.'

'They are here,' said Sophie, detaching them from a bunch of keys which, in true housewifely fashion, hung from her girdle. 'The farm servants are away in the village, or they should help you, sir.'

'We are in the habit of helping ourselves as a rule,' said one of the highwaymen, drily. 'Pray don't apologise on that score, mistress.'

Two of the men departed; five of them stalked into the farm parlour, flourishing their big hats and executing clumsy scrapings with their feet while bowing in mock fashion to the two nervous widows, who sat in one corner regarding them askance; the leader of these lawless ones dropped his cloak from his shoulders, left it trailing on the pantile floor, and made a rapid signal with his hand to Sophie to pause an instant before she entered the room.

'Treat them with fair words, and not too much strong waters,' he said, quickly; 'we have a long ride before us.'

He said it like a warning, and Sophie nodded as though she took his advice and was not ungrateful for it. Then they both went into the parlour and joined the company; and the maidservant, becoming used to the position or making the best of it, began to bustle about and wait upon their visitors, who had already drawn up their seats to the supper-table, which had been spread with good things two hours ago anticipative of the return Reuben Pemberthy to Maythorpe.

It was an odd supper-party at which Sophie Tarne presided, the highway-men insisting, with much clamour and some emphatic oaths, that they would have no old women like Mrs Tarne and Mrs Pemberthy at the head of the table. Sophie was a pretty wench, and so must do the honours of the feast.

'The young girl's health, gentlemen, with three times three, and may her husband be a match for her in good looks,' cried one admiring knight of the road; and then the toast was drunk. The ale flowed freely, and there was much laughter and loud jesting.

The man whom they called 'Guy' and 'captain' sat by Sophie's side. He ate very little, and kept a watchful eye upon his men after Stango and his companion had come in from the stable and completed the number. He exchanged at first but few words with Sophie, though he surveyed her with a grave attention that brought the colour to her cheeks. He was a man upon guard. Presently he said: 'You bear your position well. You are not alarmed at these wild fellows?'

'No – not now. I don't think they would hurt me. Besides – '

'Besides – what?' he asked, as she paused.

'I have your word for them.'

'Yes,' he answered; 'but it is only a highwayman's word.'

'I can trust it.'

'These men can be demons when they like, Mistress Pemberthy.'

Sophie did not think it worth while to inform the gentleman that her name was not Pemberthy; it could not possibly matter to him, and there was a difficulty in explaining the relationship she bore to the family.

'Why are you with such men as these?' she asked, wonderingly.

'Where should I be? Where can I be else?' he asked, lightly now; but it was with a forced lightness of demeanour or Sophie Tarne was very much deceived.

'Helping your king, not warring against him and his laws,' said Sophie, very quickly.

'I owe no allegiance to King George. I have always been a ne'er-do-well, despised and scouted by a hard father and a villainous brother or two, and life with these good fellows here is, after all, to my mind. There's independence in it, and I prefer to be independent; and danger, and I like danger. A wronged man wrongs others in his turn, mistress; and it is my turn now.'

'Two wrongs cannot make a right.'

'Oh, I do not attempt the impossible, Mistress Pemberthy.'

'What will be the end of this – to you?'

'The gallows – if I cannot get my pistol out in time.'

He laughed lightly and naturally enough as Sophie shrank in terror from him. One could see he was a desperate man enough, despite his better manners; probably as great an outcast as the rest of them, and as little to be trusted.

'That is a dreadful end to look forward to,' she said.

'I don't look forward. What is the use – when *that* is the prospect?'

'Your father – your brothers – '

'Would be glad that the end came soon,' he concluded. 'They are waiting for it patiently. They have prophesied it for the last five years.'

'They know then?'

'Oh yes; I have taken care that they should know,' he answered, laughing defiantly again.

'And your mother – does she know?'

He paused, and looked at her very hard.

'God forbid.'

'She is – '

'She is in heaven, where nothing is known of what goes on upon earth.'

'How can you tell that?'

'There would be no peace in heaven otherwise, Mistress Pemberthy; only great grief, intense shame, misery, despair, madness, at the true knowledge of us all,' he said, passionately. 'On earth we men are hypocrites and liars, devils and slaves.'

'Not all men,' said Sophie, thinking of Reu Pemberthy.

'I have met none other. Perhaps I have sought none other – all my own fault, they will tell you where my father is; where,' he added, bitterly, 'they are worse than I am, and yet, oh, so respectable.'

'You turned highwayman to – to – '

'To spite them, say. It is very near the truth.'

'It will be a poor excuse to the mother, when you see her again.'

'Eh?'

But Sophie had no time to continue so abstruse a subject with this misanthropical freebooter. She clapped her hand to her side and gave a little squeak of astonishment.

'What is the matter?' asked Captain Guy.

'My keys! They have taken my keys.'

And, sure enough, while Sophie Tarne had been talking to the captain, someone had severed the keys from her girdle and made off with them, and there was only a clean-cut black ribbon dangling at her waist instead.

'That villain Stango,' exclaimed the captain. 'I saw him pass a minute ago. He leaned over and whispered to you, Kits. You remember?'

'Stango?' said Kits, with far too innocent an expression to be genuine.

'Yes, Stango; you know he did.'

'I dare say he did. I don't gainsay it, captain, but I don't know where he has gone.'

'But *I* will know,' cried the captain, striking his hand upon the table and making every glass and plate jump thereon. 'I will have no tricks played here without my consent. Am I your master, or are you all mine?'

And here, we regret to say, Captain Guy swore a good deal, and became perfectly unheroic and inelegant and unromantic. But his oaths had more effect upon his unruly followers than his protests, and they sat looking at him in a half-sullen, half-shamefaced manner, and would have probably succumbed to his influence had not attention been diverted and aroused by the reappearance of Stango, who staggered in with four or five great black bottles heaped high in his arms. A tremendous shout of applause and delight greeted his return to the parlour.

'We have been treated scurvily, my men,' cried Stango, 'exceedingly scurvily; the best and strongest stuff in the cellar has been kept back from us. It's excellent – I've been tasting it first, lest you should all be poisoned; and there's more where this come from – oceans more of it!'

'Hurrah for Stango!'

The captain's voice was heard once more above the uproar, but it was only for a minute longer. There was a rush of six men towards Stango; a shouting, scrambling, fighting for the spirits which he had discovered; a crash of one black bottle to the floor, with the spirit streaming over the polished boards, and the unceremonious tilting over of the upper part of the supper-table in the ruffians' wild eagerness for drink.

'To horse, to horse, men! Have you forgotten how far we have to go?' cried the captain.

But they had forgotten everything, and did not heed him. They were drinking strong waters, and were heedless of the hour and the risks they ran by a protracted stay there. In ten minutes from that time Saturnalia had set in, and pandemonium seemed to have unloosed its choicest specimens They sang, they danced, they raved, they blasphemed, they crowed like cocks, they fired pistols at the chimney ornaments, they chased the maidservants from one room to another, they whirled round the room with Mrs Tarne and Mrs Pemberthy, they would have made a plunge at Sophie Tarne for partner had not the captain, very white and stern now, stood close to her side with a pistol at full cock in his right hand.

'I shall shoot the first man down who touches you,' he said, between his set teeth.

'I will get away from them soon. For heaven's sake – for mine – do not add to the horror of this night, sir,' implored Sophie.

He paused.

'I beg your pardon,' he said, in a low tone of voice, 'but – but I am powerless to help you unless I quell these wolves at once. They are going off for more drink.'

'What is to be done?'

'Can you sing, Mistress Pemberthy?'

'Yes, a little; at least, they say so,' she said, blushing at her own self-encomium.

'Sing something – to gain time. I will slip away while you are singing, and get the horses round to the front door. Do not be afraid.'

'Gentlemen,' he cried, in a loud voice, and bringing the handle of his pistol smartly on the head of the man nearest to him to emphasise his discourse, 'Mistress Pemberthy will oblige the company with a song. Order and attention for the lady!'

'A song! a song!' exclaimed the highwaymen, clapping their hands and stamping their heels upon the floor. And then, amid the pause which followed, Sophie Tarne began a plaintive little ballad in a sweet, tremulous voice, which gathered strength as she proceeded.

It was a strange scene awaiting the return of Reuben Pemberthy, whose tall form stood in the doorway before Sophie had finished her sweet, simple rendering of an old English ballad. Reuben's round blue eyes were distended with surprise, and his mouth, generally very set and close, like the mouth of a steel purse, was on this especial occasion, and for a while, wide open. Sophie Tarne stood singing her best to amuse this vile and disorderly crew, who sat or stood around the room half drunk, and with glasses in their hands, pipes in their mouths, and the formidable, old-fashioned horse-pistols in their pockets!

And who was the handsome man, with the long, black, flowing hair, and a pale face, standing by Sophie's side – his Sophie – in a suit of soiled brocade and tarnished lace, with a Ramillie cocked hat under his arm and a pistol in his hand? The leader of these robbers, the very man who had stopped him on the king's highway three hours ago and taken every stiver which he had brought away from Barnet; who had, with the help of these other scoundrels getting mad drunk on his brandy, taken away his horse and left him bound to a gate by the roadside because he would not be quietly robbed, but must make a fuss over it and fight and kick in a most unbecoming fashion, and without any regard for the numbers by whom he had been assailed.

'I did not think you could sing like that,' said the captain, quietly and in a low voice, when Sophie had finished her song, and a great shout of approval was echoing throughout the farm and many hundred yards beyond it.

'You have not got the horses ready,' said Sophie, becoming aware that he was still at her side. 'You said – you promised – '

'I could not leave you while you were singing. Did you know that was my mother's song?'

'How should I know that?'

'No – no. But how strange – how – ah! there is your brother at the door. I had the honour of meeting Master Pemberthy of Finchley earlier this evening, I think. A brave young gentleman; you should be proud of him.'

'My bro – oh! it is Reu. Oh Reu, Reu, where have you been? Why did you not come before to help us – to tell us what to do?' And Sophie Tarne ran to him and put her arms round his neck and burst into tears. It was not a wise step on Sophie's part, but it was the reaction at the sight of her sweetheart, at the glimpse, as it were, of deliverance.

'There, there, don't cry, Sophie; keep a stout heart!' he whispered. 'If these villains have robbed us, they will not be triumphant long. It will be my turn to crow presently.'

'I – I don't understand.'

'I can't explain now. Keep a good face – ply them with more drink – watch me. Well, my friends,' he said, in a loud voice, 'you have stolen a march upon me this time; but I've got home, you see, in time to welcome you to Maythorpe and share in your festivity. I'm a Pemberthy, and not likely to cry over spilled milk. More liquor for the gentlemen, you wenches, and be quick with it. Captain, here's to you and your companions, and next time you catch a Pemberthy, treat him more gently in return for a welcome here. More liquor, girls; the gentlemen are thirsty after their long ride.'

Reuben drank to the healths of the gentlemen by whom he was surrounded; he was very much at home in his own house, very cool and undismayed, having recovered from his surprise at finding an evening party being celebrated there. The highwaymen were too much excited to see anything remarkable in the effusion of Reuben Pemberthy's greeting; these were lawless times, when farmers and highwaymen were often in accord, dealt in one another's horses, and drove various bargains at odd seasons and in odd corners of the market-places; and Reuben Pemberthy was not unknown to them, though they had treated him with scant respect upon a lonely country road, and when they were impressed by the fact that he was riding homeward with well-lined pockets after a day's huckstering. They cheered Mr Pemberthy's sentiments, all but the captain, who regarded him very critically, although bowing very low while his health was drunk.

'My cousin and my future bride, gentlemen will sing you another song; and I don't mind following suit myself, just to show there is no ill feeling between us; and our worthy captain, he will oblige after me, I am sure. It may be a good many years before we meet again.'

'It may,' said the captain, laconically.

'I – I cannot sing any more, Reuben,' cried Sophie.

'Try, Sophie, for all our sakes; our home's sake – the home they would strip, or burn to the ground, if they had only the chance.'

'Why do you wish to keep them here?' Sophie whispered back to him.

'I was released by a troop of soldiers who were coming in this direction,' he said, hurriedly. They have gone on toward Finchley in search of these robbers, but, failing to find them, they will return here as my guests till morning. That was their promise.'

'Oh!'

Sophie could not say more. Reuben had left her side, and was talking and laughing with Stango as though he loved him.

'Your sweetheart, then, this cock o' the game?' said the captain to Sophie, as he approached her once more.

'Yes.'

' "I had need wish you much joy, for I see but little toward it," as the poet says,' he remarked, bluntly. 'He will not make you a good husband.'

'You cannot say that.'

'It's a hard face that will look into yours, mistress, and when trouble comes, it will not look pleasantly. You are going to sing again? I am glad.'

'You promised to go away – long since.'

'I did. But the host has returned, and I distrust him. I am waiting now to see the end of it.'

'No – no – I hope not. Pray go, sir.'

'Is there danger?'

'Yes.'

'I thought so. I am fond of danger, I have told you. It braces me up; it – why are you so pale?'

'You have been kind to me, and you have saved me from indignity. Pray take your men away at once.'

'They will not go, and I will not desert them.'

'For my sake – do!'

'A song! a song! No more love-making tonight, captain. A song from the farmer's pretty lass!' cried out the men.

And then Sophie began to sing again, this time a love-song, the song of a maiden waiting for her soldier boy to come back from the wars; a maiden waiting for him, listening for him, hearing the tramp of his regiment approaching. She looked at Captain Guy as she sang, and with much entreaty in her gaze, and he looked back at her from under the cock of his hat, which he had pulled over his brows; then he wavered and stole out of the room. Kits was at the door, still with his mug of brandy in his hand. Guy seized him by the ear and took him out with him into the fresh air, where the white frost was and where the white moon was shining now.

'The soldiers are after us and know where we are, Kits. Pitch that stuff away.'

'Not if – '

'And get the horses ready – quick! I will be with you in a moment.'

He walked along the garden path in front of the big old farm, swung wide the farm gates, and propped them open. Then he went down on all fours and put his ear to the frost-bound country road and listened. 'Yes,' he added, 'two miles away, and coming on sharp. Why not let them come? What does it matter how soon?' He strode back, however, with quick steps. Five minutes afterwards he was at the door of the farm parlour again, with his cloak over his shoulder and his riding-whip in his hand.

'Boys, the redcoats are upon us!' he shouted. 'Each man to his horse.'

'We are betrayed then!'

'We won't go and leave all the good things in this house,' cried Stango. 'Why, it's like the Bank of England upstairs, and I have the keys. I – '

'Stango, I shall certainly put a bullet through your head if you attempt to do anything more save to thank our worthy host for his hospitality and give him up his keys. Do you hear?' he thundered forth. 'Will you hang us all, you fool, by your delay?'

The highwaymen were scurrying out of the room now, a few in too much haste to thank the givers of the feast, the others bowing and shaking hands in mock burlesque of their chief. Stango had thrown down the keys and run for it.

'Sorry we must leave you, Master Pemberthy,' said the captain, 'but I certainly have the impression that a troop of horse soldiers is coming in this direction. Pure fancy, probably; but one cannot risk anything in these hard times. Your purse, sir, which I took this afternoon – I shall not require it. Buy Mistress Sophie a wedding with it. Good-night.'

He bowed low, but he did not smile till he met Sophie's frightened looks; then he bowed still lower, hat in hand, and said good-night with a funny break in his voice and a longing look in his dark eyes that Sophie did not readily forget.

It was all like a dream after the highwaymen had put spurs to their horses and galloped away from Maythorpe Farm.

*   *   *

It will be fifteen years come next wintertime since the 'Minions of the Moon' held high carnival at the farm of Reuben Pemberthy. Save that the trees about the homestead are full of rustling green leaves and there is sunshine where the white frost lay, the farm looks very much the same; the great thatched roof has taken a darker tinge, and all the gold in it has turned to grey, and the walls are more weather-beaten than of yore; but it is the old farm still, standing 'foursquare', with the highroad to Finchley winding over the green hill yonder like a great, white, dusty snake. Along the road comes a horseman at full speed, as though anxious to find a shelter before nightfall, for the king's highway in this direction is no safer than it used to be, and people talk of Abershaw and Barrington, and a man with sixteen strings to his hat, who are busy in this direction. But the days are long now, and it wants some hours before sundown when the traveller leaps from his horse and stands under the broad eaves of the porch, where the creepers are growing luxuriantly and are full of fair white flowers.

The traveller is a good horseman, though he has passed the heyday of his youth. It is not for some three minutes afterwards that his manservant, hot and blown and powdered thick with dust, comes up on horseback after him and takes charge of his master's steed. The master is a man of forty years or more, and looking somewhat older than his years, his hair being very grey. He stoops a little between the shoulders too when off his guard, though he can look straight and stalwart enough when put to it. He is very dark – a fiercer sun than that which shines on England has burned him a copper colour – and he has a moustache that Munchausen might have envied.

He knocks at the door, and asks if Master Reuben Pemberthy can be seen at a moment's notice. The maidservant looks surprised, but says, 'My mistress is within, sir.'

'Reuben Pemberthy's wife, that is,' he mutters, pulling thoughtfully at his long moustache; 'ah, well, perhaps she will see me.'

'What name shall I say?'

'Sir Richard Isshaw; but she will not know the name.'

He stands in the hall, looking about him critically; his manservant, still mounted, goes slowly back towards the roadway with his master's horse and his own, where he remains in waiting. Presently, Sir Richard Isshaw is shown into the farm parlour, very cool and full of shadow, with great green plants on the broad recesses of the open window, and bees buzzing about them from the outer world.

A young woman in deep widow's weeds rises as he enters, and makes him one of those profound courtesies which were considered appropriate for the fair sex to display to those of rank and honour in the good old days when George was king. Surely a young woman still, despite the fifteen years that have passed, with a young supple figure and a pleasant unlined face. Eighteen years and fifteen only make thirty-three, and one can scarcely believe in time's inroads looking upon Sophie Pemberthy. The man cannot. He is surprised and he looks at her through tears in his dark eyes.

'You asked to see Mr Reuben Pemberthy,' she says, sadly. 'You did not know that –'

'No, I did not know,' he says, a little huskily; 'I am a stranger to these parts; I have been long abroad.'

'May I enquire the nature of your errand, Sir Richard?' she asks, in a low voice. 'Though I am afraid I cannot be of any service as regards any business of the farm.'

'How is that?' he asks, steadily keeping gaze upon her.

'The farm passes to Mr Pemberthy's cousin in a few days' time.'

'Indeed! Then you –'

He pauses halfway for a reply, but it is long in coming. Only the humming of the bees disturbs the silence of the room.

'Then you leave here?' he concludes at last.

'Yes. It is only the male Pemberthys who rule,' she says.

'Your – your children?'

'My one little boy, my dear Algy, died before his father. It was a great disappointment to my husband that he should die. We female Pemberthys,' she says, with a sudden real bright little smile that settles down into sadness again very quickly, 'do not count for a great deal in the family.'

'How long has Mr Pemberthy been dead?'

'Six months.'

'You are left poor?' he says, very quickly now.

'I – I don't think you have a right to ask me such a question, sir.'

'I have no right,' he replies. 'These are foreign manners. Excuse them, please; don't mind me.'

Still he is persistent.

'From son to son's son, and the women left anywhere and anyhow – that is the Pemberthy law, I expect. I have seen the workings of such a law before. Not that I ought to complain,' he adds, with a forced laugh – a laugh that Mrs Pemberthy seems suddenly to remember – 'for I have profited thereby.'

'Indeed!' says the farmer's widow, for the want of a better answer at the moment.

'I am a younger son; but all my brothers have been taken away by wars or pestilence, and I am 'sent' for in hot haste – I, who had shaken the dust of England from my feet fifteen years ago.'

'Fifteen years?'

'Almost. Don't you recollect the last time I was in this room?'

'You – in this room, Sir Richard?'

'Yes; try and remember when that was. I only come to look at the old place and you, just for once, before I go away again. Try and think, Mistress Pemberthy, as I used to call you.'

She looks into the red, sunburnt face, starts, blushes and looks away.

'Yes, I remember. You are – '

'Well?'

'Captain Guy!'

'Yes, that is it; Richard Guy Isshaw, younger son, who went wholly to the bad – who turned highwayman – whom *you* saved. The only one out of the eight – the rest were hanged at Tyburn and Kennington, poor devils – and I thought I would ride over and thank you, and see you once more. Your husband would have hanged me, I dare say – but there, there, peace to his soul.'

'Amen,' whispers Sophie Pemberthy.

'You saved me; you set me thinking of my young mother, who died when I was a lad and loved me much too well; and you taught me there were warm and loving hearts in the world; and when I went away from here I went away from the old life. I cannot say how that was; but,' shrugging his shoulders, 'so it was.'

'It was a call,' said Sophie, piously.

'A call to arms, for I went to the wars. And what is it now that brings me back here to thank you – an old, time-worn reprobate, turned soldier and turned respectable! – what is it?'

'I don't know.'

'Another call, depend upon it. A call to Maythorpe, where I expected to find a fat farmer and his buxom partner and a crowd of laughing boys and girls; where I hoped I might be of help to some of them, if help were needed.

And,' he adds, 'I find only you – and you just the same fair, bright girl I left behind me long ago.'

'Oh no.'

'It is like a dream; it is very remarkable to me. Yes, it's another call, Mistress Pemberthy, depend upon it.'

And it is not the last call, either. The estate of Richard Isshaw lies not so many miles from Maythorpe Farm that a good long ride cannot overcome the distance between them. And the man turned respectable – the real baronet – is so very much alone and out of place in his big house that he knows not what to do.

And Mistress Pemberthy is very much alone too, and going out alone into the world, almost friendless, and with only two hundred pounds and perhaps the second-best bed – who knows? – as her share of her late loving, but rather hard and unsympathetic, husband's worldly goods.

And folks do say, Finchley way, that pretty Mistress Pemberthy will be Lady Isshaw before the winter sets in, and that it will be exactly fifteen years since these two first set eyes upon each other.

ANTHONY TROLLOPE

Anthony Trollope, the quintessential Victorian novelist whose dozens of books illuminate virtually every aspect of late nineteenth century England, was born in London on 24 April 1815. His father failed as a barrister and his mother, Frances Trollope, successfully turned to writing in order to improve their finances. At the age of nineteen Trollope embarked on a career as a civil servant in London's General Post Office. In 1841 he was transferred to Ireland, where he lived for the next eighteen years. In 1844 he married Rose Heseltine, who became a trusted literary assistant once he began to write. Trollope's first book was published in 1847, but it was not until 1855 that he achieved commercial success with *The Warden*, the initial volume in a six-book series about clerical life in and around the fictional cathedral town of Barchester. In October 1859 he returned to England and quickly became part of London's literary life. With *Can You Forgive Her?* in 1865 he launched the Palliser novels, a new series about politics. Trollope resigned from the postal service late in 1867 to become editor of *Saint Paul's Magazine*. The next year he made an unsuccessful bid for a seat in Parliament. In the final years of his life he travelled extensively. Anthony Trollope died on 6 December 1882, a month after suffering a paralysing stroke.

Returning Home

It is generally supposed that people who live at home – good domestic people, who love tea and their armchairs, and who keep the parlour hearth-rug ever warm – it is generally supposed that these are the people who value home the most, and best appreciate all the comforts of that cherished institution. I am inclined to doubt this. It is, I think, to those who live farthest away from home, to those who find the greatest difficulty in visiting home, that the word conveys the sweetest idea. In some distant parts of the world it may be that an Englishman acknowledges his permanent resting place; but there are many others in which he will not call his daily house, his home. He would, in his own idea, desecrate the word by doing so. His home is across the blue waters, in the little northern island, which perhaps he may visit no more; which he has left, at any rate, for half his life; from which circumstances, and the necessity of living, have banished him. His home is still in England, and when he speaks of home his thoughts are there.

No one can understand the intensity of this feeling who has not seen or felt the absence of interest in life which falls to the lot of many who have to eat their bread on distant soils. We are all apt to think that a life in strange countries will be a life of excitement, of stirring enterprise, and varied scenes; that in abandoning the comforts of home, we shall receive in exchange more of movement and of adventure than would come in our way in our own tame country; and this feeling has, I am sure, sent many a young man roaming. Take any spirited fellow of twenty, and ask him whether he would like to go to Mexico for the next ten years! Prudence and his father may ultimately save him from such banishment, but he will not refuse without a pang of regret.

Alas! it is a mistake. Bread may be earned, and fortunes, perhaps, made in such countries; and as it is the destiny of our race to spread itself over the wide face of the globe, it is well that there should be something to gild and paint the outward face of that lot which so many are called upon to choose. But for a life of daily excitement, there is no life like life in England; and the farther that one goes from England the more stagnant, I think, do the waters of existence become.

But if it be so for men, it is ten times more so for women. An Englishman, if he be at Guatemala or Belize, must work for his bread, and that work will fund him in thought and excitement. But what of his wife? Where will she find excitement? By what pursuit will she repay herself for all that she has left behind her at her mother's fireside? She will love her husband. Yes; that at least! If there be not that, there will be a hell, indeed. Then she will nurse her children, and talk of her – home. When the time shall come that her promised return thither is within a year or two of its accomplishment, her thoughts will all be fixed on that coming pleasure, as are the thoughts of a young girl on her first ball for the fortnight before that event comes off.

On the central plain of that portion of Central America which is called Costa Rica stands the city of San José. It is the capital of the republic – for Costa Rica is a republic – and, for Central America, is a town of some importance. It is in the middle of the coffee district, surrounded by rich soil on which the sugar-cane is produced, is blessed with a climate only moderately hot, and the native inhabitants are neither cut-throats nor cannibals. It may be said, therefore, that by comparison with some other spots in which Englishmen and others are congregated for the gathering together of money, San José may be considered as a happy region; but, nevertheless, a life there is not in every way desirable. It is a dull place, with little to interest either the eye or the ear. Although the heat of the tropics is but little felt there on account of its altitude, men and women become too lifeless for much enterprise. There is no society. There are a few Germans and a few Englishmen in the place, who see each other on matters of business during the day; but, sombre as life generally is, they seem to care little for each other's company on any other footing. I know not to what point the aspirations of the Germans may stretch themselves, but to the English the one idea that gives salt to life is the idea of home. On some day, however distant it may be, they will once more turn their faces towards the little northern island, and then all will be well with them.

To a certain Englishman there, and to his dear little wife, this prospect came some few years since somewhat suddenly. Events and tidings, it matters not which or what, brought it about that they resolved between themselves that they would start immediately – almost immediately. They would pack up and leave San José within four months of the day on which their purpose was first formed. At San José a period of only four months for such a purpose was immediately. It creates a feeling of instant excitement, a necessity for instant doing, a consciousness that there was in those few weeks ample work both for the hands and thoughts – work almost more than ample. The dear little wife, who for the last two years had been so listless, felt herself flurried.

'Harry,' she said to her husband, 'how shall we ever be ready?' And her pretty face was lighted up with unusual brightness at the happy thought of so much haste with such an object. 'And baby's things too,' she said, as she thought of all the various little articles of dress that would be needed. A journey from San José to Southampton cannot in truth be made as easily as one from London to Liverpool. Let us think of a month to be passed without any aid from the washerwoman, and the greatest part of that month amidst the sweltering heats of the West Indian tropics!

In the first month of her hurry and flurry Mrs Arkwright was a happy woman. She would see her mother again and her sisters. It was now four years since she had left them on the quay at Southampton, while all their hearts were broken at the parting. She was a young bride then, going forth with her new lord to meet the stern world. He had then been home to look for a wife, and he had found what he looked for in the younger sister of his partner. For he, Henry Arkwright, and his wife's brother, Abel Ring, had established themselves together in San José. And now, she thought, how there would be another meeting on those quays at which there should be no broken hearts; at which there should be love without sorrow, and kisses, sweet with the sweetness of welcome, not bitter with the bitterness of parting. And people told her – the few neighbours around her – how happy, how fortunate she was to get home thus early in her life. They had been out some ten – some twenty years, and still the day of their return was distant. And then she pressed her living baby to her breast, and wiped away a tear as she thought of the other darling whom she would leave beneath that distant sod.

And then came the question as to the route home. San José stands in the middle of the high plain of Costa Rica, halfway between the Pacific and the Atlantic. The journey thence down to the Pacific is, by comparison, easy. There is a road, and the mules on which the travellers must ride go steadily and easily down to Punta Arenas, the port on that ocean. There are inns, too, on the way – places of public entertainment at which refreshment may be obtained, and beds, or fair substitutes for beds. But then by this route the traveller must take a long additional sea voyage. He must convey himself and his weary baggage down to that wretched place on the Pacific, there wait for a steamer to take him to Panama, cross the isthmus, and reship himself in the other waters for his long journey home. That terrible unshipping and reshipping is a sore burden to the unaccustomed traveller. When it is absolutely necessary – then indeed it is done without much thought; but in the case of the Arkwrights it was not absolutely necessary. And there was another reason which turned Mrs Arkwright's heart against that journey by Punt' Arenas. The place is unhealthy, having at certain seasons a very bad name – and here on their outward journey her husband had been taken ill. She had never ceased to think of the fortnight she had spent there among uncouth strangers, during a portion of which his life had trembled in the balance. Early, therefore, in those four months she begged that she might not be taken round by Punt' Arenas. There was another route. 'Harry, if you love me, let me go by the Serapiqui.' As to Harry's loving her, there was no doubt about that, as she well knew.

There was this other route by the Serapiqui River, and by Greytown. Greytown, it is true, is quite as unhealthy as Punt' Arenas, and by that route one's baggage must be shipped and unshipped into small boats. There are all manner of difficulties attached to it. Perhaps no direct road to and from any city on the world's surface is subject to sharper fatigue while it lasts. Journeying by this route also, the traveller leaves San José mounted on his mule, and so mounted he makes his way through the vast primeval forests down to the banks of the Serapiqui River. That there is a track for him is of course true; but it is simply a track, and during nine months of the twelve is so deep in mud that the mules sink in it to their bellies. Then, when the river has been reached, the traveller seats him in his canoe, and for two days is paddled down – down along the Serapiqui, into the San Juan River, and down along the San Juan till he reaches Greytown, passing one night at some hut on the riverside. At Greytown he waits for the steamer which will carry him the first stage on his road towards Southampton. He must be a connoisseur in disagreeables of every kind who can say with any precision whether Greytown or Punt' Arenas is the better place for a week's sojourn.

For a full month Mr Arkwright would not give way to his wife. At first he all but conquered her by declaring that the Serapiqui journey would be dangerous for the baby; but she heard from someone that it could be made less fatiguing for the baby than the other route. A baby had been carried down in a litter strapped on to a mule's back. A guide at the mule's head would be necessary, and that was all. When once in her boat the baby would be as well as in her cradle. What purpose cannot a woman gain by perseverance? Her purpose in this instance Mrs Arkwright did at last gain by persevering.

And then their preparations for the journey went on with much flurrying and hot haste. To us at home, who live and feel our life every day, the manufacture of endless baby-linen and the packing of mountains of clothes does not give an idea of much pleasurable excitement; but at San José, where there was scarcely motion enough in existence to prevent its waters from becoming foul with stagnation, this packing of baby-linen was delightful, and for a month or so the days went by with happy wings.

But by degrees reports began to reach both Arkwright and his wife as to this new route, which made them uneasy. The wet season had been prolonged, and even though they might not be deluged by rain themselves, the path would be in such a state of mud as to render the labour incessant. One or two people declared that the road was unfit at any time for a woman – and now the river would be much swollen. These tidings did not reach Arkwright and his wife together, or at any rate not till late amidst their preparations, or a change might still have been made. As it was, after all her entreaties, Mrs Arkwright did not like to ask him again to alter his plans; and he, having altered them once, was averse to change them again. So things went on till the mules and the boats had been hired, and things had gone so far that no change could then be made without much cost and trouble.

During the last ten days of their sojourn at San José, Mrs Arkwright had lost all that appearance of joy which had cheered up her sweet face during the last few months. Terror at that terrible journey obliterated in her mind all the happiness which had arisen from the hope of being soon at home. She was thoroughly cowed by the danger to be encountered, and would gladly have gone down to Punt' Arenas had it been now possible that she could so arrange it. It rained, and rained, and still rained, when there was now only a week from the time they started. Oh! if they could only wait for another month! But this she said to no one. After what had passed between her and her husband, she had not the heart to say such words to him. Arkwright himself was a man not given to much talking, a silent thoughtful man, stern withal in his outward bearing, but tender-hearted and loving in his nature. The sweet young wife who had left all, and come with him out to that dull distant place, was very dear to him – dearer than she herself was aware, and in these days he was thinking much of her coming troubles. Why had he given way to her foolish prayers? Ah, why indeed? And thus the last few days of their sojourn in San José passed away from them. Once or twice during these days she did speak out, expressing her fears. Her feelings were too much for her, and she could not restrain herself. 'Poor mamma,' she said, 'I shall never see her!' And then again, 'Harry, I know I shall never reach home alive.'

'Fanny, my darling, that is nonsense.' But in order that his spoken word might not sound stern to her, he took her in his arms and kissed her.

'You must behave well, Fanny,' he said to her the day before they started. Though her heart was then very low within her, she promised him that she would do her best, and then she made a great resolution. Though she should be dying on the road, she would not complain beyond the absolute necessity of her nature. She fully recognised his thoughtful tender kindness, for though he thus cautioned her, he never told her that the dangers which she feared were the result of her own choice. He never threw in her teeth those prayers which she had made, in yielding to which he knew that he had been weak.

Then came the morning of their departure. The party of travellers consisted of four besides the baby. There was Mr Arkwright, his wife, an English nurse, who was going to England with them, and her brother, Abel Ring, who was to accompany them as far as the Serapiqui River. When they had reached that, the real labour of the journey would be over.

They had eight mules; four for the four travellers, one for the baby, a spare mule laden simply with blankets, so that Mrs Arkwright might change in order that she should not be fatigued by the fatigue of her beast, and two for their luggage. The portion of their baggage had already been sent off by Punt' Arenas, and would meet them at the other side of the Isthmus of Panama.

For the last four days the rain had ceased – had ceased at any rate at San José. Those who knew the country well, would know that it might still be raining over those vast forests; but now as the matter was settled, they would hope for the best. On that morning on which they started the sun shone fairly, and they accepted this as an omen of good. Baby seemed to lie comfortably on her pile of blankets on the mule's back, and the face of the tall Indian guide who took his place at that mule's head pleased the anxious mother.

'Not leave him ever,' he said in Spanish, laying his hand on the cord which was fastened to the beast's head; and not for one moment did he leave his charge, though the labour of sticking close to him was very great.

They had four attendants or guides, all of whom made the journey on foot. That they were all men of mixed race was probable; but three of them would have been called Spaniards, Spaniards, that is, of Costa Rica, and the other would be called an Indian. One of the Spaniards was the leader, or chief man of the party, but the others seemed to stand on an equal footing with each other; and indeed the place of greatest care had been given to the Indian.

For the first four or five miles their route lay along the high road which leads from San José to Punt' Arenas, and so far a group of acquaintances followed them, all mounted on mules. Here, where the ways forked, their road leading through the great forests to the Atlantic, they separated, and many tears were shed on each side. What might be the future life of the Arkwrights had not been absolutely fixed, but there was a strong hope on their part that they might never be forced to return to Costa Rica. Those from whom they now parted had not seemed to be dear to them in any especial degree while they all lived together in the same small town, seeing each other day by day; but now – now that they might never meet again, a certain love sprang up for the old familiar faces, and women kissed each other who hitherto had hardly cared to enter each other's houses.

And then the party of the Arkwrights again started, and its steady work began. In the whole of the first day the way beneath their feet was tolerably good, and the weather continued fine. It was one long gradual ascent from the plain where the roads parted, but there was no real labour in travelling. Mrs Arkwright rode beside her baby's mule, at the head of which the Indian always walked, and the two men went together in front. The husband had found that his wife would prefer this, as long as the road allowed of such an arrangement. Her heart was too full to admit of much speaking, and so they went on in silence.

The first night was passed in a hut by the roadside, which seemed to be deserted – a hut or rancho as it is called in that country. Their food they had, of course, brought with them; and here, by common consent, they endeavoured in some sort to make themselves merry.

'Fanny,' Arkwright said to her, 'it is not so bad after all; eh, my darling?'

'No,' she answered; 'only that the mule tires one so. Will all the days be as long as that?'

He had not the heart to tell her that as regarded hours of work, that first day must of necessity be the shortest. They had risen to a considerable altitude, and the night was very cold; but baby was enveloped among a pile of coloured blankets, and things did not go very badly with them; only this, that when Fanny Arkwright rose from her hard bed, her limbs were more weary and much more stiff than they had been when Arkwright had lifted her from her mule.

On the second morning they mounted before the day had quite broken, in order that they might breakfast on the summit of the ridge which separates the two oceans. At this spot the good road comes to an end, and the forest track begins; and here also, they would, in truth, enter the forest, though their path had for some time been among straggling trees and bushes. And now, again, they rode two and two, up to this place of halting, Arkwright and Ring well knowing that from hence their labours would in truth commence.

Poor Mrs Arkwright, when she reached this resting-place, would fain have remained there for the rest of the day. One word, in her low, plaintive voice, she said, asking whether they might not sleep in the large shed which stands there. But this was manifestly impossible. At such a pace they would never reach Greytown; and she spoke no further word when he told her that they must go on.

At about noon that day the file of travellers formed itself into the line which it afterwards kept during the whole of the journey, and then started by the narrow path into the forest. First walked the leader of the guides, then another man following him; Abel Ring came next, and behind him the maid-servant; then the baby's mule, with the Indian ever at its head; close at his heels followed Mrs Arkwright, so that the mother's eye might be always on her child; and after her her husband; then another guide on foot completed the number of the travellers. In this way they went on and on, day after day, till they reached the banks of the Serapiqui, never once varying their places in the procession. As they started in the morning, so they went on till their noonday's rest, and so again they made their evening march. In that journey there was no idea of variety, no searching after the pleasures of scenery, no attempts at conversation with any object of interest or amusement. What words were spoken were those simply needful, or produced by sympathy for suffering. So they journeyed, always in the same places, with one exception. They began their work with two guides leading them, but before the first day was over one of them had fallen back to the side of Mrs Arkwright, for she was unable to sit on her mule without support.

Their daily work was divided into two stages, so as to give some hours for rest in the middle of the day. It had been arranged that the distance for each day should not be long – should be very short as was thought by them all when they talked it over at San José; but now the hours which they passed in the saddle seemed to be endless. Their descent began from that ridge of which I have spoken, and they had no sooner turned their faces down upon the mountain slopes looking towards the Atlantic, than that passage of mud began to which there was no cessation till they found themselves on the banks of the Serapiqui River. I doubt whether it be possible to convey in words an adequate idea of the labour of riding over such a path. It is not that any active exertion is necessary – that there is anything which requires doing. The traveller has before him the simple task of sitting on his mule from hour to hour, and of seeing that his knees do not get themselves jammed against the trees; but at every step the beast he rides has to drag his legs out from the deep clinging mud, and the body of the rider never knows one moment of ease. Why the mules do not die on the road, I cannot say. They live through it, and do not appear to suffer. They have their own way in everything, for no exertion on the rider's part will make them walk either faster or slower than is their wont.

On the day on which they entered the forest – that being the second of their journey – Mrs Arkwright had asked for mercy, for permission to escape that second stage. On the next she allowed herself to be lifted into her saddle after her midday rest without a word. She had tried to sleep, but in vain; and had sat within a little hut, looking out upon the desolate scene before her, with her baby in her lap. She had this one comfort, that of all the travellers, she, the baby, suffered the least. They had now left the high grounds, and the heat was becoming great, though not as yet intense. And then, the Indian guide, looking out slowly over the forest, saw that the rain was not yet over. He spoke a word or two to one of his companions in a low voice and in a patois which Mrs Arkwright did not understand, and then going after the husband, told him that the heavens were threatening.

'We have only two leagues,' said Arkwright, 'and it may perhaps hold up.'

'It will begin in an hour,' said the Indian, 'and the two leagues are four hours.'

'And tomorrow,' asked Arkwright.

'Tomorrow, and tomorrow, and tomorrow it will still rain,' said the guide, looking as he spoke up over the huge primeval forest.

'Then we had better start at once,' said Arkwright, 'before the first falling drops frighten the women.' So the mules were brought out, and he lifted his uncomplaining wife on to the blankets which formed her pillion. The file again formed itself, and slowly they wound their way out from the small enclosure by which the hut was surrounded, out from the enclosure on to a rough scrap of undrained pasture ground from which the trees had been cleared. In a few minutes they were once more struggling through the mud.

The name of the spot which our travellers had just left is Carablanco. There they found a woman living all alone. Her husband was away, she told them, at San José, but would be back to her when the dry weather came, to round up the young cattle which were straying in the forest. What a life for a woman! Nevertheless, in talking with Mrs Arkwright she made no complaint of her own lot, but had done what little she could to comfort the poor lady who was so little able to bear the fatigues of her journey.

'Is the road very bad?' Mrs Arkwright asked her in a whisper.

'Ah, yes; it is a bad road.'

'And when shall we be at the river?'

'It took me four days,' said the woman.

'Then I shall never see my mother again,' and as she spoke Mrs Arkwright pressed her baby to her bosom. Immediately after that her husband came in, and they started.

Their path now led away across the slope of a mountain which seemed to fall from the very top of that central ridge in an unbroken descent down to the valley at its foot. Hitherto, since they had entered the forest, they had had nothing before their eyes but the trees and bushes which grew close around them. But now a prospect of unrivalled grandeur was opened before them, if only had they been able to enjoy it. At the bottom of the valley ran a river, which, so great was the depth, looked like a moving silver cord; and on the other side of this there arose another mountain, steep but unbroken like that which they were passing – unbroken, so that the eye could stretch from the river up to the very summit. Not a spot on that mountainside or on their side either was left uncovered by thick forest, which had stood there untouched by man since nature first produced it.

But all this was nothing to our travellers, nor was the clang of the macaws anything, or the roaring of the little congo ape. Nothing was gained by them from beautiful scenery, nor was there any fear from the beasts of prey. The immediate pain of each step of the journey drove all other feelings from them, and their thoughts were bounded by an intense desire for the evening halt.

And then, as the guide had prophesied, the rain began. At first it came in such small soft drops that it was found to be refreshing, but the clouds soon gathered and poured forth their collected waters as though it had not rained for months among those mountains. Not that it came in big drops, or with the violence which wind can give it, beating hither and thither, breaking branches from the trees, and rising up again as it pattered against the ground. There was no violence in the rain. It fell softly in a long, continuous, noiseless stream, sinking into everything that it touched, converting the deep rich earth on all sides into mud.

Not a word was said by any of them as it came on. The Indian covered the baby with her blanket, closer than she was covered before, and the guide who walked by Mrs Arkwright's side drew her cloak around her knees. But such efforts were in vain. There is a rain that will penetrate everything, and such was the rain which fell upon them now. Nevertheless, as I have said, hardly a word was spoken. The poor woman, finding that the heat of her cloak increased her sufferings, threw it open again.

'Fanny,' said her husband, 'you had better let him protect you as well as he can.'

She answered him merely by an impatient wave of her hand, intending to signify that she could not speak, but that in this matter she must have her way.

After that her husband made no further attempt to control her. He could see, however, that ever and again she would have slipped forward from her mule and fallen, had not the man by her side steadied her with his hand. At every tree he protected her knees and feet, though there was hardly room for him to move between the beast and the bank against which he was thrust.

And then, at last, that day's work was also over, and Fanny Arkwright slipped from her pillion down into her husband's arms at the door of another rancho in the forest. Here there lived a large family adding from year to year to the patch of ground which they had rescued from the wood, and valiantly doing their part in the extension of civilisation. Our party was but a few steps from the door when they left their mules, but Mrs Arkwright did not now as heretofore hasten to receive her baby in her arms. When placed upon the ground, she still leaned against the mule, and her husband saw that he must carry her into the hut. This he did, and then, wet, mud-laden, dishevelled as she was, she laid herself down upon the planks that were to form her bed, and there stretched out her arms for her infant. On that evening they undressed and tended her like a child; and then when she was alone with her husband, she repeated to him her sad foreboding.

'Harry,' she said, 'I shall never see my mother again.'

'Oh, yes, Fanny, you will see her and talk over all these troubles with pleasure. It is very bad, I know; but we shall live through it yet.'

'You will, of course; and you will take baby home to her.'

'And face her without you! No, my darling. Three more days' riding, or rather two and a half, will bring us to the river, and then your trouble will be over. All will be easy after that.'

'Ah, Harry, you do not know.'

'I do know that it is very bad, my girl, but you must cheer up. We shall be laughing at all this in a month's time.'

On the following morning she allowed herself to be lifted up, speaking no word of remonstrance. Indeed she was like a child in their hands, having dropped all the dignity and authority of a woman's demeanour. It rained again during the whole of this day, and the heat was becoming oppressive as every hour they were descending nearer and nearer to the sea level. During this first stage hardly a word was spoken by anyone; but when she was again taken from her mule she was in tears. The poor servant-girl, too, was almost prostrate with fatigue, and absolutely unable to wait upon her mistress, or even to do anything for herself. Nevertheless they did make the second stage, seeing that their midday resting place had been under the trees of the forest. Had there been any hut there, they would have remained for the night.

On the following day they rested altogether, though the place at which they remained had but few attractions. It was another forest hut inhabited by an old Spanish couple who were by no means willing to give them room, although they paid for their accommodation at exorbitant rates. It is one singularity of places strange and out of the way, like such forest tracks as these, that money in small sums is hardly valued. Dollars there were not appreciated as sixpences are in this rich country. But there they stayed for a day, and the guides employed themselves in making a litter with long poles so that they might carry Mrs Arkwright over a portion of the ground. Poor fellows! When once she had thus changed her mode of conveyance, she never again was lifted on to the mule.

There was strong reason against this day's delay. They were to go down the Serapiqui along with the post, which would overtake them on its banks. But if the post should pass them before they got there, it could not wait; and then they would be deprived of the best canoe on the water. Then also it was possible, if they encountered further delay, that the steamer might sail from Greytown without them, and a month's residence at that frightful place be thus made necessary.

The day's rest apparently did little to relieve Mrs Arkwright's sufferings. On the following day she allowed herself to be put upon the mule, but after the first hour the beasts were stopped and she was taken off it. During that hour they had travelled hardly over half a league. At that time she so sobbed and moaned that Arkwright absolutely feared that she would perish in the forest, and he implored the guides to use the poles which they had prepared. She had declared to him over and over again that she felt sure that she should die, and, half-delirious with weariness and suffering, had begged him to leave her at the last hut. They had not yet come to the flat ground over which a litter might be carried with comparative ease; but nevertheless the men yielded, and she was placed in a recumbent position upon blankets, supported by boughs of trees. In this way she went through that day with somewhat less of suffering than before, and without that necessity for self-exertion which had been worse to her than any suffering.

There were places between that and the river at which one would have said that it was impossible that a litter should be carried, or even impossible that a mule should walk with a load on his back. But still they went on, and the men carried their burden without complaining. Not a word was said about money or extra pay – not a word, at least by them; and when Arkwright was profuse in his offer, their leader told him that they would not have done it for money. But for the poor suffering señora they would make exertions which no money would have bought from them.

On the next day about noon the post did pass them, consisting of three strong men carrying great weights on their backs, suspended by bands from their foreheads. They travelled much quicker than our friends, and would reach the banks of the river that evening. In their ordinary course they would start down the river close upon daybreak on the following day; but, after some consultation with the guides, they agreed to wait till noon. Poor Mrs Arkwright knew nothing of hours or of any such arrangements now, but her husband greatly doubted their power of catching this mail dispatch. However, it did not much depend on their exertions that afternoon. Their resting-place was marked out for them, and they could not go beyond it, unless indeed they could make the whole journey, which was impossible.

But towards evening matters seemed to improve with them. They had now got on to ground which was more open, and the men who carried the litter could walk with greater ease. Mrs Arkwright also complained less, and when they reached their resting-place on that night, said nothing of a wish to be left there to her fate. This was a place called Padregal, a cacao plantation, which had been cleared in the forest with much labour. There was a house here containing three rooms, and some forty or fifty acres round it had been stripped of the forest trees. But nevertheless the adventure had not been a prosperous one, for the place was at that time deserted. There were the cacao plants, but there was no one to pick the cacao. There was a certain melancholy beauty about the place. A few grand trees had been left standing near the house, and the grass around was rich and park-like. But it was deserted, and nothing was heard but the roaring of the congos. Ah me! Indeed it was a melancholy place, as it was seen by some of that party afterwards.

On the following morning they were astir very early, and Mrs Arkwright was so much better that she offered to sit again upon her mule. The men, however, declared that they would finish their task, and she was placed again upon the litter. And then with slow and weary step they did make their way to the river bank. It was not yet noon when they saw the mud fort which stands there, and as they drew into the enclosure round a small house which stands close by the riverside, they saw the three postmen still busy about their packages.

'Thank God!' said Arkwright.

'Thank God, indeed!' said his brother. 'All will be right with you now.'

'Well, Fanny,' said her husband, as he took her very gently from the litter and seated her on a bench which stood outside the door. 'It is all over now – is it not?'

She answered him by a shower of tears, but they were tears which brought her relief. He was aware of this, and therefore stood by her, still holding her by both her hands while her head rested against his side. 'You will find the motion of the boat very gentle,' he said; 'indeed there will be no motion, and you and baby will sleep all the way down to Greytown.' She did not answer him in words, but she looked up into his face, and he could see that her spirit was recovering itself.

There was almost a crowd of people collected on the spot, preparatory to the departure of the canoes. In the first place there was the commandant of the fort, to whom the small house belonged. He was looking to the passports of our friends, and with due diligence endeavouring to make something of the occasion by discovering fatal legal impediments to the further prosecution of their voyage, which impediments would disappear on the payment of certain dollars. And then there were half a dozen Costa Rican soldiers, men with coloured caps and old muskets, ready to support the dignity and authority of the commandant. There were the guides taking payment from Abel Ring for their past work, and the postmen preparing their boats for the further journey. And then there was a certain German there, with a German servant, to whom the boats belonged. He also was very busy preparing for the river voyage. He was not going down with them, but it was his business to see them well started. A singular looking man was he, with a huge shaggy beard, and shaggy uncombed hair, but with bright blue eyes, which gave to his face a remarkable look of sweetness. He was an uncouth man to the eye, and yet a child would have trusted herself with him in a forest.

At this place they remained some two hours. Coffee was prepared here, and Mrs Arkwright refreshed herself and her child. They washed and arranged their clothes, and when she stepped down the steep bank, clinging to her husband's arm as she made her way towards the boat, she smiled upon him as he looked at her.

'It is all over now, is it not, my girl?' he said, encouraging her.

'Oh, Harry, do not talk about it,' she answered, shuddering.

'But I want you to say a word to me to let me know that you are better.'

'I am better – much better.'

'And you will see your mother again; will you not; and give baby to her yourself?'

To this she made no immediate answer, for she was on a level with the river, and the canoe was close at her feet. And then she had to bid farewell to her brother. He was now the unfortunate one of the party, for his destiny required that he should go back to San José alone – go back and remain there perhaps some ten years longer before he might look for the happiness of home.

'God bless you, dearest Abel,' she said, kissing him and sobbing as she spoke.

'Goodbye, Fanny,' he said, 'and do not let them forget me in England. It is a great comfort to think that the worst of your troubles are over.'

'Oh, she's all right now,' said Arkwright. 'Goodbye, old boy' – and the two brothers-in-law grasped each other's hands heartily. 'Keep up your spirits, and we'll have you home before long.'

'Oh, I'm all right,' said the other. But from the tone of the voices, it was clear that poor Ring was despondent at the thoughts of his coming solitude, and that Arkwright was already triumphing in his emancipation.

And then, with much care, Fanny Arkwright was stowed away in the boat. There was a great contest about the baby, but at last it was arranged that at any rate for the first few hours she should be placed in the boat with the servant. The mother was told that by this plan she would feel herself at liberty to sleep during the heat of the day, and then she might hope to have strength to look to the child when they should be on shore during the night. In this way therefore they prepared to start, while Abel Ring stood on the bank looking at them with wishful eyes. In the first boat were two Indians paddling, and a third man steering with another paddle. In the middle there was much luggage, and near the luggage so as to be under shade, was the baby's soft bed. If nothing evil happened to the boat, the child could not be more safe in the best cradle that was ever rocked. With her was the maid-servant and some stranger who was also going down to Greytown.

In the second boat were the same number of men to paddle, the Indian guide being one of them, and there were the mails placed. Then there was a seat arranged with blankets, cloaks and cushions for Mrs Arkwright, so that she might lean back and sleep without fatigue, and immediately opposite to her her husband placed himself. 'You all look very comfortable,' said poor Abel from the bank.

'We shall do very well now,' said Arkwright.

'And I do think I shall see mamma again,' said his wife.

'That's right, old girl – of course you will see her. Now then, we are all ready.' And with some little assistance from the German on the bank, the first boat was pushed off into the stream.

The river in this place is rapid, because the full course of the water is somewhat impeded by a bank of earth jutting out from the opposite side of the river into the stream; but it is not so rapid as to make any recognised danger in the embarkation. Below this bank, which is opposite to the spot at which the boats were entered, there were four or five broken trees in the water, some of the shattered boughs of which showed themselves above the surface. These are called snags, and are very dangerous if they are met with in the course of the stream; but in this instance no danger was apprehended from them, as they lay considerably to the left of the passage which the boats would take. The first canoe was pushed off by the German, and went rapidly away. The waters were strong with rain, and it was pretty to see with what velocity the boat was carried on some hundred yards in advance of the other by the force of the first effort of the paddle. The German, however, from the bank holloaed to the first men in Spanish, bidding them relax their efforts for awhile; and then he said a word or two of caution to those who were now on the point of starting.

The boat then was pushed steadily forward, the man at the stern keeping it with his paddle a little farther away from the bank at which they had embarked. It was close under the land that the stream ran the fastest, and in obedience to the directions given to him he made his course somewhat nearer to the sunken trees. It was but one turn of his hand that gave the light boat its direction, but that turn of the hand was too strong. Had the anxious master of the canoes been but a thought less anxious, all might have been well; but, as it was, the prow of the boat was caught by some slight hidden branch which impeded its course and turned it round in the rapid river. The whole lengths of the canoe was thus brought against the sunken tree, and in half a minute the five occupants of the boat were struggling in the stream.

Abel Ring and the German were both standing on the bank close to the water when this happened, and each for a moment looked into the other's face. 'Stand where you are,' shouted the German, 'so that you may assist them from the shore. I will go in.' And then, throwing from him his boots and coat, he plunged into the river.

The canoe had been swept round so as to be brought by the force of the waters absolutely in among the upturned roots and broken stumps of the trees which impeded the river, and thus, when the party was upset, they were at first to be seen scrambling among the branches. But unfortunately there was much more wood below the water than above it, and the force of the stream was so great that those who caught hold of the timber were not able to support themselves by it above the surface. Arkwright was soon to be seen some forty yards down, having been carried clear of the trees, and here he got out of the river on the farther bank. The distance to him was not above forty yards, but from the nature of the ground he could not get up towards his wife, unless he could have forced his way against the stream.

The Indian who had had charge of the baby rose quickly to the surface, was carried once round in the eddy, with his head high above the water, and then was seen to throw himself among the broken wood. He had seen the dress of the poor woman, and made his effort to save her. The other two men were so caught by the fragments of the boughs, that they could not extricate themselves so as to make any exertions; ultimately, however, they also got out on the farther bank.

Mrs Arkwright had sunk at once on being precipitated into the water, but the buoyancy of her clothes had brought her for a moment again to the surface. She had risen for a moment, and then had again gone down, immediately below the forked trunk of a huge tree; had gone down, alas, alas! never to rise again with life within her bosom. The poor Indian made two attempts to save her, and then came up himself, incapable of further effort.

It was then that the German, the owner of the canoes, who had fought his way with great efforts across the violence of the waters, and indeed up against the stream for some few yards, made his effort to save the life of that poor frail creature. He had watched the spot at which she had gone down, and even while struggling across the river, had seen how the Indian had followed her and had failed. It was now his turn. His life was in his hand, and he was prepared to throw it away in that attempt. Having succeeded in placing himself a little above the large tree, he turned his face towards the bottom of the river, and dived down among the branches. And he also, after that, was never again seen with the life-blood flowing round his heart.

When the sun set that night, the two swollen corpses were lying in the commandant's hut, and Abel Ring and Arkwright were sitting beside them. Arkwright had his baby sleeping in his arms, but he sat there for hours, into the middle of the long night, without speaking a word to anyone.

'Harry,' said his brother at last, 'come away and lie down. It will be good for you to sleep.'

'Nothing ever will be good again for me,' said he.

'You must bear up against your sorrow as other men do,' said Ring.

'Why am I not sleeping with her as the poor German sleeps? Why did I let another man take my place in dying for her?' And then he walked away that the other might not see the tears on his face.

It was a sad night, that at the commandant's hut, and a sad morning followed upon it. It must be remembered that they had there none of those appurtenances which are so necessary to make woe decent and misfortune comfortable. They sat through the night in the small hut, and in the morning they came forth with their clothes still wet and dirty, with their haggard faces and weary stiff limbs, encumbered with the horrid task of burying that loved body among the forest trees. And then, to keep life in them till it was done, the brandy flask passed from hand to hand; and after that, with slow but resolute efforts, they reformed the litter on which the living woman had been carried thither, and took her body back to the wild plantation at Padregal. There they dug for her her grave, and repeating over her some portion of the service for the dead, left her to sleep the sleep of death. But before they left her, they erected a pallisade of timber round the grave, so that the beasts of the forest should not tear the body from its resting-place.

When that was done Arkwright and his brother made their slow journey back to San José. The widowed husband could not face his darling's mother with such a tale upon his tongue as that.

The Mistletoe Bough

'Let the boys have it if they like it,' said Mrs Garrow, pleading to her only daughter on behalf of her two sons.

'Pray don't, mamma,' said Elizabeth Garrow. 'It only means romping. To me all that is detestable, and I am sure it is not the sort of thing that Miss Holmes would like.'

'We always had it at Christmas when we were young.'

'But, mamma, the world is so changed.'

The point in dispute was one very delicate in its nature, hardly to be discussed in all its bearings, even in fiction, and the very mention of which between mother and daughter showed a great amount of close confidence between them. It was no less than this. Should that branch of mistletoe which Frank Garrow had brought home with him out of the Lowther woods be hung up on Christmas Eve in the dining-room at Thwaite Hall, according to his wishes; or should permission for such hanging be positively refused? It was clearly a thing not to be done after such a discussion, and therefore the decision given by Mrs Garrow was against it.

I am inclined to think that Miss Garrow was right in saying that the world is changed as touching mistletoe boughs. Kissing, I fear, is less innocent now than it used to be when our grandmothers were alive, and we have become more fastidious in our amusements. Nevertheless, I think that she made herself fairly open to the raillery with which her brothers attacked her.

'*Honi soit qui mal y pense*,' said Frank, who was eighteen.

'Nobody will want to kiss you, my lady Fineairs,' said Harry, who was just a year younger.

'Because you choose to be a Puritan, there are to be no more cakes and ale in the house,' said Frank.

'Still waters run deep; we all know that,' said Harry.

The boys had not been present when the matter was decided between Mrs Garrow and her daughter, nor had the mother been present when these little amenities had passed between the brothers and sister.

'Only that mamma has said it, and I wouldn't seem to go against her,' said Frank, 'I'd ask my father. He wouldn't give way to such nonsense, I know.'

Elizabeth turned away without answering, and left the room. Her eyes were full of tears, but she would not let them see that they had vexed her. They were only two days home from school, and for the last week before their coming, all her thoughts had been to prepare for their Christmas pleasures. She had arranged their rooms, making everything warm and pretty. Out of her own pocket she had bought a shot-belt for one, and skates for the other. She had told the old groom that her pony was to belong exclusively to Master Harry for the holidays, and now Harry told her that still waters ran deep. She had been driven to the use of all her eloquence in inducing her father to purchase that gun for Frank, and now Frank called her a Puritan. And why? She did not choose that a mistletoe bough should be hung in her father's hall when Godfrey Holmes was coming to visit him. She could not explain this to Frank, but Frank might have had the wit to understand it. But Frank was thinking only of Patty Coverdale, a blue-eyed little romp of sixteen, who, with her sister Kate, was coming from Penrith to spend the Christmas at Thwaite Hall. Elizabeth left the room with her slow, graceful step, hiding her tears – hiding all emotion, as latterly she had taught herself that it was feminine to do. 'There goes my lady Fineairs,' said Harry, sending his shrill voice after her.

Thwaite Hall was not a place of much pretension. It was a moderate-sized house, surrounded by pretty gardens and shrubberies, close down upon the River Eamont, on the Westmoreland side of the river, looking over to a lovely wooded bank in Cumberland. All the world knows that the Eamont runs out of Ullswater, dividing the two counties, passing under Penrith Bridge and by the old ruins of Brougham Castle, below which it joins the Eden. Thwaite Hall nestled down close upon the clear rocky stream about halfway between Ullswater and Penrith, and had been built just at a bend of the river. The windows of the dining-parlour and of the drawing-room stood at right angles to each other, and yet each commanded a reach of the stream. Immediately from a side of the house steps were cut down through the red rock to the water's edge, and here a small boat was always moored to a chain. The chain was stretched across the river, fixed to the staples driven into the rock on either side, and the boat was pulled backwards and forwards over the stream without aid from oars or paddles. From the opposite side a path led through the woods and across the fields to Penrith, and this was the route commonly used between Thwaite Hall and the town.

Major Garrow was a retired officer of engineers, who had seen service in all parts of the world, and who was now spending the evening of his days on a small property which had come to him from his father. He held in his own hands about twenty acres of land, and he was the owner of one small farm close by, which was let to a tenant. That, together with his half-pay, and the interest of his wife's thousand pounds, sufficed to educate his children and keep the wolf at a comfortable distance from his door. He himself was a spare thin man, with quiet, lazy, literary habits. He had done the work of life, but had so done it as to permit of his enjoying that which was left to him. His sole remaining care was the establishment of his children; and, as far as he could see, he had no ground for anticipating disappointment. They were clever, good-looking, well-disposed young people, and upon the whole it may be said that the sun shone brightly on Thwaite Hall. Of Mrs Garrow it may suffice to say that she always deserved such sunshine.

For years past it had been the practice of the family to have some sort of gathering at Thwaite Hall during Christmas. Godfrey Holmes had been left under the guardianship of Major Garrow, and, as he had always spent his Christmas holidays with his guardian, this, perhaps, had given rise to the practice. Then the Coverdales were cousins of the Garrows, and they had usually been there as children. At the Christmas last past the custom had been broken, for young Holmes had been abroad. Previous to that, they had all been children, excepting him. But now that they were to meet again, they were no longer children. Elizabeth, at any rate, was not so, for she had already counted nineteen winters. And Isabella Holmes was coming. Now Isabella was two years older than Elizabeth, and had been educated in Brussels; moreover she was comparatively a stranger at Thwaite Hall, never having been at those early Christmas meetings.

And now I must take permission to begin my story by telling a lady's secret. Elizabeth Garrow had already been in love with Godfrey Holmes, or perhaps it might be more becoming to say that Godfrey Holmes had already been in love with her. They had already been engaged; and, alas! they had already agreed that that engagement should be broken off!

Young Holmes was now twenty-seven years of age, and was employed in a bank at Liverpool, not as a clerk, but as assistant-manager, with a large salary. He was a man well to do in the world, who had money also of his own, and who might well afford to marry. Some two years since, on the eve of leaving Thwaite Hall, he had with low doubting whisper told Elizabeth that he loved her, and she had flown trembling to her mother. 'Godfrey, my boy,' the father said to him, as he parted with him the next morning, 'Bessy is only a child, and too young to think of this yet.' At the next Christmas Godfrey was in Italy, and the thing was gone by – so at least the father and mother said to each other. But the young people had met in the summer, and one joyful letter had come from the girl home to her mother. 'I have accepted him. Dearest, dearest mamma, I do love him. But don't tell papa yet, for I have not quite accepted him. I think I am sure, but I am not quite sure. I am not quite sure about him.'

And then, two days after that, there had come a letter that was not at all joyful. 'Dearest Mamma – It is not to be. It is not written in the book. We have both agreed that it will not do. I am so glad that you have not told dear papa, for I could never make him understand. You will understand, for I shall tell you everything, down to his very words. But we have agreed that there shall be no quarrel. It shall be exactly as it was, and he will come at Christmas all the same. It would never do that he and papa should be separated, nor could we now put off Isabella. It is better so in every way, for there is and need be no quarrel. We still like each other. I am sure I like him, but I know that I should not make him happy as his wife. He says it is my fault. I, at any rate, have never told him that I thought it his.' From all which it will be seen that the confidence between the mother and daughter was very close.

Elizabeth Garrow was a very good girl, but it might almost be a question whether she was not too good. She had learned, or thought that she had learned, that most girls are vapid, silly and useless – given chiefly to pleasure-seeking and a hankering after lovers; and she had resolved that she would not be such a one.

Industry, self-denial, and a religious purpose in life, were the tasks which she set herself; and she went about the performance of them with much courage. But such tasks, though they are excellently well adapted to fit a young lady for the work of living, may also be carried too far, and thus have the effect of unfitting her for that work. When Elizabeth Garrow made up her mind that the finding of a husband was not the only purpose of life, she did very well. It is very well that a young lady should feel herself capable of going through the world happily without one. But in teaching herself this she also taught herself to think that there was a certain merit in refusing herself the natural delight of a lover, even though the possession of the lover were compatible with all her duties to herself, her father and mother, and the world at large. It was not that she had determined to have no lover. She made no such resolve, and when the proper lover came he was admitted to her heart. But she declared to herself unconsciously that she must put a guard upon herself, lest she should be betrayed into weakness by her own happiness. She had resolved that in loving her lord she would not worship him, and that in giving her heart she would only so give it as it should be given to a human creature like herself. She had acted on these high resolves, and hence it had come to pass – not unnaturally – that Mr Godfrey Holmes had told her that it was 'her fault'.

She was a pretty, fair girl, with soft dark-brown hair, and soft long dark eyelashes. Her grey eyes, though quiet in their tone, were tender and lustrous. Her face was oval, and the lines of her cheek and chin perfect in their symmetry. She was generally quiet in her demeanour, but when moved she could rouse herself to great energy, and speak with feeling and almost with fire. Her fault was a reverence for martyrdom in general, and a feeling, of which she was unconscious, that it became a young woman to be unhappy in secret – that it became a young woman, I might rather say, to have a source of unhappiness hidden from the world in general, and endured without any detriment to her outward cheerfulness. We know the story of the Spartan boy who held the fox under his tunic. The fox was biting into him, into his very entrails; but the young hero spake never a word. Now

Bessy Garrow was inclined to think that it was a good thing to have a fox always biting, so that the torment caused no ruffling to her outward smiles. Now at this moment the fox within her bosom was biting her sore enough, but she bore it without flinching.

'If you would rather that he should not come I will have it arranged,' her mother had said to her.

'Not for worlds,' she had answered. 'I should never think well of myself again.'

Her mother had changed her own mind more than once as to the conduct in this matter which might be best for her to follow, thinking solely of her daughter's welfare. 'If he comes they will be reconciled, and she will be happy,' had been her first idea. But then there was a stern fixedness of purpose in Bessy's words when she spoke of Mr Holmes, which had expelled this hope, and Mrs Garrow had for a while thought it better that the young man should not come. But Bessy would not permit this. It would vex her father, put out of course the arrangements of other people, and display weakness on her own part. He should come, and she would endure without flinching while the fox gnawed at her.

That battle of the mistletoe had been fought on the morning before Christmas Day, and the Holmeses came on Christmas Eve. Isabella was comparatively a stranger, and therefore received at first the greater share of attention. She and Elizabeth had once seen each other, and for the last year or two had corresponded, but personally they had never been intimate. Unfortunately for the latter, that story of Godfrey's offer and acceptance had been communicated to Isabella, as had of course the immediately subsequent story of their separation. But now it would be almost impossible to avoid the subject in conversation. 'Dearest Isabella, let it be as though it had never been,' she had said in one of her letters. But sometimes it is very difficult to let things be as though they had never been.

The first evening passed over very well. The two Coverdale girls were there, and there had been much talking and merry laughter, rather juvenile in its nature, but on the whole none the worse for that. Isabella Holmes was a fine, tall, handsome girl; good-humoured and well disposed to be pleased; rather Frenchified in her manners, and quite able to take care of herself. But she was not above round games, and did not turn up her nose at the boys. Godfrey behaved himself excellently, talking much to the major, but by no means avoiding Miss Garrow. Mrs Garrow, though she had known him since he was a boy, had taken an aversion to him since he had quarrelled with her daughter; but there was no room on this first night for showing such aversion, and everything went off well.

'Godfrey is very much improved,' the major said to his wife that night.

'Do you think so?'

'Indeed I do. He has filled out and become a fine man.'

'In personal appearance, you mean. Yes, he is well-looking enough.'

'And in his manner, too. He is doing uncommonly well in Liverpool, I can tell you; and if he should think of Bessy – '

'There is nothing of that sort,' said Mrs Garrow.

'He did speak to me, you know – two years ago. Bessy was too young then, and so indeed was he. But if she likes him – '

'I don't think she does.'

'Then there's an end of it.' And so they went to bed.

'Frank,' said the sister to her elder brother, knocking at his door when they had all gone upstairs, 'may I come in – if you are not in bed?'

'In bed,' said he, looking up with some little pride from his Greek book; 'I've one hundred and fifty lines to do before I can get to bed. It'll be two, I suppose. I've got to mug uncommon hard these holidays. I have only one more half, you know, and then – '

'Don't overdo it, Frank.'

'No; I won't overdo it. I mean to take one day a week, and work eight hours a day on the other five. That will be forty hours a week, and will give me just two hundred hours for the holidays. I have got it all down here on a table. That will be a hundred and five for Greek, forty for Algebra – ' and so he explained to her the exact destiny of all his long hours of proposed labour. He had as yet been home a day and a half, and had succeeded in drawing out with red lines and blue figures the table which he showed her. 'If I can do that, it will be pretty well; won't it?'

'But, Frank, you have come home for your holidays – to enjoy yourself!'

'But a fellow must work nowadays.'

'Don't overdo it, dear; that's all. But, Frank, I could not rest if I went to bed without speaking to you. You made me unhappy today.'

'Did I, Bessy?'

'You called me a Puritan, and then you quoted that ill-natured French proverb at me. Do you really believe your sister thinks evil, Frank?' and as she spoke she put her arm caressingly round his neck.

'Of course I don't.'

'Then why say so? Harry is so much younger and so thoughtless that I can bear what he says without so much suffering. But if you and I are not friends I shall be very wretched. If you knew how I have looked forward to your coming home!'

'I did not mean to vex you, and I won't say such things again.'

'That's my own Frank. What I said to mamma, I said because I thought it right; but you must not say that I am a Puritan. I would do anything in my power to make your holidays bright and pleasant. I know that boys require so much more to amuse them than girls do. Good-night, dearest; pray don't overdo yourself with work, and do take care of your eyes.'

So saying she kissed him and went her way. In twenty minutes after that, he had gone to sleep over his book; and when he woke up to find the candle guttering down, he resolved that he would not begin his measured hours till Christmas Day was fairly over.

The morning of Christmas Day passed very quietly. They all went to church, and then sat round the fire chatting until the four o'clock dinner was ready. The Coverdale girls thought it was rather more dull than former Thwaite Hall festivities, and Frank was seen to yawn. But then everybody knows that the real fun of Christmas never begins till the day itself be passed. The beef and pudding are ponderous, and unless there be absolute children in the party, there is a difficulty in grafting any special afternoon amusements on the Sunday pursuits of the morning. In the evening they were to have a dance; that had been distinctly promised to Patty Coverdale; but the dance would not commence till eight. The beef and pudding were ponderous, but with due efforts they were overcome and disappeared. The glass of port was sipped, the almonds and raisins were nibbled, and then the ladies left the room. Ten minutes after that Elizabeth found herself seated with Isabella Holmes over the fire in her father's little book-room. It was not by her that this meeting was arranged, for she dreaded such a con-strained confidence; but of course it could not be avoided, and perhaps it might be as well now as hereafter.

'Bessy,' said the elder girl, 'I am dying to be alone with you for a moment.'

'Well, you shall not die; that is, if being alone with me will save you.'

'I have so much to say to you. And if you have any true friendship in you, you also will have so much to say to me.'

Miss Garrow perhaps had no true friendship in her at that moment, for she would gladly have avoided saying anything, had that been possible. But in order to prove that she was not deficient in friendship, she gave her friend her hand.

'And now tell me everything about Godfrey,' said Isabella.

'Dear Bella, I have nothing to tell – literally nothing.'

'That is nonsense. Stop a moment, dear, and understand that I do not mean to offend you. It cannot be that you have nothing to tell, if you choose to tell it. You are not the girl to have accepted Godfrey without loving him, nor is he the man to have asked you without loving you. When you write me word that you have changed your mind, as you might about a dress, of course I know you have not told me all. Now I insist upon knowing it – that is, if we are to be friends. I would not speak a word to Godfrey till I had seen you, in order that I might hear your story first.'

'Indeed, Bella, there is no story to tell.'

'Then I must ask him.'

'If you wish to play the part of a true friend to me, you will let the matter pass by and say nothing. You must understand that, circumstanced as we are, your brother's visit here – what I mean is, that it is very difficult for me to act and speak exactly as I should do, and a few unfortunate words spoken may make my position unendurable.'

'Will you answer me one question?'

'I cannot tell. I think I will.'

'Do you love him?' For a moment or two Bessy remained silent, striving to arrange her words so that they should contain no falsehood, and yet betray no truth. 'Ah, I see you do,' continued Miss Holmes. 'But of course you do. Why else did you accept him?'

'I fancied that I did, as young ladies do sometimes fancy.'

'And will you say that you do not, now?' Again Bessy was silent, and then her friend rose from her seat. 'I see it all,' she said. 'What a pity it was that you both had not some friend like me by you at the time! But perhaps it may not be too late.'

I need not repeat at length all the protestations which upon this were poured forth with hot energy by poor Bessy. She endeavoured to explain how great had been the difficulty of her position. This Christmas visit had been arranged before that unhappy affair at Liverpool had occurred. Isabella's visit had been partly one of business, it being necessary that certain money affairs should be arranged between her, her brother, and the major. 'I determined,' said Bessy, 'not to let my feelings stand in the way; and hoped that things might settle down to their former friendly footing. I already fear that I have been wrong, but it will be ungenerous in you to punish me.' Then she went on to say that if anybody attempted to interfere with her, she should at once go away to her mother's sister, who lived at Hexham, in Northumberland.

Then came the dance, and the hearts of Kate and Patty Coverdale were at last happy. But here again poor Bessy was made to understand how terribly difficult was this experiment of entertaining on a footing of friendship a lover with whom she had quarrelled only a month or two before. That she must as a necessity become the partner of Godfrey Holmes she had already calculated, and so much she was prepared to endure. Her brothers would of course dance with the Coverdale girls, and her father would of course stand up with Isabella. There was no other possible arrangement, at any rate as a beginning.

She had schooled herself, too, as to the way in which she would speak to him on the occasion, and how she would remain mistress of herself and of her thoughts. But when the time came the difficulty was almost too much for her.

'You do not care much for dancing, if I remember?' said he.

'Oh yes, I do. Not as Patty Coverdale does. It's a passion with her. But then I am older than Patty Coverdale.' After that he was silent for a minute or two.

'It seems so odd to me to be here again,' he said. It was odd; she felt that it was odd. But he ought not to have said so.

'Two years make a great difference. The boys have grown so much.'

'Yes, and there are other things,' said he.

'Bella was never here before; at least not with you.'

'No. But I did not exactly mean that. All that would not make the place so strange. But your mother seems altered to me. She used to be almost like my own mother.'

'I suppose she finds that you are a more formidable person as you grow older. It was all very well scolding you when you were a clerk in the bank, but it does not do to scold the manager. These are the penalties men pay for becoming great.'

'It is not my greatness that stands in my way, but –'

'Then I'm sure I cannot say what it is. But Patty will scold you if you do not mind the figure, though you were the whole board of directors packed into one. She won't respect you if you neglect your present work.'

When Bessy went to bed that night she began to feel that she had attempted too much. 'Mamma,' she said, 'could I not make some excuse and go away to Aunt Mary?'

'What now?'

'Yes, mamma; now; tomorrow. I need not say that it will make me very unhappy to be away at such a time, but I begin to think that it will be better.'

'What will papa say?'

'You must tell him all.'

'And Aunt Mary must be told also. You would not like that. Has he said anything?'

'No, nothing – very little, that is. But Bella has spoken to me. Oh, mamma, I think we have been very wrong in this. That is, I have been wrong. I feel as though I should disgrace myself, and turn the whole party here into a misfortune.'

It would be dreadful, that telling of the story to her father and to her aunt, and such a necessity must, if possible, be avoided. Should such a necessity actually come, the former task would, no doubt, be done by her mother, but that would not lighten the load materially. After a fortnight she would again meet her father, and would be forced to discuss it. 'I will remain if it be possible,' she said; 'but, mamma, if I wish to go, you will not stop me?' Her mother promised that she would not stop her, but strongly advised her to stand her ground.

On the following morning, when she came downstairs before breakfast, she found Frank standing in the hall with his gun, of which he was trying the lock. 'It is not loaded, is it, Frank?' said she.

'Oh dear, no; no one thinks of loading nowadays till he has got out of the house. Directly after breakfast I am going across with Godfrey to the back of Greystock, to see after some moor-fowl. He asked me to go, and I couldn't well refuse.'

'Of course not. Why should you?'

'It will be deuced hard work to make up the time. I was to have been up at four this morning, but that alarum went off and never woke me. However, I shall be able to do something tonight.'

'Don't make a slavery of your holidays, Frank. What's the good of having a new gun if you're not to use it?'

'It's not the new gun. I'm not such a child as that comes to. But, you see, Godfrey is here, and one ought to be civil to him. I'll tell you what I want you girls to do, Bessy. You must come and meet us on our way home. Come over in the boat and along the path to the Patterdale road. We'll be there under the hill about five.'

'And if you are not, we are to wait in the snow?'

'Don't make difficulties, Bessy. I tell you we will be there. We are to go in the cart, and so shall have plenty of time.'

'And how do you know the other girls will go?'

'Why, to tell you the truth, Patty Coverdale has promised. As for Miss Holmes, if she won't, why you must leave her at home with mamma. But Kate and Patty can't come without you.'

'Your discretion has found that out, has it?'

'They say so. But you will come; won't you, Bessy? As for waiting, it's all nonsense. Of course you can walk on. But we'll be at the stile by five. I've got my watch, you know.' And then Bessy promised him. What would she not have done for him that was in her power to do?

'Go! Of course I'll go,' said Miss Holmes. 'I'm up to anything. I'd have gone with them this morning, and have taken a gun if they'd asked me. But, by the by, I'd better not.'

'Why not?' said Patty, who was hardly yet without fear lest something should mar the expedition.

'What will three gentlemen do with four ladies?'

'Oh, I forgot,' said Patty innocently.

'I'm sure I don't care,' said Kate; 'you may have Harry if you like.'

'Thank you for nothing,' said Miss Holmes. 'I want one for myself. It's all very well for you to make the offer, but what should I do if Harry wouldn't have me? There are two sides, you know, to every bargain.'

'I'm sure he isn't anything to me,' said Kate. 'Why, he's not quite seventeen years old yet!'

'Poor boy! What a shame to dispose of him so soon. We'll let him off for a year or two; won't we, Miss Coverdale? But as there seems by acknowledgement to be one beau with unappropriated services – '

'I'm sure I have appropriated nobody,' said Patty, 'and didn't intend.'

'Godfrey, then, is the only knight whose services are claimed,' said Miss Holmes, looking at Bessy. Bessy made no immediate answer with either her eyes or tongue; but when the Coverdales were gone, she took her new friend to task.

'How can you fill those young girls' heads with such nonsense?'

'Nature has done that, my dear.'

'But nature should be trained; should it not? You will make them think that those foolish boys are in love with them.'

'The foolish boys, as you call them, will look after that themselves. It seems to me that the foolish boys know what they are about better than some of their elders.' And then, after a moment's pause, she added, 'As for my brother, I have no patience with him.'

'Pray do not discuss your brother,' said Bessy. 'And, Bella, unless you wish to drive me away, pray do not speak of him and me together as you did just now.'

'Are you so bad as that – that the slightest commonplace joke upsets you? Would not his services be due to you as a matter of course? If you are so sore about it, you will betray your own secret.'

'I have no secret – none at least from you, or from mamma; and, indeed, none from him. We were both very foolish, thinking that we knew each other and our own hearts when we knew neither.'

'I hate to hear people talk of knowing their hearts. My idea is that if you like a young man, and he asks you to marry him, you ought to have him. That is, if there is enough to live on. I don't know what more is wanted. But girls are getting to talk and think as though they were to send their hearts through some fiery furnace of trial before they may give them up to a husband's keeping. I am not at all sure that the French fashion is not the best, and that these things shouldn't be managed by the fathers and mothers, or perhaps by the family lawyers. Girls who are so intent upon knowing their own hearts generally end by knowing nobody's heart but their own; and die old maids.'

'Better that than give themselves to the keeping of those they don't know and cannot esteem.'

'That's a matter of taste. I mean to take the first that comes, so long as he looks like a gentleman, and has not less than eight hundred a year. Now Godfrey does look like a gentleman, and has double that. If I had such a chance I shouldn't think twice about it.'

'But I have no such chance.'

'That's the way the wind blows; is it?'

'No, no. Oh, Bella, pray, pray leave me alone. Pray do not interfere. There is no wind blowing in any way. All that I want is your silence and your sympathy.'

'Very well. I will be silent and sympathetic as the grave. Only don't imagine that I am cold as the grave also. I don't exactly appreciate your ideas; but if I can do no good, I will at any rate endeavour to do no harm.'

After lunch, at about three, they started on their walk, and managed to ferry themselves over the river. 'Oh, do let me, Bessy,' said Kate Coverdale. 'I understand all about it. Look here, Miss Holmes. You pull the chain through your hands – '

'And inevitably tear your gloves to pieces,' said Miss Holmes. Kate certainly had done so, and did not seem to be particularly well pleased with the accident. 'There's a nasty nail in the chain,' she said. 'I wonder those stupid boys did not tell us.'

Of course they reached the trysting-place much too soon, and were very tired of walking up and down to keep their feet warm before the sportsmen came up. But this was their own fault, seeing that they had reached the stile half an hour before the time fixed.

'I never will go anywhere to meet gentlemen again,' said Miss Holmes. 'It is most preposterous that ladies should be left in the snow for an hour. Well, young men, what sport have you had?'

'I shot the big black cock,' said Harry.

'Did you indeed?' said Kate Coverdale.

'And here are the feathers out of his tail for you. He dropped them in the water, and I had to go in after them up to my middle. But I told you that I would, so I was determined to get them.'

'Oh, you silly, silly boy,' said Kate. 'But I'll keep them for ever. I will indeed.' This was said a little apart, for Harry had managed to draw the young lady aside before he presented the feathers.

Frank had also his trophies for Patty, and the tale to tell of his own prowess. In that he was a year older than his brother, he was by a year's growth less ready to tender his present to his lady-love, openly in the presence of them all. But he found his opportunity, and then he and Patty went on a little in advance. Kate also was deep in her consolations to Harry for his ducking; and therefore the four disposed of themselves in the manner previously suggested by Miss Holmes. Miss Holmes, therefore, and her brother, and Bessy Garrow, were left together in the path, and discussed the performances of the day in a manner that elicited no very ecstatic interest. So they walked for a mile, and by degrees the conversation between them dwindled down almost to nothing.

'There is nothing I dislike so much as coming out with people younger than myself,' said Miss Holmes. 'One always feels so old and dull. Listen to those children there; they make me feel as though I were an old maiden aunt, brought out with them to do propriety.'

'Patty won't at all approve if she hears you call her a child.'

'Nor shall I approve if she treats me like an old woman,' and then she stepped on and joined the children. 'I wouldn't spoil even their sport if I could help it,' she said to herself. 'But with them I shall only be a temporary nuisance; if I remain behind I shall become a permanent evil.' And thus Bessy and her old lover were left by themselves.

'I hope you will get on well with Bella,' said Godfrey, when they had remained silent for a minute or two.

'Oh, yes. She is so good-natured and light-spirited that everybody must like her. She has been used to so much amusement and active life, that I know she must find it very dull here.'

'She is never dull anywhere – even at Liverpool, which, for a young lady, I sometimes think the dullest place on earth. I know it is for a man.'

'A man who has work to do can never be dull; can he?'

'Indeed he can; as dull as death. I am so often enough. I have never been very bright there, Bessy, since you left us.'

There was nothing in his calling her Bessy, for it had become a habit with him since they were children; and they had formerly agreed that everything between them should be as it had been before that foolish whisper of love had been spoken and received. Indeed, provision had been made by them specially on this point, so that there need be no awkwardness in this mode of addressing each other. Such provision had seemed to be very prudent, but it hardly had the desired effect on the present occasion.

'I hardly know what you mean by brightness,' she said, after a pause. 'Perhaps it is not intended that people's lives should be what you call bright.'

'Life ought to be as bright as we can make it.'

'It all depends on the meaning of the word. I suppose we are not very bright here at Thwaite Hall, but yet we think ourselves very happy.'

'I am sure you are,' said Godfrey. 'I very often think of you here.'

'We always think of places where we have been when we were young,' said Bessy; and then again they walked on for some way in silence, and Bessy began to increase her pace with the view of catching the children. The present walk to her was anything but bright, and she bethought herself with dismay that there were still two miles before they reached the ferry.

'Bessy,' Godfrey said at last. And then he stopped as though he were doubtful how to proceed. She, however, did not say a word, but walked on quickly, as though her only hope was in catching the party before her. But they also were walking quickly, for Bella was determined that she would not be caught.

'Bessy, I must speak to you once of what passed between us at Liverpool.'

'Must you?' said she.

'Unless you positively forbid it.'

'Stop, Godfrey,' she said. And they did stop in the path, for now she no longer thought of putting an end to her embarrassment by overtaking her companions. 'If any such words are necessary for your comfort, it would hardly become me to forbid them. Were I to speak so harshly you would accuse me afterwards in your own heart. It must be for you to judge whether it is well to reopen a wound that is nearly healed.'

'But with me it is not nearly healed. The wound is open always.'

'There are some hurts,' she said, 'which do not admit of an absolute and perfect cure, unless after long years.' As she said so, she could not but think how much better was his chance of such perfect cure than her own. With her, so she said to herself, such curing was all but impossible; whereas with him, it was as impossible that the injury should last.

'Bessy,' he said, and he again stopped her on the narrow path, standing immediately before her on the way, 'you remember all the circumstances that made us part?'

'Yes; I think I remember them.'

'And you still think that we were right to part?'

She paused for a moment before she answered him; but it was only for a moment, and then she spoke quite firmly. 'Yes, Godfrey, I do; I have thought about it much since then. I have thought, I fear, to no good purpose about aught else. But I have never thought that we had been unwise in that.'

'And yet I think you loved me.'

'I am bound to confess I did so, as otherwise I must confess myself a liar. I told you at the time that I loved you, and I told you so truly. But it is better, ten times better, that those who love should part, even though they still should love, than that two should be joined together who are incapable of making each other happy. Remember what you told me.'

'I do remember.'

'You found yourself unhappy in your engagement, and you said it was my fault.'

'Bessy, there is my hand. If you have ceased to love me, there is an end of it. But if you love me still, let all that be forgotten.'

'Forgotten, Godfrey! How can it be forgotten? You were unhappy, and it was my fault. My fault, as it would be if I tried to solace a sick child with arithmetic, or feed a dog with grass. I had no right to love you, knowing you as I did; and knowing also that my ways would not be your ways. My punishment I understand, and it is not more than I can bear; but I had hoped that your punishment would have been soon over.'

'You are too proud, Bessy.'

'That is very likely. Frank says that I am a Puritan, and pride was the worst of their sins.'

'Too proud and unbending. In marriage should not the man and woman adapt themselves to each other?'

'When they are married, yes. And every girl who thinks of marrying should know that in very much she must adapt herself to her husband. But I do not think that a woman should be the ivy, to take the direction of every branch of the tree to which she clings. If she does so, what can be her own character? But we must go on, or we shall be too late.'

'And you will give me no other answer?'

'None other, Godfrey. Have you not just now, at this very moment, told me that I was too proud? Can it be possible that you should wish to tie yourself for life to female pride? And if you tell me that now, at such a moment as this, what would you tell me in the close intimacy of married life, when the trifles of every day would have worn away the courtesies of guest and lover?'

There was a sharpness of rebuke in this which Godfrey Holmes could not at the moment overcome. Nevertheless he knew the girl, and understood the workings of her heart and mind. Now, in her present state, she could be unbending, proud, and almost rough. In that she had much to lose in declining the renewed offer which he made her, she would, as it were, continually prompt herself to be harsh and inflexible. Had he been poor, had she not loved him, had not all good things seemed to have attended the promise of such a marriage, she would have been less suspicious of herself in receiving the offer, and more gracious in replying to it. Had he lost all his money before he came back to her, she would have taken him at once; or had he been deprived of an eye, or become crippled in his legs, she would have done so. But, circumstanced as he was, she had no motive to tenderness. There was an organic defect in her character, which no doubt was plainly marked by its own bump in her cranium – the bump of philomartyrdom, it might properly be called. She had shipwrecked her own happiness in rejecting Godfrey Holmes; but it seemed to her to be the proper thing that a well-behaved young lady should shipwreck her own happiness. For the last month or two she had been tossed about by the waters and was nearly drowned. Now there was beautiful land again close to her, and a strong pleasant hand stretched out to save her. But though she had suffered terribly among the waves, she still thought it wrong to be saved. It would be so pleasant to take that hand, so sweet, so joyous, that it surely must be wrong. That was her doctrine; and Godfrey Holmes, though he hardly analysed the matter, partly understood that it was so. And yet, if once she were landed on that green island, she would be so happy. She spoke with scorn of a woman clinging to a tree like ivy; and yet, were she once married, no woman would cling to her husband with sweeter feminine tenacity than Bessy Garrow. He spoke no further word to her as he walked home, but in handing her down to the ferry-boat he pressed her hand. For a second it seemed as though she had returned this pressure. If so, the action was involuntary, and her hand instantly resumed its stiffness to his touch.

It was late that night when Major Garrow went to his bedroom, but his wife was still up, waiting for him. 'Well,' said she, 'what has he said to you? He has been with you above an hour.'

'Such stories are not very quickly told; and in this case it was necessary to understand him very accurately. At length I think I do understand him.'

It is not necessary to repeat at length all that was said on that night between Major and Mrs Garrow, as to the offer which had now for a third time been made to their daughter. On that evening, after the ladies had gone, and when the two boys had taken themselves off, Godfrey Holmes told his tale to his host, and had honestly explained to him what he believed to be the state of his daughter's feelings. 'Now you know all,' said he. 'I do believe that she loves me, and if she does, perhaps she may still listen to you.' Major Garrow did not feel sure that he 'knew it all'. But when he had fully discussed the matter that night with his wife, then he thought that perhaps he had arrived at that knowledge.

On the following morning Bessy learned from the maid, at an early hour, that Godfrey Holmes had left Thwaite Hall and gone back to Liverpool. To the girl she said nothing on the subject, but she felt obliged to say a word or two to Bella. 'It is his coming that I regret,' she said; 'that he should have had the trouble and annoyance for nothing. I acknowledge that it was my fault, and I am very sorry.'

'It cannot be helped,' said Miss Holmes, somewhat gravely. 'As to his misfortunes, I presume that his journeys between here and Liverpool are not the worst of them.'

After breakfast on that day Bessy was summoned into her father's book-room, and found him there, and her mother also. 'Bessy,' said he, 'sit down, my dear. You know why Godfrey has left us this morning?'

Bessy walked round the room, so that in sitting she might be close to her mother and take her mother's hand in her own. 'I suppose I do, papa,' she said.

'He was with me late last night, Bessy; and when he told me what had passed between you I agreed with him that he had better go.'

'It was better that he should go, papa.'

'But he has left a message for you.'

'A message, papa?'

'Yes, Bessy. And your mother agrees with me that it had better be given to you. It is this – that if you will send him word to come again, he will be here by Twelfth Night. He came before on my invitation, but if he returns it must be on yours.'

'Oh, papa, I cannot.'

'I do not say that you can, but think of it calmly before you altogether refuse. You shall give me your answer on New Year's morning.'

'Mamma knows that it would be impossible,' said Bessy.

'Not impossible, dearest.'

'In such a matter you should do what you believe to be right,' said her father.

'If I were to ask him here again, it would be telling him that I would – '

'Exactly, Bessy. It would be telling him that you would be his wife. He would understand it so, and so would your mother and I. It must be so understood altogether.'

'But, papa, when we were at Liverpool – '

'I have told him everything, dearest,' said Mrs Garrow.

'I think I understand the whole,' said the major; 'and in such a matter as this I will not give you counsel on either side. But you must remember that in making up your mind, you must think of him as well as of yourself. If you do not love him, if you feel that as his wife you should not love him, there is not another word to be said. I need not explain to my daughter that under such circumstances she would be wrong to encourage the visits of a suitor. But your mother says you do love him.

'I will not ask you. But if you do – if you have so told him, and allowed him to build up an idea of his life-happiness on such telling, you will, I think, sin greatly against him by allowing a false feminine pride to mar his happiness. When once a girl has confessed to a man that she loves him, the confession and the love together put upon her the burden of a duty towards him, which she cannot with impunity throw aside.' Then he kissed her, and bidding her give him a reply on the morning of the new year, left her with her mother.

She had four days for consideration, and they went past her by no means easily. Could she have been alone with her mother, the struggle would not have been so painful; but there was the necessity that she should talk to Isabella Holmes, and the necessity also that she should not neglect the Coverdales. Nothing could have been kinder than Bella. She did not speak on the subject till the morning of the last day, and then only in a very few words. 'Bessy,' she said, 'as you are great, be merciful.'

'But I am not great, and it would not be mercy.'

'As to that,' said Bella, 'he has surely a right to his own opinion.'

On that evening she was sitting alone in her room when her mother came to her, and her eyes were red with weeping. Pen and paper were before her, as though she were resolved to write, but hitherto no word had been written.

'Well, Bessy,' said her mother, sitting down close beside her; 'is the deed done?'

'What deed, mamma? Who says that I am to do it?'

'The deed is not the writing, but the resolution to write. Five words will be sufficient, if only those five words may be written.'

'It is for one's whole life, mamma. For his life, as well as my own.'

'True, Bessy, that is quite true. But equally true whether you bid him come or allow him to remain away. That task of making up one's mind for life, must at last be done in some special moment of that life.'

'Mamma, mamma; tell me what I should do.'

But this Mrs Garrow would not do. 'I will write the words for you if you like,' she said, 'but it is you who must resolve that they shall be written. I cannot bid my darling go away and leave me for another home, I can only say that in my heart I do believe that home would be a happy one.'

It was morning before the note was written, but when the morning came Bessy had written it and brought it to her mother.

'You must take it to papa,' she said. Then she went and hid herself from all eyes till the noon had passed. 'Dear Godfrey,' the letter ran, 'Papa says that you will return on Wednesday if I write to ask you. Do come back to us, – if you wish it. Yours always, Bessy.'

'It is as good as though she had filled the sheet,' said the major. But in sending it to Godfrey Holmes, he did not omit a few accompanying remarks of his own.

An answer came from Godfrey by return of post; and on the afternoon of the sixth of January, Frank Garrow drove over to the station at Penrith to meet him. On their way back to Thwaite Hall there grew up a very close confidence between the two future brothers-in-law, and Frank explained with great perspicuity a little plan which he had arranged himself. 'As soon as it is dark, so that she won't see it, Harry will hang it up in the dining-room,' he said, 'and mind you go in there before you go anywhere else.'

'I am very glad you have come back, Godfrey,' said the major, meeting him in the hall.

'God bless you, dear Godfrey,' said Mrs Garrow; 'you will find Bessy in the dining-room,' she whispered; but in so whispering she was quite unconscious of the mistletoe bough.

And so also was Bessy, nor do I think that she was much more conscious when that introduction was over. Godfrey had made all manner of promises to Frank, but when the moment arrived, he had found the moment too important for any special reference to the little bough above his head. Not so, however, Patty Coverdale. 'It's a shame,' said she, bursting out of the room, 'and if I'd known what you had done, nothing on earth should have induced me to go in. I won't enter the room till I know that you have taken it out.' Nevertheless her sister Kate was bold enough to solve the mystery before the evening was over.

EDITH WHARTON

Edith Wharton was born in 1862 into a prominent and wealthy New York family. In 1885 she married a Boston socialite; the couple travelled frequently and settled in France in 1907, but the marriage was unhappy and they divorced in 1913. On her trips to Europe, Wharton became a close friend of the novelist Henry James. Her first major novel was *The House of Mirth* (1905); many short stories, travel books, memoirs and novels followed, including *Ethan Frome* (1911), *The Reef* (1912) and *The Age of Innocence* (1920). Wharton was decorated for her humanitarian work during the First World War. She died in France in 1937.

A Coward

'My daughter Irene,' said Mrs Carstyle (she made it rhyme with *tureen*), 'has had no social advantages; but if Mr Carstyle had chosen – ' she paused significantly and looked at the shabby sofa on the opposite side of the fireplace as though it had been Mr Carstyle. Vibart was glad that it was not.

Mrs Carstyle was one of the women who make refinement vulgar. She invariably spoke of her husband as *Mr Carstyle* and, though she had but one daughter, was always careful to designate the young lady by name. At luncheon she had talked a great deal of elevating influences and ideals, and had fluctuated between apologies for the overdone mutton and affected surprise that the bewildered maidservant should have forgotten to serve the coffee and liqueurs *as usual*.

Vibart was almost sorry that he had come. Miss Carstyle was still beautiful – almost as beautiful as when, two days earlier, against the leafy background of a June garden-party, he had seen her for the first time – but her mother's expositions and elucidations cheapened her beauty as signposts vulgarise a woodland solitude. Mrs Carstyle's eye was perpetually plying between her daughter and Vibart, like an empty cab in quest of a fare. Miss Carstyle, the young man decided, was the kind of girl whose surroundings rub off on her; or was it rather that Mrs Carstyle's idiosyncrasies were of a nature to colour everyone within reach? Vibart, looking across the table as this consolatory alternative occurred to him, was sure that they had not coloured Mr Carstyle; but that, perhaps, was only because they had bleached him instead. Mr Carstyle was quite colourless; it would have been impossible to guess his native tint. His wife's qualities, if they had affected him at all, had acted negatively. He did not apologise for the mutton, and he wandered off after luncheon without pretending to wait for the diurnal coffee and liqueurs; while the few remarks that he had contributed to the conversation during the meal had not been in the direction of abstract conceptions of life. As he strayed away, with his vague oblique step, and the stoop that suggested the habit of dodging missiles, Vibart, who was still in the age of formulas, found himself wondering what life could be worth to a man who had evidently resigned himself to travelling with his back to the wind; so that Mrs Carstyle's allusion to her daughter's lack of advantages (imparted while Irene searched the house for an undiscoverable cigarette) had an appositeness unintended by the speaker.

'If Mr Carstyle had chosen,' that lady repeated, 'we might have had our city home' (she never used so small a word as town) 'and Ireen could have mixed in the society to which I myself was accustomed at her age.' Her sigh pointed unmistakably to a past when young men had come to luncheon to see *her* .

The sigh led Vibart to look at her, and the look led him to the unwelcome conclusion that Irene 'took after' her mother. It was certainly not from the sapless paternal stock that the girl had drawn her warm bloom: Mrs Carstyle had contributed the highlights to the picture.

Mrs Carstyle caught his look and appropriated it with the complacency of a vicarious beauty. She was quite aware of the value of her appearance as guaranteeing Irene's development into a fine woman.

'But perhaps,' she continued, taking up the thread of her explanation, 'you have heard of Mr Carstyle's extraordinary hallucination. Mr Carstyle knows that I call it so – as I tell him, it is the most charitable view to take.'

She looked coldly at the threadbare sofa and indulgently at the young man who filled a corner of it.

'You may think it odd, Mr Vibart, that I should take you into my confidence in this way after so short an acquaintance, but somehow I can't help regarding you as a friend already. I believe in those intuitive sympathies, don't you? They have never misled me –' her lids drooped retrospectively – 'and besides, I always tell Mr Carstyle that on this point I will have no false pretences. Where truth is concerned I am inexorable, and I consider it my duty to let our friends know that our restricted way of living is due entirely to choice – to Mr Carstyle's choice. When I married Mr Carstyle it was with the expectation of living in New York and of keeping my carriage; and there is no reason for our not doing so – there is no reason, Mr Vibart, why my daughter Ireen should have been denied the intellectual advantages of foreign travel. I wish that to be understood. It is owing to her father's deliberate choice that Ireen and I have been imprisoned in the narrow limits of Millbrook society. For myself I do not complain. If Mr Carstyle chooses to place others before his wife it is not for his wife to repine. His course may be noble – Quixotic; I do not allow myself to pronounce judgement on it, though others have thought that in sacrificing his own family to strangers he was violating the most sacred obligations of domestic life. This is the opinion of my pastor and of other valued friends; but, as I have always told them, for myself I make no claims. Where my daughter Ireen is concerned it is different –'

It was a relief to Vibart when, at this point, Mrs Carstyle's discharge of her duty was cut short by her daughter's reappearance. Irene had been unable to find a cigarette for Mr Vibart, and her mother, with beaming irrelevance, suggested that in that case she had better show him the garden.

The Carstyle house stood but a few yards back from the brick-paved Millbrook street, and the garden was a very small place, unless measured, as Mrs Carstyle probably intended that it should be, by the extent of her daughter's charms. These were so considerable that Vibart walked back and forward half a dozen times between the porch and the gate before he discovered the limitations of the Carstyle domain. It was not till Irene had accused him of being sarcastic and had confided in him that 'the girls' were furious with her for letting him talk to her so long at his aunt's garden-party, that he awoke to the exiguity of his surroundings; and then it was with a touch of irritation that he noticed Mr Carstyle's inconspicuous profile bent above a newspaper in one of the lower windows. Vibart had an idea that Mr Carstyle, while ostensibly reading the paper, had kept count of the number of times that his daughter had led her companion up and down between the syringa bushes; and for some undefinable reason he resented Mr Carstyle's unperturbed observation more than his wife's zealous self-effacement. To a man who is trying to please a pretty girl there are moments when the proximity of an impartial spectator is more disconcerting than the most obvious connivance; and something about Mr Carstyle's expression conveyed his good-humored indifference to Irene's processes.

When the garden-gate closed behind Vibart he had become aware that his preoccupation with the Carstyles had shifted its centre from the daughter to the father; but he was accustomed to such emotional surprises, and skilled in seizing any compensations they might offer.

2

The Carstyles belonged to the all-the-year-round Millbrook of paper-mills, cable-cars, brick pavements and church sociables, while Mrs Vance, the aunt with whom Vibart lived, was an ornament of the summer colony whose big country-houses dotted the surrounding hills. Mrs Vance had, however, no difficulty in appeasing the curiosity which Mrs Carstyle's enigmatic utterances had aroused in the young man. Mrs Carstyle's relentless veracity vented itself mainly on the 'summer people', as they were called: she did not propose that anyone within ten miles of Millbrook should keep a carriage without knowing that she was entitled to keep one too. Mrs Vance remarked with a sigh that Mrs Carstyle's annual demand to have her position understood came in as punctually as the taxes and the water-rates.

'My dear, it's simply this: when Andrew Carstyle married her years ago – heaven knows why he did; he's one of the Albany Carstyles, you know, and she was a daughter of old Deacon Ash of South Millbrook – well, when he married her he had a tidy little income, and I suppose the bride expected to set up an establishment in New York and be hand-in-glove with the whole Carstyle clan. But whether he was ashamed of her from the first, or for some other unexplained reason, he bought a country-place and settled down here for life. For a few years they lived comfortably enough, and she had plenty of smart clothes, and drove about in a victoria calling on the summer people. Then, when the beautiful Irene was about ten years old, Mr Carstyle's only brother died, and it turned out that he had made away with a lot of trust-property. It was a horrid business: over three hundred thousand dollars were gone, and of course most of it had belonged to widows and orphans. As soon as the facts were made known, Andrew Carstyle announced that he would pay back what his brother had stolen. He sold his country-place and his wife's carriage, and they moved to the little house they live in now. Mr Carstyle's income is probably not as large as his wife would like to have it thought, and though I'm told he puts aside a good part of it every year to pay off his brother's obligations, I fancy the debt won't be discharged for some time to come. To help things along he opened a law office – he had studied law in his youth – but though he is said to be clever I hear that he has very little to do. People are afraid of him: he's too dry and quiet. Nobody believes in a man who doesn't believe in himself, and Mr Carstyle always seems to be winking at you through a slit in his professional manner. People don't like it – his wife doesn't like it. I believe she would have accepted the sacrifice of the country-place and the carriage if he had struck an attitude and talked about doing his duty. It was his regarding the whole thing as a matter of course that exasperated her. What is the use of doing something difficult in a way that makes it look perfectly easy? I feel sorry for Mrs Carstyle. She's lost her house and her carriage, and she hasn't been allowed to be heroic.'

Vibart had listened attentively.

'I wonder what Miss Carstyle thinks of it?' he mused.

Mrs Vance looked at him with a tentative smile. 'I wonder what *you* think of Miss Carstyle?' she returned,

His answer reassured her.

'I think she takes after her mother,' he said.

'Ah,' cried his aunt cheerfully, 'then I needn't write to *your* mother, and I can have Irene at all my parties!'

Miss Carstyle was an important factor in the restricted social combinations of a Millbrook hostess. A local beauty is always a useful addition to a Saturday-to-Monday house-party, and the beautiful Irene was served up as a perennial novelty to the jaded guests of the summer colony. As Vibart's aunt remarked, she was perfect till she became playful, and she never became playful till the third day.

Under these conditions, it was natural that Vibart should see a good deal of the young lady, and before he was aware of it he had drifted into the anomalous position of paying court to the daughter in order to ingratiate himself with the father. Miss Carstyle was beautiful, Vibart was young, and the days were long in his aunt's spacious and distinguished house; but it was really the desire to know something more of Mr Carstyle that led the young man to partake so often of that gentleman's overdone mutton. Vibart's imagination had been touched by the discovery that this little huddled-up man, instead of travelling with the wind, was persistently facing a domestic gale of considerable velocity. That he should have paid off his brother's debt at one stroke would have been to the young man a conceivable feat; but that he should go on methodically and uninterruptedly accumulating the needed amount, under the perpetual accusation of Irene's inadequate frocks and Mrs Carstyle's apologies for the mutton, seemed to Vibart proof of unexampled heroism. Mr Carstyle was as inaccessible as the average American parent and led a life so detached from the preoccupations of his womankind that Vibart had some difficulty in fixing his attention. To Mr Carstyle, Vibart was simply the inevitable young man who had been hanging about the house ever since Irene had left school; and Vibart's efforts to differentiate himself from this enamored abstraction were hampered by Mrs Carstyle's cheerful assumption that he *was* the young man, and by Irene's frank appropriation of his visits.

In this extremity he suddenly observed a slight but significant change in the manner of the two ladies. Irene, instead of charging him with being sarcastic and horrid, and declaring herself unable to believe a word he said, began to receive his remarks with the impersonal smile which he had seen her accord to the married men of his aunt's house-parties; while Mrs Carstyle, talking over his head to an invisible but evidently sympathetic and intelligent listener, debated the propriety of Irene's accepting an invitation to spend the month of August at Narragansett. When Vibart, rashly trespassing on the rights of this unseen oracle, remarked that a few weeks at the seashore would make a delightful change for Miss Carstyle, the ladies looked at him and then laughed.

It was at this point that Vibart, for the first time, found himself observed by Mr Carstyle. They were grouped about the debris of a luncheon which had ended precipitously with veal stew (Mrs Carstyle explaining that poor cooks *always* failed with their sweet dish when there was company) and Mr Carstyle, his hands thrust in his pockets, his lean baggy-coated shoulders pressed against his chair-back, sat contemplating his guest with a smile of unmistakable approval. When Vibart caught his eye the smile vanished, and Mr Carstyle, dropping his glasses from the bridge of his thin nose, looked out of the window with the expression of a man determined to prove an alibi. But Vibart was sure of the smile: it had established, between his host and himself, a complicity which Mr Carstyle's attempted evasion served only to confirm.

On the strength of this incident Vibart, a few days later, called at Mr Carstyle's office. Ostensibly, the young man had come to ask, on his aunt's behalf, some question on a point at issue between herself and the Millbrook telephone company; but his purpose in offering to perform the errand had been the hope of taking up his intercourse with Mr Carstyle where that gentleman's smile had left it. Vibart was not disappointed. In a dingy office, with a single window looking out on a blank wall, he found Mr Carstyle, in an alpaca coat, reading Montaigne.

It evidently did not occur to him that Vibart had come on business, and the warmth of his welcome gave the young man a sense of furnishing the last word in a conjugal argument in which, for once, Mr Carstyle had come off triumphant.

The legal question disposed of, Vibart reverted to Montaigne: had Mr Carstyle seen young So-and-so's volume of essays? There was one on Montaigne that had a decided flavour: the point of view was curious. Vibart was surprised to find that Mr Carstyle had heard of young So-and-so. Clever young men are given to thinking that their elders have never got beyond Macaulay; but Mr Carstyle seemed sufficiently familiar with recent literature not to take it too seriously. He accepted Vibart's offer of young So-and-so's volume, admitting that his own library was not exactly up-to-date.

Vibart went away musing. The next day he came back with the volume of essays. It seemed to be tacitly understood that he was to call at the office when he wished to see Mr Carstyle, whose legal engagements did not seriously interfere with the pursuit of literature.

For a week or ten days Mrs Carstyle, in Vibart's presence, continued to take counsel with her unseen adviser on the subject of her daughter's visit to Narragansett. Once or twice Irene dropped her impersonal smile to tax Vibart with not caring whether she went or not; and Mrs Carstyle seized a moment of tête-à-tête to confide in him that the dear child hated the idea of leaving, and was going only because her friend Mrs Higby would not let her off. Of course, if it had not been for Mr Carstyle's peculiarities they would have had their own seaside home – at Newport, probably: Mrs Carstyle preferred the tone of Newport – and Irene would not have been dependent on the *charity* of her friends; but as it was, they must be thankful for small mercies, and Mrs Higby was certainly very kind in her way, and had a charming social position – for Narragansett.

These confidences, however, were soon superseded by an exchange, between mother and daughter, of increasingly frequent allusions to the delights of Narragansett, the popularity of Mrs Higby, and the jolliness of her house; with an occasional reference on Mrs Carstyle's part to the probability of Hewlett Bain's being there as usual – hadn't Irene heard from Mrs Higby that he was to be there? Upon this note Miss Carstyle at length departed, leaving Vibart to the undisputed enjoyment of her father's company.

Vibart had at no time a keen taste for the summer joys of Millbrook, and the family obligation which, for several months of the year, kept him at his aunt's side (Mrs Vance was a childless widow and he filled the onerous post of favorite nephew) gave a sense of compulsion to the light occupations that chequered his leisure. Mrs Vance, who fancied herself lonely when he was away, was too much engaged with notes, telegrams and arriving and departing guests, to do more than breathlessly smile upon his presence, or implore him to take the dullest girl of the party for a drive (and would he go by way of Millbrook, like a dear, and stop at the market to ask why the lobsters hadn't come?); and the house itself, and the guests who came and went in it like people rushing through a railway station, offered no points of repose to his thoughts. Some houses are companions in themselves: the walls, the bookshelves, the very chairs and tables, have the qualities of a sympathetic mind; but Mrs Vance's interior was as impersonal as the setting of a classic drama.

These conditions made Vibart cultivate an assiduous exchange of books between himself and Mr Carstyle. The young man went down almost daily to the little house in the town, where Mrs Carstyle, who had now an air of receiving him in curl-papers, and of not always immediately distinguishing him from the piano-tuner, made no effort to detain him on his way to her husband's study.

3

Now and then, at the close of one of Vibart's visits, Mr Carstyle put on a mildewed Panama hat and accompanied the young man for a mile or two on his way home. The road to Mrs Vance's lay through one of the most amiable suburbs of Millbrook, and Mr Carstyle, walking with his slow uneager step, his hat pushed back, and his stick dragging behind him, seemed to take a philosophic pleasure in the aspect of the trim lawns and opulent gardens.

Vibart could never induce his companion to prolong his walk as far as Mrs Vance's drawing-room; but one afternoon, when the distant hills lay blue beyond the twilight of overarching elms, the two men strolled on into the country past that lady's hospitable gateposts.

It was a still day, the road was deserted, and every sound came sharply through the air. Mr Carstyle was in the midst of a disquisition on Diderot, when he raised his head and stood still.

'What's that?' he said. 'Listen!'

Vibart listened and heard a distant storm of hoof-beats. A moment later, a buggy drawn by a pair of trotters swung round the turn of the road. It was about thirty yards off, coming toward them at full speed. The man who drove was leaning forward with outstretched arms; beside him sat a girl.

Suddenly Vibart saw Mr Carstyle jump into the middle of the road, in front of the buggy. He stood there immovable, his arms extended, his legs apart, in an attitude of indomitable resistance. Almost at the same moment Vibart realised that the man in the buggy had his horses in hand.

'They're not running!' Vibart shouted, springing into the road and catching Mr Carstyle's alpaca sleeve. The older man looked around vaguely: he seemed dazed.

'Come away, sir, come away!' cried Vibart, gripping his arm. The buggy swept past them, and Mr Carstyle stood in the dust gazing after it.

At length he drew out his handkerchief and wiped his forehead. He was very pale and Vibart noticed that his hand shook.

'That was a close call, sir, wasn't it? I suppose you thought they were running.'

'Yes,' said Mr Carstyle slowly, 'I thought they were running.'

'It certainly looked like it for a minute. Let's sit down, shall we? I feel rather breathless myself.'

Vibart saw that his friend could hardly stand. They seated themselves on a tree-trunk by the roadside, and Mr Carstyle continued to wipe his forehead in silence.

At length he turned to Vibart and said abruptly: 'I made straight for the middle of the road, didn't I? If there *had* been a runaway I should have stopped it?'

Vibart looked at him in surprise. 'You would have tried to, undoubtedly, unless I'd had time to drag you away.'

Mr Carstyle straightened his narrow shoulders. 'There was no hesitation, at all events? I – I showed no signs of – avoiding it?'

'I should say not, sir; it was I who funked it for you.'

Mr Carstyle was silent: his head had dropped forward and he looked like an old man.

'It was just my cursed luck again!' he exclaimed suddenly in a loud voice.

For a moment Vibart thought that he was wandering; but he raised his head and went on speaking in more natural tones.

'I dare say I appeared ridiculous enough to you just now, eh? Perhaps you saw all along that the horses weren't running? Your eyes are younger than mine; and then you're not always looking out for runaways, as I am. Do you know that in thirty years I've never seen a runaway?'

'You're fortunate,' said Vibart, still bewildered.

'Fortunate? Good God, man, I've *prayed* to see one: not a runaway especially, but any bad accident; anything that endangered people's lives. There are accidents happening all the time all over the world; why shouldn't I ever come across one? It's not for want of trying! At one time I used to haunt the theatres in the hope of a fire: fires in theatres are so apt to be fatal. Well, will you believe it? I was in the Brooklyn Theatre the night before it burned down; I left the old Madison Square Garden half an hour before the walls fell in. And it's the same way with street accidents – I always miss them; I'm always just too late. Last year there was a boy knocked down by a cable-car at our corner; I got to my gate just as they were carrying him off on a stretcher. And so it goes. If anybody else had been walking along this road, those horses would have been running away. And there was a girl in the buggy, too – a mere child!'

Mr Carstyle's head sank again.

'You're wondering what this means,' he began after another pause. 'I was a little confused for a moment – must have seemed incoherent.' His voice cleared and he made an effort to straighten himself. 'Well, I was a damned coward once and I've been trying to live it down ever since.'

Vibart looked at him incredulously and Mr Carstyle caught the look with a smile.

'Why not? Do I look like a Hercules?' He held up his loose-skinned hand and shrunken wrist. 'Not built for the part, certainly; but that doesn't count, of course. Man's unconquerable soul, and all the rest of it . . . well, I was a coward every inch of me, body and soul.'

He paused and glanced up and down the road. There was no one in sight.

'It happened when I was a young chap just out of college. I was travelling round the world with another youngster of my own age and an older man – Charles Meriton – who has since made a name for himself. You may have heard of him.'

'Meriton, the archaeologist? The man who discovered those ruined African cities the other day?'

'That's the man. He was a college tutor then, and my father, who had known him since he was a boy, and who had a very high opinion of him, had asked him to make the tour with us. We both – my friend Collis and I – had an immense admiration for Meriton. He was just the fellow to excite a boy's enthusiasm: cool, quick, imperturbable – the kind of man whose hand is always on the hilt of action. His explorations had led him into all sorts of tight places, and he'd shown an extraordinary combination of calculating patience and reckless courage. He never talked about his doings; we picked them up from various people on our journey. He'd been everywhere, he knew everybody, and everybody had something stirring to tell about him. I dare say this account of the man sounds exaggerated; perhaps it is; I've never seen him since; but at that time he seemed to me a tremendous fellow – a kind of scientific Ajax. He was a capital travelling-companion, at any rate: good-tempered, cheerful, easily amused, with none of the been-there-before superiority so irritating to youngsters. He made us feel as though it were all as new to him as to us: he never chilled our enthusiasms or took the bloom off our surprises. There was nobody else whose good opinion I cared as much about: he was the biggest thing in sight.

'On the way home Collis broke down with diphtheria. We were in the Mediterranean, cruising about the Sporades in a felucca. He was taken ill at Chios. The attack came on suddenly and we were afraid to run the risk of taking him back to Athens in the felucca. We established ourselves in the inn at Chios and there the poor fellow lay for weeks. Luckily there was a fairly good doctor on the island and we sent to Athens for a sister to help with the nursing. Poor Collis was desperately bad: the diphtheria was followed by partial paralysis. The doctor assured us that the danger was past; he would gradually regain the use of his limbs; but his recovery would be slow. The sister encouraged us too – she had seen such cases before; and he certainly did improve a shade each day. Meriton and I had taken turns with the sister in nursing him, but after the paralysis had set in there wasn't much to do, and there was nothing to prevent Meriton's leaving us for a day or two. He had received word from some place on the coast of Asia Minor that a remarkable tomb had been discovered somewhere in the interior; he had not been willing to take us there, as the journey was not a particularly safe one; but now that we were tied up at Chios there seemed no reason why he shouldn't go and take a look at the place. The expedition would not take more than three days; Collis was convalescent; the doctor and nurse assured us that there was no cause for uneasiness; and so Meriton started off one evening at sunset. I walked down to the quay with him and saw him rowed off to the felucca. I would have given a good deal to be going with him; the prospect of danger allured me.

' "You'll see that Collis is never left alone, won't you?" he shouted back to me as the boat pulled out into the harbour; I remembered I rather resented the suggestion.

'I walked back to the inn and went to bed: the nurse sat up with Collis at night. The next morning I relieved her at the usual hour. It was a sultry day with a queer coppery-looking sky; the air was stifling. In the middle of the day the nurse came to take my place while I dined; when I went back to Collis's room she said she would go out for a breath of air.

'I sat down by Collis's bed and began to fan him with the fan the sister had been using. The heat made him uneasy and I turned him over in bed, for he was still helpless: the whole of his right side was numb. Presently he fell asleep and I went to the window and sat looking down on the hot deserted square, with a bunch of donkeys and their drivers asleep in the shade of the convent-wall across the way. I remember noticing the blue beads about the donkeys' necks . . . Were you ever in an earthquake? No? I'd never been in one either. It's an indescribable sensation . . . there's a Day of Judgement feeling in the air. It began with the donkeys waking up and trembling; I noticed that and thought it queer. Then the drivers jumped up – I saw the terror in their faces. Then a roar . . . I remember noticing a big black crack in the convent-wall opposite – a zig-zag crack, like a flash of lightning in a wood-cut . . . I thought of that, too, at the time; then all the bells in the place began to ring – it made a fearful discord . . . I saw people rushing across the square . . . the air was full of crashing noises. The floor went down under me in a sickening way and then jumped back and pitched me to the ceiling . . . but where *was* the ceiling? And the door? I said to myself: *We're two storeys up – the stairs are just wide enough for one* . . . I gave one glance at Collis: he was lying in bed, wide awake, looking straight at me. I ran. Something struck me on the head as I bolted downstairs – I kept on running. I suppose the knock I got dazed me, for I don't remember much of anything till I found myself in a vineyard a mile from the town. I was roused by the warm blood running down my nose and heard myself explaining to Meriton exactly how it had happened . . .

'When I crawled back to the town they told me that all the houses near the inn were in ruins and that a dozen people had been killed. Collis was among them, of course. The ceiling had come down on him.'

Mr Carstyle wiped his forehead. Vibart sat looking away from him.

'Two days later Meriton came back. I began to tell him the story, but he interrupted me.

' "There was no one with him at the time, then? You'd left him alone?"

' "No, he wasn't alone." '

' "Who was with him? You said the sister was out." '

' "I was with him." '

' " *You were with him?*" '

'I shall never forget Meriton's look. I believe I had meant to explain, to accuse myself, to shout out my agony of soul; but I saw the uselessness of it. A door had been shut between us. Neither of us spoke another word. He was very kind to me on the way home; he looked after me in a motherly way that was a good deal harder to stand than his open contempt. I saw the man was honestly trying to pity me; but it was no good – he simply couldn't.'

Mr Carstyle rose slowly, with a certain stiffness.

'Shall we turn toward home? Perhaps I'm keeping you.'

They walked on a few steps in silence; then he spoke again.

'That business altered my whole life. Of course I oughtn't to have allowed it to – that was another form of cowardice. But I saw myself only with Meriton's eyes – it is one of the worst miseries of youth that one is always trying to be somebody else. I had meant to be a Meriton – I saw I'd better go home and study law . . .

'It's a childish fancy, a survival of the primitive savage, if you like; but from that hour to this I've hankered day and night for a chance to retrieve myself, to set myself right with the man I meant to be. I want to prove to that man that it was all an accident – an unaccountable deviation from my normal instincts; that having once been a coward doesn't mean that a man's cowardly . . . and I can't, I can't!'

Mr Carstyle's tone had passed insensibly from agitation to irony. He had got back to his usual objective stand-point.

'Why, I'm a perfect olive-branch,' he concluded, with his dry indulgent laugh; 'the very babies stop crying at my approach – I carry a sort of millennium about with me – I'd make my fortune as an agent of the Peace Society. I shall go to the grave leaving that other man unconvinced!'

Vibart walked back with him to Millbrook. On her doorstep they met Mrs Carstyle, flushed and feathered, with a card-case and dusty boots.

Edith Wharton

'I don't ask you in,' she said plaintively to Vibart, 'because I can't answer for the food this evening. My maid-of-all-work tells me that she's going to a ball – which is more than I've done in years! And besides, it would be cruel to ask you to spend such a hot evening in our stuffy little house – the air is so much cooler at Mrs Vance's. Remember me to Mrs Vance, please, and tell her how sorry I am that I can no longer include her in my round of visits. When I had my carriage I saw the people I liked, but now that I have to walk, my social opportunities are more limited. I was not obliged to do my visiting on foot when I was younger, and my doctor tells me that to persons accustomed to a carriage no exercise is more injurious than walking.'

She glanced at her husband with a smile of unforgiving sweetness.

'Fortunately,' she concluded, 'it agrees with Mr Carstyle.'

The Moving Finger

The news of Mrs Grancy's death came to me with the shock of an immense blunder – one of fate's most irretrievable acts of vandalism. It was as though all sorts of renovating forces had been checked by the clogging of that one wheel. Not that Mrs Grancy contributed any perceptible momentum to the social machine: her unique distinction was that of filling to perfection her special place in the world. So many people are like badly composed statues, overlapping their niches at one point and leaving them vacant at another. Mrs Grancy's niche was her husband's life; and if it be argued that the space was not large enough for its vacancy to leave a very big gap, I can only say that, at the last resort, such dimensions must be determined by finer instruments than any ready-made standard of utility. Ralph Grancy's was in short a kind of disembodied usefulness: one of those constructive influences that, instead of crystallising into definite forms, remain as it were a medium for the development of clear thinking and fine feeling. He faithfully irrigated his own dusty patch of life, and the fruitful moisture stole far beyond his boundaries. If, to carry on the metaphor, Grancy's life was a sedulously cultivated enclosure, his wife was the flower he had planted in its midst – the embowering tree, rather, which gave him rest and shade at its foot and the wind of dreams in its upper branches.

We had all – his small but devoted band of followers – known a moment when it seemed likely that Grancy would fail us. We had watched him pitted against one stupid obstacle after another – ill-health, poverty, misunderstanding and, worst of all for a man of his texture, his first wife's soft insidious egotism. We had seen him sinking under the leaden embrace of her affection like a swimmer in a drowning clutch; but just as we despaired he had always come to the surface again, blinded, panting, but striking out fiercely for the shore. When at last her death released him it became a question as to how much of the man she had carried with her. Left alone, he revealed numb withered patches, like a tree from which a parasite has been stripped. But gradually he began to put out new leaves; and when he met the lady who was to become his second wife – his one *real* wife, as his friends reckoned – the whole man burst into flower.

The second Mrs Grancy was past thirty when he married her, and it was clear that she had harvested that crop of middle joy which is rooted in young despair. But if she had lost the surface of eighteen she had kept its inner light; if her cheek lacked the gloss of immaturity her eyes were young with the stored youth of half a lifetime. Grancy had first known her somewhere in the East – I believe she was the sister of one of our consuls out there – and when he brought her home to New York she came among us as a stranger. The idea of Grancy's remarriage had been a shock to us all. After one such calcining most men would have kept out of the fire; but we agreed that he was predestined to sentimental blunders, and we awaited with resignation the embodiment of his latest mistake. Then Mrs Grancy came – and we understood. She was the most beautiful and the most complete of explanations. We shuffled our defeated omniscience out of sight and gave it hasty burial under a prodigality of welcome. For the first time in years we had Grancy off our minds. 'He'll do something great now!' the least sanguine of us prophesied; and our sentimentalist emended: 'He *has* done it – in marrying her!'

It was Claydon, the portrait-painter, who risked this hyperbole; and who soon afterward, at the happy husband's request, prepared to defend it in a portrait of Mrs Grancy. We were all – even Claydon – ready to concede that Mrs Grancy's unwontedness was in some degree a matter of environment. Her graces were complementary and it needed the mate's call to reveal the flash of colour beneath her neutral-tinted wings. But if she needed Grancy to interpret her, how much greater was the service she rendered him! Claydon professionally described her as the right frame for him; but if she defined she also enlarged, if she threw the whole into perspective she also cleared new ground, opened fresh vistas, reclaimed whole areas of activity that had run to waste under the harsh husbandry of privation. This inter-action of sympathies was not without its visible expression. Claydon was not alone in maintaining that Grancy's presence – or indeed the mere mention of his name – had a perceptible effect on his wife's appearance. It was as though a light were shifted, a curtain drawn back, as though, to borrow another of Claydon's metaphors, Love the indefatigable artist were per-petually seeking a happier 'pose' for his model. In this interpretative light Mrs Grancy acquired the charm which makes some women's faces like a book of which the last page is never turned. There was always something new to read in her eyes. What Claydon read there – or at least such scattered hints of the ritual as reached him through the sanctuary doors – his portrait in due course declared to us. When the picture was exhibited it was at once acclaimed as his masterpiece; but the people who knew Mrs Grancy smiled and said it was flattered. Claydon, however, had not set out to paint *their* Mrs Grancy – or ours even – but Ralph's; and Ralph knew his own at a glance. At the first confrontation he saw that Claydon had understood. As for Mrs Grancy, when the finished picture was shown to her she turned to the painter and said simply: 'Ah, you've done me facing the east!'

The picture, then, for all its value, seemed a mere incident in the unfolding of their double destiny, a footnote to the illuminated text of their lives. It was not till afterward that it acquired the significance of last words spoken on a threshold never to be recrossed. Grancy, a year after his marriage, had given up his town house and carried his bliss an hour's journey away, to a little place among the hills. His various duties and interests brought him frequently to New York but we necessarily saw him less often than when his house had served as the rallying-point of kindred enthusiasms. It seemed a pity that such an influence should be withdrawn, but we all felt that his long arrears of happiness should be paid in whatever coin he chose. The distance from which the fortunate couple radiated warmth on us was not too great for friendship to traverse; and our conception of a glorified leisure took the form of Sundays spent in the Grancys' library, with its sedative rural outlook, and the portrait of Mrs Grancy illuminating its studious walls. The picture was at its best in that setting; and we used to accuse Claydon of visiting Mrs Grancy in order to see her portrait. He met this by declaring that the portrait *was* Mrs Grancy; and there were moments when the statement seemed unanswerable. One of us, indeed – I think it must have been the novelist – said that Claydon had been saved from falling in love with Mrs Grancy only by falling in love with his picture of her; and it was noticeable that he, to whom his finished work was no more than the shed husk of future effort, showed a perennial tenderness for this one achievement. We smiled afterward to think how often, when Mrs Grancy was in the room, her presence reflecting itself in our talk like a gleam of sky in a hurrying current, Claydon, averted from the real woman, would sit as it were listening to the picture. His attitude, at the time, seemed only a part of the unusualness of those picturesque afternoons, when the most familiar combinations of life underwent a magical change. Some human happiness is a landlocked lake; but the Grancys' was an open sea, stretching a buoyant and illimitable surface to the voyaging interests of life. There was room and to spare on those waters for all our separate ventures; and always beyond the sunset, a mirage of the fortunate isles toward which our prows bent.

2

It was in Rome that, three years later, I heard of her death. The notice said 'suddenly'; I was glad of that. I was glad too – basely perhaps – to be away from Grancy at a time when silence must have seemed obtuse and speech derisive.

I was still in Rome when, a few months afterward, he suddenly arrived there. He had been appointed secretary of legation at Constantinople and was on the way to his post. He had taken the place, he said frankly, 'to get away'. Our relations with the Porte held out a prospect of hard work, and that, he explained, was what he needed. He could never be satisfied to sit down among the ruins. I saw that, like most of us in moments of extreme moral tension, he was playing a part, behaving as he thought it became a man to behave in the eye of disaster. The instinctive posture of grief is a shuffling compromise between defiance and prostration; and pride feels the need of striking a worthier attitude in face of such a foe. Grancy, by nature musing and retrospective, had chosen the role of the man of action, who answers blow for blow and opposes a mailed front to the thrusts of destiny; and the completeness of the equipment testified to his inner weakness. We talked only of what we were not thinking of, and parted, after a few days, with a sense of relief that proved the inadequacy of friendship to perform, in such cases, the office assigned to it by tradition.

Soon afterward my own work called me home, but Grancy remained several years in Europe. International diplomacy kept its promise of giving him work to do, and during the year in which he acted as *chargé d'affaires* he acquitted himself, under trying conditions, with conspicuous zeal and discretion. A political redistribution of matter removed him from office just as he had proved his usefulness to the government; and the following summer I heard that he had come home and was down at his place in the country.

On my return to town I wrote him and his reply came by the next post. He answered as it were in his natural voice, urging me to spend the following Sunday with him, and suggesting that I should bring down any of the old set who could be persuaded to join me. I thought this a good sign, and yet – shall I own it? – I was vaguely disappointed. Perhaps we are apt to feel that our friends' sorrows should be kept like those historic monuments from which the encroaching ivy is periodically removed.

That very evening at the club I ran across Claydon. I told him of Grancy's invitation and proposed that we should go down together; but he pleaded an engagement. I was sorry, for I had always felt that he and I stood nearer Ralph than the others, and if the old Sundays were to be renewed I should have preferred that we two should spend the first alone with him. I said as much to Claydon and offered to fit my time to his; but he met this by a general refusal.

'I don't want to go to Grancy's,' he said bluntly. I waited a moment, but he appended no qualifying clause.

'You've seen him since he came back?' I finally ventured.

Claydon nodded.

'And is he so awfully bad?'

'Bad? No: he's all right.'

'All right? How can he be, unless he's changed beyond all recognition?'

'Oh, you'll recognise *him*,' said Claydon, with a puzzling deflection of emphasis.

His ambiguity was beginning to exasperate me, and I felt myself shut out from some knowledge to which I had as good a right as he.

'You've been down there already, I suppose?'

'Yes; I've been down there.'

'And you've done with each other – the partnership is dissolved?'

'Done with each other? I wish to God we had!' He rose nervously and tossed aside the review from which my approach had diverted him. 'Look here,' he said, standing before me, 'Ralph's the best fellow going and there's nothing under heaven I wouldn't do for him – short of going down there again.' And with that he walked out of the room.

Claydon was incalculable enough for me to read a dozen different meanings into his words; but none of my interpretations satisfied me. I determined, at any rate, to seek no further for a companion; and the next Sunday I travelled down to Grancy's alone. He met me at the station and I saw at once that he had changed since our last meeting. Then he had been in fighting array, but now if he and grief still housed together it was no longer as enemies. Physically the transformation was as marked but less reassuring. If the spirit triumphed the body showed its scars. At five-and-forty he was grey and stooping, with the tired gait of an old man. His serenity, however, was not the resignation of age. I saw that he did not mean to drop out of the game. Almost immediately he began to speak of our old interests; not with an effort, as at our former meeting, but simply and naturally, in the tone of a man whose life has flowed back into its normal channels. I remembered, with a touch of self-reproach, how I had distrusted his reconstructive powers; but my admiration for his reserved force was now tinged by the sense that, after all, such happiness as his ought to have been paid with his last coin. The feeling grew as we neared the house and I found how inextricably his wife was interwoven with my remembrance of the place: how the whole scene was but an extension of that vivid presence.

Within doors nothing was changed, and my hand would have dropped without surprise into her welcoming clasp. It was luncheon-time, and Grancy led me at once to the dining-room, where the walls, the furniture, the very plate and porcelain, seemed a mirror in which a moment since her face had been reflected. I wondered whether Grancy, under the recovered tranquillity of his smile, concealed the same sense of her nearness, saw perpetually between himself and the actual her bright unappeasable ghost. He spoke of her once or twice, in an easy incidental way, and her name seemed to hang in the air after he had uttered it, like a chord that continues to vibrate. If he felt her presence it was evidently as an enveloping medium, the moral atmosphere in which he breathed. I had never before known how completely the dead may survive.

After luncheon we went for a long walk through the autumnal fields and woods, and dusk was falling when we re-entered the house. Grancy led the way to the library, where, at this hour, his wife had always welcomed us back to a bright fire and a cup of tea. The room faced the west, and held a clear light of its own after the rest of the house had grown dark. I remembered how young she had looked in this pale gold light, which irradiated her eyes and hair, or silhouetted her girlish outline as she passed before the windows. Of all the rooms the library was most peculiarly hers; and here I felt that her nearness might take visible shape. Then, all in a moment, as Grancy opened the door, the feeling vanished and a kind of resistance met me on the threshold. I looked about me. Was the room changed? Had some desecrating hand effaced the traces of her presence? No; here too the setting was undisturbed. My feet sank into the same deep-piled Daghestan; the bookshelves took the firelight on the same rows of rich subdued bindings; her armchair stood in its old place near the tea-table; and from the opposite wall her face confronted me.

Her face – but *was* it hers? I moved nearer and stood looking up at the portrait. Grancy's glance had followed mine and I heard him move to my side.

'You see a change in it?' he said.

'What does it mean?' I asked.

'It means – that five years have passed.'

'Over *her* ?'

'Why not? – Look at me!' He pointed to his grey hair and furrowed temples. 'What do you think kept *her* so young? It was happiness! But now –' he looked up at her with infinite tenderness. 'I like her better so,' he said. 'It's what she would have wished.'

'Have wished?'

'That we should grow old together. Do you think she would have wanted to be left behind?'

I stood speechless, my gaze travelling from his worn grief-beaten features to the painted face above. It was not furrowed like his; but a veil of years seemed to have descended on it. The bright hair had lost its elasticity, the cheek its clearness, the brow its light: the whole woman had waned.

Grancy laid his hand on my arm. 'You don't like it?' he said sadly.

'Like it? I – I've lost her!' I burst out.

'And I've found her,' he answered.

'In *that*?' I cried with a reproachful gesture.

'Yes; in that.' He swung round on me almost defiantly. 'The other had become a sham, a lie! This is the way she would have looked – does look, I mean. Claydon ought to know, oughtn't he?'

I turned suddenly. 'Did Claydon do this for you?'

Grancy nodded.

'Since your return?'

'Yes. I sent for him after I'd been back a week –' He turned away and gave a thrust to the smouldering fire. I followed, glad to leave the picture behind me. Grancy threw himself into a chair near the hearth, so that the light fell on his sensitive variable face. He leaned his head back, shading his eyes with his hand, and began to speak.

'You fellows knew enough of my early history to guess what my second marriage meant to me. I say guess, because no one could understand – really. I've always had a feminine streak in me, I suppose: the need of a pair of eyes that should see with me, of a pulse that should keep time with mine. Life is a big thing, of course; a magnificent spectacle; but I got so tired of looking at it alone! Still, it's always good to live, and I had plenty of happiness – of the evolved kind. What I'd never had a taste of was the simple inconscient sort that one breathes in like the air . . .

'Well – I met her. It was like finding the climate in which I was meant to live. You know what she was – how indefinitely she multiplied one's points of contact with life, how she lit up the caverns and bridged the abysses! Well, I swear to you (though I suppose the sense of all that was latent in me) that what I used to think of on my way home at the end of the day was simply that when I opened this door she'd be sitting over there, with the lamplight falling in a particular way on one little curl in her neck . . . When Claydon painted her he caught just the look she used to lift to mine when I came in – I've wondered, sometimes, at his knowing how she looked when she and I were alone. How I rejoiced in that picture! I used to say to her, "You're my prisoner now – I shall never lose you. If you grew tired of me and left me you'd leave your real self there on the wall!" It was always one of our jokes that she was going to grow tired of me –

'Three years of it – and then she died. It was so sudden that there was no change, no diminution. It was as if she had suddenly become fixed, immovable, like her own portrait: as if Time had ceased at its happiest hour, just as Claydon had thrown down his brush one day and said, "I can't do better than that."

'I went away, as you know, and stayed over there five years. I worked as hard as I knew how, and after the first black months a little light stole in on me. From thinking that she would have been interested in what I was doing I came to feel that she *was* interested – that she was there and that she knew. I'm not talking any psychical jargon – I'm simply trying to express the sense I had that an influence so full, so abounding as hers couldn't pass like a spring shower. We had so lived into each other's hearts and minds that the consciousness of what she would have thought and felt illuminated all I did. At first she used to come back shyly, tentatively, as though not sure of finding me; then she stayed longer and longer, till at last she became again the very air I breathed . . . There were bad moments, of course, when her nearness mocked me with the loss of the real woman; but gradually the distinction between the two was effaced and the mere thought of her grew warm as flesh and blood.

'Then I came home. I landed in the morning and came straight down here. The thought of seeing her portrait possessed me and my heart beat like a lover's as I opened the library door. It was in the afternoon and the room was full of light. It fell on her picture – the picture of a young and radiant woman. She smiled at me coldly across the distance that divided us. I had the feeling that she didn't even recognise me. And then I caught sight of myself in the mirror over there – a grey-haired broken man whom she had never known!

'For a week we two lived together – the strange woman and the strange man. I used to sit night after night and question her smiling face; but no answer ever came. What did she know of me, after all? We were irrevocably separated by the five years of life that lay between us. At times, as I sat here, I almost grew to hate her; for her presence had driven away my gentle ghost, the real wife who had wept, aged, struggled with me during those awful years . . . It was the worst loneliness I've ever known. Then, gradually, I began to notice a look of sadness in the picture's eyes; a look that seemed to say: "Don't you see that *I* am lonely too?" And all at once it came over me how she would have hated to be left behind! I remembered her comparing life to a heavy book that could not be read with ease unless two people held it together; and I thought how impatiently her hand would have turned the pages that divided us! – So the idea came to me: "It's the picture that stands between us; the picture that is dead, and not my wife. To sit in this room is to keep watch beside a corpse." As this feeling grew on me the portrait became like a beautiful mausoleum in which she had been buried alive: I could hear her beating against the painted walls and crying to me faintly for help . . .

'One day I found I couldn't stand it any longer and I sent for Claydon. He came down and I told him what I'd been through and what I wanted him to do. At first he refused point-blank to touch the picture. The next morning I went off for a long tramp, and when I came home I found him sitting here alone. He looked at me sharply for a moment and then he said: "I've changed my mind; I'll do it." I arranged one of the north rooms as a studio and he shut himself up there for a day; then he sent for me. The picture stood there as you see it now – it was as though she'd met me on the threshold and taken me in her arms! I tried to thank him, to tell him what it meant to me, but he cut me short.

' "There's an up train at five, isn't there?" he asked. "I'm booked for a dinner tonight. I shall just have time to make a bolt for the station and you can send my traps after me." I haven't seen him since.

'I can guess what it cost him to lay hands on his masterpiece; but, after all, to him it was only a picture lost, to me it was my wife regained!'

4

After that, for ten years or more, I watched the strange spectacle of a life of hopeful and productive effort based on the structure of a dream. There could be no doubt to those who saw Grancy during this period that he drew his strength and courage from the sense of his wife's mystic participation in his task. When I went back to see him a few months later I found the portrait had been removed from the library and placed in a small study upstairs, to which he had transferred his desk and a few books. He told me he always sat there when he was alone, keeping the library for his Sunday visitors. Those who missed the portrait of course made no comment on its absence, and the few who were in his secret respected it. Gradually all his old friends had gathered about him and our Sunday afternoons regained something of their former character; but Claydon never reappeared among us.

As I look back now I see that Grancy must have been failing from the time of his return home. His invincible spirit belied and disguised the signs of weakness that afterward asserted themselves in my remembrance of him. He seemed to have an inexhaustible fund of life to draw on, and more than one of us was a pensioner on his superfluity.

Nevertheless, when I came back one summer from my European holiday and heard that he had been at the point of death, I understood at once that we had believed him well only because he wished us to.

I hastened down to the country and found him midway in a slow convalescence. I felt then that he was lost to us and he read my thought at a glance.

'Ah,' he said, 'I'm an old man now and no mistake. I suppose we shall have to go half-speed after this; but we shan't need towing just yet!'

The plural pronoun struck me, and involuntarily I looked up at Mrs Grancy's portrait. Line by line I saw my fear reflected in it. It was the face of a woman who knows that her husband is dying. My heart stood still at the thought of what Claydon had done.

Grancy had followed my glance. 'Yes, it's changed her,' he said quietly. 'For months, you know, it was touch and go with me – we had a long fight of it, and it was worse for her than for me.' After a pause he added: 'Claydon has been very kind; he's so busy nowadays that I seldom see him, but when I sent for him the other day he came down at once.'

I was silent and we spoke no more of Grancy's illness; but when I took leave it seemed like shutting him in alone with his death-warrant.

The next time I went down to see him he looked much better. It was a Sunday and he received me in the library, so that I did not see the portrait again. He continued to improve and toward spring we began to feel that, as he had said, he might yet travel a long way without being towed.

One evening, on returning to town after a visit which had confirmed my sense of reassurance, I found Claydon dining alone at the club. He asked me to join him and over the coffee our talk turned to his work.

'If you're not too busy,' I said at length, 'you ought to make time to go down to Grancy's again.'

He looked up quickly. 'Why?' he asked.

'Because he's quite well again,' I returned with a touch of cruelty. 'His wife's prognostications were mistaken.'

Claydon stared at me a moment. 'Oh, *she* knows,' he affirmed with a smile that chilled me.

'You mean to leave the portrait as it is then?' I persisted.

He shrugged his shoulders. 'He hasn't sent for me yet!'

A waiter came up with the cigars and Claydon rose and joined another group.

It was just a fortnight later that Grancy's housekeeper telegraphed for me. She met me at the station with the news that he had been 'taken bad' and that the doctors were with him. I had to wait for some time in the deserted library before the medical men appeared. They had the baffled manner of empirics who have been superseded by the great Healer; and I lingered only long enough to hear that Grancy was not suffering and that my presence could do him no harm.

I found him seated in his armchair in the little study. He held out his hand with a smile.

'You see she was right after all,' he said.

'She?' I repeated, perplexed for the moment.

'My wife.' He indicated the picture. 'Of course I knew she had no hope from the first. I saw that' – he lowered his voice – 'after Claydon had been here. But I wouldn't believe it at first!'

I caught his hands in mine. 'For God's sake don't believe it now!' I adjured him.

He shook his head gently. 'It's too late,' he said. 'I might have known that she knew.'

'But, Grancy, listen to me,' I began; and then I stopped. What could I say that would convince him? There was no common ground of argument on which we could meet; and after all it would be easier for him to die feeling that she *had* known. Strangely enough, I saw that Claydon had missed his mark . . .

5

Grancy's will named me as one of his executors; and my associate, having other duties on his hands, begged me to assume the task of carrying out our friend's wishes. This placed me under the necessity of informing Claydon that the portrait of Mrs Grancy had been bequeathed to him; and he replied by the next post that he would send for the picture at once. I was staying in the deserted house when the portrait was taken away; and as the door closed on it I felt that Grancy's presence had vanished too. Was it his turn to follow her now, and could one ghost haunt another?

After that, for a year or two, I heard nothing more of the picture, and though I met Claydon from time to time we had little to say to each other. I had no definable grievance against the man and I tried to remember that he had done a fine thing in sacrificing his best picture to a friend; but my resentment had all the tenacity of unreason.

One day, however, a lady whose portrait he had just finished begged me to go with her to see it. To refuse was impossible, and I went with the less reluctance that I knew I was not the only friend she had invited. The others were all grouped around the easel when I entered, and after contributing my share to the chorus of approval I turned away and began to stroll about the studio. Claydon was something of a collector and his things were generally worth looking at. The studio was a long tapestried room with a curtained archway at one end. The curtains were looped back, showing a smaller apartment, with books and flowers and a few fine bits of bronze and porcelain. The tea-table standing in this inner room proclaimed that it was open to inspection, and I wandered in. A *bleu poudre* vase first attracted me; then I turned to examine a slender bronze Ganymede, and in so doing found myself face to face with Mrs Grancy's portrait. I stared up at her blankly and she smiled back at me in all the recovered radiance of youth. The artist had effaced every trace of his later touches and the original picture had reappeared. It throned alone on the panelled wall, asserting a brilliant supremacy over its carefully chosen surroundings. I felt in an instant that the whole room was tributary to it: that Claydon had heaped his treasures at the feet of the woman he loved. Yes – it was the woman he had loved and not the picture; and my instinctive resentment was explained.

Suddenly I felt a hand on my shoulder.

'Ah, how could you?' I cried, turning on him.

'How could I?' he retorted. 'How could I *not* ? Doesn't she belong to me now?'

I moved away impatiently.

'Wait a moment,' he said with a detaining gesture. 'The others have gone and I want to say a word to you. – Oh, I know what you've thought of me – I can guess! You think I killed Grancy, I suppose?'

I was startled by his sudden vehemence. 'I think you tried to do a cruel thing,' I said.

'Ah – what a little way you others see into life!' he murmured. 'Sit down a moment – here, where we can look at her – and I'll tell you.'

He threw himself on the ottoman beside me and sat gazing up at the picture, with his hands clasped about his knee.

'Pygmalion,' he began slowly, 'turned his statue into a real woman; *I* turned my real woman into a picture. Small compensation, you think – but you don't know how much of a woman belongs to you after you've painted her! – Well, I made the best of it, at any rate – I gave her the best I had in me; and she gave me in return what such a woman gives by merely being. And after all she rewarded me enough by making me paint as I shall never paint again! There was one side of her, though, that was mine alone, and that was her beauty; for no one else understood it. To Grancy even it was the mere expression of herself – what language is to thought. Even when he saw the picture he didn't guess my secret – he was so sure she was all his! As though a man should think he owned the moon because it was reflected in the pool at his door –

'Well – when he came home and sent for me to change the picture it was like asking me to commit murder. He wanted me to make an old woman of her – of her who had been so divinely, unchangeably young! As if any man who really loved a woman would ask her to sacrifice her youth and beauty for his sake! At first I told him I couldn't do it – but afterward, when he left me alone with the picture, something queer happened. I suppose it was because I was always so confoundedly fond of Grancy that it went against me to refuse what he asked. Anyhow, as I sat looking up at her, she seemed to say, "I'm not yours but his, and I want you to make me what he wishes." And so I did it. I could have cut my hand off when the work was done – I dare say he told you I never would go back and look at it. He thought I was too busy – he never understood . . .

'Well – and then last year he sent for me again – you remember. It was after his illness, and he told me he'd grown twenty years older and that he wanted her to grow older too – he didn't want her to be left behind. The doctors all thought he was going to get well at that time, and he thought so too; and so did I when I first looked at him. But when I turned to the picture – ah, now I don't ask you to believe me; but I swear it was *her* face that told me he was dying, and that she wanted him to know it! She had a message for him and she made me deliver it.'

He rose abruptly and walked toward the portrait; then he sat down beside me again.

'Cruel? Yes, it seemed so to me at first; and this time, if I resisted, it was for *his* sake and not for mine. But all the while I felt her eyes drawing me, and gradually she made me understand. If she'd been there in the flesh (she seemed to say) wouldn't she have seen before any of us that he was dying? Wouldn't he have read the news first in her face? And wouldn't it be horrible if now he should discover it instead in strange eyes? – Well – that was what she wanted of me and I did it – I kept them together to the last!' He looked up at the picture again. 'But now she belongs to me,' he repeated . . .

The Quicksand

I

As Mrs Quentin's victoria, driving homeward, turned from the park into Fifth Avenue, she divined her son's tall figure walking ahead of her in the twilight. His long stride covered the ground more rapidly than usual, and she had a premonition that, if he were going home at that hour, it was because he wanted to see her.

Mrs Quentin, though not a fanciful woman, was sometimes aware of a sixth sense enabling her to detect the faintest vibrations of her son's impulses. She was too shrewd to fancy herself the one mother in possession of this faculty, but she permitted herself to think that few could exercise it more discreetly. If she could not help overhearing Alan's thoughts, she had the courage to keep her discoveries to herself, the tact to take for granted nothing that lay below the surface of their spoken intercourse: she knew that most people would rather have their letters read than their thoughts. For this super-feminine discretion Alan repaid her by – being Alan. There could have been no completer reward. He was the key to the meaning of life, the justification of what must have seemed as incomprehensible as it was odious, had it not all-sufficingly ended in himself. He was a perfect son, and Mrs Quentin had always hungered for perfection.

Her house, in a minor way, bore witness to the craving. One felt it to be the result of a series of eliminations: there was nothing fortuitous in its blending of line and colour. The almost morbid finish of every material detail of her life suggested the possibility that a diversity of energies had, by some pressure of circumstance, been forced into the channel of a narrow dilettanteism. Mrs Quentin's fastidiousness had, indeed, the flaw of being too one-sided. Her friends were not always worthy of the chairs they sat in, and she overlooked in her associates defects she would not have tolerated in her bric-à-brac. Her house was, in fact, never so distinguished as when it was empty; and it was at its best in the warm fire-lit silence that now received her.

Her son, who had overtaken her on the doorstep, followed her into the drawing-room, and threw himself into an armchair near the fire, while she laid off her furs and busied herself about the tea-table. For a while neither spoke; but glancing at him across the kettle, his mother noticed that he sat staring at the embers with a look she had never seen on his face, though its arrogant young outline was as familiar to her as her own thoughts. The look extended itself to his negligent attitude, to the droop of his long fine hands, the dejected tilt of his head against the cushions. It was like the moral equivalent of physical fatigue: he looked, as he himself would have phrased it, dead-beat, played out. Such an air was so foreign to his usual bright indomitableness that Mrs Quentin had the sense of an unfamiliar presence, in which she must observe herself, must raise hurried barriers against an alien approach. It was one of the drawbacks of their excessive intimacy that any break in it seemed a chasm.

She was accustomed to let his thoughts circle about her before they settled into speech, and she now sat in motionless expectancy, as though a sound might frighten them away.

At length, without turning his eyes from the fire, he said: 'I'm so glad you're a nice old-fashioned intuitive woman. It's painful to see them think.'

Her apprehension had already preceded him. 'Hope Fenno – ?' she faltered.

He nodded. 'She's been thinking – hard. It was very painful – to me, at least; and I don't believe she enjoyed it: she said she didn't.' He stretched his feet to the fire. 'The result of her cogitations is that she won't have me. She arrived at this by pure ratiocination – it's not a question of feeling, you understand. I'm the only man she's ever loved – but she won't have me. What novels did you read when you were young, dear? I'm convinced it all turns on that. If she'd been brought up on Trollope and Whyte-Melville, instead of Tolstoy and Mrs Ward, we should have now been vulgarly sitting on a sofa, trying on the engagement ring.'

Mrs Quentin at first was kept silent by the mother's instinctive anger that the girl she has not wanted for her son should have dared to refuse him. Then she said, 'Tell me, dear.'

'My good woman, she has scruples.'

'Scruples?'

'Against the paper. She objects to me in my official capacity as owner of the *Radiator*.'

His mother did not echo his laugh.

'She had found a solution, of course – she overflows with expedients. I was to chuck the paper, and we were to live happily ever afterward on canned food and virtue. She even had an alternative ready – women are so full of resources! I was to turn the *Radiator* into an independent organ, and run it at a loss to show the public what a model newspaper ought to be. On the whole, I think she fancied this plan more than the other – it commended itself to her as being more uncomfortable and aggressive. It's not the fashion nowadays to be good by stealth.'

Mrs Quentin said to herself, 'I didn't know how much he cared!' Aloud she murmured, 'You must give her time.'

'Time?'

'To move out the old prejudices and make room for new ones.'

'My dear mother, those she has are brand-new; that's the trouble with them. She's tremendously up-to-date. She takes in all the moral fashion-papers, and wears the newest thing in ethics.'

Her resentment lost its way in the intricacies of his metaphor. 'Is she so very religious?'

'You dear archaic woman! She's hopelessly irreligious; that's the difficulty. You can make a religious woman believe almost anything: there's the habit of credulity to work on. But when a girl's faith in the Deluge has been shaken, it's very hard to inspire her with confidence. She makes you feel that, before believing in you, it's her duty as a conscientious agnostic to find out whether you're not obsolete, or whether the text isn't corrupt, or somebody hasn't proved conclusively that you never existed, anyhow.'

Mrs Quentin was again silent. The two moved in that atmosphere of implications and assumptions where the lightest word may shake down the dust of countless stored impressions; and speech was sometimes more difficult between them than had their union been less close.

Presently she ventured, 'It's impossible?'

'Impossible?'

She seemed to use her words cautiously, like weapons that might slip and inflict a cut. 'What she suggests.'

Her son, raising himself, turned to look at her for the first time. Their glance met in a shock of comprehension. He was with her against the girl, then! Her satisfaction overflowed in a murmur of tenderness.

'Of course not, dear. One can't change – change one's life . . .'

'Oneself,' he emended. 'That's what I tell her. What's the use of my giving up the paper if I keep my point of view?'

The psychological distinction attracted her. 'Which is it she minds most?'

'Oh, the paper – for the present. She undertakes to modify the point of view afterward. All she asks is that I shall renounce my heresy: the gift of grace will come later.'

Mrs Quentin sat gazing into her untouched cup. Her son's first words had produced in her the hallucinated sense of struggling in the thick of a crowd that he could not see. It was horrible to feel herself hemmed in by influences imperceptible to him; yet if anything could have increased her misery it would have been the discovery that her ghosts had become visible.

As though to divert his attention, she precipitately asked, 'And you – ?'

His answer carried the shock of an evocation. 'I merely asked her what she thought of *you*.'

'Of me?'

'She admires you immensely, you know.'

For a moment Mrs Quentin's cheek showed the lingering light of girlhood: praise transmitted by her son acquired something of the transmitter's merit. 'Well – ?' she smiled.

'Well – you didn't make my father give up the *Radiator*, did you?'

His mother, stiffening, made a circuitous return: 'She never comes here. How can she know me?'

'She's so poor! She goes out so little.' He rose and leaned against the mantelpiece, dislodging with impatient fingers a slender bronze wrestler poised on a porphyry base, between two warm-toned Spanish ivories. 'And then *her* mother – ' he added, as if involuntarily.

'Her mother has never visited me,' Mrs Quentin finished for him.

He shrugged his shoulders. 'Mrs Fenno has the scope of a wax doll. Her rule of conduct is taken from her grandmother's sampler.'

'But the daughter is so modern – and yet – '

'The result is the same? Not exactly. *She* admires you – oh, immensely!' He replaced the bronze and turned to his mother with a smile. 'Aren't you on some hospital committee together? What especially strikes her is your way of doing good. She says philanthropy is not a line of conduct, but a state of mind – and it appears that you are one of the elect.'

As, in the vague diffusion of physical pain, relief seems to come with the acuter pang of a single nerve, Mrs Quentin felt herself suddenly eased by a rush of anger against the girl. 'If she loved you – ' she began.

His gesture checked her. 'I'm not asking you to get her to do that.'

The two were again silent, facing each other in the disarray of a common catastrophe – as though their thoughts, at the summons of danger, had rushed naked into action. Mrs Quentin, at this revealing moment, saw for the first time how many elements of her son's character had seemed comprehensible simply because they were familiar: as, in reading a foreign language, we take the meaning of certain words for granted till the context corrects us. Often, as in a given case, her maternal musings had figured his conduct, she now found herself at a loss to forecast it; and with this failure of intuition came a sense of the subserviency which had hitherto made her counsels but the anticipation of his wish. Her despair escaped in the moan, 'What *is* it you ask me?'

'To talk to her.'

'Talk to her?'

'Show her – tell her – make her understand that the paper has always been a thing outside your life – that hasn't touched you – that needn't touch *her*. Only, let her hear you – watch you – be with you – she'll see . . . she can't help seeing . . . '

His mother faltered. 'But if she's given you her reasons – ?'

'Let her give them to you! If she can – when she sees you . . . ' His impatient hand again displaced the wrestler. 'I care abominably,' he confessed.

On the Fenno threshold a sudden sense of the futility of the attempt had almost driven Mrs Quentin back to her carriage; but the door was already opening, and a parlor-maid who believed that Miss Fenno was in led the way to the depressing drawing-room. It was the kind of room in which no member of the family is likely to be found except after dinner or after death. The chairs and tables looked like poor relations who had repaid their keep by a long career of grudging usefulness: they seemed banded together against intruders in a sullen conspiracy of discomfort. Mrs Quentin, keenly susceptible to such influences, read failure in every angle of the upholstery. She was incapable of the vulgar error of thinking that Hope Fenno might be induced to marry Alan for his money; but between this assumption and the inference that the girl's imagination might be touched by the finer possibilities of wealth, good taste admitted a distinction. The Fenno furniture, however, presented to such reasoning the obtuseness of its black-walnut chamferings; and something in its attitude suggested that its owners would be as uncompromising. The room showed none of the modern attempts at palliation, no apologetic draping of facts; and Mrs Quentin, provisionally perched on a green-rep Gothic sofa with which it was clearly impossible to establish any closer relations, concluded that, had Mrs Fenno needed another seat of the same size, she would have set out placidly to match the one on which her visitor now languished.

To Mrs Quentin's fancy, Hope Fenno's opinions, presently imparted in a clear young voice from the opposite angle of the Gothic sofa, partook of the character of their surroundings. The girl's mind was like a large light empty place, scantily furnished with a few massive prejudices not designed to add to anyone's comfort but too ponderous to be easily moved. Mrs Quentin's own intelligence, in which its owner, in an artistically shaded half-light, had so long moved amid a delicate complexity of sensations, seemed in comparison suddenly close and crowded; and in taking refuge there from the glare of the young girl's candour, the older woman found herself stumbling in an unwonted obscurity. Her uneasiness resolved itself into a sense of irritation against her listener. Mrs Quentin knew that the momentary value of any argument lies in the capacity of the mind to which it is addressed, and as her shafts of persuasion spent themselves against Miss Fenno's obduracy, she said to herself that, since conduct is governed by emotions rather than ideas, the really strong people are those who mistake their sensations for opinions. Viewed in this light, Miss Fenno was certainly very strong: there was an unmistakable ring of finality in the tone with which she declared, 'It's impossible.'

Mrs Quentin's answer veiled the least shade of feminine resentment. 'I told Alan that, where he had failed, there was no chance of my making an impression.'

Hope Fenno laid on her visitor's an almost reverential hand. 'Dear Mrs Quentin, it's the impression you make that confirms the impossibility.'

Mrs Quentin waited a moment: she was perfectly aware that, where her feelings were concerned, her sense of humour was not to be relied on. 'Do I make such an odious impression?' she asked at length, with a smile that seemed to give the girl her choice of two meanings.

'You make such a beautiful one! It's too beautiful – it obscures my judgement.'

Mrs Quentin looked at her thoughtfully. 'Would it be permissible, I wonder, for an older woman to suggest that, at your age, it isn't always a misfortune to have what one calls one's judgement temporarily obscured?'

Miss Fenno flushed. 'I try not to judge others – '

'You judge Alan.'

'Ah, *he* is not others,' she murmured, with an accent that touched the older woman.

'You judge his mother.'

'I don't; I don't!'

Mrs Quentin pressed her point. 'You judge yourself, then, as you would be in my position – and your verdict condemns me.'

'How can you think it? It's because I appreciate the difference in our point of view that I find it so difficult to defend myself – '

'Against what?'

'The temptation to imagine that I might be as *you* are – feeling as I do.'

Mrs Quentin rose with a sigh. 'My child, in my day love was less subtle.' She added, after a moment, 'Alan is a perfect son.'

'Ah, that again – that makes it worse!'

'Worse?'

'Just as your goodness does, your sweetness, your immense indulgence in letting me discuss things with you in a way that must seem almost an impertinence.'

Mrs Quentin's smile was not without irony. 'You must remember that I do it for Alan.'

'That's what I love you for!' the girl instantly returned; and again her tone touched her listener.

'And yet you're sacrificing him – and to an idea!'

'Isn't it to ideas that all the sacrifices that were worth while have been made?'

'One may sacrifice oneself.'

Miss Fenno's colour rose. 'That's what I'm doing,' she said gently.

Mrs Quentin took her hand. 'I believe you are,' she answered. 'And it isn't true that I speak only for Alan. Perhaps I did when I began; but now I want to plead for you too – against yourself.' She paused, and then went on with a deeper note: 'I have let you, as you say, speak your mind to me in terms that some women might have resented, because I wanted to show you how little, as the years go on, theories, ideas, abstract conceptions of life, weigh against the actual, against the particular way in which life presents itself to us – to women especially. To decide beforehand exactly how one ought to behave in given circumstances is like deciding that one will follow a certain direction in crossing an unexplored country. Afterward we find that we must turn aside for the obstacles – cross the rivers where they're shallowest – take the tracks that others have beaten – make all sorts of unexpected concessions. Life is made up of compromises: that is what youth refuses to understand. I've lived long enough to doubt whether any real good ever came of sacrificing beautiful facts to even more beautiful theories. Do I seem casuistical? I don't know – there may be losses either way . . . but the love of the man one loves . . . of the child one loves . . . that makes up for everything . . .'

She had spoken with a thrill which seemed to communicate itself to the hand her listener had left in hers. Her eyes filled suddenly, but through their dimness she saw the girl's lips shape a last desperate denial: 'Don't you see it's because I feel all this that I mustn't – that I can't?'

3

Mrs Quentin, in the late spring afternoon, had turned in at the doors of the Metropolitan Museum. She had been walking in the park, in a solitude oppressed by the ever-present sense of her son's trouble, and had suddenly remembered that someone had added a Beltraffio to the collection. It was an old habit of Mrs Quentin's to seek in the enjoyment of the beautiful the distraction that most of her acquaintances appeared to find in each other's company. She had few friends, and their society was welcome to her only in her more superficial moods; but she could drug anxiety with a picture as some women can soothe it with a bonnet.

During the six months that had elapsed since her visit to Miss Fenno she had been conscious of a pain of which she had supposed herself no longer capable: as a man will continue to feel the ache of an amputated arm. She had fancied that all her centres of feeling had been transferred to Alan; but she now found herself subject to a kind of dual suffering, in which her individual pang was the keener in that it divided her from her son's. Alan had surprised her: she had not foreseen that he would take a sentimental rebuff so hard. His disappointment took the uncommunicative form of a sterner application to work. He threw himself into the concerns of the *Radiator* with an aggressiveness that almost betrayed itself in the paper. Mrs Quentin never read the *Radiator*, but from the glimpses of it reflected in the other journals she gathered that it was at least not being subjected to the moral reconstruction which had been one of Miss Fenno's alternatives.

Mrs Quentin never spoke to her son of what had happened. She was superior to the cheap satisfaction of avenging his injury by depreciating its cause. She knew that in sentimental sorrows such consolations are as salt in the wound. The avoidance of a subject so vividly present to both could not but affect the closeness of their relation. An invisible presence hampered their liberty of speech and thought. The girl was always between them; and to hide the sense of her intrusion they began to be less frequently together. It was then that Mrs Quentin measured the extent of her isolation. Had she ever dared to forecast such a situation, she would have proceeded on the conventional theory that her son's suffering must draw her nearer to him; and this was precisely the relief that was denied her. Alan's uncommunicativeness extended below the level of speech, and his mother, reduced to the helplessness of dead-reckoning, had not even the solace of adapting her sympathy to his needs. She did not know what he felt: his course was incalculable to her. She sometimes wondered if she had become as incomprehensible to him; and it was to find a moment's refuge from the dogging misery of such conjectures that she had now turned in at the museum.

The long line of mellow canvases seemed to receive her into the rich calm of an autumn twilight. She might have been walking in an enchanted wood where the footfall of care never sounded. So deep was the sense of seclusion that, as she turned from her prolonged communion with the new Beltraffio, it was a surprise to find she was not alone.

A young lady who had risen from the central ottoman stood in suspended flight as Mrs Quentin faced her. The older woman was the first to regain her self-possession.

'Miss Fenno!' she said.

The girl advanced with a blush. As it faded, Mrs Quentin noticed a change in her. There had always been something bright and bannerlike in her aspect, but now her look drooped, and she hung at half-mast, as it were. Mrs Quentin, in the embarrassment of surprising a secret that its possessor was doubtless unconscious of betraying, reverted hurriedly to the Beltraffio.

'I came to see this,' she said. 'It's very beautiful.'

Miss Fenno's eye travelled incuriously over the mystic blue reaches of the landscape. 'I suppose so,' she assented; adding, after another tentative pause, 'You come here often, don't you?'

'Very often,' Mrs Quentin answered. 'I find pictures a great help.'

'A help?'

'A rest, I mean . . . if one is tired or out of sorts.'

'Ah,' Miss Fenno murmured, looking down.

'This Beltraffio is new, you know,' Mrs Quentin continued. 'What a wonderful background, isn't it? Is he a painter who interests you?'

The girl glanced again at the dusky canvas, as though in a final endeavour to extract from it a clue to the consolations of art. 'I don't know,' she said at length; 'I'm afraid I don't understand pictures.' She moved nearer to Mrs Quentin and held out her hand.

'You're going?'

'Yes.'

Mrs Quentin looked at her. 'Let me drive you home,' she said, impulsively. She was feeling, with a shock of surprise, that it gave her, after all, no pleasure to see how much the girl had suffered.

Miss Fenno stiffened perceptibly. 'Thank you; I shall like the walk.'

Mrs Quentin dropped her hand with a corresponding movement of withdrawal, and a momentary wave of antagonism seemed to sweep the two women apart. Then, as Mrs Quentin, bowing slightly, again addressed herself to the picture, she felt a sudden touch on her arm.

'Mrs Quentin,' the girl faltered, 'I really came here because I saw your carriage.' Her eyes sank, and then fluttered back to her hearer's face. 'I've been horribly unhappy!' she exclaimed.

Mrs Quentin was silent. If Hope Fenno had expected an immediate response to her appeal, she was disappointed. The older woman's face was like a veil dropped before her thoughts.

'I've thought so often,' the girl went on precipitately, 'of what you said that day you came to see me last autumn. I think I understand now what you meant – what you tried to make me see . . . Oh, Mrs Quentin,' she broke out, 'I didn't mean to tell you this – I never dreamed of it till this moment – but you *do* remember what you said, don't you? You must remember it! And now that I've met you in this way, I can't help telling you that I believe – I begin to believe – that you were right, after all.'

Mrs Quentin had listened without moving; but now she raised her eyes with a slight smile. 'Do you wish me to say this to Alan?' she asked.

The girl flushed, but her glance braved the smile. 'Would he still care to hear it?' she said fearlessly.

Mrs Quentin took momentary refuge in a renewed inspection of the Beltraffio; then, turning, she said, with some reluctance: 'He would still care.'

'Ah!' broke from the girl.

During this exchange of words the two speakers had drifted unconsciously toward one of the benches. Mrs Quentin glanced about her: a custodian who had been hovering in the doorway sauntered into the adjoining gallery, and they remained alone among the silvery Vandykes and flushed bituminous Halses. Mrs Quentin sank down on the bench and reached a hand to the girl.

'Sit by me,' she said.

Miss Fenno dropped beside her. In both women the stress of emotion was too strong for speech. The girl was still trembling, and Mrs Quentin was the first to regain her composure.

'You say you've suffered,' she began at last. 'Do you suppose *I* haven't?'

'I knew you had. That made it so much worse for me – that I should have been the cause of your suffering for Alan!'

Mrs Quentin drew a deep breath. 'Not for Alan only,' she said. Miss Fenno turned on her a wondering glance. 'Not for Alan only. *That* pain every woman expects – and knows how to bear. We all know our children must have such disappointments, and to suffer with them is not the deepest pain. It's the suffering apart – in ways they don't understand.' She breathed deeply. 'I want you to know what I mean. You were right – that day – and I was wrong.'

'Oh,' the girl faltered.

Mrs Quentin went on in a voice of passionate lucidity. 'I knew it then – I knew it even while I was trying to argue with you – I've always known it! I didn't want my son to marry you till I heard your reasons for refusing him; and then – then I longed to see you his wife!'

'Oh, Mrs Quentin!'

'I longed for it; but I knew it mustn't be.'

'Mustn't be?'

Mrs Quentin shook her head sadly, and the girl, gaining courage from this mute negation, cried with an uncontrollable escape of feeling: 'It's because you thought me hard, obstinate narrow-minded? Oh, I understand that so well! My self-righteousness must have seemed so petty! A girl who could sacrifice a man's future to her own moral vanity – for it *was* a form of vanity; you showed me that plainly enough – how you must have despised me! But I am not that girl now – indeed I'm not. I'm not impulsive – I think things out. I've thought this out. I know Alan loves me – I know *how* he loves me – and I believe I can help him – oh, not in the ways I had fancied before – but just merely by loving him.' She paused, but Mrs Quentin made no sign. 'I see it all so differently now. I see what an influence love itself may be – how my believing in him, loving him, accepting him just as he is, might help him more than any theories, any arguments. I might have seen this long ago in looking at *you* – as he often told me – in seeing how you'd kept yourself apart from – from – Mr Quentin's work and his – been always the beautiful side of life to them – kept their faith alive in spite of themselves – not by interfering, preaching, reforming, but by – just loving them and being there – ' She looked at Mrs Quentin with a simple nobleness. 'It isn't as if I cared for the money, you know; if I cared for that, I should be afraid – '

'You will care for it in time,' Mrs Quentin said suddenly.

Miss Fenno drew back, releasing her hand. 'In time?'

'Yes; when there's nothing else left.' She stared a moment at the pictures. 'My poor child,' she broke out, 'I've heard all you say so often before!'

'You've heard it?'

'Yes – from myself. I felt as you do, I argued as you do, I acted as I mean to prevent your doing when I married Alan's father.'

The long empty gallery seemed to reverberate with the girl's startled exclamation – 'Oh, Mrs Quentin –'

'Hush; let me speak. Do you suppose I'd do this if you were the kind of pink-and-white idiot he ought to have married? It's because I see you're alive, as I was, tingling with beliefs, ambitions, energies, as I was – that I can't see you walled up alive, as I was, without stretching out a hand to save you!' She sat gazing rigidly forward, her eyes on the pictures, speaking in the low precipitate tone of one who tries to press the meaning of a lifetime into a few breathless sentences.

'When I met Alan's father,' she went on, 'I knew nothing of his – his work. We met abroad, where I had been living with my mother. That was twenty-six years ago, when the *Radiator* was less – less notorious than it is now. I knew my husband owned a newspaper – a great newspaper – and nothing more. I had never seen a copy of the *Radiator* ; I had no notion what it stood for, in politics – or in other ways. We were married in Europe, and a few months afterward we came to live here. People were already beginning to talk about the *Radiator*. My husband, on leaving college, had bought it with some money an old uncle had left him, and the public at first was merely curious to see what an ambitious, stirring young man without any experience of journalism was going to make out of his experiment. They found first of all that he was going to make a great deal of money out of it. I found that out too. I was so happy in other ways that it didn't make much difference at first, though it was pleasant to be able to help my mother, to be generous and charitable, to live in a nice house, and wear the handsome gowns he liked to see me in. But still it didn't really count – it counted so little that when, one day, I learned what the *Radiator* was, I would have gone out into the streets barefooted rather than live another hour on the money it brought in . . . ' Her voice sank, and she paused to steady it. The girl at her side did not speak or move. 'I shall never forget that day,' she began again. 'The paper had stripped bare some family scandal – some miserable bleeding secret that a dozen unhappy people had been struggling to keep out of print – that *would* have been kept out if my husband had not – Oh, you must guess the rest! I can't go on!'

She felt a hand on hers. 'You mustn't go on, Mrs Quentin,' the girl whispered.

'Yes, I must – I must! You must be made to understand.' She drew a deep breath. 'My husband was not like Alan. When he found out how I felt about it he was surprised at first – but gradually he began to see – or at least I fancied he saw – the hatefulness of it. At any rate he saw how I suffered, and he offered to give up the whole thing – to sell the paper. It couldn't be done all of a sudden, of course – he made me see that – for he had put all his money in it, and he had no special aptitude for any other kind of work. He was a born journalist – like Alan. It was a great sacrifice for him to give up the paper, but he promised to do it – in time – when a good opportunity offered. Meanwhile, of course, he wanted to build it up, to increase the circulation – and to do that he had to keep on in the same way – he made that clear to me. I saw that we were in a vicious circle. The paper, to sell well, had to be made more and more detestable and disgraceful. At first I rebelled – but somehow – I can't tell you how it was – after that first concession the ground seemed to give under me: with every struggle I sank deeper. And then – then Alan was born. He was such a delicate baby that there was very little hope of saving him. But money did it – the money from the paper. I took him abroad to see the best physicians – I took him to a warm climate every winter. In hot weather the doctors recommended sea air, and we had a yacht and cruised every summer. I owed his life to the *Radiator*. And when he began to grow stronger the habit was formed – the habit of luxury. He could not get on without the things he had always been used to. He pined in bad air; he drooped under monotony and discomfort; he throve on variety, amusement, travel, every kind of novelty and excitement. And all I wanted for him his inexhaustible foster-mother was there to give!

'My husband said nothing, but he must have seen how things were going. There was no more talk of giving up the *Radiator*. He never reproached me with my inconsistency, but I thought he must despise me, and the thought made me reckless. I determined to ignore the paper altogether – to take what it gave as though I didn't know where it came from. And to excuse this I invented the theory that one may, so to speak, purify money by putting it to good uses. I gave away a great deal in charity – I indulged myself very little at first. All the money that was not spent on Alan I tried to do good with. But gradually, as my boy grew up, the problem became more complicated. How was I to protect Alan from the contamination I had let him live in? I couldn't preach by example – couldn't hold up his father as a warning, or denounce the money we were living on. All I could do was to disguise the inner ugliness of life by making it beautiful outside – to build a wall of beauty between him and the facts of life, turn his tastes and interests another way, hide the *Radiator* from him as a smiling woman at a ball may hide a cancer in her breast! Just as Alan was entering college his father died. Then I saw my way clear. I had loved my husband – and yet I drew my first free breath in years. For the *Radiator* had been left to Alan outright – there was nothing on earth to prevent his selling it when he came of age. And there was no excuse for his not selling it. I had brought him up to depend on money, but the paper had given us enough money to gratify all his tastes. At last we could turn on the monster that had nourished us. I felt a savage joy in the thought – I could hardly bear to wait till Alan came of age. But I had never spoken to him of the paper, and I didn't dare speak of it now. Some false shame kept me back, some vague belief in his ignorance. I would wait till he was twenty-one, and then we should be free.

'I waited – the day came, and I spoke. You can guess his answer, I suppose. He had no idea of selling the *Radiator*. It wasn't the money he cared for – it was the career that tempted him. He was a born journalist, and his ambition, ever since he could remember, had been to carry on his father's work, to develop, to surpass it. There was nothing in the world as interesting as modern journalism. He couldn't imagine any other kind of life that wouldn't bore him to death. A newspaper like the *Radiator* might be made one of the biggest powers on earth, and he loved power, and meant to have all he could get. I listened to him in a kind of trance. I couldn't find a word to say. His father had had scruples – he had none. I seemed to realise at once that argument would be useless. I don't know that I even tried to plead with him – he was so bright and hard and inaccessible! Then I saw that he was, after all, what I had made him – the creature of my concessions, my connivances, my evasions. That was the price I had paid for him – I had kept him at that cost!

'Well – I *had* kept him, at any rate. That was the feeling that survived. He was my boy, my son, my very own – till some other woman took him. Meanwhile the old life must go on as it could. I gave up the struggle. If at that point he was inaccessible, at others he was close to me. He has always been a perfect son. Our tastes grew together – we enjoyed the same books, the same pictures, the same people. All I had to do was to look at him in profile to see the side of him that was really mine. At first I kept thinking of the dreadful other side – but gradually the impression faded, and I kept my mind turned from it, as one does from a deformity in a face one loves. I thought I had made my last compromise with life – had hit on a *modus vivendi* that would last my time.

'And then he met you. I had always been prepared for his marrying, but not a girl like you. I thought he would choose a sweet thing who would never pry into his closets – he hated women with ideas! But as soon as I saw you I knew the struggle would have to begin again. He is so much stronger than his father – he is full of the most monstrous convictions. And he has the courage of them, too – you saw last year that his love for you never made him waver. He believes in his work; he adores it – it is a kind of hideous idol to which he would make human sacrifices! He loves you still – I've been honest with you – but his love wouldn't change him. It is you who would have to change – to die gradually, as I have died, till there is only one live point left in me. Ah, if one died completely – that's simple enough! But something persists – remember that – a single point, an aching nerve of truth. Now and then you may drug it – but a touch wakes it again, as your face has waked it in me. There's always enough of one's old self left to suffer with . . . '

She stood up and faced the girl abruptly. 'What shall I tell Alan?' she said.

Miss Fenno sat motionless, her eyes on the ground. Twilight was falling on the gallery – a twilight which seemed to emanate not so much from the glass dome overhead as from the crepuscular depths into which the faces of the pictures were receding. The custodian's step sounded warningly down the corridor. When the girl looked up she was alone.

Roman Fever

From the table at which they had been lunching two American ladies of ripe but well-cared-for middle age moved across the lofty terrace of the Roman restaurant and, leaning on its parapet, looked first at each other and then down on the outspread glories of the Palatine and the Forum, with the same expression of vague but benevolent approval.

As they leaned there a girlish voice echoed up gaily from the stairs leading to the court below. 'Well, come along, then,' it cried, not to them but to an invisible companion, 'and let's leave the young things to their knitting,' and a voice as fresh laughed back: 'Oh, look here, Babs, not actually knitting – ' 'Well, I mean figuratively,' rejoined the first. 'After all, we haven't left our poor parents much else to do.. . .' At that point the turn of the stairs engulfed the dialogue.

The two ladies looked at each other again, this time with a tinge of smiling embarrassment, and the smaller and paler one shook her head and coloured slightly. 'Barbara!' she murmured, sending an unheard rebuke after the mocking voice in the stairway.

The other lady, who was fuller, and higher in colour, with a small determined nose supported by vigorous black eyebrows, gave a good-humoured laugh. 'That's what our daughters think of us.'

Her companion replied by a deprecating gesture. 'Not of us individually. We must remember that. It's just the collective modern idea of mothers. And you see – ' Half guiltily she drew from her handsomely mounted black handbag a twist of crimson silk run through by two fine knitting needles. 'One never knows,' she murmured. 'The new system has certainly given us a good deal of time to kill; and sometimes I get tired just looking – even at this.' Her gesture was now addressed to the stupendous scene at their feet.

The dark lady laughed again, and they both relapsed upon the view, contemplating it in silence, with a sort of diffused serenity which might have been borrowed from the spring effulgence of the Roman skies. The luncheon hour was long past, and the two had their end of the vast terrace to themselves. At its opposite extremity a few groups, detained by a lingering look at the outspread city, were gathering up guidebooks and fumbling for tips. The last of them scattered, and the two ladies were alone on the air-washed height.

'Well, I don't see why we shouldn't just stay here,' said Mrs Slade, the lady of the high colour and energetic brows. Two derelict basket chairs stood near, and she pushed them into the angle of the parapet, and settled herself in one, her gaze upon the Palatine. 'After all, it's still the most beautiful view in the world.'

'It always will be, to me,' assented her friend Mrs Ansley, with so slight a stress on the 'me' that Mrs Slade, though she noticed it, wondered if it were not merely accidental, like the random underlinings of old-fashioned letter writers.

'Grace Ansley was always old-fashioned,' she thought; and added aloud, with a retrospective smile: 'It's a view we've both been familiar with for a good many years. When we first met here we were younger than our girls are now. You remember!'

'Oh, yes, I remember,' murmured Mrs Ansley, with the same undefinable stress – 'There's that head-waiter wondering,' she interpolated. She was evidently far less sure than her companion of herself and of her rights in the world.

'I'll cure him of wondering,' said Mrs Slade, stretching her hand toward a bag as discreetly opulent-looking as Mrs Ansley's. Signing to the headwaiter, she explained that she and her friend were old lovers of Rome, and would like to spend the end of the afternoon looking down on the view – that is, if it did not disturb the service! The headwaiter, bowing over her gratuity, assured her that the ladies were most welcome, and would be still more so if they would condescend to remain for dinner. A full-moon night they would remember . . .

Mrs Slade's black brows drew together, as though references to the moon were out of place and even unwelcome. But she smiled away her frown as the headwaiter retreated. 'Well, why not! We might do worse. There's no knowing, I suppose, when the girls will be back. Do you even know back from where? I don't!'

Mrs Ansley again coloured slightly. 'I think those young Italian aviators we met at the embassy invited them to fly to Tarquinia for tea. I suppose they'll want to wait and fly back by moonlight.'

'Moonlight – moonlight! What a part it still plays. Do you suppose they're as sentimental as we were?'

'I've come to the conclusion that I don't in the least know what they are,' said Mrs Ansley. 'And perhaps we didn't know much more about each other.'

'No, perhaps we didn't.'

Her friend gave her a shy glance. 'I never should have supposed you were sentimental, Alida.'

'Well, perhaps I wasn't.' Mrs Slade drew her lids together in retrospect; and for a few moments the two ladies, who had been intimate since childhood, reflected how little they knew each other. Each one, of course, had a label ready to attach to the other's name; Mrs Delphin Slade, for instance, would have told herself, or anyone who asked her, that Mrs Horace Ansley, twenty-five years ago, had been exquisitely lovely – no, you wouldn't believe it, would you! though, of course, still charming, distinguished . . . Well, as a girl she had been exquisite; far more beautiful than her daughter, Barbara, though certainly Babs, according to the new standards at any rate, was more effective – had more edge, as they say. Funny where she got it, with those two nullities as parents. Yes; Horace Ansley was – well, just the duplicate of his wife. Museum specimens of old New York. Good-looking, irreproachable, exemplary. Mrs Slade and Mrs Ansley had lived opposite each other – actually as well as figuratively – for years. When the drawing-room curtains in No 20 East Seventy-Third Street were renewed, No 23, across the way, was always aware of it. And of all the movings, buyings, travels, anniversaries, illnesses – the tame chronicle of an estimable pair. Little of it escaped Mrs Slade. But she had grown bored with it by the time her husband made his big coup in Wall Street, and when they bought in upper Park Avenue had already begun to think: 'I'd rather live opposite a speakeasy for a change; at least one might see it raided.' The idea of seeing Grace raided was so amusing that (before the move) she launched it at a woman's lunch. It made a hit, and went the rounds – she sometimes wondered if it had crossed the street, and reached Mrs Ansley. She hoped not, but didn't much mind. Those were the days when respectability was at a discount, and it did the irreproachable no harm to laugh at them a little.

A few years later, and not many months apart, both ladies lost their husbands. There was an appropriate exchange of wreaths and condolences, and a brief renewal of intimacy in the half shadow of their mourning; and now, after another interval, they had run across each other in Rome, at the same hotel, each of them the modest appendage of a salient daughter. The similarity of their lot had again drawn them together, lending itself to mild jokes, and the mutual confession that, if in old days it must have been tiring to 'keep up' with daughters, it was now, at times, a little dull not to.

No doubt, Mrs Slade reflected, she felt her unemployment more than poor Grace ever would. It was a big drop from being the wife of Delphin Slade to being his widow. She had always regarded herself (with a certain conjugal pride) as his equal in social gifts, as contributing her full share to the making of the exceptional couple they were: but the difference after his death was irremediable. As the wife of the famous corporation lawyer, always with an international case or two on hand, every day brought its exciting and unexpected obligation: the impromptu entertaining of eminent colleagues from abroad, the hurried dashes on legal business to London, Paris or Rome, where the entertaining was so handsomely reciprocated; the amusement of hearing in her wake: 'What, that handsome woman with the good clothes and the eyes is Mrs Slade – the Slade's wife! Really! Generally the wives of celebrities are such frumps.'

Yes; being the Slade's widow was a dullish business after that. In living up to such a husband all her faculties had been engaged; now she had only her daughter to live up to, for the son who seemed to have inherited his father's gifts had died suddenly in boyhood. She had fought through that agony because her husband was there, to be helped and to help ; now, after the father's death, the thought of the boy had become unbearable. There was nothing left but to mother her daughter; and dear Jenny was such a perfect daughter that she needed no excessive mothering. 'Now with Babs Ansley I don't know that I should be so quiet,' Mrs Slade sometimes half-enviously reflected; but Jenny, who was younger than her brilliant friend, was that rare accident, an extremely pretty girl who somehow made youth and prettiness seem as safe as their absence. It was all perplexing – and to Mrs Slade a little boring. She wished that Jenny would fall in love – with the wrong man, even; that she might have to be watched, out-manoeuvred, rescued. And instead, it was Jenny who watched her mother, kept her out of draughts, made sure that she had taken her tonic . . .

Mrs Ansley was much less articulate than her friend, and her mental portrait of Mrs Slade was slighter, and drawn with fainter touches. 'Alida Slade's awfully brilliant; but not as brilliant as she thinks,' would have summed it up; though she would have added, for the enlightenment of strangers, that Mrs Slade had been an extremely dashing girl; much more so than her daughter, who was pretty, of course, and clever in a way, but had none of her mother's – well, 'vividness', someone had once called it. Mrs Ansley would take up current words like this, and cite them in quotation marks, as unheard-of audacities. No; Jenny was not like her mother. Sometimes Mrs Ansley thought Alida Slade was disappointed; on the whole she had had a sad life. Full of failures and mistakes; Mrs Ansley had always been rather sorry for her . . .

So these two ladies visualised each other, each through the wrong end of her little telescope.

2

For a long time they continued to sit side by side without speaking. It seemed as though, to both, there was a relief in laying down their somewhat futile activities in the presence of the vast Memento Mori which faced them. Mrs Slade sat quite still, her eyes fixed on the golden slope of the Palace of the Caesars, and after a while Mrs Ansley ceased to fidget with her bag, and she too sank into meditation. Like many intimate friends, the two ladies had never before had occasion to be silent together, and Mrs Ansley was slightly embarrassed by what seemed, after so many years, a new stage in their intimacy, and one with which she did not yet know how to deal.

Suddenly the air was full of that deep clangour of bells which periodically covers Rome with a roof of silver. Mrs Slade glanced at her wristwatch. 'Five o'clock already,' she said, as though surprised.

Mrs Ansley suggested interrogatively: 'There's bridge at the embassy at five.' For a long time Mrs Slade did not answer. She appeared to be lost in contemplation, and Mrs Ansley thought the remark had escaped her. But after a while she said, as if speaking out of a dream: 'Bridge, did you say! Not unless you want to . . . But I don't think I will, you know.'

'Oh, no,' Mrs Ansley hastened to assure her. 'I don't care to at all. It's so lovely here; and so full of old memories, as you say.' She settled herself in her chair, and almost furtively drew forth her knitting. Mrs Slade took sideways note of this activity, but her own beautifully cared-for hands remained motionless on her knee.

'I was just thinking,' she said slowly, 'what different things Rome stands for to each generation of travellers. To our grandmothers, Roman fever; to our mothers, sentimental dangers – how we used to be guarded!; to our daughters, no more dangers than the middle of Main Street. They don't know it – but how much they're missing!'

The long golden light was beginning to pale, and Mrs Ansley lifted her knitting a little closer to her eyes. 'Yes, how we were guarded!'

'I always used to think,' Mrs Slade continued, 'that our mothers had a much more difficult job than our grandmothers. When Roman fever stalked the streets it must have been comparatively easy to gather in the girls at the danger hour; but when you and I were young, with such beauty calling us, and the spice of disobedience thrown in, and no worse risk than catching cold during the cool hour after sunset, the mothers used to be put to it to keep us in – didn't they!'

She turned again toward Mrs Ansley, but the latter had reached a delicate point in her knitting. 'One, two, three – slip two; yes, they must have been,' she assented, without looking up.

Mrs Slade's eyes rested on her with a deepened attention. 'She can knit – in the face of this! How like her . . . '

Mrs Slade leaned back, brooding, her eyes ranging from the ruins which faced her to the long green hollow of the Forum, the fading glow of the church fronts beyond it, and the outlying immensity of the Colosseum. Suddenly she thought: 'It's all very well to say that our girls have done away with sentiment and moonlight. But if Babs Ansley isn't out to catch that young aviator – the one who's a *marchese* – then I don't know anything. And Jenny has no chance beside her. I know that too. I wonder if that's why Grace Ansley likes the two girls to go everywhere together! My poor Jenny as a foil – !' Mrs Slade gave a hardly audible laugh, and at the sound Mrs Ansley dropped her knitting.

'Yes – ?'

'I – oh, nothing. I was only thinking how your Babs carries everything before her. That Campolieri boy is one of the best matches in Rome. Don't look so innocent, my dear – you know he is. And I was wondering, ever so respectfully, you understand . . . wondering how two such exemplary characters as you and Horace had managed to produce anything quite so dynamic.' Mrs Slade laughed again, with a touch of asperity.

Mrs Ansley's hands lay inert across her needles. She looked straight out at the great accumulated wreckage of passion and splendour at her feet. But her small profile was almost expressionless. At length she said, 'I think you overrate Babs, my dear.'

Mrs Slade's tone grew easier. 'No; I don't. I appreciate her. And perhaps envy you. Oh, my girl's perfect; if I were a chronic invalid I'd – well, I think I'd rather be in Jenny's hands. There must be times . . . but there! I always wanted a brilliant daughter . . . and never quite understood why I got an angel instead.'

Mrs Ansley echoed her laugh in a faint murmur. 'Babs is an angel too.'

'Of course – of course! But she's got rainbow wings. Well, they're wandering by the sea with their young men; and here we sit . . . and it all brings back the past a little too acutely.'

Mrs Ansley had resumed her knitting. One might almost have imagined (if one had known her less well, Mrs Slade reflected) that, for her also, too many memories rose from the lengthening shadows of those august ruins. But no; she was simply absorbed in her work. What was there for her to worry about! She knew that Babs would almost certainly come back engaged to the extremely eligible Campolieri. 'And she'll sell the New York house, and settle down near them in Rome, and never be in their way . . . she's much too tactful. But she'll have an excellent cook, and just the right people in for bridge and cocktails . . . and a perfectly peaceful old age among her grandchildren.'

Mrs Slade broke off this prophetic flight with a recoil of self-disgust. There was no one of whom she had less right to think unkindly than of Grace Ansley. Would she never cure herself of envying her! Perhaps she had begun too long ago.

She stood up and leaned against the parapet, filling her troubled eyes with the tranquillising magic of the hour. But instead of tranquillising her the sight seemed to increase her exasperation. Her gaze turned toward the Colosseum. Already its golden flank was drowned in purple shadow, and above it the sky curved crystal clear, without light or colour. It was the moment when afternoon and evening hang balanced in midheaven.

Mrs Slade turned back and laid her hand on her friend's arm. The gesture was so abrupt that Mrs Ansley looked up, startled.

'The sun's set. You're not afraid, my dear?'

'Afraid – ?'

'Of Roman fever or pneumonia! I remember how ill you were that winter. As a girl you had a very delicate throat, hadn't you?'

'Oh, we're all right up here. Down below, in the Forum, it does get deathly cold, all of a sudden . . . but not here.'

'Ah, of course you know because you had to be so careful.' Mrs Slade turned back to the parapet. She thought: 'I must make one more effort not to hate her.' Aloud she said: 'Whenever I look at the Forum from up here, I remember that story about a great-aunt of yours, wasn't she? A dreadfully wicked great-aunt?'

'Oh, yes; Great-Aunt Harriet. The one who was supposed to have sent her young sister out to the Forum after sunset to gather a night-blooming flower for her album. All our great-aunts and grandmothers used to have albums of dried flowers.'

Mrs Slade nodded. 'But she really sent her because they were in love with the same man – '

'Well, that was the family tradition. They said Aunt Harriet confessed it years afterward. At any rate, the poor little sister caught the fever and died. Mother used to frighten us with the story when we were children.'

'And you frightened me with it, that winter when you and I were here as girls. The winter I was engaged to Delphin.'

Mrs Ansley gave a faint laugh. 'Oh, did I! Really frightened you? I don't believe you're easily frightened.'

'Not often; but I was then. I was easily frightened because I was too happy. I wonder if you know what that means?'

'I – yes . . . ' Mrs Ansley faltered.

'Well, I suppose that was why the story of your wicked aunt made such an impression on me. And I thought: "There's no more Roman fever, but the Forum is deathly cold after sunset – especially after a hot day. And the Colosseum's even colder and damper." '

'The Colosseum – ?'

'Yes. It wasn't easy to get in, after the gates were locked for the night. Far from easy. Still, in those days it could be managed; it was managed, often. Lovers met there who couldn't meet elsewhere. You knew that?'

'I – I dare say. I don't remember.'

'You don't remember? You don't remember going to visit some ruins or other one evening, just after dark, and catching a bad chill! You were supposed to have gone to see the moon rise. People always said that expedition was what caused your illness.'

There was a moment's silence; then Mrs Ansley rejoined: 'Did they? It was all so long ago.'

'Yes. And you got well again – so it didn't matter. But I suppose it struck your friends – the reason given for your illness. I mean – because everybody knew you were so prudent on account of your throat, and your mother took such care of you . . . You had been out late sightseeing, hadn't you, that night?'

'Perhaps I had. The most prudent girls aren't always prudent. What made you think of it now?'

Mrs Slade seemed to have no answer ready. But after a moment she broke out: 'Because I simply can't bear it any longer – '

Mrs Ansley lifted her head quickly. Her eyes were wide and very pale. 'Can't bear what?'

'Why – your not knowing that I've always known why you went.'

'Why I went – ?'

'Yes. You think I'm bluffing, don't you? Well, you went to meet the man I was engaged to – and I can repeat every word of the letter that took you there.'

While Mrs Slade spoke Mrs Ansley had risen unsteadily to her feet. Her bag, her knitting and gloves, slid in a panic-stricken heap to the ground. She looked at Mrs Slade as though she were looking at a ghost.

'No, no – don't,' she faltered out.

'Why not? Listen, if you don't believe me. "My one darling, things can't go on like this. I must see you alone. Come to the Colosseum immediately after dark tomorrow. There will be somebody to let you in. No one whom you need fear will suspect" – but perhaps you've forgotten what the letter said?'

Mrs Ansley met the challenge with an unexpected composure. Steadying herself against the chair she looked at her friend, and replied: 'No; I know it by heart too.'

'And the signature? "Only your D.S." Was that it? I'm right, am I? That was the letter that took you out that evening after dark?'

Mrs Ansley was still looking at her. It seemed to Mrs Slade that a slow struggle was going on behind the voluntarily controlled mask of her small quiet face. 'I shouldn't have thought she had herself so well in hand,' Mrs Slade reflected, almost resentfully. But at this moment Mrs Ansley spoke. 'I don't know how you knew. I burned that letter at once.'

'Yes; you would, naturally – you're so prudent!' The sneer was open now. 'And if you burned the letter you're wondering how on earth I know what was in it. That's it, isn't it?'

Mrs Slade waited, but Mrs Ansley did not speak.

'Well, my dear, I know what was in that letter because I wrote it!'

'You wrote it?'

'Yes.'

The two women stood for a minute staring at each other in the last golden light. Then Mrs Ansley dropped back into her chair. 'Oh,' she murmured, and covered her face with her hands.

Mrs Slade waited nervously for another word or movement. None came, and at length she broke out: 'I horrify you.'

Mrs Ansley's hands dropped to her knees. The face they uncovered was streaked with tears. 'I wasn't thinking of you. I was thinking – it was the only letter I ever had from him!'

'And I wrote it. Yes; I wrote it! But I was the girl he was engaged to. Did you happen to remember that?'

Mrs Ansley's head drooped again. 'I'm not trying to excuse myself . . . I remembered . . .'

'And still you went?'

'Still I went.'

Mrs Slade stood looking down on the small bowed figure at her side. The flame of her wrath had already sunk, and she wondered why she had ever thought there would be any satisfaction in inflicting so purposeless a wound on her friend. But she had to justify herself.

'You do understand? I'd found out – and I hated you, hated you. I knew you were in love with Delphin – and I was afraid; afraid of you, of your quiet ways, your sweetness . . . your . . . well, I wanted you out of the way, that's all. Just for a few weeks; just till I was sure of him. So in a blind fury I wrote that letter . . . I don't know why I'm telling you now.'

'I suppose,' said Mrs Ansley slowly, 'it's because you've always gone on hating me.'

'Perhaps. Or because I wanted to get the whole thing off my mind.' She paused. 'I'm glad you destroyed the letter. Of course I never thought you'd die.'

Mrs Ansley relapsed into silence, and Mrs Slade, leaning above her, was conscious of a strange sense of isolation, of being cut off from the warm current of human communion. 'You think me a monster!'

'I don't know . . . It was the only letter I had, and you say he didn't write it.'

'Ah, how you care for him still!'

'I cared for that memory,' said Mrs Ansley.

Mrs Slade continued to look down on her. She seemed physically reduced by the blow – as if, when she got up, the wind might scatter her like a puff of dust. Mrs Slade's jealousy suddenly leaped up again at the sight. All these years the woman had been living on that letter. How she must have loved him, to treasure the mere memory of its ashes! The letter of the man her friend was engaged to. Wasn't it she who was the monster?

'You tried your best to get him away from me, didn't you? But you failed; and I kept him. That's all.'

'Yes. That's all.'

'I wish now I hadn't told you. I'd no idea you'd feel about it as you do; I thought you'd be amused. It all happened so long ago, as you say; and you must do me the justice to remember that I had no reason to think you'd ever taken it seriously. How could I, when you were married to Horace Ansley two months afterward? As soon as you could get out of bed your mother rushed you off to Florence and married you. People were rather surprised – they wondered at its being done so quickly; but I thought I knew. I had an idea you did it out of pique – to be able to say you'd got ahead of Delphin and me. Kids have such silly reasons for doing the most serious things. And your marrying so soon convinced me that you'd never really cared.'

'Yes. I suppose it would,' Mrs Ansley assented.

The clear heaven overhead was emptied of all its gold. Dusk spread over it, abruptly darkening the Seven Hills. Here and there lights began to twinkle through the foliage at their feet. Steps were coming and going on the deserted terrace – waiters looking out of the doorway at the head of the stairs, then reappearing with trays and napkins and flasks of wine. Tables were moved, chairs straightened. A feeble string of electric lights flickered out. A stout lady in a dustcoat suddenly appeared, asking in broken Italian if anyone had seen the elastic band which held together her tattered Baedeker. She poked with her stick under the table at which she had lunched, the waiters assisting.

The corner where Mrs Slade and Mrs Ansley sat was still shadowy and deserted. For a long time neither of them spoke. At length Mrs Slade began again: 'I suppose I did it as a sort of joke – '

'A joke?'

'Well, girls are ferocious sometimes, you know. Girls in love especially. And I remember laughing to myself all that evening at the idea that you were waiting around there in the dark, dodging out of sight, listening for every sound, trying to get in – of course I was upset when I heard you were so ill afterward.'

Mrs Ansley had not moved for a long time. But now she turned slowly toward her companion. 'But I didn't wait. He'd arranged everything. He was there. We were let in at once,' she said.

Mrs Slade sprang up from her leaning position. 'Delphin there! They let you in! Ah, now you're lying!' she burst out with violence.

Mrs Ansley's voice grew clearer, and full of surprise. 'But of course he was there. Naturally he came – '

'Came? How did he know he'd find you there? You must be raving!'

Mrs Ansley hesitated, as though reflecting. 'But I answered the letter. I told him I'd be there. So he came.'

Mrs Slade flung her hands up to her face. 'Oh, God – you answered! I never thought of your answering . . . '

'It's odd you never thought of it, if you wrote the letter.'

'Yes. I was blind with rage.'

Mrs Ansley rose, and drew her fur scarf about her. 'It is cold here. We'd better go . . . I'm sorry for you,' she said, as she clasped the fur about her throat.

The unexpected words sent a pang through Mrs Slade. 'Yes; we'd better go.' She gathered up her bag and cloak. 'I don't know why you should be sorry for me,' she muttered.

Mrs Ansley stood looking away from her toward the dusky mass of the Colosseum. 'Well – because I didn't have to wait that night.'

Mrs Slade gave an unquiet laugh. 'Yes, I was beaten there. But I oughtn't to begrudge it to you, I suppose. At the end of all these years. After all, I had everything; I had him for twenty-five years. And you had nothing but that one letter that he didn't write.'

Mrs Ansley was again silent. At length she took a step toward the door of the terrace, and turned back, facing her companion.

'I had Barbara,' she said, and began to move ahead of Mrs Slade toward the stairway.

The Long Run

I

It was last winter, after a twelve years' absence from New York, that I saw again, at one of the Phil Cumnors' dinners, my old friend Halston Merrick.

The Cumnors' house is one of the few where, even after such a lapse of time, one can be sure of finding familiar faces and picking up old threads; where for a moment one can abandon oneself to the illusion that New York humanity is less unstable than its bricks and mortar. And that evening in particular I remember feeling that there could be no pleasanter way of re-entering the confused and careless world to which I was returning than through the quiet, softly-lit dining-room in which Mrs Cumnor, with a characteristic sense of my needing to be broken in gradually, had contrived to assemble so many friendly faces.

I was glad to see them all, including the three or four I did not know, or failed to recognise, but had no difficulty in classing as in the tradition and of the group; but I was most of all glad – as I rather wonderingly found – to set eyes again on Halston Merrick.

He and I had been at Harvard together, for one thing, and had shared there curiosities and ardours a little outside the current tendencies: had, on the whole, been freer and less amenable to the accepted. Then, for the next few years, Merrick had been a vivid and promising figure in young American life. Handsome, free and fine, he had wandered and tasted and compared. After leaving Harvard he had spent two years at Oxford. He then accepted a private secretaryship to our ambassador in England, and came back from this adventure with a fresh curiosity about public affairs at home, and the conviction that men of his kind didn't play a large enough part in them. This led, first, to his running for a state senatorship which he failed to get, and ultimately to a few months of intelligent activity in a municipal office. Soon after a change of party had deprived him of this post he published a small volume of rather hauntingly delicate sonnets, and, a year later, an odd uneven brilliant book on municipal government. After that one hardly knew where to look for his next appearance; but chance rather disappointingly solved the problem by killing off his father and placing Halston at the head of the Merrick Iron Foundry at Yonkers.

His friends had gathered that, whenever this regrettable contingency should occur, he meant to dispose of the business and continue his life of free experiment. As often happens in such cases, however, it was not the moment for a sale, and Merrick had to take over the management of the foundry. Some two years later he had a chance to free himself, but when it came he did not choose to take it. This tame sequel to an inspiriting start was slightly disappointing to some of us, and I was among those disposed to regret Merrick's drop to the level of the merely prosperous. Then I went away to my big engineering job in China, and from there to Africa, and spent the next twelve years out of sight and sound of New York doings.

During that long interval I learned of no new phase in Merrick's evolution, but this did not surprise me, as I had never expected from him actions resonant enough to be heard across the globe. All I knew – and this surprised me – was that he had never married, and that he was still in the iron business. All through those years, however, I never ceased to wish, in certain situations and at certain turns of thought, that Merrick were in reach, that I could tell this or that to Merrick. I had never, in the interval, found anyone with just his quickness of perception and just his sureness of touch.

After dinner, therefore, we irresistibly drew together. In Mrs Cumnor's big easy drawing-room cigars were allowed, and there was no break in the communion of the sexes; and, this being the case, I should have sought a seat beside one of the ladies who so indulgently suffered our presence. But, as generally happened when Merrick was in sight, I found myself steering straight for him past all the minor ports of call.

There had been no time, before our passage to the dining-room, for more than the barest expression of delight at meeting, and our seats had been at opposite ends of the longish table, so that we got our first real look at each other in the screened secluded sofa-corner to which Mrs Cumnor's vigilance now tactfully directed us.

Merrick was still handsome in his long swarthy way: handsomer perhaps, with thinnish hair and graver lines, than in the young excess of his good looks. He was very glad to see me and expressed his gladness in terms of the same charming smile; but as soon as we began to talk I felt a change. It was not merely the change that years and experience and altered values bring. There was something more fundamental the matter with Merrick: something dreadful, unforeseen, unaccountable. Merrick had grown conventional and dull.

In the face of his frank pleasure in seeing me I was ashamed, at first, to analyse the nature of the change; but presently our talk began to flag – fancy a talk with Merrick flagging! – and self-deception became impossible as I watched myself handing out platitudes with the unconvinced gesture of a salesman offering something "equally good". The worst of it was that Merrick – Merrick, who had once felt everything! – didn't seem to feel any lack of spontaneity in my remarks, but clung to me in speech and look with a harrowing faith in the resuscitating power of our past. It was as if he treasured the empty vessel of our friendship without perceiving that the last drop of its essence had gone dry.

I am putting all this in exaggerated terms. Through my surprise and disappointment there glowed a certain sense of well-being in the mere physical presence of my old friend. I liked looking at the way his thin dark hair broke away from the forehead, at the tautness of his smooth brown cheek, the contemplative backward tilt of his head, the way his brown eyes mused upon the scene through indolently lowered lids. All the past was in his way of looking and sitting, and I wanted to stay near him, and knew that he wanted me to stay, but the devil of it was that neither of us knew what to talk about.

It was this difficulty which caused me, after a while, since I could not follow Merrick's talk, to follow his eyes in their slow circuit of the room.

At the moment when our glances joined, his happened to have paused on a lady seated at some distance from our corner. Immersed, at first, in the satisfaction of finding myself again with Merrick, I had been only negatively aware of this lady, as of one of the few persons present whom I did not know, or failed to remember. There was nothing in her appearance or attitude to challenge my indifference or to excite my curiosity: I don't suppose I should have looked at her at all if I had not noticed that my friend was doing so.

She was a woman of about forty-seven, with fair faded hair and a young figure. Her smoke-grey dress was handsome but ineffective, and her pale and rather serious face wore a small unvarying smile which might have been pinned on with her ornaments. She was one of the women in whom the years show rather what they have taken than what they have bestowed, and only on looking closely did one see that what they had taken must have been exceptionally good of its kind.

Phil Cumnor and another man were talking to her, and the very intensity of the attention she bestowed on them betrayed the straining of rebellious thoughts. She never let her eyes stray or her smile drop; and at the proper moments I saw she was ready with the proper sentiment.

The party, like most of those that Mrs Cumnor gathered about her, was not composed of exceptional beings. The people of the old New York set were not exceptional: they were in fact mostly cut on the same neat, convenient and unobtrusive pattern; but they were often exceedingly 'nice'. And this obsolete quality marked every look and gesture of the lady I was scrutinising.

While these reflections were passing through my mind I was aware that Merrick's eyes were still turned in the same direction. I took a cross-section of his look and found in it neither surprise nor absorption, but only a certain sober pleasure just about at the emotional level of the rest of the room. If he were looking at the lady in question it was only, his expression seemed to say, because, all things considered, there were fewer reasons for looking at anybody else.

This made me wonder what were the reasons for looking at her: and as a first step toward enlightenment I said: 'I'm sure I've seen the lady over there in grey – '

Merrick, with a slight effort, detached his eyes and turned them on me in a wondering look.

'Seen her? You know her.' He paused for my response. ' Don't you know her? It's Mrs Reardon.'

I wondered that he should wonder, for I could not remember, in the Cumnor group or elsewhere, having known anyone of the name he mentioned.

'But perhaps,' he continued, 'you hadn't heard of her marriage? You knew her as Mrs Trant.'

I gave him back his stare. 'Not Mrs Philip Trant?'

'Yes; Mrs Philip Trant.'

'Not Paulina?' I insisted.

'Yes – Paulina,' he said, with a just perceptible delay before the name.

In my stupefaction I continued to stare at him, instead of turning my gaze toward the lady whose identity was in dispute.

He averted his eyes from mine after a moment, and I saw that they had strayed back to her. 'You find her so changed?' he asked.

An odd note in his voice acted as a warning signal, and I tried to reduce my astonishment to less unbecoming proportions. 'I don't find that she looks much older.'

'No. Only different?' he suggested, as if there were nothing new to him in my perplexity.

'Yes – awfully different,' I confessed.

'I suppose we're all awfully different. To you, I mean – coming from so far?'

'I recognised all the rest of you,' I said, hesitating. 'And she used to be the one who stood out most.'

There was a flash, a wave, a stir of something deep down in his eyes. 'Yes,' he said. 'That's the difference.'

'I see it is. She – she looks worn down. Soft but blurred, like the figures in the tapestry behind her.'

He glanced at her again, as if to test the exactness of my analogy.

'Life wears everybody down, I suppose,' he said.

'Yes – except those it makes more distinct. They're the rare ones, of course; but she was rare.'

He stood up suddenly, looking old and tired. 'I believe I'll be off. I wish you'd come down to my place for Sunday . . . No, don't shake hands – I want to slide away while they're not looking.'

We were standing near the door of the inner drawing-room, and I placed myself before him to say a last word and screen his retreat.

'You will come down, won't you?' he repeated. 'I want to see you. There'll be no one else.' He had backed away to the threshold and was turning the noiseless door-knob. Even Mrs Cumnor's door-knobs had tact and didn't tell!

'Of course I'll come,' I promised warmly. In the last ten minutes he had begun to interest me again.

'All right. Goodbye.' Half through the door he paused to stammer: ' – She remembers you. You ought to speak to her.'

'I'm going to. But tell me a little more.' I thought I saw a shade of constraint on his face, and did not add, as I had meant to: 'Tell me – because she interests me – what wore her down?' Instead, I asked: 'How soon after Trant's death did she remarry?'

He seemed to require an effort of memory to recall the date. 'It was seven years ago, I think.'

'And is Reardon here tonight?'

'Yes; over there, talking to Mrs Cumnor.'

I looked across the broken lamplit groupings and saw a large glossy man with straw-coloured hair and a red face, whose shirt and shoes and complexion seemed all to have received a coat of the same expensive varnish.

As I looked there was a drop in the talk about us, and I heard Mr Reardon pronounce in a big booming voice: 'What I say is: what's the good of disturbing things? Thank the Lord, I'm content with what I've got!'

'Is that her husband? What's he like?'

'Oh, the best fellow in the world,' said Merrick, going.

2

Merrick had a little place at Riverdale, where he went occasionally to be near the Iron Works, and where he hid at weekends when the world was too much with him.

Here he awaited me on the following Saturday afternoon, and at tea-time I found myself with him in a pleasant careless setting of books and prints and faded parental furniture.

We dined late, and smoked and talked afterward in his low-ceilinged book-walled study till the terrier on the hearth-rug stood up and yawned for bed. When we took the hint and picked up our candles in the hall I felt not that I had found the old Merrick again, but that I was on his track, had come across traces of his passage here and there in the thick jungle that had grown up between us. But I had an odd poignant feeling that when I finally came on the man himself he might be dead . . .

As we started up the shallow country stairs he turned with one of his abrupt shy movements, and walked back into the study.

'Wait a bit!' he called to me.

I waited, and he came out in a moment carrying a limp folio.

'It's typewritten. Will you take a look at it? I've been trying to get to work again,' he lamely explained, thrusting the manuscript into my hand.

'What? Poetry, I hope?' I exclaimed.

He shook his head with a gleam of derision. 'No – just general considerations. The fruit of fifty years of inexperience.'

He showed me to my room and said good-night.

The following afternoon – it was a mild winter day with soft wet gusts, I remember – we took a long walk inland, across the hills, and I said to Merrick what I could of his book. Unluckily there wasn't much to say. The essays were judicious, polished and cultivated, but they lacked the freshness and audacity of his youthful work. I tried to conceal my opinion behind the usual ambiguities, but he broke through these feints with a quick thrust to the heart of my meaning.

'It's worn down – blurred? Like the figures in the Cumnors' tapestry?'

I hesitated. 'It's a little too damned resigned,' I said.

'Ah,' he exclaimed, 'so am I. Resigned.' He switched the bare brambles by the roadside. 'A man can't serve two masters.'

'You mean business and literature?'

'No; I mean theory and instinct. The grey tree and the green. You've got to choose which fruit you'll try; and you don't know till afterward which of the two has the dead core.'

'How can anybody be sure that only one of them has?'

'I'm sure,' said Merrick sharply.

We turned back to the subject of his essays, and I was astonished at the detachment with which he criticised and demolished them. Little by little, as we talked, his old perspective, his old standards came back to him, but with the difference that they no longer seemed like functions of his mind but merely like attitudes assumed or dropped at will. He could still, with an effort, put himself at the angle from which he had formerly seen things; but it was with the effort of a man climbing mountains after a sedentary life in the plain.

I tried to cut the talk short, but he kept coming back to it with nervous insistence, forcing me into the last retrenchments of hypocrisy, and anticipating the verdict I held back. I perceived that a great deal – immensely more than I could see a reason for – had hung for him on my opinion of his book.

Then, as suddenly, his insistence broke and, as if ashamed of having forced himself so long on my attention, he began to talk rapidly and uninterestingly of other things.

We were alone again that evening, and after dinner, wishing to efface the impression of the afternoon, and above all to show that I wanted him to talk about himself, I reverted to the subject of his work. 'You must need an outlet of that sort. When a man's once had it in him, as you have – and when other things begin to dwindle –'

He laughed. 'Your theory is that a man ought to be able to return to the Muse as he comes back to his wife after he's ceased to interest other women?'

'No; as he comes back to his wife after the day's work is done.' A new thought came to me as I looked at him. 'You ought to have had one,' I added.

He laughed again. 'A wife, you mean? So that there'd have been someone waiting for me even if the Muse decamped?' He went on after a pause: 'I've a notion that the kind of woman worth coming back to wouldn't be much more patient than the Muse. But as it happens I never tried – because, for fear they'd chuck me, I put them both out of doors together.'

He turned his head abruptly and looked past me with a queer expression at the low grey-panelled door at my back. 'Out of that very door they went – the two of 'em, on a rainy night like this: and one stopped and looked back, to see if I wasn't going to call her – and I didn't – and so they both went . . .'

3

'The Muse?' said Merrick, refilling my glass and stooping to pat the terrier as he went back to his chair – 'well, you've met the Muse in the little volume of sonnets you used to like; and you've met the woman too, and you used to like her; though you didn't know her when you saw her the other evening . . .

'No, I won't ask you how she struck you: I know. She struck you like that stuff I gave you to read last night. She's conformed – I've conformed – the mills have caught us and ground us: ground us, oh, exceedingly small!

'But you remember what she was: I saw at once that you remembered. And that's the reason why I'm telling you this now . . .

'You may recall that after my father's death I tried unsuccessfully to sell the Works. I was impatient to free myself from anything that would keep me tied to New York. I don't dislike my trade, and I've made, in the end, a fairly good thing of it; but industrialism was not, at that time, in the line of my tastes, and I know now that it wasn't what I was meant for. Above all, I wanted to get away, to see new places and rub up against different ideas. I had reached a time of life – the top of the first hill, so to speak – where the distance draws one, and everything in the foreground seems tame and stale. I was sick to death of the particular set of conformities I had grown up among; sick of being a pleasant popular young man with a long line of dinners on my engagement list, and the dead certainty of meeting the same people, or their prototypes, at all of them.

'Well – I failed to sell the Works, and that increased my discontent. I went through moods of cold unsociability, alternating with sudden flushes of curiosity, when I gloated over stray scraps of talk overheard in railway stations and omnibuses, when strange faces that I passed in the street tantalised me with fugitive promises. I wanted to get away, among things that were unexpected and unknown; and it seemed to me that nobody about me understood in the least what I felt, but that somewhere just out of reach there was someone who did, and whom I must find or despair . . .

'It was just then that, one evening, I saw Mrs Trant for the first time.

'Yes: I know – you wonder what I mean. I'd known her, of course, as a girl; I'd met her several times after her marriage to Trant; and I'd lately been thrown with her, quite intimately and continuously, during a succession of country-house visits. But I had never, as it happened, really seen her till then . . .

'It was at a dinner at the Cumnors', I remember; and there she was, in front of the very tapestry we saw her against the other evening, with people about her, and her face turned from me, and nothing noticeable or different in her dress or manner; and suddenly she stood out for me against the pinkish-smoky background, and for the first time I saw a meaning in the stale phrase of a picture's walking out of its frame. For you've noticed, haven't you, that most people are just that to us: pictures, furniture, the inanimate accessories of our little island-area of sensation? And then sometimes one of these graven images moves and throws out live filaments toward us, and the line they make draws us across the world as the moon-track seems to draw a boat across black water . . .

'Well, there she stood; and as this queer sensation came over me I felt that she was looking steadily at me, that her eyes were voluntarily, consciously resting on me with the weight of a deep interrogation.

'I went over and joined her, and she turned silently and walked with me into the music-room. Earlier in the evening someone had been singing, and there were low lights there, and a few couples still sitting in those confidential corners of which Mrs Cumnor has the art; but we were under no illusion as to the nature of these presences. We knew that they were just painted in, and that the whole of sentient life was in us two, and flowing back and forward between us in swift innumerable streams. We talked, of course; we had the attitudes, even the words, of the others: I remember her telling me her plans for the spring and asking me politely about mine! As if there were the least sense in plans, now that this thing had happened to us!

'When we went back into the drawing-room I had said nothing to her that I might not have said to any other woman of the party; but when we said goodbye I knew we should see each other the next day – and the next . . .

'That's the way, I take it, that nature has arranged the beginning of the great enduring loves; and likewise of the little epidermal flurries. And how's a man to know where he is going?

'From the first, I own, my feeling for Paulina Trant seemed to me a grave business; but then I knew that the enemy is given to producing that illusion. Many a man – I'm talking of the kind with imagination – has thought he was seeking a soul when all he wanted was a closer view of its tenement. And I tried – honestly tried – to make myself think I was in this case. Because, in the first place, I didn't just then, want a big disturbing influence in my life; and because I didn't want to be a dupe; and because Paulina Trant was not, according to hearsay, the kind of woman for whom it was worth while to bring up the big batteries . . .

'But my resistance was only half-hearted. What I really felt – all I really felt – was the flood of joy that comes of heightened emotion. She had given me that, and I wanted her to give it to me again. That's as near as I've ever come to analysing my state in the beginning.

'I knew her story, as no doubt you know it: the current version, I mean. She had been poor and fond of enjoyment, and she had married that pompous monolith Philip Trant because she needed a home, and perhaps also because she wanted a little luxury. Queer how we sneer at women for wanting the thing that gives them half their grace!

'People shook their heads over the marriage, and divided, prematurely, into Philip's partisans and hers: for no one thought it would work. And they were almost disappointed when, after all, it did. She and her wooden consort seemed to get on well enough. There was a ripple at one time over her close friendship with young Jim Dalham, who was always with her during a summer at Newport and an autumn in Italy; then the talk died out, and she and Trant were seen together, as before, on terms of apparent good-fellowship.

'This was the more surprising because, from the first, Paulina had never made the least attempt to change her tone or subdue her colours. In the grey Trant atmosphere she flashed with prismatic fires. She smoked, she talked subversively, she did as she liked and went where she pleased, and danced over the Trant prejudices and the Trant principles as if they'd been a ball-room floor; and all without apparent offence to her solemn husband and his cloud of cousins. I believe her frankness and directness struck them dumb. She moved like a kind of primitive Una through the virtuous rout, and never got a fingermark on her freshness.

'One of the finest things about her was the fact that she never, for an instant, used her plight as a means of enhancing her attraction. With a husband like Trant it would have been so easy! He was a man who always saw the small sides of big things. He thought most of life compressible into a set of by-laws and the rest unmentionable; and with his stiff frock-coated and tall-hatted mind, instinctively distrustful of intelligences in another dress, with his arbitrary classification of whatever he didn't understand into 'the kind of thing I don't approve of', 'the kind of thing that isn't done' and – deepest depth of all – 'the kind of thing I'd rather not discuss', he lived in the service of a shadowy moral etiquette, of which the complex rites and awful penalties had cast an abiding gloom upon his manner.

'A woman like his wife couldn't have asked a better foil; yet I'm sure she never consciously used his dullness to relieve her brilliancy. She may have felt that the case spoke for itself. But I believe her reserve was rather due to a lively sense of justice, and to the rare habit (you said she was rare) of looking at facts as they are, without any throwing of sentimental lime-lights. She knew Trant could no more help being Trant than she could help being herself – and there was an end of it. I've never known a woman who 'made up' so little mentally . . .

'Perhaps her very reserve, the fierceness of her implicit rejection of sympathy, exposed her the more to – well, to what happened when we met. She said afterward that it was like having been shut up for months in the hold of a ship, and coming suddenly on deck on a day that was all flying blue and silver . . .

'I won't try to tell you what she was. It's easier to tell you what her friendship made of me; and I can do that best by adopting her metaphor of the ship. Haven't you, sometimes, at the moment of starting on a journey, some glorious plunge into the unknown, been tripped up by the thought: 'If only one hadn't to come back'? Well, with her one had the sense that one would never have to come back; that the magic ship would always carry one farther. And what an air one breathed on it! And, oh, the wind, and the islands, and the sunsets!

'I said just now "her friendship"; and I used the word advisedly. Love is deeper than friendship, but friendship is a good deal wider. The beauty of our relation was that it included both dimensions. Our thoughts met as naturally as our eyes: it was almost as if we loved each other because we liked each other. I'm inclined to think that the quality of a love may be tested by the amount of friendship it contains, and in our case there was no dividing line between loving and liking, no disproportion between them, no barrier against which desire beat in vain or from which thought fell back unsatisfied. Ours was a robust passion that could give an open-eyed account of itself, and not a beautiful madness shrinking away from the proof . . .

'For the first months friendship sufficed us, or rather gave us so much by the way that we were in no haste to reach what we knew it led to. But we were moving there nevertheless, and one day we found ourselves on the borders. It came about through a sudden decision of Trant's to start on a long tour with his wife. We had never foreseen such a possibility: he seemed rooted in his New York habits and convinced that the city's whole social and financial machinery would cease to function if he did not keep an eye on it through the columns of his morning paper and pronounce judgement on it in the afternoon at his club. But something new had happened to him. He caught a cold, which was followed by a touch of pleurisy, and instantly he perceived the intense interest and importance which ill-health may add to life. He took the fullest advantage of it. A complaisant doctor recommended travel, insisted on a winter in a warm climate; and suddenly, the morning paper, the afternoon club, Fifth Avenue, Wall Street, all the complex phenomena of the metropolis, faded into insignificance, and the rest of the terrestrial globe, from being a mere geographical hypothesis, useful in enabling one to determine the latitude of New York, acquired reality and magnitude as a factor in the convalescence of Mr Philip Trant.

'His wife was absorbed in preparations for the journey. It took an army to mobilise him, and weeks before the date set for their departure it was almost as if she were already gone.

'This foretaste of separation showed us what we were to each other. Yet I was letting her go – and there was no help for it, no way of preventing it. Resistance was as useless as the vain struggles in a nightmare. She was Trant's and not mine: a part of his luggage when he travelled as she was part of his household furniture when he stayed at home . . .

'The day she told me that their passages were taken – it was on a November afternoon, in her drawing-room in town – I turned away from the tea-table and, going to the window, stood looking out at the torrent of traffic interminably pouring down Fifth Avenue. I watched the senseless machinery of life revolving in the rain and mud, and tried to picture myself performing my small function in it after she had gone from me.

' "It can't be – it can't be!" I exclaimed.

' "What can't be?"

'I came back into the room and sat down by her. "This – this – " I hadn't any words. "Two weeks!" I said. "What's two weeks?"

'She answered vaguely, something about their thinking of Spain for the spring –

' "Two weeks – two weeks!" I repeated. "And the months we've lost – the days that belonged to us!"

' "Yes," she said, "I'm thankful it's settled."

'Our words seemed irrelevant, haphazard. It was as if each were answering a secret voice and not what the other was saying.

' "Don't you feel anything at all?" I remember bursting out at her. As I asked it the tears were streaming down her face. I felt angry with her, and was almost glad to note that her lids were red and that she didn't cry becomingly. I can't express my sensation to you except by saying that she seemed part of life's huge league against me. And suddenly I thought of an afternoon we had spent together in the country, on a ferny hillside, when we had sat under a beech tree, and her hand had lain palm upward in the moss, close to mine, and I had watched a little black-and-red beetle creeping over it . . .

'The bell rang, and we heard the voice of a visitor and the click of an umbrella in the umbrella-stand.

'She rose to go into the inner drawing-room, and I caught her suddenly by the wrist. "You understand,' I said, "that we can't go on like this?"

' "I understand," she answered, and moved away to meet her visitor. As I went out I heard her saying in the other room, "Yes, we're really off on the twelfth."

4

'I wrote her a long letter that night, and waited two days for a reply.

'On the third day I had a brief line saying that she was going to spend Sunday with some friends who had a place near Riverdale, and that she would arrange to see me while she was there. That was all.

'It was on a Saturday that I received the note and I came out here the same night. The next morning was rainy, and I was in despair, for I had counted on her asking me to take her for a drive or a long walk. It was hopeless to try to say what I had to say to her in the drawing-room of a crowded country-house. And only eleven days were left!

'I stayed indoors all the morning, fearing to go out lest she should telephone me. But no sign came, and I grew more and more restless and anxious. She was too free and frank for coquetry, but her silence and evasiveness made me feel that, for some reason, she did not wish to hear what she knew I meant to say. Could it be that she was, after all, more conventional, less genuine, than I had thought? I went again and again over the whole maddening round of conjecture; but the only conclusion I could rest in was that, if she loved me as I loved her, she would be as determined as I was to let no obstacle come between us during the days that were left.

'The luncheon-hour came and passed, and there was no word from her. I had ordered my trap to be ready, so that I might drive over as soon as she summoned me; but the hours dragged on, the early twilight came, and I sat here in this very chair, or measured up and down, up and down, the length of this very rug – and still there was no message and no letter.

'It had grown quite dark, and I had ordered away, impatiently, the servant who came in with the lamps: I couldn't bear any definite sign that the day was over! And I was standing there on the rug, staring at the door, and noticing a bad crack in its panel, when I heard the sound of wheels on the gravel. A word at last, no doubt – a line to explain . . . I didn't seem to care much for her reasons, and I stood where I was and continued to stare at the door. And suddenly it opened and she came in.

'The servant followed her with a lamp, and then went out and closed the door. Her face looked pale in the lamplight, but her voice was as clear as a bell.

' "Well," she said "you see I've come."

'I started toward her with hands outstretched. "You've come – you've come!" I stammered.

'Yes; it was like her to come in that way – without shame, without dissimulation, without explanations or excuses. It was like her, if she gave at all, to give not furtively or in haste, but openly, deliberately, without stinting the measure or counting the cost. But her quietness and serenity disconcerted me. She did not look like a woman who has yielded impetuously to an uncontrollable impulse. There was something almost solemn in her face.

'The awe of it stole over me as I looked at her, suddenly subduing the huge flush of gratified longing.

' "You're here, here, here!" I kept repeating, like a child singing over a happy word.

' "You said," she continued, in her grave clear voice, "that we couldn't go on as we were – "

' "Ah, it's divine of you!" I broke in, and held out my arms to her.

'She didn't draw back from them, but her faint smile said, "Wait," and lifting her hands she took the pins from her hat, and laid the hat on the table.

'As I saw her dear head bare in the lamplight, with the thick hair waving away from the parting, I forgot everything but the bliss and wonder of her being here – here, in my house, on my hearth – I can show you, yet, the exact spot where she was standing.

'I drew her over to the fire, and made her sit down in the chair where you're sitting, and knelt down by her, and hid my face on her knees. She put her hand on my head, and I was happy to the depths of my soul.

' "Oh, I forgot – " she exclaimed suddenly. I lifted my head and our eyes met. Hers were smiling.

'She reached out her hand, opened the little bag she had tossed down with her hat, and drew a small object from it. "I left my trunk at the station," she said. "Here's the check. Can you send for it?"

'Her trunk – she wanted me to send for her trunk! Oh, yes – I see your smile, your "lucky man!" Only, you see, I didn't love her in that way. I knew she couldn't come to my house without running a big risk of discovery, and my tenderness for her, my impulse to shield her, was stronger, even then, than masculine vanity or masculine desire. Judged from the point of view of those emotions I fell terribly short of my part. I hadn't any of the proper feelings. Such an act of romantic folly was so unlike her that it almost irritated me, and I found myself desperately wondering how I could get her to reconsider her plan without – well, without seeming to want her to.

'It's not the way a novel hero feels; it's probably not the way a man in real life ought to have felt. But it's the way I felt – and she saw it.

'She put her hands on my shoulders and looked at me with deep, deep eyes. "Then you didn't expect me to stay?" she asked, half-smiling.

'I caught her hands and pressed them close to me, stammering out that I hadn't dared to dream . . .

' "You thought I'd come – just for an hour?"

' "How could I dare think more? I adore you, you know, for what you've done! But it would be known if you – if you stayed on. My servants –

everybody about here knows you. I've no right to expose you to the risk."
She made no answer, and I went on tenderly: "Give me, if you will, the next
few hours: there's a train that will get you to town by midnight. And then
we'll arrange something – in town – where it's safer for you – easily
managed . . . It's beautiful, it's glorious of you to have come; but I love you
too much – I must take care of you and think for you – "

'I don't suppose it ever took me so long to say so few words, and though
they were profoundly sincere they sounded unutterably shallow, irrelevant
and grotesque. She made no effort to help me out, but sat silent, listening
with her meditative smile. "It's my duty, dearest, as a man," I rambled on.
"The more I love you the more I'm bound – "

' "Yes; but you don't understand," she interrupted.

'She rose as she spoke, and I got up also, and we stood and looked at each
other.

' "I haven't come for a night; if you want me I've come for always," she said.

'Here again, if I give you an honest account of my feelings, I shall write
myself down as the poor-spirited creature I suppose I am. There wasn't, I
swear, at the moment, a gram of selfishness, of personal reluctance, in my
feeling. I worshipped every hair of her head – when we were together I was
happy, when I was away from her something was gone from every good
thing; but I had always looked on our love for each other, our possible
relation to each other, as such situations are looked on in what is called
society. I had supposed her, for all her freedom and originality, to be just as
tacitly subservient to that view as I was: ready to take what she wanted on the
terms on which society concedes such taking, and to pay for it by the usual
restrictions, concealments and hypocrisies. In short, I supposed that she
would 'play the game' – look out for her own safety and expect me to look
out for it. It sounds cheap enough, put that way – but it's the rule we live
under, all of us. And the amazement of finding her suddenly outside of it,
oblivious of it, unconscious of it, left me, for an awful minute, stammering at
her like a graceless dolt . . . Perhaps it wasn't even a minute; but in it she had
gone the whole round of my thoughts.

' "It's raining," she said, very low. "I suppose you can telephone for a
trap?"

'There was no irony or resentment in her voice. She walked slowly across
the room and paused before the Brangwyn etching over there. "That's a
good impression. Will you telephone, please?" she repeated.

'I found my voice again, and with it the power of movement. I followed
her, and dropped at her feet. "You can't go like this!" I cried.

'She looked down on me from heights and heights. "I can't stay like this,"
she answered.

'I stood up and we faced each other like antagonists. "You don't know," I
accused her passionately, "in the least what you're asking me to ask of you!"

' "Yes, I do: everything," she breathed.

' "And it's got to be that or nothing?"

' "Oh, on both sides," she reminded me.

' "Not on both sides. It isn't fair. That's why – "

' "Why you won't?"

' "Why I cannot – may not!"

' "Why you'll take a night and not a life?"

'The taunt, for a woman usually so sure of her aim, fell so short of the mark that its only effect was to increase my conviction of her helplessness. The very intensity of my longing for her made me tremble where she was fearless. I had to protect her first, and think of my own attitude afterward.

'She was too discerning not to see this too. Her face softened, grew inexpressibly appealing, and she dropped again into that chair you're in, leaned forward, and looked up with her grave smile.

' "You think I'm beside myself – raving? (You're not thinking of yourself, I know.) I'm not: I never was saner. Since I've known you I've often thought that this might happen. This thing between us isn't an ordinary thing. If it had been we shouldn't, all these months, have drifted. We should have wanted to skip to the last page – and then throw down the book. We shouldn't have felt we could trust the future as we did. We were in no hurry because we knew we shouldn't get tired; and when two people feel that about each other they must live together – or part. I don't see what else they can do. A little trip along the coast won't answer. It's the high seas – or else being tied up to Lethe wharf. And I'm for the high seas, my dear!"

'Think of sitting here – here, in this room, in this chair – and listening to that, and seeing the light on her hair, and hearing the sound of her voice! I don't suppose there ever was a scene just like it . . .

'She was astounding – inexhaustible; through all my anguish of resistance I found a kind of fierce joy in following her. It was lucidity at white heat: the last sublimation of passion. She might have been an angel arguing a point in the empyrean if she hadn't been, so completely, a woman pleading for her life . . .

'Her life: that was the thing at stake! She couldn't do with less of it than she was capable of; and a woman's life is inextricably part of the man's she cares for.

'That was why, she argued, she couldn't accept the usual solution: couldn't enter into the only relation that society tolerates between people situated like ourselves. Yes: she knew all the arguments on that side: didn't I suppose she'd been over them and over them? She knew (for hadn't she often said it of others?) what is said of the woman who, by throwing in her lot with her lover's, binds him to a life-long duty which has the irksomeness without the dignity of marriage. Oh, she could talk on that side with the best of them: only she asked me to consider the other – the side of the man and woman who love each other deeply and completely enough to want their lives enlarged, and not diminished, by their love. What, in such a case – she reasoned – must be the inevitable effect of concealing, denying, disowning the central fact, the motive power of one's existence? She asked me to picture the course of such a love: first working as a fever in the blood, distorting and deflecting everything, making all other interests insipid, all other duties irksome, and then, as the acknowledged claims of life regained their hold, gradually dying – the poor starved passion! – for want of the wholesome necessary food of common living and doing, yet leaving life impoverished by the loss of all it might have been.

' "I'm not talking, dear – " I see her now, leaning toward me with shining eyes: "I'm not talking of the people who haven't enough to fill their days, and to whom a little mystery, a little manoeuvring, gives an illusion of importance that they can't afford to miss; I'm talking of you and me, with all our tastes and curiosities and activities; and I ask you what our love would become if we had to keep it apart from our lives, like a pretty useless animal that we went to peep at and feed with sweetmeats through its cage?"

'I won't, my dear fellow, go into the other side of our strange duel: the arguments I used were those that most men in my situation would have felt bound to use, and that most women in Paulina's accept instinctively, without even formulating them. The exceptionalness, the significance, of the case lay wholly in the fact that she had formulated them all and then rejected them . . .

'There was one point I didn't, of course, touch on, and that was the popular conviction (which I confess I shared) that when a man and a woman agree to defy the world together the man really sacrifices much more than the woman. I was not even conscious of thinking of this at the time, though it may have lurked somewhere in the shadow of my scruples for her; but she dragged it out into the daylight and held me face to face with it.

' "Remember, I'm not attempting to lay down any general rule," she insisted; "I'm not theorising about Man and Woman, I'm talking about you and me. How do I know what's best for the woman in the next house? Very likely she'll bolt when it would have been better for her to stay at home. And it's the same with the man: he'll probably do the wrong thing. It's generally the weak heads that commit follies, when it's the strong ones that ought to; and my point is that you and I are both strong enough to behave like fools if we want to . . .

' "Take your own case first – because, in spite of the sentimentalists, it's the man who stands to lose most. You'll have to give up the Iron Works: which you don't much care about – because it won't be particularly agreeable for us to live in New York: which you don't care much about either. But you won't be sacrificing what is called a 'career'. You made up your mind long ago that your best chance of self-development, and consequently of general usefulness, lay in thinking rather than doing, and, when we first met, you were already planning to sell out your business, and travel and write. Well! Those ambitions are of a kind that won't be harmed by your dropping out of your social setting. On the contrary, such work as you want to do ought to gain by it, because you'll be brought nearer to life-as-it-is, in contrast to life-as-a-visiting-list . . . "

'She threw back her head with a sudden laugh. "And the joy of not having any more visits to make! I wonder if you've ever thought of that? Just at first, I mean; for society's getting so deplorably lax that, little by little, it will edge up to us – you'll see! I don't want to idealise the situation, dearest, and I won't conceal from you that in time we shall be called on. But, oh, the fun we shall have had in the interval! And then, for the first time we shall be able to dictate our own terms, one of which will be that no bores need apply. Think of being cured of all one's chronic bores! We shall feel as jolly as people after a successful operation."

'I don't know why this nonsense sticks in my mind when some of the graver things we said are less distinct. Perhaps it's because of a certain iridescent quality of feeling that made her gaiety seem like sunshine through a shower . . .

' "You ask me to think of myself?" she went on. "But the beauty of our being together will be that, for the first time, I shall dare to! Now I have to think of all the tedious trifles I can pack the days with, because I'm afraid – I'm afraid – to hear the voice of the real me, down below, in the windowless underground hole where I keep her . . . "

' "Remember, again, please, it's not Woman, it's Paulina Trant, I'm talking of. The woman in the next house may have all sorts of reasons – honest reasons – for staying there. There may be someone there who needs her badly: for whom the light would go out if she went. Whereas to Philip I've been simply – well, what New York was before he decided to travel: the most important thing in life till he made up his mind to leave it; and now merely the starting-place of several lines of steamers. Oh, I didn't have to love you to know that! I only had to live with him . . . If he lost his eye-glasses he'd think it was the fault of the eye-glasses; he'd really feel that the eye-glasses had been careless. And he'd be convinced that no others would suit him quite as well. But at the optician's he'd probably be told that he needed something a little different, and after that he'd feel that the old eye-glasses had never suited him at all, and that that was their fault too . . . "

'At one moment – but I don't recall when – I remember she stood up with one of her quick movements, and came toward me, holding out her arms. "Oh, my dear, I'm pleading for my life; do you suppose I'll ever want for arguments?" she cried . . .

'After that, for a bit, nothing much remains with me except a sense of darkness and of conflict. The one spot of daylight in my whirling brain was the conviction that I couldn't – whatever happened – profit by the sudden impulse she had acted on, and allow her to take, in a moment of passion, a decision that was to shape her whole life. I couldn't so much as lift my little finger to keep her with me then, unless I were prepared to accept for her as well as for myself the full consequences of the future she had planned for us . . .

'Well – there's the point: I wasn't. I felt in her – poor fatuous idiot that I was! – that lack of objective imagination which had always seemed to me to account, at least in part, for many of the so-called heroic qualities in women. When their feelings are involved they simply can't look ahead. Her unfaltering logic notwithstanding, I felt this about Paulina as I listened. She had a specious air of knowing where she was going, but she didn't. She seemed the genius of logic and understanding, but the demon of illusion spoke through her lips . . .

'I said just now that I hadn't, at the outset, given my own side of the case a thought. It would have been truer to say that I hadn't given it a separate thought. But I couldn't think of her without seeing myself as a factor – the chief factor – in her problem, and without recognising that whatever the experiment made of me, that it must fatally, in the end, make of her. If I couldn't carry the thing through she must break down with me: we should have to throw our separate selves into the melting-pot of this mad adventure and be 'one' in a terrible indissoluble completeness of which marriage is only an imperfect counterpart . . .

'There could be no better proof of her extraordinary power over me, and of the way she had managed to clear the air of sentimental illusion, than the fact that I presently found myself putting this to her with a merciless precision of touch.

' "If we love each other enough to do a thing like this, we must love each other enough to see just what it is we're going to do." '

'So I invited her to the dissecting-table, and I see now the fearless eye with which she approached the cadaver. "For that's what it is, you know," she flashed out at me, at the end of my long demonstration. "It's a dead body, like all the instances and examples and hypothetical cases that ever were! What do you expect to learn from that? The first great anatomist was the man who stuck his knife in a heart that was beating; and the only way to find out what doing a thing will be like is to do it!"

'She looked away from me suddenly, as if she were fixing her eyes on some vision on the outer rim of consciousness. "No: there's one other way," she exclaimed; "and that is, not to do it! To abstain and refrain; and then see what we become, or what we don't become, in the long run, and draw our inferences. That's the game that almost everybody about us is playing, I suppose; there's hardly one of the dull people one meets at dinner who hasn't had, just once, the chance of a berth on a ship that was off for the Happy Isles, and hasn't refused it for fear of sticking on a sand-bank!

' "I'm doing my best, you know," she continued, "to see the sequel as you see it, as you believe it's your duty to me to see it. I know the instances you're thinking of: the listless couples wearing out their lives in shabby watering places, and hanging on the favour of hotel acquaintances; or the proud quarrelling wretches shut up alone in a fine house because they're too good for the only society they can get, and trying to cheat their boredom by squabbling with their tradesmen and spying on their servants. No doubt there are such cases; but I don't recognise either of us in those dismal figures. Why, to do it would be to admit that our life, yours and mine, is in the people about us and not in ourselves; that we're parasites and not self-sustaining creatures; and that the lives we're leading now are so brilliant, full and satisfying that what we should have to give up would surpass even the blessedness of being together!"

'At that stage, I confess, the solid ground of my resistance began to give way under me. It was not that my convictions were shaken, but that she had swept me into a world whose laws were different, where one could reach out in directions that the slave of gravity hasn't pictured. But at the same time my opposition hardened from reason into instinct. I knew it was her voice, and not her logic, that was unsettling me. I knew that if she'd written out her thesis and sent it me by post I should have made short work of it; and again the part of me which I called by all the finest names: my chivalry, my unselfishness, my superior masculine experience, cried out with one voice: "You can't let a woman use her graces to her own undoing – you can't, for her own sake, let her eyes convince you when her reasons don't!"

'And then, abruptly, and for the first time, a doubt entered me: a doubt of her perfect moral honesty. I don't know how else to describe my feeling that she wasn't playing fair, that in coming to my house, in throwing herself at my head (I called things by their names), she had perhaps not so much obeyed an irresistible impulse as deeply, deliberately reckoned on the dissolvent effect of her generosity, her rashness and her beauty . . .

'From the moment that this mean doubt raised its head in me I was once more the creature of all the conventional scruples: I was repeating, before the looking-glass of my self-consciousness, all the stereotyped gestures of the "man of honour" . . . Oh, the sorry figure I must have cut! You'll understand my dropping the curtain on it as quickly as I can . . .

'Yet I remember, as I made my point, being struck by its impressiveness. I was suffering and enjoying my own suffering. I told her that, whatever step we decided to take, I owed it to her to insist on its being taken soberly, deliberately –

'("No: it's 'advisedly', isn't it? Oh, I was thinking of the Marriage Service," she interposed with a faint laugh.)

' – that if I accepted, there, on the spot, her headlong beautiful gift of herself, I should feel that I had taken an unmanly advantage of her, an advantage which she would be justified in reproaching me with ever afterward; that I was not afraid to tell her this because she was intelligent enough to know that my scruples were the surest proof of the quality of my love; that I refused to owe my happiness to an unconsidered impulse; that we must see each other again, in her own house, in less agitating circumstances, when she had had time to reflect on my words, to study her heart and look into the future . . .

'The factitious exhilaration produced by uttering these beautiful sentiments did not last very long, as you may imagine. It fell, little by little, under her quiet gaze, a gaze in which there was neither contempt nor irony nor wounded pride, but only a tender wistfulness of interrogation; and I think the acutest point in my suffering was reached when she said, as I ended: "Oh, yes, of course I understand."

' "If only you hadn't come to me here!" I blurted out in the torture of my soul.

'She was on the threshold when I said it, and she turned and laid her hand gently on mine. "There was no other way," she said; and at the moment it seemed to me like some hackneyed phrase in a novel that she had used without any sense of its meaning.

'I don't remember what I answered or what more we either of us said. At the end a desperate longing to take her in my arms and keep her with me swept aside everything else, and I went up to her, pleading, stammering, urging I don't know what . . . But she held me back with a quiet look, and went. I had ordered the carriage, as she asked me to; and my last definite recollection is of watching her drive off alone in the rain . . .

'I had her promise that she would see me, two days later, at her house in town, and that we should then have what I called "a decisive talk"; but I don't think that even at the moment I was the dupe of my phrase. I knew, and she knew, that the end had come . . .

5

'It was about that time,' Merrick went on after a long pause, 'that I definitely decided not to sell the Works, but to stick to my job and conform my life to it.

'I can't describe to you the rage of conformity that possessed me. Poetry, ideas – all the picture-making processes stopped. A kind of dull self-discipline seemed to me the only exercise worthy of a reflecting mind. I had to justify my great refusal, and I tried to do it by plunging myself up to the eyes into the very conditions I had been instinctively struggling to get away from. The only possible consolation would have been to find in a life of business routine and social submission such moral compensations as may reward the citizen if they fail the man; but to attain to these I should have had to accept the old delusion that the social and the individual man are two. Now, on the contrary, I found soon enough that I couldn't get one part of my machinery to work effectively while another wanted feeding; and that in rejecting what had seemed to me a negation of action I had made all my action negative.

'The best solution, of course, would have been to fall in love with another woman, but it was long before I could bring myself to wish that this might happen to me . . . Then, at length, I suddenly and violently desired it; and as such impulses are seldom without some kind of imperfect issue I contrived, a year or two later, to work myself up into the wished-for state . . . She was a woman in society, and with all the awe of that institution that Paulina lacked. Our relation was consequently one of those unavowed affairs in which triviality is the only alternative to tragedy. Luckily we had, on both sides, risked only as much as prudent people stake in a drawing-room game; and when the match was over I take it that we came out fairly even.

'My gain, at all events, was of an unexpected kind. The adventure had served only to make me understand Paulina's abhorrence of such experiments, and at every turn of the slight intrigue I had felt how exasperating and belittling such a relation was bound to be between two people who, had they been free, would have mated openly. And so from a brief phase of imperfect forgetting I was driven back to a deeper and more understanding remembrance . . .

'This second incarnation of Paulina was one of the strangest episodes of the whole strange experience. Things she had said during our extraordinary talk, things I had hardly heard at the time, came back to me with singular vividness and a fuller meaning. I hadn't any longer the cold consolation of believing in my own perspicacity: I saw that her insight had been deeper and keener than mine.

'I remember, in particular, starting up in bed one sleepless night as there flashed into my head the meaning of her last words: 'There was no other way'; the phrase I had half-smiled at at the time, as a parrot-like echo of the novel-heroine's stock farewell. I had never, up to that moment, wholly understood why Paulina had come to my house that night. I had never been able to make that particular act – which could hardly, in the light of her subsequent conduct, be dismissed as a blind surge of passion – square with my conception of her character. She was at once the most spontaneous and the steadiest-minded woman I had ever known, and the last to wish to owe any advantage to surprise, to unpreparedness, to any play on the spring of sex. The better I came, retrospectively, to know her, the more sure I was of this, and the less intelligible her act appeared. And then, suddenly, after a night of hungry restless thinking, the flash of illumination came. She had come to my house, had brought her trunk with her, had thrown herself at my head with all possible violence and publicity, in order to give me a pretext, a loophole, an honourable excuse for doing and saying – why, precisely what I had said and done!

'As the idea came to me it was as if some ironic hand had touched an electric button, and all my fatuous phrases had leapt out on me in fire.

'Of course she had known all along just the kind of thing I should say if I didn't at once open my arms to her; and to save my pride, my dignity, my conception of the figure I was cutting in her eyes, she had recklessly and magnificently provided me with the decentest pretext a man could have for doing a pusillanimous thing . . .

'With that discovery the whole case took a different aspect. It hurt less to think of Paulina – and yet it hurt more. The tinge of bitterness, of doubt, in my thoughts of her had had a tonic quality. It was harder to go on persuading myself that I had done right as, bit by bit, my theories crumbled under the test of time. Yet, after all, as she herself had said, one could judge of results only in the long run.

'The Trants stayed away for two years; and about a year after they got back, you may remember, Trant was killed in a railway accident. You know fate's way of untying a knot after everybody has given up tugging at it!

'Well – there I was, completely justified: all my weaknesses turned into merits! I had "saved" a weak woman from herself, I had kept her to the path of duty, I had spared her the humiliation of scandal and the misery of self-reproach; and now I had only to put out my hand and take the reward I deserved.

'I had avoided Paulina since her return, and she had made no effort to see me. But after Trant's death I wrote her a few lines, to which she sent a friendly answer; and when a decent interval had elapsed, and I asked if I might call on her, she answered at once that she would see me.

'I went to her house with the fixed intention of asking her to marry me – and I left it without having done so. Why? I don't know that I can tell you. Perhaps you would have had to sit there opposite her, knowing what I did and feeling as I did, to understand why. She was kind, she was compassionate – I could see she didn't want to make it hard for me. Perhaps she even wanted to make it easy. But there, between us, was the memory of the gesture I hadn't made, forever parodying the one I was attempting! There wasn't a word I could think of that hadn't an echo in it of words of hers I had been deaf to; there wasn't an appeal I could make that didn't mock the appeal I had rejected. I sat there and talked of her husband's death; of her plans, of my sympathy; and I knew she understood; and knowing that, in a way, made it harder . . . The doorbell rang and the footman came in to ask if she would receive other visitors. She looked at me a moment and said, 'Yes,' and I stood up and shook hands with her and went away.

'A few days later she sailed for Europe, and the next time we met she had married Reardon . . . '

6

It was long past midnight, and the terrier's hints became imperious.

Merrick rose from his chair, pushed back a fallen log and put up the fender. He walked across the room and stared a moment at the Brangwyn etching before which Paulina Trant had paused at a memorable turn of their talk. Then he came back and laid his hand on my shoulder.

'She summed it all up, you know, when she said that one way of finding out whether a risk is worth taking is not to take it, and then to see what one becomes in the long run, and draw one's inferences. The long run – well, we've run it, she and I. I know what I've become, but that's nothing to the misery of knowing what she's become. She had to have some kind of life, and she married Reardon. Reardon's a very good fellow in his way; but the worst of it is that it's not her way . . .

'No: the worst of it is that now she and I meet as friends. We dine at the same houses, we talk about the same people, we play bridge together, and I lend her books. And sometimes Reardon slaps me on the back and says: 'Come in and dine with us, old man! What you want is to be cheered up!' And I go and dine with them, and he tells me how jolly comfortable she makes him, and what an ass I am not to marry; and she presses on me a second helping of poulet Maryland, and I smoke one of Reardon's good cigars, and at half-past ten I get into my overcoat and goloshes, and walk back alone to my rooms . . . '

MRS HENRY WOOD

Mrs Henry Wood, neé Ellen Price, was born in Worcester in 1814, the daughter of a manufacturer. A spinal disease confined her to bed or a sofa for most of her life. She married Henry Wood, a shipping agent living in France, but returned to England with him in 1860. After his death in 1866 she settled in London, and wrote for magazines. Her second published novel, *East Lynne* (1861), had an almost unparalleled success. She never rose above the commonplace in her many novels, but showed some power in the analysis of character in her anonymous *Johnny Ludlow* stories (1874–80). In 1867 she bought the monthly *Argosy*, which she edited, and her novels went on appearing in it long after her death.

The Self-Convicted

I

It was a wild, boisterous evening at the commencement of winter. The wind, howling in fearful gusts, swept the earth as with a whirlwind, booming and rushing with a force seldom met with in an inland county. The rain descended in torrents, pattering against the window-panes, especially against those of a solitary farmhouse, situated several miles from the city of Worcester. In fact, it seemed a battle between the wind and the rain which should treat the house most roughly, and the wind had the best of it. It roared in the chimneys, it shook the old gables on the roof, burst open the chamber casements, and fairly unseated the weathercock from its perch on the barn. The appearance of the dwelling would seem to denote that it belonged to one of the middle class of agriculturists. There was no finery about it, inside or out, but plenty of substance. A large room, partaking partly of the parlour, partly of the hall, and somewhat of the kitchen, was the general sitting-room; and in this apartment, on this same turbulent Friday evening, sat, knitting by firelight, a middle-aged lady, homely, but very neat, in her dress.

'Eugh!' she shuddered, as the wind roared and the rain dashed against the windows, which were only protected by inside shutters, 'what a night it is! I wish to goodness Robert would come home.'

Laying down her knitting, she pushed the logs together on the hearth, and was resuming her employment, when a quiet, sensible-looking girl, apparently about one or two and twenty, entered. Her features were not beautiful, but there was an air of truth and good-nature pervading them more pleasing than beauty.

'Well, Jane,' said the elder lady, looking up, 'how does she seem now?'

'Her ankle is in less pain, mother,' was the reply, 'but it appears to me that she is getting feverish. I gave her the draught.'

'A most unfortunate thing!' ejaculated Mrs Armstrong. 'Benjamin at home ill, and now Susan must get doing some of his work, that she has no business to attempt, and falls down the loft, poor girl, and sprains her ankle. Why could she not have trusted to Wilson? I do believe,' broke off Mrs Armstrong, abruptly, and suspending her knitting to listen, 'that your father is coming. The wind howls so that one can scarcely hear, but it sounds to me like a horse's hoofs.'

'I do not think it is a horse,' returned Jane. 'It is more like someone walking round to the house-door.'

'Well, child, your ears are younger than mine; it may be as you say.'

'I hope it is not Darnley! ' cried Jane, involuntarily.

'Jane,' rebuked her mother, 'you are very obstinate to persist in this dislike of a neighbour. A wealthy young man with a long lease of one of the best farms in the county over his head is not to be sneezed at. What is there to dislike in James Darnley?'

'I – I don't know that there is anything particularly to dislike in him,' hesitated Jane, 'but I cannot see what there is to like.'

'Don't talk foolishly, but go and open the door,' interposed Mrs Armstrong. 'You hear the knocking.'

Jane made her way to the house-door, and, withdrawing the chain and bolt, a rush of wind, a shower of rain, and a fine-looking young man sprang in together. The latter clasped Jane round the waist, and – if the truth must be told – brought his lips into contact with hers.

'Hush, hush, Ronald,' she whispered; 'my mother is in the hall alone; what if she should hear!'

'I will fasten the door,' was all the answer she received. And Jane disengaged herself, and walked towards the hall.

'Who is it?' asked Mrs Armstrong, as her daughter reappeared. 'Mr Darnley?'

'It is Ronald Payne,' answered Jane, in a timid voice.

'Oh!' said Mrs Armstrong, in a very short tone. 'Get those shirts of your father's, Jane, and look to the buttons; there they lie, on the sideboard. And light the candles: you cannot see to work by firelight.'

'How are you, Mrs Armstrong?' enquired the young man, in cheerful tones, as he entered and seated himself on the opposite side of the large fireplace. 'What an awful night! I am not deficient in strength, but it was as much as I could do to keep my feet coming across the land.'

'Ah!' said Mrs Armstrong, plying her knitting-needles with great energy; 'you would have been better at home.'

'Home is dull for me now,' was the answering remark of Ronald Payne. 'Last winter my poor mother was alive to bear me company, but this, I have no one to care for.'

'Go upstairs, Jane, and see if Susan has dropped asleep,' interrupted Mrs Armstrong, who did not seem to be in the most pleasant humour, 'and as you will have the beds to turn down tonight, you can do that.'

Jane rose, and departed on her errand.

'And lonely my home is likely to be,' continued Ronald, 'until I follow good example and marry.'

'It would be the very thing for you, Mr Payne,' replied the lady. 'Why don't you set about it?'

'I wish I dare. But I fear it will take time and trouble to win the wife I should like to have.'

'There's a great deal of trouble in getting a wife – a good one; as for the bad ones, they are as plentiful as blackberries. There have been two or three young blades wanting to be after Jane,' continued the shrewd Mrs Armstrong, 'but I put a stop to them at once, for she is promised already.'

'Promised!' echoed Ronald.

'Of course she is. Her father has promised her to Mr Darnley; and a good match it will be.'

'A wretched sacrifice,' exclaimed Payne, indignantly. 'Jane hates him.'

'How do you know that?' demanded Mrs Armstrong, sharply.

'I hate him too,' continued the excited Ronald. 'I wish he was a thousand miles away.'

And the conversation continued in this strain until Jane returned, when another loud knocking at the house-door was heard above the wind.

'Allow me to open it,' cried Mr Payne, starting up; and a second stranger entered the sitting-room.

'How are you, Mr Darnley? I am very glad to see you,' was the cordial salutation of Mrs Armstrong, 'Come to the fire; and, Jane, go and draw a tankard of ale. Susan has managed to sprain her ankle tonight, and cannot stir a step,' she explained. 'An unlucky time for it to happen, for our indoor man went home ill three days ago, and is not back yet. Did you ever know such weather?'

'Scarcely,' returned the newcomer. 'As I rode home from the fair, I thought the wind could not be higher, but it gets worse every hour.'

'You have been to the fair, then?'

'Yes. I had a heavy lot of stock to sell. I saw Mr Armstrong there; he was buying, I think.'

'I wish he would make baste home,' was Mrs Armstrong's answer. 'It is not a desirable night to be out in.'

'A pretty prospect for going to Worcester market tomorrow!' observed Darnley.

'But need you go?'

'I shall go if it rains cats and dogs,' was the gentleman's reply. 'My business today was to sell stock – tomorrow, it will be to buy.'

Jane entered with the silver tankard, its contents foaming above its brim like a mountain of snow, and placed it on a small, round table between the two young men. They sat there, sipping the ale occasionally, now one, now the other, but angry words passed continually between them. Darnley was fuming at the evident preference Jane accorded to his rival, and Payne fretted and chafed at Darnley's suit being favoured by Mr and Mrs Armstrong. They did not quite come to a quarrel, but it was little short of it, and when they left the house together, it was in anything but a cordial humour.

'Jane, what can have become of your father?' exclaimed Mrs Armstrong, as the door closed upon the two young men. 'It is hard upon ten o'clock.

How late it will be for him to go to Wilson's: he will have, as it is, to knock him up, for the man must have been in bed an hour ago.'

Now it is universally known that farmers in general, even the most steady, have an irresistible propensity to yield to one temptation – that of taking a little too much on a fair or market night. Mr Armstrong was not wholly exempt from this failing, though it was rare indeed that he fell into the snare. For a twelvemonth, at least, his family had not seen him the worse for liquor; yet, as ill-luck would have it, he came in on this night stumbling and staggering, his legs reeling one way, and his head flying another. How he got home was a mystery to Mrs Armstrong; and to himself also, when he came to his senses. As to making him comprehend that an accident had befallen Susan, and that in consequence he was wanted to go and tell some one of their outdoor men to be at the house early in the morning, it was not to be thought of. All that could be done with him was to get him upstairs – a feat that was at length accomplished.

'This is a pretty business, Jane!' cried the indignant Mrs Armstrong. 'You will be obliged to milk the cows in the morning, now.'

'Milk the cows!' returned Jane, aghast at the suggestion.

'What else can be done? Neither you nor I can go to tell Wilson at this time of night, and in such a storm; and the cows must be milked. You can milk, I suppose?'

'Oh, mother!' was Jane's remonstrance.

'I ask if you can milk?' repeated Mrs Armstrong, impatiently – she was by far too much put out to speak otherwise.

'I have never tried since I was a child,' was Jane's reply. 'I sometimes used to do it then, for pastime.'

'Then, my dear, you must do it once for use. It would be a mercy,' continued the excited lady, 'if all the public-houses and their drinkables were at the bottom of the sea.'

Jane Armstrong was a girl of sound sense and right feeling. Unpalatable as the employment was, she nevertheless saw that it was her duty, under the present circumstances, to perform it; so she quietly made up her mind to the task, and requested her mother to call her at the necessary hour in the morning.

They were highly respectable and respected people, Robert Armstrong and his wife, though not moving in the sphere exclusive to gentlefolks. Jane had been brought up well. Perfectly conversant with all household duties, her education in other respects would scarcely have disgraced the first lady in the county – for it must be remembered that education then was not what it is now – and her parents could afford to spend money upon their only child. Amply she repaid them by her duty and affection. One little matter only did they disagree upon, and that not openly. Very indignant was Mrs Armstrong at Ronald Payne's presuming to look up to her, and exceedingly sore did she feel with Jane for not checking this presumption. But she could urge nothing against Ronald, excepting that he was a poor, rather than a rich man, and that the farm he rented was regarded as an unproductive one. His pretensions created a very ill-feeling towards him in Mrs Armstrong's mind, for she believed, that but for him, her daughter would consent to marry the wealthy James Darnley, and so become mistress of his splendid farm.

Before it was light the next morning Jane left the house with her milk-pail. Only the faintest glimmer of dawn was appearing in the east. There was no rain, and the wind had dropped to a calm; but it was a cold, raw morning. Jane wrapped her woollen shawl closely round her, and made good speed.

The field in which the cowsheds were situated was bounded on the left by a lonely lane, leading from the main road. It branched off in various directions, passing some of the farmhouses. Jane had reached the field, and was putting down her milk-pail, when a strange noise on the other side of the hedge caused her to start and listen.

A violent struggle, as for life or death, was taking place. A voice, that was certainly familiar to her, twice called out 'Murder!' with a shriek of agony, but heavy blows, seemingly from a club or other formidable weapon, soon silenced it, and someone fell to the earth amidst moans and groans of anguish.

'Lie there, and be still!' burst forth another voice, rising powerfully over the cries. 'What! you are not finished yet! I have lain in wait for ye to a pretty purpose if ye be to escape me now. One! two! three!' and Jane shuddered and turned sick as she listened, for each sentence was followed by a blow upon the prostrate form. The voice was totally strange to Jane – one that she had never heard in her life – and shocking blasphemy was mingled with the words.

Ere silence supervened, Jane, half stupefied with horror and fear, silently tore her thick shoes off her feet, leaving them where they were, in her agitation, and stole away on the damp path, gathering her clothes about her, so that not a sound should betray her presence to those on the other side. As she widened the distance between herself and that fearful scene, her speed increased; she flew, rather than ran, and entered her father and mother's bedroom to fall senseless on the floor.

Later in the morning, when broad daylight had come, a crowd stood around the murdered man. The face was bruised and blood-stained, and the head had been battered to death; but there was no difficulty in recognising the features of James Darnley. His pockets were turned inside out, having been rifled of their contents, and a thick, knotted stick, covered with blood and hair, lay by his side. It was supposed he had had a heavy sum about him in his pockets, but all had been abstracted.

And now came a question, first whispered amongst the multitude, but repeated louder and louder by indignant voices: 'Who is the murderer?'

'Ronald Payne,' was the answer, deliberately uttered by a bystander. 'I have just heard it from Mrs Armstrong's own lips. They were at her house last night quarrelling and contending, and she knows he is the murderer.'

'Ronald Payne!' echoed the crowd, with one universal accent of surprise and incredulity.

'As God is my judge,' cried the unhappy young man – for he was also present – 'I am innocent of this deed!'

'You have long been upon ill terms,' retorted the before-mentioned bystander – and it may be remarked that he was an acquaintance of Payne's who had never borne anything but kind feeling towards him. Yet now, so gratifying is it to the vain display and pride of human nature to be mixed up with one of these public tales of horror, he suddenly became his vehement accuser. 'Mrs Armstrong says that you left her house bickering with each other; and she heard you assert, before he was present, that you hated him, and wished he was a thousand miles away.'

'That is all true,' answered Ronald, turning his clear eye to the crowd, who now began to regard him with doubt. 'We *were* bickering one with the other at Mrs Armstrong's last night; not quarrelling, but talking at each other; but no ill words passed between us after we left the house. We walked peaceably together, and I left him at his own door. I never set eyes upon him afterwards till I saw him here with you, lying dead.'

Words of doubt, hints of suspicion, ran through the multitude, headed by the contumacious bystander: and Robert Payne's cheeks, as he listened, burnt like fire.

'How can you think I would have a hand in such an awful deed!' he indignantly exclaimed. 'Can you look in my face and believe me one capable of committing murder?'

'Faces don't go for nothing, sir,' interposed the constable, Samuel Dodd, who had come bustling up and heard the accusation made; 'we don't take 'em into account in these matters. I am afeared, sir, it's my duty to put the 'an'cuffs on you.'

'Handcuffs on me!' exclaimed Ronald, passionately.

'You may be wanted, sir, at the crowner's quest, and perhaps at another tribune after that. It is more than my office is worth to let you be at large.'

'Do you fear I should attempt to run away?' retorted Ronald.

'Such steps have been heered on, sir,' answered the constable; 'and my office is give me, you see, to prevent such.'

The idea of resistance rose irresistibly to the mind of Ronald Payne; but his better judgement came to his aid, and he yielded to the constable, who was calling on those around to help to secure him in the king's name – good old George III.

'I resign myself to circumstances,' was his remark to the officer, 'and will not oppose your performing what is your apparent duty. Yet, oh! believe me,' he added, earnestly, 'I am entirely innocent of this foul deed – as innocent as can be. I repeat, that I never saw James Darnley after I left him at his own house last night; and far from quarrelling during our walk home, we were amicably talking over farming matters.'

When the constable had secured his prisoner in the place known as the 'lock-up', he made his way to Mr Armstrong's, intensely delighted at all the excitement and stir, and anxious to gather every possible gossip about it, true or untrue. Such an event had never happened in the place since he was sworn in as constable. In Farmer Armstrong's hall were gathered several people, Sir John Seabury, the landlord of that and the neighbouring farms, standing in the midst.

Sir John was an affable man, and, as times went, a liberal landlord. It happened that he was then just appointed high sheriff of Worcestershire for the ensuing year, his name having been the one pricked by the king.

When the constable entered, all faces were turned towards him. Several voices spoke, but Sir John's rose above the rest.

'Well, constable, what news?'

'He's in the lock-up, sir,' was Mr Sam Dodd's reply; 'and there he'll be, safe and sound, till the crowner holds his quest.'

'Who is in the lock-up?' asked Sir John, for the parties now present were not those who had been at the taking of Payne: *they* had flocked, one and all, to the 'lock-up', crowd-like, at the heels of the constable and his prisoner. And Sir John Seabury, having but just entered, had not heard of Mrs Armstrong's suspicion.

'Him what did the murder, sir,' was the constable's explanatory answer, who had reasoned himself to the conclusion, as rural constables were apt to do in those days, that, because some slight suspicion attached to Payne, he must inevitably have committed it. 'And he never said a word,' exulted Mr Dodd, 'but he held out his hands for the 'an'cuffs as if he knowed they'd fit. He only declared he waren't guilty, and walked along with his head up, like a lord, and not a bit o' shame about him, saying that the truth would come out sooner or later. It's a sight to see, gentlemen, the brass them murderers has, and many on 'em keeps it up till they's a-ridin' to the drop.'

'How was it brought home to him? – who is it?' reiterated the baronet.

'It's young Mr Payne,' answered the officer, wiping his face, and then throwing the handkerchief into the hat, which stood on the floor beside him.

'Mr Payne!' repeated Sir John Seabury, in astonishment; whilst Jane, never for a moment believing the words, but startled into anger, stood forward, and spoke with trembling lips.

'What are you talking about, constable? what do you mean?'

'Mean, miss! Why, it were young Mr Payne what did the murder, and I have took him into custody.'

'The constable says right,' added Mrs Armstrong. 'There's not a doubt about it. He and Darnley were disputing here all last evening, and they left with ill-feeling between them. Who else can have done it?'

But she was interrupted by Miss Armstrong; and it should be explained that Jane, having just risen from the bed where they had placed her in the morning, had not until this moment known of the accusation against Payne. She turned to Sir John Seabury; she appealed to her father; she essayed to remonstrate with her mother; her anger and distress at length finding vent in hysterical words.

'Father! Sir John! there is some terrible mistake. Mother! how can you stand by and listen? I told you the murderer was a stranger – I *told* you so: what do they mean by accusing Ronald Payne?'

Jane might have held her tongue, for instilled suspicion is a serpent that gains quick and sure ground, and perhaps there was scarcely one around her who did not think it probable that Payne was the guilty man. They listened to Jane's reiterated account of the morning's scene to which she had been an ear-witness; to her assertion that it was impossible Ronald Payne could have been the murderer; but they hinted how unlikely it was, that in her terror, she was capable of recognising or not recognising voices; and she saw she was not fully believed.

She found herself, subsequently, she hardly knew how, in their best parlour – a handsome room and handsomely furnished – alone with Sir John Seabury. She had an indefinite idea, afterwards, that in passing the door she had drawn him in. He stood there with his eyes fixed on Jane, waiting for her to speak.

'Oh, Sir John! Sir John!' she cried, clinging to his arm in the agitation of the moment as she might cling to that of a brother, 'I see I am not believed; yet indeed I have told the truth. It was a stranger who murdered Mr Darnley.'

'Certainly the voice of one we are intimate with is not readily mistaken, even in moments of terror,' was Sir John Seabury's reply.

'It was an ill voice, a wicked voice; a voice that, independently of any accessory circumstances, one could only suppose belonged to a wicked man. But the language it used was awful: such that I had never imagined could be uttered.'

'And it was a voice you did not recognise?'

'It was a voice I could not recognise,' returned Jane, 'for I had never until then heard it.'

Sir John looked keenly at her. 'Is this rumour correct that they have been now hinting at,' he whispered – 'you heard it as well as I – that there was an attachment between you and Ronald Payne? and that there was ill-feeling between him and Darnley in consequence?'

'I see even you do not believe me,' cried Jane, bursting into tears. 'There *is* an attachment between us: but do you think I would avow such attachment for a murderer? The man whom I heard commit the deed was a stranger,' she continued earnestly; 'and Ronald Payne was not near the spot at the hour.'

'There is truth in your face, Miss Armstrong,' observed Sir John, gazing at her

'And truth in my heart,' she added.

And before he could prevent her, she had slipped towards the ground, and was kneeling on the carpet at the feet of Sir John.

'As truly as that I must one day answer before the bar of God,' she said, clasping her hands together, 'so have I spoken now: and according to my truth in this, may God deal then with me! Sir John Seabury, do you believe me?'

'I do believe you, my dear young lady,' he answered, the conviction of her honest truth forcing itself upon his mind. 'And however this unfortunate business may turn out for Ronald Payne, in my mind he will be from henceforth an innocent and a wronged man.'

'Can your influence not release him?' enquired Jane. 'You are powerful.'

'Impossible. I could do no more than yourself. He is in the hands of the law.'

'But you can speak to his character at the coroner's inquest?' she rejoined. 'You know how good it has always been.'

Sir John kindly explained to her that all testimonials to character must be offered at the trial, should it be Payne's fate to be committed for one.

When further enquiries came to be instituted, it was found that Darnley had been roused from his slumbers, and called out of his house, about half an hour, perhaps less, before the murder was committed. The only person deposing to this fact was his housekeeper – a most respectable woman, who slept in the room over her master. She declared that she had been unable to sleep in the early part of the night, feeling nervous at the violence of the wind; that towards morning she dropped asleep, and was awakened by a noise, and by some one shouting out her master's name. That she then heard her master open his window, and speak with the person outside, whoever it was; and that he almost immediately afterwards went downstairs, and out at the house-door.

'Who was it?' asked all the curious listeners. 'And what did he want with Darnley?'

The housekeeper did not know. She thought the voice was that of a stranger; at any rate it was one she did not recognise. And she could not say what he wanted, for she had not heard the words that passed: in fact, she was but half awake at the time, and had thought it was one of the farm-servants.

The coroner's inquest was held, and the several facts already related were deposed to. Mrs Armstrong's evidence told against, Jane's for, the prisoner. No article belonging to the unfortunate James Darnley had been found, saving a handkerchief, and that was found in the pocket of Ronald Payne. He accounted for it in this way. He left his own pocket-handkerchief, he said, a red silk one, by accident that night on the table at Mrs Armstrong's – and this was proved to be correct; that when he and Darnley got out, the wind was so boisterous they could not keep their hats on. Darnley tied his handkerchief over his. Payne would have done the same, but could not find his, so he had to hold his hat on with his hand. That when Darnley entered his house, he threw the handkerchief to his companion, to use it for the same purpose the remainder of his way, he having farther to go than Darnley. And, finally, Payne asserted that he had put the handkerchief in his pocket upon getting up that morning, intending to return it to Darnley as soon as he saw him.

The handkerchief was produced in court. It was of white lawn, large and of fine texture, marked in full, 'James Darnley'.

'He was always a bit of a dandy, poor fellow,' whispered the country rustics, scanning the white handkerchief: 'especially when he went a-courting.'

Ronald Payne, as one proof of his innocence, stated that he was in bed at the time the murder was committed. A manservant of his, who slept on the same floor as himself, also deposed to this; and said that a labourer came to the house with the news that a man had been found killed, before his master came downstairs. But upon being asked whether his master could not have left his bedroom and the house in the night, and have subsequently returned to it without his knowledge, he admitted that such might have been the case; though it was next to a 'moral impossibility' – such were his words – for it to have been done without his hearing.

But what was the verdict? – 'Wilful murder by person or persons unknown;' for the jury and the coroner did not find the evidence sufficiently strong to commit Payne for trial. So he left the court a discharged man, but *not*, as the frequent saying runs, without a stain upon his character. Although the verdict, contrary to general expectation, was in his favour, the whole neighbourhood believed him guilty. And from that moment, so violent is popular opinion, whether for good or for ill, he was exposed to nearly all the penalties of a guilty man. A dog could scarcely have been more badly treated than was he; and, so far as talking against him went, Mrs Armstrong headed the malcontents.

2

So matters went on till the month of February. In the quiet dusk of one of its evenings, Jane Armstrong crept away from her house, and, taking a direction opposite to that where the murder was committed, walked quickly until her father's orchard was in view. Crossing the stile of this, she turned to the right, and there stood Ronald Payne.

'This is kind of you, Jane,' he said, as he seated her upon the stump of a felled tree, and placed himself beside her. 'God bless you for this!'

'It is but little matter, Ronald, to be thanked for,' she replied. 'Perhaps it is not exactly what I ought to do, coming secretly to meet you here, but – '

'It is a great matter,' he interrupted, bitterly. 'I am now a proscribed man; a thing for boys to hoot at. It requires some courage, Jane, to meet a murderer.'

'I *know* your innocence, Ronald,' she answered, as, in all confiding affection, she leaned upon his bosom, while her tears fell fast. 'Had you been tried – condemned – executed, I would still have testified unceasingly to your innocence.'

'I sent for you here, Jane,' he resumed, 'to tell you my plans. I am about to leave this country for America. Perhaps I may there walk about without the brand upon my brow.'

'Oh, Ronald!' she ejaculated, 'is this your fortitude? Did you not promise me to bear this affliction with patience, and to hope for better days?'

'Jane, I did so promise you,' replied the unhappy young man; 'and if it were not for that promise, I should have gone long ago: but things get worse every day, and I can no longer bear it. I believe if I remained here I should go mad. See what a life mine is! I am buffeted – trampled down – spat upon – shunned – jeered – deserted by my fellow-creatures; not by one, but by all: save you, Jane, there is not a human being who will speak with me. *I* would not so goad another, were he even a known murderer, whilst I am but a suspected one. I have not deserved this treatment – God knows I have not!' And suddenly breaking off, he bent down his head, and, giving way to the misery that oppressed him, for some moments sobbed aloud like a child.

'Ronald, dearest Ronald,' she entreated, 'think better of this for my sake. Trust in – '

'It is useless, Jane, to urge me,' he interrupted. 'I cannot remain in England.'

Again she tried to combat his resolution: it seemed useless. But, unwilling to give up the point, she wrung a promise from him that he would well reconsider the matter during the following night and day; and, agreeing to meet him on the same spot the next evening, she parted from him with his kisses warm on her lips.

'Where can Jane be?' exclaimed Mrs Armstrong, calling out, and looking up and down the house in search of her. 'Robert, do you know?'

Mr Armstrong knew nothing about it.

The lady went into the kitchen, where the two indoor servants were seated at their tea.

'Susan – Benjamin, do you know anything of Miss Jane?'

'She is up there in the orchard with young Mr Payne, ma'am,' interposed Ned, the carter's boy, who stood by.

'How do you know?' demanded Mrs Armstrong, wrathfully.

'Because I brought her a message from him to go there. So I just trudged up a short while ago, and there I see 'em. He was a-kissin' of her or something o' that.'

'My daughter with *him*!' cried Mrs Armstrong, her face crimson, whilst Susan overbalanced her chair in her haste to administer a little wholesome correction to the bold-speaking boy. 'My daughter with a murderer!'

'That's why I went up,' chimed in the lad, dodging out of Susan's way. 'I feared he might be for killin' Miss Jane as he killed t'other, so I thought I'd watch 'em a bit.'

Away flew Mrs Armstrong to her husband, representing the grievance with all the exaggeration of an angry woman. Loud, stinging denunciations from both greeted Jane upon her entrance, and she, miserable and heart-broken, could offer no resistance to the anger of her incensed parents. It was very seldom Mr Armstrong gave way to passion; never with Jane; but he did that night: and she, terrified and sick at heart, promised compliance with his commands never to see Ronald Payne again.

Here was another blow for the ill-fated young man. Whether he had wavered or not, after his previous interview with Jane, must remain unknown, but he now determined to leave England, and without loss of time. He went to Sir John Seabury, and gave up the lease of his farm. It was said that Sir John urged him to stop and battle out the storm; but in vain. He disposed privately of his stock and furniture, and by the first week in March was on his way to Liverpool.

It was on the following Saturday that Jane Armstrong accompanied her father and mother to Worcester. She seemed as much like a person dead as alive; and Susan said, in confidence to a gossip, that young Mr Payne's untoward fate was breaking her heart. The city, in the afternoon, wore an aspect of gaiety and bustle far beyond that of the customary market-day, for the judges were expected in from Oxford to hold the assizes: a grand holiday then, and still a grand show for the Worcester people. Jane and her mother spent the day with some friends, whose residence was situated in the London Road, as it is called, the way by which the judges entered the city. It has been mentioned that the high sheriff for that year was Sir John Seabury; and, about three o'clock, he went out with his procession to meet the judges, halting at the little village of Whittington until they should arrive.

It may have been an hour or more after its departure from the city that the sweet, melodious bells of the cathedral struck out upon the air, giving notice that the cavalcade had turned and was advancing; and, in due time, a flourish of trumpets announced its approach. The heralds rode first, at a slow and stately pace, with their trumpets, preceding a double line of javelin men in the sumptuous liveries of the Seaburys, their javelins in rest, and their horses, handsomely caparisoned, pawing the ground. A chaise, thrown open, followed, containing the governor of the county gaol, his white wand raised in the air; and then came the sheriff's carriage, an equipage of surpassing elegance, the Seabury arms shining forth on the panels, and its four stately steeds prancing and chafing at the deliberate pace to which they were restrained.

It contained only one of the judges, all imposing in his flowing wig and scarlet robes. The Oxford assizes not having terminated when he left, he had hastened on to open court at Worcester, leaving his learned brother to follow. Opposite to him sat Sir John Seabury, with his chaplain in his gown and bands, and as Jane stood with her mother and their friends at the open window, the eye of their affable young landlord caught hers, and he leaned forward and bowed: but the smile on his face was checked, for he too surely read the worn and breaking spirit betrayed by Jane's. Some personal friends of the sheriff followed the carriage on horseback; and, closing the procession, rode a crowd of Sir John's well-mounted tenants, the portly person of Mr Armstrong conspicuous in the midst. But when Mrs Armstrong turned towards her daughter with an admiring remark on the pageantry, Jane was sobbing bitterly.

Mrs and Miss Armstrong left their friends' house, when tea was over, on their way to the inn used by Mr Armstrong at the opposite end of the town. They were in High Street, passing the Guildhall – Jane walking dreamily forwards, and her mother gazing at the unusual groups scattered about it, though all signs of the recent cavalcade had faded away – when Samuel Dodd, the constable, met them. He stood still, and addressed Jane.

'I think we have got the right man at last, Miss Armstrong. I suppose it will turn out, after all, that you were right about young Mr Payne.'

'What has happened?' faltered Jane.

'We have took a man, miss, on strong suspicions that he is the one what cooked Mr Darnley. We have been upon the scent this week past. You must be in readiness, ladies, for you'll be wanted at the trial, and it will come on next Tuesday or Wednesday. You'll get your summonses on Monday morning.'

'Good heart alive, constable!' cried the startled Mrs Armstrong. 'You don't mean to say that Ronald Payne was innocent!'

'Why, ma'am, that have got to be proved. For my part, I think matters would be best left as they is, and not raked up again. He have been treated so very shameful if it should turn out that he warn't guilty.'

It was even as the constable said. A man had been arrested and thrown into the county gaol at Worcester charged with the wilful murder of James Darnley

3

Late on Tuesday evening, Mr and Mrs Armstrong, with their daughter, drove into Worcester, to be in readiness for the next day's trial. It was a dull, rainy evening, and Jane leaned back in the carriage, almost careless as to what the following day would bring forth, since Ronald Payne had gone away for ever.

At about five minutes past nine in the morning, the presiding judge took his seat on the bench. The crowded, noisy court was hushed to silence, the prisoner was brought in, and the trial began.

The chief fact against the accused was that the pocket-book, with its contents, known to have been in Darnley's possession on the ill-fated morning, had been traced to the prisoner. The bank-notes he had changed away, and a silver pencil-case that was in it he had pledged. All this he did not deny; but he asserted that he had found the pocket-book hid in the hedge, close to the spot, when he had been prowling about there a few hours subsequent to the murder. It *might* be as he said; and counsel chattered wisely to each other, saying there was no evidence to convict him.

The last witness called was Jane Armstrong, and her sensible, modest, and ladylike appearance prepossessed everyone in her favour. She gave her testimony clearly and distinctly. The deadly struggle she had heard; the groans of the victim, and his shrieks of murder; the words uttered by the assailant; the blows which had been dealt, and the fall of the murdered man – all she separately deposed to. Still the crime was not brought home to the prisoner. Jane thought her testimony was over, and was waiting for her dismissal from the witness-box, when the counsel for the prosecution addressed her.

'Look around you, young lady: can you point out anyone present as the murderer?'

She looked attentively round the court, but as she had not *seen* the murderer on the dark morning, the effort was vain. But, though she felt it was fruitless, she once more gazed minutely and carefully at the sea of faces around her – at the prisoner's amongst the rest; and turning again to the judge, she shook her head.

At this moment a voice was heard, rising harshly above all the murmur of the court. Jane's back was towards the speaker, and she did not know from whom it came, but the tones thrilled upon her ear with horror, for she recognised them instantaneously. They were addressed to the judge.

'My lord, she's going to swear away my life.'

'*That's the man!*' uttered Jane, with the startling earnestness of truth. 'I know him by his voice.'

The prisoner – for he had been the speaker – quailed as he heard her, and an ashy paleness overspread his face. The judge gazed sternly, but somewhat mournfully, at him, and spoke words that are remembered in Worcester unto this day.

'Prisoner, *you have hanged yourself.*'

The trial proceeded to its close. A verdict of guilty was returned against the prisoner: and the judge, placing on his head the dread black cap, pronounced upon him the extreme sentence of the law.

Before he suffered, he confessed his guilt, with the full particulars attending it. It may be remembered that on the stormy evening when the chief actors in this history were introduced to the reader, the unfortunate James Darnley spoke of having just returned from a neighbouring fair. At this fair, it seemed, he had entered a public-house, and finding there some farmers of his acquaintance, he sat down with them to drink a glass of ale. In the course of conversation he spoke of the stock, cattle, etc., he had just sold, and the sum he had received for it, the money being then – he himself gratuitously added – in his breeches-pocket. He mentioned also his intended journey to Worcester market the following day, and that there his business would be to buy.

The wretched man, afterwards his murderer, was present amongst various other strangers which a fair is apt to collect together, and he formed the diabolical project of robbing him that night; but by some means or other the intention was frustrated. How, was never clearly ascertained, but it was supposed through Darnley's leaving for home at an unusually early hour, that he might be in time to pay a visit to the house of Miss Armstrong. The villain, however, was not to be so baulked. Rightly judging that Darnley would not remove his money from his breeches-pocket, as he would require it at Worcester market the following day, he made his way to his victim's house in the early dark of the ensuing winter's morning, and knocked him up. A strange proceeding, the reader will say, for one with the intentions he held. Yes. There stood James Darnley shivering at his chamber-window, suddenly roused from a sound sleep by the knocking; and there, underneath, stood one in the dark, whose form he was unable to distinguish; but it seemed a friendly voice that spoke to him, and it told a plausible tale. That Darnley's cows had broken from their enclosure and were strolling away, trespassing, and that he would do well to rise and hasten to them.

With a few cordial thanks to the unknown warner, with a pithy anathema on his cows, Darnley thrust on his knee-breeches – *the* breeches, as his destroyer had foreseen – and his farm jacket: went downstairs, and departed hastily on his errand. The reader need be told no more.

This was the substance of his confession; and on the appointed day he was placed in the cart to be drawn to execution. At that period, the gallows consecrated to Worcester criminals was erected on Redhill, a part of the London Road situated about midway between Worcester and Whittington; and here he was executed. An exhibition of the sort generally attracts its spectators, but such an immense assemblage has rarely been collected in Worcester, whether before or since, as was gathered together to witness the show on the day of his execution.

In proportion as the tide had turned against Ronald Payne, so did it now set in for him. The neighbourhood, one and all, took shame to themselves for their conduct to an innocent man, and it was astonishing to observe how quick they were in declaring that they must have been fools to suspect the kind-hearted, honourable fellow could be guilty of murder. Mrs Armstrong's self-reproaches were keen: she was a just woman and she knew that she had treated him with bitter harshness. Sir John Seabury, however, did not waste words in condolence and reproaches, as did the others: he dispatched a trusty messenger to Liverpool, in the hope of catching Payne before he embarked for a foreign land; and, as vessels in those times did not start every day, as steamers do in these, he was successful.

4

It was a beautiful afternoon in the middle of March. The villagers were decked out as for a holiday; garlands and festoons denoted that there was some unusual cause for rejoicing; and the higher class of farmers and their wives were grouped together, conversing cheerfully. Jane Armstrong stood by her mother, a happy flush upon her pleasing countenance. It was the hour of the expected return of Ronald Payne, and a rustic band of music had gone forth to meet the stage-coach.

Everybody was talking, nobody listening; the buzz of expectation rose louder and louder; and soon the band was heard returning, half of it blowing away at 'See the Conquering Hero Comes', the other half (not having been able to agree amongst themselves) drumming and whistling 'God Save the King'. Before the audience had time to comment on the novel effect of this new music, horses' heads were seen in the distance, and not the heavy coach, as had been expected, but the open barouche of Sir John Seabury came in sight, containing himself and Ronald Payne.

Ronald was nearly hugged to death. Words of apology and congratulation, of excuse and good-will, of repentance and joy, were poured into his ear by all, save Jane; and she stood away, the uncontrollable tears coursing down her face. It was plain, in a moment, that he bore no malice to any of them: his brow was as frank as ever, his eye as merry, his hands as open to clasp theirs. He was the same old Ronald Payne of months ago.

'Ronald Payne!' exclaimed Mrs Armstrong, standing a little before the rest: 'I was the first to accuse you; I was the foremost to rail at and shun you; let me be the most eager to express my painful regret, and so far – which is all I can do – make reparation. For the future, you shall not have a more sincere friend than myself.'

'And allow me, Mr Payne, to be the second to speak,' added Sir John; 'although I have no apology to make, for I never believed you guilty, as you know; but all these good people did, and it is useless, you are aware, to run against a stream. As some recompense for what you have suffered, I hereby offer you a lease of the farm and lands rented by the unfortunate James Darnley. It is the best vacant farm on my estate. And – a word yet: should you not have sufficient ready money to stock it, I will be your banker.'

Ronald Payne grasped in silence the offered hand of his landlord. His heart was too full to speak; but a hum of gratification from those around told that the generosity was appreciated.

'But, Mr Armstrong,' continued Sir John, a merry smile upon his countenance; 'is there no other recompense you can offer him?'

Jane was now standing amongst them, by Ronald's side, though not a word had yet passed between them. His eyes fondly sought hers at the last words, but her glowing countenance was alike turned from him and from Sir John Seabury.

'Ay, by all that's right and just, there is, Sir John!' burst forth good Farmer Armstrong. 'He deserves her, and he shall have her; and if my wife still says no, why I don't think she is any wife of mine.'

Sir John glanced at Mrs Armstrong, waiting no doubt for her lips to form themselves into the negative; but they formed themselves into nothing, excepting an approving smile cast towards Ronald Payne.

'And with many thanks, grateful thanks – which I am sure *he* feels – for your generous offer of being his banker, Sir John,' continued Mr Armstrong, 'you must give me leave to say that it will not now be needed. My daughter does not go to her husband portionless.'

'You must let me have notice of the time, Miss Armstrong,' whispered Sir John, as he leaned forward and took her hand; 'for I have made up my mind to dance at your wedding.'

But the secret was not confined to Sir John Seabury alone. The crowd had comprehended it now; and suddenly, as with one universal voice, the air was rent with shouts. 'Long live Ronald Payne and his fair wife when he shall win her! Long life and happiness to Mr and Mrs Ronald Payne!'

Mr North's Dream

I

The house stood in the midst of extensive grounds in one of the many suburbs of South London, a green lawn dotted with shrubs lying before the front-entrance. Land was at a discount there in the old days, and Mr North had bought the place for a comparatively small sum. He was a man of some consideration in the city, of high commercial and private character, well regarded by his fellow-merchants.

The lawn lay steeped in the lovely twilight of a midsummer evening. The moon glittered on the leaves of the laurels; the flowers, closing their petals, threw out their sweet scent, so that the air was rich with perfume. It was wafted to the open glass-doors of a small sitting-room, where stood a young girl; and her heart, as she inhaled it, grew more rapturously joyful than it had been before, if such a thing were possible.

It was Millicent Carden, the niece of Mr North's wife, and his ward. A merry, guileless, loving girl of seventeen; not quite eighteen yet; gay, careless, sweet-tempered. Her face was fair and refined, with a bright bloom just now on the delicate features; her light brown hair, unconfined by comb and fashion, fell in silken curls. Mrs North had gone out that night, taking her daughters, Frances and Amy. Mr North, his son and his nephew, Archie, were in the dining-room, for they had been delayed in the City, and came home late. The glow on Millicent's face was only a reflection of the glow that illumined her heart; nay, her whole being. For she had learned to love one with a strange fervour; and in such a nature as hers – deep, silent, ardent – love changes the whole current of life, and is as a very ray snatched from Eden.

The room-door opened and someone came in. Millicent did not turn; she stood where she was, and began to hum a tune carelessly; but her pulses leaped up with a bound, and the cheeks' glow increased to crimson.

'Why, Millicent! I thought you were going with the rest.'

Ah, she could turn calmly now. The colour faded.

The pulses became sober again. It was only John North.

'I did not care to go, John. And your mother thought we should be too many.'

'Then I hope my mother made an apology for leaving you. Frances or Amy might have stayed at home.'

'Frances and Amy are ages older than I. Don't look so solemn, John: it was my own wish to remain; I proposed it myself. Is my uncle not going?'

'Yes. But not with me: later. He has some – matters to settle first with Archibald. I'll go out this way, I think. Good-night to you, cousin mine.'

John North had made the pause in reference to the matters his father had to settle with Archibald. Miss Carden had thought nothing of it. If she had momentarily thought there was anything strange in the words, it was the name Archibald – for she had never heard him called anything but Archie. She watched John North cross the lawn in his evening dress. He was a tall, fine man of three-and-twenty, and had just been made a partner with his father. The young lady stepped out on the gravel and silently executed a dancing-step.

'You good old John! As if I should want to go when they did not invite *him*! As if I would go, unless my aunt had made me! I fancied John suspected something last week, though,' she pursued, more thoughtfully, bringing her dance to a conclusion; 'he looked so hard at us that evening when he came up and saw us in the laurel walk. Oh, how beautiful the night is! how lovely everything is in the whole world!'

Stooping, she plucked one of the sweet June roses, and put it within the folds of her light summer dress, her hands and arms looking so fragile and faultless in the moonlight. Then she stepped back indoors, and stood gazing out on the fair scene. Things were so still! Not a sound broke the solitude; the railways, with their shrieks and turmoil, had not quite cut up the place then. As the light in the west grew darker and the moon brighter, the nightingales began their song in the neighbouring trees; the twinkling stars came out in their canopy; the light on the laurels turned to silver. Insensibly the girl herself broke softly into melody. Six months before, Archie North had given her *Lalla Rookh*; she had soon learned its seductive songs by heart.

> There's a bower of roses by Bendemeer's stream,
> And the nightingale sings round it all the day long;
> In the time of my childhood 'twas like a sweet dream
> To sit in the roses, and hear the bird's song.

The striking of the clock interrupted her. Ten. Ten! Why, what could they be about so long in the dining-room? With a light step, she went along the gravel walks, and so round to the dining-room window.

It was closed. Closed that hot summer night: and her uncle, Mr North, was so fond of air, having the windows always open, except in the dead of winter! Millicent looked into the lighted room, and what she saw caused her heart to beat wildly.

Archie North stood against the wall; his arms folded, his head bowed, his good-looking face inflamed with tears, his whole aspect one of humiliation – of intense shame. He was as tall as his cousin John, but younger – only twenty. Only twenty! And exposed at that age, without a home (excepting lodgings), to the snares and temptations of a London life! On the table lay some papers; they looked like bills; and Mr North stood opposite Archie, talking, with his right hand outstretched, and an awful look of severity upon his face. Millicent turned sick with undefined fear, and crept back to the little room. What could the shame be?

The dining-room door opened, and voices were heard in the hall. Millicent, trembling from head to foot, looked out of this room cautiously. Archie had taken up his hat and a light overcoat that he wore to protect his clothes from the summer dust.

'Never attempt again to cross my threshold,' Mr North was saying, in the cold stern tone of an irrevocable decree. 'You are a disgrace to the name North, and I cast you off for ever from me and mine.'

Archie went out without an answering word, and North shut the hall-door upon him. Then he crossed the hall and went up the stairs, his boots creaking. Mr North's boots always creaked; it had a pompous sound, like himself, for he was a pompous man. He was dark, upright, portly, with a head well thrown back; eminently respectable, eminently self-important: doing his business strictly, as respectable men like to do; a large subscriber to charities, a good husband and father; but, in the midst of it all, very hard.

Millicent went back to the open window, and saw Archie North crossing the lawn, the light coat swung on his arm. Was he going away for ever? With a heart sick to faintness, with a mental confusion that seemed to put everything into a tumult, she ran after him, conscious of nothing but the moment's impulse.

'Archie! Archie!'

Archie North turned round. He was not her cousin; was not in fact related to her. If he had begun to love her, however deeply and enduringly, he knew it must all be at an end now.

'What is the matter, Archie?'

'I thought you were out tonight, Millicent.'

'No. The others went; I did not care to go. My uncle is angry with you: what is it?'

'Angry!' he repeated, as if the word were a perfect mockery to illustrate Mr North's state of feeling towards him. 'Yes; he is angry.'

'But you have not deserved it.'

'I have deserved it all; and worse.'

With his hand upon her shoulder he went back across the lawn to the room she had quitted. Standing just within the open window, he looked down upon her while he spoke. The moonlight played upon his troubled face, hard now almost as his uncle's, and lighted up the blue eyes that seemed filled with nothing but a dogged obstinacy.

'I am going away, Millicent. London can no longer hold me, so a distant quarter of the globe must do so. I have been upon the wrong track this long time. God forgive me! I never meant it to come to this.'

She tried to speak, but not a word came in answer. Her lips were white, her throat beating.

'On my soul, I had resolved to do better! – to set about redeeming the past. For your sake, Millicent; for your sake. And I should have carried it out, heaven helping me. When I am far away, my darling; when they tell you wicked stories of me – and yet not wicked in one sense, for they are true – remember this: it was *you* who awoke me to better things. It has been just one faint glimmer of light in a dark career: dark before; doubly dark after, for that's what it will be. God bless you, Millicent.'

He clasped her to him with a close pressure and kissed her unresisting face, down which the tears were flowing. What Millicent said she did not fully know at the time, and never remembered afterwards; confused words of redeeming the past, of allowing her fortune to help him to redeem it.

'No, no,' he said, with a kind of harsh laugh. 'I am a great blackguard, Millicent, but not quite so bad a one as that. Thank you for the thought,' he added, holding her two hands in his, and looking down into her eyes as she stood before him. 'Thank you, *my darling*, for all; thank you, above all, for your love. I do not suppose – bear with me one moment – that we shall ever meet again on this side the grave. If I can redeem things over yonder – but I'd better say nothing of that. My lot will probably be downwards; you will become the wife of some happy man, and the mother of his children. Fate deals out her prizes equally. Fare you well; fare you well for ever.'

With his coat on his arm as before, he went swinging across the lawn again, leaving Millicent ready to die of the moment's agony. And yet it all seemed so unreal! At the gate, lingering amidst the shrubs that surrounded it, and looking out for him, was John North.

'I couldn't go, Archie, in the uncertainty,' he said, coming forth into the moonlight. 'How has it ended?'

'How should it end?' returned Archie. 'There was only one way.'

'You are discarded?'

'Of course I am discarded. Sent adrift. Your father is a harsh man in anything that touches his respectability, or his name. Nine City magnates out of every ten might have done just the same.'

'What shall you do?'

'What I can. He has not been all hardness. He said something about giving me a fresh start in life: paying my passage to Australia, and transmitting fifty pounds, to be touched on my landing there. I am to meet him tomorrow. I don't grumble, John; I've deserved all I've got, and more. I shall see you, old fellow, once again before I start.'

A late omnibus passed. Archie North hailed it, and mounted on the top; and John went away quickly to the neighbouring house, that evening keeping festival.

Poor Millicent! She was dragging herself and her misery upstairs, when her uncle came suddenly out of his room in evening dress. She turned swiftly into a niche in the wall, and stood there until he had passed.

Archibald North set sail for Australia. There was no mystery made about him or his ill-doings, and Millicent heard what the rest heard. He had not been guilty of any crime; had not robbed his uncle's cash-box, or forged his name: but he had been an excessively prodigal sinner on his own score, and come to general grief; he had made an ocean of disreputable debts, and altogether gone to the bad.

'And he had the opportunity of doing so well!' cried Mr North, making severe comments in the bosom of his family. 'I gave him a stool in my counting-house; I invited him here frequently; and this has been my reward! What he might have gone on to but for my providential discovery of his sins, I shudder to think of. Henceforth let his name be as though we had never known him.'

And it was so.

2

Six years went by, and the seventh was quickly passing. Mr North and his children prospered and prospered; the ill-doing nephew had never been heard of, and was quite forgotten. Mrs North was dead; Amy had married; but with the exception of those two losses, the inmates of the old home were the same.

It was Christmas Eve, and bitter weather; ice and frost without, ruddy warmth and comfort within. The dessert-table was drawn to the fire in the dining-room, and Mr North and his son sat there. John was deep in the pages of a review he had brought home from town, but Mr North was only reading the faces in the fire, and sipping his port wine at intervals. He saw the face of his dead wife, whom he mourned sincerely, if soberly; he saw that of his absent daughter, who had a happy home of her own; he saw that of his younger son, also married and flourishing. Mr North's own face was smooth, after the manner of a man who has a calm conscience and a heavy balance-sheet – and he had both. His ledgers showed increase upon increase: on the other side he had dispensed largely to Christmas charities, public and private. Had Mr North's thoughts been laid bare, they would have been seen to ignore altogether a sense of sin, and to run very much after the bent of a certain Pharisee: 'I am thankful that I am not as other men are.' Mr North believed himself to be supremely good: he fully thought he was going swimmingly on the road that leads direct to heaven.

He saw other faces in the fire, besides those mentioned; his son John's, who was sitting beside him; and Millicent Carden's. He was wishing they would form a union with each other, those two; he had wished it for some time. Millicent was of age now. In accordance with her father's will, she did not attain her majority until she was twenty-four; and Mr North had then formally resigned to her his trusteeship, informing her at the same time that she was worth twenty thousand pounds, well invested. Had he been John, he should have proposed to her years ago; time and again he had felt inclined to say a prompting word; but he knew how much better these things work when left alone. Millicent had been ill in the summer with fever – and she did not seem to have recovered her entire strength.

'You will be thirty in a few months, John,' suddenly observed Mr North, breaking the silence.

John looked up from his review. 'Yes; getting quite a middle-aged man.'

'Not that yet. It will come, though, for years creep on us imperceptibly. Why don't you marry?'

Mr John North cut two pages of his book before replying. 'I don't know that anyone would have me.'

'What nonsense, John! In your case it would be only to ask and have. But if you *don't* ask, why of course – '

Mr North did not finish the sentence. John laughed, but did not attempt to pursue the subject. His father looked at him.

'Yes, sir, though you may laugh, many would answer "Yes" to the asking of John North. But there's one, above all the rest, whom I should wish you to choose.'

'Why, who's that?' returned John, in some surprise.

'You need not go far to find her. Millicent Carden.'

John North returned to his review again with a slight smile. And it vexed his father.

'Have you no better answer than that to give me?'

'I should not care to marry Millicent. She is my cousin, you know.'

'And what though she is your cousin?' indignantly spoke Mr North. 'She has twenty thousand pounds.'

John cut his review.

'And she is one of the best and nicest girls that the whole world contains. Don't be a fool, John.'

'She is a sweet girl; a charming girl,' came the ready assent. 'But I have not thought of her as a wife.'

'Think now, then.'

The silence, and the impassive look on his son's face, did not seem to promise well for the proposition. Was Mr North going to be thwarted in his hope? – the vexation the doubt brought showed him how surely he had been indulging it.

'Make up your mind to marry, and take Millicent,' urged Mr North impressively. 'My blessing shall be upon it. John, I have hoped for this union a long while: cherished the thought. I believe.'

John North grew serious then. He closed the book, leaving the paper-knife between its pages.

'I am sorry for that, sir; very sorry to disappoint you, if you have indeed cherished it. I had no idea you were doing anything of the sort. Putting myself entirely out of the question, I am sure Millicent would not have me. She would not have anyone.'

'She is well again.'

'Her health I was not thinking of, but her inclination. I have never exchanged a word with her upon the subject, but I am convinced her intention is not to marry. Millicent had her little romance years ago: and wore it out.'

'Why, what do you mean?' cried Mr North. 'Would you insinuate that Millicent was ever in love?'

'Yes; unhappily. With Archie North.'

Mr North stared at his son, as if he were unable at once to take in the words. There was scorn in his eye, contempt in his tone, when he answered. 'In love with Archie North! Why, she was a child when he went away.'

'Oh no, she was not: a girl of seventeen or eighteen is as capable of love as a woman of thirty; perhaps more so. Father, I know I am right. And Archie was in love with her.'

'Archie, the reprobate!' apostrophised the elder man: and the utter condemnation of the tone, the hatred it expressed, served to prove that the offending nephew had never been forgiven – no, not in the least degree. 'At any rate, if it be as you say, though I doubt it, she has had time to forget her fancy,' added Mr North. 'I would rather say her folly.'

'Quite time. But I do not think she has done it.'

'And you would make this an objection to asking her to be your wife? – a child's passing fancy! I should have given you credit for more sense.'

'Pardon me, sir, I did not say so. My own wishes, for or against, need not be brought into the discussion at all. What I said was, that Millicent would not have me, though I did ask her: and I am sure she would not.'

John North opened the book again as he spoke, and went on cutting its leaves. For some little time he had been indulging a day-dream of his own, but it was not connected with Millicent. Mr North tossed off the glass of port at his elbow, and said no more. He had never thought his clever business son so near a fool; and he intended to prove him one.

In the pretty garden-room, where you once saw Millicent Carden, you may see her still. The family often sat there. The window was closed now, the warm green curtain fell across its shutters in ample folds; the fire burnt clear and bright; the tea waited on the table, and Millicent sat ready to make it. Miss North had gone to a neighbour's to help in dispensing the prizes from a Christmas tree which she had for some days been assisting to adorn.

She sat at the table, waiting for her uncle and cousin to come in. But ah, how altered! Scarcely a trace remained of the winsome, happy girl of seventeen, to whom her boy-lover had bidden so abrupt and miserable an adieu six years and a half before. She wore a soft dress of light-grey cashmere, and a close white-net cap, very pretty, but almost as simple as that of a Quakeress. No ornament, excepting a gold chain and some fine lace at her wrists. After the summer's fever, her hair grew so thin that they cut it close, and she had to wear caps: it was growing again now, but she wore the caps still. The features were delicate as of yore: the deep hazel eyes more thoughtful. She looked like one who has passed through tribulation.

For the first time the thought struck Mr North, as he came in to tea, proving how slow we are, for the most part, to take up indications of the familiar, everyday life by which we are surrounded. In the subdued meek manner, the quiet face, the unobtrusive attire, so void of fashion and frivolity, Mr North saw reason to think his son was right. His unobservant eyes, closed hitherto, were rudely opened.

'But she has had time, and to spare, to forget the folly,' he thought. 'Even its remembrance must have long ago passed away. John would win her for the asking.'

John sat by her now, just as usual. But, as Mr North noted their manners to each other, so entirely that of brother and sister, a slight doubt arose to Mr North, or rather would have arisen, but that he drove it back again.

'You look tired, Millicent.'

'Do I? I am not tired; although Frances and I have had a busy day, giving away the things. The poor people are all so grateful to you, uncle.'

Mr North received the gratitude as his due. He deemed himself quite an earthly angel, in the matter of charity. 'All right,' he said in answer, 'I hope none have been forgotten.'

'If Millicent's tired, it must be at our keeping her waiting so long for tea,' cried John. 'It's half-past nine o'clock.'

'Time you went for Frances, John,' she said.

'I am going. Those mites were to be put to bed at nine, and she said she did not care to remain after that. She is fond of children, is Frances.'

He rose to go out as he spoke; but opened the door again, and said a word to Millicent, who nodded an answer. 'I shall be ready, John.'

Mr North, buried in his own reflections, did not observe it. He was making up his mind to speak to Millicent, and have that absurd question set at rest that John had started. He could not believe it yet; the longer he thought of it the more ridiculous it seemed. And yet he hesitated, lest he might do harm – harm to John's remote chance of succeeding.

The tea-things were sent away, and Millicent took out her work; some slippers she was working for John. Mr North sat on in indecision.

'Another Christmas Eve, Millicent!' he said, when he at length turned to her. 'The years steal upon us, my dear.'

'They do, uncle.'

'I have been thinking tonight – one gets thoughtful at Christmastide – that it is time you were married.'

Millicent looked at him, some wonder in her eyes; and a smile stole over her sweet face.

'You should say that to Frances, uncle. It is her turn first; she is ever so much older than I am.'

'Oh, Frances,' he slightingly said. 'My opinion is she does not think of marriage. She lets her chances slip.'

'Neither do I think of it, uncle.'

'Nonsense,' he testily responded; 'I shall insist upon your marrying. I mean, I wish you to do it.'

'No living person has a right to insist on my course of action,' was the firm answer. 'Not even you, uncle; I am my own mistress. Forgive me for saying it.'

Mr North's face darkened. 'A fable was whispered to me – as a fable I regarded it – that some – some – what shall I call it? – some love nonsense had lain between you and that miserable nephew of mine, who was a disgrace to his name.'

A change passed over her face. The eyelids quivered, the mouth grew sad and pale. Mr North watched the signs.

'Millicent! was it so? Answer me, child. Surely you can answer? It must be as a thing dead and buried now.'

'Yes; I cared for him. And he for me.'

'But you do not care still? You cannot.'

'Perhaps not. I suppose not. I think he must be dead,' she continued, a kind of weariness in her tone. 'He would have been back ere now if he had lived.'

'Back!' cried the scandalised man, 'back! He'd know better than to venture back here. Why!' looking condemningly at her, '*you* would not have countenanced him had he returned?'

'Yes, I should. Stay a moment, uncle; don't be angry with me. But for believing him to be dead, I could not say this to you; I could not speak of him; I have thought he must be dead – oh, for these three years past. But had he come back with his – his wrongdoings – redeemed; hoping, purposing to do well in the future, I would have welcomed him, and helped him in it. Let it pass; why should the discussion arise?'

'And it is for this man's sake – dead, though you admit he probably is – that you deliberately say you will never marry? Shame upon you, Millicent! I am thankful your poor aunt is not alive to hear it.'

'I did not say I should never marry,' she meekly returned, and her tone was full of pain and contrition, as if accepting as her due the shame he cast on her. 'I would not marry now; no one living could tempt me to do so; but I cannot answer for what I may do in the future – in years to come. The probabilities are that I never shall marry; still, I cannot answer for it. We all change so, uncle; as you must know.'

It seemed so complete a check to any hope for his son that Mr North was angered beyond repression. He called Archie sundry hard names, recapitulating his committed sins and offences, in a far more comprehensive manner than Millicent had heard in the days of the trouble. She listened without comment, folding up the slipper and putting it away, until his wrath had expended itself and he was fain to cease. Then she spoke.

'Yes, uncle; I dare say it was all very true, miserably true; but you know he might not have continued so. There is such a thing as young men awaking to the errors of their course and entering on a better.'

Mr North would have answered that there was no chance of the young man under discussion awaking to the error of his, but his niece had left the room. She came back with her bonnet on: at which he looked surprised. She and Frances had wished to go to a Christmas Eve service at a church close by, and John had promised to take them. Even while she was explaining this, they came for her.

Mr North remained alone. Matters through life had gone so smoothly with him that he could not bear to be crossed. It tried both himself and his temper. He knocked the fire about, he paced the room, he walked into the hall in his restlessness. A good, domesticated girl like Millicent, and twenty thousand pounds, slipping through his favourite son's fingers! Mr North dashed open the front-door, seeking a breath of the cold fresh air to cool his hot and angry brow.

It was colder than he thought for; flakes of snow had begun to fall, and there was some ice on the doorstep; indeed Mr North slipped upon it, and he would have measured his length on the ground but for the extended arm of some visitor, who had approached the door, and saved him. Mr North threw his own arm around the pillar, while he took breath and recovered his equanimity.

'Merciful powers! I was all but down!'

'It is my uncle!' cried an answering voice. 'I was not quite sure of it, sir, until you spoke. May I come in?'

To say that Mr North recoiled in some terror; to say that he gazed at the speaker in alarm, would not be to say much. *Was* it his nephew, Archie, standing there, or was it not? With the past conversation turning on Archie North, with his mind full of him, Mr North for one single moment fancied he was being deceived by some spectral vision, and backed into the hall.

Archie followed him and shut the door. It was not the Archie of former days, strong, active, buoyant, but a sort of broken-down man, who was lame, and walked with the help of a stick. Mr North, seeming almost as if he really fled from a phantom, backed yet again into the parlour he had quitted: Archie and his stick went after him.

There ensued a scene. A scene little fitted for the blessed Christmastide about to dawn. When Mr North had once taken in the fact that it was his nephew in real flesh and blood, and not a deception of fancy, his passion burst out. Archie had come at an unlucky time; but for his uncle's mind having first been freshly embittered against him, he might have met with a less harsh reception.

The traveller strove to explain his appearance and a little of the past. For six years he had been working manfully in Australia: all his bad habits, his careless ways eradicated; he had earned his living, but not enough to put by anything of consequence – great luck did not attend him. A changed man, yearning for home and friends, he had determined to return to the old country, where he could equally earn a competence; and he set sail. The ship, when she had arrived very near her destination, was wrecked on the coast of the Isle of Wight; and Archie had received an injury on the rocks, from which he was slowly recovering. It had detained him, and exhausted his available funds. He had written an account of this to Mr North, which letter he supposed would have been delivered that morning, bringing the news that he was following close upon it.

All this he essayed to explain. Mr North did not catch a word of it; he had not seen any letter. He put up his hands and stormed at Archie; he drove him forth, calling him very hard names in the process; he told him he did not know him henceforth, and never had known him since that wicked time seven years ago. Finally he closed the hall-door upon him; and the unhappy wanderer limped away across the lawn.

Mr North sat down by the fire to recover himself. He believed he had done a righteous thing in discarding the once bad man; and his own passion he excused to himself. One cannot be always watchful, says the plastic conscience. Snatches of Archie's explanation stole into his mind now imperfectly, though he had not seemed to hear any of it at the time; amidst them a confused reminiscence of his having said he had only eighteenpence in the world.

'And that's more than he deserves,' quoth Mr North, savagely. 'How dared he come back with his disgrace! How dared he show himself at my –'

A tremendous ring at the hall-bell cut short the speech. Mr North started up with an evil cry of rage; he thought the fellow had come back again, and he hastened across the hall to drive him away, calling out to his servants that he would answer the door himself. And he opened it.

But he was wrong. The postman stood there, and put a letter into his hand.

'You are late,' growled Mr North.

'Yes, sir, the delivery is heavy tonight; and the roads are slippery; one has to walk with caution.'

The letter was from Archie; the one he had supposed would have been already received. Mr North flung it on the table in a climax of passion, and let it lie there.

The joyous peal of church bells broke upon his ear, ringing in Christmas. Mr North remembered how his wife, in her last Christmas, when she was sitting in that very chair close to his elbow, had remarked that she could fancy they spoke the words, 'Peace on earth, goodwill toward men.' There was not much peace, or goodwill either, in Mr North's heart this evening.

He heard the children entering; taking up the letter, he thrust it into his pocket out of sight, unopened. The only wonder was that he did not put it effectively away from sight on the fire. Spiced wine, cake, and other good things were brought in; and they sat round the red coals, talking pleasantly, quite unconscious that Mr North's plumage had been ruffled. Millicent sat by her uncle; she put her hand on his arm as it lay on the elbow of the chair, as if she would intimate that the little rupture between them was over and forgotten.

'I wish you had gone with us, uncle; I think you would have liked it. The singing was so good, and the sermon beautiful. It only lasted ten minutes, but it was full of love and peace. He asked us how we could expect God's love to reach us if we did not love our fellow-creatures; he said this was the season for putting away evil passions and hatred, and for receiving the loving spirit of Christ into our hearts, who had done so much for us.'

'What sort of a night is it?' responded Mr North, his tones testy and impatient – as if there were something in Millicent's words that grated on his temper.

'Snowing,' answered John. 'We shall have a white Christmas.'

Mr North went to rest with the others; and by that time, what with the fire and the good things he had taken, he was in a tolerably genial good humour. But he could not get to sleep. Down deep in his conscience something sharp was stinging and pricking and making itself inconveniently felt. Tossing and turning from side to side, it was four o'clock in the morning before he lost consciousness.

And he woke up at six. He awoke with a great horror within, and trembling without. He sat up in bed and stared out into the darkness; and only discovered by degrees that what he had gone through was a dream, and not reality.

It was a dream that shook him to the core; a vivid scene so like life; and the terror, the dismay, the remorse that overwhelmed him were so indisputably felt – felt still in all their agony, now that he was wide awake – that Mr North for the moment verily thought it must have been a vision sent to him, like the visions of old in the days of the patriarchs.

He had dreamed over again the scene of the past night, or very much of it – of the return of Archibald North and his thrusting him out. He further dreamed that he had gone forth to pursue him with his anger, and went stamping up hill and down dale unable to discover him. Suddenly he found himself in a roadside field, about half a mile from his own home; and there, by the pond, he saw Archie lying dead, his upturned face calm and serene, pale but pleasant to look upon, as if its owner had passed to a happy rest. All in a moment the most intense remorse took possession of Mr North as he gazed: he thought that he himself was also dead, and was about to answer for his sins. One that looked like an angel, clad in dazzling white, stood there with a severe and pitying countenance; severe in its condemning anger, pity for him, for the man who had forfeited peace for ever. 'Pardon, Lord, pardon!' he had cried out in his desperate anguish, knowing all the time that pardon was impossible; and a soft, sweet, mournful wail had sounded in his ear as the answer: 'Inasmuch as ye did it not to one of the least of these, ye did it not to Me.'

Mr North awoke. Horror lay on his heart; drops, as of death agony, on his brow. It was some time before he could believe he was yet in this state of existence. It was much longer before he could in the least overcome the agitation that shook his soul.

In all reactions, such as this, the feelings necessarily run into exaggeration. The harshness of the previous night appeared to Mr North in the worst possible light; a heinous crime; a sin that perhaps even yet, although the world was his still, he might never find forgiveness for. It stared him in the face in all the vivid colouring that newly-awakened remorse wears. Ay, and not only this last act, but the whole course of his doings by Archibald, in the years gone by, came rolling before him as waves in a sea of fire.

'His own brother's son! his own brother's son!' were the words that kept beating their burthen on his brain. His brother whom he had loved very dearly when they were boys together; and who, when dying, had asked him to take care of his boy Archie. How had Mr North responded to the dying prayer? It is true he had given Archie a stool in his counting-house, and told him he would get on if he took care, but he had not held out a hand to save him from sin. He had left him to find lodgings where he could, abandoning him (he saw it now) to the perils of a London life. And when Archie went wrong (and it was nearly a matter of course that he would go wrong) and his tribulations were laid bare he had hurled him forth upon the world, unforgiven. Those tribulations of poor Archie's were as nothing to the dire tribulations that rent his uncle now. And the refrain kept on and on, repeating itself for ever – 'His own brother's son! his brother's son!'

So certainly did Mr North appear to have seen the dead body lying by the pond, every little particular being as clear as a witnessed scene, that, but for the sense of shame that lay in attending to a dream, he would have got up and gone to the spot. As it was, he lay still until daylight. Drawing his blind aside, he saw that the ground was covered with snow; but not a deep snow; and the sky now looked tolerably clear. Perhaps a more miserable man than Mr North, when he dressed himself, was not to be found that day in London. God had shown the self-righteous Pharisee his sin.

The children (he was apt to call them children still, as we all do, however old they may grow) came up to kiss him as he entered the breakfast-room, Frances first. 'Dear papa! I wish you a happy Christmas, and a great many of them!' And so they all followed: and Mr North groaned inwardly by way of answer.

What a room of luxury it was! a bright and blazing fire, a sumptuous breakfast. Tea and coffee in their silver pots, savoury meats warm and cold; the pâté de foie gras, sent to his orders direct from Strasburg, forming the centre dish. All this for him, the hard, selfish man, and for his children; but where was his brother's son?

He could not eat. John asked him if he had a headache, and he answered yes; and when breakfast was over he turned his chair to the fire. Where was he? With only eighteenpence in his pocket, how could he find food and shelter? That the calamity he dreamed of had not happened, Mr North felt sure of now, since no news had come, for the pond was within view of the road, and anyone lying near it could not fail to be seen.

When left alone, he drew the letter from his pocket and opened it. It contained an account of Archie's life in Australia; of his shipwreck and injury on the coast of the Isle of Wight; just what he had wished to tell the previous night. 'Do not, my dear uncle, think I am coming back to be a burden on you, or to disgrace you,' it concluded. 'Disgrace and folly, thank Heaven, I left behind in England, when that severe lesson was read to me just six years and six months ago. I have a little money (it is a good thing I did not bring it with me) lodged in the hands of some Australian merchants, who have a branch house in London, and I shall soon be earning more. They have offered me a lucrative post in their London house, which I think I shall accept. I know how justly angry you were with me when I went away; but I hope you will forgive and receive the prodigal son, and let me spend a happy Christmas Day with you all in the dear old home. I am not quite up to travelling yet, but I must come; I have set my heart upon it. Do you remember the cake that Amy used to make to be cut after dinner on Christmas Day, with a gold and an iron ring in it? Do you remember the hopes and fears as to who should get the rings? – and the laughing and the fun? I hope the cake is an institution still. I would not miss it this year for the world, and so I shall come – and send on this letter to prepare my way for me. Dear uncle! the random boy has become a steady man; the scapegrace has put away folly for wisdom. You will not refuse to welcome him!'

Mr North held the letter in his hand, and gazed at its writing (that such a thing should have to be told of him!) until his tears dropped fast upon it. It was so different from what he expected; it was no begging letter, this. And he had turned him out with harsh words. Where was he? – where was he? Mr North put on his hat and went down the road, as if to take a little walk before service. No; the pond lay there still enough, but Archibald was not lying beside it.

They went to church; and Mr North did his best to hide from others that he could not attend to the prayers. Peace on earth and goodwill to men! What had he to do with it now? Oh, he seemed very very far from Him whom the angels heralded with those glorious words. It was as if a great gulf had sprung up between him and heaven. He did not dare to stay for the sacrament, and he wondered how worthy in God's sight he must have been on the past Christmas Days to partake of it. Not a single cry for forgiveness went up from his closed lips; his sense of sin lay too heavily upon him.

They dined at four; it had been the Christmas hour when the children were young, and it was never altered. There was no cake now; somehow sobriety in the later years had fallen upon them, and Amy, who was the cake-maker, had gone. She and her husband were to have dined there this day, but had been prevented from doing so. The only guests were two young ladies, orphans, one of whom (she was only a governess) made John North's day-dream. And he meant to tell her so, though he foresaw it would bring disappointment to his father.

It was a well-spread board: the turkey a prize; the plum-pudding rich; the wine good; but Mr North could scarcely swallow a morsel; every mouthful seemed to choke him, every drop to chill him. Sitting alone in the little garden-room before dinner, he had lived over the interview of the previous night; he had lived over (oh, worse than all) the dream. An unpleasant superstition was beginning to creep upon him – he who had never been given to superstition in all his life – that the dream must have come to him as a foreshadowing of the truth, and that Archibald was really dead.

Perhaps he was in the pond, instead of beside it? A horror broke over Mr North at the sudden thought, just as it had broken when awaking from the dream. An awful dread that it was so took possession of him; a conviction so sure that he looked upon it as a prevision. No wonder he could not eat any dinner!

But, if it had not been for his own preoccupation, he must have seen that some unusual emotion was stirring Millicent. She wore her little net cap, but the cheeks it shaded were crimson, the eyes had a sweet light of expectation; her blue silk dress was nearly as gay as the dresses of yore. Little did Mr North suspect that Millicent had read the letter. In his troubled state he had contrived to drop it in the morning, before going to the pond; Frances had picked it up, read it, thinking it no breach of faith, and shown it to Millicent. But they kept their own counsel, and concluded that the evident perturbation of Mr North must be connected with this.

He could not sit there. His brother's son! his own brother's son! Making some inaudible excuse of headache, of not wanting dessert, he left the table at the close of dinner, and stole out of the house by a side-door, very much as though he were going to a funeral. That Archibald was in the pond seemed to have grown into a certainty – perhaps had thrown himself in, broken-hearted, after that cruel reception – and Mr North could not keep from it. It drew him to it with a sort of fascination, just as surely and helplessly as he felt that he was drifting farther and farther away from heaven.

The snow was falling again; the air keen; and Mr North had to walk slowly and carefully along the road, because of the ice, until he turned into the field. Crunching the snow beneath his feet, he paced round and round the pond and strained his eyes into it; and saw nothing. But for the utter despair that lay upon him, the lively sense of guilt in the sight of God, a petitioning cry had gone up to heaven that there might be no one lying beneath the waters. With the morrow he would confess to Archibald's visit and have the pond dragged. How bear the suspense until then? How bear it?

He took the field way home; the snow was less dangerous than the ice; and by and by dragged his weary limbs through a gate in the remote part of his own grounds into which the fields opened. Scarcely had he done this when a groan broke upon his ear. A groan, and then another; and then something like a faint voice, speaking faint words.

'Halloa! what's that?' called out Mr North.

'Uncle! Is it you?'

With a rush as of burning heat coursing through all his veins, Mr North turned to the spot, and saw Archie lying in a sort of dry ditch or dyke. He was not dead: but he would surely have died, left there another night. The explanation was simple. On his way to an inn up the road, where he thought he might sleep, when driven forth the previous night, he had taken the more sheltered and well-remembered path through the grounds, in preference to the slippery highway. Awkward from his lameness, deceived by the snow, he had wandered from the path, missed his footing at the edge of the dyke, and had fallen into it. Upon essaying to rise, he found he could not do so; he believed his leg was broken. Too far off to attract attention, though he had called at intervals until strength and voice were exhausted, there he had lain ever since.

Mr North was not of a demonstrative nature; but there may arise moments in all men's lives where emotion has more or less its way. He could not get to Archie in the dyke without stooping in the most inconvenient fashion, but he held one uplifted hand between his, clasping it tenderly, as a fond mother may clasp her little child's.

'If you can find one or two men, uncle, just to carry me to the inn and to get a surgeon?'

To the inn, indeed! No, no. Mr North bounded along the path to his home at a faster rate than he had tried since his days of youth and slenderness. The tears were raining from his eyes at the mercy vouchsafed to him; and in the thankfulness that his sin was not irredeemable, his mouth, like the publican's of old, could once more open: 'God be merciful to me, a sinner!'

They carried Archie in. The surgeon was there and did what was necessary, and said he would want good nursing. Mr North gently answered that he would be tended as his own son. Millicent was admitted then. Their hands met, their eyes looked straight into each other's, and they knew that the boy and girl love had lasted in all its brightness; that sadness and separation were now over.

'To think that he should have lain there for eighteen hours with nothing to eat!' lamented Miss North, who was of a practical turn of mind.

'But I didn't, Frances,' spoke up Archie. 'I had by chance a hard biscuit in my pocket, and ate it this morning.'

'After all, it has been a blessed Christmas Day,' murmured Mr North to himself that night in his bedchamber, as he reverently knelt down by his bedside. 'Glory to God in the highest, and on earth peace; goodwill toward men!'

VIRGINIA WOOLF

Virginia Woolf was born in 1882, the youngest daughter of the Victorian writer Leslie Stephen. After her father's death, Virginia moved with her sister Vanessa (later Vanessa Bell) and her brothers Thoby and Adrian to 46 Gordon Square, which was to be the first meeting place of the Bloomsbury Group. Virginia married Leonard Woolf in 1912, and together they established the Hogarth Press. Virginia also published her first novel, *The Voyage Out*, in 1912, and she subsequently wrote eight more, several of which are considered classics, as well as two books of seminal feminist thought. Woolf suffered from mental illness throughout her life and committed suicide in 1941.

The Legacy

'For Sissy Miller.' Gilbert Clandon, taking up the pearl brooch that lay among a litter of rings and brooches on a little table in his wife's drawing-room, read the inscription: 'For Sissy Miller, with my love.'

It was like Angela to have remembered even Sissy Miller, her secretary. Yet how strange it was, Gilbert Clandon thought once more, that she had left everything in such order – a little gift of some sort for every one of her friends. It was as if she had foreseen her death. Yet she had been in perfect health when she left the house that morning, six weeks ago; when she stepped off the kerb in Piccadilly and the car had killed her.

He was waiting for Sissy Miller. He had asked her to come; he owed her, he felt, after all the years she had been with them, this token of consideration. Yes, he went on, as he sat there waiting, it was strange that Angela had left everything in such order. Every friend had been left some little token of her affection. Every ring, every necklace, every little Chinese box – she had a passion for little boxes – had a name on it. And each had some memory for him. This he had given her; this – the enamel dolphin with the ruby eyes – she had pounced upon one day in a back street in Venice. He could remember her little cry of delight. To him, of course, she had left nothing in particular, unless it were her diary. Fifteen little volumes, bound in green leather, stood behind him on her writing table. Ever since they were married, she had kept a diary. Some of their very few – he could not call them quarrels, say tiffs – had been about that diary. When he came in and found her writing, she always shut it or put her hand over it. 'No, no, no,' he could hear her say. 'After I'm dead – perhaps.' So she had left it him, as her legacy. It was the only thing they had not shared when she was alive. But he had always taken it for granted that she would outlive him. If only she had stopped one moment, and had thought what she was doing, she would be alive now. But she had stepped straight off the kerb, the driver of the car had said at the inquest. She had given him no chance to pull up . . . Here the sound of voices in the hall interrupted him.

'Miss Miller, sir,' said the maid.

She came in. He had never seen her alone in his life, nor, of course, in tears. She was terribly distressed, and no wonder. Angela had been much more to her than an employer. She had been a friend. To himself, he thought, as he pushed a chair for her and asked her to sit down, she was scarcely distinguishable from any other woman of her kind. There were thousands of Sissy Millers – drab little women in black carrying attaché cases. But Angela, with her genius for sympathy, had discovered all sorts of qualities in Sissy Miller. She was the soul of discretion; so silent; so trustworthy, one could tell her anything, and so on.

Miss Miller could not speak at first. She sat there dabbing her eyes with her pocket handkerchief. Then she made an effort.

'Pardon me, Mr Clandon,' she said.

He murmured. Of course he understood. It was only natural. He could guess what his wife had meant to her.

'I've been so happy here,' she said, looking round. Her eyes rested on the writing table behind him. It was here they had worked – she and Angela. For Angela had her share of the duties that fall to the lot of a prominent politician's wife. She had been the greatest help to him in his career. He had often seen her and Sissy sitting at that table – Sissy at the typewriter, taking down letters from her dictation. No doubt Miss Miller was thinking of that, too. Now all he had to do was to give her the brooch his wife had left her. A rather incongruous gift it seemed. It might have been better to have left her a sum of money, or even the typewriter. But there it was – 'For Sissy Miller, with my love.' And, taking the brooch, he gave it her with the little speech that he had prepared. He knew, he said, that she would value it. His wife had often worn it . . . And she replied, as she took it almost as if she too had prepared a speech, that it would always be a treasured possession . . . She had, he supposed, other clothes upon which a pearl brooch would not look quite so incongruous. She was wearing the little black coat and skirt that seemed the uniform of her profession. Then he remembered – she was in mourning, of course. She, too, had had her tragedy – a brother, to whom she was devoted, had died only a week or two before Angela. In some accident was it? He could not remember – only Angela telling him. Angela, with her genius for sympathy, had been terribly upset. Meanwhile Sissy Miller had risen. She was putting on her gloves. Evidently she felt that she ought not to intrude. But he could not let her go without saying something about her future. What were her plans? Was there any way in which he could help her?

She was gazing at the table, where she had sat at her typewriter, where the diary lay. And, lost in her memories of Angela, she did not at once answer his suggestion that he should help her. She seemed for a moment not to understand.

So he repeated: 'What are your plans, Miss Miller?'

'My plans? Oh, that's all right, Mr Clandon,' she exclaimed. 'Please don't bother yourself about me.'

He took her to mean that she was in no need of financial assistance. It would be better, he realised, to make any suggestion of that kind in a letter. All he could do now was to say as he pressed her hand, 'Remember, Miss Miller, if there's any way in which I can help you, it will be a pleasure . . . '

Then he opened the door. For a moment, on the threshold, as if a sudden thought had struck her, she stopped.

'Mr Clandon,' she said, looking straight at him for the first time, and for the first time he was struck by the expression, sympathetic yet searching, in her eyes. 'If at any time,' she continued, 'there's anything I can do to help you, remember, I shall feel it, for your wife's sake, a pleasure . . .'

With that she was gone. Her words and the look that went with them were unexpected. It was almost as if she believed, or hoped, that he would need her. A curious, perhaps a fantastic idea occurred to him as he returned to his chair. Could it be that, during all those years when he had scarcely noticed her, she, as the novelists say, had entertained a passion for him? He caught his own reflection in the glass as he passed. He was over fifty; but he could not help admitting that he was still, as the looking-glass showed him, a very distinguished-looking man.

'Poor Sissy Miller!' he said, half laughing. How he would have liked to share that joke with his wife! He turned instinctively to her diary. 'Gilbert,' he read, opening it at random, 'looked so wonderful . . . ' It was as if she had answered his question. Of course, she seemed to say, you're very attractive to women. Of course Sissy Miller felt that too. He read on. 'How proud I am to be his wife!' And he had always been very proud to be her husband. How often, when they dined out somewhere, he had looked at her across the table and said to himself, She is the loveliest woman here! He read on. That first year he had been standing for Parliament. They had toured his constituency. 'When Gilbert sat down the applause was terrific. The whole audience rose and sang: "For he's a jolly good fellow." I was quite overcome.' He remembered that, too. She had been sitting on the platform beside him. He could still see the glance she cast at him, and how she had tears in her eyes. And then? He turned the pages. They had gone to Venice. He recalled that happy holiday after the election. 'We had ices at Florians.' He smiled – she was still such a child; she loved ices. 'Gilbert gave me a most interesting account of the history of Venice. He told me that the Doges . . . ' she had written it all out in her schoolgirl hand. One of the delights of travelling with Angela had been that she was so eager to learn. She was so terribly ignorant, she used to say, as if that were not one of her charms. And then – he opened the next volume – they had come back to London. 'I was so anxious to make a good impression. I wore my wedding dress.' He could see her now sitting next old Sir Edward; and making a conquest of that formidable old man, his chief. He read on rapidly, filling in scene after scene from her scrappy fragments. 'Dined at the House of Commons . . . To an evening party at the Lovegroves. Did I realise my responsibility, Lady L. asked me, as Gilbert's wife?' Then, as the years passed – he took another volume from the writing table – he had become more and more absorbed in his work. And she, of course, was more often alone . . . It had been a great grief to her, apparently, that they had had no children. 'How I wish,' one entry read, 'that Gilbert had a son!' Oddly enough he had never much regretted that himself. Life had been so full, so rich as it was. That year he had been given a minor post in the government. A minor post only, but her comment was: 'I am quite certain now that he will be Prime Minister!' Well, if things had gone differently, it might have been so. He paused here to speculate upon what might have been. Politics was a gamble, he reflected; but the game wasn't over yet. Not at fifty. He cast his eyes rapidly over more pages, full of the little trifles, the insignificant, happy, daily trifles that had made up her life.

He took up another volume and opened it at random. 'What a coward I am! I let the chance slip again. But it seemed selfish to bother him with my own affairs, when he has so much to think about. And we so seldom have an evening alone.' What was the meaning of that? Oh, here was the explanation – it referred to her work in the East End. 'I plucked up courage and talked to Gilbert at last. He was so kind, so good. He made no objection.' He remembered that conversation. She had told him that she felt so idle, so useless. She wished to have some work of her own. She wanted to do something – she had blushed so prettily, he remembered, as she said it, sitting in that very chair – to help others. He had bantered her a little. Hadn't she enough to do looking after him, after her home? Still, if it amused her, of course he had no objection. What was it? Some district? Some committee? Only she must promise not to make herself ill. So it seemed that every Wednesday she went to Whitechapel. He remembered how he hated the clothes she wore on those occasions. But she had taken it very seriously, it seemed. The diary was full of references like this: 'Saw Mrs Jones . . . She has ten children . . . Husband lost his arm in an accident . . . Did my best to find a job for Lily.' He skipped on. His own name occurred less frequently. His interest slackened. Some of the entries conveyed nothing to him. For example: 'Had a heated argument about socialism with B.M.' Who was B.M.? He could not fill in the initials; some woman, he supposed, that she had met on one of her committees. 'B.M. made a violent attack upon the upper classes . . . I walked back after the meeting with B.M. and tried to convince him. But he is so narrow-minded.' So B.M. was a man – no doubt one of those 'intellectuals', as they call themselves, who are so violent, as Angela said, and so narrow-minded. She had invited him to come and see her apparently. 'B.M. came to dinner. He shook hands with Minnie!' That note of exclamation gave another twist to his mental picture. B.M., it seemed, wasn't used to parlourmaids; he had shaken hands with Minnie. Presumably he was one of those tame working men who air their views in ladies' drawing-rooms. Gilbert knew the type, and had no liking for this particular specimen, whoever B.M. might be. Here he was again. 'Went with B.M. to the Tower of London. . . . He said revolution is bound to come . . . He said we live in a Fool's Paradise.' That was just the kind of thing B.M. would say – Gilbert could hear him. He could also see him quite distinctly – a stubby little man, with a rough beard, red tie, dressed as they always did in tweeds, who had never done an honest day's work in his life. Surely Angela had the sense to see through him? He read on. 'B.M. said some very disagreeable things about – ' The name was carefully scratched out. 'I told him I would not listen to any more abuse of – ' Again the name was obliterated. Could it have been his own name? Was that why Angela covered the page so quickly when he came in? The thought added to his growing dislike of B.M. He had had the impertinence to discuss him in this very room. Why had Angela never told him? It was very unlike her to conceal anything; she had been the soul of candour. He turned the pages, picking out every reference to B.M. 'B.M. told me the story of his childhood. His mother went out charring . . . When I think of it, I can hardly bear to go on living in such luxury . . . Three guineas for one hat!' If only she had discussed the matter with him, instead of puzzling her poor little head about questions that were much too difficult for her to understand! He had lent her books. Karl Marx, *The Coming Revolution*. The initials B.M., B.M., B.M., recurred repeatedly. But why never the full name? There was an informality, an intimacy in the use of initials that was very unlike Angela. Had she called him B.M. to his face? He read on. 'B.M. came unexpectedly after dinner. Luckily, I was alone.' That was only a year ago. 'Luckily' – why luckily? – 'I was alone.' Where had he been that night? He checked the date in his engagement book. It had been the night of the Mansion House dinner. And B.M. and Angela had spent the evening alone! He tried to recall that evening. Was she waiting up for him when he came back? Had the room looked just as usual? Were there glasses on the table? Were the chairs drawn close together? He could remember nothing – nothing whatever, nothing except his own speech at the Mansion House dinner. It became more and more inexplicable to him – the whole situation; his wife receiving an unknown man alone. Perhaps the next volume would explain. Hastily he reached for the last of the diaries – the one she had left unfinished when she died. There, on the very first page, was that cursed fellow again. 'Dined alone with B.M. . . . He became very agitated. He said it was time we understood each other . . . I tried to make him listen. But he would not. He threatened that if I did not . . . ' the rest of the page was scored over. She had written 'Egypt. Egypt. Egypt,' over the whole page. He could not make out a single word; but there could be only one inter-pretation: the scoundrel had asked her to become his mistress. Alone in his room! The blood rushed to Gilbert Clandon's face. He turned the pages rapidly. What had been her answer? Initials had ceased. It was simply 'he' now. 'He came again. I told him I could not come to any decision . . . I implored him to leave me.' He had forced himself upon her in this very house. But why hadn't she told him? How could she have hesitated for an instant? Then: 'I wrote him a letter.' Then pages were left blank. Then there was this: 'No answer to my letter.' Then more blank pages; and then this: 'He has done what he threatened.' After that – what came after that? He turned page after page. All were blank. But there, on the very day before her death, was this entry: 'Have I the courage to do it too?' That was the end.

Gilbert Clandon let the book slide to the floor. He could see her in front of him. She was standing on the kerb in Piccadilly. Her eyes stared; her fists were clenched. Here came the car . . .

He could not bear it. He must know the truth. He strode to the telephone. 'Miss Miller!'

There was silence. Then he heard someone moving in the room. 'Sissy Miller speaking' – her voice at last answered him.

'Who,' he thundered, 'is B.M.?'

He could hear the cheap clock ticking on her mantelpiece; then a long drawn sigh. Then at last she said: 'He was my brother.'

He *was* her brother; her brother who had killed himself. 'Is there,' he heard Sissy Miller asking, 'anything that I can explain?'

'Nothing!' he cried. 'Nothing!'

He had received his legacy. She had told him the truth. She had stepped off the kerb to rejoin her lover. She had stepped off the kerb to escape from him.

Kew Gardens

From the oval-shaped flowerbed there rose perhaps a hundred stalks spreading into heart-shaped or tongue-shaped leaves halfway up and unfurling at the tip red or blue or yellow petals marked with spots of colour raised upon the surface; and from the red, blue or yellow gloom of the throat emerged a straight bar, rough with gold dust and slightly clubbed at the end. The petals were voluminous enough to be stirred by the summer breeze, and when they moved, the red, blue and yellow lights passed one over the other, staining an inch of the brown earth beneath with a spot of the most intricate colour. The light fell either upon the smooth, grey back of a pebble, or the shell of a snail with its brown, circular veins, or falling into a raindrop, it expanded with such intensity of red, blue and yellow the thin walls of water that one expected them to burst and disappear. Instead, the drop was left in a second silver grey once more, and the light now settled upon the flesh of a leaf, revealing the branching thread of fibre beneath the surface, and again it moved on and spread its illumination in the vast green spaces beneath the dome of the heart-shaped and tongue-shaped leaves. Then the breeze stirred rather more briskly overhead and the colour was flashed into the air above, into the eyes of the men and women who walk in Kew Gardens in July.

The figures of these men and women straggled past the flowerbed with a curiously irregular movement, not unlike that of the white and blue butterflies who crossed the turf in zigzag flights from bed to bed. The man was about six inches in front of the woman, strolling carelessly, while she bore on with greater purpose, only turning her head now and then to see that the children were not too far behind. The man kept this distance in front of the woman purposely, though perhaps unconsciously, for he wished to go on with his thoughts.

Fifteen years ago I came here with Lily, he thought. We sat somewhere over there by a lake and I begged her to marry me all through the hot afternoon. How the dragonfly kept circling round us: how clearly I see the dragonfly and her shoe with the square silver buckle at the toe. All the time I spoke I saw her shoe and when it moved impatiently I knew without looking up what she was going to say: the whole of her seemed to be in her shoe. And my love, my desire, were in the dragonfly; for some reason I thought that if it settled there, on that leaf, the broad one with the red flower in the middle of it, if the dragonfly settled on the leaf she would say 'Yes' at once. But the dragonfly went round and round: it never settled anywhere – of course not,

happily not, or I shouldn't be walking here with Eleanor and the children –
'Tell me, Eleanor. D'you ever think of the past?'

'Why do you ask, Simon?'

'Because I've been thinking of the past. I've been thinking of Lily, the woman I might have married . . . Well, why are you silent? Do you mind my thinking of the past?'

'Why should I mind, Simon? Doesn't one always think of the past, in a garden with men and women lying under the trees? Aren't they one's past, all that remains of it, those men and women, those ghosts lying under the trees. . . one's happiness, one's reality?'

'For me, a square silver shoe buckle and a dragonfly – '

'For me, a kiss. Imagine six little girls sitting before their easels twenty years ago, down by the side of a lake, painting the water-lilies, the first red water-lilies I'd ever seen. And suddenly a kiss, there on the back of my neck. And my hand shook all the afternoon so that I couldn't paint. I took out my watch and marked the hour when I would allow myself to think of the kiss for five minutes only – it was so precious – the kiss of an old grey-haired woman with a wart on her nose, the mother of all my kisses all my life. Come, Caroline, come, Hubert.'

They walked on the past the flowerbed, now walking four abreast, and soon diminished in size among the trees and looked half transparent as the sunlight and shade swam over their backs in large trembling irregular patches.

In the oval flowerbed the snail, whose shell had been stained red, blue, and yellow for the space of two minutes or so, now appeared to be moving very slightly in its shell, and next began to labour over the crumbs of loose earth which broke away and rolled down as it passed over them. It appeared to have a definite goal in front of it, differing in this respect from the singular high-stepping angular green insect who attempted to cross in front of it, and waited for a second with its antenna trembling as if in deliberation, and then stepped off as rapidly and strangely in the opposite direction. Brown cliffs with deep green lakes in the hollows, flat, blade-like trees that waved from root to tip, round boulders of grey stone, vast crumpled surfaces of a thin crackling texture – all these objects lay across the snail's progress between one stalk and another to his goal. Before he had decided whether to circumvent the arched tent of a dead leaf or to breast it there came past the bed the feet of other human beings.

This time they were both men. The younger of the two wore an expression of perhaps unnatural calm; he raised his eyes and fixed them very steadily in front of him while his companion spoke, and directly his companion had done speaking he looked on the ground again and sometimes opened his lips only after a long pause and sometimes did not open them at all. The elder man had a curiously uneven and shaky method of walking, jerking his hand forward and throwing up his head abruptly, rather in the manner of an impatient carriage horse tired of waiting outside a house; but in the man these gestures were irresolute and pointless. He talked almost incessantly; he smiled to himself and again began to talk, as if the smile had been an answer. He was talking about spirits – the spirits of the dead, who, according to him, were even now telling him all sorts of odd things about their experiences in Heaven.

'Heaven was known to the ancients as Thessaly, William, and now, with this war, the spirit matter is rolling between the hills like thunder.' He paused, seemed to listen, smiled, jerked his head and continued: 'You have a small electric battery and a piece of rubber to insulate the wire – isolate? – insulate? – well, we'll skip the details, no good going into details that wouldn't be understood – and in short the little machine stands in any convenient position by the head of the bed, we will say, on a neat mahogany stand. All arrangements being properly fixed by workmen under my direction, the widow applies her ear and summons the spirit by sign as agreed. Women! Widows! Women in black – '

Here he seemed to have caught sight of a woman's dress in the distance, which in the shade looked a purple black. He took off his hat, placed his hand upon his heart, and hurried towards her muttering and gesticulating feverishly. But William caught him by the sleeve and touched a flower with the tip of his walking-stick in order to divert the old man's attention. After looking at it for a moment in some confusion the old man bent his ear to it and seemed to answer a voice speaking from it, for he began talking about the forests of Uruguay which he had visited hundreds of years ago in company with the most beautiful young woman in Europe. He could be heard murmuring about forests of Uruguay blanketed with the wax petals of tropical roses, nightingales, sea beaches, mermaids, and women drowned at sea, as he suffered himself to be moved on by William, upon whose face the look of stoical patience grew slowly deeper and deeper.

Following his steps so closely as to be slightly puzzled by his gestures came two elderly women of the lower middle class, one stout and ponderous, the other rosy-cheeked and nimble. Like most people of their station they were frankly fascinated by any signs of eccentricity betokening a disordered brain, especially in the well-to-do; but they were too far off to be certain whether the gestures were merely eccentric or genuinely mad. After they had scrutinised the old man's back in silence for a moment and given each other a queer, sly look, they went on energetically piecing together their very complicated dialogue:

'Nell, Bert, Lot, Cess, Phil, Pa, he says, I says, she says, I says, I says, I says – '

'My Bert, Sis, Bill, Grandad, the old man, sugar, Sugar, flour, kippers, greens, Sugar, sugar, sugar.'

The ponderous woman looked through the pattern of falling words at the flowers standing cool, firm, and upright in the earth, with a curious expression. She saw them as a sleeper waking from a heavy sleep sees a brass candlestick reflecting the light in an unfamiliar way, and closes his eyes and opens them, and seeing the brass candlestick again, finally starts broad awake and stares at the candlestick with all his powers. So the heavy woman came to a standstill opposite the oval-shaped flower bed, and ceased even to pretend to listen to what the other woman was saying. She stood there letting the words fall over her, swaying the top part of her body slowly backwards and forwards, looking at the flowers. Then she suggested that they should find a seat and have their tea.

The snail had now considered every possible method of reaching his goal without going round the dead leaf or climbing over it. Let alone the effort needed for climbing a leaf, he was doubtful whether the thin texture which vibrated with such an alarming crackle when touched even by the tip of his horns would bear his weight; and this determined him finally to creep beneath it, for there was a point where the leaf curved high enough from the ground to admit him. He had just inserted his head in the opening and was taking stock of the high brown roof and was getting used to the cool brown light when two other people came past outside on the turf. This time they were both young, a young man and a young woman. They were both in the prime of youth, or even in that season which precedes the prime of youth, the season before the smooth pink folds of the flower have burst their gummy case, when the wings of the butterfly, though fully grown, are motionless in the sun.

'Lucky it isn't Friday,' he observed.

'Why? D'you believe in luck?'

'They make you pay sixpence on Friday.'

'What's sixpence anyway? Isn't it worth sixpence?'

'What's "it" – what do you mean by "it"?'

'Oh, anything – I mean – you know what I mean.'

Long pauses came between each of these remarks; they were uttered in toneless and monotonous voices. The couple stood still on the edge of the flowerbed, and together pressed the end of her parasol deep down into the soft earth. The action and the fact that his hand rested on the top of hers expressed their feelings in a strange way, as these short insignificant words also expressed something, words with short wings for their heavy body of meaning, inadequate to carry them far and thus alighting awkwardly upon the very common objects that surrounded them, and were to their inexperienced touch so massive; but who knows (so they thought as they pressed the parasol into the earth) what precipices aren't concealed in them, or what slopes of ice don't shine in the sun on the other side? Who knows? Who has ever seen this before? Even when she wondered what sort of tea they gave you at Kew, he felt that something loomed up behind her words, and stood vast and solid behind them; and the mist very slowly rose and uncovered – Oh, Heavens, what were those shapes? – little white tables, and waitresses who looked first at her and then at him; and there was a bill that he would pay with a real two-shilling piece, and it was real, all real, he assured himself, fingering the coin in his pocket, real to everyone except to him and to her; even to him it began to seem real; and then – but it was too exciting to stand and think any longer, and he pulled the parasol out of the earth with a jerk and was impatient to find the place where one had tea with other people, like other people.

'Come along, Trissie; it's time we had our tea.'

'Wherever *does* one have one's tea?' she asked with the oddest thrill of excitement in her voice, looking vaguely round and letting herself be drawn on down the grass path, trailing her parasol, turning her head this way and that way, forgetting her tea, wishing to go down there and then down there, remembering orchids and cranes among wild flowers, a Chinese pagoda and a crimson-crested bird; but he bore her on.

Thus one couple after another with much the same irregular and aimless movement passed the flowerbed and were enveloped in layer after layer of green-blue vapour, in which at first their bodies had substance and a dash of colour, but later both substance and colour dissolved in the green-blue atmosphere. How hot it was! So hot that even the thrush chose to hop, like a mechanical bird, in the shadow of the flowers, with long pauses between one movement and the next; instead of rambling vaguely the white butterflies danced one above another, making with their white shifting flakes the outline of a shattered marble column above the tallest flowers; the glass roofs of the palm house shone as if a whole market full of shiny green umbrellas had opened in the sun; and in the drone of the aeroplane the voice of the summer sky murmured its fierce soul. Yellow and black, pink and snow white, shapes of all these colours, men, women, and children were spotted for a second upon the horizon, and then, seeing the breadth of yellow that lay upon the grass, they wavered and sought shade beneath the trees, dissolving like drops of water in the yellow and green atmosphere, staining it faintly with red and blue. It seemed as if all gross and heavy bodies had sunk down in the heat motionless and lay huddled upon the ground, but their voices went wavering from them as if they were flames lolling from the thick waxen bodies of candles. Voices. Yes, voices. Wordless voices, breaking the silence suddenly with such depth of contentment, such passion of desire, or, in the voices of children, such freshness of surprise; breaking the silence? But there was no silence; all the time the motor omnibuses were turning their wheels and changing their gears; like a vast nest of Chinese boxes all of wrought steel turning ceaselessly one within another the city murmured; on the top of which the voices cried aloud and the petals of myriads of flowers flashed their colours into the air.

The Mark on the Wall

Perhaps it was the middle of January in the present year that I first looked up and saw the mark on the wall. In order to fix a date it is necessary to remember what one saw. So now I think of the fire; the steady film of yellow light upon the page of my book; the three chrysanthemums in the round glass bowl on the mantelpiece. Yes, it must have been the winter time, and we had just finished our tea, for I remember that I was smoking a cigarette when I looked up and saw the mark on the wall for the first time. I looked up through the smoke of my cigarette and my eye lodged for a moment upon the burning coals, and that old fancy of the crimson flag flapping from the castle tower came into my mind, and I thought of the cavalcade of red knights riding up the side of the black rock. Rather to my relief the sight of the mark interrupted the fancy, for it is an old fancy, an automatic fancy, made as a child perhaps. The mark was a small round mark, black upon the white wall, about six or seven inches above the mantelpiece.

How readily our thoughts swarm upon a new object, lifting it a little way, as ants carry a blade of straw so feverishly, and then leave it. . . If that mark was made by a nail, it can't have been for a picture, it must have been for a miniature – the miniature of a lady with white powdered curls, powder-dusted cheeks, and lips like red carnations. A fraud of course, for the people who had this house before us would have chosen pictures in that way – an old picture for an old room. That is the sort of people they were – very interesting people, and I think of them so often, in such queer places, because one will never see them again, never know what happened next. They wanted to leave this house because they wanted to change their style of furniture, so he said, and he was in process of saying that in his opinion art should have ideas behind it when we were torn asunder, as one is torn from the old lady about to pour out tea and the young man about to hit the tennis ball in the back garden of the suburban villa as one rushes past in the train.

But as for that mark, I'm not sure about it; I don't believe it was made by a nail after all; it's too big, too round, for that. I might get up, but if I got up and looked at it, ten to one I shouldn't be able to say for certain; because once a thing's done, no one ever knows how it happened. Oh! dear me, the mystery of life; the inaccuracy of thought! The ignorance of humanity! To show how very little control of our possessions we have – what an accidental affair this living is after all our civilisation – let me just count over a few of the things lost in one lifetime, beginning, for that seems always the most mysterious of losses – what cat would gnaw? what rat would nibble? – three pale blue canisters of book-binding tools. Then there were the bird cages, the iron hoops, the steel skates, the Queen Anne coal-scuttle, the bagatelle board, the hand organ – all gone, and jewels, too. Opals and emeralds, they lie about the roots of turnips. What a scraping paring affair it is to be sure! The wonder is that I've any clothes on my back, that I sit surrounded by solid furniture at this moment. Why, if one wants to compare life to anything, one must liken it to being blown through the Tube at fifty miles an hour – landing at the other end without a single hairpin in one's hair! Shot out at the feet of God entirely naked! Tumbling head over heels in the asphodel meadows like brown-paper parcels pitched down a shoot in the post office! With one's hair flying back like the tail of a race-horse. Yes, that seems to express the rapidity of life, the perpetual waste and repair; all so casual, all so haphazard . . .

But after life. The slow pulling down of thick green stalks so that the cup of the flower, as it turns over, deluges one with purple and red light. Why, after all, should one not be born there as one is born here, helpless, speech-less, unable to focus one's eyesight, groping at the roots of the grass, at the toes of the Giants? As for saying which are trees, and which are men and women, or whether there are such things, that one won't be in a condition to do for fifty years or so. There will be nothing but spaces of light and dark, intersected by thick stalks, and rather higher up perhaps, rose-shaped blots of an indistinct colour – dim pinks and blues – which will, as time goes on, become more definite, become – I don't know what . . .

And yet that mark on the wall is not a hole at all. It may even be caused by some round black substance, such as a small rose leaf, left over from the summer, and I, not being a very vigilant housekeeper – look at the dust on the mantelpiece, for example, the dust which, so they say, buried Troy three times over, only fragments of pots utterly refusing annihilation, as one can believe.

The tree outside the window taps very gently on the pane . . . I want to think quietly, calmly, spaciously, never to be interrupted, never to have to rise from my chair, to slip easily from one thing to another, without any sense of hostility, or obstacle. I want to sink deeper and deeper, away from the surface, with its hard separate facts. To steady myself, let me catch hold of the first idea that passes . . . Shakespeare . . . Well, he will do as well as another. A man who sat himself solidly in an armchair, and looked into the fire, so – A shower of ideas fell perpetually from some very high heaven down through his mind. He leant his forehead on his hand, and people, looking in through the open door – for this scene is supposed to take place on a summer's evening – But how dull this is, this historical fiction! It doesn't interest me at all. I wish I could hit upon a pleasant track of thought, a track indirectly reflecting credit upon myself, for those are the pleasantest thoughts, and very frequent even in the minds of modest mouse-coloured people, who believe genuinely that they dislike to hear their own praises. They are not thoughts directly praising oneself; that is the beauty of them; they are thoughts like this:

'And then I came into the room. They were discussing botany. I said how I'd seen a flower growing on a dust heap on the site of an old house in Kingsway. The seed, I said, must have been sown in the reign of Charles I. What flowers grew in the reign of Charles I? I asked – (but, I don't remember the answer). Tall flowers with purple tassels to them perhaps.' And so it goes on. All the time I'm dressing up the figure of myself in my own mind, lovingly, stealthily, not openly adoring it, for if I did that, I should catch myself out, and stretch my hand at once for a book in self-protection. Indeed, it is curious how instinctively one protects the image of oneself from idolatry or any other handling that could make it ridiculous, or too unlike the original to be believed in any longer. Or is it not so very curious after all? It is a matter of great importance. Suppose the looking glass smashes, the image disappears, and the romantic figure with the green of forest depths all about it is there no longer, but only that shell of a person which is seen by other people – what an airless, shallow, bald, prominent world it becomes! A world not to be lived in. As we face each other in omnibuses and underground railways we are looking into the mirror; that accounts for the vagueness, the gleam of glassiness, in our eyes. And the novelists in future will realise more and more the importance of these reflections, for of course there is not one reflection but an almost infinite number; those are the depths they will explore, those the phantoms they will pursue, leaving the description of reality more and more out of their stories, taking a knowledge of it for granted, as the Greeks did and Shakespeare perhaps – but these generalisations are very worthless. The military sound of the word is enough. It recalls leading articles, cabinet ministers – a whole class of things indeed which as a child one thought the thing itself, the standard thing, the real thing, from which one could not depart save at the risk of nameless damnation. Generalisations bring back somehow Sunday in London, Sunday-afternoon walks, Sunday luncheons, and also ways of speaking of the dead, clothes, and habits – like the habit of sitting all together in one room until a certain hour, although nobody liked it. There was a rule for everything. The rule for tablecloths at that particular period was that they should be made of tapestry with little yellow compartments marked upon them, such as you may see in photographs of the carpets in the corridors of the royal palaces. Tablecloths of a different kind were not real tablecloths. How shocking, and yet how wonderful it was to discover that these real things, Sunday luncheons, Sunday walks, country houses, and tablecloths, were not entirely real, were indeed half phantoms, and the damnation which visited the disbeliever in them was only a sense of illegitimate freedom. What now takes the place of those things I wonder, those real standard things? Men perhaps, should you be a woman; the masculine point of view which governs our lives, which sets the standard, which established Whitaker's Table of Precedency, which has become, I suppose, since the war, half a phantom to many men and women, which soon, one may hope, will be laughed into the dustbin where the phantoms go, the mahogany sideboards and the Landseer prints, Gods and Devils, Hell and so forth, leaving us all with an intoxicating sense of illegitimate freedom – if freedom exists. . .

In certain lights that mark on the wall seems actually to project from the wall. Nor is it entirely circular. I cannot be sure, but it seems to cast a perceptible shadow, suggesting that if I ran my finger down that strip of the wall it would, at a certain point, mount and descend a small tumulus, a smooth tumulus like those barrows on the South Downs which are, they say, either tombs or camps. Of the two I should prefer them to be tombs, desiring melancholy like most English people, and finding it natural at the end of a walk to think of the bones stretched beneath the turf . . . There must be some book about it. Some antiquary must have dug up those bones and given them a name . . . What sort of a man is an antiquary, I wonder? Retired colonels for the most part, I dare say, leading parties of aged labourers to the top here, examining clods of earth and stone, and getting into correspondence with the neighbouring clergy, which, being opened at breakfast time, gives them a feeling of importance, and the comparison of arrowheads necessitates cross-country journeys to the county towns, an agreeable necessity both to them and to their elderly wives, who wish to make plum jam or to clean out the study, and have every reason for keeping that great question of the camp or the tomb in perpetual suspension, while the colonel himself feels agreeably philosophic in accumulating evidence on both sides of the question. It is true that he does finally incline to believe in the camp; and, being opposed, indites a pamphlet which he is about to read at the quarterly meeting of the local society when a stroke lays him low, and his last conscious thoughts are not of wife or child, but of the camp and that arrowhead there, which is now in the case at the local museum, together with the foot of a Chinese murderess, a handful of Elizabethan nails, a great many Tudor clay pipes, a piece of Roman pottery, and the wine-glass that Nelson drank out of – proving I really don't know what.

No, no, nothing is proved, nothing is known. And if I were to get up at this very moment and ascertain that the mark on the wall is really – what shall we say? – the head of a gigantic old nail, driven in two hundred years ago, which has now, owing to the patient attrition of many generations of housemaids, revealed its head above the coat of paint, and is taking its first view of modern life in the sight of a white-walled fire-lit room, what should I gain? – Knowledge? Matter for further speculation? I can think sitting still as well as standing up. And what is knowledge? What are our learned men save the descendants of witches and hermits who crouched in caves and in woods brewing herbs, interrogating shrew-mice and writing down the language of the stars? And the less we honour them as our superstitions dwindle and our respect for beauty and health of mind increases. . . Yes, one could imagine a very pleasant world. A quiet, spacious world, with the flowers so red and blue in the open fields. A world without professors or specialists or housekeepers with the profiles of policemen, a world which one could slice with one's thought as a fish slices the water with his fin, grazing the stems of the water-lilies, hanging suspended over nests of white sea eggs. . . How peaceful it is down here, rooted in the centre of the world and gazing up through the grey waters, with their sudden gleams of light, and their reflections – if it were not for Whitaker's *Almanack* – if it were not for the Table of Precedency!

I must jump up and see for myself what that mark on the wall really is – a nail, a rose-leaf, a crack in the wood?

Here is nature once more at her old game of self-preservation. This train of thought, she perceives, is threatening mere waste of energy, even some collision with reality, for who will ever be able to lift a finger against Whitaker's Table of Precedency? The Archbishop of Canterbury is followed by the Lord High Chancellor; the Lord High Chancellor is followed by the Archbishop of York. Everybody follows somebody, such is the philosophy of Whitaker; and the great thing is to know who follows whom. Whitaker knows, and let that, so Nature counsels, comfort you, instead of enraging you; and if you can't be comforted, if you must shatter this hour of peace, think of the mark on the wall.

I understand Nature's game – her prompting to take action as a way of ending any thought that threatens to excite or to pain. Hence, I suppose, comes our slight contempt for men of action – men, we assume, who don't think. Still, there's no harm in putting a full stop to one's disagreeable thoughts by looking at a mark on the wall.

Indeed, now that I have fixed my eyes upon it, I feel that I have grasped a plank in the sea; I feel a satisfying sense of reality which at once turns the two Archbishops and the Lord High Chancellor to the shadows of shades. Here is something definite, something real. Thus, waking from a midnight dream of horror, one hastily turns on the light and lies quiescent, worshipping the chest of drawers, worshipping solidity, worshipping reality, worshipping the impersonal world which is a proof of some existence other than ours. That is what one wants to be sure of . . . Wood is a pleasant thing to think about. It comes from a tree; and trees grow, and we don't know how they grow. For years and years they grow, without paying any attention to us, in meadows, in forests, and by the side of rivers – all things one likes to think about. The cows swish their tails beneath them on hot afternoons; they paint rivers so green that when a moorhen dives one expects to see its feathers all green when it comes up again. I like to think of the fish balanced against the stream

like flags blown out; and of water-beetles slowly raiding domes of mud upon
the bed of the river. I like to think of the tree itself: first the close dry
sensation of being wood; then the grinding of the storm; then the slow,
delicious ooze of sap. I like to think of it, too, on winter's nights standing in
the empty field with all leaves close-furled, nothing tender exposed to the
iron bullets of the moon, a naked mast upon an earth that goes tumbling,
tumbling, all night long. The song of birds must sound very loud and
strange in June; and how cold the feet of insects must feel upon it, as they
make laborious progresses up the creases of the bark, or sun themselves
upon the thin green awning of the leaves, and look straight in front of them
with diamond-cut red eyes. . . One by one the fibres snap beneath the
immense cold pressure of the earth, then the last storm comes and, falling,
the highest branches drive deep into the ground again. Even so, life isn't
done with; there are a million patient, watchful lives still for a tree, all over
the world, in bedrooms, in ships, on the pavement, lining rooms, where men
and women sit after tea, smoking cigarettes. It is full of peaceful thoughts,
happy thoughts, this tree. I should like to take each one separately – but
something is getting in the way. . . Where was I? What has it all been about?
A tree? A river? The Downs? Whitaker's *Almanack*? The fields of asphodel? I
can't remember a thing. Everything's moving, falling, slipping, vanishing . . .
There is a vast upheaval of matter. Someone is standing over me and saying –

'I'm going out to buy a newspaper.'

'Yes?'

'Though it's no good buying newspapers. . . Nothing ever happens. Curse
this war; God damn this war! . . . All the same, I don't see why we should
have a snail on our wall.'

Ah, the mark on the wall! It was a snail.

The Shooting Party

She got in and put her suitcase in the rack, and the brace of pheasants on top of it. Then she sat down in the corner. The train was rattling through the Midlands, and the fog, which came in when she opened the door, seemed to enlarge the carriage and set the four travellers apart. Obviously M. M. – those were the initials on the suitcase – had been staying the weekend with a shooting party. Obviously, for she was telling over the story now, lying back in her corner. She did not shut her eyes. But clearly she did not see the man opposite, nor the coloured photograph of York Minster. She must have heard, too, what they had been saying. For as she gazed, her lips moved; now and then she smiled. And she was handsome: a cabbage rose; a russet apple; tawny; but scarred on the jaw – the scar lengthened when she smiled. Since she was telling over the story she must have been a guest there, and yet, dressed as she was out of fashion as women dressed, years ago, in pictures, in sporting newspapers, she did not seem exactly a guest, nor yet a maid. Had she had a basket with her she would have been the woman who breeds fox terriers; the owner of the Siamese cat; someone connected with hounds and horses. But she had only a suitcase and the pheasants. Somehow, therefore, she must have wormed her way into the room that she was seeing through the stuffing of the carriage, and the man's bald head, and the picture of York Minster. And she must have listened to what they were saying, for now, like somebody imitating the noise that someone else makes, she made a little click at the back of her throat. 'Chk.' Then she smiled.

*   *   *

'Chk,' said Miss Antonia, pinching her glasses on her nose. The damp leaves fell across the long windows of the gallery; one or two stuck, fish shaped, and lay like inlaid brown wood upon the window panes. Then the trees in the Park shivered, and the leaves, flaunting down, seemed to make the shiver visible – the damp brown shiver.

'Chk.' Miss Antonia sniffed again, and pecked at the flimsy white stuff that she held in her hands, as a hen pecks nervously rapidly at a piece of white bread.

The wind sighed. The room was draughty. The doors did not fit, nor the windows. Now and then a ripple, like a reptile, ran under the carpet. On the carpet lay panels of green and yellow, where the sun rested, and then the sun moved and pointed a finger as if in mockery at a hole in the carpet and stopped. And then on it went, the sun's feeble but impartial finger, and lay upon the coat of arms over the fireplace – gently illumined – the shield, the pendant grapes, the mermaid, and the spears. Miss Antonia looked up as the light strengthened. Vast lands, so they said, the old people had owned – her forefathers – the Rashleighs. Over there. Up the Amazon. Freebooters. Voyagers. Sacks of emeralds. Nosing round the island. Taking captives. Maidens. There she was, all scales from the tail to the waist. Miss Antonia grinned. Down struck the finger of the sun and her eye went with it. Now it rested on a silver frame; on a photograph; on an egg-shaped baldish head, on a lip that stuck out under the moustache; and the name 'Edward' written with a flourish beneath.

'The King . . .' Miss Antonia muttered, turning the film of white upon her knee – 'had the Blue Room,' she added with a toss of her head as the light faded.

Out in the King's Ride the pheasants were being driven across the noses of the guns. Up they spurted from the underwood like heavy rockets, reddish-purple rockets, and as they rose the guns cracked in order, eagerly, sharply, as if a line of dogs had suddenly barked. Tufts of white smoke held together for a moment; then gently solved themselves, faded, and dispersed.

In the deep cut road beneath the hanger, a cart stood, laid already with soft warm bodies, with limp claws, and still lustrous eyes. The birds seemed alive still, but swooning under their rich damp feathers. They looked relaxed and comfortable, stirring slightly, as if they slept upon a warm bank of soft feathers on the floor of the cart.

Then the Squire, with the hang-dog stained face, in the shabby gaiters, cursed and raised his gun.

*   *   *

Miss Antonia stitched on. Now and then a tongue of flame reached round the grey log that stretched from one bar to another across the grate, ate it greedily, then died out, leaving a white bracelet where the bark had been eaten off. Miss Antonia looked up for a moment, stared wide eyed, instinctively, as a dog stares at a flame. Then the flame sank and she stitched again.

Then, silently, the enormously high door opened. Two lean men came in, and drew a table over the hole in the carpet. They went out; they came in. They laid a cloth upon the table. They went out; they came in. They brought a green-baize basket of knives and forks; and glasses; and sugar casters; and salt cellars; and bread; and a silver vase with three chrysanthemums in it. And the table was laid. Miss Antonia stitched on.

Again the door opened, pushed feebly this time. A little dog trotted in, a spaniel nosing nimbly; it paused. The door stood open. And then, leaning on her stick, heavily, old Miss Rashleigh entered. A white shawl, diamond fastened, clouded her baldness. She hobbled; crossed the room; hunched herself in the high-backed chair by the fireside. Miss Antonia went on stitching.

'Shooting,' she said at last.

Old Miss Rashleigh nodded. She gripped her stick. They sat waiting.

* * *

The shooters had moved now from the King's Ride to the Home Woods. They stood in the purple ploughed field outside. Now and then a twig snapped; leaves came whirling. But above the mist and the smoke was an island of blue – faint blue, pure blue – alone in the sky. And in the innocent air, as if straying alone like a cherub, a bell from a far hidden steeple frolicked, gambolled, then faded. Then again up shot the rockets, the reddish-purple pheasants. Up and up they went. Again the guns barked; the smoke balls formed; loosened, dispersed. And the busy little dogs ran nosing nimbly over the fields; and the warm damp bodies, still languid and soft, as if in a swoon, were bunched together by the men in gaiters and flung into the cart.

* * *

'There!' grunted Milly Masters, the housekeeper, throwing down her glasses. She was stitching, too, in the small dark room that overlooked the stable yard. The jersey, the rough woollen jersey, for her son, the boy who cleaned the church, was finished. 'The end 'o that!' she muttered. Then she heard the cart. Wheels ground on the cobbles. Up she got. With her hands to her hair, her chestnut-coloured hair, she stood in the yard, in the wind.

'Coming!' she laughed, and the scar on her cheek lengthened. She unbolted the door of the game room as Wing, the keeper, drove the cart over the cobbles. The birds were dead now, their claws gripped tight, though they gripped nothing. The leathery eyelids were creased greyly over their eyes. Mrs Masters the housekeeper, Wing the gamekeeper, took bunches of dead birds by the neck and flung them down on the slate floor of the game larder. The slate floor became smeared and spotted with blood. The pheasants looked smaller now, as if their bodies had shrunk together. Then Wing lifted the tail of the cart and drove in the pins which secured it. The sides of the cart were stuck about with little grey-blue feathers, and the floor was smeared and stained with blood. But it was empty.

'The last of the lot!' Milly Masters grinned as the cart drove off.

* * *

'Luncheon is served, ma'am,' said the butler. He pointed at the table; he directed the footman. The dish with the silver cover was placed precisely there where he pointed. They waited, the butler and the footman.

Miss Antonia laid her white film upon the basket; put away her silk; her thimble; stuck her needle through a piece of flannel; and hung her glasses on a hook upon her breast. Then she rose.

'Luncheon!' she barked in old Miss Rashleigh's ear. One second later old

Miss Rashleigh stretched her leg out; gripped her stick; and rose too. Both old women advanced slowly to the table; and were tucked in by the butler and the footman, one at this end, one at that. Off came the silver cover. And there was the pheasant, featherless, gleaming; the thighs tightly pressed to its sides; and little mounds of breadcrumbs were heaped at either end.

Miss Antonia drew the carving knife across the pheasant's breast firmly. She cut two slices and laid them on a plate. Deftly the footman whipped it from her, and old Miss Rashleigh raised her knife. Shots rang out in the wood under the window.

'Coming?' said old Miss Rashleigh, suspending her fork.

The branches flung and flaunted on the trees in the Park.

She took a mouthful of pheasant. Falling leaves flicked the window pane; one or two stuck to the glass.

'The Home Woods, now,' said Miss Antonia. 'Hugh's lost that. Shooting.' She drew her knife down the other side of the breast. She added potatoes and gravy, brussels sprouts and bread sauce methodically in a circle round the slices on her plate. The butler and the footman stood watching, like servers at a feast. The old ladies ate quietly; silently; nor did they hurry themselves; methodically they cleaned the bird. Bones only were left on their plates. Then the butler drew the decanter towards Miss Antonia, and paused for a moment with his head bent.

'Give it here, Griffiths,' said Miss Antonia, and took the carcase in her fingers and tossed it to the spaniel beneath the table. The butler and the footman bowed and went out.

'Coming closer,' said Miss Rashleigh, listening. The wind was rising. A brown shudder shook the air; leaves flew too fast to stick. The glass rattled in the windows.

'Birds wild,' Miss Antonia nodded, watching the helter-skelter.

Old Miss Rashleigh filled her glass. As they sipped their eyes became lustrous like half precious stones held to the light. Slate blue were Miss Rashleigh's; Miss Antonia's red, like port. And their laces and their flounces seemed to quiver, as if their bodies were warm and languid underneath their feathers as they drank.

'It was a day like this, d'you remember?' said old Miss Rashleigh, fingering her glass. 'They brought him home – a bullet through his heart. A bramble, so they said. Tripped. Caught his foot . . .' She chuckled as she sipped her wine.

'And John . . .' said Miss Antonia. 'The mare, they said, put her foot in a hole. Died in the field. The hunt rode over him. He came home, too, on a shutter . . .'

They sipped again.

'Remember Lily?' said old Miss Rashleigh. 'A bad 'un.' She shook her head. 'Riding with a scarlet tassel on her cane . . .'

'Rotten at the heart!' cried Miss Antonia.

'Remember the colonel's letter. Your son rode as if he had twenty devils in him – charged at the head of his men. Then one white devil – ah hah!'

She sipped again.

'The men of our house,' began Miss Rashleigh. She raised her glass. She held it high, as if she toasted the mermaid carved in plaster on the fireplace. She paused. The guns were barking. Something cracked in the woodwork. Or was it a rat running behind the plaster?

'Always women . . .' Miss Antonia nodded. 'The men of our house. Pink and white Lucy at the Mill – d'you remember?'

'Ellen's daughter at the Goat and Sickle,' Miss Rashleigh added.

'And the girl at the tailor's,' Miss Antonia murmured, 'where Hugh bought his riding breeches, the little dark shop on the right . . .'

' . . . that used to be flooded every winter. It's his boy,' Miss Antonia chuckled, leaning towards her sister, 'that cleans the church.'

There was a crash. A slate had fallen down the chimney. The great log had snapped in two. Flakes of plaster fell from the shield above the fireplace.

'Falling,' old Miss Rashleigh chuckled. 'Falling.'

'And who,' said Miss Antonia, looking at the flakes on the carpet, 'who's to pay?'

Crowing like old babies, indifferent, reckless, they laughed; crossed to the fireplace, and sipped the sherry by the wood ashes and the plaster, until each glass held only one drop of wine, reddish purple, at the bottom. And this the old women did not wish to part with, so it seemed; for they fingered their glasses, as they sat side by side by the ashes; but they never raised them to their lips.

'Milly Masters in the still room,' began old Miss Rashleigh. 'She's our brother's . . .'

A shot barked beneath the window. It cut the string that held the rain. Down it poured, down, down, down, in straight rods whipping the windows. Light faded from the carpet. Light faded in their eyes, too, as they sat by the white ashes listening. Their eyes became like pebbles, taken from water; grey stones dulled and dried. And their hands gripped – their hands like the claws of dead birds – gripping nothing. And they shrivelled as if the bodies inside the clothes had shrunk.

Then Miss Antonia raised her glass to the mermaid. It was the last drop; she drank it off. 'Coming!' she croaked, and slapped the glass down. A door banged below. Then another. Then another. Feet could be heard trampling, yet shuffling, along the corridor towards the gallery.

'Closer! Closer!' grinned Miss Rashleigh, baring her three yellow teeth.

The immensely high door burst open. In rushed three great hounds and stood panting. Then there entered, slouching, the Squire himself in shabby gaiters. The dogs pressed round him, tossing their heads, snuffling at his pockets. Then they bounded forward. They smelt the meat. The floor of the gallery waved like a wind-lashed forest with the tails and backs of the great questing hounds. They snuffed the table. They pawed the cloth. Then, with a wild neighing whimper, they flung themselves upon the little yellow spaniel who was gnawing the carcass under the table.

'Curse you, curse you!' howled the Squire. But his voice was weak, as if he shouted against a wind. 'Curse you, curse you!' he shouted, now cursing his sisters.

Miss Antonia and Miss Rashleigh rose to their feet. The great dogs had seized the spaniel. They worried him, they mauled him with their great yellow teeth. The Squire swung a leather knotted tawse this way and that way, cursing the dogs, cursing his sisters, in the voice that sounded so loud yet so weak. With one lash he curled to the ground the vase of chrysanthemums. Another caught old Miss Rashleigh on the cheek. The old woman staggered backwards. She fell against the mantelpiece. Her stick, striking wildly, struck the shield above the fireplace. She fell with a thud upon the ashes. The shield of the Rashleighs crashed from the wall. Under the mermaid, under the spears, she lay buried.

The wind lashed the panes of glass; shots volleyed in the Park and a tree fell. And then King Edward, in the silver frame, slid, toppled, and fell too.

*   *   *

The grey mist had thickened in the carriage. It hung down like a veil; it seemed to put the four travellers in the corners at a great distance from each other, though in fact they were as close as a third-class railway carriage could bring them. The effect was strange. The handsome, if elderly, the well-dressed, if rather shabby woman, who had got into the train at some station in the Midlands, seemed to have lost her shape. Her body had become all mist. Only her eyes gleamed, changed, lived all by themselves, it seemed; eyes without a body; eyes seeing something invisible. In the misty air they shone out, they moved, so that in the sepulchral atmosphere – the windows were blurred, the lamps haloed with fog – they were like lights dancing, will o' the wisps that move, people say, over the graves of unquiet sleepers in churchyards. An absurd idea? Mere fancy! Yet after all, since there is nothing that does not leave some residue, and memory is a light that dances in the mind when the reality is buried, why should not the eyes there, gleaming, moving, be the ghost of a family, of an age, of a civilisation dancing over the grave?

The train slowed down. Lamps stood up. They were felled. Up they stood again as the train slid into the station. The lights blazed. And the eyes in the corner? They were shut. Perhaps the light was too strong. And of course in the full blaze of the station lamps it was plain – she was quite an ordinary, rather elderly, woman, travelling to London on some ordinary piece of business – something connected with a cat, or a horse, or a dog. She reached for her suitcase, rose, and took the pheasants from the rack. But did she, all the same, as she opened the carriage door and stepped out, murmur 'Chk, Chk,' as she passed?

Together and Apart

Mrs Dalloway introduced them, saying you will like him. The conversation began some minutes before anything was said, for both Mr Serle and Miss Arming looked at the sky and in both of their minds the sky went on pouring its meaning though very differently, until the presence of Mr Serle by her side became so distinct to Miss Anning that she could not see the sky, simply, itself, any more, but the sky shored up by the tall body, dark eyes, grey hair, clasped hands, the stern melancholy (but she had been told 'falsely melancholy') face of Roderick Serle, and, knowing how foolish it was, she yet felt impelled to say: 'What a beautiful night!'

Foolish! Idiotically foolish! But if one mayn't be foolish at the age of forty in the presence of the sky, which makes the wisest imbecile – mere wisps of straw – she and Mr Serle atoms, motes, standing there at Mrs Dalloway's window, and their lives, seen by moonlight, as long as an insect's and no more important.

'Well!' said Miss Anning, patting the sofa cushion emphatically. And down he sat beside her. Was he 'falsely melancholy', as they said? Prompted by the sky, which seemed to make it all a little futile – what they said, what they did – she said something perfectly commonplace again: 'There was a Miss Serle who lived at Canterbury when I was a girl there.'

With the sky in his mind, all the tombs of his ancestors immediately appeared to Mr Serle in a blue romantic light, and his eyes expanding and darkening, he said: 'Yes.

'We are originally a Norman family, who came over with the Conqueror. That is a Richard Serle buried in the Cathedral. He was a knight of the garter.'

Miss Arming felt that she had struck accidentally the true man, upon whom the false man was built. Under the influence of the moon (the moon which symbolised man to her, she could see it through a chink of the curtain, and she took dips of the moon) she was capable of saying almost anything and she settled in to disinter the true man who was buried under the false, saying to herself: 'On, Stanley, on' – which was a watchword of hers, a secret spur, or scourge such as middle-aged people often make to flagellate some inveterate vice, hers being a deplorable timidity, or rather indolence, for it was not so much that she lacked courage, but lacked energy, especially in talking to men, who frightened her rather, and so often her talks petered out into dull commonplaces, and she had very few men friends – very few intimate friends at all, she thought, but after all, did she want them? No. She had Sarah, Arthur, the cottage, the chow and, of course, *that*, she thought, dipping herself, sousing herself, even as she sat on the sofa beside Mr Serle, in *that*, in the sense she had coming home of something collected there, a cluster of miracles, which she could not believe other people had (since it was she only who had Arthur, Sarah, the cottage, and the chow), but she soused herself again in the deep satisfactory possession, feeling that what with this and the moon (music that was, the moon), she could afford to leave this man and that pride of his in the Serles buried. No! That was the danger – she must not sink into torpidity – not at her age. 'On, Stanley, on,' she said to herself, and asked him: 'Do you know Canterbury yourself?'

Did he know Canterbury! Mr Serle smiled, thinking how absurd a question it was, how little she knew – this nice quiet woman who played some instrument and seemed intelligent and had good eyes, and was wearing a very nice old necklace – knew what it meant. To be asked if he knew Canterbury. When the best years of his life, all his memories, things he had never been able to tell anybody, but had tried to write – ah, had tried to write (and he sighed) – all had centred in Canterbury; it made him laugh.

His sigh and then his laugh, his melancholy and his humour, made people like him, and he knew it, and yet being liked had not made up for the disappointment, and if he sponged on the liking people had for him (paying long calls on sympathetic ladies, long, long calls), it was half bitterly, for he had never done a tenth part of what he could have done, and had dreamed of doing, as a boy in Canterbury. With a stranger he felt a renewal of hope because they could not say that he had not done what he had promised, and yielding to his charm would give him a fresh start – at fifty! She had touched the spring. Fields and flowers and grey buildings dripped down into his mind, formed silver drops on the gaunt, dark walls of his mind and dripped down. With such an image his poems often began. He felt the desire to make images now, sitting by this quiet woman.

'Yes, I know Canterbury,' he said reminiscently, sentimentally, inviting, Miss Anning felt, discreet questions, and that was what made him interesting to so many people, and it was this extraordinary facility and responsiveness to talk on his part that had been his undoing, so he thought often, taking his studs out and putting his keys and small change on the dressing-table after one of these parties (and he went out sometimes almost every night in the season), and, going down to breakfast, becoming quite different, grumpy, unpleasant at breakfast to his wife, who was an invalid, and never went out, but had old friends to see her sometimes, women friends for the most part, interested in Indian philosophy and different cures and different doctors, which Roderick Serle snubbed off by some caustic remark too clever for her to meet, except by gentle expostulations and a tear or two – he had failed, he often thought, because he could not cut himself off utterly from society and the company of women, which was so necessary to him, and write. He had involved himself too deep in life – and here he would cross his knees (all his movements were a little unconventional and distinguished) and not blame himself, but put the blame off upon the richness of his nature, which he compared favourably with Wordsworth's, for example, and, since he had given so much to people, he felt, resting his head on his hands, they in their turn should help him, and this was the prelude, tremulous, fascinating, exciting, to talk; and images bubbled up in his mind.

'She's like a fruit tree – like a flowering cherry tree,' he said, looking at a youngish woman with fine white hair. It was a nice sort of image, Ruth Anning thought – rather nice, yet she did not feel sure that she liked this distinguished, melancholy man with his gestures; and it's odd, she thought, how one's feelings are influenced. She did not like *him*, though she rather liked that comparison of his of a woman to a cherry tree. Fibres of her were floated capriciously this way and that, like the tentacles of a sea anemone, now thrilled, now snubbed, and her brain, miles away, cool and distant, up in the air, received messages which it would sum up in time so that when people talked about Roderick Serle (and he was a bit of a figure) she would say unhesitatingly: 'I like him,' or 'I don't like him,' and her opinion would be made up for ever. An odd thought; a solemn thought; throwing a green light on what human fellowship consisted of.

'It's odd that you should know Canterbury,' said Mr Serle. 'It's always a shock,' he went on (the white-haired lady having passed), 'when one meets someone' (they had never met before), 'by chance, as it were, who touches the fringe of what has meant a great deal to oneself, touches accidentally, for I suppose Canterbury was nothing but a nice old town to you. So you stayed there one summer with an aunt?' (That was all Ruth Anning was going to tell him about her visit to Canterbury.) 'And you saw the sights and went away and never thought of it again.'

Let him think so; not liking him, she wanted him to run away with an absurd idea of her. For really, her three months in Canterbury had been amazing. She remembered to the last detail, though it was merely a chance visit, going to see Miss Charlotte Serle, an acquaintance of her aunt's. Even now she could repeat Miss Serle's very words about the thunder. 'Whenever I wake, or hear thunder in the night, I think "Someone has been killed." ' And she could see the hard, hairy, diamond-patterned carpet, and the twinkling, suffused, brown eyes of the elderly lady, holding the teacup out unfilled, while she said that about the thunder. And always she saw Canterbury, all thundercloud and livid apple blossom, and the long grey backs of the buildings.

The thunder roused her from her plethoric middle-aged swoon of indifference; 'On, Stanley, on,' she said to herself; that is, this man shall not glide away from me, like everybody else, on this false assumption; I will tell him the truth.

'I loved Canterbury,' she said.

He kindled instantly. It was his gift, his fault, his destiny.

'Loved it,' he repeated. 'I can see that you did.'

Her tentacles sent back the message that Roderick Serle was nice.

Their eyes met; collided rather, for each felt that behind the eyes the secluded being, who sits in darkness while his shallow agile companion does all the tumbling and beckoning, and keeps the show going, suddenly stood erect; flung off his cloak; confronted the other. It was alarming; it was terrific. They were elderly and burnished into a glowing smoothness, so that Roderick Serle would go perhaps to a dozen parties in a season and feel nothing out of the common, or only sentimental regrets, and the desire for pretty images – like this of the flowering cherry tree – and all the time there stagnated in him unstirred a sort of superiority to his company, a sense of untapped resources, which sent him back home dissatisfied with life, with himself, yawning, empty, capricious. But now, quite suddenly, like a white bolt in a mist (but this image forged itself with the inevitability of lightning and loomed up), there it had happened; the old ecstasy of life; its invincible assault; for it was unpleasant, at the same time that it rejoiced and rejuvenated and filled the veins and nerves with threads of ice and fire; it was terrifying. 'Canterbury twenty years ago,' said Miss Anning, as one lays a shade over an intense light, or covers some burning peach with a green leaf, for it is too strong, too ripe, too full.

Sometimes she wished she had married. Sometimes the cool peace of middle life, with its automatic devices for shielding mind and body from bruises, seemed to her, compared with the thunder and the livid apple blossom of Canterbury, base. She could imagine something different, more like lightning, more intense. She could imagine some physical sensation. She could imagine –

And, strangely enough, for she had never seen him before, her senses, those tentacles which were thrilled and snubbed, now sent no more messages, now lay quiescent, as if she and Mr Serle knew each other so perfectly, were, in fact, so closely united that they had only to float side by side down this stream.

Of all things, nothing is so strange as human intercourse, she thought, because of its changes, its extraordinary irrationality, her dislike being now nothing short of the most intense and rapturous love, but directly the word 'love' occurred to her, she rejected it, thinking again how obscure the mind was, with its very few words for all these astonishing perceptions, these alternations of pain and pleasure. For how did one name this? That is what she felt now, the withdrawal of human affection, Serle's disappearance, and the instant need they were both under to cover up what was so desolating and degrading to human nature that everyone tried to bury it decently from sight – this withdrawal, this violation of trust, and, seeking some decent acknowledged and accepted burial form, she said: 'Of course, whatever they may do, they can't spoil Canterbury.'

He smiled; he accepted it; he crossed his knees the other way about. She did her part; he his. So things came to an end. And over them both came instantly that paralysing blankness of feeling, when nothing bursts from the mind, when its walls appear like slate; when vacancy almost hurts, and the eyes petrified and fixed see the same spot – a pattern, a coal scuttle – with an exactness which is terrifying, since no emotion, no idea, no impression of any kind comes to change it, to modify it, to embellish it, since the fountains of feeling seem sealed and as the mind turns rigid, so does the body; stark, statuesque, so that neither Mr Serle nor Miss Anning could move or speak; and they felt as if an enchanter had freed them, and spring flushed every vein with streams of life, when Mira Cartwright, tapping Mr Serle archly on the shoulder, said: 'I saw you at the Meistersinger, and you cut me. Villain,' said Miss Cartwright, 'you don't deserve that I should ever speak to you again.' And they could separate.

ISRAEL ZANGWILL

Israel Zangwill was born in London in 1864. His family, Russian Jews, lived in the Jewish quarter of Whitechapel. After receiving both an English and a Jewish education, he studied at the University of London. Having left teaching for a career in journalism, he generated much popular interest as a writer and a literary editor. His best-known novel, *Children of the Ghetto*, was published in 1892. The work had considerable impact in the non-Jewish world, giving the English reader a jarring glimpse of the poverty-stricken life of London's Jewish community. Zangwill's productivity ranged over many literary genres. He wrote a number of unsuccessful plays. In 1908 he published a volume of poetry, *Blind Children*, followed by another, *Italian Phantasies*, in 1910. He translated into English a quantity of religious poetry which he published in *Selected Religious Poems* (1903). In the early 1890s Zangwill joined the Lovers of Zion movement in England and later was involved with Theodor Herzl in founding the World Zionist Organisation. He took part in the first seven Zionist congresses and became renowned as an impassioned orator. When the prospects of Jewish settlement in Palestine became more clearly defined at the end of World War 1, Zangwill returned to the Zionist effort and took an active part in soliciting the Balfour Declaration. He died in 1926.

The Woman-Beater

I

She came 'to meet John Lefolle', but John Lefolle did not know he was to meet Winifred Glamorys. He did not even know he was himself the meeting-point of all the brilliant and beautiful persons assembled in the publisher's Saturday Salon, for although a youthful minor poet, he was modest and lovable. Perhaps his Oxford tutorship was sobering. At any rate his head remained unturned by his precocious fame, and to meet these other young men and women – his revered seniors on the slopes of Parnassus – gave him more pleasure than the receipt of 'royalties'. Not that his publisher afforded him much opportunity of contrasting the two pleasures. The profits of the Muse went to provide this room of old furniture and roses, this beautiful garden a-twinkle with Japanese lanterns, like gorgeous fire-flowers blossoming under the white crescent moon of early June.

Winifred Glamorys was not literary herself. She was better than a poetess, she was a poem. The publisher always threw in a few realities, and some beautiful brainless creature would generally be found the nucleus of a crowd, while Clio in spectacles languished in a corner. Winifred Glamorys, however, was reputed to have a tongue that matched her eye; paralleling with whimsies and epigrams its freakish fires and witcheries, and, assuredly, flitting in her white gown through the dark balmy garden, she seemed the very spirit of moonlight, the subtle incarnation of night and roses.

When John Lefolle met her, Cecilia was with her, and the first conversation was triangular. Cecilia fired most of the shots; she was a bouncing, rattling beauty, chockful of confidence and high spirits, except when asked to do the one thing she could do – sing! Then she became – quite genuinely – a nervous, hesitant, pale little thing. However, the suppliant hostess bore her off, and presently her rich contralto notes passed through the garden, adding to its passion and mystery, and through the open French windows, John could see her standing against the wall near the piano, her head thrown back, her eyes half-closed, her creamy throat swelling in the very abandonment of artistic ecstasy.

'What a charming creature!' he exclaimed involuntarily.

'That is what everybody thinks, except her husband,' Winifred laughed.

'Is he blind then?' asked John with his cloistral *naïveté*.

'Blind? No, love is blind. Marriage is never blind.'

The bitterness in her tone pierced John. He felt vaguely the passing of some icy current from unknown seas of experience. Cecilia's voice soared out enchantingly.

'Then, marriage must be deaf,' he said, 'or such music as that would charm it.'

She smiled sadly. Her smile was the tricksy play of moonlight among clouds of faerie.

'You have never been married,' she said simply.

'Do you mean that you, too, are neglected?' something impelled him to exclaim.

'Worse,' she murmured.

'It is incredible!' he cried. 'You!'

'Hush! My husband will hear you.'

Her warning whisper brought him into a delicious conspiracy with her. 'Which is your husband?' he whispered back.

'There! Near the casement, standing gazing open-mouthed at Cecilia. He always opens his mouth when she sings. It is like two toys moved by the same wire.'

He looked at the tall, stalwart, ruddy-haired Anglo-Saxon. 'Do you mean to say he – ?'

'I mean to say nothing.'

'But you said – '

'I said "worse".'

'Why, what can be worse?'

She put her hand over her face. 'I am ashamed to tell you.' How adorable was that half-divined blush!

'But you must tell me everything.' He scarcely knew how he had leapt into this role of confessor. He only felt they were 'moved by the same wire'.

Her head drooped on her breast. 'He – beats – me.'

'What!' John forgot to whisper. It was the greatest shock his recluse life had known, compact as it was of horror at the revelation, shamed confusion at her candour, and delicious pleasure in her confidence.

This fragile, exquisite creature under the rod of a brutal bully!

Once he had gone to a wedding reception, and among the serious presents some grinning Philistine drew his attention to an uncouth club – 'a wife-beater' he called it. The flippancy had jarred upon John terribly: this intrusive reminder of the customs of the slums. It grated like Billingsgate in a boudoir. Now that savage weapon recurred to him – for a lurid instant he saw Winifred's husband wielding it. Oh, abomination of his sex! And did he stand there, in his immaculate evening dress, posing as an English gentleman? Even so might some gentleman burglar bear through a salon his imperturbable swallow-tail.

Beat a woman! Beat that essence of charm and purity, God's best gift to man, redeeming him from his own grossness! Could such things be? John Lefolle would as soon have credited the French legend that English wives are sold in Smithfield. No! it could not be real that this flower-like figure was thrashed.

'Do you mean to say – ?' he cried. The rapidity of her confidence alone made him feel it all of a dreamlike unreality.

'Hush! Cecilia's singing!' she admonished him with an unexpected smile, as her fingers fell from her face.

'Oh, you have been making fun of me.' He was vastly relieved. 'He beats you – at chess – or at lawn-tennis?'

'Does one wear a high-necked dress to conceal the traces of chess, or lawn-tennis?'

He had not noticed her dress before, save for its spiritual whiteness. Susceptible though he was to beautiful shoulders, Winifred's enchanting face had been sufficiently distracting. Now the thought of physical bruises gave him a second spasm of righteous horror. That delicate rose-leaf flesh abraded and lacerated!

'The ruffian! Does he use a stick or a fist?'

'Both! But as a rule he just takes me by the arms and shakes me like a terrier. I'm all black and blue now.'

'Poor butterfly!' he murmured poetically.

'Why did I tell you?' she murmured back with subtler poetry.

The poet thrilled in every vein. 'Love at first sight,' of which he had often read and often written, was then a reality! It could be as mutual, too, as Romeo's and Juliet's. But how awkward that Juliet should be married and her husband a Bill Sykes in broadcloth!

2

Mrs Glamorys herself gave 'At Homes', every Sunday afternoon, and so, on the morrow, after a sleepless night mitigated by perpended sonnets, the love-sick young tutor presented himself by invitation at the beautiful old house in Hampstead. He was enchanted to find his heart's mistress set in an eighteenth-century frame of small-paned windows and of high oak-panelling, and at once began to image her dancing minuets and playing on virginals. Her husband was absent, but a broad band of velvet round Winifred's neck was a painful reminder of his possibilities. Winifred, however, said it was only a touch of sore throat caught in the garden. Her eyes added that there was nothing in the pathological dictionary which she would not willingly have caught for the sake of those divine, if draughty moments, but that, alas! it was more than a mere bodily ailment she had caught there.

There were a great many visitors in the two delightfully quaint rooms, among whom he wandered disconsolate and admired, jealous of her scattered smiles, but presently he found himself seated by her side on a 'cosy corner' near the open folding-doors, with all the other guests huddled round a violinist in the inner room. How Winifred had managed it he did not know, but she sat plausibly in the outer room, awaiting newcomers, and this particular niche was invisible, save to a determined eye. He took her unresisting hand – that dear, warm hand, with its begemmed artistic fingers – and held it in uneasy beatitude. How wonderful! She – the beautiful and adored hostess, of whose sweetness and charm he heard even her own guests murmur to one another – it was her actual flesh-and-blood hand that lay in his – thrillingly tangible. Oh, adventure beyond all merit, beyond all hoping!

But every now and then, the outer door facing them would open on some new-comer, and John had hastily to release her soft magnetic fingers and sit demure, and jealously overhear her effusive welcome to those innocent intruders, nor did his brow clear till she had shepherded them within the inner fold. Fortunately, the refreshments were in this section, so that once therein, few of the sheep strayed back, and the jiggling wail of the violin was succeeded by a shrill babble of tongues and the clatter of cups and spoons. 'Get me an ice, please – strawberry,' she ordered John during one of these forced intervals in manual flirtation; and when he had steered laboriously to and fro, he found a young actor beside her *their* hands dispart. He stood over them with a sickly smile, while Winifred ate her ice. When he returned from depositing the empty saucer, the player-fellow was gone, and in remorse for his mad suspicion he stooped and reverently lifted her fragrant fingertips to his lips. The door behind his back opened abruptly.

'Goodbye,' she said, rising in a flash. The words had the calm conventional cadence, and instantly extorted from him – amid all his dazedness – the corresponding 'Goodbye.' When he turned and saw it was Mr Glamorys who had come in, his heart leapt wildly at the nearness of his escape. As he passed this masked ruffian, he nodded perfunctorily and received a cordial smile. Yes, he was handsome and fascinating enough externally, this blonde savage.

'A man may smile and smile and be a villain,' John thought. 'I wonder how he'd feel, if he knew I knew he beats women.'

Already John had generalised the charge. 'I hope Cecilia will keep him at arm's length,' he had said to Winifred, 'if only that she may not smart for it someday.'

He lingered purposely in the hall to get an impression of the brute, who had begun talking loudly to a friend with irritating bursts of laughter, speciously frank-ringing. Golf, fishing, comic operas – ah, the Boeotian! These were the men who monopolised the ethereal divinities.

But this brusque separation from his particular divinity was disconcerting. How to see her again? He must go up to Oxford in the morning, he wrote her that night, but if she could possibly let him call during the week he would manage to run down again.

'Oh, my dear, dreaming poet,' she wrote to Oxford, 'how could you possibly send me a letter to be laid on the breakfast-table beside *The Times*! With a poem in it, too. Fortunately my husband was in a hurry to get down to the City, and he neglected to read my correspondence.' (The unchivalrous blackguard, John commented. But what can be expected of a woman-beater?) 'Never, never write to me again at the house. A letter, care of Mrs Best, 8A Foley Street, WC, will always find me. She is my maid's mother. And you must not come here either, my dear handsome head-in-the-clouds, except to my At Homes, and then only at judicious intervals. I shall be walking round the pond in Kensington Gardens at four next Wednesday, unless Mrs Best brings me a letter to the contrary. And now thank you for your delicious poem; I do not recognise my humble self in the dainty lines, but I shall always be proud to think I inspired them. Will it be in the new volume? I have never been in print before; it will be a novel sensation. I cannot pay you song for song, only feeling for feeling. Oh, John Lefolle, why did we not meet when I had still my girlish dreams? Now, I have grown to distrust all men – to fear the brute beneath the cavalier . . . '

Mrs Best did bring her a letter, but it was not to cancel the appointment, only to say he was not surprised at her horror of the male sex, but that she must beware of false generalisations. Life was still a wonderful and beautiful thing – *vide* poem enclosed. He was counting the minutes till Wednesday afternoon. It was surely a popular mistake that only sixty went to the hour.

This chronometrical reflection recurred to him even more poignantly in the hour that he circumambulated the pond in Kensington Gardens. Had she forgotten – had her husband locked her up? What could have happened? It seemed six hundred minutes, ere, at ten past five she came tripping daintily towards him. His brain had been reduced to insanely devising problems for his pupils – if a man walks two strides of one and a half feet a second round a lake fifty acres in area, in how many turns will he overtake a lady who walks half as fast and isn't there? – but the moment her pink parasol loomed on the horizon, all his long misery vanished in an ineffable peace and uplifting. He hurried, bare-headed, to clasp her little gloved hand. He had forgotten her unpunctuality, nor did she remind him of it.

'How sweet of you to come all that way,' was all she said, and it was a sufficient reward for the hours in the train and the six hundred minutes among the nursemaids and perambulators. The elms were in their glory, the birds were singing briskly, the water sparkled, the sunlit sward stretched fresh and green – it was the loveliest, coolest moment of the afternoon. John instinctively turned down a leafy avenue. Nature and Love! What more could poet ask?

'No, we can't have tea by the Kiosk,' Mrs Glamorys protested. 'Of course

I love anything that savours of Paris, but it's become so fashionable. There will be heaps of people who know me. I suppose you've forgotten it's the height of the season. I know a quiet little place in the High Street.' She led him, unresisting but bemused, towards the gate, and into a confectioner's. Conversation languished on the way.

'Tea,' he was about to instruct the pretty attendant.

'Strawberry ices,' Mrs Glamorys remarked gently. 'And some of those nice French cakes.'

The ice restored his spirits, it was really delicious, and he had got so hot and tired, pacing round the pond. Decidedly Winifred was a practical person and he was a dreamer. The pastry he dared not touch – being a genius – but he was charmed at the gaiety with which Winifred crammed cake after cake into her rosebud of a mouth. What an enchanting creature! How bravely she covered up her life's tragedy!

The thought made him glance at her velvet band – it was broader than ever.

'He has beaten you again!' he murmured furiously. Her joyous eyes saddened, she hung her head, and her fingers crumbled the cake. 'What is his pretext?' he asked, his blood burning.

'Jealousy,' she whispered.

His blood lost its glow, ran cold. He felt the bully's blows on his own skin, his romance turning suddenly sordid. But he recovered his courage. He, too, had muscles. 'But I thought he just missed seeing me kiss your hand.'

She opened her eyes wide. 'It wasn't you, you darling old dreamer.'

He was relieved and disturbed in one.

'Somebody else?' he murmured. Somehow the vision of the player-fellow came up.

She nodded. 'Isn't it lucky he has himself drawn a red-herring across the track? I didn't mind his blows – you were safe!' Then, with one of her adorable transitions, 'I am dreaming of another ice,' she cried with roguish wistfulness.

'I was afraid to confess my own greediness,' he said, laughing. He beckoned the waitress. 'Two more.'

'We haven't got any more strawberries,' was her unexpected reply. 'There's been such a run on them today.'

Winifred's face grew overcast. 'Oh, nonsense!' she pouted. To John the moment seemed tragic.

'Won't you have another kind?' he queried. He himself liked any kind, but he could scarcely eat a second ice without her.

Winifred meditated. 'Coffee?' she queried.

The waitress went away and returned with a face as gloomy as Winifred's. 'It's been such a hot day,' she said deprecatingly. 'There is only one ice in the place and that's Neapolitan.'

'Well, bring two Neapolitans,' John ventured.

'I mean there is only one Neapolitan ice left.'

'Well, bring that. I don't really want one.'

He watched Mrs Glamorys daintily devouring the solitary ice, and felt a certain pathos about the parti-coloured oblong, a something of the haunting sadness of 'The Last Rose of Summer'. It would make a graceful, serio-comic triolet, he was thinking. But at the last spoonful, his beautiful companion dislocated his rhymes by her sudden upspringing.

'Goodness gracious,' she cried, 'how late it is!'

'Oh, you're not leaving me yet!' he said. A world of things sprang to his brain, things that he was going to say – to arrange. They had said nothing – not a word of their love even; nothing but cakes and ices.

'Poet!' she laughed. 'Have you forgotten I live at Hampstead?' She picked up her parasol. 'Put me into a hansom, or my husband will be raving at his lonely dinner-table.'

He was so dazed as to be surprised when the waitress blocked his departure with a bill. When Winifred was spirited away, he remembered she might, without much risk, have given him a lift to Paddington. He hailed another hansom and caught the next train to Oxford. But he was too late for his own dinner in Hall.

3

He was kept very busy for the next few days, and could only exchange a passionate letter or two with her. For some time the examination fever had been raging, and in every college poor patients sat with wet towels round their heads. Some, who had neglected their tutor all the term, now strove to absorb his omniscience in a sitting.

On the Monday, John Lefolle was good-naturedly giving a special audience to a muscular dunce, trying to explain to him the political effects of the Crusades, when there was a knock at the sitting-room door, and the scout ushered in Mrs Glamorys. She was bewitchingly dressed in white, and stood in the open doorway, smiling – an embodiment of the summer he was neglecting. He rose, but his tongue was paralysed. The dunce became suddenly important – a symbol of the decorum he had been outraging. His soul, torn so abruptly from history to romance, could not get up the right emotion. Why this imprudence of Winifred's? She had been so careful heretofore.

'What a lot of boots there are on your staircase!' she said gaily.

He laughed. The spell was broken. 'Yes, the heap to be cleaned is rather obtrusive,' he said, 'but I suppose it is a sort of tradition.'

'I think I've got hold of the thing pretty well now, sir.' The dunce rose and smiled, and his tutor realised how little the dunce had to learn in some things. He felt quite grateful to him.

'Oh, well, you'll come and see me again after lunch, won't you, if one or two points occur to you for elucidation,' he said, feeling vaguely a liar, and generally guilty. But when, on the departure of the dunce, Winifred held out her arms, everything fell from him but the sense of the exquisite moment. Their lips met for the first time, but only for an instant. He had scarcely time to realise that this wonderful thing had happened before the mobile creature had darted to his bookshelves and was examining a Thucydides upside down.

'How clever to know Greek!' she exclaimed. 'And do you really talk it with the other dons?'

'No, we never talk shop,' he laughed. 'But, Winifred, what made you come here?'

'I had never seen Oxford. Isn't it beautiful?'

'There's nothing beautiful *here*,' he said, looking round his sober study.

'No,' she admitted; 'there's nothing I care for here,' and had left another celestial kiss on his lips before he knew it. 'And now you must take me to lunch and on the river.'

He stammered, 'I have – work.'

She pouted. 'But I can't stay beyond tomorrow morning, and I want so much to see all your celebrated oarsmen practising.'

'You are not staying over the night?' he gasped.

'Yes, I am,' and she threw him a dazzling glance.

His heart went pit-a-pat. 'Where?' he murmured.

'Oh, some poky little hotel near the station. The swell hotels are full.'

He was glad to hear she was not conspicuously quartered.

'So many people have come down already for Commem,' he said. 'I suppose they are anxious to see the generals get their degrees. But hadn't we better go somewhere and lunch?'

They went down the stone staircase, past the battalion of boots, and across the quad. He felt that all the windows were alive with eyes, but she insisted on standing still and admiring their ivied picturesqueness. After lunch he shamefacedly borrowed the dunce's punt. The necessities of punting, which kept him far from her, and demanded much adroit labour, gradually restored his self-respect, and he was able to look the uncelebrated oarsmen they met in the eyes, except when they were accompanied by their parents and sisters, which subtly made him feel uncomfortable again. But Winifred, piquant under her pink parasol, was singularly at ease, enraptured with the changing beauty of the river, applauding with childish glee the wild flowers on the banks, or the rippling reflections in the water.

'Look, look!' she cried once, pointing skyward. He stared upwards, expecting a balloon at least. But it was only 'Keats's little rosy cloud', she explained. It was not her fault if he did not find the excursion unreservedly idyllic.

'How stupid,' she reflected, 'to keep all those nice boys cooped up reading dead languages in a spot made for life and love.'

'I'm afraid they don't disturb the dead languages so much as you think,' he reassured her, smiling. 'And there will be plenty of love-making during Commem.'

'I am so glad. I suppose there are lots of engagements that week.'

'Oh, yes – but not one per cent come to anything.'

'Really? Oh, how fickle men are!'

That seemed rather question-begging, but he was so thrilled by the implicit revelation that she could not even imagine feminine inconstancy, that he forebore to draw her attention to her inadequate logic.

So childish and thoughtless indeed was she that day that nothing would content her but attending a 'viva', which he had incautiously informed her was public.

'Nobody will notice us,' she urged with strange unconsciousness of her loveliness. 'Besides, they don't know I'm not your sister.'

'The Oxford intellect is sceptical,' he said, laughing. 'It cultivates philosophical doubt.'

But, putting a bold face on the matter, and assuming a fraternal air, he took her to the torture-chamber, in which candidates sat dolefully on a row of chairs against the wall, waiting their turn to come before the three grand inquisitors at the table. Fortunately, Winifred and he were the only spectators; but unfortunately they blundered in at the very moment when the poor owner of the punt was on the rack. The central inquisitor was trying to extract from him information about à Becket, almost prompting him with the very words, but without penetrating through the duncical denseness. John Lefolle breathed more freely when the Crusades were broached; but, alas, it very soon became evident that the dunce had by no means 'got hold of the thing'. As the dunce passed out sadly, obviously ploughed, John Lefolle suffered more than he. So conscience-stricken was he that, when he had accompanied Winifred as far as her hotel, he refused her invitation to come in, pleading the compulsoriness of duty and dinner in Hall. But he could not get away without promising to call in during the evening.

The prospect of this visit was with him all through dinner, at once tempting and terrifying. Assuredly there was a skeleton at his feast, as he sat at the high table, facing the Master. The venerable portraits round the hall seemed to rebuke his romantic waywardness. In the common-room, he sipped his port uneasily, listening as in a daze to the discussion on free will, which an eminent stranger had stirred up. How academic it seemed, compared with the passionate realities of life. But somehow he found himself lingering on at the academic discussion, postponing the realities of life. Every now and again, he was impelled to glance at his watch; but suddenly murmuring, 'It is very late,' he pulled himself together, and took leave of his learned brethren. But in the street the sight of a telegraph office drew his steps to it, and almost mechanically he wrote out the message: 'Regret detained. Will call early in morning.'

When he did call in the morning, he was told she had gone back to London the night before on receipt of a telegram. He turned away with a bitter pang of disappointment and regret.

4

Their subsequent correspondence was only the more amorous. The reason she had fled from the hotel, she explained, was that she could not endure the night in those stuffy quarters. He consoled himself with the hope of seeing much of her during the long vacation. He did see her once at her own reception, but this time her husband wandered about the two rooms. The cosy corner was impossible, and they could only manage to gasp out a few mutual endearments amid the buzz and movement, and to arrange a rendez-vous for the end of July. When the day came, he received a heart-broken letter, stating that her husband had borne her away to Goodwood. In a postscript she informed him that 'Quicksilver was a sure thing'. Much correspondence passed without another meeting being effected, and he lent her five pounds to pay a debt of honour incurred through her husband's 'absurd confidence in Quicksilver'. A week later this horsey husband of hers brought her on to Brighton for the races there, and hither John Lefolle flew. But her husband shadowed her, and he could only lift his hat to her as they passed each other on the Lawns. Sometimes he saw her sitting pensively on a chair while her lord and thrasher perused a pink sporting-paper. Such tantalising proximity raised their correspondence through the Hove Post Office to fever heat. Life apart, they felt, was impossible, and, removed from the sobering influences of his cap and gown, John Lefolle dreamed of throwing everything to the winds. His literary reputation had opened out a new career. The Winifred lyrics alone had brought in a tidy sum, and though he had expended that and more on dispatches of flowers and trifles to her, yet he felt this extravagance would become extinguished under daily companionship, and the poems provoked by her charms would go far towards their daily maintenance. Yes, he could throw up the university. He would rescue her from this bully, this gentleman bruiser. They would live openly and nobly in the world's eye. A poet was not even expected to be conventional.

She, on her side, was no less ardent for the great step. She raged against the world's law, the injustice by which a husband's cruelty was not sufficient ground for divorce. 'But we finer souls must take the law into our own hands,' she wrote. 'We must teach society that the ethics of a barbarous age are unfitted for our century of enlightenment.' But somehow the actual time and place of the elopement could never get itself fixed. In September her husband dragged her to Scotland, in October after the pheasants. When the dramatic day was actually fixed, Winifred wrote by the next post deferring it for a week. Even the few actual preliminary meetings they planned for Kensington Gardens or Hampstead Heath rarely came off. He lived in a whirling atmosphere of express letters of excuse, and telegrams that transformed the situation from hour to hour. Not that her passion in any way abated, or her romantic resolution really altered: it was only that her conception of time and place and ways and means was dizzily mutable.

But after nigh six months of palpitating negotiations with the adorable Mrs Glamorys, the poet, in a moment of dejection, penned the prose apophthegm, 'It is of no use trying to change a changeable person.'

5

But at last she astonished him by a sketch plan of the elopement, so detailed, even to band-boxes and the Paris night route via Dieppe, that no further room for doubt was left in his intoxicated soul, and he was actually further astonished when, just as he was putting his hand-bag into the hansom, a telegram was handed to him saying: 'Gone to Hamburg. Letter follows.'

He stood still for a moment on the pavement in utter distraction. What did it mean? Had she failed him again? Or was it simply that she had changed the city of refuge from Paris to Hamburg? He was about to name the new station to the cabman, but then, 'letter follows'. Surely that meant that he was to wait for it. Perplexed and miserable, he stood with the telegram crumpled up in his fist. What a ridiculous situation! He had wrought himself up to the point of breaking with the world and his past, and now – it only remained to satisfy the cabman!

He tossed feverishly all night, seeking to soothe himself, but really exciting himself the more by a hundred plausible explanations. He was now strung up to such a pitch of uncertainty that he was astonished for the third time when the 'letter' did duly 'follow'.

'Dearest,' it ran, 'as I explained in my telegram, my husband became suddenly ill' – (if she had only put that in the telegram, he groaned) – 'and was ordered to Hamburg. Of course it was impossible to leave him in this crisis, both for practical and sentimental reasons. You yourself, darling, would not like me to have aggravated his illness by my flight just at this moment, and thus possibly have his death on my conscience.' (Darling, you are always right, he said, kissing the letter.) 'Let us possess our souls in patience a little longer. I need not tell you how vexatious it will be to find myself nursing him in Hamburg – out of the season even – instead of the prospect to which I had looked forward with my whole heart and soul. But what can one do? How true is the French proverb, "Nothing happens but the unexpected"! Write to me immediately Poste Restante, that I may at least console myself with your dear words.'

The unexpected did indeed happen. Despite draughts of Elizabeth-brunnen and promenades on the Kurhaus terrace, the stalwart woman-beater succumbed to his malady. The curt telegram from Winifred gave no indication of her emotions. He sent a reply-telegram of sympathy with her trouble. Although he could not pretend to grieve at this sudden providential solution of their life-problem, still he did sincerely sympathise with the distress inevitable in connection with a death, especially on foreign soil.

He was not able to see her till her husband's body had been brought across the North Sea and committed to the green repose of the old Hampstead churchyard. He found her pathetically altered – her face wan and spiritualised, and all in subtle harmony with the exquisite black gown. In the first interview, he did not dare speak of their love at all. They discussed the immortality of the soul, and she quoted George Herbert. But with the weeks the question of their future began to force its way back to his lips.

'We could not decently marry before six months,' she said, when definitely confronted with the problem.

'Six months!' he gasped.

'Well, surely you don't want to outrage everybody,' she said, pouting.

At first he was outraged himself. What! She who had been ready to flutter the world with a fantastic dance was now measuring her footsteps. But on reflection he saw that Mrs Glamorys was right once more. Since providence had been good enough to rescue them, why should they fly in its face? A little patience, and a blameless happiness lay before them. Let him not blind himself to the immense relief he really felt at being spared social obloquy. After all, a poet could be unconventional in his *work* – he had no need of the practical outlet demanded for the less gifted.

6

They scarcely met at all during the next six months – it had, naturally, in this grateful reaction against their recklessness, become a sacred period, even more charged with tremulous emotion than the engagement periods of those who have not so nearly scorched themselves. Even in her presence he found a certain pleasure in combining distant adoration with the confident expectation of proximity, and thus she was restored to the sanctity which she had risked by her former easiness. And so all was for the best in the best of all possible worlds.

When the six months had gone by, he came to claim her hand. She was quite astonished. 'You promised to marry me at the end of six months,' he reminded her.

'Surely it isn't six months already,' she said.

He referred her to the calendar, recalled the date of her husband's death.

'You are strangely literal for a poet,' she said. 'Of course I *said* six months, but six months doesn't mean twenty-six weeks by the clock. All I meant was that a decent period must intervene. But even to myself it seems only yesterday that poor Harold was walking beside me in the Kurhaus Park.' She burst into tears, and in the face of them he could not pursue the argument.

Gradually, after several interviews and letters, it was agreed that they should wait another six months.

'She *is* right,' he reflected again. 'We have waited so long, we may as well wait a little longer and leave malice no handle.'

The second six months seemed to him much longer than the first. The charm of respectful adoration had lost its novelty, and once again his breast was racked by fitful fevers which could scarcely calm themselves even by conversion into sonnets. The one point of repose was that shining fixed star of marriage. Still smarting under Winifred's reproach of his unpoetic literality, he did not intend to force her to marry him exactly at the end of the twelve-month. But he was determined that she should have no later than this exact date for at least 'naming the day'. Not the most punctilious stickler for convention, he felt, could deny that Mrs Grundy's claim had been paid to the last minute.

The publication of his new volume – containing the Winifred lyrics – had served to colour these months of intolerable delay. Even the reaction of the critics against his poetry, that conventional revolt against every second volume, that parrot cry of over-praise from the very throats that had praised him, though it pained and perplexed him, was perhaps really helpful. At any rate, the long waiting was over at last. He felt like Jacob after his years of service for Rachel.

The fateful morning dawned bright and blue, and as the towers of Oxford were left behind him he recalled that distant Saturday when he had first gone down to meet the literary lights of London in his publisher's salon. How much older he was now than then – and yet how much younger! The nebulous melancholy of youth, the clouds of philosophy, had vanished before this beautiful creature of sunshine whose radiance cut out a clear line for his future through the confusion of life.

At a florist's in the High Street of Hampstead he bought a costly bouquet of white flowers, and walked airily to the house and rang the bell jubilantly. He could scarcely believe his ears when the maid told him her mistress was not at home. How dared the girl stare at him so impassively? Did she not know by what appointment – on what errand – he had come? Had he not written to her mistress a week ago that he would present himself that afternoon?

'Not at home!' he gasped. 'But when will she be home?'

'I fancy she won't be long. She went out an hour ago, and she has an appointment with her dressmaker at five.'

'Do you know in what direction she'd have gone?'

'Oh, she generally walks on the heath before tea.'

The world suddenly grew rosy again. 'I will come back again,' he said. Yes, a walk in this glorious air – heathward – would do him good.

As the door shut he remembered he might have left the flowers, but he would not ring again, and besides, it was, perhaps, better he should present them with his own hand than let her find them on the hall table. Still, it seemed rather awkward to walk about the streets with a bouquet, and he was glad accidentally to strike the old Hampstead church, and to seek a momentary seclusion in passing through its avenue of quiet gravestones on his heathward way.

Mounting the few steps, he paused idly a moment on the verge of this green 'God's-acre' to read a perpendicular slab on a wall, and his face broadened into a smile as he followed the absurdly elaborate biography of a rich, self-made merchant who had taught himself to read. 'Reader, go thou and do likewise,' was the delicious bull at the end. As he turned away, the smile still lingering about his lips, he saw a dainty figure tripping down the stony graveyard path, and though he was somehow startled to find her still in black, there was no mistaking Mrs Glamorys. She ran to meet him with a glad cry, which filled his eyes with happy tears.

'How good of you to remember!' she said, as she took the bouquet from his unresisting hand, and turned again on her footsteps. He followed her wonderingly across the uneven road towards a narrow aisle of graves on the left. In another instant she had stooped before a shining white stone, and laid his bouquet reverently upon it. As he reached her side, he saw that his flowers were almost lost in the vast mass of floral offerings with which the grave of the woman-beater was bestrewn.

'How good of you to remember the anniversary,' she murmured again.

'How could I forget it?' he stammered, astonished. 'Is not this the end of the terrible twelve-month?'

The soft gratitude died out of her face. 'Oh, is *that* what you were thinking off?'

'What else?' he murmured, pale with conflicting emotions.

'What else! I think decency demanded that this day, at least, should be sacred to his memory. Oh, what brutes men are!' And she burst into tears.

His patient breast revolted at last. 'You said *he* was the brute!' he retorted, outraged.

'Is that your chivalry to the dead? Oh, my poor Harold, my poor Harold!'

For once her tears could not extinguish the flame of his anger. 'But you told me he beat you,' he cried.

'And if he did, I dare say I deserved it. Oh, my darling, my darling!' She laid her face on the stone and sobbed.

John Lefolle stood by in silent torture. As he helplessly watched her white throat swell and fall with the sobs, he was suddenly struck by the absence of the black velvet band – the truer mourning she had worn in the lifetime of the so lamented. A faint scar, only perceptible to his conscious eye, added to his painful bewilderment.

At last she rose and walked unsteadily forward. He followed her in mute misery. In a moment or two they found themselves on the outskirts of the deserted heath. How beautiful stretched the gorsy rolling country! The sun was setting in great burning furrows of gold and green – a panorama to take one's breath away. The beauty and peace of nature passed into the poet's soul.

'Forgive me, dearest,' he begged, taking her hand.

She drew it away sharply. 'I cannot forgive you. You have shown yourself in your true colours.'

Her unreasonableness angered him again. 'What do you mean? I only came in accordance with our long-standing arrangement. You have put me off long enough.'

'It is fortunate I did put you off long enough to discover what you are.'

He gasped. He thought of all the weary months of waiting, all the long comedy of telegrams and express letters, the far-off flirtations of the cosy corner, the baffled elopement to Paris. 'Then you won't marry me?'

'I cannot marry a man I neither love nor respect.'

'You don't love me!' Her spontaneous kiss in his sober Oxford study seemed to burn on his angry lips.

'No, I never loved you.'

He took her by the arms and turned her round roughly. 'Look me in the face and dare to say you have never loved me.'

His memory was buzzing with passionate phrases from her endless letters. They stung like a swarm of bees. The sunset was like blood-red mist before his eyes.

'I have never loved you,' she said obstinately.

'You – !' His grasp on her arms tightened. He shook her.

'You are bruising me,' she cried.

His grasp fell from her arms as though they were red-hot. He had become a woman-beater.

A Rose in the Ghetto

One day it occurred to Leibel that he ought to get married. He went to Sugarman the Shadchan forthwith.

'I have the very thing for you,' said the great marriage broker.

'Is she pretty?' asked Leibel.

'Her father has a boot-and-shoe warehouse,' replied Sugarman, enthusiastically.

'Then there ought to be a dowry with her,' said Leibel, eagerly.

'Certainly a dowry! A fine man like you!'

'How much do you think it would be?'

'Of course it is not a large warehouse; but then you could get your boots at trade price, and your wife's, perhaps, for the cost of the leather.'

'When could I see her?'

'I will arrange for you to call next Sabbath afternoon.'

'You won't charge me more than a sovereign?'

'Not a groschen more! Such a pious maiden! I'm sure you will be happy. She has so much way-of-the-country [breeding]. And of course five per cent on the dowry?'

'H'm! Well, I don't mind!' Perhaps they won't give a dowry, he thought with a consolatory sense of outwitting the Shadchan.

On the Saturday Leibel went to see the damsel, and on the Sunday he went to see Sugarman the Shadchan.

'But your maiden squints!' he cried, resentfully.

'An excellent thing!' said Sugarman. 'A wife who squints can never look her husband straight in the face and overwhelm him. Who would quail before a woman with a squint?'

'I could endure the squint,' went on Leibel, dubiously, 'but she also stammers.'

'Well, what is better, in the event of a quarrel? The difficulty she has in talking will keep her far more silent than most wives. You had best secure her while you have the chance.'

'But she halts on the left leg,' cried Leibel, exasperated.

'*Gott in Himmel!* Do you mean to say you do not see what an advantage it is to have a wife unable to accompany you in all your goings?'

Leibel lost patience.

'Why, the girl is a hunchback!' he protested, furiously.

'My dear Leibel,' said the marriage broker, deprecatingly shrugging his shoulders and spreading out his palms, 'you can't expect perfection!'

Nevertheless Leibel persisted in his unreasonable attitude. He accused Sugarman of wasting his time, of making a fool of him.

'A fool of you!' echoed the Shadchan, indignantly, 'when I give you a chance of a boot-and-shoe manufacturer's daughter? You will make a fool of yourself if you refuse. I dare say her dowry would be enough to set you up as a master tailor. At present you are compelled to slave away as a cutter for thirty shillings a week. It is most unjust. If you only had a few machines you would be able to employ your own cutters. And they can be got so cheap nowadays.'

This gave Leibel pause, and he departed without having definitely broken the negotiations. His whole week was befogged by doubt, his work became uncertain, his chalk marks lacked their usual decision, and he did not always cut his coat according to his cloth. His aberrations became so marked that pretty Rose Green, the sweater's eldest daughter, who managed a machine in the same room, divined, with all a woman's intuition, that he was in love.

'What is the matter?' she said, in rallying Yiddish, when they were taking their lunch of bread and cheese and ginger-beer amid the clatter of machines, whose serfs had not yet knocked off work.

'They are proposing me a match,' he answered, sullenly.

'A match!' ejaculated Rose. 'Thou!' She had worked by his side for years, and familiarity bred the second person singular. Leibel nodded his head, and put a mouthful of Dutch cheese into it.

'With whom?' asked Rose.

Somehow he felt ashamed. He gurgled the answer into the stone ginger-beer bottle, which he put to his thirsty lips. 'With Leah Volcovitch!'

'Leah Volcovitch!' gasped Rose. 'Leah, the boot-and-shoe manufacturer's daughter?'

Leibel hung his head – he scarce knew why. He did not dare meet her gaze. His droop said 'Yes.' There was a long pause.

'And why dost thou not have her?' said Rose. It was more than an enquiry; there was contempt in it, and perhaps even pique.

Leibel did not reply. The embarrassing silence reigned again, and reigned long.

Rose broke it at last. 'Is it that thou likest me better?' she asked.

Leibel seemed to see a ball of lightning in the air; it burst, and he felt the electric current strike right through his heart. The shock threw his head up with a jerk, so that his eyes gazed into a face whose beauty and tenderness were revealed to him for the first time. The face of his old acquaintance had vanished; this was a cajoling, coquettish, smiling face, suggesting undreamed-of things.

'*Nu*, yes,' he replied, without perceptible pause.

'*Nu*, good!' she rejoined as quickly.

And in the ecstasy of that moment of mutual understanding Leibel forgot to wonder why he had never thought of Rose before. Afterwards he remembered that she had always been his social superior.

The situation seemed too dream-like for explanation to the room just yet. Leibel lovingly passed a bottle of ginger-beer, and Rose took a sip, with a beautiful air of plighting troth, understood only of those two. When Leibel quaffed the remnant it intoxicated him. The relics of the bread and cheese were the ambrosia to this nectar. They did not dare kiss; the suddenness of it all left them bashful, and the smack of lips would have been like a cannon-peal announcing their engagement. There was a subtler sweetness in this sense of a secret, apart from the fact that neither cared to break the news to the master tailor, a stern little old man. Leibel's chalk marks continued indecisive that afternoon, which shows how correctly Rose had connected them with love.

Before he left that night Rose said to him, 'Art thou sure thou wouldst not rather have Leah Volcovitch?'

'Not for all the boots and shoes in the world,' replied Leibel, vehemently.

'And I,' protested Rose, 'would rather go without my own than without thee.'

The landing outside the workshop was so badly lighted that their lips came together in the darkness.

'Nay, nay; thou must not yet,' said Rose. 'Thou art still courting Leah Volcovitch. For aught thou knowest, Sugarman the Shadchan may have entangled thee beyond redemption.'

'Not so,' asserted Leibel. 'I have only seen the maiden once.'

'Yes. But Sugarman has seen her father several times,' persisted Rose. 'For so misshapen a maiden his commission would be large. Thou must go to Sugarman tonight, and tell him that thou canst not find it in thy heart to go on with the match.'

'Kiss me, and I will go,' pleaded Leibel.

'Go, and I will kiss thee,' said Rose, resolutely.

'And when shall we tell thy father?' he asked, pressing her hand, as the next best thing to her lips.

'As soon as thou art free from Leah.'

'But will he consent?'

'He will not be glad,' said Rose, frankly. 'But after mother's death – peace be upon her – the rule passed from her hands into mine.'

'Ah, that is well,' said Leibel. He was a superficial thinker.

Leibel found Sugarman at supper. The great Shadchan offered him a chair, but nothing else. Hospitality was associated in his mind with special occasions only, and involved lemonade and 'stuffed monkeys'.

He was very put out – almost to the point of indigestion – to hear of Leibel's final determination, and plied him with reproachful enquiries.

'You don't mean to say that you give up a boot-and shoe-manufacturer merely because his daughter has round shoulders!' he exclaimed, incredulously.

'It is more than round shoulders – it is a hump!' cried Leibel.

'And suppose? See how much better off you will be when you get your own machines! We do not refuse to let camels carry our burdens because they have humps.'

'Ah, but a wife is not a camel,' said Leibel, with a sage air.

'And a cutter is not a master tailor,' retorted Sugarman.

'Enough, enough!' cried Leibel. 'I tell you, I would not have her if she were a machine warehouse.'

'There sticks something behind,' persisted Sugarman, unconvinced.

Leibel shook his head. 'Only her hump,' he said with a flash of humour.

'Moses Mendelssohn had a hump,' expostulated Sugarman, reproachfully.

'Yes, but he was a heretic,' rejoined Leibel, who was not without reading. 'And then he was a man! A man with two humps could find a wife for each. But a woman with a hump cannot expect a husband in addition.'

'Guard your tongue from evil,' quoth the Shadchan, angrily. 'If everybody were to talk like you Leah Volcovitch would never be married at all.'

Leibel shrugged his shoulders, and reminded him that hunchbacked girls who stammered and squinted and halted on left legs were not usually led under the canopy.

'Nonsense! Stuff!' cried Sugarman, angrily. 'That is because they do not come to me.'

'Leah Volcovitch *has* come to you,' said Leibel, 'but she shall not come to me.' And he rose, anxious to escape.

Instantly Sugarman gave a sigh of resignation. 'Be it so! Then I shall have to look out for another, that's all.'

'No, I don't want any,' replied Leibel, quickly.

Sugarman stopped eating. 'You don't want any?' he cried. 'But you came to me for one?'

'I – I – know,' stammered Leibel. 'But I've – I've altered my mind.'

'One needs Hillel's patience to deal with you!' cried Sugarman. 'But I shall charge you, all the same, for my trouble. You cannot cancel an order like this in the middle! No, no! You can play fast and loose with Leah Volcovitch, but you shall not make a fool of me.'

'But if I don't want one?' said Leibel, sullenly.

Sugarman gazed at him with a cunning look of suspicion. 'Didn't I say there was something sticking behind?'

Leibel felt guilty. 'But whom have you got in your eye?' he enquired, desperately.

'Perhaps you may have someone in yours!' naïvely answered Sugarman.

Leibel gave a hypocritic long-drawn 'U–m–m–m! I wonder if Rose Green – where I work – ?' he said, and stopped.

'I fear not,' said Sugarman. 'She is on my list. Her father gave her to me some months ago, but he is hard to please. Even the maiden herself is not easy, being pretty.'

'Perhaps she has waited for someone,' suggested Leibel.

Sugarman's keen ear caught the note of complacent triumph.

'You have been asking her yourself!' he exclaimed, in horror-stricken accents.

'And if I have?' said Leibel, defiantly.

'You have cheated me! And so has Eliphaz Green – I always knew he was tricky! You have both defrauded me!'

'I did not mean to,' said Leibel, mildly.

'You *did* mean to. You had no business to take the matter out of my hands. What right had you to propose to Rose Green?'

'I did not,' cried Leibel, excitedly.

'Then you asked her father!'

'No; I have not asked her father yet.'

'Then how do you know she will have you?'

'I – I know,' stammered Leibel, feeling himself somehow a liar as well as a thief. His brain was in a whirl; he could not remember how the thing had come about. Certainly he had not proposed; nor could he say that she had.

'You know she will have you,' repeated Sugarman, reflectively. 'And does *she* know?'

'Yes. In fact,' he blurted out, 'we arranged it together.'

'Ah, you both know. And does her father know?'

'Not yet.'

'Ah, then I must get his consent,' said Sugarman, decisively.

'I – I thought of speaking to him myself.'

'Yourself!' echoed Sugarman, in horror. 'Are you unsound in the head? Why, that would be worse than the mistake you have already made!'

'What mistake?' asked Leibel, firing up.

'The mistake of asking the maiden herself. When you quarrel with her after your marriage she will always throw it in your teeth that you wished to marry her. Moreover, if you tell a maiden you love her, her father will think you ought to marry her as she stands. Still, what is done is done.' And he sighed regretfully.

'And what more do I want? I love her.'

'You piece of clay!' cried Sugarman, contemptuously. 'Love will not turn machines, much less buy them. You must have a dowry. Her father has a big stocking; he can well afford it.'

Leibel's eyes lit up. There was really no reason why he should not have bread and cheese with his kisses.

'Now, if *you* went to her father,' pursued the Shadchan, 'the odds are that he would not even give you his daughter – to say nothing of the dowry. After all, it is a cheek of you to aspire so high. As you told me from the first, you haven't saved a penny. Even my commission you won't be able to pay till you get the dowry. But if *I* go I do not despair of getting a substantial sum – to say nothing of the daughter.'

'Yes, I think you had better go,' said Leibel, eagerly.

'But if I do this thing for you I shall want a pound more,' rejoined Sugarman.

'A pound more!' echoed Leibel, in dismay. 'Why?'

'Because Rose Green's hump is of gold,' replied Sugarman, oracularly. 'Also, she is fair to see, and many men desire her.'

'But you have always your five per cent, on the dowry.'

'It will be less than Volcovitch's,' explained Sugarman. 'You see, Green has other and less beautiful daughters.'

'Yes, but then it settles itself more easily. Say five shillings.'

'Eliphaz Green is a hard man,' said the Shadchan instead.

'Ten shillings is the most I will give!'

'Twelve and sixpence is the least I will take. Eliphaz Green haggles so terribly.'

They split the difference, and so eleven and threepence represented the predominance of Eliphaz Green's stinginess over Volcovitch's.

The very next day Sugarman invaded the Green workroom. Rose bent over her seams, her heart fluttering. Leibel had duly apprised her of the round-about manner in which she would have to be won, and she had acquiesced in the comedy. At the least it would save her the trouble of father-taming.

Sugarman's entry was brusque and breathless. He was overwhelmed with joyous emotion. His blue bandana trailed agitatedly from his coat-tail.

'At last!' he cried, addressing the little white-haired master tailor; 'I have the very man for you.'

'Yes?' grunted Eliphaz, unimpressed. The monosyllable was packed with emotion. It said, 'Have you really the face to come to me again with an ideal man?'

'He has all the qualities that you desire,' began the Shadchan, in a tone that repudiated the implications of the monosyllable. 'He is young, strong, God-fearing – '

'Has he any money?' grumpily interrupted Eliphaz.

'He *will* have money,' replied Sugarman, unhesitatingly, 'when he marries.'

'Ah!' The father's voice relaxed, and his foot lay limp on the treadle. He worked one of his machines himself, and paid himself the wages so as to enjoy the profit. 'How much will he have?'

'I think he will have fifty pounds; and the least you can do is to let him have fifty pounds,' replied Sugarman, with the same happy ambiguity.

Eliphaz shook his head on principle.

'Yes, you will,' said Sugarman, 'when you learn how fine a man he is.'

The flush of confusion and trepidation already on Leibel's countenance became a rosy glow of modesty, for he could not help overhearing what was being said, owing to the lull of the master tailor's machine.

'Tell me, then,' rejoined Eliphaz.

'Tell me, first, if you will give fifty to a young, healthy, hard-working, God-fearing man, whose idea it is to start as a master tailor on his own account? And you know how profitable that is!'

'To a man like that,' said Eliphaz, in a burst of enthusiasm, 'I would give as much as twenty-seven pounds ten!'

Sugarman groaned inwardly, but Leibel's heart leaped with joy. To get four months' wages at a stroke! With twenty-seven pounds ten he could certainly procure several machines, especially on the instalment system. Out of the corners of his eye he shot a glance at Rose, who was beyond earshot.

'Unless you can promise thirty it is waste of time mentioning his name,' said Sugarman.

'Well, well – who is he?'

Sugarman bent down, lowering his voice into the father's ear.

'What! Leibel!' cried Eliphaz, outraged.

'Sh!' said Sugarman, 'or he will overhear your delight, and ask more. He has his nose high enough, as it is.'

'B–b–b–ut,' sputtered the bewildered parent, 'I know Leibel myself. I see him every day. I don't want a Shadchan to find me a man I know – a mere hand in my own workshop!'

'Your talk has neither face nor figure,' answered Sugarman, sternly. 'It is just the people one sees every day that one knows least. I warrant that if I had not put it into your head you would never have dreamt of Leibel as a son-in-law. Come now, confess.'

Eliphaz grunted vaguely, and the Shadchan went on triumphantly: 'I thought as much. And yet where could you find a better man to keep your daughter?'

'He ought to be content with her alone,' grumbled her father.

Sugarman saw the signs of weakening, and dashed in, full strength: 'It's a question whether he will have her at all. I have not been to him about her yet. I awaited your approval of the idea.' Leibel admired the verbal accuracy of these statements, which he had just caught.

'But I didn't know he would be having money,' murmured Eliphaz.

'Of course you didn't know. That's what the Shadchan is for – to point out the things that are under your nose.'

'But where will he be getting this money from?'

'From you,' said Sugarman, frankly.

'From me?'

'From whom else? Are you not his employer? It has been put by for his marriage day.'

'He has saved it?'

'He has not *spent* it,' said Sugarman, impatiently.

'But do you mean to say he has saved fifty pounds?'

'If he could manage to save fifty pounds out of your wages he would be indeed a treasure,' said Sugarman. 'Perhaps it might be thirty.'

'But you said fifty.'

'Well, *you* came down to thirty,' retorted the Shadchan. 'You cannot expect him to have more than your daughter brings.'

'I never said thirty,' Eliphaz reminded him. 'Twenty-seven ten was my last bid.'

'Very well; that will do as a basis of negotiations,' said Sugarman, resignedly. 'I will call upon him this evening. If I were to go over and speak to him now, he would perceive you were anxious, and raise his terms, and that will never do. Of course you will not mind allowing me a pound more for finding you so economical a son-in-law?'

'Not a penny more.'

'You need not fear,' said Sugarman, resentfully. 'It is not likely I shall be able to persuade him to take so economical a father-in-law. So you will be none the worse for promising.'

'Be it so,' said Eliphaz, with a gesture of weariness, and he started his machine again.

'Twenty-seven pounds ten, remember,' said Sugarman, above the whir.

Eliphaz nodded his head, whirring his wheel-work louder.

'And paid before the wedding, mind.'

The machine took no notice.

'Before the wedding, mind,' repeated Sugarman. 'Before we go under the canopy.'

'Go now, go now!' grunted Eliphaz, with a gesture of impatience. 'It shall all be well.' And the white-haired head bowed immovably over its work.

In the evening Rose extracted from her father the motive of Sugarman's visit, and confessed that the idea was to her liking.

'But dost thou think he will have me, little father?' she asked, with cajoling eyes.

'Anyone would have my Rose.'

'Ah, but Leibel is different. So many years he has sat at my side and said nothing.'

'He had his work to think of. He is a good, saving youth.'

'At this very moment Sugarman is trying to persuade him – not so? I suppose he will want much money.'

'Be easy, my child.' And he passed his discoloured hand over her hair.

Sugarman turned up the next day, and reported that Leibel was unobtainable under thirty pounds, and Eliphaz, weary of the contest, called over Leibel, till that moment carefully absorbed in his scientific chalk marks, and mentioned the thing to him for the first time. 'I am not a man to bargain,' Eliphaz said, and so he gave the young man his tawny hand, and a bottle of rum sprang from somewhere, and work was suspended for five minutes, and the 'hands' all drank amid surprised excitement. Sugarman's visits had prepared them to congratulate Rose; but Leibel was a shock.

The formal engagement was marked by even greater junketing, and at last the marriage day came. Leibel was resplendent in a diagonal frockcoat, cut by his own hand; and Rose stepped from the cab a medley of flowers, fairness, and white silk, and behind her came two bridesmaids – her sisters – a trio that glorified the spectator-strewn pavement outside the synagogue. Eliphaz looked almost tall in his shiny high hat and frilled shirt-front. Sugarman arrived on foot, carrying red-socked little Ebenezer tucked under his arm.

Leibel and Rose were not the only couple to be disposed of, for it was the thirty-third day of the Omer – a day fruitful in marriages.

But at last their turn came. They did not, however, come in their turn, and their special friends among the audience wondered why they had lost their precedence. After several later marriages had taken place a whisper began to circulate. The rumour of a hitch gained ground steadily, and the sensation was proportionate. And, indeed, the rose was not to be picked without a touch of the thorn.

Gradually the facts leaked out, and a buzz of talk and comment ran through the waiting synagogue. Eliphaz had not paid up!

At first he declared he would put down the money immediately after the ceremony. But the wary Sugarman, schooled by experience, demanded its instant delivery on behalf of his other client. Hard pressed, Eliphaz produced ten sovereigns from his trousers-pocket, and tendered them on account. These Sugarman disdainfully refused, and the negotiations were suspended. The bridegroom's party was encamped in one room, the bride's in another, and after a painful delay Eliphaz sent an emissary to say that half the amount should be forthcoming, the extra five pounds in a bright new Bank of England note. Leibel, instructed and encouraged by Sugarman, stood firm.

And then arose a hubbub of voices, a chaos of suggestions; friends rushed to and fro between the camps, some emerging from their seats in the synagogue to add to the confusion. But Eliphaz had taken his stand upon a rock – he had no more ready money. Tomorrow, the next day, he would have some. And Leibel, pale and dogged, clutched tighter at those machines that were slipping away momently from him. He had not yet seen his bride that morning, and so her face was shadowy compared with the tangibility of those machines. Most of the other maidens were married women by now, and the situation was growing desperate. From the female camp came terrible rumours of bridesmaids in hysterics, and a bride that tore her wreath in a passion of shame and humiliation. Eliphaz sent word that he would give an IOU for the balance, but that he really could not muster any more current coin. Sugarman instructed the ambassador to suggest that Eliphaz should raise the money among his friends.

And the short spring day slipped away. In vain the minister, apprised of the block, lengthened out the formulae for the other pairs, and blessed them with more reposeful unction. It was impossible to stave off the Leibel-Green item indefinitely, and at last Rose remained the only orange-wreathed spinster in the synagogue. And then there was a hush of solemn suspense, that swelled gradually into a steady rumble of babbling tongues, as minute succeeded minute and the final bridal party still failed to appear. The latest bulletin pictured the bride in a dead faint. The afternoon was waning fast. The minister left his post near the canopy, under which so many lives had been united, and came to add his white tie to the forces for compromise. But he fared no better than the others. Incensed at the obstinacy of the antagonists, he declared he would close the synagogue. He gave the couple ten minutes to marry in or quit. Then chaos came, and pandemonium – a frantic babel of suggestion and exhortation from the crowd. When five minutes had passed a legate from Eliphaz announced that his side had scraped together twenty pounds, and that this was their final bid.

Leibel wavered; the long day's combat had told upon him; the reports of the bride's distress had weakened him. Even Sugarman had lost his cock-sureness of victory. A few minutes more and both commissions might slip through his fingers. Once the parties left the synagogue, it would not be easy to drive them there another day. But he cheered on his man still: one could always surrender at the tenth minute.

At the eighth the buzz of tongues faltered suddenly, to be transposed into a new key, so to speak. Through the gesticulating assembly swept that murmur of expectation which crowds know when the procession is coming at last. By some mysterious magnetism all were aware that the *bride* herself – the poor hysteric bride – had left the paternal camp and was coming in person to plead with her mercenary lover.

And as the glory of her and the flowers and the white draperies loomed upon Leibel's vision his heart melted in worship, and he knew his citadel would crumble in ruins at her first glance, at her first touch. Was it fair fighting? As his troubled vision cleared, and as she came nigh unto him, he saw to his amazement that she was speckless and composed – no trace of tears dimmed the fairness of her face, there was no disarray in her bridal wreath.

The clock showed the ninth minute.

She put her hand appeallingly on his arm, while a heavenly light came into her face – the expression of a Joan of Arc animating her country.

'Do not give in, Leibel!' she said. 'Do not have me! Do not let them persuade thee! By my life, thou must not! Go home!'

So at the eleventh minute the vanquished Eliphaz produced the balance, and they all lived happily ever afterward.

The Grey Wig

I

They both styled themselves 'Madame', but only the younger of the old ladies had been married. Madame Valière was still a *demoiselle*, but as she drew towards sixty it had seemed more *convenable* to possess a mature label. Certainly Madame Dépine had no visible matrimonial advantages over her fellow-lodger at the Hôtel des Tourterelles, though in the symmetrical cemetery of Montparnasse (Section 22) wreaths of glass beads testified to a copious domesticity in the far past, and a newspaper picture of a *chasseur d'Afrique* pinned over her bed recalled – though only the uniform was the dead soldier's – the son she had contributed to France's colonial empire. Practically it was two old maids – or two lone widows – whose boots turned pointed toes towards each other in the dark cranny of the rambling, fusty corridor of the sky-floor. Madame Dépine was round, and grew dumpier with age; 'Madame' Valière was long, and grew slimmer. Otherwise their lives ran parallel. For the true madame of the establishment you had to turn to Madame la Propriétaire, with her buxom bookkeeper of a daughter and her tame baggage-bearing husband. This full-blooded, jovial creature, with her swart moustache, represented the only Parisian success of three provincial lives, and, in her good-nature, had permitted her decayed towns-women – at as low a rent as was compatible with prudence – to shelter themselves under her roof and as near it as possible. Her house being a profitable warren of American art-students, tempered by native journalists and decadent poets, she could, moreover, afford to let the old ladies off coffee and candles. They were at liberty to prepare their own *déjeuner* in winter or to buy it outside in summer; they could burn their own candles or sit in the dark, as the heart in them pleased; and thus they were as cheaply niched as anyone in the gay city. *Rentières* after their meticulous fashion, they drew a ridiculous but regular amount from the mysterious coffers of the Credit Lyonnais.

But though they met continuously in the musty corridor, and even dined – when they did dine – at the same *crémerie*, they never spoke to each other. Madame la Propriétaire was the channel through which they sucked each other's history, for though they had both known her in their girlish days at Tonnerre, in the department of Yonne, they had not known each other. Madame Valière (Madame Dépine learnt, and it seemed to explain the frigidity of her neighbour's manner) still trailed clouds of glory from the service of a princess a quarter of a century before. Her refusal to wink at the princess's goings-on, her austere, if provincial, regard for the *convenances*, had cost her the place, and from these purpureal heights she had fallen lower and lower, till she struck the attic of the Hôtel des Tourterelles.

But even a haloed past does not give one a licence to annoy one's neighbours, Madame Dépine felt resentfully, and she hated Madame Valière as a haughty minion of royalty, who kept a cough, which barked loudest in the silence of the night.

'Why doesn't she go to the hospital, your princess?' she complained to Madame la Propriétaire.

'Since she is able to nurse herself at home,' the opulent-bosomed hostess replied with a shrug.

'At the expense of other people,' Madame Dépine retorted bitterly. 'I shall die of her cough, I am sure of it.'

Madame showed her white teeth sweetly. 'Then it is you who should go to the hospital.'

2

Time wrote wrinkles enough on the brows of the two old ladies, but his frosty finger never touched their glossy brown hair, for both wore wigs of nearly the same shade. These wigs were almost symbolic of the evenness of their existence, which had got beyond the reach of happenings. The church calendar, so richly dyed with figures of saints and martyrs, filled life with colour enough, and fast-days were almost as welcome as feast-days, for if the latter warmed the general air, the former cloaked economy with dignity. As for Mardi Gras, that shook you up for weeks, even though you did not venture out of your apartment; the gay serpentine streamers remained round one's soul as round the trees.

At intervals, indeed, secular excitements broke the even tenor. A country cousin would call upon the important Parisian relative, and be received, not in the little bedroom, but in state in the mustily magnificent salon of the hotel – all gold mirrors and mouldiness – which the poor country mouse vaguely accepted as part of the glories of Paris and success. Madame Dépine would don her ponderous gold brooch, sole salvage of her bourgeois prosperity; while, if the visitor were for Madame Valière, that *grande dame* would hang from her yellow, shrivelled neck the long gold chain and the old-fashioned watch, whose hands still seemed to point to regal hours.

Another break in the monotony was the day on which the lottery was drawn – the day of the pagan god of luck. What delicious hopes of wealth flamed in these withered breasts, only to turn grey and cold when the blank was theirs again, but not the less to soar up again, with each fresh investment, towards the heaven of the hundred thousand francs! But if ever Madame

Dépine stumbled on Madame Valière buying a section of a *billet* at the lottery agent's, she insisted on having her own slice cut from another number. Fortune itself would be robbed of its sweet if the 'princess' should share it. Even their common failure to win a sou did not draw them from their freezing depths of silence, from which every passing year made it more difficult to emerge. Some greater conjuncture was needed for that.

It came when Madame la Propriétaire made her début one fine morning in a grey wig.

3

Hitherto that portly lady's hair had been black. But now, as suddenly as darkness vanishes in a tropic dawn, it was become light. No gradual approach of the grey, for the black had been equally artificial. The wig is the region without twilight. Only in the swart moustache had the grey crept on, so that perhaps the growing incongruity had necessitated the sudden surrender to age.

To both Madame Dépine and Madame Valière the grey wig came like a blow on the heart.

It was a grisly embodiment of their secret griefs, a tantalising vision of the unattainable. To glide reputably into a grey wig had been for years their dearest desire. As each saw herself getting older and older, saw her complexion fade and the crow's-feet gather, and her eyes grow hollow, and her teeth fall out and her cheeks fall in, so did the impropriety of her brown wig strike more and more humiliatingly to her soul. But how should a poor old woman ever accumulate enough for a new wig? One might as well cry for the moon – or a set of false teeth. Unless, indeed, the lottery – ?

And so, when Madame Dépine received a sister-in-law from Tonnerre, or Madame Valière's nephew came up by the excursion train from that same quiet and incongruously christened townlet, the Parisian personage would receive the visitor in the darkest corner of the salon, with her back to the light, and a big bonnet on her head – an imposing figure repeated duskily in the gold mirrors. These visits, instead of a relief, became a terror. Even a provincial knows it is not *convenable* for an old woman to wear a brown wig. And Tonnerre kept strict record of birthdays.

Tears of shame and misery had wetted the old ladies' hired pillows, as under the threat of a provincial visitation they had tossed sleepless in similar solicitude, and their wigs, had they not been wigs, would have turned grey of themselves. Their only consolation had been that neither outdid the other, and so long as each saw the other's brown wig, they had refrained from facing the dread possibility of having to sell off their jewellery in a desperate effort of emulation. Gradually Madame Dépine had grown to wear her wig with vindictive endurance, and Madame Valière to wear hers with gentle resignation. And now, here was Madame la Propriétaire, a woman five years younger and ten years better preserved, putting them both to the public blush, drawing the hotel's attention to what the hotel might have overlooked, in its long habituation to their surmounting brownness.

More morbidly conscious than ever of a young head on old shoulders, the old ladies no longer paused at the *bureau* to exchange the news with Madame or even with her black-haired bookkeeping daughter. No more lounging against the newel under the carved torch-bearer, while the journalist of the fourth floor spat at the Dreyfusites, and the poet of the *entresol* threw versified vitriol at perfidious Albion. For the first time, too – losing their channel of communication – they grew out of touch with each other's microscopic affairs, and their mutual detestation increased with their resentful ignorance. And so, shrinking and silent, and protected as far as possible by their big bonnets, the squat Madame Dépine and the skinny Madame Valière toiled up and down the dark, fusty stairs of the Hôtel des Tourterelles, often brushing against each other, yet sundered by icy infinities. And the endurance on Madame Dépine's round face became more vindictive, and gentler grew the resignation on the angular visage of Madame Valière.

4

'*Tiens!* Madame Dépine, one never sees you now.' Madame la Propriétaire was blocking the threshold, preventing her exit. 'I was almost thinking you had veritably died of Madame Valière's cough.'

'One has received my rent, the Monday,' the little old lady replied frigidly.

'*Oh! la! la!*' Madame waved her plump hands. 'And La Valière, too, makes herself invisible. What has then happened to both of you? Is it that you are doing a penance together?'

'*Hist!*' said Madame Dépine, flushing.

For at this moment Madame Valière appeared on the pavement outside bearing a long French roll and a bag of figs, which made an excellent lunch at low water. Madame la Propriétaire, dominatingly bestriding her doorstep, was sandwiched between the two old ladies, her wig aggressively grey between the two browns. Madame Valière halted awkwardly, a bronze blush mounting to match her wig. To be seen by Madame Dépine carrying in her meagre provisions was humiliation enough; to be juxtaposited with a grey wig was unbearable.

'Maman, maman, the English monsieur will not pay two francs for his dinner!' And the distressed bookkeeper, bill in hand, shattered the trio.

'And why will he not pay?' Fire leapt into the black eyes.

'He says you told him the night he came that by arrangement he could have his dinners for one franc fifty.'

Madame la Propriétaire made two strides towards the refractory English monsieur. '*I* told you one franc fifty? For *déjeuner*, yes, as many luncheons as you can eat. But for dinner? You eat with us as one of the family, and *vin compris* and *café* likewise, and it should be all for one franc fifty! *Mon Dieu!* it is to ruin oneself. Come here.' And she seized the surprised Anglo-Saxon by the wrist and dragged him towards a painted tablet of prices that hung in a dark niche of the hall. 'I have kept this hotel for twenty years, I have grown grey in the service of artists and students, and this is the first time one has demanded dinner for one franc fifty!'

'*She* has grown grey!' contemptuously muttered Madame Valière.

'Grey? She!' repeated Madame Dépine, with no less bitterness. 'It is only to give herself the air of a *grande dame!*'

Then both started, and coloured to the roots of their wigs. Simultaneously they realised that they had spoken to each other.

5

As they went up the stairs together – for Madame Dépine had quite forgotten she was going out – an immense relief enlarged their souls. Merely to mention the grey wig had been a vent for all this morbid brooding; to abuse Madame la Propriétaire into the bargain was to pass from the long isolation into a subtle sympathy.

'I wonder if she did say one franc fifty,' observed Madame Valière, reflectively.

'Without doubt,' Madame Dépine replied viciously. 'And fifty centimes a day soon mount up to a grey wig.'

'Not so soon,' sighed Madame Valière.

'But then it is not only one client that she cheats.'

'Ah! at that rate wigs fall from the skies,' admitted Madame Valière.

'Especially if one has not to give dowries to one's nieces,' said Madame Dépine, boldly.

'And if one is mean on New Year's Day,' returned Madame Valière, with a shade less of mendacity.

They inhaled the immemorial airlessness of the staircase as if they were breathing the free air of the forests depicted on its dirty-brown wallpaper. It was the new atmosphere of self-respect that they were really absorbing. Each had at last explained herself and her brown wig to the other. An immaculate honesty (that would scorn to overcharge fifty centimes even to *un Anglais*), complicated with unwedded nieces in one case, with a royal shower of New Year's gifts in the other, had kept them from selfish, if seemly, hoary-headedness.

'Ah! here is my floor,' panted Madame Valière at length, with an air of indicating it to a thorough stranger. 'Will you not come into my room and eat a fig? They are very healthy between meals.'

Madame Dépine accepted the invitation, and entering her own corner of the corridor with a responsive air of foreign exploration, passed behind the door through whose keyhole she had so often peered. Ah! no wonder she had detected nothing abnormal. The room was a facsimile of her own – the same bed with the same quilt over it and the same crucifix above it, the same little table with the same books of devotion, the same washstand with the same tiny jug and basin, the same rusted, fireless grate. The wardrobe, like her own, was merely a pair of moth-eaten tartan curtains, concealing both pegs and garments from her curiosity. The only sense of difference came subtly from the folding windows, below whose railed balcony showed another view of the quarter, with steam-trams – diminished to toy trains – puffing past to the suburbs. But as Madame Dépine's eyes roved from these to the mantelpiece, she caught sight of an oval miniature of an elegant young woman, who was jewelled in many places and corresponded exactly with her idea of a princess!

To disguise her access of respect, she said abruptly, 'It must be very noisy here from the steam-trams.'

'It is what I love, the bustle of life,' replied Madame Valière, simply.

'Ah!' said Madame Dépine, impressed beyond masking-point, 'I suppose when one has had the habit of courts –'

Madame Valière shuddered unexpectedly. 'Let us not speak of it. Take a fig.'

But Madame Dépine persisted – though she took the fig. 'Ah! those were brave days when we had still an emperor and an empress to drive to the *Bois* with their equipages and outriders. Ah, how pretty it was!'

'But the president has also' – a fit of coughing interrupted Madame Valière – 'has also outriders.'

'But he is so bourgeois – a mere man of the people,' said Madame Dépine.

'They are the most decent sort of folk. But do you not feel cold? I will light a fire.' She bent towards the wood-box.

'No, no; do not trouble. I shall be going in a moment. I have a large fire blazing in my room.'

'Then suppose we go and sit there,' said poor Madame Valière.

Poor Madame Dépine was seized with a cough, more protracted than any of which she had complained.

'Provided it has not gone out in my absence,' she stammered at last. 'I will go first and see if it is in good trim.'

'No, no; it is not worth the trouble of moving.' And Madame Valière drew her street-cloak closer round her slim form. 'But I have lived so long in Russia, I forget people call this cold.'

'Ah! the princess travelled far?' said Madame Dépine, eagerly.

'Too far,' replied Madame Valière, with a flash of Gallic wit. 'But who has told you of the princess?'

'Madame la Propriétaire, naturally.'

'She talks too much – she and her wig!'

'If only she didn't imagine herself a powdered marquise in it! To see her standing before the mirror in the salon!'

'The beautiful spectacle!' assented Madame Valière.

'Ah! but I don't forget – if she does – that her mother wheeled a fruit-barrow through the streets of Tonnerre!'

'Ah! yes, I knew you were from Tonnerre – dear Tonnerre!'

'How did you know?'

'Naturally, Madame la Propriétaire.'

'The old gossip!' cried Madame Dépine – 'though not so old as she feigns. But did she tell you of her mother, too, and the fruit-barrow?'

'I knew her mother – *une brave femme*.'

'I do not say not,' said Madame Dépine, a whit disconcerted. 'Nevertheless, when one's mother is a merchant of the four seasons – '

'Provided she sold fruit as good as this! Take another fig, I beg of you.'

'Thank you. These are indeed excellent,' said Madame Dépine. 'She owed all her good fortune to a *coup* in the lottery.'

'Ah! the lottery!' Madame Valière sighed. Before the eyes of both rose the vision of a lucky number and a grey wig.

6

The acquaintanceship ripened. It was not only their common grievances against fate and Madame la Propriétaire: they were linked by the sheer physical fact that each was the only person to whom the other could talk without the morbid consciousness of an eye scrutinising the unseemly brown wig. It became quite natural, therefore, for Madame Dépine to stroll into her 'princess's' room, and they soon slid into dividing the cost of the fire. That was more than an economy, for neither could afford a fire alone. It was an easy transition to the discovery that coffee could be made more cheaply for two, and that the same candle would light two persons, provided they sat in the same room. And if they did not fall out of the habit of companionship even at the *crémerie*, though 'two portions for one' were not served, their union at least kept the sexagenarians in countenance. Two brown wigs give each other a moral support, are on the way to a fashion.

But there was more than wigs and cheese-parings in their *camaraderie*. Madame Dépine found a fathomless mine of edification in Madame Valière's reminiscences, which she skilfully extracted from her, finding the average ore rich with noble streaks, though the old tirewoman had an obstinate way of harking back to her girlhood, which made some delvings result in mere earth.

On the Day of the Dead, Madame Dépine emerged into importance, taking her friend with her to the Cemetery Montparnasse to see the glass flowers blooming immortally over the graves of her husband and children.

Madame Dépine paid the omnibus for both (inside places), and felt, for once, superior to the poor 'princess', who had never known the realities of love and death.

7

Two months passed. Another of Madame Valière's teeth fell out. Madame Dépine's cheeks grew more pendulous. But their brown wigs remained as fadeless as the cemetery flowers.

One day they passed the hairdresser's shop together. It was indeed next to the tobacconist's, so not easy to avoid whenever one wanted a stamp or a postcard. In the window, amid pendent plaits of divers hues, bloomed two wax busts of females – the one young and coquettish and golden-haired, the other aristocratic in a distinguished grey wig. Both wore diamond rosettes in their hair and ropes of pearls round their necks. The old ladies' eyes met, then turned away.

'If one demanded the price!' said Madame Dépine (who had already done so twice).

'It is an idea!' agreed Madame Valière.

'The day will come when one's nieces will be married.'

'But scarcely when New Year's Day shall cease to be,' the 'princess' sighed.

'Still, one might win in the lottery!'

'Ah! true. Let us enter, then.'

'One will be enough. You go.' Madame Dépine rather dreaded the *coiffeur*, whom intercourse with jocose students had made severe.

But Madame Valière shrank back shyly. 'No, let us both go.' She added, with a smile to cover her timidity, 'Two heads are better than one.'

'You are right. He will name a lower price in the hope of two orders.' And, pushing the 'princess' before her like a turret of defence, Madame Dépine wheeled her into the ladies' department.

The *coiffeur*, who was washing the head of an American girl, looked up ungraciously. As he perceived the outer circumference of Madame Dépine projecting on either side of her turret, he emitted a glacial, '*Bonjour, mesdames.*'

'Those grey wigs – ' faltered Madame Valière.

'I have already told your friend.' He rubbed the American head viciously.

Madame Dépine coloured. 'But – but we are two. Is there no reduction on taking a quantity?'

'And why then? A wig is a wig. Twice a hundred francs are two hundred francs.'

'One hundred francs for a wig!' said Madame Valière, paling. 'I did not pay that for the one I wear.'

'I well believe it, madame. A grey wig is not a brown wig.'

'But you just said a wig is a wig.'

The *coiffeur* gave angry rubs at the head, in time with his explosive phrases. 'You want real hair, I presume – and to your measure – and to look natural – and *convenable!*' (Both old ladies shuddered at the word.) 'Of course, if you want it merely for private theatricals – '

'Private theatricals!' repeated Madame Dépine, aghast.

'A *comédienne*'s wig I can sell you for a bagatelle. That passes at a distance.'

Madame Valière ignored the suggestion. 'But why should a grey wig cost more than any other?'

The *coiffeur* shrugged his shoulders. 'Since there are fewer grey hairs in the world – '

'*Comment!*' repeated Madame Valière, in amazement.

'It stands to reason,' said the *coiffeur*. 'Since most persons do not live to be old – or only live to be bald.' He grew animated, professorial almost, seeing the weight his words carried to unthinking bosoms. 'And since one must provide a fine hairnet for a groundwork, to imitate the flesh-tint of the scalp, and since each hair of the parting must be treated separately, and since the natural wave of the hair must be reproduced, and since you will also need a block for it to stand on at nights to guard its shape – '

'But since one has already blocks,' interposed Madame Dépine.

'But since a conscientious artist cannot trust another's block! Represent to yourself also that the shape of the head does not remain as fixed as the dome of the Invalides, and that – '

'*Eh bien*, we will think,' interrupted Madame Valière, with dignity.

8

They walked slowly towards the Hôtel des Tourterelles.

'If one could share a wig!' Madame Dépine exclaimed suddenly.

'It is an idea,' replied Madame Valière. And then each stared involuntarily at the other's head. They had shared so many things that this new possibility sounded like a discovery. Pleasing pictures flitted before their eyes – the country cousin received (on a Box and Cox basis) by a Parisian old gentle-woman *sans peur* and *sans reproche*; a day of seclusion for each alternating with a day of ostentatious publicity.

But the light died out of their eyes as Madame Dépine recognised that the 'princess's' skull was hopelessly long, and Madame Valière recognised that Madame Dépine's cranium was hopelessly round. Decidedly either head would be a bad block for the other's wig to repose on.

'It would be more sensible to acquire a wig together, and draw lots for it,' said Madame Dépine.

The 'princess's' eyes rekindled. 'Yes, and then save up again to buy the loser a wig.'

'*Parfaitement*,' said Madame Dépine. They had slid out of pretending that they had large sums immediately available. Certain sums still existed in vague stockings for dowries or presents, but these, of course, could not be touched. For practical purposes it was understood that neither had the advantage of the other, and that the few francs a month by which Madame Dépine's income exceeded Madame Valière's were neutralised by the superior rent she paid for her comparative immunity from steam-trams. The accumulation of fifty francs apiece was thus a limitless perspective.

They discussed their budget. It was really almost impossible to cut down anything. By incredible economies they saw their way to saving a franc a week each. But fifty weeks! A whole year, allowing for sickness and other breakdowns! Who can do penance for a whole year? They thought of moving to an even cheaper hotel; but then in the course of years Madame Valière had fallen three weeks behind with the rent, and Madame Dépine a fortnight, and these arrears would have to be paid up. The first council ended in despair. But in the silence of the night Madame Dépine had another inspiration. If one suppressed the lottery for a season!

On the average each speculated a full franc a week, with scarcely a gleam of encouragement. Two francs a week each – already the year becomes six months! For six months one can hold out. Hardships shared are halved, too. It will seem scarce three months. Ah, how good are the blessed saints!

But over the morning coffee Madame Valière objected that they might win the whole hundred francs in a week!

It was true; it was heartbreaking.

Madame Dépine made a reckless reference to her brooch, but the 'princess' made a gesture of horror. 'And wear your heart on your shawl when your friends come?' she exclaimed poetically. 'Sooner my watch shall go, since that at least is hidden in my bosom!'

'Heaven forbid!' ejaculated Madame Dépine. 'But if you sold the other things hidden in your bosom – '

'How do you mean?'

'The royal secrets.'

The 'princess' blushed. 'What are you thinking of?'

'The journalist below us tells me that gossip about the great sells like Easter buns.'

'He is truly below us,' said Madame Valière, witheringly. 'What! sell one's memories! No, no; it would not be *convenable*. There are even people living – '

'But nobody would know,' urged Madame Dépine.

'One must carry the head high, even if it is not grey.'

It was almost a quarrel. Far below the steam-tram was puffing past. At the window across the street a woman was beating her carpet with swift, spasmodic thwacks, as one who knew the legal time was nearly up. In the tragic silence which followed Madame Valière's rebuke, these sounds acquired a curious intensity.

'I prefer to sacrifice the lottery rather than honour,' she added, in more conciliatory accents.

9

The long quasi-Lenten weeks went by, and unflinchingly the two old ladies pursued their pious quest of the grey wig. Butter had vanished from their bread, and beans from their coffee. Their morning brew was confected of charred crusts, and as they sipped it solemnly they exchanged the reflection that it was quite equal to the coffee at the *crémerie*. Positively one was safer drinking one's own messes. Figs, no longer posing as a pastime of the palate, were accepted seriously as *pièces de resistance*. The spring was still cold, yet fires could be left to die after breakfast. The chill had been taken off, and by midday the sun was in its full power. Each sustained the other by a desperate cheerfulness. When they took their morning walk in the Luxembourg Gardens – what time the blue-aproned Jacques was polishing their waxed floors with his legs for broom-handles – they went into ecstasies over everything, drawing each other's attention to the sky, the trees, the water. And, indeed, of a sunshiny morning it was heartening to sit by the pond and watch the wavering sheet of beaten gold water, reflecting all shades of green in a restless shimmer against the shadowed grass around. Madame Valière always had a bit of dry bread to feed the pigeons withal – it gave a cheerful sense of superfluity, and her manner of sprinkling the crumbs revived Madame Dépine's faded images of a princess scattering New Year largess.

But beneath all these pretences of content lay a hollow sense of desolation. It was not the want of butter nor the diminished meat; it was the total removal from life of that intangible splendour of hope produced by the lottery ticket. Ah! every day was drawn blank now. This gloom, this gnawing emptiness at the heart, was worse than either had foreseen or now confessed. Malicious fate, too, they felt, would even crown with the *grand prix* the number they would have chosen. But for the prospective draw for the wig – which reintroduced the aleatory – life would scarcely have been bearable.

Madame Dépine's sister-in-law's visit by the June excursion train was a not unexpected catastrophe. It only lasted a day, but it put back the grey wig by a week, for Madame Choucrou had to be fed at Duval's, and Madame Valière magnanimously insisted on being of the party: whether to run parallel with her friend, or to carry off the brown wig, she alone knew. Fortunately, Madame Choucrou was both short-sighted and colour-blind. On the other hand, she liked a *petit verre* with her coffee, and both at a separate restaurant. But never had Madame Valière appeared to Madame Dépine's eyes more like the 'princess', more gay and polished and debonair, than at this little round table on the sunlit boulevard. Little trills of laughter came from the half-toothless gums; long gloved fingers toyed with the liqueur glass or drew out the old-fashioned watch to see that Madame Choucrou did not miss her train; she spent her sou royally on a hawked journal. When they had seen Madame Choucrou off, she proposed to dock meat entirely for a fortnight so as to regain the week. Madame Dépine accepted in the same heroic spirit, and even suggested the elimination of the figs: one could lunch quite well on bread and milk, now the sunshine was here. But Madame Valière only agreed to a week's trial of this, for she had a sweet tooth among the few in her gums.

The very next morning, as they walked in the Luxembourg Gardens, Madame Dépine's foot kicked against something. She stooped and saw a shining glory – a five-franc piece!

'What is it?' said Madame Valière.

'Nothing,' said Madame Dépine, covering the coin with her foot. 'My bootlace.' And she bent down – to pick up the coin, to fumble at her bootlace, and to cover her furious blush. It was not that she wished to keep the godsend to herself – one saw on the instant that *le bon Dieu* was paying for Madame Choucrou – it was an instantaneous dread of the 'princess's' quixotic code of honour. La Valière was capable of flying in the face of providence, of taking the windfall to a *bureau de police*. As if the inspector wouldn't stick to it himself! A purse – yes. But a five-franc piece, one of a flock of sheep!

The treasure-trove was added to the heap of which her stocking was guardian, and thus honestly divided. The trouble, however, was that, as she dared not inform the 'princess', she could not decently back out of the meatless fortnight. Providence, as it turned out, was making them gain a week. As to the figs, however, she confessed on the third day that she hungered sore for them, and Madame Valière readily agreed to make this concession to her weakness.

10

This little episode coloured for Madame Dépine the whole dreary period that remained. Life was never again so depressingly definite; though curiously enough the 'princess' mistook for gloom her steady earthward glance, as they sauntered about the sweltering city. With anxious solicitude Madame Valière would direct her attention to sunsets, to clouds, to the rising moon; but heaven had ceased to have attraction, except as a place from which five-francs fell, and as soon as the 'princess's' eye was off her, her own sought the ground again. But this imaginary need of cheering up Madame Dépine kept Madame Valière herself from collapsing. At last, when the first red leaves began to litter the gardens and cover up possible coins, the francs in the stocking approached their century.

What a happy time was that! The privations were become second nature; the weather was still fine. The morning gardens were a glow of pink and purple and dripping diamonds, and on some of the trees was the delicate green of a second blossoming, like hope in the heart of age. They could scarcely refrain from betraying their exultation to the Hôtel des Tourterelles, from which they had concealed their sufferings. But the polyglot population seething round its malodorous stairs and tortuous corridors remained ignorant that anything was passing in the life of these faded old creatures, and even on the day of drawing lots for the wig the exuberant hotel retained its imperturbable activity.

Not that they really drew lots. That was a figure of speech, difficult to translate into facts. They preferred to spin a coin. Madame Dépine was to toss, the 'princess' to cry *pile ou face*. From the stocking Madame Dépine drew, naturally enough, the solitary five-franc piece. It whirled in the air; the 'princess' cried *face*. The puff-puff of the steam-tram sounded like the panting of anxious fate. The great coin fell, rolled, balanced itself between two destinies, then subsided, *pile* upwards. The poor 'princess's' face grew even longer; but for the life of her Madame Dépine could not make her own face other than a round red glow, like the sun in a fog. In fact, she looked so young at this supreme moment that the brown wig quite became her.

'I congratulate you,' said Madame Valière, after the steam-tram had become a far-away rumble.

'Before next summer we shall have yours too,' the winner reminded her consolingly.

II

They had not waited till the hundred francs were actually in the stocking. The last few would accumulate while the wig was making. As they sat at their joyous breakfast the next morning, ere starting for the hairdresser's, the casement open to the October sunshine, Jacques brought up a letter for Madame Valière – an infrequent incident. Both old women paled with instinctive distrust of life. And as the 'princess' read her letter, all the sympathetic happiness died out of her face.

'What is the matter, then?' breathed Madame Dépine.

The 'princess' recovered herself. 'Nothing, nothing. Only my nephew who is marrying.'

'Soon?'

'The middle of next month.'

'Then you will need to give presents!'

'One gives a watch, a bagatelle, and then – there is time. It is nothing. How good the coffee is this morning!'

They had not changed the name of the brew: it is not only in religious evolutions that old names are a comfort.

They walked to the hairdresser's in silence. The triumphal procession had become almost a dead march. Only once was the silence broken.

'I suppose they have invited you down for the wedding?' said Madame Dépine.

'Yes,' said Madame Valière.

They walked on.

The *coiffeur* was at his door, sunning his aproned stomach, and twisting his moustache as if it were a customer's. Emotion overcame Madame Dépine at the sight of him. She pushed Madame Valière into the tobacconist's instead.

'I have need of a stamp,' she explained, and demanded one for five centimes. She leaned over the counter babbling aimlessly to the proprietor, postponing the great moment. Madame Valière lost the clue to her movements, felt her suddenly as a stranger. But finally Madame Dépine drew herself together and led the way into the hairdresser's. The proprietor, who had re-entered his parlour, re-emerged gloomily.

Madame Valière took the initiative. 'We are thinking of ordering a wig.'

'Cash in advance, of course,' said the *coiffeur*.

'*Comment!*' cried Madame Valière, indignantly. 'You do not trust my friend!'

'Madame Valière has moved in the best society,' added Madame Dépine.

'But you cannot expect me to do two hundred francs of work and then be left planted with the wigs!'

'But who said two hundred francs?' cried Madame Dépine. 'It is only one wig that we demand – today at least.'

He shrugged his shoulders. 'A hundred francs, then.'

'And why should we trust you with one hundred francs?' asked Madame Dépine. 'You might botch the work.'

'Or fly to Italy,' added the 'princess'.

In the end it was agreed he should have fifty down and fifty on delivery.

'Measure us, while we are here,' said Madame Dépine. 'I will bring you the fifty francs immediately.'

'Very well,' he murmured. 'Which of you?'

But Madame Valière was already affectionately untying Madame Dépine's bonnet-strings. 'It is for my friend,' she cried. 'And let it be as *chic* and *convenable* as possible!'

He bowed. 'An artist remains always an artist.'

Madame Dépine removed her wig and exposed her poor old scalp, with its thin, forlorn wisps and patches of grey hair, grotesque, almost indecent, in its nudity. But the *coiffeur* measured it in sublime seriousness, putting his tape this way and that way, while Madame Valière's eyes danced in sympathetic excitement.

'You may as well measure my friend too,' remarked Madame Dépine, as she reassumed her glossy brown wig (which seemed propriety itself compared with the bald cranium).

'What an idea!' ejaculated Madame Valière. 'To what end?'

'Since you are here,' returned Madame Dépine, indifferently. 'You may as well leave your measurements. Then when you decide yourself – Is it not so, monsieur?'

The *coiffeur*, like a good man of business, eagerly endorsed the suggestion. 'Perfectly, madame.'

'But if one's head should change?' said Madame Valière, trembling with excitement at the vivid imminence of the visioned wig.

'*Souvent femme varié*, madame,' said the *coiffeur*. 'But it is the inside, not the outside of the head.'

'But you said one is not the dome of the Invalides,' Madame Valière reminded him.

'He spoke of our old blocks,' Madame Dépine intervened hastily. 'At our age one changes no more.'

Thus persuaded, the 'princess' in her turn denuded herself of her wealth of wig, and Madame Dépine watched with unsmiling satisfaction the stretchings of tape across the ungainly cranium.

'*C'est bien*,' she said. 'I return with your fifty francs on the instant.'

And having seen her 'princess' safely ensconced in the attic, she rifled the stocking, and returned to the *coiffeur*.

When she emerged from the shop, the vindictive endurance had vanished from her face, and in its place reigned an angelic exaltation.

12

Eleven days later Madame Valière and Madame Dépine set out on the great expedition to the hairdresser's to try on the wig. The 'princess's' excitement was no less tense than the fortunate winner's. Neither had slept a wink the night before, but the November morning was keen and bright, and supplied an excellent tonic. They conversed with animation on the English in Egypt, and Madame Dépine recalled the gallant death of her son, the *chasseur*.

The *coiffeur* saluted them amiably. Yes, mesdames, it was a beautiful morning. The wig was quite ready. Behold it there – on its block.

Madame Valière's eyes turned thither, then grew clouded, and returned to Madame Dépine's head and thence back to the grey wig.

'It is this one?' she said dubiously.

'*Mais, oui.*' Madame Dépine was nodding, a great smile transfiguring the emaciated orb of her face. The artist's eyes twinkled.

'But this will not fit you,' Madame Valière gasped.

'It is a little error, I know,' replied Madame Dépine.

'But it is a great error,' cried Madame Valière, aghast. And her angry gaze transfixed the *coiffeur*.

'It is not his fault – I ought not to have let him measure you.'

'Ha! Did I not tell you so?' Triumph softened her anger. 'He has mixed up the two measurements!'

'Yes. I suspected as much when I went in to enquire the other day; but I was afraid to tell you, lest it shouldn't even fit *you*.'

'Fit *me*!' breathed Madame Valière.

'But whom else?' replied Madame Dépine, impatiently, as she whipped off the 'princess's' wig. 'If only it fits you, one can pardon him. Let us see. Stand still, *ma cherie*,' and with shaking hands she seized the grey wig.

'But – but – ' The 'princess' was gasping, coughing, her ridiculous scalp bare.

'But stand still, then! What is the matter? Are you a little infant? Ah! that is better. Look at yourself, then, in the mirror. But it is perfect! A true princess,' she muttered beatifically to herself. 'Ah, how she will show up the fruit-vendor's daughter!'

As the 'princess' gazed at the majestic figure in the mirror, crowned with the dignity of age, two great tears trickled down her pendulous cheeks.

'I shall be able to go to the wedding,' she murmured chokingly.

'The wedding!' Madame Dépine opened her eyes. 'What wedding?'

'My nephew's, of course!'

'Your nephew is marrying? I congratulate you. But why did you not tell me?'

'I did mention it. That day I had a letter!'

'Ah! I seem to remember. I had not thought of it.' Then briskly: 'Well, that makes all for the best again. Ah! I was right not to scold *monsieur le coiffeur* too much, was I not?'

'You are very good to be so patient,' said Madame Valière, with a sob in her voice.

Madame Dépine shot her a dignified glance. 'We will discuss our affairs at home. Here it only remains to say whether you are satisfied with the fit.'

Madame Valière patted the wig, as much in approbation as in adjustment. 'But it fits me to a miracle!'

'Then we will pay our friend, and wish him *le bon jour*.' She produced the fifty francs – two gold pieces, well sounding, for which she had exchanged her silver and copper, and two five-franc pieces. 'And *voilà*,' she added, putting down a franc for *pourboire*, 'we are very content with the artist.'

The 'princess' stared at her, with a new admiration.

'*Merci bien*,' said the *coiffeur*, fervently, as he counted the cash. 'Would that all customers' heads lent themselves so easily to artistic treatment!'

'And when will my friend's wig be ready?' said the 'Princess'.

'Madame Valière! What are you saying there? Monsieur will set to work when I bring him the fifty francs.'

'*Mais non*, madame. I commence immediately. In a week it shall be ready, and you shall only pay on delivery.'

'You are very good. But I shall not need it yet – not till the winter – when the snows come,' said Madame Dépine, vaguely. '*Bonjour*, monsieur;' and, thrusting the old wig on the new block, and both under her shawl, she dragged the 'princess' out of the shop. Then, looking back through the door, 'Do not lose the measurement, monsieur,' she cried. 'One of these days!'

13

The grey wig soon showed its dark side. Its possession, indeed, enabled Madame Valière to loiter on the more lighted stairs, or dawdle in the hall with Madame la Propriétaire; but Madame Dépine was not only debarred from these dignified domestic attitudes, but found a new awkwardness in bearing Madame Valière company in their walks abroad. Instead of keeping each other in countenance – *duo contra mundum* – they might now have served as an advertisement for the *coiffeur* and the *convenable*. Before the grey wig – after the grey wig.

Wherefore Madame Dépine was not so very sorry when, after a few weeks of this discomforting contrast, the hour drew near of the 'princess's' departure for the family wedding; especially as she was only losing her for two days. She had insisted, of course, that the savings for the second wig were not to commence till the return, so that Madame Valière might carry with her a present worthy of her position and her port. They had anxious consultations over this present. Madame Dépine was for a cheap but showy article from the Bon Marché; but Madame Valière reminded her that the price-lists of this enterprising firm knocked at the doors of Tonnerre. Something distinguished (in silver) was her own idea. Madame Dépine frequently wept during these discussions, reminded of her own wedding. Oh, the roundabouts at Robinson, and that delicious wedding-lunch up the tree! One was gay then, my dear.

At last they purchased a tiny metal Louis-Quinze timepiece for eleven francs seventy-five centimes, congratulating themselves on the surplus of twenty-five centimes from their three weeks' savings. Madame Valière packed it with her impedimenta into the carpet-bag lent her by Madame la Propriétaire. She was going by a night train from the Gare de Lyon, and sternly refused to let Madame Dépine see her off.

'And how would you go back – an old woman, alone on these dark November nights, with the papers all full of crimes of violence? It is not *convenable*, either.'

Madame Dépine yielded to the latter consideration; but as Madame Valière, carrying the bulging carpet-bag, was crying '*La porte, s'il vous plait*' to the *concierge*, she heard Madame Dépine come tearing and puffing after her like the steam-tram, and, looking back, saw her breathlessly brandishing her gold brooch. '*Tiens!*' she panted, fastening the 'princess's' cloak with it. 'That will give thee an air.'

'But – it is too valuable. Thou must not.' They had never 'thou'd' each other before, and this enhanced the tremulousness of the moment.

'I do not give it thee,' Madame Dépine laughed through her tears. '*Au revoir, mon amie.*'

'*Adieu, ma cherie!* I will tell my dear ones of my Paris comrade.' And for the first time their lips met, and the brown wig brushed the grey.

14

Madame Dépine had two drearier days than she had foreseen. She kept to her own room, creeping out only at night, when, like all cats, all wigs are grey. After an eternity of loneliness the third day dawned, and she went by prearrangement to meet the morning train. Ah, how gaily gleamed the kiosks on the boulevards through the grey mist! What jolly red faces glowed under the cabmen's white hats! How blithely the birds sang in the bird-shops!

The train was late. Her spirits fell as she stood impatiently at the barrier, shivering in her thin clothes, and morbidly conscious of all those eyes on her wig. At length the train glided in unconcernedly, and shot out a medley of passengers. Her poor old eyes strained towards them. They surged through the gate in animated masses, but Madame Valière's form did not disentangle itself from them, though every instant she expected it to jump at her eyes. Her heart contracted painfully – there was no 'princess'. She rushed round to another exit, then outside, to the gates at the end of the drive; she peered into every cab even, as it rumbled past. What had happened? She trudged home as hastily as her legs could bear her. No, Madame Valière had not arrived.

'They have persuaded her to stay another day,' said Madame la Propriétaire. 'She will come by the evening train, or she will write.'

Madame Dépine passed the evening at the Gare de Lyon, and came home heavy of heart and weary of foot. The 'princess' might still arrive at midnight, though, and Madame Dépine lay down dressed in her bed, waiting for the familiar step in the corridor. About three o'clock she fell into a heavy doze, and woke in broad day. She jumped to her feet, her overwrought brain still heavy with the vapours of sleep, and threw open her door.

'Ah! she has already taken in her boots,' she thought confusedly. 'I shall be late for coffee.' She gave her perfunctory knock, and turned the door-handle. But the door would not budge.

'Jacques! Jacques!' she cried, with a clammy fear at her heart. The *garçon*, who was pottering about with pails, opened the door with his key. An emptiness struck cold from the neat bed, the bare walls, the parted wardrobe-curtains that revealed nothing. She fled down the stairs, into the *bureau*.

'Madame Valière is not returned?' she cried.

Madame la Propriétaire shook her head.

'And she has not written?'

'No letter in her writing has come – for anybody.'

'*O mon Dieu!* She has been murdered. She *would* go alone by night.'

'She owes me three weeks' rent,' grimly returned Madame la Propriétaire.

'What do you insinuate?' Madame Dépine's eyes flared.

Madame la Propriétaire shrugged her shoulders. 'I am not at my first communion. I have grown grey in the service of lodgers. And this is how they reward me.' She called Jacques, who had followed uneasily in Madame Dépine's wake. 'Is there anything in the room?'

'Empty as an eggshell, madame.'

'Not even the miniature of her sister?'

'Not even the miniature of her sister.'

'Of her sister?' repeated Madame Dépine.

'Yes; did I never tell you of her? A handsome creature, but she threw her bonnet over the mills.'

'But I thought that was the princess.'

'The princess, too. Her bonnet will also be found lying there.'

'No, no; I mean I thought the portrait was the princess's.'

Madame la Propriétaire laughed. 'She told you so?'

'No, no; but – but I imagined so.'

'Without doubt, she gave you the idea. *Quelle farceuse!* I don't believe there ever was a princess. The family was always inflated.'

All Madame Dépine's world seemed toppling. Somehow her own mistake added to her sense of having been exploited.

'Still,' said Madame la Propriétaire with a shrug, 'it is only three weeks' rent.'

'If you lose it, I will pay!' Madame Dépine had an heroic burst of faith.

'As you please. But I ought to have been on my guard. Where did she take the funds for a grey wig?'

'Ah, the brown wig!' cried Madame Dépine, joyfully. 'She must have left that behind, and any *coiffeur* will give you three weeks' rent for that alone.'

'We shall see,' replied Madame la Propriétaire, ambiguously.

The trio mounted the stairs, and hunted high and low, disturbing the peaceful spider-webs. They peered under the very bed. Not even the old block was to be seen. As far as Madame Valière's own chattels were concerned, the room was indeed 'empty as an eggshell.'

'She has carried it away with the three weeks' rent,' sneered Madame la

Propriétaire. 'In my own carpet-bag,' she added with a terrible recollection.

'She wished to wear it at night against the hard back of the carriage, and guard the other all glossy for the wedding,' Madame Dépine quavered pleadingly, but she could not quite believe herself.

'The wedding had no more existence than the princess,' returned Madame la Propriétaire, believing herself more and more.

'Then she will have cheated me out of the grey wig from the first,' cried Madame Dépine, involuntarily. 'And I who sacrificed myself to her!'

'*Comment!* It was your wig?'

'No, no.' She flushed and stammered. 'But *enfin* – ' and then, 'Oh, heaven! my brooch!'

'She has stolen your brooch?'

Great tears rolled down the wrinkled, ashen cheeks. So this was her reward for secretly instructing the *coiffeur* to make the 'princess's' wig first. The 'princess', indeed! Ah, the adventuress! She felt choking; she shook her fist in the air. Not even the brooch to show when her family came up from Tonnerre, to say nothing of the wig. Was there a God in the world at all? Oh, holy Mother! No wonder the trickstress would not be escorted to the station – she never went to the station. No wonder she would not sell the royal secrets to the journalist – there were none to sell. Oh! it was all of a piece.

'If I were you I should go to the *bureau de police!*' said Madame la Propriétaire.

Yes, she would go; the wretch should be captured, should be haled to gaol. Even her half of the Louis-Quinze timepiece recurred to poor Madame Dépine's brain.

'Add that she has stolen my carpet-bag.'

The local *bureau* telegraphed first to Tonnerre.

There had been the wedding, but no Madame Valière. She had accepted the invitation, had given notice of her arrival; one had awaited the midnight train. The family was still wondering why the rich aunt had turned sulky at the last hour. But she was always an eccentric; a capricious and haughty personage.

Poor Madame Dépine's recurrent 'My wig! my brooch!' reduced the official mind to the same muddle as her own.

'No doubt a sudden impulse of senescent kleptomania,' said the superintendent, sagely, when he had noted down for transference to headquarters Madame Dépine's verbose and vociferous description of the traits and garments of the runagate. 'But we will do our best to recover your brooch and your wig.' Then, with a spasm of supreme sagacity, 'Without doubt they are in the carpet-bag.'

15

Madame Dépine left the *bureau* and wandered about in a daze. That monster of ingratitude! That arch-adventuress, more vicious even than her bejewelled sister! All the long months of more than Lenten rigour recurred to her self-pitiful mood, that futile half-year of semi-starvation. How Madame Valière must have gorged on the sly, the rich eccentric! She crossed a bridge to the Île de la Cité, and came to the gargoyled portals of Notre Dame, and let herself be drawn through the open door, and all the gloom and glory of the building fell around her like a soothing caress. She dropped before an altar and poured out her grief to the Mother of Sorrows. At last she arose, and tottered up the aisle, and the great rose-window glowed like the window of heaven. She imagined her husband and the dead children looking through it. Probably they wondered, as they gazed down, why her head remained so young.

Ah! but she was old, so very old. Surely God would take her soon. How should she endure the long years of loneliness and social ignominy?

As she stumbled out of the cathedral, the cold, hard day smote her full in the face. People stared at her, and she knew it was at the brown wig. But could they expect her to starve herself for a whole year?

'*Mon Dieu!* Starve yourselves, my good friends. At my age, one needs fuel.'

She escaped from them, and ran, muttering, across the road, and almost into the low grey shed.

Ah! the morgue! Blessed idea! That should be the end of her. A moment's struggle, and then – the rose-window of heaven! Hell? No, no; the Madonna would plead for her; she who always looked so beautiful, so *convenable*.

She would peep in. Let her see how she would look when they found her. Would they clap a grey wig upon her, or expose her humiliation even in death?

'A–a–a–h!' A long scream tore her lips apart. There, behind the glass, in terrible waxen peace, a gash on her forehead, lay the 'princess', so uncanny-looking without any wig at all, that she would not have recognised her but for that moment of measurement at the hairdresser's. She fell sobbing before the cold glass wall of the death-chamber. Ah, God! Her first fear had been right; her brooch had but added to the murderer's temptation. And she had just traduced this martyred saint to the police.

'Forgive me, *ma cherie*, forgive me,' she moaned, not even conscious that the attendant was lifting her to her feet with professional interest.

For in that instant everything passed from her but the great yearning for love and reconciliation, and for the first time a grey wig seemed a petty and futile aspiration.

The Silent Sisters

They had quarrelled in girlhood, and mutually declared their intention never to speak to each other again, wetting and drying their forefingers to the accompaniment of an ancient childish incantation, and while they lived on the paternal farm they kept their foolish oath with the stubbornness of a slow country stock, despite the alternate coaxing and chastisement of their parents, notwithstanding the perpetual everyday contact of their lives, through every vicissitude of season and weather, of sowing and reaping, of sun and shade, of joy and sorrow.

Death and misfortune did not reconcile them, and when their father died and the old farm was sold up, they travelled to London in the same silence, by the same train, in search of similar situations. Service separated them for years, though there was only a stone's throw between them. They often stared at each other in the street.

Honor, the elder, married a local artisan, and two and a half years later, Mercy, the younger, married a fellow-workman of Honor's husband. The two husbands were friends, and often visited each other's houses, which were on opposite sides of the same sordid street, and the wives made them welcome. Neither Honor nor Mercy suffered an allusion to their breach; it was understood that their silence must be received in silence. Each of the children had a quiverful of children who played and quarrelled together in the streets and in one another's houses, but not even the street affrays and mutual grievances of the children could provoke the mothers to words. They stood at their doors in impotent fury, almost bursting with the torture of keeping their mouths shut against the effervescence of angry speech. When either lost a child the other watched the funeral from her window, dumb as the mutes.

The years rolled on, and still the river of silence flowed between their lives. Their good looks faded, the burden of life and child-bearing was heavy upon them. Grey hairs streaked their brown tresses, then brown hairs streaked their grey tresses. The puckers of age replaced the dimples of youth. The years rolled on, and Death grew busy among the families. Honor's husband died, and Mercy lost a son, who died a week after his wife. Cholera took several of the younger children. But the sisters themselves lived on, bent and shrivelled by toil and sorrow even more than by the slow frost of the years.

Then one day Mercy took to her deathbed. An internal disease, too long neglected, would carry her off within a week. So the doctor told Jim, Mercy's husband.

Through him, the news travelled to Honor's eldest son, who still lived with her. By the evening it reached Honor.

She went upstairs abruptly when her son told her, leaving him wondering at her stony aspect. When she came down she was bonneted and shawled. He was filled with joyous amaze to see her hobble across the street and for the first time in her life pass over her sister Mercy's threshold.

As Honor entered the sick-room, with pursed lips, a light leapt into the wasted, wrinkled countenance of the dying creature. She raised herself slightly in bed, her lips parted – then they shut tightly, and her face darkened.

Honor turned angrily to Mercy's husband, who hung about impotently. 'Why did you let her run down so low?' she said.

'I didn't know,' the old man stammered, taken aback by her presence even more than by her question. 'She was always a woman to say nothin'.'

Honor put him impatiently aside and examined the medicine bottle on the bedside table.

'Isn't it time she took her dose?'

'I dessay.'

Honor snorted wrathfully. 'What's the use of a man?' she enquired, as she carefully measured out the fluid and put it to her sister's lips, which opened to receive it, and then closed tightly again.

'How is your wife feeling now?' Honor asked after a pause.

'How are you, now, Mercy?' asked the old man awkwardly.

The old woman shook her head. 'I'm a-goin' fast, Jim,' she grumbled weakly, and a tear of self-pity trickled down her parchment cheek.

'What rubbidge she do talk!' cried Honor, sharply. 'Why d'ye stand there like a tailor's dummy? Why don't you tell her to cheer up?'

'Cheer up, Mercy,' quavered the old man, hoarsely.

But Mercy groaned instead, and turned fretfully on her other side, with her face to the wall.

'I'm too old, I'm too old,' she moaned, 'this is the end o' me.'

'Did you ever hear the like?' Honor asked Jim, angrily, as she smoothed his wife's pillow. 'She was always conceited about her age, settin' herself up as the equals of her elders, and here am I, her elder sister, as carried her in my arms when I was five and she was two, still hale and strong, and with no mind for underground for many a day. Nigh three times her age I was once, mind you, and now she has the imperence to talk of dyin' before me.'

She took off her bonnet and shawl. 'Send one o' the kids to tell my boy I'm stayin' here,' she said, 'and then just you get 'em all to bed – there's too much noise about the house.'

The children, who were orphaned grandchildren of the dying woman, were sent to bed, and then Jim himself was packed off to refresh himself for the next day's labours, for the poor old fellow still doddered about the workshop.

The silence of the sick-room spread over the whole house. About ten o'clock the doctor came again and instructed Honor how to alleviate the patient's last hours. All night long she sat watching her dying sister, hand and eye alert to anticipate every wish. No word broke the awful stillness.

The first thing in the morning, Mercy's married daughter, the only child of hers living in London, arrived to nurse her mother. But Honor indignantly refused to be dispossessed.

'A nice daughter you are,' she said, 'to leave your mother lay a day and a night without a sight o' your ugly face.'

'I had to look after the good man, and the little 'uns,' the daughter pleaded.

'Then what do you mean by desertin' them now?' the irate old woman retorted. 'First you deserts your mother, and then your husband and children. You must go back to them as needs your care. I carried your mother in my arms before you was born, and if she wants anybody else now to look after her, let her just tell me so, and I'll be off in a brace o' shakes.'

She looked defiantly at the yellow, dried-up creature in the bed. Mercy's withered lips twitched, but no sound came from them. Jim, strung up by the situation, took the word. 'You can't do no good up here, the doctor says. You might look after the kids downstairs a bit, when you can spare an hour, and I've got to go to the shop. I'll send you a telegraph if there's a change,' he whispered to the daughter, and she, not wholly discontented to return to her living interests, kissed her mother, lingered a little, and then stole quietly away.

All that day the old women remained together in solemn silence, broken only by the doctor's visit. He reported that Mercy might last a couple of days more. In the evening Jim replaced his sister-in-law, who slept perforce. At midnight she reappeared and sent him to bed. The sufferer tossed about restlessly. At half-past two she awoke, and Honor fed her with some broth, as she would have fed a baby. Mercy, indeed, looked scarcely bigger than an infant, and Honor only had the advantage of her by being puffed out with clothes. A church clock in the distance struck three. Then the silence fell deeper. The watcher drowsed, the lamp flickered, tossing her shadow about the walls as if she, too, were turning feverishly from side to side. A strange ticking made itself heard in the wainscoting. Mercy sat up with a scream of terror. 'Jim!' she shrieked, 'Jim!'

Honor started up, opened her mouth to cry 'Hush!' then checked herself, suddenly frozen.

'Jim,' cried the dying woman, 'listen! Is that the death spider?'

Honor listened, her blood curdling. Then she went towards the door and opened it. 'Jim,' she said, in low tones, speaking towards the landing, 'tell her it's nothing, it's only a mouse. She was always a nervous little thing.' And she closed the door softly, and pressing her trembling sister tenderly back on the pillow, tucked her up snugly in the blanket.

Next morning, when Jim was really present, the patient begged pathetically to have a grandchild with her in the room, day and night. 'Don't leave me alone again,' she quavered, 'don't leave me alone with not a soul to talk to.' Honor winced, but said nothing.

The youngest child, who did not have to go to school, was brought – a pretty little boy with brown curls, which the sun, streaming through the panes, turned to gold. The morning passed slowly. About noon Mercy took the child's hand, and smoothed his curls.

'My sister Honor had golden curls like that,' she whispered.

'They were in the family, Bobby,' Honor answered. 'Your granny had them, too, when she was a girl.'

There was a long pause. Mercy's eyes were half-glazed. But her vision was inward now.

'The mignonette will be growin' in the gardens, Bobby,' she murmured.

'Yes, Bobby, and the heart's-ease,' said Honor, softly. 'We lived in the country, you know, Bobby.'

'There is flowers in the country,' Bobby declared gravely.

'Yes, and trees,' said Honor. 'I wonder if your granny remembers when we were larruped for stealin' apples.'

'Ay, that I do, Bobby, he, he,' croaked the dying creature, with a burst of enthusiasm. 'We was a pair o' tomboys. The farmer he ran after us cryin' "Ye! ye!" but we wouldn't take no gar. He, he, he!'

Honor wept at the laughter. The native idiom, unheard for half a century, made her face shine under the tears. 'Don't let your granny excite herself, Bobby. Let me give her her drink.' She moved the boy aside, and Mercy's lips automatically opened to the draught.

'Tom was wi' us, Bobby,' she gurgled, still vibrating with amusement, 'and he tumbled over on the heather. He, he!'

'Tom is dead this forty year, Bobby,' whispered Honor.

Mercy's head fell back, and an expression of supreme exhaustion came over the face. Half an hour passed. Bobby was called down to dinner. The doctor had been sent for. The silent sisters were alone. Suddenly Mercy sat up with a jerk.

'It be growin' dark, Tom,' she said hoarsely, ' 'haint it time to call the cattle home from the ma'shes?'

'She's talkin' rubbidge again,' said Honor, chokingly. 'Tell her she's in London, Bobby.'

A wave of intelligence traversed the sallow face. Still sitting up, Mercy bent towards the side of the bed. 'Ah, is Honor still there? Kiss me – Bobby.' Her hands groped blindly. Honor bent down and the old women's withered lips met.

And in that kiss Mercy passed away into the greater silence.

Hopes and Dreams

The morning of the Great White Fast broke bleak and grey. Esther, alone in the house save for the servant, wandered from room to room in dull misery. The day before had been almost a feast-day in the ghetto – everybody providing for the morrow. Esther had scarcely eaten anything. Nevertheless she was fasting, and would fast for over twenty-four hours, till the night fell. She knew not why. Her record was unbroken, and instinct resented a breach now. She had always fasted – even the Henry Goldsmiths fasted, and greater than the Henry Goldsmiths! QC's fasted, and peers, and prize-fighters and actors. And yet Esther, like many far more pious persons, did not think of her sins for a moment. She thought of everything but them – of the bereaved family in that strange provincial town; of her own family in that strange distant land. Well, she would soon be with them now. Her passage was booked – a steerage passage it was, not because she could not afford cabin fare, but from her morbid impulse to identify herself with poverty. The same impulse led her to choose a vessel in which a party of Jewish pauper immigrants was being shipped farther west. She thought also of Dutch Debby, with whom she had spent the previous evening; and of Raphael Leon, who had sent her, via the publishers, a letter which she could not trust herself to answer cruelly, and which she deemed it most prudent to leave unanswered. Uncertain of her powers of resistance, she scarcely ventured outside the house for fear of his stumbling across her. Happily, every day diminished the chance of her whereabouts leaking out through some unsuspected channel.

About noon, her restlessness carried her into the streets. There was a festal solemnity about the air. Women and children, not at synagogue, showed themselves at the doors, pranked in their best. Indifferently pious young men sought relief from the ennui of the day-long service in lounging about for a breath of fresh air; some even strolled towards the Strand, and turned into the National Gallery, satisfied to reappear for the twilight service. On all sides came the fervent roar of prayer which indicated a synagogue or a *chevrah*, the number of places of worship having been indefinitely increased to accommodate those who made their appearance for this occasion only.

Everywhere friends and neighbours were asking one another how they were bearing the fast, exhibiting their white tongues and generally comparing symptoms, the physical aspects of the Day of Atonement more or less completely diverting attention from the spiritual. Smelling-salts passed from hand to hand, and men explained to one another that, but for the deprivation of their cigars, they could endure Yom Kippur with complacency.

Esther passed the ghetto school, within which free services were going on even in the playground, poor Russians and Poles, fanatically observant, fore-gathering with lax fishmongers and welshers; and without which hulking young men hovered uneasily, feeling too out of tune with religion to go in, too conscious of the terrors of the day to stay entirely away. From the interior came from sunrise to nightfall a throbbing thunder of supplication, now pealing in passionate outcry, now subsiding to a low rumble. The sounds of prayer that pervaded the ghetto, and burst upon her at every turn, wrought upon Esther strangely; all her soul went out in sympathy with these yearning outbursts; she stopped every now and then to listen, as in those far-off days when the Sons of the Covenant drew her with their melancholy cadences.

At last, moved by an irresistible instinct, she crossed the threshold of a large *chevrah* she had known in her girlhood, mounted the stairs and entered the female compartment without hostile challenge. The reek of many breaths and candles nearly drove her back, but she pressed forwards towards a remembered window, through a crowd of bewigged women, shaking their bodies fervently to and fro.

This room had no connection with the men's; it was simply the room above part of theirs, and the declamations of the unseen cantor came but faintly through the flooring, though the clamour of the general masculine chorus kept the pious *au courant* with their husbands. When weather or the whims of the more important ladies permitted, the window at the end was opened; it gave upon a little balcony, below which the men's chamber projected con-siderably, having been built out into the back-yard. When this window was opened simultaneously with the skylight in the men's synagogue, the fervid roulades of the cantor were as audible to the women as to their masters.

Esther had always affected the balcony: there the air was comparatively fresh, and on fine days there was a glimpse of blue sky, and a perspective of sunny red tiles, where brown birds fluttered and cats lounged and little episodes arose to temper the tedium of endless invocation; and farther off there was a back view of a nunnery, with visions of placid black-hooded faces at windows; and from the distance came a pleasant drone of monosyllabic spelling from fresh young voices, to relieve the ear from the monotony of long stretches of meaningless mumbling.

Here, lost in a sweet melancholy, Esther dreamed away the long grey day, only vaguely conscious of the stages of the service – morning dovetailing into afternoon service, and afternoon into evening; of the heavy-jowled woman behind her reciting a jargon-version of the Atonement liturgy to a devout coterie; of the prostrations full-length on the floor, and the series of impassioned sermons; of the interminably rhyming poems, and the acrostics with their recurring burdens shouted in devotional frenzy, voice rising above voice as in emulation, with special staccato phrases flung heavenwards; of the wailing confessions of communal sin, with their accompaniment of sobs and tears and howls and grimaces and clenchings of palms and beatings of the breast. She was lapped in a great ocean of sound that broke upon her consciousness like the waves upon a beach, now with a cooing murmur, now with a majestic crash, followed by a long receding moan. She lost herself in the roar, in its barren sensuousness, while the leaden sky grew duskier and the twilight crept on, and the awful hour drew nigh when God would seal what He had written, and the annual scrolls of destiny would be closed, immutable. She saw them looming mystically through the skylight, the swaying forms below, in their white grave-clothes, oscillating weirdly backwards and forwards, bowed as by a mighty wind.

Suddenly there fell a vast silence; even from without no sound came to break the awful stillness. It was as if all creation paused to hear a pregnant word.

'Hear, O Israel, the Lord our God, the Lord is One!' sang the cantor frenziedly.

And all the ghostly congregation answered with a great cry, closing their eyes and rocking frantically to and fro: 'Hear, O Israel, the Lord our God, the Lord is One!'

They seemed like a great army of the sheeted dead risen to testify to the Unity. The magnetic tremor that ran through the synagogue thrilled the lonely girl to the core; once again her dead self woke, her dead ancestors that would not be shaken off lived and moved in her. She was sucked up into the great wave of passionate faith, and from her lips came, in rapturous surrender to an overmastering impulse, the half-hysterical protestation: 'Hear, O Israel, the Lord our God, the Lord is One!'

And then in the brief instant while the congregation, with ever-ascending rhapsody, blessed God till the climax came with the sevenfold declaration, 'The Lord, He is God', the whole history of her strange, unhappy race flashed through her mind in a whirl of resistless emotion. She was overwhelmed by the thought of its sons in every corner of the earth proclaiming to the sombre twilight sky the belief for which its generations had lived and died – the Jews of Russia sobbing it forth in their pale of enclosure, the Jews of Morocco in their *mellah*, and of South Africa in their tents by the diamond mines; the Jews of the New World in great free cities, in Canadian backwoods, in South American savannahs; the Australian Jews on the sheep-farms and the gold-fields and in the mushroom cities; the Jews of Asia in their reeking quarters begirt by barbarian populations. The shadow of a large mysterious destiny seemed to hang over these poor superstitious zealots, whose lives she knew so well in all their everyday prose, and to invest the unconscious shunning sons of the ghetto with something of tragic grandeur. The grey dusk palpitated with floating shapes of prophets and martyrs, scholars and sages and poets, full of a yearning love and pity, lifting hands of benediction. By what great high roads and queer byways of history had they travelled hither, these wandering Jews, 'sated with contempt', these shrewd eager fanatics, these sensual ascetics, these human paradoxes, adaptive to every environment, energising in every field of activity, omnipresent like some great natural force, indestructible and almost inconvertible, surviving – with the incurable optimism that overlay all their poetic sadness – Babylon and Carthage, Greece and Rome; involuntarily financing the Crusades, out-living the Inquisition, illusive of all baits, unshaken by all persecutions – at once the greatest and meanest of races? Had the Jew come so far only to break down at last, sinking in morasses of modern doubt, and irresistibly dragging down with him the Christian and the Moslem; or was he yet fated to outlast them both, in continuous testimony to a hand moulding incomprehensibly the life of humanity? Would Israel develop into the sacred phalanx, the nobler brotherhood that Raphael Leon had dreamed of, or would the race that had first proclaimed – through Moses for the ancient world, through Spinoza for the modern – 'One God, one Law, one Element,' become, in the larger, wilder dream of the Russian idealist, the main factor in 'One far-off divine event to which the whole Creation moves'?

The roar dwindled to a solemn silence, as though in answer to her questionings. Then the ram's horn shrilled – a stern long-drawn-out note, that rose at last into a mighty peal of sacred jubilation. The Atonement was complete.

The crowd bore Esther downstairs and into the blank indifferent street. But the long exhausting fast, the fetid atmosphere, the strain upon her emotions, had overtaxed her beyond endurance. Up to now the frenzy of the service had sustained her, but as she stepped across the threshold on to the pavement she staggered and fell. One of the men pouring out from the lower synagogue caught her in his arms. It was Strelitski.

*   *   *

A group of three stood on the saloon deck of an outward-bound steamer. Raphael Leon was bidding farewell to the man he reverenced without discipleship, and the woman he loved without blindness.

'Look!' he said, pointing compassionately to the wretched throng of Jewish emigrants huddling on the lower deck and scattered about the gang-way amid jostling sailors and stevedores and bales and coils of rope; the men in peaked or fur caps, the women with shawls and babies, some gazing upwards with lacklustre eyes, the majority brooding, despondent, apathetic. 'How could either of you have borne the sights and smells of the steerage? You are a pair of visionaries. You could not have breathed a day in that society. Look!'

Strelitski looked at Esther instead; perhaps he was thinking he could have